ALICE WORTH BOX SET

LISA EDMONDS

City Owl Press

This book is a work of fiction. Names, characters, places, and incidents either are products of the author's imagination or are used fictitiously. Any resemblance to actual events or locales or persons, living or dead, is entirely coincidental and not intended by the author.

ALICE WORTH BOX SET
Books 1 - 3 and Bonus Novella

CITY OWL PRESS
www.cityowlpress.com

All Rights reserved. Except as permitted under the U.S. Copyright Act of 1976, no part of this publication may be reproduced, distributed, or transmitted in any form or by any means, or stored in a database or retrieval system, without the prior consent and permission of the publisher.

Copyright © 2018 by Lisa Edmonds.

Cover Design by Mibl Art and Tina Moss. All stock photos licensed appropriately.

Author Photo by Madison Hurley Photography.

Edited by Heather McCorkle.

For information on subsidiary rights, please contact the publisher at info@cityowlpress.com.

Print Edition ISBN: 978-1-949090-18-5

Digital Edition ISBN: 978-1-949090-17-8

Printed in the United States of America

PRAISE FOR LISA EDMONDS

"Edmonds's prose is energetic...Alice is both spunky and self-deprecating, with incredibly advanced magical powers...There is promise in Edmonds's melding of the supernatural and the everyday."
— *Publishers Weekly*

"Alice is a pretty badass heroine who has potential to be one of my favorite in the genre. She takes a beating, heals herself, and goes back into the fray. The plot is fast-paced and revolves around an excellent magical mystery with earth shattering consequences should something go askew. I loved Alice's backstory and learning how this world works. I look forward to seeing what is in store for Alice in the next book."
— *All Things Urban Fantasy*

"Edmonds's suspenseful second urban fantasy novel is just as action-packed and entertaining as the first... Edmonds has an eye for both detail and entertaining characters, and her story is fun and energetic... Readers will enjoy this installment and look forward to more in the continuing saga of Alice Worth."
— *Publishers Weekly*

"What a cracking read...ages since I read a new fantasy story that's gripped me like this, that I so enjoyed. It's up there with my favourite reads and I hope Lisa is hard at work with the next book."
— *Jeannie Zelos Book Reviews*

"There is NOTHING better than finding a fantastic new paranormal series. *Lisa Edmonds* has started a series that grabbed and held my attention...Heart of Malice successfully shows me the new world as it's experienced. With a little info here...and a little info there, I wasn't bombarded all at once and I got to see it all live and in action."
— *Stacey is Sassy*

"Add everything together, great writing, great characters, interesting pasts, and great plotting, I can't wait to read more! Highly recommend!"
— *Librarian, Penny Noble*

"A nice mystery wrapped up in suspense and a few hotties to top it off! A perfect way to describe Heart of Fire—a paranormal romance with a set of characters that pull the reader into the story."
— *InD'tale, Jacey Lee*

"Lisa Edmonds has made an instant fan of me. I look forward to reading the next case that requires Alice's special set of skills."
— *The Reading Cafe*

"The Alice Worth series quickly turned into a must-read series for me. As soon as you think you have a handle on what she can do, another level of power is revealed. She truly is a bad-ass and it's amazing to witness what she can do. As with book one, I didn't want to stop reading when the book ended. I look forward to seeing what book three will bring to the table."
— *Urban Fantasy Investigations*

"Alice is the type of Heroine I live to read about and scour the net looking for others of her ilk. Tough, no-nonsense, a bit damaged, yet so real and full of compassion and needing love yet afraid of it when it finds them. Edmonds can't get book three out fast enough as far as I am concerned."
— *Boundless Book Reviews*

"10 New Urban Fantasy Series You Need to Read: Alice Worth is a Mage Private Investigator with a ghost sidekick and some really cool magic. She can conjure a cold fire whip! There are vampires and werewolves and all our favorite old school UF elements. I wish more people were talking about this series."
— *Vampire Book Club*

THE ALICE WORTH SERIES

BY LISA EDMONDS

Heart of Malice

Just For One Night (Short Story)

Blood Money (Novella)

Heart of Fire

Heart of Ice

HEART OF MALICE

BOOK 1

1

I was just finishing my second beer when someone leaned down to whisper in my ear. "Want to do something insane?"

As pickup lines went, it wasn't half bad.

I set my glass on the bar and looked up. He was dark-haired, gorgeous, and tall, dwarfing me by almost a foot—and at five-six plus heels, I wasn't exactly short. I took a moment to savor the close-up view of his impressively muscled chest and let my appreciation show in my voice when I answered, "Absolutely."

He drained the last of his bourbon and tossed a crisp hundred on the bar next to our empty glasses. "Then let's get out of here."

I let him help me slide down off my barstool. His eyes moved approvingly from my tall boots to my thighs and over my short dress to my cleavage, where they paused for a moment before meeting my gaze. "Scott," he said and held my jacket while I put it on.

I smiled up at him. "Alice."

"Nice to meet you, Alice." He offered his hand, and I took it. We plowed through the crowded bar toward the front door.

When we finally emerged on the sidewalk, I tucked my arm through Scott's and fell in step beside him. Despite the cold, he didn't need a coat; I felt his warmth even through my leather jacket. He smelled smoky and woodsy, like a forest fire.

"What's on the agenda?" I asked as we strolled along Ninth Street, past a dozen bars and late-night cafés.

"Have you ever flown the 101?"

I laughed. "I've *driven* the Pacific Coast Highway. I didn't know you could fly it."

He grinned at me. "In my car, we can."

"Let's do it." I squeezed his arm. "Where are you parked?"

"Up ahead a couple of blocks."

The March wind was bitterly cold on my bare legs. Though we walked quickly, within minutes, I was shivering.

"Come on—we're almost there." Scott squeezed me against his side with an enormous arm.

"How did you manage to get parking down here on a Saturday, anyway?" I asked, pouting a bit. "I'm all the way over on Fulton, in a pay lot."

"I know the guy who owns McGovern's Steakhouse," Scott replied. "He lets me park in his alley whenever I'm here."

"Well, that sure is convenient."

Scott flashed me a smile. We were in front of McGovern's, which was already closed for the night. At one a.m., there weren't many pedestrians around. It was cold enough that anyone who was out was in a hurry to get where they were going, and the most popular bars were back in the direction we'd come from. Where Scott was parked, there was nothing but long-closed restaurants and shops. I saw one other couple about a block behind us, wrapped in long coats, their heads down as they talked quietly, but no one else was in sight. The sharp staccato sound of my boot heels echoed as we walked.

Finally, we rounded the corner and started into the alley behind the steakhouse. It was a relief to be out of the wind. Ahead, by the light of a single streetlight, I saw a black Porsche 911 Turbo parked in front of a large sign that read Authorized Vehicles Only.

"Nice car," I remarked as we approached it.

"Thanks," he said, and punched me.

I felt him tense up and managed to turn a fraction of a second before he swung, so his massive fist connected with my side instead of my stomach.

Pain exploded in my ribs. I gasped and hit Scott's chest with both hands. Magic flared, and he flew backward into the side of the restaurant, leaving a man-sized crater in the brick wall. He landed in a crouch with a snarl, his eyes blazing bright red.

My left side hurt so badly it was hard to think for a moment, and I wondered if he'd broken any ribs. I held my side and spooled my earth magic. Green flames sparked on my skin as a five-foot-long whip-like stream of cold fire emerged from my right hand. I lashed the Porsche's front tire, and it split with a loud *bang* and the hiss of air escaping. I smiled grimly. No quick getaways for him.

"Bitch," Scott growled. His voice was deeper and more gravelly now that he was no longer pretending to be human. "My car!"

"I guess you won't be flying the 101 anytime soon," I said. "And by the way, that's a terrible line."

The half demon glowered at me. Above us, the streetlight buzzed and flickered. "What do you want?" he demanded.

"You're coming with me. I've got a Court summons with your name on it."

His eyes glowed brighter with anger. "I don't answer to the *humans*," he snarled.

The corner of my mouth turned up. "No, the *other* Court."

Scott hissed. I tensed and shifted my weight, ready for him to attack.

Instead, the bastard ran.

I cursed and took off down the alley after him, feeling a burst of sharp pain in my side with every step. My boots and short dress might have worked well to catch his attention in the bar, but they were far from ideal for a foot chase. By the time I reached the end of the alley, Scott was already almost a full block ahead of me.

As we ran down the deserted sidewalk, headed farther from the relative safety of the bar district and possible witnesses, I set my jaw and blocked out the pain. Scott Grierson was not getting away from me tonight, not after all he had done.

Up ahead, Scott darted across the street. Between gasping breaths, I groaned. He was headed for Fields Park. If I lost sight of him in there, he was gone.

I put on an extra burst of speed, breaking into a full sprint. Half-demons were larger and stronger than humans, but it was heavy muscle mass. They might get off to a fast start, but they weren't built for running long distances. By the time Scott ran through the gates of the park, I'd cut the distance separating us in half.

The moon, a day from being full, hung bright in the clear sky, and I could see my quarry ahead of me, his steps crunching in the gravel path.

Scott heard me gaining on him and suddenly veered off the main path toward some trees. I cut across the grass, hoping to intercept him before he found cover. Behind me, I thought I heard running footsteps back near the gate but couldn't turn to look. If he had an accomplice, I'd deal with that when I had to; right now I couldn't chance him getting away.

When I got within twenty feet, I raised my hands. White magic sparked on my palms, and I unleashed a gust of air that sent the half-demon sprawling into the grass with a surprised grunt.

Scott rolled to his feet with a growl and turned to face me. His eyes glowed brightly in the darkness. "Who sent you?"

I stopped ten feet away, breathing hard. "I'm here because of Maggie."

"Who?" I couldn't see his expression clearly, but his tone sounded genuinely puzzled, and it infuriated me.

"Maggie Hill, the girl you picked up a month ago from the same bar we were just in."

Scott grinned. Unfortunately for them, a lot of women had found his smile to be charming. Of course, they hadn't seen it paired with his red eyes—at least, not until it was too late. "Was that her name? I had no idea."

My jaw clenched so hard that it hurt. "Did you know *any* of their names? Maggie? Alison? Katie?"

"Nope," Scott said with a shrug. "Honestly, I didn't care. I don't even know what *your* name is."

Suddenly, his arm moved.

A flash of metal glinted in the moonlight and I lashed out with my cold-fire whip. The bright green arc of lightning intercepted the blade in midair and sent it flying back in the direction it came from.

And buried it to the hilt in the half-demon's right eye.

It was over in a heartbeat. For a moment, Scott remained upright, his single red eye wide open in surprise. Then he fell backward and landed on the grass with a solid *thump*.

I approached him warily, my whip still crackling at my side. The half-demon was dying. His remaining eye stared up at me, glowing faintly. Dark blood ran from his right eye socket, where a four-inch knife handle protruded. His mouth moved, but nothing came out.

My fingers itched to pull the knife out and put it through his other eye. Instead, I crouched next to him as my whip coiled back into my hand and vanished. Disappointment left a bitter taste in my mouth. He didn't deserve a quick death; it should have been slow and painful. Maggie deserved that, at least.

"My name," I told him coldly, "is Alice."

Scott exhaled in a long, rattling wheeze. His eye dimmed, then went dark.

I sat on the grass next to the body while I caught my breath. Pain lanced through my side, and the chill of the night started to seep into me. Running had made me sweat, and now the wind felt icy on my damp skin.

My jaw ached from clenching my teeth, and my fingers dug into the ground in frustration. "Damn it, Alice," I chastised myself. When Scott threw the knife, I'd acted to defend myself, drawing on years of training that had become instinct. Unfortunately, as a result, he'd escaped justice, and now instead of presenting him to the Vampire Court as my prisoner, he would have to be tried *ex mortem*. I hoped the Hills could at least find some answers and closure from that.

Time to call the vamps to come get the body. I reached into my pocket for my phone.

I heard footsteps running from the tree line a half second before two flashlight beams blinded me. "SPEMA! Hands on your head!" The voice was loud and male, its tone unmistakable. My night had just gone from bad to infinitely worse.

Slowly, I pulled my hand out of my pocket, showed that it was empty, and clasped my hands on top of my head, half expecting to hear gunshots ring out and bracing for bullets that never came. Through the glare of the flashlights, I saw two dark figures in long coats, both pointing guns at me.

"My name is Alice Worth," I said calmly over the pounding of my heart. "I'm a licensed private investigator and a registered earth and air mage. My ID is in my wallet in the left pocket of my jacket."

"Do not move," the other agent, a woman, warned me.

I kept my hands on my head as the larger of the two shadows moved the beam of his flashlight to point at Scott Grierson's face. He swore and walked over to check the half-demon's pulse. "Dead. Goddammit, did you have to kill him?"

I blinked. I wasn't dumb enough to admit anything—even self-defense—in front of two federal agents, but the frustration and anger in his tone made me think these two hadn't just happened to be taking a late-night walk in the park.

I looked closer at them, and then it clicked. "You were following us, back on Ninth," I said slowly. "Why?"

No reply, not that I'd really expected one. These two federal agents were the "couple" I'd seen as we walked from the bar to Scott's car. I remembered hearing footsteps behind me on the path in the park. Had the agents seen and heard the entire thing? And who had they been following: Scott, or me?

The male agent held me at gunpoint while his partner walked around behind me. She was a few inches taller than me, built solidly, wearing a long coat over a dark suit. "On your feet, slowly," she ordered me. I heard metal clinking.

Carefully and a bit stiffly, I stood. She grabbed my left wrist and twisted my arm down behind my back. The movement made pain flare in my side. "You're under arrest," she said, closing a spell cuff on my wrist. She pulled my right arm down and cuffed it too.

The instant the first cuff closed on my wrist, my magic was suppressed, and I jerked in the agent's grip as the dampening spell settled on my skin like an itchy blanket. The discomfort made my stomach churn.

Once I was cuffed, the female agent recited the Miranda warning, and I acknowledged with a simple yes that I understood my rights.

She went through my pockets, starting with my wallet. "Alice Evelyn Worth," she told her partner. "Mage private investigator's license, SPERA registration, and current permits. Are you carrying any weapons or spells?"

"Air magic healing spell and spell cuffs in my right pocket," I said. "No weapons."

When my arms started to ache, I laced my fingers together and tried not to pull on the cuffs. They drained your strength if you did, which was why I'd planned to use a pair on Scott. They worked well to restrain half-demons, vampires, and others with superhuman strength. Between the cuffs and a sleep spell, I should have been able to get Scott Grierson to the vamps without much trouble. I glared at the half-demon's body. I ought to have just dropped him the instant we got into the alley instead of waiting until we were completely out of sight from the street. The consequences of my hesitation grew more dire by the second.

The agent continued the search, dropping each item, including my cell phone, in the grass as she went through my jacket pockets. Then she frisked me very efficiently and thoroughly. When her hand slid over my ribs, I had to bite the inside of my cheek to keep from flinching.

The male agent, who had been crouching next to Scott's body, stood and came over. He was well over six feet tall and blond, wearing a long coat and dark suit like his partner. He picked up my wallet and read through its contents for himself.

"Alice Worth," he said quietly, as if to himself. Then he looked at me, his eyes hard. "Why were you with him?" he asked, hooking his thumb at the body.

I kept my mouth shut. If I had the right to remain silent, I was going to use it.

The male agent looked over my shoulder at his partner behind me. Whatever unspoken conversation they had, he didn't like it. His scowl deepened, and he stared at me. I fixed my gaze on his chin and stayed still, even though the discomfort of the spell cuffs and the pain in my side made me want to shuffle my feet.

Finally, he grunted, pulled out his own identification, and stuck it under my nose. "Special Agent Lake of the Supernatural and Paranormal Entity Management Agency," he said brusquely. "My partner is Special Agent Parker. We believe Mr. Grierson might have been involved in a series of disappearances in the area."

I said nothing.

A muscle moved in Lake's square jaw. "Since August of last year, we have six cases of young women going missing. A few days ago, we obtained camera footage from an ATM that showed the latest victim, Maggie Hill, on the night she disappeared, with a male suspect we believe to be Grierson. If you have any information tying him to these disappearances, or know anything about the whereabouts of these women, now is the time."

I thought about it. As with most supes and mages, my distrust of SPEMA agents ran deep. They had nearly limitless power and authority, and we had so few rights. I was acutely aware that Lake and Parker could haul me off and I would disappear into one of the Agency's supe prisons, never to be seen or heard from again. I'd killed Grierson in self-defense—by accident, really—but it would be difficult to prove that. As such, I wasn't particularly inclined to say anything.

The longer I stayed silent, the angrier Lake got. He stepped closer to loom over me.

"I can take you down to our office, if you'd be more comfortable talking to me there," he said grimly. We both knew my comfort didn't figure into the equation, and the odds of me walking back out of the Agency office were slim at best. "I want some answers. I've got six families waiting for news, and so help me, if you know what happened and you're not telling me, I will find a way to get it out of you."

I stared at him, my face blank. He'd gone from intimidation to explicit threats in a blink. Neither was anything new to me. If he expected me to be rattled, he was destined to be disappointed. I'd spent the first twenty-four years of my life being threatened with—and suffering—far worse torments than he could even begin to imagine.

"Forget it," Parker said. "She isn't going to tell us anything. Let's go." She yanked on my cuffed wrists, and I barely suppressed a wince.

Lake held up his hand and met my gaze. The anger in his eyes faded, replaced with grim determination. He sighed. "We saw what happened," he told me.

From behind me, Parker made a disgusted noise. She let go of my arm and stepped back, as if to distance herself from Lake.

"We overheard you tell him that you were here because of Maggie, and we heard him confess to taking the girls," Lake said. "We saw him throw the knife. You didn't mean to kill him; you were protecting yourself. If I take those cuffs off you, will you tell me what you know?"

"For God's sake, Lake," Parker exploded. "You can't do that."

"I can and I will," Lake snapped. "You want to go back and tell them we don't know where their girls are?"

Parker stayed silent.

"Do you?" Lake demanded.

"No, but—"

"Take the cuffs off." Lake glowered at Parker. A full minute passed.

Apparently Lake won the staring contest, because suddenly I heard a jingle of keys. I braced myself, but when the cuffs came off, the surge of released magic caused me to stagger before Lake caught me by my left arm.

Before I could stop myself, I grimaced at the pain in my side as my weight pulled on my arm. "Are you injured?" Lake's eyes narrowed as he looked me over.

"No." I pulled away from him and forced myself to stand up straight. "Just stiff from the cuffs." If he thought I was hurt, he might try to force me to go to the hospital, and that was something I had to avoid.

Lake looked like he wasn't sure he believed me, but luckily for me, he was more interested in Grierson than any bumps or bruises—or cracked ribs—that I might have. "Tell me what you know."

I'd thought at first that Lake's change in attitude was simply a tactic to get me to talk, but he looked sincere. Grierson was dead, and as far as the agent knew, so were his chances of finding out where Maggie and the other girls were. My instincts were telling me that Lake cared far more about finding them than about throwing me in prison for accidentally killing a half-demon.

My only way out of this might be to tell him what I knew. I was about to take a very big—and very uncharacteristic—gamble with my freedom and my life. "Two weeks ago, I was hired by Maggie Hill's parents to look for their missing daughter. They were frustrated by the lack of progress the task force was making, and thought a private investigator might be more successful."

Behind me, Parker made a derisive sound. My eyes narrowed, and Lake gave her a quelling look. "How did you connect Maggie to Grierson?" he asked.

"I canvassed all of the bars Maggie's friends said she liked to visit and got nothing, just like the cops did. I started checking other bars close to her apartment and didn't have much luck until I got to the bar we were in tonight. The bartender there said Maggie had been in a couple of times, and he thought he remembered her with a flashy guy who liked to brag about his car. I got a physical description and a first name. I staked out the area for a couple of nights until I saw a guy matching the description parking his Porsche in the alley behind the steakhouse. I followed him home that night. This was about a week ago."

"That was before we got the surveillance footage." Parker's tone made it clear she wasn't happy I had identified their suspect before they did.

I continued. "Once I had Grierson's name and address, I did some digging into his background. It didn't take long to figure out that he was half-demon; I'd already guessed it from his size."

As I talked, Lake wrote in a little notebook. He paused at the last, his eyes narrowing at me. "Why didn't you pass his information on to the police or SPEMA?"

"At that point, it wasn't anything more than a possible lead. I needed something that would tie Grierson to Maggie, or to one of the other girls. I hoped I could find physical evidence I could give to the police."

"*Did* you find any evidence?"

"How familiar are you with magic trace, Agent Lake?"

Parker snorted.

Lake's mouth compressed into a grim line. "Parker, Mr. Grierson's vehicle and the alley behind McGovern's are a crime scene. I need you to head there and request a CSU."

"I can't leave you here alone with a suspect," Parker said. "It's against regulations."

"She's not a suspect; she's a witness. I'll call in for additional agents and a second CSU," Lake told her. "We'll be fine here in the meantime. Go secure the other scene."

Seething, Parker spun around and headed off in the direction of the park gate. Lake watched her go, then turned back to me. "I'll have to report this soon. She'll be sending more agents out here." In other words, get to the point.

I tucked my cold hands into my jacket pockets. "Maggie and the rest of the girls went missing the day before a full moon. I suspected the timing might indicate some sort of ritual magic. I went to Grierson's house to look around. When I got close enough, I could sense traces of what felt like a demon summoning. It was strong enough that I could sense it through the house wards, which meant if I was right, Grierson had summoned a very powerful demon."

It was hard to tell in the moonlight, but I thought Lake looked pale. "What did you do then?"

"The house wards were strong enough that if I tried to unweave or break them, he would know immediately. I asked an acquaintance to come with me and try scrying, to see if he could see anything that might have taken place in the house." I'd cashed in a big favor to get Michael to do it.

A pause. "What am I going to find in that house, Ms. Worth?"

"Not what you were hoping to find," I told him. "You'll need to unweave or break Grierson's house wards first. You'll find a basement with black wards. Make sure you bring a strong blood mage, and be aware that it will take some time to get through."

"What's in the basement?" Lake demanded.

"A very large summoning circle. Grierson was summoning his father from the demon realm and using the girls' blood to bring him over on the night of the full moon."

"When the boundary between the demon realm and ours is thinnest."

"Yes."

Another pause. "Did Grierson kill the girls to bring his father over?"

I hesitated.

"Tell me," the agent commanded, stepping back up into my personal space.

Despite our height difference, I didn't move away. "Grierson used their blood for the summoning circle. When the demon appeared, he ate them."

Lake staggered back like I'd hit him.

When Michael saw what happened to Maggie, he'd vomited, packed up his scrying mirror, and told me never to call him again. He wouldn't even let me take him home; he called a cab and walked away without a backward glance.

"I'm not sure you'll find any physical evidence showing that the girls died in the basement," I said as Lake visibly reeled. "He probably used a burner spell to clean up the blood, but you may find something else that puts the victims in his house—hair, fingerprints, maybe bone fragments." Michael had told me enough before he walked off for me to know that Maggie hadn't died quickly. Demons liked to play with their food.

Lake stared at me. "Please tell me the Hills don't know how she died."

"No," I said, and he looked relieved. "I told them she was sacrificed as part of a summoning ritual, and it was over quickly."

"What were you going to do with Grierson?"

"At the request of Maggie's parents, I was going to turn him over to the vampires. The Hills believed, as did I, that the best chance for them—and the rest of the families—to get justice was in Vampire Court. They wanted him punished, and the vampires have the facilities to ensure he wouldn't have known an hour of peace for the rest of his long and miserable life. I didn't want Grierson dead; I wanted him to suffer."

If Lake was taken aback by that, he didn't show it. "If he did clean the basement with a burner spell, there might not be any physical evidence left. The Vampire Court could have been the only chance for a conviction. None of the magic-related evidence would have been admissible in human court." He seemed to be reasoning out loud to himself. I let him think.

Finally, Lake turned to me. "All of the victims had long, dark hair and were similar in height and body type. We speculated it was the work of a serial killer."

"I don't think you were wrong," I told him. "He selected his victims based on their appearance. It's possible that if you dig into his past, you'll find the woman he hated, who he felt he needed to kill over and over again. He needed blood for the summoning, but he didn't need to feed the girls to his father. He enjoyed watching them suffer."

After a moment, Lake said, "You went into that bar and used yourself as bait, knowing you were his type. You risked your life to get justice for Maggie and the other girls." I could see grudging respect in his eyes.

I stayed quiet.

Lake turned back to Grierson's body, his face set. "You need to leave. The official report is going to say that we confronted Grierson in the alley and then chased him into the park, where he died resisting arrest. I don't need to tell you that saying anything to the contrary would be inadvisable."

"What about your partner?"

"Parker's report will match mine. I'll be visiting with the Hills privately. Other than sending them a bill for your services, I don't think there's any need for you to have further contact with them, do you?" His tone made it clear that it would be in my best interest to agree.

Ah, there it was: that trademark SPEMA arrogance. It was a good reminder that when it came down to it, even someone like Lake, who obviously cared a great deal about getting justice for Grierson's victims, had no trouble letting me know exactly who had the power in this scenario. I'd identified a serial killer, risked my life to capture him, and revealed what had happened in Grierson's basement, but it was Lake calling all the shots.

If he was worried that I wanted publicity, I could at least dispel that notion. "You can have the credit; I don't care about any of that. If everything had gone according to plan, no one outside the Vampire Court would have ever known I was involved, except the Hills."

"Good." Lake bent down and picked up my phone, healing spell, cuffs, and a few other items Parker had dropped on the ground, and handed them to me, along with my wallet. "Take your stuff and go."

I put my possessions back in my pockets and paused, looking at Grierson's body. It was just beginning to sink in that I had killed him. He was far from the first person to die by my hand, but at least I had no doubt he'd deserved his fate. So many others hadn't. I took a shaky breath.

Lake had his phone out. "What are you waiting for?"

I turned on my heel and headed for the main gate. Behind me, I heard Lake barking orders into his phone. I resisted the urge to hold my side as I walked, even though each step sent a bolt of pain through my ribs. The moon disappeared behind the clouds and I shivered.

Nausea surged, and I paused just outside the park gate, leaning against a lamppost while I swallowed hard. It was the closest I'd come in five years to getting caught. Part of me wanted to run, to put as much distance between myself and Lake as I could, but I forced myself to walk calmly and not attract attention.

My car was six blocks away, eight if I took a route that completely avoided Parker and the alley behind McGovern's, which seemed like a good idea. My feet and calves were starting to hurt, but I could make it. I'd go home, use a healing spell on my ribs, and crawl into bed.

In my mind, in an endless loop, I saw the glint of a blade and the bright green flash of my cold fire, and heard the sound of Grierson's knife going into his brain. I wrapped my arms around my middle and walked, my boot heels echoing like gunshots on the empty street.

2

TWO WEEKS LATER

"The worst part about being a ghost," the ghost confided, "is that you don't get to pick who you end up haunting. I know that seems counterintuitive, but there's a system. Of course, you can put in a request, but there are a ton of forms to fill out, which is a bitch if you're noncorporeal. By the time all the paperwork goes through, what usually ends up happening is you get someone from the priority list—the list of people who deserve to have a demented spirit running around ruining their lives. And that," he added happily, clicking his long, pointed fingernails together, "is how I ended up here with you."

"Fantastic." I sighed.

All three of the ghost's faces were hideous. One visage was alight with excitement, his red goat eyes with their slit pupils zipping around my office, taking in the economical furnishings. Another set of eyes, so black that they seemed more like holes than actual eyes, focused on my MPI license where it hung, slightly crooked, on the wall above my head. The third set, the multifaceted eyes of a spider set in an arachnid head, were fixed on my face. His black robes moved as though hordes of beetles crawled on his body beneath the silk. An unidentified purplish-black goo dripped from his fangs. I had to give him credit: he was thoroughly gruesome.

I blew out a breath. "Look, nothing personal, but I'm probably going to have you exorcised. I can't afford to have a ghost on the payroll; the supe insurance alone would *kill* me."

Three sets of angry eyes focused on my face. "Is that supposed to be a joke about me being dead? Because I find that to be in particularly poor taste."

"Honestly, I really don't care."

Two monstrous mouths fell open in shock. One was full of rows of very sharp, jagged teeth, while in the other, spider fangs clacked in consternation. The third face—the one with the black-nothingness eyes—had no mouth. He'd probably been expecting a much different reaction, based on the form he'd chosen to take. I might not be his first haunting, but I was going to be his last. I had no use for petty ghosts who got their kicks trying to make living humans miserable, even if I had earned my spot on the "priority list."

Some would say that threatening exorcisms or making puns about death to a ghost was cruel, but I'd never really gotten the hang of being nice.

While the ghost sputtered in indignation, I picked absently at the underside of my new desk. A particularly disgruntled client with surprisingly powerful telekinetic powers threw a fit in my office a little over a week ago, and I was still trying to get repairs completed and the furniture replaced. The remains of the old desk, along with pretty much everything else that had been in the office, were now in the dumpster out back. The large cabinet behind my desk, a heavily warded antique, was the only piece of furniture to withstand the dwarf's tantrum. The sole other survivor was my framed mage private investigator license, though it looked a bit worse for wear.

The ghost finally recovered his power of speech and gave me a truly grotesque arachnid smile. "I see you're an MPI, Alice Evelyn Worth," he said silkily. "Surely someone in your line of work has use for someone with particular...talents?"

I scoffed. "How long were you in the Null since your last haunting? Ghosts aren't a new thing anymore. If I need to get results, I'd have better luck summoning a demon, or hiring one of those crazy half-vamps, a dhampir. At least people are scared of them. You. Are. Not. Scary."

The ghost's red goat eyes flared in anger. I met his gaze without fear. He wasn't the first nightmare-form ghost to show up in my life, and I'd dispatched all the others as quickly as they'd arrived. There wasn't anything he could do or say that would make me want to keep him around.

Of course, just as I thought that, he proved me wrong.

The ghost raised his clawed hand. Bright blue-and-green flames danced along his fingertips.

Drawing on my air magic, I threw up a protective circle around me and my chair just as my desk—and everything on it and in it—went up in cold bluish-green flames. In seconds, there was nothing left but ash.

It was my turn to be momentarily speechless. "Well, that's different," I said finally.

Turns out, the ghost had a very particular set of skills—skills that had apparently put him at odds with someone who decided he didn't need to be walking around alive anymore.

Now rather intrigued, I poured myself a cup of coffee from the coffeepot that had, thankfully, been sitting on the little table behind me and not on the second desk I watched get destroyed in the past week. I used my desk generally to make my office look more professional, and to create a psychological barrier between myself and my clients. I'd been forced several times to use a desk as a shield, and twice as weapon. The new desk hadn't been around long enough to be used as any of those things.

The ghost looked disappointed that I wasn't all that upset about the loss of my desk and its contents, but I'd long ago ceased to worry about the destruction of office furniture. When you're a PI specializing in the paranormal and supernatural, it didn't pay to get attached to office décor. Not all my clients left satisfied, and the nature of my business often brought angry supes of various species to my door—which, though heavily warded, has had to be replaced six times in three years. I wasn't very popular with the building's management.

The ghost watched me sip my coffee. I couldn't help but notice he was smirking. The spider mouth might also be sneering, but it was hard to tell. Well, I still planned to have him exorcised, so that ought to wipe those smiles right off. He'd thrown me a pretty epic curveball with the speed and precision of his cold fire, though, and I was curious about his past. If nothing else, I'd be adding to my knowledge of ghost abilities, and that was worth fifteen minutes of talking with this dead jerk.

"Tell me about yourself," I said. With no desk to put it on, I held my coffee cup and made unflinching eye contact with my uninvited guest.

The ghost's goat eyes sparkled with something like humor. Strangely enough, most ghosts found their situation funny, even when their deaths were violent and unexpected. I had yet to figure out why this would be the case. My working theory was that being in the Null for any length of time made them all a little unhinged.

"My name is...Malcolm," the ghost said slowly, as if recalling his own name took a moment. "I was a mage."

I snorted and gestured toward the pile of ash that had once been a perfectly respectable secondhand desk. "No shit."

He made a raspy, wheezing noise that I realized was laughter. While his goat head was speaking to me, the other two sets of eyes went back to looking around my office. The three pairs of eyes looking in different directions were starting to make me feel queasy.

"What kind of mage?" I asked.

"Earth," he said, confirming my suspicions. The cold fire was unique to earth mages. Then he surprised me again. "And water."

My eyebrows raised, despite my intention to stay only mildly interested. "Earth *and* water? That's very unusual."

I carefully opened my shields enough to get a better sense of the ghost's magic. I recognized the cool blue of his water magic and the peaceful green of earth magic. His aura sizzled along my senses. I realized he was definitely a high-level mage, and well trained; his control of his cold fire was precise.

"Unusual enough for me to end up on a good payroll," Malcolm was saying as my senses turned outward again. "It was a good living, for a while." He stopped talking, and the goat's eyes wandered over to look out the window. Since it looked out on the dirty bricks of the building next door, I figured he wasn't lost in the view.

"Let me guess," I said. All three sets of eyes suddenly focused on my face. "Everything was great at first. Then they started asking you to do things you didn't like, then things you didn't want to do, then things you'd swore you'd never do, and then things that made you not be able to sleep at night or look at yourself in the mirror. And then...." I stopped. I noticed that my hands had clenched and forced them to relax.

"And then, I died."

I nodded. These days, it was a common story.

"I worked for Darius Bell." For a moment, the ghost sounded almost proud, but then his shoulders slumped. I was sure at one point he'd been honored to be a part of Bell's cabal, one of the most powerful, wealthy, and well-connected on the West Coast. Hard on the heels of that flash of pride would be the recollection that his boss had him killed—and that for all his hard work and loyalty, he was rewarded with what had probably been a very unpleasant exit from this plane of existence.

The ghost—who I was grudgingly starting to think of as Malcolm, despite every effort not to, damn it—settled in to tell his story. Apparently tired of the effort it took to maintain all three nightmarish countenances, he suddenly re-formed with a single human face and head, with spiky, blond hair and bright blue eyes. His robes turned into a button-up shirt and jeans. His claws retracted into his sleeves, then pushed back out as normal, even delicate-looking human hands.

Transformation complete, he peered at me through the wire frames of quite unnecessary glasses—after all, who'd ever heard of a nearsighted ghost? The affectation was almost quirky, and completely unexpected after the gruesomeness of his nightmare form. I had no idea whether this was how Malcolm appeared when he was alive, but now he looked like a cute librarian.

The total package, I had to admit, was not unpleasant—you know, for a dead guy.

"I went to work for Darius right out of college," Malcolm said. "Well, I say that, but it's not really true. I left college to work for him. Two semesters to go before I had my chemistry degree and probably a decent career as a research chemist, and I let a recruiter hand me a signing bonus and the next thing I knew, I was signing a ten-year contract and moving across the country."

I whistled. A ten-year contract *and* a signing bonus? Malcolm must have had some serious talent. I looked at my noncorporeal guest with new respect.

I felt a familiar hollowness when I thought of the years I spent as a mage for my grandfather's cabal: the sleepless nights, the misery, the blood—both literal and metaphorical—on my hands. Even now, I could see the telltale signs of blood magic in my aura that even the strongest spellwork couldn't hide completely. If it weren't for my spelled tattoos, my bloody history would be visible for any ghost or sensitive to see.

I wrapped my hands around my mug and refocused my attention on Malcolm's face. Behind those superfluous glasses, Malcolm's eyes looked...concerned? Troubled? I raised my eyebrows, waiting for him to continue his story, and hoping he couldn't see anything in my aura but the light smudges of someone who'd only dabbled in blood magic once or twice.

Malcolm went on. "At first, they gave me the best assignments: bringing rain to crops that needed it, enriching the ground for farmers, shoring up land for housing developments, nothing bad or even questionable. I felt good about the work I did. I spent the first year wondering where all those horror stories about the cabals came from. I finally decided the stories were made up by anti-magic activists and people who weren't good enough to work for the cabals. I really believed it was all lies. God, I was so stupid." He hung his head.

I stayed silent. In a weird way, I envied Malcolm's lost innocence; as the granddaughter of Moses Merrum Murphy, I'd never had the luxury of *not* knowing the truth about the cabals. My earliest memories of magic involved the suffering of others, and always—*always*—the pursuit of profit and power, the two things Moses Murphy and Darius Bell and pretty much every other cabal leader, or Davo, lived for.

While there were certainly plenty of smaller cabals out there that had no interest in criminal activities and whose members used their magic to help rather than harm, all of the very powerful ones were organized crime syndicates. These cabals, like any other criminal organization, ran on brutal efficiency, demanded unwavering loyalty, and cared about two things: money and power. There were a dozen major cabals in the US and a host of smaller ones, each run by a powerful Davo and his or her lieutenants. Like the

Mafia, cabals made money through various criminal enterprises. Mages bound to cabals did whatever was required to make these ventures profitable.

Malcolm was speaking again. "So, after about a year of getting the cushy, easy jobs, they started me on the ones I didn't really like very much: causing droughts and floods, destabilizing the ground under particular building projects, disrupting shipping routes. Then they came to me with the rough stuff: landslides, washouts, attacks on construction sites and building projects owned by other cabals. People were hurt. People died. I tried to refuse, but that contract...." He rubbed his wrists with recollected pain, and my own wrists throbbed in sympathy.

I remembered all too well the agony of trying to break a contract once I had been forced to accept it, the crippling white-hot lashes of pain that scoured my body whenever I tried to refuse to carry out an assignment. Even now, just *hearing* the word *contract* still brought on nausea at unexpected moments.

"It got worse and worse," Malcolm continued. "By that time, I realized the stories about the cabals were true—and they weren't even close to the worst things they were responsible for. But something tells me," he said, regarding me much too closely for my own comfort, "that you know that just as well as I do."

"What I know or don't know is none of your business, ghost," I snapped, setting my forgotten mug down on the side table so hard that lukewarm coffee sloshed over the side. I stood.

Malcolm's eyes went suddenly wide with fear. The familiar power of my magic surged and swirled around me. Unlike Malcolm's brightly colored earth and water magic, mine was black and red and purple, dark and malevolent and dangerous. Without me having to consciously call for it, the energy spooled around my fists, waiting to be unleashed.

"Blood magic," he whispered. If it was possible for a ghost to turn pale, Malcolm was doing it.

And now he knew how I got on that priority list.

The midmorning sunshine poured in through my office windows, glittering on dust particles in the air. The light was diffused as it passed through my guest and made strange, indistinct shadows on the floor. We stood unmoving, Malcolm frozen in place with fear, and me struggling to get control of my anger.

It took nearly a full minute, but I pulled the magic back inside myself, and the residual energy faded. When my arms finally stopped prickling, I breathed deeply, sat back down in my chair, and looked across the pile of ash at Malcolm.

Despite his initial fear, he looked calmer now that I no longer seemed like an immediate threat. It occurred to me then that his death could have been at the hands of a blood mage, and that my loss of control might have triggered some very unpleasant memories.

Malcolm eyed me with obvious unease. "I'm sorry I upset you."

"It's fine." I started cleaning up the spilled coffee with a handful of Kleenex. Malcolm waited silently.

Finally, I dropped the gloppy, wet tissues into the trash can and turned back to him. "So, they were giving you assignments you didn't want...," I prompted.

Malcolm nodded. "I had no choice but to do what they told me. I belonged to the cabal for ten years, but I didn't make it that long, obviously. By my fourth year, I was fighting them every step of the way. I'd developed a tolerance for the pain, and it was taking them longer and longer to get me to comply. Sometimes I'd be unconscious for days and they'd end up having to use a different mage who wasn't as strong. I told them I wanted different work or I wanted out of my contract. This went on for another year."

I was surprised Malcolm resisted his contract so openly for that long and survived as long as he did. It was a testimony to how talented he was that a) he'd been strong enough to resist the power of the contract, and b) that the cabal had been unwilling to kill him for resisting. To the end, I doubted Bell really wanted to kill Malcolm. A strong mage with both earth and water magic was a rare gem, one that any Davo would be very reluctant to part with.

"So what finally got you killed?" I asked.

Despite the bluntness of my question, he laughed a little. "Well, that's pretty direct," he said. "I guess they finally got tired of my shit, figured out that I wasn't going to stop fighting. They handed me over to a blood mage. Three days later, I was dead."

I was right, then: he'd been killed by a blood mage. A normal person probably would have felt guilty for unleashing blood magic in front of a ghost who had died that way, but thanks to my grandfather, I had never really been any kind of a normal person. The best I could come up with was some empathy. Those three days had probably felt like three hundred years. I was willing to bet Malcolm had welcomed death in the end; after even an hour with a blood mage, many would. I knew that from personal experience.

Suddenly, realization hit me. "Wait...how are you here?" I asked in confusion. "How did you end up bound to *me*, instead of Bell's cabal?"

Malcolm shook his head. "I don't know. I was under contract when I died, so I should be back at the cabal." He shuddered. Bound ghosts were often simply "stored" in spell crystals and foci, where their energy could be used in spellwork and continuously drained like magical self-charging batteries. It was a horrible fate for any mage. "Unless Darius freed me, but why would he do that?"

"I have no idea. I can't imagine he would let a mage as powerful and skilled as you be unbound."

"But what other explanation is there?" Malcolm asked. "It's got to be punishment of some sort, but I can't think of a scenario where being a bound ghost isn't worse than coming back as a haunt. Sorry about that, by the way," he added.

I shrugged. "Not your fault."

"Maybe he expected me *not* to come back as a ghost, and instead end up in the Underworld. Considering the things I did, I can't imagine that would be very pleasant for me."

I sat back and thought.

Why would Darius Bell do something as unheard of as let a mage's ghost be unbound? Malcolm's theory of punishment was possible, I supposed; death wasn't necessarily the end of suffering. Ghosts, unless exorcised, remained incorporeally on earth, tied to a person or place, tormented by their inability to connect with their loved ones or find peace and rest. If exorcised, they went to the Underworld, but, as Malcolm said, there was no guarantee he'd find any peace or rest there. I didn't know the extent of the things he did while working for the cabal, but I could guess. There were a lot of theories, few of them cheerful, about what happens to those in the afterlife who caused suffering in this one, even if they were coerced into doing so.

So had Bell freed Malcolm so he would be unbound? If so, why? Had he wanted to ensure Malcolm ended up in the Underworld? He could just as easily have destroyed Malcolm's essence completely, wiping him out of existence, but it would mean Malcolm would no longer be suffering. So if punishment was the goal, I could see some kind of logic in sentencing Malcolm to a noncorporeal afterlife.

But somehow it didn't seem right. To say cabal mages never got their contracts nullified and their ghosts unbound would be an understatement. What was less frequent than never? Was there a word for that? Never*er*? Never*est*? That was how often it happened. So this had to be an extraordinary circumstance.

I raised my eyes to look at Malcolm, who clearly shared my unease. "You don't think it's punishment."

"I don't, not in the way you're thinking. It's something else. There's a plan for you. It may involve more suffering—in fact, it almost certainly does—but it's not as simple as just condemning you to being a ghost and haunting someone like me." I fell silent.

Malcolm's face went blank, but I could feel his disquiet as if it was my own. For some reason I couldn't quite articulate, there was something very disturbing about Malcolm's story, beyond the obvious parts about the things he was forced to do while under contract, or his terrible death at the hands of a blood mage. I couldn't shake the feeling there was something going on in Bell's cabal, and that Malcolm being bound to me was a clue to it, which meant I wasn't going to be exorcising Malcolm now or anytime soon, not until I had some answers.

I stood, and Malcolm floated back a few inches. "Well," I said with a sigh, "welcome to Looking Glass Investigations. You're the newest member of the team."

3

Article 1, Section 34.1 of the Supernatural and Paranormal Entity Registration Act stated that I had seventy-two hours to register my new ghost with SPEMA. That, I believed quite sincerely, was going to be a problem. If Bell had indeed given Malcolm his freedom so that the mage would return to earth as a ghost, then he would be watching the Agency's registration system for his name to pop up, and then the entire cabal would be on my doorstep. I had a bad feeling nothing would keep them from taking both of us. It would likely mean either my death, my undeath, or my return to the cabal I'd escaped five years ago. Obviously, I wasn't going to be making that call to the Agency.

"How long have you been dead?" I asked Malcolm, hands on my hips, as I thought about what to do with the pile of ash that had been my desk and its contents.

"Um, I don't know." I glanced at him with raised eyebrows. "Things have been a little crazy," he said defensively. "I wasn't really thinking clearly when I died, and it's not like I had a watch or a calendar. What's the date?"

I told him. He stared at me, clearly stunned. "Two...no, almost three years? I've been gone that long?"

"Apparently." I turned away to give him some space to process that revelation. I went to the storage closet and emerged with a broom, dustpan, and bucket. I'd long ago given up on having carpet in my office and resorted to bare, stained concrete. What it lacked in aesthetics it made up for in convenience when it came to cleaning up the inevitable messes my visitors tended to leave behind. There were other benefits as well; my second sight revealed the shimmer of the circle I'd inlaid into the floor around my chair. The ash had settled around it in a semicircle, the only visible hint of the circle's existence.

"Let me—" Malcolm started to reach for the broom, then stopped with a grimace. "I'm sorry about the mess," he said instead.

"Don't worry about it." I swept ash into the dustpan and then dumped it into the bucket. There really wasn't as much ash as you might think there would be; magical fires didn't tend to leave as much behind as mundane ones. Even entire houses and all their contents could be consumed and leave less ash than would fill the bucket I was using. Memory flooded through me, despite my best efforts to keep those images locked away. My fingers tightened on the broom handle, and for a moment, it was hard to breathe.

"Are you all right?" Malcolm floated a little closer.

"I'm fine," I said shortly, focusing on sweeping. You could never get it all, though, really, I thought absently. I'd have to clean it with more than just a broom or mop to remove the traces of Malcolm's magic. I didn't need anyone knowing I'd had a high-level earth and water mage in my office, much less a dead one.

Once the ash was swept up, I put the dustpan and broom into the bucket and left it sitting in the middle of the floor where the desk had been. "I need to get rid of this," I told Malcolm. "If we're going to keep you off the radar as long as possible, there can't be any of your magic trace left behind, so try not to incinerate anything else. If you do, just use basic earth magic. That's easy enough to disperse."

"Do you think it's possible to hide me from Darius and his people?"

I made a face. "Honestly, I'm not sure how long we can keep you under wraps. I'm not about to register you with the Agency, but that doesn't guarantee your—our—secret is safe."

It occurred to me that the consequences of breaking one of SPERA's most strictly enforced laws would probably mean I'd never see daylight again if we were caught, and if the rumors were true, I'd probably be begging for death before it was all over. I saw a flash of a blood-splattered room and heard an echo of my own screams. Ice seemed to form in my veins, and suddenly my vision tunneled and again it was hard to get a breath.

"...Sit down! Sit down!" Malcolm was saying, as if from a long way away. I found my chair and sat, bending over to put my head between my knees. I focused on breathing deeply and slowly. The ghost hovered a few feet away.

Finally, I raised my head to look at Malcolm. I don't know what my face looked like, but he flitted back a few feet in that way ghosts could move when they got really spooked—so to speak. I smiled mirthlessly at my pun, and something in my expression made him flit again.

"This could be a death sentence for me," I said quietly. "And there are rumors that there are punishments for ghosts as well, not just exorcism. I've heard there are traps that capture the ghost, and...." I paused. "Blood mages designed the traps to torment the ghosts. I don't know the details, but we can assume it would be better for us both if we stay far away from SPEMA."

Malcolm looked anguished.

"If it comes down to it, I'll try to have you exorcised before they can catch you. If that's not possible, I can discorporate you."

His eyes widened as he realized what I meant. My own special set of blood-mage skills included the permanent dispersal of a ghost's noncorporeal form. It wasn't something I did very often, and I'd only ever discorporated wraiths and poltergeists. They were so far gone by that point, they didn't know what was happening to them, but Malcolm would be self-aware enough to know.

I spoke quietly but purposefully. "It would mean a one-way trip to the Underworld, but some might say that would be preferable to ending up in one of those traps. I need to know ahead of time if that's what you want, because we may not have time to think or talk if the Agency or a cabal catches us. I'll have a few seconds at most, just long enough to—"

"Do it," Malcolm broke in. "If it comes to that, send me on. I don't know what will happen to me down there, but I know I don't want to spend eternity in a trap, or back at the cabal being used as a focus." He stopped as realization dawned. "But if you spend those last few seconds taking care of *me*, you won't be able to do anything to defend yourself. They'll take you."

I didn't tell him that I had one final option standing between me and the tortures of the Agency or a cabal. Inside my left leg, a so-called "divine wind" spell was carved into my femur. Only the most sensitive and focused X-ray would be able to spot it, and it couldn't be sensed before I invoked it. It was basically my nuclear option, and one I would never use unless I had no hope of escape. I knew it was a better alternative than the suffering I would have to look forward to at the hands of either the Agency or a cabal. And if my grandfather ever caught me...well, nuking myself would be the only choice. At least I would take a lot of them with me when I went, in true kamikaze style.

I resisted the urge to glance down at my leg and shrugged with a nonchalance I certainly didn't feel. "Odds are, if they catch on to us, they'll send a small army. I'm strong, but not strong enough to take on the kind of combined firepower they'd send. The best I can do is try to keep you from being caught. At some point, we need to figure out why Bell gave you your soul back."

I had no earthly idea how we were going to do that, but what the hell; it was a Wednesday, and I always came up with lofty goals on Wednesdays.

My phone beeped a reminder that I had a downtown lunch appointment with a potential client at noon. I turned to my new ghost companion. "We've got to head out. Can you leave the office and hang out unseen in the hallway for a moment? I need to clean up in here."

Malcolm nodded and vanished. I waited until I could sense that he had gone past my wards before pulling some of the energy to me that had spindled earlier. I focused on the little tickle in my senses that represented the remaining traces of Malcolm's earth and water magic. "*Obliterate*."

The metaphysical blast that radiated out from me would have staggered a less powerful mage, but long years of practice and training kept me steady as the wave swept through my office, taking apart Malcolm's handiwork and dispersing it. The atoms weren't gone, of course; magic still obeyed physical laws. In less than a heartbeat, no trace of ash remained, in the bucket, on any surface, or in the air. In a few minutes, even the trace of his energy would disperse.

The air felt heavy and smelled like ozone, as it always did when I used magic in an enclosed space. I peeked into the bucket for a visual confirmation of what my senses already told me: the ash was capital-G *Gone*.

I stuck the cleaning supplies back in the closet, grabbed my messenger bag, and locked up the office. I could feel Malcolm's presence nearby, like a gentle, distinctly blue-green pressure in my mind, but he stayed invisible as we traveled down the elevator to the parking garage below the office building. Neither of us said a word until we were in my car and on our way out of the garage.

Finally, I gave voice to what had been going through my head. "I have a spell that should mask your energy. To other mages, you should feel like a nonmagical spirit. If you don't attract attention to yourself, it should hold up fine, but I don't have time to do the spellwork right now. To find something that will withstand scrutiny, I'm going to have to do some work. Depending on what this case is, I might be able to look into that tonight. You're going to have to stay invisible until we can work something up."

"How do we keep other mages or ghosts from sensing me in the meantime?" Malcolm's voice was quiet, either because he wasn't manifesting physically, or from apprehension, or both.

"I have a thought," I said slowly. "But you may not like it."

When I walked into Janie's Downtown Café forty-five minutes later, I walked in alone. I told the hostess my name and said I was meeting someone.

She glanced down at her notepad, then pointed. "Redhead in the third booth from the back. She's been here fifteen minutes already." There was clear disapproval in her tone.

I glanced up at the clock and frowned. I wasn't late; it was only just noon. I'd intended to be here ten minutes ago, but construction caused me to have problems finding a place to park. Plus there had been the matter of dealing with Malcolm....

I resisted the urge to touch my right earring and headed for the booth she'd indicated. "Natalie Newton?"

A petite young woman in an emerald-green shirt and khakis looked up, startled. "Yes? Are you Alice?"

"That's me." I sat down across from my client and studied her. Her hair was a remarkably bright red. A smattering of freckles made her look younger than she was. I guessed her at about twenty-five. She was very thin. Her hands played with her teacup while she fidgeted under my gaze. I sensed no magical ability in her.

"How can I help you?" I asked. "Your message indicated that you're worried about some missing items."

Natalie dropped her eyes to the table and sighed, rubbing her forehead. "Yes, that's right." Her voice was as thin as the rest of her. "My grandmother passed away about three months ago." She paused.

I'm not very good at social cues, but even I could figure that one out. I murmured, "I'm sorry," and she nodded graciously.

"Thank you. It was a car accident; a drunk driver swerved over the center line and hit her. My grandmother raised me after my parents died when I was ten, and I'm an only child, so...it was hard." Her eyes filled with tears.

I waited. No one had come by to ask if I wanted something to drink, so while Natalie was sniffling and wiping her eyes, I waved at a server and mimicked drinking a cup of coffee. She gave me a quick smile and headed for a coffeepot.

Finally, Natalie cleared her throat. "My grandmother left me everything. I have three aunts and an uncle and some cousins, but they hadn't really spent much time around Grandma for years, so...." She shrugged. "I was surprised, since I thought I'd be dividing things with the rest of the family, but her will was pretty clear. I own the house and everything in it, as well as her money." She didn't sound happy about it. Inherited money was often bittersweet, but I got the impression there was more to Natalie's unhappiness than just her grandmother's death.

"How is the rest of the family taking the news about the will?" I asked as the waitress brought my coffee.

Natalie made a face. "Some of them aren't taking it well at all. My aunt Elise hired an attorney to argue that my grandmother wasn't of sound mind when she made the will, which is such a terrible thing to say about her own mother." Her eyes filled with tears again. "I don't think anything will come of it, since there are plenty of folks who will testify that she was thinking very clearly. In the meantime, my grandmother's lawyer got me a restraining order to keep them out of the house, but it's not Elise's lawsuit I'm worried about."

She took a long drink of hot tea and looked at the cup like she wished it held something a lot stronger. "I think one of my aunts or uncles has stolen things from my house. And...." She swallowed hard, coughed a little, and looked away. When she met my eyes again, there was real fear in her gaze. "I think I'm being poisoned."

I sat back and looked at her more closely. Her hands trembled with more than just emotion, her eyes looked dull and listless, and I saw that instead of healthy pink, the skin under her fingernails was white and bloodless, as if her circulation was poor. Clearly something was wrong, but it could be as much anxiety and grief over her grandmother as anything else. "What makes you think you're being poisoned?"

She gestured at her body. "I've lost almost twenty pounds in the last few months, and it's not because I don't eat. Or *try* to eat, at least. I'm always nauseous, and often I can't seem to keep anything down. I've been to four doctors, and they all run tests and then tell me it's a stomach bug and it will pass. I know what they're thinking: I'm depressed about my grandmother, I'm worried about my aunt's lawsuit, I'm making myself sick. But I swear to you that's not what's happening."

Natalie leaned forward and reached out, as if she wanted to grab my hand. I picked up the coffee mug and took a drink. Generally speaking, I don't like to be touched.

If Natalie felt slighted, she didn't let on. Instead, she took a drink from her own cup, her hands shaking. Finally, she said, "I don't care if you don't believe me either, but I just want someone to take me seriously, and no one else will listen to what I'm saying. That's how I ended up calling you; the last private investigator I called told me that I might be better off talking to a PI who specializes in unusual cases, and I got your number from the Internet. I'm willing to pay you to find out what's going on. I need to know if I'm really being poisoned, and by whom. And why, although I can guess," she added bitterly. "I loved my grandmother, and I love our home, and the things we shared. My aunt and the rest of them don't care about Grandma at all. All they want is the money, and all they see when they look at the house and what's in it is what they could sell it for."

"You said some things were missing," I said. "What's missing? Valuables?"

"Not really, not in the way most people would think. It's books that are missing." She looked at me like she expected me to scoff at her. I got the feeling others had.

Some people wouldn't be concerned about missing books, but I was intrigued. There were all kinds of books: books that educated, books you read at the beach or on planes, books that sold bad advice...and books that could level whole cities. I wasn't psychic, but I had an inkling that the missing books weren't celebrity memoirs. Suddenly Natalie's grandmother and her house were a lot more interesting.

Finally, a harried-looking server came by to see about food orders. Natalie made a little face and ordered a salad with chicken, dressing on the side. I ordered my usual: a grilled cheese and bowl of tomato soup.

After the server left to put in our orders, I turned my attention back to Natalie. "I'd like to come take a look at the house, especially the place where the missing books were kept, and we can talk more about the rest."

Natalie's eyes got big. "You believe me?" she asked hopefully, and I could see in her expression that my belief meant a lot more to her than I thought it would.

I imagined myself in her place, going from doctor to doctor, being told not to worry, that it was just a stomach bug that would pass; week after week, month after month of no one listening. It must have felt very hopeless and lonely and frustrating. Still, I tried to be as honest with potential clients as I could be. "I'm not sure of anything yet."

Her face fell.

I held up my hand. "I am certainly willing to believe your intuition may be right," I added. "I think we have...special senses sometimes, and that we don't listen to our instincts as much as we should. So if you think there is something going on here, I'll help you find out for sure."

As fast as she'd withdrawn, Natalie's face lit up with pure happiness. "Thank you." Her eyes filled with tears again. She cleared her throat as our server brought the food and we focused on our lunch.

I attacked my sandwich and soup like a starving werewolf, but Natalie, despite her flash of joy, only picked at her salad. She watched me eat with undisguised envy. It probably didn't say anything good about me that even her obvious misery didn't affect my appetite. I'd only had a piece of toast for breakfast, and doing the kind of magic required to clean up after Malcolm, plus capturing and hiding his energy in the earring dangling from my right ear, had drained me somewhat.

Thinking about my ghost, I felt the urge to fiddle with my earring, and once again I forced myself not to draw any attention to it. I'd used my crystal earrings to smuggle magical energy, spells, and even a fragment of a poltergeist once. (That was a long story that involved the destruction of several cars, a storage building, and a small section of a local cemetery.) This was the first time I'd hidden a ghost in one of them. I'd spent many hours crafting the earrings by hand to be both pretty and functional. Unless someone physically touched my right earring, there would be no way to know a powerful ghost resided in it.

I used the last bites of sandwich to mop up what was left of my soup. Natalie had eaten about a fourth of her salad and given up, sipping her water while I ate. When I finished, I pushed away the soup bowl and reached for the check.

Natalie snatched it up. "Let me. It's the least I can do for you listening to me."

"Thank you." As Natalie handed her credit card to the server, I asked, "Are you available to go back to your house right now and have me look around?"

"Absolutely." A little life came back into her pale face as she signed the receipt. We stood, I slung my bag over my shoulder, and we turned to leave.

At that moment, the front door of the café opened and three SPEMA agents walked in.

For mundane humans, their presence was supposed to be reassuring, or so I have been told. For this reason, most agents displayed their credentials and wore Agency jackets or vests everywhere they went. Their visibility was designed to give people a sense of security in a dark and scary world full of monsters and magic and things that went bump in the night.

For supes and mages, however, agents were far from comforting; on their word, someone could be hauled away in spell cuffs, or even put down on the spot if deemed a danger to citizens' property or their safety. It didn't take much to be labeled a threat and killed. It was most common with supes like shifters, vamps, half-demons, and dhampirs, but it happened to mages too.

I evaluated the newcomers in a split second with the practiced eye of someone who had spent her entire life avoiding contact with agents whenever possible. Their body language was natural and relaxed. While the blond man in front spoke to the hostess and held up four fingers, the other two scanned the room, not as if they were looking for anyone in particular, but just keeping an eye on their surroundings. My conclusion: it was simply lunchtime for them as well.

Time to make a casual exit via the side door. I turned to Natalie. "Where are you parked?"

"Two streets over, on Powell."

Drat; that was in the direction of the front door. "Well, I'm in the garage. Walk with me? I'll take you to your car."

"Sounds good!" Natalie followed me as I wove between the tables toward the garage entrance.

Just as we made it through the lunchtime crowd and approached the side door, it jingled open.

Special Agent Lake stood inside the door, three feet in front of me, his hand on the door handle and eyes locked on my face.

4

As Moses Murphy's granddaughter, I never had the luxury of anonymity—not from the public, the Agency, or anyone else. Even as a child, I was famous, and feared. My face was known, even if the extent of my skills was a closely guarded secret. Moses kept me on a short leash, cultivating my mystique by leaking information now and then, teasing outsiders with hints and rumors about what his granddaughter was capable of doing.

I remained in the public eye until my escape. I moved across the country, established a new identity, earned my MPI license, and redefined myself in a world that hated and distrusted my kind. I had to leave behind the name and the face that were so well known to so many. Alice Worth bore little to no resemblance to the deceased granddaughter of Moses Murphy, physically or otherwise.

In my new life, I kept my head down and avoided all publicity and contact with SPEMA. Anonymity was key to my survival. Being instantly recognized by a SPEMA agent was not in the plan.

Lake's stare became impersonal. Apparently, we were going to pretend not to know each other, which was fine with me.

"Sorry, wasn't looking where I was going," I said politely.

"Not a problem." Lake studied us for a moment, then stepped aside to hold the door open for us to walk past him into the alley. Behind me, I heard the door close.

The tension faded from my shoulders with every step away from the diner. "I think I'm parked on the fourth level," I told Natalie, heading to the garage elevator. "I'll drop you at your car and follow you back to your house."

"Thanks!" Natalie hummed quietly to herself as we took the elevator up.

I ferried Natalie to her car in my blue Toyota, a nondescript three-year-old sedan that worked well for surveillance. To my surprise, she drove a bright red Mustang convertible, which was definitely not the type of vehicle I thought she would be driving. I followed her out of the downtown area and toward the west side of the city.

As I drove, I thought about Special Agent Lake. Two days after Grierson's death in Fields Park, SPEMA announced the half-demon the media had dubbed the "Full Moon Stalker" died trying to elude capture. The public reacted with predictable horror at the news that Grierson had sacrificed the six known victims as part of demon-summoning rituals. Lake and Parker appeared on a handful of national news channels for bringing Grierson's reign of terror to an end. I watched one of their interviews on CNN. Lake looked uncomfortable in the spotlight, but Parker seemed more than happy to take the credit for catching Grierson.

I never did send an invoice to the Hills. I don't know what Lake said to them, but they mailed me a sizable check anyway. I made a donation to a women's shelter in Maggie's name and sent flowers to her memorial service.

After a fifteen-minute drive, Natalie turned into the driveway of a tidy single-story house, and I parked at the curb.

There was a Lexus SUV parked in the driveway when we arrived. The back window featured several stickers representing extremist anti-magic organizations and anti-supe hate groups. Fantastic.

Natalie parked next to the SUV and flew out of her car to confront a middle-aged bleach-blonde in a lime-green designer track suit. The woman stood on the front porch holding a high-end digital camera. I watched for a moment to gauge their interaction.

When Natalie started yelling, I decided it was time to find out what was going on. I grabbed my bag and exited my car.

"You have no right to be here," Natalie shouted as I strode across the yard. "The court has ordered you to stay off my property. Get out of my house!"

"I am not *in your house*," the woman said, in a snotty tone I would have thought was impossible for someone who was not sixteen years old. "I am on the porch of *my mother's house*, and by the time my lawyers and I are done, you won't be living in it."

This must be Aunt Elise. "Excuse me," I said loudly.

The woman turned on me. "Who the hell are you?"

"An order of protection prohibits you, your vehicles, and your agents from stepping foot on or in property owned by Ms. Newton. At this moment, you are in violation of the law and I am dialing the police." I held up my phone and began hitting buttons.

"Who is this?" the woman demanded of Natalie.

"I am Ms. Newton's representative." I advanced on Natalie's unwelcome guest with an expression that caused her to step back before I got within ten feet of the porch. "I have one more number to push before I hit Call, so you have approximately five seconds to get out of here before you'll be needing bail money."

Elise glared daggers at me. "This is my mother's house," she hissed, but she headed toward her SUV.

"What's on the camera?" I asked.

Elise clutched it to her chest. "None of your business," she spat. Then she saw my crystal jewelry and her face switched from fury to terror and back to fury as she put two and two together and rounded on her niece. "Who is this *freak* you're bringing into my mother's house?" she screeched. "I won't allow it!"

I hit Call on my phone and waved it. Elise's face turned tomato red as she sputtered expletives. I stared at her impassively. I'd looked full demons in the face and been flayed alive by a blood mage, so the wrath of a soccer mom didn't faze me in the least.

I acted like someone had answered the phone while it rang in my empty office. "Yes, this is MPI number 230492-394." I rattled off my license number. "I would like to report a violation of a protection order—"

"*Bitch!*" Elise screamed and hurled a small potted plant at me before running to her SUV. I flicked out a finger and used a tiny stream of air magic to soften the plant's landing so that it came to rest unharmed in the grass three feet to my right. Elise jumped into her SUV, slammed the door, and backed out of the driveway, narrowly missing my car. She flipped me off and shouted a few more curses out her open window before peeling out, tires squealing.

I sighed and joined Natalie on the porch. She sat on the front step, sobbing.

I stuck my phone in my bag, returned the plant to where it belonged, and leaned against the porch railing while my client cried herself out. It took a while.

Finally, Natalie wound down. Sniffling, she got up and unlocked the front door. I paused outside the threshold, getting a sense of the place.

Someone who had lived here was *definitely* magical. Judging by the faded magic I could sense, I was betting it was the recently deceased grandmother. Odd that Natalie had no such talents; they usually ran in families. There were wards on the house, but they had faded without upkeep from their creator.

I touched the doorframe gently, running my fingers along its smooth wooden surface. I closed my eyes and listened to the house.

It sang. It was beautiful. There had been a lot of love within these walls.

"What are you doing?" Natalie's voice was curious.

Slowly, I opened my eyes and looked at the young woman as she stood, still shaken, in the entryway to the home her grandmother had left to her. Strangely—since such sentimentality was very unlike me—I felt compelled to do what I could to find the secrets of this house and protect both it and Natalie from those who would wish them harm. This house had told me it was worth saving—that they were *both* worth saving.

"Listening to the house. May I come in?" I asked.

She looked surprised. "Do you have to have permission, like a vampire?"

"No," I replied, smiling despite myself. "It's just polite to ask. And also, incidentally, it's not true about vampires either."

She paled.

Looking around Natalie's living room, I wondered if she had changed much of anything after her grandmother's death.

The deceased had been very fond of cats, it would seem; in addition to four actual cats living there, the décor was cat-themed. There were cat sculptures, cat paintings, cat knickknacks, cat-shaped rugs, cat refrigerator magnets, photographs of cats in cat-shaped picture frames, and even a wall-mounted grandfather clock with different breeds of cats as the hours. Normally this level of obsession would have irritated me, but for some reason, it didn't. It was like a peek into a world of a sweet, cat-loving, old granny I'd certainly never known.

The grandmother's room had been kept more or less the same since her passing; Natalie confessed a reluctance to clean it out and use it as her own. I made a noncommittal sound. Due to my unique upbringing, I lacked not only social etiquette but also most of the sentimentality that seemed to make life difficult for those who were more sensitive. The master bedroom was much larger and had its own bathroom. From my perspective, it would be a better room for Natalie to live in.

The master suite also connected directly to the library, the room I was most excited to see. Natalie opened the door and walked inside. I started to follow her in—

—and was promptly knocked on my ass with a hard *zap* of magic that singed my shirt, sucked the air out of my lungs, and left me seeing honest-to-God stars.

Startled, Natalie yelped as I fell. Since she was nonmagical, she could not have seen or felt the bolt that hit me; it would have just looked like I ran into an invisible wall and went down.

Dazed, I propped myself up on my hands and wheezed.

The library door pulsed with wards that had been dormant probably since the grandmother's death. They'd flared to life with my attempt to unknowingly trespass, and now I could feel them sizzling on my skin.

The power of the wards was enormous. That probably meant the library had been where the grandmother practiced her craft and kept important books. It would be warded with the strongest whammies she could cook up—spells that would not have faded as easily as those around the house. The wards seemed designed to permit passage to specific individuals, since Natalie was able to come and go freely.

I was furious with myself for not being more cautious. Even though I hadn't sensed any magic inside the house, I should have used a spell to detect hidden wards. In fact, I was lucky I hadn't blundered into deadly black wards. Mistakes like that can cost a mage her life.

Natalie was speaking to me. "Are you all right? What happened? Did you faint?"

"I'm fine, I'm fine," I said crossly, embarrassed by my carelessness. I swatted her hands away and hauled myself to my feet, shaking my head to clear the cobwebs. Damn it, my shirt was ruined. There was a scorched two-inch hole just to the left of my breastbone. Double damn. Through the hole, I saw an angry red burn over my heart. *Triple* damn. If I'd walked into those wards right after the grandmother's death, right now I'd be hanging out in the afterlife with her.

I suddenly had way more respect for Natalie's grandmother, and a hell of lot of questions. First, I had to see if I could untangle these wards so I could get into the library.

"Um, Alice? Ms. Worth?"

I'd almost forgotten about Natalie, who looked at the hole in my shirt in confusion.

Well, even *I* knew this would be an awkward and possibly very upsetting conversation. In a situation like this, there was only one thing to do.

"Do you have any coffee?"

Much to my dismay, Natalie was a tea drinker and did not have so much as a single coffee bean in the house.

Some time later, after we'd consumed an entire pot of tea and I'd eaten several homemade oatmeal-raisin cookies, Natalie sat in stunned silence in the living room, a cat in her lap and two others on the back of the couch next to her.

I sat in an armchair across from my client, holding a bag of frozen peas to the burn on my chest and waiting for her to process what I'd told her. It was a lot to think about, I supposed, wiping cookie crumbs off my ruined shirt.

Finally, Natalie stirred and rubbed her forehead. "So...my grandmother was a mage."

"Yes," I said, somewhat impatiently. "She had very strong skills with air magic, and possibly fire. I need to take a closer look at the wards on the library to know for sure."

Natalie frowned. "I thought mages only had one kind of magic."

"Most do," I told her. "Magic of any kind is rare; they say less than a half a percent of humans have it. Of those, almost all have only one of the four types of natural magic —earth, water, air, or fire—but some have two kinds. I have both earth and air. Some mages have what's called blood magic."

"That's death magic, right?" Natalie said.

I hesitated. "It's highly volatile dark magic, and it's illegal, but it's not necessarily 'death magic.' It has other uses."

Natalie was quiet for a bit. "This is a lot to take in. It's not that I don't believe you...."

"I understand," I said, even though I didn't. Magic just *was* for me; it wasn't a thing to be believed or not. "If she never showed any of her abilities to you, and kept them so well hidden that her family didn't know, she did it for a reason, possibly to avoid the kind of reaction we saw today from your aunt."

"Oh my God, my aunt." Natalie's eyes widened. "Her *own mother* was a mage, and she hates supes and mages so much."

I shrugged. "People are ignorant. They're afraid of what they don't understand. There's a lot of anti-supe propaganda out there that people like your aunt believe. Maybe if she'd known about your grandmother, she'd think differently, but who knows. Prejudice and bigotry aren't logical."

"Aunt Elise *cannot* know about this," Natalie said vehemently. "If she did, she'd burn this house to the ground."

I thought about Elise's hateful eyes and didn't disagree. "Well, she won't hear about it from me, but if she came here with someone who was sensitive, they could tell the house has wards. That wouldn't prove your grandmother was a mage," I added at Natalie's sudden look of panic. "Lots of non-mages have protective wards on their houses; it's more effective than hiring an alarm company. If someone encountered the wards on the library, though, they'd know for sure someone who lived here was a mage. They might think it was your grandmother, or they might suspect it was you."

Natalie looked terrified, but she needed to know the truth. Hiding it from her could only do more harm than good.

"Here's my thought. I need to examine the wards on the library closely to understand them. If I can take them down, I will, then replace them with my own. That should divert suspicions. I can also put wards on the house to help prevent any more trespassers from getting in, including your aunt."

Natalie looked hopeful. "Really? That's great!" She paused. "Will it hurt her?"

I considered the possibilities. There were aversion spells, or even stronger options, if you wanted to take a more aggressive approach to home defense. My mind conjured up an image of Aunt Elise going up in a bright green fireball, and my mouth twitched. "Not too much," I said finally. "At least, not unless she gets overly enthusiastic about getting in the house. In that case, she might get a nasty surprise."

Natalie grinned. "Good."

Two hours later, I sat down on the grandmother's bed and wiped sweat off my forehead. While the house wards were easy to take down and replace with my own, the wards protecting the library were another thing altogether. The spellwork was exquisitely complex.

I discovered her grandmother had set the wards so Natalie could come and go safely through them. The intensity of their defense was based on the strength of the mage trying to cross them, which confirmed my initial evaluation that those wards would have killed me if I'd walked into them when they were at full power. Anyone without magical ability would feel an aversion to the library, which probably meant the rest of the family would simply avoid going in without giving it much thought. Whatever was in that library was both magical and worth killing for, but not something the grandmother feared Natalie would find.

Of course, all this begged the question of how someone would have gotten in there to steal the books Natalie said were missing, but I'd cross that ward when I came to it.

I had to admit unraveling the wards by myself would take at least a day. Conveniently, I'd recently made the acquaintance of a ghost who also happened to be a very strong mage. I was willing to bet he was at least decent with spellwork.

I took a piece of chalk from my pocket and drew a circle around myself on the floor, then removed my right earring and held it in the palm of my right hand. Against my skin the earring buzzed as if it held a very slight electrical charge. "*Release.*"

"*Holy shit!*" Malcolm yelled.

I jumped. Malcolm, still in his cute librarian ghost form, stood in my circle, looking shocked. I broke the circle with the toe of my boot, and he flitted back away from me, half disappearing into the grandmother's neatly made bed.

"Holy shit!" he shouted again.

"Hey, buddy," I said. "How are you doing?"

Malcolm flew around the room, a ghostly whirlwind. "That...freaking...*sucked*," he declared as he zipped around. Trying to keep track of him made my eyes cross. "It was so dark. It felt like forever, or a second, or both. I don't know!" He came to a stop in front of me. "*Please* don't put me back in there," he begged. "It was awful. There has got to be another way."

"I'll try to think of an alternative. But hey, in the meantime, you wanna help me with something?"

Malcolm paused to take a closer look at the hole in my shirt. "What happened to you? That looks nasty."

"It could have been a *lot* worse." I gestured over my shoulder at the doorway to the library.

That brought an end to his snit. "Whoa," he said in awe, gliding over to take a look at the wards. As a ghost, they would be evident to him, like neon signs. "This is grade-A work. Kind of faded," he muttered to himself. "They must have been *intense.*" He sounded impressed.

"Hey, Alice? Who are you talking to?" Natalie appeared in the doorway to the bedroom, steaming mug of tea in hand, looking around the room as if she thought someone was hiding.

Well, hell, in for a penny.... I walked over to where Malcolm was reading the wards and grabbed his arm. I funneled energy into him, and Malcolm went from invisible to partially opaque. "Natalie, this is my ghost, Malcolm. Malcolm, meet Natalie Newton, my client."

Natalie stared at Malcolm. After a moment's hesitation, Malcolm waved.

Natalie walked over and sat on her grandmother's bed. "Wow," she said weakly. "This has been a *day*."

I let go of Malcolm's arm and he went invisible again, but Natalie sat on the bed and watched me have a one-sided conversation with thin air.

After about ten minutes of careful scrutiny, the ghost pronounced that together he and I could dismantle the wards in a couple of hours.

"I need to rest for a bit," I said. "That zap earlier really got me, and that was on top of all the other magic I've used."

"Take all the time you need." Malcolm's eyes were on Natalie. "So, what's her story?"

"We can talk about that later," I said, frowning at him. Natalie, who could only hear my side of the conversation, looked puzzled. "He's asking about you."

"Oh, he hasn't been here all along?" Natalie asked.

"Well, he was, but not in a form where he could listen."

"Damn right I wasn't," Malcolm griped.

I glared. "Well, that's gratitude."

He looked abashed. "Sorry. I know you're doing your best for me, but...."

"I know it was rough," I said. "If there is any other way to hide you, I'll try to think of options."

"Why does he have to hide?" Natalie asked.

I debated how much to tell her and decided on a portion of the truth. "He's in hiding from someone who wants him for a reason we don't understand. So if anybody ever asks you about Malcolm, you never saw him."

"Saw who?" Natalie quipped.

"Exactly."

Malcolm grinned. "I like her. She's cool."

"Settle down, Ghost of Don Juan." I lowered myself to the floor and folded my legs with practiced ease. I placed my hands on my knees and began to breathe deeply and evenly, closing off outside distractions as I sought the calm, centered core of myself that would help me focus on the serious business of unraveling someone else's wards.

For whatever reason, that calm center was difficult to find. I supposed it had something to do with the surprise arrival of a mage's ghost, a narrow escape from SPEMA agents, and a new client with a loud-mouthed bigot of an aunt and a mysterious magical grandmother with near-deadly wards.

It took several minutes, but I was finally able to relax. I meditated until I felt sure I was prepared to do the dangerous work ahead of us, and then I opened my eyes.

Natalie was curled up on her grandmother's bed. At first I thought she was asleep, but her eyes were open and she seemed to be looking through the open door into the library. I might have been imagining it, but I thought she seemed to have a bit more color in her face and sparkle in her eyes than earlier in the day.

Malcolm was still examining the wards, his fingers moving as he formulated a strategy for unraveling them.

"What was your grandmother's name?" I asked, my voice breaking the silence of the room.

Natalie jumped. "Morrison. Betty Morrison."

The name didn't ring any bells. I got up and stretched. Natalie rose as well. "You should probably go into the other part of the house, just in case."

She looked disappointed. "I was hoping to watch you work. Will it really be dangerous?"

I considered. "Probably not for you, since the wards were tuned to let you in and out, but everything we're going to be doing will be invisible to you since you aren't a mage. If you want to stay in the room with us, I'd be more comfortable if you would at least sit over there to the side, away from the wards."

"Okay." Natalie moved to the far side of the room and sat.

Malcolm hovered next to me. When I slipped into my second sight, I saw the complex runes connected by threads that pulsed like power lines. The wards formed a perimeter around the library at floor level, with additional reinforcement around the doorway. The wards were orange and white, the signature colors of fire and air magic.

Faint black threads were the last remaining evidence of how deadly the wards had once been. It wasn't hard to imagine that anyone running into them when they were at full strength might have been reduced to a smoking ruin. Betty Morrison had been playing hardball. I rubbed my chest.

"How do you want to do this?" Malcolm asked.

I contemplated the wards and the threads connecting them. "Could you break it?"

He tilted his head, considering. "Maybe, but honestly, I'm not comfortable doing that. It looks like there is a *lot* of energy still stored up in there. There's no telling what it will do if we break the ward, since the person who set it isn't here anymore to control the flare. We might level the house, or take out the entire neighborhood. If we cast a circle strong enough to contain the surge of energy, we'd have to tap a ley line to hold it, and that would attract a lot of attention we definitely don't need."

I sighed. "That was my assessment too. An unweaving would probably work best. That's gonna take a while." I rolled my neck and shoulders to loosen myself up. "Give me a minute to get focused, then find me."

I closed my eyes and opened the tiniest chink in my shields. The wards buzzed on the edge of my senses like a hive of bees. Slowly, I reached out with my magic to feel the threads of Betty's wards.

The fabric of the wards pulsed in a tapestry of runes and power. I observed the threads, feeling my way through them to understand the patterns. I sifted through the wards like fingers moving through the finest beach sand. The wards were works of art, and I regretted having to destroy them.

As my shields lowered, I could sense Malcolm's magic. It was lovely, colorful and light, with none of the darkness mine held. His magic was like a symphony playing Beethoven. By comparison, mine sounded like a bunch of xylophones falling down the stairs. With a jolt, I realized I was actually jealous of a ghost.

As quickly as the feeling flared, I squashed it. Now was *not* the time. Even faded by time and lack of maintenance, Betty's wards could be dangerous, even deadly if we lost control over them during the unweaving. I had to stay focused. Everything else would have to wait.

Slowly, painstakingly, I slowed the sifting of the sand until I could feel individual grains. Vaguely, I was aware of Malcolm following my lead. I focused my senses on a single mote of power. Using my own magic, I slipped inside it and pulled gently, and it fell apart with a tiny pulse of energy and a sound like a distant chime. Somewhere near and yet in another universe, I heard and felt another chime as Malcolm took apart a different thread. It tugged on my awareness, like someone gently pulling at a single hair and then letting go.

Two grains of sand gone from the beach. I focused on my task while somewhere on the edge of my awareness, Malcolm did the same. The wards began to fall.

5

Hours later, I hugged the toilet in the master bathroom and heaved miserably. My stomach felt like it was full of razors, and I tasted blood. I was aware Malcolm was hovering nearby while Natalie stood outside the bathroom door, but I didn't care much about either of those things.

The moment the last thread of Betty's wards disintegrated, agony and nausea ripped through me, sending me fleeing on rubbery legs toward the nearest bathroom, half-blind with pain. I barely had time to slam the door closed and fall on my knees in front of the toilet before I threw up everything I'd eaten today, and then it felt like I threw up everything I'd eaten in the last week. The spasms that racked my body were so violent, I was surprised my shoes didn't come up too.

"Alice, what should I do?" Malcolm's hands felt ice-cold on my shoulders.

Blinded by pain and sickness, I flailed at him. "Get away!" Another spasm tore at me. This time, I threw up mostly blood. Dimly, I thought, *Shit...that* cannot *be good.*

Through the haze, the rational part of my mind figured out that I had triggered a curse hidden within the wards designed to punish anyone who tried to disassemble the library's protections. Curses and spells concealed within other spells, commonly known as landmines, were one of the most dangerous hazards mages faced when interacting with unknown spellwork, since they were virtually undetectable until tripped.

This landmine didn't seem to have affected Malcolm; it was possible it simply did not include noncorporeal beings as targets. I couldn't really think about it very much right now. The pain was endless.

I heard Natalie through the door, asking if she should call for an ambulance.

"No," I rasped. "No," I said again, louder, so she could hear me. I convulsed and vomited blood so violently that it splattered across the toilet and floor. I spat several times and wiped my mouth with the back of my hand. "No ambulance. I will...be...okay," I managed to say. I hoped she heard me.

A minute passed, and though I dry-heaved and spat up more blood, the worst of the vomiting seemed to have passed. The pain was lessening by degrees. I flushed the toilet again and lay down on the cold tile of the bathroom, shivering with shock. My vision had gone gray, and vertigo made the bathroom spin around me.

The bathroom door swung open. "Oh my God," Natalie said, horrified. After a moment, I heard soft noises and water running, and then a cool, wet washcloth began cleaning my face.

I had no strength or will to move, so I let her clean me up a little while sensation crept back into my limbs. I didn't realize I'd closed my eyes until water trickled over one eyelid. I opened my eyes and was somewhat surprised I could see again.

Natalie appeared, a bloody washcloth in her hand, her eyes wild with fear. "Can you hear me?"

I took a ragged breath and whispered, "Yes."

"What happened?" Natalie wiped my face gently with a different, cleaner washcloth. "I don't know what to do to help you."

"You...don't have to do...anything," I said, my voice gaining some strength. "I will be okay."

She looked incredulous. "There is blood *everywhere*." I thought she might be on the verge of losing it completely.

I tried to move but stopped when it felt like broken glass ripped through my stomach. I moaned and curled up in a ball. "Don't call anyone," I whispered. "I just... need to rest." Then I let go and passed out.

The next time I opened my eyes, the pain in my stomach had faded to a dull ache. For a moment, I was disoriented and confused, my mind a jumble of fractured memories and pain. I remembered lying on the cold tile in the bathroom, but what was under me felt warm and soft.

When the fog cleared a bit, I realized I was on the floor in Betty's bedroom, wrapped in a thick cocoon of heavy blankets and quilts. I turned my head and saw Natalie sitting on a pillow next to me, her back against the bed. She was focused on her phone, tapping on the screen and frowning.

I felt a jolt of fear. "Who are you calling?"

She jumped and dropped her phone with a clatter. "Nobody!" she said, sounding defensive, scared, and angry all at once. "I was reading what to do for someone in shock that didn't involve calling 9-1-1." She stared at me pointedly.

I closed my eyes. "Okay." I cleared my throat gently. It was still raw and painful from vomiting. The gross taste in my mouth defied description. "Okay," I repeated, opening my eyes again to look at her. "I just...can't go to a hospital." They'd run tests, call SPEMA—or, if I was really unlucky, my grandfather—and I'd disappear.

Natalie picked up her phone and put it on the bed behind her. I noticed she was even paler than before. My condition must have really frightened her. "I'm glad you're awake," she said. "I didn't know how long you'd be out. You were shivering so badly, I got every blanket in the house and wrapped you up in them." She gestured at my blanket nest.

"Thank you." I felt weak but clearheaded, which was good. I'd half expected to wake up dead. "I'm sorry about the mess in your bathroom. When I can get up and around, I'll clean it up." The way my arms and legs felt, it might be a little while before I was mobile, though.

"Don't worry about it. It's clean."

I sighed. "Oh. I am so—"

"I didn't do it," Natalie interrupted me. "The ghost did."

Welp, I was completely awake now. "Malcolm?"

She nodded.

I looked around the room and saw my ghost hovering near the door to the library—a doorway no longer blocked by wards. He looked like he'd expended a lot of energy. "Did you use magic to clean the bathroom?"

Malcolm shrugged. "I had to. I didn't know when you were going to wake up, and all that blood...." He shook his head.

"Thank you." My blood could never be left behind. It could be used against me and was one of the few things that could connect my current life as Alice Worth to my real identity. Despite my order to not call an ambulance, Natalie might have done just that if my condition hadn't improved, and Malcolm had done his best to protect me.

The windows were dark, and it occurred to me that I had no sense of how much time had passed. "What time is it?"

"About eleven o'clock," Natalie told me. "You've been unconscious for almost three hours."

Whoa. So the unweaving of the wards had taken something like four hours, then I'd been knocked out by what I was now sure were the remains of a landmine, no doubt put in place by Betty and designed to bring an abrupt and agonizing end to the life of anyone brave or foolish enough to try and dismantle her wards. My admiration of Betty's skill rose another couple of notches, along with some other less pleasant emotions arising from the fact I'd been hurt twice in one day since coming into contact with the dead woman's magic.

I started to wonder if all the cutesy cat crap in the house was camouflage. Who was Natalie's grandmother? Why would she put black wards around her library, then double down by hiding a death curse within them? And what the hell was in that library?

I tested my arms and legs and found that strength was creeping back into them. I started peeling back layers of quilts and realized I was in my bra and underwear. "Where are my clothes?"

"Soaking in cold water," Natalie said. "They were really bloody. I'll get you something to wear."

"How did I get into the bedroom?"

"I rolled you onto a blanket, then slid you across the floor into the bedroom. I wish I could have put you in bed, but I couldn't pick you up."

"Thank you for what you did," I told her sincerely. I realized Natalie was sweating and looking a little unfocused. "Are you okay?"

"I don't know. I don't feel very good." She shivered hard.

"Alice—" Malcolm began, his voice urgent.

Natalie gasped and white magic flared around her hands for a split second before it vanished. She sagged back against the bed, her eyes wide with panic.

"She's a mage!" I shouted at Malcolm as I kicked frantically to get myself loose from the blankets that were tangled around my legs. "Malcolm, knock her out and drain her! *Right now!*"

Malcolm got to Natalie just as she shrieked and an orange fireball erupted from her hands. I dove to one side to avoid it and heat rolled over me.

Natalie's cry cut off abruptly. When I looked back, she was on the floor, unconscious, and Malcolm's hands were on her shoulders, draining her magic as fast as he could pull it. He began to glow.

I finally freed myself from the blankets and staggered to my feet, dizzy and achy. I was cold but didn't have time to worry about trying to find clothes. "Do we need a circle?"

"I don't think so," Malcolm said tersely. "I'm almost done."

"Did you hit her with a sleep spell?"

"Yes." Malcolm drifted back from Natalie's body. He was so bright from the surge of energy, I had to squint a bit. "She's drained for now, but we need to bind her magic. A blood magic spell would be stronger than my earth or water magic."

"I'm low on magical energy right now, but I think I have enough to bind her." I knelt beside Natalie and used a hidden edge in my ring to open my right index finger, then pulled down the back of her shirt to expose her right shoulder blade. I drew a rune on her back in my blood and used most of my remaining energy to bind her magic. My blood hummed with power, then the mark faded.

I used the bed to push myself to my feet, and Malcolm and I looked down at Natalie as she slept.

"It looks like Granny Betty isn't the only person in the family with a secret," I said.

"Do you think she knows anything about her magic?"

I shook my head. "I don't believe she knows. I'm thinking Betty found a way to hide Natalie's magical ability from everyone, including Natalie."

"Why would Betty not want Natalie to know about her own powers?"

I shrugged. "Could be lots of reasons. Betty hid her abilities well, probably to stay off the Agency's registry. Maybe Betty was worried Natalie would screw up and out the whole family so she cast a suppression spell—more likely a shitload of layered spells—to bury Natalie's abilities so deep that even Natalie doesn't know she has them. Then Betty died without releasing the spell or telling Natalie the truth."

I had a new emotion to add to my complicated feelings toward Betty: disgust. What did she think would happen if Natalie's magic escaped the binding spells?

Malcolm moved over next to me. "Those would have to be some powerful spells. I mean, *seriously* powerful. And why are some of those powers breaking out now?"

"It might have something to do with the fact Betty's wards are fading and we just finished unweaving the wards on the library. There was a lot of power in those wards." I pressed my hands to my aching stomach. "Maybe some of that power was anchoring the binding spells on Natalie. We disrupted them, and now the cat's out of the bag." I glanced around at all the cat décor. "So to speak."

Betty's magic had been impressive, and she'd been an expert at wielding it, as the library wards and the pain in my chest and stomach could attest. How much power did Natalie have?

"We've stumbled into a mess here." Malcolm gave voice to the thoughts in my head. "What are we going to do?"

I sighed and rubbed the bridge of my nose. "We have a couple of choices." I was startled to notice how easily I'd started using the pronoun *we*. "Worst-case scenario, unweaving the wards started a process and Natalie's powers will manifest in full, like a dam breaking."

"That could be bad."

I snorted. "Yeah. If she's got as much power as Betty did, and it flares, she could level the house, or worse. She'll have no control, no discipline, no training. SPEMA will put her down. The only question is how much destruction she'll cause before they nuke her, and how much collateral damage there will be when they do."

Malcolm looked stricken.

"Best case," I continued, "her powers manifest slowly enough that someone can train her." Who the hell that person might be, I had no idea. I didn't even know anyone who could—or *would*—take on an adult whose magical abilities had been suppressed her entire life. I'd have to find someone powerful and trustworthy enough to control Natalie's magic until she could. I sighed. I'd have more luck finding a unicorn, and no one had seen one of those on this side of the fae realm in more than a hundred years.

"Well, we know she has both fire and air magic, but how much she has, I don't know. It was a small flare, but for all we know, she's as strong as her grandmother."

I realized Malcolm was very studiously avoiding looking at me in my underwear. I glanced down at myself. "I need clothes. I'm going to find something to wear and get my go-bag out of my car so I can clean up."

"While you're doing that, I'll start working on the library wards. You don't look like you have much magical energy left."

"I don't. The binding spell took about everything I had." As Malcolm moved over to the library door, I went in search of clothes. A few minutes later, wearing one of Natalie's T-shirts and a pair of her yoga pants, I hurried barefoot out to my car, got the black duffel bag out of the backseat, and returned to the house.

I used the toiletries in my go-bag to shower, and then put on jeans and a comfy T-shirt that advertised a great local supe band with a half-demon lead singer named Cam who'd shared my bed for a sizzling-hot six weeks. After I was clean and dressed and had brushed my teeth, I felt almost human again.

When I returned to the bedroom, Malcolm was putting wards on the library. He was focused on his work, so I sat cross-legged on the bed and gently rubbed my sore abdomen as I watched him. His fingers were quick and deft, forming runes and symbols, stringing them together, and then layering the strands. He was using earth magic only, and I couldn't see or sense anything that might lead anyone to believe they were placed by anyone other than a strong earth mage. It was exquisite workmanship.

By the time he finished with the wards, it was almost three a.m. I had gone from sitting up to lying down on the bed. When Malcolm finally turned around, his energy looked somewhat depleted, but he looked like he had enough left for me to pull from. I might not be powerless for much longer if he could be talked into sharing with me.

I'm not usually one for compliments, but I had to give him credit. "The wards are incredible. Some of the best I've ever seen."

Malcolm smiled. "Perimeter wards are one of my specialties."

I sat up slowly to avoid strain on my sore stomach. "Looks like mostly aversion spells, but the defenses are going to hit mages pretty strong."

He glanced back at the wards. "Yeah, I figured we want to keep anyone out who has magical ability, until we know what's in there." He paused. "Do you want me to set it so that Natalie can pass?"

I thought about it, then shook my head. "We better not, until we know how much magic she has. We don't know what Betty left in the library."

Now I had a decision to make, and I found I wanted Malcolm's opinion on it. "Should we put the stronger spells in?"

He looked at me. "Like the ones that almost killed you?"

"Yeah." We were silent for a moment. "There's something in there that Betty was willing to kill to protect. Until we know what it is—or was—I'm wondering if we need to up the threat level on the wards."

Malcolm went quiet and frowned while he gave that some serious thought. "If I funnel enough energy into these wards, and we maintain them, they'll incapacitate up to a half dozen mages trying to get in at once. If you want black wards and landmines, that's not something I can do—not something I *will* do. I did enough for Darius. I'm done with death."

I rubbed my face. I could do them, if I had enough energy. I didn't even need my blood magic; my air magic was strong enough that I could replicate both the black wards that had burned me and the landmine I'd tripped during the unraveling. I was running on fumes, however. Time to test our partnership. "If you let me siphon energy from you, I can set the wards."

Malcolm and I stared at each other. I had no idea what he was thinking about me or my request. It had been a rough day for both of us. He'd been threatened with exorcism and stuck in an earring. I took two big hits from deadly wards and now I was as low on magic as I could ever remember being.

I let him think.

Finally, Malcolm made a decision. "If you take enough energy from me to do what you need to do, I'll be very weak for a while. You'll have to hide me and protect me until I get my strength back." He looked at my earring with a grimace.

I took a deep breath and slid off the bed. "I will try to figure out a better way to hide you. I can't promise it will be much of an improvement, but maybe there's another option. For now, we've got to get these wards up, and then I'm going to go out."

"Go out?" He glanced at the clock. "By the time you do all that, it will be four o'clock in the morning."

"I know. It's cutting it close, but as long as I get there by five, he'll still be there."

"Who will be where?"

"I've gotta go see a vampire."

"A vampire? What vampire?"

"His name is Charles Vaughan. He's a member of the Vampire Court."

Malcolm flitted back in surprise. "You know a member of the Vampire Court?"

"I've worked for them for a couple of years. Charles is a friend. More importantly, he's a broker."

"A broker? Of what?"

"Treasures and secrets, mostly." I smiled. "Charles likes to say that he buys and sells only things that are priceless. Also, he knows people who know people. If we're going to find a master mage to teach Natalie how to control her magic, I'll need his help."

"Okay," Malcolm said finally. "I guess we better do this, huh?"

I took Malcolm's arm, closed my eyes, and reached out with my senses until I felt the hum of his magic. I began to draw it into myself, slowly at first, then faster as our connection opened wider.

Malcolm's magic tasted sweet and pure, like rain. I felt parched, like I'd been stranded in the desert for days without water, and had to fight not to siphon every drop. When I felt him getting weak, I closed the connection between us and released his arm.

Energy rose and crashed within me like an ocean wave breaking on a beach. I kept my eyes closed and allowed it to settle into me, soaking into my bones. Even when it was at rest in my skin, I felt buoyant, lighter on my feet.

I opened my eyes. Malcolm hovered in front of me, almost invisible. He opened his mouth, tried to speak, then shook his head. I hadn't left him with enough energy to communicate.

I reached out my hand and he took it.

I'm sorry. I took too much, I thought at him.

His eyes widened in surprise at hearing my voice in his head. He focused on me and thought back, *It's okay. I should probably...rest.*

With my other hand, I reached up and touched my earring. "*Contain.*" The spell flared, and Malcolm vanished. The earring buzzed; the ghost was in residence.

The room felt emptier without Malcolm's presence. I shook my head. *Don't be ridiculous,* I thought. *Stay focused.*

Upgrading the library wards didn't take long; I knew the spellwork well enough to do it in my sleep. I upped the aversion spells for nonmagical intruders and then set black wards for magical trespassers.

I frowned at the door to the library. I really wanted to know what was in there, but I wasn't about to go into Betty's library low on magic. The woman had put black wards around it and woven a death curse into them. Who knew what was waiting in there?

For now, I needed to put Natalie in bed and get to Hawthorne's before Charles went to sleep for the day. My client was such a tiny thing, but I was still weak and sore. As a result, it was embarrassingly difficult and painful to hoist her up onto the bed and get her under the covers. I took her shoes off and tucked her in.

I replaced Malcolm's sleep spell with a compulsion that would wear off in about six hours. Natalie murmured and snuggled deeper under the covers. Because of the spells, she'd wake a little confused, and probably with no memory of her magic breaking free. That was good, because I really didn't need her to panic when she woke up.

I found a pad and pen on the nightstand and jotted a quick note: *You fell asleep while we were working, so I put you in bed. We're still working on making the library safe, so don't try to go in there yet. I'll give you a call in the afternoon. Alice.*

I propped the note up on the nightstand where she'd see it, made sure I had all my belongings, and locked the door on my way out. After I checked to make sure the house wards were up, I headed to my car and took off for Hawthorne's.

6

Hawthorne's was one of the few bars I really enjoyed frequenting. Named for a famous literary friend of its owner, it sat in the trendy neighborhood known as The Heights, in the middle of a block of very expensive retail lofts all owned by Charles Vaughan. Its patrons tended to be late twenties and older, professional types more likely to be discussing stock portfolios over expensive bourbon than sports over beers.

Since Hawthorne's was open until dawn, it was popular with both human night owls and nocturnal supes. Despite the diverse clientele, things generally stayed peaceful. There were two main reasons for that: Adri and Bryan, two of Charles's enforcers who often worked as security to keep an eye on the crowd downstairs while their employer conducted business in his offices above.

When I walked up, Adri stood at the door checking IDs. As always, the tall woman wore all black—black turtleneck, black pants, black boots—with her shoulder-length, brown hair in a ponytail. With her height, her striking features, and a body toned by mixed martial arts and free climbing, it was impossible not to feel intimidated next to her, even if you didn't know she could pick a grown man up and toss him across the room.

"Alice." She greeted me with a half hug.

I squeezed her back with real affection. "How are you, Adri?"

"It's a slow night. It's good to see you, *chica*. You here for fun or business?"

I sighed. "Business, unfortunately. Is Charles in?"

"He is. Go talk to Bryan."

"You're a doll," I told her.

She snorted and waved me in.

The inside of Hawthorne's, like its owner, radiated subtle elegance: all dark wood, low lights, and brass fixtures. Patrons took up only about half of the tables and booths, talking in low murmurs over the sound of clinking glasses and Eddie Money on the jukebox.

Pete, the manager and my favorite bartender, was pouring out shots in a long row on the bar. He grinned as I came up. "How you doing, Alice?"

"Doing okay, Pete. How have you been?"

"Not too bad." He finished pouring the last shot with a flourish and slid the bottle back onto the shelf behind him. "What can I get you?" A waitress put the shots on her tray and headed off to distribute them.

I started to ask for a beer, then shrugged mentally. All things considered, I thought I deserved a real drink. "Scotch. The good stuff."

Pete reached up to the top shelf as I slid onto a barstool. He poured me two fingers of whisky and pushed the glass over.

I took an appreciative sip. "Is Bryan around?"

A hand the size of a catcher's mitt landed on my shoulder. I somehow managed not to drop my drink and screech as Bryan's laugh rolled through the bar. "Damn it, Bryan, don't do that!" I scolded him, giving his massive bicep a punch that hurt my hand but only made him laugh harder. I scowled and nursed my drink.

"Mr. Vaughan is meeting with a client," Bryan said when he finished laughing at my expense. His voice sounded like boulders rolling down a mountainside. "If you can wait, I'll let him know you're here and take you up when he's available."

"Not a problem." I jerked my chin toward the back of the bar. "I'll be over there whenever he's ready."

My favorite booth was in the corner, where I could sit with my back to the wall and watch the bar. There wasn't much light in the back, and the lamp that hung over the table hadn't worked in ages, which was why it tended to be a popular booth for couples, or solitary souls trying not to be noticed. I sipped my Scotch and retreated into the shadows, staring off into the distance while my mind wandered.

My solitude lasted for all of about five minutes before a deep voice interrupted my thoughts. "Can I join you?"

I looked up.

The tall, dark-haired newcomer wore jeans and a button-up shirt and held a bottle of craft beer. Ruggedly handsome and muscular with about two days' worth of stubble, he had the casual confidence of a man used to hearing yes to that question. As delectable as he looked, what I liked most was the way the corners of his eyes crinkled when he smiled, as if he smiled a lot.

Despite the flutter in my stomach, I took a drink of my whisky and gave him a level stare just this side of unfriendly.

Apparently undaunted, he propped an elbow on the back of the seat across from me and raised his eyebrows.

I should say no. Then again, it had been a long day, and he wasn't the worst-looking man in the bar. "Why not."

He grinned and dropped into the seat opposite mine. "I'm Sean."

I hesitated. "Alice."

"Hi, Alice." Sean set his beer down on the table and stuck out his hand.

I stared at him and thought about how the last time a man tried to pick me up in a bar, he ended up dead with a knife in his eye.

Sean waited.

I reached out and shook his hand briefly. His skin was very warm.

"What are you drinking?" he asked.

I saluted him with my glass. "Dalwhinnie."

He looked surprised, but pleasantly so. "Rough day?"

"You could say that."

"I know what you mean." Sean leaned back in the booth, stretching out. His right leg brushed against mine. "Sorry," he said. He didn't look all that sorry. I was pretty sure he'd done it on purpose. Maybe it was the Scotch talking, but I didn't really mind. "I had to work overtime, didn't get off till three. Then I didn't feel like staying home, so I decided to go out for a drink."

"Where do you work?"

"I own a private security firm." I liked that he didn't say it as if I was supposed to be impressed. "One of my employees called in sick for the second time this week and I had to cover his shift. I think he's got a new girlfriend." He laughed and I smiled. "So, tell me about yourself, Alice. What do you do?"

I took a drink to give myself a moment to think. Normally I claimed to be an administrative assistant if anyone asked, since most people started peppering me with annoying questions if I told them I was a mage private investigator. If he was private security, though, he probably wouldn't be all that awed with my job, or ask me how many vamps I'd staked—three—or if I'd ever seen a full demon—yes, right before I sent him back where he came from. "I'm an MPI."

"Wow, I never would have guessed."

I gave him a flat look. "Why? Because I'm female?"

"Not at all." Sean smiled good-naturedly. "I actually know several female mage PIs. We have a couple on retainer as consultants, but all the ones I know are ex-law enforcement, and you don't strike me as a LEO."

I took that as a compliment.

He finished off his beer. "So what's keeping you up tonight? Working late on a case?"

"I was," I said. "Client meeting ran late. I decided to stop by to see…a friend."

"Oh?" Sean looked around the bar. "Is she…or he…joining you here?" He was plainly wondering if I was meeting a date.

"Sort of." I glanced around for Bryan but didn't see him. I supposed that meant Charles was still in his meeting and wasn't ready for me. "I guess he'll be around at some point." I shrugged. Part of me was impatient, wanting to talk to Charles about finding a master mage to help with Natalie, but I found myself enjoying Sean's company.

I raised my glass and drained the rest of my Scotch. I caught Pete's eye and pointed at Sean's beer, holding up two fingers. He gave me a thumbs up, grabbed two bottles from the cooler, uncapped them, and headed our way.

As Pete put the beers down in front of us, Sean spoke up. "Thanks. You can put her drinks on my tab."

"Oh no," I said. "That's not necessary."

"Please, let me—"

Pete looked back and forth between us, his eyebrows raised.

"No, thank you," I said. "I've got it." I didn't want any misunderstandings between us. Men who buy drinks for women in bars near closing time get certain expectations. Sometimes soon I'd be leaving him sitting at the table whenever Bryan came back to get me, and that would be that.

"Okay, okay." Sean held up his hands in surrender. "Just thought I'd offer."

"I appreciate it."

Pete took Sean's empty bottle and my glass away and returned to the bar. I asked

Sean what brands of craft beer he liked, and we talked microbrews for a while. As I was telling him about a popular local beer I enjoyed, I noticed him studying me intently, his brow furrowed.

I broke off in midthought. "What?" I asked.

"Alice, are you hurt?"

I frowned. "Why do you ask?"

"You've been flinching, and you're holding your stomach like you're in pain."

I realized my arm was wrapped around my sore abdomen and I hadn't even noticed I was doing it. I moved my left hand on top of the table and straightened. "I'm fine."

"What happened?"

I lifted one shoulder in a careful half shrug. "I ran into some black wards at my client's home earlier in the evening and tripped a landmine hidden in the spellwork."

I watched several emotions—surprise, anger, then alarm—cross Sean's face as he processed what I told him. "Black wards *and* a landmine? Aren't those both deadly?"

I shook my head. "Not always. These were just very...intense. I survived."

"Do you need to go to a hospital?" Sean looked me over, I think for visible injuries.

"Seriously, I'm fine," I insisted. "No permanent damage. I was lucky. I know better than to just walk into a room without checking."

"I'm a security consultant," Sean reminded me. "Can I do anything to help? Was the person who set the wards arrested?"

I shook my head. "Really, I can't talk about it. Client confidentiality."

Sean looked unconvinced, but he sat back, apparently willing to let it go, at least for now.

Despite how self-conscious it made me, I appreciated both his concern and that he took my word that I was all right. Since my parents' murder when I was eight, I hadn't had anyone to fuss over me when I was hurting. Even now, five years after my escape from my grandfather, I didn't spend much time around what few friends I had, and wasn't used to others worrying about me. The only people I counted as friends were Adri, Bryan, Pete, and maybe Charles, if a vampire could be said to be anyone's friend. The longest dating relationship I'd had was with Cam, the singer, and that was pretty much just sex. My fear of being found out kept me from getting close to people.

Looking across the booth at Sean, I suddenly felt lonely. I'd long ago accepted my isolation as a condition of being in hiding. It wasn't like me to feel maudlin about it, but to my horror, my eyes burned with angry tears. I hoped the bar was too dark for him to see them.

I took a drink and stared absently in the general direction of the front door. I caught sight of Adri turning away a pair of teenage boys. They watched with wide eyes as she tore their fake IDs in half twice and handed them the pieces. The offenders slunk away, dejected, and Adri smirked, leaning against the doorway. She caught my eye and winked.

"Alice?"

I blinked.

Sean was leaning toward me again. I got the impression he'd been talking, and I hadn't heard a word he'd said. "I'm sorry, I spaced out for a minute. What did you say?"

"I was asking what was wrong."

I forced a little laugh and glanced at my phone. If I was going to see Charles, it would have to be soon; dawn was an hour away. "Like I said, it's been a long day. I'm not sure my friend is going to have time to see me tonight, and I'm starting to get tired. I'm just not the best company right now."

Sean reached out. I started to pull back, then forced myself to be still as his hand covered mine.

I'm so tired of being afraid. The vehemence of my own thought startled me.

"You okay?"

"Yes. I'm all right." I curled my fingers around his and his grip tightened.

The part of my brain that was always on guard, always worried about giving myself away, wanted to yank my hand back, but the warmth of his skin felt good. It occurred to me that the stress of the day—Malcolm's troubling story, a run-in with Special Agent Lake, two close calls with Betty's wards, and Natalie's magic manifesting unexpectedly—had left me feeling out of sorts. On another night, I'd probably have told Sean to go away. I might never have told him what I did for a living, or let him hold my hand. Knowing that on an intellectual level didn't change how good his touch felt, however, or how much I appreciated having a good-looking man show interest in me.

Sean brushed my palm with his fingertips. "Is your friend not coming?"

"I'm not sure. He said he'd be along, but...." I shrugged. "It's getting really late."

"Or early, depending on how you look at it," Sean joked. "The sun will be up soon."

"I know." I finished my beer and toyed with the bottle.

We studied each other. "What are your plans if your friend doesn't show?" Sean asked finally.

"No plans per se. Probably just home to bed."

The subtext hung in the air between us like a chandelier.

"I'd like to take you home," Sean said.

My brows shot up. So much for subtext.

Sean chuckled at my expression. "You seem like the sort of woman who doesn't play games. You've probably already decided if you're interested in me or not. Now that I've gotten to know you a bit, I thought I'd take the direct approach and see what happened."

I nailed him with a look. "What do you think you know about me?"

Sean leaned forward, meeting my gaze—and my challenge—head-on. "You're a private detective. You work hard, you're loyal to your clients, and you aren't afraid of the risks that come with the job or going in where others fear to tread. You're tough, and other people's respect is important to you. You don't like to be the center of attention, but you want the person you're with to listen when you talk. You're on constant alert. I bet if I asked you to close your eyes and describe every person in here, you could do it. And you enjoy good Scotch, good beer, and good music."

I tilted my head. "Leaving the other items aside for the moment, how do you know what kind of music I like?"

"I've been watching your reactions to the songs that played while we've been sitting here. You liked Guns N' Roses, scoffed at Starship, and lost your train of thought twice while listening to 'Purple Rain.' That tells me a lot about you right there."

"It *is* a great song," I mused.

"Alice."

We both looked up. *Way* up.

Bryan stood at the booth, looking at our hands with raised eyebrows. Suddenly self-conscious, I pulled back from Sean and put my hands in my lap. "Yes?"

"Mr. Vaughan sends his regrets. Unfortunately, he won't have time to see you tonight. Unless it's an emergency?"

I thought about that. Charles and I had known each other for almost five years, but you had to be very careful around vampires. The situation with Natalie probably didn't qualify as the kind of emergency that would justify pulling him out of his meeting, and if he got angry with me, he might not help me.

I sighed and shook my head. "Not an emergency, Bryan, but if you could get me in to see him tomorrow night, I would appreciate it. I have a situation where I need his advice."

"I'll put you on the schedule and text you a time," Bryan said. "Do you need a lift home?"

I wasn't drunk, but the Scotch and the beer on an empty stomach had given me a buzz and I knew I wasn't okay to drive. I frowned.

Sean spoke up. "I was just about to offer Alice a ride home."

Bryan focused on Sean. "Oh?" He managed to pack a lot of suspicion and distrust into that one word.

Sean returned his gaze, totally unfazed, then both men looked at me. I had a decision to make.

Bryan could get someone to take me home. Probably Pete, or either he or Adri if I hung out while they closed.

Or I could call a cab.

Or I could do something completely irresponsible and ask a security consultant with beautiful eyes to give me a ride home.

What the hell. "If you could take me home, I'd really appreciate it," I told Sean. He grinned.

Bryan didn't look happy about my choice. "Call up here when you get home. We'll drop your car off in a few hours."

"You are such a sweetie. I'll go settle up with Pete." I slid out of the booth and walked to the bar.

"You headed out?" Pete asked me as he ran my credit card.

"Yep." I filled out the receipt, left a generous tip, and handed him my key. "That's for my car. Bryan said he'd drop it off in a bit."

Pete stuck the key in his pocket, then printed off Sean's tab. Sean handed him a twenty and a ten and told him to keep the change.

"Thanks, buddy." Pete dropped the tip into the jar before turning to grab a bottle from the beer cooler.

"After you." Sean gestured grandly at the front door. We said good night to Adri as we passed.

Sean's car was a silver Mercedes, and he'd managed to get a parking spot right near the door. I sank back into the leather seat and buckled in. Sean put my address into the car's navigation system, and we were off.

We chatted about music as the car glided smoothly and quietly through the nearly deserted city streets toward my neighborhood on the east side. I leaned my head back and closed my eyes as Sean talked. Despite my interest in what he was saying, I found myself drifting.

I jolted awake when I felt Sean's hand on my arm. "We're here," he said softly.

I looked out the windshield and rubbed my eyes. We were parked in my driveway. It was a twenty-five-minute drive from Hawthorne's to my house, and apparently I'd been asleep for most of it. The car's engine was off. I got the feeling we might have been here for a couple of minutes before he'd woken me up.

I stretched and something popped in my back. "Sorry I fell asleep," I murmured, fumbling around for the door handle.

"It's okay." I heard the smile in his voice. "Your snore is adorable."

I gasped and turned back to face him. "I do *not* snore!"

We stared at each other in the faint blue light from the dashboard. In the east, I could see streaks of orange and red on the horizon. Dawn was breaking. Desire stirred the air like a fan.

I'm not sure who made the first move, but we suddenly closed the distance between us. Sean's kiss was hungry, and his stubble scoured the skin around my mouth. I ran my fingers through his thick hair and held on as the kiss deepened. When our tongues met, it felt like a shock ran through my body. He pressed me back against the seat, his hands coming up to touch my face. The warmth in my belly from the Scotch moved lower and I made a little sound.

When we came up for air, Sean held my chin. His eyes looked very bright in the early dawn light. "Do you want to go in?"

I took a moment to consider. That guarded part of my brain was still voting that I end the evening here and now, but my hormones were redlining and my desire was drowning out the anxiety. Besides, I had a lot of built-up tension and stress from the day that I wouldn't mind working out of my system. "Let's go inside."

Sean kissed the tip of my nose. We got out of the car and I led him up the sidewalk to the porch.

As I unlocked the door, I ran my fingertips along the doorframe to lower the house wards. I opened the door and stepped inside with Sean behind me. I shut the door and raised the wards again. They would let us out, but anyone trying to get in would get a nasty surprise.

I switched on the light in the foyer and Sean looked around. I'd bought the house, a beautiful but neglected Victorian, for far less than it was worth when I first arrived in the city. The previous owner had passed away, and his children lived out of state and didn't want to deal with fixing it up before they sold it. The neighborhood wasn't fancy, but it was quiet. After extensive renovations, the house was beautiful, if simply furnished.

I turned to put my bag on the small table by the door. Sean wrapped his arms around me and trailed kisses up my neck from my shoulder to my jaw. As I leaned back against him, he burrowed his face into my hair and inhaled deeply. I shivered and turned around to take his hand. "Upstairs."

Sean let me lead the way. When we got to the landing, he followed me down the short hall to my bedroom.

We stood in the middle of the room, looking at each other in the light from the streetlight. He really was a fine-looking man.

Suddenly, Sean twitched, as if he'd just thought of something. "Call the bar."

"What?"

"You were supposed to call the bar to let them know you got home safely," he reminded me.

Oh. Right. I dug my phone out of my pocket, pulled up my contacts list, and scrolled down to the *H*'s.

The phone rang four times, then: "Yes." A familiar rumble.

"Hey, Bryan, I'm home."

"He dropped you off?"

I looked at Sean. "Yep," I lied.

"Are your house wards up?"

"Yep."

"You going to bed?"

"Yep." That's me, the witty conversationalist.

A pause. "Good. We'll drop your car off in about an hour. I'll text you about seeing Charles tonight."

"Thanks. Good night."

"Good night, Alice."

I ended the call, put the phone on my nightstand, and looked at Sean.

"Why did you tell him I dropped you off?" he asked, his voice mild. I couldn't tell what he was thinking.

I shrugged. "None of his business either way." I leaned down and unzipped my right boot, then slid my foot out. I did the same with the left, then pushed them aside.

Sean watched me silently. There was something fierce in his eyes, and I liked the intensity of his gaze. He waited for me to make a move, to let him know what I wanted.

So I did.

I grabbed a handful of his shirt and pulled him to me. Sean crushed my body to his and lifted me. I wrapped my legs around his hips and clung to him, kissing him hungrily. He took a couple of steps forward and we dropped onto the bed. My hands fumbled at the buttons on his shirt while he slid his hands up over the skin of my stomach. He helped me get my T-shirt off over my head, and then I went back to unbuttoning his shirt. My fingers were clumsy from urgency.

Evidently, I was taking too long. He made an impatient noise and pulled his shirt and undershirt off, revealing a muscular chest that looked like it belonged on the cover of one of those cheap romance novels. I stared at him in wonder.

He paused, looking down at me. "What's wrong?"

"Not a thing." I gently raked my fingernails across the flesh of his hard stomach, leaving scratches I couldn't see in the dim light. He made a growly noise and kissed me hard while he lifted my torso and unhooked my bra. It went flying and suddenly his mouth moved from my lips to my right breast. My back arched and I moaned as he licked my nipple, then gently sucked, watching me as he teased me with his tongue.

I wanted his skin on mine, but his jeans were out of my reach and I made a complaining sound.

Sean chuckled and rose, unbuttoning my jeans. I wiggled as he pulled them off, leaving me in my underwear. He stood above me, shirtless, jeans riding low on his hips, looking me over like a starving man in front of a five-course meal.

I stretched my arms above my head and looked at him through half-closed eyes, running my bare foot up his leg. "Are you waiting for a formal invitation?"

In a flash, he was back on top of me, pinning my hands to the bed while his mouth teased first my right breast, then my left. His hands slid down to my hips as I trembled. It had been months since I'd been touched.

I felt a tug on my Wonder Woman underwear and looked down. Sean was sliding them off slowly, his eyes on mine, looking for permission. In answer, I raised myself up a little and he grinned, and then the underwear was gone too. When his gaze moved down and settled between my thighs, I blushed.

Sean moved up my body to kiss me. "You are so fucking beautiful," he said roughly.

I started to make a snarky comment about him not having to pile on the compliments since I'd already invited him to my bed, but then he did something with his fingers that made me forget what I was going to say. Sean's mouth trailed down my throat, and his tongue moved slowly down my abdomen to my navel, where he gently tugged on my belly-button piercing with his teeth. When I moaned, he slid down the bed, bent his head, and licked me.

I cried out, arching my back. The resulting pain in my stomach was no match for the pleasure. I clutched his head with my hands, my fingers in his hair, as he raised my hips and caressed me with his tongue.

Soon, I was shuddering under his touch. I felt like if he wasn't inside me soon, I'd lose my mind. I tried to pull him up, but he refused to budge. The pleasure was too intense, and I was reduced to begging. "Please. *Please*."

I felt him move away and heard the sound of his shoes falling on the floor, then a zipper and the rustling of clothes. When I opened my eyes, he was naked, and I swear my heart skipped a beat at the sight of him.

"Condom," I said breathlessly, reaching for him. There was no chance of me getting pregnant, but it was always best to be safe.

He produced a small square packet as if by magic, rolled the condom onto himself, and returned to the bed. Despite his attentions, it had been a while and he was a tight fit. He groaned and I screamed again, my nails digging into his shoulders. Starbursts filled my vision as I wrapped my legs around him. I cried out, but it sounded like someone else. I'd never felt anything so good in my entire life.

A wonderful pressure began to build low in my abdomen. I opened my eyes and looked at him. He was sweaty and gorgeous in the morning light, his eyes on my face, watching me closely as I moved beneath him.

Suddenly, in the midst of the passion, a bolt of fear made my stomach clench. The nagging worry I'd managed to drown out earlier was back at the worst possible time. I was afraid of being found, of being caught, of losing control and being vulnerable. I went from delirious with desire to guarded and tense. I was suddenly unable to lose myself in the moment, and the climax that had begun to build faded. I closed my eyes in despair and my grip on Sean's biceps loosened.

His movement slowed. "Alice?"

I opened my eyes.

Sean bent down to press his lips to my ear. "Let go," he told me, moving his hips in some magical way that made me cry out. "Let go. I've got you." He kissed my ear, then bit it.

I looked into his eyes. Maybe he saw my fear; he seemed to be able to read me pretty well. "I've got you," he said again, this time with more force in his voice. He cupped my face with his hand and held my gaze. "Let go. Come for me, beautiful girl." He shifted position a bit, catching my knees with his forearms. My gasps turned into one long cry.

As the rush of pleasure swept over me, I let go of my fear, my anger, and the worry I would be found, and did something I had never done before: I threw off the tight control I kept over my magic, and as Sean began to shudder, my magic poured out of me and rushed around us in a hurricane of green-and-white energy. I thought I heard things crashing in the background as he groaned, but I didn't care. I lost myself in the storm.

Sean collapsed onto his forearms to keep from putting all his weight on me. My magic drew back inside me and settled into my core. Through the haze, I could feel that my energy level was nearly back to normal. Good sex can build magical energy quickly, and that was *very* good sex.

I was still breathing hard, my heart racing. Sean looked down at me, his eyes dark with passion, and nuzzled my neck. "Holy shit," he breathed into my ear. "I don't know what just happened, but that was incredible."

I couldn't have spoken if my life depended on it, but I definitely agreed with his assessment.

We lay there for a few minutes to catch our breath, then Sean slowly disengaged and got up while I stayed where I was. He disappeared into the bathroom. I heard the toilet flush and the sound of water running in the sink.

He returned to the bedroom, still naked, and pulled the covers back. He scooped me up and I squawked. He laughed and settled me into the bed, then climbed in beside me and pulled the covers over us. He drew me close to snuggle with my head on his chest.

My exhaustion had been replaced with contentment. I lay in bed and listened to Sean's heartbeat.

"What are you smiling about?" he asked, pressing a kiss to the top of my head.

"Your heart is going a million miles an hour." I tilted my head up to look at him. "And it's hot under the covers. You're like a furnace."

He grinned and flipped the comforter back so we were just covered by the sheet.

"Ahhhh, that's much better," I murmured with a sigh.

My brain slowly came back online. I saw my bedroom and sat bolt upright in shock.

Unleashed, my magic had swept through the room like a tornado. Clothes were everywhere. Everything that had been on top of my dresser or hanging on the wall was on the floor. My lamp and hamper were turned over. The files from my nightstand were scattered across the room.

Sean sat up next to me. "I take it this isn't something that happens around here very often?" he teased.

"Um, no. This would be a first for me."

Sean looked smug then. *Men.* I rolled my eyes.

We settled back into the bed, and he wrapped his arms around me. It was officially morning; I heard cars going by outside as my neighbors headed off to work. Daylight streamed through the window. I stretched, but from the bed I couldn't reach the curtains. Sean reached up and pulled them closed and the room fell into near-darkness.

"Do you want me to stay?" Sean asked.

I couldn't see his face, but he didn't really sound like he wanted to leave. I was hardly a dewy-eyed romantic who demanded her lovers stick around afterward, but it might be nice to go to sleep with someone warm in my bed. My stomach still ached, and I was rattled from the run-in with the landmine.

"If you don't have any place you need to be, you're welcome to stay," I told him.

"I don't have to be anywhere." Now that we had recovered somewhat and cooled off a bit, I was starting to feel chilly. Without being asked, he pulled the comforter back up over us. "One of the benefits of owning the company is that I have flexible hours most days. I don't have to be in the office today until a meeting at three." He rubbed his stubbly chin on the top of my head, and the bristles scratching my scalp felt good. "We can sleep in if you want."

"I do want." I yawned and rolled over onto my other side. Sean spooned up behind me, fitting his body against my curves. I let him wrap his arm around me and pull me close.

As good as the sex was, and as much as I appreciated that he seemed to really care that it was as satisfying for me as it was for him, Sean was a one-night stand. A damn fine one, though, and with any luck, after we'd slept, he'd have at least one more chance to show off his skills before I sent him on his way.

Just before sleep pulled me under, I remembered my earrings. I took them out, stretched over the edge of the bed, and tossed them lightly onto the nightstand before settling back into the warmth of Sean's arms. I felt his breath on the back of my neck.

As I was drifting off, Sean whispered, "Sweet dreams, Alice."

Good night. I wasn't sure if I thought it or said it. Between one heartbeat and the next, I was sound asleep.

7

WHEN I WAKE UP, I WILL BE A DIFFERENT PERSON.

In a city a thousand miles from where I grew up and two thousand miles from where I am headed, I stand in front of a mirror looking at my face for the last time.

In a few minutes, a plastic surgeon will begin the long and painful process of turning me into Alice Worth, an unremarkable earth and air mage who is about to move to the West Coast to start a new life. My face will be completely different. This me, the one in the mirror, will be gone forever. I am trying to figure out how I feel. I should be scared, I suppose. Maybe relieved or angry. Instead, I just feel numb.

After the night I left the cabal compound, it took me nearly a week to get here and another week before I found a plastic surgeon who could be trusted to do the work I needed. The surgeon is a mage whose family was killed by a cabal. He knows who I am and he wants to help.

There is a picture taped to the mirror of the real Alice Worth. I run my fingertips over my face, feeling my forehead, my eyes, my nose, my lips, my chin, and try to imagine looking into the glass and seeing that other woman looking back at me. Somehow, I already feel like this isn't my face anymore, like it's been on too long already. I'm impatient to have it be gone so I can start recovering. It will be at least another week before I am able to resume my run across the country to my final destination.

Although I have heard nothing to make me think I am being pursued, and the news is filled with images of my grandfather openly grieving over my death, I can't help but feel like danger is nipping at my heels. I want to be moving on, but this stop is necessary. I can go no farther wearing this face.

There is a quiet knock on the door. It's the surgeon, asking if I am ready.

I've been ready for this moment for as long as I can remember.

As I lie back on the table, the surgeon asks again if I am sure I want to do this. With no hesitation, I tell him yes. I look at the world as Moses Murphy's granddaughter one last time, and then an ocean of soft darkness sweeps me away.

I woke to the unfamiliar sensation of a very large, very warm body pressed up against my backside and an arm curled around my middle. Sean was nuzzling my neck. He'd opened the curtains a bit to let some afternoon sunlight into the room. I blinked fuzzily at the clock on the nightstand to see it was a little after one. I'd had about six hours of sleep and felt pretty good. I yawned and started to stretch.

Agony flared in my stomach, and I gasped and curled into a ball. Either my sore abdominal muscles had tightened up and they were simply cramping, or it was actual injuries from the landmine I'd triggered. The pain made me breathe in short, panting breaths.

"Alice, what's wrong?" Sean was wide awake in an instant. "You're hurt."

I gritted my teeth and managed not to whimper.

He looked at my stomach, but there was nothing to see. The injury, whatever it was, was on the inside. I focused on breathing through the pain, and it started to recede.

"The wards...from yesterday," I finally managed to say. "It's just a muscle cramp. I'm okay."

Sean made a snarly noise. "You keep saying you're fine and you're okay, but it's pretty clear you're not." He sounded angry. "I can smell blood. You may be bleeding internally."

I froze and looked at him—like, really, really looked at him.

In the daylight, I could see a faint gold sheen over his eyes that reflected the light in a way no human eye did. Add that to his muscular physique, body temperature, tendency to rub his face against me, and ability to smell an internal injury, and....

"Werewolf?" I guessed.

Sean went perfectly still. We stared at each other.

A number of emotions were visible on his face: worry, anger, and...fear? What was he afraid of, that I'd turn on him? I supposed it was a legitimate concern for a werewolf these days, when we were all afraid of each other and the Agency.

I sighed and gingerly rubbed my abdomen where the pain had faded to soreness, like I'd done too many sit-ups. I wasn't worried that Sean was a werewolf. If it were nearer the full moon, I might have been concerned, but as it was, I doubted he'd be going furry on me. Since a bite from a werewolf in wolf form was the only way to contract the virus, I was more bothered by the pain in my stomach and the possibility of internal injuries.

Sean cleared his throat. "Should I leave?"

Carefully, so I didn't strain my stomach muscles, I turned so I could face him. His arms were still around me, but he looked grim.

I took his face in my hands and kissed him.

At first, he didn't respond; I think I surprised him. Then he kissed me back with a hunger that took my breath away. When we separated, he met my gaze with dark eyes that shone gold. How I'd missed the signs last night, I had no idea. I must have been too preoccupied with the events of the day.

Sean touched my face. "So you're not angry?"

I shook my head. "I don't care that you're a werewolf. Sure, I'd have preferred it if you'd told me last night, but it wouldn't have changed anything. It's not like I can catch it from having sex with you."

That made him relax a little, but he looked concerned as he placed his hand carefully on my stomach. "What kind of wards did you walk into yesterday? What magic could hurt you like this?"

I debated what I could tell him without breaching client confidentiality. "The wards were set by a woman who died a couple of months ago. When I walked into them, they did this." I pointed to the burn on my chest. It was still red, and it hurt the way burns did: a steady, hot, stinging sensation that hadn't faded much since last night.

Sean paled. "That's right over your heart."

"Yep. The wards were designed to kill. I was lucky they had faded."

He stared at me.

I kept talking. "I needed to take down the wards for my client. The unweaving went fine, but apparently there was a landmine, and it got me." He didn't say anything. "I threw up a lot, and some of it was blood. That's probably what you're smelling. Honestly, I don't think I'm actually still bleeding internally—"

Sean lost it.

I squeaked as he wrapped his arms around me and pulled me against his body with a growl. He was careful not to hold me too tightly, though his arms felt like steel. "I want to kill the person who hurt you."

"You can't; she's dead already," I said into his chest. "I don't need a protector, Sean. I'm not looking for someone to take care of me, or fight my battles for me."

"I know, but I'm an alpha. My instinct is to protect..." He hesitated. "People who are injured."

"Females and the weak," I corrected him. "I know. I'm familiar enough with werewolves to understand that, but I'm not part of your pack, or yours to protect. I'm just your one-night stand."

Sean pulled back. "Is that what this is?" He looked startled, as if that hadn't been anything close to what he expected me to say. I wondered if he was used to women who got emotionally attached to one-night stands. He wouldn't have to worry about that with me; emotional attachments weren't really my thing.

I patted his chest affectionately. "Sean, we both had a good time, but I don't have any illusions about how this goes."

Sean's expression went flat. "How do you think 'this' goes?"

I ran my hands over his chest, scratching him lightly with my nails, and he made that growly sound I liked. "We lie here for a while longer, since neither of us has to be anywhere immediately, then we have sex again because you're that damn good at it, and then we part company with good feelings and good memories."

Sean leaned close to me. Before I realized what he was doing, he inhaled deeply. I recoiled, taken aback by his suddenly very werewolf behavior. "What I'm smelling isn't old injuries from yesterday. I'm pretty sure you *are* still bleeding internally. You need medical attention, Alice."

I put my hands on my aching stomach and knew he was right. "I have healing spells," I told him with a sigh. "Give me a minute." I started to slide off the bed.

"Do you need help?"

I shook my head and stood, heading for my bathroom. "This won't take long. There's another bathroom down the hall if you need to use it." I went in and closed the door.

After I used the toilet, I dug around in a drawer and took out my first aid kit, a small wooden box with runes carved on all sides. The runes were spells that hid the energy stored within. I traced three runes on the lid, then opened it. Inside the box were crystals containing healing spells of various strengths, color-coded from light green—minor injury—to dark purple—possibly fatal wound. I took out a green crystal, held it gently against the burn on my chest, braced myself, and said, "*Helios.*"

Magic flared and I sucked in a breath as the spell went to work on the burn. It felt like a hundred tiny needles were stabbing me. The sensation lasted for about thirty seconds before fading. When I took my hand away, the burn was gone, leaving a faint scar. I set the crystal aside to be respelled when I had time.

Whatever the landmine had done to my insides, it was going to take a stronger spell to fix it. I rooted around in the box and came up with a mid-range blue crystal. This one was going to hurt. Mindful of Sean in the next room, I turned on the shower to help mask any sounds and grabbed a hand towel. I sat down on the bath mat next to the tub, pressed the crystal against my stomach, and invoked the spell.

I stuffed the towel into my mouth to muffle my cries. Now the needles were inside me, and it felt like they were ripping through my insides as the spell went to work on the damage. This much pain from the healing spell meant there really were significant internal injuries. I'd always thought healing spells should feel good, not hurt, but no one had ever been successful at creating one that wasn't painful. I bit down on the towel and tried to be quiet.

Minutes crawled by. When the pins-and-needles sensation finally faded, I dropped the empty spell crystal on the rug and pushed myself to my feet using the side of the tub. My stomach felt tender in the way that recently healed injuries do. I put the box away in the drawer, washed my face and rinsed my mouth, and turned off the shower.

When I opened the bathroom door, Sean was sitting on the edge of the bed, looking very tense. He'd probably heard enough to know that the healing spells had hurt. He stood and looked me over. "Are you all right?"

"I am now. All healed." I wrapped my arms around his neck and kissed him warmly. He relaxed against me and kissed me back.

We returned to the bed, and Sean pulled me into his arms. My fingers traced over his shoulders, feeling the definition of his muscles. His hands moved up my back, caressing.

"Where did you get these scars?" he asked.

I stiffened. The scars on my back were from another lifetime. My phoenix tattoo covered most of the damage, but the lines were still visible if you looked closely. Healing spells and even plastic surgery could only do so much. The only thing that might heal them completely would be slicing the scars off and pouring vampire blood over the wounds, but I had no desire to undergo that particularly extreme measure.

"I used to know some bad people," I said.

He stilled. "How bad?"

"Very bad." I moved my head so my lips were against his neck. The smell of him eased the tension in my shoulders. I wondered absently if alphas gave off calming pheromones.

"I saw the scars while you were asleep." Sean's fingers traced the lines. "I assume healing spells were used...after?"

"Yes. A lot of them, for a long time." My voice was level.

He took a deep, involuntary breath. "And these scars remain?"

Intensive healing spells could heal most severe injuries with minimal or no scarring. Right now, he was imagining how bad the wounds had been for the spells to have been unable to heal me completely. I didn't have to imagine anything; I'd been conscious for all of it. I knew my back looked butchered when the blood mage had finished with me. For it to look as good as it did now was nothing short of miraculous.

I was suddenly cold. I wanted heat and to be distracted from the memories, and I knew one sure way to get both.

I drew his hand up to my mouth so I could lightly bite his fingers, and he made a snarly wolf sound that sparked an instant reaction. I was suddenly very aware of my breasts brushing against his chest. I reached down and stroked him gently.

Sean groaned and shifted on the bed. "Alice—"

I nipped his bottom lip and his eyes turned gold. I pushed him onto his back and moved to my hands and knees so I could lick slowly across his chest. He reached for me, but I moved away and bent over him, teasing him with my mouth and tongue and making him writhe. I found I liked having an alpha werewolf at my mercy.

He moved so quickly, all I saw was a blur. One second I was leaning forward to draw him into my mouth again, and the next I was on my back and he was on top of me, his hand between my thighs, and I was crying out. Blissful minutes later, I was gasping and screaming and trying to pull away from him, but he held me tight until I stopped shuddering.

When I opened my eyes, Sean looked at me with an expression of such fierce passion that I went still. "Condoms?"

"Nightstand. Bottom drawer," I panted.

The drawer opened, the box tore, a packet crinkled, and then Sean was back. "Up," he commanded, raising me and turning me over onto my stomach.

I resisted, self-conscious about my scars in the daylight, but then he was kissing my back and suddenly I didn't care anymore. He pulled me onto my hands and knees, his hands on my hips, and then he pushed into me from behind. I arched my back with a cry.

He moved carefully and gently. It was wonderful, but I wanted and needed something else. "Harder," I gasped. "Faster."

He bent over to run his lips across my back and I shuddered. "Are you sure?" His voice was deep and growly and it made me crazy. "Your stomach...."

"I'm healed," I told him breathlessly. "Please, Sean. Please don't go slow."

His fingers dug into my hips hard enough to leave bruises and suddenly the brakes were off. I grabbed the bedding as hard as I could as he growled—a deep, rumbling werewolf growl—that almost sent me over the edge. I forgot about everything else as the pleasure rose toward a crescendo. I called his name over and over and begged him to go even faster.

This time, I had none of the second thoughts that held me back last night. He reached around to stroke me and I came with a wail. A heartbeat later, he snarled and emptied himself inside me. We fell over onto the bed, gasping for breath.

"Oh my God," Sean rasped.

"Mmm-hmmm."

I lay on the bed while he went to the bathroom to clean up. He had, I thought appreciatively, a thoroughly magnificent butt.

When Sean came back, he climbed onto the bed and wrapped his arms around me. "I'm glad I went to Hawthorne's last night," he said, biting my earlobe gently.

I laughed. "Me too. And I'm glad Charles was too busy to see me. This turned into a really fantastic night—well, a really fantastic day."

"What brought you in to see the vampire?"

"A matter related to one of my cases." I shrugged lazily and glanced at the clock. "It's almost two. Don't you have to be at work at three?"

He groaned. "Are you kicking me out of bed?"

"We have to get up at some point. You've got to get to work, and I'm supposed to be getting a text about seeing Charles tonight. And I've got a client to see." And a ghost to check on, though I didn't mention that.

"You did get a couple of messages."

"What? Why didn't you wake me up?" I scooted away from him to grab my phone off the nightstand.

"I thought you needed your sleep."

I sat cross-legged on the bed and checked my messages. There were two. The first one was from Bryan, who'd texted me around eight a.m. *Meeting with Mr. V at midnight. Car is out front, key in the mailbox. Sean Maclin's car is in your driveway.*

Shit. I'd told them Sean had dropped me off. Now Bryan knew that not only had I lied, but that Sean had stayed with me. My face burned.

"What is it?" Sean watched me, frowning.

"Nothing." Damn it, I didn't answer to Bryan for anything, least of all my sex life. It was none of his business if Sean stayed with me. I supposed I shouldn't have lied, but Bryan had pushed me about whether or not Sean had dropped me off and maybe I resented him acting like it was any of his business. I wasn't really clear on my motives for lying. In any case, I would have to face Bryan tonight at Hawthorne's in order to see Charles. Fantastic.

Also, Sean's last name was Maclin. Good to know. Bryan must have had someone run the tags of the vehicle when they saw it in the driveway. Maybe he was concerned about my safety, but whatever his reason, it felt like an egregious invasion of my privacy.

I scowled and fired back a terse text: *Ok will meet C at midnight.*

"Alice?"

I looked up from my phone. "Bryan texted me a meeting time for Charles when he came by. He was wondering why your car was parked in my driveway. And your last name is Maclin."

Sean sat up. "And you told him I dropped you off."

"Yes."

"Is this going to cause problems?"

"Why should it? I don't owe anyone an explanation for who I sleep with."

Again Sean looked surprised. Then he grinned.

"What?" I asked.

"I don't think I've ever met anyone quite like you before, Alice."

"You're probably right."

He laughed. I smiled briefly.

The second text was from Natalie. *Hi! Saw your note. Sorry I fell asleep. Call when you get a chance.* She signed the message with a smiley face.

I blew out a relieved breath. It looked like she didn't remember anything about manifesting any magic.

Sean moved over to me on his hands and knees and kissed me so hard that I dropped my phone. "What was that?" I asked breathlessly.

"I have to go to work, but at the risk of being cliché, I'd really like to see you again."

"In what way?" If he was interested in working out a bang-buddy arrangement, I would be willing to consider it.

"How about tonight, after your meeting with Vaughan? I'll be off work. We can have some drinks and talk about beer and music or whatever else is on your mind."

I stared at him. "You're talking about an actual date."

Sean's mouth quirked. "Yes, an *actual date*. What we do after that—if anything—is up to you."

"I'm not really looking for a relationship," I told him.

"Me neither, but I think we both had a good time. I'd like to get to know you better. How about one date, and then you decide where we go from there."

The sex had been very satisfying, and it was a tempting offer, but there was something in Sean's eyes that made me wary. I'd invited him into my bed thinking we were on the same page about this being a one-night deal. Maybe we'd started out that way, but it looked like he might be on a different page now, possibly a whole other chapter, and I wasn't even sure my book had that chapter in it.

Still, I could try to let him down easy. "Let me think about it."

He gave me a wolfish smile. "Did I not pass the audition?"

I was quiet for a few moments. "I thought we were clear about the plan for how this would go."

"Plans can change."

"Not mine." Mine was simple: stay cautious, stay under the radar, stay alive.

Sean leaned forward. "Give me a chance to change your mind."

"I said I would think about it."

He got up and started pulling on his clothes. I shamelessly watched the reverse striptease and couldn't help but feel a little sad when he was dressed.

As he sat on the bed putting on his shoes, he turned to me. "Well, you know my last name, but I don't know yours."

I hesitated but saw no reason not to tell him. He had my address; he could find out easily for himself. "Worth."

"Alice Worth." He finished tying his shoes. "Can I have your number, Alice?"

I tilted my head and considered. "Why don't you give me yours? If you need to get me a message, you can call Hawthorne's, and they'll see that I get it."

"You don't give an inch." Strangely, he was grinning.

"Nope."

Sean gave me his number and I put it in my phone under Wolf. He saw the nickname and laughed.

He rose, then bent down to give me a sizzling kiss. When he drew back, his eyes were gold. It occurred to me to wonder if the wolf in him enjoyed the idea of a chase. Too bad for him that I had no intention of playing along.

He moved his lips to my ear. "Give me a call," he said softly.

"Maybe."

He went to the door of my room, then turned back. We looked at each other.

"Have a good day at work, Alice," he said finally.

"You too, Sean."

He hesitated, as if he wanted to say something else, and then he was gone.

8

I showered and washed my hair. When I got out, I wrapped myself in a bathrobe and spent several minutes straightening the mess left behind by this morning's magical hurricane. I stacked my files, put my dirty clothes back in the hamper, returned the scattered items to my nightstand and dresser, and hung the pictures back on the wall.

After I got dressed and dried and braided my hair, I ate a sandwich while setting out a replacement change of clothes for my go-bag.

With my preparations finished, I called my client.

"Hello!" Natalie's greeting was warm and cheerful. I felt a pang of guilt that she had no memory of what had happened last night. "How are you feeling? I've been so worried about you."

"Doing fine," I told her. "I'm ready to come take a look at that library."

"I'm glad you're okay. I haven't tried to go in there."

"I'm sorry about that, but until we know what's going on, I think we'd better err on the side of caution."

"Good thinking. I can't believe I was living in this house for so long with those wards." I could hear the fear and anger in Natalie's voice. I could understand the feeling; even knowing the wards had been keyed not to harm her, anyone not used to being around magic would have good reason to be afraid of spells designed to kill without warning or mercy. Hell, I'd been using magic since I was four and blood magic since I was twelve, and it was enough to rattle me.

"Well, it made for an interesting afternoon. What time should I come over?"

"Whenever you want. I'm here all day."

"I'm about ready to head out. I can be there in about an hour."

"Awesome." A pause. "Is Malcolm coming?"

"Yes. He's going to help me with the wards. See you in a few."

We said good-bye and disconnected. I put on my jewelry: rings, charm bracelet—

with assorted spells—and a monogram necklace with a pendant shaped like the letter *A*.

Time to let my new sidekick out. I picked up my crystal earrings from the tray on the nightstand. I could feel Malcolm's energy buzzing in my palm. Yesterday, unsure of how much energy would be discharged, I'd used a circle to contain Malcolm when I released him, but it hadn't been necessary. Today, I simply held the earring and said, "*Release*."

With a yell, Malcolm popped into existence three feet in front of me. The wave of magic staggered me back a half step. Unlike yesterday, when he'd been disoriented and near frantic, today he just looked surprised. He also looked far more substantial than he did before. Hmm. I suddenly wondered if he'd gotten a boost at the same time I did when I was having sex with Sean. I'd been wearing the earrings and it seemed logical. I flushed.

"Hey, Alice." Malcolm moved back and forth slowly. "I feel...different, more solid and much stronger. Did you try another spell?"

"Sorta." He categorically did *not* need to know where the energy boost had come from. "Was it less rough on you this time?"

"Yes." He looked relieved. "It feels like it's only been a few minutes this time. The time before...." He shuddered. "It felt like forever, and like a split second too, if that makes any sense. It really messed with my head."

I tried to wrap my brain around that and couldn't. "I'll have to take your word for it. I'm glad it wasn't as bad this time. I'll look into a different spell as soon as I get a chance."

"So how long was I in there?"

"It's tomorrow afternoon. After I put you in the earring, I went to meet the vamp, but he was busy. I'll be seeing him tonight. Then I, uh, got some sleep, called Natalie to let her know we're on our way over, and here you are."

"Cool." Malcolm moved around the room. "So this is your house?"

"Yes." I gave him a quick tour of the upstairs, then grabbed the stack of clothes that were going in my go-bag and headed downstairs, Malcolm floating behind me. I showed him around the main floor—living room, kitchen, laundry room/downstairs bathroom, storage room—and then pointed at the basement door. "That's my library and my spellwork area. We'll be spending a lot of time down there."

"Right on." Malcolm stared at the door and whistled low. "Whoa."

I realized he was seeing the wards. I'd poured a lot of time, energy, and blood into those wards. They were the strongest and most intricate I'd ever made. Even the best mages wouldn't be able to get in. There were layers of deadly landmines strung throughout the spells. Trying to break the wards directly would mean death for the mage or mages who tried. Nuking the wards with focused energy would level the house and kill everyone in it. My basement was as secure as I could make it.

Malcolm looked at me with a combination of fear and respect. "Holy shit. I thought Betty's wards were intense. How long did it take you to do this?"

"The foundation spells took three days and eight pints of blood. The rest of the basic spells took about a week. I've been adding on to it and pouring energy into it since I moved in almost five years ago."

"It's incredible," Malcolm said reverently. "All that energy, and yet I couldn't even sense it from upstairs." He drifted forward, his fingers moving as if he was envisioning the process I'd used to layer the spells. "I've never seen anything like it. I *see* the energy, but I can't *feel* it. I can't even begin to understand the spells you're using to mask the trace. Unbelievable."

"Well, I couldn't very well let anyone sense the energy. It would be a beacon so bright, they'd see it from space. You're not even seeing the strongest and most deadly wards."

"What?" Malcolm's eyes widened.

"There are secondary spells hidden in landmines. Even if a team of mages came in here and tried to unweave the spells, they'd hit the landmines and release the cascades." Cascades were spells that triggered a series of other, more powerful spells, like an avalanche. There were even more surprises hidden in the cascades: divine wind spells designed to travel back to the heart of whichever cabal attempted to break my wards and cause maximum destruction. If my library went—even if I went with it—I'd be going out with a very big bang.

Malcolm was silent for a long time. "With skills and power like this, you would be the most powerful mage in just about any cabal in the country," he said finally. He drifted back toward me and stopped close enough that I felt his energy buzzing. "There is no way any cabal would let you go. I know you used to belong to one; you knew what I was talking about when I was telling you about my past. At first I thought you'd completed your contract and negotiated a release, but there's no way." His eyes searched my face. "You feel like a mid-level mage, but you aren't, are you?"

I said nothing.

Malcolm's brows drew together and his anger prickled on my skin. "Alice—"

"No," I said in a cold, flat tone.

He closed his mouth.

"I belonged to a cabal. Now I don't. The rest of what happened isn't a story I can share with you, not right now, maybe not ever. You know better than most people what the cabals are capable of. Now you know at least some of what *I'm* capable of." I gestured at the wards protecting my basement. "Perhaps you can fill in some of the blanks for yourself, or at least hazard a guess."

I took a step toward him, despite the sizzle of his energy on my skin. It hurt, but I was no stranger to pain. I'd felt little else since I was four years old. "You're one of the best mages I've ever met. I think we can have a good long-term partnership. I want to know what's in Betty's library and what books were stolen from her. I want to know how strong Natalie's magic is and find her a mentor if she wants one. Big picture, I want to know what Darius Bell is up to and how you ended up bound to me. But from here on, you have to understand that my past is off-limits. No questions, no poking around. It's not personal, but I will protect myself. If those wards tell you anything, it's that I am not someone you'd want to cross."

Malcolm's mouth opened and closed several times. I stepped back.

Finally, he regained his power of speech. "Well, at least we cleared *that* up." He sighed—purely an affectation, as ghosts didn't breathe. "I get it. No questions."

"Good. We need to head over to Natalie's house." I put on my leather jacket and turned to gather my things.

"Wait, I do have one question."

I paused, my arms full. "Yes?"

"The blood in the foundation spells—all eight pints of it—it isn't yours."

I turned and gave him the kind of smile that made people twitch. "I never said it was."

Malcolm flitted back so fast, he passed through the couch and the coffee table and ended up over near the fireplace. "Okay then." He sounded strangled. "I'm glad we could have this talk."

"Come on, Malcolm." I opened the front door. "Let's go see a woman about some missing books."

The drive over to Natalie's house was more or less silent. When I parked in her driveway, I could feel the wards. They felt as strong as they had when I'd left. At some point, Natalie would be able to maintain them, but that would be a while yet, and that was assuming I could find someone to teach her.

I had to find Natalie a mentor, but I also had to be very careful. If she had strong magic like her grandmother, she'd be worth good money to a cabal. A mage without scruples would sell her out in a heartbeat. At the same time, I was hiding from the cabals. I couldn't very well go around making inquiries, but Charles could. As a broker and a member of the Vampire Court, he was powerful and connected. I was betting he would know someone who could train Natalie and wouldn't sell her out.

Was there any reason to doubt Charles? I thought back over all my dealings with him. He was ruthless, certainly; all vampires were. The older they were, the less human they became. Charles wasn't all that old by vamp standards; he'd fought in the Revolutionary War as an adolescent, which meant he'd been turned sometime around 1800. As a member of the Vampire Court and a successful businessman, he excelled in reading people, making alliances, and staying ahead of the competition. Could I trust him with Natalie's life? I'd been so certain last night, but now, in the cold light of day and looking at the home Betty had shared with her granddaughter, I started to wonder.

The X factor was how much power Natalie had. If she had a lot, it would make her a powerful bargaining chip, and for a vamp, that might be too irresistible of a prize if he needed something to establish an alliance with a cabal. Of course, if her power was mid-level or lower, she wouldn't be worth selling out.

"Are we going in?" Malcolm's voice made me jump. I realized we'd been sitting in front of Natalie's house for almost ten minutes while I thought through the problem.

"In a minute. I need your opinion." I laid it out for him. "Thoughts?"

"I definitely agree that we need to know how strong she is," Malcolm said. "If she's powerful, you're right—telling the vamp about her might not be a good idea. If she's mid-level or below, we're probably safe talking to him."

I nodded. It was great having a partner to talk things through with, especially when he agreed with my plan.

"I vote we tell Natalie the truth and let her decide," he added. "I think she needs to know what's going on and make an informed decision. I'm not sure we have the right to determine how much she gets to know about herself."

"You're right. If it were me, and I found out someone had been keeping this kind of information from me, I'd be furious. I'm worried about how she'll take the news, but she deserves to know."

"I think the best thing to do is tell her what we know, give her the options, and see what she wants to do. Hell, she may want us to bind her power completely. There are a lot of people who don't want any part of magic. There are a lot of days when I'd give anything not to have it. I suffered a lot because of my 'gift.'" He sounded bitter.

"Do you really wish you had been born without magic?"

A long pause. Then the ghost in my car said, "Honestly? Yes."

I sat back in my seat and tried to imagine my life without magic. No cabal, no blood magic. No Agency to fear. My parents would still be alive. I thought about all the pain I had endured since the day when I was four and my magic manifested and my grandfather saw in me the potential to be the strongest mage in the family's history.

I rubbed my face. It didn't matter if I didn't want the magic or not; I had it. I couldn't change anything about my past. The dead would stay dead. As an MPI, I tried to help people, as if I could do enough good to somehow make up for what I'd done for the cabal. It wasn't enough, but it was all I could do.

"Let's go talk to Natalie," I said finally.

Once we were inside, Malcolm went visible again. Because he'd drawn energy from Natalie the night before, she could hear him now. What surprised me was that she could sort of see him too, probably thanks to the power boost.

Natalie sat on the couch, I took the chair, and Malcolm floated three feet to my left. She was looking right at him. "I can see the outline of someone," she said in wonder. "Like when you stare at a geometric pattern and then a blank wall, and your eyes still see the pattern."

I pulled a folder out of my bag. "Before we get started, we should write up a contract and talk about payment. I should have done it yesterday, but things got unexpectedly...busy."

Natalie's hand flew to her mouth. "I am so sorry! I forgot completely about that. Let's do it now."

We spent about twenty minutes going over the contract. She argued when I told her I wasn't invoking the "extraordinary circumstances with personal injury" clause after what happened last night. I insisted that my burn and ruined shirt were my fault, but I let her talk me into adding a bonus for the landmine mishap. We agreed on a retainer and a daily rate plus expenses, and she wrote me a check and signed the papers.

With the legalities out of the way, it was time for The Talk. "Natalie, before I start working on the library, there's something we need to discuss. What's the last thing you remember from last night?"

She thought about it. "You'd been hurt by the wards," she said slowly. "I wrapped you in blankets and Malcolm was going to put new wards on the library. And then I... fell asleep?" She frowned. "That doesn't seem right. How did I fall asleep in the middle of all that?"

"You didn't." She blinked at me in confusion. "Some pretty strange stuff happened last night. I'm going to tell you everything, but you might find it a little upsetting."

"Just tell me!" Natalie demanded.

I told her about her fire and air magic suddenly manifesting, how Betty had suppressed her magic, and how I'd bound it again before tucking her into bed.

By the time I finished, Natalie was pacing around the living room, her arms wrapped around her middle. She looked mad and scared. I wasn't sure what would help her, so I waited.

Finally, she turned to face me. "What am I supposed to do?" she demanded. "Yesterday I found out my grandmother was a powerful mage who left killer wards behind when she died. I saw you hurt twice from what she did. Now you tell me I have magic too, but that my grandmother put spells on me so I wouldn't know I had it."

Malcolm and I waited quietly while she struggled to process what I'd told her. Finally, she dropped back onto the couch and sighed. "Okay, I can deal with this. Tell me what we need to do."

Briefly, I outlined the problem. "I'm pretty sure we can keep your magic bound. If you want no part of this life, I'm about ninety percent certain I can keep your magic from manifesting. I think the reason it flared last night is that Betty's spells weren't maintained after she passed away. They might have been tied to the library wards; I'm not sure."

I suddenly had a revelation. "You know how you told me you thought you were being poisoned because you've been sick and losing weight? I'm wondering if your magic trying to escape the binding spells might be causing you to be ill."

She looked shocked. "You really think so?"

"It's a possibility. Have you felt better today?"

She thought about it. "Well, yes, I guess I have. I ate a big sandwich for lunch, and normally I'm not that hungry. I thought it was because I got a good night's sleep." Suddenly she seemed more energized. "Well, *that's* a relief! One less thing to worry about. I guess nobody is really trying to kill me after all!"

"I'm not sure I'm right; it's just a theory for now," I said before she could get too excited. "The binding spell I put on you is tied to our wards, which are at full strength, so your situation should be stabilized for a while."

"Will the spell always be tied to the wards?" Natalie bit her lip.

"No. There's another way. A better way."

"How?"

"A tattoo." I pushed up my right sleeve and pulled down the back of my shirt to show her some of my own tattoos, including a dragon coiled around my upper arm and the phoenix on my back. "A tattoo can hold a spell pretty much indefinitely. It wouldn't have to be very big—maybe two inches square. Your own aura will power the spell."

"Would it have to be a particular design?"

I shook my head. "There would be runes, but a good mage tattoo artist can make them practically invisible within most any design. You could get pretty much whatever you want and put it wherever you want. I can take you to the mage who did my tattoos."

"You said ninety percent." Natalie seized on something I said earlier. "Why not a hundred percent?"

"Unfortunately, every spell has counterspells, and I can't anticipate every possibility. Most government buildings are protected by wards that disrupt spells, even ones anchored by tattoos. If you crossed one, the binding might fail. If you ever touched a null—"

"What's a null?"

"A null is a mage who can drain someone else's energy by touching them. They're not common, but they're out there. If you bumped into one on the street, you'd lose some or all of your magic and the suppression spell would fail. If you didn't get to me or someone soon to redo the spells, your magic would be uncontrolled as it regenerated."

Natalie closed her eyes.

"If you're looking for guarantees, I can't give them to you," I said. "That's life, pretty much. You'll be as safe—and nonmagical—as anyone can make you, if you decide that's what you want."

"And if I don't want it bound?" Natalie opened her eyes and stared at me. She might be tiny, but she was feisty.

"You'll need training. First, I need to know for sure what kind of magic you have, and how strong you are. Once I know that, I can find someone to take you on as an apprentice. You'll learn how to control your magic and use it. You don't have to become a practicing mage. Your life won't have to change much. Once you learn control, it will be just like any other ability, like being able to paint or sing." Well, that was oversimplifying things, but the gist was true.

"How do we find out how strong my magic is?"

"Two choices. I can put you back in a sleep spell and Malcolm and I will find out, rebind you, and wake you up to tell you. Second option: you stay awake and find out at the same time we do."

"Which do you recommend?"

"It's up to you. One thing you might want to think about is that you have no memory of having magic, of how it feels. I can imagine it might be frightening for you if you're awake when we release the binding spells, which is why I suggested you be asleep. You might prefer to make the decision without the memory of being afraid."

Natalie was quiet. "How long can I think about this?"

"As long as you need," Malcolm said. "Your magic is bound. I know Alice would prefer that we at least find out today what kind of magic you have and how strong you are, but really it's up to you. If you want to do that today, and then decide later whether or not to bind the magic permanently, that's okay. For whatever it's worth, if it were me, I'd at least want to know that about myself before I made any long-term decisions."

Natalie took a deep breath. "Okay, let me think about this."

I stood up. "In the meantime, Malcolm and I are going to take a look at the library."

"I'm going to make some tea. You want some?"

"Sure."

Malcolm and I headed back to the master bedroom, and Natalie went to the kitchen.

We looked at the wards we'd put on the library the night before. I could see the beautiful green lines of Malcolm's spellwork and the darker colors of my own magic.

"What are you thinking?" Malcolm asked.

"I'm thinking we need strong containment wards. Whatever's in there, we don't want it getting out."

"I can do that. Can you take down your wards?"

I reached out and brushed my fingertips over the doorframe and my wards fell. Malcolm's fingers moved quickly, and in a few minutes, the library perimeter hummed with a strong containment spell. Nothing short of the magical equivalent of a nuke was getting out.

"Whew," Malcolm said. "I feel like I have so much more power today. Whatever spell you used, I like it."

Yeah, I like it too. I didn't say a thing.

I took a deep breath and opened the door to Betty's library.

9

YESTERDAY, WHEN I TRIED TO WALK INSIDE, BETTY'S WARDS SWATTED ME LIKE A FLY. Today, I felt only the prickle of the containment spell as I stepped across the threshold and flipped on the light.

The windowless library was as large as Betty's bedroom. Three of the walls were floor-to-ceiling bookcases. A heavy antique desk with matching file cabinet and a love seat took up the fourth wall.

The floor was hardwood, like the master bedroom, but a large rug lay in the center of the room. I felt a distinctive itchiness and a sudden urge to back away and walk around it. I gritted my teeth, lifted a corner of the rug, and flipped it back, revealing an inscribed circle. Even though Betty had been gone for months, it still hummed with stored energy. My fingers went numb from touching the spelled rug.

Natalie appeared in the doorway, a mug in her hands.

"Don't try to come inside," I told her.

"I never knew that was there." She stared at the circle. "I never even thought to look under the rug."

"There's an aversion spell on the rug." I rubbed my tingly fingers on my jeans. "She didn't want you to look."

Natalie sighed. "Here's your tea."

I came to the door and took it. "Thank you. Where were the missing books?"

She peered into the room and pointed, staying clear of the doorway. "Bottom shelf, second bookcase on the right. You see how the books all have gaps between them? It looks like someone took some books and then spread the rest of them out so there wasn't a big hole. I know that shelf was stuffed full."

"When did you notice the gap?"

She frowned and thought. "I'd say about two weeks ago, but I can't say for certain when they might have disappeared. All these books and papers were my grandmother's. Most of my books are on my e-reader or in the bookcase in my room. I've really never looked at any of these books. There's no reason to."

The sudden flat quality of her voice made me look at her in surprise, then stare suspiciously at the bookcases. I immediately got a strong feeling that I didn't need to look at any of the books.

I scowled. "Aversion spells on the bookcases too. Malcolm, would you be so kind?"

"No problem." After checking for hidden spells, Malcolm went to work unweaving the aversion spells in the library, starting with the rug, and then moving on to the bookcases.

"Start with the shelf where the books are missing." He dutifully went to the bookcase Natalie indicated.

I turned back to my client and sipped my tea. "With those spells in place, I'm surprised you even noticed the books were missing."

She pursed her lips and thought. "I was sitting in the love seat reading. I remember I just saw it out of the corner of my eye and thought it looked wrong. All those shelves were always crammed full. I used to tease my grandmother about it because she always bought more and never seemed to give any away." She smiled at the memory.

"That's probably why it worked. The aversion spells kept you from looking at the books directly or too closely until the last few days, but out of the corner of your eye, your subconscious saw what the spells kept your conscious mind from seeing. Without her here to maintain the spells, they probably lost some of their power. There's really no telling when the books might have been taken. It could have been any time in the last three months."

"How did someone get past the wards?" She asked the question that had been bugging the hell out of me. "And the aversion spells on the bookcase?"

Malcolm piped up. "I think I can answer that. Something I noticed last night but forgot to mention in all the excitement, but here it is again." He motioned me over to the bookcase, then held out his hand.

I closed my fingers around his. I felt a moment of disorientation, and then he was showing me what he was seeing in his mind. Betty's aversion spells had exclusions: herself, obviously, and one other. At first, it looked like Betty's own magical signature, but I realized it was slightly different. This person's fire magic was stronger than Betty's, his or her air magic weaker. The magic was so similar, though, I knew it had to be a close relative: a parent, sibling, or child. I closed my eyes and reached for that strand of magic, committing it to memory so that if I encountered it again, I would recognize it.

When I was done, I let go of Malcolm's hand and staggered, suddenly out of his head and back into mine. "Go ahead and unweave the aversion spells." Malcolm got to work, and I rejoined Natalie at the door. "Are Betty's parents still alive?"

"No, they died a long time ago."

"Does she have any brothers or sisters?"

"One brother and one sister, my great-aunt Helen and my great-uncle Robert. They're both in their late seventies."

"What about your aunts and uncles?"

Natalie narrowed her eyes. "What's this about?"

"Someone else in your family is a mage with the same skills as your grandmother. As far as I can tell, the spells haven't been disturbed since your grandmother passed away, so whoever is the mage is probably the same person who took the books. So tell me about your aunts and uncles."

She rubbed her forehead. "Well, there's Elise, of course, who you met yesterday, but there's no way *she's* a mage. All I ever heard about from her was how evil mages are, about how all supes should be put in camps or killed on sight. She joined a bunch of those anti-supe hate groups years ago."

"Still, I'd better check her out. She could be hiding behind all that hot air." I doubted it, though. Elise's hate seemed pretty sincere.

Natalie shrugged. "Her name is Elise Browning. I've got her address."

"Who else?"

"My mom had two other sisters and a half brother: Deborah Mackey, Kathy Adams, and Peter Eppright. He was my grandmother's son from her first marriage. They all live in the city."

"I'll get their addresses from you and start checking them out. Any guesses as to which of them it might be?"

Natalie shook her head. "Honestly, no. If you'd asked me that yesterday, I'd have said none of them could possibly be mages, but it's becoming increasingly apparent that I don't know nearly as much about my family as I thought. What will we do when we figure out who stole the books?"

"Well, we'll find out what they took, and why. They're *your* books, so we'll try to get them back. At some point, you need to decide what to do with Betty's books." I gestured at the library. "You could keep them, or put them in storage, or sell them to collectors. If we find Betty's spellbooks, you might want to save those in case you want to hand those down." Spellbooks were usually family heirlooms. Even if Natalie didn't want her magic, someone else in the family might want those books. I coveted them myself.

I went to the bookcase where the missing books had been kept and knelt in front of the bottom shelf. I closed my eyes and reached out tentatively, focusing on what my senses might be able to tell me about the books that were still here, and the ones that weren't.

As I lowered my shields and stretched out my senses, I gasped as a punch of residual power and a wave of orange, gray, and black magic rolled over me. Dimly, I heard Malcolm asking if I was all right, but I couldn't answer. I had to focus on not being swept away. I could feel my knees on the hardwood floor in the library, and that physical sensation kept me grounded. If I could ride it out, I'd be able to extricate myself.

It took a lot of effort to think, but I was able to make some sense of what was happening. I was caught up in the echo of something incredibly powerful that had been in the library at one time but wasn't here anymore. The magic trace, as formidable as it was, felt diminished. If this was the amount of energy it had left behind, I shuddered to think what the actual object might feel like.

Slowly, the power receded, like a tide going out, and I started to surface. I became aware of my body, especially the pain in my knees from kneeling on the floor. My neck had a cramp from my head hanging down for so long.

The low, indistinct sounds I'd been hearing were becoming recognizable as voices. Now that the power wasn't rushing through me anymore, I raised my shields slowly, and my hearing and vision cleared.

"Alice, can you hear me?" Malcolm's voice came from somewhere near my left shoulder. He sounded worried but calm.

"I can hear you," I mumbled. I took a deep breath and raised my head.

Malcolm hovered nearby, but not close enough to have gotten caught up in the same surge of energy that had snagged me.

"What did you see?" I asked him.

"There was a massive power surge from the area of the bottom shelf. It was like nothing I've ever seen before. I thought I saw fire magic, but most of the trace was black and gray. I don't even know what that is."

"Yeah, me neither." I looked at the books on the bottom shelf. I saw Bradshaw's *History of Fire Magic*, *Air Magic and Storm Cycles* by Ann Lewis, and a bunch of other unremarkable texts. I ran my fingers carefully over each of the books. It felt like they had soaked up some of the power that had swept over me, but none of them were the source of it.

I stacked the books on the floor and hunkered down to look at the shelf itself, running my fingertips along the bottom edge of the bookcase. About six inches from the left side of the shelf, it felt like I ran my fingers over a razor.

"Ow!" I jerked back, looking at my hand. I expected to see blood, but there was nothing. What the hell?

"Malcolm, can you see anything right here?" I pointed.

Malcolm bent down next to me. "It looks like a blood ward lock. Hang on." His fingers danced in the air. "It's been opened, but the spell is still in place. Just a second." I felt a puff of magic. "Okay, it's gone."

I reached back in and felt around carefully. This time, instead of a sharp pain, I felt a raised edge. I lifted up and a lid opened, revealing a compartment hidden in the bottom of the bookcase. The lid was covered with runes that looked like an intricate containment spell, designed to shield whatever was in the compartment from being sensed when the lid was closed.

"Well, whatever was in here, it's gone now." I sat back on my heels. "It looks like they took something out of this compartment and a couple of books, then rearranged the shelf to hide the fact that anything had been taken. Since it doesn't look like any of the spells have been broken, whoever took the stuff was the person who these wards were designed to allow in."

Natalie pulled the wooden chair over from the other side of the bedroom and settled in to watch us work. "So, one of my aunts or my uncle."

"It looks like it." I pushed myself onto my hands and knees, then staggered to my feet. "Ugh. Jeez." I shook my head to clear it. "Whatever was in that compartment, it's a hell of a thing. I hope whoever took it can contain it."

"What could they want with it?" Natalie asked.

I shrugged. "Hard to tell until we know what it is. Your grandmother had it well hidden, but somehow this mystery mage knew about it and came and took it, we can assume after Betty died. Whatever it is, it's extremely powerful. I'd feel a lot better if I knew what it is, and what they intend to do with it."

"Me too," Malcolm said. "How do you want to go about looking for it?"

"Well, we've got a definite list of suspects." I glanced at Natalie. "How are you doing with all of this?"

"Honestly, a lot better than I thought I would be," my client said. "I think the big shock was finding out about my grandmother. The rest of this is just...." She shrugged. "My grandmother was a mage, I've got some weird magic situation going on, and someone in my family broke into my house and stole some mysterious *thing* out of my grandmother's library. Oh, and my grandmother's magic could have killed you." She made a *pfffft* sound. "I guess I'm all out of surprise at this point."

"Speaking of, any thoughts on what you want to do about your magic?" Malcolm asked.

"Whenever you're ready, I'm ready to find out what kind of magic I have. At least then I'll have enough information to be able to make a decision about my future."

I looked at Natalie. Yesterday, she'd been pale and fragile-looking; today, there was color in her cheeks, and though she was still painfully thin, there was an aura of vitality that hadn't been there before. I hoped I was right about her deteriorating health being tied to the weakening spell that bound her magic.

I gave her a smile. "I'm really glad to hear it. You want to do it now?"

She finished off her tea. "Sure, no time like the present, right?"

"You want to use the circle in here?" Malcolm asked.

I glanced at the floor. "No. Too many residual spells in here, and I don't trust anyone else's circles but mine. And yours," I amended. "Let's go into the bedroom again."

We stepped out of the library. I looked at Malcolm. "What do you think? I draw the circles, you power them?" He was still super-powered; might as well take advantage of it.

"Sounds like a plan," Malcolm said.

I pulled out my chalk and got to work, drawing a nested set of three circles. I was reasonably certain we'd be fine with just one, but I was cautious enough to have two backups in case things got out of hand. I'd had just about enough of surprises in this house.

"Let's do this," I said.

Natalie, who'd been sitting on the bed while I worked, stood. "Stand in the center of the circle," I told her. She moved into place and fidgeted.

I gestured at the circles I'd drawn. "The first thing I'm going to do is close this circle. When I do, you'll feel a tingle, like a small electric charge, but it's harmless. Then I'll charge the circle so it's strong enough to contain your magic. You'll feel the tingle get stronger. Malcolm is going to be out there to close and charge the other circles if we need to."

Natalie looked at Malcolm. He grinned and waved. "He's waving at you," I said.

She let out a nervous laugh. "Then what?"

"Once this circle is ready, I'll remove your grandmother's binding spells from you, leaving just my own. When her spells break, you'll feel a...pop, I guess is the best word for it. Nothing will happen because my spells will still be there. Then I'll start letting your magic out."

"What will that feel like?"

I thought about that. "For me, it feels like I'm exhaling. It feels wonderful. It will feel weird to you since you've never done it before, but if I do a good job with my spells, it will be gradual, like breathing out."

"Will I be able to hurt you?" Her eyes were wide.

"No," I said, though there was a chance. Uncontrolled magic was never safe for anyone, but I needed Natalie calm and feeling as secure as possible so she didn't panic. Panic would be bad. "I'll be protected within my circle, and with my own spell. Nothing you can do can hurt me."

Malcolm frowned at me. I gave my head a tiny shake to tell him not scare her.

I continued with my explanation. "Once your magic is freed at least partway, I'll be able to tell how strong you are. Then I'll bind your magic again until you make a decision about what to do, and we'll break the circle. Are you with me?"

Natalie took a couple of deep breaths, then nodded. "Okay. I'm ready. Let's do it."

"Okay. Here we go." I activated the protection spell on my bracelet, then closed the center circle around Natalie. She gasped.

"How does it feel?" I asked her.

She was quiet for a moment. "It feels so weird, like an electric charge, but really faint. It doesn't hurt at all." She looked immensely relieved.

"I did tell you it wouldn't. Now I'm going to charge the circle." I closed my eyes and reached out so I could feel the circle. In deference to Natalie, I transferred the energy slowly.

She sucked in a breath but stayed quiet as the power built. When I was happy with its energy level, I stopped the transfer and opened my eyes to check on my client.

Natalie's red hair floated in the air from the charge in the circle. "That feels amazing," she breathed. "It's like standing on a power line. Oh, I can see why people do this," she blurted out.

I laughed. "Malcolm, you ready?"

"Yep." Malcolm was in the third circle, ready to close it at a moment's notice if Natalie's magic broke out of hers.

"Natalie?"

"Let's do it." Her eyes were huge but she held her ground.

"Stand still. Here we go." I closed my eyes and reached out toward Natalie with my mind. Slowly, I lowered my shields and focused my senses toward my client. I could clearly see my binding spell as well as her grandmother's layered spells. They were degrading quickly. Some of the strands were sickly gray-green. Suddenly, my theory about the binding spells being the cause of Natalie's mystery illness was almost a certainty.

I began plucking at the strands of Betty's binding spells. They were weak and began falling apart faster than I could unweave them. In a few seconds, my gentle pulling tore clean through them like someone had taken a knife and cut them away. Natalie yelped in surprise.

"Are you all right?" Malcolm asked.

"Y-yes," she said. "Was that my grandmother's spells?"

"Yes." I opened my eyes. "Now I'm going to start removing mine. You're going to feel the magic coming out of you. Try to stay calm, and remember that you can't be hurt by your own magic, and you can't hurt me. Deep breaths."

I began unweaving my binding spells. After the first few strands fell away, I started to feel the magic rising in a breath of warmth with strands of cool white.

"Fire magic," I said quietly, knowing Malcolm would hear me. "And air as well."

"As we thought." Malcolm was equally quiet.

Natalie made little fearful sounds.

"You're doing fine. Everything's good. Stay relaxed." The magic I could sense dammed up behind my spell didn't feel like an overwhelming amount of power. I found myself hoping that would be the case. Natalie would probably be happier as a low-level mage.

I felt a rush of heat and air, and Natalie gasped.

I opened my eyes. Magical fire and air swirled around Natalie in the center circle. It was mild, but her eyes were wide with terror. "You're fine. It won't hurt you."

Natalie wasn't hearing me. Panic shone in her eyes. She was losing it.

"Natalie, don't—"

Several things happened pretty much simultaneously. Malcolm sensed trouble and closed the third circle. Natalie stumbled and hit her circle, which discharged energy and somehow broke instantly, releasing her fire and air magic into the larger second circle where I stood. Even protected by my spell, I felt the heat as the firestorm raged around us.

Startled by the power surge, Natalie shrieked and flailed blindly, striking me in the stomach. I saw a flash of telltale bright yellow just before I collapsed in a heap, my magic snuffed out like a candle.

In a split second of clarity, I realized Natalie was a null, and a strong one. I'd had no way of knowing that until now, and it was going to cost me big-time.

With no magic to sustain it, my protection spell failed. In the next heartbeat, Natalie's binding spell broke, and the full force of her fire and air magic tore free and roared through the circle—

—where, without a drop of magic in me, I was completely unprotected, and in the middle of an inferno.

10

I screamed and pulled my leather jacket up and over the top of my head, trying to shield my head and face. "*Malcolm!*"

Fire scorched my skin and heat seared my nose and throat, the agony so intense that I almost passed out immediately. I clung to consciousness, desperately trying to think of anything I could do to save myself before I burned to death, but with no magic, I was defenseless.

I sensed an enormous impact of magic that felt like I'd been hit by an invisible bus. Natalie's screaming cut off abruptly, and the fiery maelstrom was suddenly gone. I couldn't see anything. I didn't know if the fire had blinded me or I was just in shock.

From the darkness, I heard Malcolm shouting my name. Something ice-cold hit my right shoulder and fresh agony surged. I tried to scream, but nothing came out. Malcolm's voice rose, and the cold feeling spread through my body, a wave of liquid ice followed by red-hot needles and then numbness. Whatever part of my brain was still functioning recognized an earth-magic healing spell. A second spell hit my left shoulder and I cried out, a pathetic, broken sound.

After that, all I could do was writhe on the floor while Malcolm's spells hit me one after another, trying to save my life. The numbness and pins-and-needles sensations rolled through my body in turns. When I had a moment of peace, I wondered what had happened to Natalie, but then another wave of pain hit and I couldn't care anymore. Finally, mercifully, I blacked out.

I floated in darkness for what felt like a very long time, surfacing for brief moments just long enough to overhear indistinct sounds and feel intense pain.

Eventually, somehow, I was able to stay conscious for a few minutes. Above me, Malcolm floated, almost transparent. "Alice?" His voice was faint. "You've got to get help. I'm too drained to do any more healing spells. I don't know if you're going to make it if we don't get someone over here."

It took a few moments for me to process what he was saying. I realized I was sprawled on the bedroom floor. From where I lay, I could see my phone in my bag next to the library door. It wasn't very far, but I had no idea if I could make it. Every part of me that hadn't been somewhat protected by my jacket radiated agony, and all the skin I could see was red and splotchy. My brain refused to believe what I was seeing, or that I had nearly burned to death.

Slowly, I rolled onto my stomach and began pulling myself across the floor. Every movement brought searing pain. I lost consciousness several times.

Finally, I got to my bag. With swollen fingers, I managed to pull my phone out and drop it on the floor. I held down the button until the screen turned on, then I dragged my fingertip across the screen to unlock the phone. It took three tries.

When I got to the main screen, I used a numb finger to tap the Contacts button. I wanted to find the number for Hawthorne's, but my eyesight was fading. At the last moment, I saw Wolf, the most recent contact I had created, and in desperation tried to touch the green icon next to it.

My head hit the floor next to my phone. From beyond the growing darkness, I heard someone asking if anyone was there.

"Help," I whispered.

I thought I heard a voice say "Alice?" but it might have been wishful thinking. I fell into oblivion.

An eternity later, I surfaced again, roused by a surge of magic that ripped through my brain like talons.

I heard shouting and heavy footsteps, and then a male voice, growly and familiar. "Jesus. Alice?" Somehow, the werewolf had found me.

Gently, slowly, Sean rolled me over onto my back. I tried to open my eyes but couldn't. I sensed him leaning close as his fingertips pressed into my wrist, searching for a pulse. I moaned.

"Thank God." Strong arms scooped me up off the floor and I cried out in pain. "I'm taking you to a hospital."

"No." I kicked weakly. "No hospital. Malcolm...."

"Who is Malcolm?" Sean jerked, and I heard a vicious-sounding snarl. "Who's here?"

"Ghost," I whispered. "Help Malcolm...."

"Help him how?" Sean demanded.

Malcolm spoke. "Help me save her."

Sean jumped at the disembodied voice. "Where are you?"

"I'm right next to you," the ghost snapped. "I need to pull energy from you."

"Do it! Help her!" Sean ordered.

I summoned up enough strength to talk. "No hospital, Malcolm."

"I won't let him take you," Malcolm promised. Sean growled.

Malcolm said something else, but I was fading again and couldn't hear him. I felt an impact on my shoulder and another wave of cold rushed through me, followed by the white-hot needles of another healing spell, and then darkness again.

I had to be alive. You couldn't hurt this much and be dead.

I opened my eyes. Pain. I closed them again. That hurt too. Breathing also hurt. My throat was agonizingly dry.

I sensed movement behind me, and it felt like someone was sanding the skin off my back. I whimpered.

The motion stopped immediately. "Allie?"

I was momentarily confused by the nickname, but I recognized Sean's voice. I opened my eyes and blinked groggily, trying to figure out where I was.

After a moment, I realized I was in Betty's bed, under a mountain of blankets. A bleary glance revealed a familiar arm wrapped around my waist from behind, and that I was wearing a blue nightgown. The soft cotton was probably the best clothing for me to be wearing under the circumstances, but it still felt like the harshest sandpaper. Instead of the severe burns I'd seen before, my skin looked pink and felt sensitive and tight, like I had an all-over sunburn.

I'd been burned with uncontrolled fire and air magic, and I was really damn lucky to be alive and still have skin on my bones. I tried to sense my own magic, but there was nothing there. *Oh, right. Natalie freaking nulled me.* I was *not* getting paid enough for this shit. It might be time to invoke that personal injury clause in our contract. I felt dizzy and closed my eyes.

"Alice?" It was Malcolm.

"Let her sleep," Sean growled from behind me.

Malcolm's voice was patient and nonthreatening. He must have dealt with angry werewolves before. "She's been unconscious for five hours. I need to know what to do to help her."

I forced my eyes open. Malcolm floated in front of me. "Hey," I rasped.

The ghost touched my shoulder. I felt a light tingle of magic, and then he withdrew. "How do you feel?"

I took a deep breath. "Hurts," I said, my voice scratchy. I coughed.

"I know." Malcolm sounded grim. "Natalie nulled you, and your binding spell failed."

"I remember fire." I coughed again. "Water?"

Sean got out of the bed and disappeared in the direction of the kitchen.

"What happened?" I asked my ghost sidekick.

Malcolm looked relieved when Sean was gone. I was sure dealing with an alpha werewolf in protective mode had been difficult. "When Natalie nulled your spells and her magic escaped, I broke your circle, knocked her out, and drained her magic to make healing spells as fast as I could. You went into shock, I kept pulling magic and energy out of Natalie for healing spells until she was drained and so was I. You woke up and managed to call Sean."

I closed my eyes.

Footsteps approached. "Allie, here's some water."

I didn't want water. I was hurting and deeply shaken by how close I'd come to death. Hot tears slid from my eyes, burning like acid on my face.

Gentle fingertips tried to wipe away the tears, but even Sean's light touch was too much. Ignoring the agony of the nightgown scraping my tender skin, I rolled over and turned my back to them, burrowing under the blankets and shaking with pain and shock.

Sean swore. Footsteps moved around the bed. "Allie, you have to drink some water."

"Leave me alone." I meant to sound mean and threatening, but it came out choked and teary. Damn it, couldn't I just be left alone?

Apparently not. I felt the blankets lifted and then Sean got into bed next to me. "Drink the water, Alice." This time it was an order. Alphas don't make requests; they give commands, and they expect to be obeyed.

Well, *I* don't take orders, not anymore. I opened my eyes and glared. Sean was giving me the full-on alpha stare, gold eyes and all, and it made me furious. "Don't order...me around," I told him flatly. Anger gave me strength, and the tears dried up.

Sean's face softened, and his eyes went back to normal. "I'm sorry. I know you're hurting. Please, will you drink some water?" He held out a plastic cup with a straw sticking out of it.

Reluctantly, I leaned forward and drank. The tap water was room temperature, but it tasted like heaven. "Easy, don't make yourself sick," Sean murmured.

As slowly as I could, I drank every drop, then lay back down. Sean set the cup on the floor and gathered me carefully in his arms. I felt acutely uncomfortable. Cuddling together earlier in private was one thing, but now we were in Betty Morrison's bed in Natalie's house, and Malcolm was in here watching us.

"How did you find me?" I asked hoarsely.

Sean stiffened at my tone, though he didn't move away. "I was at work when I got your call. By the time I realized it was you needing help, you'd lost consciousness again. I called a buddy of mine to track your phone. When I got here, your car was out front, but there was no answer at the door. I came in and found you burned to holy hell in here on the floor. After Malcolm got you stabilized, I found something for you to wear and put you in bed so he could keep healing you for as long as we could."

My brain was having trouble catching up. "You came in through the house wards?"

"Yeah, he got a good zap." Malcolm floated into view. "He was bleeding from the nose and ears for a while."

For the first time, I saw blood splattered on the shoulders and front of Sean's green polo shirt just above the lettering that read *Maclin Security*. There were streaks of dried blood below his ears. Getting through the wards had cost him.

"Thank you." My voice was a dry whisper. "I'm sorry I got you mixed up in this."

"Don't be," Sean told me. "I'm glad you're alive. When I saw you, I thought you were dead. I wanted to take you to a hospital, but I guess you can't go to one." His eyes searched my face, looking for an explanation.

"No hospital," I insisted.

Malcolm spoke. "Alice, I gotta be honest with you...if Sean hadn't gotten here when he did, I'm not sure I would have been able to save you. As it was, we used so many healing spells back-to-back that your blood pressure was through the roof. We were worried you'd stroke out if I did any more. If you hadn't stopped seizing, I don't know what else we could have done."

"I told you—" I started to say.

"I know," Malcolm interrupted me. "I know, no hospital, no doctors, but damn it, you were *dying*."

I closed my eyes and dropped my head onto the pillow. "Where's Natalie?"

"She's asleep in her room," Malcolm said. "I used some of Sean's energy to replace the binding spell on her and he put her in bed. She'll probably be asleep until the morning."

"What time is it?"

"Almost midnight," Sean told me.

I jerked. "Charles!"

"Don't worry about that," Sean said. "I'll call and tell them you can't make it."

"I can do it. Can you get me my phone? I think it's over by the library door."

"Okay." Sean slid out of bed again.

I turned to Malcolm. "What's your assessment of Natalie's magic?"

"Mid-level fire, low-to-mid-level air," Malcolm replied. That had been my analysis too, before the proverbial shit hit the fan. "The nulling thing is rare, though. I've known mages who could null, but not as fast as she does. It takes time to drain someone, usually. She can null instantly, and break circles with a touch."

"Tell me about it," I griped.

Sean handed over my phone. I tried to sit up but didn't have the strength. I gave up and fumbled around with the phone, finally getting it unlocked and finding the number for the bar.

Three rings and then Pete answered. "Hawthorne's." I heard voices, laughter, and glasses clinking in the background. It sounded like a busy night.

"Hey, Pete, it's Alice."

"Hey, girl. You still coming in to see us this evening?" Only on VST—Vampire Standard Time—would midnight be considered "evening."

"I don't think I can make it in. I had a little…accident."

A pause, and then the background noise disappeared as Pete stepped into a back room. "Alice, are you okay? You sound like you're in bad shape."

"I'm okay."

Sean growled.

"I *will be* okay," I amended, though I had no idea why I was appeasing Sean. "But I'm not going anywhere tonight. Please extend my apologies to Charles. I'd like to reschedule for tomorrow night, if I can."

"Should I ask Adri to come over and help you?"

I hesitated, debating how to answer. Finally, I said, "I'm not alone. Someone is here."

Another pause. "Who's with you? The werewolf?"

Beside me, Sean went very still.

"Yes. What the hell, Pete? Are you keeping tabs on me now?"

"I'm not keeping tabs on you. We were concerned when you told Bryan you'd been dropped off, but Maclin's car was still in your driveway when we came by with your car. Bryan checked the house, but when everything was quiet, we assumed you'd invited him in."

Sean's face was like granite. The thought Bryan had been snooping around in my yard this morning while Sean and I were inside asleep was enough to make me see red.

"Whether or not I invited him in is none of Bryan's business, or yours," I told Pete through gritted teeth. "Stay out of my personal life."

"Okay, Alice," Pete said quietly. "I'll tell Bryan you won't be in tonight, and he'll let you know when Mr. Vaughan will be available."

"Thank you."

"Good night."

I dropped the phone on the bed and closed my eyes. Whatever energy I'd had was suddenly gone. I felt completely drained, in more ways than one. I could barely move, but things needed to be done, and then I was going home. I wanted out of this house.

I opened my eyes, then pushed myself up until I was sitting. My arms shook and my tender skin hurt, but I blocked it out.

"Out of the bed," I told Sean.

He blinked at me.

"Scoot. Off." I made a shooing motion.

Looking confused, Sean got up. His expression switched from bewildered to angry a second later when I started inching toward the edge of the bed. "Stay there. Tell me what you want, and I'll get it."

I waved him back. "I need to get up. I can't just lie here."

Sean and Malcolm started to argue. If I'd had any magic, I'd have zapped them both. "Stop," I said, holding up a shaking hand. "Just stop, both of you." I swung my legs over the side of the bed, closed my eyes, and waited for the room to stop spinning.

"Allie, for God's sake," Sean said, exasperated.

I opened my eyes and glared at him. "I want to go home. Are the circles still on the floor?"

"Yes," Malcolm said.

"I need to clean those up. Somebody get me a wet towel." I started to get off the bed.

"Stay on the bed," Sean said, then added, "Please," when I glowered at him. "I'll clean up your circles." He stalked off to the bathroom.

"How much energy do you have left?" I asked Malcolm.

"Not much, but I'll give you what I can, and maybe that will get you on your feet and home."

"What kind of shape is Natalie in?" I asked as Sean came back with a wet towel. He began wiping the floor on the other side of the bed, his jaw clenched and anger rolling off him in waves. It occurred to me that he was probably feeling helpless, and that was not an emotion alphas dealt with very well.

"She's fine," Malcolm said. "She's been out since I knocked her out."

"Shit," I breathed. "She's going to be a mess. I'll have to leave her a note again and hope she's calm enough in the morning that I can talk to her. She'll probably think she killed me." I watched Sean cleaning the floor and despised how powerless I was.

I looked at Malcolm. He read my expression and floated over to me. "Do it."

When I touched his arm, I thought, *Thank you for saving my life. I owe you.*

Malcolm smiled at me. *Don't worry about it. I owe you more than I can ever repay for hiding me from Darius.* His face grew serious. *You have some of my magic signature now, since I used so many healing spells on you. You'll have to be careful so that no one senses it.*

All right. I closed my eyes and felt for Malcolm's magic. It was very weak. I slowly pulled energy from him into myself. There wasn't much for me to take; just enough to put him in my earring and maybe raise and lower my house wards.

When I opened my eyes, I could only see his outline; otherwise, he was completely transparent. I touched my earring, protected from the fire by its own spells, and in a heartbeat, he was contained. I could barely feel the earring buzz. I took a deep breath and stood.

I staggered, and in a flash Sean was there to hold me up. "I'm okay," I said in a voice that shook. "Give me a minute."

Sean touched my cheek gently, and even that was painful. "You're *not* okay. I can see how badly you're hurt. There's nothing wrong with letting others help you."

I looked around for the pad and pen I'd used the night before. Shrugging out of Sean's grip, I walked slowly to the nightstand, using the bed to hold myself up, then scrawled another note with trembling hands: *Good morning. Don't worry and don't panic—I'm fine. Give me a call when you're up. Alice.*

I looked down and sighed. I didn't have the energy to change clothes, and it would probably hurt like hell anyway. Screw it; I'd go home in the nightgown.

"Can you grab my bag and my phone?" I asked Sean. He picked them up. Barefoot, I shuffled to the bedroom door, and Sean turned the light off. We moved down the hall at a snail's pace. When we got to Natalie's room, I could hear her snoring lightly. Sean put the note on her nightstand.

I was dead on my feet, but I kept moving like I was on autopilot. We went out the front door and Sean locked it behind us. The wards still felt at full power. I looked at Sean and shook my head. Going through them must have really hurt.

From the front steps, I looked at my car sitting in Natalie's driveway. It felt like a lifetime ago when I'd parked here this afternoon and sat talking to Malcolm. Sean's Mercedes was parked at the curb. The cool air felt good on my hot skin.

"Allie?"

"Yeah?" I realized I was swaying on my feet.

"I'll drive you home in your car. If that's all right," he added.

I appreciated that he was sort of asking. "Okay."

"Okay?" He looked surprised I wasn't arguing.

Things began to get very fuzzy, and I suddenly felt cold all over. "I think you'd better—" I started to say, and then the sidewalk rushed up toward my face and everything went dark.

11

I rocked back and forth on a boat as someone gently wiped my forehead with a cold, wet cloth.

"Mmmrrrph?"

"Hey, baby. Wake up." Sean sounded really worried. But what were we doing on a boat?

I forced my eyes open and blinked a couple of times to bring my surroundings into focus. As it turned out, we were *not* on a boat. We were on the front porch swing at my house, and I was curled up in Sean's lap while he swayed us back and forth slowly with his feet. He had a bottle of cold water and was using his shirt to cool my face.

I blinked slowly, and time seemed to jump forward several minutes by the time I opened my eyes again.

Sean put the wet shirt on the swing. "Can you hear me?"

"Yes." My voice sounded like dry leaves on a sidewalk.

He kissed my forehead, visibly relieved. "Do you think you can lower the wards?"

I thought about it. I was awfully comfy, but I didn't know how long we'd been sitting out here, and Sean probably wasn't comfortable. "I think so," I murmured. "Help me up."

Instead, Sean stood up effortlessly with me in his arms and brought me over to the front door. I tried to reach out, but my arm just flopped uselessly. I frowned at my hand and tried again, but I had no strength. He stepped right up next to the door, and the energy from the wards ran over our skin like an electric current. I was able to touch the house. A little nudge, and the wards fell.

In a flash, Sean had the door unlocked and we were inside, and he kicked the door shut. I was so depleted, the ambient energy of the house wards felt like an invisible, prickly blanket.

"Can you put the wards back up?" he asked me.

"Yes." I reached out to touch the doorframe and focused with extreme difficulty. I got them back up, but it took everything I had. I went limp in Sean's arms, my head falling back while my vision went dark. I made a little noise and started to fade out again.

"No, no, no," he chanted to himself, shifting me so my head flopped onto his chest instead of hanging limply back over his arm. "Come on, Allie, stay with me now. Shit, I shouldn't have even asked about the damn wards."

He rushed through the foyer, up the stairs, and into my room before I could really process what was going on.

He got me under the covers and stripped down to his boxers. The bed dipped as he climbed in next to me and pulled me against his hot, bare skin.

I shivered uncontrollably. "C-cold," I told him, my teeth chattering.

"I know, baby." His mouth was pressed into my hair. "Hold on to me."

Okay, I could live with the nickname Allie, but that was twice now. "Don't c-call me 'b-baby,'" I mumbled, thumping his chest with my fist.

Sean snorted softly. He probably thought it was funny that I was burned to a crisp and bitching at him for calling me "baby." I'd have been mad if I wasn't so wretchedly cold. I buried my face into the side of his neck, and the smell of him was comforting.

We lay like that for a long time, me shivering and him holding me to share his heat. I was so cold that even his werewolf body temperature wasn't warm enough to drive away the chill.

I drifted in and out while he talked to me. I couldn't understand a word he said, but his tone was quiet and soothing. At some point, I cried for a while, though I wasn't exactly sure why. Eventually, I slept.

About an hour before dawn, I woke feeling marginally better, though my skin still felt tight, and I couldn't close my swollen hands into fists or move without serious pain.

Sean dozed, curled around me protectively. He looked exhausted. I reflected on how he'd come looking for me and forced his way through the house wards to get to my side, then let Malcolm use his energy for healing spells. He'd driven me home, sat on the porch until I woke up to let us in, carried me upstairs, and held me for hours while I shivered and cried and slept.

As I looked at him, I felt something strange and unfamiliar stirring in a part of me I thought was dead. I tried to remind myself that alpha werewolves were not boyfriend material, and I was not girlfriend material. I was a haunted house, and not the fun kind you visited on Halloween for cheap thrills. The scars on my back were nothing compared to the ones on the inside.

I realized with a start that Sean's eyes were open and he was watching me. "Did I wake you up?" he asked.

"No." I hesitated. I should tell him to go.

"What's wrong?" Sean brushed my chin with his fingertips.

He was so warm. "I don't want you to go." The words just tumbled out of my mouth before I could stop them.

He kissed me so gently that I barely felt it. "I don't want to go either, so that's fine. Just rest." He tried to hold my hand, but pain made me hiss and he quickly let go. "I'm sorry. Is there anything I can do to help you? Can Malcolm—"

I shook my head. "Malcolm's drained to nothing. Can you get my healing spells for me? There's a wooden box in my second drawer in the bathroom. Don't open it; just bring it to me."

"Okay." Sean carefully unwound himself from around me and slid out of bed. He went to the bathroom and returned with my first aid kit. He knelt next to me on the bed and looked at the box. "It's beautiful. What are these carvings?"

"Runes to keep anyone from sensing the spells inside." I took the box from him and traced three runes on its lid before opening it.

Sean watched as I used my swollen fingers to paw through the spells, then awkwardly lifted out a purple crystal. I closed the box and set it aside. I knew I needed a strong healing spell, and this was the second-strongest in the box. I also knew it was going to hurt, and that was going to make a certain werewolf very unhappy.

I tried to sound as clinical as possible. "This is a powerful healing spell. I'm pretty sure it will be enough to heal the burns and the rest of the damage, but it's going to be painful. I don't know if you've ever seen one used, so I just wanted you to know what to expect so you're not surprised. Don't touch me until the spell is done."

A muscle moved in Sean's jaw. "Will it be worse than the ones Malcolm used earlier?"

I considered. "Probably. Those were earth magic. Blood magic is more intense. Maybe you should go downstairs while I do this."

Sean's gaze turned steely. "If you can stand it, so can I."

"Okay. Give me some space, then, and get the trash can for me in case I need it."

Reluctantly, Sean moved to the edge of the bed and scooted the wastebasket closer.

I pulled up one side of the nightgown and grabbed one of my pillows. Before I had too much time to tense up, I held the crystal to my abdomen and invoked the spell. "*Helios.*"

Magic hit me like a freight train. I put the pillow over my face to muffle my hoarse screams as what felt like liquid ice and burning acid rolled through my body. Instinct made me want to throw the source of the pain across the room, and it took every ounce of my willpower not to. I squashed the pillow to my face as hard as I could and panted out breaths between shrieks as the crystal pulsed, discharging its healing energy into my body in waves. My skin tingled as the magic went to work. I hadn't used a strong healing spell in a while, and it hurt every bit as badly as I remembered.

Finally, an eternity later, the pulses began to slow, signaling that the spell was completing its work. As the waves began to ease and numbness set in, I took the pillow off my face. Through the fog of pain and healing magic, I heard a low, reverberating sound.

It took me a full ten seconds to realize it came from Sean.

He was pacing back and forth next to the bed and growling, his hands clenched into fists, his eyes bright gold. At that moment, he looked much closer to wolf than man. I felt a little stab of fear, though I knew it was the instinct to protect, not harm, that was calling his wolf close to his skin.

When he saw me looking at him, he stopped pacing and came to the side of the bed, leaning on it with both hands. "Is it done?"

I felt a whisper of magic from the crystal, then stillness as the last of its healing power gave out. I dropped the empty crystal on the bed. "Now it's done." My voice cracked.

Sean was shaking with the effort of holding himself back. "Did it work?"

I moved carefully, testing my limbs. I couldn't see my skin well in the darkness, but the pain and tightness of the burns were gone. I was achy and nauseous, but it didn't feel like I was going to throw up, thankfully. "I think it worked."

In a flash, Sean was on the bed and pulling me into his arms. "That was just about the worst fucking thing I've ever had to stand by and watch," he growled into my hair, squeezing me so tightly that my bones creaked. "You don't know how hard it was not to take that thing away from you."

"You know you can't interfere with a spell when it's working." His chest muffled my voice. "It's over. Now I'm all better."

He made a strangled sound. "A few hours ago, you were close enough to Death to look him in the eye. Then you went through a healing spell that looked like it hurt as much as a werewolf's first shift, and now you're 'all better.' How can you be so calm about this?"

I couldn't tell him how many times I'd looked Death in the eye, or how many strong healing spells I'd had to withstand over the years. I might not have had much use for them after I escaped my grandfather's cabal, but during the twenty years I was under its control, I'd teetered on the edge of the abyss many times, only to be yanked back unwillingly into the land of the living. Alice Worth hadn't had nearly as many run-ins with Death, but Moses Murphy's granddaughter was no stranger to the coldness of his scythe.

"I've used healing spells before," I told him.

He stilled, probably remembering the scars on my back. "I guess you have."

I moved the first aid box to the floor next to the bed and put the empty crystal on the nightstand. I got up, stretched carefully, then went to my dresser for pajamas. I grabbed a pair and changed into them in the bathroom.

When I came back out, Sean raised the covers in a silent invitation. I climbed in next to him, and he wrapped himself around me, as much for his own comfort as mine, I thought. In moments, I fell into a deep, dreamless sleep.

I woke midmorning to my phone blaring. I groaned, untangling myself from Sean to roll over and grab it from the nightstand. I rubbed my eyes, looked at the screen, and tried to sound alert when I answered. "Morning, Natalie."

I heard her sobbing. "Alice, I'm so sorry. Are you okay?"

"I'm fine. I got a little singed, but I'm okay."

Beside me, Sean growled. I elbowed him in the ribs and he grunted.

Natalie sniffled. "Are you sure?"

"Yes." I stifled a grimace as I shifted to a more comfortable position on the bed and my sore muscles protested. Sean watched me like a hawk for signs of distress. "How do *you* feel?"

She made a sound like a half laugh, half sob. "Like I've got the worst hangover I've had since college. I could barely get out of bed."

"You'll probably feel a little weak for a day or two. We bound your magic again, so you're safe. I do have some good news on that front. You have fire and air magic, like your grandmother, but your power is low-to-mid-range, which is easier to learn to control. Also, it keeps you off the cabals' radar." I paused.

"What else?" Natalie prodded.

"You have an additional ability that's unusual. Do you remember what I told you about nulls?"

"Mages who can drain other people's magic?"

"Yes. You're a null."

"What's unusual about that? You said there are lots of them."

"It's unusual because you can do it so quickly. A lot of mages can drain someone else's energy, but it takes a while. Your ability is lightning fast, and you do it instinctually. You drained me just by touching me." She gasped. "It's fine—I'm recovering well enough, but it's one more thing that you'll need to learn to control. *If* you decide to learn, that is."

She went quiet. Sean rubbed my back and it felt really good.

"Don't make a decision right now when you're upset. We've got time. Your binding spell will hold for as long as you need to decide what to do. You can do something for me, though."

She took a deep breath. "What can I do?"

"If it's okay with you, I'll swing by your house with Malcolm. We'll double-check to make sure there aren't any more spells in the library, and then I'd like you to look through your grandmother's papers and books to see if she has anything that might indicate what was in that hidden compartment. In the meantime, I'm going to track down your aunts and uncle and try to figure out which one of them has been in your house. I'll need whatever information you have on them, like addresses, phone numbers, work info, photos, et cetera."

"I can do that," she said. Her voice sounded stronger. Giving her a project to work on helped her cope. "I'll have it for you when you get here."

"Great. I'll head over in about an hour." We disconnected and I flopped back in the bed.

Sean lay on his side and propped his head on his hand. "Sounds like a busy day."

"It'll be nice to do some actual *investigating* today. I don't want to tempt fate, but I sincerely hope I'm done with the near-death experiences for a while."

"Knock on wood," Sean said and rapped my skull lightly with his knuckles.

"Ha-ha."

We lay in my bed for a while, me on my back staring at the ceiling, Sean on his side facing me. It was a comfortable silence.

"What are you thinking about?" he asked finally.

I thought about different ways to answer that question, then settled on simply "You."

"What about me?"

"Well, for one thing, you got your wish."

"What wish?"

I gave him a wry smile. "To see me again."

He shook his head. "This was about as far from what I was hoping for as it can get." He paused. "Having said that...do I get a date?"

"You don't give up, do you?"

"No." The wolfish smile was back. "How about tonight?"

I sat up and leaned back against my headboard, putting some distance between us. "Do you think I owe you a date?"

"I don't think you owe me anything," Sean stated. "But I was hoping you might think it was at least worth considering."

"I told you yesterday I would think about it."

He gave me a look. "You and I both know you'd already decided."

He had me there. I didn't insult him by denying it.

"I get that you're cautious," he said. "I'm sure I would be too, if I'd been through whatever you've been through. I'd like to know what I need to do or say for you to give me a chance."

Sean could have reminded me of everything he'd done for me since I called him for help yesterday, but he didn't. He looked sincere when he told me I didn't owe him anything for saving my life. He was persistent, but I understood the value of single-mindedness; my own stubbornness had kept me alive more times than I cared to count. He was an alpha, but other than a brief moment last night when he'd tried to order me to drink water, he hadn't tried to control me. All those things were certainly in his favor, along with the great sex, the sense of humor, and our shared love of music and craft beer.

Unfortunately, on the other side of the equation was my life, and that was a pretty big consideration. It was a lot to risk for a slim chance at happiness.

Sean watched me for clues as to where my deliberations were headed. I thought I had a pretty good poker face, but he was probably even better than me at reading microexpressions. He sat up, looking resigned.

The sunlight coming through the window revealed dried blood on his neck and ears. The man had suffered and bled to save me. No one had done anything like that for me in a very long time, and that had to be worth something.

I took a deep breath. "You asked what you could do to prove yourself."

Sean tilted his head. "Yes."

"How long have you been in the security business?"

"Almost twenty years."

I blinked. He didn't look more than thirty-five, but shifters aged more slowly than humans. He must be in his early forties, then. "Permits and licenses current?"

"All of them."

"Willing to sign a nondisclosure and confidentiality agreement?"

His mouth twitched. "Is this a job interview?"

"Of a sort."

"Then, yes."

I was quiet. Sean waited.

Finally, I said, "Here's my offer. I have a full day ahead of me, as you heard. Come with me."

"In what capacity?"

"Colleague."

He grinned. "Colleague, huh?"

"That's the offer. I've got to do some work at my client's home, then track down four people who might have taken something from her house, something that might be dangerous."

He turned serious. "How dangerous?"

"I'm not sure yet. It's a magical item of some sort, possibly an object of power, or a focus. I'm still looking into that." I sighed. "Of course, this is all assuming you can take a day off from work. Is that even an option?"

"Already taken care of. I told my business partner last night that I wouldn't be in. He's got everything covered. I thought you might need me today."

I stiffened. "'Need' you?"

Sean's eyes darkened. "Yes, *need* me. When I texted Ron last night, I was holding you on your front porch and you were unconscious. You'd been burned, gone into shock, and were unresponsive for five hours. I thought you might be dying in my arms. You'd made it very clear I couldn't take you to the hospital—for reasons I haven't even asked about, I might add—so I sat there helpless, listening to you breathe and waiting to see if you would live or die."

I shifted uncomfortably. "Sean—"

"Alice, let me say this, please."

I waited.

"I took the day off in case you still hadn't woken up, or you needed someone to take care of you, even though you hate relying on anyone's help and get really unreasonably angry about it. Fortunately, thanks to Malcolm and me and the healing spells, you're well enough to drag yourself out of bed and carry on with this investigation, and I'm free to be a part of your day, as a *colleague*. And despite your tendency to think the worst of me and my intentions, I'd rather be with you than anywhere else right now."

I was shocked by the vehemence in Sean's words. I felt torn between my resentment and guilt for not thinking more about what he'd gone through.

I didn't do well with guilt; it made me angry. I spent so long under the cabal's control, the two emotions went hand in hand for me: shame over the things I did, combined with fury at my grandfather and his lieutenants for forcing me to make people suffer. On some level, I knew Sean didn't deserve my anger, but I felt guilty, and that made me mad. I didn't need any more guilt. I carried so much already, sometimes it crushed me flat.

On top of that, I was rattled by his statement that he'd rather be with me than anywhere else. This one-night stand was evolving into something that scared me.

My isolation began when I was eight years old and my grandfather murdered my parents—not that I had many friends before that, but after they died, I had no one. Twenty-one lonely years later, maybe I didn't have to be alone anymore. Everything Sean had done for me made me think that maybe I could allow him to try to earn my trust.

"I'm sorry," I said finally. "If you still want to come with me, you can." I didn't want it to sound like I was reluctantly granting him a boon, but I think that's how it came out.

Sean didn't look happy. "You don't sound very enthusiastic about it."

"I'm used to being on my own," I admitted. "And you're right: I don't like relying on other people, or needing help. I'm unreasonable about it, and I'm liable to try to take your head off at any time for no good reason. Sometimes I'm rude, and I'm no good at being friendly because I've never had many friends. They were just one more thing that could be used against me by the people who wanted to control me."

Sean's eyes softened, and he reached out to comfort me. I moved away, which clearly frustrated him. "I'm not looking for sympathy; I'm just stating facts. I'm trying to figure out if I can trust you, and maybe letting you come with me today will help me answer that question. Knowing all that, if you want to go with me and find out the hard way how difficult I am to be around, then let's do it."

Sean and I looked at each other. I had no idea what he was thinking. I half expected him to get up and leave.

Instead, he stretched and grinned at me. "So who gets the shower first?"

12

I got the shower first while Sean went down to my car for his go-bag. I dropped the wards to let him go in and out without getting fried—again—and shut myself in the bathroom.

I took off my pajamas, stood in front of the mirror, and looked myself over. My skin looked normal, with no sign of burns. My head and face had thankfully been protected by my jacket, but my hair was a horror show; it had come out the braid I'd put it in yesterday and was sticking out wildly in all directions. Gah. If Sean hadn't run screaming at the sight of that mess, maybe he was tougher than I already gave him credit for.

I climbed into the shower with a wide-tooth comb and spent ten minutes just trying to unsnarl the colony of rats' nests that was my hair. It was painful and required a lot of swearing and conditioner. Finally clean and detangled, I wrapped my hair in a towel and myself in a bathrobe, brushed my teeth, and stuck my first aid kit back in the bathroom drawer before returning to the bedroom.

I found Sean lying on the bed in his boxers, chest bare and fingers laced behind his head. I took a moment to appreciate the mouthwatering view. From the gleam in his eyes, he was well-aware of the effect he was having on me.

"Is there any hot water left?" he asked, raising an eyebrow.

"Yes," I grumped. "Get in there before I change my mind and leave you behind."

"Yes, ma'am." He sprang out of bed and picked me up around the waist, kissing me so thoroughly, my toes curled. Then he put me down and went into the bathroom with his bag.

After the door closed and the shower came on, I checked my phone. There was a text message from Bryan that Charles would be busy tonight, but I could meet with him tomorrow night at ten. I texted him back that I'd be there.

I was already dressed by the time Sean stepped out of the bathroom wearing a black polo shirt and khakis. "Any idea where my jacket and boots are?" I asked.

Sean turned grim. "Your clothes were nothing but rags. Even the jacket and boots were pretty much destroyed."

I closed my eyes and sighed. "Those were my favorite boots. Son of a bitch." I went into my closet for my backup pair, then sat on the bed to put them on.

Sean started shaving in the bathroom. I realized he was the first man to do so, and that made me pause. I wasn't sure why it seemed so significant to me. Maybe because I'd never encouraged a man to stick around before? Hard to say. I found I liked watching him shave as I got ready and wondered what that meant.

I finished zipping up my boots, then put on my charm bracelet, rings, and monogram necklace. I picked up Malcolm's earring for the first time since last night and it buzzed in my hand. He at least had regenerated much of his magic; I, on the other hand, had been nulled so completely that I had almost none, and I hated how vulnerable it made me feel. I thought about having sex with Sean, simply to restore my magic. I watched him washing the rest of the shaving cream off his face and decided even I couldn't be that cold-blooded.

I left Malcolm where he was for now and put the earrings on. Sean was finished in the bathroom, so I traded places with him and put on my makeup and french-braided my damp hair while he packed up his dirty clothes and toiletries. In a few minutes, we were both ready. I stuck my phone in my bag and we headed out.

By the time we got in the car, we'd agreed to stop at Moe's, a fast-food place I liked that was between my house and Natalie's. I adjusted the driver's seat, which had been pushed all the way back to accommodate Sean's height, and we were off. If Sean's instincts were rebelling against being in the passenger seat, he didn't let on. It was a point in his favor.

I turned on the radio as background noise. "So, tell me about yourself," I invited as I drove.

"What would you like to know?"

"How old are you?"

"Forty-two." Which was about what I'd figured.

"Where were you born?"

"Here—well, on a farm not too far from here. My brother and his family live there now, with my parents." Sean seemed entirely comfortable answering questions. I tried to feel as comfortable asking them. As someone who was intensely private about her life, it was hard to feel at ease asking someone else to reveal personal details.

I really wanted to know if he'd been born a werewolf or been bitten, but that wasn't something you asked. He'd tell me himself if he wanted to. I asked about his security company instead.

"My friend Ron Dormer and I worked together for a different security company for about five years," Sean told me. "Then we decided to start our own business. It took a couple of years to build up a decent client base, but now we've got about thirty full-time employees, plus about two dozen part-timers. Our office is downtown, on Decatur near the park."

I pictured the area. "I know where that is. What kind of work do you do?"

"The personal security division does short-term bodyguard or security work. Our installation division sets up surveillance and security systems."

"And your friend who tracks cell phones?"

"Cyro's not an on-the-books employee. He's more of a consultant who works on a cash-only basis."

"With that kind of illegal equipment, I guess he would."

"He does more than track phones. I provided security for a woman last year who was going through a particularly nasty divorce. Her husband was abusive and threatening to take their kids out of the country. Cyro did some digging into the husband's financials, and it turned out he was laundering money for a cabal. Cyro sent the info to the Feds, and problem solved. Guy's doing twenty in federal prison, and the kids are safe with their mom."

"Good for him. Sounds like Cyro is a good man to know, and not someone you'd want to cross."

"That's for sure. He likes to see justice done, and he has the technology and expertise to make it happen."

"Interesting."

Sean glanced at me. "What are you thinking?"

"Not a thing."

His eyes narrowed. "Your tone sounded like you were thinking about something or someone in particular where some justice is needed."

"Nope."

Sean snorted. I ignored him and turned into the drive-thru at Moe's. I ordered a breakfast sandwich and coffee. He opted for three double bacon cheeseburgers, two large orders of home fries, and a large soda. I wondered if he planned to eat it all or if he'd ordered extra thinking I might need it. We focused on eating rather than conversation as I drove to Natalie's house.

By the time I pulled into her driveway, we'd finished all our food. I resisted the urge to steal from Sean's fries; his werewolf metabolism needed the calories after giving up so much of his energy healing me. He looked like he could have eaten more.

I knocked on the front door, and Natalie answered it. She looked pale—not surprising, after what happened yesterday—but her expression lightened when she saw me standing on the porch, as if she hadn't believed I was all right until she saw me with her own eyes. "I'm so glad to see you." She stepped back to let us inside. "I really thought I'd killed you."

"I'm okay." Sean looked like he wanted to say something, but I gave him a look and he changed his mind. "It was close, but we were fine."

Natalie looked at Sean. "Hi, I'm Natalie," she said, sticking out her hand. He shook it.

Oops. I'd forgotten they'd never actually met. "Natalie, this is Sean, my colleague. Sean, Natalie Newton, my client. Sean was over here last night to help with the...cleanup."

"Oh." Natalie's cheeks turned pink. "Well, I'm so sorry about yesterday. It was entirely my fault. Alice is very kind to not blame me for everything that's happened in this house. Thank you for helping."

"Not a problem," Sean said, though something in his eyes made me think he wasn't happy with Natalie's role in yesterday's events.

To distract him, I got down to business. "Do you have the info on your aunts and uncle?"

Natalie led the way into the kitchen and handed me a piece of paper that had been waiting on the counter. On it were the names, addresses, phone numbers, and work information for our suspects. I scanned the list.

"Did I forget anything?" Natalie asked.

"Nope, this looks good. Thank you. We'll start checking them out today. In the meantime, I think Malcolm and I will take a look in the library again." I stuck the sheet in my bag.

"Would you like some tea?" Natalie asked us.

"I would," I said.

"Sure," Sean added.

I headed down the hall, Sean trailing along behind me.

When we got to Betty's bedroom, I flipped on the light and gasped. The floor was badly charred, but there was an irregular unburned shape in the middle of the scorched area. I went cold when I realized that must have been where my body had lain. I'd been too out of it to notice the damage last night. The blood drained from my face.

"Allie?" Sean touched my arm lightly. "Are you all right?"

The sight of the burned floor paralyzed me. It was easier to pretend I hadn't been so badly injured when I didn't have to see the evidence of what happened.

Suddenly, the lingering smell of fire magic and burned wood and the scorched outline of a body catapulted me back in time to another house, where two similar body-shaped burns, one larger, one smaller, were plainly visible, as was the fact they'd been holding on to each other and died where they'd fallen. A terrified eight-year-old girl stood over the ash on the floor, shaking and crying, next to an old man with cruel eyes.

"The floor will have to be replaced." My voice sounded strange, distant, like someone else was talking.

Sean's hand wrapped around my arm. "Hey."

I pulled away. When I looked at him, I knew my eyes showed the darkness in my head. "What are you remembering?" he asked me softly.

"Nightmares." I didn't want to talk about it. I turned away from him and touched Malcolm's earring. "*Release.*"

Malcolm appeared a few feet in front of me. This time, he didn't yell, and I didn't stumble backward from the force of his aura. We must be getting better at this.

He looked at me, clearly relieved. "Alice, I am so glad to see you up and around."

"I'm glad to *be* up and around." My voice still sounded a little off. "We need to check the library for any more spells before we let Natalie back in there."

Malcolm's eyes flicked to Sean and back. "You have a new partner?"

"I'm her *colleague*," Sean said, humor evident in his tone.

"It's temporary," I said. Sean shot me an irritated look that I ignored. "Let's check out the library."

Walking around the burned section of the floor, I opened the library door and flipped on the light switch. With a flick of my fingers, I dropped our perimeter wards. "Can you raise the containment wards again?" I asked Malcolm. Sean stayed outside the library, watching us through the open door.

Malcolm raised them. "What are we looking for?"

"I've asked Natalie to search through Betty's books and papers to see if there's anything that might indicate what was taken from that compartment. I want to make sure there aren't any spells or booby traps in here that she might trigger while she's looking, so we need to be thorough. Betty was tricky."

"Got it. You want to do that side, and I'll check over here?" Malcolm gestured to the wall to our left. I went to the right.

I started at the top of the bookcase. I raised my hand above my head, closed my eyes, and lowered my shields. I passed my hand slowly along the books, reaching out with my senses. I felt extremely low levels of air and fire magic, probably echoes left from the last time Betty had handled the books. When I cleared the top shelf, I moved to the next one, and the next. Across the room, Malcolm was doing the same.

We moved slowly and carefully. I cleared the first bookcase and moved to the second one. About halfway through the third shelf, I felt a spark of strong magic on a particular book. I carefully pulled it from the shelf. It was a very old book, stuck in among a bunch of newer texts on magical theory. Its cover and spine were blank, but inside a spidery handwriting covered the lined pages. A journal, perhaps? I set it aside and continued.

We made our rounds of the library, and then I checked the desk and file cabinet and found nothing while Malcolm double-checked the floor. The library appeared to be clean of spells.

At some point, Natalie had come with tea for Sean. When I finished with the desk, he was drinking from a large mug and sitting in the hard-backed chair in Betty's bedroom.

I swayed on my feet, shaky from having my shields down and senses wide open for so long. Sean watched me as I wiped my forehead with the back of my hand and took the journal to the love seat.

On the first page, Betty had written her full name: *Elizabeth Ann Finchley Eppright Morrison*. Below that was an incantation. I had no idea what it would trigger and obviously did not read it aloud.

I flipped through the pages. It looked like this was part of Betty's spell book, but all of the spells it contained were for her air magic. It looked like she kept her fire and blood magic spells recorded separately. I hadn't seen any other spell books. None of the other books in the library carried as much residual energy as this one, and even it was fairly light. I wondered if that meant that Betty had been focusing on her fire and blood magic before she died. Were the other spell books what had been taken from the compartment? Or were they the books that were missing from the bottom shelf, and the item from the compartment something else entirely?

I told Malcolm what I'd found, and my theories about the rest of Betty's spells. We looked back through all the books, but nothing we saw looked or felt like another spell book.

"I bet someone took them," Malcolm said, echoing my thoughts, when we'd come up empty from our second search of the library. "They were probably on that bottom shelf."

"Still no idea what was in that compartment." I collapsed back onto the loveseat to catch my breath. "We need a name for it so we don't have to keep saying 'whatever was in that compartment.'"

"We could call it the MacGuffin," Malcolm suggested.

"The what?"

"You know, the MacGuffin. That's what Hitchcock called the mystery objects in his movies that the characters were always after, like the microfilm James Mason was smuggling in *North by Northwest*."

I stared at him. "Okay. Fine. It's the MacGuffin."

"Excellent." Malcolm was pleased. Sean regarded us with his eyebrows raised, clearly amused.

Natalie appeared, holding a mug of tea. "Is it safe to come in?"

"Yes," I said.

Tentatively, Natalie stepped over the threshold and frowned. "I felt something."

"A containment ward, in case we triggered a spell in here, but everything seems neutralized," Malcolm told her.

"Oh. Good." Natalie handed me the tea and I took it gratefully. The hot liquid helped settle my stomach. "So I should look through the desk and the file cabinet?"

"Yes. It looks like there are a lot of papers in both." I held up the book I'd found. "We found one of your grandmother's spell books, but the other ones are missing. They might have been taken from the bottom shelf. We're not sure, but we need to try and find out what the MacGuffin is."

"The what?"

I made a face at Malcolm. "You explain it." I heaved myself up off the love seat and left the library, moving into the master bedroom to stand next to Sean while Malcolm explained the esoteric reference to Natalie. She was either fascinated by Malcolm's film history knowledge or doing a good job of feigning interest.

I didn't want to stay in Betty's bedroom with the burns on the floor. "Whoever was in here, we don't want them to be able to get back in this room. Malcolm, can you set up wards on the library that allow us and Natalie in and out and no one else?"

"Sure."

I turned on my heel and left the master bedroom with Sean in my wake.

When I got to the living room, I pulled the paper Natalie had given me out of my bag and looked at it. I was relieved my hands were steady. The flashback to my parents' murder had unnerved me. I needed to focus on looking for the person who had gotten into Natalie's house and taken the books and the MacGuffin from the library. There was no time for the horrors of the past to be sneaking up on me.

Sean stepped up next to me. "What's the plan?"

"I need to get within touching distance of these people in order to sense who has magic. I should be able to recognize their magical signature based on the wards that were set in the library if I can get skin contact with them for a few seconds."

Sean read the list over my shoulder. I started to bristle, then reminded myself to relax. He was a professional colleague with valuable advice.

"Well, this guy is an insurance agent." He pointed at Peter's name and info. "They meet with people all day long. Kathy is a real estate agent. Aren't we in the market for a new house?" He grinned at me, and I smiled.

Maybe this "colleague" thing wasn't so bad after all.

Elise and Deborah would be a little trickier. They were both housewives, and Elise had already met me. I might need a disguise for that one. I could either try to catch them at home or follow them and try to bump into them while they were running errands.

"Who do we want first?" Sean asked.

I considered. "Well, the insurance agent should be easy enough to get in to see. How about we call up for an appointment?" I pulled out my phone and called his office.

Once I got past the automated phone system, a cheerful secretary came on the line. "Eppright Insurance. This is Mandy."

"Hello. My name is Audrey," I told her, using one of my aliases. "My fiancé and I recently moved to the city, and we're looking for a local insurance agent for our home and cars. We wondered if Mr. Eppright might be available to meet with us?"

"Of course!" I heard computer keys clicking in the background. "When are you available?"

"We're free this afternoon, unless that's too soon."

"I have a two o'clock available."

I checked my watch. It was almost one. Plenty of time. "We can make it."

I gave her my fake name—Audrey Talbot—and a posh address in one of the city's newer gated communities. When she asked, I told her my fiancé's name was Sean and managed to say it without coughing. Much.

"We'll see you soon!" the receptionist chirped. We disconnected.

Sean grinned again. "Promoted from temporary colleague to fiancé in less than a day," he teased. "I must be doing something right."

"You definitely do *something* right. Keep up the good work, and I might be able to talk the boss into offering you a better position. With benefits."

A gold sheen rolled over Sean's eyes. "Tell the boss I am committed to the quality of my work, and I look forward to proving it in any *position* she wants me in."

A wave of heat settled low in my belly. I made a little sound and shuffled my feet.

Sean growled low in his throat and nuzzled the back of my neck. "You smell like sex," he whispered, lips against my skin.

I shivered and stepped away from him. Sean had that distinctly male self-satisfied look that made me simultaneously want to punch him and pull him down to the floor.

Fortunately, Natalie came walking into the room to save me from my hormones. "Malcolm's finishing up the wards. There's a lot of stuff in the desk and cabinet. What should I be looking for?"

I cleared my throat and avoided Sean's fiery gaze. "Hard to say. We don't know what was in the compartment, but your grandmother's fire and blood magic spell books seems to be missing too. So anything that refers to fire or blood magic, an object of power, or really, anything that just seems weird to you."

"This all seems pretty weird to me." She thought about it for a moment, then added, "But way less weird than it would have seemed two days ago."

I laughed at that. "I bet."

Natalie smiled. "You want some more tea?"

"We're going to be heading out to go see your uncle. What do you think of him?"

"We're not very close." Natalie leaned against the doorway. "As I said, he was my grandmother's only child from her first marriage, and I don't think he ever felt entirely comfortable around my mom or my aunts because he was nine or ten when his dad died and my grandmother remarried and his stepsisters were all so much younger. I always got the impression that he felt like a fifth wheel. My mom used to tell me that after he moved out to go to college, he didn't really come around that often."

A quick online search revealed that Eppright had no social media presence, but he'd been in the newspaper a year ago. I studied the picture. Peter Eppright appeared to be in his late fifties. He was posing with two other local businessmen, all wearing tuxedos and toasting champagne glasses.

I used my phone to pull up the location of Eppright's office, which was partway across town. It would probably take us close to a half hour to get there. "We'd better leave soon." I headed back toward the library.

When I got to Betty's bedroom, Malcolm was standing inside the library, finishing the wards. I marveled at their beauty as he wove the spells together to form a perimeter around the entire room. No rookie mistakes with Malcolm. Inexperienced and poorly trained mages often warded around doorways and windows, since those were obvious points of ingress, but walls, floors, and ceilings could be broken through, which is why *good* wards run around the perimeter of the room, top and bottom, blocking all four walls, floor, and ceiling.

I recognized my own magic signature in the wards, along with Malcolm's and Natalie's, which granted us free passage. It looked like they were set to incapacitate any trespassers. I thought about upping the ante but wondered if there was much point. Betty had tried to protect the library's contents with wards so deadly, they'd nearly taken me out months after her death, but it hadn't been enough; the MacGuffin and the books were gone, taken by one of the two people Betty thought she could trust. Malcolm's wards would knock out anyone who tried to get into the library. At this point, doing more seemed like closing the proverbial barn door long after the horses were gone.

Malcolm finished his work. "What do you think?" he asked, gesturing with both hands at the room.

"Looks damn good." I stepped over the threshold. "I had a thought. Can you add to the containment spell and make this a 'safe' room for Natalie?"

Malcolm frowned. "What are you thinking?"

"Here's what I want. If Natalie's magic breaks free of her binding spells, I'm wondering if we can set a containment spell so she could come in here. The spell would confine her magic and keep her from either destroying the house or attracting unwanted attention, and then drain her magic into the wards."

Malcolm was thinking. "So long as she doesn't touch the wards and accidentally null them, it will work. I can do it. It's going to take some time, though."

"Sean and I are going to check out Peter Eppright and see if he's our mage. Why don't I leave you here to work on the spells and we'll be back?"

Malcolm looked surprised and then nervous. I realized we hadn't parted company since he'd popped into my office two days ago. "You can sense me wherever I am, right?" I asked.

He nodded slowly. "You're like a beacon, but then again, I've never been very far from you."

"I know, but distance shouldn't matter. I speak from experience on this one. We could be in different states and you'd still be able to find me without too much trouble."

Malcolm looked a little less anxious. "Okay. No problem. We have to get used to this sometime." He sounded like he was talking to himself more than me. "Go on and go. I'll work on these wards while you're gone."

"Okay. Back soon."

I stepped out of the library and led Sean back down the hall to the living room, where Natalie sat on the couch with a cat in her lap. I told her Malcolm was staying to work on the library wards.

"Should I go back there and keep him company?"

I shook my head. "He's going to be focused for a while. He might come back in here when he's done, though. Hopefully he doesn't scare you too badly when he does."

Natalie laughed. "I'll have to remember he's here so I don't do anything embarrassing."

I grabbed my bag and headed out with Sean. I went to my trunk, opened it, and dug around in the large duffel I keep back there as an emergency disguise kit. I swapped out my crystal jewelry for a nice pair of gold hoop earrings. From inside a zippered pouch, I pulled out a sparkly ring and slipped it onto my left hand.

Sean looked at the ring. "You keep a spare engagement ring in your trunk?"

"It's just cubic zirconia. I had to investigate a bridal shop a few months ago." I closed the trunk and we got in my car.

I followed the GPS instructions across the city to Eppright Insurance and parked in front of the next building over.

"We keep the story simple," I said as we walked toward his office. "Just got engaged a month ago and moved to the city from Los Angeles. I'll do the emergency phone call ruse if he gets too pushy."

"Sounds like a plan." Sean opened the door and we stepped inside Eppright Insurance.

13

A young brunette receptionist with a name tag identifying her as Mandy sat behind a large L-shaped desk right beside the door. A man and a woman in business casual chatted near the door of an open office. No one else waited in the lobby, but I could hear voices down the hall.

"Hi, can I help you?" Mandy asked.

"I'm Audrey Talbot," I said. "We have a two o'clock appointment?"

"Of course!" Mandy grabbed a clipboard and some forms and handed them to me with a smile. "Have a seat in the lobby and fill these out so Mr. Eppright has a better idea of your needs, and he'll call you in a few minutes."

I took the clipboard and went to sit in the small lobby. Sean got two cups of water from the cooler and came to sit next to me as I tapped the pen and looked over the questionnaire.

"Seems pretty standard," Sean said, glancing at the paperwork.

I started filling out our fake contact information, then moved on to the more detailed questions. As I was reaching the end of the questionnaire, a man's deep voice said, "Sean? Audrey?"

We looked up. Peter Eppright wore a button-up shirt, slacks, and designer shoes. He glanced at me, then focused his attention on Sean, beaming and holding out his hand. At another time, being dismissed might have annoyed me, but in this scenario, having Eppright's attention on Sean would work in my favor. While he was busy schmoozing with my fake fiancé, I would be taking the measure of his magic.

He shook Sean's hand first, then turned to me, almost as an afterthought.

I lowered my shields, smiled brightly, and reached out. His handshake was strong. A frisson of familiar magic trickled over my hand: air and fire, but only a trace. I drew on it gently. Eppright's smile faltered, as if he'd sensed something, but when I withdrew and raised my shields, it was back up to full strength. The entire exchange took about three seconds.

"Please follow me," Eppright said, gesturing at the hallway. Sean and I fell in step behind him as he led us past cubicles and offices to the end of the hall and a large corner office. "Have a seat." We settled into the guest chairs while he sat behind his desk.

I wanted to parse what I'd sensed about Peter Eppright's magic, but first I had a part to play. "Thanks so much for seeing us today," I said to Natalie's uncle, handing over our clipboard. "We didn't get quite all the way through."

"No problem, no problem," Eppright said, waving it away as unimportant. "It's just to give me an idea of what we might able to do for you." He looked over the questionnaire, and I took the opportunity to think about what I'd felt.

There was no doubt he was Betty's son. His magic felt very similar to hers, but was it the *same* magical signature from the library wards and the spell on the secret compartment? Perhaps, but he had so little magical energy, it was practically nonexistent. The signature in the wards felt strong. Still, I wasn't ready to dismiss Eppright as a suspect quite yet.

Eppright finished reading through the questionnaire. He must have liked what he saw, because he leaned forward in his chair. "I can see you are building a wonderful life together," he said, looking at my ring and then back to Sean. "And you need to protect everything you've both worked so hard for. I'm sure I can set you up with the best policies so you can sleep well at night knowing you're safe."

"We're just getting moved in," Sean lied with a smile so charming that even Eppright seemed to fall under its spell. "We don't have a whole lot of time here today because we have to be at another appointment by three o'clock, but we wanted to meet you and see if this was the right agency to handle our insurance needs."

Eppright's eyes widened. We'd dangled a tantalizing prize in front of him to get us in the door, and he had no intention of letting us walk out without signing on the dotted line.

Sure enough, Eppright quickly reached into his desk and started pulling out forms. "Well, we can certainly start by discussing home coverage and make a follow-up appointment for a complete review."

Sean leaned back comfortably and propped one ankle on his knee, fingers laced over his flat stomach. Eppright sucked in his gut and I hid my smile behind my water cup.

"I'm sure you understand this is not the kind of decision a man in my position is going to make in a half hour," Sean said to Eppright, still with that easygoing smile. "Our assets are extensive. We met with Rick Marshall yesterday."

I didn't know who that was, but Eppright's face went grim at the name.

"I have to be honest with you, though; I wasn't all that impressed with him," Sean added. The insurance agent relaxed. "My friends in town speak highly of you, Peter, and I'd like to think I'm a good judge of character."

"What business are you in, Sean?" Eppright asked.

"Risk management," Sean replied without missing a beat. "So, as you might imagine, I'm a cautious man. After all, there's nothing more important than protecting what's mine." He gave my hand an affectionate pat. He noticed my eyes narrow minutely, and the corners of his mouth twitched. "Tell me about your services," Sean urged.

Eppright launched into a lengthy recitation of the various types of products offered by his company. My eyes glazed over almost immediately, but Sean looked engrossed, asking questions and making notes on his fancy phone. While Eppright was intently focused on selling Sean on his company, I eased my shields open and focused on Natalie's uncle.

His air and fire magic were nearly identical to the magical signature in the library wards at Natalie's house, but something about it felt off. It *wasn't* exactly the same, I decided. It was a subtle difference, like having more versus less cinnamon in a recipe. Whoever the unknown mage was, it was someone closely related to Eppright, but it wasn't him.

I raised my shields. I didn't realize I sighed in relief until I noticed Eppright and Sean were looking at me. Sean's eyebrows were raised.

"Sorry," I murmured, rubbing my forehead. "I've suddenly got the *worst* headache."

"Oh, babe," Sean said, and the way he said it made me feel warm all the way down to my toes. "I'm sorry," he said to Eppright. "She's not feeling well. Can we continue this conversation another day? I need to take care of my fiancée."

Eppright looked disappointed but forced a smile. "Of course. I hope you feel better soon."

"Thank you," I said.

We got up to leave, but Eppright turned to his computer, clicking quickly. "I have a few appointments open tomorrow and Monday," he told Sean. "What time would be convenient for you to come back?"

Sean glanced at me. I tried to telegraph to him with my eyes that Eppright was not our guy. He gave me a nearly imperceptible nod. "We are booked solid until next week," he told Eppright. "But we have next Thursday afternoon open."

Eppright clicked keys. "Thursday at one, then?"

"Absolutely." Sean pretended to note the appointment in his phone.

"I hope I can count on you not to make any final decisions until we get a chance to really talk," Eppright said with an amiable smile and reached out for a handshake.

Sean shook his hand and I followed suit. The mage who'd been in Natalie's house had been strong. With my shields up, I felt no magic from Eppright at all. We could cross him off our list of suspects.

Eppright led us back down the hall to the lobby. I feigned my headache until we were out the front door.

Once we were inside the car, Sean said, "No joy?"

I explained what I'd felt from Eppright. "So it's going to be someone close to him, but it's not him," Sean said.

"Pretty much." I turned the key in the ignition.

"Well, we couldn't expect it to be the first person on the list," Sean said with far too much cheer. "That would have been too easy. At least I only had to sit through about ten minutes of sales pitch before you got us out of there."

I winced. "Sorry about that."

He grinned. "It's okay. I'll let you make it up to me at some point." His eyes glinted and my cheeks got hot. "It drives me crazy when you blush," he said and leaned over to kiss me. I lost track of time for a bit.

When we came up for air, I was out of breath. "You're pretty good at this undercover stuff," I told him. "Who was that guy you baited him with?"

"Huh? Oh, Rick Marshall." Sean shrugged. "He owns one of the big insurance agencies in town. We talked to them about insurance back when Ron and I started our company. So who do we want next?"

I pulled out Natalie's list. "How about Kathy the real estate agent? Fancy a look at a nice three-bedroom, two-bath in a good school district?" I typed Kathy's name into Google.

"Met you two days ago, and now we're engaged and house-hunting. My mama warned me about women like you," Sean teased.

I snorted. "Please. Your mama didn't know there *were* women like me out there, or she'd have never let you out of the...." My voice drifted off and I stared at my phone.

"What?" Sean asked.

I held up my phone so he could see it, and he whistled. "We're gonna need a change of clothes," he said. "And we need to switch cars."

The type of homes Kathy Adams sold were not the kind I would ever be in the market for. All of the houses listed on her website were valued at two million dollars and up.

Sean and I looked over the listings and chose a lovely mansion in a gated community—three stories, six bedrooms, five and a half bathrooms, listed for almost three million dollars. Lower-end, by Kathy's standards, but it looked like it had been listed for a while, and that probably meant she'd jump at the chance to get it sold.

I called Kathy's office and got put through to her assistant. I introduced myself as Audrey Keller and told her my fiancé and I were very interested in the house but we'd need to see it soon, preferably today. The assistant perked right up, and in a moment I was speaking to Kathy herself.

"I am so glad to hear you're interested in the Cherry Tree Lane property," Kathy told me. "My afternoon is pretty packed—"

"I know this is late notice, but my fiancé and I are taking the jet back to LA tonight—"

"—but I've just had a cancellation at four thirty," she said quickly. "Will that work for you?"

I checked the time. It would be tight, but we could make it. "Yes. Shall we meet you at the house?"

"Absolutely! I will see you then!"

Kathy hung up. I threw the car into reverse. "Are we closer to your house or mine?"

"Yours," Sean said. "Let's roll."

I broke every speed limit on the way to my house. When we arrived, I whipped into my driveway, parked, and dashed to the front door. I got the wards down and the door open in record time, then sprinted up the stairs. I went to my closet, grabbed my Armani suit and my Louboutin heels and handbag, and went to the bathroom. I stripped, refreshed my makeup, put on red lipstick, dabbed on some perfume, and changed my hairstyle from a french braid to a french twist. I swapped out my jewelry for real diamond earrings, then put on the suit and stepped into the heels.

I glanced in the mirror. The suit was dark blue pinstripe, and I wore it with a scoop-neck off-white silk top. Not bad for a ten-minute change. I blotted my lipstick and headed out.

Sean was waiting by the front door. When I appeared on the stairs, he looked positively gobsmacked. I grinned and headed down the steps, one hand on the railing for balance in the four-inch heels.

When I got to the bottom, I struck a pose. "Do I clean up good?"

"You look beautiful." I liked the way he looked at me when he said it.

I headed for the door, keys in hand. "Should we pick up your car next, or head to your place?"

"Let's get the car. It's on the way to my house. You want to ride with me to my place, or drive separately?"

"I'll ride with you." I locked up, raised the wards, and we were off to Natalie's.

At Natalie's house, we moved our stuff to Sean's car and took off. As he drove, I transferred my wallet and a few key items from the messenger bag to the handbag. It appeared Sean lived near Hawthorne's in The Heights.

By the time Sean parked in his driveway, my handbag was full and the messenger bag was on the floor in the backseat. As we got out, I studied the house.

It was two stories and all brick, with a three-car garage and a fenced backyard. There was a large black truck in the garage, and the third spot held a pair of jet skis on a trailer. I pictured him bare-chested riding a jet ski and nearly tripped over my own feet.

Inside, the house had a definite bachelor-pad feel. I smiled at the framed vintage concert posters on the walls.

"Do you want something to drink?" Sean asked.

"No, I'm good."

"I'll go change, then. Feel free to look around." Sean disappeared, leaving me in the kitchen.

I looked over his posters and music memorabilia while I waited. When I moved to the living room, I found a gigantic television and a state-of-the-art home theater system. I surprised myself by imagining us sitting on the couch watching a movie or playing video games.

The family pictures in the living room featured an older couple who were probably Sean's parents, and several other families I took to be Sean's siblings and their kids. On the mantelpiece I found a family photo. It looked like it had been taken in a park on a sunny day. Sean was standing with his parents while his siblings and their families flanked them. Everyone was smiling.

I wondered what it would be like to come from a big, happy family. I'd never had any brothers or sisters; my mother had told me once, not long before she died, that she'd always wanted at least three children but feared losing them to her father as she had lost me. I looked at the picture of Sean's family and felt a little stab of jealousy.

I heard footsteps behind me, turned, and stared.

Nothing could have prepared me for the sight of Sean in a silver-blue suit. I didn't know much about men's suits, but it looked expensive and perfectly tailored. My brain literally went blank.

Sean stood in the middle of the living room, one hand in his pocket, and grinned at me. Damn that man for knowing exactly how good he looked.

Finally, I cleared my throat and got my legs moving to walk over to him. "Well, you look *okay*." I brushed some imaginary lint off his lapel.

Sean caught my hand and raised my fingers to his lips. "You've got to stop looking at me like that." He pulled me toward the door to the garage. "Let's go, before I say to hell with this real estate agent and ruin our fancy clothes."

We got back in the Mercedes. Sean put the Cherry Tree Lane address into the car's GPS and we took off. I noticed him glancing at my legs as he drove and smiled to myself.

As we headed toward the east side, Sean seemed to be thinking hard about something. Finally, he asked, "How long have you been in the city?"

"About five years."

"Have you been a private investigator since you got here?"

"I worked for another MPI for a year and a half before I got my license. I've been self-employed ever since."

"What kind of work do you usually do?"

"A little of everything: magic tracing, spellwork and wards, summonings and banishments, tracking of magical objects. I also do mundane work like missing persons, skip traces, insurance fraud, background checks, and cheating spouse/divorce stuff. That's my least favorite type of case, but sometimes it's just about paying the bills."

"You work with anybody?"

"Just Malcolm. Other than that, nobody." I shrugged. "I like working for myself. It keeps things simple."

"I can see that." A long pause. Then: "I'm trying to figure out what I can ask about, and what I can't."

"Anything about the last couple of years here in the city, you can ask, and I'll probably answer. Nothing from before."

"Okay." Sean navigated through some heavy traffic before we got on the highway to head east out of the city. "This one might be off-limits, but can I assume the reason you can't go to a hospital is connected to whatever happened before you arrived in the city?"

I shifted uncomfortably in my seat. I'd asked questions of Sean on the way to Natalie's house and he'd answered them, but I couldn't reciprocate. He could never know anything about my life before I'd arrived in the city, and there were some things I would not—could not—discuss. It wasn't fair, but that was how it had to be. My life depended on it.

I decided on part of the truth. "There are some anomalies in my magic that I need to keep secret. I can't leave my blood anywhere, and I can't go to a hospital. I need to stay clear of SPEMA and anyone from a cabal, and there's not much more I can say about it." I paused, then added softly, "I'm sorry."

"It's okay." Sean squeezed my knee and his touch relaxed me. "I understand. I won't push you. If I ask something you don't want to answer, just tell me."

"Thank you."

We made the rest of the drive in silence. We turned onto Cherry Tree Lane at four twenty-five and found the house with no trouble. Sean parked in the driveway behind a white Land Rover. "Are you ready for this?" he asked.

"Definitely." We got out of the car and headed up the walk to the front door.

The door opened before we even got to the porch. "Welcome!" Kathy Adams called out to us. Her practiced eye looked us over, saw the shiny new Mercedes, and decided we looked the part. Her smile was even more radiant than Eppright's had been, and that was saying something. She ushered us inside and closed the door.

I could see the family resemblance to Natalie, though Kathy's perfectly coiffed auburn hair framed a narrow, almost hawk-like face, and her green eyes glinted with cool calculation. A hint of crow's-feet put her in her midforties. Her eager smile grew wider as she reached out to shake Sean's hand.

I dropped my shields and focused my senses as she turned that big, fake smile to me, hand outstretched. The instant our hands touched, I felt a tiny flare of very low-level air magic and no fire magic at all.

A sudden wave of dizziness made me stagger and almost fall. With my magic and energy still depleted, focusing my senses so intently was taking its toll.

Sean caught me by the arm. "Audrey! Are you all right?" It took me a moment to realize he was calling me by my alias.

I got my shields in place. Everything was a little out of focus and my head pounded, but I gave Kathy my best smile and stepped away from Sean. "I tripped. Such a klutz."

Kathy frowned and looked down at the spanish tile in the foyer, obviously trying to figure out what I could have possibly tripped on.

"New shoes," I told her, sticking my right foot out to show off my Louboutins, which she dutifully admired. "We're Sean and Audrey. What a cute little house!" I said, moving past her and looking around.

Kathy blinked at my "cute little house" comment but was immediately back on her game. "It may be small," she said agreeably, "but the space is amazingly well-designed. It's an open plan, so it feels like it's twice as big." And she was off, leading us farther into the house, going on about natural light and vaulted ceilings and other realtor-type talk.

Sean hung back. "You okay?"

"I'm good," I told him. "Just feeling a little run-down." He squeezed my hand and we hurried to catch up with Kathy.

As the realtor walked us around the house, I let Sean take the lead as he'd done with Eppright, engaging her in conversation and asking questions while I focused on sensing her magic.

Like Eppright, Kathy was not an exact match to the magical signature in the library wards. Hers was similar, but not as close of a match as her half brother's. We were in the right ballpark but still not the right person.

Once I realized Kathy wasn't our suspect, it was time to bring an end to our tour. My knees were getting wobbly.

As we walked into the master suite, which was as big as the entire top floor of my house and overlooked the pool and guest house, Kathy beamed. "Well? What do you think?" she asked us, gesturing at the enormous bedroom.

"It's lovely." I gave her a sad smile.

Kathy's smile faded. "What's wrong?" she asked anxiously.

"It's just too small for us," I said, shaking my head and wishing I could sit down. "I really thought, with the open floor plan, it would feel bigger, but...."

Sean put his arm around my waist to hold me up. At first, I resisted; it felt possessive, and I didn't want him to think I was relying on him, but I was cold and light-headed. I reluctantly leaned against him and he squeezed me gently.

"We did see some other larger homes on your website. I actually liked the one on Pinehurst quite a bit better than this one," Sean told her.

Kathy perked up again and led us back to the front door. "Oh, yes! That house is *lovely*." And listed for a million more than this one was. "Would you like to see it? I can arrange a walk-through for tomorrow."

"We'll be in Los Angeles for a couple of days." Sean pulled me tighter against his side as I swayed. "If you're available when we get back, we would definitely like to see it."

Sean took Kathy's card. She encouraged us to call her when we returned to the city. We promised we would, shook her hand again, and made our escape.

Sean helped me into the passenger side of his car. I leaned my head back and closed my eyes.

Sean got in, and I felt him throw his suit jacket into the backseat. "Are you all right?"

It was a moment before I could respond. "Yes." My voice sounded wispy.

Sean sighed. "Why do I bother to ask?" He touched my hand. "You're cold again."

I took a deep breath. "I'm just tired." He put the car in gear, pulled through the circular driveway, and accelerated away down Cherry Tree Lane. "It took a lot of energy to check the library this morning, and I've been running on fumes ever since. I just need to rest for a bit."

"It seems like you were asking too much of yourself to do all this today." Sean cleared his throat. "Not that I would have told you that, of course."

I snorted.

Sean drove in silence. Once we were on the highway, he asked, "Where are we headed?"

I thought about that, then sighed. "We need to check in with Malcolm and Natalie. I wish I felt up to tracking down Deborah and/or Elise today, but I don't."

"So swing by Natalie's house and pick up the ghost, then what?"

"After that, I need to go home. I'm just too worn out to think about doing anything else today." The rhythm of the tires on the road made me sleepy, and I let myself drift.

"What about tomorrow?" Sean asked suddenly.

"What about it?" I murmured, half dozing.

"I could take another personal day."

I opened my eyes and looked at him as he drove. It was rush hour, but we were driving back toward the city and the traffic wouldn't be bad until we got into town. The outbound lanes were bumper-to-bumper with folks headed home at the end of the day. "I appreciate it, but I'll be fine, and I'm sure you need to get back to work. I did enjoy having you along today. It's been fun, and that's not something I get to say very often during an investigation."

Despite my earlier misgivings, I *had* liked working with Sean. We'd fallen into an easy, comfortable partnership. He was a natural at undercover work, and I had no doubt having him with me today had made it easier to get access to both Peter Eppright and Kathy Adams. The thought of tracking down Elise and Deborah on my own tomorrow suddenly seemed unappealing.

Sean was talking. I turned my attention back to him. "I've got a lot of PT built up. Hell, now that I think about it, I haven't taken a vacation in over a year. Today was the most fun I've had in a long time. I'd much rather do undercover work with you than coordinate bodyguards for a client, or supervise the installation of a camera system at a law office, which is what I had on the schedule for tomorrow. Someone else can do that shit. I want to put on a disguise and help you find a secret mage and a MacGuffin."

I had to laugh, despite the turmoil in my head. "I'm still not clear on what a MacGuffin is exactly, but it seemed to make Malcolm's day to let him call it that, so I guess we're sticking with it. Seems like the least I can do after...after yesterday." And just like that, the mood went from light to serious.

Sean squeezed my knee. "Why don't we pick up Malcolm and go from there? We don't have to decide anything right this minute."

I sighed, leaned my head back, and closed my eyes again. "Okay."

For five years, I'd feared if I let myself depend on someone else in any way, I would lose the edge that kept me alive long enough to escape the cabal. After spending the past few days with Malcolm and Sean, however, I was starting to think that maybe having colleagues—or whatever Sean and I might be to each other—could be a strength rather than a weakness.

Or maybe I was just tired of being so afraid all the time. The problem was, after a lifetime of fearing everything and everyone around me, I wasn't sure I knew any other way to be.

14

I sent Natalie a text that we were on our way, and Sean drove us to my client's house while I dozed in the passenger seat. When we arrived, I was able to get out of the car and walk up to her door on my own power.

Before we could knock, Natalie opened the door. "Come on in. Malcolm's in the living room. Would you guys like anything to eat or drink?"

"No, thank you," I said as we stepped inside. "Sorry it took longer than I thought to get here."

"It's okay, no problem." Natalie waved her hand and took us to the living room.

Malcolm looked up from where he was studying a chess board with a game in progress. He looked at me closely and frowned. "Hey, you guys look nice. What did you find out?"

"Neither of the people we talked to are who we're looking for, but the mage is definitely in the family. Both Peter and Kathy's magic felt very similar. It must be either Deborah or Elise. Did you get those spells set up in the library?"

"Yep. You want to see?"

"Definitely."

We all went back toward Betty's bedroom. This time I was more prepared for the sight and smell of the burned floor and was able to ignore it to focus on the library wards.

"Wow. Beautiful work," I breathed, looking at the spellwork. I could see the spells that would contain Natalie's magic, as well as the spells that would drain it into the perimeter wards. "Well done, Malcolm."

"Thanks. It took a little while, but I'm pretty happy with the result."

"Did you tell her what the spells do, and that she needs to avoid touching the walls so she doesn't null the wards?" I sidled away from the group to sit on the edge of the bed.

"Yes, he did," Natalie said. "And I really appreciate that you've done this for me.

Knowing I have a 'safe room' to go to if I lose control of my magic makes me feel so much better."

Malcolm and Sean were watching me. "Alice, you look exhausted," the ghost stated.

"I'm fine," I said, at the same moment Sean said, "She's barely able to walk."

I glared at Sean. "*She's* right here, and perfectly capable of speaking for herself."

Malcolm looked unhappy. He floated over to me. "You should have asked me to share some energy with you before you left," he told me, holding out his arm. "Here."

"No."

Malcolm blinked at me. "What?"

"I'm not going to keep draining you every time I'm depleted," I told him flatly. "You're not a battery, Malcolm."

"That's not—"

I didn't want to have this argument in front of Sean and Natalie. "Malcolm, we can talk about this later. I appreciate the offer, but no."

Natalie's expression was dark. "You're still hurt from yesterday." She bit her lip. "I'm dangerous."

"No." I started to get up.

She held up her hands to stop me. "Yes. I'm dangerous, because I don't know how to control my magic. I wish my grandmother was here to explain why she did this to me, but I guess it doesn't matter now. I've decided I want training."

"Are you sure?" I asked.

"Yes. I've been talking to Malcolm, and he told me about the things you can use fire and air magic to do. Plus, I was so scared when my magic got loose yesterday. I need to be able to control it so I'm not afraid of that happening again. I'm done being afraid."

"Okay. It may take a little while, but I'll start looking for a teacher." I turned to Malcolm. "Did you test the containment spell?"

"Not yet."

Sean growled quietly. "We're not waiting around for that. You're going home."

I stiffened. "I'll go when I want to go. The containment spell—"

"Does not need to be tested tonight," Malcolm interrupted. "You can bring me back here tomorrow and we'll do it then. Nat's fine in the meantime. Sean's right; you need to rest. You look like roadkill."

I crossed my arms. "You realize you are scoring no points with me with comments like that."

"Totally rude, Mal." Natalie frowned in the ghost's general direction.

"Sorry," Malcolm said to me. "But seriously, you do."

I pushed myself to my feet. "Fine. I'll come by in the morning to drop off Malcolm so he can test the containment spell, if that's okay. When he's done with that, you can start looking through your grandmother's files while I check on Deborah and Elise."

"Thank you, Alice." Suddenly, Natalie launched herself forward to give me a hug. "You've been so awesome."

I patted her awkwardly on the back and extricated myself from her embrace. "No problem. I'll be back in the morning." I glanced at Malcolm.

He groaned. "Earring time, huh?"

"It's the safest thing to do for now."

"Okay," he said, sighing. "See you soon, Nat."

"See you, Mal," she said with a smile.

I touched my earring and invoked the spell. "*Contain*." Malcolm vanished, and my earring buzzed.

"Does that hurt him?" Natalie asked.

"Not at all," I assured her. "It's kind of like being asleep."

"Okay. Well, I guess I'll hear from you in the morning." Natalie escorted us to the front door.

"I'll text you," I promised, and she closed the door behind us.

As soon as the door clicked shut, I took a step and stumbled.

Sean swung me up into his arms before I could argue. "That's it; we're going home *now*."

"Only because I say we are," I countered, but my retort didn't quite match the shakiness of my voice.

Sean sighed and carried me down the sidewalk to where we were parked at the curb. "Your car or mine?"

When I didn't immediately answer, he brought me over to his Mercedes and sat me on the hood.

I rested my weight carefully on the car and looked up at him. "You can't stay the night with me."

Sean gave me a long-suffering look. "Once again, you're assuming I have ulterior motives. I'm only thinking about getting you home and making sure you have what you need when you get there."

"All I'm going to need is my bed. I'll be asleep the minute my head touches the pillow. I need to recharge."

He hesitated. "I read somewhere that there's another, faster way to regenerate magical energy." He tilted my chin up and looked into my eyes. "Is it true?"

"It's true," I admitted.

Sean ran his thumb lightly over my lower lip. "Then why are you sending me home when I could be helping you?"

I opened my mouth to say something sarcastic about his motivations for offering me some sexual healing, but the seriousness in his eyes made me reconsider my response. "Because Malcolm is not a battery and neither are you," I said instead.

"You regenerated your magic with me the first time we were together."

"Yes, I did. That was part of the plan, when I invited you home with me."

He seemed neither surprised nor upset by my admission. "And now?"

"Now the plan's changed."

He absorbed that. "Speaking of plans, what did you decide about tomorrow?"

I tilted my head back, bracing myself with my hands on the hood of the car. Above the trees, the three-quarter moon shone against a darkening sky. Sean's wolf would be feeling restless, no doubt. I wondered where he and his pack went on the full moon, and what he looked like in wolf form. I was suddenly full of questions about him, and it was a strange feeling.

"I'll be ready at eight o'clock," I said finally.

Sean grinned. "Eight o'clock it is. Come on, Sleeping Beauty. Let's get you home." He held out his hand and I took it.

When Sean knocked on my door at precisely eight a.m. the next morning, he'd opted for a green button-up shirt that brought out the gold flecks in his dark brown eyes, and khakis that fit very, very well. I looked him over appreciatively before my eyes zeroed in on the enormous cup of coffee and bag of donuts in his hands.

"Now you're just buttering me up," I said after I'd inhaled a warm donut and drunk half the coffee in three large gulps. "And rather shamelessly, I might add."

He grinned. "Is it working?"

"Well, it doesn't hurt."

Sean snorted as he backed down my driveway. I snarfed another donut. "Hungry?" he teased.

I hadn't eaten anything since our late breakfast the day before. When I got home, I'd gone straight to bed and slept for eleven hours. "Famished. This coffee is fantastic."

"It's from a little coffee shop near my house," Sean said. "We heading to Natalie's?"

"Yep. We're going to drop Malcolm off, then go track down Natalie's other two aunts." I licked some frosting off my fingers.

"How'd you sleep?"

"Like a log."

"And your magic? Back to normal?"

"Getting there." It would take several days for my magic to regenerate completely on its own, but he didn't need to know that. "You were able to take the day off again without any problems?"

"No problems, though my partner Ron thinks I've been replaced by a pod person, since the 'real' Sean hasn't taken two workdays off in a row in a very long time."

"What's a 'pod person'?"

Sean stopped at a red light. "You're kidding. *Invasion of the Body Snatchers?*"

"Haven't seen it." I chomped into another donut.

Sean widened his eyes in mock horror, then stepped on the gas when the light turned green. "That's a classic. I can see we'll have to have a movie night very soon."

His casual remark caused me to pause with the donut halfway to my mouth. *Movie night.* I'd never had a movie night. For Sean, it was as unremarkable as buying coffee; for me, it would be a completely new experience, one of many I might be facing in the near future. My stomach knotted, and I dropped the half-eaten donut back into the bag.

Sean slowed down to make a turn and glanced at me. "What's wrong?"

"Nothing." How could I possibly explain why the idea of having a movie night caused me anxiety? There wouldn't be any easy way to justify how I'd managed to get to the age of twenty-nine without ever going to someone's house to watch a movie. It was another reminder of how difficult it would be to have any kind of relationship when I had to keep so much of myself hidden.

"Not having second thoughts already, are you?" Sean's voice sounded like he was teasing, but his shoulders looked tense.

"No." I realized my voice sounded like it was made up of second thoughts. I cleared my throat. "No," I repeated, more firmly. I'd made a decision, and I was going ahead with it.

"Okay." Sean took my hand.

I tried to pull away. "Don't—I'm all sticky from the donuts."

He grinned and squeezed tighter. "I don't care."

We dropped Malcolm off at Natalie's, then Sean and I headed to Deborah Mackey's house. As he drove, I reached into the small duffel bag at my feet and pulled out a baseball cap and a pair of large sunglasses.

Sean glanced at the cap. His mouth turned down.

"I know," I said. "But it's part of the ruse."

Sean's grip tightened on the steering wheel until his knuckles turned white. He didn't say anything. We drove in silence for a while.

Deborah lived on a typical west-side residential street. Sean pulled to the curb diagonally across from her house. According to Natalie's information sheet, Deborah and her husband Lawrence were childless. Their house was quiet. There was a new BMW parked out front.

"What's the plan?" Sean asked.

I dug out a clipboard. "Petition ruse. I'm a volunteer going door-to-door meeting people and collecting signatures."

"Signatures for what?"

"In this case, Prop 87."

Sean growled. "Well, that explains the hat."

I took his hand and squeezed it. If it passed, the proposed law would require vamps, shifters, and other supes to notify the neighborhood when they moved in, and would allow cities to designate certain areas, like around schools and churches, as supe-free zones. It was blatantly racist and horribly unfair. I was suddenly struck by the thought that if Prop 87 became law, Sean would have to reveal his werewolf identity to his neighbors, potentially making him a target of anti-supe hate groups like the one whose hat I was wearing.

"I'm sorry," I told him. "Maybe this isn't the best idea."

"No, it's fine. There are a limited number of ways to meet strangers and shake their hands. It's a good plan." Tension prickled on my skin as his anger disrupted his natural shields, and his emotions bled over to me.

I gave him a minute to deal with his fury while I took out a blank petition sheet and fastened it to the clipboard. I filled in the top with the information about the proposition, the date, and—after a quick Internet search—the state representative for this district.

"It's what they do to *sex offenders*, Allie," Sean snarled.

"I know." I swallowed hard around the lump in my throat. I'd signed a petition opposing Prop 87 and gone to rallies against it. Even though mages weren't included among those who were directly affected by the proposition, there was a good chance they'd be added to the list at some point. Today, shifters, half-demons, and vamps; tomorrow, mages like me.

"We can't go directly to their house; it's in the middle of the block," I said quietly. "We need to start at the corner."

Without a word, Sean eased back onto the street and reparked at the end of the block. I pulled out a small bag of pins and picked out a couple representing other anti-supe groups. I put them on my bag. I didn't ask Sean to put any on, and he didn't offer.

"You can stay in the car," I told him as we got out of the car.

"We're in this together." Sean shut the door hard enough to make me jump.

I slung my bag across my chest and adjusted my jacket. Clipboard in hand, I marched resolutely up to the first house on the block with Sean next to me. I rang the doorbell, plastered a perky smile on my face, and became Audrey Talbot, anti-supe crusader.

Ten minutes later, I was brimming with hidden rage, but I had my first two signatures from the couple who owned that house. They both had very strong opinions on supes, and they absolutely did not want any in their neighborhood. The husband confided they were members of Humans First, a radical "Human rights" organization that advocated creating walled-off reservations for supes and keeping them away from humans.

Sean made a few comments but let me do most of the talking. His jaw was clenched so tightly that I worried it would break.

We walked back to the sidewalk and stood silently, looking at each other. Sean reached out and I took his hand, recognizing his need for warmth and physical contact. The tautness in his shoulders made mine ache.

I drew him to me and kissed him. His body felt like caged violence. "Go back to the car," I told him, my voice ragged. "It's not going to get any better."

Those beautiful brown eyes turned stony. It wasn't in his nature to back away from anything, no matter what it might cost him emotionally. "Let's just do this," he said.

We went to the next house and had much the same experience, except I cut the couple off after a few minutes, telling them we wanted to get to as many houses as we could today. The elderly woman in the third house declined to sign and gave us an earful about the evils of prejudice and racism. I turned and left with tears burning in my eyes.

There was no answer when we knocked at the next house. I steeled myself and headed up the sidewalk toward the Mackeys' home.

Just as we were halfway to their front door, it opened and Peter Eppright, Deborah's half brother, walked out. Behind him in the doorway stood a slim middle-aged woman I recognized from Natalie's photo as Deborah. Neither looked very happy.

Beside me, I heard Sean mutter, "Shit." My sentiments exactly.

Nothing to do but soldier on. I summoned up a big, cheery smile and marched up to the porch. "Peter!"

Eppright looked at me, then at Sean, and recognition dawned. "Sean and...Audrey?" he asked in surprise.

Sean stepped forward to shake Eppright's hand and gave him a manly clap on the shoulder that almost made the older man stagger. "Peter, how are you?"

Deborah looked back and forth between us. "Sean and Audrey came to see me yesterday about some insurance," Eppright said to his half sister.

"What a small world!" I chirped. "Do you live here?"

"It's my sister's house," Eppright told us. "I was just leaving."

"I hope we haven't caught you at a bad time," Sean said.

Deborah stepped out onto the porch. "What do you want?"

I launched into a shortened version of my spiel about Prop 87, pointing to my various pins and waving the clipboard for emphasis. Eppright paused to listen.

"So, I was hoping to get your signature on this petition showing your support for protecting our neighborhoods," I concluded, shoving the clipboard at Deborah.

"Sure," she said hesitantly and took it and the pen from me.

As she was filling in her name and information, I opened my senses and focused on her, trying to sense if she had any magic. Almost none, I determined almost immediately. Like Kathy, she had only a trace of air magic and no fire magic at all. I'd know better after I shook her hand, but I was ready to cross Deborah off the suspect list.

She finished filling in her information and handed the clipboard back. I stuck out my hand. "Thank you so much for helping us today."

After a hesitation, she reached out and shook. A slight tickle of magic, barely enough to register. Definitely part of Betty's family—the magical signature was familiar—but not the person whose signature was in the library's wards.

I gave her a bright smile. "Have a wonderful day."

"You too."

Eppright walked with us down the sidewalk. "Are we still on for that meeting next week?"

"Absolutely." Sean shook Eppright's hand again. "We'll be there."

Eppright climbed into his BMW as we walked over to the next house. Deborah stayed on her porch. I gave them both a cheerful wave and rang the doorbell. Eppright backed out of Deborah's driveway and headed down the street.

The front door opened, and it was a young mother holding a baby on her hip.

"Hi! I'm Audrey with the Human Defense League...."

Out of the corner of my eye, I watched Deborah go inside her house. We went through the motions with the mom, who was joined at the door by two more small children. I could see she was totally frazzled and didn't push her for a signature. I wouldn't have even knocked on her door if we weren't being watched.

When the baby started wailing, Sean and I made our escape and headed back to the car.

When we were inside, I took off the offending baseball cap and pins and stuffed them out of sight into the duffel bag. "That was not ideal."

Sean's laugh was so loud and sudden that it startled me. "Definitely *not* ideal, but I think he bought it."

"I didn't see any indication he suspected us of anything, but we'll have to use a different ruse for Elise."

Sean pulled away from the curb. I put Elise Browning's home address into his car's navigation system and settled back into my seat.

"I take it Deborah's not our mage?" he asked.

"Nope." I told him what I'd sensed.

"That leaves Elise, then."

I grimaced. "Yeah, but I'm having a hard time believing she's a strong mage."

"She's the only sibling left," Sean pointed out. "It *has* to be her, right?"

"I guess," I said doubtfully.

"So what's the plan for Elise, then, if not the petition ruse?"

"Good question. Let's drive by her house and get an idea of what we have to work with."

As Sean drove, I got to work on my disguise. I used bobby pins to secure my hair tightly to my head, then put on a blonde wig. I used my fingers to comb through the wig hair and used the mirror on my sun visor to make sure it looked natural and my own hair wasn't visible. I put on a different pair of sunglasses, a sparkly pair that looked more like something the blonde would wear, and took off my jacket.

"I like you better as a brunette," Sean said, watching the transformation out of the corner of his eye.

"Good."

He laughed.

Elise lived on the northeast side of the city in a fancier area than her sister. I saw the SUV I'd seen at Natalie's house parked in the open garage of a large three-story home, along with a Mercedes and a Land Rover. A sticker on the Land Rover indicated that their children attended a very expensive prep school. Natalie had said that Elise's husband, Ray, owned a construction company. Business must be good for them to afford such a large home, private-school tuition, and three vehicles on a single salary.

Sean drove down the street slowly as I tried to see if there was any obvious way to gain entry to Elise's home. Nothing jumped out at me, and this wasn't the kind of street where we could park and watch the house waiting for her to leave. Nice neighborhoods like this meant people noticed strange cars and unfamiliar people lurking around.

"Lost dog," Sean said suddenly.

"Huh?"

"Lost dog," he repeated. "Our dog got away from us when we were walking it. We're going door-to-door asking if anyone has seen it."

I grinned. "That could actually work." We continued down the street, turned the corner, and parked. I went online and browsed pictures of yellow Labs. I saved several to my phone and decided to call the dog Mal. Sean laughed.

I put on a different ball cap over my blonde hair—this one representing the city's basketball team—and we headed out on foot. By the time we were getting close to Elise's house, I had real tears in my eyes over the plight of our poor lost dog. Sean seemed to be enjoying playing the role of worried dog owner.

We were in the yard next door to Elise's house, showing them the dog pictures, when Natalie's aunt came outside with two little dogs of her own on leashes.

"Elise!" Her neighbor, a pretty young woman named Tracee—"with two *E*'s!"—hollered and waved her over. We were in business.

Elise came over, looking irritated. "Hey, Tracee. What's going on over here?"

Her dogs bounced and barked their heads off at Sean. He stared at them, and I saw a glint of gold in his eyes. The dogs went silent and hunkered to the ground. I coughed to hide my smile.

"These poor folks' dog got away from them," Tracee said. "Show her the pictures."

I sniffled and obediently held up my phone. "His name is Mal. He broke the leash and ran in this direction. I'm so desperate to find him before he gets hit by a car. Have you seen him?" I stuck the phone under her nose.

Meanwhile, I focused my senses on Elise. I was shocked at what I felt.

Nothing. No magic at all.

"I haven't seen your dog." Elise seemed completely unmoved by my sniffling.

"Your dogs are so sweet." I reached down to pet one of them.

Elise grabbed my hand. "Don't—they might bite you."

Even with her touching me, I felt nothing. Elise was not the mage who had been in the library—not even close.

Which left me with exactly *zero* suspects. What the hell?

15

I backed away from Elise and her dogs. I didn't have to fake looking tragic; my last lead had gone nowhere. "Well, if anybody sees our dog, please call us. My number is on his tag."

Tracee assured me she'd call. Elise didn't say anything; she was too busy trying to keep her little dogs from biting Tracee.

I headed back to the car, Sean beside me. "So?" he asked as we walked.

"It's not her."

Sean frowned. "How is that possible? You said it has to be one of them."

I rubbed my forehead. "It wasn't Peter, Kathy, Deborah, or Elise. All of them have weak or no magical ability. I would have *sworn* it was one of Betty's children. When I touched Peter, Kathy, and Deborah, I can sense that their magic is almost identical to the signature in the wards. It *has* to be one of them, but it isn't!" We got into Sean's car. I pulled off my hat and wig and tossed them into the duffel bag on the floor. "I don't understand this at all."

"Could the mage be one of Natalie's cousins?" Sean started the car.

I shook my head. "The magic was almost identical to Betty's. I'd have bet any amount of money the mage was one of her children. I'm trying to figure out what I'm doing wrong here. It makes no sense. Maybe Natalie found something in Betty's papers." I pulled my phone out and called my client.

"Hey, Alice," she said with far too much cheer, considering how my morning was going.

"Are the wards finished and tested?" I asked. "Have you had a chance to start looking through Betty's files?"

"Malcolm is working on the library wards, so I haven't gone in there yet. We still need to test the containment spell. How are you doing?"

"I struck out," I confessed. "I've contacted your uncle and all of your aunts, and none of them are the mage who was in your library."

A pause. "I thought you said it had to be one of them."

"I thought it did."

Natalie hummed a bit. "What about my grandmother's sister and brother?"

"It's possible," I mused. "You said they live nearby?"

"Yes. Should I text you their addresses?"

"That would be great. We can check them out this afternoon."

"Give me a few minutes to find the information—it's probably in my grandmother's address book."

"Thanks, Natalie."

"No problem!"

We disconnected. I picked up my empty coffee cup and looked at it wistfully.

Sean chuckled and pulled away from the curb. "Where are we going?" I asked.

"I saw a coffee shop a couple of blocks from here. Might as well take a little break while we wait."

It was almost fifteen minutes before Natalie texted me the addresses of her great-aunt Helen and great-uncle Robert. In the meantime, since it was nearing lunchtime, I bought us some much-needed caffeine and sandwiches at the coffee shop. Sean tried to pay, arguing that since he was buying three sandwiches that it should be his treat, but I was insistent. It seemed only fair, since he'd bought breakfast and he'd been doing most of the driving. I added a cherry turnover to the order when I saw Sean eyeballing it in the dessert case.

We settled in to eat at a table on the coffee shop's patio. Sean seemed to have recovered from the unpleasantness of the petition ruse. In between bites, he brought up *Invasion of the Body Snatchers* again and launched into a rather interesting explanation of how many of the science fiction films of the fifties, sixties, and seventies were thinly veiled references to the fear of communism. I ate my lunch and listened to him talk.

Sean Maclin, alpha werewolf and security consultant, was kind of nerdy. I liked it.

When Natalie's text finally came in, along with her apology for the delay, we looked up the addresses. Robert Finchley lived in an assisted-living facility in Springtown, a suburb about an hour's drive away. Helen Matson lived another hour farther away from the city, in a town called Hope.

"Who do you want first?" Sean finished his coffee and the last bite of sandwich number three. I was just finishing my half sandwich and still had most of my fruit salad to go. I was a little in awe of his appetite.

"Might as well start with Robert in Springtown."

Sean took the opportunity to respond to some work e-mails while I finished my food. We threw away our trash and got back in the car. Sean put Finchley's address in his GPS and headed out.

"Do you want me to do some of the driving?" I asked. "I feel bad that you've been chauffeuring me all over the city for the past day."

"I don't mind it. I drive for clients all the time." He paused. "And it's hard for me to ride shotgun."

"I understand." An alpha needed to be in control, and the past few days hadn't been easy on him in that regard. As much as it rankled me to be in the passenger seat, I could live with it for the rest of today. After that, we'd see. I didn't much care for riding shotgun either.

Sean talked more about movies during the drive to Springtown. He was already making plans for several double-feature movie nights.

When Sean finally turned into Pine Ridge Resort Village forty-five minutes later, my jaw dropped. I saw what looked like a nine-hole golf course, tennis courts, multiple pools, a network of shady sidewalks connecting brick townhouses, and dozens of very spry-looking seniors out and about on the grounds as we parked in front of the building marked Office.

"The old guy's not doing too badly here," Sean said as we got out.

"No freaking kidding." We entered the office and approached the reception desk.

"Can I help you?" a young red-haired nurse asked us.

"We'd like to see Robert Finchley," I said.

"Can I see your identification?"

Sean and I both gave her our driver's licenses. The nurse recorded our information, then handed them back, along with two guest badges on lanyards. We put them on.

The nurse checked the computer. "Unit 5B. Go out this door, then turn right. It will be the third building on your left."

We thanked her and headed back outside. "I don't think my parents would go for a place like this," Sean said as we walked. "But if it ends up that one or both of them need to move to a retirement community, this isn't so bad."

I wondered if he was fishing for information about my parents, but his tone seemed casual. "It's pretty far from your standard nursing home, that's for sure," I said.

We traded cheery hellos with several residents on our way to Finchley's townhouse. We found 5B easily, and I rang the doorbell. To my surprise, the door opened almost immediately.

The white-haired gentleman who answered held a cane in one hand, but he looked remarkably energetic for a man of nearly eighty. "The front office called ahead to say I had some visitors." His voice was strong, and his eyes were bright. "I'm Robert. What can I do for you?"

I smiled and held out my hand. "My name is Alice Worth. I'm a private investigator. This is Sean Maclin, my colleague."

It was Finchley's turn to be surprised. "Well, my goodness." He reached out to take my hand and eyed me with interest. "How exciting."

I lowered my shields as our hands touched and felt a flare of air magic. Mid-level, I thought—not weak like Betty's children. Interesting. I felt no fire magic, however, and was quickly sure Robert was not the mystery mage. He *was* a mage, though, and that made me wonder what he might know about the family's magic.

"Why don't you come in?" Finchley said, stepping aside.

Sean and I entered the spotless house. "Can I get you some iced tea?" Finchley asked.

We declined. The elderly man led us to a small sunroom off the living room, and we settled into a wicker love seat while Finchley lowered himself into an armchair. "How can I help you, Miss Worth?"

"I was hired by your grand-niece, Natalie Newton, to look for some books that have gone missing from your sister Betty's personal library."

Finchley's bushy eyebrows drew together. "I see," he said heavily. "Of course, you won't mind if I call my niece to verify that you are who you say you are?"

"Please do. I have her number handy, if you need it."

"I appreciate that." Finchley reached for a cordless telephone, and I read Natalie's number off for him as he punched in the numbers. We waited as the phone rang.

When Natalie answered, our host said, "Natalie, good afternoon. This is your Uncle

Robert." Finchley looked at me. "I have some surprise visitors today. I wonder if you could tell me who they are?"

Finchley listened. "And these people…they know about your grandmother's *library*?" Finchley asked, his voice hardening. If the family had taken such pains to keep their magic secret, I could well imagine he would not be happy about the information getting out.

I couldn't hear Natalie's response, but it was lengthy. Her tone sounded urgent and apologetic.

Whatever Natalie said, it seemed to mollify Finchley. He exchanged a few pleasantries with her, then hung up.

"My niece seems to think you're trustworthy." The older man nailed me with a hard look. "I have to say I'm less than thrilled you know about our family's private business."

"My contract with Natalie includes a confidentiality agreement. Beyond that, I'm a mage myself," I told him frankly. "I have no love for SPEMA, and I violate SPERA regulations more than I follow them. I assure you, no one will ever hear about your family's secret from me."

Finchley looked at Sean. "And you, Mr. Maclin?"

Sean didn't hesitate. "I'm a shifter." I was surprised he volunteered that information, but Finchley didn't even blink. "Like Alice, I have no use for the Agency, and I've signed a confidentiality agreement."

Our forthrightness softened Finchley's expression, and the tension left his shoulders. "I appreciate your honesty," he said gruffly, leaning back in his chair and reaching for a glass of iced tea on the table beside him. "It hasn't been easy, obviously, to keep our family out of SPEMA's records."

"Is that why Betty bound Natalie's magic?" I asked.

Finchley started. "She never told me about that. That poor girl. I suppose Betty's binding spells failed?"

"They did, but luckily, I was there when it happened."

The old man sighed. "I wish I could say I was surprised my sister would do something like that, but I suppose I'm not. Betty was always cautious. We've all had to be careful, of course, but she was always so worried we'd be found out. I don't understand why she didn't want Natalie to know she had magic, though. No one in our family has ever been bound once they were old enough to learn control."

"We certainly haven't come across any explanations so far. Natalie has requested I find someone to train her, and I'm working on that. In the meantime, I've bound her magic and warded her house, as well as the library, to protect what's in there." I watched him closely as I said it.

Finchley's look of bewilderment looked genuine. "The books? Betty's spell books, certainly, but I don't think anything else in there is particularly valuable. We want to keep outsiders away, of course." He paused. "You said something has gone missing from the library. What's missing?"

"Something Betty had in a hidden compartment in the bottom of one of the bookcases. We're not sure what it was. Any ideas?"

"None at all," Finchley said, and I believed him. "My sister and I didn't talk about magic; no one in our family does. I suppose it's always been something of a taboo subject. The need for secrecy, you see. It's not always easy to tell who might be listening."

"I understand. Other than Betty, Natalie, and yourself, who else in the family has magic?"

Finchley looked at me, saying nothing.

As a good-faith gesture, I decided to put another card on the table. "Whoever took the item from Betty's library has strong magic. I first suspected one of her children, but I've been able to eliminate them."

Finchley smiled. "As you've eliminated me, I suspect, with that long handshake."

"Yes." I smiled back.

"Well, if you've contacted my nieces and nephew, you know they have little or no magic. Natalie's mother, God rest her soul, had air magic, but not much. Is Natalie's magic strong?"

"No."

"Thank God for that," Finchley said. "It's better that way."

I didn't comment on that. "What about your sister, Helen?"

Finchley looked thoughtful. "Helen has air and fire magic, like Betty. It's not strong, but she does have it. Are you going to visit her as well?"

"I think so." My ears perked up. It looked like we were headed to Hope after all. "Can you think of anything else I might need to know about Betty that could help us figure out what she had hidden in her library?"

Finchley thought about that, then shook his head. "I really can't. As I said, we never spoke about magic. Whatever it was, I suppose she took that secret to her grave." He regarded me. "What magic do you have, Miss Worth?"

"Air and earth."

"Earth magic," he said wistfully. "I was always so envious of Betty's fire. My own magic seemed so dull by comparison." My skin prickled as a warm breeze swirled through the room, then vanished. Sean started and Finchley winked at me.

I glanced around and spotted a shelf full of small antique apothecary bottles. Finchley appeared to collect them. "May I?" I asked, pointing at the shelf.

He raised his bushy eyebrows. "Help yourself."

I fetched one of the bottles and brought it over to our host, pulling out the stopper. Finchley and Sean leaned forward to watch.

I held out my right hand, and a tendril of green flame rose from my palm. It snaked into the bottle, then coiled into a spiral. I murmured an incantation, and the flame brightened for a moment before dimming to a soft green glow. I stoppered the bottle and handed it to Finchley.

"Give it a little energy once a week to keep it charged. If you need a bright light, the spell is '*Luminous.*' The flare lasts for about a minute."

"It's beautiful." Finchley lifted the bottle to peer at the spiral flame. "An amazing construction, and you did it so easily."

"Lots of practice," I said with a ghost of a smile. I'd had many lonely hours locked in my rooms in the cabal compound to master cold-fire forms. The luminary spell was one of my favorites.

Finchley set the bottle on his side table and rose from his chair. Sean stood as well.

"Thank you for visiting me," Finchley said. "It was surprisingly pleasant to talk about magic with you."

"We appreciate you taking the time to visit with us," I told Natalie's great-uncle as we followed him back to the front door. "My condolences on the loss of your sister."

"Betty was a good person," Finchley said. "I'm sorry Natalie never knew about her magic, but I suppose my sister thought it was for the best. I'm glad she knows now, and that you were there to help her." He took my hand and squeezed it.

Sean and I said our good-byes, and Finchley closed the door behind us as we headed down the walkway.

"That was incredible," Sean said.

"What was?"

"The fire in the bottle. I've never seen anything like that. I didn't even know it was possible."

"Had a lot of downtime when I was a kid." I shrugged.

I caught Sean's look of surprise out of the corner of my eye and realized I'd just casually referenced my life prior to arriving in the city. I turned away from him to watch a tennis game in progress.

We turned in our guest IDs at the office and returned to the car. "Are we bound for Hope?" Sean asked as we got in and shut the doors.

"It looks like it. Robert said Helen has both fire and air magic, same as the signature in the wards."

"He said her magic wasn't strong, though," Sean pointed out as he headed out of the Pine Ridge parking lot.

"He might be mistaken or have been misled about how strong her magic is. We'll just have to find out for ourselves."

"He's probably calling her to let her know we're coming," Sean commented.

"More than likely," I sighed. "Can't be helped. Hopefully, she'll be willing to talk to us."

She wasn't.

Sean and I stood on Helen Matson's porch, talking to her closed front door. "Mrs. Matson—" I began.

"My brother said you were nosing around, asking about Betty," came the querulous voice from inside the house. "I have nothing to say to you. Go away."

I met Sean's gaze, then glanced at the door. Somehow, he got my meaning and turned to the door, unleashing a category-five smile. I hoped Helen Matson was still peering through the peephole, though I worried the sheer force of his grin might be too much for the old lady's heart. "Mrs. Matson, my name is Sean Maclin. Ms. Worth and I certainly don't want to bother you, but your great-niece Natalie hired us to track down some items that have gone missing from Betty's library."

As Sean was speaking and hopefully drawing Helen's attention away from me, I closed my eyes, lowered my shields, and reached out with my senses.

Sensing magic without skin contact is a very different—and much more difficult—process. Sean and Helen's voices faded into a faint murmur as I focused on the older woman's energy, which was muffled but not concealed by the walls of her home. I had to pass through the physical barrier to reach her, and it took effort. I was able to sense Helen's magic, but it was indistinct. I lowered my shields more and concentrated harder.

Finally, I sensed air and fire magic, as Finchley had said, but it was low-level, and distinctly different from the signature in the library wards. Helen Matson was not the mystery mage.

I must have swayed or started to fall, because suddenly Sean's hands were around my upper arms, holding me up. I raised my shields, took a deep breath, and opened my eyes.

"Are you all right?" Sean asked me.

I blinked at him, struggling to make my eyes focus on his face. "I'm okay. It's harder when I can't touch someone." It didn't help that I wasn't completely recovered from being nulled.

From behind the door, I heard Helen's voice. "What's going on out there? Both of you, get off my property before I call the police."

"We're leaving," I said. "Sorry to have bothered you." I turned on shaky legs. Sean guided me back to the car, loading me into the passenger seat before he got into the driver's side.

"That's a negative, then?"

"It's a negative." I rubbed my eyes. "We're out of suspects. *Again*."

Sean squeezed my hand. "You'll figure it out. Rest for a bit while I drive us back."

"Let's head to Natalie's house. With any luck, she'll have found something helpful in Betty's files."

A wreck on the highway added almost an hour to the drive back to the city. By the time we got back to Natalie's house, it was well after six o'clock.

Malcolm had tested the containment spell on the library and pronounced it ready to go. Natalie was looking through the files in Betty's desk but hadn't found anything yet that was magic-related.

When I explained our visits to Robert Finchley and Helen Matson had come up empty, Natalie became understandably frustrated.

"I don't know what to say," I told her. "I'm still certain the magic signature in the wards belongs to a close relative of your grandmother. Keep looking through those files, and I'll work on the magic angle some more."

"I'll look," Natalie promised. "If I find anything that looks like it might be interesting, I'll let you know."

I turned to my ghost. "Earring time again, Malcolm."

He sighed.

"Tomorrow's Sunday," I said. "It's going to be my day off. At the top of my to-do list is working on a masking spell for you."

"That is very good news," Malcolm said, visibly relieved.

Once Malcolm was contained in my earring, Sean and I said good-bye to Natalie and walked to his car.

Sean leaned against the driver's door. "What are your plans for the evening?"

"I have a meeting with Charles Vaughan at ten. I'm going home to relax for a couple of hours and clear my head."

Sean looked disappointed. I knew he was hoping for that date he'd been campaigning for. I'd considered it earlier in the day, but after eleven hours in his company, I needed some space and a chance to think about what I was going to say before I talked to Charles.

Speaking of which.... "I do have a favor to ask, if it's feasible."

"Name it."

"I'm going to ask Charles for help finding a teacher for Natalie." I explained my reasoning for involving the vampire in the search.

"Asking a vampire for help is risky," Sean said, his brow furrowing. "He'll want something in return, obviously—I'm pretty sure the phrase 'quid pro quo' was coined by a vamp."

"Probably," I agreed. "I'm going to make some offers, but I have to be prepared for the possibility he may demand something I'm not willing to give."

His eyes darkened. "What do you need from me?"

I'd been pondering that off and on for the better part of the day and had come up with a plan I thought would help me avoid a confrontation with Charles that might force me to reveal the power of my magic. "A kind of backup. I text you when I go into the meeting, then text when I leave."

Sean looked thoughtful. "Bringing someone along with you signifies fear and weakness, but this demonstrates confidence and forethought. It's proactive, but more defensive. If you're having to tell him you have an ally awaiting an all-clear message, the situation has already gone south. The idea is to avoid that in the first place."

"That's a good point," I acknowledged. It was odd to hear Sean speak not as a lover or colleague, but as a werewolf alpha, used to navigating complex and often dangerous political waters. "Do you have another suggestion?"

"Vampires respect power plays and alliances. I can make you an ally of the Tomb Mountain Pack. If Vaughan threatens you or attacks, he's taking on the entire pack. Even a member of the Vampire Court would avoid that unless there was no other choice. This way, you go in as an associate of my pack. It's a move he'll understand and respect. You'll be protected, but you won't lose face."

It was my turn to think. "In return, I'll be expected to aid your pack if asked to do so?"

Sean looked surprised. "So you're familiar with the concept of pack ally?"

"Yes." I didn't elaborate. My grandfather's cabal was affiliated with two werewolf packs, so shifter politics was nothing new to me. "How will we formalize my status as pack associate?"

"I'll write you a letter you can display and present as needed," Sean said. "In the meantime, since Vaughan is a vampire, my suggestion is that I mark you with my blood. He'll understand what that means from the moment you walk into his office without you having to say a word."

An alliance with the Tomb Mountain Pack, even if it was temporary, was undeniably professionally beneficial to me. I was certainly getting the better end of the deal. "Either party can rescind the alliance with notice?"

"Standard clause," Sean assured me.

"Done. How should we do this?"

Sean produced an engraved pocketknife. He opened it, then drew the blade across the pad of his thumb. Blood welled. "Hold out your hands, palms up."

I obeyed.

Using his thumb, Sean rubbed blood onto the insides of both of my wrists. Without being asked, I pulled my hair to the side and tilted my head. He drew his thumb across my neck at the shoulder, marking me as an ally of his pack.

Instead of stepping back, Sean cupped the back of my neck with his hand. "You're off tomorrow?"

"Yep. I owe Malcolm a masking spell, and if I don't do laundry soon, I might run out of clothes."

Sean's eyes glinted. "That doesn't sound like such a bad thing to me."

I rolled my eyes.

He chuckled and released me. "What's your schedule look like for the next couple of days?"

I shook my head. "I really don't know at this point. That's one of the downsides of PI work."

"I understand. Private security isn't much different. But if we can make it work, I'd like to see you next week."

"I'd like that." I glanced down at his hand. "I was going to offer you a Band-Aid, but it looks like you don't need it."

Sean held up his thumb. The cut was already healing. In twenty minutes, there would be no sign of the wound.

He leaned down to give me a kiss, pulling me close with one hand on my hip. It was a very nice kiss: undemanding, yet full of promise.

When we broke apart, he nuzzled my neck and inhaled my scent. I shivered at the feeling of his breath on my skin. "Be safe," he said quietly. "You can still text me when you're done, if you want."

"It might be late."

"I'll be up." He gave me a wolfish grin. "I tend to be fairly nocturnal."

I laughed. "No doubt."

He gave me a kiss on the cheek, then stepped back. "Have a good night, Allie."

"You too, Sean."

He got into his car and waited until I was in mine with the engine started before he waved and drove away.

16

I'd hoped to sit and chat with Adri before my meeting with Charles, but she was at the door checking IDs when I arrived at Hawthorne's and it was a busy night. We exchanged quick hellos and I went inside to find a table and a much-needed drink.

I squeezed in at the bar and flagged Pete down to order a beer. He slid it over to me, took my money, and gave me a quick smile before turning to grab a bottle of vodka off a shelf. I took my drink and headed toward my usual booth, hoping to find it empty.

To my disappointment, it was occupied by a lone man, sitting back in the shadows where I usually took refuge. I sighed and started back toward the bar.

A familiar voice stopped me. "Ms. Worth."

I turned around.

The man in the shadows leaned forward into the light. It took a moment for me to recognize him in civilian clothes, but I'd know those ice-blue eyes anywhere.

"Special Agent Lake," I said, startled. "I wouldn't have thought this would be your scene." I wasn't sure what Lake's scene *would* be, but a supe bar owned by a vampire seemed an unlikely place for a SPEMA agent to be spending his off-hours.

"Hawthorne's has the finest selection of bourbon in the city." Lake raised his glass. "The owner is a connoisseur, or so I've been told."

"That he is," I murmured.

He regarded me with raised eyebrows. "Are you acquainted with the owner?"

Before I could answer, I felt someone come up next to me. Even in my high-heeled boots, Bryan towered over me. "Miss Alice," he rumbled. "Am I interrupting?"

"Not at all," I said, hoping my relief didn't show. "Am I wanted upstairs?"

"You are."

Lake studied me. I might have been imagining it, but I thought the fact I was here to see Charles Vaughan might have piqued the SPEMA agent's interest and raised his estimation of me by several degrees—neither of which pleased me. I would rather Lake forget about me altogether.

"Enjoy your bourbon," I told him.

"I'm sure I will." A small smile turned up the corners of Lake's mouth.

I turned to follow Bryan's enormous back through the crowd, depositing my beer bottle in a trash can as I passed. The enforcer and I walked down the hall and through a door marked *Private*.

As we started up the stairs, I said quietly, "You know he's a fed."

Bryan glanced at me. "We are aware. Agent Lake comes in every few weeks, has one drink of good bourbon, and then leaves."

"Anybody know why?"

"No."

"Hmm."

We climbed three flights of stairs, went through another, much heavier door, and entered another world.

The floor above the bar was soundproofed. I knew there was music blaring downstairs, but I couldn't hear a thing. The carpet was thick, the lighting dim. It was the kind of understated elegance that would appeal to a vampire.

I'd first met Charles when I worked for Mark Dunlap. Mark was a longtime associate of the Vampire Court, doing investigative work for them. Most mages steer clear of the fangy undead, since mage blood is particularly tasty for vamps. Some are able to absorb magical energy that way, enhancing their own innate powers, and drinking mage blood can become addictive. There was a lot of mutual respect between Mark and the Court, though, and since I had no particular objection, we'd ended up doing a lot of work for them. It was lucrative as well; the vamps wanted discretion, and they were willing to pay premium rates for it.

When I left Mark's firm, I was no longer on retainer for them, but Charles had hired me on a per-job basis to do some work for his businesses and the Court when Mark wasn't available. I'd proven myself to be trustworthy and capable. Charles started inviting me up to his office for a drink—liquor, not blood—from time to time when I was in Hawthorne's. He told me my bluntness was a refreshing break from the lies, evasions, and machinations of vamp politics.

Charles had also made it clear he wouldn't mind a roll in the hay, but so far I'd managed to steer clear of that particular minefield. I figured if he was that determined, he'd have pressed the issue by now, so maybe his overtures were just one more way for a two-hundred-year-old vamp to pass the time.

I checked my reflection in the mirror in the hall. I'd dressed up for my meeting in slim black slacks, an emerald-green, cowl-neck sweater, and high-heeled ankle boots, and pulled my hair up. A pair of dangly, gold earrings danced above my shoulders.

"You look very nice," Bryan said.

"Why, thank you, Bryan." I patted his arm. "We mustn't keep him waiting, I guess."

He led me down the hall to a set of double doors on the end, where two guards almost as large as him stood at attention. He knocked twice with a fist the size of a football.

From inside, I heard Charles's voice: "Come in."

Bryan opened the heavy door and stepped aside so I could enter Charles Vaughan's office.

"Hello, Alice." Charles stood and came around his enormous desk to meet me. As usual, the strikingly handsome, dark-haired vampire wore an expensive, tailored suit cut to flatter his lean physique and a watch that probably cost almost as much as my house.

He would forever appear to be in his early thirties, though no one looking into those ageless eyes would mistake him for a young man. His dark suit, hair, and eyes contrasted sharply with his pallor, but his coloring looked vamp-healthy, meaning he'd probably fed already this evening. His skin, when he took my hands, felt characteristically cool to the touch.

As he bent to kiss my cheek, he inhaled almost soundlessly, then chuckled softly. My pack alliance had been noted.

Charles sat back down, and I sank into a leather armchair across from him. Bryan closed the door and took up a position next to it.

The vampire closed a file on his desk and folded his hands on top of it. "I hoped I might have time to honor your request for a consultation on Thursday, but as I am sure Mr. Smith told you, my meeting ran very late."

"Not a problem at all," I said. "I figured it was a long shot anyway, just dropping in unannounced. Rude of me, really, but I was out and about and thought I'd risk it."

"Scotch?" Charles gestured at his extensive private bar.

"No, thank you. But if you have water, I'd love some."

He nodded at Bryan, who went to the bar and pulled out a glass bottle of imported artisanal water. He opened it, wrapped the cold bottle in a cloth napkin, and handed it to me. I sipped the fancy water. The label said its contents were filtered through natural lava rocks in a particular region of Iceland. I couldn't tell the difference between it and what you got out of a vending machine, but what did I know?

"I hope you are recovered from your recent misadventures," Charles said.

"I am, thanks. I ran into some black wards on Wednesday night, and on Thursday, I had a spell fail and got burned by uncontrolled magic."

His eyebrows raised. "Horrifying. Your job is dangerous at the most unexpected times."

"There's always an unpredictable element when magic is involved. Even the best of us can be surprised. The case I'm currently working on started out pretty straightforward but has quickly turned...interesting."

"It would seem so, if you encountered both black wards and uncontrolled magic in a single day," Charles said. "I am pleased to see you survived."

"It was a near thing, both times," I confessed. "It's been a rough couple of days."

"And yet, you drink water. Are you sure I cannot tempt you with a fifty-year single malt Scotch? I have looked forward to sharing a glass with someone who appreciates such a fine whisky."

A fifty-year-old single malt was an offer I couldn't refuse. "Well, if you insist."

"Mr. Smith, two glasses of the Glenfiddich, if you would."

We paused the conversation to watch with appropriate reverence as Bryan took out the bottle, unstoppered it, and poured us each two fingers of Scotch. We toasted each other and sipped. I closed my eyes to better appreciate the taste and smoothness of the whisky.

"Excellent." Charles clearly enjoyed both his drink and my reaction. "Simply superb."

"Definitely the best I've ever had. Thank you very much for sharing it with me."

"It is my pleasure."

We savored the Scotch a bit more, then Charles asked, "Have you had any contact with Mark Dunlap recently?"

I blinked in surprise. "No, we haven't spoken in years."

"He was puzzled by your decision to work independently, and hurt, I think."

"I know." I pondered my Scotch. "But I like being my own boss."

"Surely it has been difficult to establish yourself as a new investigator," Charles commented. "Mark has an excellent reputation and connections in both the supernatural and mundane worlds. He told me you did not attempt to steal any of his clients when you left."

"I wanted to leave Mark on good terms," I said a bit defensively. "I had no intention of poaching his clients. I'd still be friendly today if it were up to me, but Mark made it pretty clear he had no interest in talking to me."

"Perhaps it is presumptuous for me to say this, but I think you might find Mark's attitude has mellowed." He turned his glass in his hands, watching the light reflecting in the amber liquid. "Recently, he mentioned he had heard only good reports on your work. I detected a certain...regret regarding how you parted company."

"Interesting." On the one hand, part of me still smarted when I thought of the way Mark had reacted when I'd told him I was leaving, but years had passed, and perhaps it was time to let that go. I wasn't sure what kind of relationship we'd have these days. Were we colleagues? Competitors? It was hard to say exactly. Should I pick up the phone and call him? Then again, he could have called me at any point in the past three years if he was feeling regretful.

Finally, I said, "Well, the next time you speak with Mark, tell him I said hello."

"I will do that. What brings you to me this evening?"

I sipped my Scotch. "I came across an interesting situation and thought you might have some insights."

"How can I help?" Charles leaned back in his chair.

I weighed my words carefully, as was always prudent when dealing with vampires. "I met a young woman who has low-level magic, but a family member bound her, probably when she was very young, and until a few days ago, she had no idea she or anyone in her family had any such abilities."

He raised an elegant eyebrow. "How distressing for her."

"It was quite a shock." I smiled at the understatement. "She has no control over her magic. Because the family member who bound her passed away unexpectedly a few months ago, the binding spells began to fade, which is how we came to discover her hidden talent."

"Ah, I understand. The 'uncontrolled magic' accident you experienced on Thursday."

"Yes. I was able to bind her magic again, so things are good for now, but she's decided she wants to learn how to control and use her magic."

"I am glad to hear it. One should always embrace one's natural abilities. What is the problem?"

"The problem is that her family has avoided any attention from either the cabals or SPEMA and she'd like to keep it that way. Since she's an adult, her magic is at full strength. She needs a strong fire and air mage who can teach her to control her magic, someone who isn't part of a cabal, and who can be trusted not to rat her out to the Agency."

"And my role in this?"

I leaned forward. "You know a lot of people, and you're an excellent judge of character. I was hoping you could find someone who would be a good mentor, and who wouldn't sell her out for favors or money."

Charles looked pleased at my praise. "It is a tall order to find someone honorable these days," he mused. "It is fortunate her power is not strong. She is less of a prize."

"I had the same thought. She's low-level air, mid-level fire. It's nothing a cabal would pay much for; mages of her power level are a dime a dozen. She does have null abilities, but there's nothing unique about that." Okay, I was fudging a little there, since Natalie could null a mage almost instantly and break circles simply by touching them, but he didn't need to know that.

Charles steepled his fingers. "I will need to make discreet inquiries. It may take some time to find the best candidates. Let me ask this: why not become her mentor yourself?"

"A couple of reasons. First, I don't have time," I admitted. "My schedule is completely erratic because of my job. She'll need someone to spend a *lot* of time with her, especially in the beginning, and I can't afford to take time off. Second, I don't have fire magic, and she really needs to work with someone with the same abilities she has. Third, I have no experience with training a new mage, much less an adult with fully developed power. I would suck at it."

Charles chuckled. "I doubt, my dear, if you 'suck' at anything magic-related at all, but your reasoning is sound. A second question: why not ask around for a mage to train her, rather than come to me?"

Time to be careful. Charles had no idea of my background, or that I was anything more than the mid-level air and earth mage I made myself out to be, and I needed to avoid saying anything that might cause him to suspect otherwise.

"It's mainly a matter of expediency," I said, going for partial truth. "You know more people already than I could meet in a year, and you know them well enough to know if they meet the requirements. No one I know would fit the bill."

"Perfectly logical." Charles finished the last of his Glenfiddich and contemplated his glass. "One must savor such a fine Scotch slowly, and resist the urge to drink it so frequently that it becomes commonplace." He looked at me. "So, now that I know your request, what do you offer in exchange?"

Ah, yes, the proverbial deal with the devil. Money—unless it was in significant quantities—held little interest for wealthy vampires. Their preferred currency was favors. "I have a few possibilities in mind," I said.

"I cannot wait to hear these possibilities." Charles's lips twitched in a hint of a smile.

I raised one finger. "I offer my investigative services in exchange for your time and effort in locating an appropriate mentor for my client. A single employment contract, with prenegotiated duration limit."

He tapped his steepled fingers together and regarded me with half-lidded eyes. "Perhaps."

I raised a second finger. "My expertise in wards and spellwork. I have several new and highly complex wards I can discuss in more detail if you wish. One or more projects, depending on power levels and intricacy involved."

"Including black wards, if I require them?"

"Under specific conditions that I would have to preapprove."

"Understood. Any other offers?"

I blinked at him, rather surprised he didn't jump at the opportunity to have me create wards for him. "Did you have something particular in mind?"

"I do, in fact." Charles leaned forward, his hands folded on his desk. His gaze was suddenly very direct. "I require something very particular indeed."

I began to get an *oh shit* feeling. "Yes?"

"I would like to drink from you, Alice."

I stared.

Charles's eyes never left mine. "I have known you for almost five years, and never in that time have I tasted your blood. I have never asked, but this is something I have long desired. In return for finding a mentor for your client, I require one drink of your blood, at a time and place to be chosen by you, but within the next month. I am not asking for any intimacy beyond the bite, unless you wish it."

Anxiety surged inside me, but I squashed it and concentrated on keeping my breathing and heartbeat even and slow. One did not show fear in front of a vampire; they found it arousing. Charles could *not* be allowed to drink from me. He would instantly know I was no mid-level mage. Natalie's magic made her no trophy; I, on the other hand, was a great prize. I couldn't count on our history to protect me from being auctioned off to the highest-bidding cabal.

I looked at Charles and tried to keep my emotions off my face. He'd feel my alarm, but I hoped he'd chalk that up to a fear of being bitten. "I'm no one's cattle," I said quietly, using the slang term for a vamp's food supply.

Behind me, I heard Bryan shift closer to us at my tone. As far as he knew, I was little threat, but his job was to protect Charles. If it came down to it, Bryan would kill me before he'd let me harm the vampire.

"I would not ask you to be," Charles said. "Nor would I *want* you to be. It is a one-time arrangement."

"I've never allowed any vampire to drink from me." I was surprised at how calm my voice sounded. "I have no plans to do so."

"Even if it is I who does it, and you dictate the terms?" He looked mildly surprised at my reaction. For a normally poker-faced vamp, "mild surprise" was the equivalent of being flabbergasted. I supposed Charles thought I would have no objection to donating a meal, since I'd shown no previous aversion to being around vamps.

Many people craved the bite of a vampire. It could be intensely pleasurable, if the vampire wished it to be. No vampire ever had to go hungry; there were willing donors who happily lined up around the block for the chance to be breakfast, lunch, dinner, or a midnight snack. Countless men and women would climb over each other for a chance at what I was turning down.

How on earth could I extricate myself from this without arousing Charles's suspicion and anger?

"I can't," I told him. "I'm honored you'd ask this of me, Charles, but I won't be a blood meal, for anyone, for any reason."

Charles studied my face. I tried to keep my expression neutral.

Finally, he spoke. "Then I am afraid I cannot help you." His voice was calm, perfectly dispassionate.

My mouth fell open. "Because I won't let you drink my blood, you won't help me find someone to teach my client?"

"Yes."

"Why not?" The question popped out before I could stop it. It sounded far too much like a challenge. My fingers tightened on my glass.

Charles didn't move, though a muscle in his jaw twitched. I swallowed, my mouth suddenly dry.

"I do not owe you any explanation," he said finally, his voice still cold. "But perhaps I will say that I have asked so little, and your refusal has...hurt my feelings."

Oh God. I hurt the feelings of a two-hundred-year-old vampire. I didn't wet my pants, but it was a near thing. My flat refusal was a slap in the face, and I had no way to better explain myself that wouldn't expose my secrets. I'd probably lost an employer and an ally. No more late-night drinks at Hawthorne's.

Because to leave any of the very expensive Scotch would add insult to injury, I drained what little remained and gently set my glass down on the desk. Slowly, I rose, keeping my hands in plain sight. I did nothing that could be read as threatening, very aware of the vampire in front of me and the enforcer at my back.

"I'm sorry," I said softly. The vampire said nothing.

Carefully, I backed toward the door. Charles remained motionless, his eyes on me. I suddenly felt like a gazelle under the watchful stare of a lion.

Just as Bryan reached to open the door for me, Charles spoke. "A moment."

I paused. "Yes?"

Charles rose but stayed behind his desk. "I will contact you soon about a project for the Court that requires wards: a new facility, one hour from the city. If you are available, it will be a lucrative contract."

"Thank you."

"Good night."

"Good night."

Charles remained standing as Bryan opened the door of the office. I backed into the hall, and the door closed in my face.

I'd originally intended to return to the bar after the meeting for another drink or two, and maybe a chat with Adri, but I was rethinking that plan. Despite Charles's parting comments regarding a potential contract from the Court—comments that may or may not have been designed to deescalate a tense situation—the thought of dealing with the noisy, boisterous Saturday-night crowd downstairs was suddenly unappealing.

I returned to the main floor. As I weaved through the crush of people, I noticed Lake was gone and a couple had taken his place in the back corner booth.

I slipped out the front door, giving Adri a quick wave as I passed. It wasn't until I was halfway home that I started to feel the tension seeping out of my shoulders.

When I parked in my driveway, I fired off a quick text: *Home*. I stuck the phone in my pocket and got out of the car, heading for my front door.

The phone beeped as I unlocked my door. I went inside, locked the door, and went to the kitchen for a glass of water.

Wolf: Meeting went well?

I texted back, then headed for the stairs, cup in hand.

Me: No. We could not agree on terms.

The response came back in seconds. *Are you all right?*

Me: Unharmed.

Wolf: What did he ask for?

Me: Long story. Will tell you when I see you.

A few minutes went by. I went upstairs and started taking off my clothes and jewelry.

Beep.

Wolf: I have Monday and Tuesday evenings clear as of now. Dinner Monday?
Me: Maybe. Good night.
Wolf: Good night, Allie. Sweet dreams.

    I plugged in my phone, stripped, and used soap and water to wash Sean's blood off my wrists and neck. As I changed into pajamas and climbed into bed, I realized I was smiling. With a growl, I turned over to put my back to the phone, curled up under the covers, and fell asleep.

17

Sunday morning, I rolled out of bed at eight and headed to the bathroom to shower. I dried my hair, dressed quickly, and released Malcolm from my earring.

"What's the plan for today?" Malcolm trailed behind me down the stairs.

"Today we're going to work on your masking spell." I went into the kitchen, fired up the coffeepot, and made myself some toast with grape jelly for breakfast.

With my travel mug filled with the nectar of the gods, I led Malcolm to the door to my basement. "Come here. I need to let the basement wards know you're allowed to pass."

Once Malcolm's energy signature was integrated into the wards, I flipped on the light, opened the door, and led the way down the stairs.

Malcolm's form shimmered a bit as he passed through the barrier, and he grimaced. "Oof. That felt intense. So much power."

At the bottom of the steps, he paused to look around.

To the right was my library. It was modest, about half the size of Betty's. When I escaped my grandfather's cabal, I left with only my scars and the half-burned clothes on my back. My personal library at the cabal compound had been massive, and it was one of the hardest things to leave behind. I'd begun building a new library the moment I arrived in the city, but it was a slow process. Spelled bookcases, carved with protection runes, ran around the outside of the room, with a large wooden table in the middle.

To the left was my spell-crafting and summoning area. Another heavy table stood against the wall. Chalk, papers, crystals, little tubes of henna, and jewelry-making materials were scattered on top of it. Four large, heavily warded oak storage cabinets against the back wall contained a variety of implements and supplies, from crystals to athames. The floor had three concentric circles inlaid into the concrete.

Malcolm studied the cabinets. "What's with those two cabinets on the end there?"

"Don't touch those."

Malcolm snorted. "No shit. Those are serious black wards. What's in there?"

"It's where I keep all my blood magic materials."

"Oh, that explains the wards. Wouldn't want anybody finding that stuff."

I went to the library and started scanning through the books. "I'm looking for how to mask your magical energy so you being a mage ghost is less noticeable," I said, hunting for helpful volumes.

Malcolm drifted over next to me. "Seems like a masking spell might work, if we can make it so anyone who senses me thinks all I have is low-level earth or water magic."

"I don't know how to make a masking spell that will work on a noncorporeal being," I confessed.

"It's not that different than a spell for a living person. I think I can show you."

We worked for most of the day on Malcolm's masking spell, taking a few breaks to chat and rest while we refined the spellwork.

Storing him in the earring helped hide him, but it occurred to me it wasn't fair of me to expect him to stay in there all the time. When I'd first put him in the earring, it was supposed to be a temporary arrangement, but then I'd let this case—and other things—distract me from working on the spell that was needed to obscure his identity. I'd been stashing him in there for my convenience and letting him out when I needed help, which was inexcusably selfish. I felt guilty about it and told him so.

"No worries," Malcolm said with way more understanding than I thought I deserved. "Since the minute I showed up in your office, you've been working nonstop on this case, and you've been injured a couple of times. There really hasn't been any chance for you to work on this spell, but we're doing it now, and that's all that matters."

"Thanks for being so patient."

Malcolm shrugged. "Hey, I've got time. It's not like I'm getting any older here."

When I was sure he was joking, I laughed. I'd had a dream about the cabal the night before, and it was a grim reminder about what he'd gone through. He seemed pretty stable for somebody who had died that way. Unlike some ghosts who go completely bonkers in the Null and come back to earth as wraiths, poltergeists, or just plain deranged, he seemed to have made it back with his sanity intact. I wondered if that was due to his strong magical abilities.

"Hey, you in there?" Malcolm interrupted my musings.

I blinked at him. "Sorry. Got lost in thought for a minute. You were saying?"

"I was saying I think I might have figured it out." He showed me the spellwork he'd been working on. It was similar to the spell I'd used to mask my own magic and pass myself off as a low-level air mage while I was recovering from plastic surgery on my face. He'd modified it to work on a noncorporeal body and to make himself seem like he had a low amount of water magic only.

"Hmm." I pondered the spell. "It might work."

"Only one way to find out."

I reached out to take Malcolm's arm with my left hand and used my right to trace the spell in the air. In moments, his energy signature muted and transformed. I added the additional disguising spell, wove it through the masking spell, and invoked both. Then I released his arm.

I could immediately sense the difference in Malcolm's energy signature. While before I could sense strong earth and water magic, now I would have sworn he was only a low-level water mage.

"Did it work?" Malcolm asked.

I remembered he wouldn't be able to feel the difference, just as I couldn't feel my own masking spell that made me seem like a mid-level air and earth mage. "Yep. I think you're officially incognito now. I guess this means less earring time for you."

"No offense, but thank God. It's weird in there."

That made me laugh. "I do want you to come up with a spell that would let you jump into the earring if you needed to. We don't know yet how well the masking spell will hold up under scrutiny, and I'd like you to have a bolt-hole of some sort in case we're out and about and encounter a strong mage or a ward that disrupts the spell."

"Makes sense. Maybe I can work on that while you figure out how to set your basement wards so they don't zap me when I cross them." He looked at me sideways.

I rolled my eyes at him. "You are such a nag. I'll work on that tomorrow. I am seriously worn out after all this work we did today. How are you not tired?"

"Um, because I'm a ghost?"

"Whatever. I'm going upstairs." I led Malcolm back up the steps to the main floor, where he braved the sizzle of the wards once more. "Sorry about that."

"It's okay. It's not like it hurts. It just feels like I'm being pulled apart a little."

I winced. "I'm not sure how much less uncomfortable I can make it without compromising the wards, but I'll look into it."

It was almost nine p.m. I threw a load of clothes into the washer, then made myself a quick dinner. As I was eating, I realized the message light on my phone was blinking. I'd missed a call from Natalie while I was doing laundry and had a voice mail.

"Hey, Alice." Natalie sounded excited. "I think maybe I found something that might help us. It's a folder of letters from a couple of years ago from a man named John West. In one of the letters, he refers to something called the *Kasten*." She spelled it. "He thanks my grandmother for agreeing to keep it. I looked through the rest of the letters, but he never mentions it again. It sounds like he and my grandmother were both in something called a harnad?"

I went cold. A harnad was an alliance of blood mages who do magic in pairs or groups to increase their power. They were extremely dangerous and had the well-deserved reputation of being ruthless. Harnads had been known to even use lifeblood—the last blood drained from a dying person, which was extremely potent—for spells and the most deadly and powerful black wards and curses. To do so was a capital crime in all fifty states, but there had been at least a dozen documented cases of the ritual being performed in the past decade, and those were just the ones that had become public knowledge.

This had the potential to be very, very bad.

Natalie was still talking, oblivious to the bomb she'd just dropped. "Anyway, I'm putting these letters on the dining table for you to look at, and I'll keep digging around. Have a good night!" *Beep.*

Malcolm and I looked at each other. "Shit," he said.

I couldn't have said it better myself.

I curled up on the couch with my laptop while Malcolm alternated between reading over my shoulder and floating around the house. I did a search for *Kasten*, but nothing came up that looked remotely useful, other than it was the German word for *box* or *chest*. I tried combining it with different search terms like *object of power* and *focus*, which were my best guesses about what it might be, but still got zilch.

After I put my clothes in the dryer, I searched for *harnad* and *Kasten* together, but all I got were news articles about harnads and websites denouncing blood magic. More than one website claimed there were at least two active harnads in the city, though not much was known about them. A local reporter believed they were responsible for a string of missing prostitutes, but the police were unconvinced.

I had no problem finding information about Betty's friend, John West. He was a high-level fire mage who lived in the city. By all accounts, he was a respected businessman who still did frequent commercial work, despite being in his seventies. I found nothing about West being a blood mage, but that wasn't surprising since blood magic was illegal.

Contacting West would be a highly dangerous proposition, since I had no desire to get myself on the radar of a member of a harnad. I leaned my head back against the couch and closed my eyes.

"What are you going to do?" Malcolm wanted to know.

"Good freaking question," I told him without opening my eyes. I briefly outlined what I'd found out about John West, the rumored local harnads, and the missing prostitutes. "Things just keep getting worse. This started out being about missing books. Now we're talking about a harnad being involved."

"If this *Kasten* doohickey belonged to the harnad, maybe they figured out who the mystery mage is and got that person to go in and get it for them," Malcolm suggested.

I'd been thinking that myself. "You're pretty good at this private investigator thing. Maybe *you* should be the PI and *I* should be the wisecracking assistant."

"That would work, except your jokes suck," Malcolm quipped.

I threw a pillow at him—they call them throw pillows, after all—and it went through him and landed over by the fireplace. "Do you think it's worth asking that reporter about the local harnads?"

"At this point, I'm not sure. I still think our best bet is figuring out who the mystery mage is and following that lead to see where it takes us."

I threw my hands up in aggravation. "Except we're out of suspects! It *has* to be one of Betty's children or siblings, but we've eliminated them all. It makes no damn sense."

"Okay, well, that's the thing. It *has* to be one of them, so either someone is capable of disguising their magic, or there's another family member we don't know about."

I rubbed my forehead. "If one of them is hiding their magic and/or disguising their energy signature, we'll need a spell that can detect a masking spell like the one we just put on you."

"I can do that, no problem."

"Awesome. Then all I'll have to do is sneak up to each of them and see if the spell triggers." I wrinkled my nose.

"Actually, I can do that easier than you," Malcolm pointed out. "I'm invisible. You can just wait in the car."

I could get used to this ghost assistant thing. "That sounds like an excellent plan, if you can design a spell that won't be triggered by the masking spell that's on you."

Malcolm gave me an insulted look. "I'm pretty sure I can do that."

"Figuring out if there's another sibling that Natalie isn't aware of might take a bit more legwork. I'm wondering if she could call Betty's lawyer tomorrow and find out."

"That's a thought. I'll work on the detection spell tonight and have it for you in the morning."

I glanced at the clock and was surprised to see it was almost midnight. "Wow. I really lost track of time. I'd better hit the hay." I hesitated, realizing I'd never "let" Malcolm out of the earring overnight. "Do you...need anything?" I asked awkwardly.

"Like what, my blankie and a bedtime story?"

I made a face at him. "Jerk."

Malcolm grinned. "No, I'm good. I'll work on the spell and maybe experiment with going out and about."

"Until we have a spell that can jump you back to me or into the earring, I don't know how comfortable I am with you going out on your own."

He scowled. "I don't need a babysitter."

"That's not how I meant it. Your masking spell isn't foolproof. We can't have anyone finding out who and what you are."

Malcolm nailed me with a hard stare. "You mean the way you can't have anyone finding out who and what *you* are?"

We eyeballed one another like two gunfighters sizing each other up in the middle of a dusty street. If a tumbleweed blew through my living room, we'd be all set.

"You can't go to a hospital, you can't let anyone get ahold of your blood, you've got multiple layers of masking spells, you don't want to ask around for a mentor for Natalie because you don't want to attract the attention of the local cabals. It doesn't take a rocket scientist to figure out that you're hiding. I'm dead, not stupid."

I kept silent.

Malcolm literally buzzed with anger, his fury intensifying by the second. "You know pretty much my whole life story, but apparently you don't trust me enough to even tell me what you're hiding from."

"No, I don't, not yet, and that's going to have to be the way it is for now, because I don't trust anyone with that information. It's not just you," I added when Malcolm started to get huffy. "I haven't told anyone about my past, and that isn't likely to change anytime soon. I value you, and I want you to be safe, which is why I'd like you to have a bolt-hole spell to get you back to the earring in case of an emergency."

I got up and headed for the stairs. "So be pissy if you want. Go out if you want; I'm not going to stop you. The house wards will let you pass. Just be careful."

I was almost halfway up the stairs when Malcolm finally spoke. "I'll make the bolt-hole spell before I go out." He still sounded angry, but there wasn't anything I could do about that.

I paused. "Thanks. Have a good night."

"You too."

I went upstairs and shut my bedroom door. It took a long time for me to fall asleep.

18

When my alarm went off Monday morning at seven thirty, I'd been lying awake in bed for almost an hour. What little sleep I'd managed to get had been plagued by nightmares about blood mages and faceless, dark figures chanting around an altar and an object I couldn't see. My restless brain bounced from one topic to the next: Natalie, Malcolm, the mystery mage, Betty, harnads, John West, the *Kasten*, and even Charles and Sean. The worst part was, they were all big question marks.

Since I already had my phone in my hand, I pulled up Natalie's number and called her before I realized it might be too early.

She picked up on the third ring. "Hi, Alice!"

I was relieved that she sounded perfectly awake. "Morning, Natalie. Sorry I'm calling so early."

"Nah, I was up. Did you get my message last night? Did any of that make sense?"

"Some of it," I hedged. "Not sure what the *Kasten* is—I'm still looking to that. A harnad is the name for a group of blood mages."

A very long pause.

"Natalie?"

For the first time since I'd met her, Natalie swore. "Are you saying my grandmother was a blood mage?"

"It looks that way," I admitted. "I'd really like to look at those letters."

"I've got them here. You can come look at them anytime. God." I wasn't sure if she was swearing or if it was a prayer. "I thought I couldn't be shocked by this anymore, but I was wrong. Do you think my grandmother killed people?"

"I don't know, but we're going to be very careful. Harnads are dangerous. Don't talk to anyone about this."

She whimpered.

"I was wondering if you could do something for me," I said.

"What do you need?"

I explained that Malcolm and I were going to see if any of her aunts or uncle were hiding their magical abilities. "In the meantime, you mentioned you were still in touch with your grandmother's attorney."

"Yes. He's helping me fight my aunt in court."

"Could you call him and ask if Betty had any other siblings or children besides the ones we know about?"

Another long pause. "If my mother had any other brothers or sisters—even half brothers or half sisters—I'd think she would have told me," Natalie said finally.

"Unless she didn't know. Maybe there was a black sheep in the family."

Natalie snorted. "At this point, anything is possible. Sure, I'll call him and ask. I'm sure the answer is no, but we might as well check."

"Thanks. Let me know what you find out. I'll keep you posted on our end."

We made plans to touch base in the afternoon and said good-bye. I rolled out of bed and headed for my bathroom to shower and brush my teeth.

When I came out of the bathroom, Malcolm was in my room.

I shrieked, jumped, and almost lost my towel. "Damn it, Malcolm, what the hell? What if I'd walked out of my bathroom naked?"

He whirled around to face the other way. "Sorry! Sorry! Shit."

"We need to have some ground rules about my bedroom." I went into the bathroom, put on my bathrobe, and came back out. "Okay, I'm decent."

Malcolm turned around. "Seriously, sorry about that."

"It's fine. What's up?"

"Couple of things. I've got the masking-spell detector ready to go. I made the bolt-hole spell for your earring, but I need to test it."

"Awesome! How—"

Malcolm vanished.

I jerked. "What the hell? Oh." I went over to the nightstand and picked up my earrings. One of them buzzed with energy. "*Release.*"

Malcolm popped into my room, looking quite pleased with himself.

"Way to go. Any idea what its range might be?"

"That I'm not sure of," Malcolm said. "In theory, range shouldn't matter since this is metaphysical, but I would like to do more testing in incremental distances before I rely on it to jump me across town."

I felt a hell of a lot better about the situation now Malcolm was able to jump into the earring in case of an emergency.

"What about a spell I could use to get *out* of the earring, instead of needing you to let me out?" he asked.

I frowned. "That is going to be more of a challenge. The earring is a heavy-duty containment spell designed from the ground up to keep its contents in and only respond to my commands. I'll have to mess with it. It's possible, I think, but it's going to take some time."

I went to my closet to find clothes. "I asked Natalie to call the lawyer to find out if she's got any other relatives we don't know about. She's not very happy about the thought of her grandmother being in a harnad." I grabbed a blue plaid shirt and a pair of jeans and emerged from the closet.

Malcolm snorted. "I can't say I blame her. Imagine if *your* grandmother was in a harnad."

My grandmother *founded* three harnads, but that was neither here nor there. "I did tell her not to talk to anyone about it, which I would think would go without saying, but better to be safe than sorry. Now shoo so I can get dressed."

Malcolm went through the door into the hall. I put on my clothes, then brushed out my hair and pulled it into a ponytail before doing my makeup and putting on my jewelry.

Once I had my boots on, I opened the bedroom door and Malcolm was waiting in the hall. "You ready to go solve this thing?" he asked.

"Absolutely," I said. "Just as soon as I get some coffee."

I figured we'd start with Elise and work our way backward up the suspect list. I hit a fast-food drive-thru for a breakfast sandwich and gigantic cup of dark roast.

"How's your cholesterol?" Malcolm's disembodied voice was sardonic.

I took a big bite of my sandwich. "No idea. Probably fine, though," I said through a mouthful of food.

"You are a classy woman."

"Shut up."

By the time we got to Elise's neighborhood, I'd finished off the sandwich and most of the coffee. I rolled past Elise's house and told Malcolm to meet me around the corner.

"Roger that," Malcolm said, and I felt his energy leave the car.

I cruised down the street, turned the corner, and pulled over to the curb. I took my phone out and pretended to be in the middle of an animated conversation, as if I'd just stopped to make a call. Several morning dog-walkers and joggers passed by my car, saw me on the phone, and moved on without paying me much attention.

It was nearly ten minutes later by the time I felt Malcolm's energy in the car. I'd started to get worried around the six-minute mark. "Boo," Malcolm said.

I put my phone in my lap. "Very funny. What took so long?"

He snorted, which was a weird sound to hear from an invisible ghost. "'Gosh, Malcolm, it's pretty cool you can detect masking spells and you can sneak up on people without them knowing since you're *invisible* and whatnot, but gee whiz, can't you work faster?'"

"Was that sarcasm? I couldn't tell."

"Yes, that was sarcasm."

"Yeah, so was that. So what took so long?"

There was a pause, during which I tried to imagine what expression was on Malcolm's face. "I had to do some 'tuning' before I could get it to work," he said finally, sounding aggravated. "But I'm 99.9 percent certain Elise is exactly what she seems: a nonmagical human. She's not hiding anything. Well, except maybe alcoholism. She was drinking wine."

I glanced at the clock on my dashboard. "At nine a.m.?"

"Yup. *Red* wine. In a coffee mug."

"Damn." I couldn't decide whether to be amused, disapproving, or impressed. "Well, that's one we can cross off the list, again." I pulled away from the curb.

"Who's next on the list?"

"Deborah Mackey."

"Sweet."

Three hours later, I was parked just down the street from Helen Matson's house in Hope, crushing candy on my phone, when Malcolm returned to the car. "You won't believe this, but it was negative too."

I shut the game off and hit the steering wheel with the heel of my hand. "This is nuts. You and I both think that energy signature on the library wards belongs to a child or sibling of Betty Morrison, but you're telling me your spell is not picking up masking spells on *any* of them?"

"Yep. We've eliminated Elise, Deborah, Kathy, and Peter, and even Robert and Helen."

"And you're sure it works?"

Malcolm sighed. "Yes, I'm sure. It picked mine up before I tuned it out. It's picking *yours* up."

"Then what the hell?"

"Maybe we should call Natalie and see what the lawyer told her."

"Good thinking." I called her cell. There was no answer, so I left a message to call me.

"What now?" Malcolm asked.

I sighed. "I guess let's go back home. I want to keep looking for info on this *Kasten* and try to figure out what the hell it is. If nothing else pans out, I might try to track down John West or call that journalist about the local harnads."

By the time we got back to my house, it was almost two and I was hungry. Malcolm went down to the basement to work on spells. I started to pull a small pizza out of the freezer, but I thought about my cholesterol and decided to make a salad instead. I grabbed a diet soda and carried my lunch downstairs.

I set out my lunch at the table in the library area and pulled a couple of books from the shelves. Malcolm was using my circles in the workspace. It looked like he was trying to set up additional bolt-hole spells that could jump him to different crystals. Not a bad idea; we could leave one here and another at the office in case of emergencies.

I ate my lunch and started thumbing through the books, looking for any references to anything called a *Kasten*. I checked the indexes in the back, then skimmed them, finding nothing. When my vision got blurry, I took a break to do more Internet searches, but nothing came up, no matter what I searched for. Even alternate spellings gave me nothing.

I went back to the books, this time looking through some of my books on fire magic. Over an hour later, I still had nothing except a headache. No call from Natalie yet either.

Malcolm, meanwhile, was jumping in and out of crystals in the work area. "I hope you don't get stuck in one of those while you're testing your spells," I told him as I headed for my storage cabinets. "Before we start using them to jump you from place to place, I need some way to get you in and out of them too."

"I'm working on that," Malcolm said, disappearing and reappearing. "Right now I can jump in and out, but there's no masking spell on the crystals, so any mage who wanders by them would be able to tell I was in there."

"Good point. We should work on that too." I went to the leftmost cabinet, traced four runes on the door, and opened it. Four of the shelves held books and notebooks, the contents of my carefully curated but limited blood magic library. These books were black market and extremely hard to find. They'd been procured through third parties and delivered to post office boxes.

I pulled out any books that dealt with harnads or objects of power used in ritual blood magic. I took the books to the library table and spread them out while Malcolm went back to his bolt-hole spells. I bent my head over my books.

Twenty minutes later, I dropped a book on the table with a yell.

Malcolm popped to my side. "What?"

I pointed to the page. "I found it!"

"Found what?"

I picked up the book, a rather dry tome on harnad history and myth, and read: "'In the year 1648, a small village in Germany was destroyed by fire. Witnesses reported that the fire moved with unnatural speed, devouring everything and everyone in the village in a matter of seconds. The fire was said to have been the work of a local harnad leader, a man named Adelbert, who had been driven from the village after suspicions of witchcraft years before.'"

"What does this have to do with—"

"I'm getting there. 'Only one family survived the fire. Adelbert warned a young woman named Alide, whom he had hoped to marry before his banishment, that he was returning to take his revenge on the town and she should take her family and leave. He told her that he was in possession of an object of power he referred to as *der Zauberkasten*, which he claimed would destroy the village.'"

"What else does it say?" Malcolm asked.

I read on. "'The Adelbert *Kasten*, as it came to be called, is often considered to be a mythical object, as no reliable sources have ever documented its existence. It has been described by various anecdotal sources as a wooden box or chest with a lid. One account from mid-eighteenth-century France references the *Kasten* as a reliquary containing bones supposedly belonging to Adelbert himself. Another report, this one recorded by a monk in eighteenth-century Germany, describes the *Kasten* as wielding enormous destructive power when filled with the lifeblood or severed body parts of mages representing all four cardinal elements: air, fire, earth, and water. Such an object would be of obvious interest to a harnad, whose members regularly practice ritual blood magic, but there is no record of the *Kasten* being used since 1748 in Europe, and never in the United States. The evidence seems to suggest that if Adelbert's *Kasten* ever existed at all, it has been lost to time.' That's all it says."

"Holy shit," Malcolm said after a moment.

We stared at each other.

"So this *Kasten* is some sort of magical weapon of mass destruction that runs on the blood or body parts of mages?" Malcolm asked. "Do we think it's possible Betty Morrison and her harnad had it and she was keeping it hidden in her bookcase?"

I rubbed my forehead. "I don't know. The person who wrote this book certainly seems to think it probably didn't really exist, but Natalie's got a letter from John West to Betty thanking her for keeping it safe. Whether that was what was in the bookcase, I don't know."

I picked up my phone and called Natalie again.

"Hey, Alice," she said breathlessly. I heard traffic sounds in the background. It sounded like she was downtown. "I'm sorry I haven't had a chance to call you. I'm having to run some errands and deal with an accountant, and it's taking all day."

"That's okay. Did you get in touch with the lawyer?"

"I left a message," Natalie replied. "He hasn't called me back yet. If I don't hear from him today, I'll call him again in the morning."

I debated telling her what I'd found out about the *Kasten*, then decided it was a conversation better had in person. "Okay, great. Let me know what you find out." We said our good-byes and hung up.

"What's the plan for the rest of the day?" Malcolm asked.

I glanced at the clock on my phone. "Well, it's almost four. Now that we know what the *Kasten* is—or might be—I think I need to know more about John West."

Malcolm floated back and forth nervously. "Well, we know he's a high-level fire mage, and if he's in a harnad, that means he's probably a high-level blood mage as well."

"I'd like to get a sense of his magic so I could recognize it again, and to know exactly what I might be up against if it turns out he's in the middle of all this." I started gathering up the books on the table.

"Are you going to use a ruse so you can shake hands with him?"

I shook my head. "I don't think that's a good idea. It worked with Peter and the others because they have low-level magic and they have no idea how to use it. West is a high-level mage. If I touched him with my shields even partially down, he'd sense me immediately. I don't want to attract the attention of anyone in a harnad, least of all a high-level fire mage."

"I could do it," Malcolm suggested. "Like I did today, with the spell detector."

I thought about it but shook my head again. "No, it's dangerous for you too. Even with the masking spell, you're still vulnerable. All I need to do is get near him and I should be able to sense his magic."

My phone rang. I glanced at the screen. *Wolf*. I remembered he'd invited me to dinner tonight and I hadn't had time to think about it today.

I answered the call. "Hi, Sean."

"Hi, Allie." I smiled at the sound of his familiar voice: deep and a little growly. "I'm leaving the office and thought I'd check in and see if you were interested in getting dinner tonight."

"I was just about to head out to check on a person of interest who's come up in the last day. It may take up most of my evening."

"Want a colleague along for the ride? You can catch me up on the situation with Vaughan."

I thought about that. As a pack associate, I did owe its alpha a summary of what had transpired at my meeting with Charles. Plus, having Sean along was good camouflage for surveilling West. "That would work. I need to be at his office before he leaves work at five, though."

"It's four now. I can be at your place in twenty. Is that enough time?"

"Should be. I'll be ready."

"See you in twenty." We disconnected.

I finished collecting the books on the table and took them over to the cabinet. Malcolm followed me.

As I was putting them back on the shelves, he said, "So this thing with the werewolf."

"There's no 'thing' with Sean. He's useful."

"'Useful,' huh?" Malcolm didn't bother to hide his skepticism. "Useful for what?"

"Professionally useful." I put up the last book and closed the cabinet. "It was easier to get access to Natalie's aunts and uncle with him posing as a colleague or fiancé. I can use his car to surveil West. My alliance with his pack strengthens my reputation in the supe community and improves my bargaining position with the vamps."

"What alliance?"

I told Malcolm about my new status as pack associate and briefly recapped my meeting with Charles as we went upstairs and into my storage room.

He was understandably concerned about my close call with Charles, but wasn't easily distracted from his original question. "Sean may be useful, but it's more than that," Malcolm said as I pinned my hair up and reached for a blonde wig. "I saw the way you smiled when the phone rang."

I slipped the wig on carefully, then adjusted it in the mirror and used my fingers to gently comb out the hair. When I was satisfied with how it looked, I slipped on a pair of thick-framed fake glasses and left the storage room, turning the light off and closing the door.

"I do like his company." I checked to make sure I had everything I needed in my bag. "He's a good colleague and a good resource. Anything else that happens is purely recreational."

Malcolm grinned. "Good for you. All work and no play makes Alice a dull girl."

I scowled at him. "Whether or not I 'play' is none of your business."

"Duly noted. But if you're planning on having 'playtime' tonight, warn me so I can go hide out at Nat's house, okay?"

Aggravated, I dove at him, magic sparking on my fingertips. With a laugh, he vanished.

19

Forty-five minutes later, Sean and I were parked outside a small office building just east of downtown, reading online reviews of John West's investment company and news stories about his fire magic. Most of the comments on the stories were from local contractors who had used his services. A couple of fire departments had hired him to help manage some wildfires, and apparently he'd saved a lot of lives and property.

To hear the city's fire chief tell it, John West was a hero who'd fearlessly walked into a wildfire and controlled it so it could be contained. I did an Internet search for the incident and found news footage. Sean and I watched in stunned silence.

"I can see why you're keeping your distance on this one," Sean said after we'd seen the video twice. "Have you ever seen anyone control that much fire at once?"

"Yes." My grandfather could, not that he'd ever used it to help anyone. "But it's very rare. As much as I'd like to avoid him and anyone else in his harnad, if there is one, forewarned is forearmed. If I end up having to meet him, I don't want to go in blind."

"That is true, though in this case, I'm not sure how much good it might do you."

I stayed quiet and watched the video again.

On the way to West's office, I'd told Sean about my meeting with Charles and the vampire's demand for my blood. Though his hands tightened on the steering wheel until it creaked, his only comments were professional and neutral. I'd also told him who we thought West might be—a blood mage and member of a local harnad—but didn't mention the *Kasten*. If that was what was missing from Betty's library, and it was an object of power, the fewer people who were aware of its existence, the better, until Malcolm and I knew more about it.

Once the video ended, I read up more on West's bio while we waited. As five o'clock approached, lights started turning off in the various offices and people started pouring out of the building. I didn't see any sign of John West until ten after, when he suddenly came out the front door.

"That's him," I said to Sean.

Despite being in his seventies, West looked lean, like a runner, with silver hair brushed back from hard, blue eyes that reminded me of my grandfather's cold gaze. The fire mage scanned the parking lot as he walked briskly to a black BMW, laid his suit jacket carefully across the backseat, and climbed into the driver's seat.

Sean started his car and fell in behind him, keeping his distance as we battled rush-hour traffic on our way north of town. I knew West's house was on the east side, so I wondered where we were going. It was probably too much to hope that he was headed to a harnad meeting.

When he finally turned through the gates of the art museum, Sean asked, "What are we doing here?"

"No idea." I thought the museum normally closed at six, but the parking lot still had quite a few cars in it. West parked, put his suit jacket back on, and headed into the museum.

"He may be meeting somebody," Sean commented.

"Could be." I checked my wig in the mirror on the visor, unfastened my seat belt, and opened my door. Sean and I exited the car. I slung my bag over my shoulder, and we headed into the museum.

When we stepped inside, I scanned the enormous lobby and spotted West heading toward the auditorium. An easel beside the reception desk advertised a special presentation tonight by an art historian on the Italian High Renaissance.

"Are you here for the lecture?" the woman behind the desk asked us cheerfully.

West went into the auditorium, so it looked like we were. I paid for our admission, and Sean and I put museum stickers on our shirts.

When we got to the auditorium, I spotted John West holding a glass of wine and looking over a spread of hors d'oeuvres.

Sean and I went to the cash bar. He bought water for me and a beer for himself, and then we browsed the long table of bite-sized appetizers. Food and drinks in hand, we staked out a spot along the wall where I could keep an eye on West as Sean chatted about his day. West spoke to no one; unlike most of the other attendees, he stood off by himself, sipping his wine.

A few minutes before six, people started to move to the seats. We managed to snag the seats behind West. I put my bag and jacket in the seat next to mine. The auditorium was only about a third full, but I didn't want anyone sitting down next to us.

A museum employee came out, and I half listened as she welcomed everyone to the museum and said a few words about the evening's speaker, an art historian named Dr. Jacob Altman. I pictured a dusty old man with horn-rimmed glasses carrying an overflowing briefcase.

When the presenter came out, however, I was surprised that Dr. Altman was an enthusiastic young man with unruly hair and Converse sneakers. Instead of an old, battered briefcase, he carried a MacBook Pro that he connected at the lectern, and fired up a very modern PowerPoint.

As the art historian lectured us on the finer points of High Renaissance art, I watched John West. The older man seemed to be listening intently and taking notes in a small notebook. It was looking more and more like he was simply here to learn about a bunch of sixteenth-century painters I'd never heard of.

When the presentation was well underway and I was certain West's attention was focused on the lecture, I closed my eyes and concentrated on his magical energy as it buzzed against the edges of my senses. Slowly, I reached out with my mind.

White-hot fire screamed through the crack in my shields like a blowtorch through tissue paper. The sheer power of West's magic blazed through my brain in a shockwave that felt like it would take off the back of my skull. The energy level was nearly incomprehensible. My senses shut down, and my arms and legs went rigid with strain. I had to raise my shields or risk permanent damage.

It took an excruciatingly long time and every ounce of strength I had to raise my tattered shields and block him out.

When awareness returned, I realized I was half slumped in my chair and sweating profusely. I heard a strange sound I slowly recognized as applause; apparently, the presentation was over. I had no idea how much time had passed while I was semiconscious; it might have been as much as ten or fifteen minutes. The audience was filing out of the auditorium.

My entire body hurt as if all my nerve endings had been seared, but the agony was receding like a tide going out. As the fog lifted and my vision cleared, I became aware of a different kind of pain. Sean was gripping my right wrist tightly enough to bruise, and probably had been for a while, judging by the ache.

When I looked at him, his eyes shone gold. "Allie," he said roughly. "Tell me you can hear me."

I stared at him uncomprehendingly. I heard the words, but they weren't connecting with anything. I wondered if I'd shorted something out in my brain.

A blank stare wasn't the response Sean was looking for. As West finished collecting his belongings and stood, heading for the exit, Sean gripped my chin and leaned closer. His eyes glowed. "Alice," he said, and a little shiver of something ran down my spine. "Wake up and talk to me."

It felt like someone took their hand and brushed away the cobwebs. Somehow, though I wasn't a shifter, Sean had been able to use his alpha influence to help me recover. I shuddered and exhaled a long, shaky breath. As my straining muscles suddenly relaxed, I fell forward against his chest, making a pained noise when my nose hit his sternum.

Sean tipped my chin up to look me in the eyes as I rubbed my nose. "You with me now?"

"I'm with you." My voice still sounded a little thin, but at least I could think clearly.

"Give yourself a minute," Sean said. "West went into the men's room."

How he'd seen that with his focus on me, I had no idea, but I was grateful for the extra few minutes to clear my head and regain muscle control.

By the time West exited the bathroom, Sean and I were making our way toward the auditorium doors. My legs were wobbly, but I was walking on my own.

We followed West back out to the parking lot. "You doing okay?" Sean asked as we got in the car.

"I feel much better." I put my bag on the floor and buckled in.

West left the lot, heading east, and Sean followed at a distance. As he drove, I thought about what I'd felt. John West was, by far, the most powerful fire mage I had ever encountered, and that was saying something. West made my grandfather's fire magic feel like a birthday candle by comparison. Perhaps more chilling, West's blood magic would likely be as strong or stronger than his fire magic. I thought of what my grandfather could do with his fire magic, and then imagined someone stronger, and with high-level blood magic too. I felt nauseous.

I knew what I wanted to know about West's magic, but it wasn't going to help me sleep any easier.

West drove back to his house. After a brief debate, I opted not to stay and watch his house, having no real reason to right now, other than my curiosity about his harnad. We headed home.

When we arrived, Sean pulled into my driveway and parked. Before he could say anything, I said, "I know you said you wanted to go out to dinner, but how would you feel about just ordering a pizza and maybe watching a movie here? I know my TV isn't as big as yours, but we could stream something."

"I was hoping to take you out to this great steakhouse I like, and then maybe for a walk down by the...." Sean trailed off, reading my expression. "What are you thinking when you get that look in your eyes?"

I wasn't sure what look he was referring to, but what I was thinking was that I'd never been on a real, formal date—not the kind he was describing. I hadn't been picked up and taken to dinner, or for a romantic walk. It would be difficult, or impossible, to explain why something so seemingly innocuous felt so terrifying. I tried to figure out what to say.

"Hey." Sean smiled and leaned over to kiss me. "It would be very much okay to order a pizza and watch a movie," he told me when we broke apart. "I can't think of anything I'd rather do."

Sean grabbed his go-bag out of the trunk while I lowered the house wards, unlocked the door, and went inside. I put my stuff down by the door and went around turning on lights while he changed into casual clothes in the downstairs bathroom. I grew puzzled when I sensed Malcolm wasn't in the house, but remembered his comment about going to Natalie's in case Sean and I needed privacy. I smiled to myself.

Once Sean changed into jeans and a vintage Allman Brothers T-shirt, we ordered our pizza, and then I showed him around the house. He was impressed with the renovations I'd designed. We talked home remodeling for a bit, until our tour took us to the door to the basement.

I paused a few feet from the threshold. I'd never let anyone but Malcolm into my basement, but for some reason, I wanted to show it to Sean. "The basement is my library and spellwork area. Don't ever let anyone touch the door or try to go into the basement without me. The wards could kill them. At the very least, they'd be incapacitated."

"Understood."

I drew a series of four runes on the doorframe. "What was that?" Sean asked.

"Think of it like a security code. Give me your hand."

After a moment's hesitation, Sean reached out. I took his hand in mine, placed my index finger along his, and touched the doorframe. Sean twitched when the wards gave him a little zap. "It's tasting you," I murmured, and I traced two more runes on the doorway with our fingers.

A frisson of magic ran through us, and Sean sucked in a breath. "Wow."

"The wards know you as a friend now." I released his hand and reached for the doorknob. "It will be uncomfortable to cross the threshold, but you won't get knocked out. I'd say brace yourself, but it won't be as bad as when you broke through Natalie's house wards."

"That hurt," Sean said.

I laughed. "Yeah, I bet. We've both been on the wrong end of some wards lately." I flipped on the basement lights and breathed deeply as I pushed through the invisible wall of magic to start down the stairs ahead of Sean. Behind me, Sean grunted, but he didn't falter or stagger. Either werewolf strength or werewolf pride, or a combination of both, I thought.

When he was through, I led him down the steps. At the bottom, he stopped and looked around the basement, taking it all in.

I spread my arms out. "Welcome to my lair, Mr. Maclin."

He stayed on the stair landing. "What's safe down here and what's not?"

"That's a smart question to ask. When dealing with mages and their private spaces, it's always a good idea to assume there are spells all around. In this case, you have been designated an official 'friendly' presence, so most of the spells and wards in here will be uncomfortable but not harmful to you."

"Most, huh?" Sean looked like a man standing in the middle of a minefield. "So what shouldn't I touch?"

I pointed to the storage cabinets. "The last two cabinets on the left have black wards. If you touch them, they will kill you."

Sean stared at me.

"The rest of the cabinets are safe to you, but like the threshold upstairs, it will be uncomfortable."

He looked like he was still processing the fact there were spells in the room that would kill someone. I could only imagine what his reaction would be if he knew what the basement's perimeter wards were capable of doing.

He cleared his throat. "Should I even ask what's in those cabinets on the left?"

"Dangerous magic stuff."

"'Dangerous magic stuff,'" Sean repeated. "Okay. The security consultant in me wonders if the contents are explosive."

I shrugged. "Not particularly, but all magic is volatile, even earth and air magic."

"Other than the fire in the bottle you made the other day, I haven't really gotten to see much of your magic." He started to lean against the wall, but the sizzle of the wards made him move away. "I feel like a kid asking this, but is there anything you can show me?"

I grinned. "Show and tell? I can do that. Come with me." I walked to the circles on the floor. Cautiously, he followed me. "Stand in the center circle." He stepped into it and I stood outside it.

"What are you going to do?"

I winked. "It's a surprise. Don't worry; you're perfectly safe in there." I closed both his circle and mine and they blazed with energy.

He jerked. "I can feel it."

"Good. Now watch." I raised my hands in front of me. They erupted in bright green fire.

He made a startled sound. "Are you all right?"

"Of course." I turned my hands and moved closer so he could see the flames caressing my skin but not burning me. "Cold fire. Earth magic." I drew the fire slowly up my arms and let it spread over my upper body. It took focus because I hadn't done this in a while, but I knew it looked incredible. I didn't get much opportunity to show off my fancy tricks. The bright green fire danced along my arms.

"That's beautiful," Sean breathed, watching the fire move. "How much control do you have over it?"

In answer, I pulled the fire back to my right hand, then flicked my wrist. The fire became a short rope about five feet long. The rope coiled through the air, the flames dancing. I twirled it over my head, cowgirl style, and it snapped out in front of me like a whip before coiling back into my hand.

Sean applauded. I laughed and pulled the fire back down to the tip of my right index finger. I blew on my finger and the fire went out, only to flare up on my left hand as if I'd blown it there.

It was a corny trick, but Sean grinned. I broke his circle with my hand. "Come here." He walked up close to me. "Hold out your index finger."

He held up his left—not his right, I noticed, which would have been his trigger finger. I murmured an invocation and traced a spell in the air. "Don't move." I touched my finger to his.

His eyes widened as the green flame spread to the tip of his index finger. "It's cold," he said in wonder.

I drew my hand back, and a small green flame continued to burn on his finger.

He raised his eyebrows. "Are you going to put this out?"

"Nope, but *you* can. Blow on it."

He looked at me.

"Blow on it," I repeated.

He blew, and the flame went out.

"Now, focus on your finger, envision the flame, snap your thumb and index finger together, and say, '*Frio*.'"

Sean awkwardly snapped his fingers. "*Frio*." The tip of his index finger burst into green flame. "Whoa." He stared at his hand.

I watched him admire the tiny flame. "It's a simple spell. I can take it off, or it will fade by itself in about a week."

He blew on his finger and the flame went out, then he brought it back. "Holy shit, this is awesome." He blew out the flame.

I laughed. "I guess I'll just leave it, then. But remember: always use your powers for good. Now for the big finale." I closed his circle, isolating him inside, and my hands flamed up again.

This time, as I held on to my earth magic for the fire, I brought up my air magic. An impossible breeze came up, blowing my hair back from my face. I continued to draw on the air magic until it whipped around the inner circle where I stood, contained on the inside by Sean's circle and on the outside by mine.

He watched the wind blowing my hair as the green flames on my hands danced. "Incredible."

"You ain't seen nothin' yet. Stay in your circle." *Showtime.*

I took a deep breath, exhaled, and my entire body went up in green flame.

"Allie!" he shouted, fear in his voice.

"I'm all right." I held my arms out to feel the wind on my body. Then, as the wind whipped around me furiously, I opened the valve and poured green fire from every square inch of my body.

In an instant, the circle where I stood became an inferno of cold fire. Blown by the wind, the firestorm raged in my circle while Sean stood safe in the eye of a hurricane. His mouth hung open.

I tilted my head back and closed my eyes and let the fire and air pour out of me. Like I'd told Natalie, using magic felt wonderful, like that first stretch when you wake up in the morning. There was a great pleasure to using magic, if you stayed the hell away from the cabals and were able to use it to help instead of harm.

Letting the magic flow out of me felt so good, I could have stood like that for a long time, but I remembered Sean was watching and waiting. I opened my eyes.

He was up next to the barrier of the inner circle, as close as he could get to me and my firestorm. His expression was a combination of awe, admiration, and something else I couldn't quite interpret, but that might have been hunger, and not for food.

"Do you trust me?" I asked him.

He didn't hesitate. "Yes."

I murmured an invocation, reached out, and grabbed his hand. The inner circle fell, and the inferno raged around us as I held his hand in mine, his body protected by a spell. He stood frozen as his brain struggled to process that he was standing, unhurt, in the middle of a firestorm that felt cold instead of hot.

I drew him to me and kissed him. The hunger I'd seen in his eyes was in his kiss. It took my breath away.

While my lips were pressed to his, I pulled both my air and earth magic back into myself. The wind began to fade, and the fire dwindled. By the time the kiss ended, the flames were gone, and the air was still.

Sean touched his forehead to mine. He was breathing heavily, but I was calmer than I'd been in days. I felt purified.

"Good enough for show and tell?" I teased.

"Holy shit, yes." He wrapped me in his arms.

I rested my head against his chest. "Next time, I'll do something *really* cool."

His laugh filled the basement.

The pizza arrived not long after we went back upstairs. I let Sean flip through my vinyl collection while I got napkins and beers and set up our dinner on the coffee table in the living room.

As I sat on the couch to take off my boots, he fired up the turntable and I heard a familiar sound like a heartbeat. I grinned. "Excellent choice."

"Just when I thought the evening couldn't get any better, I find out you've got *Dark Side of the Moon* on vinyl," Sean said, dropping onto the sofa and grabbing a piece of pizza. "If you've got *The Wizard of Oz*, we're in business."

"I thought that was an urban legend."

"It's not. They really do sync."

We ate pizza and drank our beers and listened to Pink Floyd. I ate two slices and lay down on the couch with my head in Sean's lap while he "wolfed" down the rest of the pizza. When the first side of the record ran out, we were both too comfortable and full of pizza to get up and flip it over. Sean ran his fingers through my hair, gently working out the tangles from the windstorm downstairs. I closed my eyes and relaxed.

After a while, he asked, "Where do things stand with your case?"

"I've eliminated all the known suspects *again*." I told him about Malcolm's masking spell detector and our visits to Natalie's family earlier in the day. "What West's involvement is, I'm not sure, but finding out more about him and this harnad he was supposedly in with Betty is probably the next step."

I didn't have to see his face to know the idea wasn't making him happy, but he didn't object. Instead, he said, "Thanks for including me in today's adventures."

"I'm not sure anything we did today could be categorized as 'adventures.'" I shifted on the couch and looked up at him. "But there's still time to make things interesting."

His eyes glinted. "What did you have in mind?"

"For starters, how about this?" I rolled to my feet, then straddled his lap. His hands gripped my hips as I kissed him, then bit his lower lip. He growled.

I moved my lips across his jaw to his ear, tracing its contours with the tip of my tongue before plunging it inside. He jerked like I'd shocked him and growled again. I bit his earlobe and he groaned. "Allie."

I went back to kissing him, feeling the hard length of him between us as I moved against him. Sean ran his hands up under my shirt and over my ribs to cup my breasts. I gasped when his thumbs stroked my nipples through my bra.

I pulled my shirt off over my head and took his face in my hands.

His eyes glowed like golden lanterns. "Are you sure?"

"Absolutely," I told him.

He made a snarly noise, and suddenly my bra tore in half and his mouth was on me. "Hey," I said weakly.

"I'll buy you another one," he growled, then bit down. I cried out and dug my nails into his shoulders, my head falling back.

I heard him whisper something as he snapped his fingers, and when I looked back, he was tracing a line down my breastbone with the tiny, cold flame on his finger. I whimpered as the cold, tingly sensation shot through me like an arrow.

Sean held up his spelled finger. "This has possibilities," he mused.

I blew out the flame and reached for his belt. "You're overdressed."

Sean stood, his hands under my butt. "Put your legs around my waist," he instructed me. "We're going upstairs."

I locked my ankles behind his back and kissed him as he carried me upstairs. When we got to my room, he tossed me carefully onto the bed. I raised myself up on my elbows to watch as he took off his T-shirt and shoes. He reached for his belt.

"Come here," I ordered.

To my surprise, he obeyed. I undid his belt, then unfastened and unzipped his pants. His breathing sped up as I pushed his jeans and boxers down to free him.

Sean sucked in a breath when I wrapped my hand around him and stroked gently. I leaned forward and took him into my mouth. He groaned as I moved in a steady rhythm that made him fight for control.

Soon, Sean was breathing heavy, and his fingers dug into my shoulders. "Stop, stop," he said roughly, and I released him from my mouth. "Clothes off."

I stood and took off my socks, then slid my jeans and underwear off as one. I reached into my nightstand drawer for a condom, tossed it on the bed, and looked at him with an arched eyebrow. "Why aren't you naked?"

In a second, Sean was out of his jeans and boxers. With a throaty growl, he leaped and took me down onto the bed, his mouth on mine. I hooked my leg around his hip and arched up against his body in a blatant demand that made him chuckle.

Instead of unwrapping the condom, he pushed my leg to the side and reached down between us. I writhed underneath him and bit his shoulder. He kissed me again, muffling my cries with his mouth. I started to shudder.

"That's it," he murmured against my lips. "Come for me, Allie."

I was vaguely aware of my own voice calling his name as everything fractured around me in a wave of intense pleasure. A moment later, I heard the condom packet tear. In a single movement, he grabbed my hip, sank his teeth into the flesh of my shoulder, and thrust into me.

I threw my head back and screamed. He buried his face in my neck as he moved. I dug my nails into his back as he adjusted his angle and speed, driving me back toward the edge.

He rose above me, his eyes bright gold, predatory and hungry, beautiful and dangerous. "Allie," he growled. "Release your magic."

I intended to, but first, I wanted more than merely physical intimacy. I closed my eyes and dropped my shields, focusing on Sean.

Suddenly, my mind filled with images, smells, and sounds. I saw flashes of moonlight, of teeth and fur, trees and a grassy field, and smelled forest and earth. I heard a howl so beautiful that it brought tears to my eyes.

Then I saw myself, my head thrown back and eyes closed, gasping for air, the sheen of sweat on my skin, and I knew I was seeing through Sean's eyes, and feeling what he felt. Our combined pleasure was so intense, I thought I would black out.

Everything came apart in a rush. Sean's movements caught the crest of my bliss and stoked it higher. My magic tore free in a burst that felt far stronger than when we'd been together before. Once again, I heard things crashing in my room. I opened my eyes and saw the green-and-white hurricane was infused with golden, primal shifter magic, Sean's power mixed with my own.

Our magic rolled through us in a wave. Above me, Sean groaned and began to shudder. I cried out as he made a sound that was part shout, part howl, and collapsed on top of me. My inner muscles twitched around him, and he jerked and snarled.

"Did you just *growl* at me?" I asked, reaching up to push sweaty hair back from his forehead.

"Maybe." He rolled on to his side and pulled me tightly against him. "Are you all right?"

I felt so much better than *all right*. "Yes," I replied breathlessly.

My shoulder stung. I reached up to touch it, and my fingers came away smeared with red.

Sean froze. "I hurt you."

I kissed him, tugging gently on his lip with my teeth. "It's all right. I like a little pain with my pleasure."

He looked stunned. "I've never done that before. I'm sorry."

"I bit you first," I pointed out, kissing the mark my teeth had left on his shoulder. "You were just returning the favor."

"I shouldn't have—"

"Sean, shut up."

He shut up.

A few minutes later, I said, "Was this how you were hoping the evening would go?"

He nuzzled my hair. "I'd be lying if I said no, but for the record, I really did want to take you to dinner, and for a walk along the riverfront, and maybe for some ice cream, first."

This man thought I was worth taking to dinner and out for ice cream. I felt a stab of disbelief mixed with wonder. "Maybe next time."

He jerked, pulling back from me.

"What?"

He looked confused. "I thought...." He shook his head as if to clear it and pulled me close again.

"So there will be a next time?" he asked finally.

"I'd like there to be a next time."

"So would I." He ran his fingers over my hip, tracing the line of tattooed stars that ran from my upper left thigh to my rib cage. "Speaking of which...."

My eyes widened.

Some wonderful time later, Sean held me close as I lay on top of him and we gasped for air.

"I need you so much, I can't even think," he said, his lips against my ear. "I can't get enough of you, and it's making me crazy."

"We can be crazy together," I told him. "It's more fun that way."

20

At a little after midnight, we lay on the bed in a tangle of arms and legs. Most of the bedding was on the floor, along with pretty much everything else in my room.

As it turned out, the rumors of werewolf stamina were *not* exaggerated. I was well past the point of exhaustion, but judging by the now-familiar glint in Sean's eyes, he was, almost unbelievably, thinking about another round, and I was thinking seriously about whether I would survive it.

Before either of us could do anything about that, however, my phone beeped. Sean had brought our phones upstairs in case he got a call from work, then abandoned them on top of the dresser. They were now somewhere on the floor.

When I groaned and started to move, he wrapped his arm around me and pulled me close, removing all doubt as to whether he was recovering. "Leave it," he growled into my ear. "You're mine until the morning."

"It might be an emergency," I pointed out. "Nobody texts this late at night with good news."

He grumbled but let me go. I slid out of bed, wincing slightly, then started pawing through the debris on the floor. I finally found my phone under some clothes.

To my surprise, there was a text message from Adri. *Mr. V would like to meet tonight to discuss a time-sensitive project that requires your expertise. Can you come to Hawthorne's?*

I frowned and texted back. *Busy tonight. Can it wait till tomorrow?*

Adri: Mr. V believes it cannot.

I made a face. *What time?*

The response was immediate. *As soon as possible. Mr. V awaits your arrival.*

Well, that sounded serious—and potentially very lucrative. I mentally applied a multiplier to my usual Court rate and fired back a reply. *ETA 1 hour.*

Sean sat up. "What's going on?"

"Text from Adri. Charles has an urgent project and wants to meet." I tossed my phone on the bed and headed for the bathroom.

Sean was off the bed and in front of me in a blink. "Is this a trap?"

I shook my head. "I doubt it. He mentioned the other night that there was a project coming up." I was reasonably certain Charles had no plan to demand a meal or take one by force; my alliance with Sean's pack protected me, and beyond that, my abilities made me a valuable asset both to him personally and the Vampire Court. I doubted he would risk losing that resource by biting me.

"I don't like it. Not after what happened Saturday night."

I shrugged and continued into the bathroom, turning on the shower. "Come with me." I stepped into the tub and slid the curtain closed. "You can stay downstairs in the bar while I meet with Charles."

The curtain moved, and Sean stepped into the shower with me. I raised my eyebrows.

He gave me a toothy smile that brought back a rush of pleasant memories. "I can wash your back."

"Don't make me turn this shower on cold," I warned him.

He laughed and reached for my bottle of shower gel. "I'll be on my best behavior," he promised. "The sooner we get this meeting over with, the sooner we can come back to bed." His eyes gleamed, and I very much doubted he was thinking about sleeping. Truth be told, neither was I. I hoped this new project wouldn't take long to discuss. By the time we got back, I figured I'd have my second wind, and then we'd see exactly what it took to wear out an alpha werewolf.

Almost exactly an hour later, we parked down the street from Hawthorne's and strolled up the sidewalk to the door, where Bryan was checking IDs.

"Evening, Miss Alice," he boomed. "Here to see Mr. Vaughan?"

"Yes. Is he ready for me?"

"Adri will come get you in a few minutes." Bryan glanced at my companion. "Mr. Maclin should plan to wait for you in the bar. Vampire/shifter politics are touchy these days. The appearance of favoritism might cause problems." He stepped aside to let us pass.

Despite it being two a.m. on a Monday night, the bar was busy. I sent Sean to find us a table while I went to say hello to Pete.

Pete grinned when he saw me walking up, but the smile fell off when he spotted Sean behind me. *What the hell is up with that?* I wondered.

"Hey, Alice," he said. "How are you doing tonight?"

"Doing great, Pete. Just wanted to say hi. We're going to try to find a table."

"What are you drinking? I'll send it over."

I ordered two bottles of a craft beer I liked, and Pete said he had to get them out of the cooler in the back. I went to find Sean and finally spotted him at a standing table by the window.

As we stood together at the table, Sean rested his hand on my hip. I stepped away slightly to put a little distance between us, and Sean's hand fell away. Despite our physical intimacy and how content I was to be in his company, I wasn't anyone's territory. Sean looked frustrated, but he leaned down to kiss my temple and I let him.

When AC/DC came on the jukebox, Sean and I started talking about favorite rock albums. I was mounting a passionate defense of the Eagles' *Hell Freezes Over* when a server appeared with our beers.

"I guess I don't know much about recent developments in local vamp/shifter politics," I said, drinking my beer. "Is there something going on in particular, or is just the usual intrigues?"

"Nothing specific going on that I'm aware of. There are three large werewolf packs in the area—mine and two others—and a half dozen smaller packs, plus the cats, though they're more of a loose-knit clan. Everyone's looking to make alliances, and the vamps have more power and influence than any other group. Since Vaughan is on the Vampire Court, it would probably be prudent for him not to be seen meeting privately with any of the pack alphas. The other alphas might take offense, and who knows what the cats might do. They're weird."

I laughed at that. "Such a *wolf* thing to say, disparaging the cats," I teased.

"It's not disparaging if it's true," Sean griped. "They *are* weird."

We drank our beers and listened to the music. I caught Sean looking strangely at me a couple of times, but didn't have a chance to ask him about it before I saw Adri heading toward me, weaving through the crowd with a dancer's grace. She caught my eye.

"I'm heading up." I gave Sean a quick kiss. "I'll be back."

"I'll be here."

Adri seemed preoccupied and said little on our way upstairs. Despite my earlier certainty that Charles was not a threat, Adri's silence was making me uneasy. On the other hand, maybe her mood had nothing to do with me.

When we arrived at Charles's office, she knocked twice, then opened the door without waiting for a response.

Charles rose when we entered. For a moment, I thought I saw something—anger, maybe—in his eyes, but it was gone before I could figure it out. "Thank you for coming on such short notice," he said. "Can I offer you a drink?"

"I'm good for now." I settled into the guest chair while Adri stood off the side—not by the door as usual, which I thought was odd. "You said you had a project you needed to discuss right away."

Charles sat down behind his desk and looked at me silently. I raised my eyebrows.

Finally, he spoke. "I must confess that I have asked you to meet under false pretenses. There is no such project."

I stared at him, my stomach knotting. "Then why am I here?"

"I apologize for the subterfuge, but it was necessary, for reasons that will become apparent." He folded his hands on top of his desk. "In the past few hours, I have been made aware of information that concerns you. Despite our...disagreement...on Saturday evening, because we have known one another for some time, I felt it was imperative to pass it on to you immediately, hence the urgent summons."

My uneasiness gave way to full-blown apprehension. "Go on."

"I understand you are in the company of Sean Maclin of the Tomb Mountain Pack."

"Yes," I said.

"I believe you met him for the first time in the bar last week."

"That's true." Where was he going with this?

"Forgive me for noticing, but it would appear you have become lovers."

Incensed, I stood, forgetting in my shock that I needed to avoid making any abrupt movements. Adri was suddenly beside me. "How the *hell*—"

"I can smell him on you," Charles said matter-of-factly.

Goddamned vampire senses. I blushed and hated myself for it. "What of it?"

Charles rose from his desk and came around to stand in front of me. "Maclin leads a strong pack and has a good reputation, but he is unmated, which is unusual for an alpha at his age. Werewolf packs require an alpha pair to remain stable. His lack of a mate is causing dissension and insecurity in the pack, and the other packs sense the turmoil and are circling. Recently, Maclin's beta advised him that he must find a mate, or he risks losing his pack, either to infighting or opportunistic attacks from rivals."

I felt sick to my stomach.

"The beta suggested some possible mates for him, including a female from a smaller pack, which would bring about an alliance many believe would be advantageous. According to one of the pack members, who visited our bar this night and spoke to Pete, Maclin declined the offer to mate with this female, stating that he wishes instead to find a mage, preferably a strong one, and infect her with the werewolf virus. He believes such a woman would make an ideal alpha female for the pack, protecting it from possible attacks from other packs, and discouraging challengers from within."

Charles said something else, but I didn't hear him. I thought of Sean's face, his eyes, his smile. How he held me when I was hurting. The way he looked at me while we had sex. The heat of his touch. How he'd broken through house wards to get to me, and rearranged his entire work schedule to spend two days by my side.

"I need you so much, I can't even think," he'd said.

The bastard. He'd sought me out in the bar and slept with me because he needed a mate to keep control of his pack. He planned to bite me, turn me into a werewolf, and make me his alpha female.

I felt a surge of fury so raw, so ferocious, that for a moment I went blind with rage. Blood magic sizzled on my skin, threatening to break loose and destroy Charles's office and everything in it. I closed my eyes so the vampire couldn't see them glow. With herculean effort, I pulled the magic back and regained control.

Charles moved toward me. "Alice?"

I took two deep breaths and waited until I knew my eyes were back to normal before opening them. "Thank you for telling me." My voice was so cold, it made Charles seem warm and fuzzy by comparison. Adri watched me warily. "I need to go downstairs and tell Sean that our...date...is over. We came together in his car. Is there someone who can give me a ride home?"

"Ms. Smith will take you." Charles glanced at Adri. Whatever instructions he gave her through their telepathic bond, her eyes hardened perceptibly.

He regarded me. "We will speak again."

I nodded, and Adri opened the door to the office. When we were down the hall, she said quietly, "There is a direct exit to the parking garage."

"I'm not going down the back stairs." I pushed open the door to the main staircase and it banged against the wall.

We returned to the bar. The music and cacophony of voices were almost painful after the silence of the upper floor. Weaving my way through the crowd, I spotted Sean before he saw me. He was still at the table, leaning against it, drinking a beer. Two empty bottles sat in front of him. As I watched, a cute blonde came up to him. He shook his head and said something, and she moved on.

Sean looked up. Our eyes met through the crowd, and for a heartbeat, the bar noise faded away. He set his beer down immediately and moved to intercept me, his eyes darkening. I was aware of Adri behind me, close enough to intervene if needed, but far enough away to give us the illusion of privacy.

Sean's gaze flicked to Adri and then back to me. "What's wrong?"

"I have to go." My voice could have cut glass. "Feel free to stay. Adri's going to give me a ride home."

Something shadowy and dangerous flashed in his eyes. "Just like that?"

Anger made my skin feel like it was on too tight. I wanted to confront him, but this was not the place. Not in public, not with so many witnesses—or potential collateral damage—around us. "I have business I need to take care of."

Sean's eyes narrowed. He looked at Adri again, this time with open suspicion. "What's going on?"

"I don't have time to do this with you right now. We'll talk later." I started to walk away.

He grabbed my arm. "Allie, wait." Magic crackled on my skin, and he flinched.

Adri took a step forward.

I met Sean's gaze. "Take your hand off me."

Sean let go. I felt a strange spike of something like hurt and anger that made me take an involuntary step back. I shook my head to clear it, then looked at Adri. "Let's go," I said.

I turned on my heel and walked out.

Adri took me home in a black Audi SUV. She seemed content to drive quietly, and I had no idea what to say. My fury had gone from red-hot to icy-cold, the glacial calm allowing me to think clearly. I knew now why Pete reacted the way he did to Sean being with me tonight.

Unbidden, images of the past few days, of Sean, tumbled through my brain. I felt like the world had been yanked out from under my feet and I was dangling over a long fall into nothing.

He wanted to turn me into a werewolf. My shoulder hurt where he'd bitten me.

Adri stopped for a red light. "Are you all right?"

"Yes." I turned away to look out the window.

"Do you want to talk about it?"

"No."

"Okay." A pause, then: "I'm sorry, Alice."

I said nothing. The light turned green. Adri drove on.

A few minutes later, she pulled into my driveway and parked. "Do you need anything?"

"I'm fine. Thank you for the ride home."

"Do you want me to come in?"

I shook my head. "I'm tired. I'm going to bed."

She squeezed my hand. "Call me if you need me. You've got my number."

"Have a good night."

"You too."

I got out of the SUV and headed for the front steps. Adri waited until I was inside before she started backing down the drive. I waved at her through the front window and watched as she drove away. I let the curtain fall back in place and stood in the foyer of my house.

I pulled my shirt off over my head to see the bite mark on my shoulder. What I'd regarded earlier as a souvenir of a passionate roll in the hay now looked more like a sinister brand. The light from the kitchen revealed a pizza box and two empty beer bottles on my coffee table, right where we'd left them. I knew if I went upstairs, my bed would smell like us. I might have been imagining it, but I thought I caught a hint of Sean's scent—aftershave and forest—in the air. He'd gotten past my defenses—not by much, but enough to become a presence in my home, all on a foundation of lies.

My fury erupted out of me like a volcano, and this time, I made no attempt to hold it back. My blood magic became a violent red, black, and purple storm with my body in the center. In seconds, the walls of the foyer were stripped bare of pictures, the small table by the door reduced to kindling, the curtain ripped from its rod and shredded. The overhead light fixture burst in a hailstorm of broken glass. The magic I'd accidentally unleashed in front of Malcolm when we'd first met was nothing compared to this. That had been a trickle from a faucet. This was Niagara Falls.

I roared inside while the magic tore through and around me. I wanted to burn down the world.

I realized I was angry less at Sean than at myself. *This is what happens when you trust someone even a little bit*, I raged in my head. *You can trust no one, not ever, you brainless, fucking idiot.* Furious at my own stupidity, I went to my knees and smashed my fists as hard as I could into the tile. My knuckles split. I did it again. Blood splattered across the floor, and I felt bones crunch.

I stayed on my knees, head hanging, eyes closed.

Through the fog, I heard a crash and realized the door to my coat closet had been ripped off its hinges. With enormous difficulty, I pulled the magic back into myself before I tore down my own house. My skin hummed like I was holding on to a high-voltage wire. I shuddered and bent over, resting my forehead on the tile, my head between my arms. For several long minutes, the only sound was the pounding of my heart and my ragged breathing.

I must have seemed like easy prey that night at Hawthorne's, alone and injured from my run-in with Betty's wards. I'd probably put up more of a fight than Sean had anticipated, but in the end, he'd almost suckered me into believing, if only for a moment, I could be worth something to someone for more than my magic—that I was deserving of kindness and caring for who I was, instead of what I could do.

You'd think I'd know better by now.

Out front, a car door slammed. I jerked upright with a sound that might have been a snarl. Moments later, heavy footsteps crossed the porch and a fist banged on the door, three loud booms that made it shake and the wards sizzle. "Alice!" Sean shouted. "Alice, are you hurt?"

At the sound of his voice, magic sparked on my fingertips as a cold wind blew over me.

I struggled to get my feet. My hands throbbed in time to my pulse, but the pain was distant, muted. I wrapped my shirt around my hands and staggered to the door in my bra and blood-spattered jeans. "Go away." I barely recognized my own voice. "Leave me alone and don't come back."

"I don't understand," Sean protested. "What the hell happened?"

"Someone told me some important information about your pack and how much you need a mate." I leaned my forehead against the door and the wards crackled on my skin. "Suddenly, these last few days, everything you said and did from the moment we met, it all made sense."

"It's not like that," Sean said. "I wasn't even thinking about that when I met you."

"Even if that's true, which I don't believe, I know you thought about it later, or you wouldn't have been so persistent. Don't lie to me, Sean."

"Allie—"

"Don't call me that!" I shouted, then lowered my voice. "You don't get to call me that ever again. You lied to me. You screwed me and you lied to me so you could turn me into a werewolf to be your mate."

A long silence. "Who told you that?" It was a growl.

"It doesn't matter. What matters is, it's not going to happen. Stay the hell away from me, or I will burn you."

Sean swore. "If you won't let me in, at least open the door so we can talk face-to-face. I'll stay on the porch and you can stay behind your wards, but I deserve the chance to explain."

"You don't 'deserve' a damn thing," I told him. "I deserved the truth from the beginning, and all I got was lies. But I've learned—or *re*learned—some important lessons because of this, so I guess I owe you some kind of thanks for reminding me why I can't trust anyone."

"Alice, please." I heard a soft thump, like Sean was bumping his head or his fist against the door. "I would never have turned you into a werewolf against your will. If you lower your shields, you'll be able to feel I'm telling the truth."

Shock left me speechless for a several heartbeats. "What does that mean?"

Silence.

"Sean, tell me what the hell that means!" I demanded.

"We have a metaphysical link," Sean said finally, sounding resigned. "I can sense your emotions, and you can sense mine."

Suddenly, I remembered the odd looks he'd been giving me all night, and the strange feeling of hurt and anger I'd felt at the bar. I went ice-cold all over.

Sean must have created a link between us when we'd slept together tonight. It was the first step in establishing a mating bond, and he'd done it without my knowledge, or my consent. The violation made me physically sick.

Up until that moment, a part of me still wondered if Charles had been wrong about Sean's motivation for pursuing me. Now I felt those last bits of doubt vanish.

"What were you going to do, take me as your mate against my will? Hold me down and bite me if I wouldn't be turned voluntarily? Rape me?"

"Of course not. What kind of man do you think I am?"

I snorted. I couldn't believe he had the balls to sound outraged after all his lying and scheming. "I really don't know what kind of man you are. I thought I did, but clearly, I was wrong."

"I can feel that you're in pain. Who hurt you?"

I ignored him. "I fell right into your trap, but I've wised up. Now go. Don't call me, don't come looking for me. We're done. Go back to your pack and find yourself a werewolf female and leave me the hell alone."

"Goddammit, Alice, at least give me a chance to explain before you do this."

"Go. Away." I was getting tired of saying it.

Silence. Then: "What the hell are *you* doing here?" he snarled.

I frowned in confusion. Then I heard another voice outside, as cold as Sean's was hot with anger. "I am here to ensure Alice's safety."

Charles Vaughan had come to my house. A member of the Vampire Court had left the security of his office and crossed the city to protect me. A dozen emotions clashed inside me, fear strongest among them.

"Alice doesn't need any protection from me," Sean growled.

"We have good reason to think otherwise."

"Are you behind this?" Sean demanded. "What lies have you been telling her?"

Footsteps on the front steps. "I have told her no lies." It sounded like Charles had joined Sean on the porch.

"Someone has," Sean retorted. "I don't know what your game is, Vaughan, but I'm going to find out."

"Are you threatening me, wolf?" Charles's voice was low and very, very dangerous, the sound of a predator. It triggered something primal in some deep part of my brain, making me tremble. I had never heard Charles use that tone before, and hoped I never would again.

What was scaring me more, however, was the prospect of Charles and Sean coming to blows on my front porch. It could be war between the Vampire Court and Sean's pack, and I would be caught in the middle of a massive shitstorm. My anonymity would be blown in an instant. I had to get them away from each other and my home.

"Get out of here, Sean," I said through the door. "Just go."

"I'm not going anywhere," Sean said. "The vampire goes, and then you and I are going to talk."

I heard an inhuman hissing sound that I realized had come from Charles. *Oh no.*

"Sean, leave *now*," I said desperately. "I will talk to you later, but you need to go."

"I'm not leaving." Sean's voice was an octave lower than normal.

"You will vacate the premises or I will remove you," Charles told him. "I will not permit you to bite Alice."

Sean snarled. "For the last time, I *never* had any plans to turn her into a fucking werewolf!"

"You lie," Charles said.

Sean's growl made the hair stand up on my arms. A pulse of magic sizzled against my house wards, and the growl turned into a howl of fury. To my horror, I heard fighting erupt on the other side of the door.

With bloody, numb hands, I dropped my house wards and fumbled to unlock the deadbolt. Before I could open the door, the front window exploded as a vampire and a huge gray-and-black wolf smashed through it.

21

I SCREAMED AND TURNED AWAY AS SHARDS OF GLASS PELTED ME, RIPPING INTO MY arms, back, and face.

The sounds of snarling and crashing caused me to shake my head and try to focus on what was happening. My vision was blurry and red; I realized glass had cut my face and blood was running into my eyes. I wiped it away as best I could and saw the fight had moved past me into my living room. The vampire and wolf moved so quickly, I had a hard time seeing what was happening, other than a gray-and-blue blur demolishing everything in sight.

"Stop!" I shouted and stumbled toward them. They were both a hundred times faster and stronger than I was, but I couldn't just let them destroy everything I owned.

Massive arms wrapped around me and held me back. "You're hurt." Bryan must have come in when I wasn't looking. "You have to stay back, or you could get killed."

"I have to stop them," I said stupidly, struggling in his grip.

"It won't last much longer. The wolf is weakened by the speed of his shift, and Mr. Vaughan is faster."

Bryan was obviously seeing something I wasn't, because it sure as hell didn't look as if—

Like someone pushed Pause in the middle of a fight scene, it was abruptly over. The sudden silence startled me.

In the middle of my wrecked living room, Charles stood over the wolf's limp body. He was fully vamped out, eyes pure black and fangs extended. His suit had been shredded by teeth and claws. Blood seeped from about a dozen lacerations, but they were already healing. I could see that the wolf—Sean—was still breathing but unconscious. Broken furniture, electronics, pictures, and glass were everywhere.

Adri came in, talking urgently into her headset in a low voice. I caught the words "cleanup," "tranquilizer," "cage," and "van" through the buzzing in my ears.

Charles's gaze shifted from the wolf to me. "Alice, you are injured."

I could see bloody cuts all over my arms, chest, and legs, and it felt like some of the wounds still had glass imbedded in them. I was standing in front of Charles, Adri, and Bryan in my bra, but was too much in shock to care.

"I'll be all right," I told him. Bryan's massive hands were under my elbows, holding me up with surprising gentleness.

Charles took a few steps toward me. I realized I was covered in fresh blood, and my heart was pounding. I was basically ringing the dinner bell, and he suddenly looked hungry.

With effort, I fought back my sudden fear. "Charles, don't come any closer," I said firmly. "I'm not on the menu tonight."

Adri and Bryan tensed. The hands on my arms tightened. I wasn't sure if Bryan would help Charles or me if the vampire lost control and attacked, and I wasn't going to wait to find out.

Bright green cold fire burst from my hands and ran up my arms. In a blink, Bryan released me and jumped away.

"Everyone stay back," I warned them. I moved until I had the wall behind me and could see Charles and his enforcers. Broken glass crunched under my boots.

Charles gazed at my cold fire, his expression somewhere between awe and appraisal. As I watched, his eyes began to return to normal, and his fangs disappeared. It was a remarkable—and chilling—display of control.

"I apologize," he said finally. "I forgot myself. You have my word I will not harm you."

We stared at each other. I read sincerity in his eyes. Slowly, the cold fire drew back to my hands and vanished.

Charles's eyes narrowed. "Alice, your shoulder."

I picked up my shirt and used it to cover the bite mark as my face grew hot. "It's nothing."

His gaze moved to my bloody and swollen hands, and his frown became thunderous. "Who is responsible for these injuries?"

I had no intention of discussing this with Charles, especially not in front of Adri and Bryan. "It's none of your business."

He looked at the blood splattered on the tile and the extensive damage to the foyer, and then back at my hands. I saw disbelief in his eyes as realization dawned. "You have done this to yourself."

Adri inhaled sharply.

My eyes stung with angry tears. Humiliated, I went on the attack. "Why the hell are you here, Charles?"

His eyes flashed silver. "Mr. Smith and I followed the werewolf when he left Hawthorne's. We believed he posed a danger to you, and it would appear we were correct."

"He says he never intended to turn me into a werewolf," I said quietly, almost to myself.

"Of course he would deny it," Charles said. "To bite someone against their will is a capital offense in both human and shifter courts."

When I stayed silent, Adri spoke up. "I have a team on its way to take the wolf into custody, sir," she told Charles.

"The window must be replaced immediately."

"I'll take care of it." Adri started scrolling through her phone.

I glared at Charles. "I don't need you to do anything for me."

"I will arrange for someone to come immediately to fix the window. Your home must be secure."

"Make sure I get the bill," I told him. "I don't want you to buy me anything."

He regarded me. "Alice, as I am at least partially responsible for the damage, I ask that you allow me to pay for the window."

"Fine," I conceded.

Adri made a call and began speaking quietly to someone about getting a window company out to my house immediately.

I shivered hard and fought back a wave of dizziness. When I glanced down, I saw blood forming a small puddle around my feet.

When I looked up, Charles was in front of me. I hadn't even seen or heard him move. Gently, he raised my hands. The movement made fresh pain surge, and I grimaced at the sight of my bloody, swollen knuckles. I couldn't make a fist with my left hand. In my blind rage, I might have actually broken something.

"I think you have," Charles said. I realized I'd spoken aloud. "Will you let me heal your injuries?"

"How?" My eyes narrowed.

"A few ounces of my blood will suffice."

"What will you want in return?" I remembered his request to drink from me and feared he would try to revisit that demand.

"Nothing. This gift of healing is freely given."

I sighed and hung my head for a moment. "All right."

"Will you permit Ms. Smith to assist you in removing the glass? You will need help to reach the wounds on your back."

I couldn't argue with that. "Okay." I started toward the stairs, then paused. "What will you do with Sean?"

Charles looked at the unconscious wolf. "He will be sedated and taken to a holding cell at Hawthorne's," he told me. "He shifted and attacked me, causing these injuries to you, and that cannot go unpunished. I will contact his pack and apprise them of the situation. For now, you must tend to your wounds. Ms. Smith, please go with her."

I shuffled across the floor to the foot of the stairs. I paused with one foot on the bottom step, looking at the wolf in the middle of my wrecked living room. I noticed then that my record player had somehow survived the destruction. *Dark Side of the Moon* was still on the turntable where we'd left it. I closed my eyes.

"Alice, do you need help up the stairs?" Adri asked me.

I looked up toward the second floor. I felt weakened and dizzy, but I shook my head. "I can make it," I said and began to climb.

When I got to the door to my room, I looked back at the trail of blood I'd left behind me. I couldn't leave my blood lying around, not with Charles and his people here. With difficulty, I crouched to put my fingertips in the blood on the floor. "Fire in the hole!" I hollered. I assumed Adri was warning Charles telepathically about what I was about to do.

"*Burn.*" With a *whoosh*, an air magic burner spell flashed through my upstairs hallway, down the stairs, and into the foyer of my house, reducing all my blood to a fine layer of white ash.

From downstairs, I heard Bryan's familiar rumble: "What the hell was that?"

I smiled grimly and pushed myself upright using the wall as leverage. "Okay," I told Adri. "Let's do this."

It took well over an hour to pull all the pieces of glass out of my face, scalp, back, arms, and legs. I had to comb glass out of my hair. My bathroom looked like a scene from a slasher movie by the time we finished. Adri stripped off my clothes and put me in the shower to rinse off the blood. I used a burner spell to clean up the blood in the bathroom and my bedroom, and Adri swept up the broken glass and ash while I sat naked in the tub.

When the floor was clean, I asked Adri to change my bedding. She did so without comment and took the other bedding downstairs to the laundry room. When she came back, she wrapped me in my bathrobe and got me to my bed, where I curled up on top of the quilt. I was bleeding from a dozen deep cuts that throbbed painfully, and my hands hurt so badly it was hard to think clearly. I was glad Sean and I had taken the time to straighten my room before we left; the thought of Adri—and Charles—seeing it in such disarray would have been more humiliation than I could have dealt with tonight.

Charles appeared in the doorway of my bedroom, presumably responding to Adri's telepathic summons. For a moment, I saw a flash of something that might have been tenderness when he saw me lying on the bed. It faded and his face became impassive once more.

Adri stepped outside the bedroom and closed the door as Charles came to sit on the edge of my bed. Someone must have brought him a change of clothes; his tattered and bloody suit was gone, and he was elegant once again.

"You are very pale," Charles told me, removing his suit jacket.

"Look who's talking," I shot back.

Charles chuckled. As he unfastened his cufflink and rolled up his sleeve, I suddenly felt terribly awkward.

He touched my face, his cool fingertips brushing my cheek. I closed my eyes.

When I opened them again, Charles's fangs were visible. He used them to pierce his wrist and blood welled up. He raised his wrist toward my mouth. "Drink from me."

Before I lost my nerve, I reached for his arm, brought it to my lips, and covered the wound with my mouth.

The first taste was of blood, coppery and cool, but somehow not unpleasant. I sucked gently on the wound, and sensation exploded in my mouth, spreading rapidly through my body. I closed my eyes as it rolled through me in a warm wave of intense pleasure. I swallowed again, and this time it felt so good that I shuddered. Strange sensations flared in a dozen places on my body. Charles gently brushed my hair back from my face, his arm still at my mouth. I swallowed again.

A few ounces, I thought hazily. Surely that had been enough. I ran my tongue over his skin to lick up the last of his blood. I heard a moan. It might have been him or it might have been me.

Charles's arm moved away from my mouth. From beyond the bliss, I felt my hands spasm and I cried out. Cool hands were resting on top of mine, holding me still with my arms against my chest while things moved under my skin in my hands and wrists. I suddenly felt as if ants were running over my skin as my cuts began to heal. Charles held me as I whimpered and squirmed.

When my head finally cleared, I opened my eyes. Charles was leaning over me, his hands still covering mine. I looked dazedly up at him. "Did it work?" My tongue felt thick.

"Yes." Charles held up my hands so I could see them. I stared at them in wonder. The skin was unbroken, the swelling gone. I flexed them experimentally, marveling at how the fingers opened and closed without pain. Vampire blood had painful healing spells beat by a mile.

Charles settled back, rolling his shirtsleeve back down and neatly fastening the cuff. His arm was already healed, the skin unblemished.

I sat up and kept looking at my knuckles. "Amazing," I said, more to myself than to him. I pulled the collar of my robe aside to see that no sign of Sean's bite or any of the cuts remained. "What's going on downstairs?"

"The wolf has been taken to Hawthorne's," Charles said. "The window is being replaced and the glass cleaned up. My crew is cleaning your floor. Within a few minutes, the work will be complete."

I gave him a small smile. "Thank you."

Charles watched me swing my legs over the side of the bed. I felt cool air on my skin and realized the bathrobe had come untied at some point, and I was naked beneath it.

Charles reached out toward me, his eyes on mine. Given the way he'd been looking at me minutes earlier, I expected him to touch me, and, strangely, I wasn't sure how I would respond. I was surprised when he gently pulled the robe closed and held it while I tied the belt. Then he stood and drew me to my feet.

"Are you well?" Charles still held on to my hands.

"I feel good." I pulled free of his grip. "Thank you for everything."

His expression became distant for a moment, then he looked at me. "My people have finished their work downstairs. You may raise your house wards."

I laid my palm against the wall. In moments, the wards crackled with their familiar intensity.

When I opened my eyes, Charles stood next to me. "Do you wish me to leave someone here to watch the house?"

I shook my head. "No. You've got Sean in custody. My wards are up, and I'm fine."

"Very well." He hesitated, then bent down to kiss my cheek. "Sleep well, Alice."

"You too, Charles."

He went to the door of my room and opened it. Adri waited on the other side. She looked at Charles, and then at me with a thoughtful expression.

"Good night, Adri," I said. "Thank you for your help."

"Anytime, Alice."

She and Charles headed down the stairs. Moments later, I felt a tingle from the wards when they left.

I stripped off my bathrobe and changed into pajamas. Then I brushed my teeth and fell into bed, pulling the covers up to my chin. In minutes, I was sound asleep.

22

I'D BEEN SCREAMING FOR HOURS.

My voice was nothing more than a hoarse rasp. My throat must have been raw, but I couldn't feel anything anymore. Maybe I'd shorted out whatever part of my brain processed pain. It took long enough.

I'd been kept hanging on a metal rack for most of the day so the blood mage had full access to my naked body, though she'd focused most of her attention on my back this time. During rare moments of coherent thought, I wondered if my grandfather had ordered her not to damage any part of me that might be visible. Moses had to maintain the fiction that his granddaughter obeyed his every command, that she never hesitated to unleash her terrible magic according to his wishes. There could be no hint that she resisted him. He'd had people killed for even mentioning the possibility.

They said my heart stopped twice. I'd wanted to die, but like everything else I'd ever wanted, I didn't get it. They brought me back each time. The floor was littered with expended spell crystals and empty blood bags from transfusions. I'd probably bled out three times over.

I'd experienced it often enough to know I was in shock. I felt ice-cold and I was shaking so badly it looked like I was having a seizure. I'd been taken down from the rack and dumped facedown on a cot that was bolted to the floor. My wrists and ankles were manacled to the frame with spell cuffs. The metal edges cut my skin and rattled against the cot as I shook. Someone had thrown a sheet over my bare ass and legs. It had once been white but now was mostly red. My thirst was painful, but no one had offered me water.

Though shock kept me from feeling much of anything, I strongly suspected there was no skin left on my back. Odd sensations made me think things were exposed that shouldn't have been. I wondered how many healing spells it would take to fix me this time.

I'd been alone in the soundproofed torture room for a very long time. I faded in and out, though I never really lost consciousness, thanks to the spells. Perhaps they were waiting for me to bleed out, or for shock to stop my heart. I'd have wished for it if I didn't know they'd just bring me back again. Dying hurt, but coming back always hurt worse.

The heavy door swung open. My grandfather appeared, accompanied by the blood mage and one of his favorite lieutenants, a snake of a man named Kade. I felt a weak surge of something through the numbness: hate. Kade was a sadist. He supervised most of my torture sessions, and he usually became aroused watching me bleed. At least the other lieutenants acted like it was just a job and maintained a kind of clinical distance. Kade took a lot of pleasure in his work.

Moses strode across the room, walking through the blood without even looking at it. He didn't flinch in the slightest at the sight of my body or the amount of blood on the floor and walls and ceiling. But why would he? He'd have inflicted the damage himself if he'd had anything more than mid-level blood magic. Handing my punishment over to a high-level blood mage had been merely a practical decision.

"Exceptional work, as always," my grandfather said to the blood mage as they came to stand over me. "I was able to observe some of the session between meetings."

"Thank you, Davo," the blood mage said. Her gaze swept over my body like an artist surveying her work. She was clearly pleased with her efforts.

"Your precision has improved." Moses looked me over. "There is almost no skin remaining, and yet she is conscious. Remarkable."

The mage made a murmuring sound. I stared fixedly into space, avoiding eye contact with my grandfather and trying not to notice the obvious bulge in the front of Kade's pants.

"There is, however, significant muscle damage," Moses added in that same casual tone.

The blood mage appeared unconcerned. "Healing spells will repair the damage."

She failed to see the shark fin in the water, but Kade and I both spotted the signs. He tensed. I did not. The blood mage was dead already; she just didn't know it.

"Muscle damage requires extensive and lengthy use of healing spells," my grandfather said. "Our timeline for this project is quite inflexible. She won't be recovered before the priority deadline has passed."

The blood mage was becoming aware that she was in trouble and took a step back. "Davo, it was unclear—"

That was as far as she got. My grandfather's hand whipped out, and a coil of fire wrapped around the blood mage's neck. Her scream was piercing, and I smelled burning flesh.

"This is an unacceptable loss of revenue, and if we fail to meet the schedule, it will damage our reputation," Moses said with that same calm voice as the blood mage writhed and shrieked on the end of his fire rope. I didn't flinch. What was she experiencing that I hadn't at her hands, and for hours at a time? "Despite your skills, you continue to lack the kind of attention to detail I require in my employees. I made the timetable clear to you when you received the assignment."

The blood mage finally lost consciousness. The coil of fire released her neck, and she hit the floor in a heap, her throat a charred mess. The smell was terrible, but I was glad for the silence.

Kade stepped away to call someone to come get the mage. My grandfather looked at me. He might as well have been looking at a piece of trash on the side of the road. There was absolutely nothing in his eyes. Looking into them was like looking into hell.

"Her stupidity and your stubbornness are going to cost me a lot of money." That was the only warning I got before he brought the heel of his boot down on my back. Agony whited out my vision and I sank toward oblivion, but I could not pass out because of the blood mage's spells. I found I was still able to scream some more after all.

23

I came awake with a scream that sounded like it was ripped out of my soul. With a sob, I curled up on my side, drawing my knees up to my chest, and began to shake. I swore I could still feel my grandfather's boot heel on the middle of my back.

It had been months since I'd had a nightmare that intense. It didn't take a psychiatrist to figure out what had brought on such vivid memories; Adri had spent the better part of an hour digging glass out of my back. The pain and blood from last night was more than enough to remind me of the horrors of what my grandfather had done to me.

I stumbled to the bathroom to wash my face. I was about to put toothpaste on my toothbrush when my phone rang.

It was Adri. "You must never sleep," I told her after we'd said hello to each other.

"I'm headed home. Mr. Vaughan requested I call you in the morning to let you know where things stand, but I didn't want to wake you too early."

I was quiet. "How is Sean?" I asked finally.

"Mr. Maclin is healing well. He'll be our guest for a few days. Mr. Vaughan informed the pack of his whereabouts, and his beta saw for himself that he's unharmed and being kept in comfortable conditions."

"What do you plan to do with him?"

Adri's tone was businesslike, which I appreciated. "Since he suffered no serious injury, Mr. Vaughan has decided not to file a grievance with the Were Ruling Council. He suggested you go before the council and demand a judgment against Mr. Maclin for the seriousness of your injuries and the damages to your home."

"I don't want anything from Sean," I stated. "The less I have to think about him at this point, the better. I'd rather pay for the repairs myself than drag this out."

"It would be Mr. Vaughan's honor to represent you," Adri informed me. "You'd have no contact with Mr. Maclin at all."

"Please tell Charles I appreciate his offer, but I just want all of this behind me. The sooner Sean and I have nothing to do with each other, the sooner we can both move on."

After a beat, I asked, "Has Sean said anything about…the situation?" I didn't know why I inquired or why it mattered to me in the least.

Adri didn't seem surprised at my question. "Once Mr. Maclin shifted back to human form, he was extremely upset you were hurt, and he wouldn't be calm until we convinced him that you were healed. He's also insisting he had no intention of infecting you with the werewolf virus, or claiming you as his mate against your will, though he admits you share a metaphysical link."

I scowled.

"We've been told the link will dissolve on its own given time, as long as you have no further contact with Mr. Maclin." Adri paused. "He asked that we tell you that he would still like the chance to explain himself."

"You can tell him that you delivered the message and there's nothing he has to say that I want to hear." I was pleased at how steely my voice sounded, though I felt a sharp ache somewhere in the middle of my chest.

"I will do that." Another pause. "You doing okay with all of this?"

"I'll be all right. It's not like I was in love with him, or anything close to it." I paused, then added, "He should have known I'm not prey."

"I understand."

We fell quiet.

"Oh, I almost forgot," Adri said finally. "Mr. Vaughan began making inquiries last night to find a teacher for your client."

"Really? I thought…."

"He's apparently changed his mind about requesting your blood. I believe he'll ask you to upgrade the wards on one of his storage facilities instead."

"Please tell him thank you, and that I'll be happy to work on the wards. Just tell me when and where and what kind."

"I will. Have a good day, Alice."

"You too, Adri. Go get some sleep."

I put the phone down, lay back on the bed, and closed my eyes.

My heart felt bruised. I was glad Charles was keeping Sean in custody for a couple of days, so I wouldn't have to worry about him showing up on my doorstep. Despite everything, there was a part of me that wondered if Sean had been telling the truth when he'd claimed he had no plans to turn me into a werewolf. Maybe it was unfair of me not to hear him out.

Even if that was true, I reminded myself, there was no place for me in Sean's life. He was an alpha werewolf in need of a mate, and that wasn't going to change. Until Charles had explained the situation, I hadn't really thought of Sean's role as an alpha and how different it was from a pack werewolf.

More importantly, he'd initiated a mating bond with me without my permission, and I didn't think that was something I was going to be able to forgive or forget. It was best we made a clean break. For both our sakes, I hoped by the time his involuntary seclusion was over, Sean would come to the same conclusion.

Wanting to distract myself from thoughts about Sean, I called Natalie.

She answered immediately, her voice cheerful. "Alice! No answer from the lawyer yet, so I left him another message. How are you?"

"Doing well, Natalie. Have you had any luck finding out more about our missing item?"

"The MacGuffin?" Natalie teased. I made a face at Malcolm's goofy nickname for the *Kasten*. "Nothing yet. I just got started on the papers in her desk, though. There's a lot more to go through. I'll try to get finished this afternoon."

I remembered my earlier conversation with Adri. "By the way, I'm in the process of finding you a teacher. I hope to have some news on that soon too."

"Awesome," Natalie said. "I'm actually getting kind of excited about it."

"I'm really glad to hear that. Let me know if you find anything, and I'll keep you posted." We said our good-byes and disconnected.

I took a long shower, scrubbing myself until I could no longer imagine I smelled Sean on my skin. I dried my hair and dressed.

When I opened my bedroom door, Malcolm waited on the other side. "Where have *you* been?" I asked.

"At Natalie's, giving you some space. What the hell happened downstairs? Were we robbed?"

I leaned against the doorframe and told him about my visit to Hawthorne's, what Charles told me about Sean's pack problems and his plan to turn me into a werewolf, what happened at my house, and Sean being held in Charles's custody.

Malcolm was flitting around in a rage. "That son of a bitch. I'm so sorry, Alice."

I shrugged. "He still claims he had no intention of infecting me, but he *did* initiate a bond without telling me about it. Even if he didn't want to turn me into a werewolf, an alpha has to have a werewolf mate, so it was basically doomed from the start."

"He did save your life after Natalie burned you, and he took care of you afterward. I suppose that's worth something. Though if he wanted you for his mate, that would explain why he was so strongly motivated to get through the wards. I can't believe he was going to bite you."

I headed down the hall to the stairs, Malcolm trailing along behind me. "I guess it doesn't matter anymore. He's Charles's problem for a couple of days while he calms down. After that, if he does come around, I'll just have to make it clear he needs to stay away from me."

"You need to get some silver."

I paused in the middle of the stairs, then continued on. "I hope it doesn't come to that," I said softly. "But you're probably right. I have silver, though. I guess I need to start carrying it."

When I got to the main floor of the house, I stopped and stared.

My front window had been replaced with a lovely piece of decorative fixed glass that looked frightfully expensive even without adding in the cost of having a window company come out in the middle of the night. The bevels in the glass cast rainbows of light across the foyer. The floor was spotlessly clean, and I didn't see or sense any trace of ash or my blood anywhere.

My living room was virtually empty. The books that had been in the bookcases were stacked neatly on the floor. The broken furniture, my smashed television, and the rest of the debris were gone. Only the couch and the record player remained. How they had avoided getting destroyed, I had no idea.

I went to the basement door. When I looked at my wards, I could see the golden thread that represented Sean. I yanked it out. The wards rippled, then went still. I opened the door, and Malcolm and I went downstairs.

I went to one of the cabinets, traced runes on the door, then opened it. I pulled out two small silver throwing knives and a wrist sheath from one of the cabinets, then I took out a box of silver bullets, my gun, and an empty magazine. Malcolm watched silently as I loaded the magazine with the bullets.

I felt sick at the thought of shooting Sean, but if he did intend to bite me and turn me into a werewolf, I'd do it without hesitation, even if it brought the entire Tomb Mountain Pack down on my head. My only hope in that case would be to get to the Were Ruling Council before the pack got to me and explain that Sean had attempted to bite me against my will.

There was a slim chance my strong blood magic would be able to burn the werewolf virus from my body if I did get bitten—I'd heard of it happening before—but I was certainly not going to bank on that. My best defense was silver.

While I finished loading the magazine, I told Malcolm what I'd sensed from John West at the art museum the night before.

He was justifiably troubled. "We knew he was strong, but from what you're saying, West might not just be a member of the harnad. He might be its leader."

"I'm starting to think that too. In that case, he could draw on the power of the other members to enhance his own blood magic."

"Not someone you'd want to have to face."

I snorted. "No kidding."

I went back upstairs to make coffee and toast an english muffin, then returned to the basement to look through my blood magic books for any more references to the *Kasten*. Other than the one I'd shown Malcolm yesterday, I didn't see any more mentions of the box, though a few of the books described other objects of power with similar characteristics. I made some notes on those, hoping I'd learn something that might help me better understand what the *Kasten* was—if indeed that's what had been in Betty's library—and what it might be able to do. Malcolm worked on his masking spells in the work area.

Shortly before lunch, Natalie texted that she was looking through the last of the papers in the desk. We made plans for me to come over later in the afternoon to look at the letters she'd found from John West, once she'd had a chance to look through the rest of Betty's files.

By two o'clock, I was bleary-eyed and my back was killing me. I leaned back in my chair for a few minutes and watched Malcolm jump in and out of his bolt-hole crystals.

I was reaching for another book when it felt like something kicked me in the head and I fell over. My chin hit the table and I bit my tongue. I ended up on the floor, staring up dazedly and tasting blood.

As the ringing in my ears faded, I could hear Malcolm calling my name. "What the hell was that?" he demanded. "I felt a surge of magic, and then you fell out of your chair."

I tried to think, but my brain was fuzzy. "I don't know. It almost felt like my house wards broke, but they're fine." I frowned. "Did someone try to get past my wards?"

"That wouldn't have affected me," he pointed out. "The only wards I've been working on—"

"—Are at Natalie's house," I finished. "Did someone just break Natalie's house wards?" I struggled to my feet, reaching for my phone. My call to Natalie went straight to voice mail. I didn't bother to leave a message.

"We've got to get to Natalie's house," I said. "Right the hell now. Can you jump there?"

Malcolm shook his head. "No, but I can get there a lot faster than you. Meet you there." He vanished.

I took thirty seconds to cram my blood magic books back into the cabinet. Then I grabbed my phone, my bag, and my gun on the way out the door.

24

I might not be able to move as fast as a ghost, but I could haul ass in my car. I got to Natalie's house in less than fifteen minutes.

Even from the street, I could tell her house wards were broken. It felt like something was scraping against my brain, and the feeling got worse the closer I got to the house. By the time I reached the porch, I was staggering. The wards hadn't just been broken; they'd been ripped apart with brute force.

I managed to get to the house and place my palm against the doorframe. I brought down the broken wards, and the disorientation and pain vanished. I straightened up shakily and tried the front door. It was unlocked.

Inside, it didn't look like anything was out of place. Whatever happened, it happened quickly. "Malcolm?"

Malcolm appeared next to me. He flitted back and forth so rapidly, it hurt my eyes. "She's gone. There's blood in Betty's room."

"Shit." Just outside the library door, there was a large smear of blood on the floor. I wondered if Natalie was trying to get to the safety of the library, where the wards would have protected her, but someone got her just before she crossed the threshold.

"Whatever happened here, we missed it." Malcolm flitted so fast I could barely see him. "Someone took her."

"Can you sense her?"

Malcolm stopped, closed his eyes, and concentrated. He vanished for a moment, then reappeared, then vanished again, then came back.

"I can't," he said finally. "Something is blocking me. She must be spelled or inside a ward. Whatever it is, it's got to be strong."

I cursed. The library wards ran over my skin like an electric current. Whoever had come into Natalie's home, they hadn't broken them. I wondered if that was because there was nothing in the library they needed anymore, if the wards had proven too strong for them to break, or if they figured someone would feel the house wards break and come to investigate.

I put my hands on my hips. "Natalie said she had the letters from West on the dining table, but they weren't there. I'm guessing they were taken too."

Malcolm moved next to me. "Can you track her with blood magic?"

I glanced at the blood on the floor. "Maybe. The longer the blood sits there, the harder it gets. If she's protected by a masking or protection spell or ward, it gets even harder. I'll need some of the things from my basement. I'll get what I need to do the spells and be back as soon as I can."

"I'll stay here in case whoever took her comes back."

"Be careful." I shut the front door of Natalie's house and hurried to my car.

My thoughts raced as I drove back to my house. Why take Natalie now? Malcolm and I had used his spell detector on Natalie's aunts and uncle, but I didn't see how any of them could have been aware we'd done that since Malcolm was invisible. Even if they had, none of them were the mystery mage. I was pretty sure John West hadn't noticed us tailing him last night.

I almost hit a parked car when a sudden realization struck me.

Son of a bitch. The lawyer.

I'd asked Natalie to call Betty's lawyer and find out if her grandmother had any other children besides the ones we knew about. Hours after leaving another message for him, Natalie was gone. Was there a connection? If the mystery mage wasn't one of the siblings Malcolm and I had checked out, then there *had* to be another family member. It made sense. Maybe Natalie's calls to the lawyer had spooked someone, and they'd come to shut her up.

I didn't know the lawyer's name, but I'd bet it was in the paperwork on Betty's desk. I'd find it when I got back to Natalie's house, and if my blood magic wasn't able to locate Natalie, Malcolm and I would pay him a visit. If he knew who had Natalie, he'd tell me.

When I parked in my driveway, I left everything but my keys in the car so my hands would be free to carry what I needed for the blood magic ritual.

I was so focused on getting in and out of the house as quickly as possible that it took me way too long to realize Peter Eppright was standing five feet away in the shadows under my carport, and that he was pointing a gun at me.

I stared at him for a full second before reacting. I lashed his right hand with my cold-fire whip. He yelled in pain and dropped his gun, bending over to cradle his hand. I reached into my car to grab my gun off the passenger seat just as I heard a footstep crunch in the gravel behind me.

Something smashed into the back of my head, and everything went black.

The digital clock on my nightstand read 3:35 a.m. I sat cross-legged on the floor inside a circle. In front of me were three large jars filled with my blood and a spell crystal into which I was draining almost every last drop of my magic. Anyone monitoring me—which they certainly were, as I was under surveillance almost every minute of every day—would see me working ritual blood magic for my grandfather. They would not be able to see the jars or the spell crystal. I'd spent many hours crafting the circle. It was a powerful obfuscation spell, one of the most difficult I had ever attempted.

Tonight was the culmination of almost a year of planning and preparing, waiting for the right time, for the right type of contract. When my grandfather was hired by a smaller cabal to wipe out their competitor, it was the perfect opportunity for me to put my escape plan into action. Of course, I couldn't readily accept the assignment or that would have aroused suspicion, so I'd initially refused to obey my grandfather's command. I hoped Moses wouldn't suspect I'd relented too soon. I had to balance how much torture I could take with how much I would have to recover for my plan to work.

The attack would require an enormous amount of energy, which was what I had been waiting for. I had been instructed to perform the ritual tonight, when the targets would all be at a location that was less well-protected than their compound. Everything had been carefully planned. It was a shame it was about to go completely sideways.

I'd drained as much of my blood into the jars as I dared. It had to be an enormous amount, and full of magic, for this to work. When it was dispersed by the explosion, my grandfather would have to believe I had been killed. I'd been thinking about this for almost a year. Now, in the moment, I was very calm, almost detached. It was almost certainly mainly the blood loss, but the rest was cold resolve. Either I would be free, or I would be dead. There were no other alternatives. Knowing that made it easier.

I funneled all of my magic into the spell crystal until all I had left was a tiny amount of blood magic.

I opened the jars and poured their contents into the circle. The coppery scent turned my stomach. The smell of my blood was inexorably tied to torture by my grandfather, the recently deceased blood mage, and others. Tonight it would be the key to my escape—I hoped.

The blood ran across the floor in wide rivers. I left the jars where they were. There would be nothing left of them, or the room I was in.

I used a small knife to cut four runes into my forearm with quick precision. A blood-magic protection and obfuscation spell flared over my body, powered by the last of my blood magic. It had to hold or I was going to be dead in about five seconds.

I closed my eyes. Blood magic flared around me.

I don't remember the actual blast. One second, I was standing in my room. I blinked, and I was outside.

I lay in the courtyard, surrounded by burning debris. An enormous fireball billowed from a giant hole in the side of the compound where my rooms used to be. My hearing was gone, but I saw red flashing lights and knew every alarm in the compound was going off. People in black uniforms were running everywhere, some toward the blaze, some toward my grandfather's apartment, the library, and the storage areas.

No one saw me on the ground, staring dazedly at the ruined section of the compound where I'd been kept prisoner for most of my life. The obfuscation spell was holding for now, but only fumes of my magic remained to keep it going. Once it failed, I'd be visible. I had another spell in my pocket, but it was an emergency backup and I couldn't use it until I was well outside the compound walls.

I sat up and pain took my breath away. The protection spell had saved my life, but my left arm was broken at the elbow. I staggered to my feet, holding my arm against my body, and focused as well as I could to avoid bumping into anyone as I made my way through the chaos and smoke to the main gate.

Behind me, there was a second explosion; apparently, the fire had reached something volatile. I smiled grimly. Maybe the whole damn compound would burn to the ground. It was probably too much to hope for. It wouldn't destroy the cabal, but it would certainly cripple it for a while.

The guard at the gate was shouting into his radio as the heavy double doors beside the gate opened. More uniformed men and women came pouring in—they'd been outside the gates on patrol and had been called in to help. They wouldn't open the main gate; if it was an attack, that would put the compound at risk, but the small personnel doors could be opened to let in reinforcements.

I waited for my chance. When the guards stopped coming through, I slipped out and began running. Every step jostled my broken arm, but I held it as steady as possible and moved as quickly as I could through the woods surrounding the compound. I had to put as much distance between myself and that place as I was able to before blood loss and exhaustion rendered me visible and vulnerable.

Somehow, I made it the three miles from the compound to the state highway before I could go no farther. My vision was graying, and I was reduced to crawling the last few hundred yards. I'd hoped to use one of the disguise spells in my pockets and get a ride from a passing motorist, but I couldn't even stand up, much less wave anyone down.

I spotted a culvert under the highway. On my knees and one hand, my left arm held against my body, I crawled inside the drainpipe and crept back into the darkness, half burying myself under leaves. Luckily, it hadn't rained lately, and the drainpipe was dry.

Despite the warm summer night, I was shivering from shock and pain. With fumbling fingers, I dug into my pocket and felt around for the healing spell I'd brought. It was the largest of the spell crystals in my pocket; the others were mainly disguise and masking spells, plus a suicide spell that would burn my body to ash. The latter was the only one in my pocket that was distinctly cube-shaped. I was careful not to grab it by mistake.

My fingers closed around the healing spell. I had to hope no one came near this area and sensed its use before the magic trace dissipated. I knew I was risking being caught, but I also knew there was a real chance I would die from shock and blood loss if I didn't do something. I hadn't come this far to die now. I'd already gone all-in. What was one more gamble?

I pulled the crystal from my pocket, stuck it inside my bra so it would stay against my skin even if I passed out, and invoked the spell.

Magic hit my chest like a sledgehammer, and I spun off into darkness. My last thought was of freedom.

25

Awareness returned slowly, as if I had to surface from a great depth.

I'd gone through so many torture sessions in my life that it had become second nature to play possum upon first waking. Feigning unconsciousness had worked in my favor more than once. I held perfectly still, breathed slowly and evenly, and tried to figure out what the hell was going on.

The first sensations I had were disorientation and tremendous pain. The latter seemed to be coming from the back of my head. Had I fallen? I tried to remember, but everything was fuzzy. I dimly recalled going to Natalie's house after someone broke her house wards. Blood on the floor in Betty's room. Malcolm trying to find her using their connection and failing. Driving back to my house. Then...nothing. The pain in my head indicated I'd been attacked.

That hypothesis was supported by the fact I was tied up and gagged. I felt a surge of fear when I realized I was splayed out on a hard surface. My left wrist and ankles were tied with rope, but my right wrist was fastened with a spell cuff. I reached for my magic, but it was dampened completely. It took everything I had to breathe slowly through the terror. It felt like I was back at the cabal, held in restraints for torture.

I had been basically rendered helpless, and the fear began to give way to rage.

I heard movement to my right. "You can open your eyes now."

The male voice was familiar, but I couldn't place it. I didn't react.

"Miss Worth, please. You've been awake for several minutes."

I finally recognized the voice: Peter Eppright. *What the hell?*

I opened my eyes and blinked, waiting for what I was seeing to make sense.

It looked like I was in a half-finished office building. I saw scaffolding, clear plastic sheets, boxes of drop cloths, stacks of sheet rock, huge spools of cables, and tables covered with hand tools. There were lights on stands set up around us. The rest of the building was dark. It must be night.

I lay on top of a large wooden table in my bra and underwear. All of my weapons and jewelry were gone, even my belly-button piercing. I was miserably cold.

I glared at Eppright, who stood about four feet away near a smaller table covered with a black cloth. His right hand and wrist were wrapped in gauze. I got a sudden flash of him standing under my carport with a gun. I didn't think I'd been shot, but how had I ended up here? Whatever was going on, he was clearly in on it.

I heard a sound from the darkness and turned my head to look. It was a mistake.

Nausea surged. Vomit filled my mouth and sinuses, and I couldn't get any air. I made desperate noises and tried to breathe through my nose, but that caused me to aspirate vomit into my lungs.

Eppright started cursing. He untied my gag and left wrist, lifted my upper body, and turned me awkwardly onto my right side so I could vomit off the table onto the floor. As I was desperately trying to breathe, I noticed a leather cord tied around my left wrist with several spell crystals on it. I wondered what its purpose was. I saw a second table next to mine, but it was empty.

"What's going on?"

It was a woman's furious voice. If I hadn't been trying not to choke to death on my own vomit, I would have looked to see who it was. My brain felt too big for my skull. Definitely a concussion. The fact I was having a hard time thinking clearly and had been unconscious for at least several hours were very bad signs.

"She started to choke," Eppright told the woman, who stood behind him and out of my line of sight. "You said we needed her alive."

I threw up again, then started coughing up bits of stuff that had gone into my lungs.

"You should have thought of that before you and that idiot bashed her skull in," the woman said.

I decided I didn't recognize her voice at all. Also, I'd like to know which "idiot" hit me on the head so I could return the favor. My eyeballs throbbed in time with my pulse.

"That was Ray." Eppright looked a little green, hopefully due to my vomit.

"Clean that up," she ordered. I wished she would move so I could see her. She sounded like she was in charge of whatever the hell was going on. My brain started to catch up. Was this the mystery mage? With the cuff on, I couldn't sense her magic.

He looked like he wanted to refuse her order, but thought better of it. "Are you done?" he demanded.

I coughed up some vomit out of my burning lungs and spat it in his face.

He jerked back, but not in time, and my glob of spit hit him on the forehead. Eppright's face turned bright red as he pulled back his bandaged fist to punch me. I didn't give him the satisfaction of cowering.

"Stop!" the woman snapped. Furious, Eppright obeyed, dropping his fist to his side. She stepped around him and I got my first look at her.

She looked like she was in her mid-to-late fifties, but in good shape for her age. She wore slacks and a light blue shirt, her ash-blonde hair pulled back in a neat ponytail. She looked vaguely familiar, though I'd have sworn I'd never seen her before. Then I realized she looked a lot like Betty.

"So you're Betty's other daughter." My voice was hoarse from throwing up.

Eppright used a drop cloth to clean up my vomit. I winked at him and he clenched his fists so tightly that his knuckles turned white.

The woman looked surprised. "Well, aren't you smart." She didn't sound sarcastic. "I'm Amelia Wharton. Formerly Amelia Eppright."

I glanced at Peter. "Brother?"

"Yes."

I made a face. "My condolences."

Eppright flushed again.

"Now, don't be rude," Amelia said. "I can understand why you're upset, but there's no reason we can't all be civil."

My eyebrows went up. I was beginning to think Amelia might not be all there. There was something off about her tone—a kind of detachment, like she was discussing the weather report, not standing over someone she'd had kidnapped and tied up.

Kidnapped. That triggered a memory. My brain still felt entirely too sluggish. "Where's Natalie?" I asked.

Amelia glanced at her watch. "They should be bringing her here in a few minutes."

"Is she all right?"

Amelia shrugged. "She's alive."

"That is *not* the right answer," I retorted. "She's done nothing wrong. She's your *niece*."

She looked at me with flat, expressionless eyes that reminded me of my grandfather's empty gaze. Amelia, like my grandfather, did not care about human life. She was a psychopath, just like him. Whatever she was planning, I wasn't going to be able to appeal to any kind of a conscience to get us out of this.

"I must say, I am impressed by your spellwork," she said. "Natalie's magic is better bound now than it was when Betty was alive. Judging by the burn mark on the floor in her bedroom, it must have gotten loose at some point."

"Yes." No sense revealing any details. "Why do you call your mother by her first name? Why didn't Natalie know you existed?"

I saw a flash of emotion in Amelia's eyes: pure hate. Then it vanished, as if it had never been there. "Betty sent me away when I was six years old and Peter was two. My magic developed very early, and she found it impossible to bind completely. Rather than raise me, she sent me to a...facility in Oregon. I lived there until I was twelve, and then I was sent to live in a group home in South Dakota."

"I don't understand. Betty was a strong mage."

"I was stronger. Even at six years old, she couldn't control me. She was concerned I would use my magic in public and expose her. She was hiding our magic from her husband, so she sent me away."

It was equally possible Betty had recognized her daughter's psychopathy, I thought, looking at Amelia's flat stare. This didn't seem like the time to pry into that, though. "If you hated your mother so much, why did you come back?"

Amelia smiled, but it didn't reach her eyes. "Five years ago, my harnad in Portland heard a rumor that Betty had come into possession of Adelbert's *Kasten*. It seemed impossible, but I had to find out. No one has seen it in more than a century."

"So you showed up on her doorstep, or what?"

"Yes. The prodigal daughter, returned." Her tone was dry.

"And she trusted you?"

"Not at all, but I could see she felt some guilt over abandoning me, so I used that. I showed her that I was a strong blood mage, and that I could make her harnad stronger."

"She brought you into her harnad?" I was having a hard time believing Betty would trust her daughter enough to let her join her alliance of blood mages. I'd known her five minutes and I didn't trust her one little bit.

"After some persuasion from John West," Amelia said. "I showed John how powerful I was, and he wanted me to join. Plus, after I figured out I was his daughter and I made Betty tell him, all he wanted was to know me. The poor man never had any other children, apparently."

The pieces were falling into place. Amelia was the daughter of Betty and the powerful fire mage John West. Peter was actually her half brother, the son of Betty's first husband. No wonder their magic felt similar, but Amelia's was so strong and the other siblings' magic so weak.

"So you came back for the *Kasten*?" I scoffed. "It's a myth."

"It's not a myth," she countered. "It's very real, as a lot of people are about to find out. I've been waiting a long time for this day. I wish Betty could be here too, but the bitch died before I had everything in place."

"What exactly are you planning here? And what's Tweedle*dumb*'s role in all of this?" I glanced at her half brother.

He looked like he would love nothing more than to strangle me with his bare hands. The feeling was mutual. My head was killing me.

Amelia patted Eppright's arm. "Peter is key to everything. Without him, none of this would be possible."

Eppright preened.

I would have rolled my eyes, but they hurt too much. "Then what the hell am *I* doing here?" I asked the obvious question.

"At first, I was simply curious as to how much you'd found out by snooping around Betty's house and visiting my brother and sisters. Until Natalie asked William today if Betty had had any other children, I wasn't worried." I assumed William was the lawyer. "But when he called to warn me, I realized my complacency had nearly cost me everything. William helped me get Natalie at her home. I had Peter and Ray Browning intercept you at your house and bring you here. Unfortunately, we had to get rid of William. He became too much of a liability."

I was sickened by her casual admission of murder. "How did you manage to get Betty to give you passage through her library wards?"

Amelia looked surprised. "Well, well. I clearly underestimated you from the beginning. That explains why you were visiting my brother and sisters, and why you had Natalie ask if Betty had any other children—you were looking for whoever besides Betty could pass through the wards."

"So you somehow tricked Betty into allowing you into her library. Then after Betty was dead, you waited until Natalie was out, and came in and took the *Kasten* and Betty's spell books?"

Before Amelia could reply, I heard voices. Out of the darkness, a small group approached us. I saw Deborah, Kathy, and a large man I didn't recognize. He was carrying something over his shoulder wrapped in a blanket. I saw a flash of red hair inside the blanket and felt ice in my veins. Natalie.

Deborah avoided looking at me, but Kathy gave me a big, ugly smile. "Well, hello, *Audrey*," she said in a singsong voice. "So nice to see you again. Still looking to buy a house?"

"Oh, you know," I said casually, "it's really a buyer's market right now. I'm not rushing into anything."

Her eyes narrowed. "Where's your friend?" She turned to Amelia. "She wasn't alone when she came to see me."

"The werewolf?" Amelia said.

I stiffened. How the hell did they know who Sean was?

"He won't be able to find her. The obfuscation spell she's wearing and the blood ward will block any magical or metaphysical links."

I glanced down. Sure enough, there was a dark stain on the floor in a large circle around the table I was on. The circle was about fifteen feet wide and contained both of the large tables and the smaller, cloth-covered table. I hadn't been able to sense the ward because of the spell cuff. Between that and the spell I was wearing on my wrist, there was no way for Malcolm or Sean to find me, even if Sean hadn't been in Charles's custody.

Charles.

For a moment, I felt a flare of hope, but it quickly died. Without drinking my blood, he wouldn't be able to sense my location. There was no rescue coming. I'd have to get out this by myself. Fair enough; I was used to being on my own.

"Put her on the other table," Amelia instructed the man carrying Natalie.

He grunted and dropped the rolled-up bundle with a thud that made me wince.

"Ray," Amelia scolded.

"Sorry." He didn't sound like he meant it.

So this was Ray, Elise's husband, the asshole who'd bashed in the back of my head. "Why isn't your wife here?" I asked him.

Ray scowled at me. "She doesn't believe in using magic," he said shortly. He unrolled the blanket, revealing Natalie's unconscious body. She looked extremely pale, and there was a bloodstain on her shirt near her shoulder blade.

"What did you do to her?" I demanded.

"Shut up." Ray started tying Natalie to the table with rope. On her left wrist was a leather bracelet like mine.

I looked at Amelia for an answer.

She gestured at Natalie. "I had to use magic to knock her out, as well as an obfuscation spell to prevent you from locating her. Her magic and your binding have been reacting badly to my spells. It can't be helped. I don't have time to make new ones."

"Then let me do it," I said. "It's killing her."

Amelia gave me another one of those cold smiles. "Do you think I'm stupid? You won't be using your magic here today. Tie her arm down again," she said to Ray.

I had really, really been hoping they would forget about my untied left arm. As Ray moved toward me, I fought him off for a few seconds. Then Eppright backhanded me across the face, my head hit the table, and I blacked out.

26

I wasn't out for long—a few minutes at most. When I came to, Ray was tying my arm down again. When he saw me looking at him, he gave my wrist a vicious twist and something popped. I shrieked and gagged.

"Ray." Amelia's voice was sharp. He stepped back from the table and sneered at me. I lay still and focused on not throwing up again.

When the nausea subsided, I still wanted to know what the hell was going on. "Okay, I get why I'm here and why Amelia is here." My words sounded slurred. My vision was blurry and I tried to focus. "But what are the rest of you doing?"

"We're Amelia's harnad," Deborah said primly. "We're here to allow her to draw energy from us for the box."

I blinked at Amelia in confusion. "*They're* your harnad?"

She gave me a calculating smile. "Of course. They're my family."

"But you can't be in a harnad," I told Kathy. "You aren't a blood mage."

"Of course I am," Kathy said as if I was slow. "Amelia and I are sisters."

"That's not how it works. You and Deborah have only very weak air magic. Peter is a low-level fire and air mage. Harnads only include very strong blood mages, which *none* of you are."

"Alice, Alice." Amelia shook her head. "Lies will not help you here. We are a family of blood mages. Betty never wanted us to use our magic. She wanted all the power for herself, but now we will become the most powerful cabal in the country with the *Kasten*. No one will *ever* cross us again." She gestured at her half siblings. "Please, step inside the circle so we can begin."

Kathy and Deborah joined Ray and Eppright inside the blood ward. Amelia traced a rune in the air and the ward flared.

"I'm telling you, you're not her harnad," I insisted, looking at the three half siblings and Elise's dumb thug of a husband. "I don't know what she's up to, or what she's told you, but you are not blood mages—only *she* is."

"Shut up," Eppright snarled. "Or I'll shove that gag down your throat and let you choke on it this time."

I shut up. I wasn't going to be able to convince them of anything. They didn't know enough about magic to know it wasn't possible for them to be blood mages or in a harnad. She'd duped them completely.

What the hell was Amelia up to? She'd probably promised to share power with them, but somehow I doubted that would actually happen. I didn't believe a word of this "family" crap she was spewing. That woman didn't care one iota about her half sisters and half brother. If anything, she probably despised them since Betty had abandoned her and raised them.

I narrowed my eyes at Amelia and then at the cloth-draped table where, I presumed, the *Kasten* awaited. What was it the book had said? That the *Kasten* had to be filled with the blood or body parts of mages representing all four elements?

I looked at Amelia in horror. She smiled at me. "*Religo!*"

Despite the dampening of the spell cuff, I felt a wave of magic prickle over my skin. My cuff protected me from Amelia's binding spell, but Kathy, Deborah, Ray, and Peter were not so lucky. All four were frozen in place where they stood. Awareness and fear shone in their eyes, but they were immobilized.

Amelia patted me on the hand. "Relax, dear. You're just a bystander for now."

She went to the covered table and pulled back the cloth. On it sat an old wooden chest about the size of a shoebox, a small ritual knife, two spell books that were probably Betty's, and a long black robe. Rune carvings covered the box. Amelia put the robe on and picked up the knife, cutting the pad of her thumb. She smeared her blood across the lid of the box and recited an incantation. It sounded like German.

"You're going to kill them all," I said.

"Yes." Amelia's voice was emotionless. "Greedy fools. Kathy's husband spends money faster than she can make it, and Deborah and her husband have nothing saved for their retirement. Peter owes his bookie a hundred grand. Ray and Elise are so far in debt, with their house and their cars and private school tuition, he was all too eager to join us. It might be the only time he would have been better off listening to my idiot half sister. All any of them want is power and money."

"And you don't?" I said skeptically.

"Of course I do, but what I want the most is revenge. I can't get to Betty, but I can do this." She used the knife to gesture at the four terrified people standing frozen around us. "I can wipe out her family, everyone she loved after she turned her back on me. Then I'll burn the city down. There won't be a single person or cabal who can stand against me. If I fill the *Kasten* with the lifeblood of an entire family, it will be the most unstoppable object of power the magical world has ever known."

I didn't know how much I believed that, but if the legends were true, I couldn't let her unleash the *Kasten* on the city. I doubted I had much chance of reasoning with her, but I had to try. It was either that or lie here and watch her kill five people. I might not like Natalie's extended family very much, but they were still human beings. I'd seen enough suffering and death in my lifetime.

"What makes you think the *Kasten* will be as powerful as you think? Everything I read said it's a myth."

Amelia caressed the box. "Our harnad in Portland had a letter written by a mage in 1843. He described a story told to him by his father, who had witnessed a mage wield the power of the *Kasten* filled with the blood of a father, mother, and three children. It laid waste to more than ten square miles. Imagine what one filled with the lifeblood of an entire extended family would do. Four siblings, their spouses, their children, and grandchildren. And Betty's brother and sister, and her precious granddaughter." She sneered at Natalie.

I went cold at the way she casually described killing children. "So, old legends? That's all you've got?" I challenged her. "What if it doesn't work? You'd have killed all these people for nothing."

"Not for nothing," Amelia countered, picking up the box and the knife and moving toward Peter Eppright. "Even if the *Kasten* isn't even powerful enough to start a campfire, wherever Betty is, she gets to watch her entire family die. It's enough for me." She stopped in front of Eppright. His eyes were full of panic. "*Kneel*," she commanded.

All four of them crashed to their knees on the concrete floor, compelled to obey by her spell.

I struggled against my cuff and ropes to no avail.

Amelia murmured an invocation, traced runes on the lid of the *Kasten*, and opened the box. I felt a whisper of power that I recognized immediately from Betty's library; this was what had been hidden in the bookcase, behind the blood ward. The inside was stained black.

I began pulling on the rope that bound my left wrist. It hurt, but I hoped Ray might have been careless in his haste to tie me up. I twisted and pulled, trying not to attract Amelia's attention. I couldn't feel any give at all, but I kept trying.

With one quick movement, Amelia cut Peter Eppright's throat.

Blood spurted out across the floor. His eyes were wide and horrified, but he remained immobile. Amelia stood to the side for a moment, watching the blood arc through the air without so much as a blink, and then she raised the *Kasten* to catch it.

Warm blood ran down my fingers from where the rope on my left wrist had cut through the skin. Maybe the blood would make it easier to slip out.

I didn't dare look at my hand and tip Amelia off to what I was doing, so instead I watched Peter Eppright bleed out and die. It seemed to take forever, but in reality it probably took less than a minute. I felt the moment he died; it was like a frisson of energy across my skin. The *Kasten* now contained the lifeblood of one member of Betty's family. There were four more in the circle, awaiting their turn.

Amelia stepped away from Eppright's body, which, grotesquely, was still upright on its knees despite being dead. I stared at her, hoping she wouldn't notice the blood dripping from my left hand. Her face was serene.

"Blood magic is the most peaceful feeling," she said, breathing deeply. She touched Eppright's body and it fell over, hitting the floor with a wet *thump*.

Then she turned to Elise's husband Ray, who was facing me. When she slit his throat, hot blood sprayed across my stomach and legs before Amelia moved the *Kasten* between us. I flinched and continued pulling on my ropes, watching Amelia smile and hold the wooden box while Ray's lifeblood drained into it. I kept my face impassive, but inside I was screaming curses. I'd wanted him to suffer for hurting me, but this...this was a nightmare.

It took longer for Ray to die, but in the end, the life faded from his eyes and my skin tingled. More lifeblood for the triple-damned *Kasten*. At Amelia's touch, his body joined Eppright's on the blood-splattered floor.

I looked at Kathy and Deborah, and then at Natalie, still lying unconscious on the other table. "What's my part in all of this? I'm not a part of the family."

"You're actually very important," Amelia informed me. "Imagine how glad I was to sense that you have water magic. No one in our family is a water mage."

I blinked. "I'm not a water mage."

She shook her head at me. "No point in lying, dear. Not now." She walked to Kathy and casually cut her throat.

I clenched my teeth as the blood fountained from Kathy's slim neck and Amelia lifted the box to catch it. "I'm not a water mage," I repeated. "I have air and earth magic and that's all."

Amelia ignored me and watched Kathy's lifeblood drain into the *Kasten*.

I desperately tried to think, despite the pounding in my head and the nausea. I didn't understand why she was insisting I had water magic. I'd never....

Wait.

I remembered something Malcolm had said several days ago, after he'd had to use a dozen healing spells to save my life. He'd said I'd carry some of his magic as a result. Shit, I *did* have water magic—only a trace, but it might be enough. Thanks to me, Amelia would be able to give the *Kasten* everything it needed to unleash destruction on a massive scale.

I seethed and continued pulling on the rope on my left wrist as another tingle ran over my skin. Kathy was dead. A moment later, she fell to the floor.

Something started to slide over my left hand. The leather cord holding the masking and obfuscation spells had gotten slippery enough with blood that I might be able to slide it off. I scraped my wrist against the edge of the table, trying to push it over the big part of my hand, but it was stuck. I pulled harder.

If I could get the cord off, Malcolm might be able to sense me, at least enough to get close, since the blood ward wasn't specifically designed to obscure my aura like the obfuscation spells were. It was likely Charles knew I was missing by now. If I could somehow break Amelia's blood ward, someone would be able to find me quickly. I didn't know if I could break the ward without getting my spell cuff off, but one problem at a time.

I kept my attention on Amelia so she wouldn't suspect I was trying to get my hand free.

"Isn't the box full yet?" I asked her. Deborah's eyes were so full of fear, horror, and grief that I could hardly stand to look at her.

"It can't be filled." Amelia's voice sounded dreamy, her eyes unfocused. "Its capacity is endless, like its power."

The cord slid off. I caught it so it didn't fall to the floor, then tossed it up and onto the table where it was hidden by my body. The obfuscation spell was gone. Hopefully Malcolm would be on his way. Now I had to get out of this spell cuff and break the blood ward.

Sure. No problem.

My left wrist was streaming blood now from cuts made by the rope. If Amelia was paying attention to me instead of slitting throats, she'd have noticed the small puddle forming on the floor near my table. Instead, she stood with her eyes closed, swaying back and forth, presumably entranced by the power of the *Kasten*.

I twisted my left wrist just so, and the rope went slack and started to slide over my hand. My wrist was shredded, and I could barely feel my fingers.

I had a few seconds to plan at the most. If I got my left hand free, I might be able to undo the spell cuff if it wasn't the kind that required a key. Once I had my magic, Amelia was fucking toast.

Even if I couldn't get the cuff off, I might still be able to break her blood ward. It might only be down for a short time, but it might be long enough for Malcolm and whoever else was looking to find me. That was a lot of "mights," but I didn't think I had much of a choice. Amelia was heading over to Deborah, and once she was dead, then she'd be ready to cut Natalie's throat and mine. It was now or never. I was done watching people die.

I slipped my left hand out of the rope, twisted my upper body, and looked at the spell cuff on my right wrist. Hallelujah, no key required; it was the kind with two latches.

"No!" Amelia shouted. I ignored her and focused on making my numb fingers unfasten the latches. I had to get the damn cuff off or I was dead.

Just as I flicked open the second catch on the cuff, Amelia attacked, slashing me with her knife. The blade cut across my chest and blood spilled out. I shrieked and swung wildly with my left arm as I shook the cuff off my right wrist.

The second the cuff fell off, my magic roared through me like a dam had broken, and I made no attempt to hold back the surge of power. I threw my head back and screamed. The sheer force of my unleashed magic caused Amelia to stumble backward and fall, splashing blood from the *Kasten* onto her.

I fought to pull my magic back into myself and get it under control, but it was harder than it should have been; my head was pounding because of the damn concussion. I tried to move before I remembered my feet were still tied. I used my earth magic to burn the ropes off.

I staggered to my feet just as Amelia cut loose with a flash of air and fire magic. I barely had time to throw up a quick protective circle. She attacked again with a stronger blast, breaking my circle, and fire scoured my body. I screamed and lashed out with my cold-fire whip. It seared Amelia across the chest and knocked her down again. Her shriek of pain was music to my ears.

I realized Natalie was unprotected, lying unconscious on her table. As Amelia struggled to get to her feet, I threw up another circle, this one much stronger, and staggered over to Natalie. With a heave, I pushed her table over so it was between us and Amelia and made my circle larger to cover us both. The other mage blasted my circle with fire, but this time, it held.

I yanked the spell bracelet off Natalie's wrist. She was deathly pale, her breathing shallow. Amelia's spells were killing her. I didn't have time to unweave them, but if I unbound Natalie's null magic, it might disrupt the spells and keep her alive. I pulled at the threads of the binding spell and removed the one that kept her null magic contained. Yellow magic flared briefly, and Amelia's spells fractured.

Amelia sent another wave of fire, stronger than the last. My circle wavered but held. It wouldn't protect us for long, though. I needed to drop the damn blood ward and call in the cavalry. I'd hand Amelia over to the vamps.

With my right hand, I wiped across my chest, gathering up as much of my blood as I could. I steeled myself, broke my protective circle, and lunged for the blood ward. Behind me, Amelia screeched in fury.

I shoved my bloody hand into Amelia's ward and pushed energy into it, chanting "*Obliterate, obliterate, obliterate,*" until it broke with a surge that made me stagger. I wiped my foot through the ward on the floor and smeared my blood across it so she couldn't close it again. Now maybe Malcolm and Charles could find me.

I turned around and realized Amelia was right behind me. The light glinted off the edge of her knife as it arced toward my heart.

I stumbled backward, but I was dazed and disoriented from breaking the blood ward and moved too slowly. Screaming incoherently in rage, Amelia buried the blade in my chest, just above my right breast.

I stared dumbly at the knife for several confused seconds before Amelia yanked it out. My feet slid out from under me and I collapsed.

As I slumped against a large crate, Amelia picked up the *Kasten*. With the knife in one hand and the box in the other, she walked toward me. I tried to use my earth or air magic to push her back, but I was too dizzy and weakened to do more than raise a gentle breeze and a few paltry green flames.

With my lifeblood, she would have all four kinds of natural magic. If the legends were true, she would wield the *Kasten* and destroy the city, killing everyone in her path. With it, she might become the most powerful blood mage in modern history.

No.

There was no Malcolm. No Charles. There was only me here to stop her.

I forced myself to think. What could I do? I was having trouble breathing; my lung was probably punctured. Blood pumped out of the stab wound in my chest at an alarming rate. I wasn't going to be able to put up much of a physical fight. I didn't know if she would try to slit my throat or just catch the blood coming out of my chest. All I knew was that I was not going to give up yet.

I looked up at the half-finished building we were in. If I could spool enough earth magic, I could bring the building down on her. On us. Let's see the bitch get out of that one. I smiled and coughed up some blood.

Natalie and I might survive, if we were lucky. If not, at least we'd take her with us.

Amelia knelt in front of me, knife poised, and rested the *Kasten* in my lap. It looked like she was going to slit my throat after all.

I started spooling my earth magic. She either didn't notice or didn't care.

Amelia leaned close to me. "I enjoyed this. It's rare I find someone so near my own skill level. I'm almost sorry to have to kill you."

"Fuck off," I mumbled, which would have been more impressive if it hadn't come out in a bloody gurgle.

She opened the *Kasten*. Despite having its contents splashed around several times, the box was still full of blood. The power it gave off was enormous.

"Leave it be," Amelia said. "There's nothing for you to do now." I realized she was referring to my spooling earth magic.

She was wrong about that; I could bring down the building. Either she didn't think I could or she didn't think I would. I certainly didn't want to, but I didn't think I had much choice.

I looked down. My bloody hands tingled with the power of my earth magic, but I wasn't sure it was going to be strong enough or fast enough. I put my palms on the floor and prepared to shove every last ounce of magic I had kindled into the concrete.

I caught movement out of the corner of my eye and glanced up. To my shock, Natalie, pale and shaken, was standing behind Amelia. She gestured at me as if to say, *What should I do?*

Amelia raised the knife.

"Just touch her," I whispered.

Amelia paused, her blade an inch from my jugular, and stared at me. "What?"

I'd been on the receiving end of Natalie's nulling once, but I'd never seen anyone hit with it before. When Natalie's hands came down on Amelia's shoulders, the flare of bright yellow magic seared my eyes. Amelia screamed in anger and panic, and I felt a strange pulling sensation on the edge of my senses, like I was too close to the big drain at the bottom of a pool. Natalie's powerful nulling magic sucked Amelia dry in an instant.

With a cry of rage, Amelia staggered to her feet, knife in hand. She might be nulled, but she was far from defenseless.

"Look out," I rasped.

Natalie dodged the knife as Amelia lunged. As the older woman stumbled, off-balance, Natalie reached for a stack of short metal pipes, grabbed one, and swung it two-handed at Amelia's head.

The pipe connected with Amelia's skull with a sickening, wet *crunch*. She went down, and I seriously doubted she'd be getting up again.

Natalie dropped the pipe and stared at Amelia's body. "Oh God."

Before I could speak, a wave of gray-and-black magic swept over me, and a surge of pure power whited out my vision. The *Kasten* had lost its host and moved on to the strongest mage in the vicinity.

As if in a dream, I stuck my hand into the box. The blood felt thick and warm. In the bottom, I felt small, knobby objects that I realized were finger bones. *Adelbert*.

Hallo, meine Liebe. The voice in my head sounded like it originated in the depths of hell.

Power coursed up my right arm and through my body. It was the most incredible feeling I'd ever experienced, and with it came the desire and the power to annihilate. I could destroy the building, the city, the world, and I wanted to.

I closed my eyes. The *Kasten* showed me a vision of my mother, beautiful and gentle. My mother, who promised me that soon she and my father would take me away from my grandfather to a place where he'd never find us. My mother, whose own father had burned her alive, along with my father, when the guard she'd bribed to help her get me out of the compound betrayed her. I saw my mother and father, two piles of ash, on the floor of their house. My grandfather had taken me to see them when it was over so I could see what happened to people who crossed him.

Then the *Kasten* showed me my grandfather. Moses Murphy sat in his office, reading an offer from a prospective client. People were to die. Moses had only to agree to a price. He would never stop killing, unless someone stopped him.

Grief and rage rose within me like a tidal wave. I could level the compound, kill everyone in it. Moses would be dead. I could burn him to ash, and I could stand in front of him when I did it. I would be free forever. The *Kasten* offered it to me as a gift, and I wept in joy at the thought.

Then I would destroy everything and everyone else who stood against me. I would bring the world to its knees.

No. I wanted no one on their knees, not ever.

Ja, the *Kasten* said. Somehow, though I'd never spoken a word of German, I could understand it. *We will have vengeance. All will suffer for what was done to you. Take us and destroy*.

No, I am not a destroyer. I struggled but sank further into the darkness that was spreading through my brain.

Alice. I heard a different voice in my mind. It was gentle, like a caress. *Alice, come back.*

I opened my eyes. My brain processed a series of images, like a slideshow.

My right hand was wrist-deep in the blood in the *Kasten*. My left arm was wrapped around the box, holding it against my stomach.

Charles crouched in front of me, his hands on my bloody, burned legs, fangs extended, eyes solid black. Somehow, he had found me within minutes of the blood ward falling. He must have been nearby when I broke it. I wasn't sure I liked the covetous way he was looking at the box on my lap.

Amelia lay dead on the floor next to him in a puddle of her own blood. I felt nothing at the sight, not even satisfaction.

Natalie stood next to Bryan, her eyes as wide as saucers. Malcolm floated on the other side of her, looking at me and the box in horror.

I was burned again. Blood pumped sluggishly out of the stab wound in my chest. I should be dead, but I wasn't. I knew the box was keeping me alive so we could become the Destroyer.

I never needed to fear again. The *Kasten* would free me.

I would become a monster. I'd run away from the cabal so I didn't become one.

His eyes shining silver, Charles reached for the box. The *Kasten* struck with a bolt of black-and-gray magic that knocked him back several feet and left a scorched and bloody gash on his chest.

Natalie shrieked. Bryan was instantly at the vampire's side, but Charles held up his hand and stared at the *Kasten*.

"*Fass mich nicht an,*" I heard myself say, my voice flat. "*Ich bin für dich nicht da du Toter.*" *Do not touch me. I am not for you, dead man.*

Unlike me, Charles apparently spoke German. "*Was willst du?*" the vampire asked me, his voice hard. *What do you want?*

"*Rache,*" I rasped.

Revenge.

The *Kasten* showed me a vision of endless devastation, of blackened earth and mountains of corpses. I understood then that Adelbert's thirst was unquenchable. I could not just use the *Kasten* to kill my grandfather; once released, Adelbert would control me. Through me, he would destroy everything in his path.

If I gave in to what the box wanted—what this terrible part of me wanted—I might as well be dead. As badly as I wanted Moses to die for everything he had done, I couldn't surrender my soul to this darkness. I couldn't unleash the *Kasten* on the world.

And yet, I couldn't just let go of the box either. No one else should have this kind of power. Charles wanted it. Others would kill to possess it. There was no choice here; the *Kasten* must be destroyed.

I met Charles's gaze and coughed up more blood. "Thank you for finding me," I whispered.

The vampire's eyes widened almost imperceptibly. He recognized a good-bye when he heard one. He reached out cautiously to touch my foot, and I heard his voice in my head: *Alice, no!*

I closed my eyes and shoved every ounce of magical energy I had down my right arm into the black void that was the soul of the *Kasten*. *Die*, I ordered it.

From deep within the emptiness came a roar of fury: *NO. YOU WILL DIE.*

I'm already dying, I said simply. *And I'm taking you with me.*

The only response was a wordless scream out of the darkness.

The *Kasten* lived on the life energy of those whose blood made it whole. I felt familiar magical traces: Amelia Wharton, Peter Eppright, Ray Browning, Kathy Adams. My own. Beyond that, deep in the core of the box, I sensed a dark malevolence, a spirit so filled with hate and malice that it made me shudder.

Adelbert's enduring evil was the soul of the *Kasten*.

I had not used my blood magic to kill in a very long time, not since I left the cabal, but I still remembered how. I reached into the vile nothingness at the center of the *Kasten* and ripped out its heart with a single power word.

The darkness receded. With a howl of rage, the box died.

I let out a long, gurgling sigh. Without the *Kasten*'s poison in my veins, I felt completely at peace. Amelia was dead. Natalie and Deborah were alive. Despite the power it had offered me, I'd resisted long enough to destroy the *Kasten*. This was going to be a giant mess, but it was going to be someone else's job to clean it up.

I realized I was no longer sitting up. At some point, I'd fallen over and was now lying on my back on the cold concrete floor. A face appeared above mine, but I couldn't see who it was.

My heart stuttered in my chest. I didn't think I was breathing anymore, but that was all right. Maybe it was time to rest. Some part of me was breaking free.

Strong arms gathered me up and cradled me like a child. Something cool and delicious filled my mouth and ran down my chin. Vampire blood.

You must live, Alice. Drink from me. Charles's voice in my mind was urgent.

I couldn't obey. *Tired.*

I know. Drink.

...

I was too far gone to frame a thought.

Alice, you are not permitted to die.

Arrogant vampire. As if it was up to him.

I used my last bit of strength to comfort Charles with my mind. It was all I could do. Then I slipped away.

27

I WOKE IN AN UNFAMILIAR BED TO THE SOUND OF AN ARGUMENT.

"Your anger is unwarranted." Charles's voice was quiet and calm.

"It's been almost a week, Vaughan," Sean growled, also in undertone. It sounded like they were on the other side of the room. "A *week* you've kept me waiting to see her."

I could not open my eyes, or move, or speak. That should have frightened me, but strangely I felt entirely contented. I lay still and listened to the steady beeping of a heart monitor, the soft whirring sounds of machines, and the voices of Sean and Charles.

"Your presence would have done nothing to improve her condition," the vampire replied. "As you can see, she is comfortable and well cared for."

"Damn it, that's not the point and you know it," Sean snarled. "I had the right to see her as soon as you knew the accusations against me weren't true. The Were Ruling Council cleared me three days ago, and still you turned me away."

"I am aware of the council's findings, but Alice is under my protection here, and I had no intention of permitting you access to her until *I* was personally satisfied the allegations were false."

"And it took you three extra days to come to that conclusion?"

"If it had taken a year, I would not have risked her safety by allowing your presence one day too soon," Charles countered. "If you care for her as much as you claim, you would understand my diligence."

"I didn't come here to argue with you; I came to see Alice. If you'll leave, I'd like a few minutes with her."

A long silence. "Speak of nothing that will trouble her," Charles said at last. "If she can hear you, I would not have her be distressed."

"I will keep that in mind," Sean said icily.

A door closed. Footsteps approached my bed, and Sean took my hand. His skin felt almost painfully hot.

"You're so cold." Sean's voice was rough. He brushed hair back from my face, his fingers lingering on my cheek. "Damned vampires. I'll tell them to turn the heat up in here. You shouldn't be so cold."

Minutes passed. Sean rubbed my arms, warming me.

"I spoke to the nurse, and she said hearing familiar voices might help you find your way back," Sean said finally. "I don't know if you can hear me, but I'm here. I want you to know I found the source of the allegations that I planned to turn you into a werewolf. One of my wolves, Mike Holleman, wanted to take over my pack, but he knew there was no way he could win a challenge. He started spreading rumors that I planned to bite a woman to make her my mate, thinking I would be arrested or shot dead. It was one of Mike's buddies who told the bartender, Pete. After reviewing the evidence, the Were Ruling Council cleared me immediately of all charges, though apparently it took far longer to convince Vaughan that the whole thing was false."

Sean began rubbing my hands. "He wouldn't let me in to see you until now. I've been here every day for the last week, but this is the first time I've gotten to see you except through a video monitor. You're at Hawthorne's, but you probably guessed that."

Another pause.

"I have a lot more I need to say to you, but I'm going to wait until you're awake." Sean held my hand in both of his. "Allie, wake up. I know you're there. Just open your eyes, damn it." His voice was tight with frustration and grief. "Open your eyes and *look at me*."

My fingers moved. Sean froze.

It was nothing more than the slightest twitch, but I *moved*. I was elated.

"Allie, I can feel you," he breathed. "Do it again, baby. Squeeze my hand."

For a long moment, nothing happened. Sean's hope washed over me through the link that stretched between us.

My fingers tightened again.

The warmth of his happiness was a welcome feeling after my long, lonely wandering in the darkness. "Now I know you can hear me," Sean said softly. "It's time to wake up, baby. You've been asleep long enough."

I sent a blast of annoyance down our link and felt his surprise. "Don't call me baby," I murmured. My lips barely moved, and the sound was softer than a whisper, but his werewolf ears heard me.

Sean raised my hand to his lips and pressed a kiss to my knuckles. I managed a ghost of a smile before sleep took me away again.

The next time I woke up, it was the middle of the night, and there was a vampire in my bed.

"Alice?"

With effort, I rolled my head on the pillow to look at him in the moonlight spilling through my windows. Charles lay on his side, facing me. I noticed he wore a button-up shirt and khakis, and his feet were bare. I'd never seen him dressed so casually.

"Ch...Charles." My voice was hoarse from disuse.

"I am here, Alice. I feared you would wake during the day when I could not be with you, but Ms. Smith was here so that you were not alone. You were cared for at Hawthorne's until early this evening. Once your condition improved, I believed you would be more comfortable in your own home."

I frowned. "But...the wards?"

"Your ghost was able to adjust the wards to permit us to enter." Charles took my hand. "I am glad you are back with us."

"Glad...to be alive. How did you...find me?"

"The werewolf sensed the attack on you through your link. Since he was still in my custody at the time, he and Ms. Smith went to your house immediately and attempted to find out what had happened to you. They found your blood in your driveway, but you were gone. Maclin recognized Peter Eppright's scent from your previous meeting, but they had no idea where you had been taken. Once your ghost arrived, he was able to communicate with the werewolf and tell him of Ms. Newton's kidnapping. When I woke at sunset, I tasted the trace of your blood found at your home and attempted to locate you, but it was so degraded by then that beyond a general sense that you were on the east side of the city and alive, I was unsuccessful. The wards hiding you were too strong."

Charles tucked my hair behind my ear. "Maclin was driving around the area, trying to reach you through your link or catch your scent, and I was attempting to locate you when I felt you break one of the spells. I still could not sense your exact location, but we were close when you broke the blood ward. We arrived soon after, but it was almost too late."

His gaze was troubled. "You went into cardiac arrest. Maclin arrived and performed CPR. Once we resuscitated you, we brought you back to Hawthorne's for medical care."

"Thank you for taking care of me." It was getting easier to speak, thank goodness. "What have I missed?"

"The building where you were held was a site belonging to Browning Construction," Charles told me. "We removed everything belonging to you, Ms. Newton, and Ms. Newton's grandmother, and your ghost dispersed your magic trace. I arranged a fire that consumed the building and destroyed much of the evidence."

I stared at him in shock.

"At this time, the police and coroner's office believe Amelia Wharton sacrificed Browning, Eppright, and Kathy Adams as part of a blood magic ritual, then lost control of the power she had gathered and burned the building down, killing herself. The case has not been closed, but unless additional evidence surfaces, I believe your involvement will remain unknown."

"What about Deborah Mackey?"

"While I feel certain Ms. Newton can be relied upon not to divulge your secret, especially as she would then be implicating herself in Wharton's death, I doubted Mrs. Mackey could be trusted. I glamoured her, and she remembers nothing of knowing Wharton or going to the construction site that night. It was, I believe, the best course of action, besides leaving her to perish in the fire. Your ghost was most insistent you would not have permitted her to die."

"Malcolm was right about that," I said. "Enough people died there."

"Then I made the correct choice." Charles's brow furrowed. "A man by the name of John West has been making discreet inquiries about the fire. There is some concern, as West seems to suspect there were at least one or two other mages present at the ritual who are not accounted for among the dead. As your ghost dispersed all magic traces other than Wharton's, how he came to this conclusion is not clear, nor is his involvement in these events."

Slowly, with frequent pauses to catch my breath, I explained how I'd been taken from my house by Peter Eppright and Ray Browning, who Amelia Wharton was, what she was doing with the *Kasten*, and why John West was involved. When I described how Adelbert and the *Kasten* had attempted to take control of me, Charles's face grew even more grim.

By the time I finished the story, I was breathless and covered in a cold sweat. Who knew talking could be so exhausting?

Charles touched my face. "You must rest. Your strength will return."

"I'm a little surprised to be so weak. You saved me with your blood, didn't you?" When I woke the morning after being cut by window glass, I felt fully recovered; this time, I felt as wrung out as a dishrag.

"It took a significant amount of my blood just to save your life. You had a deep stab wound, significant blood loss, a punctured and collapsed lung, first- and second-degree burns, a skull fracture, a severe concussion, a fractured wrist, broken ribs—"

"Broken ribs?" I didn't remember that.

"From chest compressions."

"Oh."

"I was concerned too much of my blood might have long-term effects. We used primarily human blood transfusions once the major injuries were healed, which is why you are weak."

I tilted my head to look at him. "What long-term effects were you worried about?"

"At first, I feared you might become a dhampir, since you had already consumed my blood just the night before. Once that danger was past, it was possible more blood could create a permanent telepathic bond between us. You might be able to broadcast thoughts and emotions as well, and there would surely be a dramatic increase in your libido."

I blinked at that. "Well, I definitely want to skip the first three, but that last thing might not be a complete disaster."

With a cool fingertip, Charles traced a line down my forehead and nose to my lips and chin. "A *dramatic* increase," he repeated.

I spent a few moments thinking about what would constitute a *dramatic* increase. "Well, it's just as well, I suppose. I wouldn't want to go around wanting to f—"

I was abruptly silenced by his mouth on mine.

Charles's lips were as cool as the rest of him, but the kiss was anything but chilly. His hunger was its own warmth. I'd never kissed a vampire before, but he didn't taste any different from any other man.

Heat blazed through me as my body responded to his touch, and I moaned. If there was anything in the world I wanted more than Charles at that moment, I didn't know what it was.

Through the haze of desire, I felt a strange sensation, as if something was nagging at me. Even as my body was responding to the feeling of Charles's hands on me, I was starting to realize something was terribly wrong. Charles was dangerous. I didn't want him touching me, or kissing me. My body was betraying me because of the blood he'd shared with me. My brain screamed to get away, even as I pulled at his clothes and dug my nails into his flesh. *No*, I thought desperately, as his cool hand slid under my pajama top. *No, I don't want this*. If he heard my thoughts, he ignored them.

Charles's blood might be powerful, but there was one emotion in me that was stronger. Fear of being victimized was at the core of my being. It rose in me like a tidal wave and broke his influence.

I took a ragged breath and looked up at the vampire. His eyes were silver. "Charles, stop."

"You are afraid, Alice." Charles's voice was low, almost a purr. "It is arousing."

"Well, it's *not* arousing to me," I snapped. Anger was clearing the fog of desire away. "Take your hands off me. I'm not thinking clearly. You know that what you're doing isn't fair."

"I never claimed to be fair, my dear," he said, lowering his head.

"But you've always been honorable," I said quickly, before his lips could touch mine. "There's nothing honorable in taking advantage of a woman whose judgment is impaired, or ignoring her when she says no. And have you forgotten my alliance with Sean's pack? An assault on me is an assault on the pack."

Charles chuckled, flashing his fangs. "Oh, yes, your alliance. 'Well played,' as they say." He rose smoothly from the bed and tucked in his shirt, stepping into a pair of Italian loafers. I wrapped my arms around myself.

Charles crouched at the side of the bed, his face level with mine. "Soon you will come to me," he said, and his voice made me shiver. "You may say what you feel is because of the blood I shared with you, but we both know it is not true. You fear me, but you desire me as well." He stood and looked down at me. "Sweet Alice," he murmured.

He moved to the bedroom door and opened it, then vanished into the darkness.

I slept for a few more hours and woke just before dawn, feeling surprisingly clearheaded and alert. Instead of getting up, however, I lay in bed and tried not to think too much about Amelia Wharton and the horrors I'd witnessed at the construction site.

Though I tried to distract myself, I kept coming back to John West. The thought of West digging around made me nervous. I wasn't sure how he had been able to tell there had been any other mages at the construction site once it had burned down, unless he was able to sense the magic Malcolm used to remove my blood and trace. If it was Malcolm's magic he was tracking, that was still very dangerous since Malcolm was bound to me and I carried some of his magic within me.

Not long after sunrise, I thought I heard a car pull into my driveway. When the engine shut off and a car door slammed, I rolled out of bed and went to the window. I recognized the silver Mercedes even before I saw who was walking up the sidewalk.

Sean.

I froze, my hand on the curtain. After he'd spoken to me while I was in a coma, I knew we needed to talk about where things stood between us. I'd felt his truthfulness when he said he'd never intended to turn me into a werewolf. There was still the matter of him being an alpha in need of a mate, though, and the metaphysical link he'd created without my permission.

I'd planned on talking to Sean about all that when I was ready, but it looked like he was done waiting for me to call. Never mind I'd only been out of a coma for all of—I glanced at the clock—five hours.

Sean looked up and saw me at the window. A surprisingly overt parade of emotions moved across his face: relief, anger, determination.

I could claim I was exhausted and ask him to come back another day, but I didn't want to be a coward about this. It wasn't like the conversation would get any easier if I put it off.

I heaved a sigh and held up a finger, indicating I would be down in a minute. Sean nodded and pointed at the porch.

As I was debating whether to put on a robe or get dressed, my phone rang. Someone had plugged it in and left it on the nightstand. The screen said *Bryan Smith*. "Hello?"

"Do you require assistance?" Bryan's voice was a deep rumble.

I frowned.

"Alice? Do you need us to come to your house?"

"What? No, why would I?"

"Sean Maclin is at your house," Bryan said.

I glared at the phone as if the enforcer could see me. "How the hell do you know that? Are you people *watching* me?"

A pause. "Mr. Vaughan is concerned about your safety. We are monitoring your visitors."

My face grew hot. "Well, you can tell *Mr. Vaughan* when he wakes up that this surveillance had better be gone by tomorrow. And no, I do *not* require assistance. I can take care of my own damn self."

I threw the phone on my bed in disgust and stomped over to my dresser for clothes, then stuck my feet into flip-flops and braided my hair. Good enough. Anyone who showed up unexpectedly at my house at the crack of dawn got what they got.

I yanked my bedroom door open and walked straight into Malcolm; like, literally *into* Malcolm.

We both yelped and jumped back. I shuddered and rubbed my arms. "Son of a bitch!"

"Sorry!" Malcolm flitted around the upstairs hallway. "Damn it, sorry. I was about to tell you Sean is here."

"Yeah, I know. I'm going down to talk to him." I walked around him and headed for the stairs.

"Are you sure?" Malcolm trailed after me.

"Yes, I'm sure!"

"Jeez. You're really grouchy when you wake up from a coma."

I sighed. "Sorry." I explained about Bryan's phone call.

Malcolm did not look happy. "The vampire's spying on you, huh? What are you going to do about that?"

"First off, get someone in here to check for hidden cameras and microphones, that's for damn sure." I stomped down the stairs. "And you are going to fix those wards so Charles and his people can't get back in here."

The ghost followed me. "I'll do that right now. You want backup with the werewolf?"

I squared my shoulders. "No, I want privacy. We have to get this over with."

"Okay, Alice. I'll be downstairs. Summon me if you need me." Malcolm disappeared through the basement door.

Before I chickened out, I marched to the door, opened it, and came face-to-face with Sean.

He wore a faded Rolling Stones T-shirt that stretched across his broad chest, jeans that fit very well, and sneakers. "Hello, Allie."

I hadn't seen him—not in human form—since I left him standing in Hawthorne's more than a week ago. It felt like eons since that night, and yet, when I looked at him, I felt a surge of something so powerful that it hit me like a physical blow.

To cover my reaction, I moved over to the porch swing and sat down. That made me think of the night I'd been burned by Natalie's magic, and how he'd held me on the swing while I was unconscious. I scrubbed my face with my hands.

"Allie?"

I peeked through my fingers. Sean was crouched in front of me. "What's going on?" he asked me.

I blew out a breath. "I don't know, Sean. I really don't. I thought you wanted to turn me into a werewolf. I watched three people get their throats cut, and I was helpless to do anything about it. I damn near died trying to save the city from a crazy woman with a box full of mage blood. I was in a coma for a week. Charles has people watching my house. It's a lot to process."

Sean stared at me. "Well, when you put it that way, it *does* sound like you've got a lot on your mind," he said finally.

Despite everything, that made me smile.

He put his hands on my knees, his eyes turning serious. "We need to talk."

"I know. But first, thank you for saving my life at the construction site."

Sean looked grim. "When the blood ward fell, I was several miles away. When I got there, Bryan was holding you and Vaughan was trying to get you to drink his blood, but you were already...." He paused. "I hoped you would use our link to reach out to me and tell me where you were, but you never tried."

I was startled. "It never occurred to me," I confessed. "I doubt it would have worked through the blood ward, anyway, but you got there in time to save my life." I hesitated, then covered his hands with mine and squeezed. "I heard you speaking to me while I was asleep. Thank you for not giving up on me. It just took me a while to find my way back."

"So you heard what I told you about Mike?"

"I heard you. Are you going to have any more problems with this guy?"

"No. He's dead."

I blinked.

Sean's face was hard. "I confronted him the day after the construction site murders. He challenged me and lost. Two of his buddies stepped up after him. They're dead too." He looked at me. "Does that bother you?"

"No." I'd seen my share of challenges when I was part of my grandfather's cabal. I remembered how Sean had looked in wolf form, and my mind conjured up an image of him fighting another wolf to the death. It would have been bloody and vicious. His werewolf physiology meant he healed quickly, but three fights was a lot, even for an alpha. "I'm glad you're all right."

Sean took my hands. "You must have spent some time around a pack at some point," he said, his eyes searching my face. "Most people aren't this calm when they find out they're alone with someone who recently killed three people."

I didn't comment on the first part of his statement. "You killed them in a fair challenge," I said, raising my shoulder in a half shrug. "They were trying to kill you. I know what it means to be an alpha." I'd assumed Sean had fought and killed numerous times as a wolf; alphas didn't get—or keep—that position by popular vote. "Mike gave you no choice. He sealed his own fate when he tried to get you killed."

"I tried to tell you it was a lie."

I shifted uncomfortably. "I know."

Sean pinned me with his stare. "I walked through Natalie's house wards when you called me. I helped Malcolm save your life. I held you and kept you from hurting yourself when you were delirious and hallucinating."

I'd hallucinated after being burned? I didn't remember that at all. Neither he nor Malcolm had ever said anything to me about it.

While I was still trying to wrap my brain around that news, Sean continued. "I did all those things because you are worth it, and I wouldn't hesitate to do them again. I let you set all the limits and call all the shots while we were working. You say you know what it means to be an alpha, but I'm not sure you know how difficult it was to let someone else have that much control. Believe me when I say that I have never done anything like that before." His gaze was fierce. "Before I met you, I never *wanted* to do anything like that for anyone who wasn't part of my pack. And despite everything we went through and everything I've done, you never gave me a chance."

I said nothing. What could I say? He was right.

Sean wasn't going to let me get away with silence. "Didn't I deserve the benefit of the doubt, Allie?"

"Yes, you did. I'm sorry I didn't give you the chance to explain. I was so angry that I couldn't think."

"I can understand that." Sean squeezed my hands. "My guess is that up to now, you've probably known a lot more betrayal and lies than people you could trust."

He wasn't wrong about that either, but that wasn't a topic I was interested in discussing.

Sean rose, then sat on the porch swing next to me. "What happened between you and Vaughan last night, after you woke up?"

I looked at him.

"Did he hurt you?" When I didn't immediately respond, Sean's eyes turned bright gold. "He did," he snarled. "Tell me."

"He didn't hurt me. He kissed me and...wanted more. I said no, and he left."

"It was more than that," Sean said flatly. "I felt you through our link earlier. That's one of the reasons I came over."

I scowled. "Were you eavesdropping on me?"

Sean shook his head. "Not on purpose. I had the link wide open while you were in the coma, trying to sense you. I closed it when Adri Smith texted me that you were awake, but my shields must have gone down while I was asleep. I thought at first it was a dream, but then I realized what I was sensing. I felt your desire, and then I felt your terror. I knew you were with Vaughan. I was throwing clothes on to come over here when the fear subsided."

"He healed me with his blood. I wasn't thinking clearly, and I asked him to leave."

"But not before he scared you so badly that I felt it all the way across town. He didn't want to take no for an answer, did he?"

"I took care of it. It's over. I don't want a repeat of what happened over here a week ago."

Sean's anger prickled on my skin. "The vampire and I have unfinished business," he informed me.

My stomach lurched. "He was wrong about you and your supposed plan to infect me. Please don't—"

"That's not all of it," Sean said. "I'd have confronted him earlier, but he had you until last night and I'm not going to jeopardize you again. I underestimated Vaughan's ruthlessness last time. I won't repeat that mistake."

"What do you mean?" I asked with a frown.

"Vaughan deliberately pushed me through your window."

I stared at him.

"I had no intention of letting our...disagreement endanger you. I was trying to take the fight into the yard. Vaughan maneuvered us in front of the window, then pushed me through it." Sean's eyes became amber fire. "Even if he was just trying to use your wards to injure me, he *knew* you were standing right there. I don't know if he wanted you injured or if he simply had no regard for your safety, but I can tell you that he did it on purpose."

I tried to remember the scene the night Charles confronted Sean at my house. Sean *had* come through the window first, but when I replayed it in my head, the wolf's body had its back to the window. Charles would have been in position to take the fight through the window and into my house.

My thoughts raced. Why would Charles have wanted to injure me? He'd implied Sean was responsible for my wounds, thus further driving the wedge between us, and he'd held Sean in custody, effectively preventing Sean from warning me. Charles had offered to heal me that night, knowing his blood would influence me. I'd certainly lowered my guard around him after that. He'd played me like a violin, and I hadn't even realized it.

Cold fingers closed around my heart. Charles had several opportunities to taste my blood: before the burner spell turned it to ash, from my driveway after Ray Browning hit me on the head, when I'd been bleeding at the construction site, and then while I lay defenseless in a coma. If Charles had bitten me while I slept, I wouldn't know; vampires didn't leave fang marks unless they intended to brand their cattle.

In any case, if he'd tasted my blood, he knew I was no mid-level mage. There was a good chance my identity as Alice Worth had been irrevocably compromised, at least as far as Charles was concerned.

There was little I could do about it at this point except stay the hell away from him and make sure his prediction about us being lovers never came true.

"Allie, I'm sorry. It's my fault. I should have protected you better."

"It's not your job to protect me." My voice sounded mechanical, flat. "I knew he was a threat. If it's anyone's fault, it's mine."

"If he ever touches you again, I'll kill him," Sean stated.

"If he ever touches me again without my permission, you won't have to." I spent more than twenty years belonging to a cabal, with no control over my own body, and nearly died to regain my autonomy. I'd be damned if I'd let Charles, or anyone, take that away from me again.

We looked at each other.

"You mean that," Sean said.

"I do."

Sean didn't ask how it was possible I could kill Charles; he simply accepted it as fact. Maybe I shouldn't have been surprised by his confidence in me, but I was.

I took a deep breath. "I have a couple of things I have to say."

"Say them."

"You're an alpha werewolf. You have to have a werewolf mate, and soon, or you could lose your pack. I'm not a werewolf, and I never will be. There's no future for us together."

"My mate doesn't have to be a werewolf."

I felt like my world had just tilted ninety degrees.

"Traditionally, yes, the alpha pair are both shifters, but there's no written law that says that has to be the case. In fact, there are a number of alphas with nonshifter mates. Several are mages. It's not unprecedented."

I looked him in the eye and lowered my shields to feel the link that stretched between us. It was thin and fragile but still strong enough to sense him. "Did you seek me out because I'm a mage and you want a mage for a mate?"

Sean met my gaze and didn't blink. "No."

Truth. I relaxed minutely.

Sean continued. "I saw you at the bar, and I thought you were the most beautiful woman there. I wanted to be with you for the night. By the next morning, I knew I wanted more than just one night."

Truth. Now I had to ask the hard questions.

"You created a link between us without my permission. Just when I thought I could trust you this much"—I held up my thumb and index finger a centimeter apart —"you tried to make me your mate without me knowing. That's not something I'm going to be able to get past, not very easily. Why did you do it?"

Sean rubbed his face. When he looked back at me, his eyes were troubled. "I didn't intend to form a link with you. When we were together here that last night, it felt like you were in my head. I don't know why it happened; I must have lowered my shields and reached out to you without realizing I'd done it. My wolf recognized a strong female he thought would be a good mate and created the link. I sensed something new in my head, like a door opening up, but I didn't understand what it meant, not until later that night. Suddenly, I could feel your emotions, and then I realized what had happened."

Truth.

I leaned back in the swing and stared at him. Acting on instinct, I had lowered my shields to feel closer to Sean during the most intimate moments of making love. I should have known that with magic and metaphysics, there could always be unexpected outcomes. His wolf had simply responded to my presence in Sean's mind.

I felt like someone had kicked me in the stomach.

"I screwed up not telling you about the link the minute I figured it out," Sean said. "I don't know if you'll believe me, but I was going to tell you as soon as we got back here from the bar."

I barely heard him over the rush of guilt I sensed through the link. I'd decided not to tell him at the time about lowering my shields, worried he would be upset I had seen some of his memories. My instinct was always not to volunteer information that could be used against me. I'd learned that the hard way. I wasn't in the cabal anymore, though, and Sean was not my grandfather. I swallowed hard.

"Allie? What are you thinking?"

"It's my fault, Sean," I blurted out. "The link is my fault."

"What? How is it your fault?"

"When I...." I cleared my throat. "When we were having sex, I lowered my shields.

I wanted to feel what you were feeling. I saw little flashes of memories, of you as a wolf running through the woods at night. Nothing specific—just glimpses, really—and I saw myself through your eyes for a few seconds."

Sean looked stunned. "Why didn't you tell me?"

"I thought you'd be angry that I accidentally read your mind." I looked away. "I should have said something. It's just...."

To my surprise, Sean took my hands in his. "Thank you, Allie."

Confused, I frowned at him. "For what?"

"For being honest and telling me about what you saw. I wish you'd told me then, but I can understand why you didn't. Now at least I know why it happened."

I was silent.

"Alice?" he prodded.

"I don't get it," I said.

"You don't get what?"

"What you could possibly see in me."

Sean stared at me.

"I had sex with you, then I kicked you to the curb with no intention of ever calling you. After you nearly killed yourself getting through Natalie's house wards to save me, I made you work for the dubious privilege of a date with me. Then I dumped you like last week's garbage the second someone told me something about you that I immediately believed, instead of giving you the benefit of the doubt, or letting you explain yourself. I blamed you for a link I caused, and I almost let myself get seduced by a vampire whose ulterior motives have ulterior motives. I'm an asshole *and* an idiot."

Sean said nothing.

I kept going. "I'm rude, secretive, and stubborn, and I have massive trust issues."

Sean waited. "Are you done?" he asked me finally.

I thought about it. "Honestly, I'm a mess, but you know that by now, which is why I have *no idea*—"

For the second time today, I was interrupted by a kiss.

This time, however, my desire wasn't tempered by fear—only by my uncertainty over why Sean Maclin, alpha werewolf, wanted to put up with me and my shit. It was not enough, however, to make me want to stop, not even close. And if Charles's people were watching, well, so much the better. I hoped they reported it all back to him, every last detail.

Sean pulled back, his eyes flashing.

"What?" I asked, breathless.

"I can feel your confusion. You really don't know how incredible you are, do you?"

I scoffed.

Sean leaned forward until his forehead touched mine, his eyes glowing softly. "You are brave, strong, beautiful, and *literally* magical."

I snorted inelegantly. "One out of four."

"*Four* out of four," he corrected me. "I'm an alpha. We're always right."

I laughed.

"What now?" he asked.

I thought about it. "Why don't you come inside. I still have my turntable and my couch. We can listen to side two of *Dark Side of the Moon* and figure out where we go from here."

Sean kissed the tip of my nose. "Sounds like a plan."

28

THE NEXT MORNING, I WAS SITTING IN NATALIE'S LIVING ROOM WITH A CAT IN MY lap and another on the arm of the chair. My client was curled up on the couch across from me. We both had mugs of tea.

Natalie told me how Betty's lawyer, William Benson, showed up on her doorstep with Amelia, who tore apart the house wards and took her out with a spell just before she could get to the safety of the library.

"That's what we figured," I said. "Malcolm and I both felt when your wards went down, but by the time we got to your house, you were already gone."

Natalie rubbed her arms. "I don't remember anything until I woke up tied to the table. I could see Amelia standing over you, and Peter, Ray, and Kathy were dead. Deborah was frozen, like a statue, and there was blood everywhere. I was in such a daze, I barely remember getting myself untied."

"You were incredible," I told her sincerely. "If it weren't for you, we'd both probably be dead. Nice work with the pipe, by the way. You've got a hell of a swing."

"I paid for my art history degree with a softball scholarship," she said, wrapping her arms around her knees. "Never thought it would save my life."

Benson had vanished without a trace; what Amelia had done with him, I had no idea. His disappearance had been in the local news, but so far, no one had connected him with the construction site murders.

"How are you doing with all of this?" I asked.

Natalie blew out a breath. "I'm doing okay today," she said. "Sometimes it's hard to believe that I actually...killed someone." She swallowed hard. "But she murdered three people, and she was about to kill you and me too. I know I didn't have any choice. I've been talking about it with Malcolm, and that helps."

Malcolm had been spending a lot of time at her house lately. Considering what Natalie had been through in the past couple of weeks, having a ghost as her new best friend seemed strangely appropriate.

Natalie shifted on the couch. "The hardest part was lying to the detective who came by. I hated to lie, but the vampire, Mr. Vaughan, explained it was best if I said I didn't know anything about Amelia or what happened."

The more I heard about how Natalie was dealing with everything, the more impressed I was with her newfound moxie. The Natalie who sat in front of me today was very different from the one I'd met two weeks ago at Janie's Downtown Café. Since learning about her grandmother's magic and her own abilities, and especially after what she'd done to save our lives at the construction site, Natalie had toughened up considerably.

"I have some good news for you," I told her. "I'm going to be interviewing a couple of potential mentors for you in the next few days. With any luck, I'll find someone to help you with your magic soon."

"I'm glad," Natalie said. "Are you sure you can't do it? I'd be so much more comfortable with you."

"I would if I could, but I don't have fire magic, and you really need someone who has the same kind of magic you do. I'll stay in touch, though, and keep track of how your training is going." I smiled at her. "I'm excited for you. I look forward to seeing you show off your skills."

It occurred to me then that Natalie had never gotten to see real magic up close; she'd seen it almost kill me twice, and Amelia killed three of her relatives to get more of it. For her, it was still a scary unknown. I hesitated, then asked, "Do you want to come over to my house sometime this week and see some cool magic?"

"Sure!" She lit up and looked at me hopefully. "Can you show me something now?"

I held out my right hand, palm up, and a tendril of bright green flame spiraled up. Natalie gasped in wonder. I spun the single flame into a small fireball, then blew gently, sending it floating across toward her.

She watched it move, her eyes wide with awe. "Will I be able to do this?"

"That's earth magic. You have fire magic. You'll be able to do that, but your fire will be hot instead of cold." I crooked my fingers and the fireball zipped back to me. I let it grow until it consumed my entire hand. We sat and watched the bright green flames dance.

"That's incredible," Natalie said. "It's so beautiful."

I looked into the flames. "Yes, it is."

Finally, I drew the magic back into my hand, and the fire went out.

"How long before I can do things like that?" Natalie asked.

"It will take a while," I told her honestly. "Learning control takes time and hard work, but children learn to control their magic. You will too. I'll find you the best teacher I can."

"Thank you, Alice. For everything."

"You're welcome." I got up and went to the kitchen.

As I was standing at the sink rinsing out my mug, I glanced out the window.

And froze.

A familiar black BMW was parked across the street. Inside, behind the dark-tinted glass, I saw a single figure, sitting motionless, as if watching the house.

"Shit," I breathed.

The car glided smoothly away from the curb and drove past Natalie's house, only to make a three-point turn and come back. I moved away from the window as the BMW rolled slowly past my car, as if John West wanted a good look at it. Then the car took off down the street, paused at the stop sign, and disappeared around the corner.

A few days later, I was sitting on my couch in the middle of the afternoon, holding a mug of coffee that had long since gone cold and staring blankly at my empty living room.

For days, I'd barely slept. Nightmares left me restless and prowling the house at night. I'd gotten so crabby from lack of sleep that Malcolm had taken refuge at Natalie's house. I was letting my voice mail take my calls. I had two messages from Adri, three from Sean, two from Natalie, and a couple from my office line that were probably potential clients. They sat untouched in my inbox.

At a little after two, I heard heavy footsteps on my porch and someone knocked on my front door.

I frowned and made no move to get up. I wasn't expecting visitors and had no desire to talk to anyone. Besides, I hadn't showered or even brushed my hair and I was wearing pajamas and a robe.

More knocking, much louder this time. It sounded like someone's fist. My frown deepened. "Go away," I muttered. Apparently, whoever it was couldn't take a hint.

My phone rang. Listlessly, I picked it up and glanced at the screen: *Adri Smith*. Damn it, were they still watching my house? I thought I'd made it clear I didn't appreciate being spied on.

With a snarl that would have made a werewolf proud, I swiped at the phone's screen, rejecting the call. I stomped to the front door and peered through the peephole.

When I saw who was on my porch, I froze.

"Ms. Worth, please open the door." The voice was calm, with an authoritative tone that set my teeth on edge.

Reluctantly, I turned the deadbolt and opened the door.

If Special Agent Lake was taken aback by my dishevelment, or the fact I was wearing pajamas at two o'clock in the afternoon, he didn't let on. His eyes swept over me analytically before meeting my gaze. "Good afternoon, Ms. Worth," he said, reaching into his inside jacket pocket for his identification. "I'm sure you remember me."

"I do, but I'd like to see your credentials anyway." The last time he'd shown them to me, I'd had a flashlight in my face and hadn't been able to read them.

Lake flipped open the leather wallet and held it up. The top section contained the SPEMA seal and next to it, his photo and name: Special Agent Trent Lake. Below was his shield. I looked at the picture for a moment, then studied the man as he returned his ID to the inside pocket his suit jacket.

No coat today; it was warm and sunny, and he wore a dark gray suit with a blue tie that matched his eyes. Up close and in the light of day, I could see a faint scar on his chin and another that had split his left eyebrow. In my bare feet, I felt dwarfed by his size.

I stood in my doorway and regarded him with a distinctly unwelcoming stare. "What brings you to my door, Agent Lake?"

Lake gave me a smile that was surprisingly charming. "Can we go inside?"

"Nope, not unless you have a warrant."

The smile faded. "I'm not an enemy, Ms. Worth."

That was debatable. "You're not a friend, either." I stepped out onto the porch and pulled the door closed behind me. "Where is Agent Parker today?"

"At a crime scene." He was watching me closely. "The local police have called us in to help with the investigation into the murders at the Browning Construction site."

I probably deserved an Oscar for the mildly interested expression I gave him. "I heard about that. Really awful. Mages like this Amelia Walker give all of us a bad name."

"Wharton," Lake corrected me.

His gaze was intense, but I didn't blink. "Oh. Wharton. Right." I shrugged. "I'd never heard of her before she was in the news. I thought I read somewhere that she was from Portland."

"That's what it looks like. You're sure you didn't know her?"

I frowned, feigning puzzlement. "I'm sure," I assured him. "I don't know anybody in Portland. Plus, I stay away from blood mages. They're dangerous."

Lake stared at me, saying nothing.

I raised my eyebrows and leaned back against the doorframe. "Any particular reason why you'd think I'd know a blood mage from Portland?"

"I wondered, since the victims were all related to your client, Natalie Newton." I saw a flash in Lake's eyes that said, *Gotcha*.

I blinked at him innocently. *You've got nothing, Lake*. "That is true. Both Natalie and I were very surprised—and horrified—by what happened to her uncles and aunt. I'm sure Natalie told you she never met or heard of Amelia Wharton. Neither had I, until I saw it on the news." I tilted my head. "How did you know Natalie was one of my clients?"

"We've been speaking to members of the extended family, gathering background information on the victims. When I met with Ms. Newton yesterday, I remembered seeing you together at Janie's Café downtown, and she told me she'd hired you to put wards around her home."

"Ah," I said, mentally applauding Natalie for successfully bluffing Lake. "You've got a good memory for faces, Agent Lake."

"It comes in handy in investigative work. As a private detective, I'm sure you agree." The smile was back. If I didn't know it was nothing more than an interrogation technique, I might have been fooled by it.

"Oh, definitely." I regarded him. "I'm sorry I can't help you with your current investigation. I didn't know Amelia Wharton."

"But you *did* know Natalie's aunts and uncles," Lake said.

I strongly suspected he was fishing, trying to catch me off guard. I declined to bite the hook. "I spoke to a couple of them, very briefly, while I was looking for the person who had attempted to enter Natalie's home without her knowledge. I wouldn't say I 'know' any of them."

"So you spoke to the victims?" Lake pounced on that. "Why didn't you mention that?"

"I only spoke to Peter Eppright and Kathy Adams for a few minutes. Once I determined they hadn't gotten into her home, I had no further contact with them."

"How did you know they hadn't been in her house?"

"Interested in my investigative techniques, Agent Lake?"

"Simply curious."

I shrugged. "It was rather straightforward, actually. Whoever crossed the wards left magic trace behind. No one in Natalie's family has magic, so it was easy enough to rule them out. We've suspended the investigation pending any new information." I met his gaze without flinching. He might suspect my involvement, but there was zero evidence tying me to the construction site. As long as I kept my cool, he had nothing.

Lake reached into his pocket. I tensed, but he only pulled out a card and handed it to me. "If you think of anything that might help us, please give me a call. My cell number is on there."

I tucked the card into the pocket of my robe. "I'll certainly do that," I lied.

We looked at each other. His gaze was sharp. Mine was guileless.

Finally, Lake squared his shoulders. "All right. Have a good afternoon." He turned to leave.

Just as I reached for the doorknob, Lake turned back, one foot on the porch steps. "Oh, one more question."

His casual tone immediately put me on alert. "Yes?"

"When I ran into you at the café, I noticed your earrings. Where did you get them? I remember thinking my sister would love a pair like that."

I shrugged. "I made them."

"I see." Lake dug in his pocket and pulled something out. "Did they look something like this?" He held out his hand, stepping back up onto the porch so I could see what he was holding.

My earring.

It was sooty, the wire bent, the crystal cracked and dark, but I recognized it just the same. Apparently, so had Lake.

I remembered how when I came to at the construction site, all my jewelry was gone, removed by either Amelia or Peter Eppright. Charles had told me they'd taken everything of mine and Natalie's from the crime scene before the fire, but it appeared they'd missed at least one piece of my jewelry, and Lake had found it.

I frowned and looked at the earring. "Sort of, but mine had little beads at the top. Not all crystal jewelry is the same, you know."

Lake's gaze was razor-sharp. "I'm pretty sure this is yours, Ms. Worth. Guess where I found it."

"It's not my earring," I told him flatly. "I have mine."

"Then let's see them."

I narrowed my eyes. "Agent Lake, I don't have to show you anything." I did have another pair, actually—not exactly the same, but very similar—but I would be damned if this man was going to bully me into getting them.

He shifted his feet, planting himself more firmly in place on my porch. "Show me your earrings and I'll go."

Despite our height difference, I refused to be intimidated. "You'll go anyway, since you don't have a warrant."

We stared at each other.

"Ms. Worth, I'm starting to think you know something about what happened to those people."

"Agent Lake, I'm starting to think you're grasping at straws," I countered. "That is *not* my earring, I have *never* been to that construction site, and I *do not know* anything more than what I have told you."

It occurred to me then that Lake having my earring in his pocket wasn't exactly procedure. If he was treating it as evidence, it should be in an evidence bag, its chain of custody clearly preserved. It looked more like he'd found the earring while poking around in the debris and decided to do a little independent investigation.

The corners of my mouth twitched when realization dawned. If he told anyone how he knew me, it might jeopardize the official story of how Scott Grierson, the half-demon "Full Moon Stalker," ended up dead in the park with a knife through his eye. Lake and Parker had already taken credit for bringing an end to Grierson's killing spree; there was no room in their tidy narrative for my involvement. So Agent Lake was in a bit of a pickle: he suspected it was my earring but couldn't tell anyone why he thought that. No one would believe he remembered it from a chance encounter between strangers in a café weeks ago.

I met Lake's gaze. "I'm sorry I don't have any information that might help you. I'm sure Amelia Wharton was nothing more than a sick, delusional woman who murdered three people in some bizarre blood magic ritual and then died when she lost control of it and brought the building down on herself."

Lake seemed to be weighing my words. "It would help our investigation a great deal to have corroboration from someone who was there," he said finally. "If someone was merely a witness—or an intended victim—there would be no reason for that person to fear prosecution, or even have their name released." His piercing blue gaze took in the shadows under my eyes, my tangled hair, and the robe I'd thrown on over my pajamas because actually getting dressed seemed like too much effort.

I didn't like the way he was looking at me, as if he could see the nightmares in my head. My expression grew cold. "I'm sure it would, but just looking at the scene on the news, it seems unlikely anyone got out of there alive."

"Or at least, nobody got out unscathed." Lake glanced meaningfully at the burned remains of my earring.

"Well, it's been lovely chatting with you." I turned toward my front door. "Best of luck in your investigation."

"I know you were there, Ms. Worth."

I spun back around.

Lake held up his hand to stop my angry retort. "I may not be able to prove it yet, and maybe there's nothing more to what happened than, as you say, a woman who sacrificed three victims and lost control of the ritual. But that's twice now you've been in the middle of something big here in the city. I think it would be in my best interest to keep an eye on you from now on."

"I'm just a private investigator. I'm nobody." My heart pounded so loudly, I feared he could hear it. "I'm not worth your time."

"I disagree. I think you are. See you around, Alice Worth."

With that threat hanging in the air, Lake turned and headed down the steps toward the unmarked black SUV parked at the curb, tucking my earring back into his pocket as he walked.

I went inside, slammed the door, and locked it. Then I thumped my forehead against the doorframe and took a deep, shaky breath.

See you around, Alice Worth.

Fantastic.

THE END

Thank you for reading! Did you enjoy?

Please Add Your Review! And turn the page for bonus novella, BLOOD MONEY, in the Alice Worth series!

BLOOD MONEY

BONUS NOVELLA

PROLOGUE

BECAUSE SHE OFTEN FOUND HERSELF WORKING LATE, ATTORNEY CHRISTINE FOREMAN took care to park in the well-lit parking garage next to her office building, though it cost an arm and a leg compared to other options in the area. As the daughter of a cop, she knew to always be alert and aware of her surroundings, even checking under her car before approaching it and never letting her guard down for even a moment, especially when preparations for the next day's hearings kept her in the office past ten. She had belts in both jiu-jitsu and aikido and had always been the sort to punch first and ask questions later.

Which was why when the man attacked her from behind, she was ready.

She heard running footsteps just before he struck, giving her enough time to twist in his grasp and jam a stun gun into his side and pull the trigger. He grunted and stiffened, and she had a moment to be grateful she'd been carrying her weapon out and ready, despite teasing by coworkers and years of late-night walks like this one that had been entirely uneventful.

And then he ripped the stun gun from her grip, crushed it with one hand, and bit down hard on her neck.

The pain was excruciating. Christine screamed and drove her elbow into the attacker's gut with all her strength. When he didn't react, she clawed at him like a wild animal, gouging his face, hands, and arms with her nails, but he didn't seem to notice. His arms, hard as iron, crushed her against his body, making it difficult to breathe. The pain intensified and she felt a strange pulling sensation where he was biting her.

Realization was slow in coming, but as her head buzzed and he dragged her down to the concrete next to her car, still gnawing and sucking at her throat, Christine finally put two and two together.

A vampire.

Her screams grew thin and gurgling and her arms were heavy, but still she fought. Nothing she did seemed to affect him in any way. All she could see of him was longish dark hair and his eyes, which were glowing bright red. She tried to remember if she'd ever heard of a vampire with red eyes, but it was becoming increasingly difficult to think or move.

She pushed feebly at the vampire's shoulders. "Stop, please," she pleaded.

The pain faded, replaced by a wonderfully warm feeling. Thinking he'd released her, she murmured, "Thank you."

The lights in the parking garage dimmed. How strange, Christine thought. The lights were supposed to stay on until morning. Surely it wasn't dawn yet. And where was Dan, the security guard who patrolled the garage? Had he become a victim too?

Dimly, she felt another pull at her neck and realized the vampire was still drinking, but she was no longer angry or afraid. Her hands slid from his arms and fell to her sides.

Christine thought of her parents, both of whom had been gone for years. She supposed she'd see them soon.

She thought about Daniel, her fiancé. She'd once thought she loved him, but in the last few months, she'd become increasingly aware he would never love her as much as he loved money. She'd considered breaking off their engagement, though it would make her brother furious. Alex had pushed her at Daniel to begin with, seeing the potential benefit in forging a connection between their families and businesses. Now there would be no marriage. She was surprised to feel no regret about that. It was possible she'd only ever agreed to the engagement to make Alex happy—not that he was, or had ever been really happy.

Deep in her gut, something began to burn—something that felt like a ferocious hunger. Christine couldn't remember ever feeling so hungry before in her life. She'd canceled dinner plans with Alex in order to work late.

What a strange time to remember I missed dinner, she thought absently. The hunger grew, even as her vision faded.

She thought about Alex.

Her brother despised all supes, but he'd always reserved a special level of hatred for vampires. And now his own sister had been attacked by one.

Alex, Christine thought as darkness descended.

Hungry, some other part of her brain said.

That was her last coherent thought for a very long time.

1

It was the perfect night for a hunt.

In the moonlight, the blood trail looked almost purple-black and nearly invisible on the asphalt. It led from a broken security gate, across a small parking lot, and down a narrow passageway between two warehouses. Smeared bloody handprints marked the walls, as if someone had been staggering as they walked.

A tall, dark-haired man in a black T-shirt, military-style BDU pants, and a tactical vest stepped out of the darkness and into the passageway. He wore an array of weapons, including a large handgun and several blades, all black. In his right hand he carried a black stake with a hilt. The light revealed a long scar on the left side of his face that had narrowly missed his eye.

The man crouched to touch the blood on the pavement. He scanned the path through the crates and other discarded packaging items stacked along the sides of the warehouses. He listened carefully to the sound of the river nearby and the distant clinking of the chain-link fence as it swayed in the wind.

A door creaked.

Slowly, the man rose, his eyes fixed on the source of the noise. Despite his large body and heavy boots, he moved silently through the shadows, gripping the stake.

Tension rippled across his shoulders as he approached a door on the left that hung slightly ajar. The blood trail continued through the doorway and disappeared. There was a bloody handprint on the doorframe.

The man placed his hand on the door and paused, his brow furrowed in concentration as he listened for any noises inside the warehouse. Hearing none, he threw the door open and dashed inside, disappearing into the darkness.

"Cut!" The director's voice echoed between the buildings.

A half-dozen crew members appeared from behind the warehouse. The cameramen wheeled their equipment toward the other end of the passageway, where the director and his assistants waited next to the van that served as their mobile production studio. The door of the van rolled open, revealing the sound tech.

"Got some real good shots and angles on that take, Danny," the lead cameraman, Hank, said as they joined the rest of the crew. "The lighting's much better than I thought it would be. Adding that one directional light helped the blood really shine."

Before the director could reply, a shorter man with spiky platinum hair emerged from a black rental Escalade parked behind the van. He approached them, phone in hand. "Where's Jack?" he demanded.

Danny sighed and jerked his chin toward the passageway. "Still in the warehouse."

The producer scowled at his phone and sent a short text message. "What the hell is he doing in there?"

Danny shrugged wearily. "I don't know, Leonard. Maybe looking for vampires."

Ignoring him, Leonard headed down the passageway. "Jack!" he called.

The man known as Sergeant Jack Justice emerged from the open doorway. "What?"

Leonard pointed accusingly at the stake in Justice's hand. "Why are you using that? I told you, the silver one scored much better with test audiences."

"And I told *you* I can't use a silver stake on a hunt," Justice replied, his voice edged with annoyance. "Day or night, shiny metal catches the light." He flipped the stake in his hand. "Matte black finish blends into the shadows. Amateurs are flashy, Leonard. Professionals know not to use shiny weapons. That's how they stay alive long enough to become professionals."

"You could at least use the silver stake when you're shooting reenactments like this," the producer argued.

"No, I could not," Justice countered. "My contract states that I have final say on my equipment, and my final say is that I do not carry silver stakes, period."

"Our ratings are slipping." Leonard waved his phone in Justice's face. The taller man didn't bother to try to read what was on the screen. "It was the Des Moines job that did it. The fanghead was too young, too scared. You killed him too quickly. The reviews are *devastating*, Jack. There are people out there who love your show who *sympathized* with that biter. It was all wrong. We should have added some threats in post instead of leaving the audio like it was. I let Danny talk me into thinking people would love to hear the fanghead begging. Instead, they feel sorry for him!" Leonard threw up his hands. "I should have known better."

Justice shook his head. "I don't think adding a threatening voice would have been very convincing. Anybody could see the vamp was scared, not angry."

"Let *them* worry about that," Leonard said, waving his hand dismissively at the production crew standing near the van. "We've got to do better, Jack."

"*We've* got to do better?" Justice's brows drew together. His grip tightened on the stake's hilt.

"*You've* got to do better," Leonard replied, oblivious to the other man's irritation. "We're heading into a crisis. There's a new vamp-hunter show about to premiere."

"Which one?" Justice asked. "There's what, three new shows that are rip-offs of mine?"

"I don't care about the other two, but *Night Hawk* is going to be a problem for us. A big problem."

"I don't see why." Justice shrugged. "Julia Myles is a police academy dropout with no qualifications and zero experience. She won't catch a single vamp and her show will get cancelled after one season, if not—"

"Don't be an idiot," Leonard snapped. "You've seen the promos. You know damn well she didn't get her own vampire-hunting show because of her credentials. She got it because of *these*." He cupped his hands obscenely in front of his chest. "She's wearing a leather cat suit and hooker boots and she's carrying *shiny silver stakes* and she has blonde hair and big tits. She's going to blow our show out of the water and you and I both are going to end up unemployed."

"I won't be unemployed." Justice slid the stake into specially designed loops on his pant leg and crossed his arms, his biceps straining the fabric of his T-shirt. "I was a vampire hunter for eight years before I signed on to do this series. I'll still be a vampire hunter when the series is over."

"My point is that we've got to up the ante around here," Leonard continued as if Justice hadn't spoken. "I get why you have to do this, filming yourself 'hunting,' since the crew can't be there when you actually catch the vamp, but you're playing it too safe. We need more drama. More risks."

Justice said nothing.

"You always dart them or immobilize them with the stun net. I think we need to figure out a way for the net to fail."

Justice studied him. "If the net fails, it's likely I, along with everyone on the set, would be killed."

Leonard waved his hands. "Then maybe it blinks out for a second so the fanghead *almost* escapes and then we switch it back on."

"A vampire can escape the net in less than a second."

"You're not helping here," the producer said testily. "I'm trying to come up with ways to make this show better. We need more danger, more close calls. They can get tits on that other show, but they won't get the kind of danger they'll get on *Sergeant Justice*. We need bigger, meaner fangheads who almost escape. We need surprises and scares. We can only do the same episode so many times before people get tired of seeing you track down the biter, net them, and stake them over and over."

"That's the job."

Leonard stared at him. "You're not hearing me, Jack. I know it's the job, but this is a *show*. This is what pays your bills and mine, so we better come up with some ways to make it more interesting before Julia fucking Cat-Suit steals all your viewers and you end up with no series, doing the *paso doble* on some B-list celebrity dancing show."

He stomped off, heading back toward his Escalade, texting angrily.

When he was well out of earshot, Hank joined Justice by the warehouse door. "Danny says that last take is good, so we'll probably wrap up for tonight and let you hunt."

"Good. I want to get to work." Justice watched Leonard get into the passenger side of the Escalade and start shouting at someone on his phone. "What have you heard about possible sightings around town?"

Hank lowered his voice and turned his back to where the director was conferencing with the rest of the crew about the next day's shooting schedule. "I talked to some folks down at one of the homeless camps who said a rogue's been seen several times at the city park about six blocks from where Foreman's sister was attacked. It's the best lead I've come up with."

Justice grunted. "That's good. What about our bait?"

"Yeah, we're good to go on that. Found a hooker who'll do what she's told. We'll give her booze, cut her up a little, and put her on a bench in the park like we did with that girl in Charleston. If the rogue's around, it won't be able to resist the smell of that much blood. Then you can dart him, net him, and take him to Foreman." Hank made an appreciative sound. "Guy's got a real hard-on to watch you torture the fanghead who bit his sister. You should show him the video of what you did to the one in Biloxi."

"That reminds me: Foreman wants video," Justice said. "You up for making some overtime money?"

"Hell, yeah," Hank said instantly. "What's the setup? Is this just for Foreman personally, or is he thinking about distribution?"

"He was asking about production and editing, so it looks like he's planning to distribute."

"There's a huge market for vamp torture on the dark web." Hank glanced back the rest of the crew and lowered his voice again. "Most of them are fake as shit, though, and the production values are garbage. I can do lights, sound, camera, the works on this one. It'll be legendary."

"No one can know it's me," Justice warned.

"No problem, man, no problem," Hank said hurriedly. "I know the angles and I can fix anything in post that might hint that it's you. I got your back, you know that. Just focus on finding that rogue and let's make some money."

One of the production assistants approached them. "Jack, there's a big group of fans outside the main gate asking for autographs. Do you have time—"

"No." Justice shouldered his way past the PA and headed for a black truck parked next to the director's van.

The PA scurried after him. "Maybe a few autographs? They've been waiting a while."

When Justice didn't reply, Danny asked, "How did they know we were here?"

The PA hesitated. "Leonard may have tweeted about it."

Danny muttered a string of curses. "Jack, maybe you'd better—"

"I'm hunting," Justice snapped over his shoulder. "Maybe later."

"Call me if you need the crew," Danny called as Justice reached his truck.

The vampire hunter grunted an acknowledgement, climbed in, and shut his door. The truck rumbled to life and headed toward a side entrance, away from the fans chanting his name at the main gate.

Danny turned to Hank. "Are you going back to the hotel?"

The cameraman shook his head. "I'm going to check out a club I saw earlier, have some fun."

"Don't get so wasted that you can't run a camera if he calls us out to a scene," Danny warned him. "And keep your phone on."

"Yeah, okay. Later." Hank headed for his rental car.

When he was out of earshot, the PA turned to the director. "Something's up, Danny. I swear I heard Hank say something to Jack about making money."

"We're all here to make money, Ash," Danny said. "I'm sure it was something to do with the show. You know Leonard's got a bug up his ass about the ratings."

"Yeah, about that." The PA glanced at the producer's SUV and lowered her voice. "Leonard asked me if there was any way to rig up a kill switch for Jack's stun net so one of us could switch it off and on, give the vamp a 'fighting chance' to escape, make things more dramatic."

"Holy shit," Danny said involuntarily. "What did you tell him?"

"I told him no, of course. I said that even if I *could* do it I wouldn't, because if the vamp got loose it might kill all of us, including him."

"And what did he say to that?"

"He yelled about that new vamp hunter show and stormed off. I'm worried he's going to do something stupid and get us all killed."

Danny pinched the bridge of his nose. "I'll talk to him."

"Don't tell him I told you," Ash pleaded. "He'll fire me."

"I won't tell him. I'm just glad Jack keeps such a close eye on his equipment. That makes it hard for Leonard to do anything to it."

"Thanks, Danny. See you back at the hotel."

"See you." The director climbed into the van with the sound tech and Ash went to help the second cameraman load his gear.

As the crew packed up their equipment, Steve, the other PA, used a hose to wash the blood he'd placed earlier off the asphalt and the walls of the warehouse. He worked methodically, his head bobbing to the beat of the music playing in his earbuds.

Twenty feet above, a slim man crouched unnoticed on the edge of the roof, his dark clothing making him nearly invisible against the night sky. Slowly, he rose and moved silently across the warehouse roof to the other side, where he jumped to the ground, landing easily and without a sound.

A second man, much larger and wearing all black, emerged from behind a pile of empty crates. "Is it as bad as you feared?"

"Worse," Charles Vaughan replied grimly. "We must leave."

Bryan Smith, Charles's head of security, stayed close to his employer as they moved through the shadows toward a damaged section of fence and their vehicle parked on the next block.

As they walked, Charles described the conversation he'd overheard between Justice and the cameraman.

"Should we alert local law enforcement to step up patrols in the area around the park to discourage Justice from planting his bait?" Bryan held the chain-link aside.

The vampire shook his head as he slipped through the opening ahead of the enforcer. "No. Increased police presence may simply force them to move to another location. It is better for us to know where they are."

"What's the plan, then?"

"I will ask Amira to take her Hunters to the park area. If a rogue is nearby, they will find him. In the meantime, Amira will ensure Justice's 'bait' comes to no harm."

They reached the black SUV. Bryan opened the back door and Charles climbed in.

As the SUV glided smoothly through nearly deserted streets, Charles said, "While Amira hunts, I would like to meet with the other members of the Court who are currently in the city."

"And what do we do about Foreman wanting to pay someone to torture a vampire?" Bryan wanted to know.

Charles's eyes glowed silver. "As long as I am able to prevent it, there will be no torture of vampires in our city. Please extend an invitation for the others to join me at Hawthorne's as soon as possible. We must plan."

2

THE VAMPIRE WAS BEGGING.

"Please," he lisped. He was so young, he hadn't yet learned to speak clearly around his fangs. His arms and legs twitched as though he was trying to fight or run, but the stun net ensured his efforts were in vain.

Jack Justice stared down at the vampire on the pavement and spun a stake in his hand, saying nothing.

The vampire saw the stake and redoubled his efforts to fight the effects of the stun net. It emitted a pulse of magic and left him nearly immobilized. "Please," he said again, his voice barely audible.

"Did those kids you bit at the lake beg like this?" Justice asked. In the dim streetlight, his gray eyes glinted. "Did they beg you not to hurt them?"

The vampire said nothing.

"You remember how they begged, don't you?" Justice said, towering over the vampire, who stared up at him, wide-eyed. "You didn't care. Your kind never does."

"I was just hungry," the vampire moaned. "Please, I was so careful. I only drank a little."

Justice crouched. The vampire struggled to squirm away, but the stun net emitted another pulse. "By the authority granted to me by this state and in accordance with local and state criminal codes, I execute you for your crimes."

"Wait," the young vampire cried.

Ignoring him, Justice swung his arm high and then down, driving the stake through the vamp's ribcage and into his heart with a meaty crunch of flesh and bone.

The young vamp had a half-second to react, his mouth opening wide in a silent scream of agony before his body crumbled into ash.

Justice picked up his stake, dusted it off, and stood. He pushed up his left shirtsleeve to reveal several neat rows of scars. Without flinching, he used the razor-sharp point of the stake to cut another tick mark into his flesh, then wiped the blade on his pants and returned it to the holster on his thigh.

The camera zoomed in on the thin line of blood trickling down his arm, then pulled back to frame him standing half in shadow over the ash. The screen went black.

As the end credits rolled, Charles paused the video. He set the remote control on the conference table, picked up his glass of Scotch, and drained the last of its contents.

Ossun, a Persian vampire sitting to Charles's left, broke the silence. "He kills for pleasure and profit. It is blood money, not justice."

On Charles's right, the third member of the Vampire Court in the room, Niara, spoke in her usual soft Shona accent. "This man is now in the city?"

"Yes." Charles reached for the crystal decanter in the middle of the table and poured himself two more fingers of Scotch. "He was filming an episode in Charleston but ended that job early at the behest of Alexander Foreman, who provided a private jet to transport Justice and his entourage directly here. They arrived this morning at eight and staged a press conference on the tarmac at the airport."

The significance of the timing wasn't lost on anyone in the room. "During daylight, so no member of the Court could be there," Niara said. "Was a Court daytime representative not in attendance?"

Charles stoppered the decanter. "The Court was specifically *disinvited* to the event, but several of our security personnel were undercover in the crowd to provide us with a detailed account. The video is available should you wish to view it."

"What steps have we taken to respond to Foreman's actions?" Niara asked.

"Valas prepared a statement reaffirming our commitment to apprehending the rogue vampires and holding both them and their maker accountable for these attacks. The statement was presented on our behalf shortly after Foreman's press conference by Ezekiel Monroe."

The others nodded. It was common for the head of the Vampire Court to communicate to the public via her trusted daytime representative and spokesperson.

David Noble, another member of the Court, rose and moved to the small bar on the far side of the room, where he selected a bottle of wine and a glass. "What do we know of this man Justice?"

Charles picked up the remote and switched the large wall screen to Justice's dossier. "The man calling himself 'Sergeant Jack Justice' is really Keith Cornwall, a former Army Ranger. He is forty-one years old, unmarried, and has been a SPEMA-certified vampire hunter-for-hire for the past ten years. His scripted reality show, *Sergeant Justice*, premiered two years ago and remains immensely popular, especially among so-called 'Human rights' organizations."

Niara studied the report. "His kill count stands at thirty-six?"

Charles shook his head. "We have good reason to believe the number is actually much higher. Thirty-six sanctioned executions, perhaps, but it is rather an open secret that Jack Justice's services are for hire and that many of his kills are not legal."

"This Court allows a known murderer not only to operate freely, but to be rewarded and venerated by the public and human law enforcement alike?" David demanded.

"Without proof, we have little legal recourse, as you know," Niara reminded him. "Even if we *had* proof, it is unlikely he would be prosecuted and even less likely he would be convicted. We know of three cases in the past year alone where the killer was acquitted despite ample evidence of guilt."

"Perhaps I was not speaking of legal actions." David returned to the conference table, wineglass in hand. "There are other avenues. We need not be hindered by human law when it fails to offer us the same protections as human citizens."

Silence. It was an old argument, one that no one else in the room wanted to revisit.

"Valas has ruled on this matter," Charles said finally, when neither of the other vampires spoke. "Jack Justice is not to be targeted. While he is within our territory, he will be watched. If he is indeed committing unsanctioned murders, we will see him prosecuted for it. Any attack on Mr. Justice is likely to create far more problems than it would solve."

"I obey the head of the Court, of course," David said with a deferential half-bow, though Valas was not present. As always, the vampires presumed anything they said would travel back to her ears.

"Alexander Foreman's actions in this matter are most unfortunate," Ossun said.

"On that we can all agree," David commented. "Foreman has a long and well-documented history of supporting anti-supe organizations and has spoken many times of his hatred of vampires in particular."

"Have we any news of his sister's whereabouts?" Niara inquired.

"None since the night she was bitten," Charles said. "It is likely she is responsible for the attack on the parking structure security guard. Fortunately, the man survived, but he is in a medically induced coma and has been unable to speak to anyone."

"Was there no surveillance footage of either attack?" Ossun asked.

Charles's eyes glowed with anger. "The surveillance footage was erased before either we or law enforcement were able to obtain a copy. The building's head of security claimed there was a 'glitch' in their system."

"Foreman's doing, no doubt," David said darkly. "He would not want any video to become public that showed his sister being bitten and then rising as a vampire before attacking the security guard."

"If indeed she was responsible for that attack," Ossun said. "As a newly risen vampire, she must have attacked others beside the guard."

"There have not any reports of attacks," Charles pointed out. "It is likely the victims have not yet been found. It is impossible for a newly risen vampire to have fed only once in two days without becoming mad with hunger. Valas has reached out to Foreman to offer her assistance, but he refused to acknowledge that his sister is now a vampire. He speaks of her as though she is truly dead."

Niara said, "He has become a zealot, one we must watch closely."

"We have yet to determine the person responsible for siring these rogues, or the purpose of allowing newly risen vampires with no control over their bloodlust to roam the city unchecked," David said, sipping his wine. "One hopes their master simply met with an untimely end and his or her young were released."

"An unlikely scenario, as no master would make a half-dozen new vampires at once with any hope of caring for and controlling them all," Ossun observed.

Charles tapped the tabletop. "Until we have one of the rogues in custody or can identify their master—or masters—we must face the more plausible explanation that someone is siring new vampires without the Court's knowledge or consent and releasing them on purpose."

"To what end?" Ossun demanded. "No good can come of this. It brings nothing but negative attention, and now it has brought the nation's most famous vampire killer to the city, with nearly *carte blanche* from local authorities to hunt and kill. How many of us believe this man who calls himself Justice will target only the rogues?"

"Not I," David said. "He will kill whomever he finds, if he believes himself beyond the law."

Niara said nothing, but she clearly agreed with David.

"Worse still, some of his most dedicated followers have named themselves as 'deputy' vampire hunters and are roaming the streets looking for the rogues or any other vampires to target for retribution," Ossun continued. "We must protect ourselves. This can only lead to more violence."

Charles set his glass on the table. "All vampires in the city must be cautious. Young vampires should be quartered with their masters and fed only by donors whose consent has been registered and notarized. Valas asks that you pass these instructions on to all vampires in your line."

"I will not live in fear," David snapped.

"To live prudently is not to live in fear," Niara said before Charles could reply. "We have spoken before of our concern for young vampires allowed to find their own food sources too soon. Some masters forget what it is like to be newly risen, how the thirst can overwhelm and steal one's control. Valas's request is reasonable."

"More than reasonable," Ossun agreed. "But keeping young vampires in their masters' homes will not solve our problem."

Charles nodded. "That is true. We must capture a rogue if we are to have any chance of identifying the master responsible for their making."

"All our efforts to do so for the past two weeks have been unsuccessful," David pointed out. "There is no pattern to the attacks, no way to predict where and when they will occur. We have nothing but poor-quality surveillance footage and no living witnesses. We do not know even how many rogues there are."

"Even so, a rogue must be captured. Christine Foreman must be found. All our efforts must now focus on this." Charles shut off the wall screen. "The Court's resources will be reallocated. We will request assistance from the Chicago Court if necessary."

Niara blinked. David sat up straighter and Ossun's head tilted slightly. For normally unflappable vampires, these tiny movements were the equivalent of shouts of alarm.

"Surely not," David protested. "Our bargaining position with Chicago would be irrevocably weakened. Elizabeth never offers help without receiving far more in return than she gives."

"Then we must ensure that Chicago's help is not required and resolve this crisis quickly," Charles replied. "Valas has no desire to request assistance, but she recognizes the seriousness of what we face."

David finished his wine and set the glass on the table as the others sat silently.

Charles rose. "I suggest you all return to your homes. I will keep you informed of our progress in the investigation."

Ossun and David departed with their security details. Bryan Smith stationed himself in front of the door to the conference room, a silent sentinel whose enormous shoulders brushed the sides of the doorway. Niara's enforcer, Nadya, stood against the wall, watching the room.

"You are troubled," Niara said once the door had closed behind the others.

Charles reseated himself and poured another glass of Scotch as she moved around behind his chair to place her hands on his shoulders. "These attacks are troubling," he said.

Niara bent so her lips were near his ear. "You may fool the others, but you do not fool me," she murmured, her breath cool against his skin. Her scent, a combination of cinnamon and wine, teased his nose. "There is more you know that you do not share with us."

"If that is true, it would be at Valas's request and in the interest of the Court."

"My sister is not here, so she hunts tonight." Niara took his glass. She sipped the Scotch, then placed the glass back in his hand. "Amira will find one of these rogues and our questions will be answered, though we may not like what we discover."

Charles said nothing.

Her lips brushed his cheek. "Will you come to my home once your business here is concluded?"

"If time allows," Charles said. "I must make arrangements to expand our search for the rogues."

"Even if your arrival is just before dawn, please join me. I hope not to sleep alone." She trailed her fingers up his arms.

Vamp-fast, he caught her hand and pressed a kiss into her palm. "I have rarely known you to sleep alone, Nia."

Her laugh was the most pleasant thing Charles had heard in quite some time, and it accomplished the seemingly impossible: it took some of the tension out of his shoulders.

"That is true," she said lightly. "Perhaps I shall say I will leave room for you." She slipped her hand from his grasp and headed for the door. "May your meetings be productive and your hunt successful, *mudiwa*," she said over her shoulder as Bryan opened the door.

"I will see you soon," Charles said. The women departed and Bryan closed the door after them.

Charles studied the amber liquid in his glass, rubbing his thumb absently through the faint mark left behind by Niara's lips.

Even the promise of sharing her bed wasn't enough to offset the bitter taste of watching "Sergeant Jack Justice" kill a young vampire whose neglectful master let him out to feed freely much too soon. The teenage victims had survived their wounds, but in Iowa, as with most Midwestern states, nonconsensual bites—even if not fatal—were a capital crime. The locals called in Justice and his crew to find the culprit.

What the show had *not* disclosed was how the now-deceased young vampire had been handed over to Justice by his master without argument and without consulting the Chicago Court, under whose jurisdiction and at whose discretion the master lived. Rumors had reached Valas that Elizabeth, the head of the Chicago Court, had dealt with the negligent master quickly and severely. Charles assumed that meant either true death or punishment that would have made true death preferable.

And while the show depicted Justice supposedly tracking, cornering, and netting the young vampire, the truth was that the victim—for Charles found it difficult to think of the young vampire as anything but a victim—had been handed over in restraints. Justice, or perhaps members of his entourage, had dumped the vampire in the alley, thrown a stun net over him, and staked him on camera, broadcasting his execution to an audience of millions.

The young vampire's fear and begging for mercy had aroused sympathy among viewers and galvanized some protests against the show and the cable network that produced it, but as far as most humans were concerned, the only salient facts were that the dead vampire had bitten two teenagers without their consent and law enforcement had tasked Justice with meting out the maximum punishment allowable by law for that crime.

And now this man and his media circus were in his city, hunting vampires on his streets, not in the name of justice, but for the purpose of torturing them. Charles hissed and drank.

Bryan moved to stand across the table from his employer. "Amira sent word that the cameraman placed an unconscious woman on a bench in the park near the garage where Christine Foreman was attacked. The scent of blood is strong. She suspects the woman has minor wounds, inflicted for the purpose of drawing in any nearby vampires. It's a tactic Justice has been known to use before."

Charles's eyes lit up silver. *And they call* us *monsters,* he thought. "And the vampire hunter?"

"He's set up about fifty yards downwind with a rifle. Amira believes it's loaded with darts of some sort."

Charles recalled overhearing a reference to darts during the conversation between the cameraman and Jack Justice. "We must ascertain what these darts contain. Normal tranquilizers and paralytic agents would have little to no effect on vampires. I am troubled by the possibility that someone may have developed a drug capable of incapacitating us."

"I'll have one of the researchers follow up." Bryan sent a quick text, then read an incoming message. "Amira and two of her Hunters are watching the park while her enforcers are searching the area. If any rogues are drawn in by the scent of blood, they'll be contained and brought in." His expression darkened. "She also reports police patrols seem to be avoiding the area around the park."

Charles wasn't surprised by the news. "Foreman may have made arrangements with the chief of police to allow Justice to hunt without interference. They are quite good friends, from what I understand."

"They certainly share the same attitudes about vampires and other supes, that's for damn sure. I've heard rumors the chief attended Daylighters meetings regularly before he was elected." Bryan studied Charles. "You didn't tell the others about Foreman's plan to torture a rogue or that Amira and her Hunters are watching Justice and searching for the rogues."

"No, I did not." Charles drained his Scotch and set the glass on the table.

"Do you have reason to believe someone on the Court is involved in these attacks?"

"I have...a feeling," Charles admitted. "It is little more than a suspicion and I have no evidence yet with which to support my theory, but it is enough for me to be judicious with the information in our possession."

"Valas shares your suspicions?"

"She does, but we cannot make an accusation without proof. Perhaps—"

Bryan's phone buzzed with an incoming message. The enforcer read the screen. "Leah, Amira's head of security, says a group of about a dozen self-appointed 'deputy vampire hunters' armed with stakes and other weapons is approaching the park."

Charles was on his feet instantly. "It is against federal law for anyone other than a SPEMA-certified vampire hunter to carry a stake. Where are the police?"

"Nowhere to be seen," Bryan said.

"Advise Leah that we are on our way to the park and request she and Amira meet us." As they headed for the conference room door, Charles reached out mentally to

Adri Smith, another of his enforcers who was currently downstairs in the bar. *Ms. Smith, we are leaving now. Meet us in the garage.*

Her response was immediate: *Yes, sir.*

Charles and Bryan took the stairs down to the garage level so quickly that they were little more than blurs on the building's surveillance system. They emerged into the underground parking area only a few seconds before a second door opened and Adri appeared, also at a run. She gave her brother a quick nod before heading for a black SUV.

Thirty seconds later, Adri drove up the ramp and out the rolling door that led to the alley behind Hawthorne's. As the heavy door rolled closed behind them and the SUV accelerated, Bryan checked his mobile phone and said, "Leah reports the vigilantes appear to be searching the area."

No group of untrained humans would be any match for a vampire, even a young one. While Charles had worried that Jack Justice might be able to catch one of the rogues for the purposes of torture and execution, now he had a new concern: what would happen if the vigilantes actually located a rogue. It would likely be a slaughter, and the end of peaceful attempts to locate and apprehend the rogues and their maker.

"We are less than ten minutes away," Adri stated.

"Update on Justice?" Charles asked Bryan.

"Leah says he appears to be packing up and abandoning his post. Once he clears the scene, Amira will see that the woman he used as bait is taken to a hospital."

A familiar icy chill touched his mind just before Valas's voice interrupted his thoughts. The head of the Vampire Court did not waste time with greetings. *Charles, you may act on behalf of the Court in this matter. We must de-escalate the situation immediately. I am placing a call to the director of the local SPEMA office. If the city police will not act, federal agents will.*

Amira has advised you of the situation? Charles asked.

Yes. Valas's voice belied her fury. *This man Justice brings mob rule to our city.*

He is here because one of us has created these rogues and allowed them to attack humans, Charles replied. *Justice would not be here were it not for these attacks. It is the rogue-maker who must answer for these acts of violence.*

Her anger seared him. *You must see that the vigilantes come to no harm until law enforcement arrives. If you must choose between the lives of the humans and capturing the rogue alive, protect the humans.*

Valas's logic was obvious: though they needed to catch a rogue in order to identify his or her maker, that was less important than ensuring no more humans were attacked or killed. Tonight, a dozen vigilantes were on the street searching for vampires to stake. If there was another attack, there would be mobs. The police had done nothing thus far to dissuade the vigilantes from hunting; Charles very much doubted they would do much to oppose larger groups.

Perhaps we should contact the chief ourselves, Charles suggested. *He should remember that it is humans who are likely to be injured if they confront a vampire. Anti-vigilante laws are in place to protect humans. Regardless of his motives, it is humans he endangers by refusing to act.*

I am sure the chief is well aware, but I will remind him. Valas paused. *Amira says Justice appears to be heading toward the park's south gate to intercept the vigilantes.*

Charles made a decision. "Head for the south side of the park," he instructed Adri. In his head, he told Valas, *Please ask Amira to watch the vigilantes until we arrive.*

I will do so, Valas replied. The chill in his mind dissipated as she severed their connection.

He informed his enforcers that both Amira and Justice were headed to meet the vigilantes.

"Will Justice lead them or ask them to disperse?" Bryan asked.

Charles shook his head. "I think it unlikely he is interested in working with drunken amateurs who are more likely to get him killed than help him."

Adri pulled to a stop on a side street two blocks from the park. She remained in the driver's seat with the engine running as Charles and Bryan exited the vehicle and slipped through the shadows toward the park's south gate.

The sound of voices grew louder as they neared the entrance. They took cover behind a large tree and observed.

A group of men ranging in age from their early twenties to late fifties were standing about thirty feet from the gate, talking loudly among themselves. It appeared they were arguing about how to proceed with their search. A few wanted to split up to cover more ground, while others advocated staying together "for safety." Several looked around nervously. All carried homemade stakes that appeared to be broken pieces of broom handles or other similar tools. There was a fair chance at least a few of the vigilantes were carrying concealed guns.

The breeze shifted, bringing with it the stench from the large trash bin near the gate mixed with the scents of fear, cheap cologne, body odor, and alcohol from the would-be vigilantes. Enhanced senses were one of a vampire's greatest assets, but in situations such as this Charles would have gladly accepted a less-sensitive nose if it would spare him from the olfactory assault of urban smells and sub-standard hygiene.

In the midst of those odors, however, he detected the unmistakable scent of steel, oil, and gunpowder. At least a few of them *were* armed. While a standard bullet might wound or temporarily incapacitate in the case of a head shot, a silver bullet to the heart could be fatal. It was unlikely any of them had expensive and hard-to-obtain silver rounds, but the possibility could not be ignored.

A muscular man wearing a sleeveless T-shirt despite the cold night stepped to the front of the group. His massive biceps bore tattoos identifying him as a former Marine. Charles noted that he carried an actual tactical stake similar to those Jack Justice used. They were illegal for non-professionals, but were available on the black market.

"If you cows want to stay here and bend your necks go ahead, but I came here to hunt fangheads," he said, handling the stake as though he had practiced with it. Unlike the rest of the group, this man had the potential to be a threat. Beside Charles, Bryan came to the same conclusion and tensed, watching the Marine.

The reference to the slang term for a vampire's food supply elicited angry responses. One man mooed and gave the Marine his middle finger. "I ain't no cattle," another yelled. "Let's go!" He turned to the others. "If you're scared, go home!"

The scent of fear grew stronger, but no one turned back. The group headed toward the park gate with the Marine in the lead. Bryan and Charles followed the vigilantes, moving unseen along the trees that lined the park fence.

Look at these idiots, Bryan said in Charles's head as one of the men dropped his makeshift stake with a clatter. He fumbled to pick it up as it rolled toward the edge of the sidewalk.

Even a drunken idiot could score a lucky hit to a vampire's heart with a sharp stick,

Charles reflected as the man reclaimed his weapon and brandished it. There were a dozen such idiots with sharp sticks in the group.

It would only take one to kill him.

3

A FAMILIAR SCENT TEASED CHARLES'S NOSE JUST BEFORE AMIRA STEPPED INTO VIEW from behind the large stone pillar marking the entrance to the park, blocking the group's path. Her fangs were visible and her copper-colored eyes glowed softly in the light from the streetlamp. The men halted. The smell of fear increased dramatically.

Unlike her sister Niara, who favored brightly colored dresses and complex hairstyles, Amira wore clothing better suited to quick movements and hand-to-hand fighting: slim black pants, a black sleeveless top, and boots. Tonight, her hair was a halo of natural curls.

Another familiar scent in the air told him that Leah, Amira's head of security, was nearby, behind a tree to their right.

"You should not be here," Amira said, addressing the Marine who led the group. "The search for the rogues is best left to those who are qualified to hunt them."

"Who the hell are you?" The man who had seconded the Marine's call to action stepped forward to join their leader, gripping his makeshift wooden stake.

"I am Amira of the Vampire Court," she said with a slight bow, never taking her eyes off the group. "I ask you all to return to your homes. You should not risk your lives in this way."

"How do we know *you're* not a rogue?" someone called out.

Even the stoic Marine winced perceptibly at the absurdity of the question. A small smile turned up the corners of Amira's mouth. "The fact I am standing here speaking to you rather than simply tearing out your throats should be evidence enough, but if you require further proof you may call the Court or your own police department and they can confirm my identity."

Charles's nose twitched as a new and unwelcome scent drifted over from the direction of the group. The vigilantes exchanged glances, probably also detecting the smell and wondering which of them had urinated in fear.

Amira's smile faded. "For your own safety, please discontinue this ill-advised course of action. Court operatives, along with law enforcement, are seeking the rogues. They will be found and brought to justice."

"I don't think you have any plans to apprehend them," the second man argued. "If you did, you'd have caught them by now. For all we know, you're the ones behind this." The others muttered agreement.

"The Court has as much reason to stop these attacks as anyone, as such violence brings harm to us as well," Amira countered. "It is only a matter of time before the rogues are caught, but you will not be the ones to do it, with no training and such inadequate weapons. If you are lucky, you will not find one of the rogues. If you are very unlucky you will find one, and then you will be dead."

Several in the group took a step back, but the Marine, the second man, and most of the others held their ground.

The Marine spoke. "How about we show you just how adequate our weapons are?" He spun the stake in his hand, the same way Jack Justice had done. Charles wondered if he was a fan of the show, or if military weapons training now included the handling and use of stakes.

Amira shook her head. "I am many times faster and stronger. You would not be able to injure me."

The Marine's face darkened. His grip tightened on the stake. "You're pretty sure of yourself."

"She has every right to be."

At the sudden voice, everyone in the group—including the Marine—jumped. A few swore involuntarily.

Jack Justice emerged from behind a tree about five feet from where Leah was still hidden. His arrival had gone unnoticed by all of the humans. The vampires and their enforcers, however, had noticed him approaching not long after Amira had intercepted the would-be vigilantes.

Justice wore the same black clothing he'd been wearing during the shoot in the warehouse district. In addition to the weapons he'd had on earlier, he was carrying a rifle on his back. Charles caught a strange chemical smell from the rifle he did not recognize. The prospect that Justice was armed with darts that could incapacitate a vampire was quite troubling.

As Justice moved to stand midway between Amira and the group of vigilantes, Charles detected another scent, this one easily recognizable: silver, and lots of it. As little threat as the others presented, Justice was a real danger.

The would-be vigilantes looked at Justice with a mixture of awe and fear. Even the Marine seemed star-struck. No one spoke, but a few of the men had their phones out and were surreptitiously taking photos.

Justice gave them a hard stare. "You disrupted my attempt to apprehend a rogue. I've always been very clear that vampire hunting is a job for professionals, not drunks with broken broom handles."

Many in the group looked abashed, but the Marine and his companion didn't back down. "The vamps aren't doing shit to find the rogues and the cops can't find them," the second man said. "We want to help."

"All you're going to do is get yourselves killed," Justice said flatly. "If I don't catch a rogue tonight because I'm here dealing with you and it kills someone, you've gotten that person killed too."

The Marine spoke up. "Some of us have lost family members to fangheads. You can't ask us to do nothing while they attack and kill humans on our streets."

Justice regarded him. "I'm sorry for your loss, but you can't do anything to avenge your loved ones if you're dead. With some training, you might be a professional hunter." He reached into one of the pockets in his pants and took out a card. He offered it to the Marine, who approached and took it. "Until then, the best way for all of you to help catch the rogues is to ask around about sightings and get that information to me."

"We can do more than call in tips," the second man protested. "We can help you. You said you'd set a trap for a rogue. We could—"

Justice's eyes flashed. "I am not going to repeat myself again. Leave vamp hunting to the professionals. You don't even know enough to know when you're in danger. None of you knew this one was watching you."

Amira smiled, flashing her fangs.

"And there's another vampire here as well, behind you." Justice gestured toward the tree where Charles and Bryan stood. With another round of cursing, the group turned.

Having lost his advantage, Charles motioned for Bryan to stay hidden and stepped out into the light.

The vampire and the vampire hunter studied each other. Charles sensed judicious wariness from Justice, but not fear. He also sensed hate, unsurprisingly, but unlike the unchecked animosity of the vigilantes, Justice's was a cold, calculating loathing. It made him all the more dangerous.

"Charles Vaughan, also of the Vampire Court," Charles said. "Your reputation precedes you, Mr. Justice." He put a slight emphasis on the *Mr.* and let his tone indicate what aspect of Justice's reputation he was referring to.

"As does yours." Justice turned and addressed the Marine. "If either of these vampires had been rogues, you would all be dead now. Ask around about sightings, tell me what you find out, and let *me* hunt."

Apparently, the revelation that not one but *two* vampires had been watching their group without their knowledge was enough to convince even the Marine that he was out of his depth. The large man straightened. "Yes, sir." He gestured at the group. "You heard him. Let's go."

As they began to leave, someone asked, "Can we get a selfie with you, Sergeant Justice?"

Justice stared at him.

"Never mind. Maybe some other time," the man said quickly, putting away his phone.

Grumbling, the group departed, heading for Ninth Street and the bar district where, no doubt, they had hatched their plan to go vampire hunting. Amira joined Charles and they watched the men leave.

When they were more than a block away, Charles turned to Justice. "We are aware you are in the city at the behest of Alexander Foreman. On behalf of the Vampire Court, I formally request that you capture, rather than execute, any rogues you may find and turn them over to us so that we may ascertain their origin."

"I operate according to regulations established by SPEMA," Justice said. "My mandate from them is to track, apprehend, and execute the rogues. Any change to that has to come from their office."

"And what is the nature of your agreement with Mr. Foreman?" Amira inquired.

"I don't have an agreement with Mr. Foreman," Justice said, lying with practiced ease. Charles sensed the falsehood, but did not let on that he knew Justice's statement to be untrue. Information was leverage, as he had said on more than one occasion.

"You arrived on Foreman's private jet less than eight hours after the attack on his sister," Amira pointed out. "He was present this morning at your news conference."

"Commercial travel is difficult for someone who carries weapons that can't be checked," Justice countered. "Normally the network arranges a jet, but it was unavailable. Mr. Foreman provided our transportation. That is the extent of our agreement."

Again, his lies grated along Charles's nerves. "We will contact SPEMA and request your agreement with them be amended. In the meantime, should you capture a rogue, we ask that you contact the Court immediately so we may dispatch personnel to your position and take the rogue into custody." Charles took a red card embossed with gold from his pocket and held it out.

Justice accepted the card and glanced at it. "If I receive notice from SPEMA that changes my mission, I will do so. Until then, I'll proceed under my current instructions."

"It is in the interest of all that we ascertain the source of these rogues so we may hold him or her accountable for these attacks and prevent more from occurring." Charles said. "If you stake the rogue rather than capture it, we cannot identify its maker. If your primary concern is human life rather than your kill count, you will help us, regardless of any other agreements you may have made."

Justice's steel-gray eyes flashed. "A staked rogue won't be killing any more humans."

"A staked rogue-maker makes no more rogues," Amira countered.

The vampire hunter's eyes narrowed. "You intend to execute the vampire responsible for making these rogues?"

"Our law is quite clear," Charles said. "The rogue-maker will face justice for these crimes. Once their guilt is proven, he or she may choose the stake or the sun."

"And the rogues?"

"Rogues who have not caused death may be spared, if they can be controlled by a master. If they cannot be controlled, or if they have killed, they too will die."

"Any vampires who attack humans should die," Justice stated.

"That may well be your personal philosophy, but in this state, the law condemns only vampires who kill. The rogues are not capable of knowing right from wrong or controlling their impulse to feed, which is why it is their maker who is ultimately responsible for the attacks."

"A rabid animal doesn't know right from wrong and can't control what they do or who they attack, but if it bites humans, you put the animal down." Justice's fingers moved as if he was spinning a stake.

"Your analogy is inaccurate and insulting. A vampire is a person, not an animal," Amira said coldly.

Justice said nothing, but his expression made it clear that he disagreed.

Charles found it unlikely that any rogue Justice captured would be turned over to the Court alive, regardless of instructions from SPEMA. Justice could simply claim the vampire had attempted to escape and he was forced to stake it.

Though lawyers working on behalf of vampires had repeatedly requested that SPEMA require hunters to wear body cameras, the agency had balked, claiming the cameras could endanger the hunters by giving away their movements. Hunters had threatened to cease operations if any such policy was implemented. To Charles and others, their resistance—and SPEMA's unwillingness to require body cameras—indicated not only that hunters misused their authority, but that SPEMA was aware of it and reluctant to reign them in.

Charles's eyes shone with a soft silver light. "On behalf of the Court, I warn you unequivocally that we will not tolerate any unsanctioned murders of vampires, nor any actions that exceed the lawful limits set by SPEMA and this state. If you do not turn over a captured rogue as required by SPEMA, not only will we see you are prosecuted for interfering with an investigation, but you will be directly responsible for any further attacks that could have been prevented by identifying the rogue-maker."

"The only ones responsible for these attacks are fangheads," Justice said without noticeable emotion. "The rogues, their maker, and the Court that allows them to roam the city streets unchecked are the guilty parties. I'm here to clean up your mess. How I do it is not up to you. You had your chance; now it's my turn."

An SUV pulled to a stop next to the sidewalk. "Oh my God, it's really him!" a young woman exclaimed. "Sergeant Justice! Hi! Can we take your picture?" Without waiting for an answer, she raised her phone and pointed it at him. Several others in the SUV followed suit, talking excitedly.

Down the street, two news vans turned the corner and raced toward the park. Charles recognized them as belonging to local news stations.

Justice's fury increased as the vans approached. Amira disappeared into the park with Leah, leaving Charles and Bryan with the vampire hunter.

"It would appear your admirers have alerted the public to your whereabouts," Charles said.

"Apparently so." Justice backed toward the park entrance. "Find the rogues and their maker, Vaughan, or the mobs will get bigger and they'll be knocking on your door next."

"Remember my warning," Charles said. "Follow the law, Mr. Cornwall. There will be no torture or unsanctioned murders of vampires in my city."

Something flashed in Justice's steely eyes, and for the first time Charles sensed a hint of fear. The hunter spun on his heel and jogged off into the park.

Before the news vans could reach them, Charles and Bryan slipped away.

A block away from the SUV, Amira and Leah appeared from around the corner of a building.

"He is watched," Amira said without preamble, in response to Charles's unspoken question. "Valas ordered round-the-clock surveillance. Wherever he goes, he will be followed. I have already contacted Valas and related our conversation with Justice," she added. "She will be contacting SPEMA directly to request that Justice apprehend the rogues and turn them over to us rather than executing them."

Leah, a tall brunette, spoke. "If Justice captures a rogue in the meantime, what are our orders?"

Amira's displeasure was evident in soft copper glow of her eyes. "Valas has made it clear that we cannot overtly interfere with Justice as long as he is following SPEMA protocols and regulations. If he violates them, however, we can act. If he attempts to capture or execute any vampire who is not a rogue, or attempts to execute a rogue once SPEMA orders him to hold them for us, we can intervene."

"And the drug contained in Justice's darts?" Charles asked.

Amira shook her head. "I do not recognize its smell. I have assigned a researcher to find out what it is. In the meantime, we should attempt to obtain one of these darts."

"It will be difficult," Charles said. "I doubt he is careless with his equipment."

Amira smiled, showing her fangs. "I consider it a welcome challenge. He is a worthy adversary."

"What will you do now?" he asked.

"Leah and I will continue our hunt for the rogues, with the help of my Hunters. I will alert you immediately when we have news."

"Thank you." Charles inclined his head. "I wish you success."

"You as well, Charles," Amira said.

She and Leah headed back toward the park as Charles and Bryan returned to the SUV.

Once they were inside, Adri caught Charles's eye in the rearview mirror. "Where to, sir?"

"Back to Hawthorne's, please," he said, settling back into the seat. "I have an appointment with a potential client in less than an hour."

"The woman who's looking to buy the Etruscan relic?" Adri asked as she headed back toward the Heights. "Does she know about the other buyers?"

"Not yet." Charles smiled at the thought of the bidding war to come. It promised to be vicious, dangerous, and quite diverting, as all four of the potential buyers were avid collectors with far more money and pride than sense. The scheming, bribery, threats, and plotting were sure to make the coming weeks interesting. The profit from the eventual sale was almost an afterthought compared to the competition between the bidders—and at the center of it all, Charles pulled all the strings and made them dance.

There really was no better profession for a vampire of Charles's disposition than that of a broker specializing in magical objects and antiquities. Of the many occupations he had pursued in two hundred years, it was by far the most continually rewarding—both financially and personally.

More than one of his clients had asked him what items he bought for his own collection. For the sake of appearances, Charles kept a small collection of paintings, sculptures, and artifacts he could show to select clientele, but none of the items in what he referred to as his "public" gallery were of value to him. The public gallery was part of his persona, a bit of fakery that satisfied the curiosity of clients without revealing anything of himself.

His private collection, on the other hand, would reveal far too much, which was why no eyes other than his ever saw it.

"And after the meeting?" Adri wanted to know. "Where will you sleep tonight?"

Charles considered his primary options: Hawthorne's, his own residence, or Niara's home. The latter offered the promise of a pleasant diversion, but he was restless. Thoughts of his private collection—of one item in particular—made it difficult to accept Niara's offer tonight. She would not take offense if he decided to go home. Unlike human females, who demanded loyalty and monogamy, Niara simply welcomed him to her bed when he desired to share it, and wished him well when he slept or sought pleasure elsewhere. Their understanding was delightfully uncomplicated.

"Once my meeting with Ms. Collins is finished, I will return to my own home," Charles said finally, noting Bryan's surprise. His head of security had no doubt expected him to accept Niara's invitation. On another night, he would have done so, but tonight he needed something more than even the pleasures Niara could offer.

Not long before dawn, with his meetings completed and the situation with the rogues still weighing heavily on his mind, Charles sat in a chair in the private underground apartment beneath his residence, wearing a robe. In his hands he held a small portrait in a battered wooden frame.

Unlike many painted portraits from the turn of the nineteenth century, it did not depict a wealthy woman in her sitting room with her children. Instead, it showed a young woman with long, dark hair tied back with a ribbon, reading her Bible in a garden, her finger on the page as she read. She wore an embroidered apron over her long dress. In the background, Charles's sharp eyes found three small shadows, peeking playfully at him from behind narrow trees.

Clients who saw his public gallery would not have been impressed by the portrait. It was amateurish, certainly; the woman's face was indistinct, the perspective not quite right, the colors faded by time. But if Charles were to speak honestly, he would say it was the most valuable item he owned. Were his home to catch fire and he could save only one possession, it would be this small portrait, and the rest of it be damned... though perhaps he would ask Bryan to save the Monet.

He picked up a glass of wine from the table at his elbow and sipped it. Ordinarily he would have ended his night with one of his best whiskies, but she had never approved of strong drink. Wine was permissible in moderation, however, so he had one glass of a fine merlot, its taste enhanced by a few drops of fresh blood.

Already he could sense the approach of day in his bones. It was a familiar sensation, a survival instinct that warned the undead to seek shelter and safety far from sunlight before sleep rendered them insensible until the following sunset. Though some younger vampires jokingly referred to the feeling as "Last Call," for Charles it still conjured memories of the early years after he was first turned, when shelter and safety were difficult to find, and every sleep carried with it the very real possibility of never waking again if someone were to find his lair or betray him.

These days, surrounded by security and high walls, Charles felt fairly certain he was safe and would rise again at sunset, but it was impossible to forget the fear. One could deny it, ease it with alcohol, distract oneself with pleasure...but the fear remained. It might diminish, but it would never go away. The young ones feared less now because in their early years, they'd had less to fear.

Charles finished the last of his wine. He rose smoothly and moved to the wall, to a specially designed climate-controlled safe. He placed the portrait carefully on a shelf next to an old wooden cross, a handkerchief yellowed with age, and several similarly odd items. He closed the door firmly. The soft whirring of the lock engaging was audible only to vampire hearing.

With the safe locked against prying eyes, Charles crossed the room to the enormous bed. He draped his robe precisely over a chair and lay down, his body fitting neatly into a slight indentation created by many nights of sleeping in the same spot.

Though he was a frequent visitor to Niara's bedroom and many others, he had never invited any lover here. There were other bedrooms in the house for those activities. This room—this bed—was his.

And hers.

His fingers slid over the velvet coverlet, reaching out toward the left side of the bed as if seeking something or someone. Finding nothing, he returned his hand to his side and stared up at the ceiling.

The lights in the room dimmed, signaling the approach of dawn—as if the heaviness in his limbs wasn't enough of a warning. He grew colder and his vision faded. Beyond the walls of his home, the first rays of the sun appeared on the eastern horizon.

Emma, he thought.

And then all was darkness.

4

The next night, Charles woke at sunset, bathed, dressed, and enjoyed a light breakfast from the throat of a raven-haired earth mage named Miranda.

Within an hour of waking, he was on his way to Hawthorne's, reading a report of the day's events.

"Any news from Amira or Leah?" Adri asked, catching Charles's eye in the rearview mirror.

He consulted the report. "Leah says Jack Justice did not locate any rogues last night and returned to his hotel shortly after dawn, where he stayed and slept until just before noon. He and the production team filmed some scenes in several locations during the afternoon and evening."

"Do we have his current location?" Bryan asked.

Charles skimmed the rest of Leah's message. "He is currently searching an area near a city park where a number of homeless individuals are known to camp during the night."

Bryan drummed his fingers on his knee. "Where the rogue sightings were reported?"

Charles nodded. "No reports of armed vigilantes thus far, which is—"

He broke off as a sudden chill touched his mind. Valas spoke urgently. *Charles, your presence is required at Northbourne immediately. Amira's Hunters have captured a rogue vampire. They are coming here now.*

We are on our way, he replied. Out loud, he said, "Ms. Smith, we are needed at Northbourne."

"Yes, sir." Adri made an illegal U-turn in the middle of the street and accelerated in the direction of Vampire Court headquarters.

Charles reached out again to Valas. *What information do we have about the captured rogue?*

A brief pause, indicating Valas had been speaking to someone before turning her attention back to him. *Her identity is as yet unknown. The Hunters followed a blood trail and found her severely wounded in an abandoned building near the park you visited last night. They believe she was injured in a fall onto a fence. Though she was able to tear herself free, she lost too much blood and is too young to heal without assistance.*

Despite the grim news about the rogue's condition, Charles felt a measure of hope. *Has her scent provided any useful information about her master?*

Amira reports that she bears no scent of her maker.

He hissed. *Impossible.*

Indeed. Valas's voice in his head was tinged with anger. *I am assured it is so. Perhaps it is a result of the symbols.*

What symbols?

She bears symbols in her flesh. We will see them ourselves when they arrive at Northbourne.

Were any of the symbols familiar?

I am told they are mage symbols, but their meanings are unclear.

Charles weighed several options in the space of a second and came to a decision. *We will require assistance from a mage outside the Court to understand the symbols.*

You are referring to the mage private investigator?

Yes.

I concur. You will make the arrangements?

Of course. He glanced out the window. *We are fifteen minutes from the manor.*

Another pause. *Amira has brought the rogue. Join us in the holding cells when you arrive.* The chill dissipated as Valas ended their connection.

Charles turned to Bryan, sitting at his right. "A rogue has been apprehended and is being taken to Northbourne. Mark Dunlap is needed there immediately."

Bryan took out his phone. "Should I send a car for him?"

"Yes, and notify Dunlap of their ETA so he is prepared for their arrival. We have no time for delays."

Charles settled back as Bryan made the arrangements for transporting Dunlap and Adri raced through nearly deserted streets toward the headquarters of the Vampire Court.

His short-lived elation at the news of a captured rogue had given way to a combination of frustration, curiosity, and uneasiness at the news about the lack of scent and presence of mage symbols on the rogue. It was an unexpected and most unwelcome development in an already difficult situation. He hoped Dunlap would be able to unravel the meaning behind the symbols.

If not, Charles feared the attack on Christine Foreman and the chaos caused by Jack Justice's arrival were merely a taste of things to come.

They passed few other vehicles on their way to Northbourne. Even on a weeknight Charles would have normally expected some traffic, but the rogue attacks meant many people were staying home. With the roads clear, Adri made the drive in just under twenty minutes.

When she braked sharply well ahead of Northbourne's drive, Charles looked up from his phone and saw several dozen protestors assembled in front of the gate. Most carried signs and wore T-shirts and hats with anti-vampire slogans. One large banner read *Vampires are Murderers*.

Two sheriff's department SUVs were parked nearby, their windows down and headlights off. The deputies had been assigned to watch the protestors and ensure their demonstration remained peaceful. Adri raised a hand as she drove past, but neither of the deputies returned the greeting.

From a legal standpoint, Northbourne and the property surrounding it belonged to the Vampire Court. While the authority of the sheriff's department ended at the property line, the manor—like the headquarters of the Chicago, New York, Atlanta, and New Orleans Courts—fell under the jurisdiction of the federal Supernatural and Paranormal Entity Management Agency, or SPEMA.

"There's twice as many out here tonight as last night," Adri said as she turned into the driveway and slowed to a stop in front of the retractable barricades. "I see a lot of Human Future and Daylighters shirts, too."

"I saw Don Hall of the Daylighters interviewed on the news this morning." Bryan watched the crowd as it slowly parted in front of the SUV. "He said membership in the Daylighters organization has skyrocketed since the attacks. He talked more about that than the attacks themselves."

"A more cynical person might think he was happy about the attacks," Adri said, her eyes on the gate in front of them as the barricades slid down into the ground. "They've been good business for hate groups, that's for sure."

Charles had watched Hall's interview upon waking and come to the same conclusion. And while he agreed with Valas that any action taken against Alex Foreman, Jack Justice, or anti-supe leaders like Don Hall would do more harm than good, he shared his fellow Court members' loathing for them.

The massive gate began to swing open. As Adri drove slowly through the opening in the crowd, the protestors shouted and cursed, their voices muffled by the thick doors and windows of the SUV. Several threw water bottles and other items as the SUV passed. The deputies made no move to intervene.

Black-clad enforcers emerged from behind the gate to keep the protestors back. Once the SUV passed through the opening, the enforcers retreated and the gate swung closed.

Adri drove quickly down the quarter-mile-long driveway that led to the mansion that served as the headquarters of the Vampire Court of the Northwestern United States.

The stately home, with its five-story domed atrium and multiple underground levels, had once belonged to a shipping magnate. The Vampire Court had purchased it in 1900 and more than a century of renovations and alterations had completely changed the interior while leaving the exterior virtually untouched.

Adri pulled through the circular drive and parked directly in front of the wide front steps. Charles was out of the SUV before it came to a complete stop, Bryan right behind him.

Just as his foot touched the bottom step, a blast of cold and fury nearly made him stumble. As he regained his footing, he reached out to the head of the Court. *Valas? We are here. What has happened?*

Her only response was wordless rage.

As one of the Court enforcers opened the front door, the building trembled under their feet. Valas was angry—very, very angry.

"Was that from Valas?" Bryan asked, startled.

"I am afraid so," Charles replied, and they ran.

Mark Dunlap strode into the conference room, set his briefcase down, shook Charles's hand briskly, and said, "I hope that coffee is for me."

Charles gestured at the tray on the table. "Please, help yourself."

With an appreciative grunt, the burly mage private investigator poured himself a mug of coffee, added a splash of creamer, and sat down in the chair closest to the tray. As Dunlap pulled a notepad and pen from his briefcase, Charles studied the other man.

As always, Dunlap wore a long-sleeved plaid shirt, jeans, and work boots. While some members of the Court found his casual attire disrespectful, Charles was far more concerned with the quality of his work, which was exemplary. Dunlap had been an MPI for nearly thirty years and had operated as an independent investigator for the Vampire Court for the last ten. Now in his early fifties, he owned the second-largest private investigation firm in the city and both his attention to detail and discretion were beyond reproach. It was those attributes Charles needed, as well as some of the PI's more specialized magic-related skills.

Dunlap disliked small talk, another trait Charles appreciated, especially now. As the investigator uncapped his pen, Charles activated the wall-mounted screen. Jack Justice's profile appeared.

Dunlap looked up at the screen and scowled. "That prick."

"You are aware of the recent attacks in the city?"

"The rogues? Of course." Dunlap took a long drink of coffee, draining half the mug at once. Charles, who didn't care for coffee, very nearly grimaced. "I figured you'd be holed up working out your strategy for dealing with Justice and his traveling circus, especially after what happened to Christine Foreman and the nonsense down by the park last night."

"Others are searching for Foreman's sister and monitoring Mr. Justice. My focus is on finding and capturing the rogues before more attacks occur, and before Justice—or anyone else—summarily executes them."

"Which would leave you with no way of figuring out who made them." Dunlap set his mug down. "You have any success tracking them down?"

"In a manner of speaking."

Dunlap's bushy eyebrows went up. "How can I help?"

Charles deliberately tapped the table with two fingers. At this prearranged signal, Dunlap's expression became distant and Charles sensed a rise of magic. "*Sub rosa*," Dunlap murmured.

Wards flared, isolating the conference room and preventing eavesdropping. Dunlap was only a mid-level mage, but his air magic was sufficient to provide additional security for conversations like the one they were about to have.

At Charles's gesture, Bryan opened a cabinet and took out a wine bottle made of dark glass and covered with runes, its opening sealed with a glass stopper also covered with symbols. He placed it carefully on the table and stepped back.

Dunlap leaned forward to study the bottle. "What's this?"

"A captured rogue," Charles said, somewhat dryly. "Hunters tracked a severely injured rogue and brought her to Northbourne. Within minutes of her arrival, however, she died."

"So this bottle is full of her ashes?" Dunlap shook his head. "That was good thinking, grabbing one of the bottles you use to store vampire blood and pouring her in there, but even if you did it immediately, magic dissipates quickly. Its usefulness is probably close to zero for any sort of trace."

"Even so, we must try. Many lives may depend on our success." Charles slid a folder across the table. "There is more."

Dunlap flipped the folder open and stared. "Christ almighty."

Slowly, he picked up a small stack of eight-by-ten photos and spread them out on the table, picking up each one and studying it closely.

Charles gestured at the pictures. "Fortunately, prior to her death, we were able to take photos of the rogue. As you can see, her flesh bore runes we believe to be mage symbols. Some were drawn with henna and others were tattooed or cut into her flesh."

"Hard to see the details of the symbols with all the blood and the light wasn't great." Dunlap held up one of the photos and squinted. "Are her eyes red, or is that a trick of the light?"

"They were red."

"Red eyes? What the hell does that mean?"

Charles nearly snarled. "We do not know."

"Can your people do anything to enhance the images?"

"They are attempting to do so. In the meantime, what can you determine from these photos?"

"Not a hell of a lot, frankly. You see this symbol here?" Dunlap held up a photo of the rogue's mangled torso and pointed to a rune just below her right breast. "That's earth magic, but this one beneath it looks like blood magic. I'm seeing spellwork I don't recognize, and without the body it's going to the damn difficult to suss out what all this means. I hate to say it, but it's beyond my abilities."

It was not the pronouncement Charles wanted to hear. "And the ashes in the bottle?"

"A different kind of problem, but same answer. You need an earth mage, preferably one with some knowledge of blood magic symbology. Even then, it's a tall order."

Charles was well aware he was asking for a miracle. The situation left him little choice. "Do you know of someone who could meet our needs in this matter?"

Dunlap took a deep breath. "I may. I have a new trainee investigator working for me who is as good with wards and spellwork as anyone I've ever seen, and she's not the sort to back away from a challenge. If you're needing some answers, she might just be the one to get them for you."

Charles frowned. "You would suggest the Court entrust this investigation to a trainee?"

"Normally I wouldn't, but she isn't your typical trainee." Dunlap paused, weighing his words.

Charles sensed uncharacteristic reserve in the usually forthright investigator. Not deceit, he decided, but a reluctance combined with what might be protectiveness. Interesting.

Though a fierce advocate for his investigators and the interests and security of his company, Dunlap had never before shown any kind of personal attachment to an employee. Charles wondered if Dunlap was having an affair with this new trainee. Humans tended to become emotionally attached to lovers; it would explain his hesitation. Charles found Dunlap's wife Sharon to be particularly disagreeable, and Dunlap would hardly be the first middle-aged man to seek the pleasures of a younger woman.

Finally, Dunlap cleared his throat and continued. "She's only been with me a few months, but I'll tell you what I told my wife: if I had to choose one person from my firm to have my back, it would be her. She's young, but you wouldn't know it to talk to her. Nothing rattles this woman. She learns fast, follows instructions, and has the kind of instincts you usually only get when you've been doing this for a long time, or you've gone through the kind of bad times that teach you real hard lessons." He hesitated, then added, "She had kind of a wild past back in Chicago, but she seems to have left that life far behind her. I wouldn't recommend her for this if I had any kind of reservations about either her abilities or her discretion."

As Dunlap spoke, Charles revised his assessment of the relationship between the Court's lead investigator and his new trainee. Dunlap's protectiveness was more fatherly; he was concerned for the trainee's safety but confident in her abilities. Charles had worked with him long enough to respect his assessment, though he still had reservations about hiring a young trainee for such a dangerous and sensitive assignment—especially after hearing Dunlap allude to a "wild past." In Charles's experience, few people truly left their pasts behind them.

"What is this trainee's name?" he asked.

"Alice Worth."

Charles glanced at Bryan, who moved to a laptop at the far end of the conference table. A number of clicks and a few seconds later, the screen on the wall switched from Jack Justice's dossier to a different page.

Dunlap raised his mug in a salute. "You already have her information, I see."

Charles barely heard him. His attention was on the screen.

In addition to her basic information, there were four photos. Two were posed—her driver's license and MDI identification badge pictures—and the other two were candid shots taken by someone sent by the Court. She had been photographed leaving the MDI building and again at what was probably her home, sitting on what appeared to be a back porch.

She was beautiful, but that wasn't what had caused Charles to pause. It was her eyes: dark, shadowed, haunted. The dossier listed her age as twenty-four, but those were not the eyes of someone so young.

He steepled his fingers and studied the photos. She'd managed to force an uncertain smile for the MDI badge but her expression looked as though she had not wanted her picture taken. She wore the same uncomfortable look in her driver's license photo, though in that earlier picture, taken not long after her arrival in the city, she appeared thinner and even more guarded.

In the candid shot taken in the MDI parking lot, she was looking around suspiciously, as if worried about a surprise attack. Given the photo had been taken during broad daylight and Charles knew MDI to be located in a fairly safe area, her apprehension was telling. Perhaps she feared the ghosts of her former life would follow her to her new home.

The photo taken in the backyard, however, captured another side of Dunlap's trainee. It was an unguarded moment, with no trace of the wariness or disquiet of the other photos. In the privacy and safety of her home, no doubt protected by its wards, Alice Worth looked almost blissful. Her head was tipped back and she was staring up at the sky, a glass of something that might have been whiskey in her hand. The contrast between the photos was startling.

Charles remembered Dunlap was waiting on his answer. "What can you tell me of this 'wild past'?" he asked.

Dunlap settled into his chair. "I'm sure you've got it all in the file, but the short version is that Alice had a good life and showed a lot of promise until her parents were killed in a boating accident when she was twenty-one. They say everyone copes differently with loss, but Alice went from straight-A pre-med college student to party girl almost overnight. Her parents left her a fortune and she blew through most of it pretty quickly."

"Alcohol? Drugs?" Charles asked.

Dunlap shrugged. "By all accounts, if it got you high, she used it. There were DUIs, arrests for trespassing and public intoxication, even a charge of contempt for failure to appear. The family attorney made a lot of money keeping her out of jail. It went on like that for almost two years. Then one day, poof—she disappeared."

At this, Charles turned his full attention to the investigator. "She disappeared? For how long?"

"More than a month."

"Did the police investigate?"

Dunlap sighed. "By that point, she'd burned all her bridges with what little family she had and all of her old friends hadn't had much to do with her in a long time. There was no one to file a report. By the time anyone knew she'd been missing for weeks, she turned back up, stone-cold sober. She told the freeloaders who'd been living in her house to hit the bricks, sold everything she owned, and moved out here for a fresh start."

Charles sorted through the idioms and thought he had at least a good idea of what Dunlap had said. "And how did this rather colorful young woman end up in your employ? She hardly seems the type you would hire, or someone who would pursue a career as an MPI."

Dunlap smiled. "I had an opening for a trainee. We've got more business than we can handle these days and I thought it was time to take someone on and train 'em up the right way. She showed up for the interview looking like she'd been through hell and back and told me she wanted to help people." His smile faded. "I've interviewed a lot of applicants over the years and heard a lot of reasons for wanting to become an MPI and that's the first time someone told me they wanted to help others. Maybe my wife is right and I'm a sentimental old fart, but it got to me. I hired her."

Charles pondered the photos again. "Where was she during the month she was missing?"

"She says the bender to end all benders and she doesn't remember most of it. She hit rock bottom. Then something happened that set her straight."

"Which was?"

Dunlap took a drink of coffee. "She saw someone die and realized if she didn't stop doing what she was doing, she'd end up dead too."

Charles's eyes narrowed. "Do you believe her?"

"I do believe her," the other man stated emphatically. "Maybe she's fudging on a few of the details, but I believe the story. In any case, she's been with me almost six months now and I think she may turn out to be one of the best investigators I've ever had. She wants to put all that in her past and I'm going to let her."

"And her magic?"

"Mid-level earth, mid-level air," Dunlap said.

Charles read his expression. "Earth and air only?"

"That's how she's registered." The investigator cleared his throat and poured more coffee, avoiding eye contact.

Dunlap didn't say so, but he clearly suspected Alice Worth had blood magic. Charles hoped it was true. If she did, it would increase the chances of using the trace from the ashes to find the rogue's maker. Even without blood magic, however, a mid-level earth mage should be able to match the trace to its source, assuming there was enough remaining. She might also be able to interpret the runes on the rogue's body.

"Time is against us," Charles said. "Alice Worth must come to Northbourne now. I will send a car." He gestured at Bryan, who took out his phone and began to text.

Dunlap put down his coffee. "Let me go with the driver to pick her up. Alice is liable to be hostile if your people show up on her doorstep in the middle of the night saying she's supposed to go with them. Someone's likely to get hurt."

Angered that Dunlap would think a member of his security detail would harm a Court asset, Charles snapped, "My enforcer would not injure her."

Dunlap snorted. "It's your enforcer I'm worried about, Vaughan. Alice can take care of herself." He paused. "One thing: she prefers not to shake hands. If you offer and she declines, I didn't want you to think she's being rude or that she has anti-vampire feelings."

"She prefers an alternate form of greeting?"

"She prefers to avoid any sort of physical contact. With anyone. It's just one of her...quirks."

Charles tilted his head. "To what do you attribute this unusual 'quirk'?"

Dunlap sighed and rose from the table. "I haven't asked and she hasn't said, but those kinds of quirks are usually the result of abuse. Add in the rest of her habits and I'm guessing something very bad happened to her, maybe during that month she was missing, maybe before. In any case, please try to remember that she's going to help you catch your rogue-maker and I apologize in advance for anything she may say or do that rubs you the wrong way."

Sir, are we certain it's advisable to include this woman in our investigation? Bryan's voice in his head was disapproving.

We seem to have little choice, Charles replied. Out loud, he said, "Very well. Bring your trainee in, Mr. Dunlap. We shall see what she can do."

5

Charles spent the next hour reading Alice Worth's Court dossier, compiled when she'd joined MDI. It was standard practice for all employees of any business that worked for the Court. Most such files went untouched except for periodic updates, unless that person came to the attention of the Court.

Alice's file was extensive and contained the information Dunlap had described, but in greater detail. There were copies of newspaper articles about the wealthy Worth family dating from Alice's childhood, an announcement on the occasion of her high school graduation, and a few pieces about the family at significant Chicago-area social events. Alice's life had certainly been one of privilege.

And then came the boating accident. A yacht full of drunken revelers collided with the Worths' boat and killed both Henry and Laura Worth. Alice, then in her last year of college, was miraculously not seriously injured, suffering only a broken arm and minor burns.

As Dunlap had said, Alice's fall from grace began only weeks after her parents' funeral. There were stories about alcohol- and drug-fueled parties, DUIs, and out-of-control behavior in public. Over the course of two years, Alice went from promising pre-med student to strung-out drug addict.

And then she disappeared for a month, only to come back as a changed woman.

Soon after her return, she'd sold her parents' home, divested all her remaining assets, and moved halfway across the country, severing all ties to her former life. She'd bought a modest house, invested her remaining savings, and gotten a job with MDI, where she'd been working for the past six months, training to become a licensed mage private investigator.

The more he read, the more Charles was convinced there was more to the story. That month-long vanishing act and sudden behavior change troubled him. Was it possible she had truly "hit rock bottom," as Dunlap said, and had a moment of clarity that caused her to change her ways? It was certainly plausible, but Charles's instincts told him he needed to know more.

He told himself it was because no one who worked for the Court should have any secrets that might make them vulnerable to extortion, but he found himself staring at the photo of Alice on her back porch. Strangely, it was that photo of her gazing at the sky like a woman enjoying freedom for the first time that convinced him Alice's story was more complex than what was contained in her dossier.

"I want a full background check," he told Bryan after he'd finished reading the file. "Assign our best researcher."

"Is the file incomplete?" Bryan asked as he texted.

"It is insufficient. In particular, I wish to know more about this missing month."

Bryan sent a second text. A reply came back almost immediately. "The background check is underway," he reported, reading from the screen. "We'll be notified when it's complete, or if any information is uncovered that the researcher deems urgent." His phone buzzed again. "Their vehicle is ten minutes out."

"Thank you." Charles collected the photos of the rogue and tucked them into the folder.

At just after midnight, someone knocked on the conference room door. Charles turned off the wall-mounted screen, hiding Alice Worth's dossier from view. He gave Bryan a nod.

Bryan opened the conference room door. Adri stepped into the room. "Sir, Mr. Dunlap and Ms. Worth." She gestured for her companions to enter.

As Charles rose, Dunlap walked in, followed by Alice. Bryan closed the door behind them as Adri left to check on the status of the enhanced photos.

Visitors to the Vampire Court were expected, if not required, to dress appropriately. Business casual or evening wear was rather the minimum expectation, even for an unexpected middle-of-the-night summons. Either Alice Worth was unaware of this expectation or she had decided, like her boss, to ignore it. Charles wagered on the latter.

She wore a leather jacket over a purple shirt, jeans, and tall boots, and her long dark hair was pulled back in a neat French braid. Her makeup was minimal, her jewelry simple: a monogram pendant in the shape of the letter *A*, crystal earrings, and a charm bracelet with a half-dozen smaller crystals. A messenger bag hung across her chest, leaving her hands free.

Once inside the conference room, Alice moved to put the wall at her back. Her eyes swept the room, assessing each person with a disconcerting speed and efficiency. Charles had the distinct impression she had automatically catalogued all items in the room for either weapon or threat potential. His enforcers followed the same habit, but as a result of years—or decades—of training and experience. Where and why would a trainee MPI with Alice's privileged background have learned such behaviors? Bryan's eyes narrowed, indicating he shared Charles's reservations.

When Alice's dark eyes met his, Charles saw only curiosity and professional detachment, with perhaps a hint of judicious reserve, rather than the usual apprehension of someone meeting a master vampire and member of the Vampire Court. She did not fear him, and that did not sit well with him.

Charles came around the conference table to greet her. "Ms. Worth, a pleasure to meet you," he said, extending his hand and flashing his fangs. He sensed dismay and anger from Dunlap at the deliberate provocation.

He expected fear, anger, shock, or irritation—or some combination thereof—from Alice in response to his challenge. Given her youth and the guarded demeanor he had seen in her photos, he also expected her to acquiesce and accept his handshake, perhaps in bad grace.

Instead, to his surprise and annoyance, he sensed, of all things, amusement. Her eyes twinkled as she leaned forward in a perfectly executed bow. "The pleasure is mine," she said.

The Court rules of conduct required that he return her greeting in kind. He withdrew his proffered hand and gave her a perfunctory half-bow, the prescribed response by a member of the Court to a guest who had shown formal deference with a lower bow.

He had been outmaneuvered in his own territory, in front of his head enforcer. Infuriated, he attempted to sense her magic and got another surprise.

Nothing.

He sensed nothing, when he should have felt the cool white of her air magic and the peaceful green of earth magic, if not also the delicious searing red of blood magic that never failed to arouse him. Her shields were incredibly strong. That meant years of training.

The only way to sense her magic would be to attempt to disrupt her shields, but he was reluctant to do so, as it might reveal his ability to sense emotions and he preferred to use that to his advantage without her knowledge. It was likely she was on her guard for a first meeting with a member of the Vampire Court. She would not always be so alert. There would be other opportunities.

A small, almost mocking smile turned up the corners of her mouth, as if she suspected he'd attempted to sense her magic and failed. Few would dare smirk in front of a master vampire. Her impudence both angered and interested him. It had been a very long time since any human had dared to defy him so openly.

His opening gambits having failed, Charles changed his approach. He gestured grandly at the tray of refreshments that had been laid out prior to their arrival. "I apologize for the late-night summons. You are welcome to coffee and food."

Both guests poured mugs of coffee, but while her boss took two pastries, Alice declined to accept any food. She added cream and sugar to her coffee, then sat beside Dunlap as Charles resumed his seat at the head of the table.

At Charles's signal, Dunlap again raised the *sub rosa* ward. Alice looked at Charles expectantly.

"Mr. Dunlap has familiarized you with the situation with the rogues, as I requested?" Charles asked her.

She nodded. "I've been following the news of the attacks, like everyone else. I'm sure you're all very concerned about interference from Jack Justice."

"To put it mildly," Charles said. "I am hopeful that with your help, we may be able to resolve the crisis before Justice and his entourage have the opportunity to turn the city into their hunting ground."

Her eyebrows went up. "With *my* help?"

Briefly, Charles explained how one of the rogues had been tracked and captured, then died shortly after arriving at Northbourne.

"You didn't give her blood to heal her wounds?" Her tone was disapproving.

"We were deeply concerned by the symbols in her flesh," he told her coldly. "We did not know what they were or how the magic might affect anyone who shared blood with her."

"That's what wards and nulling spells are for," she pointed out, unfazed by his glower. "Were you not able to get a mage here in time?" She read his expression and tilted her head. "Or are you not sure if you can trust the mages who work for you?"

If Dunlap was blunt to a fault, he had nothing on Alice's candor. "Until we know more about the rogue-maker, his or her mage accomplice, and the symbols, I am loathe to trust anyone with the information in our possession," Charles said.

"Probably a good idea." She finished her coffee and poured another cup. "Good coffee," she added, as if that was significant to her.

Adri arrived then with a thick red folder. Charles glanced through the enhanced photos, then handed the folder to Alice. She opened the folder and examined the first photo.

And Charles's suspicions about her murky past became certainties.

The first image in the stack was a close shot of the young vampire's mangled torso, bloody and gruesome, with exposed bones and internal organs. Most people would have reacted as Dunlap had, with shock and revulsion or even nausea. Alice Worth did not so much as flinch.

As she studied the photo, Charles recalled something Dunlap had said when he'd first described Alice: *She has the kind of instincts you usually only get when you've been doing this for a long time, or you've gone through the kind of bad times that teach you real hard lessons.*

At the time, he had discounted Dunlap's assessment, especially after hearing and reading about her privileged life and drug-fueled self-destructive behavior. Now, however, he was beginning to reconsider. There was nothing in Alice's file that would explain her lack of reaction to the photos. Whatever had occurred during that missing month, it was more significant than the story she'd given Dunlap.

One by one, Alice studied the pictures and arranged them on the table to recreate the spellwork as best she could. As Bryan remained on guard at the door, Charles, Adri, and Dunlap watched as she followed the symbols, tracing runes with her fingertip, her lips pursed in concentration.

Finally, Alice said, "I see two complete spells and fragments of at least four others." Her tone was professional and confident. "The runes on her left shoulder appear to be a masking spell. If this was on a mage, it would be for the purpose of disguising his or her magic. In this context, I would imagine it was designed to prevent you from catching the scent of whoever sired her."

"I did not know such a thing was possible," Charles said, displeased both by the spell's function and that he had been forced to admit a lack of knowledge.

She shook her head. "I've never seen it used in this way. Only a high-level blood mage would be able to do the spellwork. That's also true of the second complete spell, which appears to be a modified sleep spell."

Dunlap leaned down to get a closer look at the runes she was indicating. "Not possible. Sleep spells don't work on vampires."

"I said 'modified,'" Alice reminded him. "Ordinary sleep spells don't, but this one is designed to either keep the vampire in daytime sleep or force them to sleep on command. It looks like the sleep spell required the blood of the vampire's maker for it to work, which makes sense, since a master can compel a young vampire to sleep."

Charles's eyes narrowed. "That information is not common knowledge."

"It's not a secret," she replied. "And it's logical. A master would need the ability to control a very young vampire if his or her bloodlust took over. I understand that normally that ability diminishes within the first few months, so I presume this spell would extend that time frame indefinitely."

"And the other partial spells?" he asked.

She made a face. "'Partial' is the key word. Without seeing the entire spells, I'd only be guessing and there are too many possibilities. The one exception might be this one." She traced a set of runes on the vampire's stomach that had been partly destroyed when she'd had torn herself free from the fence. "This is a guess, mind you, but there's a good chance it's a kind of summoning spell."

Charles's brow furrowed. "Such as one would use to summon a spirit or demon?"

She nodded. "Similar. The spelled vampire would feel an irresistible pull, like a magnet, no matter where they were in relation to the mage who'd spelled them. And in answer to your next question, it would be possible to make one that would work on a vampire, *if* the vampire's maker provided the blood to anchor the spell. I've only got part of the spellwork here, but if it was done right, either the master or the mage could use the spell to summon the rogue. It's damaged, obviously, so they wouldn't have been able to recall her after she was injured even if she'd been in a condition to travel."

"So they could let her loose to attack someone, then bring her back in afterward?" Dunlap asked. "That might explain why you've had such a hard time tracking the rogues or finding one running around. It almost sounds like the rogues are being deployed and recalled."

Charles was getting answers to his questions about the symbols on the rogue and he didn't like any of them. "Is this spellwork difficult?"

"Very difficult work," Alice said immediately. "Also very time-consuming and draining. What I'm seeing would require skill and many years of training, and probably experience with working with vampires. Specialized and modified spells like these are far from common. You might have to look close to home to find the mage responsible."

He had feared as much. "Do you have a theory as to why the rogue's eyes are red?"

"That's probably from the blood magic spells. I've not seen that before with a vampire, but we're in uncharted territory here."

"What else can you determine from the photos?" Dunlap asked.

Alice sighed. "That's about it, I think. I'll be able to tell you more once I get my hands on the rogue's ashes, maybe sense the trace of the mage who did the spellwork or even the vampire who sired her. Where are the ashes? Time is ticking and the longer we wait, the less trace there will be."

Charles studied her. "You are aware you are operating as an agent of the Court and that everything you see and hear is confidential?"

"Yes, Mark told me that in the SUV," she said impatiently. "Give me something to sign if you have to, but let's not take our time about it."

Charles was beginning to see why Dunlap liked her; her personality was very like her employer's. He was certain few others on the Court would appreciate her brusque manner and lack of deference, but little else mattered at the moment besides finding out who was making the rogues.

At Charles's signal, Bryan retrieved the bottle from a cupboard and set it on the table.

Alice studied the bottle. "This wasn't designed to preserve trace necessarily, just life energy. It was the best you could do under the circumstances, I suppose." She sighed.

"Indeed," Charles informed her icily. "We preserved her remains in this way because these ashes represent our best chance at identifying the vampire who sired the rogues. Once it has lost the last of its trace, we will have nothing."

Alice rotated the bottle slowly, examining the runes etched into the glass. "Whose runes are these?"

"A mage who works for the Court." Charles eyed her, wondering if he had made a mistake by following Dunlap's recommendation to bring such a young and inexperienced MPI into the investigation. She had done well interpreting the symbols on the rogue, but sensing magic trace was quite different—and quite difficult, even for mages with many years of training and experience. "Once the seal is broken, the trace will dissipate," he reminded her.

"I understand." Her voice was edged with irritation.

Alice's manner remained altogether much too casual for his liking. Did she not understand the seriousness of the situation? Or was she simply supremely confident in her abilities? Adri and Bryan exchanged a look, clearly sharing his unease.

Alice picked up the bottle. "Do you need privacy to work?" Dunlap asked her.

She shook her head. "No, but stay back, and anyone here with magic needs to keep it to themselves until I'm done."

Her fingers moved as if she was playing the piano in midair as she explored the spellwork on the bottle. Charles sensed a faint frisson of magic as the spells broke.

Without hesitation, Alice pulled the glass stopper from the bottle. She swore softly and poured the ashes out into her hand. They spilled over her palm and onto the table.

Charles was at her side in a blink but it was too late. He was certain she had just destroyed their only evidence and opened his mouth to order them both to leave.

Before he could speak, Alice dropped her shields and her magic danced on the edges of his senses in a swirl of white and green. To his surprise and disappointment, he did not sense any blood magic. Why had Dunlap implied she was a blood mage? Or was her blood magic hidden so well that he could not sense it?

She gasped softly. Charles sensed faint echoes of dark magic from the ashes. They teased the very edge of his awareness and then vanished. There had been almost no trace left and now it was gone.

Charles wanted to smash the table in frustration. He'd known the ashes offered little chance of a lead, but he'd hoped they could be used to find the rogues or their maker. The bitter taste returned to his mouth, ten times worse than before.

Alice took a deep breath, exhaled, and set the bottle down. She carefully poured the ash she'd been holding onto the table and wiped her hand with a tissue before placing it gently next to the ash. She regarded the little pile with sadness, as if she thought of it as someone's remains rather than simply ashes or evidence. It was surprisingly unguarded and sentimental for the decidedly brusque mage. Then the moment was gone and her face was a cold mask once more.

He expected her to apologize for the failure or to tell him there had been too little of the trace left for anyone to use.

Instead, she squared her shoulders and turned to face him. "Okay, I've got good news and bad news. The bad news is that it *was* a masking spell designed to obscure the trace from whoever sired her and it worked, mostly. I got a hint of the maker's trace, but it won't be strong enough for me to track."

Charles studied her. "If you came into physical contact with the rogue-maker, would you be able to recognize the trace?"

Her eyes darkened. She squashed her fear quickly, but not before he had confirmation that the aversion to physical contact Dunlap had described went deeper than mere idiosyncrasy. "I might," she said shortly, her voice flat. "Skin contact increases the chances. No guarantees."

"And the good news?" Dunlap interjected, moving a protective half-step closer to his trainee.

"I know who did the spellwork on the rogue."

Charles's eyes lit up silver. "You know the name of the blood mage who has done this?" He gestured at the photos on the table.

She shook her head. "Not their name, no." She picked up the now-empty bottle and waved it at him. "Whoever did the spellwork on this is the same person who spelled the rogue. Your big bad rogue-making blood mage is under your own roof."

6

ALICE'S STATEMENT WAS GREETED WITH SILENCE.

Charles was the first to speak. "You are mistaken."

His statement caused a flash of resentment that she didn't bother to hide. "I am *not* mistaken." She pointed at the bottle and then at the pile of ash on the table. "*This* trace matches *that* trace."

"Then the trace from the bottle must have bled over into the ash," Charles stated.

She shook her head. "No, it didn't. The spells on the bottle are specifically designed *not* to affect the contents. I know what I'm sensing."

"Clara McKnight has worked as a mage for the Court for more than twenty years," Dunlap said. Disbelief warred with anger in his voice. "I've known her even longer than that. Alice, are you sure?"

"Yes, I'm sure," she said testily. "I wouldn't say it otherwise. You think I'd throw around an accusation like that in front of a member of the Court if I wasn't sure?"

"Perhaps you wish to impress us," Charles said.

"It wouldn't be very impressive if I was wrong, would it?" Alice retorted.

"Rather the opposite, in fact." Charles crossed his arms. "Your interpretation of the spellwork on the rogue appeared competent, but I find it difficult to believe that Ms. McKnight would collude to create violent rogues."

"Then why didn't you ask *her* to tell you what these spells are?" she shot back. "Why didn't you show *her* the ash?"

When Charles didn't reply, she spread her hands to indicate the conference room. "I don't see her up here and I have no doubt she's nearby, so that would have been a much faster option than sending someone to bring me in. So you *don't* know for sure that you can trust her, and if that's the case, maybe you have a personal reason for being so defensive."

Charles's eyes blazed. Alarmed, Dunlap moved to stand partially in front of Alice and shot her a warning look, which was met with a lack of emotion that even Charles found mildly disturbing.

"Mr. Vaughan, she may not have phrased it very diplomatically, but Alice made a fair point," Dunlap said. "I wondered myself why you didn't involve Clara. I don't think she's behind this, but if on some level you don't trust her, then we have to be sure. Alice's word is enough for me to be concerned."

Charles glanced at Adri. "Where is Ms. McKnight presently?"

The enforcer looked up from her phone. "Lower level, in her work area. She's been here since eleven o'clock."

Charles took the bottle from Alice's hand. "We will go now and determine whether or not she is involved."

"Let's take these," Alice said, gathering up the photos on the table. "See what she tells you they mean."

"You are not coming with us," Charles told her.

She raised an eyebrow and continued stacking the photos. "Suit yourself, but you're about to confront a blood mage on her turf. She's bound to have spells and wards all around. I don't know what kind of fail-safes you have in place, but going in there without mage backup is downright foolish."

She put the photos in the folder and turned to face him. "If I'm wrong, I'll owe you all an apology. Maybe she'll see something in the spellwork I missed and I'll learn something. But If I'm right, she could turn you all into pâté and there wouldn't be a damn thing you could do about it."

"You are not a blood mage," Charles pointed out. "What if anything could you do against one if we *were* attacked?"

Alice ignored the first part of his statement. "Don't underestimate air and earth magic, Mr. Vaughan. If the shit hits the fan, you're better off with us there than without us."

Dunlap gave him an apologetic look. At some point, Alice's employer would have to have a word with his trainee about her language, but for now there were more pressing matters to attend to than Alice Worth's lack of manners.

"Fine." Charles gestured at the door. "You will accompany us, if for no other reason than to offer Ms. McKnight your apology in person."

"Let's hope that's how this turns out," Dunlap said grimly, picking up the folder of photos and following Alice to the door.

As they descended several flights of stairs to the first underground level of Northbourne via a seldom-used staircase, Charles mulled the enigma that was Alice Worth.

She was crass and rude, and yet familiar with the finer points of Vampire Court etiquette. She'd grown up wealthy and privileged, but had the guarded instincts of a trained fighter. She'd thwarted his attempts to assert control, then given them honest answers to their questions about the spellwork on the rogue. She was a sea of contradictions around an island of mystery and a challenge that appealed to him despite her thorny disposition.

During their walk downstairs, Alice was on high alert, watching her surroundings for potential danger. Given she and Dunlap were in the headquarters of the Vampire Court and under his personal protection, Charles found her concern insulting.

Sensing his annoyance, Adri addressed the edgy mage. "You are safe here and well-guarded, Ms. Worth."

"Call me Alice," the younger woman said, scanning for hidden threats in every corner and shadow. "It's no reflection on your abilities as a bodyguard. Since none of us are entirely sure who to trust right now, just think of me as another pair of eyes keeping a lookout."

Her simple logic left Charles both irritated and mildly amused, despite the gravity of the situation. It was, he suspected, likely to be a frequent reaction to her almost compulsive forthrightness.

Dunlap, for his part, seemed torn between almost fatherly pride in Alice's interpretations of the photographed spells, nervousness that she would push Charles too far, and unease about Clara McKnight's possible involvement in the rogues. He stayed at Alice's side during their walk. Charles noticed he was careful not to brush against her.

As the group reached the first basement level and proceeded down a long hallway, Charles sensed a spike of uneasiness from Alice. Perhaps she was uncomfortable at being underground. It was a common phobia among humans, and not without some justification.

Though not gifted with the ability to sense emotions, Dunlap was aware his trainee was acutely uncomfortable and attempted to distract her by pointing out some of the antiques and tapestries on display.

"Impressive, isn't it?" he asked her, gesturing at a particularly ornate vase.

She glanced at the vase. Charles got the impression she was assessing it not for its beauty, but as a potential weapon. "It certainly is," she said.

Alice's unease grew as they went farther away from the staircase. Charles found himself slowing slightly and allowing Bryan to lead the group as he fell into step next to her. "Regardless of the outcome of our meeting with Ms. McKnight, you and Dunlap will both leave here safely," he said quietly. "I give you my word."

He was not surprised when her disquiet remained unabated. "I'll drink to that when I'm back home," she muttered.

"What will you drink?" he asked, curious.

Startled, she looked up at him, her dark brown eyes searching his face. For what, he wasn't sure. "I like a good Scotch whisky, neat," she said reluctantly.

He smiled, careful not to flash his fangs, and let his eyes glow softly. It was a smile many women had found irresistible. "I have an extensive collection of fine Scotch. Perhaps we will raise a glass when this case is concluded."

To his annoyance, she seemed unaffected by his flirtation. "Maybe." Her tone indicated that she thought it unlikely.

At the end of the hall, the group stopped in front of a pair of ornately carved doors. Alice stepped to the side and put her back to the wall, as if concerned about a preemptive attack from inside.

"This Clara McKnight doesn't know about me, right?" she asked Dunlap.

He shook his head. "No, I haven't mentioned you to her."

She smiled. "Good."

"Why do you ask this?" Charles demanded.

"Just until we know for sure what's going on, how about you introduce me simply as Mark's assistant?" she suggested. "No need for her to know I'm a mage. We can keep that in our back pocket in case it comes in handy."

Charles gave her a nod. "Very well."

Bryan placed his hand on a scanner next to the doors and the lock deactivated. He opened the door and Adri led the group through the doorway. Bryan closed the door behind them.

When the lock engaged with a heavy *thunk*, Alice looked sharply at Charles. Vexed, he reminded her, "I gave you my word you will leave here safely."

"I will burn this building down if you try to keep me here," she said flatly.

Dunlap made a startled sound. Both Adri and Bryan moved closer, flanking Charles. The vampire and his enforcers made for an imposing group, but Alice faced them defiantly, undaunted.

Charles was unsure if a mid-level earth and air mage could cause destruction on that level, but the expression on Dunlap's face indicated he thought it was more than possible. Whether she could do so was a question Charles very much wanted an answer to, but she clearly believed she could.

It would be madness to destroy the headquarters of the Vampire Court, but Alice's threat did clarify the cause of her uneasiness: not a fear of being underground per se, but of captivity. He filed that away as useful information and raised his hand as a visible signal to his enforcers to stand down. "That will not be necessary. You will not be held here tonight against your will."

A wry smile twisted the corner of her mouth. "Not tonight."

"Not tonight," he agreed.

He saw a flash of what might have been a genuine smile. "I appreciate the honesty." She glanced down the hall. "Your mage is down here?"

"Yes. The second door on the left. You will comport yourself as Mr. Dunlap's assistant unless I request otherwise."

"Got it."

The small group approached the door to Clara McKnight's workshop. Charles sensed the mage at work inside. She was quite worried about something; what, he did not know.

He reached out with his mind and touched hers. *Ms. McKnight.*

He sensed surprise and a hint of fear, not unexpected since he had no doubt startled her. *Mr. Vaughan? Am I needed upstairs?*

I am outside your workshop door. I require your assistance on an urgent matter.

A pause, and then she replied, *One moment. I'm working on a spell. Give me a minute to dispel it and lower the containment wards.*

Thank you.

A few moments later, Charles felt a frisson of magic as the wards on the workshop dropped. Clara McKnight opened the door.

The slim middle-aged brunette wore jeans and a loose long-sleeved shirt, her feet bare. A streak of chalk was visible on her forehead. "Mr. Vaughan," she greeted him, then smiled warmly when she saw Dunlap. "Mark! I didn't know you were here! How are you?"

"Doing great, Clara," Dunlap replied, with no hint of suspicion in his voice, though he didn't return her smile. "Sorry to interrupt your work."

"Not a problem at all." Clara spotted Alice. "Who have you brought with you?"

Dunlap gestured. "This is my new assistant, Alice. We were working late when Mr. Vaughan asked me to come up here, so I thought I'd bring her along, introduce her to him, let her see what Northbourne looks like."

"Nice to meet you, ma'am," Alice said meekly.

Charles was stunned by her transformation. Her confrontational attitude had vanished. When he wasn't looking, she'd slipped on a pair of thick-rimmed glasses she must have had tucked in her bag. Her shoulders hunched slightly and she avoided their gazes, scuffing the toe of her boot on the stone floor. If he hadn't spent the past half-hour with the real Alice, he would never have believed this shy young woman would have been capable of smirking in his face.

A consummate actress, he thought. *Fascinating.*

Clara turned her attention back to Charles, uninterested in Dunlap's seemingly mousy assistant. "What can I help you with, Mr. Vaughan?"

He took the red folder from Dunlap and held it up. "Can we step inside?"

"Of course, of course, come in." Clara stepped back and held the door open for the group to file in, then closed it behind them.

Bryan stood by the door and Adri stayed at Charles's side as they moved into her work area. Alice stuck close to Dunlap, maintaining her scared-girl persona, but Charles noted how her eyes scanned every inch of the room before focusing on Clara.

The main room was dominated by three large circles inlaid in the floor, currently marked with complex rings of hand-drawn chalk runes. Tables and cabinets lined the back wall, covered with implements ranging from chalk to tubes of henna and stacks of books.

The other half of the front room was empty except for a long table partially covered with more stacks of books. A hallway led into the private apartment behind the work area, where Clara sometimes slept when her duties kept her at Northbourne for extended periods.

"Would you like to sit?" Clara asked, gesturing at the table. "I apologize for the mess. I can clear some space."

"Thank you, but that will not be necessary. Our time is rather limited." Charles studied her. "I am sure you are aware of the recent attacks by rogue vampires and our unsuccessful attempts to capture a rogue and determine who is siring them."

Clara shook her head sadly. "I've been following the news, of course. The entire situation is unfortunate. Have there been any developments?"

Charles sensed only Clara's typical professional detachment; no guilt, no deceit, and no indication of any involvement with the rogues.

Annoyed that he had allowed a young, inexperienced trainee to cause him to question the loyalty of one of the Court's most trusted employees, he glanced at Alice, ready to show his displeasure and demand an apology for wasting their time.

She was studying Clara closely, her eyes narrowed.

Despite his irritation, there was something about the deadly serious way Alice was scrutinizing Clara that caused him to hold his tongue. She appeared to be focused on Clara's arms, hidden by the long sleeves of her shirt. It wasn't unusual for Clara to wear such a shirt; the humans who lived and worked in Northbourne frequently complained that the ambient temperature was colder than was preferred.

Charles found himself wondering why Alice was so focused on Clara's arms. Was she sensing something? He tried to catch her eye, but she was watching Clara and didn't look his way. Without having bitten her or being in physical contact, he couldn't contact her telepathically to ask what she thought might be hidden under Clara's long sleeves.

She suspects something, sir, Adri said in his head. *But I can't tell what it is.* Her irritation matched his own.

Charles's jaw tightened. Would there ever be any interaction with Alice that did not involve frustration?

He refocused his attention on Clara. He was accustomed to sensing and seeing affection from her when they spoke. Though it had been some time since he had last bitten her and even longer since he'd last desired her, humans—even powerful blood mages—were overly sentimental about bedmates. Though he'd requested that she not demonstrate such feelings in front of others, Clara had been unwilling or unable to hide her adoration, even in meetings with members of the Court. She seemed not to understand that his interest in her began and ended with the taste and effect of her blood.

He was, therefore, quite surprised and somewhat relieved to see none of the usual fondness in Clara's expression when she looked at him. Perhaps his last remonstration had finally persuaded her to maintain more professional decorum.

"Ms. McKnight," he said, "The reason we have come to see you this evening is to ask for your assistance."

"How can I help you, sir?" Clara asked. He thought he heard something odd in her tone, something that sounded almost like bitterness, but he sensed no anger or animosity, so he decided he must have been mistaken.

He opened the folder, selected one of the photographs—one that showed the rogue's mangled upper body and face—and presented it to her. "I would like your opinion on this."

If Alice's reaction had been strangely detached, Clara's was just as he had expected: shock, horror, and disbelief.

She gasped and stared, holding the photo as her other hand went to her mouth. "Oh no," she whispered, clearly sickened. "This is horrible. This poor girl. Wait, was this photo taken in one of the cells downstairs?"

"It was," Charles said. "Earlier tonight, she was found severely injured and brought to Northbourne."

"Where is she now?" Clara asked anxiously. "Can I see her?"

"Unfortunately, she died from her injuries shortly after these pictures were taken."

Clara sighed. "Oh, that's too bad. I suppose you weren't able to tell who sired her."

"For some reason, we were unable to detect the scent of her maker," Charles told her. "It is most perplexing. We thought perhaps it was the result of the spellwork on her body."

"I don't know of any spell that could obscure the scent of a vampire's maker, but if you couldn't identify the maker by smell, maybe you're right. I suppose it's the only explanation."

"What can you tell us about the spells you see?" he asked.

Clara studied the photo, then took another from the stack that showed a close-up of the rogue's torso. She grimaced. "Well, this one here on her shoulder might be the masking spell that hid her maker's scent," she said finally. "It's quite strange and I can't be certain just from the photograph, but I recognize elements of a masking spell. It might have had a different purpose, however—again, impossible to tell its true purpose from an image."

That was the spell Alice had identified as the masking spell, though while Alice had been quite confident of its function, Clara seemed much less sure. Was Alice's certainty merely cockiness, or was Clara's hesitation an attempt to muddy the waters? He still sensed no duplicity, though, which made the former more likely.

He pointed at the symbols Alice had identified as a modified sleep spell. "And this one?"

She pondered the spellwork. "Some kind of sleep spell, I think, but I don't know of any sleep spell that would work on a vampire or what its purpose might be. If I had a chance to try to emulate the spellwork, perhaps I could determine its purpose."

So far, Clara's responses had matched Alice's, but with far less certainty. He still sensed no duplicity. It was beginning to look like they'd come downstairs for no reason other than to corroborate Alice's interpretations. That did have some value and validated part of Alice's work, but Charles was far from pleased that Alice had almost caused him to openly accuse a Court mage of conspiring to create the rogues.

"What about this one?" Dunlap asked, pointing to the partial spell Alice had thought might have been some kind of summoning spell. Charles sensed he was still uneasy.

Clara pursed her lips. "It's not all there, but I recognize a protection spell. Yes, that's quite clearly what it is." She sounded certain.

"You're lying."

Alice's voice startled them. Charles turned to look sharply at her, but the young woman was staring straight at Clara, her eyes narrowed, her meek façade gone. If she noticed his anger, she ignored it.

Clara looked up and frowned. "Excuse me? What did you say?"

"You heard me." Alice stepped out from behind Dunlap and joined Charles at Clara's side, removing the fake glasses and tucking them in her bag. "You're lying. That's nowhere near a protection spell. It's a summoning spell and you know it."

Clara snorted. "A summoning spell on a *vampire?* There's no such thing. Mark, your assistant is out of her league, isn't she?" She sniffed. "What do *you* know about blood magic?"

Alice pointed to the photograph, her finger tracing the lines. "Those are the runes that make the spell for a summoning. They're woven with the symbols for 'vampire-maker' and 'vampire-offspring,' and *that* is the rune for 'blood mage,' which means—"

"Ridiculous," Clara snapped. "Get out of my apartment."

"—*Which means*," Alice continued, her voice hardening, "The blood mage who made these spells could summon this vampire, just like her maker."

Her face red, Clara yanked the photograph away. "You stupid girl—"

The surge of pure fury Charles sensed from Alice was almost staggering in both its suddenness and intensity. He wasn't sure if it was a result of being called "stupid" or if Clara had triggered something in particular, but in the next heartbeat Alice punched Clara squarely in the jaw.

He could have blocked the blow—vamp speed and reflexes were far faster than human speed—but Alice's claim about the symbols on the rogue and Clara's overly emotional response made him curious enough to wait and see what this altercation revealed about both women.

Clara screamed and stumbled backward.

Sir! Adri protested. Both she and Bryan wore identical expressions of shock, looking to him for instructions.

Do not interfere, he ordered.

Reluctantly, they stayed where they were.

"Alice!" Dunlap started forward, but Charles held up a hand, halting the older man's movements. Dunlap had said Alice could take care of herself.

Charles would like very much to see that for himself.

7

It had been some time since Charles had last witnessed an altercation between mages. As a precaution, he signaled Adri to have a stun net ready in case their confrontation spiraled out of control. Adri slipped the net out of the pack on her belt.

Regaining her footing, Clara swung at Alice—not with her fist, but with her fingers spread and outstretched. Her fingertips glowed bright red and Charles sensed the familiar searing heat of deadly blood magic. The magic formed a kind of blade and Clara slashed the air as if attempting to disembowel her opponent.

Charles felt a spike of dread from Dunlap. Whether it was fear of or for Alice, he wasn't sure.

White magic flared on Alice's hands, forming a shield that blocked Clara's blade. Energy discharged when their magic collided. Charles was astounded when it was Clara, not Alice, who stumbled from the whiplash of power, and even more surprised that Alice was able to block Clara's attack with air magic alone.

As the older woman stumbled, off balance, Alice grabbed Clara's sleeve at the shoulder and pulled, ripping it at the seam. The sleeve tore away, revealing her arm. It was covered from shoulder to wrist with spellwork in the form of henna tattoos.

A small blade appeared in Alice's other hand; she'd apparently already palmed it prior to confronting Clara. Before the older woman could react, Alice slashed down Clara's forearm, opening a long, shallow cut and breaking a half-dozen intricately drawn spells.

Clara shrieked and flailed, striking out with another blood magic blade, but Alice evaded her easily.

Guilt. Fear. Anger. Panic. *HE KNOWS. KILL THEM RUN RUN RUN—*

Like a dam had broken, Clara's thoughts and emotions poured out and streamed through Charles's mind. She was able to get control of her thoughts, but the damage was done.

Her eyes glowing, Clara raised her hands. Blood magic surged.

Adri threw the stun net. It came down over Clara's head and emitted a powerful surge of magic and electricity. The traitorous mage dropped in a heap.

The air was full of the scent of her blood. Charles's fangs slid out as hunger made him almost forget where he was. Clara's blood was exquisite, full of magic and smoother and more refined than the finest whisky. Even for a master vampire, its siren call was almost too powerful to resist.

As Charles stood frozen, fighting for control, Dunlap stepped forward, his eyes full of anger and sadness. "Clara, *why?*"

She didn't answer.

Regaining his composure, Charles picked up the dropped photograph of the rogue and held it up. "This is your spellwork, is it not, Ms. McKnight?"

Unable to move, Clara glared up at him, her eyes dark with hate Charles could now sense as well as see.

He crouched beside her. "You have long been a valued asset of this Court. Until this moment, I believed you incapable of inflicting this kind of suffering on another. I do not understand why you would participate in such an enterprise."

"I'm nothing but an 'asset' to you." Clara forced the words out as the stun net pulsed, keeping her immobile. "For years I let you drink my blood and slept with you and you call me an *asset*."

Charles sensed anger and disgust from Alice at Clara's accusation. Her reaction puzzled him; would she not have assumed that as a member of the Court, he would have been drinking from a powerful mage?

He focused his attention on Clara. "I do not see how your actions are related to my categorization of you as a Court asset."

"No, you wouldn't," Clara said bitterly.

"Who's the maker of the rogues, Clara?" Dunlap asked gently. "How do we keep more people from dying? Whatever your reasoning for what you've done, I don't believe for one minute that you intended for these people to die. I've known you since we were in college. I can't have been that wrong about you."

Clara flinched, shame and anger in her eyes. "The spellwork wasn't perfect," she admitted, attempting to move to a more comfortable position. The stun net pulsed again and she made a pained sound. "I couldn't keep control over them all the time. They got loose sometimes."

"Is that what happened to Christine Foreman the other night?" Dunlap asked. "One of them got loose and attacked her?"

"I would have figured out how to control them," Clara said through gritted teeth. "I just needed more time."

"What's the goal?" Alice asked. "You spelled the rogues so you and the rogue-maker could control them. Were you planning on attacking Mr. Vaughan with an army of vampires under your command?" She studied Clara's expression. "No, not just Vaughan. You had your sights on the Court itself, didn't you?"

Clara glared at her defiantly.

Charles's eyes lit up silver. "Who is the maker of the rogues? Who conspires against the Court?"

No answer.

"Why are you doing this?" Dunlap asked.

It was Alice who spoke then. "Because she loves him."

Charles frowned at her. "She does not love me," he stated. That much was plain to see, even for someone without Charles's gift of sensing emotions.

Alice sighed. "Not you, Mr. Vaughan. She loves the rogue-maker."

To his surprise, Clara didn't deny Alice's statement. Charles's fury grew—not at the loss of Clara's affections, which he'd never wanted in the first place, but that another vampire had dared intrude on his territory.

"Who is the rogue-maker?" he demanded. "Speak, and I will see you receive a fair trial before the Court."

Again, she refused to answer.

He'd hoped he would catch a hint from Clara's thoughts, but she very carefully avoided betraying her lover's identity. Fortunately, there were other ways of identification. He leaned down and inhaled deeply, expecting to catch the scent of the vampire who had usurped him, but smelled nothing from her—nothing but her blood, sweet and fiery. She stared up at him defiantly.

Perhaps Clara thought their history would shield her. It was time to remind her of whom she was dealing with—whom she had betrayed.

Charles reached out with his mind and called the darkness to him.

In a rush of dark power the shadows gathered, all but extinguishing the light and plunging the room into near-darkness. The air became thick with power and difficult to breathe. Around him, the humans cowered—even Alice. Their terror tasted sweet, especially hers.

He leaned closer so Clara could see his eyes, as black as the deepest abyss. She cringed, frozen in fear.

"Secrets have a way of getting out, dear Clara," he said. "I have but to attend any of a dozen parties, and within an hour I would know the name of every sub-par lover whose bed you have shared since we parted ways. This is not gossip. This is treason. When I pull this from you, it will not be with a glass of wine. It will be with tongs and a heated knife."

Alice's terror became horror. Her reaction pleased him. Perhaps their interactions would be more productive going forward.

Clara closed her eyes.

All magic had colors and scents. Charles was familiar with a dozen variations of magic, from the natural magic used by mages to the golden magic of shifters and the dark magic of demons and other creatures. As a vampire, he could see and sense the silver afterlife magic of ghosts and other spirits. He had even experienced the wonders of fae magic, though there had been little of it to be found for more than one hundred years, as the fae retreated further from the human world.

It was, therefore, a complete surprise when he caught a hint of a magic he did not recognize. It was red and black and carried with it the highly improbable scent of the sea. He paused, attempting to identify the type of magic and its source.

Alice raised her hands above her head, white air magic flaring with a burst of power that made them all stumble. She spun the magic into a half-moon shape and then used all her strength and even her body weight to bring it down on top of Clara.

Alice landed hard on her knees on the concrete floor as the floor blew out below where Clara had lain. The blast tossed Charles, Adri, Bryan, and Dunlap backward and set off every alarm in the building.

A fine spray of blood and body fluids tinged with magic filled the air—all that was left of Clara McKnight.

With one massive blow and with no explanation, Alice had apparently vaporized the Court's longtime blood mage—and along with her, very likely any chance of discovering the identities of her co-conspirators and the rogue-maker.

Alice remained on her hands and knees next to the six-foot hole in the floor, pale and shaken. Dust and bits of concrete, rock, and marble rained down from the gaping hole into the level below them.

Vamp-fast, Charles flashed across the room and picked Alice up by her throat. "What have you done?" he thundered, his eyes blazing.

"*Don't touch me!*" Alice screamed. She struck him in the chest with her palms and Charles found himself flying backward again, propelled by a blast of magic—the last of Alice's air magic, judging by the way she collapsed to the floor, her eyes dazed and unfocused.

As he started back toward her, Dunlap's shout stopped him. "Vaughan, wait! She just saved all of us!"

Charles paused. Alice huddled on the floor, shaking uncontrollably.

A chill touched his mind. *Charles, what has happened?* Valas demanded.

Rather than take the time to explain the events of the past few minutes, Charles simply shared his memory with the head of the Court.

Valas's response was a combination of anger and puzzlement. *Why has Alice Worth done this?*

I do not know. I will find out.

At the door, Bryan was speaking to the cadre of enforcers who responded to the apparent explosion. Adri was guarding Alice, spell cuffs in hand. "Should I arrest her?" she asked Charles.

Dunlap went to Alice's side. "Don't cuff her," he said, crouching next to his trainee. "She just saved our lives."

"Explain," Charles ordered.

He'd addressed Dunlap, but it was Alice who answered. "She had a divine wind spell," she said, her voice cracking. She was so pale that Charles thought she might be on the verge of passing out from the amount of magic she'd expended. "All I did was contain the blast. She killed herself."

"A suicide spell?" Charles asked. He had heard of such spells, but had never seen one used nor had he been aware that one could do so much damage.

She shook her head. "Much more than simply a suicide spell. The magic in that spell is designed to travel through the magic trace of those in the vicinity and destroy everything and everyone connected to them. That much raw energy would have probably taken out a good part of the building too."

Charles recalled the unfamiliar magic he had sensed a half-second before Alice acted. "Is this true?" he demanded of Dunlap.

Dunlap nodded. "I sensed it too, but I didn't recognize what it was until it would have been way too late. Even if I'd reacted in time, I'm not strong enough to contain a spell like that. If Alice hadn't done what she did, we'd all be dead and every vampire in your line—and every enforcer who had drunk from you—would be dead too. That's how those spells work. It's a kamikaze spell. You die, but you take a lot of people with you when you go."

"She committed suicide rather than name her lover," Charles said with disdain. How like Clara to do something so melodramatic and unnecessary in the name of love. Humans were prisoners of their own fairy tales.

Ultimately, it was an empty gesture; they would uncover the identity of the rogue-maker anyway. Charles found it highly unlikely he would be moved by Clara's sacrifice.

"Like she said, you didn't give her much of a choice," Alice said. "Torture, or betray the man she loved. You backed her into a corner and she didn't see any other way out."

Dunlap sighed.

Irked, Charles flexed his fingers, remembering the feeling of her warm throat in his hand. His temper and his patience were growing short.

He had now seen and heard enough from the young mage, however, to know she would be an asset to the Court, and her well-being would be of concern to Valas. More importantly, his own interest in her was growing, and not all of it involved the things she might be able to do for the Court.

As such, he relaxed his hands and crouched next to Alice, who watched him warily. "You are young," he said softly. "And you saved many lives tonight with quick action and impressive ability. I and many others owe you a debt. For this reason, I forgive your candor and I give you our thanks."

Alice blinked at him. Several emotions flashed in her eyes: suspicion, anger, puzzlement, and yes, that damnable amusement. "You're welcome," she said finally. Just as Dunlap blew out a relieved breath, she added, "All things considered, I probably shouldn't say 'I told you so.'"

Her employer sighed again. "Alice."

"Or perhaps you should say it," Charles said. A ripple of surprise crossed the faces of the others in the room.

Alice tilted her head, her eyes narrowing, as if she suspected his motives. She was much too intuitive for his liking.

He rose smoothly. "Can you stand, or do you require assistance?"

He wasn't surprised when her eyes flashed. "I can stand," she stated.

"Good," he said briskly as she forced herself to rise. "We must seek out the rogue-maker before he becomes aware of Ms. McKnight's death."

"You have a suspect in mind?" Alice asked as she got to her feet.

"I do," Charles said. "If you would accompany us, I would like you to confirm his identity."

Dunlap started to object, but Alice smiled—not her usual smirk, but a real and almost predatory grin, worthy of a vampire. "I'm in," she said. She wiped her hand across her face and grimaced at the smear of blood and fluids on her palm. "But first, someone needs to point me toward the showers and give me some clean clothes, because this is just *gross*."

8

Despite the veil of secrecy surrounding the captured rogue and the explosion in Clara McKnight's apartment, Charles knew it was only a matter of time before word would spread and questions asked about the visits by Mark Dunlap and Alice Worth. For that reason, he made the decision—after a brief conference with Valas—to head directly to confront the suspected rogue-maker. With him would be his own personal security detail and the two mages.

The latter displeased both Bryan and Adri, but Alice had correctly pointed out with her usual bluntness that the rogue-maker's apparent alliance with a blood mage meant Charles and the others might well be facing more than physical threats and none of the mages employed by the Court could be included in the operation. More to the point, she had sensed trace from the rogue's maker, making her an indispensable asset. Whether the Smith siblings liked it or not, Alice was necessary, and Dunlap made it clear she was not going anywhere without him.

Valas approved of his decision to include them, but added two more Court enforcers to the group whose specific role was to watch the mages and put one or both of them down at the first indication of duplicity.

Even with this contingency plan in place, Bryan and Adri remained edgy. Dunlap they knew well, but as a mid-level air mage with minimal self-defense skills he would likely be a liability if they met resistance.

Alice was an unknown, a wild card, and no one knew quite what to expect from her, especially now that she had demonstrated impressive power and skill. For his part, Charles welcomed the opportunity to see what Alice could do against vampire opponents.

She'd expended a great deal of magic containing Clara's divine wind spell and seemed shaky, even limping slightly from her hard fall on the stone floor. But when Charles had inquired about her physical condition, she'd simply replied, "I'm fine" in a tone that made it clear she wasn't interested in discussing the matter further.

Despite the urgency of their mission, it was imperative they remove all traces of

Clara's blood before leaving Northbourne, as it would alert any possible conspirators to her demise. Charles retired to his private apartment to attend to this task, while Adri and Bryan went to their own quarters. Dunlap and Alice were escorted to separate guest suites by their new court minders, Carlos and Kirwin. Dunlap seemed reluctant to let Alice out of his sight, so Charles instructed their guards to take them to adjoining rooms and open the connecting doors.

When Charles emerged from his apartment, he found the rest of the group waiting in the hall. Even Alice was already there, face scrubbed clean of makeup and her damp hair in a braid. She wore her own leather jacket and boots—quickly and expertly cleaned by Court employees—but the black shirt and black pants of an enforcer. Dunlap too had been given black clothing. Even with his enhanced senses, Charles could not smell any trace of Clara or her blood on anyone in their group.

While Dunlap looked uncomfortable in the uniform of an enforcer, Charles was startled to see how much Alice's manner matched that of his security detail. In the all-black attire, Alice could almost be mistaken for one of his guards. She was focused on her surroundings and on guard against possible attacks. Given one of the Court's own mages had very recently tried to kill her, Charles could no longer fault her suspicious nature.

"Ms. Worth." He greeted her with a nod. "You are recovering well?"

Her expression flattened. "Well enough," she said shortly.

At a later time, he would give more thought to why inquiries about her physical condition were met with hostility. At the moment, they had more pressing matters to attend to.

Charles and Bryan led Alice and Dunlap down the hall with Adri at the rear. He had noticed Alice seemed slightly less suspicious of Adri than Bryan and as such instructed his most trusted female enforcer to watch their backs. It was to his advantage for Alice to be able to focus on potential threats without distraction from his own personnel. Though she did glance back at Adri a few times, she seemed less edgy than on their walk down to confront Clara.

As the group reached the main stairs, however, Charles sensed a spike of alarm from Alice. As they started down, the reason for her disquiet became evident: below them, near the front doors, Amira waited with two female Hunters, a tall redhead and a shorter brunette.

Like Amira, the Hunters wore all black. Both were relatively young, their skin almost as pale as a vampire's, with the lean and predatory look characteristic of dhampirs. Unlike enforcers, who tended to be heavily muscled and physically intimidating, half-vampires were wiry, their strength and speed less evident.

And also unlike enforcers and even other dhampirs, Hunters were single-minded trackers and, when triggered, merciless killing machines.

At the moment, under Amira's control, the women were docile. Their sharp eyes took in everything around them, including Charles and his companions as they descended the stairs.

The closer they got to the bottom of the steps, the more uneasy Alice became. Her apprehension prickled on his skin. Perhaps she feared the Hunters. Many did, and not without good reason. Strangely, however, her emotions were far more complex than mere fright.

The Hunters' eyes locked on Alice. The brunette leaned forward, a red sheen rolling over her eyes. The other hissed softly.

"Quiet," Amira commanded.

The red-haired Hunter went silent, her eyes following Alice as the group reached the main floor.

Amira smiled as the group approached. "Charles, how lovely to run into you. And you as well, Mr. Dunlap. You are looking well."

"Thank you very much," Dunlap said courteously. "May I present my newest employee, Ms. Alice Worth?"

"Yes, you certainly may." Amira held out her hand. "Ms. Worth, I am Amira of the Court."

"An honor to meet you," Alice said, her voice betraying none of the unease Charles sensed. As she had done earlier in the conference room, she bowed to Amira, who withdrew her hand and returned the bow.

Alice moved to stand next to Dunlap. The Hunters continued to stare at her.

"And where are you going with Ms. Worth and Mr. Dunlap?" Amira asked Charles.

"We are going to one of my buildings. Ms. Worth will be demonstrating her ability with wards, with Mr. Dunlap's supervision," he said for the benefit of the Court enforcers nearby. "And where are you bound this evening?"

"My Hunters and I will be searching for traces of the rogues near downtown. There are rumors of sightings in the area."

"I wish you success in your hunt," Charles said.

"And I wish you all success as well." Amira rejoined her Hunters, who were still fixated on Alice. "It was a pleasure to meet you, Ms. Worth."

"You too," Alice echoed.

As Amira and the Hunters remained inside, Bryan led their group down the front steps. Charles sensed relief from Alice when the doors closed.

Two black SUVs waited out front. "Mr. Dunlap, you will take the second vehicle," Charles said. "Ms. Smith will drive you. Ms. Worth will accompany me in the lead vehicle."

Dunlap hesitated, clearly not wanting to be separated from his trainee. "All right," he said reluctantly.

The group climbed into the Court vehicles. As the small caravan headed for the main gate, Charles glanced at Alice. She was staring straight ahead, her face unreadable. He sensed only determination and focus in her now, with no trace of the uneasiness from earlier.

"You were disturbed by the Hunters," he said.

She turned to him with a hint of a smile that didn't reach her eyes. "Didn't you expect me to be?"

Of all the possible responses he had expected, that was not one of them. How could she have known he had engineered their encounter with Amira and her Hunters?

"Our meeting in the lobby was pure happenstance," he lied, his voice cold. "It would serve no purpose for me to arrange such a spurious encounter. Our investigation is far too important to waste time on such matters."

"Very true. No time for games when lives are at stake."

Anger made his eyes glow. "You are disrespectful."

"I am, sometimes," she agreed. "For which I apologize."

Her bluntness was disconcerting. He decided that if subterfuge had failed to unnerve her, perhaps equal frankness would have more success. "I find your explanation for what transpired during the month you disappeared to be highly suspect."

He felt a flash of surprise, fear, and anger as her eyes darkened. "What's so hard to believe about it? I was desperate, miserable, dying a little more each day. I probably should have died, but I didn't. I decided I couldn't go on living that way. Something had to change."

It had the unmistakable ring of truth and yet the faint tinge of falsehood. Charles pressed for more information. "But someone *did* die, or so you told Dunlap."

If Alice was displeased or surprised that Dunlap had revealed that information, she didn't let on. "Someone did," she admitted, her eyes reflecting that same haunted look he had seen earlier in the photographs.

"Who was it?"

She smiled bitterly. "Just some girl, I suppose, another junkie who finally ran out of luck. I watched her die and I couldn't do anything to help her."

"The death of a stranger seems hardly sufficient reason for you to abandon your destructive course and overcome several years of drug addiction." Charles's tone was derisive.

Her eyes blazed and her anger seared him. "Has it been so long since you were human that you can't fathom how witnessing someone's death would be traumatic enough to cause me to want to get sober?"

Sir! Bryan's voice in his head was outraged.

I baited her deliberately, Charles replied. Out loud, he said coolly, "A vampire understands death perhaps better than most, Ms. Worth, having died once only to awaken in a body that will never know warmth again, and then dying again each and every morning."

Alice's ire faded somewhat. "That is a fair point." She turned her face to the window.

Charles's ability to sense emotions, including duplicity, had served him well for nearly two hundred years. He was not infallible, but after two centuries of honing his senses—as well as a steady diet of mage blood, which increased his sensitivity—he would have expected to be able to detect whether Alice spoke the truth when she described witnessing the girl's death. Her anger was real; of that, he had no doubt. Beyond that, he sensed no deceit.

And yet, his instincts continued to tell him there was more to the story.

The SUV slowed as the gate swung inward. The crowd of protestors had diminished significantly in the hours since Charles's arrival, leaving only a half-dozen men and women.

As their vehicle passed, one of the demonstrators spat on Alice's window. "Well, that was rude," she said, her tone light, though Charles could see nothing amusing about what had transpired. "This is because of the rogue attacks, I'm assuming?"

"Yes. Such demonstrations are not typical. Vampire-human relations in the city are generally uneventful." Charles regarded her as their SUV turned onto the main road. "You understand that anyone associated with the Court is subject to a background check. Anything that might render an employee vulnerable to blackmail or manipulation must be divulged."

She shrugged. "Makes sense. It sounds like you already know everything."

"Your story is incomplete. There is no record of you having magic when you lived in Chicago, but you registered here as an earth and air mage and clearly you received extensive training. How do you explain this?"

Strangely, she seemed more at ease with him now that he had dispensed with courtesy and simply confronted her with his questions. "I was adopted at birth. Neither of my parents had magic, but when mine showed up they hired private teachers to train me and paid whoever they needed to pay to make sure I never went into the Agency's registry." Alice's voice was matter-of-fact, almost mechanical in the way she delivered the information. "When I moved here and decided to become an MPI, I had to register my abilities."

"With so many options to choose from, why become a mage private investigator, especially when it would require you to reveal your abilities?"

"I spent most of my life being waited on hand and foot, and then I wasted a couple of years harming myself and those around me. I wanted to do something meaningful, something that would help people. I thought I could try to make up for some of the things I did." Her voice grew bitter.

"But why an investigator? There are many other occupations in which one can be of service to others," Charles pointed out. "Investigative work is often dangerous, as tonight's events prove."

"There are far too many people who use magic to harm. I wanted to use my magic for something good. I'm nosy and obstinate and I like solving puzzles. I've got a criminal record and I don't take orders well, so I can't be a cop. And I guess you could say I'm addicted to danger. That qualifies me to be an MPI and not much else."

"And why this city? You have no family here, no ties to the area." Her file had made that clear.

"Exactly. Nobody knows me. I got a fresh start, a long, long way away from the mess I left behind. I'd have gone farther, but I'd be in the ocean."

Charles recognized the last was a joke, but she delivered it in the same flat tone, as if it was rehearsed and she cared little whether it elicited a laugh.

He asked about something else that had been puzzling him. "It is notoriously difficult to quit taking drugs and become a cold turkey. How—"

She laughed, startling him. He was so entranced by her laugh that by the time he thought he might be offended that she'd laughed at him, she was speaking. "The expression is 'going cold turkey,' not *becoming* a cold turkey," she corrected him. "I went 'cold turkey' all right, and it *sucked*. No offense," she added.

Bryan made a sound that might have been a truncated chuckle.

"None was taken," Charles said. "I am familiar with that vernacular phrase. You must be exceptionally strong-willed to have quit successfully without assistance or relapse."

"I'm a stubborn bitch," she said bluntly, shocking him. "That's what kept me alive, got me out of there, brought me here. If I'd been any less stubborn I wouldn't have made it, so I won't apologize for it. I'm good with magic, good with spellwork, good with wards. Not so good at not offending people or holding back, even when I ought to."

"You should work on that aspect of your personality, particularly if you work for the Vampire Court," Bryan said, catching her eye in the rearview mirror. "If Mr. Vaughan will forgive my saying so, vampires are quick to take offense and slow to forgive."

"I'll take that under advisement," Alice said, her tone perfectly neutral. "So, where are we headed? Or do you have more questions you want to ask?"

He did indeed have more questions, but they were perhaps ten minutes away from their destination and those questions would have to wait until another time. "We are going to an establishment called Nyx."

Her brows rose. "Interesting. I haven't been there, but I know of it. You think we'll find the rogue-maker there?"

"My intelligence indicates he is there tonight." Charles couldn't keep the distaste out of his voice. "The club belongs to one of his line and he sometimes conducts business in one of the private rooms."

"Conducts business," Alice echoed, her mouth turning up slightly. "Is that what they're calling it now?" At Charles's quizzical look, she explained, "I was insinuating that you were using the phrase as a euphemism for sex."

"Not intentionally, but such activities do occur at the club."

She tilted her head. "You sound disapproving."

"I find the atmosphere at Nyx quite...garish."

"Not a fan of purple neon?" Her voice was tinged with humor.

"It is not the lighting I find objectionable."

"Surely you're not prudishly offended by consenting adults enjoying each other's company?"

He regarded her. "There are many kinds of addictions, Ms. Worth, as you well know. Nyx feeds the addictions of its employees, its patrons, and its owners."

Her smile faded. "You can't protect people, including vampires, from themselves, Mr. Vaughan. I'm sure you learned that a long time ago. If they don't get their fix at Nyx, they'll just go somewhere else, probably somewhere a lot less safe. At least there everyone who goes in does so of their own accord and leaves safely, plus or minus a pint or so."

He had not expected her response to be quite so logical. "You are very pragmatic for one so young."

"So I've been told." She turned to watch out the window as the SUV glided through empty streets toward the club.

Looking at her in the near-darkness as the streetlights flashed across her face, he was struck by how lovely she was. It was not her beauty that intrigued him, however; it was the certainty that though she had appeared to reveal much to him during their conversation, he still knew so little about her. Parts of her story felt like truth, while others seemed carefully rehearsed. That alone did not make them false; she must have recounted her story many times for many listeners, and he did not sense any deceit. And yet...and yet, he doubted. He was unaccustomed to feeling any sort of curiosity about a human woman and it left him conflicted.

Likewise, he was plagued by the thought that his ability to detect deception was failing him tonight: first with Clara, now with Alice. He'd long depended on his extraordinary senses to guide him through delicate and dangerous confrontations and the night promised more such situations. His abilities were a significant factor in his election to the Court and gave him the upper hand in business dealings. Valas had charged him with uncovering the identity of the rogue-maker largely due to his ability to sense truthfulness and deceit. If he could not rely on his own senses—if they could be tricked or rendered useless by spells—what use was he to the Court? Would clients exploit that weakness in business transactions if it became known?

He wondered whether he should ask Alice how to offset the kind of magic that had permitted Clara to mislead him. He was reluctant to reveal his weakness, but Alice and Bryan already knew he had been deceived by Clara and Kirwin was loyal.

"Tell me what kind of magic Clara used to hide her thoughts from me," he said.

"A variation on the masking spell she put on the rogue. Very complex work. Earth magic laced with your blood."

Charles's eyes silvered. "My blood is to be used only for healing and for sanctioned magic on behalf of the Court. She utilized blood designated for those purposes for her deception."

"Presumably," Alice said, her tone even and calm. "It would seem an upgrade to your security is in order."

With effort, Charles mastered his anger. "There must be some level of trust between the Court and its mages. Ms. McKnight served the Court for twenty years without a hint of questionable behavior."

"That plus your history with her made her the perfect target for your rogue-maker," Alice said. "The guy's not dumb. He read her like a book, knew exactly what to say and do to manipulate her, and turned a powerful mage into your basic Renfield. It's a shame. She was very talented."

Charles showed his fangs. "Please refrain from using that name in my presence."

"Sorry, Mr. Vaughan." Her apology was sincere. "I know she tried to cut me in half, but I have to give credit where credit is due: her spellcraft was exquisite. The only reason the spells on the rogue failed is she just hadn't perfected them yet. She was creating brand-new spellwork and that's no small feat. It's good that you documented the spells before the rogue died; you'll want one of your other court mages to be able to recognize and replicate them and come up with counterspells. If you can find an intact rogue, that would be even better, obviously."

"I presume you could sense the spells she used to obscure her thoughts. Is it possible she may have replicated those spells on the rogue-maker or other confederates?"

Alice considered. "It's possible, but with her death, those spells are going to start fading, even if they're tattooed. Which they probably aren't," she added.

"Why do you think that unlikely?"

She regarded him. "Would you willingly tattoo proof of a conspiracy against the Court into your flesh?"

"I concede the point. If the rogue-maker is spelled, how may these spells be disrupted?"

She made a face. "Wards would be one way, but since we're going into their territory rather than bringing them to ours, that's not really an option. The very nature of a masking spell is to obscure its existence, but they can be broken, either with a counterspell or by physically cutting the spell apart like I did with Clara's."

"And how does one detect these spells?"

"It's complicated spellwork," she told him. "It usually takes a couple of hours to create a spell detector and fine-tune it. We don't have a couple of hours, obviously."

"How did you detect Clara's spells?"

"I'm an earth mage, so I'm pretty well attuned to earth magic. I could tell she was using some kind of masking spells, but I wasn't completely sure what they were until I saw her lying to you and you couldn't tell."

The silence in the car was deafening.

Bryan eyed Alice in the rearview mirror. Charles caught a stray thought from his head enforcer: *Does she have a death wish?*

"In what way could you see she was lying to me?" Charles asked softly.

"That was pure human intuition," she admitted. "Maybe a woman's intuition to boot, though I'm usually not one to rely on that sort of thing. Her body language was too perfect, as if she'd practiced how she would answer those questions if she was asked. I saw resentment when she looked at you. Maybe…" Her voice trailed off.

Given her level of candor up to now, Charles was quite curious as to what she had been about to say before thinking better of it. "Finish your thought," he said.

She cleared her throat. "Maybe you rely a bit too much on your special senses and not enough on your eyes and intuition. Magic can fool your senses, but it's harder to trick your eyes or your gut. Visual obfuscation spells are damn near impossible and your gut can tell you things your senses can't. If you can't count on your senses, you have to go back to your eyes and your instincts. Be a little more human that way."

Charles was reasonably certain Dunlap had no idea that he could sense emotions, including truthfulness and deceit, and none of his enforcers would have told her. She had figured it out for herself, and after only a few hours in his company. Either her powers of observation were unusually keen or she had some extraordinary senses of her own.

"Don't worry; I'm not psychic," she said, her mouth twisting into a bitter smile, her comment almost startling him with its apparent prescience. "I just notice things."

Curious as to how she would answer, he asked, "How could you tell that I can sense truthfulness?"

"It's the way you listen to people when they talk," she said. "Not listening with your ears, but listening with something else, other senses, the way mages feel magic and spells."

"You have keen powers of observation for a human."

"I had to learn the hard way to watch people very closely. A couple of times, it was the only thing that kept me alive."

He studied her. "In Chicago?"

"Yes, in Chicago."

He ignored his senses and tried to listen to his instincts instead. It was difficult. His gut—though he nearly grimaced to refer to it as such—told him she spoke the truth. She had indeed faced great danger in Chicago. She turned back to the window.

As the SUV turned onto the street where Nyx was located, he sensed a surge of anticipation and excitement from Alice. Magic buzzed briefly on the edge of his senses before she contained it.

Many people would be nervous about confronting a vampire or group of vampires, but as he had already determined, Alice was not most people. *I'm addicted to danger*, she'd told him. There would be plenty of danger at Nyx.

"Once we reach our destination, you will obey my commands and those of my enforcers," Charles said. "Dunlap is known, but you are not. You will thus be able to blend in among the enforcers until such time as you are called upon to reveal yourself. You will engage any magic-related attacks as necessary and alert us about any threats or deceptive spells you may sense or see."

"Got it."

He thought about how best to address the issue of identifying their target, then decided bluntness would be the most likely way to get the response he desired. "I will need you to confirm the identity of the rogue-maker through physical contact. If this is something you will refuse to do, you must tell me now."

A parade of emotions flashed in her eyes: fear, anger, revulsion, and then resolve. "I'll do it," she said tonelessly. "But not for you."

He frowned. "I do not take your meaning."

"I'm not doing it as a favor to you. I'm doing it for that girl, the dead rogue."

Ordinarily, Charles would not have cared one whit about Alice's motivation as long as she did what he wanted. Given he was developing his personal dossier on her, however, this was useful insight. She looked at the rogue as a victim, and her desire to see someone punished for what had been done to her was stronger than her aversion to physical contact.

"To be clear, my agreeing to this is no guarantee of doing it again in the future," Alice added, then paused. "I want you to do something for me, though, in return."

He studied her, wondering if she would demand compensation beyond what the Court intended to pay MDI. "What is your request?"

"Find out who she was and give her family closure. Make sure they have a grave they can visit." Her voice was quiet.

He wondered if she was thinking about the nameless addict she'd seen die. A pattern was beginning to emerge in regard to who stirred her sympathy and who did not.

He filed this information away as well and inclined his head. "I will."

"Good."

The SUV pulled to a smooth stop in front of Nyx. Kirwin and Bryan exited the vehicle as a tuxedo-clad doorman emerged from the building and hurried to open Alice's door.

"Ms. Worth," Charles said.

She paused. "Yes?"

He spoke words that did not often cross his lips, but were necessary if he was to further his purpose of methodically undermining her resistance. "Thank you."

"Don't thank me yet," she said, climbing out of the vehicle and looking up at the club, her face bathed in purple light. "The night's just getting started."

9

Most patrons wishing to gain entry to Nyx waited behind a velvet rope guarded by not one but two enforcers. Upon entering, they submitted to hand searches, presented two forms of identification, and signed waivers based on which activities they were interested in pursuing while on the premises. The waivers were duly notarized and filed, and then the patrons were ushered to the main floor, where they could enjoy the staged performances before exploring the many pleasurable activities taking place on one of the other five levels—three above ground and two below.

As a member of the Court, Charles and his entourage did not enter by the front door. Instead, they were ushered quickly through the VIP entrance and into a private lounge on the first floor. Though its décor matched the rest of the ultramodern building, Charles was at least spared from having to listen to the music being played in the main stage area thanks to excellent soundproofing. Seconds after they entered, the speakers in the private lounge began playing Sinatra. Someone somewhere knew his listening preferences and that they did not include whatever was currently passing as "music" in the main room.

The lounge included a fully stocked bar. A female vampire bartender offered them drinks. Ever the well-mannered guest, Charles accepted a glass of champagne flavored with a few drops of fresh blood. Dunlap, who had been visibly relieved to see Alice alive and unharmed upon their arrival, took a bottle of German beer. The enforcers—with whom Alice stood, maintaining her cover—were offered nothing, not out of rudeness, but because as Charles's security detail, they would have declined it.

Charles could tell Dunlap wanted very much to speak to Alice, but he stood with Charles instead and did nothing that would call attention to her.

Well aware the bartender was listening, Charles engaged Dunlap in conversation about beer and asked for recommendations of brands he might add to the menu at Hawthorne's. If the bartender was relaying their conversation to her master, he would learn nothing except that Dunlap found the selection of IPAs at Hawthorne's to be inexcusably limited.

The group waited less than three minutes before a young vampire in a tuxedo hurried in. "Mr. Vaughan," he said politely with a bow. "My name is Henry. Please forgive the delay. Had we been informed of your desire to visit this evening, we would have prepared better accommodations for you and your guest."

"Your hospitality has thus far been quite adequate," Charles said.

A slight tightening of the eyes was Henry's only visible reaction to Charles's deliberate use of the adjective *adequate,* which in vampire parlance was far from complimentary.

Henry handed Charles and Dunlap embossed black leather menus. "What may we offer you this evening? May I suggest one of our exclusive packages for you, and something less exotic for Mr. Dunlap? Your enforcers may, of course, accompany you, or they are welcome to wait in an adjacent suite."

Charles gave his menu only a perfunctory glance, but Dunlap scanned his, perhaps out of curiosity. Halfway down the list, his eyes widened and he flushed, closing the cover abruptly. Charles sensed amusement from Alice at her boss's discomfort.

Charles handed their menus back. "Perhaps another time. At the moment, I wish to speak to your employers."

Henry's smile became fixed. "One moment." A pause as he contacted his master telepathically, and then he stepped to the side and gestured at the door. "This way, if you please."

With Bryan flanking him, Dunlap and Carlos behind them, and Alice, Kirwin, and Adri bringing up the rear, Charles followed Henry into the hall. Its walls were made of black glass and lined with a half-dozen unmarked doors identical to the one they'd just exited.

They passed through a set of double doors, climbed several flights of stairs, went through another set of heavy doors, and emerged onto an enclosed black-glass walkway suspended over the main floor.

From this vantage point, Charles could see the entirety of the main stage area and the audience, seated at tables surrounding the stages on all sides. The room was enormous and three stories tall, ringed with walkways at each level. Behind the black glass walls were private rooms and suites where occupants could watch the shows below when not engaged in their own activities. Electronic music filled the room, causing subtle vibrations in the glass walkway.

With his back to her, Charles was unable to see Alice's reaction to the scene below, but he felt her surprise and curiosity. Her reaction was intriguing. She seemed untroubled by the sight of vampires drinking from humans, despite her earlier disgust at hearing that Charles had been drinking from Clara. He was puzzled, as he saw little difference between his actions and those of the performers onstage, but Alice's moral code seemed full of contradictions and perhaps this was one of them.

To their left, two male vampires shared one stage. At the moment, one was drinking from the throat of a red-haired human woman wearing black lingerie and bringing her to climax simply with his bite. She thrashed in his embrace, her head flung back in ecstasy. The other vampire was biting the inner thigh of a shirtless human man reclining in a chaise lounge. Charles, who preferred his intimate activities to be more... intimate, found the entire display quite gauche.

On their right, two female vampires were performing similar acts, one with a human male and the other with a human woman.

A third female vampire, an aerial silks performer, slid down from the ceiling as their group passed, dangling upside-down thirty feet above the stage by a single leg wrapped in fabric. She paused her descent to watch them walk past, then suddenly dropped ten feet at once before stopping her fall and swaying gently. As the audience reacted with exclamations of surprise, fear, and appreciation, Charles sensed a little thrill of interest from Alice.

Even more intriguing. Was it the risky maneuver that appealed to the danger-seeking young mage, or the performer herself? Perhaps Alice's glances at Adri indicated more than simply attempts to evaluate his enforcer's threat potential.

Charles set his speculations about Alice's sexual preferences aside as they approached the end of the walkway and the luxury suite occupied by Nyx's owner, Josiah Harrison. The doors were guarded by a male dhampir. He wondered if the dhampir was always on guard or had been stationed at the door for his benefit. If the latter were true, he had to wonder at the motivation for such an ostentatious show of force to a member of the Court.

Should this confrontation escalate, you and Adri will engage the dhampir, Charles said to Bryan. *Kirwin and Carlos will guard the mages and I will deal with our hosts.*

Understood, Bryan replied. With a quick glance, he relayed Charles's instructions nonverbally to his sister. The corners of Adri's mouth turned up slightly as she eyed the dhampir. No doubt she was half-hoping for the opportunity to fight. Though Charles would never admit to such a vulgar impulse, he too would welcome the opportunity to vent his anger and frustration from the past few weeks by "engaging" the suspected rogue-maker.

The dhampir opened the doors to the suite as the group approached. He was nearly as tall as Bryan. Though not as heavily muscled, he would be almost as strong and fast as a young vampire. His enforcers routinely trained with dhampirs, however, and Charles had little doubt Bryan and Adri would hold their own.

The dhampir, his eyes glowing, hissed softly as Charles passed and flashed a bit of fang. Charles declined to comment on the insult.

Henry led them into the suite as the dhampir stepped inside and closed the doors. Bryan and Adri stayed back, positioning themselves between the half-vampire guard and the rest of the group.

Charles and Dunlap approached the two male vampires standing in front of a sofa, flanked by four enforcers.

Their guide bowed deeply. "Sirs, may I present Mr. Charles Vaughan and Mr. Marcus Dunlap, Senior."

David Noble inclined his head formally. "Charles, this is quite unexpected. You know Josiah, of course." He gestured to the dark-haired younger vampire on his right.

Josiah bowed. "Mr. Vaughan."

"Good evening, Mr. Harrison," Charles said with a nod. "I hope my arrival has not greatly inconvenienced you."

"We were about to retire to our private rooms," Nyx's owner said.

Charles thought he detected a note of hostility in Josiah's voice. Perhaps he was displeased at the interruption in his plans. Charles raised an eyebrow.

David gave the younger vampire a disapproving glance. Josiah's expression became impassive. "My apologies, Mr. Vaughan. I did not intend to appear inhospitable. You are, of course, an honored guest and we are pleased you are with us tonight." His tone was perfectly polite. "Henry informs me you saw nothing on our menu that interested you. If you could indicate what you are seeking, it would be my privilege to provide you with whatever you wish, if it is within my power to grant."

"Your offer is most cordial," Charles said. "Unfortunately, I must decline as I have Court business to discuss with David. Perhaps another time."

Henry bowed to David and departed, closing the doors to the walkway behind him.

As Josiah refilled his drink at the bar, David looked past Charles, his eyes narrowed slightly. "Charles, have you a new member of your entourage? Everyone else I know, but this one is not familiar to me."

Charles gestured for Alice to step forward. "Alice Worth, David Noble of the Vampire Court."

David extended his hand as Alice approached. After a slight hesitation, she took it.

She had her emotions as tightly locked down as she could, but Charles sensed her mental anguish when David's hand closed around hers. Her pain was so raw that he flinched ever so slightly—a reaction he had not experienced in recent memory. It caused another unfamiliar response: a pang of conscience.

He dismissed it quickly as a result of the strain of the past few weeks. Alice was an asset. Her skills made her useful for solving a problem. Her highly irrational emotional reactions were valuable information and nothing more.

Alice's pain subsided, replaced by recognition. She must have recognized David's trace. And since she had never encountered him before, there was only one way she would recognize it: from the dead rogue's ashes.

Alice caught Charles's eye for a moment as she turned to rejoin them. Though she gave no visible signal, he read her verdict in her eyes: David was the rogue-maker.

David's brow furrowed. "She does not smell of your blood, Charles, nor does she appear to be physically adequate to serve as your personal security. I do not understand her role."

"She is in training. Her skills are currently under evaluation by myself and the Court," Charles said.

"If she does not meet your needs, perhaps she may find a place in my household. You must keep me apprised of her progress."

Alice clearly—and correctly—interpreted David's interest as sexual. Her reaction was as he would have expected: disgust, distrust, and a hint of fear. As David did not react, she had apparently been able to keep those emotions off her face.

"I am told there was some excitement at Northbourne about an hour ago," David said, finally tearing his gaze away from Alice to address Charles. "I understand someone accidentally tripped a ward in one of the subbasements and caused a minor explosion. The damage is not extensive, I hope."

"A most unfortunate incident," Charles said, relieved that the news of Clara's betrayal and suicide had not yet spread. "Luckily, the damage was contained to a small area."

"I am relieved to hear that. What Court business brings you here this evening?" David inquired.

Charles straightened and spoke formally. "David Noble, I am here acting as an emissary of Valas. You are charged with the crime of producing unsanctioned offspring and allowing them to roam the city freely, causing at least a half-dozen deaths. You are also charged with collusion and conspiring against the Court. You will accompany me to Northbourne to face these charges."

David's brows rose a fraction of an inch. Over by the bar, Josiah set his drink on the counter and stared at them in apparent shock.

"On what evidence am I charged?" David's tone was curious.

"On the evidence of your co-conspirator," Charles replied. "And on the trace evidence from a rogue captured earlier tonight."

"I have not conspired with anyone against the Court," David said coolly. "Any such testimony would be false. And since I have created no rogues, your 'trace evidence' is erroneous." He turned to Dunlap. "The reason for your presence becomes clear. Your work for the Court has always proven quite excellent, Mr. Dunlap, but in this matter you are entirely mistaken if you believe me to be the source of any such trace."

"The evidence is pretty damning, Mr. Noble," Dunlap said, allowing David to assume he was the accuser, rather than Alice.

"Perhaps it damns someone, but not me," David countered.

"Your trace was recognized in the rogue you sired." Charles studied the accused rogue-maker. "The spellwork used by Clara McKnight to disguise your trace failed to hide your identity. Valas has generously granted you the opportunity to come to Northbourne of your own free will to answer these charges. It is a far better offer than you deserve."

A muscle moved in David's jaw. "You insult me with these spurious allegations."

"You deny that you are the rogue-maker?"

"I deny it categorically."

Charles sensed truthfulness from David and his anger seemed genuine, but Alice's identification, combined with his own suspicions and a new uncertainty about his senses, was sufficient cause for him to see that David answered to the Court.

He gestured at the doors. "Then return to Northbourne and explain yourself and the evidence to Valas. She awaits you."

David leveled an imperious stare at Charles. "I will speak to Valas, but I will not go to Northbourne as your prisoner. My entourage and I will travel by our own means. Josiah," he said sharply, turning toward the younger vampire standing near the bar.

All hell broke loose.

Charles detected an odd sound from above a millisecond before a half-dozen young vampires, their eyes glowing red, dropped from the ceiling and attacked in a berserker rage. Behind him, the dhampir went after Adri and Bryan.

One of the rogues landed three feet to Alice's right. Charles expected to sense and see fear from the young mage. Instead, she grinned and flicked her right hand like she was tossing a pair of dice. A six-foot rope made of bright green earth magic spiraled out of her hand.

Charles was so startled by Alice's eagerness to fight and the sight of her magical weapon that one of the rogues got a grip on his arm and sank his teeth into his shoulder.

Dunlap reacted quickly to the ambush, raising his hands and unleashing a powerful blast of air that threw two of the rogues backward and into two of David's enforcers. As the enforcers struggled with the rogues, Alice sent a third rogue airborne with her own blast of air magic. The rogue crashed through the glass wall separating their suite from the empty one next to it.

As Dunlap staggered from expending so much magic, one of David's enforcers threw a heavy lamp. It struck Dunlap a glancing blow on the side of the head and he went down in a heap. That enforcer was joined by another and they attacked Carlos and Kirwin, leaving Dunlap unconscious on the floor and undefended.

Alice dashed to Dunlap's side. She lashed out with her cold fire whip and struck one of David's enforcers, who had been rushing toward her. The whip sent him flying backward, a deep and bloody gash across his chest. As he went down with a wet gurgle, she twirled the whip above her head and lashed out again, this time very nearly taking the head off another enforcer who was coming at them. That enforcer went down as well and did not get back up.

As Alice stood guard over Dunlap, her whip crackling, Charles turned his attention to his attacker. The rogue who had attacked him was far too young to be any match for a vampire of Charles's age and experience. There was no method to his attack; he was simply frenzied with rage. Within moments, Charles tore him loose from his arm, immobilized him, and broke his neck. It was an injury that a young vampire would not heal from very quickly without help. He dropped the rogue to the carpet.

Behind him, the dhampir went down and Adri shouted in triumph as Bryan pounded his enormous fist into the half-vampire's face, attempting to render him unconscious.

The rogue Alice had thrown through the glass wall leapt onto Charles's back, her fangs sinking into the flesh of his shoulder near his neck. Charles tore her free and broke her neck with a single twist.

As the female rogue fell, one of David's enforcers went after Alice, a knife in his hand. Her back was turned, her attention on the rogues fighting to get past Kirwin and Carlos, and she did not see the attacker approaching.

In a flash, Charles intercepted the enforcer. Rather than attempt to disarm him, Charles simply crushed his hand and broke his arm.

As the man howled, Charles tossed him to Adri. Without missing a beat, she planted her boot in his gut and then kicked him squarely in the jaw. He was unconscious before he hit the carpet.

A male rogue leapt onto Bryan's back and locked his arm around the enforcer's throat, gnawing at his shoulder. Unable to breathe and in danger of having his throat crushed, the enforcer strained to pull the rogue's arm away from his neck.

Alice lashed her whip again, coiling it around a heavy stone sculpture on a table. She yanked and the sculpture flew through the air, exploding against the head of Bryan's attacker. The rogue went down and did not move, the side of his skull caved in.

"I had him," Bryan rasped, blood soaking his shirt from his torn shoulder.

Alice frowned. "Hey, I'm not expecting you to throw dollar bills at me, but a little appreciation is in order."

Bryan glowered at her.

The two remaining rogues attacked Charles at the same time. As they did so, Josiah Harrison ran toward the doors that led to the glass walkway, brushing past Alice on the way.

Alice's eyes widened. In a single fluid movement, she spun and lashed out with her whip, coiling it around Josiah's torso just as he reached the doors. She yanked sharply and the vampire ended up on the floor, wrapped in a coil of cold green fire.

With a hiss, David Noble, who had been observing the fighting from his vantage point near the wall, went for Alice, fangs bared.

With no time to carefully incapacitate the rogues, Charles smashed their heads together, pulverizing their skulls. Brain matter splattered his suit as he dropped them and met David in midair, knocking the other vampire aside and away from Alice. David hissed and started to leap at Alice again.

A sudden blast of air knocked Charles off-balance but sent David flying backward. He hit the wall and was pinned there.

Dumbfounded, Charles turned. With her right hand, Alice held Josiah Harrison wrapped in her cold fire as he thrashed against the coil of green flame. With her left, she was emitting enough air magic to hold a master vampire against the wall.

Furious, David fought to free himself, but Alice's magic held. Power crackled in the air and made Charles's skin tingle. The air smelled of ozone.

Alice was magnificent, her eyes almost iridescent with the power she was controlling. Charles had thought her air magic depleted by containing Clara McKnight's suicide spell, but clearly that was not the case.

David's two remaining enforcers went after Alice but were met by Adri and Carlos. Kirwin's left arm appeared to be broken, but he stood guard next to Alice as Adri and Carlos fought the enforcers. Bryan, his breathing labored from the damage inflicted on his throat by the rogue, stayed at Charles's side.

"Release us immediately!" David thundered.

"I'll let you go if you give me your word that you won't attack me," Alice said before Charles could respond.

David glowered.

"Your word," Charles said.

His eyes bright gold with fury, David said, "You have my word."

Charles turned to Alice. "Please release Mr. Noble."

She cut off the air magic and David landed on his feet. "Stand down," he ordered his enforcers, who reluctantly stepped back from Adri and Carlos. "Now release Josiah."

She shook her head. "Nope. He's got to answer for all of this. This is your rogue-maker, Mr. Vaughan."

"She's lying!" Josiah fought the coil of fire, to no avail. "Mr. Noble, tell her to release me!"

"Explain yourself, Miss Worth," David demanded.

"The trace I got from the captured rogue was partial," Alice said. "The masking spell Clara McKnight used to hide the identity of the vampire who made the rogue held up even after the rogue died, but I got enough of the trace to identify the rogue-maker. When I shook your hand, I recognized the trace."

"I am not the rogue-maker," David stated.

She nodded. "I know that now, and I apologize for implicating you. However, you *are* Mr. Harrison's maker, so your trace is almost identical. When I touched him, I realized it was *his* trace I sensed on the rogue, not yours."

Charles had not sensed any duplicity from Josiah, but perhaps Clara had spelled him to disguise his emotions, as Alice had suggested earlier. "Is he spelled?" Charles asked.

Alice nodded. "Probably, but I can break the spells if—"

In a single violent and desperate movement, Josiah Harrison tore free of Alice's earth magic and dashed for the windows, dealing a glancing blow to Alice's ribs as he passed.

She went down with a cry of pain that she stifled almost immediately, as if she did not want those around her to know she was hurt, or how badly. His own enforcers did the same during both training and fights, but like the habit of assessing people and surroundings for potential weapons or threats, it was a practice they had developed after years of experience. Once again, Charles wondered where and how Alice had learned that behavior.

Moving faster than the human eye could follow, David intercepted Josiah just before the younger vampire reached the glass, snatching him out of the air inches from escape. David slammed him to the floor with a hand around his throat, hard enough to break his neck with a crack that was audible to even the humans in the room. The injury was not as debilitating as it was for the rogues, who were much younger, but it would incapacitate Josiah for several minutes.

Charles offered his hand to Alice, who was struggling to rise. She waved him away and got to her feet, clearly favoring her right side where Josiah had hit her. Even a passing strike from a vampire was capable of causing serious or even fatal injuries, and Alice, despite her bravado and sharp tongue, was human and fragile.

"You are injured. Do you require medical attention?" Charles spoke quietly, recalling that she did not like to be questioned about her physical condition.

"No," she told him, the strain in her voice belying her pain. "Nothing's broken; it'll just be a hell of a bruise. I'll put some ice on it later."

Alice went to David's side and looked down at Josiah. The rogue-maker showed his fangs and hissed at her. "You've got him?" she asked.

"Yes." David's grip tightened on Josiah's throat. He looked up at one of his enforcers. "Spell cuffs."

The enforcer produced a pair and snapped them tightly onto Josiah's wrists, rendering him immobile.

David released Josiah's throat and rose to tower over the prone vampire. "You will explain why you have created these rogues."

"The humans do not fear us," Josiah rasped, his body twitching as his broken neck began to heal. "They are our food, but we treat them as equals. My rogues made them fear us."

"The rogues made humans hate us," Charles said. "Hate and fear are not the same, and neither are to our advantage."

"History has proven many times that when humans fear vampires, it is the vampires who suffer and die." David's fury made his eyes glow. "You cannot be ignorant of this, as you have seen anti-vampire violence in your lifetime. I do not understand why you believe this course of action would be beneficial to us."

"I think he's full of crap," Alice said with characteristic bluntness. "I don't doubt that he wants to be feared—he seems like the type who gets off on that—but I think the real reason for making the rogues was his plan to make a move against the Court. He needed disposable foot soldiers he could control."

Josiah glared at her and said nothing.

David's eyes glowed brighter. "Did you intend to use the rogues against me?"

"Against Valas," Josiah snarled. "She is weak. She appeases the humans, seeks their cooperation, forms *alliances*. You have said yourself that human law fails to protect us; why then should we follow someone who obeys these laws? The Court needs a different ruler, someone who will put the humans in their place."

"While I may disagree with her on occasion, Valas is the duly elected head of our Court, to whom you swore an allegiance." David's voice was cold. "You have betrayed the Court and shamed me and everyone else in my line."

"If you think Valas weak, you are much mistaken," Charles said. "You will face her judgement for your crimes."

"No, I will not." Josiah's eyes grew distant for a moment, then widened in shock and dismay.

"Nice try, but your suicide spell won't work," Alice said. "Not with those spell cuffs on, and it's already fading anyway, just like the rest of your spells. Clara's dead."

Josiah did not appear surprised or taken aback by the news. "Did she kill herself?"

"Yes."

He flashed his fangs. "Good."

Alice's rage seared Charles's senses. White magic flared on her hands and a cold wind swept through the room, startling the others.

He wondered if she was about to unleash an attack and decided, with regret, that he would have to intervene to ensure the rogue-maker lived to stand trial before Valas. As angry as she was, he expected her to lash out with her whip and perhaps try to take off Josiah's head.

Instead, the magic faded and she smiled.

It was one of the more chilling smiles Charles had seen in recent memory, a feat he would not have thought possible for a human. There was something almost predatory in the way she showed her teeth. Her cold, calculating stare appealed to him a great deal.

Neither Charles nor David intervened or objected when Alice placed her boot on Josiah's throat. He hissed in fury. Her smile widened as she applied pressure with her heel. The vampire made an involuntary *gack* sound as she compressed his windpipe.

"I want you to remember this moment," Alice said softly, bending over to look into the vampire's furious eyes. "You think you're superior, but it was a human who caught you. It's a human with her boot on your throat. Whatever the vamps do to you, it was a human who made sure you answered for your crimes. I hope that's the last thought you have right before they put the stake in your heart."

10

For a moment, the room was completely silent in the wake of Alice's words.

Josiah found enough air in his lungs to speak. "Cow," he hissed. "I'll kill you."

"Seems unlikely from where I'm standing," she said, grinding her boot a little more before stepping back, leaving the imprint of her heel in the soft flesh of his throat.

David's eyebrows rose. "Since it is now perfectly clear that you are not, in fact, a prospective personal guard, perhaps you would care to properly introduce yourself?"

She bowed stiffly, despite the pain in her injured ribs. "My name is Alice Worth. I'm an earth and air mage and I work for Mark Dunlap." She glanced at Adri, who was guarding the unconscious PI.

Dunlap groaned and opened his eyes. "Damn, that hurts," he muttered, gingerly touching the side of his head where the lamp had hit him.

As Adri helped him sit up, Dunlap looked around the room, taking in the destruction. He spotted Alice and his relief was obvious, though he appeared concerned at the way she was standing with her arm wrapped protectively around her injured side.

When he registered that it was Josiah, not David, on the floor in cuffs, Dunlap blinked. "What did I miss? Did we have the wrong guy?"

"It was my mistake, Mark," Alice admitted. "I recognized the trace from the rogue's ashes and identified Mr. Noble as its source, without considering the fact that other vampires in his line would share similar trace."

In sharp contrast to the cockiness Charles was used to seeing, she wilted under her employer's sharp gaze and he sensed shame and anger that seemed to be directed at herself. She also appeared afraid, perhaps that Dunlap might dismiss her for having made such a potentially disastrous error.

Despite her embarrassment over her mistake, Alice was visibly relieved as Adri assisted Dunlap in getting to his feet. Despite having been rendered unconscious, his injury did not seem serious.

As soon as he was standing, Dunlap squared his shoulders and faced David. "My sincere apologies for unintentionally making a false accusation against you, Mr. Noble."

The vampire's anger was evident in his tone and glowing eyes. "While Ms. Worth's mistake might be excused by her youth and inexperience, I am unsure why you and Charles were so anxious to take her word over mine."

"I make no excuses," Charles said. Though they could not share thoughts, much could be said without words. With his eyes, Charles acknowledged that he had insulted David greatly, and that he understood compensation would be expected. David's anger abated somewhat, though Charles knew the insult would not be quickly forgotten.

Out loud, Charles added, "I had harbored suspicions that the rogues might be connected to this location, based on the pattern of attacks. I was not aware that spellwork existed that might allow one of our line to hide treachery from us; therefore, it was logical to believe that either you might be the rogue-maker, or be in collusion with him." He glanced at Alice, who stood next to Dunlap. "Ms. Worth has been entirely correct in her information to this point, unmasking Mr. Harrison's co-conspirator and revealing the meaning of the spellwork on the rogue. Her initial deduction supported my own suspicions. My conclusion was entirely logical, based on the information in my possession. I am curious, however, as to why you did not intervene when the rogues attacked. I interpreted your lack of action as complicity."

David studied him. "The rogues attacked you and your people. Your people attacked my enforcers. I did not understand the purpose of the attacks or their cause. More to the point, you had just accused me of creating these abominations and allowing them to attack humans. But perhaps I should have acted, if for no other reason to ensure the rogues were subdued. For that, I do apologize." He looked around at the half-dozen rogues, lying cuffed and incapacitated on the floor. "How many rogues did you make, Josiah?"

Josiah said nothing.

"Strip him," Alice said.

Charles blinked. After a beat, David asked, "I beg your pardon?"

She gestured at Josiah. "Clara put spellwork on him that allows him to recall the rogues, as well as hide his duplicity from you. It's masked, but it's on his skin somewhere. I should be able to tell from the runes how many there are. We just need to find the markings."

"I will kill you slowly," Josiah snarled at Alice.

She rolled her eyes with characteristic derision. "A few more bad-guy clichés like that and I'll off myself for you."

At David's nod, his two remaining enforcers moved to Josiah's side. With his strength drained by the cuffs, the vampire could do nothing but threaten and swear as the enforcers produced knives and sliced through the fabric of his suit jacket, shirt, and undershirt quickly and efficiently. Alice watched them with a raised eyebrow, no doubt noting the practiced ease with which they removed the clothing from a body.

Josiah's pale torso was unmarked. The enforcers picked him up so Alice could see his sides and back, but no runes were visible. She passed her hand over his skin, searching for spellwork, but found nothing.

"Take off the rest," she said briskly.

Ignoring Josiah's furious threats, the enforcers cut away his suit pants and removed his socks and shoes, leaving the vampire in his skin. With clinical detachment, Alice passed her hand over his right leg, moving slowly from hip to foot, then walked around him and crouched again to pass her hand up his left leg.

Unable to elicit any response from Alice or the others with insults or threats, Josiah lapsed into stony silence.

When her hand reached his left thigh, she paused. "Spellwork here, for certain, but heavily masked. Let me see if I can—"

Josiah's eyes flicked to one of David's two remaining enforcers. The man went for her, blade in hand.

Charles had no time to wonder if Clara had spelled the man in order to hide his intentions from both him and David, who should have been able to sense his enforcer's treachery. The attacker was mere feet from Alice. With speed and reflexes enhanced by drinking David's blood regularly, he moved too fast for her to be able to react in time.

Vamp-fast, Charles hit the enforcer full speed, sending them both sliding across the floor. The enforcer's head smashed into the side of the solid-mahogany bar, rendering the man unconscious.

When he was certain the enforcer was no longer a threat, Charles released him and stood. Bryan locked spell cuffs on the unconscious man and picked up the blade he'd intended to use on Alice.

David had his one remaining enforcer by the throat, holding his massive body more than six inches off the floor. "You have one chance to live past tonight," he snarled into the man's face, his fangs extended and eyes bright gold. "Are you also in league with the traitors?"

"No, sir," the enforcer managed to say, his face turning purple.

David glanced at Charles. "I sense no duplicity."

"Ms. McKnight's spells apparently mask emotions," Charles told him. "We did not sense treachery from this one." He gestured at the unconscious enforcer, whose head was still lodged in the side of the partially demolished bar.

He turned to ask Alice to check the enforcer for spells, and that was when he caught a scent so intoxicating that the words died in his throat.

Alice's blood.

If Clara's blood had tasted like fine whisky to him, Alice's smelled like wine sweeter than any he recalled tasting. His fangs slid out involuntarily. If the scent had been stronger, he might have had difficulty controlling his urge to feed—and for a vampire his age, that was quite disconcerting. David's fangs were also visible, and he too appeared to be struggling to reign in his hunger.

Alice's right hand was on her neck, applying pressure to what Charles deduced was a moderate injury, judging by the amount of blood he smelled. He had thought he'd intercepted the enforcer before he could wound her, but it appeared that was not the case.

"Alice," Dunlap said worriedly, producing a handkerchief from one of the pockets in his borrowed pants. "Damn it, he got you."

"It's just a scratch," she said, taking the folded cloth. When she moved her hand, Charles saw a gash about three inches long that was bleeding profusely. She pressed the makeshift dressing to the wound. It did not seem particularly debilitating, though Dunlap hovered near his trainee, concerned despite her reassurance that the injury was not serious.

From the location of the laceration, the enforcer had clearly been attempting to inflict a fatal wound. It had been quite some time since Charles had offered his blood to any human to save their life, but he found that he would have been willing to do so to save Alice. Whether she would have accepted his help willingly was another matter, but her consent mattered little if it meant the difference between life or death. She could be as angry at him as she wished as long as she was alive.

There was no time for Charles to ponder the madness of that sentiment. David had lowered his enforcer so the man's feet were on the floor and permitted him to breathe, but the vampire's hand was still on his throat, a clear warning against any sudden or suspicious movements. The enforcer was perfectly still, well aware his life hung in the balance.

"Check him for spells," David ordered Alice, his eyes never leaving the enforcer's face.

Charles caught a flash of irritation from Alice at David's imperious tone, but to his surprise, she did not object. Likely, she still felt guilt for having initially identified David as the rogue-maker.

Dunlap, for his part, took umbrage at David issuing commands to his trainee. "Now, just a minute. She's bleeding from her throat in a room full of vampires. At least patch her up."

"Mark, I'm fine," Alice said.

Charles was surprised to hear an almost gentle note in her voice, rather than the irritation she'd expressed when Charles voiced concern over her physical condition at Northbourne. Perhaps for all her prickliness, she valued Dunlap's almost fatherly worry for her. Charles recalled that her parents were dead. It would be reasonable for her to think of Dunlap as a father figure. Her emotional connection to Dunlap was, perhaps, another possible weakness he could exploit, should the need arise.

"There is a first aid kit in the top right drawer behind the bar," the enforcer said, his voice strained.

As Charles debated whether the enforcer's suggestion could be trusted, Bryan spoke. "I've got it," he said hoarsely. He reached into one of the many pockets in his pants and produced a military-issue first-aid kit. He glanced at Charles. "With your permission?"

Charles inclined his head. "Please."

Alice watched Bryan approach. "You have much experience with those things?" she asked, indicating the kit.

"Some," Bryan rumbled. "I didn't treat many wounds that were this minor, though."

It was, oddly, the right thing to say to reassure the distrustful mage. She chuckled.

Bryan tore open the pack, took out several smaller packets, and handed them to Dunlap. "Hold these, please."

The former Army medic ripped open one of the smaller packets. The strong smell of disinfectant filled the air. "Let's see it," he said.

Carefully, Alice moved the folded handkerchief. Bryan studied the wound. "You're lucky; he missed your inner jugular by millimeters. This will need stitches or it will leave a scar."

"Just do what you can for now," she said. "I'll get it fixed up later."

Bryan cleaned the injury quickly and expertly, then handed the bloody antiseptic wipes back to Dunlap. He used a wound-sealing powder and three butterfly bandages to close the cut, then covered it with a folded rectangle of gauze and taped it down. Charles was not surprised that Alice remained stoic throughout the procedure, though her pain sizzled along his senses.

Despite Bryan's brusque manner, his hands were gentle. Charles sensed grudging respect from his enforcer at not only Alice's fortitude, but also the way she had handled herself during the fight with the rogues.

When Bryan finished, Alice collected the soiled first-aid items from Dunlap. She crumpled them, then held out her hand, the ball of trash in her palm. "*Burn.*"

The trash went up in white fire, reduced to fine ash. "Thanks," she told Bryan.

"Don't mention it," he told her.

"If you are quite finished, we still have two rather pressing matters to attend to," David Noble said, his hand still on his enforcer's throat.

"Right." Alice dusted off her hands. "It won't take me long to check Security Dude. Then I'll get back to the trace on the traitor." She glanced at Josiah, who bared his fangs at her.

"Go ahead," Dunlap told her.

She turned to David. "I need him naked to check for spellwork," she said, gesturing at the enforcer.

As David had no other personnel left to assist, Charles said, "Mr. Rodriguez, if you would."

Without a word, Carlos started removing the enforcer's clothes with clinical detachment. Alice stood nearby, waiting.

When the enforcer was nude, Alice passed her hand over his body, starting at the top of his head, looking for hidden spellwork. "Nothing on the back," she reported finally. "Turn."

David loosened his grip enough for the enforcer to rotate and face the windows.

As she stepped in front of him, her hand an inch from his chest, the enforcer caught her eye. "Andreas," he said. "Not Security Dude."

"Sorry about this, Andreas." Alice moved her hand over his arms. "It's the only way for us to be sure."

"Normally I expect at least dinner and a few drinks before a lady tells me to strip," Andreas told her.

She smiled. "If you come up clean, maybe we can revisit that sometime when we're both off the clock."

He stared stoically ahead as Alice scanned his chest, lower abdomen, and groin area. She checked his legs and even the bottoms of his feet, then stood and addressed David Noble. "I don't sense any spells. I can't guarantee I didn't miss something or that he's not in league with the others, but I'm not sensing any blood magic on him at all."

As the enforcer turned to face his employer, David asked, "Where do your loyalties lie?"

"With you, sir," Andreas said without hesitation. "Give me a stake and I'll put it in Harrison's heart right now."

"That will not be necessary. I am sure Valas will prefer to do that herself." David released him.

Andreas took a slow step back. "May I dress?" At David's nod, he quickly put his clothes back on.

Alice returned to Josiah Harrison's side. The vampire glared up at her. "Now, where were we?" she asked. "Oh, yes...I was about to tell them how many rogues you've got."

"All my rogues are here," he said.

She shook her head. "Even I can tell you're lying." She looked at David as he moved to stand across Josiah's body from her. "I am going to unweave the spellwork Clara put on him. It's the only way to know how many rogues he's controlling and break the spell that's hiding his thoughts from you."

"I understand." David frowned. "If you remove those spells, he will no longer control the rogues, correct?"

"No more so than any vampire can control his offspring," Alice told him. "Clara's spells are fading fast now that she's dead. If there are other rogues out there, they're about to slip their leashes anyway."

"How will we locate them once these spells are broken?" Charles asked.

She took a deep breath. "I should be able to locate them. I might be able to control them too. Not as well as he could, but maybe enough to keep them in one place until we can get to them."

Charles glanced at David. The older vampire studied Alice. "I was not aware that an earth mage would be capable of such a feat."

"It will be difficult and it might not work—I've never tried to do it before. But if that's our only way of finding the other rogues tonight, I'm willing to give it a try."

Dunlap spoke up. "That kind of spellwork and magic is well beyond your job description." He was plainly unhappy at the idea of letting her attempt such a risky endeavor.

She gave him a wan smile. "I figured it fell into that murky category of 'and other duties as assigned' on my contract." The smile disappeared. "You saw what he and Clara did to that woman who died at Northbourne earlier tonight, the female rogue. They carved spellwork into her body and treated her like an animal. I don't know if we can save any of these people, but I have to try."

Dunlap shook his head. "You can't save everyone, Alice."

Several emotions—pain, grief, anger—flashed in Alice's eyes before they turned flinty. "I know I can't save everyone, but this I *can* do. We can't stand here and debate all night." She looked at Charles. "I need to concentrate. Don't talk to me or touch me until I tell you it's okay to do so. I'll do my best to tell you what I'm finding out as I go." Her gaze flicked to Adri. "I need someone to watch my back while I work."

Adri was fast, but not fast enough, given the number of potential attackers in the room and how many of them were vampires. The bandage on Alice's neck was a grim reminder of how close the traitorous enforcer had come to mortally wounding her—and how close Charles had come to having to explain to Valas how he had allowed such a potentially valuable asset to be killed while under his protection. He did not desire to have any such conversation with her.

"I will stand guard," he said, joining her at Josiah's side.

Alice hesitated, clearly not entirely comfortable having him at her back.

"No one will touch you," Charles told her. "You have my word."

She gave him a tiny nod and crouched, holding her hand over Josiah's left thigh. Charles sensed her shields lowering and her magic danced on the edges of his awareness.

When her eyes lost focus, Charles realized how vulnerable she was, and why she had hesitated to let him stand beside her. Dealing with Clara's spellwork required all of her attention, leaving none to watch her surroundings.

He watched the room with Adri at his side as Bryan guarded their backs. David, with Andreas beside him, stood on Josiah's other side, watching Alice. The enforcer who had attacked Alice with a knife was still unconscious, as were the two enforcers Alice had wounded with her earth-magic whip. The six rogues were incapacitated—

four with broken necks and two with shattered skulls. The dhampir had regained consciousness. Like the others, he was immobilized by spell cuffs. All were staring fixedly at Josiah.

Alice's fingers moved in the air as she explored Clara's spellwork. "Masking and obfuscation spells," she murmured. "Layers of them, hiding his thoughts, his emotions, his betrayal, and hiding the scent of her blood." She tilted her head, her eyes half-lidded, her fingers moving as if she was playing an invisible harp. "So many spells, made with her blood and his blood too. It must have taken hours to make each one." She fell silent.

Charles could not sense the spells breaking, but he knew when the last of the obfuscation spells broke because suddenly the full force of Josiah's fury seared him. David's eyes turned bright gold, signaling that he too could now sense Josiah's hate.

"I'm working on the rogue summoning spells now," Alice said.

Several minutes went by while she worked. Dunlap's worry grew the longer she stayed silent.

Finally, she spoke. "There are eight rogues." Her voice was soft, almost dreamy. "One is deceased. Six are in this room. There is one more, a male."

"Is he in this building?" Charles asked.

A long pause. "No. He is...not nearby." She looked up at David, blinking until her eyes focused on him. "I think he's a couple of miles away, but it's hard to tell for sure."

David crouched and regarded Josiah without emotion, then addressed Alice. "What do you need to summon the last of the rogues?"

"The blood of his maker," she said.

Josiah hissed.

David held out his hand. Andreas took a blade from his boot and placed the hilt in his employer's hand. "How much do you require?" David asked.

Alice considered. "A pint will probably be sufficient, but you'd better collect two, just in case. A small ceramic pot or bowl would work best, if you have one."

As Andreas went in search of an appropriate receptacle, Alice rose stiffly and took off her leather jacket, draping it over the back of a chair. After a hesitation, she pulled her black shirt off over her head, leaving her in a modest athletic-style bra.

Charles was somewhat surprised to see a tattoo of a dragon coiled around her upper right arm. He was even more startled when the tattoo seemed to shimmer slightly. As that made no sense, however, he decided it must have been a trick of the light.

When she turned to put her shirt down, Charles saw a second tattoo, this one a spectacular phoenix across her upper back. Like the dragon, it appeared to be a recent tattoo, the colors of the ink still vibrant. The symbolism of both images was fairly clear, even to him: a fierce fighter and protector, and a firebird rising from the ashes of an old life. Though not an aficionado of tattoos, even Charles could appreciate the beauty and appropriateness of both.

A darkening area on Alice's right side indicated where Josiah had hit her during his escape attempt. Judging by the size and color of the injury, he had likely bruised or cracked a few of her ribs. Dunlap grimaced at the sight of the discoloration.

"Why are you removing your clothing?" Charles asked.

"I'll have to paint the spellwork on my skin in his blood." She shivered. "Just my arms and chest, though, so don't get too excited thinking I'm about to take off my pants."

Before Charles could formulate a response, Dunlap spoke. "You don't have to do this. You're hurt. The vamps can find the rogue."

"I've got this, Mark," Alice said firmly. "If things start to go sideways, I'll cut our connection. I'll be fine."

Andreas placed a ceramic bowl on the floor next to his employer. "Would you prefer to turn your back?" David asked her, the knife poised over Josiah's arm.

She shook her head. "I never turn my back, Mr. Noble. If I can't face it, I have no business participating in it."

"An admirable sentiment," David said, tilting his head. "One wonders how you came to believe that."

"I don't like cowards, and I don't like people who pretend their hands are clean while they force others to do their dirty work for them." She rubbed her arms. "Let's get this show on the road."

"I want you dead," Josiah snarled.

She shrugged. "Take a number."

David drew the blade across the younger vampire's pale arm. Dark blood ran into the bowl.

As the bowl began to fill, Alice crouched and dipped her finger into it. She raised her hand and studied the blood on the tip of her index finger. "I sense Clara's magic. You must have drunk from her earlier tonight. Lucky for me, since that makes this even easier."

She settled cross-legged on the floor, rolled her shoulders, and dipped her finger back into the bowl. Using the blood as paint and her flesh as the canvas, she began to draw.

11

The SUV flew over a railroad track. All four tires left the pavement for a full second before landing back on the road with a bone-jarring impact only partially cushioned by the vehicle's heavy-duty suspension. Behind them, the second SUV, carrying Kirwin and Carlos, cleared the same obstacle.

In the rear seat behind Charles, Mark Dunlap had a white-knuckled grip on the grab handle. "We can't catch that rogue if we're dead," he muttered.

From the passenger seat, Alice spoke, her voice an eerie monotone. "Turn right."

Charles and the others braced themselves as Adri took a corner on two wheels. They appeared to be headed south of the river, toward the warehouse district where Justice had been shooting scenes for his show on his first night in the city.

It had taken a half-hour for Alice to complete the intricate spellwork on her arms and torso. As she worked, enforcers working for Valas and the Court arrived at Nyx to transport the captured rogues, the dhampir, and the enforcers who had been loyal to Josiah Harrison to cells at Northbourne for interrogation. Niara would be conducting the interrogations on Valas's behalf. Charles felt no pity for traitors, but he was certain the enforcers would rue the day they had sided with Harrison against the Court.

In the meantime, Valas would be sorting out the rogues. Any who had killed would have to be executed in the presence of witnesses from SPEMA. Those who had not killed might be spared if David Noble could become their new master. At nearly five hundred years old and as Harrison's sire, David had a better-than-average chance of successfully bringing the survivors into his line.

Before David could attempt to bring them over, however, two things had to happen, according to Alice. First, the spellwork that had been carved, tattooed, and marked into their flesh must be removed; and second, Josiah Harrison had to die. The latter would take place before SPEMA witnesses as soon as Valas was satisfied that nothing more could be learned from the traitor. The former required that the spellwork be removed and the affected flesh cut from their bodies by a blood mage.

Alice had delivered the news matter-of-factly during a pause in the process of painting spellwork onto her body in Harrison's blood. While Dunlap had shuddered at the prospect, she had been clinical as she explained why the rogues' tattooed and scarred skin would have to be removed. Despite her apparent detachment, Charles sensed a variety of strong emotions, including anger, grief, and revulsion. It was the darkness in her eyes, however, that made him think that she knew quite well how horrible the process of cutting off the rogues' flesh would be.

And then he saw her back and knew it for certain.

With his focus on watching for potential threats, it was several minutes before Charles gave more than a cursory glance to Alice's back. As she worked, however, Charles found himself studying the phoenix tattoo more closely and saw what the tattoo had been designed to obscure: massive scarring on her upper back. To the untrained eye, the scars might seem relatively minor, but judging by their current appearance, they represented the last remaining visible signs of what had once been a near-fatal injury.

He'd thought at first the scars were from the boat accident that had killed her parents, but the lines were much too precise. He had only seen scars like this when a blood mage flayed skin.

Not long after he'd noticed the scars, Alice had finished the spellwork and urged an immediate departure. The revelation that she'd been tortured by a blood mage at some point in the past few years had been occupying Charles's thoughts during the drive.

"Slow down," Alice said from the front passenger seat, her voice still the strange monotone it had been since she'd invoked the spellwork and tethered herself to the remaining rogue. The bloody writing that had covered her arms, chest, and shoulders was no longer visible to the human eye, but Charles could see it shimmering with magic even in the darkness. He'd hoped to see blood magic, but she appeared to be using only earth magic to connect to the rogue.

Adri slowed the SUV to a crawl. Dunlap braced himself against the back of Charles's seat and leaned forward. "Alice, are you losing your connection to the rogue?"

"No, but we're close," she said. "I'm going to open up our connection more and try to get a clearer sense of where he is."

Dunlap's worry became something close to panic. "Alice, wait—"

Alice screamed, her back arching. The sound was piercing in the confines of the SUV. Adri pulled to the curb and Carlos, driving the second SUV, did the same.

Alice's arms flailed and she kicked violently at the underside of the dash as if trying to escape something.

"What is happening?" Charles demanded.

It was Dunlap who answered. "Something's happening to the rogue and she's feeling it too. Vaughan, tell her to cut the connection before it kills her!"

Cutting the connection would mean losing their only viable way of finding the rogue. "That is not an option," Charles said.

Dunlap's fury seared Charles's senses. "Listen here, you cold son of a—"

Charles caught an unexpected smell of blood. Strangely, it was not Alice's, or anyone else's in the vehicle. He recognized it as blood of a vampire. He could not discern the scent of the vampire's maker, which meant it was the rogue's blood he could smell.

"Jesus Christ," Dunlap said. It sounded like a prayer.

In the front seat, Alice struggled to breathe. As Charles watched, dumbfounded, a dozen bloody lacerations appeared on Alice's torso, arms, and face.

Dunlap punched the back of Charles's seat in frustration. "She'll bleed to death!"

"It is not her blood," Charles said.

"What the hell do you mean, it's not her blood?" Dunlap demanded. "It's coming out of *her!*"

"It is the rogue's blood," Charles stated, for the benefit of those in the vehicle who could not discern the difference. "How it is coming out of Ms. Worth, I do not know."

Stunned silence.

Bloody and shaking, Alice stilled. She was in great pain, Charles sensed, but forcing herself to overcome it.

"Alice?" Dunlap asked tentatively. "Alice, please cut the connection."

"We are close," Alice said, her words slurred. "Very close."

"What is happening to the rogue?" Charles asked.

Alice took a ragged breath. "Torture. He's being tortured." Tears spilled down her cheeks.

Charles's eyes went silver. "We must get to him. Ms. Worth, tell us where he is."

"Vaughan, this is killing her," Dunlap snapped.

Slowly, Alice raised a bloody hand and indicated a warehouse on the next block. "In there."

Bryan was already on his phone, looking up the information on the warehouse she was indicating. "It belongs to Foreman's company," he reported after a moment. "Just like the warehouse Justice was using to film last night."

Charles pointed to an alley on a nearby a side street. "Park there, Ms. Smith. We will approach on foot. Mr. Smith, alert the Court to our location and request additional personnel."

Adri and Carlos parked in the alley. Adri got out, opening the door for Charles. Bryan exited, folding his seat so that Dunlap could climb out of the third row before opening Alice's door.

As Charles came around the SUV, flanked by Carlos and Kirwin, Alice emerged from the vehicle on wobbly legs, her face ashen. Her wounds were significant enough to be debilitating.

Just how debilitating became clear a moment later, when Alice collapsed.

Bryan caught her, scooping her up into his arms. Charles sensed Alice's distress at being held, but it was muddled by her pain. "Put me down," she protested weakly.

"Ms. Worth, you can't walk," Bryan said, his voice surprisingly gentle. "We can move much faster this way."

Her back arched again as a burn appeared on her stomach. She suppressed a scream and turned her face toward Bryan's chest, his shirt muffling her moan. It was less an attempt to draw comfort from the enforcer as a way to hide her suffering, Charles decided.

"Alice, let go of the connection," Dunlap urged. "We know where he is now. You don't have to do this anymore."

"I have to hold him," she said, her voice barely audible. "I'm the only thing keeping him sane."

"What do you mean?" Dunlap's hand moved, as if he'd started to touch her, then thought better of it.

"We do not have time for debates." Charles turned to his people. "More personnel are en route, but we cannot wait. Ms. Smith, you will take the lead. Mr. Rodriguez, you will take the rear. We must move."

Adri headed for the warehouse with Charles and Kirwin behind her. Bryan followed, carrying Alice, with Dunlap beside him and Carlos at their backs.

As they slipped through the shadows toward the target, Charles reached out to his head enforcer with his mind. *When we enter the warehouse, you must protect Alice.*

He expected a protest. Instead, Bryan replied, *Yes, sir.* He cradled Alice carefully, trying to minimize the jostling as they ran.

Though his attention was on their surroundings, scanning the buildings and shadows for potential threats, Charles was aware that Alice was shaking and her wounds continued to bleed. They were leaving a blood trail leading directly from their vehicles to the warehouse that would have to be eliminated as soon as possible.

The group stopped out of sight of the warehouse while Adri did a quick recon. She returned with good news. "Minimal security," she told Charles. "Cameras on each corner of the building and several doors with what appear to be basic locks. There's an alarm system, but it's one we can get around without much trouble. There are three sets of tracks going into one of the vehicle entrances. It looks like one heavy SUV, a car, and a truck. I'm thinking it's probably Foreman, Justice, and the cameraman alone in there. Maybe one or two more, if Foreman has a driver and security with him."

Charles glanced at Kirwin. "Go with her and disable the alarm. Let us know when we can approach."

They disappeared in the direction of the warehouse. A few minutes later, Charles heard Adri's voice in his head. *Approach along the south side of the building. Best entry is at the far door.*

"South side," he told Carlos. The enforcer guarded their rear as Charles led the others to meet Adri and Kirwin.

Alice suppressed a scream as they reached the door. A second burn appeared slowly on her abdomen, as if whoever was causing it was taking their time and savoring the pain he was causing.

Dunlap closed his eyes. When he opened them, Charles expected him to repeat his plea for Alice to sever her connection to the rogue. Instead, the private investigator reached up tentatively and rested his hand on the top of Alice's head. "Hang in there, girl," Dunlap said, his voice tight with anger and grief. "We're going to end this now."

Alice's hands clenched into fists. "Hurry," she whispered. "His madness is growing."

From inside the warehouse, Charles heard a scream of agony that was audible only to his ears. At the same moment, Alice made a choking sound. Another burn appeared on her right cheek.

"Vaughan, *enough*," Dunlap grated. "Let's get in there before they do something to the rogue that kills Alice. What are we waiting for?"

Amira and Leah appeared from around the corner of the warehouse. Amira raised her eyebrows at the sight of Alice, bloody and pale in Bryan's arms.

Leah broke the handle off the door. "We must hurry," she said.

The group slipped into the building. The door led to a dimly lit interior hallway lined with offices, all currently dark.

Amira and Leah led the group down the hallway, following the sounds of the rogue's cries. They turned left into a short, wide hallway that ended in a set of double doors.

A fresh wound appeared on Alice's arm. From beyond the double doors, the rogue screamed.

Amira and Charles moved to the doors with the others behind them. "I will apprehend Jack Justice," Charles said softly. "Amira will attend to the injured rogue. The rest of you will deal with any other personnel. We must preserve the recordings."

Dunlap stared at him. "Preserve the *what?*"

Charles grabbed the door handles and ripped the doors from their hinges. The group entered the room beyond.

The cavernous space was virtually empty except for a few tables and chairs, some filming equipment, and a shipping container.

In the center of the space, Jack Justice, a razor-tipped stake in one hand and a glowing electric charcoal starter in the other, stood over a young male vampire. The rogue was splayed out on a low table, his wrists and ankles chained and held with spell cuffs. His dark hair was matted with blood and his body bore the same wounds as Alice's. His eyes were wild with fear and pain.

Alex Foreman sat in a chair, his tie loosened and a bottle of bourbon on a small table on his right. He gaped at the intruders, his mouth hanging open in shock. A third man, who Charles recognized as the cameraman who had arranged Justice's "bait" the night before, was operating a camera pointed at the rogue and his tormentor.

Charles crossed the room in less than a blink, moving toward Justice at the speed of lightning. Somehow, the bounty hunter dropped the nearly white-hot charcoal starter and raised the stake, aiming for Charles's heart. Charles brushed the stake aside, its edge slicing his arm before he crushed Justice's hand. The stake clattered to the concrete floor next to the charcoal starter.

Justice set his jaw and didn't make a sound, even as his hand broke. Charles knocked a second stake from his grip. It joined the hunter's primary weapon on the floor.

They locked eyes. Justice's gaze was cold. "Vaughan."

"I warned you there would not be any torture of vampires in my city," Charles said. "You will go to prison for this, Mr. Cornwall. As will you, Mr. Jeffries," he added, glancing at Hank the cameraman, who was face down next to his camera, Leah's knee in the middle of his back as she snapped cuffs on his wrists.

A familiar scent teased Charles's nose. He leaned toward Justice and inhaled. "You have been drinking vampire blood. That would explain your reflexes and why you are so successful with your hunts."

A silver blade appeared in Justice's hand, from a sheath hidden in his sleeve. Charles delivered a punch to his jaw and the bounty hunter went down, unconscious. Kirwin cuffed him and left him face down on the concrete.

Carlos hauled the handcuffed Alex Foreman to his feet and threw him back into his chair.

"As for you, Mr. Foreman, I think you will find the accommodations where you are headed to be far less pleasant than you would like," Amira said.

Foreman spat at her. "Fanghead bitch," he said, his face twisted with hate. "What right do you have to enter private property?"

Charles reached into his inner jacket pocket and withdrew a folded piece of paper. "My authorization, supplied by SPEMA. They will be taking you into custody very shortly."

Amira approached the rogue, who watched her with wide eyes. She bent to touch his forehead and the young vampire flinched. "Do not worry," she said softly. "We will care for you. You must rest." She glanced at Alice, still in Bryan's arms. "You may release him, Ms. Worth."

Alice closed her eyes. The spellwork on her skin shimmered and faded. Slowly, her wounds vanished and she went limp. Bryan's arms tightened. She didn't appear to notice.

The rogue sighed. Amira smoothed his matted hair back from his face and murmured soothingly.

Chains scraped against metal. The sound came from inside the shipping container. Charles headed for the container.

Behind him, Foreman shouted, "Stay away from there! Leave the doors locked! God damn you, *leave it locked!*" He tried to rise, but Carlos shoved him back into the chair.

Charles reached the container. "Who or what is in this container, Mr. Foreman?"

No answer.

Kirwin and Adri joined Charles. From inside the container, Charles heard the sound of chains rattling again.

Bryan placed Alice carefully on her feet. She swayed, still pale and shaky. "Are you certain there are no more rogues?" Charles asked her.

She shook her head. "If there are, Harrison wasn't spelled to control them."

Charles glanced at Adri. She gave him a nod and readied a stun net. He broke the chain and opened the doors.

And found himself rendered speechless with horror for the first time in many, many years.

"Oh my God," Dunlap breathed.

The creature huddled on the floor of the container was shackled with spell cuffs on both ankles. The cuffs were on chains that were bolted to the floor and permitted virtually no movement.

She'd once been wearing a business suit, but it was torn in a dozen places and her feet were bare. Her long hair was matted with blood and what appeared to be leaves and twigs. She was starved almost to the brink of madness, her body wasted to skin and bones, her eyes pure black.

The caged vampire stretched out a hand toward them. Considering her condition, Charles expected her to be well beyond speech, but she managed a hoarse whisper. "*Hungry.*"

Alice let out a sob and stumbled toward the container. "Who is that?"

Charles found his voice. "It is Christine Foreman."

12

THE CONCRETE FLOOR TREMBLED BENEATH THEIR FEET.

The sensation was so like Valas's fury after the death of the first captured rogue that for a moment, Charles thought the head of the Court had come to the warehouse without notifying him. He turned, expecting to see Valas, and instead found Alice standing behind him.

Her stoic façade and trademark smirk were gone and in their place was pure rage. Her body nearly vibrated with it.

Bright green earth magic sparked on her hands. The tremors grew and the building shook, sending the light fixtures above their heads swinging wildly. The windows shattered, raining glass along the walls. Metal groaned and broken bolts fell from the ceiling, clinking on the concrete.

"Alice," Dunlap said urgently. "Alice, *stop*. You're tearing the building down."

At first, Alice gave no indication that she heard him. Charles thought he might be forced to incapacitate her to prevent her from bringing the roof down on all of them.

Finally, the tremors subsided and the green magic disappeared. Alice stared at Christine, then turned toward Alex Foreman, still pinned in his chair by Carlos. "You chained your own sister and left her to slowly starve to death." Her voice was hollow.

"That *thing* is not my sister," Foreman spat. "It showed up at my house the night my sister died. I managed to put enough bullets into it that we could get it locked up until Jack could get here. He shot it full of some fanghead tranq and put it in chains."

Charles tore his gaze away from the emaciated vampire and faced her brother. "If you wished to kill her, why not simply stake her? It would have been far more merciful."

Foreman's face twisted into an expression of pure loathing. "Why would I want to be merciful to that thing?"

It took every ounce of Charles's self-control not to rip the man's head off. Experience had taught him well that nothing he or anyone else could say would change how Foreman and those like him felt about vampires.

There were countless cases of friends, lovers, and family members staking newly risen vampires. Though it was murder, Charles could at least comprehend their reasoning. He even understood Jack Justice's motivations, as cold-blooded and sadistic as they were.

But to chain one's own sister and condemn her to die slowly and agonizingly...Charles was again struck by the thought that humans were so quick to label vampires as monsters, when they were capable of acts that would turn a vampire's stomach.

The starving vampire lifted her head. "Alex, *hungry*."

Charles considered his options. As the offspring of a rogue, there was little chance Christine could be brought under the control of any master less than several hundred years old. He doubted his own blood would be powerful enough to help her. Amira's might, but she had not made any vampires in more than a century, instead focusing her energy on creating and controlling her Hunters. Ultimately, it would be Valas who would decide if Christine would live or die, but until then, the newly risen vampire needed sustenance and whatever care they could offer.

Alice's bright green earth magic spiraled out of her hand.

Charles read her intention in her eyes. Vamp-fast, he stepped between Alice and Alex Foreman. "Ms. Worth, you cannot."

Her eyes were full of pain as her magic crackled on his skin. "Please move, Mr. Vaughan."

He longed to tell her how much he wished he could allow her to feed Alex Foreman to his sister, but it would reflect poorly on him and the Court to admit to such a savage impulse. "I understand what you want to do and why you want to do it, but this is not the way," he said.

"He *chained her*," Alice pleaded. Tears spilled down her cheeks. "He chained up his own sister to watch her starve to death slowly. She needs blood, and he deserves to die."

"Perhaps he does." Charles glanced at Foreman, who stared at Alice's fire whip in shock and horror. "But vengeance and justice are not the same. He will stand trial for what he has done."

"It's not enough," she insisted. "You can't put your own family in chains. You can't torture them and enjoy their suffering and just keep going like nothing happened."

This wasn't just about what Alex Foreman had done to his sister, that much was certain. The pain in her eyes made that clear. Charles recalled the scars on Alice's back and wondered if someone in the Worth family had inflicted that torture on her. It would certainly explain her reaction not only to Christine's suffering, but to what had been done to the captured female rogue.

"You can't let her kill me," Foreman snarled.

Alice's eyes flashed. The whip crackled and the floor trembled again. "No one *lets* me do anything. Don't think that me trying to explain this to him is the same as me asking him for permission. I want him to understand. I want *you* to die."

"Alice," Charles said quietly. "We are not the monsters they believe us to be. And neither are you."

For a moment, she stared at him. A number of emotions crossed her face: anger, grief, guilt. Finally, the whip spiraled back into her hand and vanished. "Please help her," Alice said.

To Charles's surprise, Amira spoke. "I will care for her." She left the now-catatonic rogue and entered the container. She knelt beside Christine, pushed up her sleeve, and used her own fangs to open a wound on her wrist. She brought her arm to Christine's mouth. "Drink, child," she said.

With a wretched sob, Christine bit into the soft flesh of Amira's wrist and drank.

The drive from the warehouse to Alice's house took nearly a half-hour, and she had said nothing other than a terse and quite unconvincing "I'm fine" in response to Charles's inquiry about her physical condition. She stared out her window, her expression pensive.

Court vehicles had taken the last rogue and Christine Foreman back to Northbourne, where Valas would determine if either could be saved. While Mark Dunlap and Amira remained at the warehouse to speak to the SPEMA agents sent to apprehend Alex Foreman, Jack Justice, and the cameraman, Charles offered to escort Alice back to her home. Adri drove, and Carlos accompanied them.

When they were perhaps ten minutes from her house, Alice turned to Charles. "You had people watching Jack Justice, didn't you?"

He tilted his head. "Yes."

Her eyes flashed. "So how did he get hold of a rogue and torture him without you knowing?"

Charles weighed possible responses. Her question was not unexpected; it was reasonable to assume that the Court would not have allowed Jack Justice to operate in the city without surveillance.

As such, he did not insult her intelligence by attempting to lie. "We were aware that Mr. Cornwall had captured a rogue, though we did not know exactly where he had taken him. Our surveillance team was forced to withdraw to avoid detection."

"Did you know he intended to torture the rogue?" Alice's voice was cold.

"Yes."

Magic sparked on her hands and a cold wind blew through the vehicle. "Why?" she demanded. "Why let him be tortured?"

"It was necessary. Cornwall is suspected of torturing vampires in other cities, but there was no evidence with which to prosecute him. Now there is. He and Alex Foreman will go to prison for many years."

"You're ruthless." She took a deep, shuddering breath. "Please tell me you didn't know what they were doing to Christine Foreman."

Charles's eyes silvered. "No, I did not."

She shook her head. "You said you aren't the monsters Foreman thinks you are, but you let one of your own be tortured. Does the end justify the means?"

"In this case, yes." He regarded her. "Would you rather Foreman have continued to torment his sister and Jack Justice torture and kill vampires with impunity?"

Alice fell silent. "It still feels so cruel and wrong," she said finally. "And a little monstrous."

"Life presents us with few easy moral choices," Charles said. "Sometimes we must choose the lesser of two evils and be at peace with that decision."

Her mouth twisted. "And you call *me* pragmatic." She paused. "So, are you?"

"Am I what?" he asked with a frown.

"At peace with your decision."

It had been Valas's decision to permit Jack Justice to capture a rogue and take him to Alex Foreman, but Charles had not disagreed with her strategy. It was, he believed then and now, the best way to bring an end to Justice's career as a killer. "I am."

She turned back to the window. "That must be nice," she said tonelessly.

A few minutes later, Adri pulled into Alice's driveway and parked. Her home was a modest two-story Victorian. A nondescript gray Honda sedan was parked under the carport.

Charles said, "Your work tonight was exemplary. You saved many lives."

"Maybe tomorrow I'll feel good about that." Alice sounded tired. "Right now, all I can think about is Christine Foreman and what her brother did to her, and what Jack Justice did to that vamp."

"A new day will bring new perspective." Charles handed her a card with his name and a phone number embossed in gold. "I look forward to working with you again in the future, Ms. Worth."

"I figured you'd be glad to be rid of me and my bad manners," she said, tucking the card into her bag. Her light tone seemed forced.

He smiled. "Your manners could use some refinement. Perhaps we could discuss that tomorrow evening, over dinner."

She did not return his smile. "I don't date vampires, Mr. Vaughan, much less members of the Vampire Court."

"I am offering dinner, Ms. Worth, nothing more."

"You and I both know what you're offering." She unbuckled her seatbelt. "I may not have your gift for sensing emotions, but give me some credit. I caught your flirtation earlier and I'm not interested. Let's leave it at that."

"I am the sort of man who enjoys uncovering secrets." Charles let his eyes glow softly. "I will see yours laid bare."

She smiled, her eyes sparkling with the same maddening amusement he'd seen earlier in the night. "Not in this lifetime, Mr. Vaughan. Have a good night."

He had not expected her to accept his offer; in fact, he would have been quite surprised if she had. He was in no hurry to add her to his collection, however. It would take time to get past her defenses. A vampire had nothing but time.

Charles gave Carlos a nod and the enforcer got out to open Alice's door. "Very well, then. Good night, Ms. Worth."

She exited the vehicle and put her bag on her shoulder. "If you decide you want wards on your office that would disrupt spells like the one Clara used to deceive you, let me know. I might be able to whip something up. I'll let you and Mark work out the pricing."

"Thank you. I will discuss it with your employer. Sleep well."

"You too." She turned and limped across the yard toward her door.

Carlos slid into the seat beside Charles and closed his door. They watched as Alice climbed her front steps, unlocked her door, and went inside without looking back.

"Hell of a gal," Adri said appreciatively, backing down the driveway and out into the street.

"That she is." Charles settled back into his seat. "To Niara's, please, Ms. Smith."

The clock on the mantle was just chiming two a.m. when Charles sensed that his head enforcer was outside the bedroom door.

Bryan's voice in his head was apologetic. *Sir, I'm sorry for disturbing you, but I have a report from the researcher assigned to do the background check on Ms. Worth. She says it's extremely urgent.*

Charles rose from the bed and put on a robe. It had been nearly a week since he had asked for a report on Alice Worth's background, a week spent dealing with SPEMA agents, local and state law enforcement, local and national news agencies, Josiah Harrison, Alex Foreman, and Jack Justice.

Each night, he had inquired as to the status of the research, only to be told the researcher had found little more than what was already in Alice's file, and nothing that could shed more light on the month she'd been missing.

Until now.

He tied his robe and slipped quietly into the hallway, closing the bedroom door behind him.

Bryan waited in the hall, a slim red folder in his hand. He handed it to his employer.

Charles read through the contents of the folder. When he finished, he looked up at Bryan. "Did you read the report?"

Bryan shook his head. "No, sir."

"Has anyone else?"

"No, sir. Only the researcher who created it and you have seen it. She has been held at Northbourne with no contact with anyone."

"Good. Instruct Adri to wipe her computer personally and use the appropriate protocols to remove all records of her searches permanently. There cannot be any trace of this information anywhere in our system."

Bryan straightened. "Yes, sir. Do you want me to dispose of the report?"

"I will destroy it myself. Go to Northbourne and bring me the researcher."

As Bryan left, Charles opened the door and reentered the bedroom.

"Important business, *mudiwa?*" Niara stretched languidly on the oversized bed, the light from the fire dancing on her bare skin. "It must have been for your enforcer to disturb our rest."

"I do not recall that we were resting," Charles countered, crossing the room to the fireplace. He tossed the folder onto the fire. When he was sure there was nothing left, he returned to the bed.

"How intriguing," Niara said as he untied his robe and draped it neatly over a chair. "A knock at the door, an urgent conversation, mysterious papers burned to ash. You will not indulge me by sharing your secrets, I suppose?"

"Merely a matter related to an item I wish to acquire. There has been a development that requires contemplation and careful planning, but there is no need for it to distract me any further tonight." He rested a knee on the bed. "My apologies for the interruption. Shall we continue?"

"By all means." Niara trailed her fingers along the spine of the voluptuous brunette lying on her stomach between them. Still lost in a haze of pleasure, the young woman murmured something unintelligible. "What is your desire?" Niara asked him, her eyes glowing copper. "Her throat, or someplace more…intimate?"

Charles bowed slightly. "I defer to you, Nia. You know my appetites."

"That I do." Niara gently rolled their bedmate over onto her back. She bent her head, teasing the young woman's breast with delicate flicks of her tongue. The girl moaned as Niara trailed light kisses from her breast to her throat. Her blood pulsed faster in her femoral artery and Charles made a low, approving sound.

Niara carefully scraped the tips of her fangs on the delicate skin over the girl's carotid.

"Please," the young woman whispered, reaching for them both.

Magic danced on the edges of his senses and a light breeze swirled around them. Their meal tonight was a mid-level air mage, a special indulgence to celebrate Josiah Harrison's execution. Mage blood was always delicious, no matter what kind, but Charles had always particularly enjoyed the almost effervescent blood of air mages.

Especially the ones who gave him a merry chase first.

He looked down at the woman and thought of Alice, imagining her in his arsenal, picturing her in his bed. Each time she would draw him near, he would never be entirely sure whether she meant to kiss him or kill him. The thrill of it was almost intoxicating.

Not in this lifetime, she had said.

Charles smiled and allowed Niara to draw him down onto the bed. *We shall see, my dear,* he thought. *We shall see.*

EPILOGUE

FIVE YEARS LATER

In two hundred years, Charles had done business with billionaires and dock workers, presidents and poets. He'd bought and sold secrets, objects, and on rare occasions people, to and from all manner of clients.

Few made his skin crawl quite as much as the man sitting currently in his office, sipping a glass of his finest whisky and studying the artifacts in the case behind his desk with cold gray eyes.

"I am surprised you traveled here to collect the object in person," Charles said. "My couriers could have delivered it to your home in Baltimore."

The old man gestured with his glass. "It was no trouble. I've never visited your city, and this was a good excuse to see what the area has to offer."

That was, of course, a lie. Charles's sources had informed him that his visitor had in fact made several trips to the city in the past year. The same sources reported that the man was responsible for several recent violent and destructive attacks on properties owned by local cabal leader Darius Bell. Many suspected he intended to make a move on Bell's territory and use the city as his base of operations on the west coast.

Charles did not let on that he knew the old man's words to be a lie. Instead, he returned the conversation to the reason for the visit. "The item has proven to be somewhat volatile, so it is currently kept in a sealed box lined with containment spells. I am told the box should not be opened except by a very strong blood mage."

"I assure you I am well aware of the item's instability. We'll certainly handle it with the utmost care." The old man smoothed his suit jacket. "You say the object has been volatile. You haven't tried to use it, I assume?" The last was clearly a veiled threat.

"The report comes from its previous owners." Charles finished the last of his Scotch. "The item is untouched. The box was opened for my agents at its purchase to confirm that the object was inside and has not been opened since."

"Excellent." The old man finished his drink and set his glass on the table beside his chair. "Quite excellent. I'm glad to hear that."

"As I stated in our previous conversation, I cannot vouch for the power of the object or what its uses might be," Charles said. "My agent confirmed its authenticity, but its exact nature remains uncertain."

"I brought someone with me who will check to make sure its powers are what we believe them to be," the old man said. "Once our business here is concluded, we'll take possession of it and open it elsewhere."

"That is satisfactory. My attorney has prepared an agreement based on the terms we discussed previously," Charles said.

The old man tapped his fingers on the armrest of the chair. "Let's see it then."

At Charles's nod, Bryan opened the door to the hall. "Ms. Foreman? Please come in."

Christine Foreman strode into the office, briefcase in hand. She crossed to the desk, set the case down, and produced a red folder. She handed it to Charles's guest. "Your paperwork, Mr. Murphy."

Moses Murphy, head of the largest cabal on the east coast, opened the folder, glanced at the first page, and then back up at her. "A vampire attorney? How novel. How ever did you complete law school? Night classes?"

Christine's smile was brief. "I was an attorney before I became a vampire. And please, no quips about lawyers being bloodsuckers."

"Perish the thought, my dear." Murphy gave her an equally cold smile and turned his attention back to the contract.

Charles glanced at his head enforcer. *You said earlier that Alice Worth is here to see me. Is she still waiting downstairs in the bar?*

Yes, sir.

Charles glanced at the clock on his desk. *I doubt I will have time to meet with her tonight. Did she give any indication of what she wishes to discuss?*

No, sir. Bryan hesitated. *She's talking to Sean Maclin of the Tomb Mountain Pack.*

Charles stilled. *Do they know each other?*

Pete says Maclin just introduced himself. Alice invited him to sit with her.

Alice had indulged in a handful of relationships in the past few years, but none of her lovers, male or female, had given him any cause for concern as potential rivals. She enjoyed sex but wanted nothing more, ending relationships the moment her partners sought any sort of emotional connection. She remained almost as guarded and careful as she had been when she'd first arrived in the city.

Sean Maclin, however, was another story. The alpha werewolf was a successful business owner and head of the largest and strongest pack in the area. He was by all accounts kind, fair, and much loved by his pack. He might be the sort of man Alice would want for more than sex. Despite her trademark sarcasm and smirk, Alice was a wounded soul. Maclin was an alpha, programmed to defend and protect people like her. He wouldn't back away from the challenge Alice presented. Wolves enjoyed a chase.

Bryan sensed his employer's displeasure. *Do you want me to get her away from him?*

It was tempting to say yes, but Charles had to tread carefully. Any overt interference would risk the ire of Maclin's pack and the Were Ruling Council.

He also knew from personal experience that Alice was fiercely independent. She would never stand for an alpha werewolf's controlling nature or accept his protection. An alpha would not be able to put up with anyone so strong-willed, especially a female —not for long, anyway. They might have a passionate affair, but it would be short-lived.

No, Charles said finally. *We will monitor the situation. Send Carlos in, please, and let Alice know I will be pleased to meet with her tomorrow night, if her schedule allows.*

Bryan departed. Carlos came into the office and took up a position next to Charles.

Moses Murphy finished reading the contract. He signed the last page and handed the papers back to Christine. "Everything seems to be in order. I'll have the funds transferred now." He took out his phone.

Within moments, Charles's computer alerted him that payment had been received. "You may take possession of the object," Charles said. "As I mentioned previously, for safety reasons, it has been stored off-site at this address." He rose and handed Murphy a piece of paper. "You will be expected."

"Excellent." Murphy stood and extended his hand.

Charles shook it. Murphy's magic seared his skin. Most mages kept their magic hidden behind shields or even masking spells. Murphy, on the other hand, made little attempt to hide the power of his fire magic. It was an ill-mannered display of power, but Charles would expect nothing less from a man like Murphy.

Murphy buttoned his jacket and picked up his briefcase. "It's been a pleasure doing business with you, Mr. Vaughan."

"Likewise." Charles remained standing until Murphy left the office, headed down the private stairs that led directly to the parking garage beneath the building, rather than exiting through Hawthorne's.

As he picked up his empty glass, Charles heard Bryan's voice in his head. *Sir, Alice will meet with you tomorrow evening. She says she has a situation where she needs your help.*

The corners of Charles's mouth turned up. In the five years he had known her, Alice had never asked for his help, well aware that by doing so she would put herself in his debt. All of their interactions had been carefully framed as business transactions. She'd been careful for so long, keeping him at arm's length. He'd played a slow game, inviting her up to his office to sample his best Scotch, talk about her investigations, walk her through the process of starting her own business after she left MDI. He'd flirted from time to time and she rebuffed him with a smile and her trademark sarcasm. It had become a kind of running joke, as he slowly but surely got through her defenses. Now she needed his help. It was the opportunity he had been waiting for.

She is leaving with Sean Maclin, Bryan added after a pause. *He offered to take her home, and she agreed.*

The glass shattered in Charles's hand.

Christine raised her eyebrows as he used a handkerchief to collect the broken glass. "Problem, Mr. Vaughan?"

"Not at all." Charles dropped the shards of glass into the trash can and studied the cuts on his palm. They were closing and healing as he watched. "Merely an accident."

Should I stop them? Bryan asked.

No, Charles replied, wiping the blood from his hand. *Let them go.* He moved to the bar to pour himself another drink.

"I hope that's the last we see of that man," Christine said, tucking the signed contract into her briefcase. "He's vile."

"I cannot argue with that assessment of Moses Murphy's character." Charles stoppered the decanter of Scotch and returned to his desk. "One hopes Darius Bell will prevent Murphy from getting a foothold here. Bell is many things, but he is not a butcher."

"That piece he bought...what does it do?" she asked curiously.

He sipped his Scotch. "From what I understand, a blood mage can use it to trace magical signature, even trace hidden by spells."

She frowned. "So Murphy's looking for someone?"

Charles nodded. "It would appear so, someone he thinks might be well hidden." He wondered who Murphy's target might be.

Whoever it was, they were on borrowed time, no matter how well they were hidden or how far they had run.

GHOSTING 101
Note: This story takes place between *Heart of Malice* and *Heart of Fire*

The ghost was beside himself.

"Put me back!" he screeched, flinging himself repeatedly and ineffectually at the body lying face-down on the pavement like a moth battering itself against a light bulb.

This was just sad. With a sigh, I floated out of the shadows where I'd been watching this going on for the last five minutes. "Hey, buddy, that's not going to work. Give it up. You're just burning yourself out."

He whirled around and zipped toward me full-speed. I moved out of the way and he went past me, disappearing through the wall of the building.

I heard him scream from the other side of the wall and rolled my eyes. Noobs.

He reappeared, twice as fast and twice as frantic, and this time he barreled straight into me. When we collided, the ricochet of energy sent us both careening backward. I halted my momentum before I reached the other side of the alley, but he had no control over himself and went back through the wall. He screamed again.

Oh, for Pete's sake.

When he came back into the alley, eyes crazed and ready to yell again, I was waiting, my arms crossed. "Calm down," I ordered him.

That startled him out of his panicky feedback loop. He halted in mid-air. "Wait, you can see me?"

Unsurprisingly, he looked like most newly formed ghosts: a hodgepodge of body parts in a roughly human shape. It took a little time for spirits to realize they had control over their appearance, so at first they took the form their subconscious mind created, which seemed to be a jumbled manifestation of impressions about themselves. All the parts were there; they just weren't quite where they were supposed to be or in proportion to each other. He looked like a Salvador Dalí painting.

He hadn't noticed that about himself yet and I didn't think pointing it out would help him calm down, so I just waited.

"Okay, obviously you can see me," he said finally. "What's wrong with me?"

I would have thought that was fairly obvious given the large puddle of blood around the body, but this guy might not be the brightest bulb in the chandelier. "You're dead."

"What? No, I'm not. I fell and hit my head and I'm having some kind of out-of-body experience." He flitted over to his body and stared down at it.

The body was face down, so it was hard to tell much about him except he was a little heavyset and had been wearing sweatpants, a long-sleeved T-shirt, and sneakers when he died. The fact he was wearing shoes was mildly interesting given it was the middle of the night, but maybe he worked third shift.

I stopped that train of thought right there. I was not going to get pulled into this guy's crisis. No way. I had enough on my plate without additional newly dead drama.

"I read about this," he said. "I'll float around for a while and then I'll go back into my body. Man, I am going to have the *best* story to tell everybody when I wake up."

Somehow I didn't think the gentle approach was going to work with this one. "Seriously, you're dead. Look at all that blood. I'm pretty sure I can see some brains leaking out too. You're not going to wake up."

He looked closer at his head and started making a choking sound. "Oh, sweet Jesus, I can see my brain. I'm going to throw up."

"You can't throw up," I told him patiently. "You don't have a stomach anymore."

The gagging noises continued.

I sighed. "What's your name?"

"Abe," he told me between heaving sounds.

"Abe, quit it. You're not going to barf and you're annoying the hell out of me."

He turned to face me. "I might survive," he pleaded. "Doctors save people with head injuries all the time."

"Not that kind of head injury, Abe. That one's not the kind you come back from." His face fell. I softened my tone a little. "But the good news is, it wasn't the end of the line for you. You're still you; you're just more invisible now."

He mumbled something.

"What did you say?"

"Are you an angel?" he asked, his voice timid.

"Oh, for—do I *look* like an angel?"

"I don't know what an angel looks like," he sniffled. "I mean, you don't have wings, but I guess you wouldn't have to have wings."

"I guarantee you I am not an angel," I said.

He missed my dark tone as something occurred to him and his eyes widened. "Are you from—?" He looked down at the ground.

Mildly insulted, I said, "No, I am not from Hell either."

His shoulders sagged in relief. "Well, if you're not an angel and you're not a demon, what are you?"

"Same as you," I said. "I'm a ghost. My name is Malcolm."

"Malcolm what?"

"Just Malcolm."

He looked confused. "We don't get to have last names anymore?"

"You can have a last name if you want, but I don't give mine out. If someone knows your full name, or even your first and last name, they could summon you. You don't want to be summoned."

"Why not?"

"Because pretty much anyone who would summon you would not have your best interests in mind."

Fear made him flitter. "What does that mean?"

I waved my hands. "This isn't Intro to Ghosting 101, Abe. I was just trying to help you get situated. You can figure it out from here. I was on my way somewhere when I saw you."

Abe zipped over in front of me. "Please, don't leave," he said hesitantly. "I'm not...I don't know what to do."

I shrugged. "None of us do. Death is a lot like life: you just figure things out as you go and do the best you can."

"I guess I didn't do very well if I'm dead." He turned to look at his body. "How did I die?"

"Judging by the way you went splat, I'd say you fell." I looked up at the apartment building above us. "Do you recognize where we are?"

He looked up. "I'm not sure. It seems familiar, but I can't quite place it. My memory is really fuzzy."

"Not surprising. That happens a lot when you first realize you're dead, actually. I think your brain takes a little while to reboot." It looked like I was doing Ghosting 101 after all, damn it. At least he was calmer now, albeit still a jumble of body parts.

"How long did it take for your memory to come back?" Abe asked.

"My situation was a little different than yours. When I died, before I came back as a ghost, I went...somewhere else first."

"Heaven?" He sounded hopeful.

I shook my head.

After a moment, he asked, "Hell?"

I shook my head again.

He looked relieved. "What's the other thing called? Purgatory?"

"You could maybe call it that. Some people call it the Null. It's kind of like the afterlife's waiting room, except it's empty and you're in there by yourself. There isn't even any crappy music or hard plastic chairs." I tried to pull off a joke but it didn't work.

"That sounds awful," Abe said.

"It kinda was, but it's mostly a blur now, thankfully." I started to float back toward the street. "I really need to go."

"Wait, where are you going?"

"I have to check on someone."

"Who?" He followed me.

I sighed and stopped. "Just a friend."

"Is he a ghost too?"

"Her. No."

"Someone you left behind when you died?"

"Abe—"

"I don't want you to leave me, okay?" he yelled suddenly, flitting back and forth between the body on the pavement and me. "Just talk to me for a little while. Is that asking so much? I just died and I'm trying to figure out why and where I am and what's going to happen to me now. I know this whole being dead thing is old hat to you, but my blood's not even dry. Jeez, I *hope* you're not an angel because you'd be the worst angel *ever*."

I was closer to the angel of death than any angel he was thinking of, but I didn't figure it would improve the situation for me to volunteer that information. "Fine, I'll stay a couple more minutes. I'm sure Alice will be okay for a while longer without me." I wished I could be more certain of that, though. I'd already been away from the house most of the day and I was uneasy.

"Thank you." He drifted back and forth. "So, who's Alice?"

"She's a mage. I'm bound to her."

"What does that mean?"

"It's kind of complicated, but the short version is that I was sent here to haunt her. We're kind of friends now, though, so I try to keep her alive and out of trouble." I'd only been moderately successful at that so far, but I tried to be vigilant. She really didn't have anyone else she could count on these days, since the vampire had betrayed her and the thing with the werewolf went south in a big way. Of course, she'd probably object to the idea that she ever counted on anyone for anything, but I knew better.

"Why were you supposed to haunt her?"

"I don't know; they didn't tell me," I lied. "When I showed up in her office I was pretty scary, but she wasn't even afraid, just kind of irritated. First she threatened to have me exorcised—"

"Exorcised?" he interrupted. "Like in that movie with the girl with the spinning head?"

Oy. "That was a fictional demon possession. Exorcising a ghost means sending them from this plane of existence on to the afterlife, to wherever you go after this."

"Okay. Well, you're still here, so obviously she didn't do that."

"No. After we talked for a while, she offered me a job, so now I'm kind of her partner. She's a private investigator."

"Hey, that's pretty cool," Abe said, looking impressed. "Do you think she could use another ghost helping her out? I could do easy stuff for you guys."

"Like what, make coffee and do the filing?"

My sarcasm whizzed over his head. "I could follow people and spy on them. Once I get the whole ghost thing figured out, I bet I'd be good at that." He frowned. "I feel like maybe I used to do that sort of thing, actually."

"You think you used to spy on people?" Who *was* this guy? He seemed like way too much of a schmuck to be some kind of PI. I suddenly wondered if he was a stalker or a peeping Tom. I edged away from him.

"I can't remember," he said morosely. "So why do you need to go check on her? Is she in the middle of a dangerous case?"

"Not at the moment. She's kind of...between cases right now. She's been having a rough time lately. She's been in a really shitty mood for a couple of weeks, so I've been giving her some space." And she'd been drinking like a fish too, but that wasn't a detail I wanted to share with Abe the possible creep.

His eyebrow—the only one he currently had—went up. "A couple of *weeks?* That doesn't really sound like a mood. Are you sure that's not just her personality?"

"It's not her personality," I argued. "Her last case was dangerous. She actually died for a few minutes. She survived, but she's having a hard time."

"Yeah, weird how dying kind of messes you up," Abe muttered. "I'm glad I can't relate to that."

I related too, obviously. Alice had almost died at the hands of blood mage Amelia Wharton. I was pretty sure it wasn't Alice's first experience with death, but she was taking it all particularly hard. I couldn't be sure because she refused to talk about what happened or why she'd ingested more Scotch than food in the past two weeks, but I strongly suspected she had major survivor's guilt because she'd seen Wharton kill three people and had been unable to save them.

I had my suspicions about her past—which she *also* refused to talk about—but even without taking that into consideration, she was one of the biggest control freaks I'd ever met. She'd been tied up and something close to helpless for quite a while. And though she'd saved the two other people who were there—not to mention probably thousands or millions of lives if that *Kasten* doohickey had gotten loose—all she could think about was the people she hadn't been able to save. I saw it in her eyes every time she thought I wasn't watching. Guilt and anger surrounded her like a cloud.

"She also broke up with her sort-of boyfriend, and a nosy federal agent has been following her everywhere," I added. "So it's been a rough couple of weeks. I'm sure she'll be back on her feet soon, though." I sounded dubious, even to my own ears.

"On second thought, maybe I'll look for a different job," Abe said. "It sounds like your partner doesn't need any more stress right now."

I felt relieved, and then guilty when I realized I was possessive and protective of Alice. The thought of a second ghost lurking around made me jealous. Then again, I doubted Alice would let him hang around. Abe had no magic, and stalker vibe aside, no skills she'd find useful. She'd probably do what she'd threatened to do to me and send him on to the afterlife.

It was then Abe became aware of how he looked. It went about as well as I'd expected.

When his screeching and flitting started winding down, I waved my arms, trying to get his attention. "Abe. *Abe*. Come on, man—calm down."

"Don't tell me to calm down!" he shrieked. His face, head, arms, legs, torso, feet, and hands were moving around each other like some kind of nightmare kaleidoscope, so his mouth was somewhere in the vicinity of his left elbow. "They didn't put me together right!"

"If you will just listen to me for one—"

An impressive string of expletives emerged from the mouth now located in the middle of his torso, which was where his right leg should be.

I raised my voice. "Abe, I will explain how to fix this if you will stop freaking out and *calm down*."

He whizzed to a stop in front of me, still a jumble of parts. "Fine," he said, the voice coming from his right foot, which was currently on his left shoulder. "How do I fix myself?"

"You have to concentrate and envision how your body looked. Before you died," I added quickly. "Start at the top and work your way down. Focus on your head and face, then your shoulders, your arms, your chest, your waist, your legs…"

In front of me, Abe's body parts were shifting around each other, assembling themselves into a form that looked a lot closer to human, but nothing was quite lining up or matching. Time for a different tactic. "Picture a photo of yourself," I said.

Abe suddenly turned into a twelve-year-old kid in a Star Wars T-shirt, shorts, and sneakers.

"A *recent* photo, Abe."

He reformed again, this time as a forty-ish man with close-cropped brown hair, wearing a shirt and tie and slacks. "How do I look?" he asked anxiously.

"Much better."

He looked down at himself and sighed. "Do I have to go through eternity now wearing a tie?"

It wasn't as if it would actually be uncomfortable, but as someone who hated ties in life, I got it. "No. Just change the picture in your head so you're not wearing it."

The tie vanished.

"That wasn't that difficult," Abe said, floating around nervously. "How do I keep from getting mixed up again?"

"I'm no expert, but basically it seems like once I get an image of myself fixed in my head, I have to actually focus in order to change how I look. I don't think I've ever 'accidentally' changed form without meaning to once I figured that out."

"That's a relief. Hey, does that mean I can look however I want?"

Before I could answer, he reformed as Tom Cruise from *Top Gun*, complete with Navy flight suit and aviator shades. He grinned. "Awesome."

"The thing is—" I began.

He turned into Darth Vader.

"Okay, that's cool," I told him, legitimately impressed. "But you need to know that everything you do requires energy. You only have a finite amount at any given time and it regenerates slowly. When you change forms and move from place to place, you're using energy. That's why I stopped you from trying to get back into your body; you can literally use up all of your energy and go poof."

"Go poof?" Vader asked me in Abe's voice. He sounded worried.

"Yeah, go poof...as in, no more ghost Abe."

Abe reappeared in the shirt and slacks. "Am I me again?"

"Yep."

"So what happens if I go poof?"

"I'm not sure," I hedged. "I obviously haven't done it. I would think it would be similar to what happens if you're exorcised: you go on to whatever's after this."

He absorbed that. "Have you seen it happen?"

"A couple of times. It didn't look pleasant."

"Thanks for not just letting me go poof."

"You're welcome."

We hovered awkwardly for a bit. Just as I was about to wish him well and head back to Alice's house, Abe floated over to his body. "How long have I been lying here dead?"

"Time feels a little different when you're a ghost," I said. "I'm getting better at keeping track, but I've been distracted. Maybe twenty, thirty minutes?"

"Nobody's found me yet." He sounded dejected.

"It's the middle of the night and nobody's come walking past the alley since you fell. Plus you're kind of hidden behind that gate and the garbage bin. Someone will find you soon, I'm sure."

He looked at his body and then up at the building. "It looks like I fell quite a ways, though, doesn't it? I'm sure I yelled on the way down. I wonder why no one came out to check."

"Well, it's the middle of the night and everyone's got their doors and windows shut. Probably everyone was asleep."

Abe started floating upward. "Where are you going?" I asked, following him.

"I must have fallen from somewhere up here," he said, drifting higher and peering at the sliding doors of the second-floor apartment. "This one looks locked and the curtains are closed." He rose up to the third floor.

I followed, now curious despite my vow not to get involved. "Any of your memories coming back?"

"Nothing so far."

The doors of both the third and fourth-floor apartments were closed and the curtains drawn, so we floated up to the fifth floor.

"Hey, what's going on up here?" Abe asked.

The small wrought-iron balcony on the fifth floor was clearly broken, dangling from the building and held on by a few remaining bolts. The sliding door was open about two feet, but the curtain was closed, blocking our view of the inside of the apartment.

Well, it looked like we'd found the cause of Abe's fall. "I think this is where you came from," I said. "You want to go in and see if it looks familiar?"

Abe stared at the broken balcony. "Oh, come on," he yelled.

I blinked. "What's the matter?"

"You're telling me I died in a stupid *accident?* I'm dead because of *this?*"

"People die in accidents all the—" I began.

"Don't tell me people die in accidents all the time!" he hollered. "I *know* people die in accidents all the time! *I* wasn't supposed to die in an accident!"

"Why not?"

"It's so...so...pointless!"

I had no idea what to say to that at first. "A lot of deaths are pointless, Abe."

"I bet you didn't die in an accident," he said accusingly.

"No, I was murdered."

He stilled.

"By a blood mage," I added. "It took me three days to die just because he liked to take his time. So not only are there worse ways to go, there are more pointless deaths than one caused by a poorly maintained apartment balcony."

A long silence.

"Well, hell." Abe floated back and forth, looking stricken. "I'm sorry, man."

I was already regretting what I'd said. "It's okay."

"Jeez, I didn't know."

"Of course you didn't." I raised my hands. "I'm sorry, too. Of course it sucks to die in an accident. You have every right to be mad about it."

"Yeah, I'm probably going to be mad about it for a while. You did give me some perspective, though, so thank you." He looked at the apartment. "I guess I'm going to go in there and see what my life was like. Want to come in?" he asked, somewhat awkwardly.

I really wanted to get home to check on Alice, but now I was feeling guilty about the way I'd trivialized Abe's death and his feelings about it. In fact, I'd been rather harsh more or less from the minute we met and I didn't like what that might say about the kind of person I had become. Deaths used to mean more to me before I'd been a cabal stooge for four years. All that suffering—mine and others'—had affected me more than I liked to admit.

That lingering pain was one of many reasons I knew Alice had once been in similar circumstances, even though she refused to talk about it. I recognized the haunted look in her eyes and the way she sometimes had to remind herself to have human emotions and allow others to see them. One of the first things you learned in a cabal was to never let them see anything that made you happy or caused you pain, because they would use both of those things against you every chance they got.

"Sure, I'll come in," I said. "Assuming this is your place, that is."

"I guess we'll find out." Abe drifted toward the sliding glass door and disappeared into the apartment.

Despite his invitation, I hesitated. If it wasn't his apartment, I felt uncomfortable just traipsing in there. Ghosts could go just about anywhere if there weren't wards to keep us out. As far I could tell, we were basically on the honor system. I'd only met a few other ghosts in my approximately four weeks back on earth and all of them had sworn they didn't go peeking into people's homes. I certainly hadn't, but there was probably a good chance some of them did and just didn't want to admit it. It was a temptation, sure, but I kept thinking about how I would feel if some stranger was watching me and I didn't know.

I tried to not even do it on accident. I'd once surprised Alice as she was walking out of her bathroom in a towel and she was mad enough about it that I made sure never to do it again. The mood she'd been in lately, I couldn't be sure she wouldn't say to hell with trying to figure out why I'd been bound to her and just boot me to the afterlife.

"Hey, Malcolm?" Abe's voice drifted out of the apartment. "Can you come in here a second?"

His tone had me moving before he'd even finished the question. I crossed through the doors and entered the apartment.

Abe was hovering in the middle of the living room. I joined him and stared around the room, taking it all in.

Finally, I said, "There's a chance it might not have been an accident after all."

"You think?" Abe asked sardonically.

The living room and dining room were in shambles: furniture overturned, framed pictures knocked off the walls, and broken items everywhere.

The apartment was small and sparsely furnished. One entire section of the living room was devoted to a massive, U-shaped computer desk with three large screens, one of which had been knocked off and was face-down on the table. Paperwork of all shapes, sizes, and colors was scattered on the table and the floor. The desk chair was knocked over, as was one of the two chairs at the tiny dining table.

At first, I thought someone had tossed the place looking for something, but the more I looked at the carnage, the more it appeared there had been a fight or struggle that ended with Abe going out the door and onto the balcony, which collapsed. That hypothesis was supported by the sight of several demolished shelves and what appeared to be dozens of shattered teacups all over the floor.

"My cups," Abe said weakly. "Oh, no. Look at this." He seemed to be at a loss for words as he drifted over to the remains of what had apparently been an extensive collection of hand-painted teacups. "Oh, what a mess."

"Are you remembering what happened?" I asked him.

He shook his head. "No. I just...I remember loving these. They were unique. I'd been collecting them for a long time."

There were a few still left intact on the highest shelf on the wall. I floated over to look at them. I knew absolutely nothing about teacups, but they really were beautiful. Each one looked as delicate as an eggshell and was hand-painted with scenes ranging from *Alice in Wonderland* to a Thomas Kinkade-esque cottage in a forest.

I wished I had some way to take the Alice teacup to Alice as a gift. She didn't have anything from *Alice in Wonderland*, but I'd seen her smile sometimes at references to the book, so she might like something like that. I'd asked her once if she'd been named after Lewis Carroll's famous heroine, but she got a strange look in her eyes, said it had been a family name, and changed the subject.

"They're really beautiful, Abe," I said sincerely. "I wish I'd gotten to see them all, but the ones that are left are amazing."

"Thanks," he said glumly. "But who the hell came in here and trashed everything and threw me out the door?"

That was a good question. What would Alice do? She'd probably start by figuring out who Abe was and what he did for a living. I floated over to the computer desk and looked at the notes stuck to the monitors and the paperwork I could see.

"Abe Porter," I said, reading from something that looked like an invoice. "Hey, you're Abe Porter."

"I am?" He sounded uncertain.

"It looks like it." I pointed at the invoice. "You remember how you said you thought you spied on people?"

"Yeah?" He perked up a little.

"This looks like you were a forensic accountant."

A pause, then: "So I spied on people...with my computer?"

"Looks like it." I looked closer at the paper. "This invoice is from the city police department. You made a couple grand for compiling financial data on someone named Arthur Davies."

He joined me at the desk. "That doesn't ring a bell. Damn it, I wish I could remember any of this." He made a sweeping gesture to indicate the desk and all the paperwork scattered around. "I wonder if I found something out about someone and they had me bumped off."

It wasn't as farfetched of a theory as I would have thought even a few minutes ago. Forensic accountants, especially ones who do work for the cops, just might get themselves mixed up in the kind of investigation that would put a target on their backs.

Something was bugging me about that theory, though. If Abe had stumbled onto some kind of criminal dealings and someone had sent a hitman after him, the messy scene didn't look like the work of a professional. Abe didn't strike me as the sort who would put up much of a fight against anyone, much less a hired killer, and yet the apartment looked like an extended physical fight had taken place.

Then again, it didn't have to be a professional hitman; it could just as easily been some desperate person who'd gotten backed into a corner and figured his only hope of eluding justice was bumping off the poor schmuck who'd been hired to dig into his financials. Maybe they'd come in and surprised Abe working late on some project, and the two had fought until somehow the attacker got the upper hand and pushed Abe out onto the balcony, which gave way under his weight. Or maybe Abe had tried to take refuge or call for help from the balcony and it collapsed. Then the killer left, leaving Abe's body in the alley for someone to find, and hoping their secret died along with him.

Except...

I floated to the kitchen with Abe trailing behind me.

"What are you looking for?" he asked eagerly. I supposed I couldn't blame him; I could see a weird logic in being more excited about having been murdered than thinking you died in an accident.

I went to the front door and confirmed what I'd seen from across the room. "The door's locked."

"Of course it's locked," Abe said irritably. "Whoever came in here isn't going to leave it hanging open, are they?"

"That's not what I mean," I said. "The chain's on the door."

Silence.

"How did they do that?" Abe asked, confused.

"They didn't." I turned and drifted back into the living room with Abe behind me.

"I don't get it," he said as I hovered in the midst of the wrecked apartment. "The chain's on the door, so they had to have gone out the patio door."

"How did they get into the apartment?" I asked. "Would you have let someone into your apartment in the middle of the night if you didn't know them?"

"Hell no," he said automatically. "Wait...so, it was someone I *knew?*"

What was I missing? I looked around again.

When I was in college, I used to love mystery novels. I supposed this would fall into the category of a "locked room" murder, except there *was* one way in and out: the patio door. But then it was a five-story jump—or fall—and unless the killer brought climbing equipment and rappelled down without pulling the balcony the rest of the way loose, they didn't go out that way.

"When you have eliminated the impossible, whatever remains, however improbable, must be the truth," I said.

Abe frowned. "What does that mean?"

"It's something Sherlock Holmes once said to Dr. Watson."

He looked at me with an expression bordering on irritation. "Still waiting to hear what that means."

"The door is locked from the inside and nobody but you went out that patio door," I said. "So that means—"

"I didn't wreck my own damn apartment and then decide I needed to pop out for some fresh air on my clearly very poorly maintained balcony," Abe said hotly. "Someone else did this, Malcolm."

"I didn't say you did," I countered. "But I don't see how anyone else got in and out of here, do you?"

"They had to have used the patio door," he argued. "That's the only other way in and out of the apartment."

A grey striped tabby strolled out of the bedroom and across the living room. The cat sat down, looked directly up at Abe, and meowed.

"Can he see me?" Abe asked in wonder.

"Maybe," I admitted. "I've noticed that animals seem to have a weird sense for when I'm around."

"Hey, kitty," Abe said, floated down closer to the cat. "Hey, kitty-kitty."

When he got close, the cat hissed and swiped at him. Out of reflex, Abe flitted back, though the cat's paw passed harmlessly through him. "Bad cat," he said.

The cat hissed again, then raised a paw and licked it.

We watched the cat for a bit. I worried it might try to go outside, but hopefully the fluttering curtain would dissuade it from trying to venture out onto the broken balcony until someone came in here and closed the door. If I used a lot of energy, I could sometimes make little things move, but I wouldn't be able to close a sliding glass door —and I wouldn't want to compromise evidence anyway.

The cat started playing with something, batting it around and chasing it across the floor. "What's that?" Abe asked.

I floated over to look at what the cat was playing with. "It's a feather. Do you have a bird?"

He started to shake his head, then shrugged. "Honestly, I don't remember. Maybe?"

We looked in the bedroom and bathroom, which were surprisingly tidy with none of the chaos of the front rooms, but saw no sign of any bird cage. I did, however, spot two more small gray feathers in the living room, now that I knew to look for them.

Meanwhile, the cat had tired of playing with the feather and was now curled up in a small bed next to the computer desk.

I stayed in the living room as Abe floated around the apartment. He seemed to be trying to remember more about himself and what might have happened. In the meantime, I was sorting through the clues and trying to piece together a plausible scenario that explained what we saw in Abe's apartment.

Maybe if I went and got Alice, she could make heads or tails of this. I was sure the police would investigate the death as soon as Abe's body was discovered. On the other hand, maybe what Alice needed to get her out of the funk she was in was a good, old-fashioned whodunit involving a door locked from the inside, a broken balcony, an open patio door, a wrecked apartment...

...a cat...

...and a bird.

Hmm.

"Abe?" I called.

"What?" Abe asked, drifting in from the bedroom. "Did you find something?"

"I think I may have figured out what happened." I paused. "But...you probably won't like it."

"I ended up dead, so no, I'm sure I won't like it," he said, somewhat dryly. "But let's hear it."

I floated over to the computer desk, where a single gray feather lay where the cat had left it. "So, here's what I think happened."

About a half-hour later, we floated in the alley, watching the excitement below. A man taking his dog for a middle-of-the-night walk had finally found Abe's body and called the police. Suddenly the quiet neighborhood was a hive of activity, the night sky lit with flashing lights. The alley was full of cops while others were canvassing Abe's building looking for possible witnesses. Soon they'd figure out which apartment was his and then they'd have to piece together the events that led to Abe's demise.

"You think they'll figure it out?" Abe asked.

"Hopefully," I said. "The clues are there. After all, we figured it out and we're not professionals."

"Well, *I'm* not, but *you* are," Abe countered. He shook his head ruefully. "I can't believe it. What a way to go."

"Well, if they do figure it out, you're likely to become internet famous," I pointed out.

"Sure, after a pigeon flew into my apartment through an open patio door and the cat went berserk trying to catch it, and then, in an attempt to both shoo the bird back out the door and keep the cat from running after it, I went out onto my rickety old balcony that had been needing repairs for years and promptly fell to my death five stories below." He sighed. "Maybe it will make the news."

He was taking it better than I'd thought he would, really. I'd expected furious denials and more yelling, but instead he'd listened to my theory, looked around at the scene in the apartment, and come to the same conclusion I had.

The cat had seemed to watch us floating around the apartment for a while, then gone to sleep in his bed. "Can't blame him or the bird," Abe said. "It was all just an accident."

"A really bizarre accident," I agreed.

We looked down at the sound of heavy vehicle doors slamming. The medical examiner had arrived.

"They're going to flip your body over soon," I told Abe. "You probably don't want to see that."

"Yeah, I don't need that image in my head. I've already seen more than I wish I had." He shuddered.

"If it's any consolation, my memory is a lot like it was when I was alive," I said. "Things fade, even the really bad things." And wasn't I grateful for that small favor.

Together, we floated out of the alley and headed down the street away from the police cars and growing crowd of onlookers.

"Do you think I'll get a chance to move on someday?" he asked suddenly.

I debated what to say. Ghosts bound to people either gained in power or stayed relatively stable. Unbound ghosts, however, gradually diminished, eventually fading away entirely and moving on to the afterlife. Some became poltergeists or wraiths, insane spirits whose remaining time on earth was usually spent tormenting the living by moving small objects or inflicting minor wounds before they too faded.

I didn't think he needed to hear that, though. He'd had a rough night. "Yes, someday. I'm not sure when, exactly; I think it varies. Enjoy the time you have. This life can be meaningful too."

"I'll find something to do. Right now, I think I'm just going to spend some time figuring me out."

I understood. I was still figuring me out too.

"Maybe I'll see you around," he said as we came to a stop near a small park.

"I hope so," I said, and I meant it. "Take care, Abe."

"You too, Malcolm. Hey, I just thought of something."

"What?"

He grinned. "So it *was* 'fowl' play after all."

I shook my head, smiling despite myself. "That pun is a crime against humanity, Abe."

Laughing, he zipped away toward the park. I jumped home.

When I emerged from the basement, I found Alice curled up alone on the couch in the middle of the empty living room. There was a little light coming in from the kitchen, but she sat in the near-dark, a glass of whisky in her hand. My heart sank when I spotted a half-empty bottle on the floor next to her. I was pretty sure that bottle had been full yesterday.

"Hey," I said, floating over to her. "It's almost four in the morning, Alice. Shouldn't you be in bed?"

"Can't sleep," she said, sipping her whisky. "Thought I'd have a nightcap. Where have you been?"

"I was on my way back when I ran into a new ghost," I said. "I kept him company for a while, showed him the ropes."

"Oh, yeah? How did that go?"

"Pretty well. He's adjusting. It's going to take some time, but I think he'll be okay."

"That's good." She rested her glass on her knee. "How did he die?"

She listened, her drink forgotten, as I told her the story. When I described finding the feather, she smiled and I could tell she was already figuring out how poor Abe ended up lying in the alley.

"That was some dang good detective work," Alice said when I'd finished. She raised her glass to toast me and then drained it. "Poor guy. I'd hate to go that way," she added.

"He was philosophical about it in the end. He even joked that it was *fowl* play."

She groaned. "Oh God, that's so bad."

I smiled. "I know, really, really bad. But it was a good sign that he could joke about it."

Alice unfolded herself from the couch and reached for the bottle of Scotch. I worried she was going to pour another glass, but instead she took the bottle to the kitchen and stuck it in the cupboard and put the glass in the sink.

"I think I'll try to get some sleep," she told me, heading for the stairs. "I've got an appointment with a potential client at ten o'clock. Her name is Irene Miller and she thinks there might be a poltergeist in her house. You want to come with me to check it out?"

My heart soared at the thought of working on an actual case again and getting Alice out of the house and away from her liquor cabinet. "Hell yeah!"

Her eyebrows went up. "Alrighty, Mr. Enthusiasm. We'll head out around nine-fifteen. See you in the morning."

"See you," I echoed as she went up the stairs. A moment later, her bedroom door closed. I heard footsteps going into the bathroom and water running in the sink.

I flitted around the living room in excitement. We had a case! Maybe this was the beginning of things getting better around here. I hadn't had any luck getting Alice out of this funk, but maybe a case would do the trick. A poltergeist should be interesting. Then hopefully she'd get another client, and then another, and we could start putting the Wharton nightmare behind us—and the sooner the better, before either my patience or Alice's liver gave out, or both.

I had about five hours before we'd need to head out. As Alice finished in her bathroom and went to bed, I returned to the basement to work on some spells for a while, my mood light. I was looking forward to the morning for a change.

I hummed while I worked on a new ward for the house, drawing runes in the air and stringing them together. Maybe I could finish the spellwork tonight and show Alice in the morning.

"*Fowl* play," I said to myself with a chuckle. "That was a good one."

THE END

Please Add Your Review! And turn the page for HEART OF FIRE, book 2 in the Alice Worth series!

HEART OF FIRE

BOOK 2

PROLOGUE

When the half-drunk graveyard shift cook with singed eyebrows and Johnnie Walker breath says you're looking rough, you know you've got problems.

"Thanks for the coffee," I said wearily, tucking cash under my plate and heading for the door.

"Your food!" the cook hollered, gesturing with his spatula at the counter, where I'd left behind an empty coffee pot and untouched club sandwich.

"Guess I wasn't hungry after all." I pushed the door open and headed out to the parking lot.

When I'd arrived, despite it being after midnight, the only available spot in the tiny lot next to Nancy's Diner was at the back near the dumpster. I unlocked my car, tossed my bag onto the passenger seat, and started to get in.

Someone screamed.

My head whipped around. The sound cut off abruptly, but not before I was already running toward the alley on the other side of the dumpster.

When I rounded the corner, I saw what looked like three or four people fighting about twenty feet away. As I got closer and my eyes adjusted to the dim light, I realized with horror that three young men had cornered a blonde girl by a large trash bin. She kicked wildly as one of them tried to pin her against the wall and another covered her mouth while the third yanked her bag away and dumped it on the ground.

"Hey!" I yelled.

They looked up. The one who'd taken her bag dropped it and headed toward me, while the other two continued to struggle with the girl. She looked at me, her eyes huge and panicked.

"Bitch, you better get out of here," he told me. A blade glinted in his hand. It was shaking.

"I don't think so," I said, advancing. "Put your little knife away before you hurt yourself."

Twitchy raised his knife and spun it between his fingers with surprising dexterity. I was close enough now to see he wasn't trembling because he was afraid. His pupils were dilated, and despite the cool night, he was sweating. Realization dawned. He wasn't scared; he was high.

The girl suddenly screamed again. One of the other thugs swore. "She bit me!" He punched her in the jaw. She hit the pavement hard and didn't move.

I took a deep breath and said a little prayer to whoever might be listening. I was about to do something really stupid.

"Look at you losers," I taunted them. "Three of you against one girl. Is this the only way you can get any action?"

That did it. With twin snarls, the other two joined their friend, leaving the girl on the dirty pavement behind them.

"Maybe we start with you instead," the tallest of the three said. "You got a big mouth. It'll feel real good right here." He grabbed his crotch and the other two laughed.

Two of them—Twitchy and Dipstick, the tall one—had blades. The third cracked his knuckles while he leered at my chest. His hands looked bloody, from hitting either the girl or someone else earlier in the evening. All of them twitched like they were holding onto a high-voltage wire.

Three against one wasn't great, but I wasn't nearly as defenseless as they probably thought I was.

Dipstick came at me first. I waited until he was about four feet away before I flicked my right wrist in a gesture as if I were tossing a pair of dice. Bright green earth magic spiraled out of my hand. His eyes widened, but he had no time to react before I whipped the stream of cold fire through the air and lashed his knife hand. He screamed and dropped the knife, doubling over and clutching his hand. I struck again, knocking him flat, then kicked him in the jaw. He went still. One down.

Knuckles took a step back, but Twitchy advanced, his lip curled and knife raised. He turned back to his companion. "Come on!"

They rushed me.

I went for Twitchy, striking out with my whip and connecting with his chest. He staggered back but managed to hang onto his blade. Knuckles came at me from my left side, which was smart...or might have been, if my whip were my only weapon.

Knuckles took a swing at me and I ducked. My cold fire whip vanished and I hit him in the chest with both palms. A strong blast of air magic sent him flying backward ten feet to smash into the wall of the building. The impact knocked him out and he hit the pavement in a heap. Two down, one to go.

In the meantime, Twitchy was on the attack. His blade sliced across my right forearm and I cried out. Before he could strike again, I lashed out and my whip caught him across the neck. He shrieked and stumbled, dropping his knife to grab his throat. I took two steps to pick up momentum and kicked him in the groin. He doubled over with a breathless scream and I brought my knee up into his face. Cartilage crunched and he went down, blood streaming from his nose. One kick to the head, and then there were none.

Breathing hard, I looked at my arm. Blood dripped from my fingers. I couldn't see how bad the cut was in the dim light, but the tear in my sleeve was about six inches long and the wound stung.

Before I could deal with my injury, I had to make sure they stayed down until the girl and I were gone. I touched Dipstick's arm, using a "nap" spell that put him out cold for about an hour. I went to the other two and repeated the spell.

If Malcolm, my ghost sidekick, were here, he'd have asked me why I hadn't just put them to sleep as soon as I got close enough to touch them. I'd have told him I wanted the practice, but the truth was, I'd *needed* that fight to blow off steam. All the tension that had been building in my shoulders for the past week or so was gone. I felt lighter.

With the three would-be rapists taken care of, I went to check on the girl. She was still unconscious, her jaw swelling where Knuckles had hit her.

At a glance, I guessed she was a working girl: short black skirt, high heels, mesh top over a bright pink bra. The contents of her bag lay scattered around her.

While I waited for her to wake up, I unfastened one of the charms on my bracelet—a small, blue crystal—and moved until I was leaning against the wall, out of sight of the street and the diner parking lot. I pushed up my sleeve, held the crystal to my bloody right forearm, and invoked the spell. "*Helios*."

It was a mid-range air magic healing spell, the strongest I dared carry with me. I breathed deeply through the pain as the spell worked to heal the knife wound. The pins-and-needles sensation lasted for about a minute.

When at last the magic faded, I tucked the spent crystal into my pocket and looked at my arm. The cut was mostly healed, reduced to an angry red line. Another healing spell would heal the injury altogether, but I only had the one with me. I'd have to wait until I got home.

I rolled up my sleeves to hide the blood and went back to where I had been standing when my arm got cut. I crouched and put my fingertips in my blood on the pavement. "*Burn*." With a *whoosh*, white fire—my air magic—consumed my blood, leaving behind a fine gray ash that would blow away.

I went through Dipstick's pockets first. His wallet contained a few bucks in cash, no cards, and an expired driver's license identifying him as John Andrews. I put the cash in my pocket, left the wallet on the pavement next to him, and turned his jeans pockets inside out. Nothing but some loose change and a lighter.

Nothing interesting in Knuckles's pockets, either, though I confiscated about forty dollars in small bills.

I hit pay dirt with Twitchy. He had a respectable roll of cash and two small plastic bags containing marble-sized amounts of black crystals. The bags were marked with black flames. I frowned. *What the hell is this?* I wondered. What were these guys on?

I tucked the money in my pocket and the drugs in my boot and stood. Behind me, I heard a moan. When I turned, the girl was blinking and looking around, plainly confused.

I approached slowly so I didn't startle her. "Hey, are you okay?"

Her eyes widened. "Where are they?"

"They're napping." I crouched down. "You're safe."

The girl groaned and pushed herself up to lean against the brick wall. She touched her jaw gingerly. "Where did you come from?"

"I was in the parking lot at Nancy's when I heard you scream."

She looked at the three unconscious thugs in disbelief. "What are you, some kind of superhero?"

I snorted. "Hardly. I didn't know if they were trying to rob you or rape you or both, but I wasn't going to stand by and let it happen. How do you feel?"

The girl started cramming stuff back into her bag and flexed her jaw. "It doesn't feel too good, but I'll be okay. I've had worse."

"What's your name?"

She stared at me, her eyes narrowing. "Why?"

"No particular reason. I'm Alice."

"Where's your rabbit, Alice?" The girl grimaced as she started trying to stand up.

I rose. "Can't find him. Little furry bastard runs too fast."

She laughed and used the wall to push herself to her feet. "Ow, my ass," she breathed, rubbing her tailbone.

"Is anything broken?"

She shook her head. "I don't think so. Just bruises, probably. I'm Carrie."

"Hey, Carrie. Why don't you take the rest of the night off?" I dug in my pocket and handed her the cash I'd collected. "It's all they had."

Carrie grinned. "Sweet. I like you, Alice." She took the money and stuck it in her bag. "Wish I could have seen what you did. First time anyone ever came to my rescue, and I missed it."

"It wasn't all that exciting. Really, they went down pretty quickly." I reached into my boot and pulled out one of the little plastic bags. "What do you know about this stuff?"

Carrie glanced at the bag and grimaced. "Haze," she said with disgust.

"Haze?" I'd never heard of it. "Is that a new nickname for meth?"

She held out her hand. I handed her the bag and she looked at it closely. "It's not meth. This shit started showing up a couple of months back. Now it's like everybody's on it. They always mark the bags with the flames. They call it Haze or Black Fire. It's bad stuff, makes you real mean and paranoid. My old roommate took too much and jumped off a bridge."

"Wow." I stared at the little bag in surprise.

Carrie was quiet for a moment. "I'm not gonna lie: I take pills. You gotta have something to take the edge off, you know? But I don't want any part of that garbage." She handed the bag back.

"Thanks for the info."

Carrie gingerly put her bag over her shoulder. "Thanks for kicking their asses. Hope you catch that rabbit," she added with a smirk, and headed off down the alley and out of sight.

I took one last look at the thugs, then cradled my sore arm and headed back toward the parking lot, tossing the bags of Haze into the dumpster as I passed.

In my rush to get to Carrie's aid I'd left my car unlocked, but by some miracle no one had stolen it. I got in and locked the doors, wincing as I used my sore right arm to turn the key in the ignition and shift out of park.

I turned out of the lot and headed down the street, driving with my left hand while my right arm rested in my lap. I had healing spells at home that would take care of the knife wound, and then I'd have to try to get some sleep.

I sighed. I probably wouldn't have any more luck sleeping tonight than any other night in the days since I'd woken from the coma, but I always hoped.

The nightmares had to stop at some point, right?

1

ONE MONTH LATER

"Here's to another job well done," I said, raising my glass in a toast.

"Cheers," my companion said dryly.

I took a drink and leaned back in my chair, propping my bare feet up on the railing. The late April evening was unseasonably warm, and I was on my back porch in a tank top and shorts.

Malcolm hovered three feet to my right. The moonlight shone through his body, making him glow. "That's the third toast of the evening."

"So?" I ran my fingers through my long hair and rolled my neck, enjoying the warm, disconnected feeling of being drunk. "I'm celebrating. Another paycheck, another satisfied customer."

"Well, maybe not *satisfied*," the ghost pointed out. "She was pretty upset."

I waved my hand. "I found the thing; it's not my fault it didn't do what she wanted. I warned her magical objects have a mind of their own. She's lucky all she lost was her garage and a couple of trees."

"You could have been a little more understanding."

I shrugged off the rebuke and sipped my whisky. "I'm not a counselor; I'm a detective." I gently swirled the liquor in my glass. "I don't get paid to talk to people about their feelings."

Malcolm muttered something.

"What are you grumbling about?"

"Maybe you should talk to someone about *your* feelings," he said loudly.

I tipped my chair on its back legs. Malcolm drifted closer, looking anxious as I teetered precariously. "Why would I want to do that?" I asked.

"Maybe then you could figure out why you haven't slept worth a damn for a month, and why you don't eat, and why you find at least two or three things to toast almost every single night."

"You need to find something new to complain about. This is all I hear from you these days. Stop fussing at me."

"I'm not—"

"I've been working *every day*," I snapped, dropping my chair back down onto all four legs with a bang. Startled, Malcolm flitted away from me. "I've closed three cases in the past month. I'd call that a pretty big win for Team Alice." I took a drink and glared at him. "So what's the problem, exactly? I'm not *socializing* enough? I like to celebrate when things go well?"

"*Are* things going well?"

The unexpected voice caused me to jump and drop my glass. It shattered and broken glass scattered across the porch. "Son of a bitch!" I squinted into the darkness of my backyard, but saw no one. "Where the hell are you?"

Charles Vaughan stepped out of the shadows. In the moonlight, the vampire's eyes shone with a silvery light. "Good evening, Alice."

I glared at him. "How long have you been standing out there watching me?"

"A few minutes." Which could mean three minutes or thirty or anything in between.

"That was my favorite whisky glass," I complained.

"I will replace it. The question remains: are things going well for you?"

"Things are fine, Charles," I said peevishly. "Didn't you get my message?"

"If you are asking if Ms. Smith passed along the contents of your most recent text message, then yes. I had hoped you would return my calls or accept my invitation to visit my office." He moved to the bottom of the porch steps and studied me. "I have not seen you in almost a month. You appear unwell."

"Gee, thanks." I picked up the bottle of Scotch next to my chair, stared at it, then shrugged and took a swig. Dismay flashed in the vampire's eyes before his expression returned to its normal impassivity.

"What brings you out this evening?" I asked, setting the bottle in my lap.

"I was concerned. Since you completed the wards on my storage facility, you have not visited Hawthorne's. My calls have gone unanswered, my invitations declined, my job offers refused. As you seem unwilling to speak with me, I am forced to appear on your doorstep."

"I've been busy." The bottle started to tip and I caught it just before it fell off my lap. "Three cases in the past month. I got my car detailed. I haven't had one minute to myself."

Malcolm sighed.

"You know what we need?" I asked the ghost. "Perimeter wards around the property, so we get some warning when unexpected *visitors* decide to drop in. Why don't you work on that?"

He drifted toward me. "Alice…"

I took another drink from my bottle of Scotch. "Just leave me alone, would you? Please."

"Fine." He vanished.

I looked at Charles. "Drink?" I held out the bottle. It slipped from my fingers and fell.

Charles moved so fast that he blurred. He was suddenly up the steps and at my side, the bottle in his hand.

"Wow." I hiccupped. "Good catch."

"Alice." It sounded like a reproach.

We stared at each other. Finally, I held out my hand. "Either drink or give it back."

Charles tilted his head and regarded me silently. He glanced at the label, then brought the bottle to his lips. I was willing to bet the vampire had never drunk whisky straight from the bottle in his life. Still, he somehow managed to look entirely graceful while doing so.

I reached for the bottle and Charles reluctantly handed it back. I took a drink, wiped my mouth inelegantly with the back of my hand, and blinked up at him. "You didn't have to come out here. I would have called you back. Eventually. Probably."

"What has happened to you, Alice? For nearly six weeks, since you awoke from the coma, you do not sleep. You work all day and night. You drink excessively. You have lost weight. You avoid your friends, and you speak unkindly to your ghost."

I didn't need to ask how he knew all that. Somehow, Charles always seemed to know what was going on. No matter what I said or how angry I got, he maintained surveillance on my house. I didn't even bother to complain about it this time.

"I sleep," I protested, and it was kind of true. "I'm just trying to be a productive, law-abiding MPI and pay my bills."

Charles crouched by my chair. When I started to raise the bottle, he put his hand on mine. "I would like to know what troubles you."

"Why do you care? What is this, an intervention? Did Malcolm put you up to this?" I tried to pull away. "Let go of me."

"You are sufficiently inebriated," he informed me.

I bristled. "Who the hell are you to come to my house and tell me I've had too much to drink?"

"I am your friend."

"Vampires don't have friends. They have allies, they have enemies, and they have cattle for food. Which one am I?"

Charles stared at me. "You are not yourself."

"That's funny, because I feel like myself." I yanked my hand out of his grip and lifted the bottle to look at it. There was only about two inches of Scotch left in the bottom. I frowned. Had I opened this bottle yesterday or the day before? I couldn't remember.

He took the bottle from me and set it on the porch. "Give it back," I protested.

"Tell me what distresses you," he said.

"At the moment, not being able to drink in peace on my own damn porch." I started to get up to go into the house, then remembered the broken glass and my bare feet. "Shit." I wrapped my arms around my legs and rested my forehead on my knees.

I sensed movement, then heard footsteps crunching in the glass. When I raised my head, I was stunned to see Charles grab an old battered broom leaning against the wall. "What are you doing?"

"Sweeping."

I glanced toward the backyard. Somewhere in the darkness, one or more of Charles's enforcers were watching us. I wondered what they were thinking right now, seeing a two-hundred-year-old vampire in a five-thousand-dollar suit with a broom in his well-manicured hands.

"That wasn't really my favorite whisky glass," I confessed as he meticulously swept broken glass into the corner of the porch. "I have three more just like it. I think I got them at Costco or something. I have two really nice glasses someone gave me as gifts, but I don't know where they are." I realized I was babbling and closed my mouth.

Charles worked in silence. When he was satisfied no more glass was left, he leaned the broom up against the wall next to the little pile of debris.

"Thanks." I unfolded myself from my chair and stood. The porch felt like it was moving under my feet as I tottered to the railing and leaned against it. The vampire and I stared at each other.

There was a time, not so long ago, when I'd considered Charles to be an ally and a friend, or as close to one as a vampire could ever be, but things had transpired between us that made me question everything about him and his motives. I suspected he might have deliberately caused me to be injured so he could taste my blood. He'd also tried to seduce me while I was under his influence, and I'd been avoiding him ever since.

Emboldened by liquor, I decided to demand some answers. "Why do you have someone watching my house?"

"Because if I'd had surveillance in place the day Peter Eppright and Ray Browning attacked you in your driveway, you would not have been kidnapped, tortured by Amelia Wharton, possessed by the *Kasten,* and left in a coma," he said.

It was a straightforward answer as far as it went, though I'd be an idiot to accept it as the whole truth.

I frowned. "I'm not your responsibility or yours to protect. I want you to stop watching my house. I've asked you before and now I'm telling you: it needs to stop."

Charles took a step toward me. "Alice—"

"I survived this long without you looking after me," I said, my voice gaining strength. "If I need your help I'll come to you, but in the meantime call off your watchdogs."

He tilted his head. "I will discontinue the surveillance if you will tell me what troubles you."

I turned away to face my backyard, my hands on the railing. Charles moved to stand at my side. We stood in silence for a few minutes.

"You must not blame yourself for the deaths of Peter Eppright, Ray Browning, and Kathy Adams," he said. "There was nothing more you could have done to save them."

My vision went blurry. I blinked and hot tears slid down my face. Charles made a noise and reached for me.

I suddenly couldn't stand to be touched. I stumbled back, tripped over my chair, and fell. He tried to grab me, but I twisted away from him and landed hard on my side. I cried out and rolled onto my back, cradling my left arm.

"Alice!" Charles crouched next to me, looking horrified. "You are injured."

I'd just fallen down drunk in front of a two-hundred-year-old vampire, and I felt like I might be close to a breaking point. "Don't touch me. Please, just go."

"Let me help—"

"Just go!" I shouted.

He touched my face gently. "Let me help you."

I looked up into his eyes and suddenly had the crazy thought that maybe he would understand. "I keep seeing them in my dreams," I heard myself say. "I try to warn them, but no one will listen to me. I watch Amelia cut their throats and they bleed to death over and over again. I can't do anything to stop her." I closed my eyes. "There's blood everywhere. I'm drowning in it."

Cool fingers wiped away my tears. "What could you have done, other than what you did? You attempted to warn them of Amelia Wharton's intentions, but they chose not to listen. Their greed blinded them. They went to the construction site knowing she intended to kill Ms. Newton and you, and yet you did everything within your power to save them when they would not have done the same for you."

Startled, I opened my eyes.

Charles brushed hair back from my face. His gentle voice and compassionate touch made it hard to remember how dangerous he was. "Perhaps you think you did not deserve to live, that somehow you failed, but you did *not* fail. You saved the lives of Deborah Mackey and Natalie Newton. Most remarkably of all, you defeated an evil that had endured for centuries, and might have killed us all if given the chance. You saved thousands, if not millions, of lives, at great personal cost."

After a moment's pause, he continued. "I can only imagine the temptation the *Kasten* offered you, and yet you refused to become either its master or its slave. You are made of iron, Alice. You must forgive yourself for this imagined failure. More than that, you must remember not the helplessness you felt but that you were *not* helpless, that you were the least helpless person there."

I didn't know what to say. I recognized the truth in what he said, and it felt like a weight lifted off my chest.

Charles stroked my forehead. "I know to be helpless is your greatest nightmare."

"What do you know about my nightmares?" I asked, my voice rough.

"Only what I sense. When you woke from the coma, you spoke of being tied down, unable to act, and I could feel how deep your anger goes. I have seen the scars on your back. Beneath that lovely tattoo of the phoenix, your flesh tells a story of great suffering. If you were once helpless and tormented, then these events surely rekindled those memories."

I stared. "When did you get a degree in psychology?"

Charles graced me with one of his rare smiles. "In two hundred years, one comes to understand such things." He moved to his knees, unbuttoned his suit jacket, then reached for his belt.

My eyes widened. "Charles..." I began, struggling to rise without using my injured arm.

He helped me sit up. "There is no need to be concerned," he said with a hint of humor. "I assure you I have no intention of trying to seduce you on the cold concrete of your back porch."

My cheeks burned. "Sorry," I muttered.

Charles unfastened his belt and pulled his shirt out of his pants. Despite my embarrassment and his assertion that this was not a romantic overture, my breath caught. Dangerous or not, he was a very good-looking man, and he was unbuttoning his pants in front of me. After all, I was only human.

He pulled his waistband down a few inches. "You have shared your secret with me. I offer you mine in return."

He lifted his shirt to bare his pale stomach. I gasped.

A long scar ran across his lower abdomen. At first, I didn't understand; how could a vampire be scarred? Then realization dawned: it was a wound he'd received while alive, before he'd become a vampire. He'd been eviscerated, but the wound hadn't been immediately fatal. Somehow, he'd survived long enough for it to heal somewhat before he'd been turned.

"I know what it is to be helpless and afraid," he said quietly. "And what it means to bear scars."

Almost of their own accord, my fingers traced the scar. I might have imagined it, but he seemed to tremble at my touch.

With Charles's vanity, I was rather surprised he still had such a significant scar. "Why didn't you have this healed before you were turned?"

"I suspect for the same reasons you did not have your own scars healed. Having once suffered the trauma of the original injury, I could not bear to relive it. It is a reminder to me, as well, of a lesson I dare not forget."

I shivered. Before I got the phoenix tattoo, I could have had the scars sliced off my back and vampire blood poured over the wound. The skin would have healed without the scars, but having survived being flayed alive by a blood mage, I couldn't bring myself to have it done, even though I would have been unconscious for the procedure. The mere thought used to make me physically sick. Like Charles's scar, mine were also reminders of lessons learned so very well.

He lowered his shirt and my hand went back to cradling my left arm in my lap. He touched my face. "We have this in common: great darkness in our pasts, scars that we carry."

"Yes. We're survivors." Saying it out loud made the rest of the weight lift off my chest. I took a deep, full breath for what felt like the first time in ages.

Charles smiled again. "Yes, survivors," he agreed. He leaned toward me, his hand cupping my chin. Our eyes met. "Wounded, scarred, but never defeated," he murmured, and kissed me.

For a moment, the Scotch and the soft silver glow of his eyes made me forget the danger, and I lost myself in the feeling of his mouth on mine. I'd been so lonely the past month, since an argument about furniture ended with Sean Maclin walking out of my life, probably for good. It had been that long since I'd been kissed and two hundred years of practice made Charles an expert at it. I moaned softly before I could stop myself and the vampire made a noise deep in his throat that sounded almost like a purr.

The kiss deepened and a cool hand came to rest on my thigh. The hand didn't move, but it was there: an offer, an invitation, a request.

And just like that, I regained my senses. *His ulterior motives have ulterior motives*, I reminded myself. With vampires, nothing was ever what it seemed. Was his visit tonight truly out of concern for my well-being, or another carefully orchestrated attempt to get me to let down my guard? Either way, this was precisely the reason I'd avoided him for weeks.

I broke the kiss and leaned back. Charles must have felt the shift in my emotions. He took his hand off my leg and the silver in his eyes faded.

I cleared my throat. "You assured me you wouldn't try to seduce me on my porch."

"So I did," he said evenly. He tucked his shirt back into his pants, buckled his belt, and buttoned his suit jacket. He rose smoothly, as if pulled up by invisible strings.

I, on the other hand, clambered to my feet clumsily, using the chair for leverage, and cradled my arm. My hip hurt, too; I was probably going to have a hell of a bruise there. Charles watched me stand up, his face impassive, but when I swayed, his hand moved as if he were ready to catch me.

I took a few steps back. "Thank you for talking with me. It helped."

"I am relieved to hear it."

Adri Smith, one of Charles's enforcers, appeared out of the darkness and came to stand at the bottom of the porch steps. Despite her neutral expression, I was fairly certain she wasn't happy with me, though I wasn't exactly sure whether it was because of something I'd done or something I hadn't.

"I will contact you in the next few days about a project that requires wards," Charles said briskly. "I would be most appreciative if you would accept my call."

"I'll make every effort to be available." Phone calls I could handle; late-night heart-to-hearts on my back porch, not so much.

"Thank you. Good night." He turned and headed down the steps.

"Good night," I echoed.

They vanished into the darkness.

Suddenly, I jerked. "Shit!" Once again, Charles had left without agreeing to call off his surveillance.

With a growl, I grabbed the near-empty bottle of Scotch, limped inside, and slammed the door.

2

I SLEPT FOR TWELVE HOURS AND WOKE WITH THE HANGOVER FROM HELL.

"Oh, God." I rolled over and blinked groggily at the ceiling. My body hurt like I'd been beaten with socks full of rocks and I thought my head might be in actual danger of exploding. The room spun like a broken carnival ride.

"How are you feeling?"

I raised my head just enough to see Malcolm floating by my bedroom door. "Just shoot me," I groaned.

"At least you got a full night's sleep for a change. Talking to the vampire must have helped."

I put my pillow over my face. "Yeah, it helped. Go 'way."

Malcolm snickered. My crude response was muffled by the pillow.

"When you feel like getting up and around, I'll be in the basement," he said. "I've got something to show you."

"'Kay," I mumbled. I felt rather than saw Malcolm leave the room.

I lay in bed until I felt like I could stand up without falling, then staggered to the bathroom. I washed down a couple of aspirin with a cup of tap water, climbed into the shower, and stood under the spray for a long time. My left hip and elbow were bruised and sore. I thought about using healing spells on them, but decided I deserved the discomfort.

When I finally emerged from the shower, I wrapped my hair in a towel, brushed my teeth, and drank another cup of water. I still felt terrible, but at least my vision wasn't blurry anymore and my brain now seemed to be the right size for my skull. By the time I dried my hair, got dressed, and made it downstairs, the aspirin had taken the edge off the headache.

I pulled the bag from my kitchen trash can and headed outside. The late morning sun was painfully bright, and I wished I'd put on my sunglasses as I trudged around the side of the house to my garbage can. I lifted the lid and tossed the bag in.

A short, dark-haired man in a gray uniform was walking up my sidewalk, a clipboard in hand. A city utility truck was parked across the street. He waved the clipboard at me. "Excuse me."

I stopped in the yard as he veered off the sidewalk and approached. "Yes?"

"I'm with the water department," he said. His name tag read LARRY. "I don't know if you were aware, but there was some damage to the water main in this area. Have you noticed any issues with your water in the past two days?"

"I haven't noticed any problems," I said.

The hairs on the back of my neck prickled in warning. "Larry" was unnaturally stiff, like he wasn't quite sure how all his muscles worked. His dark eyes looked empty and flat. I suspected "Larry" was neither a city worker nor human.

Carefully, I lowered my shields enough to get an idea of what I might be dealing with. A familiar searing heat danced on the edges of my senses, and I caught just the slightest whiff of sulfur. The corner of my mouth turned up ever so slightly. I was surprised he was out in broad daylight; usually low demons preferred twilight or full dark. Then again, the long-sleeved uniform and cap covered most of his body, and he kept his back to the sun as much as possible.

"Larry" raised his clipboard and scrawled my street address on a piece of paper, then added "No problems" next to it and gave me a smile that didn't look quite right. "Thanks for your time." He dug in his pocket and handed me a fridge magnet shaped like a water tower. "If you ever have any problems, here's our website and phone number. Be sure to keep it handy."

"I will," I assured him. "You have a good day."

"You too." He spun on his heel and headed back across the yard toward his truck. I watched him get in, write something else on the clipboard, then drive off down the street.

When he was out of sight, I glanced at the magnet on my palm. I couldn't sense any spells on it but I'd bet real money it was anything but just a freebie magnet. "Beware demons bearing gifts," I murmured.

There was no way I was hanging onto it, much less taking it inside the house past my wards. I held out my hand. "*Burn.*"

The magnet went up in a ball of white fire. I felt a tingle and puff of dark magic, and then all that was left was ash. The magnet had been spelled, all right. To what end I didn't know, but the threat was neutralized. I took the ashes to the trash can, dumped them in, then went back inside.

After washing my hands, I took my cell phone to the living room and curled up on one end of the couch, the only piece of furniture in the room. A record player sat on a shelf, covered in dust. A couple of crates of records and several stacks of books and movies were lined up on the floor below it, equally dusty.

I had a voice mail from an unknown local number. It was date-stamped two days ago, and it was a voice I hadn't heard in years. "Alice, this is Mark Dunlap. I hope you're doing well and staying busy. If you get a chance, I'd like to speak with you. I understand from a mutual acquaintance you might be willing to at least talk things through. Also, I have an important case I'd like to discuss with you. You can get me at this number anytime." He disconnected.

To say I was startled was an understatement. I hadn't heard from Mark since the day I left his private investigator firm to start my own. I'd worked for him for eighteen months while I was getting my mage PI license. He'd expected me to stay on and hadn't taken my departure well.

The "mutual acquaintance" was probably Charles, who routinely hired Mark and his firm to do work for the Vampire Court. Charles had hinted to me a while back that Mark had expressed regret about how we'd parted company and I'd indicated I might feel ready to let bygones be bygones. I hadn't given it much thought, but hearing Mark's familiar gruff voice brought back a tidal wave of memories.

I frowned as I thought about what he'd said. "Important case" had always been Mark's sly way of referencing jobs for the Vampire Court. I could only assume his word choice had not been accidental. I wondered what case he was working on and why he wanted to discuss it with me. I recalled last night's awkward scene with Charles and grimaced. I needed to be smart and stay away from the vampire. I stored Mark's number in my phone and decided to think about calling him.

I left my phone on the couch, grabbed an apple from the fridge, and headed for the basement door.

My basement was a fortress. There were wards on top of wards on top of wards, all with deadly landmines and cascade spells designed to repel intruders. Its foundation spells required eight pints of blood, and its black wards—the deadliest kind of spellwork—would kill or incapacitate anyone who tried to breach its perimeter. I'd been working on the wards for the entire four and half years that I had been in this house. They were a masterpiece of power and intricacy, yet so well-hidden that even the most adept mage would not be able to sense them from outside the house. Only two people could cross the wards safely: myself and Malcolm.

I took a bite of my apple, opened the basement door, and pushed through the wards. "Coming down!" I hollered.

"Clear!" Malcolm called back.

It was always a good idea to warn a mage when you were about to enter their work area, in case they were in the middle of delicate spellwork. Not doing so could have serious consequences. My grandfather's cabal compound lost part of a wing for precisely that reason when I was ten. Luckily, I'd been on the other side of the compound at the time. Six people died, including the mage and the idiot who interrupted him.

I headed down the steps and shut the door behind me. The basement was divided into two areas: a library with a half-dozen floor-to-ceiling bookcases and a large reading table, and my work area, featuring a triple circle inlaid in the floor, a large work table, and five heavily warded large oak storage cabinets. Two of them contained my blood magic materials and had deadly black wards.

When I got to the bottom of the steps, I found Malcolm working with the spell crystals I'd gotten for him. He'd already created "bolt-hole" spells allowing him to jump to and between certain crystals in case of an emergency. We'd put one in my office so he could jump directly there and another here in the basement. I had one in my car and one on my charm bracelet. We hadn't used them much but I felt better knowing Malcolm could jump to safety if the poop hit the prop.

Malcolm was hiding from Darius Bell, his former employer who'd had him murdered. As such, I had not registered Malcolm with the Supernatural and Paranormal Entity Management Agency, or SPEMA, as required by federal law, so we both had a vested interest in keeping him safely hidden. Meanwhile, I was hiding from my grandfather, crime lord Moses Murphy, whose cabal I had escaped five years before by faking my death and assuming the identity of Alice Worth, a Chicago native who moved to the West Coast to start a new life after her parents' deaths. Though Malcolm had surmised that I was hiding too, he didn't know from whom or why, and I had to keep it that way—for both his sake and mine.

Malcolm paused what he was doing. "Hey, I know you've been busy, so I made you some more mid-range healing spells in case you need them." He gestured at a little pile of small white crystals on the table.

"Thank you. I made some more blood-magic healing spells the other day too, so my first-aid kit is back to fully stocked."

"Knowing you, it won't be long until you need some." Malcolm floated over to me. "What's up? You look concerned."

"The weirdest thing just happened." I told him about my demon visitor and the magnet I'd burned to ash.

Malcolm studied me. "I don't see any trace of unfamiliar magic. Whatever spell was on it, it didn't do anything to you as far as I can tell. What do you think that was about?"

"No idea," I said with a shrug, taking a bite of apple. "I didn't recognize him. What kind of spells are you working on?"

"Is that all you're going to eat?"

I made a face. "Malcolm, if you had any idea how nauseated I am right now, you'd be amazed I'm eating anything at all."

"You've lost at least ten pounds in the last month or so. You really need to take better care of yourself."

"I have not lost ten pounds."

He looked at me.

I sighed. "Fine, I'll try to eat better. Satisfied?"

"No, but this is the most reasonable you've been in a while, so I'm going to chalk it up as a win."

I rolled my eyes and went over to the work table, where a dozen small spell crystals were laid out in a row. "What's all this?"

He lit up in excitement. "I've got a new trick. Find me if you can." He vanished.

I passed my hand over the crystals one at a time, reaching out with my senses until I found him in the third crystal from the left. I picked it up and booted him out of it. *"Release."*

Malcolm appeared in front of me. "Nice. But what if I do this?" He disappeared again.

I put the crystal back on the table and passed my hand over the crystals. This time, he wasn't in any of them. Hmm. I glanced around but I didn't see any more crystals sitting out. I frowned. Had he jumped somewhere else?

After a minute, Malcolm popped into existence again. "You didn't find me, did you?" he asked smugly.

"Where did you go?"

Malcolm pointed to the first crystal on the right. "There."

I shook my head. "I would have felt you."

"Nope. That's what I've been working on: a stronger masking spell to hide me better. Try again with the same crystal." He disappeared.

I held my hand over the crystal and still felt nothing. Scowling, I put my apple core on the table, closed my eyes, and tried again. This time, I took a deep breath, exhaled, and concentrated. It was surprisingly difficult to stay focused. I realized I hadn't been practicing much for the past month. Three cases back-to-back meant I hadn't had much spare time.

I was suddenly angry with myself. That wasn't an excuse and I knew it. I couldn't afford to let my skills slip.

I took another deep breath, inhaling through my nose and out through my mouth. I did that several times, slowing my heart rate and breathing and clearing my head. I raised my hand over the crystal and focused.

Finally, on the edge of my senses, I felt the telltale buzzing. It was extremely faint, and if I hadn't known Malcolm was in the crystal, I would never have noticed it. I touched the crystal and released Malcolm.

"Took some work, didn't it?" he asked.

"Yes, it did. That's really excellent, Malcolm. Even knowing where you were, I could barely sense you. That's one of the strongest masking spells I've ever felt. How long have you been working on it?"

"The last couple of weeks." He looked closely at me. "Your aura looks better. It was kind of muddy before."

"I bet," I said with a sigh. "I haven't been working on my magic much lately. I think I need to spend some time down here and clear my head *and* my aura."

An hour later, I emerged from the basement, covered in sweat and limping.

"I'm sorry!" Malcolm said for the fourth or fifth time.

"It's *fine*," I repeated, going into the kitchen for a drink of water. I filled a cup from the sink, guzzled it, filled it again, and grabbed a bag of frozen peas from the freezer. I hobbled to the couch, flopped down, and put the bag on my left thigh, where a two-inch hole was burned in my pants. Beneath it, the skin was an angry red.

"Aren't you going to use a healing spell?" Malcolm asked, floating in front of the couch.

"Maybe later. Right now, I'm teaching myself an important lesson."

"You're teaching yourself an important lesson?" Malcolm echoed. "What, that frozen peas are good for burns?"

"No, I learned that a long time ago. I'm teaching myself what happens when you don't keep your skills up."

"I am really sorry."

"I swear, if you don't stop apologizing, I will listen to every Ozzy and Black Sabbath album I own." Malcolm hated Ozzy. "Two months ago, you'd never have been able to zap me like that. I haven't been practicing my spellwork or with my whip. You outmaneuvered me fair and square, and you weren't even moving at full speed. Don't bother trying to deny it," I added when he started to argue. "It was obvious you were holding back. If you'd really been trying, I'd be covered in burns."

"Can I at least heal that? Every time you grimace, it's making me feel guilty."

I sighed. "Okay. I guess I've probably suffered enough that I'll remember this." With a groan, I sat up, removed the bag of peas, and steeled myself. "Go for it."

Malcolm's fingers moved quickly, drawing a rune in the air. He floated over to me, held his hand above my leg, and invoked the spell. "*Integro.*"

Earth magic flared, and I sucked in a breath as the healing spell went to work. After about thirty seconds of discomfort and minor pain, the burn was gone.

"Now, if only there were a spell to fix these pants," I said grumpily. "They're about the only thing I have to wear that fits these days."

He cleared his throat and glanced meaningfully at the kitchen.

"Fine." I hauled myself to my feet and took the peas back to the freezer. I threw together a salad, grabbed a beer, and took my food to the couch.

"When are you going to buy some furniture?" Malcolm wanted to know. "It looks kind of sad in here."

I sat cross-legged on the couch, my salad bowl in my lap and my beer next to me. "Yeah, I know. It's on my to-do list." I shoveled some salad into my mouth and chased the food down with a swig of beer.

"I get why you didn't want the vampire to buy you furniture, all things considered, but why didn't you let Sean do it when he offered?" He hesitated, then added, "I never really understood how you guys ended up breaking up over furniture."

It wasn't the first time he'd asked about my fight with Sean. I'd been telling him it was none of his business, but Malcolm was clearly not going to stop asking until he got an answer.

I sighed. "First of all, we didn't break up; you can't break up if you aren't really dating. Second, he didn't *offer*. He *told* me he was going to buy me furniture and a television."

He winced.

"Third..." I paused, looking for the right words.

"Third, you don't like people doing things for you. You're kind of weird about that."

I frowned at him, but didn't disagree.

"So he tried to pull the alpha thing, and then...?"

"I told him he was acting like a bully. He said I was being 'irrational.' After that, things went downhill pretty quickly." I focused on my salad.

"So, speaking of the vampire, what did you two talk about last night?"

I eyed him. "Why do you ask?"

"You seem a little more like yourself today, so whatever he said, it must have helped get you out of the funk you've been in. I was just wondering."

"We talked about the construction site thing." I ate quietly while Malcolm floated slowly back and forth in front of the fireplace. Finally, I added, "I'm sorry I've been difficult to get along with lately."

I expected him to respond with one of his trademark snorts or a snarky comment about how I'd been difficult to get along with since the moment he first appeared in my office and I threatened to have him exorcised, but he was surprisingly serious. "It's okay. You went through some really bad stuff. Nobody expects you to bounce right back." A pause. "But the drinking is making me worry."

"I think I'll be cutting down on the drinking a bit." I held up my bruised left elbow.

Malcolm whistled. "You want me to heal that?"

I shook my head and went back to my salad. "It's a reminder."

"Why do you do that?"

I stopped with the fork halfway to my mouth. "Do what?"

"Hurt yourself—or get hurt and refuse to be healed—and say it's to teach yourself a lesson, or to help you remember something." Malcolm floated closer. "Because I have a theory."

"Don't," I said sharply. "Just...don't."

We stared at each other.

"You can talk to me about it, you know."

"No, I can't. Just drop it." I set my salad bowl aside, suddenly no longer hungry. This was the problem with having friends. They wanted things. They felt they deserved answers and explanations. Before Malcolm, before Sean, before things got complicated with Charles, no one bothered me. If I wanted to go days—or weeks—without speaking to anyone, nobody noticed or hounded me about it.

"Before you get mad at me and everyone else for worrying about you, try to remember we do it because we care." Malcolm moved back toward the fireplace. "And in case you think you were better off before we came along, keep in mind that when you're alone there's no one there to take care of you when you're hurt. Or burned. Or kidnapped, stabbed, and dying."

My ire faded. "That's a fair point," I admitted. A strange frisson of energy washed over me. "What was that?"

"Perimeter wards. Someone's pulling into the driveway. By the way, I set up perimeter wards."

I remembered sort of asking him to do that last night, but hadn't really expected him to. "Thanks."

"No problem. I had to do *something* while you slept all day." Malcolm's sarcasm was back.

I went to peek out the front window. An unfamiliar red truck with tinted windows was parked in the driveway behind my car. The driver's door opened, and Mark Dunlap stepped out, carrying a large file box.

I stared at him. I hadn't seen my former boss and mentor for more than three years. He'd been about fifty when I left his firm, but he looked like he'd aged a decade. His hair had gone from salt-and-pepper to full gray. He wore his trademark jeans and a plaid short-sleeved button-up shirt with work boots. As usual, the burly PI looked more like a construction worker.

Halfway up the sidewalk, Mark looked at the window and caught my eye.

For a moment, I was transported back five years, to the day I first stepped foot in the door of Mark Dunlap Investigations, brand new in the city and answering an ad for a low-paying trainee position. Mark Dunlap himself met me in the lobby. He shook my hand, told me his assistant was out sick with the flu, and asked me what I thought I could do. I told him I thought I could help people.

Before the interview was over, he'd offered me the job.

Now, looking at the shadows under Mark's eyes, I felt a stab of regret that we'd parted company so badly and hadn't spoken in so long. Something was chewing Mark up.

I let go of the curtain, went to the door, and lowered the house wards. By the time Mark was on the porch, I had the door open.

"Come in," I said.

3

I put the rest of my salad in the fridge and got us a couple of beers. We settled on the couch. Malcolm had disappeared into the basement.

Mark set the file box on the floor and looked around. "Bit sparse in here."

"All of my furniture got destroyed in a fight between a vampire and a werewolf." I turned sideways and tucked my legs up under me. "I haven't had time to buy new stuff yet."

Mark's eyebrows went up. "You don't say. Was the vampire anyone we know?"

"Maybe."

"Huh. Real sorry I missed that, then." He raised his beer. We clinked bottles and drank.

My former boss looked me over. It wasn't sexual—more like professional assessment. "You're looking rough."

"It's been a rough month or two. I got caught up in a case that kicked my ass a bit, but I'm getting back on my feet, I think."

"That's good to hear. Other than that, how have you been?"

"Doing okay. Business is steady."

"Still by yourself?"

"Yep." At some point I might tell him about Malcolm, but not right now. "How are things at MDI?"

Mark took another drink. "Damn good; we've got more work than we can handle. Made Kevin Garrison my partner last April and hired on two new investigators a month ago. One of 'em looks like she'll do good, but I don't think the other one has the knack. I'll give him another month, then we'll see."

I glanced at the gold band on his left hand, with its distinctive white opal signifying his air magic. "Still with Sharon?"

"Thirty years this year." He beamed.

"Congrats. That's great." I meant it. I'd always liked Sharon, a CPA who was MDI's longtime chief number-cruncher and bean-counter.

"Yeah, she's a good woman. Too good for me, probably, but who am I to tell her different?" We both grinned; it was a running joke.

Mark drained his beer. I got up, went to the kitchen, and returned with two more bottles. I uncapped one and handed it over.

"Thanks." He rested the bottle on his knee. "I'm sorry for how I treated you, Alice."

"You had every right to be upset. I should have told you what my plans were. I was afraid you'd cut me loose if you knew I planned to start my own firm when I got my license, but that's no excuse. You gave me the chance to get into the business. You trained me and watched my back. I wish I could have done things differently, but I had to leave."

"I know." Mark rubbed his chin. "At first, I was pissed because my feelings were hurt, then I started feeling bad for cutting you off. Lately, I've been feeling like an asshole."

The Mark I remembered usually preferred a direct approach. "Should we just forgive each other and be done with it?"

"If you can, I sure as hell can."

I raised my bottle and we clinked again. "Done."

We drank in companionable silence for a while. When we finished our beers, I went and got two more and a trash can for the empties.

"You still like good whisky?" Mark asked.

"Yes." Maybe too much.

"I got a bottle of Scotch from one of my clients as a gift. Not much of a whiskey drinker myself anymore. I'll bring it over next time."

"Sounds good."

Mark seemed to steel himself and I figured he was ready to talk about what was bothering him. "I left you a message," he said.

I nodded. "I just listened to it today. You said you have an important case you're working on. I'm not sure how I can help, though."

Mark hesitated. "What I'm about to tell you can't leave this room."

My stomach lurched. "Understood."

"What do you know about the missing prostitutes in the city?"

"I heard something about that. Isn't there a local reporter who thinks there have been a lot of working girls going missing?"

"Yes, Amanda Bailey. She works for the city paper. She's been investigating the case for almost a year, trying to keep people's attention on it. You know it's hard to get cops interested in a case like that. There's not much of a public outcry when hookers go missing."

I remembered reading about the missing women a while back. Bailey had published a series of articles online and in the city's print newspaper. She suspected the disappearances were connected and that a local harnad, or group of blood mages, might be involved.

I personally knew of one harnad in the city, and its leader, John West, was both a powerful blood mage and the strongest fire mage I had ever encountered. He was Amelia Wharton's father and a man I wanted to avoid.

"I read some of the articles, but it's been a while," I said. "What's the latest?"

"No one knows for sure, but there may be anywhere from twenty to thirty missing women over the past fourteen months. Amanda has been trying to track down some of the missing, but it's tough. A lot of the women are transient. A few turned up in jail or in other cities. The rest are just gone."

"So what's your involvement in this? What is the Court's interest?"

"The parents of two of the missing women believe a vampire—or group of vampires—are taking prostitutes and draining them, or keeping them as blood-slaves in some dungeon, and they've openly accused the Court of covering it up. At first, the Court wasn't all that concerned; there's no evidence to suggest the missing women are victims of vampire attacks and certainly nothing to indicate they're being held in a vamp's lair somewhere. Then some of the national news channels got wind of it and you know how they love a sensational story with blood, sex, and vampires. There have been some anti-vampire demonstrations around the city."

I stared at him, shocked. "I hadn't heard about that."

Mark looked grim. "The Court is concerned that this may get even uglier. There's no proof vamps are responsible, but nothing says they aren't, either. You and I both know that when it comes to vampires, they're guilty until proven innocent. It wouldn't take much to set people off. Most people already don't trust vampires. If even one of the girls turns up drained, the city could go off like a powder keg. We might see mobs going after any vampire they can find, like what happened in Kansas City two years ago."

"Or in Cincinnati, the year before that," I added.

"Meanwhile, the police are fixated on the vampire angle and they aren't interested in other theories. That's why I'm investigating. The Court hired me to quietly find out who, if anyone, has been taking these girls, and to get them back if any of them are still alive."

Mark finished his beer. He tossed it into the trash can and went to the kitchen to grab another. When he came back, he sat back down heavily on the couch. "I've been working on it for three weeks, and I've got shit."

"As in...?"

"As in nothing. No trace of any of the girls. It's damn hard to get working girls to tell you anything. The few who have talked to me say that this girl or that girl got into a car with a john and never came back. No one got any license plates or has much of a description of any of the cars or drivers. Sometimes the girls disappeared when they weren't working. Nobody knows anything."

"So why does Amanda Bailey, the reporter, think a local harnad has been taking the girls?"

"A roommate of one of the girls who disappeared told her that the missing girl said she had been invited to join a group of mages. A 'group of mages' is probably either a cabal or a harnad, and nobody gets randomly invited to join one, either. If she was invited to a harnad meeting, it wasn't to become a member."

"How credible is the witness?"

"She's pretty credible." Mark leaned forward. "If it's a harnad, I have to find out what's going on. These girls deserve justice, and the vamps are going to get blamed unless we find the people responsible and drop them on the steps of police headquarters."

I rubbed my face. "If it *is* a harnad taking these girls—and I'm not saying it is—it would have to be a series of individual rituals, since this has apparently been going on for at least fourteen months, and you can't store blood for ritual magic because the life energy dissipates quickly. That would be an *extremely* active harnad, though, and we haven't seen any evidence of major harnad workings in the city: no natural disasters, no infrastructure collapses, no aberrant weather patterns."

He took a long drink. "That's why I wanted to talk to you. This is the kind of help I need. That, and someone to talk to these girls and their friends. To most of them, I'm one step above a cop and a man too and they don't trust me. You might be able to get more information. You were good at that when we worked together before."

I sighed. "Mark, I agree, this is really bad, but I'm not sure I have much to offer in the way of help on this. It doesn't sound like there's much to go on."

He slammed his fist down on the arm of the couch and I jumped. "I know there's not much to go on!" he shouted. "Damn it, I've got nothing to tell the Court after three weeks on this. I need your help, Alice. I wouldn't be asking if I wasn't desperate."

"Well, that's great," I said acerbically. "Desperate times, desperate measures, huh?"

"That's not what I meant." He ran his hand through his hair in a frustrated gesture I'd seen a hundred times. "I've been intending to call you for weeks and just hadn't done it. All I wanted was to talk to you, see if we could work things out. Then all this came up, and now I need someone who knows magic, who knows that world and the vampires too. I need *you*."

He drained his beer and dropped the bottle into the trash can. "You said you've had a rough couple of months, but it's not just that, is it? Something about this case is making you skittish. It's not like you to not want to help."

I scowled. I *did* want to help, but I also wanted to stay away from John West's harnad and Charles. I was reluctant to explain either situation—the former because it would reveal my involvement in the construction site murders and the latter because I was embarrassed I'd let Charles manipulate me.

When I didn't say anything, he pushed for an answer. "Is it that there might be a harnad involved? I could understand that. Nobody wants to go around kicking hornets' nests, but these women deserve justice."

"I know they do," I said quietly. "Whether it's vampires, a cabal, or a harnad, whoever is taking these women needs to answer for it."

Mark's phone chimed. He glanced at the screen, texted back a quick reply, and then stuck it back in his pocket. "I have to go. That was Sharon, asking me to run an errand. Will you do something for me?"

"What do you need?"

He nudged the file box toward me with his foot. "Look through the files and tell me what you think. I need fresh eyes on this. Give me a direction to go. I'll take any help I can get."

"I'll look at them," I promised. "Tell Sharon I said hi."

"Will do." Mark stood and I walked him to the door. "Text me or call me anytime, day or night. You've got my number."

"I will. Keep me posted on your end."

He hesitated, then rested his hand lightly on my shoulder. When he'd hired me, I'd only been free of my grandfather's cabal for a few months and couldn't bear to be touched; even incidental contact was a source of anxiety. During the five years since, some of that had faded, and my time with Sean—brief as it was—had shown me physical contact could be a source of comfort.

I leaned into the warmth and reassurance of Mark's touch. He gave my shoulder a quick squeeze and headed down the steps.

I watched him walk to his truck, then waved as he backed down my driveway. As he drove off down the street, I went back inside.

In my living room, the file box sat where he'd left it. I sat on the couch and stared at it while I finished my beer.

I did not want to get mixed up in a Vampire Court case, and I *really* did not want to attract the attention of a harnad, especially John West's harnad, but Mark had asked for my help and I owed him. The least I could do was look at the damn files.

With a sigh, I tossed my bottle into the trash can with the rest of the afternoon's dead soldiers, went to the kitchen for a cup of water, then returned to the living room. I took the lid off the file box and starting pulling out folders.

When Malcolm came up from the basement, he found me sitting on the living room floor on a couch cushion, surrounded by stacks of files and papers. "What's all this?"

I told him about Mark's visit, the missing women, and the Vamp Court's concerns.

"Wow, that's bad," he said. "So, what's in all these files?"

I unfolded myself from the cushion, stood up, and stretched, feeling my stiff joints pop. "The brown folders are copies of Mark's notes. The loose papers clipped together are the reporter's notes, going back over a year. The red folders are the Vampire Court reports on recent anti-supe activities and hate groups."

"What have you read so far?"

I pointed to the stacks of brown folders. "I started with Mark's notes. For the past three weeks, he's been working on tracking down the women who have been reported missing. Most of the names came from Amanda Bailey and the rest from word of mouth. Mark tried to compile what information he could and piece together where and when they were last seen. There's not a lot in there. He hasn't had much luck getting witnesses to talk to him."

"How many women are missing?"

I settled back onto the cushion. "Well, there are twenty-six names on the list who haven't been accounted for. Hard to say how accurate the list is, though; there could be more who haven't been reported missing."

"Or fewer, if some of those women left town to go somewhere else," he pointed out.

"That's true, though it does seem like a lot of them left personal belongings that friends or roommates said they would never leave behind. We can probably assume the true number is somewhere upwards of twenty-six."

"Does there seem to be any pattern to when and where they go missing?"

I shook my head. "Not that Mark could see and not that I'm seeing so far. Sometimes they were last seen getting into a car with a customer; sometimes they disappeared when they weren't working. Different days, different places, different times."

I told him about the girl who disappeared after telling her roommate that she had been invited to join a group of mages.

Malcolm looked grim. "Well, I hate to say it, but that probably means a harnad is involved. It could be a cabal, though. Hard to tell without more information. Either way, it doesn't bode well."

"No, it really doesn't. I'd like to talk to the girl's roommate and get the story directly from her. I haven't gotten to her file yet."

Near the bottom of the pile, I found the folder in question, flipped it open, and found a familiar face smiling back at me. "Holy shit. Carrie."

Malcolm peered over my shoulder. "Who's Carrie?"

"You remember the girl from the alley who was being attacked by the Haze addicts?" I pointed to the picture in Mark's file. "That's her."

"Carrie Ann Davis," he read. "Disappeared two weeks ago. Looks like her roommate Zara tried to report her missing, but the cops weren't interested. She called Amanda Bailey next, who passed her name on to Dunlap."

I felt sick. It was bad enough to think about twenty-six missing women, but the situation suddenly seemed so much more real. I'd met Carrie, maybe even saved her life in the alley, and now she was gone, her fate unknown.

"You okay?" Malcolm asked.

"Yeah." I looked through the file. It contained a photo of Carrie in a bar, holding a beer and smiling. The first page listed basic info: birthdate, Social Security number, estimated height and weight, address, cell phone number, and so forth. The next page was her roommate's account of the strange story of how one of Carrie's customers had invited her to join his group of mages.

The last sheet in the file indicated Carrie had been seen around seven the night she vanished, buying cigarettes in a convenience store near her apartment. Mark had spoken to the clerk. Carrie told him she was meeting a friend and left the store walking north. No one had seen her since.

On that page, Mark had written a short note in his familiar scrawl, dated five days after her disappearance: *Called Diaz re: Carrie. No interest.*

I closed the file. One young woman's life represented by four sheets of paper and one short note. I wondered if Diaz was someone with the police. That rang a distant bell, but I couldn't figure out why.

I picked up my phone and called Mark. "Dunlap," he said gruffly.

"Hey, Mark. It's Alice. I started looking through the files you gave me."

"And?"

"I know the girl who went to meet the group of mages—well, I've met her." I gave him an abbreviated account of what happened in the alley next to Nancy's Diner.

"I'm not surprised you jumped into the middle of that, but you gotta know that wasn't real smart," Mark said when I finished. "You're lucky you came out of it with nothing more than a cut on your arm."

"Yeah, I didn't stop to think," I admitted. "But she needed help and I was pretty sure I could take them. They were too high to put up much of a fight."

"If they were on that Haze shit, you might have gotten a surprise," Mark cautioned me. "It makes people violent and unpredictable and stronger than normal. It's turning into a real problem. Between that and Black Fire, the cops have their hands full."

"What do you mean?" I frowned, remembering what Carrie had told me in the alley. "Aren't Haze and Black Fire the same thing?"

"That's what people thought at first, but they aren't. They're similar, but in addition to making users aggressive and paranoid, Black Fire seems to enhance any magic ability they might have. Suddenly, somebody who could barely summon up a spark before turns into a full-blown pyro. Last week, a guy who had nothing more than a trace of earth magic was able to knock down the wall of an electronics store and get away with twenty-five grand worth of gear. It's happening all over the city. We're in the middle of a drug-fueled, magic-enhanced crime wave."

"Whoa. I had no idea." I *seriously* needed pay more attention to current events. "Anyway, I've got more files to go through, but I wanted to tell you I'm willing to go down to the Stroll and talk to some of the women. Is there anybody down there who might be able to introduce me around?"

Mark considered. "I'm thinking Zara Anderson might help you."

"Carrie's roommate?"

"Yes. She's upset about Carrie disappearing and she's pissed at the cops for not looking into it. They don't think her disappearance is connected to the others, since she told Zara she was going to join a group of mages. In fact, they're pretty sure she's not missing at all. They think she's just joined up with some 'mage cult' and left her old life behind."

"A mage cult, huh?" I snorted. "Not that that's a real thing."

"That's what I tried to tell Ernie Diaz."

"Detective Ernie Diaz? *That's* who's investigating the missing women?"

"Yeah." Mark heaved a sigh. "They promoted him out of Property Crimes. He's with Major Crimes now and they've put him in charge of the case."

"I remember him from when I worked for you. He used to be an okay guy."

"He still is most of the time, but he's convinced it's the vamps taking the girls and he's not interested in hearing about any other theories. And he's real choosy about who he's willing to put on the list of possible victims and who doesn't qualify."

"Like Carrie."

"Yeah, like Carrie."

We were both quiet.

"Tell you what," Mark said finally. "I'll try to get a hold of Zara and see if she's able to meet you tonight. Do you want some backup down there?"

"No, I'll be fine. I won't go running into any alleys." I hesitated. "Unless I've got a good reason."

I heard the smile in Mark's voice. "That's my girl. Let me call Zara and I'll get back with you ASAP."

As we hung up, Malcolm was grinning. "What are you so happy about?" I asked.

"You're back to work."

I frowned. "I never stopped working, Malcolm. I've had three clients in the past month."

"No, you've been *doing jobs* for the past month. This is different. Now you're *back to work*."

I thought about it and realized he was right. I might have closed three cases, but I'd just been going through the motions. Despite my misgivings, I felt compelled to find out what happened to Carrie and the others. I *was* back to work, for the first time since the night I faced Amelia Wharton at the construction site.

But since getting all sentimental wasn't really my thing, I changed the subject. "I've got files to go through," I told him briskly. "You want to read along with me or do you have other stuff you have to do?"

"I'll read with you," Malcolm said, still beaming. He rubbed his hands together in anticipation. "We're getting the band back together."

We read through the rest of Mark's files. I got my laptop out and typed up some notes for myself, including a one-page list of the twenty-six women Mark and Amanda Bailey thought were missing. I added asterisks next to the thirteen who had made Diaz's much-shorter list. Next to all the names, for quick reference, I put the dates they disappeared and a brief note of where they were last seen.

We were just starting to look at Amanda Bailey's notes when Mark texted to say Zara would meet me in one hour at the apartment she shared with Carrie, then take me down to the Stroll. He sent me the address and a reminder to be careful.

I stacked up the files, printed off my list of names, and went upstairs to change. I pulled on a long-sleeved shirt, jeans, and boots, dashed on some makeup, and put on my charm bracelet with its half-dozen spell crystals.

I was back downstairs in ten minutes, stuffing a couple of granola bars into my bag and a handful of business cards into my pocket, when Malcolm appeared. "How long do you think you'll be out?" he asked.

"I really don't know. It depends on if anyone will talk to me and what I find out."

"Do you want me to come along? I could scout around, maybe see something useful."

I grabbed a bottle of water out of the fridge and stuck it in my bag. "This burning desire to tag along wouldn't have anything to do with the fact that I'm about to go talk to a bunch of working girls, would it?"

"Absolutely not," he said with injured dignity. "I'm sure I'll be so busy looking for clues, I won't even notice the ladies."

I snorted, then considered his offer. "Your masking spell is holding up well. You feel like a ghost of a low-level water mage and I think that's good enough to keep you incognito. I doubt we'll be running into any high-level mages down on the Stroll. You can come along, but if something goes down and I tell you to jump back here, you go."

"You're no fun," Malcolm complained.

"Yeah, I know." I slung my bag over my shoulder, made sure I had my phone and keys, and grabbed a jacket. "Let's go, Watson. The game's afoot."

4

Zara Anderson and Carrie Davis shared a third-floor apartment about six blocks from the Stroll. Though the outside of the building looked run-down, the inside was surprisingly tidy and smelled of pine-scented cleaner.

Zara opened the door at my knock. She appeared to be in her mid-twenties and was very tall and thin, dark-skinned, with a pierced nose and long, beaded braids. She looked me over with the sharp gaze of someone used to assessing people quickly. "You Alice?"

"That's me." I held out my hand.

After a moment, she shook it. "Come in." She stepped aside and I entered the apartment. I couldn't see Malcolm, since he'd gone invisible once we left my house, but he was nearby.

"Have a seat." Zara gestured at the futon. "I'm gonna make myself a rum and Coke. You want something to drink?"

"I'm fine." I sat down and dug a small notebook and pen out of my bag. "I appreciate you taking the time to talk with me on such short notice."

Zara returned from the tiny kitchen with her drink. She wore a long, purple tunic and jeans, and her feet were bare except for a couple of toe rings. She curled up in a threadbare armchair and regarded me with an appraising look. "So you're Wonder Woman."

I blinked.

Zara grinned. "That's what Carrie called you, you know. The woman who came out of nowhere, beat up three guys high on Haze, and saved her. She called you Wonder Woman." She laughed at my expression. "I'm not about to take some chick I don't know and ask the girls to talk to her, but Mark Dunlap explained you were the woman from the alley. I'm not sure how much I trust Dunlap, but Amanda says he's okay."

"He's a good man. For whatever it's worth, I worked for him for a couple of years before I started my own agency. I trust him."

"And I suppose, if you risked your life for Carrie, you're probably okay." Zara sipped her rum and Coke, then rested the glass on her knee. "Not many people would have done what you did."

"I do crazy things sometimes." I shrugged. "She needed help."

Zara's smile faded. "Well, it looks like she needs help again." She rubbed at the wet ring her glass had left on her jeans. "I told her not to go, but that girl, she wanted to belong to something. It sounded like bullshit, but she said they were going to make her magic stronger—"

"Wait, what?" I interrupted. "Carrie has magic?"

She shook her head. "Barely any. She has a little bit of air magic. She can blow out a candle or a lighter if she's close to it, and that's all. She always wished she was stronger, so she could work for a cabal. She did her lighter trick for a customer and he convinced her he could make her magic more powerful if she joined his group of mages. I wanted to go with her to meet him, but she said I couldn't. I should have just followed her anyway, but we had a big fight about it, and I was mad." Zara took a long drink. "Anyway, that was the last time I saw her."

"I read your statement. Can you remember anything else she might have said about the guy? His age? What kind of car he drove? Where the group met? Where she was meeting him?"

"She didn't say. I told Dunlap everything I remember." Zara slapped her knee angrily. "I should never have let her go off alone. We were supposed to watch each other's backs. Some friend I am."

"I know it probably doesn't help, but you can't do anything about the choices other people make sometimes. It's hard not to blame yourself, but you did everything you could." I thought about the way I'd blamed myself for not being able to save Natalie's aunt and uncles from Amelia Wharton and here I was dispensing the same advice Charles had given me last night. Oh, the irony.

I dug out the list of twenty-six names. "Do you know if any of these other missing women had any magic?" I got up and handed Zara the page.

She skimmed the names. "I only know six—no, seven—women on this list, including Carrie. Other than Carrie, only one other woman has any magic that I know of. Angie Clayton has a little water magic. The rest, I'm not sure—I never saw them use any, or heard them talk about it, but that doesn't mean anything."

I made a face. No connection there, either. "I read Mark's files on the missing women, but there isn't much there for most of them. Of the women on the list you knew, do you know anything about their disappearances?"

Zara went down the list and told me what she knew about the other six women. I made some notes in my notebook, but it didn't sound like she knew anything more than what was in the files I'd read.

I was beginning to see why Mark was so frustrated. Twenty-six missing women, twenty-six different leads to follow, and no apparent overlap except the fact they were all prostitutes. Most of them worked the Stroll, the city's well-known red-light district, but some had disappeared from other areas of town like the cheap motels near the airport.

"You work on the Stroll, I'm assuming?" I asked Zara.

The younger woman looked at me silently, her face unreadable.

I tilted my head. "What?"

"I'm just not used to hearing someone say that without sounding judgmental. You don't sound like you're disgusted by what I do or act like you think you're better than me."

"It's your job. I've talked to a lot of sex workers over the years, and one thing I've learned is that I don't have the right to judge anyone for what they do to put food on the table and keep a roof over their heads."

Zara gave me a small smile. "Yeah, Carrie and I both work on the Stroll. Why?"

"I'm trying to anticipate what I might be able to find out from the other girls on the Stroll, assuming any of them will talk to me."

"Some of them will; some of them won't." She shrugged. "It's their choice. If you tell them you're Carrie's Wonder Woman, that might help. I'll be with you, so that will help too. Most of us like Amanda because she's trying to help. You're kind of like another Amanda, I guess."

Before we left, I took a few minutes to search Carrie's tiny bedroom, but found nothing that looked like it might be helpful. When I returned to the living room, Zara had finished her drink and was checking social media on her phone.

"I guess I'm ready to head out, if you are," I told her.

"Let me tell the girls we're on our way." She fired off a quick text, then stuck the phone in her back pocket and stepped into a pair of purple mules that added about four inches to her already-imposing height. I suddenly felt very short. She grabbed her bag and locked the door on our way out.

"Do you want to walk or drive?" I asked, as we headed down the hallway toward the stairs.

"I'll ride with you and walk back later, if that's okay," Zara said.

"Sure."

We took the stairs down to the first floor, then went to my car, parked in the little lot next to the building. I sensed Malcolm with us as I drove the quarter-mile or so to the 900 block of South Elm, more popularly known as the start of the Stroll.

Zara suggested I park at a convenience store a block over on Ninth, despite the multiple signs warning that unauthorized vehicles would be towed. As we got out, she waved at the clerk inside, who gave her a thumbs-up. "He'll watch the car. Mario's a good guy."

I reluctantly left my Toyota in Mario's care and headed off down the street with Zara, while Malcolm drifted along behind us.

It was fairly early yet and a weeknight to boot, but there was a small group of women already gathered at the corner of Tenth and Elm. As we approached, five pairs of hard eyes turned to study me. Their expressions ranged from bored to angry and their outfits from jeans and a tank top to a Spandex minidress.

Zara introduced me to Rachel, Becca, Danielle, Shonda, and Sarah. I offered my hand to each woman in turn. Rachel, Danielle, and Shonda shook my hand without hesitation, but Becca's handshake was brief and wary and Sarah refused, crossing her arms defiantly. Still, it was a better reaction than I'd anticipated.

I opened my mouth to ask my first question, but Zara spoke first. "She's Carrie's Wonder Woman."

I blushed as the women reacted with a mix of surprise and awe. Even Sarah seemed to thaw a bit at the news.

"She talked about that night all the time," Rachel said. "*Some people* didn't believe her"—she looked sideways at Becca, who rolled her eyes—"but it was so crazy, it had to be true. You really took out three guys high on Haze all by yourself?"

"Yep," I confirmed. "But they didn't put up much of a fight, really."

"She said they had knives," Danielle said. She looked to be in her mid-thirties and wore jeans and a red bustier.

"Two of them did, but they weren't very good with them." I cleared my throat, uncomfortable being the center of attention. "I don't know if any of you have met Mark Dunlap, but he's working with Amanda Bailey, trying to find out what's been happening down here. I used to work for Mark, and I'm trying to help, too."

"We all know what's happening," Sarah snapped. "The fangheads are taking girls off the street and keeping them until they drain them dry."

"Why do you think it's vamps?" I asked.

"Of course it's the vamps." Sarah lit a cigarette and blew smoke in my face. "Who else could be so invisible? Who else could get away with this shit for this long without getting caught? The vamps own the cops—everybody knows that."

"The cops believe vamps are taking the women," I pointed out. "Amanda and Mark can't get them to even consider any other ideas."

"Yeah, but they haven't actually *arrested* anyone, have they?" Sarah countered. "Like I said, they *own* the cops."

I didn't think arguing with her was going to help the situation, so I moved on. "In any case, I would like to know what happened to these women and I want to bring them back alive if I can, so I'd like to ask if you saw any of them before they disappeared."

I dug the list out of my bag and handed it to Danielle. The women, except for Sarah, gathered around her under the streetlight. They looked over the list and Sarah smoked in sullen silence.

As I waited, I sensed a passing spirit and shivered. The trace felt like a poltergeist—cold and deranged. Usually the sensation was fleeting, but this one lingered on the edges of my senses, almost hovering. I strengthened my shields and tried to ignore the nagging feeling of wrongness.

"Why are you out here?" Sarah asked, flicking her ash onto the sidewalk.

"Mark asked me to help. With this many women missing, it seems like the more people there are working on it, the better."

She shrugged. "The cops don't even think half of 'em *are* missing. You ask me, they don't care much about the ones they *did* put on their list. I've only seen someone from the police down here maybe two, three times in the past couple months. Amanda says there's a 'task force,' but you'd never know." She put air quotes around *task force*. "Besides, Amanda said Dunlap works for the fangheads, so there ain't no way I'm gonna trust him."

"Mark's being paid by the Court to find out who's responsible for this, whether it's vamps or someone else. They want the perpetrators found more than anyone."

Sarah snorted.

"Besides that," I continued, "I've known Mark for five years. I can promise you that he may work for the Court but they don't own him. If it turns out a vamp—or a group of them—is involved, he'll see that they face justice for it."

"And you?" Sarah challenged me. "Do *you* work for the fangheads?"

"I have for several years. Mark is paying me to help him with this case." No sense denying it; they'd find out sooner or later. "But ask me who I'm working for right now."

Sarah looked at me silently.

I leaned toward her, my eyes on hers. "I'm working for Carrie."

The other women had grown quiet and were listening to us. Sarah took a drag off her cigarette, eyed me, then blew the smoke up toward the streetlight.

Danielle spoke up. "I'm not sure if this helps or not, but there's a mistake here." She pointed to a name on the list: Missy Daniels, second from the bottom, missing for almost two weeks. "This says she was last seen on the fourteenth, but I saw her on the night of the fifteenth."

I pulled my notebook out. "Do you remember seeing her leave with anyone?"

"Yeah, actually." Danielle pursed her lips thoughtfully. "I remember because it was a BMW and we don't see that kind of car down here very often." The other women nodded in agreement.

"Where were you?" I asked.

"Next block down," Danielle said, pointing. "Between Eleventh and Twelfth. The car pulled over right in front of Missy. She talked to the guy through the window for a minute, then got in. They went down the street and turned left onto Fourteenth. That was the last time I saw her."

I wrote in my notebook. "How sure are you that this was the fifteenth and not the fourteenth?"

"I was in jail on the fourteenth," Danielle said. The other women laughed.

"What was it this time, Dani?" Becca asked, bumping the older woman's hip with hers.

Danielle rolled her eyes. "Shoplifting. The owner ended up not filing charges, so they let me out the next day, the fifteenth. I saw Missy get in the BMW that night." She was quiet, then added softly, "I was mad she got a rich client."

"Do you remember what color the car was?" I asked.

"Black," she said instantly. "All black, tinted windows. I couldn't see into the car until she opened the door and the interior light came on."

"Could you see the driver?"

"Yeah. I mean, not real well, but good enough, you know? It was an older guy, gray hair, wearing a suit."

"Older man, gray hair, suit, black BMW." My stomach was sinking. "If we were able to identify a potential suspect and I came back down here with some pictures, do you think you would be able to recognize him if you saw him again?"

Danielle shrugged. "Maybe. I could try."

I glanced around at the other women. "Can anybody else add anything?"

Rachel and Shonda volunteered some information on two other women from the list, but it was secondhand and didn't sound promising. I wrote it down anyway, just in case, but my mind was on Danielle's description of Missy's customer.

I handed each of them one of my cards with my cell number on it. "Please call me if you think of anything or if you hear anything. Even something that seems unimportant might be the key to finding out what happened to your friends."

Sarah tossed her cigarette on the sidewalk and ground it out with her boot. "The cops aren't going to do shit. We figured that out a long time ago. If you and Amanda—and Mark Dunlap, I guess—don't find out what happened to them, no one will."

"It could be one of us next," Shonda said. "Any one of us."

I felt helpless in the face of their fear and hated it. "You all be careful."

Danielle handed me the list. "Thank you for helping us."

"Do you want me to walk with you back to your car?" Zara asked.

I shook my head. "No, I'll be fine. You staying?"

"Yep. Time to clock in." Zara grinned. The other women laughed.

The group split up and I headed back toward Ninth. Malcolm drifted along next to me as I walked. "Alice," he said quietly, his voice coming from my right. "Black BMW."

"I know, but there are a lot of black Beemers in the city. It's not enough to go on by itself. It might not be him."

"The reporter thinks it's a harnad," Malcolm pointed out, as I turned the corner and approached the convenience store where I'd parked my Toyota. "Harnad plus old guy in a black BMW equals—"

"Shit." I stopped short.

A tall, blond man in jeans and a leather jacket leaned casually against the driver's side of my car, arms crossed. A familiar black truck was parked three spots away from mine. Ours were the only two vehicles in the lot.

I didn't wait for Malcolm to figure out he needed to be gone. I covered my mouth with my hand and coughed. "*Home*," I muttered behind my hand.

My skin tingled as the spell sent Malcolm to the safety of my basement. I coughed again, then resumed walking and reached into my bag for my keys.

"Sounds like you've got a cold, Ms. Worth," Special Agent Trent Lake said. "Or is it allergies?"

"Don't you have cases to solve?" I asked irritably.

Lake gave me one of his annoyingly charming smiles. "Always. Never a shortage of crime in the city."

"Then why are you loitering in a convenience store parking lot, instead of off somewhere solving them?" I mimicked his pose, folding my arms and glaring at him.

Instead of moving, he settled in more comfortably against my car. "I'm off the clock. Even SPEMA agents get time off."

"So this is how you're spending it? You need a hobby, Lake. Something other than harassing me. Have you tried coin collecting or bonsai?"

"That sounds far less interesting than keeping up with your activities. What brings you down to the Stroll tonight?"

"What brings *you* down here?" I countered.

"You must be working on a new case," he continued, ignoring my question. "I understand you found Mrs. Yates's long-lost family heirloom. How did a pocket watch destroy part of her house?"

"It's a very temperamental watch, and it's very particular about how you phrase your requests. And as I told you the last half-dozen times you *just happened* to run into me in the past few weeks, I have nothing to say to you. You aren't going to get anything on me by stalking me, so you might as well give up."

"I never give up. It's one of my finer qualities."

"Be that as it may, it doesn't change the fact that you're wasting your time following me around." I jingled my keys. "Now, if you don't mind, it's late and I'm tired. Please stop leaning on my car."

His smile faded. "I asked why you're down here this evening."

"And *I* said I have nothing to say to you," I shot back. "I thought I was pretty clear about that, but maybe all that time on the gun range has damaged your hearing."

"Maybe it has," he agreed. "Help me out. What have you been hearing around here lately?"

I shrugged. "The usual. Times are tough. Weeknights are slow. There's apparently a new drug on the streets causing some problems."

He sighed. "You can't help being difficult, can you?"

"Nope. It's one of my finer qualities."

We eyeballed each other.

"Alice, you are one of the most frustrating people I have ever met," he said finally.

"Right back at ya, Lake. Now, seriously, would you move so I can leave? I've got a bitch of a headache and—wait, did you just call me Alice?"

His smile reappeared, looking more shark-like this time. "You can call me Trent."

"I don't want to call you Trent," I told him, scowling. "I want to go home and you're in my way."

"Let me buy you a cup of coffee." Lake gestured at the all-night diner down the street from the convenience store.

"No freaking way am I having coffee with you."

"Why not?"

"I can think of at least a dozen reasons. Besides, what part of 'It's late and I want to go home' do you not understand?"

"Jenny Alvarez."

"Who?"

"Missy Daniels."

I stared at him.

"Angie Clayton. Breanna Howell. Tara Fuller." He studied my face. "These names mean something to you."

I shrugged again. "A couple of them sound vaguely familiar."

Lake moved to stand in front of me. When I started to walk around him, he held out his hand. "I think we might be down here for the same reason. Am I right?"

I threw up my hands in frustration. "I have no idea why you're here, unless it's to continue your campaign of annoying me to death."

"One cup of coffee."

"No."

"Five minutes."

"No." I moved around him and unlocked my car.

"I'm trying to find out what's been happening," he said as I reached for the door handle. "And I think you want to know too."

I sighed. "Lake, I—"

"Five minutes, Alice. Not for me. For them."

I'm working for Carrie.

Damn it.

I hit the button to lock my car. "Fine; five minutes. And you're buying the coffee."

5

I made him buy me a piece of apple pie, too. With a scoop of ice cream.

Lake and I sat at a booth in the back of the Midnite Café. He leaned back, sipped his coffee, and watched me eat. I ignored him and made quick work of the pie.

When I scraped my fork on the plate to get the last of the crumbs, Lake raised his eyebrows. "You want another piece?"

I glanced longingly at the glass-covered pie stand on the front counter. "No."

Lake snorted. "You lie so well. It's as easy for you as breathing."

I poured two packets of sugar into my coffee, added some cream, and stirred it. "That sounded almost like a compliment, Agent Lake, albeit a strange one."

"More of an observation. I'm trying to figure out why your first instinct is always to lie."

Was my first instinct always to lie? I thought about it and realized Lake might have a point. "My life hasn't always been the wonderland of sunshine and kittens you see today," I told him mildly, sipping my coffee.

"I suppose not, though you started out pretty well. Born in Chicago, only child of Henry and Laura Worth, educated at one of the top prep schools in the city."

Slowly, I lowered my cup to the table.

"Attended the University of Chicago as an undergrad, pre-med," he continued. "Solid 4.0 GPA until your parents died in a boating accident when you were twenty-one. You dropped out of college, fell in with a rough crowd for a couple of years, partied too much, blew most of your inheritance, then disappeared for a while. Somehow, you ended up here, two thousand miles away, leaving all of that behind to become an MPI with a modest salary and an uncanny knack for getting involved in big cases."

"Congrats; you can use Google."

To my annoyance, he seemed immune to my sarcasm. "I was curious about you."

I was gratified my appropriated identity had held up under Lake's scrutiny. "Well, I hope you were able to satisfy your curiosity. I'd appreciate it in the future if you wouldn't dredge up ancient history. Now, you've got five minutes to say what you need to say and then I'm going home to bed."

Lake reached into his inner jacket pocket and pulled out a small notebook. He flipped it open, found the page he was looking for, then pushed it across the table. Reluctantly, I read it over.

Twenty-eight names: the twenty-six I had, plus two more. He'd put check marks next to the thirteen who were on Diaz's list. I looked up at him. "Is this supposed to mean something to me?"

"Are you going to be a complete hard-ass about this, or can we skip to the part where you tell me what you know about the missing women?"

"How about we skip to the part where you tell me what *you* know?"

He raised his hands apologetically. "I can't comment on an ongoing investigation."

I shrugged. "Ditto."

We drank our coffee. He topped off both our cups from the pot the waitress had left on the table. I added some cream to mine and stirred it noisily.

Lake caved. "Let's talk hypotheticals."

I gave him a bright smile and put down my spoon.

"Hypothetically, we've got at least twenty-eight women going missing over the past fourteen months. No apparent connection other than the fact they're all prostitutes, and there are no viable leads, which suggests a highly organized killer or group of killers." Lake dropped his voice. "It's possible we have a Green River–type serial killer in the city, averaging two victims per month. Many people suspect a vampire, or a group of vampires, of course. Those seem to be the two most likely scenarios, but no bodies have turned up."

"The police certainly seem to think it's vamps. I heard the detective in charge of the case isn't interested in any other theories."

"Our bureau chief shares Detective Diaz's opinion," he commented. "As does my partner."

As much as Lake irritated me, I disliked his partner even more. "Is that why you're down here without Agent Parker?"

"I doubt she'd care about any theories that don't involve vampires."

I raised my eyebrows. "And what about you, Agent Lake?"

"I think focusing on a suspect before we have evidence leads to tunnel vision." He eyed me over the rim of his coffee cup. "I'm curious to hear your thoughts."

"I agree there's too much on the line to assume anything right now." I finished my second cup of coffee, then put my hand over it when Lake picked up the pot to refill my mug. "No more for me. I want to be able to sleep at some point tonight."

He filled his own cup and put the pot down. "Who do you think might be responsible?"

"Why do you care what I think?"

"I'm always interested in fresh perspectives. Plus, rumor has it you're pretty good at your job."

"Be careful; such flattery will go to my head," I said wryly. "But I thought I only ended up involved in big cases because I have an 'uncanny knack' for it."

"I take it back." Out came his charming smile again. "At this point, I have to accept that it's skill, not luck, since here we are again comparing notes on a case. And like the last two times, I have the sneaking suspicion you might know at least as much—if not more—about the situation than I do." Lake tapped the list of names. "Who's taking them?"

I thought about what I wanted to say. I couldn't tip him off to my suspicions about West, but I could at least nudge him in a productive direction. "Like you said, it could be a serial killer, or it could be vamps, but it would be a bad idea to jump to any conclusions at this point."

He looked annoyed.

"But hypothetically speaking," I continued, "there might be a door number three."

"Which would be...?"

"A harnad."

Lake studied me. I gave him a bland look and sipped my water.

"The official police position is there are no active harnads in the city, unless you know differently?"

"I've heard things," I said noncommittally.

"Seen things?"

"No."

He smiled. "Lying again."

I shrugged. "Believe what you want. My point is that I don't think anyone should be so quick to dismiss the harnad theory or to blame vamps until they've investigated all the angles."

"Any suggestions on where one might start to investigate the harnad angle, if one were inclined to do so?"

"Well, you've probably heard Amanda Bailey from the *Sentinel* thinks it's a harnad, based on testimony from a witness. That might be a good place to start."

Lake pondered that. "You're referring to the girl who supposedly went to meet a group of mages, Carrie Davis." He saw my look of surprise. "I've been spending a lot of time with these case files."

"At least someone has." I didn't bother to hide the anger in my voice.

"The police have their opinions; I have mine." He put his empty mug on the table. "Besides the witness, what else makes you think this is a harnad?"

"That's all I've got for now."

The federal agent crossed his arms. "Why do I feel like that's not true?"

"I have no idea why you do anything you do." I rubbed my eyes and glanced up, looking over Lake's head.

And saw my grandfather's face.

My spine turned to ice. The surge of adrenaline was so powerful that I almost jumped out of my seat.

The television on the wall was set on a news channel. The screen showed a recent photograph of Moses, standing at the open door of a limo about to get in. He looked somehow even colder and more cruel than I remembered. His eyes bored into me, hard and gray. Below the photo, the headline read MURPHY CABAL SUSPECTED IN DEADLY ATTACKS.

Lake saw me staring and turned to look at the television.

"What attacks are they talking about?" My voice was surprisingly calm.

He turned back around. "For the last several weeks, there have been attacks on properties owned by the Bell Cabal in and around the city. From what I understand, there are about a dozen dead and at least twice that number of injuries."

My brows rose. "Why would Murphy be attacking Bell? Aren't most of his interests in the Baltimore area?"

He drained his coffee and set the empty mug down on the table. "We've had no cooperation from Bell or any of his people on the investigation, as you might imagine, but I think Murphy's softening up Bell's territory to make a move on it."

My throat was dry. "That's a scary thought. It would be war."

"A bloody one, with a lot of collateral damage, if previous cabal wars are anything to go by."

The television showed aerial footage of a burned building. The caption identified it as a warehouse belonging to one of Bell's companies. FBI and SPEMA agents in coveralls combed through the smoking ruin. A half-dozen sheet-covered bodies were lined up in the parking lot.

My thoughts whirled. It was unlikely my grandfather's move on Bell's territory had anything to do with me; he was always striking out at other large cabals with whom he did not have alliances, looking for weak spots and opportunities to expand his web. Regardless of the reason, Moses's people were moving into the city. If the takeover was successful, Moses himself wouldn't be far behind. A lead ball of fear formed in my stomach and stayed there.

Before Lake had any reason to think I was unusually interested in Moses Murphy and his cabal, I picked up my phone and checked the time. "Your five minutes are up. You want me to get the tip?"

"I've got it." He reached for his wallet as I started to slide out of the booth. "By the way," he added, "who's your client?"

"Why, Agent Lake, you know that's confidential."

"If I had to guess, I'd say it's the Vampire Court." He tucked a five under his mug as we stood. "I heard a rumor they hired someone to look into it discreetly, but that was a couple of weeks ago, and you were working on a different case then. Irene Miller's poltergeist problem, wasn't it?"

I glared at him.

"So you're new to the investigation," he continued, unfazed by my glower. "Maybe working for the Court's lead investigator, Mark Dunlap of MDI?"

I slung my bag over my shoulder and repeated what I'd said to Sarah earlier. "I'm working for the victims. The women down on South Elm would like to know what happened to their friends, and someone owes them answers."

"Some answers and some justice," Lake agreed. He gave me a card. "Call me if you hear anything."

The last time he'd handed me his card, I'd torn it up and flushed the pieces down the toilet. This time, I put his number into my contacts and tucked the card into my bag.

When I looked up, he was grinning at me. "What?" I asked with a scowl. "So I took your card. I still don't like you."

His laugh was sudden and loud. It was a nice laugh.

"Good night, Lake." I turned on my heel and headed for the door.

Lake stopped to pay our check and use the men's room, so I left alone to walk back to the convenience store. As annoyed as I was with his tendency to pop up wherever I was, I'd be lying if I said knowing he was working on this case didn't make me feel better. I was skeptical that Diaz was going to give the case the attention it deserved, and if the police wouldn't even consider the possibility a harnad was involved, then Mark, Lake, and I might be the only real chance of finding out what happened to the missing women.

When I approached the convenience store, I was relieved to see my car still parked where I'd left it. I started to dig out my keys and sighed. My headache was getting worse, and now *I* needed to use the bathroom. I said a silent prayer to the toilet gods that the store's restroom was reasonably clean and went inside.

"Hello." Mario smiled at me from atop a small ladder, where he was stocking cigarette cartons on a high shelf. "You're the driver of the blue Toyota, right?"

"Yep. Thanks for keeping an eye on it for me, Mario. I'm Alice."

"No problem, Alice. What do you need?"

"Aspirin."

He pointed to a shelf behind me. I picked up a box and set it on the counter. "Can I use your restroom?"

"Sure."

I shut myself in the bathroom and used the toilet. After I washed my hands, I dug out my phone and debated texting Mark with an update, but one look at the time and I changed my mind. It would probably be better to call him in the morning.

As I tucked the phone back into my bag, I looked at myself in the mirror and made a face. There were deep shadows under my eyes and I was almost gaunt. Yikes. No wonder Malcolm and Mark had expressed concern over my appearance. Even Charles thought I looked like I was in poor health, and that was coming from a guy who'd been undead for more than two centuries.

A bell dinged in the store, announcing a customer. I was about to reach for the doorknob when someone shouted, "Open the register! *Open it now!*"

I froze.

Mario sounded fearful but calm. "I will open it; I will open it. Please don't burn me."

The robber must have either fire or earth magic and was threatening Mario with it. *Magic-enhanced, drug-fueled crime wave*, Mark had said. It appeared I was about to get a close-up look at what he was talking about.

The robber was still shouting at Mario to open the register. It felt like hours, but was really only seconds, until Mario said, "Here's all the money. Now you go."

I heard a muffled thump. "Fill these up!"

"Fill with what?" Mario sounded confused.

"Cartons of cigarettes, you stupid asshole!" The robber's voice was increasing in pitch. He sounded young.

At first, I'd thought the robber would merely take the money and leave, but the longer he stayed, the more likely it was he would hurt or kill Mario or lose control of his magic and burn down the store with us in it. I had to do something *now*.

I reached for the doorknob as the robber shouted, "Faster! Do you think I'm playing?"

Mario cried out in pain. The robber screamed, "Hurry up! *Hurry-the-fuck-up!*"

"I'm hurrying," Mario said, sounding strained. At least he was still alive. It was up to me to see he stayed that way.

I set my bag on the floor, turned the lock gently, and eased the door open to peer out into the store.

Mario was behind the counter, stuffing cartons of cigarettes into a duffel bag. His sleeve was burned. Another bag, already full, sat on the counter.

The masked robber, in a black T-shirt, jeans, and sneakers, stood on the other side of the counter. His shaking hands blazed with orange flames. The fire magic surged and flickered with his anger.

I slipped out of the bathroom and crept along the aisle, staying low and out of sight. Mario, busy packing cartons into the bag, had his back to me. The robber was focused on what Mario was doing. Neither man saw me sneaking up on them.

I took a deep breath and dove forward. My fingers closed around the robber's upper left arm. He jerked, the fire flaring with a blast of heat that made me wince.

"*Sleep*," I commanded.

He dropped like a sack of potatoes. The fire on his hands sputtered and went out.

Alarmed, Mario dropped the bag he was holding. "Is he dead?"

I shook my head. "Not dead, just asleep. Are you okay?"

Mario raised his burned arm and grimaced. "This hurts."

"I bet. Sit down over there." I pointed to the chair behind the counter. "I'm going to get help."

I opened the front door with my shoulder, trying not to disturb any fingerprints the robber might have left, and stepped outside.

Lake's truck was still parked out front. I looked toward the street and saw the federal agent a block away, walking toward the store. I waved at him. "Lake, hurry up!"

He raised his hand and broke into a jog. I took a step forward, intending to meet him in the parking lot.

"What the hell?" A kid who looked about sixteen was staring through the front window at the scene inside the store.

"It's okay. He was trying to rob—"

The kid turned on me with a snarl. "You *bitch*! You killed my brother!" He lifted his hands, palms out, and an enormous flash of uncontrolled air magic hit me square in the middle of my chest.

I smashed through the front doors in an explosion of glass and metal, sailed across the store, and crashed through a second glass door into a room that was cold and dark. Something whacked me on the back of my head, and everything went black.

I came to lying on my side and shivering violently.

Something warm and heavy was draped over my upper body, but it felt as if I were lying on a block of solid ice and I was so cold that it was painful. My ears rang and everything hurt.

With a groan, I started to roll onto my back, but someone held me still. "Don't move. You're hurt."

I couldn't get my eyes open quite yet and my brain felt like it was stuffed with cotton, so it took me several seconds to recognize the voice. "Lake?" My voice was tight with pain. "What happened?"

"There was a robbery." His hand moved to my shoulder and squeezed gently. "You got hit with magic. Do you remember?"

Jumbled bits of memory started to organize themselves in my foggy brain. "So cold,"

I said miserably.

"You're in the walk-in cooler. I'm sorry you're cold, but I don't want to move you in case you injured your spine."

I forced my eyes open and blinked slowly, trying to focus.

In the dim light, the first object I saw clearly was Lake's shoe as he crouched next to me. I realized the heavy thing he'd draped over me was his leather jacket. I scowled and started to push it away, but it was warm and smelled good and I was freezing, so I decided to leave it be for now.

"How long was I out?" I asked.

"Just a couple of minutes."

The pain was now concentrated in the back of my head and my back. I squeezed my eyes shut and took a couple of deep breaths.

When I opened my eyes again, I looked up into Lake's worried blue gaze. "Where do you hurt?" he asked me.

"Not hurt," I informed him.

He smiled a little. "There you go, lying again." The smile faded. "You hit the wall pretty damn hard. Can you feel your legs?"

"I'm okay, Lake. Nothing's broken." I rolled slowly to my back with a pained groan. The cold floor felt good on my battered skull and back.

"Lie still," he admonished me. "If you hurt your spine or neck, you could paralyze yourself by moving around."

"I'm good." I pushed myself up, but my vision tunneled and I slid sideways down the wall.

Lake swore and eased me back down to my side. My ears were ringing again. "Stay down." His voice sounded like it was coming from a long way away. "The ambulance will be here any minute."

That cleared the cobwebs almost instantly. "I don't need an ambulance." I forced myself to sit up again, and this time I stayed upright. "I'm fine."

He held my chin and stared at me. His eyes were very blue. "You are *not* fine. You went through two glass doors and hit your head hard enough to get knocked out. You probably have a concussion and you're shocky. You're going to the hospital."

"No, I'm not." I pushed his hand away. "I've got healing spells at home. I can take care of myself."

His eyes blazed. "You aren't thinking clearly."

"I'm thinking just fine, Lake. You want me to count to one hundred by twos? Recite the alphabet backward?" I looked out past the walk-in cooler at the store. The front doors were hanging on broken hinges and glass was everywhere. "Where are the suspects?"

He sighed. "I've got them cuffed out front. Do you want to press charges for the assault?"

I started to shake my head, then thought better of it. "No. The robbery charges should be enough to keep him in jail for a while."

"How did you take out the firebug? The clerk said magic."

"Basic air-magic sleep spell. It should wear off in about six hours, unless you want me to take it off now."

Lake shook his head. "No, leave it. He'll sleep it off in a cell downtown."

"How's Mario?"

"He's going to be fine. Minor burns only."

"That's good to hear." I gathered up Lake's leather jacket and handed it to him. Using the wall for support, I slowly pushed myself to my feet. Lake hovered nearby, his brow furrowed as he watched me.

I noticed a streak of red on the wall and a small puddle on the floor at my feet where I'd been lying. Gingerly, I touched the back of my head and my fingers came away bloody.

"Alice."

I blinked up at Lake. He took me by the wrist and looked at the blood on my fingers. "Please let the paramedics take a look at you."

"It's not as bad as it looks." I wiped my fingers on my jeans and glanced at the blood on the floor. "You probably want to step back."

He frowned. "Why?"

"I'm going to clean that up."

"This is a crime scene, Alice. You can't just—"

Before he could stop me, I crouched and touched the bloodstain with my fingertips. "*Burn*." In a flash of white fire, the air magic burner spell reduced the blood on the floor and wall to ash.

His frown became a glare. "I could arrest you for that."

"You could, but you won't." When I stood up, my vision swam and I started to fall. Lake dropped his jacket and caught me.

We'd done nothing but irritate each other from the moment we met a month ago, standing over the body of the half-demon serial killer Scott Grierson. And yet, the instant Lake's arms closed around me, the feeling changed. His eyes softened and the scowl disappeared. Despite the pain in my skull and back and what was rapidly evolving into the granddaddy of all splitting headaches, I was suddenly aware of the hard muscle beneath his shirt and the warmth of him, so comforting after lying on the cold floor. I should have pushed him away and said something sarcastic, but instead my fingers tightened on his arm. Lake's gaze moved to my mouth, then back up to meet my eyes.

Outside, a squad car arrived, lights flashing. An ambulance pulled up alongside and two paramedics jumped out. Lake didn't seem to notice.

"Lake," I said softly.

"What?" His voice was a low rumble.

"Let me go."

He released me. I took a step back and leaned against the wall. "You should probably go talk to the cops who just arrived."

Lake picked up his jacket and put it on, his face unreadable. "I probably should. You'll have to give them a statement."

"I'll go sit in my car until they're ready to talk to me."

He frowned. "Can you make it to your car?"

"Sure," I said, hoping I was right. "I need to get my bag from the bathroom, though."

"Go. I'll send the detective out to see you when he gets here."

I trudged out of the walk-in cooler, my boots crunching in the broken glass, as Lake went to talk to the cops. Mario was outside, sitting in the ambulance while the paramedics treated his burned arm. I fetched my bag from the restroom, fished out a five-dollar bill, and headed for the front counter.

The kid who'd attacked me with air magic sat on the floor, handcuffed to his unconscious brother with spell cuffs that would keep either of them from using their magic. Someone, probably Lake, had taken the fire mage's mask off. Neither of them looked more than eighteen.

"Bitch," the kid snarled.

"Watch your mouth," Lake snapped from the doorway, where he was explaining the situation to a uniformed officer.

"Fuck you, fed." The kid spat on the floor next to my boot.

I ignored him, put the five on the counter, picked up the box of aspirin, took a bottle of water from a cooler, and headed outside.

An hour later, I was curled up in the passenger seat of my car, holding an ice pack to the lump on the back of my head, while I waited for the detective in charge of the case. I'd given my statement to a uniformed officer, but apparently the detective wanted to talk to me in person, and I wasn't allowed to leave until she arrived. The suspects were gone, taken downtown for booking.

I'd rejected help from the paramedics three times before they finally gave up and left. I did accept a bag of ice wrapped in a towel from Mario before his boss arrived and sent him home. The ice and the aspirin took the edge off the pain, but I wanted so badly to get home to my healing spells and my bed that I was thinking seriously about just leaving and telling the cops the detective could track me down tomorrow.

From my car, I could see Lake inside the store, talking to the store's owner. He was angry with me for refusing medical help and I was too tired and sore to worry about his feelings. I was also trying to forget about what happened in the walk-in cooler, but every time I closed my eyes, I saw his bright blue gaze and the way he'd looked at me, like he was thinking about kissing me. Maybe I really *was* concussed. It seemed like the only reasonable explanation for why I'd reacted the way I did.

I curled up tighter in the seat and tried not to wish I still had his coat. The night had gotten cold and my jacket didn't provide nearly enough warmth. I closed my eyes, rested my head against the seat, and drifted.

"Miss Worth?" A hand shook my shoulder gently. "I'm Detective Shay."

I opened my bleary eyes. The detective was petite, with short dark hair and startlingly green eyes. "I'm so sorry to keep you waiting. I had to get someone to watch my son." She peered at me. "Are you all right?"

"I'm okay," I said. "I would really like to be home in bed right now."

"I know. I'll make this as quick as I can. Do you mind if I record us?"

"No."

Detective Shay pulled out her cell phone and turned on the voice recorder. She let me tell my story, then asked questions and walked me through it again, in greater detail. We went through everything a third time, and she thanked me and turned the recorder off.

"Are you going to be all right to drive home?" Shay asked. "You're not looking so good."

That made me laugh. She looked at me quizzically. "I've been getting that a lot lately," I said wryly.

She smiled and dug into her pocket for a card. "If you think of anything else, give me a call. Thanks for waiting."

Not that I'd had much choice, but Shay was kind enough that I kept that thought to myself. "Have a good night," I told her.

She headed to the front doors of the store. With a groan, I forced myself to stumble out of the car, shut the door, and limp around toward the driver's side.

I hadn't made it very far when Lake suddenly appeared and took my elbow. "I'll drive you home."

I tried to pull away. "I'm fine."

He smiled and held on. "Yes, I know you're the baddest, but you're swaying on your feet and your eyes are unfocused and you know you shouldn't be behind the wheel."

"I don't want my car towed," I protested.

"We'll take your car. One of the officers will follow us and bring me back."

Checkmated, I let him take me back to the passenger side of my car. I got in, put the ice pack between my head and the seat, and closed my eyes.

Lake got in on the driver's side and adjusted the seat. "Keys?"

Without opening my eyes, I held them out.

A pause. "Any of these spells on your key ring going to turn me into a newt?"

"Unfortunately, no," I muttered.

He laughed softly, took the keys, and started the car. He backed carefully out of the parking spot, pulled out onto Ninth, and accelerated.

He left the radio off but hummed as he drove. I was so tired and my head hurt so badly that I was starting to feel a little delirious.

"How did you know I was down on the Stroll tonight?" I murmured, half-asleep.

"I didn't. I go down there a couple times a week, keeping an eye on things, hoping to catch a lead. I saw your car parked at the store and figured you were there for the same reason."

"Whatever. Stop following me, you jerk."

He chuckled.

The next thing I knew, he was unfastening my seatbelt. I forced my eyes open and discovered we were parked under my carport.

Lake picked up my shoulder bag and looked down at me. "Can you walk, or should I carry you?"

I muttered something about hell freezing over and swung my legs out of the car, pushing myself to my feet using the door for leverage. I carried the half-melted ice pack and bloody towel and he brought my bag. A squad car idled at the curb, waiting to take him back to the store.

I shuffled to the front steps and used the railing to drag myself up to the porch. "Keys," I said.

He put the keys in my hand. I fumbled, found the house key, and got it in the lock.

I glanced up at Lake. "I've got it from here. Thanks for the ride."

He handed me my bag. "Half-demons, blood mages, and now robbers high on Black Fire. Do you have a death wish?"

"Don't forget the fact I work for the vamps," I reminded him flippantly. "And for the fortieth time, I don't know anything about the blood mage thing."

He laughed.

I unlocked my door, stepped through the wards, and turned back.

He stood on the porch, looking at me with an expression I couldn't quite read and was too tired to figure out.

"Good night, Alice," he said finally.

"Good night, Lake." Then I shut the door and locked it.

6

"You have *got* to be kidding me."

"Mark, it's not like I planned—"

"Damn it, Alice!" I winced and held the phone away from my ear as my former boss roared at me. "You said you wouldn't do anything stupid!"

"I said no such thing," I shot back, then frowned. "Hey!"

Mark harrumphed. "Are you all right, at least?"

"Of course I am." I still had a headache, but the lump on my head and pain in my back were gone, thanks to a healing spell and more aspirin. "It was two punks high on Black Fire. They had no idea what they were doing."

A pause. "It made the morning news, you know."

I groaned.

"For the record," he added, "when I said the Court hired me to investigate *quietly*, that directive extended to you as well."

"What was I supposed to do? Let them kill the clerk and burn the place down?"

"I suppose not," Mark said grudgingly. "Well done, Wonder Woman. Speaking of, you find out anything before all this went down?"

I hesitated. After a restless night, I'd spent a good part of the morning debating whether to tell Mark about the black BMW, but I could see no other option. It was looking more and more like this investigation was going to put me on a collision course with John West.

"Alice?" Mark's voice was sharp. "What do you have?"

"I've got a possible lead." I recounted Danielle's story of the last time she'd seen Missy Daniels. "It's vague," I added. "There are probably hundreds of black BMWs driven by older white men in the city."

"It's more than we had yesterday. I knew you'd come through for me. Are you free this morning?"

"What did you have in mind?"

"I've got some paperwork for you and some information on the harnads. Can you come to my office, say, around nine thirty?"

When I didn't reply immediately, Mark made an impatient sound. "You're already working on the case. I need your signature on the forms for insurance and payroll. You know how this works."

"Mark..."

"Alice, tell me what's going on. You clearly want in on this case but something's scaring you off. I know you thought about keeping the information about the BMW to yourself, and there's more you aren't telling me. It was obvious yesterday and it's even more obvious today." He was getting angry. "We can't work like this. I need to know you aren't holding out on me."

I opened my mouth to tell him I wasn't holding out, then closed it. I couldn't lie to Mark, not about this.

"If you and I can't trust each other, who the hell *can* we trust?" he demanded.

"This isn't about whether or not I trust *you*."

Silence. "So there's someone involved you don't trust."

"This is not something I'm going to discuss over the phone."

"Come to MDI, then. We'll sort this out."

I took a deep breath and exhaled. "Forty-five minutes," I said finally. "Put the coffee on."

Walking back into Mark's firm was like stepping through a mirror into a looking-glass world that was both eerily familiar and disconcertingly different. I paused just inside the front doors, looking around in wonder.

So much was the same: the large lobby, the hallways branching off into the recesses of the office, the thick carpet Sharon had talked Mark into getting despite how difficult it was to keep clean. Even the smell was familiar.

And yet, there were many changes, from the receptionist to the cheery blue paint on the walls. Several designer sofas were grouped around a tropical aquarium. When I looked closer, I saw glossy travel magazines stacked neatly on the side tables. When I'd worked here, there were hard plastic chairs and a secondhand coffee table covered with back issues of *Field & Stream* and *National Geographic*.

"May I help you?" the receptionist asked me.

Before I could answer, Mark appeared. He must have seen me pull up out front. "Alice," he said warmly, approaching me with his hand out. I shook it, more relieved than I wanted to admit that he had come out to meet me.

"Marian, this is Alice Worth," he said to the young woman at the front desk, who rose to shake my hand. "Alice is consulting with us on a case. She started her career here and now owns her own firm."

A firm of one, I almost added, but smiled instead as Marian's eyes lit up. "That's fantastic!" she said. "Congratulations!"

Mark beamed with pride. My eyes burned.

He put his hand on my shoulder and gave it a squeeze. "We're going to be in Conference Room Three," he told Marian. "I'm expecting someone to join us later. It's on the calendar. Just bring him back when he arrives."

"Will do," Marian said, settling back in behind her desk. "It was wonderful to meet you," she added.

"Nice to meet you too," I echoed.

I followed Mark down the hall, still trying to process my feelings as we walked through a maze of familiar hallways.

Finally, Mark opened a door and ushered me into a small conference room with an oval table, six leather chairs, and a much fancier audio-visual setup than it used to have.

Mark went directly to the coffee pot, as I moved around the conference table and sat facing the door. He poured two mugs of coffee and added sugar and creamer to mine without needing to ask. I took the coffee gratefully as he sat down across from me.

"Now, tell me what you need to tell me," he said briskly.

"This room is secure?"

Mark's gaze became distant. "*Sub rosa*," he murmured. My arms tingled as a powerful ward flared. "Completely secure. Nothing's getting in or out through that ward. Talk."

I talked.

I laid it all out for him: Amelia Wharton, the construction site murders, John West, Agent Lake, and my suspicion Charles had caused me to be injured during the fight that wrecked my living room. My former boss listened quietly and drank his coffee.

When I described the vampire's aggressive attempt to seduce me after I woke from the coma, however, Mark got up and paced. A cold wind blew through the conference room, making papers flutter off the side table and the light fixtures spark. My skin prickled at the surge of magic from my former boss, a mid-level air mage with a high-level Scots-Irish temper.

When I finished, Mark was livid. "It shouldn't surprise me. I know how vamps think, how they act. I don't know why I expected better of Vaughan, but I did."

"I did too, and that was my mistake." I shifted in the chair and crossed my legs. "I'm embarrassed to say I let my guard down. Of course, I have no proof he bit me. I'm sure if I confronted him about it, he'd only deny it. No one lies better than a vampire."

"Can't argue with that." Mark returned to his chair. "I won't ask you to keep working this case knowing about Vaughan and the threat West poses to you."

"I don't want you to leave me out just because it might mean I run into West or because it's likely I'll end up in the same room as Charles. There are twenty-eight missing women, Mark. That's bigger and more important than anything I've got going on."

"It's your decision. I'll support you either way. What about this SPEMA agent? What's your read on him?"

"Lake is a smug, authoritarian asshole, just like every other SPEMA agent I've ever met." I hesitated. "But having said that, he's not fixated on the vampire angle and he might be our only ally in law enforcement if things start to go south. I think we've established some kind of détente for now. He seems to genuinely want to know what happened to the missing women, and unlike Diaz, *his* list has twenty-eight names on it."

Mark grabbed a pen. "Do you know what the two additional names are?"

I gave him the names: Jenny Alvarez and Tiana James. Mark made a note on a legal pad, then drained his coffee and got up to get more.

When he returned to his chair, he reached for an inch-thick folder. "I've got someone coming in with information about the case a little later, and we need to go over what my researcher has turned up on the harnads, but first let's take care of the paperwork."

I groaned.

MDI's freelance researcher, Caitlyn Morse, arrived at the conference room just as I finished signing the last of the forms.

Cait was a little shorter than me, with shoulder-length brown hair and cute glasses. "It's so nice to finally meet you," she told me sincerely as she put her laptop bag on the table. "Mark has told me so much about you."

I slid a glance at my former boss. "Has he? That's alarming."

Cait's laugh was loud and infectious. I found myself smiling. "It was all good," she assured me.

I raised my eyebrow skeptically.

"Well, *almost* all good," she amended as we sat down and Mark headed to the side table.

"That sounds more believable." I flipped my notebook to a clean page. "So, what can you tell me?"

She took out her laptop and opened it. "As you know, this has been going on for well over a year. There were at least sixteen women missing before the police would look into it, and even now there's not much going on with the investigation."

"So I've heard," I said. "What about the vampire angle? Does Diaz actually have anything?"

"I don't think so," Cait said.

"Then why is he so convinced it's a vampire doing it?"

"Diaz, like a lot of cops, doesn't like vamps. He knows better than to say it out loud, but I think he agrees with the Human rights folks that vampires don't have any place among us. To him, they're monsters."

"But there's no evidence implicating a vampire," I said, exasperated. "We've got circumstantial evidence pointing to harnad involvement, so you'd think they'd at least consider the possibility."

"The problem is that the police have been saying since the early nineties that there are no active harnads in the city," Mark pointed out. "You weren't here at the time, Alice, but I'm sure you heard about the Drayton harnad."

I grimaced. "I heard about it. Six children murdered, wasn't it?"

"Yes." Cait shuddered. "I was in junior high. It was sheer panic in the city. After one of the harnad mages was killed in the jail despite being in protective custody, SPEMA came in and took them all, convicted them in federal court, and sent them to the ultra-max supe prison in Colorado Springs."

"So they're afraid if they admit there *is* an active harnad here, it will set off mass hysteria again?"

"That's about the size of it." Mark gave me a nod.

"What do you know about the two harnads that are supposed to be active in the city?" I asked.

Cait glanced at her laptop. "Information is sketchy. From what I understand, there are two harnads, one smaller, one larger. The smaller harnad refers to itself as Niger Sanguis. It appears to have six to eight members and a female leader."

"*Niger Sanguis*? Black Blood?" I frowned and thought about it more. "*Sanguis* can also mean lifeblood. They probably use lifeblood in their spells and wards. Fantastic. What about the other group?"

Cait raised her hands apologetically. "I don't have a name for the larger harnad, so I've been referring to it as H2. They appear to be the more active of the two groups, with an estimated fourteen members."

I was floored. "Fourteen?" It was unusual for a harnad to be so large. That many high-level blood mages tended to result in a lot of egos battling for control and influence. Large harnads inevitably split into smaller ones, often with one faction taking out the others in spectacular fashion. I thought of John West drawing on the combined power of a dozen blood mages and felt dizzy.

Mark spoke. "Do we have any idea who the leaders of these harnads are?"

Cait shook her head. "I don't. As you might imagine, it's hard to find anything out beyond rumors. I've been digging, looking for names, but I have to be careful. The last thing I want to do is tip someone off we're onto them."

"I second that," I said. "We don't want to show our hand before we're ready to make a move. If the trail leads to H2 and we think they're behind the disappearances, we may have to act fast to have a chance of finding survivors, assuming there are any."

"Especially since we appear to be on our own with our suspicions about H2," Cait said.

I got up to get a refill on my coffee. "We may not be totally alone on that one." I told her about Lake without identifying him by name and returned to the table. "So we may have one ally at SPEMA. If we get some hard evidence they can act on, we might be able to sic the feds on H2."

"It would likely be a bloodbath," Cait said grimly.

I felt a sharp bolt of anxiety at the thought of Lake in the middle of a battle between SPEMA and H2 and wondered what the hell was wrong with me. I had no reason to worry about Lake. I told myself it was just the thought of anyone going up against high-level blood mages and left it at that.

"If we can't find probable cause for SPEMA, what is the Court prepared to do?" I asked Mark. The Court, unlike SPEMA, didn't need PC to act.

Mark and Cait exchanged a look. "That I am not sure about," Mark told me. "As usual, the vamps are pretty tight-lipped about their planning. I've spoken to Valas, and the impression I get is the Court is prepared to go in with their own forces if they believe it necessary."

I gaped. "You spoke with Valas directly?"

"In person," he said wryly. "It was not an experience I would care to repeat."

Valas was the head of the Vampire Court. Her age was unknown, but she was rumored to be more than a thousand years old and absolutely terrifying. I gulped.

"Normally, when the Court has work for me, I meet with one or more of their enforcers. Sometimes I meet with one or two of the Court if it's a particularly sensitive case. At this meeting, there were *four* Court vamps, plus Valas." Mark was grimmer than I'd ever seen him. "That should tell you how seriously they're taking this."

"And now we've got another complication," Cait said. "As if it wasn't bad enough already."

"What's that?" I asked.

"There may be another victim," Mark said. "Number twenty-nine."

She looked at him in surprise. "Twenty-nine? I thought the count was at twenty-seven."

Mark gave her the two new names I'd gotten from Lake and she made a note.

"When did this latest victim go missing?" I asked.

"Two days ago," Cait told me. "We're not sure yet if it's connected, but I've got a feeling it is. If that's true, it's a new victim profile."

"What's her name?" I dug out my list of victims as someone knocked on the door.

"Come in," Mark called. As the door swung open, he said to me, "Her name is Felicia Lowell."

"Who is she?" I asked him, writing the name at the bottom of my list.

"She's one of mine." The voice from the doorway was tense, deep, and very familiar.

I froze and looked up at the newcomer. He wore a blue button-up shirt and khakis. Dark eyes, lit from within with a soft golden glow, met mine as we stared at each other.

"Hello, Alice," he said finally.

Sean.

7

MARK AND CAIT STOOD AND MY FORMER BOSS MOVED TOWARD SEAN, HAND outstretched. "Mr. Maclin, welcome to MDI. Thanks for joining us here today."

Sean shook Mark's hand, then Cait's. "Call me Sean. Thank you for the invitation."

As Sean turned to me, I rose and held out my hand. Without hesitation, he took it. His skin was warm, his grip strong. His eyes swept over me and his mouth tightened. "It's good to see you," he said.

"You too," I murmured.

Mark looked back and forth between us. I got the distinct feeling I was going to have to answer some questions later. "Coffee?"

"Please," the werewolf said, his eyes on me. "Black."

Mark moved to the side table and I went back to my chair. Sean took the empty chair on Mark's right, leaving me alone on my side of the table. I busied myself digging in my bag for a bottle of water, while Mark brought Sean coffee and reseated himself across from me.

"We were just about to tell Alice about Felicia's disappearance," Mark told Sean as I took a long drink from my water bottle, wishing it were something stronger. "Since you're here, why don't you tell her what you know?"

Sean turned his attention to me. I took a deep breath and met his gaze. The only way to get through this was to be impersonal. If there was one thing I could do well after twenty years of torment at the hands of my grandfather, it was compartmentalize. If Sean was struggling with his emotions over seeing me, I saw no sign of it.

"Felicia is only twenty-three," Sean said. "She's unmated and has no boyfriend at the moment. Her father was killed by the alpha of their former pack, and she and her mother and younger brother came to us about four years ago. She's a substance abuse counselor with a degree in social work."

I made notes as he talked. "Where does she work?"

Sean named a local clinic. "She also does a lot of outreach. Some of her clients work on South Elm."

"Ah." I glanced at Mark. "A possible connection. She disappeared two days ago?"

"Yes," Sean said heavily. "When she didn't arrive at work as expected, her boss called her mother, who called me, and we went to her apartment. Her car and purse were there but her phone was gone and so was her house key. Nan—Felicia's mother—noticed exercise clothes seemed to be missing. It looked like maybe she went for an early morning run before work and never returned."

"Did you call the police?"

Sean's anger sizzled on my skin. "We did, and we were told an adult can go missing whenever they want. Since there was no sign of foul play, the detective told Felicia's mother she could file a missing persons report once forty-eight hours had passed. We hit forty-eight hours at nine a.m. this morning. Nan is at the police station as we speak, filling out the paperwork and speaking to a detective, but I don't think the police are going to do a damn thing about it. When they heard Felicia was a shifter, they went from marginally interested to not interested at all."

His eyes bored into mine. "When I realized Felicia has been working with clients down on the Stroll, I wondered if her disappearance could be connected. I'd heard about the Court hiring an investigator, and I contacted Mark last evening."

"The circumstances are eerily familiar," I told Mark.

"Too familiar," he agreed. He looked at Sean. "Are you able to sense her through the pack bonds?"

Sean shook his head. "No, and neither can Nan or David, her brother. I can't tell if she's behind a ward or if she's dead." Anger rolled off him and I rubbed my arms as the prickling intensified.

"If Felicia was taken by the same person or persons, it's a serious escalation," I pointed out. "They were averaging one victim every two weeks before. It was only one week between the most recent known victim and Felicia's disappearance."

"None of the other victims are shifters as far as we know," Mark pointed out.

"The fact that she's a shifter might be a coincidence," I replied. "Maybe someone spotted her down on the Stroll, followed her home, and watched for an opportunity to snatch her. It's the complete change in victim profile that's bothering me. They've jumped from high-risk, low-profile victims to a very different type of target—someone who would immediately be missed and led a low-risk lifestyle."

"Regardless, I want her found." Sean turned to Mark. "My pack and my security company are at your disposal."

"Thank you," Mark said.

"Do you have any leads?" Sean asked.

"We have some, but no clear direction right now. We got some new information last night, but it's going to require some investigation before we know if it's going to be of any help."

"I've got some of my people canvassing the area around her apartment for witnesses. Other than that, what can I do?"

Mark glanced at me. "Alice, do you want to look through Felicia's apartment to see if you can find anything that might help us?"

I nodded. "I'll go."

"I'll take you," Sean said.

"Great." I'd been aiming for a neutral tone, but what came out sounded closer to grim resignation.

"Let me know what you find." Mark finished off his coffee. "In the meantime, I'm going to look into what you and I were talking about earlier."

We rose from the table and Sean shook hands with Mark and Cait again. "Thank you for your assistance," he told them.

We filed toward the door. Mark opened it and gestured for Sean and Cait to go ahead. When I started to leave, Mark held up his hand. "One minute?"

"Sure," I said.

Mark closed the door, isolating us in the conference room while the others waited outside. "So, an ex."

"Something like that," I said with a sigh.

"Was it Maclin who tangled with Vaughan in your house?"

"Yes."

My former boss shook his head ruefully. "An alpha werewolf and a member of the Vampire Court tried to tear each other apart over you. And to think, you used to lead such a quiet life."

I glared at him. "That's not what happened. The fight was at my house, but it was wasn't *over* me."

"It sure sounds like it was." Mark held up his hands to stave off my angry retort. "Fine. Forget that. Are you going to be okay working with him?"

"Of course," I lied. "You know me; I'm all business. Are we done?"

"We're done." Mark watched as I opened the door and stepped into the hall, where Sean and Cait waited.

"Let's roll," I said to Sean, and headed down the hall toward the lobby. The others followed.

In the reception area, a tall, gray-haired woman waited by Marian's desk. It was Sharon, Mark's wife.

"Alice, welcome back." She left a stack of papers on the counter and approached me with a forced smile. "It's good to see you."

"You too, Sharon." Cait and Mark walked to the front doors, talking quietly. Sean waited next to me. "How have you been?"

"Fine, thanks for asking." Sharon's cool blue eyes watched her husband exit the building with Cait, presumably walking the researcher to her car while they finished their conversation.

As the doors closed, Sharon's smile disappeared. "You hurt him," she told me.

Sharon and I had always gotten along well before I left MDI, but it looked like those days were long gone. "That wasn't my intention," I said.

Marian was typing away at her computer, but she was obviously listening. I strongly disliked airing dirty laundry in public, but I doubted Sharon would let us move this to a private area.

"Whether it was your intention or not, that's what happened." Sharon crossed her arms. "You were more than an employee to him. He thought of you like a daughter, and you repaid him by walking away. He may have forgiven you, but I haven't."

"I'm sorry to hear that. For what it's worth, I only left because I had to. I'm grateful to Mark for everything he did for me."

"You had a strange way of showing it." Sharon regarded me. "I told him to find someone else for this, someone he could trust. He told me if I thought for one minute you wouldn't have his back, I didn't know you at all."

That sounded like Mark. "I have his back and he has mine. You have my word."

"Since I've had no luck talking him out of hiring you, I suppose that's the best I can ask for. But if anything happens to him on your watch, it's me you'll answer to."

I was starting to think this was about more than just me leaving Mark's firm, but I didn't have time right now to figure out what was behind her antagonism. "Don't threaten me, Sharon. I gave you my word and I meant it."

The front door opened and Mark came into the lobby. Sharon smiled fondly at her husband. "You get everything squared away with Cait?"

"For now." Mark looked back and forth between us. "Everything okay in here?"

"We're fine," Sharon told him.

"Just catching up," I added and glanced at Sean. "Ready to head out?"

His eyes shone gold, probably from the tension in the air. "More than ready," he said gruffly.

Mark and I shook hands. I promised to let him know what we found out, and Sean and I exited the building.

As we walked toward the parking lot, Sean asked, "Do you want to ride with me to the apartment? I can bring you back after."

"I'd rather follow you in my car. I'm not sure where I'll need to go once we're finished there." More to the point, I did not want to share a vehicle with him.

"Suit yourself, if you think you can keep up." His voice had a note of humor. He reached into his pocket for his keys and a large black SUV with heavy-duty rims beeped.

"I think I can manage to follow that tank," I said dryly. "You trade in the Mercedes?"

"Company vehicle."

"Oh. Well, see you there." I turned to walk to my Toyota, fishing around in my bag for my keys.

"Alice."

I paused, my back to him. "What?"

"Have you been sick?" he asked quietly.

"Something like that." I found my keys and started walking again. "Let's just get this over with." I unlocked my car. Behind me, Sean got into his SUV.

While I was waiting for him to back out of his parking spot, I reached into my bag and pulled out my sunglasses. "Stay cool; keep it together," I told my reflection in the rearview mirror. "Get through this, and you can go home and open that bottle of Glenfidditch you've been saving for a special occasion." It sounded like a good bargain.

Felicia Lowell's apartment was in a small complex in a quiet neighborhood on the north side. Sean unlocked the door and entered first, stopping just inside the threshold to sniff the air. "Someone's been here. I smell cigarettes and perfume."

I inhaled but didn't smell anything. Werewolf noses were far superior to human ones. "I didn't see any sign of forced entry, but you said her house key was missing. They probably just let themselves in. Does anything look different from when you were here the other day?"

He frowned. "I'm not sure. Let me look."

While Sean prowled around, I looked over Felicia's apartment. The living room was cluttered but not messy, with a sofa, papasan chair, coffee table, and small television on a stand with stacks of DVDs next to it. The coffee table was piled with health and travel magazines, and I saw a notepad with a list of possible vacation destinations.

It was evident from the contents of her kitchen that Felicia was a healthy eater. She did a lot of shopping at farmer's markets, judging by the fresh produce and meats in the fridge, all of which would be going bad in the next few days. Everything I saw indicated she'd had no plans to leave for any length of time.

When I returned to the living room, Sean was on his phone. "So you don't have it." He listened for a few moments, looking grim. "I'm sorry, Nan. I know this just makes things worse. Stay home with David. I'll let you know what we find out." He ended the call.

"What's missing?"

"Felicia's laptop and bag are gone. All of her notes for work are on the laptop, according to Nan."

"That definitely makes it sound like she was specifically targeted, possibly for something she knew or something related to her work, so this very well might be unrelated to the other disappearances."

"That's a possibility," he acknowledged. "We installed a camera across the street yesterday to keep an eye on the apartment. I didn't have anyone watching the live feed, but we should have video of whoever came in here. I'll get someone to check the video."

I blinked in surprise. "Wow. Excellent. How did you manage that?"

"We got permission from the homeowner in exchange for installing a motion-sensor light on his garage."

We stared at each other. I wondered what he was thinking and wondered why I cared.

"You—" he said.

"So—" I began at the same time.

"Go ahead," he told me.

I shook my head and headed for the bedroom. "Forget it. I'm going to keep looking around for anything that might help us while you call about the footage."

"Alice, wait."

I paused in the doorway as he joined me. My nose filled with his familiar scent, which for some reason my brain had labeled "forest." He didn't touch me, but I sensed his warmth from a foot away. I remembered the feeling of that hot skin against mine. It had been good, for as long as it had lasted.

The silence stretched out between us.

"What?" I asked finally.

"*Have* you been sick? You've lost so much weight, I barely recognized you. Your scent is different, and you seem almost...fragile."

"I'm not fragile." I flipped on the light and went into Felicia's room. "I'm a lean, mean, crime-fighting machine. I helped catch two convenience store robbers last night."

"That was you, down on Ninth?" Sean sounded surprised. "It was on the news this morning."

"Yeah, I know. I certainly didn't want to make the news. At least they didn't use my name." I started looking through the nightstand. Pens, notepads, miscellaneous junk. Nothing that looked like a flash drive or handwritten notes.

"Since when are you a vigilante? The police said they were high on Black Fire. You could have been killed."

I closed the top drawer and opened the next one. "I can take care of myself. They're in jail and I'm fine."

Sean growled. "You are *not*—"

I slammed the drawer closed, making the bedside lamp wobble. "Don't you have some phone calls to make?"

Sean turned on his heel and stalked out. I took a deep breath and exhaled as he left the apartment, not quite slamming the door on his way out.

I rolled my shoulders to relieve the tension that had been building since he walked into the conference room and refocused on searching Felicia's room. The sooner we finished looking through the apartment, the sooner I could get back to my house and that bottle of Scotch.

By the time Sean returned ten minutes later, I was sitting cross-legged on the couch, flipping through a legal pad filled with writing. "What's that?" he asked, his voice businesslike.

My response was equally impersonal. "It was the only thing I found in the bedroom that looked like it might be helpful. It was between the bed and the nightstand. I think it fell back there and whoever was in here didn't see it. It looks like case notes."

"Good work."

"Thanks."

Sean held up his phone. "I have someone back at the office looking through the footage from the surveillance camera. Hopefully we'll have something we can look at soon."

"Good."

"Anything interesting in there?"

"Nothing I can see. These notes are from the last couple of weeks, a record of what she and her clients talked about during counseling sessions." I made a face. "I'm not sure it's legal or ethical for me to be looking at these."

"No one needs to know about it. We'll make sure those notes are kept safe and given back to Felicia."

I said nothing to that, but I could tell from the look in Sean's eyes he didn't think that was likely to happen. If Felicia had been taken because of something she knew, then as soon as they had her work files, her usefulness would probably be at an end.

Sean paced around the apartment and sent a half-dozen texts and e-mails while I read through Felicia's notes. I did my best to ignore him, but his restlessness and the constant buzzing of his phone grated on my already frayed nerves.

Just as I was about to suggest he take a walk outside, Sean read an incoming text and came over to me. "We've got footage."

"Can we watch it here?"

"Yes." Sean sat next to me on the couch. He opened the video and the screen filled with a black-and-white image of the front of Felicia's apartment.

Despite the low light, the video was surprisingly clear. A few cars went by, as well as a couple of joggers. For a moment, nothing happened.

Then I saw her.

She was slim and medium height, wearing jeans, a light-colored shirt, and sneakers, her blonde hair pulled up in a ponytail and face hidden by a baseball cap. She approached the apartment from around the corner, walking briskly. As we watched, she went directly to Felicia's door, unlocked it, and slipped inside. I noted the time: 6:48 p.m. yesterday evening.

Sean fast-forwarded the video. Lights went on and off in the apartment as she searched it room by room. Finally, at 7:12, the door opened again and she emerged from the apartment with a black computer bag over her shoulder. She locked the door and headed for the sidewalk.

"I can't see her face," Sean grumbled. "That damn cap."

"Come on, come on, look up," I chanted under my breath as the woman reached the sidewalk and started walking.

A dark car stopped at the curb next to her. She went to the back door, opened it, handed the bag to someone in the back seat, and got in.

"There!" I pointed at the screen. "When she starts to get in the car. Can you zoom in?"

Sean paused the video and used the slider to run the video back. He zoomed in until the woman's half-obscured face filled the screen, then advanced the video frame-by-frame to the moment she looked toward the camera.

I sucked in a breath.

"Do you know her?" Sean demanded.

I held out my hand. He gave me the phone and I looked at it more closely. I knew her, all right. "Can you send me that image?"

Sean took his phone back, took a screenshot of the woman's face, then opened his text messages. A few moments later, my phone beeped.

I dug my phone out of my bag. The screen said *Wolf - 1 New Message*. I opened the message and looked at the photo he'd sent.

"Who is this woman?" Sean wanted to know.

"Her name is Rachel. I met her last night down on the Stroll. Here she is at seven o'clock, breaking into Felicia's apartment. I saw her a little after nine. She said she was scared, Sean. I *felt sorry* for her, and the whole time she was part of it." My voice shook with anger.

"Well, this indicates that somehow Felicia *is* connected to the other disappearances." Sean tapped his phone on his leg. "Now we've got something to go on."

I bit my lip thoughtfully. "Let me see your phone again."

Sean handed me his phone. I returned the video to its standard zoom, then ran it back to when Rachel was walking on the sidewalk. I watched the car pull up, Rachel get in, and the car pull away from the curb and disappear out of the frame. Then I ran it back and watched it again.

"What are you thinking?" Sean asked.

I paused the video, adjusted the zoom until it showed the best view of the car, and handed the phone back. "Does that look like a black BMW to you?"

Sean frowned and looked closely at the car. "Can't see the badge or the license plate from this angle, but the body shape and color look right. Traffic cams in the area might be able to get a better picture. I know someone who could help with that."

"Cyro?" I smiled a little at Sean's look of surprise. "I'm not likely to forget him, since he helped save my life." His mysterious hacker friend had tracked my cell phone when I'd been badly injured, and led Sean to me just in time.

"Who do you know who drives a black BMW?"

My smile faded as I debated what to say. Mark's contract with the Vampire Court forbade us from sharing information with anyone outside the investigation. Until I was told otherwise, I'd have to keep my suspicions about who might be driving the Beemer to myself.

"I need to talk to Mark," I told Sean.

Gold rolled over his eyes and my arms prickled from the force of his anger. "Felicia's life is at stake. This is no time for games."

"Don't accuse me of playing games with people's lives," I snapped, rising. "Whatever else you may think of me, that is one thing I have never done and will never do." My grandfather played games with lives. People were disposable to him. I might have been forced to kill for Moses, but lives meant something to me.

He stood and raised his hands. "Whatever else I—Alice, what do you think I think of you?"

"You made it pretty clear what you thought of me the last time we spoke. You called me irrational."

"And you called me a bully and worse for offering to replace the furniture I broke fighting with Vaughan," he countered.

"You didn't offer to replace it. You *told me* you were going to replace it. There's a difference!"

"I could have phrased it better, but you overreacted and I think you know that." He sighed. "Neither of us handled the situation well that day. I'm used to taking care of things and you're used to doing everything for yourself, but it shouldn't have ended the way it did. Maybe this is a chance for us to try again."

I rubbed my face. I didn't know if I wanted to try again, and I didn't have the energy right now to try to figure it out. "I'm going back to talk to Mark. It will be up to him and our contract with the Court to decide how much he passes on to you."

"Alice—"

"If you want to help, call Cyro and see if he can hack the traffic cams and get us more shots of that car leaving the neighborhood so we can confirm whose vehicle it is. Forget calling the cops about the break-in; if it's who I think it is, this is way above their pay grade. Mark and I will take care of it."

"Damn it, wait a minute."

"Take the notes. I don't see anything in here worth killing someone over." I tossed the notepad on the coffee table and headed for the door.

He moved in front of me. "Alice, let's talk."

"Let's not." I started to walk past him and we collided, knocking me off balance and into the door.

Sean grabbed my arms to steady me. "Listen to me," he began.

I was thrown against the wall hard enough to make my teeth rattle. Fingers dug into my shoulders and a cry of pain escaped before I could hold it back. My grandfather's livid face was inches from mine. "Listen to me, you stupid girl!"

Panic surged. I struck out with both hands, hitting Sean in the chest with a burst of magic. He stumbled backward, fell over the coffee table, and landed on the couch, looking surprised.

"Don't touch me. Get away." My voice sounded strangled. I bent over and put my hands on my knees as I struggled to get a breath.

"You're hyperventilating. Try to breathe slowly." He got to his feet but stayed back to give me space.

When I looked up, Sean's eyes blazed with anger that wasn't directed at me. "I'm sorry. I should have realized," he said.

"Should have realized what?" I asked raggedly.

He rejoined me at the door, his face grave. "I recognize that look in your eyes, that reaction. I've seen it in shifters who've been abused. You had a flashback. You have PTSD."

I turned and reached for the doorknob. "I'm leaving. Whatever else you need or find out, you can talk to Mark about it."

"You're still a pack associate."

I stilled.

"As the alpha of the Tomb Mountain Pack, I call on you to aid me in our search for Felicia." Sean's voice was brisk.

I gritted my teeth and turned to face him. "I'm looking for her anyway, for the Court. She's part of the case we're working. I report to Mark, not you."

"Your agreement with my pack predates your contract with MDI and the Court. I'll be happy to pull the paperwork if you want."

"What are you hoping to accomplish?" I demanded.

"I intend to use all of the resources at my disposal to find Felicia. I need your help."

"I would have helped you anyway." I opened the door and stepped outside. "I hereby submit my thirty days' notice that I am rescinding my status as pack associate."

"Duly noted. I'll need that in writing, of course. Until then, you are obligated to assist my pack in its time of need, to the best of your ability, as per our agreement."

"Fine." I headed for my car as Sean locked up the apartment.

"Where are you going?" he called to me as I walked.

"I'll meet you back at MDI." I needed a few minutes to myself to figure out how to deal with this unexpected development, and with the way my stomach fluttered every time I looked at him. I also needed coffee, and lots of it. Fortunately, I knew where to find a good coffee shop on the way, but I suspected the rest of the answers would be harder to come by.

8

"So, let me get this straight." Mark sat back in his chair and stared at us across the conference table. "One of the women you spoke with last night appears to be working with the kidnappers, we may have another BMW sighting, and my investigator was just hijacked away from me."

"I'm not hijacking her," Sean said from the seat on my right. "Alice still works for you. As an associate of my pack, Alice is part of our search for Felicia, and my *colleague*."

I shot him a withering look, which he ignored. When we'd worked together during the Amelia Wharton case, I'd referred to him as my "colleague" and it looked like he was not above throwing that back in my face.

"Your prior agreement creates a clear conflict of interest for her." Mark turned to me. "You should have disclosed you were a pack associate, Alice."

"I'm sorry. To be honest, I didn't even remember I was." After our fight, I'd stuffed Sean's letter identifying me as a pack associate in a drawer in my seldom-used office and forgotten about it.

"I want to be included in your debriefings so I can assist in the investigation," Sean told Mark.

"Our contract with the Vampire Court is very specific about who has access to what information. The Court approved Alice's involvement, but not yours."

"Check your e-mail," Sean said.

Mark frowned and reached for his phone.

Sean settled back in his chair. "Last night, I contacted the Court and spoke to Niara, asking for the Court's assistance if Felicia's case was connected to the disappearances down on the Stroll. The Court agreed to pool resources if it turned out I was right."

Mark was reading something on his phone, his expression dark.

"On the way here from Felicia's apartment, given what we saw on the surveillance video, I spoke to Juliet LaRoche, Niara's daytime representative, and confirmed Felicia's disappearance is undeniably connected. As you can see, the Court has amended your contract so I can be an active part of the investigation."

"'At the discretion of the lead investigator,' it says," Mark said, looking up. "Which is me. I don't like your power plays, Maclin, and I don't need this case to be any more difficult than it already is. And I certainly don't need my best investigator distracted in the field when we've got so many lives on the line."

They stared at each other. Sean's eyes shone gold. Mark's face was stony.

Well, this was getting us nowhere. I cleared my throat. "Gentlemen."

A heartbeat later, Mark's gaze shifted to me. "Yes, Alice?"

I'd had time to think about the situation during my drive to MDI. Once the anger wore off and I set aside my personal feelings about Sean—no small task—it occurred to me we could use this development to our advantage. "Whether we like it or not, Sean's got access to some resources that might help us."

"We have resources," Mark said stubbornly.

Sean crossed his arms. "I have a hacker who's in the city's traffic camera system as we speak, tracking that black BMW. I'm assuming that's information you'd like to have."

I sighed. "Oh, cut it out, you two. Let's be adults here. Mark, Sean has access to a hacker who can get into anything anywhere, a security company with state-of-the-art surveillance equipment, and a pack of werewolves who want to know what the hell happened to one of their own. Is he an asset, or not?"

"He would be," Mark said grudgingly. "*If* he doesn't pull any more of this going-over-my-head bullshit, and he signs some paperwork."

I turned to the werewolf next to me. "Sean, Mark is the Court's primary investigator. He's the best MPI in the city, and he knows how to run an investigation far better than you or I. Will you follow his lead?"

Sean frowned, then nodded.

I looked at Mark. "Will that do?"

"That'll do." Mark called Marian to bring the necessary forms to the conference room. Then he sat back in his chair and looked at Sean. "Well, here's what we know."

"Are you hungry?" Sean asked, turning out of MDI's parking lot and easing into traffic.

"No." I checked my e-mail on my phone and found an inquiry from a prospective client who needed wards around her home. I forwarded it to Mark to give to one of his people. I had a feeling this case was going to occupy one hundred percent of my time for the foreseeable future.

A message arrived from Mark containing a six-photo lineup of older white males I could show Danielle, to see if she could identify John West as the driver of the BMW who picked up Missy Daniels on the night of the fifteenth. It was probably a long shot to hope Danielle would be able to recognize him, but if Cyro didn't come through with info on the BMW seen leaving Felicia's apartment, her I.D. might be our only way of linking West to the disappearances.

"We need to eat," Sean said. "I've been going since before sunrise. There's a Moe's on the way. Do you want a burger?"

I looked up from my phone, irritated. "Sean, I just said I'm not hungry."

He set his jaw and drove on.

Now that he was part of the investigation with the Court's blessing, I'd had no choice but to declare a truce. I'd reluctantly agreed to share a vehicle for the afternoon, but I didn't want to be harassed about eating. I got enough of that from Malcolm.

I texted Mark to see if we had a last name and address for Rachel yet. I was impatient to go after her, but we needed a place to start. Zara—whom I'd woken up with a text message—had no idea where she lived. She said she'd ask around, but most of the women she knew would be asleep for a while yet after working all night. Mark was contacting a friend in Vice who might be able to find her through arrest records. If that didn't work out, maybe Cyro could find her.

"Can I meet Cyro?" I asked.

Sean glanced at me. "Why?"

"I've never met a hacker," I confessed. "I guess I'm just curious. What does 'Cyro' mean, anyway?"

"It's short for Cyanide Rose. I'll ask, but I doubt it will happen. Cyro's not very sociable. I've never met him."

My eyes widened. "You're kidding."

He shook his head. "He's a black-hat hacker, and wanted by a number of government agencies. He has to keep a low profile."

"How did you two cross paths?"

"Four years ago, a banker hired my company to provide security. About two weeks in, I got a call from an electronically altered voice telling me our client was the CFO for a cabal, which was not something we were aware of or we never would have taken the job. Our client and other key members of the cabal were about to get taken out by a rival and the caller warned me to pull my people out before the hit went down. That call probably saved the lives of four of my people, two of whom were wolves from my pack."

"The caller was Cyro?"

"Yes. After that, we developed a good working relationship. He charges a fortune, but he always delivers." Sean turned into the drive-thru at Moe's.

"Have you ever tried to track him down?"

"No. I doubt I could, anyway." He pulled up to the speaker and rolled down his window. "Last chance for a burger."

The smell of food made my stomach growl. I relented. "Small cheeseburger, no onions."

Sean ordered for us. When he pulled around to the window, I waved a couple of dollar bills at him. He frowned at me.

"Take it," I said crossly. "You're not buying my lunch."

With a sigh, he took the money and handed his credit card to the girl at the window. He passed me two paper bags filled with burgers and fries and we resumed our drive toward Danielle's apartment. I handed him burger number one and unwrapped my own.

By the time we arrived at Danielle's apartment at Eleventh and Maple, he had finished his werewolf-sized lunch, minus the couple of fries he'd let me sneak while he pretended not to notice.

The two-story building looked like a converted motel, with a trash-and-slime-filled hole where a pool had once been and clothes draped over the second-floor balcony railing. The windows of the office were boarded up, the door padlocked.

"You got the lineup from Mark?" Sean asked as we headed up the metal stairs to the second floor.

"Yes." I nudged a bag of trash out of the way, sending it rolling down the steps to the sidewalk below. "Oops."

Suddenly, something cold hit me in the chest, and I fell backward with a yelp. I heard disembodied laughter as I clawed desperately for the railing and missed.

Sean grabbed my wrist and jerked me upright, saving me from tumbling down the steps. "What the hell happened?" he demanded.

Wincing, I pulled free of his grip and rubbed my wrist as I looked around, but the telltale cold sensation was gone. I was sure of two things: first, it was the same poltergeist I'd sensed the night before on the Stroll, and second, it had just tried to seriously injure or kill me.

When I didn't immediately respond, Sean came down several steps so he could look me in the eye. "Are you all right?"

I thought about telling him about the ghostly attack, then decided against it. We weren't a couple anymore, but as an alpha, Sean's instincts would compel him to try to protect me anyway. Until I knew why this spirit was pursuing me, I didn't want to involve anyone else. There was nothing he could do about it in any case, and poltergeists had notoriously short attention spans. It would probably move on to another target soon enough.

"I'm okay. I tripped. Thanks for the save." I held onto the railing in case the poltergeist came back for another try as we continued our climb up the steps.

"Did I hurt your wrist?" he asked.

"No," I fibbed. It was throbbing and I could see finger marks where he'd grabbed me, but I preferred that mild discomfort over an ass-over-teakettle fall down metal stairs to a concrete sidewalk.

From the top of the stairs, we navigated a maze of trash, chairs, and broken glass to get to apartment 208 at the far end. The area in front of Danielle's apartment was swept clean and there were a couple of cheerful potted plants in her window. I knocked on the door.

We waited, but there was no answer. "She's probably still asleep." I knocked again, louder.

"Y'all looking for Danielle?"

We turned. The door to apartment 207 was open and a woman in a Seahawks T-shirt and cutoffs leaned against the doorway.

"We are," I said. "I know she's probably still asleep, but I really need to talk to her."

"She's not there. She didn't come home last night."

"Are you sure?" Sean asked.

"I'm sure. I usually hear her come in." She pointed to Danielle's front window. "And she always puts her plants outside when she gets home."

"Is it unusual for her not to be home by now?" I asked.

"Yep," the neighbor said. "Especially during the week. Weekends, she might work later in the morning and then get some breakfast with friends, but she'd be home by now even then. I've been calling her phone, but it's off. I'm actually kind of worried."

My stomach churned. "Can I get her number from you?"

"Sure. Hang on." The neighbor disappeared into her apartment and came back out with her cell phone. She read me the number and I tried calling it. The call went straight to voice mail. I left Danielle a message to call me.

I got the neighbor's name—Ashley—and gave her one of my cards. "Please ask her to give me a call on my cell. Or if you hear anything, or see anyone snooping around her place, please call me."

"Will do." Ashley stuck my card in her pocket. "Y'all take care." She went back into her apartment and closed the door.

Sean and I looked at each other. "This is not good," I said. "Rachel was there last night when Danielle described Missy getting into the BMW. What if Rachel told whoever she's working with that Danielle might be able to I.D. the driver and they took her?"

"There could be a lot of reasons why she's not home, but either way, Rachel's our next stop."

"Assuming Mark's got a lead on her." I took out another card, wrote a quick note on the back asking Danielle to call me ASAP, and slid it under the door of apartment 208. We headed back to Sean's SUV.

When we were inside the vehicle, I called Mark to report Danielle's apparent disappearance.

Mark cursed fluently and extensively. "Why didn't you ask her to I.D. West's photo last night?"

I sighed. "Two reasons. I didn't have a lineup to show her, and I didn't want to taint her memory by showing her just a picture of West. Second, I didn't want to tip my hand that we had a potential lead—and that's just as well, since Rachel was standing there listening to us."

Mark grunted. "Those are good reasons. I apologize. I should know better than to second-guess you."

"Do we have anything on Rachel yet?"

I heard Mark shuffling papers on his desk. "I finally got a call back from my friend in Vice. I have a last name—Barrow—and the address she used the last time she was arrested." Mark gave me the address.

"Excellent. We'll head over there now."

"Get a phone number if you can; we can use it to trace her movements," Mark said. "Do we have anything from the hacker yet on the BMW?"

I glanced at Sean, who shook his head. "Not yet," I told Mark. "We'll see if we can find Rachel in the meantime. I'll keep you posted." We said our goodbyes and disconnected.

Sean had already put Rachel Barrow's address into his GPS. He pulled away from the curb as I stuck my phone in the cup holder and buckled in. "It's not far," he said. "Maybe six minutes. How do you want to play it?"

"We'll go easy. I don't want to tip her off that we're onto her. We don't need anyone else doing a disappearing act, especially if she's our only known link to the kidnappers. We're following up on the conversation from last night, asking if anyone knows anything about the two new names I got from Lake. Depending on how it goes, I might mention Danielle to see if Rachel reacts."

"Who's Lake?"

Inwardly, I cursed myself. "Special Agent Trent Lake, of SPEMA," I said reluctantly.

"What does a SPEMA agent have to do with all of this?"

"He's working on the case too."

A muscle moved in Sean's jaw. "And you what, compared notes?"

"Kind of." I didn't like the dark look in Sean's eyes.

"Were you planning on telling me about his involvement?"

"No," I admitted. "Not his name, anyway. He's breaking ranks with his partner and bureau chief on this and I don't want that getting out." I explained how Lake wasn't sold on the vampire angle and was looking into the possibility that a harnad was involved.

"When did you talk to him about this?"

"Last night, after I talked to Danielle and the others on South Elm. We, uh, ran into each other and decided to get a cup of coffee."

"Before or after the convenience store robbery?"

"Before." I rested my elbow on the edge of the window and propped my chin on my hand as we passed through a residential neighborhood.

"How do you and Lake know each other?"

Something told me Sean would not react well to the news Lake had been following me around for a month and I could not tell him about my role in the death of Scott Grierson. "It's a long story."

He stopped in front of a small house with a chain-link fence and an older-model green car parked out front. "Give me the short version."

"What does it matter?"

Sean's shoulders were tense as he unfastened his seatbelt. "Because I want to know who this guy is and why you're sharing sensitive case information with him."

"I didn't say I shared sensitive case information with him," I said icily as I hopped out of the SUV and shut my door. We went through a hinged gate and approached the house via an overgrown sidewalk. "I told him he should look into the harnad angle, based on what Carrie told Zara. I didn't tell him about West or the BMW. And I guess this is the part where I remind you I don't answer to you—I answer to *Mark*. If he has no issue with me talking to Lake, neither should you."

I rang the doorbell. When there was no answer, I tried again. Finally, footsteps approached the door and it opened to reveal a sleepy-looking Rachel wearing a thin T-shirt and tiny shorts.

She blinked at us a few times. When she recognized me, her eyes widened. "Alice? What are you doing here?"

"Sorry to bother you so early," I said. "I'm following up with everyone this afternoon, making sure you got home safely and to ask if you remembered anything after we spoke last night."

Rachel's gaze shifted to Sean, and she smiled. Even without makeup and her hair tousled from rolling out of bed, she still looked good—and then there was the fact she was quite obviously not wearing a bra. Judging by Sean's grin, none of that had escaped his notice.

"And who are *you?*" Rachel asked, leaning against the door frame.

"I'm Mac." Sean held out his hand and they shook.

I cleared my throat. "So, did you remember anything?"

Rachel's eyes were on Sean. "Nope, sorry." She looked him up and down and wet her lips. Sean's grin widened.

I stifled a growl. "We've got two more missing women."

That got her attention. "Who?"

"Do you know anything about Tiana James or Jenny Alvarez?"

Relief flashed in her eyes before she managed to look regretful. "I don't know them," she said, then turned back to Sean. "I'd really like to get to know *you*, though."

Sean produced his phone. "How about you give me your number and we'll get better acquainted?"

Rachel gave him her number. I reminded myself we needed her number for tracking purposes. And why should I care whose numbers he had?

"Why don't you give me your number too?" she asked him. "Just in case you lose mine."

Sean gave her a number different from the one I had. Burner phone, probably.

My phone beeped with an incoming message. I checked it and looked at Sean. "Well, we should get going. We need to check on Danielle."

Rachel's smile faltered. If I hadn't been certain before that she'd had something to do with Danielle's disappearance, I was now. My fingertips tingled.

Rachel shivered and rubbed her arms. "Did you guys feel that wind?"

"Cold front coming through," Sean said with a smile. "You'd better get back inside, where it's warm."

Rachel winked. "Call me, Mac."

"Count on it."

"Bye." Rachel stepped back into the house and closed the door.

We headed back to the SUV. "She's definitely in on it." Sean's voice was low as we went out the gate. "I recognized her scent from Felicia's apartment."

"Mm-hmmm."

"Did you see her reaction when you said there were two new victims?" he continued as he walked around to the driver's side. "She probably thought you were going to say Danielle and Felicia."

I made a noncommittal sound and climbed into the SUV, dropping my bag on the floor and fastening my seatbelt.

Sean turned the key in the ignition. "What's wrong?"

"Nothing. I've got a headache." I rubbed my forehead.

"Too much coffee; not enough food. Should we grab something to eat on the way back? I could go for a couple of doughnuts or a bagel."

I shook my head and held up my phone, where a text message from Mark was displayed. "We need to get back to hear what Mark's got on John West and give him Rachel's phone number so we can keep track of her."

"I already sent the number to Cyro. He's on it."

"Great. Let's get to MDI." I found aspirin in my bag and took a couple with a swig of water.

He pulled away from the curb and accelerated. "You know I wasn't really flirting with her. It was the easiest way to get her number without her suspecting anything."

"Sean, it's fine. Do whatever you need to do to get Felicia back."

He drove for a few minutes. Just as I was starting to relax, he spoke. "So, you were telling me about this Agent Lake."

"I wasn't, actually, but since you won't let it go, the only salient facts are that he's not convinced it's vampires taking women from the Stroll, and that you shouldn't mention him to anyone."

"Those are the only salient facts?" he asked dryly.

"Yep."

"Your scent changes when you talk about him." His voice had a growly edge.

"No, it doesn't." I turned up the volume on the radio and stared out the window. The rest of the drive back to MDI was silent.

9

On paper, John West was a respectable businessman who, despite his age, still ran his investment company and showed no signs of wanting to retire. Thanks to his real estate holdings and investment portfolio, his net worth was estimated to be well over twenty million dollars. Cait reported some irregularities that suggested West was keeping money overseas, probably in the Caymans, but how much she couldn't be sure. Nothing too unusual about a wealthy and financially savvy person hiding wealth in a well-known tax haven, and we were after West for more than tax evasion.

While we were at MDI going over West's background with Mark and Cait, Sean got a response from Cyro consisting of a clear image of the BMW's license plate and a short note stating that no camera angle he'd found so far showed the driver or passengers. The BMW was registered to a shell company called Hampstead LLC, which he had linked back to West.

I'd only needed to see the license plate to know it was West's car. Sean and I had followed him before and I'd seen it parked across the street from Natalie Newton's house after Amelia Wharton's death.

The next step was obviously surveillance, but there we disagreed on how to proceed. Sean suggested a combination of cameras, vehicle trackers, and round-the-clock shadowing, all of which he was willing to provide. With so many lives potentially at stake, however, Mark was understandably worried that any kind of overt surveillance might be noticed and tip West off. We argued about it for a while and got nowhere. Tempers were getting short and Cait departed, leaving us to duke it out.

I'd been doing some serious thinking while Mark and Sean debated. It was several minutes before Mark noticed I'd gone silent. "Alice? What's on your mind?"

I met his eyes. "We need the *sub rosa* ward again."

He murmured the incantation and the ward flared around us.

Sean jumped at the surge of energy. "What was that?"

"Ward of silence, to prevent any kind of eavesdropping." Mark turned to me. "Let's hear it."

"First, I need your word that what I'm about to say won't leave this room."

"You have it," Mark said.

I looked at Sean. "You have my word," he told me.

I told them about Malcolm. Sean already knew about my ghost, but not that he was unregistered or that I was hiding him from not only SPEMA but also Darius Bell's cabal. Both men looked decidedly grim at the news that I was breaking federal law by not registering Malcolm, and their expressions darkened further when I said John West had sensed magic at the construction site that might be Malcolm's own trace.

"Malcolm has multiple layers of strong masking and obfuscation spells," I added. "I believe he's virtually undetectable. Even if someone like a high-level mage did sense him, he feels like the ghost of a low-level water mage."

"Are you suggesting we use Malcolm to surveil West?" Mark asked.

"I'm suggesting we *ask* him to. It's his choice, but if he'll do it, I think it's our best option. If Malcolm keeps enough distance, West won't notice him, and even if he does, he'll assume he's just a passing spirit."

"If West senses him, he might discorporate Malcolm, and that could kill you," Mark pointed out.

"I don't think he'd have any reason to discorporate Malcolm," I said while Sean looked on silently. "Mages sense ghosts all the time. I think the risk is low and it's really on Malcolm's part. If there's a risk of anything, it's that Malcolm's masking spells could be disrupted and if that happened near West, he might recognize Malcolm's magic trace from the construction site."

"And use that trace to find you," Sean said. "There has to be another option. This is too risky."

I cleared my throat. "The risk is mine and Malcolm's to take, if he's willing. I'll head home after this and ask him. If he says yes, I'll get him to West. After that, I'll go back to the Stroll and see if Danielle is there or if anyone saw her last night after I left. If I can figure out when she was last seen, we might get a lead on who took her."

"I'll come with you," Sean said.

I shook my head. "They won't talk to me if you're there."

"I'm not going to sit around doing nothing." Sean looked stubborn.

"Maybe you should call Rachel Barrow," I said.

Sean's eyes narrowed.

"She's part of this," I reminded him. "She broke into Felicia's apartment, stole her laptop, and got in John West's car. She has no magic, so she's not part of his harnad, but for some reason she's helping him. She may know where the missing women are or what happened to them. I can't see a downside to you getting to know her better. Maybe she'll let something slip or you'll see something that might help us. Maybe try to get a look at her phone, see who she's been calling."

Sean was still frowning. "I'm sure they're not dumb enough to contact her on her personal cell phone."

I rose and the others followed suit. "Headed home to talk to your ghost?" Mark asked me.

"Yes. If he's in, I'll need a location on West so I can drop off our spy. Do we have eyes on him at all?"

Mark smiled. "He's at his office now."

Sean made a snarly sound. "I don't like this."

Mark dropped the *sub rosa* ward and opened the conference room door. "Watch your back if you do meet up with Rachel," I told Sean. "If she figures out who you are, you might have someone come looking for you. She already probably sicced someone on Danielle."

"I'll ask her to meet me somewhere to talk, see what I can find out."

"To talk. Okay." I patted his arm. "Have a good *talk* with Rachel, Mac."

Mark snorted and walked down the hall. I started to follow but Sean's hand closed gently on my upper arm, halting me.

"To talk, Alice," he told me quietly as Mark disappeared around a corner. "And that's it. I have no interest in anything else."

"Judging by the way she was looking you over earlier, I'm pretty sure talking is going to be the last thing on her mind." I shook off his hand. "You don't owe me any promises."

Sean crossed his arms. "Maybe not, but I'm giving you one anyway."

I took a step back. "For the record, what you do and who you do it with is none of my business, and vice versa." I turned and walked away. He didn't follow.

Unsurprisingly, despite the danger, Malcolm jumped at the chance to spy on John West. He'd been grumpy about being sent back to the basement the previous night and feeling left out in general, so the promise of some action had him flitting around the basement in excitement.

When we'd first encountered West a month ago, Malcolm had been reluctant to go near the blood mage. In the interim, my ghost sidekick had gained a lot of confidence and layered masking spells. Still, it was a risk for both of us, and I wanted to make sure he understood he had a choice about whether or not to shadow West.

"I understand what I'm risking and I want to do it," Malcolm said firmly. "You said it yourself: odds are even if West *does* sense me nearby he won't think anything of it."

"There's something else." I filled Malcolm in on Felicia Lowell's kidnapping and Sean's subsequent involvement in the case. "As if things weren't complicated enough in my life right now."

"You ask me, you could use some werewolf *complications*."

"What do you mean?"

"Oh, come on," the ghost said impatiently. "The day after the furniture fight, you basically climbed inside a whisky bottle and have been there ever since."

I scowled. "That had nothing to do with him."

"It was mostly from the construction site stuff, sure, but Sean was part of it, too, and don't try to deny it." Malcolm floated closer. "Maybe you shouldn't be so quick to tell him to hit the bricks if he wants to talk. You two had a nice thing going there for a while. He's good for you. And you can't very well blame him for trying to take care of you. He's an alpha. It's what they do."

Time to change the subject. "How about we talk about important things, like how you're going to keep an eye on West without him noticing you're there?"

"I got this, Alice. Just tell me where he is and I'm on it."

I pulled my phone from my pocket and texted Mark. Got a 20 on JW?

MDI: *Home since 1800 hours.*

ME: *Headed there with M to surveil. Alert if 20 changes.*

MDI: *10-4. Good luck and be safe.*

I stuck my phone back in my pocket. "If you sense trouble, get out of there and jump here behind the wards. Don't try to jump to me; protect yourself first."

"I got it," Malcolm said. "No heroics."

I headed for the stairs. "Then let's roll. You've got a blood mage to spy on and I've got some working girls to talk to."

I dropped Malcolm at John West's house with a final reminder to be careful, then went back home for some peace and quiet before I went down to the Stroll. I treated myself to one glass—and one glass only—of my good Glenfidditch as a reward for having to spend the day with Sean and sat out on my back porch, sipping my drink and not wondering if he'd met up with Rachel.

I was too troubled to enjoy either the much-needed break or the whisky and ended up going back inside to read Amanda Bailey's notes on the missing women. Needless to say, my reading material did nothing to improve my mood.

I arrived at Ninth and Elm just after ten o'clock. When I drove past the convenience store, I saw the doors had been repaired and it was open for business, but the clerk inside was not Mario. Unwilling to roll the dice on getting my car towed or stolen, I ended up parking up the street in front of the Midnite Café and ordering a coffee and cherry turnover to go.

As I headed down the street toward the Stroll, Malcolm's comment about Sean being good for me kept rattling around in my head. In moments of honesty, I had to admit I was afraid of the intimacy that had developed between Sean and me and the metaphysical link we'd temporarily shared that allowed us to sense each other's emotions. The problem was, even knowing where and how I'd gone wrong, I had no idea what to do about it.

I'd finished the turnover and most of the coffee by the time I reached Tenth and Elm where Zara was waiting. Tonight, she was wearing a clingy purple dress, her braids tied back with a scarf.

"Hey," the tall woman said as I approached. "I was wondering if you were coming."

"Sorry I'm late. I stopped for coffee."

"Don't worry about it. Some of the girls have left with customers, but we can talk to the ones who are here."

"Have you seen Danielle? I've got a lineup for her to look at, to see if she might recognize the driver of the BMW who picked up Missy Daniels on the fifteenth."

Zara shook her head. "I haven't seen her." She studied me and frowned. "Should we be worried about her?"

"Maybe. I stopped by her apartment earlier today and her neighbor said she didn't come home this morning. I left messages for her to call me and haven't heard anything. Her phone is off."

Zara's face crumpled and she turned away, fighting back tears. "Damn it," she swore, her voice breaking.

I stayed quiet.

Suddenly, she spun to face me. "No one's going to care, are they?" she spat. Tears streaked down her face. "Nobody's going to look for her. She's just going to be gone, like all the others."

"Mark and I are looking. There are others looking too. We'll find them."

Zara shook her head. She sniffed and carefully wiped her eyes with her fingertips.

"When did you last see Danielle last night?" I asked.

She closed her eyes and thought. "It was probably around three. I got picked up by a customer, and she was at Twelfth with a couple of other girls. When I came back about an hour later, she was gone."

"Who was with her?"

"Shonda and Rachel."

Anger flared at the mention of Rachel's name. "Is Shonda here tonight?"

She peered down the street, then pointed. "There she is. I haven't seen Rachel yet, but she'll probably be here."

We walked silently down to Twelfth, then crossed the street to where Shonda was standing with Sarah.

As Zara and I approached, Sarah dropped her cigarette on the sidewalk and ground it out with her boot. "Who is it this time?" she asked tonelessly.

"Danielle, it looks like," Zara said.

Shonda sucked in a breath, and Sarah swore.

"Zara says you saw Danielle last night around three," I said to Shonda.

She nodded somberly. "We were talking, me and her and Rachel. Somewhere around three thirty, a red car came up and waved her over. She went with him. I had a customer not long after that. I didn't see her when I got back. I figured she got another client or she went home."

I pulled out my notebook. "Do you remember anything about the car?"

Shonda thought for a minute. "Two doors, kind of sporty. New-looking. I didn't get a look at the guy."

I wrote down the information. "And this was around three thirty?"

"Yeah, give or take." She looked around. "I don't see Rachel, but she was down here, too, last night, talking to us. Maybe she saw Danielle after that. You could ask her."

"I will if I see her." I kept my voice carefully neutral. "Can you ask around and see if anyone else saw Danielle last night after you did?"

"Sure," Shonda said. Sarah nodded.

"I'm not sure if this is related, but a substance abuse counselor who does outreach down here has recently gone missing," I said. "Do any of you know Felicia Lowell?"

"Felicia's missing?" Sarah asked.

"You know her?"

Sarah gave me a jerky nod. "I see her sometimes. She does free counseling."

I didn't want her to have to reveal anything personal in front of the other women, but they didn't seem surprised to hear Sarah was talking to a substance-abuse counselor. "She apparently went for a run two days ago and never came back," I said. "Her family has filed a missing-persons report."

"Could it be related to what's been happening down here?" Zara asked.

"I don't see how," Sarah said. "What made you ask us about her?"

"We have a mutual friend. He told me she's been doing some outreach work in the area. I figured it was just a coincidence, but I thought I'd ask and see if you guys know her."

"It has to be a coincidence." Sarah lit another cigarette with trembling hands and took a deep drag.

Shonda glanced over my shoulder and waved. "Hey, here's Rachel. You can ask her about Danielle."

I turned. Rachel was walking toward us from the direction of Ninth. She wore a leopard-print miniskirt with a black off-the-shoulder top and platform Mary Janes.

"Hey, girl," Zara said. "How was your date?"

Rachel grinned and tossed her hair. "Mac was fantastic. Funny, gorgeous, so hot. How are you not dating him, Alice?"

Hearing her talk about Sean made my teeth clench. "He's not really my type," I managed to say.

Shonda checked her makeup in a small mirror. "You had a date? Where did you go?"

Rachel waved her hands dramatically. "We went to the Carousel Bar. He bought me wine and we talked for *hours*. It was so romantic. I thought for sure we were going to end up back at his place but he got a text from work and had to leave. Next time, he's not getting away so easily. I'll tie him down if I have to. I could tell he'd totally be into that." As Zara and Shonda laughed, Rachel glanced at me. "Hey, sorry. You probably don't want to hear that about a coworker."

"Yeah, I really don't," I said tightly. And I could have told her there was zero chance Sean would be into that.

Sarah looked at me as if she could sense I didn't want to be having this conversation. "Alice says Danielle is missing."

"Oh my God," the blonde said, clapping her hand to her mouth, her eyes widening in feigned horror. "What happened?"

"I was hoping *you* might know," I said.

Rachel stared at me, fear in her eyes. "Why would *I* know anything?"

"You were talking to her last night, you and Shonda, when she got into a red car around three thirty. Did you see her after that?"

Rachel shook her head. "No. I had a customer too not too long after that and I didn't come back here afterwards. I had him drop me off up on Ninth and I went home."

I was willing to bet Rachel was lying and the driver of the red car was someone affiliated with the harnad, sent to snatch Danielle before she could identify West as the man she'd seen taking Missy.

I gave each of the women one of my cards. "Call me if you hear anything about Danielle or anything else that might help. If you see Danielle, please have her call me."

They promised they would. Rachel stepped away from the group and lit a cigarette, avoiding my gaze. I put my notebook back in my bag, said goodbye, and headed back toward the café.

I wondered what on earth Sean and Rachel could have talked about for hours. I could not imagine two people who were more different. I hoped he'd gotten some useful information, at least.

As if on cue, my phone buzzed. I fished it out of my bag and stared at the screen. *Wolf Calling*. I swiped the green button and resumed walking. "Hello."

"Alice, it's Sean."

The sound of his voice made me feel warm. "Hey. I'm down on the Stroll. I just got done talking with the girls and I'm headed back to my car."

"Want to meet somewhere and go over what we know?"

"I don't have much to report except Danielle's last customer last night drove a sporty red two-door and picked her up at Twelfth and Elm around three thirty this morning. Maybe Cyro can find some traffic cam images of the car, get a license plate." I hesitated. "You get anything useful from Rachel?"

"Not yet."

"What did you do?"

"I put a tracker on her car."

"Mark is going to be pissed."

"She helped kidnap Felicia," Sean growled. "I'm thinking about putting a bug in her house, Dunlap be damned. You don't know how hard it was to sit there and smile at her and pretend to flirt when all I could think about was whether or not Felicia is dead."

"I'm not saying you shouldn't have—" I began.

Icy fingers touched the back of my neck. I gasped and spun around, only to find the sidewalk empty.

A familiar mocking laugh drifted toward me from the direction of an alley off to my right. The poltergeist was back. "*Alissssssss*..."

Cautiously, I followed the sound, my phone forgotten in my hand as I stepped into the shadows. "What do you want?" I demanded. "Show yourself."

No response, but I could feel the poltergeist nearby. If it knew my name, this was no random encounter with a passing spirit.

"Alice!" Sean shouted.

With my eyes on the dark alley in front of me, I raised the phone to my ear. "Gotta go, Sean. I'll see you tomorrow morning."

He spoke quickly. "Do you need help?"

"No. Good night." I hit the red button and stuck the phone in my bag. "What do you want?" I asked again.

"*Alissssssss*..."

The sound came from my left. I turned and slowly lowered my bag to the pavement. "I'm in no mood for games. Either show yourself or—"

Something hit me in the stomach and I doubled over. The same unseen force picked me up and threw me sideways into the building. I hit the wall and dropped to the pavement like a sack of dog food.

Dazed and winded, I managed to roll to my hands and knees just as the poltergeist cackled and slashed my face. My cry of pain was cut off by an icy hand closing on my throat. It dragged me to my feet and smashed my head against the brick wall. Stars exploded in front of my eyes. Hot blood ran down my neck and the gashes on my face burned as the spirit dug its fingers into my throat.

Slowly, the poltergeist appeared. Unlike Malcolm, who looked fully human, she was so close to going wraith that it was difficult to see her features. A female face framed by long, pale hair, with crazed dark eyes, hovered inches from my own. I didn't recognize her.

"Alice," she hissed. "I must kill you."

I finally got enough air to ask, "Why?"

"He says you must be punished." Her fingers tightened on my throat. "He will give me your body and I will live again."

I wanted to tell her it didn't work that way and she'd been lied to, but I doubted I'd have much luck reasoning with her. "Who is he?" I croaked. "Who sent you after me?"

She cackled again. "I'll sleep with your man."

She must have seen Sean with me today at Danielle's apartment. Whatever was going on, I didn't want him dragged into it. "He's not my man."

She squeezed, cutting off my air. "Die, Alice. Die so I can live." Her grip tightened and I felt a sharp pain at the base of my skull. I'd let her manhandle me in hopes of finding out why she was attacking me, but I wasn't going to let her snap my neck.

The blood magic I'd been spooling since the moment she'd grabbed me burst from my hands. It coiled around her like a cage, holding her in place before she could disappear.

She screeched and let go of my throat, thrashing against the magical bonds. The roiling blood magic made my skin feel like it was on fire.

"Tell me who sent you," I commanded.

"*Die!*" She clawed a deep slash across my collarbone. A few inches higher, and she might have severed my jugular. My anger fed the coils and she went berserk, fighting to get at my throat.

I doubted I'd be getting any answers from her now, not in this state. I lowered my shields, looking for a clue as to who sent her after me. Within her, I found a slim black thread, a trace of magic that was dark and powerful. It was also vaguely familiar, as if I'd encountered its source or something like it recently, but couldn't remember when or where. It was not the same as the demon who'd come to my house posing as a city utility worker, but the magic was dark and sulfurous.

The demented spirit flailed against my magic and launched herself at my face, opening another gash on my forehead and barely missing my eyes.

"To hell with this," I snapped. I raked my fingers through the poltergeist's noncorporeal body and tore her apart.

She should have simply dispersed like smoke; instead, the spirit thrashed wildly and let out a piercing shriek that stabbed my eardrums like icepicks. Warm blood trickled out of my ears as her form disintegrated. It seemed to take forever until her scream faded and what was left of her vanished.

When she was gone, I snuffed out my blood magic and slid down the wall as my heart pounded and my ears ached. I'd discorporated more than a dozen poltergeists, but never one who was self-aware enough to feel pain and fear. She was unusually strong and at least moderately coherent, able to agree to attacking a living human on someone else's orders, tracking that person, and understanding the reward she was offered for doing it.

Whoever had sent her after me had funneled energy into her, stabilizing her. It appeared I had made it onto someone's hit list, but other than the magic trace I'd sensed, I had no leads on who it might be or why I had been targeted.

As the ringing in my ears faded, I noticed a loud buzzing. I staggered to my feet, found my bag, and pulled out my phone just as the call went to voice mail. The screen read *Wolf—5 Missed Calls*. I also had two text messages. The first asked if I was all right. The second said if Sean didn't hear from me in the next two minutes, he was on his way to me.

I couldn't fault him for being concerned; I was sure he'd heard me asking who was following me before I hung up on him. If our situation had been reversed, I would have been worried too.

With shaking hands, I tapped out a message: *I'm fine. No backup needed.*

The reply was almost instantaneous. *Wolf: Are you sure?*

Me: Yes. After a hesitation, I added, *False alarm.*

No response for almost a minute. I could imagine Sean on the other end, debating how to answer, whether to come looking for me anyway.

Finally, the phone beeped. *Wolf: Good night then. See you at MDI in the morning.*

I stuck the phone in my bag and stumbled out of the alley. The Midnite Café was on the next block. I slung my bag over my sore shoulder and limped toward the neon lights of the diner. My face burned and my body felt battered and bruised, my ears warm and sticky. Luckily, the sidewalk was deserted and no one inside the diner seemed to notice me.

I dug my keys out of my bag with a shaking hand and unlocked my car. The reflection in my driver's side window revealed three deep gashes across my face and wounds on my throat. My shirt was torn and bloody. I looked exactly as bad as I felt.

As I reached for my car door, an enormous figure wearing black appeared behind me. I dropped my bag and keys and spun around, my right hand erupting in green fire.

Special Agent Lake stared at me, his eyes moving from my face to my fiery hand and back again. "What happened to you?" he demanded.

I took a deep breath and extinguished my cold fire. "Why are you still stalking me?"

He took two steps forward. "I saw your car and figured you were back to talk to witnesses again. I was inside getting some coffee when I saw you walking up."

I pushed on his chest. It was like trying to move a tree. "Back off, Lake. I've had a rough night."

"You've been attacked. Are those knife wounds?" He peered at the side of my head. "Are your *ears* bleeding? What the hell is going on?"

I looked at him and didn't know what to say. For some reason, my usual ability to come up with an easy and convincing lie completely failed me. With Sean, I'd been reluctant to tell him about the poltergeist because I didn't want him to feel obligated to protect me. In Lake's case, I didn't trust him enough to tell him anything about anything.

He put his hand on the car next to my shoulder. "Talk to me, Alice. If you don't want to file a report that's your choice, but I want to know who slashed your face and why you're bleeding out the ears, and why you don't want to say who it was." He stared at me, his eyes full of fury. *Tell me whose ass I need to kick,* his expression said. The air felt heavy between us.

"I fell down some steps," I said lamely.

He stiffened. "Don't lie to me, for once."

"Don't interrogate me, for once."

"I'm not interrogating you."

"Could have fooled me." I leaned back against my car, trying to put some distance between us. "There's no reason for a SPEMA agent to be concerned. I'm going to be fine once I clean up and use a healing spell."

"I'm not asking as a SPEMA agent." His voice dropped and he cupped my face with his hand. "This is me, Trent, asking who hurt you."

"You're never *not* a SPEMA agent." His touch distracted me and I had to remind myself who I was talking to before I leaned into the warmth of his hand. "You have spell cuffs in your back pocket, a gun under your left arm, and another on your right ankle. Your credentials are in your inner jacket pocket. Don't tell me you're just Trent, Agent Lake. You're a fed. Period."

Lake's thumb ran over my bloody cheek and I shivered. "Is that really what you think? That I'm nothing but a badge?"

For almost two months, that was what I'd believed. It was far better for both of us if I continued to think of him that way. "Yes." My voice was almost steady.

The corners of his mouth turned up. "Lying again." He tipped my chin up gently and scrutinized my throat. "These marks look like someone grabbed you by the neck."

I pushed his hand away, but he caught my hand in his. "Let go," I said.

Those ice-blue eyes held mine. "I'm worried about you."

I sighed, my shoulders sagging. "Don't be. I've told you before: I'm nobody. Why you persist in thinking differently is beyond me."

"You are not nobody, Alice." His gaze turned fierce as his grip tightened on my hand. Electricity crackled between us. "No matter how much you try to convince yourself of it."

I needed to get away from him before things got any more complicated than they already were. I freed myself and backed away. "I appreciate your concern, but I'll be fine after I clean up."

I thought he was going to argue, but instead he reached for my door and opened it. "Then go home and patch yourself up. Again." He sounded resigned.

His fingers were bloody from touching my face. "Here," I said. I unbuttoned my shirt and took it off, leaving me in my tank top. I used my shirt to clean his hand as he watched me silently. When I finished, I put the ruined shirt in a plastic grocery bag and tossed it into the back seat. I suppressed a wince as I settled into the driver's seat.

He started to close my door, then paused. "Call me if you want to talk about it."

"Thank you," I said softly. "Good night."

"Good night, Alice." He shut the door and stepped back.

I buckled my seatbelt, turned the key in the ignition, and backed out onto Ninth. I gave Lake a little wave as I passed. He raised his hand, then let it fall back to his side as he watched me drive away.

10

A GOOD NIGHT'S SLEEP MIGHT HAVE DONE WONDERS FOR BOTH MY MOOD AND THE headache I couldn't seem to get rid of, but I tossed and turned all night and woke up for good around six. I rolled out of bed, took some aspirin, and stood in the shower until the pain in my skull faded to a dull throb.

By seven, I was on my way to check in with my ghost. I stopped for coffee on the way and arrived at my destination by seven thirty.

I parked down the street from West's house, turned off the car, closed my eyes, and focused on the familiar trace of blue-green magic in the corner of my brain that was my link to Malcolm. Carefully, I tugged on the thread twice, two gentle pulls that caused a few seconds of disorientation. I breathed slowly and deeply until the dizziness passed.

A few seconds after my "page," I sensed Malcolm's presence as he entered the car. "You're getting better at that," the invisible ghost said from the passenger seat area. "You didn't throw up or pass out this time."

"Hooray." I rubbed my forehead.

"You look terrible," Malcolm informed me, as if I didn't know that already. "Are you not sleeping again?"

"I had a lot on my mind." I drank some coffee. "I take it you don't have anything to report?"

"Nothing. He had no visitors and hasn't left the house. I'd love to know what he was doing, but if I crossed his wards, he'd know. I've been studying them, and I think they would disrupt my masking and obfuscation spells."

"Do what you can from the outside and follow him wherever he goes, unless it involves crossing wards. If we do end up having to get into his house, we'll go in together when we can unweave or break his wards as a team."

"Got it. I'm assuming he'll be leaving for work soon, so I'll tail him and listen in as best I can. No idea where he'll go after work, but I'll stick nearby. Where are you headed now?"

"Over to MDI to talk to Mark and Sean. We'll probably compare notes and then work out a game plan for the day. I don't want to tip West off, so I'll avoid coming by here again. If I don't hear from you, I'll assume that means no news."

Down the street, West's garage door rose and the familiar black BMW backed out toward the street. "There he is," Malcolm said. "I'd better go."

"Be careful, Malcolm."

"*You* be careful. I'm a ghost—there's not much that can hurt me. It's you I worry about."

"I'm fine," I said automatically.

He snorted. "Of course you are." The BMW headed down the street away from us. "Gotta go." I sensed him leave the car, moving off in pursuit of West's vehicle as it paused at the corner, then turned left and disappeared.

Unfortunately, my route from West's neighborhood to MDI took me close to downtown, where the morning traffic was predictably terrible. "I have not had nearly enough coffee to deal with this," I muttered, braking sharply as a man driving a Mercedes SUV cut me off and gave me the finger.

Traffic thinned out as I made it past the downtown area, but it was already past eight and I was late. I caved to temptation and turned into a Starbucks drive-thru, even though it would make me later than I already was. I needed the caffeine and sugar.

When I pulled into the MDI lot at eight twenty, both Sean's company SUV and Mark's truck were already there. With a sigh, I got out of my car and put my bag over my shoulder.

"Morning, Alice," Sean said from behind me.

I yelped and dropped my coffee. It hit the ground and splashed onto my pants and boots. I stared down at the empty cup as it rolled across the pavement.

"Shit." Sean crouched down to pick up the cup. As he stood, he added, "I'm sorry. I didn't mean to startle you. I thought you heard me walk up."

"It's fine," I said wearily.

Sean was wearing an emerald-green polo shirt and black khakis. I tried not to notice how good he looked in green, or how it brought out the gold flecks in his eyes, or the lines of hard muscles beneath the shirt. "Let me get you another cup of coffee," he said. "I'll make a quick run. What did you have?"

"Don't worry about it. Mark's got coffee." I popped my trunk and unzipped the black duffel bag that contained a change of clothes and toiletries.

"I owe you a replacement," he insisted. "And I'll pay for your dry cleaning." He reached for his wallet.

"Really, it's okay. I'll just throw them in the washer when I get home." I pulled out a pair of clean jeans and tucked them into my messenger bag. "Besides, it was my fault for not paying more attention." I shut my trunk and headed for the building.

He fell into step next to me. "I'll owe you a cup of coffee the next time we're out."

"Fair enough."

"What happened last night when you hung up on me?"

I might have known he wouldn't just let it go. "Thought I saw someone following me. Turned out I was just being paranoid."

He didn't say anything for a moment. "Easy to do, in that part of town," he said finally. "Did you not sleep well last night?"

"Yeah, I know I look terrible. Malcolm already told me."

"I didn't say you look terrible."

"That's what 'Did you not sleep well?' means," I said dryly. "But I appreciate your attempt to be diplomatic about it."

Sean tossed the cup into a trash can and reached for the front door. "What kept you awake?"

"Just couldn't sleep."

He pulled the door open and held it for me. "Thinking about the case?"

"Yup." That, and the assorted aches and pains that neither the healing spell nor the aspirin could completely banish, and wondering who had sent a poltergeist to kill me.

We walked into MDI's lobby. Marian was at the front desk. "Mr. Dunlap is in Conference Room Three," she informed us. "He said to send you back when you arrived."

"Thanks," I said.

"I'll let him know that you're on your way back," she said, reaching for the phone.

Sean and I headed down the hall. I stopped at the door to the women's restroom. "Go on ahead. I'll be there in a minute."

"I'll pour you a cup of coffee. Still cream and two sugars?"

"Yup. Find me the biggest mug they have." I pushed open the door to the bathroom. He chuckled as he continued down the hall.

I locked the door to the small bathroom and quickly changed out of my khakis and into the jeans. I wet a paper towel and scrubbed at the coffee stains, but to no avail. I sighed, rolled the pants up, and stuck them in my bag. I used the toilet, washed my hands, and headed for Conference Room Three.

I knocked on the door. Mark called out for me to enter.

Mark and Sean sat on opposite sides of the table, notepads in front of them and coffee mugs in hand. There was a full coffee cup in front of the chair next to Sean. I took a seat and pulled out my notebook.

Mark folded his hands on the table. "Let's hear what you've got."

I guzzled my coffee while I told Mark what I'd found out about Danielle's last known customer and the red two-door car that picked her up.

"I've asked Cyro to look for images of the red car," Sean told us when I finished. "So far, nothing."

I went to the coffee pot for a refill while Sean told Mark about his "date" with Rachel. As I'd predicted, Mark hit the roof when Sean told him he'd put a tracker on her car.

"The tracker is about the size of a quarter," Sean said when Mark stopped swearing. "It's the latest tech. No one's going to detect it unless they have very expensive specialized equipment and I doubt they'd be scanning Rachel's car anyway. She's probably a bit player in all this, but she's the second-best lead I've got for finding Felicia, after West."

"Maclin, you sat here and told me you'd follow my instructions," Mark snapped. "I specifically said we needed to avoid any kind of surveillance that might put the victims at risk, assuming any of them are still alive."

"You and I both know the odds of that are slim to none," Sean said. "And believe me when I say I am well aware of what's at stake here. If Felicia is dead, it will devastate my pack. I have to answer to them for what I'm doing to find her. If it were up to me, we'd be going about this very differently."

Sean's eyes went gold. When he spoke again, his voice had a growly edge. "It took every ounce of my self-control not to take Rachel Barrow out to our pack land last night and do whatever it took to get answers. Instead, I put a tracker on her car, and I'm sitting here with my thumb up my ass while my pack is questioning whether their alpha leads them or serves the Vampire Court."

Mark sat silently as I sipped my coffee and felt guilty for not thinking more about what Felicia's disappearance was doing to Sean and his pack. It would feel like they were missing a limb, especially since Felicia was young and female. If members of the pack were questioning Sean's authority, it could lead to serious trouble.

Finally, my former boss cleared his throat. "I apologize," he told Sean, surprising me. "You're in a difficult position, and I lost sight of that."

Sean gave him a grave nod.

The phone beeped. "Mr. Dunlap?" It was Marian.

Mark picked up the receiver. "What is it?" He listened, then said, "Put her through." He hit the speaker button and put the receiver down. "We have a call from Amanda Bailey."

The phone beeped twice. "Hello?" It was a woman's voice.

"Hello, Amanda," Mark said. "I'm here with two of my investigators, discussing the case."

"I'm glad I caught you," the reporter said. "I know you're busy running down leads, but I just got a call from the Catholic homeless outreach center on Sixth."

Mark's eyebrows rose. "What was the call about?"

"There's some serious concern about some homeless individuals who have gone missing over the past few months," Amanda said. "The nun I spoke to insists someone took them."

I closed my eyes. Next to me, Sean growled low.

"Has she spoken to the police?" Mark asked.

Amanda's voice was bitter. "Of course, several times, but no one will give her the time of day. I know they've got their hands full with the Haze and Black Fire users, but you'd think they'd at least be courteous to a nun. A few weeks ago, she spoke to someone in Major Crimes—a Detective Shay—who came out to talk to her, but she says no one has ever followed up, and Shay won't return her calls. The nun who called me has been following my stories about the missing women in the paper. When she couldn't get any assistance from Detective Shay, she finally called me directly to see if I could help."

Mark tapped his pen on the table. "Do we think this is related to our case?"

"It makes sense," I said. "The victim profile is similar and the outreach center is only blocks from the Stroll. If you're looking for victims who won't be missed and whose disappearances aren't likely to attract any attention from law enforcement, you can't do much better than the homeless."

"If and when this hits the news, it's going to add to the belief that vampires are taking victims off the streets," Sean said gravely.

I cleared my throat. "This is going to sound cold, but to anyone who knows vampires, if these disappearances *are* connected, this is fairly conclusive evidence it *isn't* vamps behind it. Unless they're newly risen and unable to control their bloodlust, vampires are usually very particular about who they drink from."

"It's obviously not new vamps doing it, because there would be bodies and someone would have seen the attacks," Mark said.

I nodded. "Homeless people would be near the bottom of any vamp's list of potential food sources. They may be immune to human diseases, and drugs have little to no effect on them, but every vampire I've ever known would consider drinking from a homeless person to be like eating food out of a garbage can. It would make no sense for them to do that, when they have their pick of willing blood meals who are the equivalent of filet mignon."

"Would one of you be willing to visit the outreach center and see if there's anything to this?" Amanda asked.

"We'll go down there," Mark said. "Who do we need to speak to?"

"Her name is Sister Berry," Amanda told him. "It's really Sister Mary Bernadette, but she goes by Sister Berry."

Mark made a note. "Do you have a phone number?"

Amanda read off a number and he wrote it down. "We'll look into it," Mark said.

"Thank you, Mark," Amanda said. We said our goodbyes and hung up.

Mark sat back in his chair. "Are you both available to go down there?"

I nodded. "I can go," Sean said. "I have a pack meeting tonight, but I'm free until five or so."

"I'll stay here and keep digging into John West and the harnads," Mark said. He looked at me. "I assume your ghost is tailing West today?"

"Yes. He'll let me know if anything happens we need to know about."

"Okay, then. Let's get on it." He tore out the sheet of paper that had Sister Berry's name and phone number written on it and pushed it across the table to me.

I drained the last of my coffee and stood. Caffeine and adrenaline had kicked in, clearing the cobwebs from my sleepless night, at least for the time being, but I dreaded the inevitable crash later on. I wasn't going to be much use to anyone if I didn't get some decent sleep soon.

"What's going on with you?" Mark asked. "You look ten times worse than you did yesterday."

I glared at him. "What is it with guys telling me I look like crap today?"

"Sorry." Mark reached under the table for a medium-sized gift bag. "The bottle of good Scotch I promised you."

"Excellent." I pulled back the tissue paper and peered at the wooden box. My eyebrows went up, and I grinned. "Wow, are you sure you want to give this up? This stuff is pricey."

"I don't drink whisky anymore," Mark said. "Take it."

I picked up the bag and cradled it. "You're coming home with me," I murmured.

"Did you just talk to that bottle of whisky?" Sean asked as we headed for the door.

"Yes." I sniffed. "If you appreciated good Scotch, you'd understand. Come on; let's go meet a nun."

11

Sister Berry was nothing like what I'd pictured.

"Come in," she called when I knocked on the doorway of her small office at the outreach center.

Sean and I entered the tiny room, which must have been a closet in a former life, to find a smiling woman of about forty, wearing a cheerful blue sweater and long skirt, her hair in a neat bun. Her only jewelry was a simple gold cross. She was burrowing in a box of papers and looked up when we walked in.

"You must be Alice," she said, holding out her hand.

"Yes, ma'am," I confirmed. "We spoke on the phone."

"Oh, call me Sister Berry," the nun said. She turned to Sean and shook his hand. "And you're her partner?"

"Sean Maclin," he said. "Thank you for seeing us on such short notice."

The nun set aside the box of papers and gestured for us to sit in the two plastic chairs in front of her desk. "I'm more thankful than I can say that you're here," she said earnestly, seating herself. "I've been trying for weeks to get anyone to look into this situation, but I've had no luck persuading the police that anything is wrong."

"So we've heard," I said. "You've spoken to Detective Shay, I understand."

"Once on the phone and once in person. Since then, I've called her several times, but she's only returned my call once and left me a voice mail saying she was unable to confirm these disappearances were due to foul play or there were really any disappearances at all." The nun sighed. "It's not unusual for the police to show little concern about the well-being of the people we serve here, but if I'm right and someone *is* taking these people, they deserve better than to be ignored."

"I agree," Sean said. "Why don't you tell us why you think people have been taken."

Sister Berry began looking through the paperwork on her desk. "I have a list."

A pile of folders and invoices toppled over. Sean caught the paperwork before it could slide off onto the floor and the nun smiled gratefully as he righted the stack.

"Thank you. I'd tell you that my office is usually not this disorganized, but that would be a lie, and I do try not to break a commandment if I can help it." She chuckled.

After some searching, Sister Berry found a yellow legal pad and handed it to me. On it was a list of names and nicknames, with hastily scrawled notes indicating what day each person had last been seen. Some had been crossed out, with notes like "jail" or "hospital." I flipped through the pages and counted seventeen people, ten men and seven women, whose whereabouts were unknown. The "last seen" dates ranged from six months to seven days ago.

Sean held out his hand and I passed him the notepad. "All of these people on the list are patrons here at the center?" I asked.

Sister Berry nodded. "They've all stayed here from time to time in the shelter, but we see them more often at the soup kitchen."

Sean was looking over the list. "Do you see generally the same people from day to day?"

"Yes, we do. We've gotten to know them over the months or years they've been coming in. There's always some turnover, as people cycle in and out of jail and hospitals, others arrive and leave, and some pass away, but I've seen a lot of the same people for the past four or five years, and now they're gone." She studied her folded hands. When she looked back at us, her eyes shimmered with tears. "My heart tells me something terrible is happening and I simply cannot stand by any longer and wait for the police to help."

"Can we have a copy of this list?" I asked.

"Of course. Give me a moment."

Sean handed her the list and she disappeared down the hall.

"What do you think?" he asked me quietly when we were alone.

"Gut feeling, it's connected. I think her judgment is sound. It makes sense they'd be taking homeless people, too; they're even less likely to be missed than the women from South Elm."

"But what are they taking them for?" he growled.

"That's the million-dollar question," I replied as the nun came back and handed us two copies of the list. "Sister Berry, when your patrons don't sleep here at the shelter, where do they stay?"

"Well, they're from all around the area," she said as she reseated herself. "Some sleep in alleys, in the park on Maple between Sixth and Seventh, or under overpasses. There are two larger camps: one under the Twelfth Street Bridge and another by the river where the air conditioner plant used to be." She pointed at our lists. "I put abbreviations on the list if I knew where that person stayed: 'P' for the park, '12B' for the bridge, or 'RV' for the river." She looked at us with hope in her eyes. "Will you help?"

"We'll look into it," Sean promised. "If you get any news on the missing people, let us know. We'll do the same."

We all stood. The nun came around her desk. To my surprise, she hugged both of us. My response was a little stiff, since I wasn't entirely comfortable with physical contact, but Sean seemed to sense Sister Berry sought comfort. Her obvious distress would trigger Sean's protective instincts. When she stepped back, some of the tension seemed to have drained from her. I'd always suspected Sean produced some kind of calming pheromones as part of his alpha physiology.

"If we were here around meal time, do you think anyone would be willing to talk to us?" I asked.

Sister Berry looked thoughtful. "It's possible. We're serving breakfast until eleven. You're more than welcome to visit with anyone who's willing. If you were able to help in the dining hall, that could smooth the waters a bit. We're short-handed today, so a few extra hands would be a blessing."

To my surprise, Sean immediately agreed. Ten minutes later, I was wearing a flowery apron and standing behind a warming tray, spooning scrambled eggs onto plastic cafeteria-style trays as tired men and women filed past. Mindful of our mission to establish a rapport, I put aside my discomfort at interacting with so many strangers at once and welcomed each person with a smile and a cheery greeting. Before long, my face hurt from smiling so much.

Sean, wearing an identical floral apron that somehow did not look ridiculous on him, had been recruited to refill coffee and water cups. He seemed to be striking up easy conversations with people as he moved around the room, clapping men on the shoulder and even offering side hugs to some of the older women. Unsurprisingly, a lot of the women—and a few of the men—needed several refills.

I wasn't aware I was watching him a little too much until a woman with dreadlocks and a colorful head wrap leaned toward me over the eggs and said, "Your man is gorgeous."

I blinked at her. "What? Oh, no, he's not my man. Not at all." I put eggs on her tray.

The woman made a disbelieving sound. "Girl, the way you looking at him, you ain't just friends."

From fifteen feet away where he was topping off coffee mugs at a table, Sean slid a glance in my direction and raised his eyebrows. Blasted werewolf hearing.

I narrowed my eyes at him, then turned back to the woman and gave her a big smile. "Have a great day!"

With a snort, the woman moved on to claim a cup of orange juice and headed for a table. I focused my attention on the people coming through the line and studiously ignored Sean as he made his rounds.

When things slowed down, I asked the woman serving bacon next to me to take over both stations, grabbed a pot of coffee and a pitcher of water, and wandered over to the table where the woman who'd spoken to me earlier sat with three other women. Sean sat at a table on the other side of the dining hall with four men of various ages, talking and making notes on his copy of Sister Berry's list.

"Would anyone like refills?" I inquired.

Two of the women declined, but the others asked for coffee and water. I filled their cups, then asked, "Mind if I join you?"

After a hesitation, the woman in the head-wrap gestured at the empty chair. "Sure."

I settled in and put the coffee pot and pitcher on the table. "My name is Alice." I offered my hand to each of the women. The woman I'd spoken to earlier introduced herself as Maru. The others were Berta, Joann, and Theresa.

I took a plastic cup from the stack on the middle of the table and poured myself some water. "Sister Berry asked my partner and me to look into the folks who've been disappearing around here lately."

Berta got up immediately and left the table, but the others stayed. "Don't mind her," Maru said. "She don't trust nobody who smells like a cop."

"I'm not a cop." I produced a stack of business cards from my pocket and handed one to each of the women. "I've never been a cop, actually. I'm a private investigator."

The women looked at my cards with varying degrees of skepticism. "You've talked to Sister Berry?" Maru asked.

"She said a lot of people have disappeared in the last few months. Do you know anything about that?"

Maru exchanged glances with Joann and Theresa. "Bunch'a people gone, ain't nobody know where," Maru told me as the others sat quietly. "Nothin' new about folks disappearing sometimes; you get used to it, bein' on the street. Everybody figures they been taken. People gone and left their things behind. Sometimes they leave their dogs, and we know they ain't gonna leave their dogs without finding someone to take care of them. Sometimes people leave their shit, but they ain't never leave their dogs."

The other women nodded somberly.

"Have you seen anything or anyone suspicious in the past couple of months that might help us figure out what's going on?" I asked. "Anybody lurking around where you guys stay, driving past slowly, offering people rides or work?"

"We see all those things every day," Theresa said gruffly. "Most of us are on our guard every minute. You gotta be aware, even while you're asleep. Some folks drink, do drugs...they aren't as careful, don't keep watch. Mostly it seems like those are the ones who go missing."

"Not always," Maru argued. "Bobby Jay and Rosie, they didn't trust nobody. Neither did Zoot, and they all gone."

"So you can't think of anything that might point us in a direction? Anything at all?"

Joann finished her coffee and set her cup on the table. "If we knew anything, we would have told Sister Berry when she asked, not that it would have done any good. The cops can't be bothered to look for missing homeless people. You learn pretty fast when you live on the street that your life's not worth much to anyone. Nobody cares."

"*I* care," I told her firmly. "Sister Berry cares. The people I work with care. We're going to do everything we can to find out what's going on, who's responsible, and what happened to your friends."

"We've heard that before, a dozen times over the years." Joann sounded more tired than angry. "I'm sorry if we seem rude to you, but at some point you get fed up with empty promises." She got up and left, dropping her cup in the trash and depositing her tray and silverware in the tubs for dirty dishes. Theresa followed suit, leaving me sitting alone with Maru.

I dug the list Sister Berry gave me out of my bag and slid it across the table to her. "Do you know any names of people who aren't on this list, or know the whereabouts of anyone who is unaccounted for?"

Maru looked through the list. "Everyone I know who's missing is on here." When she handed back the list, she was grave. "I ain't gonna get my hopes up. Like Joann said, we been let down too many times. But if you say you'll help, I say God bless you, and find our friends if you can." She picked up her tray and headed for the exit.

I sat alone at the table, as the dining hall emptied out and volunteers put away the breakfast leftovers and cleaned up in preparation for the lunch meal. I was so deeply lost in thought that I jumped when Sean touched my shoulder.

"Sorry," he said, sliding into the chair next to me. "I made sure you weren't holding a cup of coffee this time."

I gave him a faint smile. "I got an earful about how nobody cares about the lives of the homeless, and that was about it. You get anything helpful?"

"A couple more names of some people who went missing from the camp by the river about a month ago. Left their belongings and just disappeared. One of them left his dog."

I remembered what Maru had said. "People sometimes leave their stuff, but nobody leaves their dog."

He nodded. "I don't think we can avoid the fact that these people have been taken. Unless we can believe there are *two* separate groups out here kidnapping people, it's all part of the same problem. The question is: how are they getting them and no one sees anything?"

"Most homeless people are pretty suspicious of strangers and have fairly good instincts about who's trustworthy and who isn't. That makes me think the group who's doing this are masters at seeming nonthreatening, or they blitz-attack so fast the victims don't have a chance to put up a fight or attract anyone's attention. They've been at it at least fourteen months, so they've probably got it down to a science at this point."

"The lack of bodies is one of the most frustrating parts of all this. Bodies provide clues. I suppose that's why we don't have any, unless all these people are still alive, which seems unlikely."

I sighed. "I'm tired of having so many questions and no answers. So far, we've been using fairly conventional methods of investigation. It's time to explore other avenues."

"What are you thinking?"

"I know someone who could help us. We'll need access to Felicia's apartment and your surveillance camera has to be turned off while we're there."

Sean raised an eyebrow. "Whatever you need, I'll make it happen if you think you might be able to get us some answers. What's your plan?"

I slipped the apron off over my head and handed it to him. "If you'll say our goodbyes to Sister Berry, I'm going to step outside and make a call."

About an hour later, Sean and I were waiting in Felicia's apartment when someone knocked on the door. I opened it and came face-to-chest with a man-shaped mountain wearing a black turtleneck, black pants, and black boots. I looked up and saw my reflection in his mirrored sunglasses. "Alice Worth?" he rumbled.

"Yes?"

The man-mountain stepped aside to reveal a young man wearing a faded Tetris T-shirt and jeans. "Hey, Alice. You gonna let me in or what?" the shorter man asked.

"Hi, Adam." I moved aside so he could come in. His enormous escort stationed himself outside the door like a sentry. A black luxury SUV waited at the curb, its windows tinted so dark that I couldn't see anything other than another huge, hulking shadow in the driver's seat. The Vampire Court took the safety of their Seers very seriously.

As I closed the door, Sean rose from the couch and gave the psychic a formal nod in lieu of offering a handshake. "I'm Sean Maclin, alpha of the Tomb Mountain Pack. Thank you for coming on such short notice."

"Adam March." Our guest put his black leather duffel bag on the floor and studied me. "How you been, Alice? I haven't seen you in a couple of months."

"I'm doing okay. How much do you know about the situation?" I asked.

He shrugged. "I skimmed the reports Dunlap's been sending to the Court. Since Maclin's here, I'm guessing this is the apartment of the missing shifter."

"Her name is Felicia Lowell. We believe she's the second-most-recent victim. We're looking for leads on where she might be, and whether or not she's still alive."

"Even if it's her body we find, that would be worth a lot," Sean said.

"I'll do my best," Adam said. "You know there are no guarantees."

"We understand," I assured him. "What do you want us to do?"

"Just sit quietly somewhere so I can focus."

Sean and I sat on the couch and watched Adam as he wandered around the apartment, his hand outstretched. I knew from previous experience that he was clearing his mind of distractions and "tuning" his senses by looking for items that resonated with Felicia's unique shifter trace. He paused at the dining table, running his fingers over one of the chairs, then moved into the living room, touching the stack of travel magazines on the coffee table and the guitar on a stand in the corner of the room. His breathing was slow and measured, his eyes half-closed.

Meanwhile, Sean's growing impatience made the hairs prickle on my arms and I knew it had to be distracting for Adam. I hesitated, then slid my hand over to touch his. "Relax," I murmured.

Sean took several deep breaths and the prickling sensation faded. His fingers brushed mine. "Thanks," he said quietly.

I wanted to close my fingers around his. Instead, I pulled my hand back.

We sat silently as Adam moved around the apartment for almost twenty minutes. I was beginning to think we were going to come up empty when he suddenly stopped and turned toward me with unfocused eyes.

Slowly, I rose. "Tell me what you see," I prompted.

"Darkness." Adam looked through me. "Four people are sleeping in a dark room."

"Is Felicia one of them?"

"Yes."

Sean inhaled sharply. I kept my tone quiet and soothing. "Where is she?"

"A warehouse. Many rooms, many doors. Wards that tear flesh."

My stomach lurched. That kind of blood ward was both illegal and considered anathema among most mages.

Sean started to stand, but I signaled for him to stay where he was so he didn't break Adam's concentration. "How many people are there?" I asked.

"Dozens. I've heard them crying. There's so much fear and suffering." Tears began to trickle from Adam's eyes. "So much death."

Everything he could sense might be a clue to where Felicia and the others were being held. "What do you smell?" I asked.

Adam looked right at me. "Blood," he grated. His hand shot out and grabbed my arm. "*Save us.*"

A torrent of images poured into my brain, and the agony was instantaneous and overwhelming. Blood gushed from my nose, as my knees gave out and I dangled helplessly in Adam's iron grip. I heard Sean shouting and sensed some kind of scuffle, but I fell down a deep, dark well, leaving him behind.

I was experiencing what Adam saw and felt through his connection to Felicia, but I wasn't psychic, and my brain wasn't wired for it. It was a completely different feeling from my own Second Sight, with which I saw magic traces, wards, and spells. I might have been screaming, but my body and its condition seemed far away and unimportant compared to the horrors in Felicia's head.

Memories and sensations tumbled through my brain like rocks in a landslide: *Going for a run...a stinging pain in the back of my neck...waking up in chains...blood... screaming and begging...trying to escape...PAIN...silver chains now...so much blood...I'm dying...Mommy, please help me—*

A face above mine, cold and cruel. *Stop fighting, Felicia, or we'll have to kill you and take your brother instead.*

A room with four beds. Many more in other rooms nearby, all chained like me. The smell of blood fills my nose. We're all hurting.

We're all dying.

12

My connection to Felicia suddenly broke, and I was yanked backward through the tunnel with the abruptness of a rubber band snapping.

I hit the floor on my back, jolting me into awareness. For a horrifying moment, I thought I hadn't ended up back in my own body; my skin didn't fit and everything felt *wrong*. I tried to scream but the sound came out as a gurgle. I was choking on my own blood.

"Shit, Alice, I'm sorry," Adam said from somewhere nearby.

Someone rolled me onto my side and I coughed up some of the blood I'd aspirated. "What the hell did you do?" Sean demanded. "You almost killed her. Get him out of here." It was a snarl.

A voice rumbled, footsteps retreated, and a door slammed.

I was still coughing the blood out of my lungs. "Jesus." Sean wiped my mouth with something. "Don't die on me, Alice."

I wanted to tell him I wasn't dying but I couldn't get the words to come out. I focused on clearing my lungs and breathing. Sean kept his hand on my back as I coughed and tried not to vomit.

Finally, my head began to clear. When I opened my eyes, I found Sean on his knees on the living room floor next to me. He'd taken off his shirt and used it to wipe my mouth. His clothing and the carpet were splattered with blood. Adam was gone.

"Can you hear me?" he asked.

I managed a nod. My wrists and ankles burned, but when I glanced down at myself, I seemed to be uninjured. Phantom pains, then, left over from sharing Felicia's memories. *Silver chains*, I remembered. My inner elbows throbbed from repeated needle punctures. *Not my elbows, Felicia's*. I shivered hard.

Sean leaned over me. "Are you all right?"

I was a long, long way from all right. I hurt all over but it was difficult to separate my own current condition from my memories of Felicia's pain and suffering. The agony in my head was my own, I decided, and my nose still trickled blood.

I took Sean's shirt and pressed it to my nose. "I'll be okay," I said weakly.

His eyes blazed. "What did he do to you?"

"He didn't do it on purpose." I coughed and struggled to sit up.

He helped me sit upright. Before I could protest, he settled in with his legs around me so I could lean back against his chest. He wrapped an arm around my middle as I tipped my head forward and held the shirt to my nose.

Sean's warm breath tickled my ear. "Can you tell me what happened?"

I tried to make some sense out of my muddled thoughts. "When Adam grabbed me, I glimpsed some of what he saw through his connection to Felicia. She's alive, but in a lot of pain. I think there are others still alive, too, but I'm not sure how many."

He processed that. "How hurt are you?"

"It's just a nosebleed."

A long silence. I breathed slowly through my mouth and checked the shirt, then found a clean area and put it back to my nose. Every time I moved my head, pain stabbed me behind my eyes.

"That's the second time you've lied to me today, third if I count the text you sent me last night claiming it was all a false alarm." Sean rested his cheek against the side of my head. "Pick one of them and tell me the truth."

I hurt too much to fight about it. "Adam unintentionally shared his visions with me. I'm not a psychic, so the overload probably burst some small blood vessels in my brain."

"You hemorrhaged. In your brain." Sean's voice was even.

"It's not as bad as it sounds."

Judging by the tension in his body, he very much disagreed with me on that point. "Would a healing spell help? Do you have any with you?"

"I'll use one later, when I'm home. When I use one on my head, it feels like ants crawling in my brain. I get sick." It was bad enough to throw up in the privacy of my own home; I had no intention of doing it in Felicia's apartment, in front of Sean.

"What can I do?"

"Nothing. I'll be fine. I just need to take it easy until I can get home."

"What would have happened if I hadn't intervened?"

"A stroke, probably. Maybe worse. Thanks, by the way."

His arm tightened around my stomach. "What about last night?"

I smiled briefly. "You said to pick one."

"I was hoping you'd want to come clean on that too."

My smile faded. What could I tell him, that someone had sent a poltergeist to kill me and steal my body? Until I knew why I'd been targeted and by whom, I didn't want anyone else to put themselves at risk, especially not Sean or Malcolm.

"Not at the moment," I said finally. "Maybe later."

"I smelled blood on your bag and in your car that wasn't there yesterday. I know you were injured."

I made a face. I thought I'd cleaned my bag and car thoroughly, but obviously not well enough to fool Sean's nose.

"Whatever happened, was it related to our current case?"

"I don't think so."

"Is the situation resolved?"

"For the time being." I reached over to the coffee table, picked up my phone, and sent a quick text to Adam. *You still here?*

A few seconds later, a reply. *VCS: Yes. Waiting to hear that you're OK.*

Me: Come back in and let's talk about what you saw.
VCS: OK

"VCS?" Sean asked.

"Vampire Court Seer."

I put the shirt down. Sean stood and carried me to the couch. He propped me up with some pillows, then went to the kitchen for a wet towel. I took it from him and began to clean my face and neck. The pain in my head made my eyeballs throb.

When Adam knocked, Sean went to the door to let him in, his eyes golden.

"Take it easy," I said as he reached for the doorknob. "If I know Adam, he's probably been beating himself up since you kicked him out."

Sean didn't reply, but the glow in his eyes faded as he opened the door and stepped aside to let Adam in.

The psychic sported a split lip and swelling jaw. The man-mountain behind him glowered at Sean.

My eyes widened. "Did you punch the Vampire Court's Seer?"

Sean shut the door, leaving Adam's escort outside. "He wouldn't let you go. It was either that or break his hand to get you away from him."

"I deserved it." Adam came over and crouched so he didn't tower over me. He was pale and clearly shaken. "I'm so sorry. I don't even remember grabbing you."

"It wasn't your fault. I'll be all right." I gave him a small smile. "My head hurts like I've been waiting in line at the DMV, though."

Despite my attempt at levity, Adam flinched. "I could have killed you."

"But you didn't, so we're okay." I lowered the towel and looked up at Sean. "Is my face clean?"

"Mostly." Sean stood at my side, his arms crossed. "You missed a few spots."

I held the towel out. He found a clean section and started wiping my chin and throat.

I looked over at Adam. "We need to talk about what you saw while it's still fresh."

"If you're feeling up to it, I'm ready to talk." He glanced at Sean. "Mind if I get myself some ice from the kitchen first?"

"Go ahead."

Adam went into the kitchen and the ice maker rattled to life.

"We'll have to clean the carpet," I told Sean as he wiped my face. "I'll burn my blood, but it will leave ash."

"I'll get someone in here to clean up. Don't worry about it." He unbuttoned the top button on my bloody shirt and started cleaning my upper chest. Our eyes met and he paused. "Should I stop?"

"No," I said softly. He resumed cleaning me with the towel, his touch gentle.

Adam returned to the living room, holding an ice-filled dish towel to his mouth, just as Sean was finishing. He stood by the dining table and waited until the werewolf took the bloody towel and his shirt into the bathroom. I heard water running. Slowly, I pushed myself upright.

"Take it easy." Adam helped me adjust the pillows, careful not to touch me. "I can have some vampire blood brought here to help you heal. Mr. Vaughan has some set aside for daytime emergencies. You're on the list of approved recipients."

I started to shake my head, then decided that was a bad idea. "I have healing spells at home."

"You shouldn't wait that long," Adam argued. "Let me get the blood for you."

"I don't want Charles's help. He asks too high a price for it."

Adam looked stubborn. "It's my price to pay. I caused your injuries. Let me help."

I couldn't explain to him that I didn't want Charles's blood because I was afraid he'd be able to influence me. The fewer people who knew about our complicated situation, the better. "It was an accident, Adam. You shouldn't have to suffer because of it."

"All he'll ask for is a snack," Adam said. "I don't mind; it wouldn't be the first time I've let him drink from me. It's worse seeing you hurt, knowing I caused it."

Sean appeared in the living room, drying his hands on a towel. "Is there any blood available from Niara instead of Vaughan?" He'd evidently overheard the whole conversation.

Adam nodded. "Yes. I can get it. Would that be better?" he asked me.

Before I could answer, Sean came over to me. "Alice, let him help you."

When I started to refuse, his eyes lit up with anger. "Be reasonable. Adam caused you harm and he wants to make it right, for his sake as well as yours. You're hurting yourself *and* him by declining his help."

Malcolm was right when he'd said I disliked others doing things for me. Maybe it was because I didn't think I deserved their help, or because I didn't like feeling as if I was in someone's debt, or both.

At the same time, my refusal made Adam's guilt worse and if I knew anything, it was the torture of guilt. I couldn't do much about mine, but I could at least help Adam with his.

"If you can get Niara's blood, and all she'll ask in return is to drink from you, and you're willing, I'll do it," I said reluctantly.

Adam sent a quick text. The response came back in seconds. "It's arranged," he told me, putting his phone back in his pocket. "They'll be here in twenty-five minutes." He put the ice back to his busted lip and sat in the chair near the window. "Thank you, Alice."

"In the meantime, we need to talk about what we saw while I can still make some sense of it," I said, ready to redirect the conversation away from myself.

"You go first," Adam said. "I'd like to know what you remember."

I tried to organize the jumble of images and feelings I'd experienced in the scant seconds I'd shared Adam's visions. "I only saw a few of Felicia's memories, and they were all jumbled up. I remember she was out running, and she felt a sharp pain on the back of her neck before passing out."

"Probably a tranquilizer dart," Sean said grimly, settling onto the couch next to me.

I rubbed my forehead, struggling to think clearly through the vicious ache behind my eyes. "She woke up chained to a bed. She tried to escape and they chained her with silver."

Sean snarled.

I remembered the pain in my inner elbows. "They're taking blood from the survivors."

"For what purpose?" Sean ground out.

"I don't know." I looked at Adam. "Other than pain and fear, that's all I remember. What did you see?"

He adjusted the ice he was holding. "A warehouse. The smell of blood and disinfectant was strong, like a hospital, almost." He looked thoughtful. "I felt strong wards, but it didn't feel like there was a lot of magic being worked on the premises. If it's a harnad behind it, I'd think the magic would be thick."

"They probably have a separate location where they're doing whatever it is they're doing with all that blood." I frowned.

"What?" Sean asked me.

"It still doesn't make sense. I told Mark the other day, if the harnad were using all this blood in ritual magic, we'd know. There would be signs."

"Like what?"

"Weird weather. Seismic activity. High-level mages would be able to sense it, especially along the ley lines. Even the vamps would feel something prickly, shifters too. We'd *know*."

Sean looked at me. "Have you felt something like that before?"

"Yes, a long time ago." My grandfather's cabal compound was the epicenter of all kinds of weird and extreme weather and seismic activity. "Some people call it 'blood weather.' Once you've felt it or seen it, you'd never mistake it for anything else."

"Would you feel it even if they were working inside strong wards?" Adam asked.

"Even then," I said. "Maybe not across the city, but anyone in the vicinity would sense it."

"Maybe they're doing everything well outside the city," Sean suggested. "Out where no one will notice the magic they're using."

"Maybe," I said reluctantly. "That doesn't explain the lack of blood weather, though."

Adam jerked, like he'd just remembered something. "There was a man who threatened Felicia."

My eyes widened. *Stop fighting, Felicia.* "Yes." I frowned, trying to remember his face, and a lightning bolt of pain in my head made me wince.

"Stop straining your memory," Sean told me. "You can wrack your brain after that blood gets here and you heal yourself. Adam, can you remember this man?"

Adam had his eyes closed. "What I can see of him is more of an impression than a clear vision. I think I would recognize him if I saw a photo. Felicia might not have been fully conscious when she saw him."

Sean handed me my phone. "Pull up that six-pack Mark sent you."

I opened the lineup we'd planned to show Danielle and passed the phone back. He took it over to Adam. "Is it any of these men?"

Adam looked over the pictures carefully, then shook his head. "I don't think so. None of them look familiar. I'm not one hundred percent sure, though."

I tried to remember if the face I'd seen was John West, but my headache was getting worse, and now the room was swimming in and out of focus. I rested my head on the couch and closed my eyes.

"Alice," Sean said. I thought he was on the other side of the living room, but then he touched my cheek. "Hey."

I opened my eyes and blinked slowly but I couldn't focus. I saw two Seans leaning over me, looking worried. Everything had a strange reddish tint. The light from the windows was painfully bright and I closed my eyes again.

Sean swore. "Stay awake, Alice. Look at me."

I was so tired. "My head hurts."

"I know. Damn it, how long until they get here, Adam?"

A long pause. "Seven minutes."

"Tell them to hurry the hell up."

"I *did*."

The couch dipped as Sean sat down and gathered me in his arms. I breathed deeply, my nose against his undershirt. "Forest," I murmured.

"Is she hallucinating?" Adam asked.

"I don't know," Sean said tersely. "How badly do you think she's hurt?"

"On a scale of one to ten, I'd say probably a seven or eight. That's just an educated guess, though. She doesn't look like she was at one hundred percent to start with."

Sean's arms tightened around me. I made a protesting sound and his grip relaxed a little.

Blood trickled out of my ear. "Get me another towel," Sean said tightly.

Adam's footsteps retreated to the kitchen, then returned. Sean pressed a towel against the side of my head. "Help is coming." He kissed my forehead, his lips burning like a brand on my cold, damp skin. "Hold on."

By the time the Vamp Court courier arrived an eternity later, my head hurt like it was being crushed in a vise and I could no longer focus on anything going on around me. When the knock finally came, Adam answered the door while Sean held me. I heard indistinct voices, then the sound of the door closing.

"Here, you give it to her," Adam said.

Sean shifted me so I was sitting more upright and something pressed against my lips. It felt like the rim of an insulated travel mug. I might have laughed if my head didn't hurt so badly. I had no idea vampire blood was available in a to-go cup.

"Alice, drink," Sean urged.

Despite the pain, I resisted. I didn't want an audience. Old memories forced their way to the surface: me, handcuffed to a cot in a blood-splattered room, suffering the ravages of a strong healing spell while my grandfather, his lieutenants, and the blood mage who'd tortured me watched me scream.

"*Drink*," Sean repeated, more forcefully. "You gave Adam your word you would. If you won't do it for yourself, do it for him."

I parted my lips and warm vampire blood flowed over my tongue. Niara's blood tasted very different from Charles's, I discovered, like the difference between a shiraz and a merlot. I moaned weakly at the wave of pleasure and warmth.

"Finish it," Sean said.

I let him give me the rest of the contents of the cup. He set it aside to hold me.

The surge of heat rushed up over the top of my head, as if I were being pulled under water. Warm fingers stroked my brain inside my skull. I cried out and struggled in Sean's grip. He growled quietly.

As the strange sensations in my head faded, waves of soothing heat rolled through me as the vampire blood also healed the residual aches and pains from the poltergeist attack and the convenience store robbery. I hadn't even noticed the lingering stiffness and discomfort in my back, arms, and legs until they vanished.

When the warmth faded and my head cleared, I opened my eyes. Everything seemed brighter, more focused, like I'd been half-asleep before and was now wide awake.

Sean's eyes glowed. "How do you feel?"

"Amazing," I said, sounding breathless. "Completely amazing."

Sean's hold loosened as I stretched, testing out limbs that were suddenly lighter and pain-free. I rolled to my feet with the grace of a ballerina and looked around the room as if seeing it for the first time.

Sean and Adam watched me as if they expected something to happen. "Boo," I said with a laugh.

They exchanged a look. "You've had vampire blood before, right?" Adam asked.

"Oh, sure," I said cheerily. "I drank from Charles after I broke my hands and I got cut by all that window glass." Sean flinched. I'd never told him about that. "And then I had a lot of it when I died and they brought me back," I finished.

"Well, that explains a lot," Adam said dryly.

I pirouetted, my arms outstretched. "It didn't feel nearly this fantastic, though."

"Niara's older than Charles. You're going to feel pretty good for a couple of days."

"Awesome. I've got a lot going on and I haven't had a good night's sleep in a very long time. I could use a little extra boost."

"How long until this euphoria wears off?" Sean asked, his eyes narrowed.

"It's hard to say," Adam told him. "She only drank about six ounces, but she has no tolerance. It's weird seeing her so cheerful, isn't it?"

"That's one word for it," Sean muttered.

I didn't know why he looked so grim. It wasn't like there was anything wrong with me. "Hey, guys, stop talking about me like I'm not here." I pursed my lips. "I wonder..."

I raised my hands in front of me about two feet apart and loosed my earth and air magic. A blisteringly powerful bolt of green-and-white magic arced between my hands, electrifying the air. Both men jumped out of their seats.

I smiled, watching the magic blaze between my hands. "Now *that's* a side effect I approve of." I hadn't experienced any significant increase in power after drinking from Charles; perhaps it was only older vamps who had this effect, or maybe it was just Niara. Interesting. While the euphoria was nice, the magic boost was bound to come in handy—not to mention it felt fantastic sizzling on my hands.

"Alice."

I glanced up. Sean moved around the coffee table to stand a few feet away. "That's incredible," he said. "Does your magic feel stronger?"

"Definitely." Reluctantly, I let go of the arc and it vanished. "It feels like I stuck my fingers in a power outlet."

"That's what it felt like from over here," Adam grumbled, rubbing his arms.

I waggled my fingers threateningly at him. "Don't mess with me, Miss Cleo. I'm supercharged now."

Adam laughed. "I don't know how long this new, happier version of you is going to last, but I'm going to enjoy it."

My phone rang. I glanced at the screen and swiped the green button. "Hey, Mark," I chirped.

A pause. "Alice?"

"Yes?"

"Nothing. You just sounded different. I'm waiting for a report on the situation down at the homeless shelter."

I filled him in on what we'd found out from Sister Berry and the others at the outreach center. Then I told him about Adam's visions and what we'd seen through the connection to Felicia.

"How did you share Adam's visions?" he asked when I'd finished.

"He accidentally included me. It was kind of like a conference call."

Mark swore. Sean crossed his arms and stared at me. I raised my hand, palm up, and mouthed, *What?*

"I'm okay now," I assured my former boss as Sean frowned. "Adam had some vamp blood couriered over."

"No wonder you sound like a different person," Mark said gruffly. "It wasn't from our mutual friend, was it?"

"Nope, Niara."

A long pause.

"Mark?"

He cleared his throat. "You and I need to have a private conversation before tonight."

"Why? What's going on tonight?"

"We've been instructed to attend a meeting of the Vampire Court and deliver a progress report. Midnight tonight, at Northbourne Manor. All nine members of the Court will be in attendance."

Sean's eyebrows went up. Despite the euphoric effect of Niara's blood, my stomach lurched. Though I'd worked for the Court for the past five years, I had never stood before the entire Court when it was convened. To my knowledge, neither had Mark, though he'd been their lead investigator for more than fifteen years.

"They'll send a car for you at eleven fifteen," Mark told me. "Dress appropriately."

"Um," I said intelligently.

"It will be fine," he said. "We've been sending regular reports, so nothing they'll be hearing from us will be a surprise. From what I understand, Valas and most of the Court are satisfied with everything we've done."

I glanced at Sean, who was texting. "You and I are the only ones expected?"

"Yes. I'm sure Maclin isn't happy about that, but we're playing in the Court's sandbox here."

"Okay. You're the boss."

"And don't you forget it. Get some rest this afternoon if you can; it's going to be a long night, probably."

As good as a nap sounded, I highly doubted I'd be able to relax at all. "Wait. What did you need to tell me before tonight?"

"Go into another room."

Sean looked up from his phone and met my gaze, his face unreadable. Only the gold sheen over his eyes revealed his displeasure.

I went into Felicia's bedroom and shut the door. "Okay."

"Sorry for the secrecy, but I don't want to make things any more complicated than they already are between you and Maclin. Drinking Niara's blood has some side effects."

"I know. Up until a few minutes ago, I felt pretty amazing," I said dryly. "That seems to have worn off, though. My magic is stronger, too."

"Those are the good side effects. The thing I'm worried about—and the reason I asked you to step into another room—is that Niara's blood will give her some influence over you."

I frowned. "I figured as much, which is why—"

"—Why you chose hers rather than Vaughan's," Mark finished impatiently. "Yes, I understand that. Niara enjoys the company of women and she's expressed interest in you in the past. I never mentioned it because it didn't seem like anything would come of it, but she'll be informed you drank her blood. She may see this as an opportunity to, uh, get to know you better." He coughed uncomfortably.

Niara's sexuality wasn't news to me, but her interest was surprising. I'd certainly never sensed anything from her that would have clued me in. It was Sean's idea to use Niara's blood instead of Charles's, but I was sure he'd had no idea I'd be trading one set of complications for another that was no less thorny. It would be in my best interest to avoid contact with my benefactor until the effects of her blood wore off.

"Thanks for telling me," I said finally.

"I should have told you before."

"You had no reason to think it would become an issue. I'll be careful. What are you going to do until we're due at Northbourne?"

I heard papers shuffling in the background. "I'm going to finish up some reports and then I'll go visit those homeless camps you told me about. I know a couple of folks on the street. One of them might know something. Can you send me a copy of that list you got from the nun?"

"I'll scan it and e-mail it to you when I get back to my house." I opened the bedroom door and returned to the living room. Sean looked up from his phone as I walked by him to stand next to the couch. "Anything else we need to know?" I asked Mark.

"Nothing comes to mind. I'll text or call if I think of anything. See you tonight."

"See you then," I echoed. We disconnected.

Sean returned his phone to his pocket, his eyes dark. "My presence is not required, according to Juliet LaRoche. The Court has only invited the 'lead investigators.'"

"It sounds like it will basically be Mark and me reassuring the Court in person that we're making progress on the investigation. Doesn't seem like something I should have to put heels on for." I tried to force levity into my tone, but it didn't quite work. We were all quiet.

"It'll be fine," Adam said finally. "No worries."

I snorted. "Nope, no worries. None at all."

13

WHILE SEAN WAS ON HIS PHONE ARRANGING FOR A PROFESSIONAL CLEANING company to come to Felicia's apartment, I walked Adam out to the Court SUV. He'd put some ice in a plastic bag and wrapped it in a dish towel so he could ice his swollen jaw.

"I'm sorry for grabbing you," Adam said as we stood on the sidewalk. "I owe you, big time. You name it, it's yours, if I can make it happen."

"Thanks. If you see anything else that might help us, let me know." I jerked my chin at his duffel bag, which contained a well-read novel from Felicia's nightstand that might allow him to sense her again. He'd promised to try when he was able.

"Will do." Adam hesitated. "So, you and Maclin. Are you...?"

I made a face. "Used to be."

"I thought he was going to kill me. All things considered, I got off easy with just this." He moved the bag of ice to indicate his busted lip. "He pulled his punch, too; don't think I'm not very aware he could have taken my head off if he'd wanted to. You guys thinking about getting back together?"

"No."

Adam raised an eyebrow skeptically. "Really? I've never seen you let anyone else *touch* you, much less hold you like that. He certainly acts like he wants another chance."

"He's an alpha." I shrugged. "They're hardwired to protect females and those who've been injured. I wouldn't read too much into it."

He unwrapped the ice and used the towel to whap me on my recently healed noggin. "Alice, don't be dense."

The door to Felicia's apartment opened and Sean came out, carrying a white plastic trash bag containing the bloody towels and his shirt. He headed in our direction at a brisk walk, his eyes bright gold.

Adam gave me a look and coughed meaningfully. I glared at him and he laughed.

"The cleaning crew will be here in about ninety minutes," Sean said, joining us. "I've got time to run you to your car and then come back to meet them."

Adam waved at me. "Talk to you soon. Take care of yourself."

"You too."

Adam climbed into the back seat of the SUV and it pulled away from the curb.

I glanced down at my bloody shirt. "I'm kind of a mess."

"I've got extra shirts. You're welcome to change into one." Sean led the way to his SUV. He opened the back, put the sack of wet clothes in, took out his duffel bag, and handed it to me. "Here. Pick the one you want. I'll be there in a minute."

I took the bag back to the apartment and unzipped it on the coffee table. I picked out a polo shirt with Sean's company logo and shut myself in the bathroom, where I stripped off my shirt and used a washcloth to wash the rest of the blood off my chest.

I cleaned up the best I could, then put on Sean's shirt. It hung almost to my knees, but it was clean. I held the collar to my nose and inhaled, drinking in his familiar scent.

Irritated at myself, I wrapped the washcloth in my bloody shirt and yanked open the bathroom door.

Sean was rummaging through the duffel bag, shirtless, wearing a clean pair of unbuttoned khakis that hung rather precariously on his hips. I tried not to stare at him but failed miserably.

Sean put down the undershirt he'd just picked up and stalked toward me, a golden sheen rolling over his eyes.

I took a step back and bumped into the doorway. "Finish getting dressed," I said. "We've got to get going."

"We've got time." He tugged on the sleeve of the shirt I was wearing. "You look good in blue."

I wanted to scratch my nails across that perfect chest. "Sean, please put your shirt on," I told him, a note of desperation in my voice.

"Are you sure you want me to?" He slid his fingers down my arm, his eyes soft gold.

No. "Yes."

He smiled and the corners of his eyes crinkled. It was the first little detail I had noticed about him the night we met. He leaned closer, brushing his nose against my hair, and entwined his fingers with mine. His skin felt hot enough to burn.

He moved his head so he could look me in the eyes. "When you're done with the Vamp Court tonight, come have a drink with me."

That had "disaster" written all over it. "No."

"Why not?"

"Because." I stared into his golden eyes and lost my train of thought.

His smile widened. "Because...?"

My nose filled with the scent of forest. I dropped my shirt, pulled him to me, and kissed him.

We'd shared many kisses before this: some sweet, some demanding, some tentative, some passionate. This kiss was pure need. He pinned me against the wall and lifted me up, so I could wrap my legs around his hips as our kiss grew hungrier. When he moved just right between my thighs, it set off a shudder that ran through me and made me dig my nails into his back.

His grip tightened almost painfully on my butt, and he growled low in his throat. "Alice," he breathed into my ear, making me shiver hard. "I've missed you."

Damn it, I'd missed him too. So much.

"Put me down," I said breathlessly.

Looking surprised, Sean let me slide down until my feet reached the floor. I pushed on his chest and he stepped back.

"We need to head out," I told him shakily. "Or you won't be able to get back here before the cleaning crew arrives."

His eyes darkened. "What the hell, Alice?"

"It's the vampire blood messing with my libido." I rubbed my butt where he'd grabbed me. "I forgot about that particular side effect."

"Bullshit," he snapped.

I gaped at him. "Sean, it's a documented—"

"I know it is, but you only drank five or six ounces. That's maybe enough to lower your inhibitions, but not enough to make you do anything you don't want to do. That kiss and the fingernail marks in my back were all you."

I crossed my arms and tried not to notice the heat of his chest. "Please put on a shirt and take me to my car."

"Alice—"

"If you won't take me, I'll call Adam to come back for me." I started to walk around him.

He held out his arm, halting me. "I'll take you to your car." He went to the duffel bag and pulled on an undershirt.

I stayed where I was, watching him get dressed. "This isn't going to work," I told him as he put on a black polo shirt. "We can't work together unless we stay professional."

Sean tucked in the shirt, then buttoned his pants and buckled his belt. "*You* kissed *me*," he reminded me.

"It was a mistake."

"No, it wasn't." He was at my side in a blink. "It wasn't a mistake at all. Neither is this." He bent his head.

The first kiss was full of need; this one was full of anger. His mouth was hard and demanding. His fingers dug into my waist and I arched against him before I could stop myself. I ran my fingers through his hair and pulled just hard enough to let him know I was angry too. His teeth grazed my lip, and he growled, a deep rumble that drew a moan from me. He pressed me back against the wall, his hands sliding up under the oversize shirt to grip my waist. I wanted his hands to move higher, but he stopped and held me tight.

His mouth left mine, and those golden eyes scorched me from inches away. "The mistake is thinking you don't deserve something good in your life. You refuse to believe what's going on right now matters at least as much, if not more, than whatever's behind you." He nuzzled my neck and breathed deeply. "You want me, right here, right now, and that scares you. I want to make you forget all the bullshit in your head. I want to make you happy, but you won't let me, and that's the biggest mistake of all."

Sean let go and stepped back. I stayed upright only because I was leaning against the wall with my knees locked. I was breathing hard and shaking and I wanted him so badly that it took every ounce of my self-control to hold myself back.

"So which is it?" he asked. "Stay here and let me show you that *we* are not a mistake, or take you to your car?"

He might be right about the vampire blood, but I couldn't be sure the desire I was feeling was all mine. I was confused and angry and a little scared by how much I wanted him and how much he wanted me.

"Take me to my car, please," I said finally.

He reached down and picked up my shirt, his mouth a grim line. "Then burn your blood, and let's go."

After Sean dropped me off at MDI, I went home and put my bloody clothes in cold water to soak while I took a long shower. Once I was dressed, I made a sandwich for a late lunch and settled on the couch with my laptop and the Vamp Court files Mark had given me.

Each file represented either an anti-supe hate group or attacks against a supe or supe-owned business. I sorted the red folders into piles—one for hate groups, three for attacks—and put them in chronological order. Organizing information had always been a calming activity for me. By the time the files were stacked in order and I'd created a spreadsheet for my notes, I felt as if I were back in control.

As I read and made notes, I started to get a clearer picture of the situation, and it wasn't pretty. The heaviest files belonged to Humans First, Human Future, and The Daylighters, which were national organizations with active local chapters, but there were seven other smaller groups in the area. Each folder contained information about crimes the groups had committed (or were suspected of committing) and the CVs of their local leaders. I knew little about Rochelle Potter of Human Future or Jacob Johnson of Humans First, but Don Hall of The Daylighters was one of the city's most vocal opponents of supe rights.

A brief look at the national organizations' websites gave me a better understanding of their doctrines. Unsurprisingly, the websites featured propaganda and outright lies masquerading as fact, vitriolic hate speech, and thinly veiled calls for violence against supes. Their social media activity was mainly racist memes and more propaganda. Several of the local groups' websites didn't even bother to veil their encouragement of attacks on supes and mages. One site had a discussion forum where members could boast about what they'd done. It was hard to tell which accounts were true and which were made up, but either way the hatred was real.

Sean texted around four to report Cyro hadn't been able to find any traffic cam images of the red car that picked Danielle up the night before, which wasn't surprising. There weren't many cameras in that part of town. I made more coffee and went back to the files.

If the hate group files were bad, the records and photos of attacks against supes and supe-owned businesses were so much worse. There was a sharp increase in violence in the past year since the police had begun to openly speculate that a vampire or group of vampires were taking women from the Stroll. The attacks ranged from property damage to beatings and stabbings, including one knife attack that left a male werewolf permanently disabled.

By five, I couldn't read any more. I stacked up the files, curled up on the couch, and called Mark.

He answered almost immediately. "Dunlap."

"Hey, Mark. Have I caught you at a bad time?"

"No. I'm sitting in a van, just off Sixth near the park, keeping an eye on things. You're supposed to be resting up for tonight."

"Yeah, that's not working very well. I'm way too keyed up." I sipped my coffee. "You want some company for a while?"

"Sure." He told me where he was parked. "Leave your car over on Lescom and Third at the gas station. If anyone's lurking around out here, I don't want them seeing your car or your license plate."

"Roger that. You want me to bring you some coffee or anything?"

"That would be great. The gas station has good Danishes. I'll take two, in case you're feeling generous."

"Well, here we are again, just like old times." Mark grunted as he settled himself more comfortably in the driver's seat. "Except I don't remember getting this stiff and achy the last time we had to do this."

I poured him a cup of coffee from a thermos and handed it over. He'd already eaten the Danishes I'd brought. "Here, old man."

Mark took the coffee and snorted. "Old man my ass." He drank half the cup in one gulp. "Thanks for the coffee. You bring this from home?"

"Yup. Ground it myself, just for you."

"Fancy."

We sipped quietly and watched the park.

"You feeling okay?" Mark asked.

I glanced at him. "Sure. Why wouldn't I be?"

"I heard about what happened with Adam. You shouldn't have delayed getting help after he grabbed you."

I scowled. "Sean narc'd on me?"

"Don't get riled up. I called him to get the straight story, since I knew you'd downplay the whole thing."

"The damage was a little worse than I thought at first," I admitted. "I figured I would be fine to just wait until I got home to use a healing spell. Adam only had me for a few seconds."

"A few seconds is more than enough time to fry your brain. You know that," he scolded me.

I sighed. "I shouldn't have let him grab me."

More silence. The sun was setting. Homeless men and women trickled into the park, pushing carts or carrying backpacks, congregating in small groups. It looked like most of the park's overnight residents had decided there was more safety in numbers.

Mark shifted in his seat again. "Thanks for coming down here."

"You're welcome. It's nice to just sit and chat."

Mark grunted and finished his cup of coffee. He watched the activity in the park while I kept an eye on passing vehicles and pedestrians. Neither of us saw anything suspicious, but I jotted down a few license plates of vehicles I thought might have passed us more than once.

"I'm sorry about Sharon," he said, breaking the silence.

I shrugged. "She has every right to be concerned, I suppose, all things considered. I didn't leave your firm on the best of terms, and it's been almost four years since we've seen each other. I'm not taking it personally."

"She doesn't like that I work for the Court," Mark said, startling me. "She doesn't trust them."

"Really? I didn't realize that." I wondered if that had always been the case. I certainly hadn't picked up on any animosity when I worked for MDI, but it might explain why she'd been so antagonistic yesterday.

"It's made things difficult, as you might imagine." Mark shifted in his seat. His back popped audibly. "She's wanted me to cut ties with the Court, but I told her this was too important for me to not look into it. The Court's footing the bill, but I figure I'm working for the missing women and their families."

I smiled. "I feel the same way."

He patted my knee. "I know you do."

About twenty minutes later, as it was getting dark, Mark interrupted my thoughts. "Nothing happening here. I'm going to check on some folks I know who stay at the camp by the river."

"You want me to come with you?" I asked hopefully.

Mark turned the key in the ignition and fastened his seatbelt. "Nah, I've got this. You'd probably better be heading home to take a nap and get ready."

I groaned and reached for my bag. "I really do not want to do this," I complained.

"Join the club." Mark glanced at my thermos. "Anything left in there?"

"Yeah, quite a bit. You can have it. I'll get the thermos back from you later."

"You want a ride to your car?"

"It's only a couple of blocks." I opened the door of the van and hopped down.

"Alice." Mark's voice stopped me. "We'll get them. Maybe not today, maybe not tomorrow, but we'll get them."

We traded tired smiles. "If you need anything, call me," I said. "See you at Northbourne in a couple of hours."

I shut the door and waited as Mark pulled away from the curb. He gave me a little wave, then headed off down the street.

When the perimeter wards tingled at precisely eleven fifteen, I had been ready and anxiously pacing the living room for more than twenty minutes. I picked up my handbag and headed for the door just as someone crossed my porch and knocked loudly.

I opened my door to find Bryan Smith, Charles Vaughan's enormous security man, standing on my doorstep. Instead of his usual all-black attire, he wore a tuxedo. I had no idea they made them that big.

"Miss Alice," he boomed. "You look lovely."

"Thank you, Bryan." I stepped out onto the porch and closed the door behind me. "You don't look too shabby yourself."

My dress was royal blue, with a long, flowing skirt and an empire waist and one strap, held with a gold ring on top of my left shoulder. I'd pulled my hair up in a loose, messy bun, and wore simple diamond earrings, my charm bracelet, and my monogram pendant.

The enforcer offered me his arm, and I slid my hand into the crook of his elbow as we headed down my porch steps to the sidewalk. A stretch Hummer waited at the curb, its motor rumbling.

Bryan opened the door of the limo and helped me climb inside. I settled into the seat as he got in after me and closed the door. As soon as Bryan was seated, the limo glided away from the curb.

"Can I get you a drink?" He gestured at the minibar.

As much as I wanted a good stiff drink, I needed a clear head. "Water would be lovely."

He took a bottle of water from the small refrigerator. He uncapped it, wrapped it in a napkin, and handed it to me.

"How have you been?" I asked.

"Very busy. Improving security around Mr. Vaughan's residence and his businesses, looking into potential threats."

"Have there been any attacks?"

"None yet. We're vigilant." He studied me. "You've been avoiding Hawthorne's and Mr. Vaughan."

"I've been buried with work lately."

When Bryan snorted, he sounded like a buffalo. "So you've said." His phone buzzed, and he looked at the message, his brow furrowing.

The rest of the drive to Northbourne was silent except for the buzzing of Bryan's phone as he sent and received a dozen messages during our journey. His tension grew as we traveled to the north side of the city, but I knew there was little point in asking what he was worried about. Bryan was as cagey as his employer.

A half-hour later, the limo slowed and turned through an imposing gate. Northbourne was located just outside the city, surrounded by one hundred acres of forest and an enormous lawn featuring gardens and a complex maze I'd never attempted to navigate.

The limo glided to a smooth stop in front of the mansion. Bryan got out and came around to my side. He helped me step down onto the pavement and I looked up at the headquarters of the Vampire Court of the Northwestern United States.

Northbourne towered above us. Originally the home of a shipping magnate, it was purchased by the Court and remodeled around 1900. The wide front steps led to an impressive pair of double doors that looked like they belonged on a medieval fortress.

As we headed up the steps, the door swung open, revealing another enormous enforcer in a tuxedo. I recognized him as Adam's escort from earlier in the day. "Good evening, Miss Worth," he rumbled politely.

I gave him a tight smile. "Good evening."

Bryan and I stepped inside. The entryway was magnificent, soaring five stories above us to a rotunda. A wide staircase led up and branched left and right, while doors lined the walls, leading into the maze of hallways and rooms of the mansion. My heels clicked on the marble floor.

"Is Mark here yet?" I asked.

The enforcer closed the door. "Not yet. I've been instructed to bring you before the Court."

My stomach somersaulted. "Shouldn't we wait until Mark gets here?"

"I've been instructed to bring you before the Court," he repeated.

Bryan put his hand on mine where it rested on his arm. The message was clear: we weren't waiting for Mark. I was going to face the Court on my own.

I took a deep breath. "Let's do it."

The enforcer led me to the main staircase. We ascended to the first landing, then turned and went up the stairs on the right to the second-floor gallery. Bryan and I followed our guide down the gallery. We were not headed for the courtroom I'd been in twice before; instead, our destination appeared to be a set of double doors at the end of the corridor. I kept my head high and hoped no one could hear my heart pounding. Where the hell was Mark?

Our guide opened the doors and stepped aside. Bryan and I entered the room beyond.

It was a more elegant version of the courtroom I'd been in before. There were nine throne-like chairs arranged in a wide arc on a dais at the far end, behind a beautiful ornate table. The walls were covered with tapestries, the ceiling with painted scenes from Greek and Roman mythology. A crystal chandelier illuminated the room with a soft golden glow. Two large, empty chairs stood facing the dais. My shoes sank into carpet so deep and thick that it felt like beach sand.

Bryan and I crossed the carpet. He led me to one of the chairs that faced the dais. When I started to sit, he stopped me. "Please remain standing."

A door opened at each end of the dais and eight members of the Vampire Court filed in. The men wore suits, the women brightly colored evening wear. Each wore a medal signifying their position on the Court.

My eyes went immediately to Charles. His face was expressionless. If I'd been hoping for some measure of reassurance from him, there was none to be had. The other vampires were equally impassive as they moved soundlessly to stand beside their chairs.

The Court sat according to seniority. The empty chair in the middle belonged to Valas, who had not yet appeared. To her right sat Niara and her sister Amira. Both sisters were dark-skinned and tall, but Niara wore her hair long and braided, while Amira's was a halo of natural curls around her head. On Amira's right sat Charles, and beside him, on the end, was Ossun, a shorter, dark-haired man of Persian descent.

To Valas's left sat Peter, an older man with white hair and piercing blue eyes. To Peter's left was David Noble, tall and imposing, with a deep, booming voice and dark hair and eyes. Next to him was Friedrich. He was from Germany originally, and that was all I knew about him. On the far left sat Marin, the youngest vampire on the Court. She was petite, with long, white-blonde hair and green eyes.

I fixed my gaze on Valas's empty chair, while eight vampires stared at me. A full minute passed.

Suddenly, the doors directly behind the center chair swung open and Valas appeared, wearing a dark purple dress that contrasted sharply with the bright colors worn by Niara, Amira, and Marin. Her hair was black, and she wore it long and straight.

Vampires didn't age once they were turned, but as the decades and centuries passed, they became leaner and more predatory in appearance. Marin still looked entirely human, except for the pallor of her skin and the sharpness of her eyes.

Despite her striking beauty, Valas had the eyes and stare of a raptor. If Marin could pass as human with a little makeup, there was zero doubt the Court's head was a very old vampire. The shadows seemed to gather around her like a shroud. The hairs on my arms prickled as she stared down at me. I kept my eyes on her chair.

Finally, Valas spoke. *"Be seated."*

My legs folded as if of their own accord. I dropped inelegantly onto the chair behind me as the nine members of the Court settled into their seats and Bryan remained standing at my side. I raised my shields more and managed not to scowl. One point to Valas.

Unlike the courtroom where I had presented evidence against the half-demon Scott Grierson, everything about this room was designed to intimidate the person or persons giving testimony before the Court. The lights behind the dais, though dim, were directed at my eye level. The dais was raised and at such a distance from my chair that I was forced to look up at the Court at an angle guaranteed to leave me with a neck cramp. While they sat behind a long table, I had no such psychological or physical barrier, nor any place to rest my hands or my handbag besides my own lap. Bryan stood beside me, but his presence was not exactly reassuring. Though we were on friendly terms, there was no question who he worked for or where his loyalties lay.

I had the sudden and unwelcome feeling I was about to be tried before the Court. It occurred to me to wonder if they'd engineered a delay in Mark's arrival so they might speak to me alone, but to what end? Everything we'd done so far was by the book. Maybe this was more vampire head games, trying to catch me off guard, but I couldn't see a point to it.

I quashed my unease, raised my chin an inch, and met Valas's gaze. Her eyes were black and fathomless.

"Miss Worth." Valas's voice, though pitched low, traveled across the room with ease. "The Court welcomes you."

"Thank you for inviting me." My voice held a slight edge. "Where is Mark?"

"Mr. Dunlap has been delayed," Valas told me. "Our time is limited, so we wish to hear your account of the investigation."

"I assume you've read Mark's reports. Do you have questions I can answer? If I knew what you wanted clarification on—"

"We require a full account of your findings to this point," Niara said.

I steeled myself and looked at Niara. Her eyes, normally dark brown, were lit from within with soft amber light. *Beautiful*, I thought, then shook myself.

"I can't speak to what Mark did before I started working two days ago," I said. "I can give you a report of what we've done since then."

"Proceed." Valas's voice was brisk.

I told them everything we had discovered and done since Mark had brought me the case files. I wasn't sure if Mark had had an opportunity to submit reports about our visits to Sister Berry and the homeless outreach center, or about Adam's visions of the surviving victims, but I included that information. The vampires listened to my report, as silent and still as statues.

When I finished my report, Niara spoke again. "You suffer no ill effects from the mishap with our Seer?"

"None at all." I'd hoped to thank Niara privately, rather than alert the entire Court that I had been healed with her blood, but it appeared I would have no choice. "Please accept my thanks for the healing."

Niara smiled and I took a deep, involuntary breath at the shiver that ran down my spine. "No thanks are necessary," she said, her voice like warm chocolate. "I am extremely gratified to hear you are well. I would not have any harm befall an investigator of the Court as she works tirelessly on our behalf."

Charles leaned forward, his eyes darkening. I worried he would demand an explanation for my consumption of Niara's blood, but instead he asked about something I'd mentioned earlier. "You say you have been in contact with a SPEMA agent who is investigating the possibility of harnad involvement. Who is this agent? He is not named in Mark Dunlap's reports."

"I am not at liberty to say."

Nine pairs of angry vampire eyes focused on me. "You *will* tell us," Valas said. I sensed a push along with her words, but this time my shields were at full strength and I felt no compulsion to obey. Point to me.

I looked at Valas's left shoulder, avoiding her angry gaze. "It is my judgment that doing so may compromise this agent's ability to conduct his or her investigation, if it becomes known to other SPEMA agents that this agent might be pursuing other avenues. We have precious few allies in law enforcement, or among the public at large. I don't think it would be in our best interest to jeopardize this person, when we may need their help in the near future."

"Your reasoning is sound," Valas said. "We are displeased to have this information withheld, but we understand the need to protect this ally's identity."

"Does this investigator believe we are not to be trusted to keep the information secure?" Friedrich glowered at me, then spoke to Valas in heavily accented English. "I do not see why the identity of this agent must be hidden from *us*."

I opened my mouth to speak but Valas silenced me with a single raised finger. "Information is like water," she said to the German vampire. "It finds weaknesses and leaks with surprising ease. If Miss Worth and Mr. Dunlap believe it in the best interest of this Court for this agent to remain anonymous *for now*, then I am content to agree. We have no reason to doubt their judgment."

Ossun spoke. "And yet, despite the thoroughness of their investigation, we remain guilty in the eyes of the public and law enforcement." He stared down at me. "You have identified a clear suspect and an accomplice and yet they have not been questioned. Why can we not bring these people here and discover the whereabouts of the survivors?"

"West may be the head of a harnad of more than a dozen powerful blood mages," I said. "I don't have to tell you how much destruction a harnad that size could unleash. More critically, if he disappears, the harnad may kill all the survivors to prevent them from testifying. Besides, it's not enough for *you* to obtain a confession from West, or from Rachel Barrow, because it wouldn't be admissible in human court. We need concrete proof we can take to law enforcement."

Silence.

I continued. "The mages who are responsible need to face justice and I want the victims back *alive*." My voice carried through the room. "We need their testimony, first of all. Second, they're victims in need of rescue. Everything we've been doing is in the interest of clearing vampires of involvement, getting justice for the victims, and rescuing the survivors. I assure you we are moving as quickly—and as *deliberately*—as we can."

I met the gazes of all nine members of the Court. Some were angry, some thoughtful, others appraising.

My handbag buzzed. "Excuse me." I unzipped my bag to glance at my phone. *Lake Calling*. I frowned and sent the call to voice mail. "Sorry," I said, looking back at the Court. "What other questions can I answer for you?"

"What are your plans—" Niara began.

My phone buzzed again. I swiped the red button and rejected Lake's call.

Bryan's phone buzzed as a man in black entered from behind the dais and hurried to Valas's side. He bent to whisper in her ear.

My phone buzzed. *Lake Calling*.

Valas glanced at me as her security man spoke urgently in an undertone. Uneasiness formed a lead ball in my stomach.

I hit the green button and put the phone to my ear. "This is not a good time," I murmured.

"I need you to come to Twelfth and Whitman." Lake's voice was flat. "The alley behind the furniture store. Right now."

I expected Valas to demand that I end my call with Lake, but instead she watched me, saying nothing. "I'm in a meeting," I said. "What's this about?"

His tone gentled. "It's best if you come down here."

And that's when I knew.

It seemed as though all the air was sucked out of the room at once. I sat frozen, unable to move, my heart thudding in my ears. Deep inside my chest, something dark took hold and began to grow.

"Miss Alice," Bryan rumbled, a warning note in his voice.

Up on the dais, Valas motioned for the man who'd been whispering to her to step back and turned her attention to me. "Ms. Worth."

"Alice, did you hear me?" Lake asked. He sounded concerned.

"I'm on my way." I disconnected the call, stuck the phone in my bag, and stood. My chest felt tight, as if my fury might explode through my ribs at any moment. "I'm leaving."

Valas gestured at my chair. "Our conversation is not finished."

The pressure that had been building inside me burst through my skin. Cold green fire ignited along my arms and enveloped my upper body. Beneath my feet, the floor trembled from the force of my earth magic.

Black-clad enforcers appeared from the shadows and formed a circle around me. The vampires up on the dais stayed seated. For a long moment, no one moved.

I stared at Valas and our eyes locked. "It's finished for now," I stated. Air magic sparked on my hands. "Don't try to keep me from leaving."

Every shadow in the room seemed to gather around her as she rose to her feet. Dark magic swirled between us and the air filled with an ancient scent—something I'd never smelled before, but would from this moment associate with power.

"What is that scent?" The question spilled out before I realized I'd spoken.

Valas studied me. "I spent many days watching the mosaics being made in the Hagia Sophia. It was so new, the right to make images. Outside of the city, a man I knew owned an orchard. Such a bounty of the most delectable fruits. Have you ever had a fresh-drawn glass of blood mixed with the juice of a Byzantine pomegranate? Pomegranate seeds for Persephone; blood for the gods themselves." She leaned forward, her eyes flashing like lightning. "You have met vampires who smell like wine, like spice, like one fruit or another. Child, listen, and understand when I say, I am the whole of the orchard."

Her magic swelled until I thought I might be crushed by it. I pushed back with a burst of air magic, the bright white energy displacing the darkness, and my ears popped. Her magic withdrew, the shadows settling onto her shoulders like a mantle.

A long silence. The rest of the Court sat very still. No one breathed.

I'd gotten a taste of Valas's power and magic, and it was enough for me to know she was more than simply the oldest and most powerful vampire in the room. It was possible I could still get out of the building and away, even if she tried to prevent me. It was also equally possible we'd destroy Northbourne in the process.

Fortunately, it appeared neither of us wanted the evening to end that way.

"You may leave," Valas said. "We will speak again, once this terrible business is concluded. Mr. Smith, you will take her wherever she needs to go."

I drew my magic back beneath my skin and looked up at Valas. Perhaps I was imagining it—I almost certainly was—but I thought I saw a hint of pity in those ancient eyes.

"Thank you," I said. I grabbed my purse, gathered up my skirt, and ran.

14

WE COULDN'T GET ANYWHERE NEAR TWELFTH AND WHITMAN; POLICE CARS WITH lights flashing formed a blockade at Thirteenth and the entire block between Thirteenth and Fourteenth was full of news vans and onlookers.

Bryan pulled to the curb next to a closed coffee shop. I jumped from the SUV before it was even in park and headed for the police tape, pushing my way through the crowd.

Just as I reached the barricade, someone took my arm. "Alice."

I looked up into familiar ice-blue eyes. Lake.

I was used to seeing him in his off-hours lately, so it took me a moment to realize he was wearing a shirt and tie and a dark blue jacket with *SPEMA* emblazoned on the front and back.

Bryan came up behind me, still wearing his tux. "Who are you?" Lake asked.

"I'm with her," Bryan rumbled. "Vampire Court security."

If Lake was surprised by how I was dressed or that I had a Court escort, he didn't show it. "You'll stay outside of the tape. I'll take her back."

The two men eyed each other. I knew Bryan recognized Lake from his visits to Hawthorne's. The enforcer glanced at Lake's hand on my arm. So much for keeping Lake's identity a secret from the Court.

Finally, Bryan gave Lake a nod. "I'll wait here."

Lake lifted the tape for me. My feet felt like lead as we walked silently away from the crowd.

The entrance to the alley was blocked by more tape and three uniformed officers. One of them held up the tape for us.

A half-dozen people were crowded into the alley. Two crime scene investigators in uniform took pictures while a third made notes on a clipboard. Two men in suits wearing police department IDs talked quietly. One of them, a dark-haired man in his mid-thirties, glanced up as we entered the alley. "Alice," he said in greeting.

Dimly, I realized it was Detective Ernie Diaz, but my attention was focused on the scene in front of me.

Mark lay on his back next to an overflowing dumpster. He wore the same plaid shirt, jeans, and work boots he'd had on when I'd seen him earlier. His eyes were wide open, staring sightlessly up at the streetlight. I didn't see any wounds, but his skin was gray and bloodless. His hands had been bagged for trace evidence.

A heavyset man in medical examiner coveralls crouched near the body. He rose as we approached.

My heel caught on a crack in the pavement and I stumbled. Lake caught me by the arm. "Are you all right?"

"Who found him?" I heard myself ask.

Lake let go, but stayed close. "Two junkies. They've already been taken downtown for questioning."

"What time?"

"Just before midnight."

I looked around, but saw no cameras in the alley. That was probably why he'd been dumped here. "Where's his van?"

"What van?" Diaz asked sharply. "We have a Dodge pickup registered to him."

"He was driving a white panel van." I gave him the license plate. "It's registered to MDI."

As he wrote down the information, the other detective spoke up. His police ID read Ferguson. "The van could be the vehicle fire they had over on Third," he told Diaz. "The fire department said it was a delivery van of some kind. I'll have them take it to the lab for processing." He stepped away to make a phone call.

I approached Mark's body slowly. Lake hung back and the M.E. moved away to give me what little privacy could be had with this many people around. The detectives were tense; they didn't like someone getting close to a body, possibly compromising evidence. I gathered my skirt in one hand so it didn't touch the pavement or Mark's body and crouched carefully next to him.

I had my back to the detectives and Lake, who were conversing quietly. I let them think I was saying goodbye, but I had another, more important purpose. I did not, however, have the luxury of taking my time about it, judging by the way Diaz's eyes drilled into the back of my head. This was going to hurt.

I braced myself as best I could, touched a single fingertip lightly to Mark's cool arm, and dropped my shields.

It wasn't the agony sharing Adam's visions had been, because this was my own kind of magic, but there was so much magical trace coming at me from every direction that for a moment my senses shorted out. I ignored the pain and focused on what I needed to do.

Through my fingertip, I sensed two specific traces lingering on Mark's skin: a faded trace of air magic and strong, recent blood magic. The latter was so powerful that when I tried to follow the trace to get a better sense of the mage who'd left it, it lashed me like a whip and with my shields down, it hit me like a physical blow. I fell backward with a gasp.

Lake was at my side immediately. As he squatted next to me, I slammed my shields closed and the sudden silence in my head left me disoriented.

I swayed as his hands tightened on my upper arms. "Don't pass out," he murmured, his lips near my ear. "Get your feet under you. We're standing up."

We rose. I let him steady me, but when my head started to clear, I took a step away to show I could stand on my own.

The medical examiner joined us. "Are you lightheaded?"

"No, I'm fine," I lied. "It's just..." I looked away. I'd rather they thought I was overcome with emotion than suspected what I'd been up to.

"Do you need to sit down?" Lake asked. "We can put you in a squad car for a few minutes."

"I'll be okay." I looked at the M.E. "Cause of death?"

"Looks like a vamp. Can't confirm till I get him on the table."

I thought of Mark on an autopsy table and flinched. "Show me the bite, please."

The M.E. looked at the detectives and raised his eyebrows.

"Show her," Diaz said.

The M.E. squatted down and pulled back Mark's collar. I forced myself to bend over and look. There on his neck were two neat round holes. My vision tunneled until all I could see was that wound.

Behind me, Lake said something, but I didn't hear him. Someone else spoke and Lake responded, his voice sharp. It sounded like an argument was breaking out over jurisdiction. I was about to complicate matters considerably.

I couldn't tell them about the magic I'd sensed. It was unlikely they would believe me, and since magical evidence was not admissible in human court, most law enforcement personnel discounted it entirely. Luckily, there was more than just the trace that might lead them away from the obvious explanation for Mark's death.

"Doctor, how much blood do you think is left in his body?" I asked.

"Can't say for sure," the medical examiner said, letting go of Mark's collar as Diaz and Lake continued to argue. "Just looking at him, I'd say maybe a half a liter, probably less."

"This wasn't a vamp," I told him.

That brought an immediate end to the heated debate going on behind me. "The hell it wasn't," Diaz snapped. He was suddenly at my side as the M.E. got to his feet. Ferguson was joined by a petite woman I recognized as Detective Shay. All four of them stared at me, their faces hostile. "That's a fucking vampire bite," Diaz said.

I shook my head as Lake moved next to me. "Those holes are perfectly round. They could just as easily have been made by large-bore needles."

"There was saliva around the bite," the M.E. informed me coldly. "We ran a presumptive test. It came back as vampire saliva, not human. He's been drained."

"Then the saliva was planted. If that's the only wound, it couldn't have been a vampire. No single vampire could drain an entire body; it's not physically possible."

Doubt flashed in the M.E.'s eyes. He exchanged glances with the detectives.

I opened my mouth to argue the point, but Diaz interrupted me. "Get her out of here," he told Lake.

"You should be listening to her." Lake crossed his arms and stared at the shorter man.

Diaz didn't back down. "She *works* for the vamps; she's just trying to cover for them. We allowed you in here as a courtesy, but I'm done listening to this bullshit. Now both of you, get the hell out of my crime scene."

"You cannot be serious." I looked at the M.E., who stared back at me stonily. "You're a medical examiner; you know one vampire can't drain a body completely.

Those have to be needle marks made by someone trying to make it *look* like a vampire did this."

"Get her out of here or I'll arrest her," Diaz snapped.

"Alice, let's go," Lake said, gently taking me by the arm.

"No." I pulled against his grip, my eyes on the body on the pavement. "Mark..."

"Lake, you've got ten seconds to clear this scene before I'm calling your field office," Diaz said.

"We're leaving." Lake's suppressed anger vibrated through his hand on my arm, but he set his jaw and pulled me toward the tape barrier at the end of the alley.

Detective Ferguson stared at me with undisguised contempt as we passed. He didn't move aside, and I bumped into him. Magic sparked when my hand brushed his, and he jumped back with a startled sound. My control was slipping. I snuffed out my air magic and kept moving.

"Worth." Diaz's voice stopped me. His arms were crossed as he stared at me. "We'll be wanting to talk to you soon."

I didn't trust myself to respond, so I gave him a jerky nod and turned away. We ducked under the tape and I let Lake guide me back toward the police barricade, my steps robotic. I felt as if I were abandoning Mark in the alley and my heart hurt like someone was squeezing it in their fist.

A uniform lifted the yellow tape for us and we stepped into the crowd. I pulled out of Lake's grip. "It wasn't a vampire," I insisted.

Lake rubbed his forehead. "I believe you, but it's a local case and Diaz doesn't want SPEMA involved. We have no jurisdiction unless the locals invite us in and you heard him: he's not about to hand the case over to us."

"They won't listen to me because I work for the Court. Call the state; get them to send someone here from the Chief Medical Examiner's Office to assess the case, overrule the county M.E.'s opinion."

Lake sighed. "I can try, but they're going to be reluctant to step on a local M.E.'s toes unless I can give them something definitive. Let's go somewhere quiet and you can tell me what you know."

Bryan appeared out of the crowd and I confronted him. "Tell me you didn't know Mark was lying here dead the whole time I was asking you where he was."

He shook his head. "I found out the same time you did, Alice."

"But you knew he was missing, not 'delayed.'" I shook with anger. "Was that what all those texts were about on the way to Northbourne, and you didn't say a goddamned word?"

Bryan said nothing. He didn't have to. It was obvious the Court knew Mark was missing and had ordered him not to tell me ahead of the meeting.

I turned away from the enforcer, too furious to speak. Lake put his hand on the small of my back, offering support. I moved away and he dropped his hand to his side.

Bryan's phone buzzed. He glanced at the screen, then at me. "I'm sorry to leave you here, but I'm needed back at Northbourne."

My voice was cold. "Tell the Court whoever killed Mark tried to make it look like a vampire drained him, and it looks like the M.E. and the cops are falling for it. When this hits the news—if it hasn't already—there may be trouble."

"I'll let them know." Bryan handed me my purse. I'd left it in the SUV and not even noticed. "Get her home safe," he told Lake before disappearing into the crowd.

I glanced at the alley. A coroner's van had appeared, backed up to the crime-scene tape. As I watched, the front doors opened and two men in coveralls got out. They unloaded a stretcher with a black body bag and a sheet folded on top and disappeared into the alley.

Lake's hand closed on my arm. I realized I'd taken several steps back toward the barricade without noticing I'd moved. "Let's go, Alice. There's nothing more we can do here tonight. I'm parked just up here, on the right."

He led me through the crowd of onlookers and past the news vans. His black pickup was parked haphazardly in front of a closed accountant's office.

Mark.

I stopped and bent double, the pain so intense that I couldn't get a breath. I made a broken sound.

Lake came back and took my hand. "Come on," he said gently. "Let's get you home."

The drive to my house was a blur. At some point, I started shivering, and Lake pulled over long enough to make me put on his jacket. I wrapped it around myself and stared out the window of the truck, seeing nothing. My stomach hurt like I'd been gutted with a dull knife. I barely registered arriving home or lowering the wards to let us in.

Lake settled me on the couch and looked around my living room. "I'm not sure what I imagined your house looking like on the inside, but I didn't expect an empty room."

I realized belatedly that I'd never let him in past my wards. There was a SPEMA agent inside my house, feet away from the door to my basement, and I felt nothing about it. I felt nothing about anything.

He nudged a stack of red folders with his foot. "What's all this?"

"Confidential files. Don't touch them."

He crouched in front of me, his eyes searching my face. "Who do you think killed Dunlap?"

"Not vampires." Restlessly, I got up and headed for the kitchen with Lake trailing behind me. The gift bag containing the bottle of Scotch Mark gave me was on the counter. I reached into the bag and took out the wooden box.

"What's that?" he asked.

I held up the bottle so he could see it.

"A twenty-five-year single malt." He sounded surprised. "Nice."

"It was a gift from Mark." I grabbed a glass from a cabinet and returned to the living room, curling up on the couch and tucking my bare feet under the folds of my dress. "Sit," I told Lake.

He perched on the other end of the couch. I poured him two fingers of whisky and held out the glass. He didn't move. "Take it," I said.

He took the glass.

I lifted the bottle. "To Mark."

Lake clinked his glass against the bottle. I put the bottle to my lips and took a drink. It was excellent Scotch.

"Alice." He stared at me.

"Shut up and drink." I raised the bottle again.

He sipped and watched me. We drank in silence.

I was drunk in minutes, but Lake had barely touched his whisky. "What's wrong? Not good enough for you?" I asked him.

He rested his elbows on his knees. "If you know who's responsible for this, tell me. I want to help you."

"You can't. Not your case, not your jurisdiction, remember?"

"You told me the other night a harnad might be involved." His eyes searched my face. "You know who's behind this, don't you?"

"I don't know shit, Lake."

"Don't give me that," he snapped. "I saw you touch him right before you fell down, so I know you got something from the body. Put the bottle down and tell me what you know."

Before I could reply, the perimeter wards tingled. I scowled. "Tell them to go away."

"Tell who to go away?"

Footsteps crossed my porch and someone knocked loudly. "Whoever that is," I said, gesturing in the direction of the door. "Tell them to go away."

He put his drink down on the floor and headed for the door. I took another swig from the bottle of Scotch. The whisky made me numb and disconnected.

I heard the door open and the sound of voices: Lake's and another, deeper and a little growly. I closed my eyes and rested my head on the arm of the couch.

Lake raised his voice. "Alice, can you come to the door, please?" His tone was measured. "The alpha of the Tomb Mountain Pack is here to check on your welfare."

I stood up and walked unsteadily toward the door, my hand trailing along the wall for balance. Lake and Sean were staring each other down. When I appeared, the werewolf was visibly taken aback.

"Mark's dead." My voice sounded hollow.

His eyes glowed with anger. "I know. I tried calling you, but there was no answer."

I leaned against the doorway to steady myself. "I don't know where my phone is."

"It's in your purse, on the kitchen counter," Lake said.

I blinked at him. "Oh."

"I called Hawthorne's, and someone said you'd been taken home. I got worried and came to check on you." Sean eyed Lake, who returned his gaze impassively. "Can I have a word with you in private?"

I stepped out onto the porch. "Give us a minute," I said to Lake.

He looked at Sean, then at me, clearly reluctant to leave me alone. "I'll be inside if you need me," he said finally, and stepped back as I closed the door.

Sean sighed. "Alice, I'm sorry."

I wasn't sure if I was swaying or if I just felt as if I were. I leaned against the door. "They drained him, to make it look like a vampire did it."

"The news said it was a vampire attack, but I knew there had to be more to the story. You're sure it wasn't a vampire?"

"I'm sure." With Lake no doubt listening on the other side of the door, I couldn't tell Sean about the magic trace I'd sensed. That would have to wait until we were alone. *Harnad*, I mouthed.

He crossed his arms. "Why would they leave his body for us to find? We haven't found anyone else."

"To frame the vamps, I suppose. They left him where he'd be found right away."

He moved forward and pressed his lips to my ear, speaking so softly I could barely make out the words. "Agent Lake is watching us through the peephole."

I said nothing.

"Is there something going on between you?" Sean's voice took on an edge. "You smell like him."

I shrugged. "He gave me his coat and drove me home."

"I don't like smelling him on you."

Annoyed, I pushed him away. "Then go."

His eyes went bright gold. "Not a chance."

"Then don't get territorial," I snapped. "I'm not your territory."

He sighed. "I know you're not. How much have you had to drink?"

"What business is it of yours?"

Sean held my upper arms so he could look into my eyes. "Mark's death is not your fault. Don't punish yourself for this."

"You don't know what you're talking about." I pulled away and took two unsteady steps back.

His face hardened. "Don't tell me I don't know what I'm talking about. This isn't the first time I've seen you do this; hell, it's not even the first time *today* you've done it. Not every mistake requires that you beat yourself up, no matter what you might think."

"Just drop it, Sean."

"No, not this time. I'm tired of watching you harm yourself and run yourself into the ground over and over because you think you deserve it. It's obvious someone used to hurt you for making mistakes and you've internalized it until you punish yourself for everything. This is not your fault, Alice, not in any way."

How could Sean look me in the eye and tell me it wasn't my fault? I should have gone with Mark to the homeless camp instead of going home to nap and get ready to go see the damn vamps. I knew we were dangerously close to catching up with the harnad, and yet I let him go alone. Now he was dead. Mark had my back every time I needed him, and when he needed me, I let him down.

I reached for the doorknob. "I'm not in the mood for this right now. Please go."

His voice stopped me. "It wasn't really about the furniture, was it?"

"What?"

"That last fight. You wanted to be rid of me, because you blamed yourself for what happened at the construction site and you were hurting, so you used our disagreement about replacing your furniture as an excuse to break us up. You push people away so they can't see you're vulnerable. I should have figured it out then; if I had, I wouldn't have let you goad me into walking out, right when you needed me most. There is nothing wrong with needing help, Alice."

There was *everything* wrong with needing help, but I couldn't tell him why without telling him who I was, and that wasn't an option. "I don't need your help, Sean. I didn't then and I don't now."

"I don't believe that." He was maddeningly calm. "We shared a link. I know what you felt about me and that it scared you. I know you felt guilty. I just didn't put it all together until now."

"What do you want from me?" I demanded. His expression changed from frustration to alarm as my fists clenched. Magic rose and an unseasonably cold breeze blew over us. "For a month, I've been living on work and whisky. I've barely slept in weeks and now the closest thing I've had to a father since mine was killed was just murdered and dumped in an alley. So if you can't understand why I want to be drunk right now, you can *fuck off!*"

I took a step forward, but Scotch and magic didn't mix and a wave of dizziness made me stumble. Sean grabbed my arm as I started to fall.

I tried to pull away, but he held on. "Let go," I said.

The front door flew open behind me and Lake stepped out, gun raised. "Step. Back."

15

WE FROZE.

"Alice told you to fuck off," Lake said. "So fuck off."

I stood up slowly, easing my arm out of Sean's grip as he stared at the federal agent who was aiming a gun at his head. "Lake." Everything was a little out of focus, and I shook my head to clear it. "I'm okay. Put the gun down."

"When he backs off." Lake's eyes were fixed on Sean's face.

"No, put it down now." I reached out slowly to push his arm down. "He's not a threat. I lost my temper and tripped. We're fine."

Reluctantly, Lake lowered the gun to his side.

"Alice, are you all right?" Sean asked.

I hung onto the door frame with one hand. "I'm fine. I just need to go sit down."

"You should leave," Lake told Sean. "She's been through enough tonight."

My expression went flat. "This is my house, Agent Lake. I decide who stays and who goes. You can both leave."

"You shouldn't be alone," Lake told me, holstering his gun.

"I need some time to myself to deal with this." I stepped past him into the house.

Lake touched my arm. Sean's expression hardened. Lake either didn't notice his reaction or didn't care. "What are your plans for tonight?" the federal agent asked.

"I plan to continue to toast Mark's memory and maybe sleep later, if I can."

Lake's eyes narrowed.

"More whisky won't help," Sean told me, his eyes still on Lake.

"Maybe, maybe not." I reached for the door. "But it's all I've got right now."

"Call me if you need me," Sean said.

I shut the door.

A half-hour later, I emerged from the house and locked it behind me. A light rain had begun to fall. I raised the hood of my sweatshirt and hurried toward my car, keys in hand.

"Where are you going?"

The sudden voice made me jump and whirl around to see a man in a long coat crossing my yard. A familiar black pickup was parked across the street.

"What the hell is your problem, Lake?" I glared at him. "Why are you camped out in front of my house?"

"Because I knew you had no intention of staying home." He walked up and towered over me. He'd taken off his tie and loosened his collar. "Where are you going?" he asked again.

"None of your business." I started to walk around him.

He held out his hand. "Stop. Whatever you're about to go do, stop and think about it."

I *had* been thinking about it, since the moment I saw Mark lying dead in the alley. "I'm running out for some milk."

"At three thirty in the morning, wearing all black?"

I shrugged. "I wanted cereal, and this is all I had to wear that was clean."

"Don't bullshit me, Alice." He got in my face. "Thirty minutes ago, you were so drunk you could barely walk. How are you sober?"

That was definitely not the kind of information I'd willingly share with a federal agent. "I drank a lot of coffee," I lied. "Now get out of my way."

"Not until you tell me where you're going and what ill-advised thing you intend to do when you get there."

"You can't keep me from going, Lake." I turned to walk away.

Metal clanked behind me. By the time I recognized the sound and tried to jump out of reach, it was too late. A handcuff closed on my wrist and a second one clicked.

My mouth fell open. "What the hell do you think you're doing?"

Lake raised his left arm, lifting my right one as it dangled by the cuff around my wrist. "And don't even think about knocking me out with a sleeping spell and running, because I *will* find you and arrest you for assaulting a federal agent."

"You son of a—"

"Now," Lake said calmly. "How about we go inside and you tell me where you were going?"

I turned on my heel and headed back toward my front door, Lake at my side. The handcuff tugged at my wrist. "This is false imprisonment," I fumed as we went up the steps.

"Not at all." Lake wasn't smiling. "Supernatural and Preternatural Entity Registration Act, Article II, Section Four. An agent may hold a suspect or witness in custody for up to seventy-two hours without charge if that person is believed to be a threat to others."

"Do you think I'm a threat?"

His expression was grim. "I have no doubt you are."

I unlocked the front door and dropped my wards. He opened the door and we entered my house. He closed the door and locked it.

"Why don't you have any furniture?" he asked as we went to the kitchen.

"That's also none of your business." I led him to a cupboard, where I got out a glass and filled it with water from the sink.

Lake glanced around the kitchen. His eyes lit up when he spotted my coffeemaker. "How about some coffee?"

"Does this look like a Starbucks to you?" I started to cross my arms, then scowled. "Let me out of these cuffs. This is ridiculous."

"You told me the other night I should consider the possibility a harnad might be behind the kidnappings. I think it's time you stopped being cryptic and told me what you know."

"What I know is the medical examiner said Mark had been completely drained, but vampires can't drain their victims. As soon as the heart stops beating, the blood flow stops. Someone who dies from a vampire bite still has several pints of blood left in their body, unless they're hung upside down, or there are several vamps feeding at once, and even then, there's still some left. You saw the..." I swallowed hard. "The body. There wasn't a drop left."

Lake nodded slowly. "That is true. So, who or what is capable of draining a body dry?"

"The only person I know who could do that is a high-level blood mage."

"If you're right, that supports the theory a harnad is responsible for Mark Dunlap's murder. It doesn't necessarily mean it's connected to the missing prostitutes." He leaned against the counter next to me. "What else do you know?"

"We got a tip about some homeless people who have disappeared." I told him about Sister Berry, my visit to the outreach center—leaving out Sean's involvement—and that Mark had been watching the park before leaving to look for people he knew who might have some information. "Someone must have seen him asking questions. They took him somewhere, drained him dry, and dumped him in an alley for us to find, to make sure the vamps got blamed."

"And where were you going just now?"

"To retrace his steps and see if I could figure out who got him and where."

Lake's eyes narrowed. "I don't think that's where you were headed. I think you had a target in mind. You were moving like you had a very specific mission."

"I *am* on a mission. I want to know who killed Mark and I want to make them pay for what they did. I don't know who killed him, but I intend to find out." I raised my arm and jingled the cuffs. "I told you what you wanted to know. Take it off."

"You told me part of it. I want the rest."

"There is nothing else I can tell you."

He made a sound low in his throat that sounded like a growl. "I could arrest you for obstruction."

I gave him a half-shrug. "I suppose you could. Your partner wouldn't hesitate to do it. So what's keeping you from hauling me downtown and throwing me in a cell?"

"I don't know." He slid his hand over so it was touching mine. "Or maybe I do."

We stood silently, staring into space, not looking at each other.

"You looked beautiful in that dress," he said finally. "I shouldn't even have noticed, probably, given the circumstances, but I did." He closed his fingers around mine. "I wonder what it says about me that I think you look even more beautiful wearing burglar clothes."

"These are not burglar clothes," I informed him. "This is what I wear to go sleuthing."

"Black hoodie, black jeans, black boots." He reached into my pocket and pulled something out, holding it up. "And black gloves."

I took my glove back. "It's cold outside."

"It's not that cold." He laced his fingers through mine and turned to face me. When he spoke, his voice was strangely gentle. "Talk to me, Alice."

I tried to pull my hand away, but he held tight. "You just don't give up," I said with a sigh.

He smiled—not the deliberately charming smile he'd unleashed on me before, or its more shark-like version, but an affectionate, easy grin. "We've been over this. It's one of my finer qualities, remember?"

I huffed. "Maybe your boss at SPEMA thinks it's a positive character trait, but it's a little less endearing to have you popping up all over the place, trying to catch me doing something that might get me in trouble."

Lake tilted his head. "What have you done that might get you in trouble?"

Exasperated, I pulled free and yanked on the handcuff. "I'm going to do something that'll get me in a *lot* of trouble if you don't take off these damn cuffs."

"I'll take them off right now if you tell me where you were headed."

"I told you—"

"—A lie," he interrupted. "A convincing one, I'll give you that, but still a lie. In fact, I'd guess at least eighty percent of everything you've ever told me since the moment we met has been a lie."

"Then why the hell do you keep asking me questions?"

"Because I keep hoping one day you'll decide to tell me the truth." He took my hand again. "Forget the construction site murders. Forget whatever the hell happened to you last night outside the Midnite Café, or how you sobered up so fast when you clearly haven't brewed any coffee in here. Tell me who you think killed the man who was like a second father to you. Let me help you get justice for Mark Dunlap without getting yourself killed in the process."

"I don't know why you're so sure I'd get myself killed."

"If your target is a high-level blood mage or a harnad full of them, you're likely to end up dead. I don't want to find your body in an alley or have you disappear too."

"Mark was my mentor," I ground out. "My friend. And, yes, a second father or something close to that. I told him I would have his back, and now he's dead."

"Is that what this is? You think he died on your watch, so you're going out in the middle of the night on a suicide mission to try to kill the blood mage who murdered him?"

I said nothing.

"Silence instead of a lie; that's progress, at least." His tone was dry.

"Just go, Lake," I said dully. "Take off the damn cuffs and go home and leave me alone."

"Let's go together."

I blinked up at him. "Go where?"

"To find the blood mage." His jaw was set. "That's where you were headed, right? Let's go. I'm your backup."

"Forget it."

"Why not? You don't think I'm good enough to back you up?"

"I'm sure you would be if we were both federal agents executing a legal warrant and arresting a person suspected of murder, but that's not what would be happening. This isn't a job for SPEMA."

"It's a job for a lone vigilante who's so angry she's not thinking straight?" I opened my mouth to retort, but he continued. "And I never said I was going with you as a SPEMA agent."

"There's no other way for you to do anything."

Lake pulled out his credentials and tossed them on the counter. "What if I went with you as Trent? Not Lake, not a SPEMA agent. Just Trent."

I snorted. "This again? Even if you left behind your I.D. and your government-issued guns, you're still a fed. You think like a fed, you act like a fed, and when the chips are down, you'll react like a fed."

His expression hardened. "If that was true, I would have arrested you for killing Scott Grierson. I certainly would have turned in the earring I found at the construction site and had you hauled in for questioning. I'd have taken you downtown the night I ran into you on the Stroll the first time, when you were obviously withholding crucial information about the case. I would have taken you into protective custody when you showed up bloody and beaten the other night, or tonight for obstruction, since you clearly know who is responsible for Mark Dunlap's murder, or at least have a strong enough suspicion that you're ready to act on it. I did *none of those things*, so why do you keep trying to convince yourself that I'm nothing more than a goddamn fed?"

I stared up at him, stunned into silence.

Lake's eyes blazed. "If you ask me to, I will go with you to find the blood mage who killed your friend. I am not my badge, Alice." He pulled me against his body and lowered his mouth to mine.

The force of his kiss surprised me, though it shouldn't have. If I'd come to know anything about Lake over the past month or so, it was that he never did anything in half measures. My fingers tightened in his shirt, feeling the hardness of his chest, as his hand cupped the back of my head. He tasted perfect, like coffee and a hint of Scotch.

He pulled back to stare into my eyes. "Who am I?"

"Trent," I said softly.

He sat me on the counter so our heights were more evenly matched and nudged my knees apart. He moved between my thighs and pulled me close as his mouth returned to mine. Desire, hot and hungry, made me slip my free hand under his coat so I could slide my fingers into his waistband and tug him to me. He took my other hand in his and laced our fingers together.

I was suddenly very aware of the cuff on my right wrist and it occurred to me handcuffs could be fun. I didn't know if it was me or if my reaction was enhanced by Niara's blood, but I didn't particularly care. He was dangerous—a federal agent with the power to turn my life upside down—but in the wake of Mark's death, the danger was arousing. It made me feel alive instead of numb.

He slid a hand under my sweatshirt to curve around my waist, his fingers warm. His touch was electric and I gasped a little against his mouth at the sensation.

Lake drew back. "I've been wanting to do that for a long time." He brushed the hair back from my face, tucking it behind my ear. "So, where are we going?"

I was confused before I remembered what we'd been discussing. "You can't come with me."

Frustrated, he ran his free hand through his hair. "Why the hell not?"

I opened my mouth, a half-dozen easy lies on the tip of my tongue. Instead, I surprised myself. "Because he'll kill you."

He stared at me. "I think that was the truth. What will happen to you if you go by yourself?"

"He'll almost certainly kill me."

"If I take these cuffs off and leave you by yourself, will you still go?"

"Probably."

He kissed me, his hands on either side of my face. When he drew back, his expression was grim. "Then the cuffs stay on, and I'm not leaving."

"Take off the cuffs," I told him. "Stay, and I'll stay too."

He eyed me.

"Scout's honor." I touched his face. "Stay, so I'm not alone."

Lake reached into his pocket, withdrew his keys, and unlocked the cuffs. I flexed my wrist and made a face at the reddened lines where the metal had dug into my skin.

He put the keys and cuffs on the counter next to his credentials. "The fallout from this is going to be pretty bad. We should both try to get some sleep if we can. I know the living room is empty, but tell me you have a bed."

"I do. I also have a guest room, which also has a bed."

He looked at me, his expression unreadable.

I put my hands on my hips. "What, you thought you were going to share mine?"

Surprisingly, it didn't look like that was what he'd been thinking. "How do I know you won't disappear the minute my back is turned?" He glanced at the cuffs on the counter. I had a feeling he wasn't thinking about fun ways to use them.

I crossed my arms. "Oh, for Pete's sake. I give you my word I won't try to sneak out."

Lake regarded me. "I'll take you at your word," he said finally. "I'm not sure what to do with all this honesty."

"Don't get used to it. I'm sure it's only a temporary condition and it will wear off soon." I slid down off the counter. "If you've got a change of clothes in your truck, you might as well go get it so I can raise the house wards. Oh, and Lake?"

"Yes?"

I pointed. "Don't touch the basement door."

He raised his eyebrows. "Thanks for the warning."

I headed for the stairs. "Get your stuff. Guest room is upstairs, second door on the right. Bathroom's across the hall. Make yourself at home."

Lake went out to his truck for his bag. When he was back inside, I raised the wards and shut my bedroom door. I washed my face, brushed my teeth, and changed into pajamas before climbing into bed.

His footsteps went back and forth between the guest room and the other bathroom. Once, he paused in the hallway and I half-expected him to come to my door, but he went back to his room. I couldn't decide whether I was disappointed or relieved.

I had no business kissing a SPEMA agent, much less inviting one to my bed, but I couldn't deny that Lake was no longer just a fed to me. The realization that I had come to see him as a man scared me. I was beginning to think that at some point in the past month, his motivation for turning up wherever I was had changed, long before the scene in the walk-in cooler. I'd been too preoccupied with other things to notice.

He could have run me in a half-dozen times, but he hadn't. That in itself spoke volumes about who he was beyond the badge. Even so, I was playing with fire and the stakes got higher every minute he was in my life. He had an uncanny ability to sense when I was lying, and I had much more to hide than my involvement in the construction site murders. If Lake ever got the inkling I wasn't the same Alice Worth who'd grown up in Chicago and lost her parents in a boating accident, everything might come crashing down around my ears.

And then there was Sean, who said he wanted to make me happy, and what was I supposed to think about that?

I groaned softly and rolled over, curling into a ball under the covers.

Despite the ache in my heart and my tangled emotions, my recent lack of sleep and the events of the day left me exhausted. I was just dozing off when my door opened and soft footsteps crossed the room to my bed.

Warm lips brushed mine. "Good night, Alice."

"Good night, Lake," I murmured just before sleep took me.

A persistent buzzing dragged me from a sound sleep just after dawn. Bleary-eyed and confused, I fumbled to find my phone on the nightstand. I rubbed my eyes and tried to focus on the caller ID. The number was local, so I swiped the green button and put the phone to my ear. "Hello?" My voice was thick with sleep.

A long pause, then: "You should at least be dead too."

It took my groggy brain several seconds to recognize the voice. My stomach knotted. "Sharon?"

"You told me you would have his back." Her voice was shaking, but not with grief. With rage. "You gave me your word."

My throat closed. "I'm sorry," I choked out. "I'm so sorry."

"I wanted him to stop working for the fangheads, but he wouldn't listen." Sharon's voice was rising. "For years, I've been telling him they're dangerous. They're killers. They have no loyalty. Humans are nothing but food to them. *He wouldn't listen to me.*" It was nearly a scream.

"Vamps didn't kill him. It was the harnad."

"Don't you dare lie to me," she snarled. "The detective said he was bitten and they drained him. He told me you tried to claim it wasn't a banghead. Mark's dead and you're trying to protect *them*. You're disgusting."

"I'm not trying to protect them. If I thought it was a vampire who killed him, I'd be the first to grab a stake and go hunting. I saw the so-called 'bite' and it looked more like the holes were made by needles than fangs. Let me explain—"

She cut me off. "Save it. Your employment is terminated, effective immediately. All agreements you have with MDI are void. Do not attempt to come on our property or contact any of our employees."

I sat up in bed. "What about the investigation into the kidnapped women?"

My bedroom door swung open. Lake stood in the doorway in his undershirt and bare feet, buttoning his pants.

"As far as we are concerned, there *is* no investigation anymore. I informed the Court an hour ago that MDI is no longer affiliated with them in any way." While I was still reeling from that news, Sharon added, "Tell the fangheads justice is coming for them. After today, they won't be able to hide behind their lies anymore."

I went cold. "What is that supposed to mean?"

"There's a protest this afternoon, led by Don Hall of the Daylighters. He's invited me to speak about what happened to Mark."

"Sharon, please," I said desperately. "Mark was *not* killed by vamps. If you tell people he was, every supe-hating extremist is going to try to kill any vamp they can find and the vamps will have no choice but to protect themselves. It'll be a bloodbath."

"There's a hell of a lot more of us than there are of them," she said flatly. "I hope they all burn in hell, every last one of them." *Beep.* I looked at the screen. *Call Ended.*

Slowly, I lowered the phone. Lake moved from the doorway to the side of my bed, his face grave.

"How much did you hear?" I asked.

"Enough." He sat down next to me.

My chest felt tight. "They'll burn the city down."

"I have to go to work." He took my hand. "Promise me you won't go looking for that blood mage until I can go with you."

I shook my head. "I can't promise you that."

His gaze turned stony. "What are you going to do?"

"Whatever I have to do to find out who killed Mark before what happened in Cincinnati happens here."

His hand tightened on mine. "I was in Cincinnati three years ago—before, during, and after." I saw it in his eyes: the haunted look of someone who had witnessed the carnage firsthand. Like me, Lake had seen the worst humans could do to each other and to those who were different from them. Maybe we had more in common than I'd originally believed. The thought was unsettling.

He touched my face. I closed my eyes and leaned against his hand. When I opened them again, his gaze was piercing. "You be careful," he said.

"Of course." I gave him a fleeting smile. "When am I ever not careful?"

He snorted and rose. "Do you need to do something to let me get out through the house wards?"

I shook my head. "Not to leave."

He leaned down to kiss my cheek, then headed for the door.

"Lake?"

He turned around and waited.

I thought about a couple of things I wanted to say, but settled for, "Watch yourself."

He smiled. "Always." He disappeared down the hall. About ten minutes later, heavy footsteps went downstairs and the wards tingled as he left.

16

I dragged myself downstairs to make coffee and get my laptop. On the way back, I checked the guest room and saw Lake had made the bed before he'd left. The only hint he'd been there was a wet washcloth draped neatly on the sink, a damp hand towel, and the faint scent of his aftershave. I went back to my room and sat on the bed, leaning against the headboard and sipping my coffee as I went online.

As I'd expected, Mark's murder was big news. I was in no way prepared for the punch in the gut of seeing his picture under the headline Vampire Court Investigator Found Murdered, Drained on CNN's homepage. Worse, several stories cited "sources within the police department" as saying a vampire had killed him. While officially the department stated the investigation was ongoing and no official cause of death was yet known, both local and national news outlets, fully aware of what would get readers to click on the story, emphasized the possibility a vampire was responsible.

The anti-vamp rally was scheduled for one o'clock outside city hall. The Daylighters' website was already promoting Sharon's participation and their main page was a graphic and highly speculative account of Mark's death, blaming a vampire for draining him dry.

The story was accompanied by a gory stock photograph of a savage vampire bite that bore no resemblance whatsoever to the wound Mark had suffered. People commenting on the article assumed it was an actual photo of Mark's throat—as the Daylighters had no doubt intended—and the comments were increasingly violent and frightening. The group's leaders were whipping their followers into a frenzy ahead of today's rally.

Mark's death was like an anvil crushing my chest, but my grief and anger had evolved past the blind rage that had made me want to smash John West's wards and confront him. With the benefit of a few hours' sleep, I was seeing more clearly and what I saw was the need to take a more measured approach.

At the same time, there was no time to lose; the clock was ticking, counting down the minutes until the rally. The riots that had torn Cincinnati apart, leaving dozens of vampires, shifters, and humans dead, hundreds injured, and whole sections of the city burned to the ground, began with an anti-supe rally much like the one scheduled to begin in just a few hours.

I wanted copies of the crime scene report, the M.E.'s report, and Mark's phone records. It was still early, but I called Sean. The call went to voice mail. I left a message and took a shower.

I expected a call back fairly quickly, but forty-five minutes later, as I was getting ready to leave the house, the phone still hadn't rung. I was tempted to call again but decided against it. He might be in a meeting or driving. He'd call when he could.

In the meantime, I headed downtown, to a nondescript office building I'd visited once before. I pulled into a spot in front of the convenience store across the street. It took me only seconds to spot the familiar black BMW parked in the lot in front of the building that contained John West's investment company.

I closed my eyes and tugged on Malcolm's thread. My stomach lurched and I took deep breaths, fighting nausea and disorientation. I'd had nothing to eat since lunch yesterday, and I'd only slept a few hours, and it was taking a toll on me.

As the dizziness faded, I sensed Malcolm's familiar presence as he entered my car. "What's wrong?" the invisible ghost demanded.

"I've got some bad news." I told him about my appearance before the Vampire Court and Mark's murder.

Silence from the passenger seat. "Alice, I am so sorry," Malcolm said finally. "I don't even know what to say. I know he meant a lot to you. What can I do to help?"

"What can you tell me about West's activities yesterday?"

"He was here at the office until about five thirty. I overheard most of his meetings and phone conversations and they were all business-related, as far as I could tell. He stopped by the grocery store and then stayed home all evening. Of course, I don't know what kind of phone conversations he had while he was there, but no one came to see him. If he was involved in Mark's murder, he wasn't there himself when it happened."

That was something, at least. West could have easily ordered it done, however; without Malcolm being able to cross his wards and see and hear what went on inside the house, it severely limited how much information the ghost could gather. I needed West's phone records. I made a mental note to ask Sean about that whenever he finally called me back.

"What else have you found out since yesterday morning?" Malcolm asked.

I described our visit to the homeless shelter, Adam's discovery that Felicia and at least some of the others were alive, and recapped what I'd read on the anti-supe hate groups' websites leading up to this afternoon's rally.

"We were worried one of the missing women would turn up drained and set off a wave of anti-supe violence, but this is worse," I said. "Mark was well-respected and well-known. He's not some 'hooker' from the Stroll; he's a local businessman with a wife, children, and grandchildren. He's the perfect victim to galvanize people." I rubbed my face. "I'm running out of time. I need answers."

"Do you want me to go with you?"

I shook my head. "No, stick with West."

My phone rang. *Wolf Calling*. Finally. I swiped the green button. "Hello?"

"I'm returning your call." Sean's voice was so brusque that I almost didn't recognize it.

"Thanks for calling me back. Are you busy this morning?"

"What do you need?"

Stung, I bit back a retort and kept my tone even. "I'm obviously looking into Mark's murder. I wondered if our hacker friend could get copies of the crime scene report, the M.E.'s report, and Mark's phone records. I'm also needing John West's phone records, and soon. There's an anti-supe rally at one o'clock, and Mark's widow is going to be speaking. Things could get ugly fast if we don't find out who killed Mark and prove it wasn't a vampire."

His answer surprised me. "I understand MDI is no longer working for the Vampire Court."

"How did you hear about that?"

"MDI contacted private security and investigation agencies throughout the city this morning, urging others to join them in refusing to work for the Court."

For a moment, I was too stunned to speak. Finally, I asked, "Are you no longer part of the investigation?"

"I haven't come to a final decision yet. My priority is locating Felicia. Are you even still working for the Court now that Mark's gone?"

"I don't know," I said. "I'm not worried about that right now. I need those records. Can he get them?"

"For the right price Cyro can get anything, but it'll cost money, and the account information Mark gave me is no longer valid."

I wondered what kind of money we were talking about. What did black-hat hackers charge for this kind of thing? Surely the Court would cover the cost. That might take time to arrange, though. I thought about how much money I had in the bank and wondered if I could get an advance on my paycheck from the Court.

"I might be able to pay," I said hesitantly.

"Can't Agent Lake get you the reports you need?"

Something about the way he said it made me pause. "Lake is going to have his hands full dealing with the rally and the fallout from Mark's murder. I'm not sure he'll have time to pull strings and get the reports and time is ticking."

No reply.

I was getting irritated. "Sean, I thought we were partners on this."

"I came by your house this morning to check on you," he said.

My stomach dropped.

"I was worried. I couldn't sleep, thinking it was a mistake to leave you home by yourself, so I headed over to see you. Only you *weren't* by yourself, were you?"

"Sean—"

"Imagine my surprise when I drove past your house just in time to see *Agent Lake* leaving at dawn." His voice was cutting. "So much for needing to be alone."

"It's not what you think."

"After yesterday, I thought..." He growled. "I guess it doesn't matter what I thought. You told me what I did and who I did it with was none of your business and vice versa. You said I didn't owe you any promises. You were telling me without telling me, I suppose."

"Will you just listen for one minute?" I snapped. "He suspected I was lying when I said I was going to stay home last night, so he sat outside my house. He stopped me from trying to go after John West and he stayed the night—*in the guest room*—to make sure I didn't leave. We did not sleep together. I'm sorry you saw him leaving and jumped to a completely understandable but *completely wrong* conclusion."

Silence.

"I'm sorry for yelling at you last night," I added when he didn't reply. "That was uncalled-for. And I'm sorry Lake drew a gun on you. I'm sorry about the whole damn mess."

"Jeez," Malcolm muttered. I'd almost forgotten he was in the car. My face burned. I was never going to live this one down.

"When we were together before, I don't think you ever lied to me." Sean sounded furious. "There was a lot you didn't want to tell me, but you're entitled to your secrets, like anyone else—hell, maybe more than most. But now you've lied to me three or four times in the past day that I know of, and frankly I'm not sure what to believe."

"I have no reason to lie to you about this. Neither of us has any claim on the other. I might have told you it was none of your business, which it really isn't, but I told you the truth. Regardless, I really don't have time to argue with you about it. Mark's dead, and that rally is scheduled for less than five hours from now. Are you going to help me or not?"

He sighed. "Let me call Cyro and see what I can work out. Where are you? I can meet you."

"I'm in front of West's office right now with Malcolm, but I'm headed down to the homeless camp by the river. When I left him last night, that's where Mark was going."

"I can meet you down there in about thirty minutes."

I stared at the phone, torn between my natural impatience and aversion to feeling as if I were dependent on anyone and the knowledge we were on dangerous ground. Part of me bristled at the idea of backup, but my rational self knew it made sense not to go in alone. This was not the time to be reckless for the sake of my pride, even with my gun on me and knives in my boots. Mark had a gun, too, and they got him anyway.

"Fine," I said grudgingly. "Meet me at the convenience store at Lescom and Third."

"I'll be there as soon as I can."

My phone beeped. I checked the screen. *Bryan Smith Calling*. "I have another call. I'll see you in a few." I ended my call with Sean and answered the incoming call. "Bryan."

"Miss Alice," he rumbled. "Your presence is requested at Northbourne."

"Hang on a minute." I muted the phone. "Get back to West," I told Malcolm. "Let me know if anything happens I need to know about."

The ghost scoffed. "If you think you're getting out of telling me what the hell happened at your house last night—"

"Malcolm," I warned.

The ghost sighed. "Fine, we'll discuss it later. If you need me, summon me."

I started the car. "Be careful."

"You too." Malcolm left the car.

I unmuted Bryan's call as I backed out of my parking space. "Sorry about that," I said. "I'm investigating Mark's murder. I don't have time for meetings. I'm assuming you know about the rally this afternoon, what that might mean." I turned out of the parking lot and headed south.

"We're aware of it," Bryan said grimly. "Juliet LaRoche and Ezekiel Monroe would like to meet with you to discuss how to proceed with your investigation."

Ezekiel Monroe represented Valas's interests during daylight hours. No doubt this meeting was at her request, following MDI's decision to cut ties with the Court.

"I don't have time," I repeated. "I'm on my way to follow up on leads Mark was looking into last night before they killed him. I'm not going to waste hours driving up to Northbourne, sitting in meetings and debating, while Mark's killers are loose and the Daylighter fanatics are mobilizing for war. You can tell Ms. LaRoche and Mr. Monroe my time is better spent trying to keep mobs from coming after their bosses. Tell them to think about what happened to the vamps in Cincinnati, and then tell me if they want me to be sitting in a conference room with them or out here looking for answers."

A long pause. "I will pass along your message," he said finally.

"Do I have the Court's authorization to proceed as lead investigator?"

Another pause. I didn't hear voices, but I was sure Bryan was consulting with someone, probably LaRoche or Monroe, or both. It didn't matter to me what the answer was; I was going to find Mark's killer, with or without the Court's blessing. The only question was whether I'd have their resources at my disposal to do it.

"You are the Court's lead investigator in this matter, effective immediately," Bryan said at last. "You'll need to come to Northbourne tonight. There is protocol that must be followed, and information you'll need. In the meantime, call me if you need anything. Please keep us updated."

"Good. I'm going to go to work now." I disconnected.

I did stop for coffee and a bagel, since I could do without sleep but caffeine and at least a little bit of food were requirements. The bagel tasted like sawdust but I forced myself to eat it.

At the convenience store, I parked away from the front doors and checked my gun. I rarely carried a firearm, but I wouldn't be leaving home without it until this case was resolved.

When Sean pulled into the parking spot next to mine ten minutes later, I exited my car and opened the passenger door of his SUV. "Hey," I said neutrally.

"Hey." Sean watched as I put my bag on the floor and climbed in. He was wearing a blue button-up shirt and khakis and a shoulder holster. It looked like I wasn't the only one who thought going armed was a good idea.

The camp was only five minutes away. On the way, I finished my coffee and told Sean the timeline so far for Mark's movements the night before.

Sean turned into the parking lot of Ned's Liquor and parked toward the edge of the small lot. I took my holster from my bag and put it on my belt, tugging my jacket down over it.

"What are you carrying?" Sean asked.

".45 caliber Smith & Wesson. My standard piece."

"Enhanced rounds?"

"Silver and spelled."

He whistled. "Bet those set you back."

"They've saved my life more than once," I said as we exited the SUV. "They're standard silver rounds. I do the spellcraft myself."

Sean put on a light jacket over his shoulder rig and shut his door. I noticed a footpath that began at the edge of the parking lot and disappeared into the undergrowth. As he came around the front of the SUV, I pointed at the path. "That looks like it might take us where we need to go."

"Looks like it." Sean stopped beside me. "How are you holding up?"

"I'm okay." I hesitated. "Are we good?"

He took my hand and squeezed it. "I'm with you."

We headed for the path. It wasn't wide enough for us to walk side by side, so I went ahead and Sean followed.

"Did you hear from the Court?" he asked as we walked through the shoulder-high grass, pushing branches out of the way.

"I did. That was the call I took when I hung up with you earlier. I've been named lead investigator in Mark's stead. They wanted me to come to Northbourne for meetings."

I could hear the smile in Sean's voice when he replied. "I take it you told them to go pound sand?"

"More or less. I asked them to think about Cincinnati and then decide if they wanted me sitting in meetings or out here looking for Mark's killers." I pushed my way through some small branches, then held them aside for Sean. "Any luck getting help from Cyro?"

He took the branches from me and broke them off one-handed without noticeable effort. "He's sending the reports and phone records as soon as he can get them."

I exhaled. "What kind of deal did you have to make?"

"The expensive kind. I'll bill the Court."

My footsteps faltered. "You didn't have to do that."

"Yes, I did. We need those reports."

We. Sean and I were a *we* again. It shouldn't have mattered so much to me, but a little of the tension went out of my shoulders.

We worked our way down the path. In the distance, I could hear voices now over the sound of traffic on the nearby bridge.

We came out of the tall grass at the edge of the river camp. I'd seen it from the bridge many times, but it looked very different from the ground. There were well over two dozen shelters in the camp. Most were tents, but some were lean-to structures made from metal siding. They were nestled among the trees and against the enormous bridge supports. A small group of men and women were sitting in chairs in the middle of a small clearing, near a well-used burn barrel.

When Sean and I stepped into view, the conversation that had been taking place cut off abruptly. Two women and a man left the group, retreating to their shelters.

An older white man rose and moved toward us. "What do you want?"

I stepped forward. "Good morning. My name is Alice. I'm a friend of Mark Dunlap's."

"Don't know no one named Dunlap," the man said.

"Please." I pulled a photo from my jacket pocket and held it up so he could see it. "This is Mark. He came down here last night, maybe around eight or so. Did you see him?"

The man studied the photo. "That you in that picture with him?"

"Yes."

"You look angry."

"I didn't like having my picture taken." Despite my objections, Sharon had taken the photo of Mark and me at an MDI Christmas party not long before I left the firm.

It was the only photo I had of us together, a fact that hurt if I thought about it too much.

"We're friends and colleagues of Mark's," I said. "He was killed last night. Do you know if he was here?"

A tall, thin African-American man stood up from his seat by the barrel and approached us. "My name's Jo-Jo. What did you say your name is?"

"I'm Alice. This is Sean."

"He was here." Jo-Jo looked at the photo, then handed it back as the other man returned to his seat.

I put the photo back in my pocket and took out my notebook. "Thank you. Can you tell me what you talked about?"

"He sat with us for twenty minutes or so. We talked about our friends who've disappeared. He had a list. We gave him some more names to add to it, told him when we seen them last. Then Mary Ann told him about the van."

"What van?" Sean asked.

"The blue van." The female voice came from our left. I turned.

A tiny older woman emerged from a tent. She wore a red plaid shirt and jeans and a black knit cap over her gray hair. She walked unsteadily past a large dog who lay in front of the tent. "The blue van," she repeated, her words slurred. "It took Lucky Lou. I told Mr. Dunlap about the van."

"Do you remember anything about the van?" I asked her. "Did it have anything written on it? Any pictures?"

"White letters." She stopped next to Jo-Jo and swayed on her feet. "Plumber, it said."

"You saw it yourself?" Sean asked.

She nodded vigorously. "I did. Me and Lou went up to the liquor store and it was parked there in the lot, off to the side. Lou went down the street to buy cigarettes and I came back here. He didn't come back, not that night, not ever again."

"Did you see who was in the van?" I asked.

"Two men."

"What did they look like?"

She shrugged. "White."

"How old?"

"Young. Thirty, forty, maybe. Don't remember much about it. Wouldn't remember it at all except I asked the man in the store if they needed a plumber and he said no and I wondered why they were just sitting out there."

"What else did you tell Mark last night?" I asked them.

"We didn't know much else to tell him," Jo-Jo said. "People gone. Nobody ever see when they take 'em. Nobody care when they gone except us." He gestured at the dog, a black-and-white Husky mix, lying in front of Mary Ann's tent. "That's Lou's dog, Rogue." The dog raised his head, looked at us, then laid it back down on his front paws. "He's been waiting for Lou to get back since the night he disappeared."

"I'm sorry," I told Rogue as he looked at me with dull eyes. "I'm looking for him."

Sean approached the dog slowly, his hand outstretched. I'd seen dogs react to Sean in a variety of ways: some cowered in fear, while others barked up a storm or ran away. To my surprise, Rogue lifted his head, sniffed Sean's hand, then licked it. Sean scratched the dog's head.

"What time did Mark leave?" I asked, my eyes on Sean as he comforted Rogue.

Despite his gentle treatment of the dog, I saw tension in his neck and back. Sean was angry. Very, very angry.

"'Bout nine fifteen or so," Jo-Jo said. "He had a meeting he said he had to get to. He headed back up that path there, back toward the liquor store."

I closed my notebook. "You heard what happened to him?"

"We heard about it." He shook his head. "It's not right, none of it."

"Was anyone up there at the liquor store when he headed out last night?" I asked as Sean rose to his feet. The dog followed Sean back to me and I scratched his head.

Jo-Jo frowned. "I don't think so."

I pulled some business cards from my pocket and handed them to Jo-Jo and Mary Ann. "If anyone thinks of anything that could help us, please give me a call."

"Will do." Jo-Jo held out his hand and Sean and I both shook it.

As we turned to leave, the dog started to follow us. "Stay," Sean said quietly.

The dog turned and went back to the tent. He lay on the ground and put his head back on his paws, his gaze on Sean.

Our walk back to the parking lot was silent. I didn't know what Sean was thinking about, but my hands were shaking with a combination of grief and fury. The harnad had cut a path of death and suffering through the city. My desire for justice was swiftly being replaced by the need to inflict some commensurate level of pain and misery on those responsible. Blood magic sizzled on my skin.

"Alice," Sean said from behind me, just before we reached the end of the path and the parking lot. I stopped and turned.

I knew my eyes were glowing. So were his.

We stood facing each other, our anger and our pain plain for the other to see. As an alpha, Sean often had to mask his emotions in order to lead his pack. I had learned at an early age to do the same so they couldn't be used against me by my grandfather or his lieutenants. And yet, neither of us hid those feelings from the other. It hadn't even occurred to me to do so. That meant something, if only I could figure out what.

Sean met my gaze with eyes like golden suns. An unspoken agreement passed between us. Justice was coming for John West and his harnad.

17

WE NOW KNEW MARK HAD MADE IT TO THE CAMP AND LEFT AROUND NINE FIFTEEN. He'd been found just before midnight. It was a tight window. The draining would have taken time, a fact I was trying not to dwell on too much because it led to questions like whether he'd been conscious during the process—questions I planned on getting answers to, from the people who'd been there, right before I made sure they didn't live to regret it.

When we returned to the parking lot, I checked the front of the liquor store. Sure enough, two surveillance cameras were pointed at the parking lot. "We need that footage," I told Sean, gesturing at the cameras.

"Let's get it."

We went inside the store. It turned out Sean's company had installed the system and it took very little persuasion to get the owner to help us out. Ten minutes later, we were in a back office with Ned, the owner, staring at a small monitor. The split screen showed both views of the parking lot.

Ned, a fifty-ish man with a spectacular beard and a well-worn biker vest, ran the recording back to the night before. Sean asked him to start the video at eight thirty and took his place at the controls when a customer out front needed assistance. I stood behind his chair, watching as he ran the video forward.

At eight forty-six, a familiar white van pulled into the lot and parked off to the side, in the same spot where Sean's SUV was now. The door opened and Mark emerged.

My hand tightened on Sean's shoulder, though I didn't remember putting it there. He reached up and covered my hand with his as we watched Mark disappear out of the frame in the direction of the camp.

Sean ran the video forward. All the vehicles that entered the lot after Mark arrived were store customers, except for a police cruiser that sat for several minutes while the officer used his computer and appeared to fill out some paperwork before leaving a little after nine.

At nine twelve, Mark reappeared. Sean slowed the video to normal speed as Mark went to his van and climbed in. He sat in the van for several minutes, using his phone either to text or search online. At nine twenty, he tossed the phone onto the passenger seat, backed out, and turned left out of the parking lot. We watched as his taillights disappeared into the night.

I hadn't expected to see Mark being kidnapped out of the parking lot, but I'd certainly hoped to see something that might help us. Instead, we had visual confirmation Mark left the store at nine twenty in his van alive and well, and not much else. I sighed.

"Hey, what's that?" Sean asked suddenly.

"What's what?"

He ran the video back to just before Mark left the lot and pointed to a dark shape in the upper right corner of the screen. It was a car, parked across from the liquor store. As Mark drove away, its headlights came on and it followed Mark's van as both vehicles disappeared out of the frame.

We watched the short clip again, but the car was at the edge of the camera's range and other than the fact it was a dark-colored sedan, there wasn't much to go on. The license plate was unreadable. It wasn't a black BMW—that much was obvious from the shape of the car and besides, I knew from Malcolm that John West was home when Mark was killed.

Sean ran the recording back and we discovered the sedan arrived minutes after Mark parked at the store. He found the best view of the car and sent the image to both our phones, then took the footage between eight thirty and nine thirty and uploaded it to Maclin Security's server so we had a copy. I opened the picture on my phone and stared at it.

"I hear your wheels turning. What are you thinking?" Sean asked, rising from the desk.

I held up my phone. "Everything else aside, what do you see when you look at that car?"

Sean took my phone and studied the image. "Nondescript, heavier body, dark window tint. Could be a Crown Vic, maybe, or something like it."

"It looks like an unmarked police car."

"You're right; it does, very much so." He swore under his breath.

"Everything good in here?" Ned appeared in the doorway.

"We're good." Sean handed my phone back and shook the older man's hand. We followed him into the front of the store. "I'll send someone out to do a free software upgrade on your system," he told Ned as we went to the front door. "We appreciate your help today."

"Always glad to help. Y'all have a good day." Ned held the door for us and we exited the store.

When we were in the SUV, Sean turned to me. "So, what now?"

I gestured across the street at the empty lot. "No other security cameras around here that might have a better view of the car, which is probably not accidental. They're too smart to get caught on camera."

"Is someone with the police department mixed up in this?"

I shrugged. "Even if that *is* an unmarked car, it doesn't help us right now. The police department has dozens of them, and there's no way to tell who was driving that one last night."

"What if that's how they got him?" Sean asked. "Pulled him over somewhere where they knew there weren't any cameras, hit him with a Taser before he knew what was happening."

"It would make sense. I wondered how someone got the drop on him. He probably wouldn't have suspected a cop. It's just a theory for now, though, and not one we can afford to focus on without more evidence." I paused. "There's something else. I managed to check Mark's body for magical trace last night. I sensed two mages: one low-level air mage and one very strong blood mage."

Sean raised his eyebrows. "John West?"

I shook my head. "No, someone else, someone not quite as powerful as West, but their trace was familiar. I realized this morning that I recognized it from the wards I sensed through Adam's connection to Felicia yesterday. Whoever killed Mark also set the wards holding and hiding the victims." The blood mage was also the creator of the razor wards, which meant he or she was sadistic as well as powerful.

"So, another member of the harnad, then?"

"Probably. I doubt they'd bring in an outsider to set those wards."

Sean's phone beeped. He checked the screen, tapped some keys, and my phone buzzed. "E-mail from Cyro," he told me. "It looks like the crime scene and the medical examiner's reports. He's still working on the phone records. Apparently it's much harder to hack into the cell phone company's computers than the police department system, which is not surprising." His eyes searched my face. "Do you want to read the crime scene report, and I'll look at the M.E.'s file?"

"I appreciate the offer, but I'll read them both. Might as well start with the M.E.'s report and get that over with." I opened my messages, found the attachments Sean had forwarded, took a deep breath, and opened the autopsy report.

We read silently. The clinical language helped me stay detached. The only defects the M.E. found on Mark's body were the two holes in his neck; there was no evidence of a Taser or stungun attack or any other injuries, so there went that theory about how Mark had been incapacitated. There were also no signs of a struggle or that he had been restrained, so how he'd been taken and immobilized while being drained remained a mystery.

The report noted the amount of blood remaining in the body was so minute it could only be estimated in milliliters. There was no way to know if the victim had been conscious while being drained, the report stated. Blood work and other tests were pending and would take several days to several weeks to complete. If he'd been drugged somehow, that wouldn't show up until the tox screens came back, if at all, depending on what they'd used.

The cause of death was listed as homicide by means of exsanguination. "The wounds, while not conclusive, are consistent with the bite of a vampire," the report stated on the last page. "Lab tests confirm the presence of vampire saliva in and around the punctures. A DNA match may be possible, should a suspect be identified."

I'd hoped a closer examination of the neck wounds, combined with my objections, would lead the M.E. to at least question the presumptions he'd made last night at the scene, but no such luck. The M.E. went in looking to find proof a vampire was responsible, and that was precisely what he'd found.

It occurred to me to wonder whose saliva they had planted on Mark's body and how they'd gotten it. I dashed off a quick text message to Bryan: *Harnad may be holding a vampire prisoner. Do we have any reports of missing vamps?*

His response was immediate: *Will investigate and advise.*

I switched back to the report, flipped to the next page, and found myself staring into Mark's sightless eyes. It was a photo, a close-up of Mark's face, gray and slack in death.

My stomach heaved. I dropped the phone on the seat, fumbled for the door handle, and got out of the SUV, slamming the door. I leaned against the side of the vehicle, closed my eyes, and took several deep, ragged breaths.

I thought I was prepared to see pictures of Mark at the autopsy, but I wasn't, not even close. In the stark white light of the M.E.'s lab, Mark had been reduced to just another body on a metal table. It wasn't a photograph of a living person; it was a picture of a corpse, taken simply to document its condition. I was no stranger to death, but this was different. This was *Mark*, my friend, my mentor, the first person I'd been able to trust since my parents' murders twenty years ago.

I swallowed hard and bent over, my hands on my knees as I fought nausea. My eyes burned but the tears wouldn't come. I remained dry-eyed, even as grief made me ache.

I stayed in the parking lot until my stomach stopped churning and I could breathe slowly and evenly. I forced the pain down into a box, closed the lid, and put it away. There would be time for grief later, when those responsible for Mark's death were held accountable for it and Felicia and the rest of the survivors were rescued.

Sean looked up from his phone when I opened the door of the SUV. He seemed to know the last thing I needed was sympathy or questions. Instead, as I settled back into my seat and pulled the door closed, he held up his phone, where he'd been reading the crime scene report. "No trace on the body that didn't come from the alley. No surveillance in the area, no witnesses except the two Haze addicts who found him. No prints, no tire marks. Nothing left of the van after they burned it."

"Thanks." I picked up my phone and closed the autopsy report. I opened the crime scene report and began reading.

It didn't take long to read through it; as Sean said, the whole report boiled down to a great big *nada*. The CSI team found the remains of Mark's gun and holster in the cargo area of the van, where he never would have left them, so they had been tossed back there by whoever killed him or torched the van. There was no trace of Mark's cell phone, so presumably whoever had taken Mark had it, or had disposed of it.

"Can Cyro track Mark's phone?" I asked.

Sean shook his head. "I already asked. It's off. He's monitoring it, though, in case it gets turned on. When the phone records come in, we might at least be able to figure out where Mark was the last time it was used."

I went back to the photos of the crime scene and the burned-out van. My breath caught when I saw a close-up photo of a metal cylinder lying on the van's front floorboard and realized it was what was left of my coffee thermos.

"Alice." Sean touched my hand. "You don't have to look at all of the photos."

"Yes, I do. I have to *see* it. I owe him that much. I can't look away and pretend it was less terrible than it was."

To my surprise, Sean nodded. "I understand."

I finished looking through the photos. Something nagged at me about the report, but I couldn't figure out what it was. I flipped back through, skimming over the sketch of the scene, the CSI team's notes, the list of items found in the van, the inventory of the items Mark had on him when he was found—

Full stop.

I reopened the autopsy report and read through the list of items removed from

Mark's body: shirt, undershirt, jeans, underwear, socks, shoes, watch...and no wedding ring. His hands had been bagged at the scene or I'd have noticed it then.

"Son of a bitch," I said out loud.

Sean looked up from his phone. "What?"

"They took his wedding ring. It wasn't on him when the police got there." Anger made magic spark on my fingertips. However I might feel about Sharon, Mark hadn't taken his ring off for any reason in three decades. His wife deserved to have it.

"There could be a lot of reasons to take Mark's phone, but why take his ring?"

"Mark wore that ring for thirty years, so it would be resonant with his magic, but I don't know what good that would do them if he's dead. It doesn't make any sense."

"Could you trace it?"

I thought about it, then shook my head. "If I'd realized it was missing last night, and had some other item belonging to Mark to use as a focus, maybe, but not now. The trace will have faded too much for me to sense unless I was nearby. Damn it."

I switched back to the crime scene report and moved on to the statements of the two men who'd found the body, taken by a detective named Brody. They'd gone into the alley to go dumpster-diving, according to their accounts, and called the police to report the body. Brody noted both men were clearly under the influence of Haze, but their statements were consistent and more or less coherent. He determined there was nothing suspicious about their story and no reason to hold them. They'd been released around two in the morning.

I was about the close the file when my eyes went back to the names of the men who'd found Mark's body: Jake Travers and John Andrews. I frowned. Where did I know those names from? *How* would I know those names? I certainly hadn't crossed paths with many Haze addicts. There were no photos of them in the file, but I could swear I knew those names from somewhere.

I jerked suddenly when recognition dawned.

"What?" Sean asked.

I held up my phone and pointed to Brody's report. "I've met these assholes before," I told him. "The last time I saw them, I left them unconscious in an alley not six blocks from here, after they attacked Carrie Davis."

He stared at me. "This sounds like a story I need to hear."

I hadn't given John Andrews and Jake Travers, a.k.a. Dipstick and Twitchy, any thought since the night a month ago when I'd rescued Carrie from them. Had I not taken the time to go through their wallets that night, I never would have made the connection between Carrie's attackers and the two men who'd allegedly stumbled across Mark's body.

I told Sean the story while we sat in the liquor store parking lot. I expected him to fuss at me for taking on three drug dealers alone in an alley in the middle of the night, but he surprised me. "That was incredibly brave," he said. "And not at all unexpected, knowing what I know about you."

"That's what Mark said," I said with a sigh. "I guess I'm well-known for doing stupid shit like that on a regular basis."

Sean frowned at me. "You're well-known for trying to save people on a regular basis, at great risk to yourself. That's not stupid; it's heroic."

"Or something," I said, suddenly uncomfortable.

Sean looked thoughtful. "Should we go looking for Travers and Andrews?"

"I think so. Something feels really fishy about this. Why would a couple of drug dealers call the cops about a body they'd found? You'd think they wouldn't want any contact with police, especially if they were high. I think we need to talk to them in person." I checked the time on the dashboard clock and grimaced. "Only a few hours until the rally."

"Then we'd better get moving." He turned the key in the ignition and glanced at me. "Stop for coffee first?"

I gave him a look.

"You're right," he said, shifting gears and heading out of the parking lot. "Dumb question."

According to Brody's notes, Travers and Andrews claimed to be sharing an apartment off Seventh and Grove, a high-crime area about a half-mile from where Mark's body was found. While Sean drove us to get coffee, I located social media accounts for both men and found pictures of them. Based on their photos and posts, they were fond of video games, girls, and posing with rolls of cash and various weapons, including guns and knives.

Helpfully, they'd tagged their friend I'd dubbed "Knuckles" in several pictures. I found one that showed all three of them and sent it to Sean as we pulled into a convenience store across the street from the entrance to the apartment complex.

Sean put the SUV in park and looked at the picture I'd sent. He snorted. "These guys?"

"I know. Couple of scrawny punks. That's Andrews in the middle and Travers on the left. 'Knuckles' is Clint Ravell, on the right."

"Scrawny or not, we know at least two of them carry knives."

"And guns." I showed him some of the other pictures the trio had posted online. "I'm not going to underestimate them."

"What are we prepared to do if we find them?"

"We need answers. I'm prepared to get them."

He didn't ask how or hesitate in his response. "Then I'm with you." He glanced at the apartment complex. "But we can't do it here. Cameras on the buildings, too many witnesses. We'd need to get them to a place where we can do what we need to do. Our pack land would work. The problem is getting them out there and what to do with them after we've gotten our answers."

"If we can get them somewhere with no eyes on us, I can hit them with sleep spells and we can transport them fairly easily. Depending on what they tell us, there may not be an after."

Sean looked at me, his face unreadable.

I tilted my head. "I'm sorry, I thought we were on the same page about this. We're going to be questioning suspects using—what's the phrase?—'enhanced interrogation techniques.' If they participated in Mark's murder, I owe them a painful death. I thought you of all people would understand that."

"I understand it very well. I've killed for a lot of reasons, as you know. I suspected the same of you, though I think your reasons were very different from mine and you didn't do it by choice."

So he'd put that together. I could have denied it, told him he was wrong, but I sensed we'd come to some kind of important moment, one where I needed to know what he thought about the possibility that I was not only capable of killing but had done so many times.

Sean reached out. "Take my hand."

After a moment's hesitation, I took it.

His familiar golden shifter magic danced on the edge of my senses. Slowly, cautiously, I lowered my shields, preparing for an onslaught of power and emotions. Instead, I discovered Sean had remarkable control. Instead of the flood I'd experienced the first time we'd lowered our shields around each other—which was, admittedly, in far less controlled circumstances—Sean's emotions washed over me gently. I closed my eyes.

In my head, I saw a flash of Felicia's smile, Mark's kind face, and Rogue's empty eyes, and felt Sean's fury at what the harnad had done to them. Dozens of people—men, women, and children—flashed through my mind's eye and I sensed Sean's fierce protective instinct for his pack. I saw Lake leaving my house and gasped at the spike of jealousy, hurt, and anger created by the thought we'd slept together.

Then I saw myself through Sean's eyes in a series of fragmented memories: our reunion in Mark's conference room; my panic attack in Felicia's apartment; the morning after the poltergeist attack, when he'd smelled blood and knew I'd been injured; in his arms after sharing Adam's visions; on my porch last night, angry and drunk; and finally today, when he'd voiced what he'd long suspected about my violent past. Each memory came with emotions: I sensed worry, protectiveness, frustration, regret, self-recrimination, and understanding...but not one ounce of disapproval or condemnation.

Despite his willingness to share so much with me, I couldn't bring myself to do the same. I had too much to hide. Instead, I sent him only one image: my memory of seeing Mark lying dead in the alley. Along with it, I sent my grief, hurt, anger, and cold resolve. I also gave him a taste of my blood magic, allowing it to sear the edges of his shields, and heard his sharp intake of breath at the flash of power and pain.

I raised my shields, opened my eyes, and let go of his hand. Neither of us spoke for a while as I sorted through a strange mix of emotions. It felt as if we'd had a long, extremely honest conversation, though we hadn't said a word.

I was afraid and angry because Sean had figured out something about me and my past that I'd wanted to keep anyone from knowing. At the same time, I had an answer to the question I'd wanted to ask since the night I showed him my magic in my basement, when I'd started to wonder if there might be a place for him in my life: if he knew I was a killer and what I was capable of doing, how would he react?

The answer, it seemed, was with understanding and empathy, and I didn't know how to respond to that. I realized I'd been prepared for him to reject me but not for him to accept me. My vision of myself as a monster and a murderer was so deeply ingrained it hadn't even occurred to me Sean wouldn't react with the same disgust and hatred I heaped on myself.

Some of that must have shown on my face because Sean's eyes darkened. "Whatever you're thinking, stop," he said firmly. "I shared myself with you so you would believe me when I say I understand what it means to take lives and have no choice in the matter.

I'm not asking you to tell me about it; your secrets are your own. You know exactly how I feel about you. I think I know what you feel about me, though I'm never quite sure what, if anything, you'll allow yourself to do about it."

I wasn't sure either and this wasn't the time to try to figure it out. "I appreciate the honesty."

His mouth curved into a smile. "But—?"

"But the rally is in less than two hours and we need to find Andrews and Travers."

He glanced at the apartment complex. "If we go in there looking for them, we'll be on camera."

"I know." I opened the crime scene report on my phone and flipped to Brody's notes. The information I was looking for was at the bottom of the last page. "We've got phone numbers for both of them."

"Let's see if we can find out where they are." Sean sent the numbers off to Cyro with a request for a track. In the meantime, I texted Adam to ask if he'd been able to See anything more about Felicia's condition or where she might be.

Instead of texting, Adam called me back. "Hey, Alice. I was actually just about to call you. I've been trying to reconnect with Felicia, but now something is blocking me. I think they've added another layer to the wards, one that resists psychic contact. I don't know if something happened to tip them off about yesterday or they did it as a precaution, but I'm hitting a pretty solid wall."

I didn't need to ask to know it had hurt; I could hear it in his voice. "Thank you for trying. If you See anything that might help us, let me know." He might still have visions, even without the psychic connection.

"You know I will," he said. "I'm sorry to hear about Mark. He was a good guy."

"Thanks, Adam. Take care." We disconnected.

Sean frowned at his phone. "What's up?" I asked.

"Cyro says both phones are off."

My shoulders slumped. "So much for that idea. I wonder if that means the harnad got them, or if they're just lying low."

He hit some buttons and my phone beeped. "We do, however, have phone records for John West and Mark."

"How much did getting all these reports run?"

When he told me, I was left speechless for several seconds. Finally, I said, "I am clearly in the wrong business."

He smiled. "Sometimes I think that myself, not just from a profit standpoint, but because I'd like to know how to do the things Cyro can do."

I made a face. "On the downside, you'd be risking an extended stay at Club Fed every time, so maybe it's best we let Cyro handle it."

"Good point."

Before I opened the phone records, I shot a text off to Bryan: *Maclin Security needs account info to cover case-related expenses formerly handled through MDI.*

Less than a minute later, he replied: *Info will be sent to MS Accounts Payable.*

When I told Sean, he looked relieved. "The Court is nothing if not efficient. I'm glad to hear that's settled. I was starting to worry if we'd be able to make payroll next week at this rate. I'm kidding," he added when my eyes widened.

I frowned at him. "Jerk."

He chuckled. "Whose records do you want to look at first?"

"Let's look at Mark's."

Despite how easy and fast they made it look on television, going through phone records was tedious business, even if you knew what to look for. I found the record of Mark's communications from the night before, beginning with my call to him around five, which pinged off a tower close to the park we'd been watching. He'd exchanged a few texts with another cell I took to be Sharon's before I arrived, then nothing until after we'd parted company around eight twenty. There was a fourteen-minute phone call to Sharon just as he arrived at the liquor store.

There was another gap until nine fifteen, when he sent texts while sitting in the parking lot at Ned's Liquor. Both were to Sharon, saying he was on his way home and asking her to pick out a tie for him to wear with his suit. She texted back: *Will do. I love you.*

I love you too, he replied. That was the last outgoing message on his phone, at nine nineteen. At nine twenty, he'd left Ned's liquor, followed by the dark-colored sedan.

Beginning a little after ten, Sharon began texting asking where he was, but his phone was already off because there was no information about what tower was closest when the text arrived. At ten fifteen, having gotten no response, she began calling. The unanswered calls and texts continued until about twelve thirty, then stopped abruptly. I imagined that was when she got the news Mark's body had been found.

"There's nothing to help us here," I said around the lump in my throat. "They knew to turn his phone off so it wouldn't give away their location."

Sean squeezed my hand. "It's not surprising. We know they're careful."

West's phone records were far more extensive and we didn't have time to go through them line by line and figure out who all these people were.

"We need an analyst," I told Sean after we'd gotten a look at the size of the file and the sheer number of phone numbers and calls involved. "MDI has a good one, but that's no longer an option."

"I'm sure the Vamp Court has some good ones."

"They do," I said reluctantly.

"You can't do everything at once, Alice," Sean told me patiently. "You have to delegate. That's what a lead investigator does. Let the analysts do what they're best at, while you do what you're best at. Stop thinking like a one-person company and more like a manager of a team."

"You're right." I took a deep breath and exhaled. "Damn it, you're right." I picked up my phone and called Bryan.

He answered on the first ring. "Miss Alice."

I told him what we had and what I needed.

"Our best analyst for this kind of information is Kim Dade," he told me. "I'll put her at your disposal for the duration of this case. Send me the file. I'll send you her contact information when we're done."

"Thanks, Bryan. Any news on missing vamps?"

"We may have something," he said. "I have some people out following up on a report we received this morning. I'll let you know what we find out. What else can I do for you?"

I hesitated.

Sean touched my hand. *Delegate*, he mouthed to me.

I scowled at him, but said, "I have two persons of interest who may have information we need." I gave Bryan Travers and Andrews's names, phone numbers, and address. "I need a location on one or both of them, or their buddy Clint Ravell. I don't have an address for him."

"Location only or pick up and detain?" Bryan asked briskly.

"Pick up and detain, *quietly*. No one talks to them or touches them unless I'm there."

"Understood. Anything else?"

"If I think of anything, I'll let you know." I paused. "Are you sending people to monitor the rally?"

"Of course," Bryan said. "You're going?"

"Yes."

"Be safe."

"You too."

We hung up. Sean looked up from where he'd been sending an e-mail. "We're going to the rally?"

"You don't have to, but I need to."

"Why?"

My phone beeped with a text from Bryan containing Kim Dade's information. I saved it into my contacts and stuck my phone in the cup holder. "Because I've been so out of touch for the past month that I didn't even know about all these protests, or the assaults on supes, or the Black Fire crime wave, or the attacks on Darius Bell's cabal. I can't afford to not know what's going on, not when it affects the lives of so many people. It's not that I didn't know what groups like Humans First and the Daylighters say and believe, but I read through their Vamp Court dossiers yesterday and their websites this morning. I'm scared about what's going to happen when Sharon gets up there and tells the crowd Mark was murdered by a vampire."

Sean pulled out into traffic, heading north toward downtown. "Okay," he said, squaring his shoulders and giving me a grin. "Let's go to a riot."

18

It didn't start out as a riot; in fact, for the first half-hour or so, I thought we'd been worried for nothing.

Thousands of people packed the enormous plaza in front of city hall, many wearing Humans First or Daylighters T-shirts and carrying signs with anti-supe slogans. There were others with signs urging unity and peace, but they seemed to be outnumbered by about ten or fifteen to one.

Sean and I stood near the edge of the crowd, about midway back from the steps where the first several speakers had each taken about ten minutes to condemn Mark's murder and urge people to join one or more of the many "Human rights" groups in the area. Everything seemed calm except for a few outbursts of chanting and shouting. The conspicuous presence of riot police and heavy tactical equipment seemed to be keeping the situation under control. I saw SPEMA agents in their trademark jackets scattered around the perimeter, but no sign of Lake.

When Don Hall of the Daylighters stepped up to the microphone, however, the mood of the protesters changed. Sean felt it, too, and tension rippled across his shoulders as the crowd surged, pushing us forward.

Hall wore a dark blue suit and dark-framed glasses. He looked over the crowd, taking in the protesters and their signs, then raised his hands to quiet them. "My friends," he intoned, "I come here today with a heavy heart. One of our own citizens, a very good man who called this city home for his entire life, was slaughtered here last night and left to die in an alley, like garbage. Like *trash*."

The crowd moved restlessly.

"Mark Dunlap was a husband. A father. A grandfather. He was married for thirty years and worked long, hard hours all his life to provide for his family. He was everything you could ask a man to be and more. In all that time, he only made one single mistake: he trusted vampires and decided to work for them."

Another surge of anger from the crowd. I gritted my teeth. How dare he use Mark like this? Sean's hand found mine and squeezed.

"For years, Mark worked for the Vampire Court as an investigator. He even called some of the vampires *friends*."

Angry murmurs from the assembled protesters.

"Despite warnings from those closest to him, he believed these creatures could be trustworthy. He believed he was more than just a *human* to them. God help him, he believed they would never turn on him." Hall looked up toward the sky. When he looked back at the crowd, his gaze was intense. "He could not have been more wrong."

Shouting broke out in the crowd, loud chants of "Stake them all!" and "Kill the fangheads!" Hall stepped back from the microphone and more people took up the chants. I started to sweat.

Hall let the shouting go on for over a minute, then raised his hands and the voices quieted. "The police say they will bring the killer to justice. They say no one, *human or not*, is beyond the law. But I ask you, my friends, if that is true, then how have the vampires gotten away with *more than fifty murders* in this city in the past year and a half?"

The crowd roared.

"Son of a bitch," I hissed. Sharon must have told him about the missing homeless people.

"More than fifty murdered human women and men!" Hall shouted over the din. "You know who took them. You *all* know. And you know why no one has faced justice for it: because the police of this city fear the vampires. They won't stand up for you." He paused, then pointed to the assembled people. "*I* will stand up for you!"

The roar of the crowd became a mix of shouting and cheers. Sean muttered expletives. The police and federal agents lined up, forming a perimeter around the protesters.

That was when I saw Lake on our side of the plaza, standing with Agent Parker and another agent. He was speaking quickly into a radio, scanning the crowd for trouble. He looked past me, then his eyes zipped back to meet mine when recognition dawned. He saw Sean next to me and his jaw tightened.

Parker touched his arm and gestured at something going on behind us. Lake immediately focused on whatever it was and they headed in that direction, walking briskly. I turned my attention back to the stage.

Hall finally began quieting the crowd. "My friends," he said. "My friends, my friends." He waited until the noise died down, then continued. "Mark Dunlap's murder has left his family devastated. I have with me two members of that family who have come here today to share his memory with you." He smiled kindly toward the front of the crowd and held out his hands. "Please, everyone, welcome Mark's wife, Sharon, and his oldest son, Marcus Dunlap, Junior."

I watched as Sharon, in a black suit, and Marcus, wearing a button-up shirt and slacks, went up the steps. The Daylighters' website hadn't mentioned anything about Mark's son coming to the rally. I hadn't seen Marcus in years. He'd be about twenty-four now, I thought, and was tall and burly like his father.

Sharon was almost as tall as her son. She held onto his arm as they joined Hall behind the microphone. Hall hugged Sharon, then shook Marcus's hand and clasped his shoulder in a show of support.

Sharon stepped up to the microphone. "Thank you," she said shakily. "Thank you for coming here today. What we're doing here today is so...is so important." Her voice cracked, and she paused to collect herself.

When she spoke again, her voice was stronger, more determined. "My husband was a good man and a wonderful father. He didn't deserve what happened to him. He didn't deserve to be drained of blood and dumped in an alley, like he meant nothing. He meant everything to us." She hung her head and Hall and Marcus each reached out to comfort her with a hand on her back. I heard sniffling in the crowd.

Despite my anger at what was happening around me and Sharon's participation in it, my throat closed. Sharon's grief was real, even if her anger was misplaced.

As Sharon struggled with her tears, Hall reached out toward the audience. They broke into applause and shouts of "We love you, Sharon!"

When Sharon raised her head, the crowd quieted. She cleared her throat and continued. "Mr. Hall mentioned the horrible murders that have been terrorizing our city for the last year and a half. My husband was helping to investigate those murders. That's what he was doing last night, when they took him and killed him. I don't know what he found out, what he knew, but they killed him and left him in an alley behind a dumpster."

The crowd's fury swelled again. I closed my eyes. She'd just strongly implied that vampires killed Mark because he'd found out they were behind the murders.

Sharon raised her voice over the crowd noise. "I am asking for your help today, to help me get justice for my husband. Please don't let the police be so afraid of the vampires that they let them get away with Mark's murder and the murders of all these other people." Her voice hardened. "The vampires should be afraid of *us*, not us be afraid of *them*."

The crowd cheered.

Hall helped Sharon step back, then took her place at the microphone while Marcus held his mother with an arm around her waist.

"My friends," Hall said earnestly. "Sharon has asked for our help to get justice for her husband and for all the other victims. You may wonder how you can help. Our website lists the e-mail addresses and phone numbers of your local senior law enforcement personnel and politicians. We must work together to keep the pressure on the police until these murderers are brought to justice. Also, on our website you will find a list of local businesses owned by vampires."

I jerked. Beside me, Sean growled low in his throat.

"We ask that you refuse to do business with any of these establishments. Instead, take your money to local, *human*-owned businesses. Put no money in the fangheads' hands. Let them know you are human and proud of it!"

The crowd grew louder and we were jostled as people started pushing forward. Hall said something else, but I couldn't hear him over the shouting.

My gut churned. That list of vampire-owned businesses wasn't just a list of places to boycott; it was a list of potential targets for anyone looking to strike out at the vamps.

The police organized into lines at the perimeter of the plaza, and the SPEMA agents grouped up as the crowd surged again. Fights broke out all around us.

Up on the steps, men in suits hustled Hall, Sharon, and Marcus away from the protesters and toward SUVs parked at the curb. Hall had accomplished what he'd come here to do. His people knew when it was time to make a hasty exit and so did I. Sean and I started making our way toward the edge of the plaza.

Suddenly, I froze.

Dark, dangerous magic slid along my senses like a snake on a tree branch. I recognized it as the trace I'd detected in the poltergeist a few days before. The demon who'd sent her after me was here. Again, the magic seemed familiar, but I couldn't place it.

Slowly, carefully, I looked at the people around us but saw nothing except bodies pushing and shoving.

"Alice?" Sean said into my ear. "Alice, what is it?"

I turned my head, searching the sea of faces around me. The back of my neck prickled in warning, but when I let go of Sean's hand and spun around, I didn't see anyone staring at me.

A whiff of sulfur teased my nose and the dark magic surged. I spun again and caught a glimpse of red eyes and dark hair for a fraction of second before I lost sight of my target.

I plunged into the crowd in pursuit. Behind me, Sean shouted my name, and then he was lost in the crush of people.

A flash of red eyes to my right—I turned and it was gone. Fingertips that burned like hot coals raked across the back of my hand. I bit back a cry of pain as I whirled, but again, too slow. I heard a low laugh on my left but saw nothing but angry, shouting, rioting humans.

Sinister sulfurous magic wrapped around my throat like a tentacle and squeezed. I reached up with both hands and tore it away in a flash of white air magic that went unnoticed by the people around me. Another sepulchral laugh, and the demon magic faded.

The crowd parted just in time for me to see the fighting had spread and the police were advancing on the plaza. As they approached, someone threw a rock. It landed five or six feet in front of the line of police, but it set off a flurry of rocks, bottles, and other debris. The police raised their riot shields and an enormous armored police vehicle rumbled toward the crowd.

Pandemonium broke out. Someone's elbow hit me hard in my lower back. A poorly thrown bottle caught me just below my left eye and I staggered, almost losing my footing.

A hand closed on my arm in a vise grip. I looked up into Sean's grim face. "We have got to go, right now," he said.

I couldn't argue with that. I could no longer sense the demon's dark magic and what had begun as a peaceful protest was now a full-blown melee.

"Let's get the hell out of here," I said. So we did.

"That's turning into a shiner."

I lowered the cold pack I was holding to my left eye and glared balefully at Sean, as we sat in his SUV in the convenience store parking lot where I'd left my car that morning.

We'd come back here to regroup, after getting out of downtown just as things were getting messy. The news reported dozens of injuries and arrests at the scene of the protest, with unrest spreading to other parts of the city. So far, no attacks on vamp-owned businesses, but I suspected it was only a matter of time.

My eye hurt, but not as badly as my lower back and not even close to the pain radiating from my burned hand. I'd been hiding that injury from Sean since we left the protest.

"I wondered what you had in that cooler in the back," I said, putting the cold pack back to my eye. "I would not have guessed first aid supplies."

"They come in handy on a regular basis." Sean scanned the Daylighters' website on his phone. "It's a pretty comprehensive list they've got on here of vamp-owned businesses. I don't see Hawthorne's listed, though. They've got some of Vaughan's other properties, including the new wine bar, but not Hawthorne's or anything on that block."

"Huh." I shifted uncomfortably in my seat.

"How's your back?" Sean asked.

I grimaced. "Sore."

He reached into his jacket pocket, took out a small tube of something, and held it out.

"What's this?" I squinted at it with my good eye, but it was a plain white tube with no label.

"For your hand." Sean's voice was deceptively calm, but a muscle moved in his jaw and his eyes were bright gold.

Son of a bitch.

I raised my right hand from where it had been hidden at my side and put it in my lap. Across the back of my hand and fingers were four painful, blistering red welts several inches long.

"Take the ointment or use a healing spell," Sean said quietly. "Your choice, but pick one and do it fast."

Since I didn't have a healing spell with me that would be strong enough, I took the tube. It was cold, so it must have been in the cooler. I opened it with my stiff fingers and used my left hand to squeeze the ointment onto the burns. When the cold gel touched the wounds, the pain went white-hot and I sucked in air through my teeth.

Sean sat silently as I applied the treatment to all four burns, then took the tube from me and put the cap back on as I trembled and panted from the pain. If I'd had the option of cutting my hand off right then, I might have considered it.

Within a minute, however, the pain faded to numbness. The back of my hand cooled rapidly, then became ice-cold. That was its own kind of pain, but one I could endure much more readily than the searing heat of the burns.

"That's good stuff," I said when I could talk without my voice shaking. "I've never used anything that worked that well or that fast."

"I know a guy who knows a guy." Sean put the tube in the cup holder between us. "Tell me who did this."

"I don't know."

"Then tell me what you *do* know."

I said nothing.

"Alice, two days ago, you were attacked down on the Stroll. Today, someone came after you in broad daylight, in front of witnesses. They burned your hand, and it looks like they tried to strangle you, too. Those are just the incidents I know of."

I frowned. "Nobody tried to strangle me."

Sean reached over and flipped down my visor, tilting it so I could see my neck in the mirror. There was a dark line of bruises right where the demon magic had coiled around my throat. With my attention focused on the pain in my back and hand, I'd had no idea it was there.

"I am done being kept in the dark about this." Sean flipped the visor back up. "Who or what is after you and why?"

I shook my head. "It's nothing you need to worry about. I can take care of myself."

"I know you can take care of yourself. I'm not trying to hunt this person down on your behalf or tear them limb from limb for hurting you, as much as I'd like to do that. You've made it very clear from day one that you're not looking for a protector or someone to fight your battles for you. I'm working on accepting that, despite the fact it goes against all my instincts. All I am asking for in return is information and honesty from you."

"I'm entitled to my secrets, Sean."

"Yes, you are. I told you before I know you've got some serious shit in your past, and I'm not going to push you because we've all got things we don't want to talk about. But this isn't about your past; it's about keeping things from me right now, things affecting both of us. You were so committed to keeping me from knowing about your injury that you were willing to sit in agony for almost an hour. I waited for you to use a healing spell or tell me about what happened, but you never did, and I couldn't take how much pain you were in any longer."

He leaned toward me, his eyes fierce. "These attacks are escalating in both severity and brazenness, so someone is getting increasingly aggressive about doing you harm. I can't fight beside you if I don't know what I'm up against."

"I'm not asking you to fight beside me. It's not your fight."

"That's not your decision to make; it's mine. Sometime soon, it might not even *be* my choice if things continue to escalate. I may just end up in the line of fire, handicapped because I don't know what I'm fighting or why."

"Then maybe you need to stay clear of me until I sort this out." I was keeping Malcolm out of danger by having him watch John West; it made sense to get Sean out of harm's way too.

"Why do you do this?" He was getting angry. "Push me away? Every time we take down one barrier, you put another one up."

"Did it ever occur to you that I'm doing it to protect you?" I demanded.

The moment I said it, I knew it was the wrong thing to say. Sean's face went blank. "Do you think I need you to protect me, Alice?"

Magic rose, but it wasn't mine. Sean's eyes shone like two golden suns. He had my left wrist in his hand before I even saw him move.

The air in the SUV was suddenly thick with hot, golden shifter magic, impossibly powerful, searing my shields. My mind filled with memories, bloody and brutal. I jerked in his grip as they played in my head, overlapping each other in a jumble of violent images of vicious fighting.

Sean's wolf appeared in my mind: black and gray and enormous. He stalked across the darkness between us, with golden eyes that stared through me into my soul. He was magnificent and deadly.

The wolf leapt at me, his teeth bared.

I raised my hands and an arc of green and white lightning split the air with an audible *crack*. The lash of magic threw the wolf back and tore Sean's grip from my arm. His back hit his door hard enough to make the SUV rock back and forth. I shook my head to clear it.

Sean and I stared at each other, both breathing hard. The shifter magic faded and his eyes slowly returned to human brown.

Finally, he spoke. "If you really think you need to protect me, you know nothing about me at all."

Maybe I didn't, or maybe thinking I was keeping him at arm's length in order to protect him was just another lie I was telling myself. Maybe it was more to protect me than him.

"I only know one way to fight," I said quietly. "And that's alone."

His phone rang. He checked the screen, then answered. "This is Sean."

It was another deep male voice, with a growly edge, speaking rapidly. I watched Sean's face as he listened. His jaw tightened, and the shape of his eyes changed. Whatever he was being told, it made him worried and angry.

"I'll be there in twenty," he said when the other man stopped talking. "Call our lawyers and get them down there. No one talks to the police without Nadine or Leland present. Is that clear?"

The reply was terse.

"I'm on my way." Sean ended the call. "That was Jack, my beta. Some of the younger members of my pack got in a fight. Three of them are in jail."

"Go." I grabbed my phone and my bag with my good hand and opened my door carefully with my right. I jumped out and started to shut the door.

"Alice." He threw the SUV in reverse. "We'll finish this conversation later. Go heal yourself and watch your back. I'll call you when I'm done."

"Go," I said again, and shut the door.

He backed out fast. Seconds later, he turned out into traffic and was gone.

On the way home, I drove past the alley where Mark's body had been found. There was a memorial there with candles and piles of flowers. People were parked along the street and walking toward the memorial as I passed. It made me angry. None of them had known Mark in life; why should they get to share in the grieving for his death? Some of them wore anti-supe shirts. If they'd known Mark, they'd have known he despised those sentiments. I kept going.

I went home and used healing spells on my hand, back, and throat. The eye would have to wait until later; that many healing spells in a row left me nauseated and weakened. I used a strong blood magic healing spell on my hand, and that alone left me huddled on my bed, shaking and sweating, for more than twenty minutes.

I was in the bathroom washing my face when Malcolm crossed my house wards. "Alice, are you decent?" he called from the hallway.

"Yes." I came out of the bathroom to find the ghost flitting around my room. "What's up?"

Malcolm zipped back and forth by my bed. "Okay, so I'm tailing West and I'm staying close, but not *too* close, and he leaves work early, so I'm thinking okay, cool, maybe we're finally gonna see something, right? And—"

"*Malcolm*. Stop flitting."

He stopped right in front of me. "I do not *flit*," he huffed.

"Whatever it is you are doing, stop doing it. I can't listen to you if you're buzzing all around the room while you talk."

"Fine." He hovered in place. "I followed West in his car and we headed south of the river. He was really angry. I could feel his blood magic, like he was so furious he couldn't hold it back. He was driving like he was on his way to kick someone's ass, and then he turned around."

I blinked. "He what?"

Malcolm floated back and forth in consternation. "He just stopped, pulled into a convenience store at 28th Street South and Forrester, made a U-turn, and headed back north to his house. That's where he was when I jumped here to tell you."

I rubbed my face. "So, he was headed somewhere in the south part of town, and then he what, changed his mind? Or did he sense you?"

"I don't know," he said. "I'm pretty sure I'm almost undetectable with all these obfuscation and masking spells, but there's always a chance he sensed me and that's why he turned around. Or maybe he decided today was not a good day to go on a rampage. I don't know. I just wanted you to know what happened." He frowned. "Hey, what's with the black eye?"

"Sean and I went to that anti-vamp protest. It got a little rowdy." I hesitated. "You don't see any magic on me that shouldn't be there, do you?"

Malcolm floated close and passed his hand slowly through my aura. I shuddered at the sensation. "I don't see or sense anything. Looks clear." He floated back. "Why do you ask?"

"Thought I felt something weird at the rally, but I guess I was wrong." I sighed. "Go back to West and keep an eye on him. It's all we can do for now."

"Get some rest," Malcolm said. "You look like you're about to fall down."

"I think I might try to nap. Be careful."

"You too." Malcolm disappeared.

Once Malcolm was gone, I turned off the lights and crawled into bed. Exhausted from lack of sleep and the battering I'd taken from the healing spells, I fell asleep almost immediately.

Hours later, I woke up and stumbled into my bathroom to splash water on my face, trying to clear the cobwebs from my brain. I'd needed the nap, but I'd slept so hard and for so long that I was disoriented and unsure of not only what time it was, but also what day. I was left wondering if the nap had helped or just made things worse.

When I checked my reflection in the mirror, my eye didn't look too bad; the swelling had gone down and though there was bruising around it, it looked like it could be covered with makeup and I could avoid using another painful healing spell. That was something, at least.

When I checked my phone, I discovered it was almost nine p.m. and I had not, in fact, slept straight through until the next day. I flipped on my bedroom light, got out my laptop, and checked the local news.

And discovered the Daylighter folks had been busy putting that list of vamp-owned businesses to use.

"Shit," I breathed. Reports of vandalism were coming in from across the city and the fire department was on scene at three "suspicious" fires at businesses on the Daylighters' list. None were owned by Charles, but he could very well have been a victim of the vandalism.

My phone rang. I glanced at the screen, then answered it. "Hello, Bryan."

"Miss Alice," the enforcer rumbled.

"Are you guys all right?"

"None of Mr. Vaughan's properties have been targeted so far, and all of our personnel are safe. The same can't be said, unfortunately, for others on the Court and their people."

I sighed. "I was afraid of that."

"I'm calling for three main reasons," Bryan said. "First, we haven't located either Mr. Travers or Mr. Andrews yet. They haven't returned to their apartment, nor have their vehicles been spotted. Our resources are spread thin at the moment, but we'll continue our search. Second, Ms. Dade has compiled a preliminary report on the phone records you provided. She wants to meet to discuss her findings, which brings me to item number three: you need to come in and discuss your investigation."

"Do I need to come to Northbourne?"

"No. In fact, you should avoid Northbourne for the time being. It's become a focal point for protesters. Several hundred are gathered outside the gate, and security personnel are fully occupied securing the perimeter."

"Holy shit," I said involuntarily. "It's that bad?"

"It's bad," Bryan said grimly. "Only a few members of the Court are at Northbourne currently. Most are in their own private residences. We ask that you come to Hawthorne's and meet with Ms. Dade and Mr. Vaughan here."

I'd been avoiding Hawthorne's and Charles like the plague, but it sounded like a much better option than dealing with the mess up at Northbourne. "Is the bar open?"

"No. Mr. Vaughan is opting to remain closed until further notice."

All things considered, I thought that was a good idea. "What time should I be there?"

"Ms. Dade is on her way already and Mr. Vaughan will clear his schedule."

I glanced at the clock. "I can be there in about forty-five minutes."

"Should we send a car for you?"

"No. I'm sure I'll want to go somewhere afterward, so I'll need my car."

"Alice, you are an investigator for the Court. You are welcome to utilize a Court-owned vehicle for as long as you need it."

A Court-owned vehicle no doubt outfitted with a tracking system and audio/visual surveillance. No thanks. "I'll think about that. In the meantime, I'll head your way."

"Be safe." We ended the call.

Before I put the phone down, I thought about checking in with Sean, then decided against it. He hadn't texted or called, which probably meant he was still dealing with pack issues.

I dressed in a blue long-sleeved shirt over a black tank top, black jeans, and my favorite don't-mess-with-me boots, with my hair in a French braid. I slid knives into my boots and grabbed my bag on the way out the door.

I saw more police cars on the way to Hawthorne's than civilian vehicles. The streets were eerily deserted. When I arrived in The Heights, I drove past the closed bar and turned into a parking lot on the next block rather than be the only car parked in front of Hawthorne's. I put my holster on my belt, locked up my car, and headed for what had once been my favorite watering hole.

It was a chilly evening, but I left my jacket unzipped so I could get my gun quickly if I needed to—not that I expected to find trouble on the one-block walk to Hawthorne's, but I was on high alert for possible attacks from humans, spirits, and demons. A gun might not help me much in two out of three of those scenarios, but if any Daylighters were hanging around hoping to catch a vamp or other supe coming or going from the bar, they'd find themselves staring down the barrel of my .45.

The door opened just as I reached it. Adri gave me a tight smile. "Hey, Alice."

"Hi," I said as I walked inside. Adri shut the door and locked it.

The bar was dark and empty. I'd never been in Hawthorne's when it was closed. Only the lights behind the bar were on, but there was enough illumination that I could easily follow Adri between the tables toward the back of the bar and down a dimly lit hall to a door marked PRIVATE. Our ascent up the stairs to the second floor was silent.

I expected her to turn left toward Charles's office, but instead we went right, down the hall to a door near the end. Bryan opened it as we approached, and we entered the conference room. The space was dominated by a long wooden table ringed with twelve leather chairs. One wall was an enormous screen.

The three people at the conference table rose as we entered. Charles, in a dark gray suit, sat at the head of the table. On his left was a brunette in a red tee, black blazer, and jeans, who I took to be Kim Dade. On his right, to my surprise, was Niara, in a royal blue jumpsuit that wouldn't have looked good on anyone else. Her braided hair was arranged in an elaborate and intricate style that looked like it had taken hours to create. Vamps never let a crisis keep them from looking good.

"Alice, how lovely to see you." Charles came around the table to take my hands and kiss my cheek. It wasn't unusual for him to greet me that way when we were alone or with one of his enforcers, but he'd never before been quite so affectionate in front of others.

When Niara's brown eyes glowed, though, I thought I had a good idea why he was being so demonstrative. Fantastic. The last thing I needed to be was the prize in a tug-of-war between two members of the Vampire Court.

Then Niara moved toward me with a smile that felt like the warmth of a hundred suns, and I forgot all about Charles, Mark, Sean, and literally everything else but the pleasure and contentment promised by those amber-colored eyes.

"Alice," she murmured, reaching out to take my hand and kiss my cheek. Her lips were soft and cool as they brushed the corner of my mouth, and a shiver traveled all the way down my spine. "You have been injured, have you not?" Her fingers stroked mine as she leaned forward to speak into my ear. "You must let me heal you. Our investigator must not be distracted by pain."

"It doesn't hurt," I said absently. The word *investigator* drifted through my brain, looking for something to connect to, and it finally fell into place. *Mark. Harnad. Murders.*

Son of a bitch, she'd rolled me.

I took a slow step back. Her fingers trailed along my arm, igniting little sparks of sensation I forced myself to ignore.

"Such control." Her lips turned up in a ghost of a smile. "How remarkable."

Charles was so still he could have been made of marble. Only the faint silver glow in his eyes belied his anger. I took another, more deliberate step back and tried not to think about how much I would have liked to feel Niara's soft fingertips in other places on my body.

"If no one has any objections, I'd like to hear what Kim has to report." I was pleased my voice was steady.

The analyst, who had been waiting by her chair while our little drama played out, looked up from the tablet in her hand and raised an eyebrow. I guessed her to be in her mid-thirties. She was curvy and about my height, with shoulder-length reddish-brown hair held back in a ponytail. Her eyes twinkled as if she was thinking of a particularly funny joke. I instinctively liked her.

"By all means," Charles said.

I moved to take a seat on Kim's side of the table, a few chairs down so I could see all three of them as well as the video screen. It was a practical decision and it kept some distance between Niara and me. I was sure my choice of seat was not lost on anyone in the room.

When I was settled in, Bryan opened a bottle of water and sat it on a coaster in front of me. I smiled my thanks, then turned my attention to the analyst.

Kim did something on her tablet and the video screen on the wall lit up, displaying the emblem of the Vampire Court. It was replaced with the first page of John West's phone records, obtained by Cyro for the price of a decent used car.

"These are the records provided by Ms. Worth," she said briskly. "As you can see, West's cell sees heavy use between the hours of seven a.m. and six p.m. Monday through Friday and between seven a.m. and one p.m. on Saturday, which makes sense since it appears to be primarily for communication related to his investment business. He doesn't appear to use the texting function, which isn't surprising considering his age."

The page changed on the screen. "I began with this week's contacts and worked backward," Kim said. "Though the overall call volume is relatively high, many of the calls were made to and received from the same individuals. I compiled a list of their names. Brief background checks have been completed and I am comfortable saying there is a high probability they are clients of his investment company."

She set her tablet on the table and turned to me. "I know this isn't what you want to hear, but I'm betting West has a second mobile phone, one not registered to him or his address."

My stomach sank. "What makes you say that?"

She gestured at the screen. "The clues are there. As I said, almost all of the calls take place during what you would call normal business hours and almost none of them occur at his home or anywhere other than his place of business or a small radius around it. He has a landline phone in his residence. I took the liberty of obtaining those records, and it is so rarely used I was easily able to identify all the calls made to and from that number in the past month. Conspicuously missing from that list are what I would call 'friendly' calls. So either this guy literally has *no* friends, or they're contacting him at another number."

I sighed. "So, what you're saying is this got us nowhere?"

"Not necessarily." The screen changed to a map of the city. A red dot appeared near downtown. "That's his office," Kim told me. A blue dot lit up on the east side. "His house." Then the map lit up with yellow dots. Most of them formed a path between the red and blue dots, but others were in the north part of the city, and some in the west. "This is a map of his movements up through this evening. I can do more traffic pattern analysis, but I think this is interesting."

It took me a second, but I figured it out. "There is absolutely nothing on the south side," I said. "Wait. I know for a fact he was near 28th and Forrester this afternoon, but it's not on there."

She pointed at me. "So what does that tell us?"

"He's turning his phone off when he goes to the south side of the city." I stared at the map. "It's a big area. Mainly industrial parks and warehouses."

"Hundreds of warehouses," she confirmed. "Lots of places you could hide an operation like this and never be found."

"That's something. It gives us a place to start looking, I guess, but it's going to take a long time with an area that big."

"I can do more analysis, see if I can shrink down the search area. Have you considered tagging his car?" Kim asked.

"We considered it, but Mark was unwilling to do it. We feared if the tracker was discovered, it would endanger the surviving victims."

"And how do you stand on this issue?" Niara asked me.

My shoulders hunched under the combined weight of Felicia and the others who were still alive, as far as we knew. Mark had borne that weight for us. Now it was on me.

While I shared Mark's reluctance to risk the survivors, I was beginning to think the time for walking softly was over, not just because of Mark's death, but because the city might tear itself apart if we didn't get answers soon. The question was: could I endanger the lives of the survivors? I flashed back to watching Amelia Wharton cutting throats at the construction site and my breathing and heart rate spiked.

In a room with two vampires who were already on edge, that was not a good move. Charles's eyes went the color of moonlight and Niara's blazed with amber fire. Kim went still, her eyes on the table. I forced my breathing to slow and my heartbeat followed suit.

Kim and I jumped when my phone buzzed. I reached into my pocket and took out my phone.

Wolf: With my pack for another hour or so, then free to meet. What's your 20?

Me: Meeting with data analyst. Not sure how much longer—will text when done.

I stuck my phone back in my pocket. "Sorry about that. Where were we?"

"I think you should tag West's car," Kim said.

"Why do you say that?" I asked.

"I'm analyzing the situation; it's what I do. In my assessment, it's worth the risk. With the right tech, you can reduce the chances of it being found to practically zero. Maclin can get the tech."

It was my turn to raise an eyebrow.

She grinned. "I'm an analyst. It's my job to know all the players, all the variables. All the options."

"I'll talk to him about it. If he's got the right tech, we'll tag the car. We'll have to be ready to move fast if we get intel we can move on or the tracker is compromised."

"That's outside my area," she said. "In the meantime, I'll continue to look into the cell records and see if I can get any other helpful info." She looked at Charles. "Mr. Vaughan?"

"You are dismissed," the vampire said.

Kim rose from the table, packing away her tablet and putting her bag on her shoulder. I stood and we shook. "It was nice to meet you," she said. "Looking forward to helping you get these bastards. You get any more data you need crunched, send it on, any time day or night."

"I'll do that." I watched her go with Bryan as her escort, leaving me in the conference room with Charles, Niara, and Adri.

"So, what now?" I asked, settling back into my chair.

"Now, we wish to know what you have learned today," Charles said. "And then we will give you a brief overview of the resources we have available to assist in your investigation." He gestured, and Adri brought a folder to the table. "But first, there is paperwork to be signed."

I sighed. Of course there was.

19

An hour and a half later, the paperwork was signed, I'd given Charles and Niara a full report on the day's activities, and I'd received an overview of the kinds of help I could get from the Vamp Court, should I need it.

Mark's philosophy had always been that, even if he was investigating a case on behalf of the Court, he preferred to use his own people and resources as much as possible to maintain a critical distance and independence. He was a contractor, not an employee of the Court, and it was important that he emphasized that difference in both practice and appearance. As far as I knew, the Court had always respected the boundaries he'd established, though they tested them from time to time.

His approach made sense to me, both on principle and because I valued my independence above almost anything else. I wanted to work the same way, but it would be more of a challenge for me since I didn't have all the resources at my disposal that MDI did. If I did more work for the Court in the future, I would have to figure all that out. For now, I made notes and followed along the best I could.

By a little after midnight, I was running out of steam and the vampires could sense it.

"It grows late. We must not keep her from her bed," Niara said when I asked Charles to repeat something for the third time.

"I do not think it is *her* bed you are thinking of," Charles said dryly.

Niara's laugh was like the tinkling of bells. "Charles, you are a delight," she said, her voice tinged with mirth. She smiled at me, but I was more prepared this time and wasn't caught up in its mesmerizing warmth. "Our investigator is half-asleep. What fun could we possibly have when she is so weary?" She smiled at me. "There will be another time."

I grabbed my bag and stood. "I think I'll say good night. I'll be in touch as soon as I have something to report."

Charles and Niara rose. "Before you leave, we have not had the opportunity to express our regret over Mark's death," Charles said. "On behalf of the Court, please accept our sincere condolences on your loss."

I was still angry at having been kept in the dark that Mark was missing, but being angry at vamps for keeping secrets was like being mad at the sun for shining. It was simply what they did.

"He was a good man and a good friend." I turned to leave. "Shall we?" I asked Adri, gesturing at the door.

Niara came around the table. "I will walk you out," she said.

I wanted to glance at Charles but didn't, since I didn't want either of the vampires to think I was asking him to intercede with Niara on my behalf. I was puzzled, however. Niara was in another vampire's territory, but Charles seemed to be allowing her to openly court me right under his nose, days after that little scene on my back porch. What game were they playing, and how could I extricate myself from it?

I mustered what I hoped was a gracious smile as Adri opened the door for us. "Thank you."

Our walk down the hall was silent. When Niara and I got to the stairway door, we both reached for the handle. "Allow me," she said, to my surprise. She pushed it open and we went into the stairwell.

When I started down the stairs, she stilled me with a hand on my arm. "My dear, you are a well of grief and anger. I can help you and clear your mind of this pain."

Vampires never did anything for free, but even if she was offering to help out of the goodness of her heart, this was not a favor I wanted. "My anger helps keep me sharp. The pain motivates me."

That sounded strange when I said it out loud, but she nodded. "That I can understand," she said, her voice like music.

Niara reached up and stroked my cheek with her cool hand, her thumb brushing lightly under my bruised eye. I flinched and closed my eyes, expecting to feel pain, but instead a delicious warmth spread through me as the discomfort faded. Somehow, she was healing me simply with her touch. I hadn't known vampires could do that.

"My blood is within you," she murmured in answer to my unspoken question. "I still command it. With it, I can do many things. I can heal."

Her hands traveled down my body slowly, as if she could sense where I still ached. She caressed my hand and the last twinges of pain from the burns vanished. Her fingers moved over my lower back and the soreness disappeared. Then her hands moved to my hips and I opened my eyes.

Her gaze was amber fire. "I can also bring great pleasure."

"I am sure you can." Carefully, I put my hands on hers. They were cool, but there was nothing cold in the way she looked at me. I eased her hands off my body. She didn't resist. "I'm not free right now," I said.

"Yes, your werewolf and your federal agent. If they do not object to each other, surely they would not object to me." Her brow arched. "I am not a jealous lover."

I didn't correct her assumption about the current state of my love life. "No," I said firmly. "I'm afraid my dance card is full."

She chuckled. "I was always so fond of that phrase. Do you know why?"

I was instantly wary. "I can't imagine."

She moved so fast that I swear I didn't even see it. Suddenly I was up against the wall, her hands were on me, and her lips hovered a millimeter from mine. Her scent, like cinnamon and wine, made me shiver as she murmured, "Because there is always another time, and another dance."

She brushed her lips across mine, and then in a puff of air she was gone. The heavy soundproof door closed with a quiet thump, leaving me alone in the stairwell.

I stood with my back against the wall while my brain processed that I was not bitten, not dead, and not in Niara's bed, at least for the time being.

"I guess I'll see myself out," I said to no one in particular. It was just as well there was no one else around since my knees were not exactly steady as I went down the steps.

The downstairs seemed darker than when I'd arrived; maybe there were some streetlights that had gone out, or maybe it was just my mood.

Instead of walking straight out the front door, I detoured behind the bar and reached for the bottle of Dalwhinnie on the second-highest shelf. I poured myself two fingers of Scotch, recapped the bottle, and took my drink to my usual booth in the back corner.

"Hello, old friend," I said as I slid across the familiar seat. I leaned against the wall, stretched my legs out in front of me, and sipped my drink in the eerie silence of the bar.

I'd once been something of a fixture in this booth, but I hadn't sat in it for almost two months, since the night I'd met Sean. It felt like almost a lifetime ago when I'd sat here, nursing a glass of whisky while I waited for an audience with Charles, and a good-looking stranger interrupted my reverie to ask if he could join me.

I assumed someone was watching the bar on the surveillance cameras and expected someone—Bryan, Adri, maybe even Charles—to appear when I didn't leave, but no one came downstairs to see what I was doing or to fuss at me for helping myself to a drink. Either they were all deeply engrossed in dealing with the fallout from Mark's death, MDI's defection, and the violent protests around the city, or they were just giving me space. Either way, I was glad for the seclusion after what had been, hands down, one of the worst twenty-four hours I'd had in recent memory.

My peace and quiet was interrupted by my phone. I dug it out of my pocket and stared at the screen. *Wolf Calling.*

I was keenly aware our conversation from this afternoon had been left unfinished. Part of me wanted to apologize for saying I was trying to protect him, and part of me thought I shouldn't be sorry for trying to keep the people around me safe. He certainly wouldn't need me to protect him from most things, but a demon wasn't most things, and that was the problem. I didn't know what kind of demon I was up against, but it wasn't a lower one like the one who had come to my house, that was for damn sure. As strong as he was, I wasn't sure Sean would survive an encounter with one, and there was way too much blood on my hands already.

In my mind, I saw Sean's golden gaze staring at me. *It's not your decision; it's mine*, he'd said.

I thumped my head against the wall.

When I didn't answer, the call went to voice mail. I lowered the phone to the table, tipped my head back, and closed my eyes.

The phone rang again.

With my eyes closed, I reached for the phone, swiped at the screen, and raised it to my ear. "You'll never guess where I am."

A pause. "I can't even begin to guess," Sean said dryly.

"I'm sitting in the back corner booth at Hawthorne's with a glass of Dalwhinnie."

Silence. I wondered if he was remembering our first meeting and our first night together—the one-night stand that had somehow turned into so much more.

"I would have thought you'd had enough Scotch last night to last you for a while," he said finally.

I wondered what he would think if he saw all the empty bottles in my recycling bin at home. I finished my Scotch and set the empty glass on the table.

"You shouldn't be anywhere near Vaughan or the Vamp Court," he added. "There have been almost two dozen attacks on vampire-owned businesses this evening. Even though it wasn't on the list, it's no secret a vampire owns Hawthorne's. I'm surprised the bar is even open."

"It isn't open. I came to see Charles."

I could practically feel the prickle of Sean's anger over the phone. There was a lot of bad blood—pun intended—between him and the vampire. "Why?" he asked tightly.

"Believe it or not, it was a safer option than going to Northbourne, which is apparently Ground Zero for anti-vamp protests right now. I needed to talk to Kim Dade, the analyst, and tell Charles what we found out today." I toyed with my glass. "I know it's late, but I don't think I'll be sleeping anytime soon. Do you want to meet and go over the case?"

"Where do you want to meet?"

"I have all my case files and notes at my house. Do you want to meet there?"

"I can do that. I'm at home, so it will take me about a half-hour to get there."

"Same here. I'll leave now."

"Okay. I'll see you at your house in thirty. Be careful."

"You too." We disconnected.

I put my phone down on the table and sighed. I'd forgotten to ask how his pack was doing, but if he was able to meet me they must be all right. I'd find out more later. Empty glass and phone in hand, I slid out of the booth, put my bag over my shoulder, and headed for the bar.

Tires screeched outside and the front window exploded in a shower of broken glass. I took cover behind a tall table as something heavy landed on the floor near the window. A dark-colored van sped away down the street.

The light coming in through the broken window revealed the object on the floor: two metal pipes strapped together with zip ties, with multicolored wires connecting them. A red light blinked on one of them.

"No," I breathed.

I dropped my glass and my phone and raised my hands in front of me. Every ounce of air magic I could muster erupted from my palms in a flare of bright white a half-second before the explosion.

A wall of fire met my air magic shield and tossed me aside. I had a fraction of a second to register pain before my head hit something and then there was only darkness.

I woke up coughing and gasping for air. Smoke burned my eyes, making them water. I blinked dazedly, trying to make sense of what I was seeing.

Through the haze of pain, I realized I was in Hawthorne's and what was left of the bar was on fire. My magic had shielded me from the initial blast, but now I was buried beneath a pile of debris crushing my chest, legs, and right arm. My legs hurt, but my arm was numb. I struggled to breathe.

From beyond the beams, chunks of ceiling, and broken furniture piled on top of me, an enormous crash shook the floor. It sounded like the building was falling down.

I tried to call out for help, but my shout turned into a fit of coughing. I was dizzy and disconnected from lack of oxygen. I didn't have much time before I passed out from smoke inhalation and then died, either from suffocation or from burning to death.

Through the growing fog in my brain, I wondered why no one had come to rescue me after the bombing. Surely they'd seen me on surveillance cameras as I sat in the bar with my drink. But what if they hadn't? If they thought I left immediately, they wouldn't have any reason to check the bar for victims. I'd parked so far away they wouldn't see my car unless they were looking for it.

The floor trembled as another, louder crash shook the building. Flames surged and heat swept over me. I was running out of time.

I suddenly had an idea born of pure desperation. If Charles *had* drunk from me, we would share a telepathic bond. It would be weak, but I might be able to call for help if I could figure out how to reach him.

Charles had spoken to me mind-to-mind when we were in physical contact, but it was more a case of him sending his thoughts to me and then listening to my replies. I'd only ever communicated telepathically with Malcolm, but I'd learned how to pull my ghost to me using the magic trace connecting us. If Charles had bitten me, there would be a trace of him in my mind, somewhere. I pushed the dizziness and disorientation aside and searched for something that might be a connection to the vampire.

In a deep, dark corner of my mind, I found the tiniest thread that was strange and yet somehow terribly familiar. It was cold and gray, much different from the cool blue-green of Malcolm's trace or the hot golden thread that had once connected me to Sean.

I reached for the cold gray thread, pulled it taut with a yank that nearly sent me spinning into unconsciousness, and screamed with my mind: *Charles! Help!*

At first, I heard and felt nothing. Then, a voice in my head: *Alice?* It was Charles. He sounded surprised.

I sobbed once, relieved and horrified all at once. *Help me. I'm trapped in the bar.*

This time, the response was immediate and forceful. *We are coming for you. Five minutes.*

Another crash shook the floor. *I don't have five minutes.*

My stomach contracted almost painfully at the thought of dying alone in the ruin of Hawthorne's. If only I'd thought of the telepathic connection earlier. If only I hadn't stopped for a drink before I left. If only I'd insisted I go with Mark to the homeless camp.

It would figure my last thoughts in this life were regrets.

"No," I rasped. I'd done the impossible and escaped my grandfather's cabal compound; I could get out of this. I still had Niara's blood in me. I was a high-level air mage, damn it. No pile of debris, no matter how heavy, was going to hold me down.

Charles said something else but I shut the link between us so I could focus.

I spooled my air magic and raised my left hand, directing magic into it until the pain became almost unbearable. I closed my eyes, took a deep breath of smoky air, and struck the pile of debris with my palm, unleashing the spooled magic.

The debris blew away with a crash that I barely heard through the wave of disorientation that followed such an enormous expenditure of magical energy. I fought unconsciousness with everything I had and pushed the darkness back. When I opened my eyes, I could barely see through the thick smoke, but it was time to move.

I staggered to my feet. My legs hurt, but neither seemed to be broken. Through the smoke and piles of debris, I could see a wide hole where the front windows had once been. I had to get to that exit; there was no other choice. I tried to lift my hands, but there was something wrong with my right arm. It hung at my side, bent oddly at the elbow. There was pain, but it felt distant.

I raised my left hand and summoned what little air magic I had left. I pushed it out ahead of me, opening a path through the smoke and flames, and stumbled toward the gaping hole in the front of Hawthorne's.

Part of the ceiling collapsed, shaking the floor, and I fell to my knees, my air magic snuffing out. Fire surged around me and I screamed as it seared my back and right side. I got to my feet again and used the last ounce of air magic I had to clear a path the last dozen steps to the sidewalk.

I emerged from the burning ruin and stood on the sidewalk in a daze. The night air was cold. Sirens wailed in the distance. Behind me, something very heavy collapsed and a blast of heat rolled over me. My ears buzzed. I tried to take a breath of fresh air, but my lungs didn't seem to want to work. I could no longer feel my broken arm or the searing pain on my back and side.

"Alice!" Over the ringing in my ears, I heard someone shout my name. I turned.

Sean raced down the sidewalk, moving so quickly I was certain I was hallucinating. The buzzing grew louder. All other sounds faded away, and then even the buzzing was gone.

He reached me just as my knees gave out. I pitched forward into his arms.

There was a mouth on mine, hot and unyielding, forcing air into my lungs. My chest rose and fell several times and then the mouth moved away.

"Come on, damn it." It was a growl. "*Breathe*, Alice."

For one long terrible moment, I couldn't remember how to inhale and my chest felt as if it was being crushed under an enormous weight. Suddenly, I sucked in a lungful of deliciously cold, smoke-free air and began to cough.

Strong arms cradled my upper body and rocked me as I hacked and gasped. Through the smell of smoke, I caught the scent of forest.

I opened my eyes and looked up into Sean's bright golden gaze. Charles stood beside us. We were in the lot down the street from Hawthorne's. Sean's truck was parked next to my car, and he was on his knees, holding me. We were hidden from view by a large black SUV I recognized as belonging to Charles. Down the street, I saw red and blue flashing lights and the sky looked strangely orange. The fire must be massive.

My clothes were tattered and bloody. I vaguely recalled thinking my arm was broken and I'd been burned on my back, but nothing hurt except my chest. Charles must have given me his blood to heal me; my mouth tasted like copper and wine. Unfortunately, neither the vamp blood nor a healing spell could clear the smoke from my lungs.

"Hey," I wheezed, then broke into another coughing fit. My throat and lungs burned and it felt like there was a tight band around my ribs, keeping me from drawing in a full breath. I closed my eyes and struggled to breathe.

Heavy footsteps came running up to us. "Give her this," Charles said.

I forced my eyes open again. The vampire handed Sean a mask connected to a small portable oxygen tank that Bryan was holding. The enforcer was breathing hard, his face smudged with soot. There were medical facilities in the lower levels of Hawthorne's. Charles must have sent Bryan back in through the parking garage entrance to get the tank.

Sean put the mask over my nose and mouth. "Breathe slowly," he said, his voice tight. I forced myself to inhale the oxygen, though I could only take small breaths. Gradually, the burning in my lungs eased.

When I stopped coughing, Charles crouched next to us. Sean growled low in warning but the vampire ignored him.

I still couldn't get a full breath, but I pushed the mask aside and reached for him. "Charles."

Sean stiffened as Charles leaned over me. I touched the vampire's face with a sooty and bloody hand, leaving streaks on his pale, cool skin. I slid my hand to his neck and drew him closer. He met my gaze with eyes that shone with silvery light. Everything else faded as we stared at each other.

"You bit me," I rasped.

He tilted his head, his eyes boring into mine. "Yes."

Sean went perfectly still, his eyes flaring bright gold. A low, almost atavistic rumble started deep in his chest and the arms around me tightened. The air crackled with power from both of them.

I made a choked sound that had nothing to do with my smoke-filled lungs. "You *bastard*." I pushed my blood magic out through my fingertips like razors and ripped out Charles's throat.

Cool blood sprayed across my face and upper body as the vampire fell back, his hands on the wound. For the first time since I had met him, he looked shocked. Blood gushed down the front of his suit.

Bryan started toward me, his face darkening. Sean braced himself and snarled at him, his muscles coiled as he prepared to fight.

Unable to speak with his vocal cords torn out, Charles held out a hand.

The enforcer stopped. "Sir, she attacked you. You could have been killed."

Charles moved his hand away from the gory remains of his throat and stood smoothly. The wound was already beginning to heal; in five or ten minutes, there would be no sign it had ever existed. "If she had meant to kill me, she would have taken off my head," he said, his words garbled.

His statement was greeted with silence. I wasn't sure what Sean was thinking, but it was clear I'd just graduated from minor concern to major threat in Bryan's eyes. Within the hour, every enforcer who worked for Charles would know, and then the news would spread to the rest of the Court. I could already see the change in the way Bryan was looking at me: assessing, calculating. Respectful.

Charles gave me a small bow. How did the son of a bitch manage to look so elegant with his throat torn out and his clothes covered with blood? "We cannot linger here. This is a matter you and I will discuss privately at another time. You will proceed with your investigation in the manner we discussed. My employees will investigate this attack on my property."

I wanted very much to have the discussion about him biting me *now*, but the longer we stayed in the parking lot, the more likely we were to be spotted by passing police. Plus, I still couldn't get a full breath and felt lightheaded.

"It was a dark-colored van," I told them, my voice rough with smoke. "And a pipe bomb." I described it the best I could.

"This is very helpful," Charles said. "For now, I must speak with other members of the Court and determine our strategy for managing the situation." He handed Sean a small bag. "Here are her things. Take the tank and drive her home. See that she rests. One of my employees will deliver her vehicle within the hour. If you need additional oxygen tanks or other medical supplies, we will provide them."

Sean gave him a curt nod, gathered me in his arms, and stood. Charles headed to his SUV with Bryan at his side.

Exhaustion tugged at me. I laid my head against Sean's chest. "I don't want to get smoke and blood in your truck." My voice was little more than a whisper.

"Don't worry about it. It's seen worse." Sean brought me around to the passenger side, braced his knee against the truck, and opened the door. He lifted me inside, got me belted in, and shut the door.

In the scant moments it took for him to put the oxygen tank and duffel bag into the back seat and walk around to the driver's side, I was already half-asleep, my head drooping.

"Hey," Sean said, gently shaking my shoulder. "Stay awake, Alice, at least until I can get you home. You have to let us in past the wards." He turned the key in the ignition and the truck rumbled to life.

"Can we go to your house?"

He paused, his hand on the gearshift. "I figured you'd want to be home in your own bed while you recover."

"My house is so far away," I said. "Please. I'll just sleep on your couch." I closed my eyes and laid my head back against the seat.

Sean muttered something and threw the truck into gear. He pulled out onto the street, accelerating away from the flashing lights. I didn't know if he was headed to his house or mine, but I was too tired to care. The last thing I felt before I fell asleep was Sean's hand, squeezing mine and holding tight.

20

I woke when Sean unfastened my seatbelt and scooped me up. I blinked blearily and saw we were parked in his garage. "Your house," I murmured.

"My house," Sean confirmed. He opened the door to the kitchen and went inside. He carried me through the kitchen, past the living room, and to the stairs.

"Couch," I insisted.

"No," he said flatly, taking the steps two at a time.

At the top of the stairs, he went down a short hall and into a large bedroom that was dark except for a faint light coming from the bathroom.

"Guest room?" I asked.

"Alice, hush." He laid me gently on the bed.

"Don't," I said, grabbing at his hands. I felt dizzy and couldn't quite focus. "I'm dirty and bloody."

Sean bent over and kissed my forehead. "Do you think I care about that? Stop worrying."

He went into the bathroom and flipped on the light. Cabinets opened and closed, bottles rattled, and then I heard water running in the tub. When he came back, he sat next to me on the bed. "I don't want you to have to sleep covered in blood. Can you stay awake long enough for a bath?"

"I think so." I tried to push myself up but didn't get very far before I fell back with a frustrated sound. My breathing sounded rough and I coughed.

"Take it easy," Sean said. "I'll clean you up, if it's all right with you."

What I really wanted was to sleep, but I reeked of smoke and I could feel blood drying all over my skin and in my hair. It was uncomfortable, and more importantly, Sean didn't deserve to have to throw away all his bedding.

"Okay," I said.

Sean squeezed my hand. He unzipped my boots and chuckled when he found the knives tucked in them. He spun them expertly, one in each hand, testing their weight and balance, then set them aside. "Other than your boots, I think the rest of your clothes are a loss."

"Just get rid of them, I guess."

Sean could have just torn off what was left of my clothes; instead, he unbuttoned my shirt and eased me out of it, then took off my jeans and socks.

He paused. "Do you want to leave your top and underwear on?"

"Can't get clean with them on," I said sleepily.

He pulled my tank top off over my head, then raised my torso and unfastened my bra. He kept his eyes on mine as he took it off and set it aside. He slid my underwear off, dropped them into the pile of ruined clothing on the floor, and picked me up.

Sean carried me into the bathroom. It was all black-and-white tile, with a large glass shower and a garden tub. He tested the water temperature, adjusted the hot-water tap, and sat me down in the water. It turned gray from the soot.

He unbraided my hair, leaned me back into the water with his arm behind my shoulders, and used his free hand to rinse the blood and soot from my hair. Then he sat me up and squeezed some shampoo into my hair as the tub drained. I closed my eyes.

Sean refilled the tub with clean water as he washed my hair with gentle fingers.

"How did you find me?" I asked.

"I heard the explosion as I was leaving my house and worried it might be Hawthorne's. I got there as fast as I could. I saw your car parked in the lot and no sign of you, so I ran for the bar. Lean back."

I let him rinse my hair. When that was done, he reached for a washcloth and a bar of unscented soap. I kept my eyes closed so I didn't have to figure out whether I should look him in the eyes as he washed me. He scrubbed me gently without lingering on my breasts or anywhere else. I was torn between wishing he would and feeling grateful he didn't. Not that sex was anywhere on my radar tonight, but I couldn't help but remember other times when his hands had been on my naked body.

The hot bath was making it hard to stay awake, despite the feeling of Sean's hands on me. "I thought I was going to die," I murmured suddenly.

Silence. "But you didn't."

He left me to sit in the soapy water while he stripped off his bloody shirt and stuffed it into a garbage bag with my ruined clothes. He went into the bedroom and came back wearing pajama pants. I watched him wash his arms, face, and hair at the sink, then dry off quickly before pulling on a clean Led Zeppelin T-shirt.

Sean sat on the edge of the tub and draped a towel across his lap. He picked me up, sat me on his knees, and wrapped me in another large towel, rubbing me dry. He towel-dried my hair, then carried me into the bedroom. A long-sleeved T-shirt and a pair of drawstring pajama pants were lying on the bed.

When I was dressed in Sean's clothes, he settled me into the bed and pulled the covers up to my chin, then returned to the bathroom to drain the tub and hang the damp towels over the shower.

When it got quiet, I turned my head. He was bracing himself with both hands on the bathroom counter, head lowered and shoulders rigid with tension. He seemed angry, but I wasn't sure about what or toward whom.

He took several deep breaths before he raised his head and headed back toward the bedroom, turning off the light and plunging the room into near-darkness.

Before he could reach the bed, I was seized by a violent fit of coughing that quickly turned into a struggle for breath.

Sean swore. "The oxygen." He disappeared.

He was gone less than a minute, but by the time he came back I was gasping for air. He hurried to the side of the bed, setting the tank down. He turned a knob and held the mask to my face.

"Try to breathe slowly," he reminded me, sitting on the edge of the bed.

I inhaled the oxygen and the coughing subsided. When I was breathing normally again, Sean took the mask away and turned off the tank. "Why don't you use a healing spell?" he asked.

"Because a healing spell can't clear the smoke from my lungs any more than Charles's blood could," I rasped. "The damage is healed, but I'll have to cough the smoke and particles out the old-fashioned way."

With difficulty, I rolled onto my side, turning my back to him as he put the mask down on the nightstand. He came around to the other side of the bed and laid down on top of the covers, facing me.

We lay like that for a long time, staring at each other. There were a million things I wanted to say, but I couldn't find the words.

Finally, Sean broke the silence. "I thought I'd lost you. When I saw what was left of the bar, I was sure there was no way you'd survived...and then you walked out of the fire. I've never seen anything so terrifying and beautiful in my life."

Lake would have been grilling me about how I'd survived the blast and walked through fire and smoke. Sean didn't ask me any questions. It was enough for him that I could do those things.

I took a raspy breath. "Will you hold me?"

Sean rose, pulled back the covers, and climbed in next to me. I burrowed my face into his shirt and he held me—gently at first, then tighter as I began to shake.

When the tears started, he stayed quiet and let me weep. I cried silently and for a long time. It was the second time I had cried in front of Sean, when I hadn't cried in front of anyone else in more than a decade.

Eventually, I cried myself to sleep.

My flesh was burning.

I writhed and screamed and pulled desperately at the spell cuffs holding me in place, but they held fast, despite the blood that ran from my wrists where the metal had dug into my skin. My grandfather's slim coil of fire was wrapped around my forearm.

All I could smell was the stench of my own burning skin. The pain was bad, worse than anything I'd ever experienced. It was a big contract. Moses wanted the money, and he wanted it known his granddaughter had been the one who fulfilled it. No one would ever question my abilities again after this. He could pick and choose which contracts he accepted. He could use me as a threat against both his enemies and his allies.

The coil left my arm. I hung from the cuffs, sobbing. The skin on my arm was blistered and red and blackened.

Moses looked at me with eyes like glacier ice. My mother's eyes had been that same color, but hers were beautiful, like a winter sun. His had never held anything but the promise of misery and suffering.

I turned my head and threw up.

"Are we agreed?" he asked me. "You'll do the work?"

In the real memory, I'd said yes. He'd had me taken down and healed so I could do the spellcraft that was needed. At the time, I was fifteen years old.

In the dream, I said no.

The fire coil came back, but this time it was around my neck and it was a cold fire—the kind he'd never been able to produce. I screamed and screamed as the cold spread through me, burning me from the inside out, consuming me a little at a time, until I was nothing but pain and fire and ice.

"Alice. Alice, wake up." Sean's voice cut through the memory of pain and fire.

I rolled over onto my back, my fists clenched in the sheets and covered with a cold sweat. Sean knelt on the bed beside me. He'd apparently been in the middle of getting dressed, because his hair was still wet from a shower and he wore an undershirt and jeans, left unbuttoned.

It was the smell of him that brought me back to the present, that unmistakable scent of forest that I hadn't been able to forget, no matter how hard I tried.

"Are you all right?" he asked, brushing my hair back from my face.

"No," I choked out and reached for him.

He came to me without hesitation, his mouth finding mine and driving the chill away. Heat spread like wildfire and I pulled him on top of me, my hands sliding under his shirt and across his chest, feeling the familiar lines of his muscles as my nails dug into his skin.

Sean broke our kiss. His eyes glowed. "You almost died last night."

"All the more reason to live." I pulled his shirt off over his head, then slid my hands down his chest toward his jeans. They were out of my reach, so I hooked my toes into his waistband and pushed them down to his hips. The sight of his body was enough to make me shiver hard with desire. He was magnificent.

He resisted, moving so I couldn't push his jeans down any farther. "You're hurt."

"Charles's blood healed me. All that's left is the smoke."

"You drank more vampire blood," he reminded me.

"I know what I want," I told him, my voice husky.

He took my face in his hands and stared into my eyes. "Tell me what you want."

"I want you to make me forget all the bullshit in my head."

Sean kissed me again. I nibbled his bottom lip, drawing blood, then licked it with the tip of my tongue. Golden magic washed over us, as if I'd summoned his wolf with that single touch.

His hand slid under my top and over my ribs to my breast. His thumb ghosted over my nipple, sending an electric current through me. I gasped and arched up against him, desperate to feel his body on mine.

His touch felt controlled, as if he was holding himself back, being careful. I didn't want him to be careful. I wanted Sean to be himself, to be the alpha with his lover. I wanted to know him, the real him, not who he thought he needed to be for me.

I didn't know how to say it, so I grabbed his arms, lowered my shields just enough, and sent him what I wanted.

Sean jerked and lifted his head. "Are you sure?"

"Yes. Don't hold back, not ever again."

He tore away the shirt he'd loaned me, watching my face. Whatever he saw in my eyes must have reassured him, because he lowered his mouth to my bare breasts. I cried out and reached for him.

Lightning fast, he pinned my wrists to the bed, holding me down as he teased and tormented me with his mouth. I writhed and bucked underneath him until he moved his body on top of mine to hold me still.

As if he'd realized I was reaching a point where additional teasing would be more torture than pleasure, he let go of my wrists and ripped my borrowed pants, throwing them to the floor. He rose above me, eyes glowing, all power and danger. For the first time, I saw his wolf in his eyes when he looked at me. I reached up and touched his face. He rubbed his chin against my hand, then drew my fingers into his mouth so he could bite them lightly.

He kissed his way down my body, then slid down the bed and pushed my leg to the side, his mouth moving up my calf and thigh. It had been a long, lonely month, and no one could ever accuse Sean of lacking skill. Blissful minutes later, I shuddered and sobbed his name as waves of pleasure rolled through me. When I opened my eyes, he was above me, looking at me with such heat that I felt scorched by his eyes alone.

"Please," I said, my voice rough. "I need you."

He'd already stripped off his jeans when I wasn't looking, so there was nothing between us when his body covered mine. I held him between my thighs as he looked down at me. "Condom?" he asked.

I shook my head. "Not necessary."

He lowered his head to my breasts, teasing first one and then the other, and then he raised himself up, met my gaze, and pushed into me.

My back arched and I screamed, my fingernails digging into his forearms. He was hot, impossibly hot, and my cries were desperate and ragged as he moved, pushing me back toward the edge.

He leaned down to bury his face into the side of my neck. "Release your magic," he growled.

"Your room," I said, gasping for air. I was full of blood from two master vampires; magic sizzled on my skin, far stronger than normal, waiting to be unleashed.

He drove into me so hard that I cried out. "Don't hold back," he told me, echoing my words to him from only minutes before. "Don't hold back with me, Alice. Not ever again."

There was more to that command than just the release of my magic, but then he was moving faster and I lost all ability to think about anything other than the surge building inside me. It was so much more powerful than the first time that I felt a thrill of fear in the midst of the pleasure. I reached up and grabbed his arms just as the full force struck us both.

I threw my head back with a cry as my magic poured out like a hurricane of white and green, with threads of black, purple, and red. Sean shuddered and his golden magic blended with mine. The power of our combined magic tore through the room. I heard crashing and sounds like things breaking.

Sean leaned down and kissed me as his body pulsed inside me and our magic thundered around us. His room was being demolished but he didn't seem to care. I wrapped my arms and legs around him and we trembled and shook together.

In the past, when I'd released my magic during sex, its return to my body brought another wave of pleasure, one we shared. This time, however, it came back with a vengeance, boosted exponentially by the vampire blood I'd consumed. For Sean, it was a rush of power that raised his wolf and made him snarl and collapse onto his forearms, his breathing suddenly ragged as his eyes glowed.

I had only a brief second to brace myself before magic roared back through me like a freight train going full speed. *Too much, too fast, too strong,* my mind warned, but there was nothing I could do to stop it.

I screamed, but not with pleasure. I had a second to see Sean above me, his eyes wide, before the sheer force of it sent me plunging headlong into oblivion.

21

I came awake slowly. I hurt everywhere, as if I'd been beaten black-and-blue from head to toe. I was wrapped in someone's arms, my head tucked under his chin, my nose pressed against hot flesh that smelled like a forest in spring.

"Name of the driver?" I mumbled.

"What driver?" Sean asked, his voice a low rumble that vibrated along my skin.

I groaned. "Of the truck that hit me."

His arms tightened. "I don't know what to do to help you."

I didn't know either. "Just keep doing what you're doing."

He exhaled. "I can do that."

As more of my senses came back online, I realized we were both naked and still in his bed, though I couldn't see anything of the room since my face was turned toward his broad chest. He was wrapped around me in such a way that I wasn't sure where my body ended and his began. His body heat had seeped into me until my own temperature was closer to his, adding to the sensation we were one body instead of two. I knew this kind of closeness was comforting for shifters, but I'd always thought I would find it claustrophobic, uncomfortable, and too much like being restrained. To my surprise, I found I rather liked it.

"What day is it?" I asked him.

"It's about one o'clock in the afternoon. You've been unconscious for a little over three hours."

That magical backlash had really done a number on me. He could have said I'd been out for three days and I would have believed him.

"Has this ever happened to you before?" Sean asked.

"No, but this is the first time I've released my magic after drinking from two master vampires. If I'd had any idea it would boomerang so badly, I would have held it back."

He kissed the top of my head. "So, how do we make sure this doesn't happen again?"

"Practice."

I felt him smile. "Now *that* sounds like a plan."

"By myself, I mean. Or Malcolm can help me."

A long pause.

I sighed. "That is not what I meant. I need to practice controlling the backlash of magic. I don't have to...you know...in order to create it."

"You have to admit, it's more fun that way. Not in this case, maybe," he added quickly. "But in general."

"In general, yes, it is far more fun that way."

His fingers traced over my ribs on my right side. "You got some new ink since I saw you last. Is this a cat?"

I'd wondered when he was going to mention my new tattoo. "That's no ordinary cat. It's Bastet."

He chuckled. "I suppose as a wolf I shouldn't approve, but I can't think of a more perfect choice for you than a warrior goddess and protector." He squeezed my hand.

I squeezed back. "I'm sorry if I scared you."

"What, by screaming in agony and passing out during sex?" he asked dryly. "Please, Alice. You're going to have to do better than that to scare me after everything I've been through with you."

I smiled. "I guess, comparatively speaking, this wasn't so bad. Not even any blood involved this time. How dull for you."

"One thing I've never experienced is a dull moment with you," he said.

I laughed and was surprised that it only hurt a little. The pain was fading. I stayed where I was, however. Soon enough, we'd have to get up and face the harsh reality of the day. No one would fault me for wanting to steal a few more minutes while we could.

I sensed tension in Sean's body and guessed that he wanted to talk about some of those harsh realities. I was right. "So, what do we deal with first? The attack at the protest or the fact Vaughan bit you?"

I started to pull away, only to find he wasn't letting go. "I'm not going to hold you if you don't want me to," he said, his mouth near my ear. "But it might help you talk it out if we tried things my way, just this once."

His arms loosened, but I stayed where I was. What the hell; why not try it his way, just this once?

I told him everything: Larry the demon, the deranged spirit I'd sensed that night on the Stroll, the poltergeist assault on the stairs, the attack near the diner, and finally the demon who'd burned me at the protest. He listened quietly, his hand rubbing my back.

"Any idea how you got on this demon's shit list?" he asked when I'd finished.

"None whatsoever. I haven't run across any demons lately." Well, except for the half-demon Scott Grierson, but he was dead. "And I'm pretty sure it has nothing to do with this case, since Larry the water department demon came by before I even talked to Mark the first time."

"Is this why you've had Malcolm shadowing West for three days?"

I scowled. "We needed eyes on West. It was the best option."

"Alice."

"And it kept him out of the line of fire," I admitted. "A high-level demon could discorporate him."

"And that, in turn, could kill you."

"Not likely, but it could, though that's not why I'm trying to keep him clear of danger."

"Of course that's not why you're doing it." Sean kissed my shoulder. "But you're doing the same thing to him you did to me: taking the decision out of our hands. Malcolm's a grown-up ghost. He has the right to decide when and where to fight. I am concerned he's a vulnerability for you, but that doesn't mean he doesn't get a say in this."

"I truly do need him shadowing West unless we decide to tag his car, which is something we need to revisit."

"You know where I stand on that. I haven't changed my mind. But there's something else we have to talk about first."

I swallowed. "Charles."

It was Sean who moved then, pulling away just enough so I could see his face. There were shadows under his eyes. Despite his flip response to my apology, it was apparent he'd been worried.

He traced my jaw with his fingers. "I would kill him for you, if you weren't capable of doing it yourself."

"I don't want to kill him. That would bring the kind of trouble to my door I don't want."

"My pack will stand with you against Vaughan and the Court," Sean stated. "By biting a pack associate, Vaughan attacked all of us."

"I've already drawn blood on behalf of myself and your pack, if you'll recall. It was very nearly a fatal wound. By shifter custom, the debt is paid."

He laced his fingers through mine. "You're very calm about this; too calm, in fact. What's going on in your head?"

"I'm not as calm as I look." I let a little of my anger show in my voice. "I'm furious. I've been violated."

Sean's eyes went gold. If Charles had been within reach in that moment, I was fairly certain the vampire would have been in pieces. "All things considered, you showed restraint by not killing him outright last night."

"I thought about it. Instead, I ripped out his throat and he knows I could have killed him on the spot if I'd wanted to. That news is going to spread. I am not a passive victim. I'm no one's prey."

"There's something else, isn't there? I can see it in your eyes. There's more to this than him biting you when you were in his care."

"Yes."

He tucked my head back under his chin. "Tell me."

Partial truth time. "I'm registered as a mid-level air and earth mage, but I'm not. I'm a high-level mage with blood magic and now, because he drank from me, Charles knows it."

Sean went still. He knew the value of that kind of information, how it could be used against me. "I should kill him."

"I understand why you feel that way. Please let me deal with this part of the problem, Sean. My abilities are my secret—or they should have been."

He raised my chin to look into my eyes. "Yesterday, when I asked who was after you, you wouldn't say a word. Today, you told me far more than I ever expected. Why?"

"Charles took the information from me by force. I'm giving it to you by choice. Maybe it's about balancing the scales, or maybe it's about tearing down one more barrier." I ran my fingertips along his jaw. "Plus, I had a little time to think things over."

He caught my hand and kissed my palm. "What have you been thinking about?"

"You said the other day that you'd like to try again. I'd like that, too."

He kissed me, hard. I was suddenly acutely aware that we were both naked and certain parts of him had noticed too. His hand slid down my side to my hip and I wrapped my leg around his.

When my stomach growled, however, Sean drew back and frowned. "When did you eat last?"

"I had a bagel." I hesitated. "Yesterday morning."

"Jesus Christ, Alice." He ran a hand through his hair, making it stand straight up. He had the sexiest bedhead I'd ever seen. "What am I going to do with you?"

I ran my nails over his hip and was rewarded with a very wolf-like growl. "I have a couple of good ideas."

Despite the fact his body was clearly voting in favor of those ideas, Sean shook his head and grabbed my wrists so I couldn't continue my explorations. "You need to eat," he said firmly.

I dipped my head under his chin and nuzzled his jaw. "I can think of other things I'd rather do with my mouth."

He made a sound somewhere between a growl and a groan. "Alice Worth, you are going to eat. How do you expect to take on a harnad if you take such poor care of yourself?"

I lifted my head and glowered at him.

He rolled us over so fast that I squeaked. We ended up on the other side of the bed with him on top of me. That was more like it. I tried to reach for him and found my arms were pinned at my sides. He leaned down and kissed me so hard that I forgot everything else for a full minute.

Finally, he lifted his head, his eyes twinkling. "Take a shower, and I'll make eggs, bacon, and waffles, and a whole pot of coffee just for you."

That might have been the most romantic thing anyone had ever said to me.

I didn't get eggs, bacon, or waffles.

When I emerged from the bathroom in a towel, my hair wrapped in another, Sean was waiting for me, fully dressed and holding his phone. My go-bag was on the bed, along with the small duffel bag Charles had given him the night before.

I took one look at his face and knew our brunch plans were canceled. "What happened?"

"A couple of things. First, I just got a call from Vaughan's security man, Bryan Smith. The vamps have Clint Ravell."

"Excellent. Not as good as having Travers or Andrews, but it's a start. What else?"

"They also have two confirmed missing vamps. Smith said we'd get more info when we come in to talk to Ravell."

"And?"

His mouth turned down. "You need to call Agent Lake. He's apparently very concerned about you disappearing and has been leaving you messages. He just called me."

My eyebrows went up. "He called *you?*"

"He thought I might know where you were. I told him you were fine, but he wants to speak to you personally to make sure you're all right." Sean rolled his shoulders to relieve tension. "I know you've said nothing happened between you, but I'm not sure if I'm the 'other man' in this scenario or he is."

"We had a moment or two," I admitted. "He's a fed, but a good one. You know me and how I feel about SPEMA. I wouldn't say that lightly."

"I appreciate the honesty." Sean regarded me. "Whatever happened before, it is what it is, but last night and this morning changed things. I'm not interested in sharing you, Alice."

"I'm not interested in being shared or in having a fling with a fed, even if he *is* one of the good ones. And that goes both ways. I know it's not unusual for a shifter, especially an alpha, to have more than one lover, but that's not going to work for me."

His eyes glittered. "I figured as much when you reacted the way you did to Rachel Barrow flirting with me."

"How about how *you* reacted when I mentioned Lake that first time?" I countered. "And I don't care who flirts with you. You're a good-looking man; it's going to happen. I only care about how you respond. And if it's something that helps us with a case and I know it's just a role you're playing, I can deal with that, as long as you give me the same courtesy when I need to bat my eyelashes at someone."

"You think I'm good-looking?" He was grinning, the bastard. He knew exactly how gorgeous he was.

I shrugged. "If you're into the tall, handsome, and muscular thing, I guess."

Sean chuckled and reached into the small black duffel bag. He brought out my gun and its holster, my wallet, my keys, and my little notebook. "This was all we could salvage of the stuff you had with you. Your phone was toast."

"Thanks. I'm glad my wallet survived; I wasn't looking forward to getting all that crap replaced. I'm going to need a new phone, though."

"Already taken care of." He picked something up off the bed and held it up. It was a fancy new phone.

I shook my head. "I'll get my own."

"It's clean—no tracking software, no surveillance mods."

"That's not what I'm concerned about."

Sean eyed me. "Is this like the furniture thing? I'm still not allowed to give you anything?"

I frowned at him.

He sighed. "It was part of a batch I bought two months ago for my company. I only paid forty dollars each because we were setting up a new service contract. If it makes you feel better, you can pay me the forty bucks."

Reluctantly, I took it. He showed me how to scan my fingerprint and the screen unlocked. I had a bunch of missed calls and text messages. Some were from Bryan, two were from Kim Dade, and the rest were from Lake.

"It's the same number as the old one," Sean said. "I saved your sim card from the old phone, so you still have your contacts and old messages."

"Thank you. I'll get you the forty bucks."

He took advantage of our closeness to nuzzle my neck. "You smell good," he said, lips against my skin.

"You mean I smell like you and your soap," I teased.

He wrapped me in his arms and kissed my shoulder. "Yes, you do, and I like it."

I slid my hands around his waist and rubbed against him. "I can tell."

He held me still. "If you keep that up, we won't be getting over to see Clint Ravell for a while."

"Spoilsport." I started to move away, only to find myself crushed against his body as he kissed me.

When we came up for air, Sean said, "Get dressed. We'll have to grab something to eat on the way."

"And coffee?" I asked hopefully.

He kissed the tip of my nose. "I already made some. I'll put it in a travel mug."

I could get used to this.

With Northbourne still surrounded by protesters, the vamps were holding Ravell at a private residence belonging to Charles. We took Sean's company SUV and drove past Hawthorne's on the way.

When we turned onto the street where Charles's retail lofts were located, I gasped. The explosion and resulting fire had gutted about a third of the block. It was hard to tell what had been destroyed in the initial explosion and what had been lost due to fire, but there was nothing left whatsoever of Hawthorne's or the offices above it. How the subbasements had fared, I couldn't tell, but I was guessing not well. The feds had put up a tall chain-link fence around the entire building and investigators in coveralls combed through the ruins.

"It's not nearly as bad as it could have been," Sean said, covering my hand with his. "The explosion was near the front of the building. They saved most of the apartments. No one died, or was even seriously injured, except you."

I was relieved to hear it, but seeing the blackened ruin that was all that was left of the bar left me shaken. I pulled my hand out of Sean's and crossed my arms as we continued down the street. "I wonder if the vamps have any leads."

"From what I understand from Bryan Smith, the van was spotted by traffic cams leaving the scene. The police located it about an hour later, on fire. Apparently, it had been stolen earlier in the evening."

"No help there, then," I said with a sigh. "Unless someone takes credit for the bombing, it's going to be hard to catch whoever was behind it."

My phone rang. *Lake Calling.* I swiped the screen and put the phone to my ear. "This is Alice."

"Alice." Lake sounded relieved. "I've been calling. Are you all right?"

"I'm fine. I lost my phone and it took some time to get a replacement." All true, as far as it went.

"You heard about the bombing at Hawthorne's last night?"

"Yes. I just drove past and saw the damage. I hope they find the bastards who did it."

"Were you at Hawthorne's yesterday?"

"No."

"Were you in the area last night at all?"

On the off chance my car had been identified on traffic cams in the area, I said, "Yes. I was visiting a friend who lives in the Heights. I drove past at around ten, I think. The bar was closed."

A pause. "I was on the scene earlier today. It looks like there was someone trapped in the bar after the explosion, someone who got out by blasting their way through a large pile of debris."

"It wasn't me. I already told you I wasn't there."

"I don't believe you," Lake said, his voice frosty. "I think you're lying, but I'm not sure why."

Beside me, Sean's eyes blazed. The steering wheel creaked under his hands.

"You're free to think what you want," I said. "But no matter how many times you ask me, the answer will be the same: I wasn't there."

"Then where were you?" he demanded.

"Good-bye, Lake." I disconnected.

"For a man who's trying to get into your pants, I think he's going about it the wrong way," Sean observed, in a far more mild tone than I was expecting considering how white his knuckles were.

I shook my head. "No matter what he thinks or says, he's a fed first. That's never going to change."

That was the realization I'd come to yesterday, sometime between Lake's departure from my house and when I'd answered Sean's call at Hawthorne's. Despite our mutual attraction, the hard truth was I'd never be able to be myself around Lake for more than a few minutes at a time, and I'd be in a perpetual state of fear that he would figure out I wasn't who I claimed to be. It would be exhausting and miserable, and it would end badly. I'd be lying if I said it didn't hurt—I did like him, and Lake was a good guy underneath all that fed.

"If he decides to push it, I'll vouch for your whereabouts," Sean said.

I patted his hand. "I appreciate the offer of perjury, but I doubt it'll come to that."

Our quick stop for burgers turned into a mild argument when Sean insisted I attempt to eat a double cheeseburger and a large order of waffle fries. I managed about a third of the burger and half of the fries. Sean grumbled but finished off my food.

The house we were visiting was north of the city, only five miles or so from Northbourne. The gate swung open as we pulled up and Sean followed a long, winding driveway that ended in front of a sprawling mansion. We parked next to two other black SUVs and got out.

My boots had come out of the fire looking battered but were still wearable, thankfully. I had on the change of clothes from my go-bag, which was a green long-sleeved shirt and jeans. I had no shoulder bag anymore, so my phone was in my pocket and Sean had loaned me a Maclin Security jacket to go over my holster.

When we reached the front steps, the door opened, revealing the enforcer who had accompanied Adam to Felicia's apartment and escorted me to my meeting with the Vamp Court. "Ms. Worth," he said. "Mr. Maclin."

"What's your name?" I asked.

"Fortune."

"Is that a first or last name?"

He smiled. "Just Fortune."

Alrighty then. "Is Adri here?"

He stepped aside and we walked into the house. I felt a pang when I realized the interior reminded me of Charles's now-destroyed offices above Hawthorne's: dark wood, low light, and expensive antiques. Even if I hadn't known the house belonged to Charles, I would have been able to guess. To our right was an enormous living room with couches, cushions, and a high vaulted ceiling. In the back, a grand piano rested on a raised platform. I wondered if Charles played.

"Alice." I turned at the sound of Adri's voice. She was walking toward us down a hall, in her customary all-black attire. "I'm glad to see you've recovered."

"How's our guest?"

She smiled, and it wasn't a nice smile. "He's delightful. He's only threatened to rape me twice."

Sean made a deep rumbly noise.

"No surprise there," I said. "The first time I met him, he was robbing a girl and trying to rape her. Someone should teach him some manners."

"I would love to do so, but our instructions were not to touch him until you arrived." She glanced at Sean. "Mr. Maclin. If you'll both follow me."

Adri led us down the hall, with Fortune behind us. I could tell Sean didn't like the enforcer at his back, but we were in vamp territory and it was their playground, their rules.

At the end of the hall, we stopped at a heavy door and Adri entered a code. The door opened and we stepped into what looked like a conference room, except one wall had a large one-way mirror. In the room beyond, a wiry young man was sprawled in a chair, his leg outstretched, arms crossed over his chest.

As we entered the observation room, he was calling out, "Send that tall bitch back in here. I'll let her blow me, if she says please."

"Cocky little shit, isn't he," Adri said as Fortune closed the door to the hallway. "Most people would at least be a little intimidated by being kidnapped off a street corner and chained in a soundproof room."

"If he's on Haze, he's too high to be scared." I walked up to the window to get a good look at him.

Ravell's right ankle was cuffed to the leg of the chair and the chair was bolted to the floor. The room was otherwise bare, except for metal rings embedded in the walls, ceiling, and floor, and cameras in the corners. There was a six-inch drain in the floor, not far from the chair.

I'd spent a lot of time in rooms like the one Ravell was in and buckets of my blood had gone down drains like that one. I'd learned how to get what you want from someone who doesn't want to give it. An icy calmness settled over me.

"You gonna ask him nicely first?" Adri asked.

I eyed Ravell. Defiance oozed out of every pore. He was too high to appreciate the danger he was in and too much of a misogynist to respect anything I had to say. Mark was dead and the city was tearing itself apart. "I'm not really in the mood to ask nicely, and I don't think it would do any good anyway."

Adri arched an eyebrow, reminding me of her vampire boss. "So how do you want to play it?"

I slipped out of the jacket and put it on the table. I took the holster off my belt and my phone out of my pocket and set them down next to the jacket.

I glanced at Sean. He gave me a nod.

"Give me five minutes," I said.

When I walked into the room, Clint Ravell looked me over with blatant lust, his eyes traveling from my chest down to my boots and back again. "Damn, girl," he said, his gaze on my breasts. "You ain't the tall one, but you can come give me a ride." Then he looked up at my face and froze.

"Surprise." I lashed out with my cold-fire whip.

My aim was precise. The bright green lash caught him around the throat and he screamed. He reached up to grab the coil of fire and let go quickly when it burned his fingers.

"I have some questions," I said conversationally. "The faster and more truthfully you answer them, the sooner I walk back out of here. If you lie to me, I will separate your head from your body. Are we clear?"

"Yes!" he screeched.

"Good. Where are Jake Travers and John Andrews?"

"I don't know!" I tightened the whip and he shrieked. "I don't know!" he repeated frantically. "They disappeared yesterday. I've been calling and texting and they're just gone. Check my phone—you'll see."

"Where would they go if they were hiding?"

"I don't know! Fuck...Jake has a sister, Hailey. Maybe he went there. John's got a girlfriend named Amy."

"Amy who?"

"Amy Curry! Jesus, God..."

"What about their other friends? Give me names."

Half-sobbing, he rattled off five or six names.

"What did they have to do with killing that man they said they found in the alley?"

He frowned at me. "The guy the vampires killed?" Another shriek. "Nothing! They were walking past the alley and they saw some assholes dumping the body."

I kept my face blank. "Tell me."

"They saw two men unload a body wrapped in plastic out of this blue van and then leave it in the alley. After the van drove off, they went over to see if the dude had any money. They took his ring but they couldn't get to his wallet because they didn't want to leave fingerprints. Then they saw the fanghead bite and knew it was gonna be a big fucking deal so they called the cops."

"They're a couple of drug dealers. Why did they call it in?"

"They've got cases pending." His nose was running and he wiped it on his sleeve. "They thought if they could tell the cops about the van, it would help with their cases. Jake got part of the plate number. The cop said he'd talk to the D.A., get their charges dismissed. They told him everything and the cop let them walk out."

"Which cop?"

"I don't know! They didn't say."

It all had the unmistakable ring of truth, which meant Detective Brody had falsified his report and omitted any mention of the van, its occupants, and its license plate. I thought back to the mystery vehicle that tailed Mark from the liquor store, the one that looked like an unmarked police car. Was it Brody behind the wheel? Was he somehow involved with the harnad?

Speaking of: "Do you work for the harnad?"

"What the fuck is a harnad?"

"What do you know about the missing women from the Stroll?"

"Nothing, I swear," he said and I believed him.

"What do your friends know about it?"

"They never said nothin' to me about it, 'cept we all figured it's the vamps doing it." Ravell looked up at me, tears streaking his face. "Lady, we sell drugs, we use drugs. We bust heads for our supplier when he needs somebody to collect debts. We don't kill nobody."

"Who's your supplier?"

He stared at me. I tightened the whip, and he shrieked, "Rat Boy! Rat Boy!"

"He sounds like a great guy. If I hear about you doing anything I don't like in the future, I'm going to find Rat Boy and tell him you're a snitch."

He blanched.

"Is there anything you'd like to add, Clint? Anything you can think of that might help me find your boys?"

"No!"

I released him. His neck was bloody and blistered but he'd live. I turned and headed for the door.

Of course, he couldn't resist saying one last stupid thing. "Cunt," he spat at me.

I turned and lashed with my whip. It cut through the crotch of his jeans and sliced right through the seat of the metal chair. His scream was impressively loud and high-pitched.

I walked over and bent down so I could look him in the eye. "What did we learn today about what happens when you call women disrespectful names?"

He stared at me, his eyes like saucers. It looked like the Haze had pretty much worn off, and he was mewling.

"Don't be such a baby," I said, walking away. "I'm sure that will only take a couple of weeks to heal. You might even be able to have sex again someday."

Behind me, he started screaming curses.

The door beeped and opened as I approached. Fortune and another male enforcer I didn't recognize stepped into the room.

"He's got a boo-boo," I said.

I might have been imagining it, but I thought Fortune's buddy looked a little green. He must be new to working for the Court. I found it extremely hard to believe the little bloodletting I'd just done was anything close to the worst thing that had happened in this room in the past week alone. Despite its clean appearance, my magic told me the floor, walls, and ceiling had seen a lot of blood.

"We'll take it from here, Ms. Worth," Fortune said. They moved aside to let me pass and then closed the door behind me.

Sean and Adri waited for me in the observation room. Adri gave me a thumbs-up. "I like your style," she said. "Get in, get the answers, get out. Very efficient."

Sean leaned against the conference table, arms crossed. "There was nothing in the police report about a blue van."

"There sure wasn't, which I find *extremely* interesting. It would appear Tweedledee and Tweedle*dumb* stumbled upon Mark's body being dumped in the alley and tried to use what they saw to their advantage. Who wants to bet the detective who faked their statements called the harnad before he let them go?"

"If that's the case, I doubt we'll be seeing them again," Sean said. "The harnad has already proven they don't let potential witnesses go free for very long."

Behind me, the loud cursing cut off abruptly. I glanced through the window just in time to see Fortune tuck a used spell crystal in his pocket. He'd apparently used a sleep spell to knock Ravell out.

"We've got some leads to check out." I glanced at Adri. "We need a deep dig on a Major Crimes detective named Brody: financials, phone calls, the works."

"I'll get Kim Dade on it," she told me. "Anything else?"

"Addresses for Jake's sister Hailey and John's girlfriend Amy, and whatever you can find on the rest of those jokers he named in case neither of those leads pan out."

"You got it. We'll send them to your phone."

I jerked my head at the window to the concrete room, where Fortune and his partner were uncuffing the unconscious drug dealer. "What are you going to do with him?"

"When the vampires rise, we'll heal his neck and wipe his memory of the past twelve hours. Then he'll be dropped off in a park with a headache and his pockets turned out. He'll think he got robbed."

"So he won't remember any of this?"

She shook her head.

I made a face. "Damn, and here I thought I was making an important point he'd remember."

"He'll probably wish he *did* remember what happened when he finds the damage you did to his junk. We'll fix his neck. I see no reason to do more for him than that."

I raised my hand and she slapped me a high five. "Ow," I said, shaking my hand to ease the sting.

"Sorry," she said, but she was grinning.

22

The missing vamps turned out to be a couple, Bartholomew and Victor, two of Charles's line who owned a supe-oriented bed-and-breakfast overlooking the river north of the city. No one was sure when exactly they'd gone missing, since their staff was used to taking care of the guests and property without direct supervision from their undead bosses. Only after the vampires hadn't been seen in three nights did the staff check on their lair and found it empty.

Adri reported Charles could not reach either of them through their telepathic bond. He hadn't felt their deaths, but if they'd died behind the wards, even their master wouldn't have sensed it.

The vamps were looking into Bart and Victor's disappearance, so Sean and I focused on finding Travers and Andrews while we waited for Kim Dade to get us information about Detective Ian Brody.

Kim had finished her analysis of West's phone records and determined the calls made to and from the known cell phone were all business-related, which meant there had to be another phone we didn't know about. She had dug around and hadn't found any other number registered to either his business or home address. It was probably a burner phone—prepaid and virtually untraceable.

Despite serious misgivings, I decided it was time to put a tracker on West's car. Sean had a fancy new prototype he'd obtained from a "friend of a friend" who worked for a military contractor. It was unlikely to be noticed and almost impossible to detect, he assured me. We had to swing by Maclin Security to pick it up, and then we'd see about getting it onto West's car.

Adri was curious about the technical specs for the tracker, so as she and Sean were discussing it, I went outside to the SUV.

I was doubled over in the passenger seat, coughing, when Sean pulled his door open.

"Do you need the tank?" he asked.

I shook my head. He climbed into the SUV, shut his door, and waited while I coughed.

When I was able to get a breath, I said hoarsely, "You can head out. You don't have to wait."

"I'm going to wait until I know that you don't need the tank or other medical attention. I don't want to be in the middle of traffic when you need help."

It took a while for the coughing to subside. Finally, I huddled in my seat, exhausted and short of breath.

Sean took my hand. "I heard you coughing in the shower earlier, too. You should be in bed, recovering."

"I can't do that," I rasped. "We're close, Sean; I can feel it. If we can find Travers or Andrews, we'll get information about the blue van. Brody is working for the harnad, or they've got their hooks in him somehow. We get to them through him, or through West directly." Magic sparked on my fingers. "We're going to make them pay for what they've done."

"Yes, we will. And then we'll take a good, long vacation on a beach somewhere and leave all this behind for a while."

I blinked at him. "You want to take a vacation with me?"

"Why the hell wouldn't I?" He waved his free hand in front of us. "Picture it: a whole week in a hut on the beach, no one else in sight. Gentle ocean breezes, blue sky, palm trees, and perfect sand. And you in a bikini..." His eyes went gold.

I rolled my eyes. "Oh, sure. As soon as this is over, we'll go."

"I'm serious."

I stared at him. "No, you aren't. You're just trying to distract me from coughing."

"I am completely serious. Five days on a beach of your choice."

"Don't be ridiculous. We can't take that kind of time off."

"I haven't had a vacation in years. My business partner is practically begging me to take one."

"Well, *I* can't. I've got bills to pay and I don't have a company full of people to cover for me while I'm gone. I'm a one-woman show."

"Your paycheck from the Court will more than cover your expenses for a little while," he said matter-of-factly. "I have a pretty good idea what the vamps pay. So what's the real reason you don't want to go on vacation with me?"

"Sean, we really don't have time to talk about this right now. We've got a case to solve and people to save."

"We've got a half-hour drive to the office. Why not plan a vacation?"

"Because I want to plan how we're going to find that warehouse and get those people out and make sure everyone in the harnad gets what they deserve."

"Fine, but when this case is in the books, I am going to ask you again." He headed down the driveway. "I bet you look pretty fantastic in a bikini. Or out of a bikini." He grinned. "We could get a private beach. Swimsuits would be optional."

Despite myself, I smiled. Then I pictured Sean walking out of the water sans swim trunks, swallowed wrong, and started coughing again.

Sean started to pull to the side of the driveway, but I got the coughing under control and waved him on. "I'm good," I croaked. "I could use some water."

"On the floor behind you," he said.

I unbuckled my seatbelt and got on my knees on the seat, bending over to reach into the cooler. The SUV hit a big bump. When I glanced over my shoulder, Sean was checking out my ass. "Hey! Eyes on the road!"

I grabbed two bottles of water, reseated myself, and gave him a dirty look. He grinned unrepentantly as I buckled my seatbelt and passed him a water.

"So, how *are* we going to find the warehouse where they're keeping the survivors?" Sean asked as we turned out onto the main road.

"We've got some options. We can try to shake it out of Brody, we can hope West's tagged car leads us there, or we can ask Malcolm to look for it."

"How could Malcolm find it?"

"It's got some very distinctive wards around it. It's a big area to search, but he can move pretty fast."

"Plus, it would keep him busy and away from you in case that demon comes back."

I went silent.

"That wasn't judgment," Sean said, turning onto the highway on-ramp and accelerating. "I understand why you want to keep him safe."

"But you don't agree."

"If you're asking me if you should tell Malcolm about your demon problem, then my answer is yes."

"There are still surviving victims who need rescuing. I think Malcolm's help is better utilized looking for that warehouse."

"You could explain the situation and let him choose. You said you don't give him orders, that he has choices, despite being a bound ghost."

I bristled. "I don't give him orders."

"If you don't tell him about the demon and you just tell him about the warehouse, you aren't giving him a choice, and that's no better than giving an order."

I crossed my arms and stared out the window.

"Am I right?"

"Yes," I said softly.

"So are you going to tell him about the demon?"

"I don't know."

"Do you think he'll stay with you if you do, or go look for the warehouse?"

"I don't know."

A pause. "Do you want more coffee?"

"What do you think?"

"I think we're gonna need a bigger mug."

When we arrived at Maclin Security, Sean parked the SUV and turned to me. "You want to come in, get the fifty-cent tour?"

I shook my head. I disliked being the center of attention under the best of circumstances, and the thought of being shown around by the owner and introduced to his business partner and employees made me queasy. "You go on. I'm going to catch up on some texts."

"I'll be back in a minute, then." Sean left the engine running and got out.

When he was out of sight in the building, I coughed for a few minutes, then drank some water and checked my text messages. I deleted the ones from Lake and set it up so any future calls from him went straight to voice mail.

Kim Dade texted me addresses for Jake's sister Hailey and John's girlfriend Amy, and said she was working on compiling a dossier on Brody. I thanked her and asked her to send the information when it was ready.

Sean still wasn't back, so I went online to check the news. The bombing of Hawthorne's was the big headline, but it was only one of numerous attacks on vamp-owned businesses overnight. A few arrests had been made, but the protests continued across the city and up at Northbourne. I watched news footage of what was happening at the headquarters of the Vampire Court. Security had activated the retractable barriers in front of the entrance after someone tried to smash through the gate with a delivery truck.

When Sean got back, he was carrying a small black case. "Is that the tracker?" I asked.

He got in, put the case under his seat, and shut the door. "Two of them, in case we need to tag Brody's car too. Where to first?"

"Let's go see Malcolm."

Our drive to West's office building took us through downtown, where we got to see the protests in front of city hall and the main police building. The gathering in front of the latter was the larger of the two. One man carried a large sign with a photo of a vamp who had been burned alive. The caption read BURN EM ALL. I felt sick.

When we got to West's building, I had Sean park in the lot, away from West's car. I closed my eyes and summoned Malcolm. It was far less difficult after I'd had a decent amount of sleep and actual food.

The ghost entered the SUV a few seconds later. "Hey, Alice. Hey, Sean. Long time no see," he greeted us, his voice coming from the back seat.

"What's up, Malcolm?" Sean asked.

"Just another day of doing ghost stuff," he said cheerily. "Hey, you guys finally hooked up again. Good for you."

I sputtered. Sean grinned.

"You've got shifter trace in your aura, Alice," Malcolm pointed out. "Only one way that happens."

Sean looked smug, for some reason. Magic sparked on my fingertips.

"I guess before Alice fries both of us, I should probably ask why you're here," Malcolm said.

"We're adjusting our surveillance strategy," Sean told him. "We're putting a tracker on West's car and offering you a different job."

A pause. When Malcolm spoke again, his voice had lost its levity. "Why did you need vamp blood, Alice?" He must have sensed its trace. "And what's up with this oxygen tank back here?"

As Sean got the trackers out and synced them to his phone, I told Malcolm about the anti-vamp protests and the bombing at Hawthorne's.

The ghost was quiet for a long time.

"Malcolm?" I prompted.

"Give me a minute," was the caustic reply. "I'm processing the fact my best friend almost died last night and I'm *just now* hearing about it."

I was too stunned to respond at first. I thought about protesting that I hadn't had a chance to let him know what had happened before now, but then realized that not only was that *not* true, it hadn't even occurred to me that I needed to tell him, until it was part of explaining why we were changing the way we were tailing West.

Yes, this whole caring-about-people thing was new to me, and I'd spent the first twenty-four years of my life learning the hard way not to volunteer information about myself, but that wasn't an excuse and I knew it.

And he'd called me his best friend. My eyes stung. "I am an asshole," I said.

"Your words." He sounded pissed.

I glanced at Sean. He was looking studiously at the tracker app on his phone, so no help there.

"And why am I sensing two different vamp traces?" the ghost demanded. "I sense Charlie's blood and someone else's, someone older."

"Please don't call Charles 'Charlie,'" I said.

"*Alice.*"

I rubbed my face. "There was an incident the day before yesterday. You remember what I told you about Adam's visions of the warehouse where they're keeping the survivors?"

"Yes."

"I saw them too. He grabbed my arm. I needed healing after and a vamp named Niara provided it."

Silence.

I threw up my hands. "Look, I'm sorry. I know I am terrible about telling people things. I lie, and I keep secrets. You're right to be mad. In fact, you two can start a club for people who are mad at me. Having friends and telling people things is new for me. I'm working on getting better at it."

"She has made some strides in that area," Sean said. "It's baby steps, but it's something. Today I asked if she was okay and she said no."

"You're kidding," Malcolm said incredulously. "That's not a baby step; that's a giant freakin' leap."

"You guys are funny," I said wearily. "Totally hilari—" I started coughing and then suddenly I couldn't breathe.

Sean swore. He unbuckled his seatbelt, twisted around in his seat, and grabbed the oxygen mask. I took it and put it over my nose and mouth as oxygen hissed. I forced myself to breathe slowly and the coughing eased.

I lowered the mask to my lap, rested my head against the seat, and closed my eyes. Sean turned off the machine and took the mask from me.

"Well, now *I* feel like the asshole," Malcolm said, breaking the silence.

Sean's fingers brushed my cheek. "Are you okay?"

"I'm—"

"—*Fine,*" both men said together.

I sighed. "I was going to say 'thirsty.'"

As Sean handed me a bottle of water, Malcolm said, "So, since it's obvious you aren't going home to rest like any sane person would do in this situation, what's my new assignment?"

"You have a choice," Sean said. "You can go look for this warded warehouse where they're keeping the survivors, or you can stick around and maybe help Alice with her demon problem."

"By the way, I have a demon problem," I said.

"Oh, for Pete's sake," Malcolm said, exasperated.

In the end, after I'd explained the situation, Malcolm opted to go searching for the warehouse, as long as I promised to summon him to my side if I sensed the demon or one of his minions in my vicinity. I shared my memory of what the warehouse's wards felt like and told him we thought it was on the south side of the city, and he zipped away.

I strongly suspected he'd said something to Sean as he was leaving; Sean jumped a little and got a faraway look like someone was talking in his head. I didn't ask.

Sean stuck one of his new toys in the passenger-side wheel well of West's Beemer and then we were off, headed for the apartment of Hailey Travers, Jake's sister.

When Hailey opened the door, she took one look at us and started yelling. "I haven't seen him! Why do you people keep bothering me? I told you earlier; I haven't seen my idiot brother in months. He's on drugs and I don't want him around my kids." She slammed the door.

Sean and I exchanged glances and headed back to the SUV. "How do we interpret that?" Sean asked. "Who's been coming around looking for Jake?"

"If it's the harnad looking, that means they don't have him," I said. "Or maybe it's the cops looking for him, following up on their statements from the other night."

"She said 'you people,'" Sean pointed out as we got into the SUV. "Do we look like cops or like the sort of people who would be in a harnad?"

I shrugged and gave him the address for Amy Curry. It turned out to be a small single-family house in a working-class neighborhood, with an overgrown lawn and a two-tone pickup parked out front. We parked behind the truck and got out, picking our way cautiously up the cracked walkway toward the front porch.

Sean stopped so suddenly that I ran into him. "What's wrong?" I asked.

"I smell death," he said grimly.

Stomach knotted, I followed him up to the porch. When we got to the door, Sean used his jacket sleeve to cover his hand and tried the doorknob. The door opened.

The smell hit me like a slap across the face. I took one last deep breath of fresh air and we slipped inside and closed the door.

The living room was the crime scene. Three people—two men and a woman—were lying face down where they'd fallen, their hands tied behind their backs with zip ties. They had each been shot in the back of the head, execution style. One or more of them had emptied their bowels, either in death or in terror.

I saw the girl's face first. It was blotchy and distorted but I recognized her from the photo Kim Dade sent. "That's Amy Curry."

Sean walked around the bodies on the floor, stepping carefully. The coffee table was covered with drug paraphernalia, including a small scale, a box of little bags, and lighters.

"They made it look like a drug rip-off," I said as he crouched to look at the dead men. "Anyone walking in here is going to think they got killed for drugs and money."

"It's Jake Travers and John Andrews," Sean said as he rose. "We found them both."

My instincts told me we needed to get the hell out of Dodge, but there was one thing I had to do first. I lowered my shields, searching with my senses, and felt a familiar trace of air magic coming from another room. With Sean trailing behind me, I went to a back bedroom, following the trace.

I found what I was looking for on top of a dresser: a plain gold band with a small white opal. I picked it up and closed my eyes, drinking in this last remaining trace of Mark's familiar magic. They hadn't had time to pawn Mark's ring before the harnad got them. I supposed I should be thankful for that small favor. I stuck the ring in my pocket and we returned to the front room.

I looked at Amy Curry, a young woman who was dead because her boyfriend saw two men dumping a body in an alley. "We need to leave," I said softly.

We didn't say another word until we were back in the SUV and well away from the house. Sean drove with the window down, making little chuffing noises to clear his nose of the stench of death.

"It must have been the cops coming to see Hailey," I said. "Travers and Andrews looked like they've been dead since early yesterday morning."

"Where are we on the Brody dossier?" Sean asked, closing his window.

"Waiting on Kim Dade. She said it would be later today before she had things put together on that. It's after five now; I'll check with her if we haven't heard anything by six. Any motion from West?"

Sean checked his phone. "No, he's still at his office."

My phone rang. It was a local number. "Alice Worth."

"Ms. Worth, this is Detective Ernesto Diaz."

His tone was friendly and conversational, and it immediately put me on guard. "What can I do for you, Detective?"

"We would appreciate it if you could come down to our office and give us a statement."

I rubbed my eyes. "Would tomorrow work?"

"We would really like to talk to you this evening, if that's possible."

"I can be there in about ninety minutes, depending on traffic," I said. "Can I get into the building without having to deal with the crowd out front?"

"There's a visitors' lot on the south side of the building. Call me when you arrive and I'll come down and bring you in through the side entrance." Diaz gave me his cell number and we disconnected.

Sean eyed me. "Going into the lion's den?"

"Not much choice," I said with a sigh. "They won't stop hounding me until they get me in there, so I might as well get it over with."

"We're not that far away from the police building. Why did you say ninety minutes?"

"I need you to take me back to your house so I can get my car."

He raised his eyebrows. "Why?"

"I might be there for a couple of hours. Plus, the building has surveillance, so they'd see your vehicle dropping me off. I don't want you pulled into this if we can help it. I'll drive myself there, then meet up with you later."

Sean turned and headed toward the Heights. "It'll give me a chance to check on my troublemakers."

I slapped my forehead. "I forgot to ask you: what was that fight about yesterday?"

Sean told me the story as we drove. Apparently, the younger members of his pack were walking past a group of anti-vamp protesters when words were exchanged. It was a fistfight and no one went furry, but the cops showed up and cuffed everyone when they found out some of the fighters were shifters.

Thanks to Sean's lawyers, everyone was out of custody within hours. What had taken most of Sean's time was dealing with pack members who were upset at what they saw as an overreaction by police. Sean was angry, too, but since everyone had been released without charges, he tried to use the situation as a learning experience for his young werewolves about picking their battles.

"It's hard for them," he told me as we turned onto his street. "They've grown up in a world that romanticizes werewolves but fears and hates them too. They get angry and when you're young and angry and full of testosterone, you don't always think about the consequences of your actions."

He pulled into his driveway and parked next to my car. I slipped out of his jacket and took my keys and notebook from its pockets. "Thanks for the ride. I'll give you a call when I'm done down at the cop shop."

He leaned over the center console and kissed me. I ran my fingers through his hair and held him close. When we came up for air, he ran his nose along my hairline. "You be careful. If you feel like things are getting out of hand, walk out of there. If you need an attorney, call me."

"It ain't my first rodeo, pardner." I kissed him lightly. "I'll be fine. Go check on your wolves." I opened my door and hopped out.

"You want to take the oxygen?"

I shook my head. "I'm good." I hesitated, then reached back to touch his hand where it rested on the center console. "Thank you."

"For what?"

"For everything."

He smiled as gold rolled over his eyes. "You can thank me later. In the meantime, I'll be thinking of ways you can show your appreciation."

"I have some thoughts about that," I told him. "We'll compare later, see whose ideas sound like the most fun."

"This is the sort of challenge I like," Sean said, his eyes gleaming. I laughed and shut the door of his SUV.

Diaz and I eyeballed each other across the table. "I hope you can appreciate our position," the detective said.

"I can appreciate that you're under a lot of pressure to solve this case quickly," I replied. "That doesn't change the facts."

Diaz's partner, Ferguson, looked up from his notes and glared at me. "So far, all I've heard is guesses. I'm not hearing facts."

I drummed my fingertips on the table. "Once again, the well-documented and scientifically proven facts are that one single vamp cannot drain an entire body; it's not physically possible. Another fact: no matter how many vamps are drinking from a single body, once the heart stops, they can't drink more than a few more ounces because the blood stops pumping. The only logical conclusion is that a vamp didn't kill Mark." I raised my hands. "I'm sorry the facts aren't what you want them to be, but the longer you insist on following this line of investigation, the further it's going to take you from the real killers."

Diaz sat back and regarded me. I'd given them a detailed statement about when and where I'd seen Mark the day he was killed, and then the detective brought up what I'd said in the alley. At first, I thought he just wanted to argue, but I was beginning to wonder if some doubt was creeping into his mind about whether a vamp had killed Mark. There was something in Diaz's eyes that said he was listening.

Ferguson, however, wasn't having any. "The fact is there is a vampire bite on Mr. Dunlap's neck and vampire saliva in the wound. It is entirely consistent with a vampire bite."

"It's not entirely consistent, for the reasons I just stated," I said. "The facts definitively *exclude* a vampire bite as the cause of death. It is, however, entirely consistent with exsanguination via two large-bore needles and planted saliva."

"Is it possible that a vampire used needles to drain the body?" Diaz asked.

"Possible," I said. "But unlikely, since blood isn't just a source of nutrients for vamps. The life energy within the blood is essential for their continued existence. Stored human blood lacks that energy. Aside from jokes about vampires making 'withdrawals' from blood banks, vamps don't store human blood. It wouldn't do them much good. They need a living human donor or they might as well be drinking tap water."

It was starting to compute with Diaz; I could see it. He was adding two and two and getting four now, not three.

I'd brushed against both of them when we were walking into the interview room and hadn't sensed any residual blood magic—not that its absence cleared them of involvement with the harnad, but it moved them down the list of possible suspects within the department. I'd been hoping Brody would be Diaz's plus-one in the interview, but no such luck.

"You and Mark were looking into the women who have gone missing from the Stroll," Diaz said. "Sharon Dunlap says you both thought a harnad is taking them, not vampires. What proof do you have?"

I shook my head. "If we had proof of who took them, whether it was vamps or mages, we would have brought it to you. That's what we were hired to do."

"By the vamps," Ferguson said snidely.

"Yes, by the vamps." I looked at Diaz. "Are we done?"

He tapped his pen on the table. "For now, unless there's anything you'd like to add to your statement?"

"No."

"Then thank you for your cooperation." We rose and filed toward the door. Diaz offered me his hand and I shook it. Ferguson just looked at me.

We went down a short hall. Ferguson went left, heading into the bullpen of cubicles that were the detectives' offices. Diaz led me toward the main doors of the Major Crimes division.

A dark-haired man in a suit came in through the doors, carrying several folders. We bumped into each other as Diaz was reaching for the door.

"Sorry," I said.

"Don't worry about it," the other detective said absently. He headed for the coffeemaker as Diaz and I headed down the hall.

Our walk downstairs was silent. As we approached the side door, Diaz paused. "There aren't any harnads in the city."

"So I've heard."

Diaz hit me with that cop stare. "We'll find who killed Mark. If you find evidence that will help our investigation, you're required to turn it over to us."

"I know my job, Detective. I want these bastards caught and I want them to pay for what they've done."

He nodded once as if I'd said the right thing and reached for the side door. "Then be careful," he told me as I stepped out into the night.

"You too, Detective." The door closed behind me.

I dug my phone out as I walked to my car. I had two text messages and a voice mail. The text messages were from Sean, letting me know he was ready to meet when I was free, and Kim Dade, saying she had Brody's phone records now and was analyzing them. She'd already sent me Brody's basic info, including a picture, which was how I'd known who to bump into on my way out of the bullpen.

I hadn't sensed any residual blood magic on Brody, which probably meant he hadn't gone to the warehouse, but he'd definitely falsified the statements of Travers and Andrews, so he was involved somehow.

The voice mail was from Lake, and it was a long one: three full minutes, recorded a little over an hour before. I sighed, got in my car, and shut the door. No sense putting off listening to it. I braced myself and hit *Play*.

For several seconds, I didn't hear anything. Then I heard what sounded like a car door opening, shuffling sounds, and some muffled thumps. He must have accidentally called me without realizing it. That explained the three-minute recording.

I was about to hit *Delete* when someone spoke. "Who the hell is this guy?" I didn't recognize the voice.

Another unidentified voice, also male. "I don't know. He's out, though. Shit, this guy is huge. Help me move him so I can get his wallet."

I went cold.

More rustling, then a heavy thump. A few seconds later, one of the men swore. "He's a fed. Look."

"Why is a SPEMA agent tailing West?"

"Hell if I know. You better call in and find out what he wants us to do."

A long pause, then: "Yeah, this is Bobby. We got West, but there was this big guy in a truck watching him. We hit him with a sleep spell and he's out, but we just found out he's a fed. His I.D. says Special Agent Trent Lake, with SPEMA. What do you want us to do?"

Another long pause. I waited, my heart in my throat.

"Fine, we'll bring him to the warehouse," the man said finally. "Gary's driving the BMW and I'm driving the van, so we need someone out here pronto to drive this guy's truck unless you want someone to find it here." Pause. "No, if we lock it up, nobody'll think nothin' of it until we move it." Pause. "Okay, yeah, no problem. We'll put him in the van with West and head your way now."

"I'll pull the van around," the other man said.

"Yeah, go do that. Hey, what's this?" A loud rustling. "Shit, it's his phone! He called someone before—" The voicemail ended.

I looked at the screen. *Delete Message?*

I was breathing hard and my heart raced. Hands shaking, I carefully saved the message, then started my car and backed out of my parking space as I called Sean.

He answered on the first ring, his voice warm. "Hey, Alice. You done at the—"

"I need you to meet me right now across the street from West's office," I interrupted. "How far away are you?"

"Twenty minutes." I heard a door slam and running footsteps. "Or less."

"Make it less."

23

Sean listened to the voice mail twice, his face grim.

We were sitting in Sean's SUV, in a parking garage four blocks from West's office. By the time we got to the alley behind the convenience store where Lake was apparently watching West, it had been almost two hours since Lake's voice mail and there was no sign of West's car or Lake's truck. Bobby and Gary were long gone with West and Lake.

I'd asked Malcolm to go look for the harnad warehouse, never thinking that it was *West* who might be targeted next. Had there been a coup in the harnad, or had we been mistaken all along about who the harnad's leader was?

A quick look around confirmed there were no security cameras on the surrounding buildings that would give us a view of the alley. There were cameras on the exterior of the convenience store, but the owner told Sean they only showed the pumps. We left and went to the garage to figure out our next move.

Sean's phone reported that West's car had left the parking lot twelve minutes after the voice mail. One of Sean's employees informed us the BMW was parked on the street outside West's house. Presumably, Gary hadn't been able to cross the wards protecting the house and had opted to leave the car on the street instead.

My hands shook with adrenaline. "Why was Lake tailing West? How did he even *know* who West is?"

"I don't know." Sean did something with my phone and his beeped. "I sent myself a copy of the voice mail." He turned my phone off, pulled off its back, and removed the sim card.

"Hey!"

He stuck the phone in the cup holder. "They know who he called," he reminded me. "They have your number and probably your name. If they have the resources, they could use this phone to track you. They'll find out where you live. You can't go home." He sent someone a text and received an almost instant reply. "I've got someone heading over to watch your house."

I rubbed my face with my hands. "They took Lake to the warehouse. We have to get him, Sean. There's no way they'll let him live." I thought of what they might be doing to him and felt sick.

"Stop," Sean said, squeezing my hand. "Those thoughts won't help us find him. Focus on what we know, what we can do."

I took a deep, shaky breath and let it out. "We have to find that warehouse."

"You said Brody hadn't been there as far as you could tell, so we probably can't get it out of him. We haven't heard from Malcolm, so he hasn't found it yet. Who else knows where this damned warehouse is?"

I'd had a plan percolating in the back of my brain for several days, but it was so far out in left field that I had mentally consigned it to a drawer labeled "For Emergency Use Only." If this didn't qualify as an emergency, I didn't know what would.

"I have an idea," I said.

When Rachel Barrow opened the door, her smile was radiant. She was so focused on Sean that she didn't see me silently waiting off to the side of the porch. "Mac," she said, leaning against the doorway. "I'm so glad you finally called me back. I thought you'd forgotten about me."

Sean grinned. "I didn't forget."

He moved so fast she didn't have a chance to make a sound. In a blink, he had an arm around her throat and a hand over her mouth and they were inside the house. I entered behind them and closed the door.

Rachel's eyes widened when she saw me. She started screaming into Sean's hand.

"Be quiet, or I'll snap your neck," Sean told her.

The muffled shrieking stopped.

"I am the alpha of the Tomb Mountain Pack," Sean continued.

The blood drained out of Rachel's face.

"Felicia Lowell is one of my wolves. You were involved in her kidnapping and I would like very much to tear out your throat. You have one chance to live past tonight. You are going to do exactly as Alice tells you to do. Nod if you understand."

She nodded rapidly.

We hadn't really planned in advance to play this as "good cop/bad cop" or "nice mage/angry werewolf," but it looked like that was what was happening. I wasn't really in the mood to play the good cop, but if one of us wasn't at least marginally nice to her, she might be too scared to do what we needed her to do.

I stepped in front of her. "We know about the harnad taking the women from the Stroll for their blood. I'm betting you help them identify the best targets." I could tell from her expression that I'd guessed correctly. "You are going to make a phone call to whoever your contact is and tell them there is a new girl on the Stroll who has earth magic. Her name is Katie. She's blonde and she'll be down at Eleventh and Elm tonight."

She stared at me, her eyes wide.

Sean spoke again. "We will be listening to the conversation. If you say one thing that deviates from what Alice just told you or let on *in any way* that you are being coerced, I will break your neck, but I won't kill you. I'll take you back to my pack and let Felicia's mother and brother tear you to pieces. Are we clear?"

She nodded again.

"I'm going to move my hand now. Stay quiet."

The second Rachel could talk, she said, "They'll kill me."

"They won't," I said. "We'll make sure of it. I can promise Sean *will* kill you if you don't do as we say. I've already had to talk him out of killing you twice. I don't think he'll listen to me a third time."

Rachel made a little noise and tried to shrink away from Sean, but his arm was still on her neck. She sniffled. "I'm sorry about Felicia. She was really nice."

"Why did they take her?" I asked.

"Bobby asked me if any of the girls were shifters, said they'd pay me double if I knew any. There aren't any shifter girls on the Stroll these days; they make way more money booking online. I needed the money, so I told him about Felicia."

"Why did you break into her apartment and steal her laptop?"

Rachel didn't ask how I knew about that. "To make it look like she was taken by someone she knew at work."

Sean's eyes glowed. "How much did they pay you?"

She whimpered. "Four hundred dollars."

"So, you made two hundred dollars each time you helped them pick a target?" I asked.

"Three hundred if they had magic," she said.

"Blood money," Sean snarled. "All of it blood money."

Literally, I thought. "And Danielle? You told them she saw the driver of the black BMW, didn't you? They took her because of you."

She didn't reply, but I saw it in her eyes. She'd told them about Danielle because she thought her source of additional income might go away if Danielle had identified the driver of the BMW.

I took the anger and put it away. "Are you ready to make the call? Can you be convincing?"

She nodded. "I'll call Bobby."

I spotted her cell phone on the table and reached for it, but she shook her head. "They gave me a special phone to call him."

"Where is it?"

"In my room, in the closet. Blue shoe box."

I brought it to her. It was a prepaid phone. Sean kept his arm on her neck.

"Deep breaths," I told her. "Be calm. Make the call."

Rachel held out her hand for the phone. I turned it on and gave it to her. She unlocked it, scrolled through the contacts list to the one labeled *Pizza*, and hit Call.

The phone rang twice, and then a man answered. "Antonio's Pizza. Pick-up or delivery?"

I recognized the voice as one of the men on Lake's voicemail: Bobby, the man who'd driven West's BMW away from the scene.

"It's Rachel. I've got a pick-up for you." Rachel's voice was even and calm. I gave her a thumbs-up.

"Give me a description," Bobby said.

"Girl named Katie. Blonde, kinda tall." She eyed me. "Pretty but thin. She's been hanging at Eleventh the last couple nights. She's got magic, too."

"Why haven't you mentioned her before?"

"She's new, Bobby," Rachel said petulantly. "She used to work out by the airport, now she's down on Elm."

"How do you know she's got magic?"

I raised my hand and green fire ran along my fingertips.

Rachel nodded. "I saw her playing with little green flames on her fingers," she said. "I Googled it. Green fire is earth magic, right?"

"That's right," Bobby told her. "Blonde named Katie at Eleventh. Got it."

"You gonna get her tonight? I need some money."

"Yeah, I'll head that way in a few. After we get her, I'll drop the cash off as usual."

"Okay," Rachel said. They disconnected.

She turned the phone off and handed it to me. "How'd I do?" she asked anxiously.

"You did good," I told her. "Who should I be looking for?"

"Red two-door Mazda. Bobby's got kinda longish blond hair and usually wears a black jacket."

"How does he incapacitate them?" Sean asked.

She jumped at the sound of his voice. "A sleep spell. He told me they fall asleep and they never feel a thing."

"A lot of women may be dead because of you," I told her. "Doesn't that bother you at all? Or was it just about the money?"

"We all gotta do what we gotta do," she told me shortly. "I've been a hooker for four years. I've been beaten almost to death twice. I've been raped more times than I remember. I thought I'd get some money saved up and get out of here. Go somewhere else, start over."

"Those girls had dreams, too," Sean snarled. "Felicia dedicated her life to helping people, and you sold her for four hundred dollars."

I reached out and touched her arm. "*Sleep*."

She dropped. Sean let her go and she hit the floor hard.

We looked at each other over the unconscious body of Rachel Barrow. "What now?" Sean asked.

"Call Bryan and have him send someone to pick her up. The vamps can hold her for now, until we can turn her over to the feds. I've got to get changed."

"I would prefer to be the one getting kidnapped," Sean said.

I shrugged and applied lipstick, using the mirror on the back of the visor. "If you think you can pass as a blonde named Katie, go for it, but even if you could fool them into picking you up, you still wouldn't be able to take down the wards once you got inside the warehouse."

He growled.

I capped the lipstick and stuck it in the black vinyl handbag I'd borrowed from Rachel's closet. I'd also borrowed a shimmery, see-through shirt that tied above my waist and a red bustier. I was wearing my own jeans and boots, but had to raid Rachel's makeup and jewelry collection to round out my outfit. My blonde wig was part of the "quickie" disguise kit I kept in my trunk.

Transformation complete, I blew Sean a kiss. "How do I look?"

He laced his fingers through mine. "Brave."

I frowned at him. "Brave? I was hoping for hot, sexy, gorgeous, or something more along those lines."

"Have I mentioned that I find brave women *extremely* sexy?"

I snorted. "You just be ready to ride in with the cavalry when Malcolm shows up and tells you the wards are down," I told him, touching the spell crystal I'd tied to his wrist. "He'll jump to you and give you the all-clear. It's a good plan."

"Except for the hundred things that could go wrong." He cupped my chin. "Will you take a beach vacation with me?"

I sighed.

"I'll bring you drinks with umbrellas in them. As many as you want, whenever you want them."

I raised my eyebrows. He was offering to serve me, which was a courting ritual for shifters. "Sean, do you realize you and I have never been on an actual date? Shouldn't we do that first before we decide to take a vacation together?"

He surprised me by smiling. "I've realized this is our version of dating. Stakeouts, talking to witnesses, wearing disguises...this is how we date. We don't go out to dinner and a movie or attend the ballet after a five-course meal at La Piazza. Forget a few hours together here and there; we've had dates that lasted whole *days*, and I for one think they've generally gone pretty well."

I really hadn't thought about it that way, but the man had a point.

"So, what do you say?"

"I'll think about it," I said. "I need to go. I don't want to miss my ride."

He kissed me then, completely destroying my lipstick, but I didn't care. It was a fantastic kiss, the kind you gave someone you really liked, or someone you were afraid you might not see again. I grabbed a handful of his shirt and pulled him closer. With the console between us, it hurt my ribs, but some things were worth the pain.

When we came up for air, I kept my grip on his shirt and looked into his softly glowing eyes. "What did Malcolm say to you this afternoon before he left to go look for the warehouse?"

Sean kissed my nose. "He told me not to screw this up again."

"I don't think you screwed it up the first time." I gave him a quick kiss, then used napkins to wipe his mouth and mine. I reapplied the lipstick, put it back in my purse, and reached for the door.

"You be careful, Alice Worth," he said grimly.

"You too." I got out of the SUV, shut the door, and walked away.

Sean had parked two blocks off Elm, in case anyone was watching the Stroll. Somewhere nearby, Bryan and the rest of the Vamp Court forces were assembling, waiting for the all-clear to enter the warehouse. Once we'd secured the situation and figured out what the hell was going on, we'd alert the feds—or at least that was the plan. It all depended on what we found in the warehouse and whether Lake was still alive.

It was strange to be counting on Sean and the enforcers. I was used to doing things on my own, but this time it wasn't a one-woman job or even a one-woman/one-ghost job. I was working as part of a team. It felt...good.

When I got to Ninth and Elm, Zara was waiting for me. The much-taller woman wore a shiny silver dress, with large hoop earrings and matching cuffs around both of her toned biceps.

"Hey, you," she said, looking me over appraisingly. "Not too bad. A bit more sway in the hips, like this." She demonstrated, and we sashayed down Elm.

Sarah waited for us at Tenth. She saluted me with her cigarette and smirked at my getup. "You look good. I'd do you."

I laughed. "Thanks."

"We'll keep an eye out for the car and get the plate if we can," Zara told me. "You watch yourself."

"You too. Wish me luck, ladies." I headed off down the street toward Eleventh.

"Move your hips!" Zara called.

I waggled my butt as I walked, and Sarah snorted.

I'd been leaning up against the wall at Eleventh and Elm for almost a half-hour when I finally saw a red car approaching. I smoothed my blonde wig, gave the ends a little flip, and moved to the curb, posing with one hand on my hip.

The Mazda glided to a stop in front of me and the passenger-side window rolled down. I leaned over and peered into the car to see a thirty-something man with shoulder-length blond hair smiling at me. He was wearing a black jacket, a red T-shirt, and jeans.

I ran my hands over the car while he got a good look at my cleavage. "Hey, sugar. You looking for a date tonight?"

"I think I'm looking for you, angel," Bobby said.

I gave him my biggest smile. "I'm Katie, but I can be your angel if you want me to be."

I was very glad neither Sean nor Malcolm could hear me use that cheesy line. Sean and I had argued briefly about me wearing a wire but I vetoed it, worried I would be searched. If they found a wire, the jig would be up before I even had a chance to get into the warehouse.

"Get in, Katie," Bobby said, patting the passenger seat. "Let me take you for a ride."

I opened the door and got in. Bobby pulled away from the curb. As he drove, he slid his hand up my thigh. "Put on your seatbelt, angel."

"Where are we going?" I asked him, clicking my seatbelt.

"Just up the street," he said easily. His hand moved to my arm. I felt something hard concealed in his palm as he pressed it against my skin. "*Night*."

The sleep spell washed over me like a warm blanket, fizzling out against my natural shields. I made a surprised sound and let my head fall to the side, my eyes closed.

He let go of my arm. Something fell into the cup holder—presumably the used spell crystal—and his jacket rustled as he pulled something from his pocket.

I heard a phone ringing, and then a brusque male voice answered. "Yes?" I didn't recognize the voice, but he sounded like an older man.

"I've got the package," Bobby said.

"Any trouble?"

"No trouble. Pretty girl, like Rachel said. We're on our way. I'll be there in about twenty."

He put the phone back in his pocket and turned up the radio. Bobby liked eighties rock.

Somewhere far behind us where he wouldn't be noticed, Sean was following the Mazda via the tracker I'd slipped into the front passenger wheel-well. I tried not to worry about him. I had to focus on what I had to do to make the plan work, or Lake was a dead man—if he wasn't already.

I had a lot of experience faking unconsciousness, but Bobby didn't seem to be paying me much attention. I wondered how many women he'd taken like this from the Stroll, knocking them out and delivering them to the warehouse. I'd sensed only a trace of air magic in him, just enough to power the sleep spell, so he wasn't part of the harnad. What his role was in the operation wasn't clear, but I promised myself I would find out.

It might have only been twenty minutes from the Stroll to the warehouse, but my neck ached, and it felt like an hour before the car finally turned. The tires crunched on rough pavement, and then the car stopped.

Bobby picked up my limp arm and tied something around my wrist. A spell flared. A moment later I felt another one, as if he'd tied the same spell to himself. Then the car began to move again, slowly.

Thanks to the passkey spells on our wrists, we crossed the wards as they sizzled on my skin. Even through the spell I was wearing and my shields, I could tell the wards were powerful and very deadly. I detected many of them layered together. The aversion spells would keep most people away, and the black wards would incapacitate or kill anyone who got past the aversion spells.

I suppressed a shudder when I recognized a razor ward, and tried not to think about what would happen if the passkey spell on my wrist fell off midway through the wards. The harnad was very serious about no one getting in or out of the warehouse.

I sensed rather than saw the car pulling into the building. A large rolling door closed behind us with a heavy thud.

I was in.

Bobby took me out of the car, slung me over his shoulder, and carried me through a large room that felt and sounded cavernous. For his role in Lake's kidnapping, he deserved some payback. For groping my ass, I figured he owed me a hand.

We went through a door and down a dimly lit hallway. He stopped and opened another door, then closed it behind him. He dumped me on a cot, handcuffed me to the frame, and left me there. The door closed and his footsteps faded away down the hall. I didn't feel any wards flare around the room, and he hadn't even bothered to lock the door.

My ribs ached from being carried over his shoulder, but I lay still and waited for several minutes, listening. There was someone else in the room, but he or she was asleep or unconscious. When I was reasonably certain we were alone, I opened my eyes and peered into the darkness around me.

I was in a room with four cots, but only two were occupied: mine and one across from me. I couldn't see anything but a small figure under a sheet. The room smelled like disinfectant and bleach.

I didn't see any security cameras and I'd just been restrained with standard handcuffs. So far, so good. "Katie" was no threat to the harnad, especially not when she was knocked out by a sleep spell that was supposed to have rendered her unconscious for several hours.

I didn't have time to play it safe; Lake had been here for hours. I had to move if I wanted to get to him before they killed him. I hoped they were still trying to get information out of him. As awful as the prospect of him being tortured was, it was better than the alternative.

I sat up. When no one came running, I held the handcuff chain taut and manifested my cold-fire whip. With a single quick lash, I broke the cuff and stood to get a closer look at the room. It was bare except for the cots, which were bolted to the floor, and IV stands next to each bed. There was a doorway that led to a tiny bathroom containing a sink, a toilet, and a small shower with no door or curtain.

I checked on the person in the other bed. She was young and blonde and extremely pale and thin. She was unconscious, probably spelled, but her whole body trembled. There was an IV of clear liquid running into her hand.

Rage made me shake. *Stay focused*, I ordered myself. *We are getting these people out of here tonight, but only if you do your job.*

I gave myself one second to think about Sean, somewhere nearby with the cadre of Vamp Court forces, waiting for my signal. My fingers itched to break the wards now, but I didn't dare, not until I found Lake and figured out what was going on here and how to protect the survivors.

I took the pillows from the other beds and arranged them under the sheet and blanket on my cot, then took off the blonde wig and tucked it under the sheet until only part of it was showing. From the door, it would look like someone had put me on the cot and pulled the blankets up over me. As long as no one came over to check on me, it would buy me some time—hopefully.

I went to the door, put my ear against the wood, and listened intently. I didn't hear anything in the hallway beyond. I took a deep breath, opened the door, and peeked into the hallway.

Nothing. It was eerily silent.

I slipped out of the room and closed the door softly. The hallway was lined with doors identical to the one I had just come out of. I counted ten doors. At four cots per room, that would be forty people if all of the cots were occupied.

I wanted to look for Felicia, Danielle, and Carrie, but the longer I delayed and the more doors I opened, the more likely I was to be spotted. I needed to find Lake.

I crept down the hallway, my back against the wall, boots silent. At the end of the hall, the corridor turned left. Near the end of that hall, there were two more doors, larger and metal. My blood magic tingled as I approached.

When I reached the door on the right, I touched the door handle, then paused. I couldn't hear anything from inside the room. It might be a broom closet, for all I knew. I opened the door and slipped inside.

My eyes were used to the slightly brighter illumination in the hallway, so it took a moment for them to adjust to the dimness. Like the room I'd been left in, this one was virtually empty. Unlike my previous accommodations, this room had only one cot and it was occupied by a gray-haired man who was facing away from me.

I took two quiet steps forward. The man on the bed turned his head.

"Alice Worth," John West said. "We meet at last."

We stared at each other.

I wasn't surprised he knew who I was; he'd seen my car parked outside Natalie Newton's house after Amelia's death. It would have been easy to find out who I was from there.

He was cuffed to the cot with spell cuffs, I noticed immediately. Two sets of them, in fact: one on his left wrist and one on his left ankle. Someone wanted to make doubly sure he was completely restrained, both physically and magically. Judging by his pallor, they'd taken blood from him at least once already.

Since time was not on my side, I skipped the pleasantries and got straight to the point. "What the hell is going on, West?" I demanded in a low voice. "How'd you end up like this? Aren't you in charge of these people?"

"I was," West said. "Apparently, our group is under new management."

"How did Bobby and Gary manage to take you? Magic?"

He snorted. "Those morons don't have magic. It was a dart loaded with a paralytic." The kind they'd used to take Felicia Lowell. That was poetic justice, in any case. He looked me over. "No need to ask how *you* got in. Why are you here?"

"I came to rescue someone and shut this all down."

"How foolish of you. Who are you here to rescue?"

"A federal agent."

He sighed. "They took a federal agent?"

"Yep. He was shadowing you. When they took you, they took him, too. I'm here to make sure they regret it."

"That idiot." West's voice gained some strength. "That *imbecile*. Eighteen months we've been running this operation with no problems. Then, in the space of just a few days, Addison brings it all crashing down. I knew I should have killed him months ago."

"Who is Addison? Is that who's in charge now?"

West's eyes narrowed. "We can make a deal."

"Why would I want to make a deal with you? From where I'm standing, you're in spell cuffs and I'm free to walk out of here anytime I like and let the vamps and the feds rain justice down on all of you. They're ready to come in as soon as I drop the wards."

He raised an imperious eyebrow. "If you break those wards, you'll die. Addison's wards have landmines. And Addison is here tonight. You can't break them while he's here, not without help."

I stared at him. "Are you offering to *help?*"

"He sent people to knock me out. He cuffed me to a cot and drained my blood. He left me conscious so I could lay here and think about how he's going to kill me slowly over the next week or so, or longer if he draws it out. The members of the harnad who are loyal to me are here too, being drained. I want Addison dead. I want the members of our group who are helping him dead."

Well, that sounded like the truth, anyway, for whatever it was worth. "Why are you taking these people and draining their blood? Not for ritual magic, I know that. So why?"

He gave me a vicious smile. "So you don't know, then. Good. That's a bargaining chip for me."

I scoffed. "I can find out on my own. The answer is here, in this warehouse. I'll keep looking until I find it."

"You're on borrowed time, my dear," West said. "You can't stay out of sight forever. When Addison catches you, either you'll be dead or you'll end up like me, watching yourself die slowly. Get me out of these cuffs. I'll help you take Addison out. I'll help you bring down the wards. Then I'll disappear to a country far away from here, and you can bring in the vamp army and the feds, and you can have your justice."

I shook my head. "No deal, West. I don't know how many people died at your hands and on your watch, but you have to answer for those deaths. I'll figure out a way—"

Footsteps echoed in the hallway, approaching fast.

I dove under West's cot. He moved the sheets so they hung over the side of the bed, hiding me, just as the door swung open.

"Plotting your escape, John?" It was a man's voice, the tone mocking. The door shut and footsteps crossed the room to stand a few feet away.

"Plotting your death," West replied acerbically. "It helps me pass the time."

"You've only been here a few hours," the other man pointed out. I assumed this was the infamous Addison. I recognized his voice from Bobby's earlier phone call. "Imagine those who have been here for days. Then again, we keep them asleep most of the time and they never last more than a week or two, so they don't really have to worry about finding ways to pass the time."

"Is that blood on your shirt, Spencer?" West asked. "What stupid thing have you done now, as if killing the Vamp Court investigator wasn't bad enough?"

I'd figured this Spencer Addison was the blood mage who'd killed Mark, but hearing West talk about it so casually made my blood boil. West was obviously orchestrating this conversation for my benefit, but to what end?

"Killing Dunlap was a good move," Addison countered. "The timing was perfect. People already hated the vamps and thought they were the ones behind everything. All they needed was a sympathetic victim. The Daylighters and Humans First people are burning and bombing vamp-owned businesses. Now they're rioting outside the gates of Northbourne and the Court has no investigator."

"They have this Alice Worth, and she knows what Dunlap knew," West pointed out. "Not that *you* know what Dunlap knew, since you didn't get it out of him before he died."

My eyes filled with tears. I knew all too well how agonizing a blood mage's torture was, and yet Mark hadn't given in and told Addison what he wanted to know. I was getting answers to my questions about Mark's death, and with every answer, Addison was ensuring his hours were numbered.

"Maybe you could have done better, if you'd been the one questioning him," Addison said sardonically. "But I knew there was no sense trying to involve you because you wouldn't have done what needed to be done. I'm going to expand our operation into other cities. We may have to leave this one; even with attention focused on the vamps, it's getting too hot now, and we need more donors. Garcia wants more product."

"What do you mean, it's getting too hot? Don't tell me the Dunlap murder is backfiring on you." I could almost hear the smirk in West's voice.

"It's not your concern anymore. I'll have Worth soon. I've got her boyfriend already; it's only a matter of time before we find her."

"What boyfriend?" West pounced on that.

"Why the sudden interest?" Addison asked suspiciously.

"Because when all of your little plans fail spectacularly and it all comes down on your head, I'd like to know which idiot thing you did caused it. *I* led our harnad for more than twenty years, and no one knew we existed. *I* developed the manufacturing process and bought this warehouse. *I* had the contacts at the police department that kept us under the radar. We all made a lot of money and would have continued to do so if you hadn't gotten greedy thinking you could do better." He laughed. "You've been in charge for less than forty-eight hours and you're having to leave the city because you've made it too hot to stay. If you think you'll be able to just set up shop in some other city in another harnad or cabal's territory, you're delusional as well as stupid."

There was a long silence. Addison's blood magic sizzled on my skin, as if he'd lost control briefly. West had to know he was playing with fire, quite literally; Addison could kill him where he lay and there would be nothing West could do about it. If he was hoping I'd defend him, he was sadly mistaken.

Without another word, Addison spun on his heel and stomped out of the room, slamming the door.

Neither of us moved or said anything for several minutes. When Addison didn't return, I slid out from under the cot and got to my feet, careful to stay out of West's reach.

West adjusted his sheet and blanket. "Did you enjoy the show?"

"None of this is funny," I snapped, keeping my voice low. "And it's not a game. Who is this Garcia, and what is he buying from you? The blood or something else?"

"Addison has the temperament of a three-year-old child who isn't getting what he wants," West said, ignoring my questions. "I know what buttons to push to get him to storm out in a rage, so let's return to the previous discussion about making a mutually beneficial deal."

"No deal, West. I'd rather die breaking the wards by myself than make a deal with you."

"And your boyfriend, the fed? You'd rather let him die?"

"He's not my boyfriend and I'm not letting him die."

"Addison left the room quite angry. I've known him for more than fifteen years. When he's angry, he likes to take it out on whatever—or *whoever*—is nearby. Right now, I'm guessing that will be your fed, assuming he's even still alive."

I headed for the door, but he spoke again. "What's your plan, if you find your fed? You can't break the wards by yourself without dying. You'll be trapped here and we'll all die. Let me out and I will help you kill Addison and break the wards. It's the only way either of us survives."

West reminded me so much of my grandfather: a cold, unrepentant killer to whom lives meant nothing except as sources of potential profit. Moses Murphy had never faced justice for his crimes. I was determined that West *would* be held accountable.

"Every second you stand there is one less second your fed has to live," West said.

I pictured Lake's face, the way he'd smiled at me the night he'd handcuffed himself to me so I didn't run off and get myself killed. He was a good man. He deserved to live.

If I let West out, he'd try to kill me the second the wards broke and Addison was dead. He knew damn well I wasn't going to let him just disappear with the millions he had stashed away.

But I couldn't see any alternative, and there was no time to debate. "Hold out your cuff," I said coldly.

West held his left arm as far away from his body as possible. I manifested my cold fire whip and lashed the spell cuff. He set his jaw and didn't make a sound. The spell cuff hit the floor, broken in half. An angry red welt appeared on his forearm.

"Foot."

West held out his left leg and visibly braced himself. The green fire lashed again and the second cuff hit the floor, leaving another welt.

The dampening spell broke and West's magic was his again. It flared around him for full second before he got it under control.

West pushed himself to his feet unsteadily and swayed, his face ashen. The fact he'd already been bled by Addison might work in my favor later.

I backed toward the door. "I'm going to find the fed. I want you to hide somewhere until I come find you and then we'll break the wards and take out Addison. Where will you be?"

"You don't trust me to help you save your fed?" He was smiling, but it didn't reach his eyes.

"No, I do not. Where will you be?"

He considered. "There's a large supply closet at the other end of the hall, past the holding rooms. I'll wait for you there."

"All right." There was no sense asking for his word; it wouldn't mean anything if he gave it. I opened the door a crack and peeked out into the hallway. It was empty. "Where do you think he's holding the fed?" I asked, wondering if I could trust his answer.

"Start with the room across the hall, but let me leave first and get to the storage closet before you go exploring."

"Fine." I stood aside as West walked toward me. His gait was uneven, but his eyes were sharp. His magic crackled on the edges of my senses, like a wildfire that was barely contained. He was hobbled, but he was still powerful and deadly. Then again, so was I, and he knew it.

West slipped away down the hall and disappeared around the corner. I waited another minute to give him time to get to the closet, then stepped out into the hallway and closed the door, locking it behind me. It wouldn't gain us much time, but even a few seconds might mean the difference between life and death.

I thought of West waiting in the storage closet, presumably trying to get better control over his magic and deciding the best way to kill me at the first opportunity. I'd made a true deal with the devil. It was going to come back and bite me in the ass; the only questions were how and when.

I couldn't hear anything from the other room, but my blood magic surged as I crossed the hall and reached for the door handle. I took a deep breath and opened the door.

The smell of blood was overwhelming. I had a moment of displacement, as if I were simultaneously in two places at once: the blood mage's torture room at my grandfather's compound and this room in the harnad's warehouse. There was blood on the walls, blood on the floor, blood on the ceiling.

A bloody man in a tattered suit was slumped over in a chair in the middle of the room, his wrists and ankles cuffed to its metal frame. The cuffs had cut deeply into his skin as if he'd pulled at them trying to get away. He wasn't moving. *Please, let him be alive.*

I came into the room, pulling the door closed behind me. "Lake," I hissed.

To my relief, he raised his head. His face was bloody from multiple slashes. One eye was swollen shut. The other, ice-blue and filled with pain, focused on my face.

"Run," he grated.

An obfuscation spell broke behind me. I started to turn, but too late. Someone grabbed my shoulder and a zap of magic stunned me as a needle punctured my neck.

"I was about to give this to your boyfriend," Spencer Addison said in my ear. "But I think I'll enjoy letting him watch you die even more."

Burning acid flooded into me. I let out a choked scream, my knees buckling.

Addison let me hit the floor and stood above me, an empty syringe in his hand. He was a man of about sixty, trim, with gray hair. I recognized him as the man I'd seen in Felicia's memory, threatening to kill her and take her brother.

Addison smiled. "How do you like Black Fire?"

His face dark with rage, Lake struggled against his cuffs. "Alice," he rasped.

The burning was spreading fast. My heart raced and I couldn't get enough air, even though I was panting.

Addison nudged me with his shoe. "Thank you for saving me the trouble of finding you. Now be a good girl and die."

24

Lake lunged toward me, yanking on his cuffs. He was saying something but I couldn't hear him over the pounding of my heart and the roar of my blood in my ears. My arms and legs jerked and seized painfully.

The door flew open. I heard an urgent voice that sounded like Bobby's and caught the words "West," "cuffs," and "gone."

"Find him!" Addison shouted. He kicked me hard in the ribs and left with Bobby, slamming the door.

I managed to turn my head toward Lake. It looked like he was still saying my name, though I couldn't hear him. When he saw me looking at him, he mouthed something else. I thought it might have been *I'm sorry*.

The drug raced through my bloodstream, searing everything as it went, poisoning my body and threatening to stop my heart and lungs. My earth and air magic roared through me and I couldn't contain it all. Green flames danced over my body and the air in the room began to swirl in a kind of indoor tornado. My blood magic tore free and churned around me in a swirl of black, red, and purple. Black Fire enhanced magic and I was experiencing its effects firsthand.

There was something strange about the drug, though, something that left an echo of magic trace as it passed through my awareness. It tugged on my blood magic the way the concrete room at Charles's house and this room had, as if there was blood in the drug itself, but that wasn't possible.

Unless...unless there *was* blood in the drug.

The pieces fell into place. There was mage blood in Black Fire. That was why it enhanced the user's inherent magical ability. Somehow, West had figured out how to manufacture a drug spiked with magic—something no one else had ever done, to my knowledge.

Addison's first mistake was killing Mark. His second was seriously underestimating me. His third was assuming West was the bigger threat, and his fourth believing a massive overdose of Black Fire would simply kill me.

West was right about one thing: Addison was an idiot.

I closed my eyes. A memory surfaced of another blood-spattered room, this one at my grandfather's compound. A man in a lab coat stood over me, a syringe in his hand. My grandfather was demanding to know why the drug hadn't worked. The man in the lab coat said I had some way of neutralizing it. He couldn't make me compliant with drugs. Moses killed him in a rage.

How did you sober up so quickly? Lake had asked me the night Mark died.

Because I had a very special skill, one no one else knew about, not even Moses.

I focused on the drug in my body and unleashed my blood magic on it. The black, red, and purple magic raged through me, burning up the drug as it went. The pain was excruciating. I heard someone screaming and realized it was me.

The flames that covered my body began to fade. As my head cleared, I realized if I burned away all of the drug, I would no longer be under its influence and no longer in danger of dying, but I would be at my normal power level. I wouldn't be able to break the wards on my own without the landmines killing me.

Slowly, I drew my blood magic back. The remaining Black Fire sizzled in my veins as if I was holding an electrical charge within my own body. I thought I had been supercharged after drinking Niara's blood, but that was nothing compared to this.

I was high on Black Fire and magic, and it felt *so good.*

I opened my eyes and sat up. Everything was bright and clear. I felt powerful, invincible. Untouchable.

"Alice, your eyes," Lake said, his voice still rough.

My eyes felt hot—not the usual warm glow that signaled my blood magic was aroused, but an intense heat. I wondered if my eyes were bright gold, like Sean's when his wolf was close to his skin.

Lake knew the glowing eyes meant I was a blood mage. He watched me, not afraid, but cautious. Wary.

I rose, feeling each muscle move as I stood. I had never been so acutely aware of myself. It was like I could feel each atom, each cell, each individual hair on my body.

"I'm getting you out of here," I told Lake. My voice didn't sound like my own. As I approached, he didn't recoil from me, but he held very still as I came to stand beside him.

"I can heal some of your wounds. Brace yourself." I traced a rune in the air and held my hand in front of his chest. "*Helios.*"

The blood magic healing spell washed over him. I hadn't healed anyone in a very long time, and I had to be careful to control the power of my magic; it was so strong that too much would kill him instead.

Lake was in pain, though he was trying not to make a sound. Strong blood magic healing spells could hurt worse than the wounds they were healing. I sensed his pain but it felt distant. After about a minute, Lake leaned over and vomited.

If I'd only had my normal level of magic, I could have healed some or most of his wounds, but only at great expense to my own magic. The extra power coursing through my veins from the Black Fire overdose provided enough healing magic that I could see wounds healing all over Lake's body and my own magic remained almost unaffected.

Finally, I raised my hand and finished the spell. Lake's chest was heaving and he trembled. He was still covered in blood, but most of the wounds looked healed.

I stepped back. "Hold out your wrists so I can get to your cuffs."

He obeyed. His eyes widened when my cold fire whip spiraled out of my hand. He'd seen it once before, on the night I killed Scott Grierson, but from a distance.

I lashed out with precision and his right cuff fell off his wrist, broken neatly through. There was no welt on his skin. I hadn't had to leave burns removing West's cuffs, but I'd enjoyed doing it.

When all four of Lake's cuffs were off, he took my hand and forced himself to stand. He'd suffered enormous blood loss, and that was not something I could heal.

"You're in no shape to fight," I told him. "When things get dicey, take cover. I've got this."

"I'll do whatever I have to do." His voice was hoarse.

"I can't carry you. You have to stay on your feet and do what I say, or neither of us is getting out of here alive. Tell me you understand, or sit back down."

He put his hands on my shoulders and stared into my eyes. "How did you survive that overdose?"

I gestured at some bottles of water on a table near the door. "I'll explain later. Clean yourself up and then we need to move."

He used one bottle to wash his face and another to rinse out his mouth several times. He drank a whole bottle and half of another, and then he walked out the door. I figured it was at least eighty percent sheer willpower.

"What is this place?" Lake asked as we crept along the hallway.

"Long story. Basically, a harnad under the control of a man named John West has been kidnapping people and draining their blood. Today, Spencer Addison, a member of the harnad, kidnapped West and took over. They took you when they took West." I paused. "How did you know to follow West?"

"I've been looking into the harnad angle, like you suggested, but kept coming up empty. I finally got some information last night that West might be the leader of a large harnad group. I was watching him when I saw you and Maclin put a tracker on his car. I stayed to watch him after you left. I was calling you to ask about him when a guy tapped on my window asking for help. The next thing I knew, I woke up here."

I heard a crash and shouts coming from beyond a set of double doors that led to the section of the warehouse where Bobby had parked his car. West's voice shouted something, the words indistinct.

We reached the doors just in time to hear Addison's reply. "She's dead, John. I gave her a massive overdose of Black Fire. It's just you and me now. You know how this is going to end."

Magic surged. We heard another crash and the floor vibrated. It sounded like Addison and West had decided to start the party without me.

I turned to Lake and spoke in a whisper. "I need you to listen to me. If I don't make it out of here, you need to know what's been going on."

His set his jaw. "You're going to make it out."

"Shut up and listen." I laid it out for him: the blood, the drugs, Garcia, Andrews and Travers, Brody, Rachel Barrow, everything.

When I was done, Lake was so furious that he was cold and silent. "You'll have to fill in the blanks, find out who else was involved," I told him. "I'll do everything I can to see that you walk out of here, even if no one else does. No matter what else happens, get all of them."

He opened his mouth.

"Stop arguing and swear you'll do it," I snapped.

"I swear, Alice." He pulled me close and kissed me.

No one threw himself into a kiss more than a man who thought he might be about to die. I relished the kiss because I knew I would either die here in the warehouse or I'd be leaving with Sean. But if this was it for one or both of us, it wouldn't be so bad after a kiss like that.

When we broke apart, I looked at the double doors. Beyond them, I heard another boom and the floor shook.

"They are blood mages," I said, my voice low. "This is my part of the fight. When the magic stops flying and the wards come down, then it will be your turn."

"How will I know when the wards are down?"

My mouth twisted in a grim smile. "Don't worry. You'll know."

He took a deep breath. "Okay."

I squeezed his hand. "Ready?"

He squeezed back. "Ready."

I let go of him and hit the double doors with both hands. White magic flared and the doors blew off their hinges and disappeared into the warehouse with a loud crash.

"Nice entrance," Lake said.

"Thanks." I stepped through the doorway into the room beyond.

It was a vast area, with stacks of boxes, unused packaging and shipping equipment, and several vehicles taking up about half of the available floor space. Bobby's red Mazda was upside down and smashed, and the blond man who'd kidnapped me lay crumpled beside his car, either dead or out cold. There was a black BMW I was willing to bet belonged to Addison, and a blue van with a ladder on the roof and JOE'S PLUMBING on the side in white letters, as well as several unmarked white delivery trucks.

Addison had ducked behind a packing machine when the doors blew into the room. As we entered, he stood up and gaped at me. That moment of shock and disbelief was all I needed to blast him with enough air magic to send him flying into the wall. He hit with a thud and slid down, landing in a heap.

"I see rumors of your death were greatly exaggerated." West gave me one of his cold smiles and took a couple of steps toward Addison, apparently hoping to finish him off while the other man was dazed.

Instead, I unleashed my air magic again. West had a half-second to look startled before the magic hit and he went airborne. He smashed into the blue van, leaving a dent in the side before he hit the pavement and lay still.

"What now?" Lake asked.

I touched the crystal dangling from my belly button piercing. "*Release*."

Malcolm popped into existence a few feet in front of me. He squinted at me. "Jeez, Alice, your aura is like a supernova. What's going on?"

"We're taking out the trash. West is knocked out. Drain him completely. I don't want him to be able to light a candle when you're done." I gestured at the blood mage lying by the van.

"I'm on it." Malcolm zipped over to the van and touched West's shoulder. He began to glow.

Lake stared at me. "Am I supposed to be able to see who you're talking to?"

"Nope."

He cleared his throat. "Okay."

"I need you to find a way to restrain West in case he wakes up. Check the blue van; I'm betting they've got something in there you can use."

Lake limped over to the van, opened the back doors, and rummaged around inside. I watched Malcolm drain West until the ghost was so bright I couldn't look at him anymore.

Addison struggled to get to his feet, pushing himself up using the wall as leverage. Red and black magic spooled around his hands. "You," he ground out. "How did you survive the overdose?"

"I'm special," I said.

He released a bolt of blood magic. I held my hands in front of me and let loose my arc of magic. It absorbed his attack with a jolt that ran up my arms and made me stagger.

Addison glanced at Lake, who was trussing West up like a turkey using some kind of cable. Malcolm hovered a few feet away from Lake as he worked.

Addison sneered at me. "You can't kill me now that you've knocked West out. You can't break the wards or you'll die. And you're certainly not going to be handing me over to that half-dead fed so he can cart me off to some prison."

"That last part is true, anyway." I took a step toward him, my hands clenching into fists. "You murdered Mark. You've been killing people and draining their blood to make Haze and Black Fire. You're not going to prison."

I expected him to attack me. Instead, Addison turned and unleashed a three-foot-wide fireball of blood magic directly at Lake and Malcolm. It would kill Lake and discorporate Malcolm instantly.

No.

I reached out with my magic and did something else I wasn't supposed to be able to do: I pulled the fireball to me.

It was a gamble since I'd never attempted to absorb that much magic before, but I had no time to think. I heard Malcolm shout my name and saw Addison's look of triumph just before the fireball hit. The impact knocked me down and sent me sliding backward across the floor a good ten or fifteen feet.

I lay still, mesmerized by the sensation of being so full of magic that I could feel each individual cell of my body vibrating with it.

"Alice!" Lake yelled in warning.

Uneven footsteps approached. I rolled to a crouch.

Addison froze in mid-step, his eyes wide. The air crackled around me in a halo of green, white, black, and red magic, with traces of gold. Malcolm and Lake stared in awe.

"Who *are* you?" Addison demanded.

"I'm Mark Dunlap's friend." I hit Addison with a blast of magic that sent him tumbling through the air to smash into a large piece of packaging equipment.

As he lay stunned, I reached out with my mind and grabbed the wards protecting the building. With my Second Sight, I could see each and every thread of the wards and that they connected directly to Addison. He was controlling them and keeping them continuously powered. It was his fifth and final mistake.

Addison felt me seize the wards. He struggled to stand up, fear in his eyes. "You can't break them," he whispered.

I didn't break them; I obliterated them.

As the wards fell, each of the landmines detonated but they were as ineffectual against my Black Fire-enhanced magic as pebbles thrown at the Great Wall of China. Addison went to his knees with a shriek, bleeding from his nose and ears.

I advanced on him, his wards coiled around my fist. With a yank, I ripped Addison's razor ward out through his body. His scream turned gurgling and ended abruptly as the tangle of deadly magic sliced through him with a thick, meaty sound. Then his body fell apart.

Lake stared in stunned silence.

"Fuck me," Malcolm said reverently.

"Go get Sean," I said.

The ghost nodded and vanished.

Lake looked at the pile of flesh and rapidly expanding pool of blood that had once been Spencer Addison.

"He was going to kill all of us," I said.

"Could you not have incapacitated him?"

"No."

Lake was silent. "I don't even know you at all, do I?" he said finally. "You killed this man without blinking an eye. You did things no one should be able to do. Who are you, Alice Worth?"

"I've told you before; I'm nobody. I saved your life twice tonight. Both times I should have died, but I didn't. Maybe that's all you need to know about who I am."

"You're not going to tell me how you survived that overdose, are you?"

"No."

He sighed and looked around the warehouse. "Putting that aside for the moment, I need to figure out how to deal with this."

"When your SPEMA buddies get here, tell them what I told you about John West, Addison, and the harnad. Round up the rest of the harnad and the people who manufacture the drugs. Get Brody and whoever else is on the take at the police department. You'll solve the biggest case in the city's history. Take all the credit and leave me out of it."

He shook his head slowly.

"You'll be a hero, Lake: the man who survived torture by a blood mage, took down a harnad and a drug cartel, and saved the surviving kidnapping victims."

"You're the hero, Alice, not me."

"I'm no hero. Just finish the job and get justice for the dead."

Heavy vehicles pulled up outside, their tires crunching in the gravel. Doors opened and voices shouted commands. The cavalry had arrived.

"They'll get justice," Lake said quietly. "While you disappear back into the shadows."

I shrugged. "I like the shadows. It's where I feel most at home."

Somewhere in the back of the warehouse, a door slammed open against the wall. "Alice?" Sean called, his voice echoing. Heavily armed black-clad enforcers flooded into the warehouse, with Sean and Bryan in the lead.

Bryan led a group down the hallway toward the holding rooms. Sean stopped to check Bobby's pulse, shook his head at Lake, and came over to us.

He looked at the bloody mess on the floor and swore. "Who is that?"

"Spencer Addison," I said. "He killed Mark. He died when I broke the wards."

Sean inhaled and stared at me. "What is that I'm smelling on you?"

"Addison gave me an overdose of Black Fire, but I turned it against him and used it to break his wards."

Sean's expression was terrible. "Are you high on Black Fire?"

"Yes, she is," Malcolm said, appearing next to me. "Shit, Alice, you turned this guy into salsa. Not that he didn't have it coming, but—"

I didn't like the way they were looking at me. "I had no choice. I would have died. Lake would have died. All those people in the holding rooms would have died. It was the only way."

"Black Fire is a highly addictive drug," Lake said heavily.

"Sometimes you have to make a deal with the devil." I turned to Sean. "The survivors are down that hall. I don't know if Felicia is there; I haven't had a chance to look."

"She is," Sean said. "I can sense her through the pack bonds now that the wards are broken."

"Good. I want to find Danielle and Carrie." I headed for the holding rooms.

Sean stopped me. "What about the Black Fire?"

"It'll be out of my system soon." I shook off his hand. "Let's get Felicia and get the hell out of here."

I led Sean, Lake, and Malcolm into the hall, where the Vamp Court enforcers were standing guard. In the first room we found four people unconscious on cots. Two were survivors: a young woman and a man in his forties, both ashen and weak. The other two were mages I presumed were harnad members who had been loyal to West. They were held with two sets of spell cuffs each, as West had been. I pointed out the harnad mages to Lake.

"We'll leave them asleep for now," Lake said. "We need to get these people to a hospital and the harnad members to a secure facility."

In the next room we found two people: Danielle and another young woman. Danielle was pale but looked relatively healthy. The other woman was in such bad shape that it took me several seconds to realize who she was.

"That's Missy Daniels," I said in horror. "The victim Danielle saw being picked up in the black BMW."

The next room held three harnad mages in spell cuffs. We found Felicia alone in the fourth room.

The moment we walked into the room, the force of Sean's rage almost made me stagger. As Adam and I had seen in his visions, Felicia was restrained by her wrists and ankles with silver shifter cuffs. Her flesh was seared by the silver, and she was thin and deathly pale.

"Get her out of these cuffs," Sean ground out.

I broke the silver cuffs one at a time with my fire whip as Sean held out her arms and legs. "She needs to stay asleep until you can get her back to her family," I told Sean as he picked her up. "She's going to be in a lot of pain and be very angry and confused when she wakes up." I looked at Malcolm. "Will you go with him and break the sleep spell when they have her in a safe place?"

"I'll go with him. I can help heal her injuries on the way," Malcolm said.

Sean cradled Felicia tightly, obviously torn between needing to be with Felicia and worried about the Black Fire still burning in my veins. "Where are you going after this?" he asked.

"I'm going home. You need to take care of Felicia," I told him. "Her mother and brother must be frantic. Go. I'll be fine."

With one last look at me, Sean left at a run, Felicia in his arms and Malcolm at his side.

Lake and I continued through the holding rooms. Only about half the beds were occupied. We found the two vampires locked in a silver cage. There were sixteen survivors total, plus the seven harnad members and the vamps.

Carrie was not among them.

I stood over the unconscious body of John West with blood magic sizzling on my fists.

Footsteps came up behind me. "You can't kill him."

I didn't turn around. "That doesn't mean I can't fantasize about it."

We stood silently for a long time.

"Promise me he will never see daylight again," I said finally. "I want him buried so far underneath Colorado Springs Ultra-Max that he forgets what the sky looks like."

"I guarantee that's where he'll be until the day he dies." Lake leaned against the side of the van. He was haggard, but still on his feet somehow.

"You ready to call in your SPEMA buddies and take this operation down?"

"More than ready," he said. "We'll get the survivors to the hospital and the mages into custody. We'll have the rest of the harnad by morning and the drug ring by the end of the day."

"Everyone needs to know immediately that the vamps had nothing to do with this," I told him. "The protests and the attacks on vamps have to stop."

"I'll take care of it," he promised.

We stared at each other.

He touched my face. "Get that Black Fire out of you before you start to like it too much and forget how it was made."

I already liked it too much. "It'll be gone as soon as I get home."

"Which will be when?"

"As soon as I can get a ride." I waved at Bryan, who was headed for the warehouse door. He changed direction and joined us by the van. "Is that offer still open for the use of a Court vehicle?" I asked him.

"Yes." He studied me. "I think I'll drive."

"I think that would be a good idea," I said.

25

Bryan didn't take me home—at least, not immediately.

It didn't take long for me to figure out we were headed north and not toward my house on the east side. I had a feeling I knew where we were going.

Our destination turned out to be the mansion belonging to Charles. The gate swung open as the SUV turned into the drive. Heavily armed guards patrolled along the high brick wall. Bryan drove up the long driveway and parked in front. Another enforcer opened my door and I stepped out of the SUV.

The front door opened as we approached, revealing Adri. "Come in," she said.

"Thanks."

I followed her through the living area and past the piano to a set of French doors that opened onto a wide veranda. There were no lights on in the backyard but there was plenty of moonlight to see the man sitting alone in a wicker chair, a crystal decanter and two glasses on the table at his elbow. There were two envelopes on the table: one large and one letter-sized.

He rose as we approached, his eyes silvery. I remembered I was still wearing the see-through shirt and bustier. On another night, I might have been concerned they would send the wrong message. Tonight, I found I didn't care.

"Alice."

"Charles."

He gestured at the chair opposite his. "Please."

I sat. Adri moved to stand next to my chair as Bryan took up a position next to Charles. It appeared I now merited the presence of two enforcers instead of one.

Charles turned his attention to me. "I have received a report from Mr. Smith, but I wish to hear your account of what you found at the warehouse."

The vampire listened as I talked, his fingers steepled. When I finished, he tilted his head. "You did not mention how you came to be under the influence of Black Fire."

I shrugged. "Addison tried to kill me with it. He misjudged the dose."

"Or perhaps he misjudged *you*."

I smiled. "Perhaps."

"Perhaps *I* have misjudged you." He tapped his fingertips together. "What a vexing mystery you are, Alice."

We sat silently, watching each other. Finally, Charles looked up at his enforcers. "Leave us."

They hesitated.

"Go inside and close the doors." It was a command.

With obvious reluctance, Adri and Bryan went into the house. Bryan closed the French doors with a soft click.

Charles reached for the decanter and poured us each two fingers of whisky. He handed me a glass, then raised his. "To you and your success."

We clinked glasses. I didn't know what brand he had served me, but it was good enough to make the Scotch given to me by Mark taste like swill by comparison.

"The Court is grateful to you," Charles said. "I am to relay their thanks and give you this." He handed me the smaller envelope.

Inside was a check. I glanced at the amount and my eyebrows went up. "There seem to be a couple of extra zeroes on here."

"Consider it a well-earned bonus, for a quick resolution and with our sincere apologies for the injuries you suffered at Hawthorne's." Charles sipped his Scotch, then cradled his glass. "I have also been asked to present you with an offer of employment."

"An offer from whom?"

"From the Vampire Court. We wish to employ you as an official investigator, working full-time for the Court and representing our interests." He handed me the large envelope.

I put the envelope on the chair next to me. "I have a job. I'm not interested in working for the Court full time."

He raised an eyebrow. "I assure you our offer is quite generous."

"I'm sure it is."

"I do not wish to be indelicate, as you still grieve for your mentor, but we require a new investigator. This situation has demonstrated very clearly the need for one or more full-time employees whose priorities are not divided between the Court's interests and other matters. We have another case that will require an investigator's full attention. I believe you are an ideal choice."

"I'm willing to continue working for the Court part-time, as I've done for the past three years, but you'll have to find someone else for this." I held out the envelope.

Charles did not take it from me. "Perhaps I can offer additional incentive to consider the offer."

"I've worked very hard to become an MPI and start my own agency, and I'm not interested in giving that up."

"You should consider your position," he said. "A mage who is not who she claims to be would wish that information to remain private. She should make allies, not enemies."

I regarded him. "Blackmail, Charles?"

"Information is leverage." He finished his whisky and set the glass on the table. "I would be a poor broker if I failed to see the value of the information I have and use it to my benefit."

"To *your* benefit?"

"To the Court's benefit, of course," he corrected smoothly.

I finished my Scotch, put the glass on the table, and settled back into my chair. "If I did agree to work for the Court, what guarantee do I have you won't use this 'leverage' against me anyway, or again in the future whenever you want me to do something I don't want to do?"

"I give you my word."

"Not good enough." I leaned forward. "You bit me when I was in a coma. You had no intention of telling me what you had done until you could use it to your advantage. I once said you've always been a man of honor, but if you were you wouldn't have violated someone who was in your care. I can't trust your word, Charles."

"And yet, the situation remains unchanged. We require an investigator. I require your signature on—" Suddenly, Charles jerked in his chair, his eyes wide. He stared at me, frozen.

"Leverage *is* a valuable tool," I mused, tracing the pattern on the arm of my chair with my fingertips, leaving a barely visible trail of blood magic that dissipated like smoke. My eyes were warm and I knew they were softly glowing. "It can tilt the field in your favor or restore balance. You have information about me that's valuable to you, but now you see I have leverage too."

"What are you doing to me?" he hissed. "What is this pain?"

"You drank the blood of a high-level blood mage with a"—I chuckled—"a very particular set of skills. My blood and my magic are within you. I control my magic. I control *you*."

He strained to move, despite the daggers of magic piercing his heart. I drove them in deeper and he stilled.

"I could rip out your heart," I told him. "I could sever your spinal cord or take off your head. I could do it from four feet away, or from across the city, or from another country. You said you underestimated me. You had *no idea* by how much."

We stared at each other. I read Charles's eyes, his body language. He was thinking, calculating.

"What do you propose?" he asked finally.

"Détente. A mutually beneficial arrangement in which I continue to work for the Court on a contract basis. I'm a valuable asset, as you've no doubt concluded. Hire a full-time investigator and I'll work with him or her on jobs for you. No one needs to know what you know about my magic or that my magic can influence you."

"And how do I know you will not use this leverage against me in the future?" he asked wryly.

"I won't be anyone's slave, and I won't be anyone's master. Had you not tried to blackmail me, I would have never have done what I just did." I put the large envelope on the table. "Do we have an agreement?"

"We do."

I released him. Charles reached for the decanter. His hands were steady, but he poured three fingers' worth of the very expensive Scotch and knocked it back like he'd needed a stiff drink. When he offered to refill my glass, I shook my head and he splashed whisky into his own.

"With such a bold move, you make yourself irresistible to me," he said, stoppering the decanter. "You are powerful and calculating and surprisingly ruthless. I have seen the recording of your interrogation of Clint Ravell. Stay with me tonight, Alice. Share my bed."

"Thank you for the invitation, but no." I pushed myself to my feet. "I need to be getting home."

Charles rose as well. "Because Maclin has your heart?" There was no anger in his tone, only curiosity.

"Because I don't want to share your bed, tonight or ever."

"Ever is a very long time. Even immortal vampires do not speak in terms of never or always." He raised his hand. The French doors opened and Bryan emerged. "Alice is ready to be taken home."

Bryan gestured at the house. I picked up the small envelope, folded it neatly in half, and tucked it into my back pocket before heading inside, Bryan behind me.

As we crossed the enormous living room, I glanced back over my shoulder.

Charles was watching me. He raised his glass in a toast, a ghost of a smile on his lips. I heard his voice in my head: *Good night, Alice.*

Good night, Charles. I turned and kept walking, through the house and out the front door and into the night.

The news broke at nine o'clock that morning.

The press conference took place in front of the harnad warehouse. It was an alphabet soup of federal agencies and local law enforcement: SPEMA, DEA, ATF, FBI, SWAT, CRT. The SPEMA bureau chief was there, accompanied by Lake, who'd had a chance to shower and put on a suit, but he looked like he was barely standing. The police chief stood flanked by Detective Diaz, the deputy chief, and two federal prosecutors.

I watched the press conference on my laptop, sitting in bed. The SPEMA bureau chief laid the official story out succinctly. After a long and painstaking investigation, a joint task force had arrested thirteen members of a harnad, including its leader, who were responsible for the kidnapping and murders of at least thirty people over the past fourteen months. Nine other people had been arrested in connection with the murders, one of them an as-yet unidentified member of the police department. The DEA had raided several locations where Haze and Black Fire were being manufactured and rounded up several dozen drug suppliers and distributors. Everyone was going to be tried in federal court. There was no evidence of any vampire involvement whatsoever, and the SPEMA bureau chief was grateful to the Vampire Court for their cooperation and assistance in apprehending those responsible.

There was more, but I was having an increasingly difficult time focusing. I turned down the volume of the press conference.

"How are you feeling?" Sean asked from next to me in the bed.

He'd shown up just before dawn, having spent several hours with Felicia. When she was healed from her injuries and resting comfortably in the care of her mother and brother, he'd come to my house in my car to bring me my wallet, keys, and phone. I was surprised at how glad I was to see him.

Despite my exhaustion and the hollowness left behind after I'd burned the rest of the Black Fire from my body, I hadn't been able to sleep. We'd simply curled up together in my bed until Adri texted me about the press conference.

I opened my mouth to tell him I was fine, then closed it.

Sean sat up. "Alice?"

"I'm hurting," I said quietly.

He took my laptop and put it aside. "Where are you hurting?"

"Everywhere." I took a deep, shuddering breath. "It started about an hour ago."

His eyes darkened. "Is it the Black Fire?"

Mutely, I nodded.

He took me in his arms. I burrowed my face into his shirt but his scent failed to comfort me or ease my pain and restlessness. The need to feel that fire in my blood again was almost overwhelming.

After a few minutes of holding me while I trembled, Sean moved so he could see my face. "Do you trust me?"

"To do what?"

"To help you. Yes or no?" he prompted gently.

Did I trust him? With my heart and my secrets, no, not yet. To help me? I didn't hesitate to answer. "Yes."

Sean's eyes turned bright gold. A rush of shifter magic ran through me, making me shudder and then go limp. Everything faded away. The pain, craving, nausea, and uneasiness all disappeared and I was wonderfully warm and content. I exhaled and nestled my head against his chest.

"This is my magic," he murmured into my hair. "I can't tear down wards or make cold fire or do whatever the hell you did to Spencer Addison, but I can take this pain from you for as long as it takes until you no longer want that poison."

I drifted in blissful comfort for several minutes while he held me. Finally, I asked, "How can you do this when I'm not part of your pack?"

"I suspect because you have some of my magic and I have some of yours." He settled into the bed and pulled the covers up over us. "How about we get some sleep? I don't know about you, but I feel like I could hibernate for a while."

"Wolves don't hibernate," I reminded him, my eyes already closed.

"Have you been reading up on wolf behavior?"

"I may have read something on Wikipedia," I said sleepily.

Sean chuckled and reached up to close the curtains over the bed. I rolled onto my other side and he spooned up behind me, his arm around my middle. He nuzzled the back of my neck and pulled me close. We slept.

26

That evening, I was on my back porch with a glass of iced tea when the perimeter wards tingled, announcing a visitor.

I waited.

The back gate creaked open and closed quietly. A tall, dark-haired man in a well-tailored suit appeared from around the corner of the house. He crossed the backyard to stand about fifteen feet away. The breeze shifted and I smelled sulfur.

We watched each other in the moonlight. He was handsome in a classically aristocratic way, with the imperious bearing of a man used to power and wealth and giving orders. That wasn't my thing, but I could see why women would fall for him.

"Alice Worth," he said finally. His voice was very deep and it resonated with dark magic.

"I wondered when you'd be stopping by," I said, setting my glass on the table beside my chair.

"So you know who I am?"

"It took me a while to put it together," I admitted. "In my defense, it's been a busy week. But yes, I figured out why the trace of demon magic I kept sensing seemed so familiar. You're Scott Grierson's father."

"I am Ravan." He inclined his head formally. "I am here to seek justice for the murder of my son."

I both needed and dreaded the answer to this question. "How did you know to come looking for me?"

"At first, I believed SPEMA agents were responsible for my son's death, as they quite publicly claimed credit for the deed. However, when I visited Agent Elaine Parker, intending to avenge my son, I was informed it was you who killed him."

I'd seen Parker alive and well at the anti-vamp protest two days ago, so obviously Ravan hadn't had to torture the truth out of her. Also, she evidently hadn't felt the need to warn me there was an angry demon coming after me. I made a mental note to address both of those issues at my earliest opportunity, assuming I had the chance.

"I don't suppose it matters that I acted in self-defense," I said. "He tried to kill me."

"If you had murdered him in cold blood, you would already be dead. Instead, I wished to find out more about you first, this mage who killed my son."

"So now you've come to kill me?"

"I've come to tell you I will first kill your lovers and discorporate your ghost. Then I will kill you." He sounded matter-of-fact, as if he was discussing dinner options rather than murders.

I didn't bother to correct him about Lake being my lover; even if he did believe me, he apparently knew I cared about the federal agent and that alone would seal Lake's fate. "So that's how it is, huh?"

Ravan raised his chin. "That is how it is."

"All right." I reached out with my magic. "*Snare.*"

The force of the wards flaring felt like I'd stuck my finger into a power outlet. My backyard was suddenly a cage made of blisteringly powerful wards—including a razor ward that would tear through even a demon's hide. The wards were anchored by my house wards, which I had been enhancing for nearly five years. If Ravan tried to break them, he would die in the attempt.

Ravan roared. Luckily, the wards also prevented sound from escaping, or 911 would have been flooded with frantic calls.

His human body split open in a spray of blood and flesh that sizzled when it hit the wards. His demon form was enormous, almost ten feet tall and half as wide, with arms and legs like tree trunks. He was also unfortunately naked. My neighbors would have been thankful for the obfuscation spells that hid him from their sight if they'd known what I was sparing them from seeing.

While his human form would have looked at home in an expensive restaurant or a CEO's office, this was his true form. In this body, he had killed and eaten a half-dozen young women kidnapped by his son.

"Do you think you can hold me prisoner?" Ravan demanded. His mouth was full of jagged teeth and there were too many of them. As unpleasant as the sight was, it was still better than looking below his waist.

"I could if I wanted," I said, rising and moving to the porch railing. "I'm sure you can feel how strong those wards are. But I'm thinking about putting in some flowerbeds back there, plus you just threatened to kill people I care about, so I have to dispose of you."

"You can't kill me," the demon snarled. "Your wards are strong, but your magic alone is not enough."

The back door opened and Sean stepped out onto the porch. "She's not alone."

Ravan glowered as Sean joined me at the railing. "Alpha," the demon sneered. "Do you plan to die to defend your woman?"

"Alice is her own woman, and she doesn't need defending, as I'm sure you're already aware," Sean replied. "But if you've come for her, you'll face me as well."

Malcolm emerged from the house and hovered to my right. "Yeah, what he said." He gaped at the demon. "Why are you naked? Are you trying to scare us to death by waving that thing around?"

Ravan growled.

"Malcolm," I sighed.

"What? It's *barbed*." He tilted his head. "And a lot smaller than you'd think it would be."

The demon turned purple in indignation.

I unleashed my air magic and threw Ravan across my backyard. If I'd been able to touch him, the blast would have been more forceful, but even so I'd caught him off-guard and he hit the wards hard.

The impact stunned him. The razor ward went partway through his body before he wrenched himself free with a bellow of pain and fury. Foul-smelling black blood spurted across the grass as Ravan staggered and almost fell. His back and legs were missing large chunks of flesh.

Malcolm went invisible as he crossed the yard. He slashed the demon with a laser-like stream of air magic that opened a deep gash across his enormous chest. Ravan lashed out with a tendril of dark magic and fire but Malcolm evaded it and sliced the demon's right arm.

As Ravan tried repeatedly to strike Malcolm, who he could sense but not see, Sean dropped to his knees on the porch. I heard bones popping and shifting and a powerful surge of magic pushed me back a half-step. Moments later, an enormous black-and-silver wolf launched himself over the porch railing with a snarl.

Ravan saw Sean jump and lashed out, but the wolf dodged the demon magic and hit him full-force in a blur of teeth and claws. Malcolm took advantage of the opportunity to strike Ravan with air magic again, wounding him in the neck and making the demon stagger.

Ravan bellowed and knocked Sean off, then lashed out as the wolf was rolling to his feet. My breath caught as the tendril of dark gray magic hammered Sean back and left him dazed. Ravan took a step toward him but Malcolm attacked again, opening gashes on the demon's face and distracting his attention long enough for Sean to get on his feet. He leapt at Ravan again, and this time he got his teeth into the demon's throat.

Our plan had been for me to wound the demon with magic from a distance while Sean and Malcolm did most of the close-quarters fighting, and thus far it seemed to be working. As I watched, however, Ravan ignored Malcolm's attack and drove his basketball-sized fist into Sean's ribs with a sickening crunch. The wolf didn't let go of the demon's throat, and Ravan punched him again. The wolf whined, but still he held on.

Something happened inside me when I heard Sean's whine of pain. Before I knew what I was doing, I vaulted over the porch railing and ran at them, my blood magic spooling around my hands. Ravan saw me coming and grinned, his teeth bloody. His fist drew back to punch Sean again.

I dove at Ravan's legs. The demon tried to dodge, but as wounded as he was and with Sean still gnawing on his throat, he only managed to stagger. I grabbed his right knee with both hands and sliced through his leg with my blood magic. The demon's flesh seared my palms and I cried out.

Sean released Ravan's throat and jumped away as the demon roared and fell. Ravan lashed out, his magic striking me across my right hip. It felt like someone hit me with a lead pipe and something broke. I screamed and went down.

Sean moved in front of me, snarling and snapping his teeth at Ravan, who was struggling to rise despite the fact his right leg had been severed at the knee.

I lashed my cold-fire whip around Ravan's ravaged neck. The demon's hide was tough, but Sean had chewed through it partway already. I snapped the coil tight and pulled as hard as I could. Ravan's head rolled across the grass.

My hip was killing me and I could barely move, but the fight wasn't over. A demon could heal even that wound, given enough time and the right spells. Ravan glared at me from his disembodied head, his eyes bright red as Sean snarled at him.

There was only one way to kill a demon of Ravan's rank. Despite Sean's whine of concern, I managed to drag myself over to the demon's body and used my blood magic to slice into his chest and through his ribs. Ignoring the agony, I shoved my hand inside the demon's body, feeling my flesh burn as I pushed through his skin and the viscera underneath, searching until I found what I was looking for.

My hand emerged from the demon's chest, covered in gore and clutching the black, pulsing lump that was his heart. I reached for the power of my house wards to boost my magic. "*Burn.*"

Ravan's heart went up in burst of white fire. A moment later, his head, body, and blood followed suit. In seconds, the demon was nothing but ash scattered across the backyard.

I vomited from the pain in my hip and hands. My left palm was blistered, but my right hand and arm were badly burned almost all the way up to my elbow.

Malcolm reappeared while Sean shifted back to human.

"He didn't get you, did he?" I asked the ghost shakily, wiping my mouth with my left sleeve.

Malcolm hovered over me. "Nope, he missed me. You guys took all the hits. Oh, God, Alice—your hands."

Sean appeared in my line of sight, naked and covered with sweat. His injuries had healed when he shifted. He dropped to his knees next to me. "Where did he get you?"

"Right hip," I said, gritting my teeth.

Sean used his fingertips to gently feel around my hip. I gagged at the spike of pain. "That's fractured pretty badly." He looked up at Malcolm. "Can you heal her?"

"If she'll let me," Malcolm said. "You know how she is."

Sean squeezed my left arm, his eyes on me. "Yes, I do."

"Hey, guys, could you gang up on me some other time?" I complained.

Malcolm floated closer and held his hand over my hip. "Brace yourself."

"Alice, look at me," Sean said.

I looked up at his bright golden eyes and the pain disappeared in a rush of shifter magic. Malcolm spoke and the healing spell flared, but it was muted.

As the spells pulsed through me, my shields slipped a little and I saw Sean's wolf in the darkness between us. He was licking demon blood off his muzzle and watching me, his eyes warm and thoughtful.

I heard a voice in my head that was more growl than human. *Mate*, the wolf said.

I jerked and raised my shields instinctively, breaking Sean's influence. My movement jostled my half-healed hip and hands, and the loss of Sean's magic meant I felt Malcolm's healing spells too. The sharp pain made me whimper and I pulled out of Sean's grip.

"No," Sean said, taking my arm again. "I'm not letting you go this time." His eyes lit up once more, but I was rattled now and his magic no longer worked to take my pain away. I tried to stay quiet, but I couldn't hold back little cries as my hip and hands healed.

Finally, the healing magic faded. Malcolm floated back. "I'll let you guys talk," he said and disappeared into the house.

I sat up gingerly. My hip was sore, but the break was healed. My hands and right arm were pink and the skin felt tight, as if I had a bad sunburn. I'd have to finish healing them with a blood magic healing spell; Malcolm's magic alone wasn't strong enough.

Sean stood, lifting me to my feet by my upper arms and then steadying me when I swayed. When I was standing, he kissed my forehead. "What made you decide to let us help you with Ravan instead of facing him by yourself?" he asked.

I swallowed hard, trying to ignore the nausea caused by the healing spells. "Maybe I'm learning to like being part of a team." I hesitated, then added, "When I was at the warehouse and I heard you and the enforcers arrive, I felt safer. And you're right; it's not my call whether you fight or not, either of you. That's your decision to make."

His grin made my heart skip a beat. "That's another baby step," he teased. When I didn't smile back, he turned serious. "Whatever my wolf said to you just then, we'll deal with it. Don't put up any more barriers, Alice, that's all I ask."

"Your wolf called me his mate."

Sean sighed. "He's been drawn to you from the beginning. I'm sorry if that's threatening or frightening for you. To be honest, it's disconcerting for me. That's never happened before."

"We haven't known each other very long. How can he know he wants me as a mate?"

"The same way I knew I wanted you the first time I saw you in Hawthorne's: instinct." He tucked some loose hair behind my ear. "But we're human beings, and we're more than our instincts. There's no rush, no pressure. We have all the time in the world to figure out what we want."

I thought of my grandfather's cabal moving into the city and his war with Darius Bell, my détente with Charles, this new investigation the vamps wanted me working on, and the mystery of how Malcolm came to be bound to me, and wondered what time I really had before one or more of those things brought disaster to my door, as Agent Parker had done by revealing my identity to Ravan.

"So, Agent Parker sent him your way," Sean said, his thoughts echoing mine as we walked slowly back toward the house.

Once I'd figured out who was after me and why, I'd told Sean about my role in Scott Grierson's death and how I'd first met Lake and Parker.

"Apparently so," I grumbled as we reached the back porch. I climbed the steps slowly, trying not to wince at the ache in my hip. "I suppose, when you have a demon threatening you, you'll do what you have to do to stay alive. A heads-up would have been nice, though."

"So what are you going to do about it?" Sean asked, reaching to open the back door.

"Let's go inside. You need to get some clothes on before Malcolm gets the vapors. I need to finish healing myself. Then I'm going to call Adam March."

Sean's brow furrowed. "The Court psychic? Why?"

"You asked what I'm going to do about Parker. Well, Adam owes me a favor and I'm about to call it in."

Three days later, I was on my knees in the backyard, wedging a stone into place in what would be the border of my flowerbed. It didn't look like much now, but I had big plans for my new backyard garden. It would be more life energy, feeding my house and yard wards, if I could get it going.

A large black-and-white dog came bounding across the yard and bumped into me, dropping a stick on the ground.

"You goofball," I told my new dog, scratching his head. I picked up the stick and threw it back across the yard. Rogue ran after it with a happy bark.

I picked up another rock and put it in place, then rubbed my sore shoulders and sighed. Though I tried to distract myself with yard work, I couldn't stop my mind from wandering.

I'd asked Sean to have one of his people deliver Mark's wedding ring to Sharon. Mark's funeral had been a private, family-only service, and I was not invited. His death was still a dull ache in my gut that even the memory of killing Spencer Addison couldn't ease. The only thing that seemed to cut through the pain was drinking the Scotch Mark had given me, but I was rationing it carefully.

Yesterday, I discovered my recycling bin had been emptied. Sean hadn't said anything about all the empty liquor bottles. He was giving me the opportunity to be the one who brought it up. He might have to wait a while.

The hunger for Black Fire continued to come and go, but I was resisting thanks to Sean's help. I didn't understand how he was able to relieve my cravings, but I wasn't about to look a gift werewolf in the mouth. I'd liked the power and the rush of Black Fire too much to risk letting the need for it get the better of me.

As I was looking over the pile of stones, deciding which to place next, the perimeter wards tingled. Rogue started barking and running around the yard in circles. In addition to being unusually calm around Sean, he was extremely sensitive to wards and magic. And to ghosts, as it turned out. Anytime Malcolm was in the vicinity, the dog barked up a storm and tried to bite him. We were hoping he'd get used to Malcolm's presence soon.

"Stay," I told Rogue, pointing to the porch. He trotted up the steps and lay down on the concrete, watching me as I got to my feet and headed for the back gate.

I came around the side of the house to see a black pickup parked in my driveway and a blond man in jeans and a blue shirt on my front porch, his fist raised to knock on my door.

"Lake," I called.

He came down the porch steps and joined me. "Working in the yard?"

"Putting in a flowerbed."

His eyebrows went up. I couldn't blame him; I knew I didn't seem like the type for backyard gardening. "Need some help?" he asked. He looked like he hadn't slept well in a couple of days, and there was something in his eyes that had me worried.

"I was actually about to take a break. Come on back." I led the way through the back gate.

Lake surveyed my flowerbed-in-progress and bent down to pick up one of the stones I was using for the border. "Nice. This is a good spot. Lots of morning sunshine and afternoon shade, it looks like." He glanced at the back porch and did a double-take. "When did you get a dog?"

"That's Rogue." The dog barked at the sound of his name. "He used to belong to one of the people taken from the homeless camp by the river. The man wasn't one of the survivors, and the woman who was caring for him decided to go to a rehab program. I happened to be down there the other day, checking on the camp, and offered to adopt him."

In fact, Rogue had followed me back to my car, and Jo-Jo had laughed and said I couldn't very well *not* take him with me. I was still getting used to the idea that I had a pet for the first time in my life. Sean was ridiculously happy that I'd adopted the dog and Rogue already adored him, following him everywhere when he was at my house.

Lake smiled at Rogue, but the expression was fleeting. When he turned back to me, the darkness was back in his eyes.

"What's up, Lake?" I asked, my hands on my hips. "Is there a problem with the case against the harnad?"

"No, not as such." Lake looked at the porch again. "Can we sit?"

"Sure." I led the way to the porch as Rogue went back to running around the yard. "Can I get you something to drink? Iced tea or water?"

"I'm all right."

I sat on the porch railing and gestured at the chair. "Have a seat."

To my surprise, he settled into the chair without arguing. He was probably still weakened from blood loss.

"First, I wanted to let you know Detective Brody made a full confession to his involvement with the harnad," Lake said. "He admitted to pulling Mark Dunlap over and getting him out of the vehicle so he could be spelled by Robert Miller, who you know as Bobby. He also admitted to calling Spencer Addison about John Andrews and Jake Travers."

It was nothing I hadn't already suspected, but it still hurt to hear how Mark had been taken. "What else?"

"We found out from Jorge Garcia's people that the harnad took the shifter woman and the vampires to experiment on creating different drugs using their blood. Luckily, they weren't successful. I understand the werewolf and the vampires are recovering well."

"Yes, they are." I regarded him. "I guess the police are finding out the hard way that people don't appreciate being lied to about there not being any harnads in the city."

"SPEMA did try to warn them." Lake shook his head. "The police chief resigned this morning, as did a half-dozen other city officials. Diaz still has his job, but the lieutenant in charge of Major Crimes was fired. A lot more heads are probably going to roll before it's all over."

"Well, now the Daylighters have refocused their hate on mages. There are anti-magic protests at city hall and the police department. I don't know if you've seen it, but the list of vamp-owned businesses on the Daylighters' website is now accompanied by a list of mage-owned businesses, including mine." I paused. "I've been evicted from my office building, as of today. I have forty-eight hours to clear out my property."

He sighed. "I'm sorry, Alice."

I shrugged. "In the scheme of things, getting kicked out of my office seems unimportant. But you didn't come over here to hear about my problems. What's bugging you?"

Lake rubbed his face. "My partner was arrested yesterday."

"Parker?" My eyebrows went up. "What on earth for?"

"Falsifying evidence on a case we worked last year. Someone tipped off our bureau chief to look into it, and she confessed. Now all of her cases are under review."

"You're kidding. They don't think you had anything to do with it, do they?"

He shook his head. "No. When she was questioned, she was very clear that she'd done it without my knowledge. I asked her why she did it, and she told me because she knew the guy was guilty but we couldn't prove it. I don't know what to say. I never would have thought she'd do that."

"I'm sorry," I said sincerely. "You think you know somebody."

Lake looked up at me, his eyes searching my face. "Alice, I need to know: did you have anything to do with tipping off our bureau chief?"

"Me? Of course not. Why would you think I would?"

"Because when I went to talk to her yesterday, Parker asked if I'd seen you lately and how you were doing. When I said that as far as I knew you were fine, she said I should come check on you, just in case."

I couldn't very well tell him a psychic had told me about Parker falsifying evidence, because then I'd have to tell him Parker sent Scott Grierson's father after me. And then I'd have to explain how I'd killed the demon in my backyard, and that the touch-sensitive psychic had learned of what Parker had done by breaking into her house. No, Lake didn't need to know any of that.

"I have no idea what she meant," I said. "You know she never liked me. Maybe she was hoping I'd had an accident or something. Who knows?"

A long silence. For once, he didn't confront me about lying. Instead, he startled me. "I'm leaving, Alice."

I blinked at him. "What?"

"I've been offered a promotion. They want me to be the assistant director at the field office in Seattle."

"Lake, that's awesome! Congratulations!" I hesitated. "Why aren't you happy about it?"

"I *am* happy about it. This is something I've been working toward for a long time."

"Then what's the problem?"

He stood up and joined me at the railing. "You."

"Me?"

"I'm taking this job in Seattle because I know I can't stay here in this city with you."

Stunned, I fell silent.

"You are the most beautiful, most intriguing, and most frustrating woman I have ever met," he said, staring out into the yard. "I wanted to be with you but I couldn't get past the lies and my suspicions. By the time I decided those weren't as important as how I felt, it was too late. Sean Maclin was smarter than me, or luckier. Maybe both."

We were quiet.

"I know you aren't who you say you are," he continued. "There is nothing in Alice Worth's history to explain the things you can do or the way you killed Spencer Addison without blinking an eye. It wasn't the Black Fire or your anger over Mark Dunlap's death. You're a killer, Alice—if that's your real name. Addison wasn't your first; that much is obvious."

I didn't bother to deny it; he'd sense the lie anyway.

"I don't know who you are, but I'm not going to dig and try to find out, partially because you saved my life twice, and partially because I don't want to know. I also know I can't stay here and keep running into you, and not just because it keeps reminding me of what could have been. I took an oath to uphold the law and I've broken it a dozen times for you. One of these days you'll cross a line and I won't be able to let you walk away. I don't want to catch you doing something I'd have to arrest you for."

"I understand." Why did my voice sound funny?

He cupped my cheek with his hand. "You're not going to tell me I'm wrong about you?"

I shook my head.

"Is this another episode of honesty?" he teased.

"A short one." I managed a small smile and took his hand. "Go to Seattle, Lake. You're a good agent and a good man. I never thought I'd say that about a SPEMA agent until I met you."

"Damn it, Alice," Lake said roughly. "Will you please call me Trent?"

"Go to Seattle, Trent." I pulled him down for a sweet kiss.

In another life, we might have had something good, but not in this one. In this one, he had to go his way and I had to go mine.

When we broke apart, he rested his forehead on mine. "Did you tip my bureau chief off about Parker?"

"Don't be silly. How would I have known about something that happened before I even met you? I'm not psychic, you know."

He laughed and released me. Hand in hand, we walked down the porch steps, through the gate, and around the house.

"Keep my number," he said as we crossed the yard. "If you ever need me, I'm only a phone call or a quick flight away."

"Thank you." I kissed him on the cheek. "Good luck in Seattle."

He went to his truck. As I headed back to my flowerbed, he called out to me. "Alice."

I turned. "Yes?"

"Catch." He reached into his pocket and tossed something to me.

I caught it and looked down at my hand. In my palm was my burned earring Lake had found at the construction site.

"I thought you'd want it back." His eyes twinkled.

I shook my head. "It's still not my earring, Trent."

"Keep it anyway." He opened the door of his truck, climbed in, and shut the door.

As he backed down the driveway, he waved. I waved back, then watched as he drove off down the street and disappeared.

I tucked the earring in my pocket and returned to the backyard, closing the gate behind me.

THE END

Thank you for reading! Did you enjoy?

Please Add Your Review! And turn the page for HEART OF ICE, book 3 in the Alice Worth series!

HEART OF ICE

BOOK 3

1

As a private investigator, I'd pretended to be a lot of different people: a sex worker, a door-to-door doughnut salesperson, a tarot card reader. Hell, I'd once posed as a member of the Russian mob. This role, however, was by far the most difficult I'd ever had to play.

"It's not just the fangheads who have to die, you know." Mike Robinson, aspiring terrorist, leaned forward in eagerness. "It's mages and shifters too, and everyone who stands with them. If we're ever going to be free, we have to exterminate them all. This world was meant for humans, not creatures like that."

"I couldn't agree more," I said.

We eyed each other across his living room. Robinson was the leader of the group and the host for this meeting. The manager of a quarry thirty miles from the city, he was in his late forties and heavyset, a widower with no children and a lot of pent-up rage. He and I sat opposite each other in armchairs.

I crossed my legs and settled back. "We all want a human future, but it won't be easy and it won't happen overnight. We have to plan five steps ahead and think big-picture. That's why groups like the one I represent are always on the lookout for the kind of people who are truly committed to not just winning one battle here or there, but to winning the war."

"We are committed," Robinson assured me.

I studied the faces of the others in the room. On the sofa sat Andrew Davis and his kid brother Corey. Andrew, an A/V installation tech by day, was the group's self-described "gadget guy." He'd met Robinson in a support group for people who'd lost a loved one to a vampire attack. Unlike Robinson's wife Samantha, who'd died after being drained by a vamp, Andrew and Corey's brother Luke had *become* a vampire. Drinking blood was worse than being dead, according to his human brothers. Corey, a mechanic, had tagged along to the meeting but been quiet. While Andrew was angry about his brother's recent transition to vampire, Corey seemed to be grieving.

The fourth member of the group stood off to the side, arms crossed, biceps bulging.

He'd been standing for almost an hour without moving, expressionless and silent. Kent Stevens was a former Marine who worked at the quarry with Robinson. He'd shaken my hand when I arrived and then stationed himself near the doorway as a very large and ominous sentry. His brother had been killed by a vampire while Stevens was serving overseas in Afghanistan. If Mike Robinson and Andrew Davis's anger was visible and red-hot, Stevens's was ice-cold. For all Robinson's talk of genocide, I was pretty sure Stevens was the real menace in this room.

No doubt my driver-slash-bodyguard agreed. He stood behind me, a silent sentinel in a suit. Though Robinson and the Davis brothers glanced at my companion constantly, Stevens watched me, as if sensing I was the bigger threat, despite the size of the man standing behind me and the fact I appeared to be unarmed. It was this perceptiveness as much as anything that made me wary of him.

"We're ready to act," Robinson said. "Give us a target, or we'll find one on our own, but we want to do something. This city is the place where it starts, Ms. Day. This is where the revolution begins. People are angry after the harnad murders. They hate mages; they hate shifters. They've always hated fangheads. I heard local membership in Human rights organizations like yours is up by three hundred percent in the past two or three months. It's the perfect time to declare war."

I held up my hand. "I appreciate your enthusiasm, Mike, but as I said before, Human Future is cautious about making new affiliations. That's what has kept this side of our organization under the radar for so long, while the public front supports laws and political candidates who share our vision of a supe-free future. After this meeting, I'll go back and make my recommendations, and then we'll decide whether to bring you into the network."

Robinson drummed his fingers on the arm of his chair. "When can we expect a decision?"

"When the background checks are complete and we've had a chance to evaluate your prospects." I regarded him. "You're enthusiastic and driven. You have good leadership instincts, and I believe you have the potential to do well in an organization like ours."

Robinson preened at my praise.

I glanced at the others. "The rest of you each bring skills to the table that would be useful, but so far, all I've heard is the same kind of big talk I read in the comments section on our website, or in the online forum where we first made contact with Andrew." I raised my hands, palms up. "You claimed responsibility for quote, 'the biggest attack on the fangheads,' unquote, during the protests a month ago, but several groups have made that assertion. There were a half-dozen cases of arson, but none of them were what I'd call major attacks. For a city you argue is on the front line in the war, there doesn't seem to be much going on."

"We didn't set any of those fires." Robinson looked smug. "We bombed a business belonging to a member of the Vampire Court."

Stevens's eyes flicked to Robinson. I wondered if he was unhappy Robinson had told me that. Andrew crossed his arms, as if daring me to contradict their leader. Even Corey raised his chin defiantly.

I narrowed my eyes. "You're the third person who has told me they were responsible for that bombing."

"Bullshit," Robinson snapped, his face reddening as he pointed to the others.

"Corey obtained the van we used, Stevens built the pipe bomb, and Andrew made the detonator."

"And what did you do?" I asked, my tone skeptical.

"I chose the target and did the recon." He crossed his arms. "The bar was closed, but the building was destroyed."

I glanced at Stevens. "Why did you put ball bearings in the bomb?"

He remained impassive. "I didn't. I used silver flechettes."

That particular detail had certainly never been released to the public, but that question had tripped up others who had claimed responsibility. It would appear they were telling the truth.

I nodded slowly. "Perhaps we can find a place for you with our organization. Let me ask you this: if you had access to better weapons and better resources, what would your next target be?"

Robinson didn't hesitate. "Northbourne Manor, the headquarters of the Vampire Court."

My eyebrows went up. "That's a big target."

He smiled. "With the right people and the right weapons, it could be done. I want to be the one to do it."

"I," not "we," I noticed. Interesting.

I rose. Robinson and the Davis brothers followed suit. I extended my hand to Robinson and he shook it. His palms were damp. "I'll be in touch," I told him. "Keep a low profile for now, until you hear from me. There are a lot of feds in town, thanks to the protests and the attacks on Darius Bell's cabal. It's a lot of heat. Not a good time to be careless."

"We're never careless," Stevens said, with a note of finality in his voice that I didn't particularly care for.

I picked up my briefcase and headed for the door, with my driver in front of me and Robinson right behind us.

The meeting had gone well—better than I'd hoped, really. I wasn't home free yet, but thanks to the recording device in my briefcase, we had what we needed.

My escort reached for the doorknob.

And that's when it all went to hell.

Several things happened pretty much simultaneously.

My escort stiffened and turned toward the living room just as the lights went out.

"What the—" I began.

Someone brushed past me, knocking me aside. An explosion went off behind me and the blast felt like a punch to the side of my head. Disoriented, I staggered as the world went blindingly white for a millisecond, then pitch-black.

Blinded, confused, and unable to hear over the ringing in my ears, I stumbled and reached toward where I thought my driver was standing, but my fingers encountered nothing but air.

Somewhere in the darkness there were indistinct voices and muffled pops like distant firecrackers that some part of my brain recognized as gunshots. Without warning, a white-hot fist punched me in the upper back near my shoulder. The impact spun me around and I went down with a shriek I couldn't hear.

At first my left shoulder and arm were numb, and I wondered if someone had hit me with a pipe or a bat. Then the pain arrived and stole my breath. I curled up on my side and clutched the wound as hot blood pumped through my fingers. Apparently I'd been shot, but by whom?

I still couldn't make sense of anything, but some of my vision was coming back. Indistinct shapes moved around me in the dim light. The sounds of gunshots had ceased. I heard voices from beyond the buzzing in my ears, but they sounded like *mwaaaa mwaa mwaaa mwaaaa-mwaaa mwaaa*.

A very large shadow appeared above me. I tried to scramble away, but whoever it was had an iron grip on my leg. My earth magic spiraled out of my hand and I lashed out instinctively with my cold-fire whip.

I heard a grunt but the hand on my leg didn't let go. A face swam in and out of focus above me and I felt a jolt of recognition, but what I thought I saw didn't make any sense. Maybe I was concussed; my brain definitely felt muddled and I still couldn't string together a coherent thought.

Then another face appeared. Bright silver vampire eyes met mine and I heard Charles Vaughan's familiar voice in my head: *Alice, let us help you.*

The larger of the two shadows said something I couldn't hear, pried my fingers away from my shoulder, and ripped my suit jacket and blouse apart. He tore off his own shirt and wadded it up against the hole in my shoulder, while he lifted me and used what was left of my jacket and blouse as a bandage on the wound on my back. When he compressed my shoulder between his hands like a vise, the wave of pain made me convulse and struggle to get away, but Charles held me down. The room did a weird kaleidoscope spin and the ringing in my ears drowned out all other noises as I started to fade out.

A cool hand brushed my forehead. *Alice, look at me.* Charles's words cut through the fog of pain and dizziness and I was compelled to obey.

I opened my eyes—which was odd, since I didn't remember closing them—and met the vampire's gaze as everything else faded to background noise. My world shrank until all I could see or think about was how beautiful his eyes were. They glowed with a soft silver light as if lit with moonlight from within. The pain faded to a distant ache. I exhaled in a long sigh.

Dimly, I realized Charles had used suggestion to ease my pain. Normally I would have resisted or refused simply on principle, but the wound was bad and the agony was worse. Despite Charles's command, my eyelids were heavy and unconsciousness pulled at me.

Bryan Smith, Charles's head enforcer, said something else I couldn't understand. His tone was urgent and it galvanized the vampire into action.

Charles caressed my cheek. Bryan lifted the makeshift bandage away from my shoulder. A blade flashed and cool fingertips pushed into the gunshot wound.

Even vampire suggestion had its limits. I bit back a scream and retched. I'd experienced a lot of torture, but having someone stick their fingers into a bullet wound was pretty close to the top of my personal pain scale.

A nexus of soothing warmth and comfort formed in my shoulder, taking away the pain like a tide going out. I recognized the healing effects of vampire blood, but instead of offering me his wrist to drink from, Charles had apparently slashed his own fingers and stuck them directly into my wound. How bad was the injury if the vampire had decided drinking his blood might not heal me fast enough?

Charles withdrew his fingers from my shoulder and pulled me against his body until I was half-sitting. He tore back his sleeve, bit savagely into his wrist, and pressed his arm to my mouth. Cool blood ran down my chin. *Drink,* he told me.

I blinked slowly up at him, torn between my reluctance to put myself under his influence again and the knowledge that though the blood from his fingers had begun the healing process, my wound could kill me or leave me incapacitated in the middle of whatever was happening here. My head buzzed like it was full of bees.

Alice, drink, the vampire repeated, more forcefully. *You are losing consciousness.*

Reluctantly, I obeyed.

As I drank, the waves of pleasure and warmth that rolled through me were frighteningly intense. Things began moving in my shoulder. I moaned and struggled in Charles's arms. When he gently started to pull away, I licked his wrist to clean off the blood. The vampire made a sound low in his throat that was definitely not pain.

He held me as my bones and flesh healed and the ringing in my ears faded. It took a long time. Finally, the strange sensations subsided and my other senses returned as the blood healed the damage to my vision and inner ears.

When I opened my eyes, I discovered someone had turned on a few lights but left the house in semi-darkness, probably in deference to those of us who were still suffering the aftereffects of what I now realized had been a flash-bang grenade.

When the lights went out, I'd been almost at the front door, but now I was lying in the living room with no memory of how I'd made it there. I stared around the room, trying to process what I saw and make sense of it.

Robinson's living room was in a shambles. The large windows facing the backyard were gone, the curtains were torn down, and broken glass was everywhere. Bullet holes in the walls indicated a gun battle. The furniture was overturned and smashed as if a big fight had taken place. A half-dozen Vampire Court enforcers in black stood guard around us. Through the missing window, I saw several more in the backyard.

Charles sat on the floor with me in his lap, in a distressingly large puddle of blood that had apparently come from me. Bryan was on one knee next to us, shirtless, our blood-soaked clothes in a pile beside him. I was covered in my own blood, my jacket and shirt were gone, and my bra was held on by a few threads, but I was sitting in the middle of what looked like a war zone and that seemed more important at the moment.

Three men lay face-down and unmoving on the living room floor, their hands cuffed behind their backs. I recognized them as Robinson and the Davis brothers. They were alive but unconscious.

"Where's the other guy?" My voice sounded funny; my hearing was still messed up, or maybe it was shock and blood loss.

Bryan shook his head grimly. "Escaped."

He had a welt across his chest where my cold-fire whip had struck him. I grimaced. "Sorry," I said, gesturing at the wound.

"Don't worry about it," he rumbled, waving off my apology. "You were confused and blinded, and it will heal."

Someone crouched beside me. "Miss Alice."

I looked up at my oversized Vampire Court-assigned bodyguard. "Hey, Fortune. Oh, crap, were you hit?" His suit jacket was bloody near his right shoulder, as was his right pant leg, and he was pale.

"They're just flesh wounds. I'll be fine." He looked at Charles, his expression grim. "Sir, I failed to protect her. I offer you my blood and my resignation."

"Wait. Back up. What the hell happened?" I started to sit up but thought better of it when a wave of dizziness reminded me that my shoulder might be healed, but I'd lost a lot of blood.

Charles looked like he'd bitten into something rancid. "We intended to arrest Robinson and the others once you had obtained their confession."

His arm was still around my middle, holding me against him. I pushed at it, but he tightened his grip. "Let go."

"Don't try to stand up," Bryan advised. "You'll pass out."

As much as I hated to admit it, he was probably right. I stayed on the floor and glared at them. "Somebody needs to explain this to me," I snapped. "We had a plan, Charles. I go in, get the confession, hand it over to the feds, and they make the arrest. Why are you here?"

Charles's eyes flashed. "The Court was concerned the bombers would suspect they had been deceived and flee before the federal agents acted on our evidence."

I might have known the vamps would change the play at the last minute. I scowled. "So you decided to toss in a flash-bang and get us shot?"

"They planned to wait until we were clear of the house before coming in," Fortune told me. "Stevens cut the lights and threw the flash-bang."

So Fortune had been in on the Court's plan all along and hadn't told me. What a surprise.

"Why did he do that?" I remembered seeing Fortune turn toward the former Marine right before all hell broke loose. "What happened when the lights went out?"

Fortune looked mad enough to chew up rocks and spit out gravel. "Stevens got some kind of alert. I heard something buzz twice, like a signal. He put his hand in his pocket and the lights went out. The flash-bang was hidden in the couch next to him. He threw it before I could get to him."

Which meant he'd been close to the grenade when it went off. I winced. As much as the flash-bang had left me deaf, blind, and disoriented, it had to have hurt Fortune far worse. The enforcer's hearing and eyesight were enhanced from drinking vampire blood regularly, which meant he healed faster, but the initial detonation would have left him virtually incapacitated long enough for Stevens and the others to grab weapons.

"We came in when the banger went off," Bryan said. "In the confusion, Stevens and Robinson got a couple of shots off before we could gain control of the situation."

"Looks like it was more than a couple, unless some of those are yours," I said, gesturing at the bullet holes in the walls. "Stevens probably had some kind of perimeter alarm set up and you guys tripped it as you were making your approach."

He nodded grimly. "It would appear so."

Well, I'd have some words for Charles about being left out of the change in plans, but that could wait until we were in private. "Did you call in the feds?"

"We did," Bryan told me. "The neighbors called the police about the gunshots. There are officers outside. Agents from the ATF are on their way to take them into custody." He gestured at Robinson and the Davis brothers.

"How did Stevens get away?"

"He went out a window on the other side of the house and made it to a vehicle." Bryan's eyes blazed. He was obviously furious Stevens had escaped their net. "We have people looking for him. He won't get far."

"Good." I looked at the blood on the floor and sighed. "I can't leave that here. Get me up."

Bryan looked at Charles doubtfully.

"This amount of blood loss will be debilitating," the vampire told me, as if I hadn't already figured that out.

"I have a job to do. Just get me on my feet and I'll do the rest."

Charles stood and lifted me in one smooth motion, then held me upright when my knees tried to give out and my ears rang. Fortune stood beside us, guilt written on his features as I trembled from blood loss and the feeling of cold air on my bare skin.

Fortune took off his suit jacket and draped it over my shoulders. It was bloodstained and hung almost to my knees, but at least I was no longer standing in front of a room full of people in what was left of my bra.

I pulled out of Charles's grip and crouched carefully, putting my fingertips in the blood on the floor. "I'm going to burn this," I said.

Charles gave Bryan a nod. "Do it," the enforcer told me as some of the other enforcers moved back. Their caution was understandable but unnecessary; the burner spell would only remove traces of my blood without touching anything or anyone else.

I took a deep breath. "*Burn.*"

The spell flared, knocking me back. Charles caught me before I could land on my butt. White fire rushed across the floor and across our clothes, consuming my blood and leaving behind a thin layer of fine ash. The vampire helped me stand and held me up as ash floated down to the hardwood floor.

In the meantime, Mike Robinson was coming around. He struggled, pulling at his cuffs and swearing, his words slurred. He rolled onto his side and tried to rise, flopping like a fish.

Bryan put a hand the size of a baseball glove on Robinson's shoulder, pinning him to the floor without noticeable effort. "Stay down," he rumbled.

"Screw you," Robinson spat. He craned his neck and spotted me, standing with Charles's arm around my middle. His face twisted in rage and disgust. "*You.* You c—"

"If you wish to keep your tongue, you will be silent." Charles's voice was pure menace. A slight lisp told me the vampire's fangs were out and he was angry enough to not enunciate carefully.

Robinson made the wise choice and shut up, but hate radiated off him in almost visible waves. Unfazed, I stared back at him.

You don't need to protect me from words, Charles, I told the vampire. *Sticks and stones and large-caliber bullets may break my bones, but words will never hurt me.*

No one speaks to you in such a way in my presence, was his curt reply. His arm tightened around me.

Adri Smith, another of Charles's enforcers, came in through the front door. "Sir, the ATF agents are two minutes away."

Charles addressed Robinson. "I am Charles Vaughan, the vampire whose bar you bombed. It gives me great pleasure to see you in handcuffs. You will be handed over to federal agents momentarily."

It occurred to me rather belatedly that Charles had a second motivation for arresting Robinson and the others in person tonight, rather than simply letting the feds handle it: he'd wanted the satisfaction of putting on the cuffs himself. I couldn't say I blamed him; I'd been a part of the investigation for much the same reason. I'd almost died when they bombed Hawthorne's. If I'd been a second slower in my reaction when the bomb was thrown through the window, I'd be dead. It was worth the bullet wound to see Robinson on the floor in cuffs, his eyes widening as the reality of the situation began to sink in.

"You murdered my wife," Robinson ground out.

"I had no involvement in her death," Charles countered. "Nor did anyone of my line or any of my employees. The Court investigated your wife's murder. The vampire who killed her was unfamiliar to us and not sired by anyone on the Court. Your target had no bearing on your wife's case."

"I don't care. You all deserve to burn in hell." Robinson turned to me. "I did it for my wife. I did it for Samantha."

"No you didn't," I told him as the front door opened and four federal agents came in. "You did it for yourself."

With Charles's arm around my waist, we slowly made our way toward the front door as the feds took over.

One agent, an African-American man in a suit and ATF windbreaker, stopped us in the foyer. "Ma'am, are you injured?"

"No, just disoriented from the flash-bang," I told him, speaking too loudly, as if I was still a little deaf. Charles shook slightly. If I didn't know better, I'd have thought he was laughing silently.

The agent handed me a card and I tucked it into the pocket of my borrowed jacket. "I'm Special Agent Marshall. You'll need to come to our office to give your statement." He glanced at my attire and raised his eyebrows. "Once you're had a chance to change, of course."

"Of course," Charles interjected smoothly. "Three hours from now, at your office?" When Marshall frowned, Charles added, "She can hardly be expected to give a statement before she has recovered, Agent Marshall. Her testimony would be compromised."

I did my best to look shaky and unfocused. With the blood loss, it didn't take much acting.

Marshall relented. "Three hours," he agreed, then headed into the living room, where the other agents were conferring with each other and ignoring Robinson, who was loudly demanding a lawyer and that we be arrested for assault and false imprisonment.

Three hours is time enough to see to your medical needs and discuss your statement, Charles told me as he ushered me out the door. An SUV waited at the curb with Adri behind the wheel and Fortune at the rear passenger door, ready to open it for us.

With each step, the buzzing in my head got louder and I could no longer feel my own feet. I stumbled and almost went down. I gritted my teeth. Unless I wanted to collapse on the sidewalk in front of a dozen feds, I needed help. *Charles, I'm not going to make it to the car.*

He picked me up and moved vamp-fast to the waiting SUV. Fortune opened the door and climbed into the back seat much quicker than I would have thought possible for a man of his size. Charles handed me off to the enforcer, who laid me on the seat as his boss climbed in and shut the door.

"Ride in front," Charles told Fortune, who quickly exited through the other door and hurried around to the passenger side. He jumped in and Adri pulled away from the curb, accelerating down the street in a roar of horsepower.

Charles arranged me so my feet were propped up against the opposite door and my head was in his lap. The increased blood flow helped clear the cobwebs and the ringing faded.

He met Adri's eyes in the rearview mirror. "Call ahead to the house and have a doctor and blood transfusions waiting."

"Already done." Adri glanced at me in the mirror. "How are you doing, Alice?"

"Never better," I muttered.

Charles brushed hair back from my face. *I am sorry our change of plans led to this*, he said in my head.

I understand why you did it, but you should have included me in your plans instead of dropping me into the middle of a shooting gallery. I've earned that much.

He twitched, as if my statement had startled him. *Yes, you have. I apologize.*

An apology from a member of the Vampire Court. As if the day hadn't already been strange enough.

2

I woke up just after noon to the feeling of a large, warm body curled up behind me and a heavy weight pinning my legs.

"Hey," Sean murmured, his lips on the back of my neck.

"Hey," I echoed, my voice thick with sleep. "How long have you been here?"

"Since about ten. I didn't want to wake up you up, but I couldn't stay away once I knew you were back." He wrapped his arms around me.

"I'm awake, sort of." I yawned and smiled at the black-and-white dog lying on my feet. "Hey, Rogue."

The dog woofed and laid his head back on the bed, closing his eyes.

"When did you get home?" Sean asked.

I rubbed my eyes. "A little after dawn."

"So you've only been asleep for a few hours. Go back to sleep. We'll go downstairs." He kissed my cheek and started to pull away.

I held him back. "No, stay."

He settled back in and nestled me against his body. I was bone-tired, but it had been too long since I'd seen Sean or my dog and I couldn't have gone back to sleep now if I'd wanted to.

"You want to tell me about it?" Sean asked after a few minutes.

His werewolf nose had no doubt alerted him immediately that things had gone sideways. I was surprised he'd waited until I woke on my own to ask what had happened. The Sean I'd first known would have demanded an explanation for why I smelled like blood that was not my own, and that earlier version of me would have been annoyed and angry at being questioned. I realized neither of us were the people we'd been when we first met and was surprised that I liked the change in myself.

"Alice?" he prodded.

"Hang on," I said with a note of irritation in my voice. "I'm having a revelation."

Sean chuckled. "Isn't it a little early in your day for that? You haven't even had coffee yet."

I elbowed him in his hard stomach. He made an exaggerated *oof* sound and nuzzled my neck. "So, do you need a minute to process this revelation, or…?"

I sighed. "No, you ruined the moment."

"Sorry." He pressed a kiss into my hair. "So, things did not go well last night, I take it."

"Actually, overall, things *did* go well. We got the bombers in custody." Most of them, anyway. I wondered if they'd caught Kent Stevens yet. I'd have to text Adri and ask.

"Good, then we won't have to leave the house today." He settled in more comfortably.

"Don't you have to go to work?"

He snorted. "I haven't seen you in more than a week, Alice. I took the day off." He rubbed my arms, his hands wonderfully warm. "So, how did you end up needing vampire blood *and* a blood transfusion?"

"I can't go into details because of my contract with the Court," I reminded him. "All I can say is not everything worked like it was supposed to at the end, but I'm all right now."

He stopped rubbing my arms and just held me. "It was close, though, wasn't it?"

The old Alice would have denied it, but I was trying not to lie to Sean—at least, not unless I absolutely had to—and I'd sort of made an agreement not to tell him I was fine when I wasn't.

"Yeah, it was," I admitted.

Sean's anger prickled on my skin. He might not have demanded an explanation for my injuries, but that didn't mean he didn't want to find the person who'd hurt me and tear them apart. "I know you probably had no choice, but I don't like that you had to drink Vaughan's blood again. It gives him some influence over you and that son of a bitch is always plotting and scheming."

"I didn't have a choice about drinking his blood, but I *do* have a choice about whether I let him manipulate me afterward. If that's what he's hoping for, he's going to be sorely disappointed."

He squeezed me and kissed my temple. "So, what's on the agenda for today?"

"I planned on taking it easy and just doing some things around the house. Thanks for picking up some groceries; let me know what I owe you for that."

"You can get dinner for us later and we'll call it even." He paused. "Have you given any more thought about what you're going to do for an office?"

A month ago, I'd been evicted from my office during the height of violent anti-vamp and anti-magic protests that swept the city after it was discovered a group of mages was responsible for dozens of murders. The building's owners cited safety concerns, since several mage-owned businesses were targeted for arson and vandalism. I was having a difficult time finding anyone willing to rent me office space. The contents of my office were in storage while I figured out how I was going to deal with the situation.

Sean had offered to lease me space in the Maclin Security building, but I'd declined. It felt too much like a commitment and like I'd be mixing my professional and personal lives in a way I wasn't comfortable with.

"I don't know," I said. "Something will become available soon, I'm sure."

"There's still space available in our building if you want it," he said mildly. "Decent-size office on the first floor, with its own bathroom and a great view of the loading dock."

"Thanks. I'll keep it in mind."

He let go long enough to lean back and grab something off the nightstand and hand it to me, then pulled me back into his arms.

It was a travel brochure for a resort in the Bahamas, featuring isolated cabanas with private beaches.

I looked over the brochure. "Still wanting to take a beach vacation with me?"

Sean had wanted to go on a trip after we'd put the West-Addison harnad in jail, but within days of closing that case, the Court had hired me to help catch the bombers. I'd decided to take the job instead of the vacation and Sean had not been happy.

"Look at that sand," he murmured in my ear. "And that crystal-blue Caribbean water. Tell me you don't want to spend a week away from everything, swimming in the ocean, drinking rum punch, and lying in a hammock under the palm trees."

"It does look pretty fantastic," I admitted, folding the brochure. "Let me think about it."

He raised up on his elbow. "Let's stop thinking about it and just do it. You and I, we think too much. My pack, my company, your ghost, your work...it will all be fine while we're gone." He kissed my forehead. "Pack a bag and let's just go, Alice. Whatever we need that we don't have already, we'll buy when we get there."

"I can't go to the Bahamas; it's too far away. If something happened here, it would take too long to get back."

"What do you think might happen?"

I rubbed my face. "Anything could happen. I just...I can't go to the Bahamas. Maybe we could go to a beach somewhere closer, somewhere we could get to and from quickly, if we had to."

He sat up and leaned against the headboard. "I'd really like to know what you think might happen if you leave town. If you're worried about your house, between Malcolm and your wards and my security company, it's safer than Fort Knox. Malcolm is protected inside the house. The Court can do without you for a week; they have other people who work for them and two new full-time investigators. What are you worried about? Explain it to me so I can understand."

How could I explain how vulnerable I'd feel so far from my home and its wards? My home was my security, the first and only thing that was every truly *mine*, after twenty-four years of being a prisoner in my grandfather's cabal compound. If my grandfather ever tracked me down and I had to run, that would be one thing, but even the thought of being away for a week made my stomach churn.

"I'm not sure I can explain it," I told him finally, rolling onto my back and staring up at the ceiling. "Maybe it's irrational."

"You're never going to let me forget that, are you?" he asked wryly.

During an earlier fight over my refusal to let him buy me new furniture, I'd called him a bully and he'd called me irrational. "I wasn't referring to that," I told him, running my fingers through his hair. "Really, it *is* probably irrational of me to be afraid of going out of town."

"Is that something we can work on together?"

I took a deep breath. "Maybe we could start with something not so far away. When that goes okay, maybe something a little farther. Then, maybe the Bahamas, assuming you're not sick of me and my bullshit by then."

"I'm kind of fond of you and your bullshit." He kissed me again, more purposefully this time.

I ran my hands up under his T-shirt and over his chest, scratching him lightly with my nails. He growled low and slid a hand across my stomach where my tank top had hiked up while I slept. I shivered at his touch and pulled him half on top of me, suddenly no longer sleepy. His kiss grew hungry and his hand slipped under my top. I moaned.

Rogue raised his head and barked at us.

I laughed. "Butt out, fur-face. Sean and I need some private time."

Sean growled. Unimpressed, Rogue tilted his head, his tongue hanging out.

I threw back the covers and swung my legs over the side of the bed. "Hold that thought. I'll let him out in the backyard, and then we can—"

"Don't let him into the backyard," Sean interrupted. "There's something...weird going on back there."

I blinked at him. "In my backyard? What—?"

I didn't get to finish my question. I sensed a surge of power and a wave of magic rolled over the house. Rogue went berserk, jumping off the bed and barking. I staggered and almost fell. Despite my shields, the wave of magic left me disoriented.

Sean was off the bed and at my side in a heartbeat. "Alice!" He sat me down on the bed, his hands on my face as he stared into my eyes. "Are you all right?"

"Magic attack," I mumbled, trying to clear my head and focus.

"What do you mean, a magic attack?"

Suddenly, Malcolm was in my room. "What the hell was that?" the ghost asked.

"Did someone attack the house?" Sean demanded.

"No," Malcolm told him, floating over to me. "It feels like something big just happened, but somewhere else. Alice, you okay?"

The disorientation faded. "I'm okay. That was a massive wave of magic. Malcolm's right; something big just happened. I don't think I've ever felt anything like that."

"Let's go see if the news has anything about it," Sean suggested.

We headed downstairs. Sean turned on my new television and I went to the kitchen to make coffee. While the pot was brewing, I joined Sean, Malcolm, and Rogue in the living room. Sean had found a local station with a breaking news alert.

The anchor addressed the camera. "We have no official statements yet from either local law enforcement or federal authorities, but we are receiving reports that the magic pulse that has caused widespread disruption and minor injuries was some sort of shockwave that seems to have originated from the northeast part of the city. We have crews en route to the scene now, and will bring you more information as we receive it."

Sean turned the TV volume down as a commercial came on. "A magic shockwave? Is that possible?"

"It's possible. All magic produces energy, but to create a pulse that powerful..." I shook my head. "It had to have been a *massive* coordinated attack."

"An attack on what, though?" Sean asked. "The northeast side is mainly residential. What was the target?"

I heard the coffee pot gurgling and headed back to the kitchen. "You want a cup?"

"Definitely," Sean said.

I poured two cups of coffee, added cream and sugar to mine, and returned to the living room just as Sean was turning up the volume again.

The television showed live aerial footage of a sprawling mansion—or what was left of it. Most of the building had collapsed and it looked like the doors and windows were gone on the section that still stood. People were running from the rubble, some helping others who had been injured. A caravan of vehicles was on its way down the driveway, heading away from the ruin toward a half-dozen ambulances, fire trucks, and police vehicles parked outside an enormous gate.

The news anchor spoke. "Channel Five has learned that the epicenter of the magic pulse is a residence believed to belong to local businessman Darius Bell. As you can see from our live footage, there appears to be significant damage to the home and surrounding buildings. We have been told that emergency personnel are not being allowed to enter the property at this time. We do not yet have any information about casualties or the cause of the disaster."

I stared at the screen, dumbfounded. I could think of only one possible explanation for the devastation: after months of small-scale attacks on Bell's operation, Moses Murphy, my grandfather, had decided to declare open war by breaching Bell's wards and destroying his cabal headquarters. No wonder the shockwave had been so powerful; the blast that had broken the wards and demolished most of the building had to have been enormous.

I tried to estimate how many mages would have had to work together to create an attack on this scale. It would have to be dozens, and half or more of them would probably be incapacitated or dead after breaking the wards. I had no doubt Bell would have had landmines and cascades embedded in his wards designed to kill anyone who tried to break them. Moses had sent those mages to their deaths.

"Alice?"

I realized Sean was talking to me, and judging by his tone, it wasn't the first time he'd tried to get my attention. I tore my gaze away from the television and looked at him.

I don't know what my face looked like, but he took the coffee cups from my hands. "What's wrong?" he asked. "You're as white as a sheet. Sit down."

I remained standing, too horrified by what my grandfather had done to really process what Sean said. He set the coffee down on the floor, since I still had no other furniture other than the couch, and made me sit.

I had to say something to explain my reaction. "The wards around Bell's compound were powerful and deadly. Breaking them would have killed the mages who did it."

"What kind of magic could do that?" he asked.

"Earth magic; destabilize the ground, destroy the building. With that much power, I'm surprised any part of the house is still standing, but breaking the wards probably killed half the mages they brought in for the attack. Maybe they didn't have enough firepower left alive to finish the job."

"It had to have been the Murphy cabal." He rubbed my back. "They've been hitting Bell a lot lately. I've never seen anything like this, though." He jerked his head at the screen.

"No one has." Malcolm stared at the television. "Mages and cabals have always wondered if this kind of coordinated attack could be done, but no one's ever pulled it off until now."

"Maybe because no one was ever willing to sacrifice so many lives for one single strike." My voice was harsh.

I felt a spike of awe, horror, and anger that wasn't mine. Malcolm's emotions were leaking over to me. He floated back and forth, a sign of how unsettled he was. "Hey, you okay?" I asked him.

"I used to live there," he said quietly. "They had me in the east wing of the house for the last year I belonged to the cabal."

We watched the news for the next hour. Sean and I sat on the couch with Rogue curled up at our feet while Malcolm floated around the room, obviously upset but not wanting to talk.

It didn't take long for the national news networks to pick up the story, so Sean switched back and forth between several channels as we tried to find out what was happening. There was a lot of speculation but no real answers, other than what we could see occurring live at Bell's compound.

I wondered how long Bell's people were going to be able to keep police and federal agents from entering the property. There were dozens of them camped out on the road in front of the gate; I saw members of the ATF, FBI, SPEMA, and local and state law enforcement personnel. I supposed it was a question of how long it would take to find a judge willing to sign a warrant.

Just how much Bell did not want law enforcement poking around in his compound became evident when aerial footage of the scene showed all of Bell's people moving away from what was left of the house and heading for the gate.

I stood up and walked toward the television, Sean right behind me. "What's going on?" he asked.

"They're going to blow it up," I said.

The camp of waiting law enforcement must have come to the same conclusion, because it suddenly became a hive of activity. Men and women representing various agencies began running or taking cover behind their vehicles as the last remaining cabal personnel left the compound. The news helicopters moved to a safe distance.

Rather than the massive explosion law enforcement feared—and the news media no doubt hoped for—it was a controlled demolition that began in the center of the C-shaped building with a fireball that spread toward the ends in a series of smaller detonations. In about fifteen seconds, the entire main building was a burning ruin. Three smaller buildings went up after that, reduced quickly to smoking rubble.

"I guess they really didn't want the cops to get in there," I said when the explosions stopped.

"So, what now?" Sean asked.

"Bell will regroup and strike back at Murphy, back in Baltimore and wherever he can find anyone affiliated with the Murphy cabal. Meanwhile, Murphy's probably already on to phase two of the plan. It wouldn't surprise me if there's another attack on Bell before the day is out."

"The city's about to become a war zone," Malcolm said grimly.

I watched the burning remains of Bell's compound. "And we're all going to be caught in the middle."

Sean was hungry, so I ordered Chinese food. While we waited for it to arrive, Malcolm disappeared into the basement to deal with his complicated feelings about watching his former prison blow up, and I took a shower and got dressed.

I got back downstairs just as Sean returned from taking Rogue for a walk. "Hey, that reminds me," I said.

He unclipped the leash from Rogue's collar. "We need to talk about your backyard."

I went to the back door with Sean and Rogue behind me. As I unlocked the door, the dog growled, which surprised me. Rogue rarely growled.

When I stepped out onto the porch, I stopped and stared. "What the heck? Why is there a jungle in my backyard?"

A week ago, I'd had two large, empty flowerbeds I'd planned on filling when I got a chance. Both flowerbeds were now overflowing with plants no less than four feet tall, and some were even bigger. When I looked closer, I realized they were impossibly giant-sized versions of the flowers and plants I'd intended to grow.

And they were *moving*.

"So, I wanted to surprise you," Sean began.

I gaped at the swaying mass of vaguely menacing greenery. "Well, you nailed it."

He sighed. "You worked so hard getting these flowerbeds built and then you were too busy to plant anything, so a couple of days ago I went and bought the plants you had on your list and put them in. When I came back the next day to water the plants, they seemed bigger already, but I decided it had to be my imagination. The day before yesterday, they were huge and I realized it *wasn't* my imagination. I decided I needed to do something before the situation got any more out of hand. I tried to pull one out of the ground and it bit me."

My eyebrows shot up. "The *plant* bit you?"

He showed me his forearm. There, a few inches above his wrist, was a semi-circular scar.

I touched the scar as if to convince myself it was real. Despite all the fights he'd been in, Sean had few scars thanks to his shifter healing abilities and the ones he did have were from particularly severe injuries. And yet, somehow, a plant had wounded him badly enough to leave a scar.

While I was processing my shock, he continued, "It also made me sick for a couple of hours. It felt like I had a bad case of the flu, and I almost never get sick because of my shifter immune system. Meanwhile, the plants just kept growing and growing. Also, they eat birds. At this point, they could probably eat the dog if he got too close, or any strays that happened to get into the yard."

I headed down the porch steps and crossed my backyard with Sean at my side. As I approached, I felt a caress of dark magic and the plants leaned toward me, their leaves shivering in excitement.

"Hungry, are you?" I said dryly.

"Do you know what the hell is going on?" Sean asked.

"Oh, yes. I suppose this is my fault—well, part of it—but I didn't think you'd be doing any gardening back here. I should have warned you not to. I'm sorry you got hurt."

I reached out and one of the plants bent down toward my hand. Sean grabbed my arm. "Watch out."

"It's okay. I'm going to let them know who's boss."

Reluctantly, he let go. Wisps of black, red, and purple blood magic danced on my fingers. The plant bent down and rubbed gently against my hand like a cat.

He gaped. "What the hell?"

"This was going to be my blood garden," I said as the plant caressed my hand. "Well, I guess it still is, but it looks like my magic wasn't the only magic that got into the flowerbeds."

"Your *what* garden?"

"A garden is full of life energy. My plan was to plant a garden to help feed energy into my house wards and that I could draw from if I needed to, in case trouble came knocking at my door again. I infused the soil with my blood magic."

"When you say you 'infused' your blood magic into the soil, you mean...?"

"I mixed my blood, full of magic, with the soil. My blood and magic is in these plants."

He stared at me for a full five seconds. "So, who the hell else's magic got in here?" he asked finally.

"Whose blood did we spill back here, right before I put in the flowerbeds?"

His mouth became a grim line. "Scott Grierson's demon father, Ravan."

"Yup. Demon blood, demon magic. I burned up his blood but there must have been some residual magic left behind."

"So, now we've got demon plants." He frowned at my garden. "What are you going to do with a backyard full of bloodthirsty little Audrey Twos?"

"Audrey Twos?"

"*Little Shop of Horrors?*"

"Oh yeah, the man-eating plant. Very funny. Can I get a drop of blood?"

He eyed me.

"I need them to know that you're not food," I said.

He produced a pocketknife and cut the pad of his thumb. I smeared his blood on my fingers, then let the plant caress my hand. When I moved back, my fingers were clean. The plants made a sound like a sigh.

Sean shook his head. "Of all the weird shit I have seen in my life, this is by far the weirdest. What about the dog?"

"Don't worry; I'll make sure he's safe too. Hold out your hand."

He crossed his arms defiantly.

"Come on, you can trust me," I wheedled.

"It's not *you* I don't trust." He grudgingly let me take his hand and reach out toward the garden.

The plant leaned down and brushed against his skin. Sean held perfectly still as it ran its leaves over our entwined hands. The garden rustled.

"See? That wasn't so bad, was it?" I asked him.

He kissed my forehead. "So, you're going to keep your demon garden, huh?"

"I think so. There's a lot of power in it, and if I put wards up, no one will accidentally get eaten. Plus, it might come in handy. You never know when we might need to get rid of a body."

He stared at me.

"I'm kidding," I added.

"I kinda feel like you aren't," he said.

The wards tingled and Rogue barked inside the house. "Oh, hey, I think the food's here," I said. "Maybe the garden would like some sweet and sour chicken."

Sean snorted as we headed toward the back porch. "Better that than werewolf, mage, or dog. If there are any leftovers, the garden is welcome to them, I guess."

Behind us, the plants rustled and sighed.

3

After we ate, Sean and I spent the remainder of the afternoon and early evening watching the news and waiting for the other shoe to drop, but it never did.

I had no doubt Moses was planning another attack on Bell, but for whatever reason, he didn't strike again immediately, either because he'd lost more mages in the first attack than he'd planned to and didn't have the manpower, or because he didn't have the right target. Either way, I figured it was only a matter of time.

We found the news channel with the best coverage and turned the volume down to a murmur. Live footage of the smoldering ruins of Bell's compound—now surrounded by emergency vehicles and being doused by fire trucks—alternated with announcers recapping the events and interviewing a series of law enforcement and civilian experts on cabals and magic who offered various theories about how the attack had been planned and carried out. No one wanted to guess at how many mages had died breaking the wards, or how many were needed to destroy the compound. It didn't escape my notice that no one explicitly called out Moses as orchestrating the attack.

I took some solace from the fact my grandfather was not in the city; the news showed him making himself conspicuously visible in Baltimore while his people attacked Bell on the other side of the country. No doubt he'd sent one of his lieutenants to run things in his stead. I wondered how many of the lieutenants I'd known five years ago were still alive. Moses tended to go through them fairly quickly, and when he terminated someone's employment, it wasn't with two weeks' notice and severance pay.

I was concerned about Malcolm, who hadn't come back up from the basement, but I gave him space. He'd talk when he was ready.

As the evening wore on, I went from sitting next to Sean on the couch to lying down with my head in his lap while he rubbed my back. I was fighting sleep, but it was a losing battle, thanks to the stress of the last few weeks, getting very little rest, and being short on blood by a pint or so.

Then Sean's hand slid under my top and suddenly I was a whole lot less tired.

I rolled onto my back and looked up at him. It had gotten dark and we'd left the lights off, so the only illumination was from the TV. His eyes glowed softly. "You feel like going upstairs?" he asked.

"I dunno...I'm really comfortable," I said, feigning indifference.

He grinned and my heart skipped a beat. "Let me see if I can pique your interest," he murmured.

His hand moved under my top and stroked my stomach, making it flutter, before moving to my breast. I couldn't stop my sharp intake of breath, or the instant reaction low in my belly that made his nostrils flare and his eyes go golden.

I rolled to my feet and returned to the couch to straddle his lap, running my fingers through his hair as I kissed him deeply. He gripped my butt tightly and pulled me close, then slid his hands up my back toward my bra.

I broke our kiss and leaned back. "We should go upstairs. I don't want to scandalize Malcolm if he comes up from the basement."

"We may scandalize him anyway," he warned me, his eyes glittering. "I hope you don't expect to stay quiet. I intend to be a *very* bad wolf."

Before I could respond, Sean's phone rang from somewhere in the couch. He swore and dug in between the cushions until he found it. The screen said *Jack Hastings*.

"My beta," he said. He answered the call. "This is Sean."

I heard the growly voice on the other end say, "It's Caleb again."

I climbed off Sean's lap. He stood and paced in front of the couch as he listened. Finally, he asked, "Is he back at his apartment or with you?"

A terse response.

"Let's meet over there, then. We have to talk to him, find out what the hell is going on. I'm on the east side, so it'll take me about a half-hour to get there. Go easy on him until we find out how it started. I'm on my way." He disconnected.

I went over to him. "Pack troubles?"

"I'm sorry," he said, putting his phone in his pocket. "Caleb's a nineteen-year-old kid who got bitten while he was out running a couple of months ago and is having a hard time adjusting. We took him into our pack hoping to help him adapt, but we're not having much luck keeping him out of trouble. He keeps getting into fights and shifting in public."

I grimaced. Shifting in public was a quick way to get shot by law enforcement or an armed citizen, and behavior like that would bring a lot of trouble to Sean's pack. "Go take care of your people."

"It will probably take a while." He rubbed his face. "Damn it."

"It's okay. I'm going to turn in early and try to get a full night's sleep. Will you have to work tomorrow?"

"I have some meetings in the morning, but I'll probably be free in the afternoon," he said. "I'll text you and let you know what my schedule looks like."

"Okay. Be careful."

"You too." He kissed me thoroughly. "I'm glad you're home."

"I'm glad to *be* home." I walked him to the door, then waved from the front porch as he backed down my driveway.

I took Rogue to the front yard to do his business, then fed him in the kitchen and left him to eat dinner while I went out to the backyard and spent a half-hour putting wards around the flowerbeds to keep the dog from getting eaten. The aversion spells would keep both people and animals away while I figured out how to address my garden's dietary needs.

When the wards flared, the garden rustled. It sounded disgruntled. "No dog for you," I told the plants firmly. "And no trying to eat the werewolf either. He may be delicious, but he's mine." More unhappy rustling.

When I got back inside, I found Rogue sitting expectantly by the back door. I turned off the television and all the lights except for the one in the kitchen.

After a moment's hesitation, I opened the door to the basement and called out, "Good night, Malcolm."

"Good night," he replied. He sounded better than before, which was a relief.

I shut the door and Rogue and I went upstairs. The dog settled onto his bed by the window while I changed into pajamas.

It wasn't even ten o'clock, but I was exhausted. I brushed my teeth, turned off the lamp, and crawled into bed. In minutes, I was sound asleep.

Alice, let us in. The sharp command cut through my deep, dreamless sleep like a scythe.

I was on my feet and halfway to my bedroom door before I was awake enough to realize what I was doing.

Charles? I asked in my head, groggy and confused. The clock on my nightstand said it was a little after three.

We are outside your residence and must speak to you. Charles's voice in my head vibrated with urgency.

I threw a cardigan on over my tank top and hurried downstairs with Rogue on my heels.

Malcolm waited in the foyer. "That creepy vamp is outside. You want me to go tell Sean that he's here?"

"Not yet. Let me find out what's going on. Please stay in the basement for now."

Malcolm shimmered as he passed through the closed basement door and the wards that protected it. Just to be on the safe side, I shut Rogue in the downstairs bathroom. I dropped my house wards and opened the front door.

A black SUV was parked in my driveway. The driver's door opened and a Vampire Court enforcer I didn't know emerged. As he opened the rear door for Charles, the front passenger door opened and a tall blonde woman stepped out.

At first, I thought she was another enforcer, but she didn't come around the vehicle to stand beside Charles. Instead, she scanned the yard, then looked over the house. When her gaze finally met mine, her brow arched. In her black leather jacket and tall boots, she looked like she'd just stepped off the cover of *Badass Weekly*, and I was suddenly aware that I was wearing pajamas with sheep on them.

I didn't have a chance to worry about what my choice of sleepwear was doing to my street cred because Charles was suddenly on my porch in a puff of air. I gasped.

The front of his suit was soaked with blood and his hands and face were streaked with it. He looked livid. He was also extremely pale, even by vampire standards.

"We must get inside." His voice was flat.

I stepped back and they all filed into the house. I shut the door and locked it, then raised my wards.

When I reached for the light switch, the male enforcer snapped, "Leave the lights off." He went into the living room and yanked the curtains closed. The blonde woman took up a position near the door.

Whatever the hell was going on, I wasn't accustomed to being given orders in my own home. My eyes narrowed as I turned to the blonde woman. "Who are you?"

"Arkady Woodall, Vampire Court investigator."

So this was one of the new full-time investigators the Court had hired after I turned the job down. She looked to be about my age and was a little taller than me, with the grace and lean muscle of a fighter.

We shook hands. "Arkady?" I asked.

The corners of her mouth turned up. "Arkady."

I jerked a thumb at the enforcer looming in the living room doorway. "And who's Mr. Sunshine?"

He made a noise like truck gears grinding. "Matthias."

I turned my attention back to Charles. "What happened? Are you hurt? Where's Bryan?"

"This is not my blood. Bryan Smith has been shot and Fortune is dead," Charles said.

The words hit me like a punch in the gut. "*What?*"

"Kent Stevens ambushed our vehicle as we arrived home an hour ago." Charles shook with anger as he paced around my foyer. "We were coming from a meeting at one of my businesses. Fortune was driving and Bryan and I were in the back. When we got to the gate, it jammed instead of opening. Fortune began to retreat when Stevens opened fire with an automatic weapon. Bryan was shot six times; five bullets in his torso, and one grazed his head. Fortune was shot twice in the head. I could do nothing to save him."

I made a choked sound.

Charles stopped pacing and turned to me. His eyes were black and his fangs were out. "I was able to heal Bryan's injuries and he is resting now. Adri is with him."

Rage built inside me like a tidal wave and I struggled to rein it in. "What happened to Stevens? Tell me he's dead."

He shook his head. "He deployed countermeasures and evaded my enforcers. I had to choose between saving Bryan's life or pursuing our attacker. I chose to stay. By the time Bryan was stabilized, Stevens was gone."

"Bryan's life was more important." I took a shaky breath and tried to make sense of what Charles was telling me, but it wasn't computing. How could Fortune be dead? I'd spoken with him less than twenty-four hours ago. He'd driven me home after I was done giving my statement to Agent Marshall. He'd sat in my driveway and watched to make sure I got safely into my house before he drove away. I hadn't known him long, but I'd liked him.

Bryan, on the other hand, I had known for years. Things hadn't always been amicable between us because his loyalty was to Charles and the Court, which meant I'd been furious at him more than once, but he'd ripped off his own shirt to keep me from bleeding out on Mike Robinson's living room floor. I took a deep, shuddering breath.

"My enforcers who gave chase tell me Stevens was unusually fast and strong for a human," Charles said. "They suspect Stevens may have been drinking vampire blood."

At first, I was startled; Stevens had made no secret of his hatred of vamps, but that didn't mean he wouldn't use their blood to enhance his strength and speed. It would certainly help explain how he managed to evade capture twice. I'd credited adrenaline and training for the first escape, but two successful getaways meant the enforcers' assessment was probably accurate. I wondered if he'd been drinking expensive black-market bottled vampire blood or if he'd been draining and killing vamps we didn't know about. No doubt Charles had people already looking into that possibility.

He started pacing again. I'd never seen him so agitated. "I can find no trace of Stevens. His trail ended by the side of the road. He may have had a vehicle parked or been picked up by a confederate. The Court has dispatched Hunters to locate him. He will not be at liberty for long, and when he is found he will certainly suffer greatly for everything he has done."

I went into the kitchen and ran a towel under hot water. I brought it back to Charles, who accepted it and began cleaning the blood off his face.

"You are in danger. Stevens tried to kill you once already," he said as he scrubbed dried blood off his pale skin.

"He doesn't know who I am," I reminded him. "He only knows me as Julie Day from Denver. I assume you've got people combing the city looking for him, in addition to the feds who are looking."

"We have deployed surveillance teams to Stevens's home, the quarry where he and Michael Robinson worked, and the homes of his immediate family members and friends, as well as your home and mine. The Court has committed its resources to finding him."

"Then you've done all you can until he turns up. With so many people looking for him, he won't get far."

Charles hissed. He dropped the towel, spun, and put his fist through the wall with a force that demolished the drywall, splintered the stud behind it, and punched through to the other side. Rogue started barking and scratching at the bathroom door.

I was too startled by his uncharacteristic outburst to object before he spoke. "It is my fault," Charles snarled, his back to me. "We should not have allowed him to escape us at Robinson's house. We should have anticipated he would have an exit strategy in place and been more prepared for him to attack. I should—" He cut himself off.

I wondered if he'd been about to say that he should have left Bryan to die and chased Stevens down instead of staying behind to save his enforcer. No doubt other vampires would have done so. I wondered if he would face criticism from the Court for his decision.

Saving Bryan was the right choice, I told him through our telepathic link. Out loud, I said, "Charles, this not your fault. You can't expect to foresee every eventuality."

"There is a man dead because of me," he ground out.

"There is a man dead because of *Kent Stevens*. There is a man *alive* because of you," I corrected him as I picked up the wet towel. His hand was already healing, the cuts closing and bones knitting back together as I watched.

I took his hand and cleaned off the fresh blood. "I know you feel like you have to blame yourself and maybe I would too in your position, but we both know it's not going to help. All that matters now is catching the bastard. Put your anger into that instead of remodeling my house."

He stared at the hole in my wall as if he didn't remember making it. "I apologize for my outburst. I will have this repaired immediately."

"I know you'll take care of it."

Charles let me finish cleaning his hands. I wiped the towel down the front of his suit, but it didn't seem to make much of a difference. There was so much blood.

"Bryan will be all right." I wasn't sure if I was reassuring him or myself.

"Yes," he said firmly. "Bryan is far stronger than a normal human. He has healed and received transfusions. He will be on his feet later today and on duty by tonight."

"What about you? You're pale. You didn't even stop to change or have a meal to regain your strength before you came over here." I was surprised he hadn't brought someone in the vehicle he could drink from on the way to my house. Strange that Arkady Woodall hadn't supplied him with a meal, but perhaps that was outside the scope of her job description.

"I needed to warn you immediately that Stevens had attacked us and escaped."

"You could have sent someone else to do that, or called," I pointed out.

"Perhaps I needed to see for myself that you were safe." Charles's eyes searched my face. "Come with me until he is captured."

My stomach knotted at the thought. "No way. I'm not letting you lock me away."

"I must protect you, Alice."

"I don't need protection," I countered. "I'll be fine. Stevens has no idea who I am. He knows who *you* are. You need to stay somewhere that's well-protected until he's caught. You shouldn't even be here."

"He has proven himself to be highly resourceful. He has access to weapons and other equipment, including whatever he used to sabotage my gate. I have the ability to heal, but you do not. My home is secure; yours is not. Stevens took the time to shoot you before he escaped Robinson's house. At least permit me to give you bodyguards."

"I won't take any of your people away from protecting you. Bryan won't be back to one hundred percent for at least a couple of days. You need your guards and I'm not defenseless."

"Stevens is a killer. Refusing protection would be foolhardy. I do not think you are foolish."

I understood his desire to safeguard a Court asset from the threat Stevens represented, but I didn't need a protector, least of all one sent by the Court to stick their nose into my life, and his insistence grated on my nerves. "I can't do my job if I have a babysitter. More to the point, I'm not going to give up my freedom and my job on the off chance he's out there gunning for me."

"Based on his record and psych profile, I think it's more than an off chance he'll come looking for you," Arkady interjected.

"Even so, I'm a private investigator. I can't work if I have an entourage."

"Adri Smith has a PI license. She could accompany you," Charles said. "I would find that acceptable."

I gritted my teeth. "Adri's place is with her brother while he recovers. With Bryan injured, she's even more essential for your safety."

Charles looked stubborn. I'd have to come up with an answer to the problem before he decided to insist on doing things his way and I had to insist that he get the hell out of my house.

As much as I despised the situation, there might be an option I could live with that didn't involve having a Vampire Court enforcer dogging my every step. Dealing with this type of scenario was Maclin Security's bread and butter. Sean and I worked well together. He'd be an asset in the field, if his schedule allowed for him to take me as a client. Considering the antagonism between them, Charles might not like my idea, but it wasn't his decision to make.

"I'll ask Sean to provide security, if he has the manpower available," I told them. "You want me to have protection until Stevens is in custody, fine, but it's on my terms."

I was right; Charles plainly didn't like the idea of Sean as my bodyguard. His frown was thunderous.

"To be clear, I'm not asking your permission," I said. "This is my decision. I'm safe behind my wards for tonight. I'll call Sean in the morning and tell him the situation. If he's unavailable, I'll contact Adri and let her know what my backup plan is."

"I do not like this arrangement," Charles stated.

"Duly noted. But whatever else you may think of Sean, you can rest assured my safety will be his number-one priority." I was not happy to be forced into this, but at least it was me making the decisions and not Charles. "Please keep me updated on the manhunt."

"We will," the vampire said.

"Be safe," Arkady added.

I doubted Stevens would be able to connect "Julie Day" to me, but there was a chance. I hoped the vamps would deal with him before the former Marine could find me.

"Just catch the bastard," I told them.

"We will. He has much to answer for." Charles's eyes flashed silver.

I thought of Fortune and Bryan. Magic sparked on my fingers and a cold breeze blew over us. "Yes, he does."

It was almost four by the time Charles, Arkady, and Matthias finally left. I told Malcolm what had happened and asked him to strengthen the wards on the house and yard.

I let Rogue out into the backyard to go to the bathroom and watched him growl at the garden while it rustled ominously, then went back to bed and stared up at the ceiling, wide awake and thinking about Charles, Fortune, Bryan, and Kent Stevens. Though I tried to sleep, I was haunted by visions of Bryan, his body riddled with bullets, bleeding out on the side of the road while Stevens vanished into the night.

I thought about the fact that somewhere out there, right now, the former Marine was on the loose. Would he go after Charles? Continue with his mission to take out as many vampires as he could? Try to find me? Or would he run, knowing he was at the top of the vampires' Most Wanted list? There was nothing about Stevens that made me think he would skip town. No, he would probably find a place to hole up and then go on the offensive. As much as I didn't want to dwell on it, there was a good chance Charles and I were at the top of his hit list. As long as Charles stayed in a Vamp Court fortress, he would be virtually inaccessible. That left me.

The only people who knew Julie Day's real identity were Charles, Bryan, and Adri, and Valas and Niara of the Vampire Court. I felt reasonably certain Stevens would not be able to find me, but nagging doubt made my stomach churn.

Around five, I gave up trying to sleep and got up. I showered, dried my hair, and got dressed in a T-shirt and an old pair of jeans. I dug out a broom and dustpan and cleaned up the drywall and pieces of wood on the floor in my foyer and started a load of laundry. Rogue followed me around the house for a while, then settled into his bed in the living room and dozed.

Malcolm had been hard at work since Charles and the others left; the house wards felt supercharged and prickled on my skin. I made sure all the curtains were closed and stayed away from the windows. The knot of worry in my stomach was giving way to anger. I was already starting to feel like a prisoner in my home. I resolved to go furniture shopping today, Kent Stevens be damned.

Sean had stocked my refrigerator for me, so I actually had food to eat. I was drinking orange juice and scrambling some eggs for an early breakfast when Malcolm came up from the basement.

"Hey," he said somberly.

"Hey yourself. Nice job on the house wards."

"Nobody's getting in here. Anyone who tries is going to need a hospital or the morgue." I felt a surge of anger and magic from my ghost.

I stirred my eggs and threw in some chopped ham. "You doing okay?"

He sighed. "Yeah. Sorry I've been hiding out."

"Don't worry about it. If you need space, I understand. I know this has got to be weird for you."

"Do you know how many times I've fantasized about seeing that place destroyed?" he blurted out.

I thought about my own fantasies of watching my grandfather's cabal compound burn to the ground. "I can guess."

"I feel like I shouldn't be glad about it, but I am."

"Of course you are. They held you prisoner, tortured you to make you hurt other people, and killed you. You're entirely justified in how you feel. The only thing that could have made it better was if Bell himself died in the attack."

"How do you know he didn't?"

"Nobody panicked afterward. The evacuation was controlled, the security force didn't let anyone into the property, and the demolition went like clockwork. That says Bell is still alive and calling the shots. He's in a bunker somewhere, planning a counterstrike and waiting to see what Murphy will do next."

After a few moments, Malcolm said, "So, are you going back to work?"

"Yes. I'm not going to cower in the house. I doubt Stevens will be able to find me—there's really no way for him to connect 'Julie Day' to me. I can't be scared of him, Malcolm." I dumped the eggs on a plate.

"You're not scared of much."

Heh. It was nice that he thought so.

Malcolm went back to the basement to work. I ground some fancy coffee beans and brewed what had to be the single best-smelling pot of coffee I'd ever made in my life.

While the coffeemaker gurgled happily, I went upstairs and got my laptop. I took my coffee mug and breakfast to the couch and prepared my invoice for the Vampire Court while Rogue snoozed by the back door, lying on his back and snoring.

When I added everything up, I blinked at the total and double-checked the math to make sure I had the decimal in the right place. When the numbers added up, I sent the invoice to the Court's Accounts Payable clerk—yes, the vampires had accountants—and received a confirmation that it would be processed immediately.

By the time I put the clothes in the dryer, made my bed, and tidied the kitchen, it was after six and the sun was up. I took my phone to the living room.

I sat on the couch as I drank another cup of coffee and fumed. I didn't like having to mix my personal and professional lives yet again, but I couldn't see any better option. Finally, I decided to bite the bullet and called Sean's cell.

He answered on the second ring. "Hey, babe." His early-morning voice had a hint of growl and it made my pulse speed up.

"Hey," I said, aiming for casual. "Sorry to call while you're getting ready for work."

"What's wrong?" Sean's tone changed immediately. Evidently my voice wasn't as neutral as I'd hoped.

I sighed. No matter how I downplayed the danger, this was going to bring the overprotective alpha werewolf out in him.

"Alice, what's going on?" His voice was sharp.

"I have a…situation," I said slowly. "What's your schedule looking like today?"

4

An hour later, Sean stood in my foyer looking decidedly grim, a heavy, oversized black duffel bag in each hand and a matching backpack on his shoulder.

"It's not that big of a deal," I said for the umpteenth time as I closed the door and locked it. "This is purely a precautionary measure." I adjusted the curtain in the front window.

"Stay away from the windows," he said automatically. He noticed the hole in my wall. "What the hell happened there?"

"Charles was pretty upset. He's going to fix it."

"I should hope so." He carried his bags into the living room, where he put them down carefully on the hardwood floor. "Where's Rogue?"

"In the backyard. Don't worry; I've got wards around the garden." I went to the back door and opened it. The dog galloped inside and jumped up on Sean.

"No," Sean said firmly and pointed to the floor. "Sit."

Rogue sat, his tongue hanging out.

Sean chuckled and scratched the dog's head. He looked around the living room and sighed. "We have to get you a coffee table and some chairs. The *dog* has more furniture than you do."

Rogue went to his bed and plopped down with a heavy thump.

"I was actually planning on going furniture shopping today."

"You're not going out, not for that," Sean stated. "We can shop online and have everything delivered."

I frowned at him. "Sean Maclin, you are not going to tell me what I can and cannot do. You are not going to take over my life, and I am not buying furniture *online* without trying it out first."

He crossed his arms, straining the shoulders of his polo shirt as it stretched over his muscles. "I had a feeling you weren't giving me the straight story on this Kent Stevens, so I called Adri Smith on my way over here and she sent me his file. This is serious,

Alice. Stevens is a highly trained Marine. He got the drop on two enforcers and nearly killed both of them, and he's already shot you once."

I scowled.

Sean's gaze was intense. "You cannot hold back key information like that. I can't protect you if I don't know what I'm up against."

I had to admit he was right, but that didn't mean I had to like it. "Fine."

He cupped my cheek. "I know you hate needing help. You hate when people worry about you and you hate feeling vulnerable. I don't want to make this any harder on you than it already is, but you can't keep things back from me. You call the shots on your cases, but when it comes to keeping you safe, you're going to have to let me do my job—which I'm actually pretty good at, by the way."

The corner of my mouth turned up in a wry half-smile. "Can I get you some coffee?"

"That would be great. Then I want to hear everything you know about this guy. Adri said to tell you the Vampire Court has amended the confidentiality agreement you signed so that you can read me in on the entire operation. They're sending the paperwork over by courier for you to sign."

"Okay." I went into the kitchen and came back with two cups of coffee.

Sean was unzipping the duffel bags when I returned. My jaw fell open. "What is all that?"

"Sensors for the doors, windows, and yard. I know you have wards, but I'm going to take extra precautions. There's also a couple of panic buttons and some other goodies."

"What about the backpack?"

He unzipped it and pulled out a bulletproof vest. "It's the latest technology. It's as light as they can make them, and it will go under your clothes. They're actually pretty comfortable."

I rubbed my forehead.

"Alice." He stood, his eyes serious. "Please wear it when we go out."

At least I would be allowed to leave the house. Fantastic.

A courier arrived while Sean was bringing in the rest of his stuff. After I signed the updated confidentiality agreement, Sean and I settled on the couch with our coffee. He took out his laptop to take notes and look at the files Adri had sent.

I took a deep breath. "So, here's the story. In the days following the bombing, it became obvious that SPEMA, the FBI, and the ATF had bigger and more serious cases that needed their attention. There were riots and fires and people were getting hurt. The bombing was basically a property crime and no one was injured as far as the feds knew, so it got back-burnered in favor of more pressing cases, ones that were getting more public pressure because they involved injuries to humans."

"And so the vamps decided to solve it themselves," he guessed.

"Bingo. The only evidence besides what was left of the bomb itself was the van the bombers used, but it was stolen and burned, so other than some traffic cam footage of it leaving the crime scene, that didn't give us much. One thing the ATF did determine was the bomb's design didn't match anything in the federal database. The silver flechettes used as shrapnel were unusual, but the bomb's components were too generic to be of any help. Without physical evidence, we had to look elsewhere for leads, so we turned to the online forums."

"Whose idea was that?"

"Kim Dade, the Vamp Court data analyst who helped us catch the West-Addison harnad."

Kim and I had spent nearly two weeks combing through discussion threads looking for posts about the bombing. We ended up reading thousands of hate-filled, disturbing posts, many of which either advocated violence against vamps, mages, and supes, or boasted about actual crimes. The worst were those directed toward potential female victims. Those gave me nightmares.

It had been a rough time for Sean, as my anger mounted along with his frustration that I couldn't tell him what I was working on for the Court. I did talk to Malcolm and Adri, but the case was like a wall between Sean and me. He weathered my moodiness with the patience of a man used to dealing with a pack full of volatile werewolves.

On the plus side, we'd both enjoyed blowing off steam in the bedroom—or wherever else we happened to be when the mood struck us—so it wasn't all bad. Some mornings we'd both had to drag ourselves to work looking a little worse for wear, but it was hard to be mad about it.

Malcolm had complained about us "going at it like rabbits" until I reminded him that he'd wanted me back with Sean, so he shouldn't grumble about werewolf libido. Truth be told, I initiated sex as much as Sean, but he certainly never turned me down and I always wore out before he did.

Sean and I had installed a heavy bag in my guest room so I could take up kickboxing again. It helped me work off the lingering effects of being exposed to a meth-like drug called Black Fire. Lately, I'd needed it more to take out my fury at what Kim and I had to read in the discussion forums.

To deal with the stress, Kim had doubled up on her yoga classes. I tried that too, but there was too little punching involved for me to find it very helpful.

"You need to go punch the bag for a while?" Sean's tone was teasing, but his eyes were dark with concern.

I gave him a wry smile. "No, I'm good. Anyway, Kim and I spent a good week or so slogging through posts by bottom-feeding bigots before we found someone who claimed responsibility for the bombing. That suspect we quickly eliminated with a couple of questions. Same with the next several people who claimed responsibility. Then we found Andrew's post bragging about the bombing and I had a feeling we were onto something. He wouldn't give details, but the few he did reveal matched what we knew. We needed to make direct contact, but I couldn't do that as myself. I needed an alter ego and a plausible reason for seeking them out. So Julie Day was born, in a manner of speaking."

I described how the Vamp Court had supplied me with a complete fake identity. Julie Day supposedly worked for Human Future, a real anti-supe Human rights organization. She'd come to the city from her base of operations in Denver to meet with local activists willing to fight for the cause. It had taken some careful persuading, but Andrew finally put me in touch with Mike Robinson.

The group leader's ego made him laughably easy to manipulate with a classic "Mr. Big" sting. The operation involved baiting the alleged bombers with the possibility of joining Human Future, in hopes they'd confess to the bombing in an effort to impress me and my superiors at Human Future. It all went like clockwork, right up until it didn't.

"So, what went wrong?" Sean asked.

I explained the failed attempt to arrest the bombers. When I told him how Stevens had incapacitated us with a flash-bang and shot me, Sean's eyes blazed. "Let me see your shoulder," he said, his voice growly.

"You saw it already yesterday," I reminded him.

"Show me again."

I pulled my T-shirt off over my head. He lowered his head and ran his lips across my bare skin where I'd been shot. I shivered and moved my bra strap aside so he had unobstructed access to my shoulder, and his kisses became more insistent. He always managed to smell so good to me, that unmistakable scent of forest that made me forget everything else.

His hand slid between my thighs and rubbed along the seam of my jeans. He inhaled deeply and growled. I was suddenly acutely aware of how long it had been since we'd had sex and how much I'd missed the feeling of his hands on me.

I climbed into his lap and took his face in my hands. I kissed his mouth, then moved slowly across his jaw, enjoying the scratchiness of his stubble against my lips and chin. Sean nuzzled against me, breathing deeply. The feeling of his fingertips on my bare flesh made sparks run all the way to my toes. I moaned a little and nipped his ear. The forest scent intensified and I shivered again.

Just as I decided the rest of this conversation could wait until we ended our drought, Sean kissed me one last time and held me against his chest. "You know I want to tear your clothes off and finish what we just started, but I need to hear the rest of the story."

Clearly, I needed to work on my make-out skills if I wasn't able to distract a werewolf with sex. I sighed and moved off his lap, pulling the T-shirt back on and rearranging my clothes. "That's really all there is to tell. The Vamp Court enforcers came into the house and took out Robinson and the Davis brothers, but Stevens escaped out a back window to a vehicle he had waiting. Charles healed my wound and the feds arrived to take the others into custody. I gave the feds my statement and Fortune drove me home. That was the last time I saw him alive."

He tucked me under his arm and I rested my head on his chest. "I'm sorry about Fortune. I know you liked him. What else is bothering you about this case?"

I picked at my jeans. "Now that it's over, I expected to feel better, or at least have some satisfaction at a job well done. Instead, it feels like a completely Pyrrhic victory. Fortune is dead and Bryan almost was too. Robinson's wife is dead and so is Kent's brother. The Court is still looking into those murders but they may never know who was responsible. That's not right. It doesn't excuse what they did or what Stevens is doing, but he and Robinson have a right to be angry."

"Do you feel sorry for them?"

"For Robinson, a little. By all accounts, Samantha Robinson was a good person who was in the wrong place at the wrong time. Whatever else you can say about him, he loved her. I don't feel sorry for Andrew and Corey; their brother isn't dead or a victim of vampires, and if they can't accept him for who he is, then that's their choice and their loss. But as for Stevens..." Blood magic sizzled on my skin. Sean didn't let go, even though it had to hurt. "If the vamps get to him before the feds do, he'll never be found. I can't bring myself to feel sorry about that."

Sean growled low in his throat. "I'm pretty thoroughly disgusted with the vamps for letting Stevens get loose a second time. His training, combined with his access to military-grade weapons, means he's a very real threat. Everything points toward a very mission-oriented psychology. If he's gunning for you, we have to be concerned about that as much as his weapons ability and the fact he may have been drinking vampire blood."

I shook my head. "There's nothing linking me to Julie Day. I have no plans to go anywhere near Charles's house or any of his businesses. Stevens won't find me."

"Hopefully he won't, but we have to prepare in case he does. He's smart and resourceful, and he apparently has access to weapons and gadgets."

"That's what Charles said." I sighed and laid down on the couch, resting my head in Sean's lap.

He squeezed my hand. "Tell me what I can do to help."

"You're doing it." I closed my eyes. "It's been a rough couple of weeks."

"If you want to talk about what's on your mind, you know I'm here to listen."

"Thanks. That means a lot."

The radio on his belt beeped. "Mobile Team One to Alpha," a brisk male voice said.

Sean took the radio out. "Go ahead for Alpha."

"The temp team is gone and we're on duty."

"Ten-four." He set the radio on the arm of the couch.

"You have a mobile team outside?" I asked.

"Yes. This is a multi-person job. I need eyes watching for him while I'm protecting you up close. Vamp security will stay and watch your house while the mobile team shadows us." He read my expression. "We talked about this. You have to let me do my job."

"I understand why they're out there," I said quietly. "That's not what's bothering me. I feel crowded. I've lived alone for a long time, and all of a sudden there are people all around me, watching me."

He looked surprised, then thoughtful. "I hadn't thought of it like that, but I can see why you feel that way. I come from a big family and I'm a werewolf, so I'm used to being in a pack and I enjoy the feeling of closeness. I should have known you would be uncomfortable." He squeezed my hand.

My phone dinged. Sean dug it out of the couch cushions and handed it to me. I had a voicemail from my work number. I hit *Play* to listen to the message and heard a familiar male voice. "Hello, Alice. This is Aaron Riddell. One of my clients would like to meet with you. Please call me at your earliest convenience." He disconnected.

"Aaron Riddell of Riddell, Ives, and McAllen." Sean sounded surprised. "If not the best law firm in town, certainly the priciest. He didn't leave a number, though."

I sat up and stretched, feeling my back pop. "I've got his number; I've worked for a couple of his clients in the past."

At his expression, I added, "Don't look so astonished; some jobs are better suited for small-time MPIs than big firms. The people on Aaron's client list want small jobs handled quietly and it's hard to keep things confidential in a big firm. If he's calling me, someone's got a sticky situation they don't want anyone to know about."

He frowned. "I'm not sure how to feel about that."

"Well, *I* feel good about it. My fees are on a sliding scale and any referral I get from Aaron is automatically at the top of that scale. It will help offset the cost of the security you're providing."

He went still. "Alice, there is no way I would even think about charging you."

"And I'm not about to let you do all this for free," I countered. "This is a business arrangement. I didn't ask you to do this as a personal favor. I want invoices, time sheets, and so forth, the same as you would do for any client."

His eyes darkened. "We are keeping track of all that."

"Good."

"The Vampire Court is covering all expenses related to your security." The words were clipped.

I stood up and started to go to the window, then remembered I had to keep the curtains closed. I stopped in the middle of the room and stood with my back to him, my arms crossed.

He rose. "Are you angry because the Court is paying to provide personal security for you? Because that is ridiculous."

I spun around, but he cut me off. "Stevens escaped them not once but *twice* because they underestimated him. They feel responsible for putting you in danger and rightfully so. They may catch him an hour from now, or tomorrow, or next week, but in the meantime, they need their 'asset' kept safe." His eyes glowed softly golden. "But even if they weren't paying me a dime, I'd still be here because *I* need you to be safe. If the situation were reversed, you'd do the same."

"No, I wouldn't," I retorted. "I'd send you an invoice every single day and expect payment each Friday by noon."

We stared at each other. My lips twitched.

He chuckled and pulled me into his arms. "You are impossible," he said into my hair. "I am allowed to care about you, you know. The Court is protecting an asset. I am protecting my..." He hesitated. "My girlfriend."

I groaned. "'Girlfriend'? That makes us sound like we're in high school."

"What would you say, then?" He eyed me. "And don't say 'colleague.'"

I gave him a look. "You're not still holding a grudge about me calling you my colleague back when we first met, are you?"

"It's more like a running joke now, don't you think?"

I rolled my eyes. "I need to call Aaron back."

He sighed. "Fine, call the lawyer, but we're going to finish this conversation at some point soon."

I took my phone into the kitchen. He would be able to hear every word I said, but I could focus on the call without being distracted by my...whatever Sean was. Not boyfriend. Partner? Significant other? And what had he been about to call me, before he'd changed his mind?

I called Aaron's direct line and got his assistant, who transferred me.

When he came on the line, Aaron's voice was warm. "Alice, how are you?"

"Doing all right, Aaron. And you?"

"I'm on top of the world," the lawyer said. In the background, I could hear papers shuffling on his desk. "You busy this afternoon?"

"I just closed a big case, so I'm pretty open at the moment. What's the job?"

"I'll let my client discuss that with you. We are prepared to pay for a consultation. Same rate as before?"

"That's fine."

"I'll have a check waiting. Are you available to meet her at two?"

"Sure. At your office?"

"That would be ideal. As always, confidentiality and discretion are essential."

I hesitated. "I'll have someone with me."

"Who?" His voice sharpened.

"My personal security detail, Sean Maclin of Maclin Security."

"I know Maclin by reputation." Aaron pondered that. "I'll run it by the client, but I don't think it will be a deal-breaker as long as he agrees to the same terms of confidentiality."

"That will not be a problem."

"See you soon."

"Wait, who's the client?" I asked.

A pause. "Esther Aldridge."

My eyebrows went up. "Okay, I'll see you at two." We disconnected.

Sean came into the kitchen. "So, what's the job?"

"I don't know the details yet, but the potential client is Esther Aldridge."

"*The* Esther Aldridge?"

"Unless you know another one." I rinsed out my coffee mug and put it in the sink. "Aaron couldn't tell me what the case is about over the phone. In any case, I'll at least meet with Aldridge and get an idea of her situation before making a decision. If nothing else, it will keep me busy so I don't sit around wondering if Kent Stevens is going to pop up and shoot me again."

He jerked, his eyes shining gold. "Please don't joke about it." A muscle twitched in his jaw. "Every instinct in my body is telling me to keep you in this house until he's in custody. All I can think about is keeping you safe and how difficult it is going to be to protect you when the threat is a highly trained former Marine. My wolf is uneasy and that makes things difficult."

Though we'd only been seeing each other for a few months, Sean's wolf thought of me as his potential mate. As worried as Sean was, I could only imagine how much more displeasing the situation was for his furry half.

I put my hand on his arm and squeezed. "I'm sorry. I'm not trying to make this any harder on you than it already is."

He nuzzled my hair, which always seemed to soothe both him and his wolf. "I know you aren't. You say what you feel and you cope with everything the best way you know how."

"If I could stand to stay in my house to make this easier for you, I would, but I can't. Not after these last few weeks, and not after...everything else I've been through."

I'd been held a prisoner by my grandfather for twenty years. I'd never allow myself to be trapped again, not even if it meant Stevens might find me. Better that than give up my freedom. I couldn't explain any of that to Sean, so I shook my head to indicate that we'd run up against the part of my life that I had to keep hidden.

"It's okay. I don't need to know those secrets today." He kissed the top of my head. "If we're going out in a couple of hours, I'm going to get to work installing alarms on the windows and doors. When do we need to leave?"

"By one fifteen."

"Okay." He headed to the living room for his bag of gadgets.

I used an app on my phone to order a pizza and got my clean clothes out of the dryer. I took them upstairs and stayed out of Sean's way by puttering around cleaning for a while. When I came back down, he was finishing putting alarms on all the bottom-floor windows.

When the pizza arrived, we ate it sitting on the couch, curled up together. After the last slice was gone, I took the pile of dishes and trash to the kitchen.

I rinsed the plates, then put the trash in the can and wiped my hands on a towel. "I'm going downstairs to work on spellwork with Malcolm. I'll be back up in about an hour. Don't try to come down; if you need me, shoot me a text."

A pause. "Okay."

When we were first together, I'd given him access through my basement wards, but revoked it later and never restored his privileges. Right now, I needed a refuge, and with Sean in the house, the only place I could retreat to was the basement.

I could feel his gaze on me as I opened the basement door and the wards sizzled on my skin. "Coming down!" I called.

"Clear!" Malcolm's voice floated up to me.

I paused and looked back at Sean, where he was standing in the middle of my living room. "Hey, thank you for doing all this for me."

He smiled and some of the tension eased out of my shoulders. "Of course. Whatever you need, you know I'm here for you."

"I know." I headed down the stairs and gently closed the door behind me.

My basement was part library and part magic workshop. Like most mages, I had a collection of books on magic theory, history, and practice, Though more books were becoming available in e-reader format these days, most older and more esoteric titles were only available in hard copy. The large open space of the workshop contained several storage cabinets, a work table, and three concentric circles inlaid into the floor.

When I got to the bottom of the steps, Malcolm was in the spellwork area. "I got a call about a potential case," I told him. "Not sure what it's about yet, but I have a client meeting in a couple of hours and then I'll let you know what I find out."

"Sounds good." He met me halfway across the floor. "You doing okay?"

"I'm good. Do you have time to spar?"

"Sure. What do you want to work on?"

"It's been a while, so how about we warm up with some basic defense?"

"Okay. *En garde.*" Malcolm floated to the right. I shifted my weight and watched him closely.

Suddenly, he vanished. A flash of bright green to my left; I threw up a protective shield and Malcolm's bolt of earth magic crackled against it. I scowled and dropped the shield. "Faster, Malcolm. Don't hold ba—"

Zzzap! I yelped and staggered as his bolt hit me in the small of my back.

"Are you okay?" he asked from behind me.

I spun and lashed out with my cold fire whip. He vanished before it could touch him. Another zap to my left side. I stumbled, wincing, and reached out with my senses. I felt his presence to my right and threw up a shield just in time to intercept his magic bolt. I dropped the shield, sensed him behind me, spun, and lashed him with the whip.

"Better." Malcolm's disembodied voice seemed to be to my right. I lashed out, but the bolt hit me from the left, searing a welt across my side.

"Son of a bitch!" I yelled. I took a deep breath and grimaced, touching the burn. The pain felt good. "More," I ordered. "Faster."

"Are you sure?" He materialized in front of me, looking concerned.

"Yes. I have got to get better. My life may depend on it."

"Okay, it's on." He vanished.

I waited until I sensed him to my left, then manifested my whip again and lashed out, intercepting a bolt in midair.

"Yes!" he yelled.

I laughed. "Keep 'em coming, ghost." *Zzzap.* "Ow! Damn it! Again!"

5

I opened the basement door and staggered out into the living room.

"I thought you were working on spellwork. What on earth have you been doing?" Sean was sitting on the couch, his phone in one hand and a small black key fob in the other. He stared disbelievingly at my tattered clothes and the dozens of small burns and welts all over my body. Rogue looked up from his dog bed, chuffed softly, and went back to sleep.

"Sparring practice with Malcolm," I said breathlessly, pulling the basement door closed and stumbling toward the stairs. "I really needed to blow off some steam and work on my magic defenses."

"Do you need help?"

"Nope, I'm good." I grabbed the banister and started dragging myself up the stairs. "I'm going to clean up and heal these burns, and then we'll be ready to go."

When I looked back, he was shaking his head, his attention back on his phone. I appreciated that he wasn't fussing over me. Maybe we were making progress with that.

I was back downstairs in thirty minutes, in my Armani suit and four-inch Louboutin heels, briefcase in hand. My wounds were healed, and I'd showered, put on makeup, and pulled my hair up in a neat French twist. Simple diamond earrings and my monogram pendant completed my outfit.

Sean was waiting for me in the kitchen, wearing a Maclin Security jacket over his shoulder rig. On the counter were the bulletproof vest and a couple of key fobs.

"You look lovely," he said, kissing me on the temple.

"Gotta look the part when you go to see Aaron Riddell or they won't let you past the front lobby. What's all this?"

He held up one of the key fobs. "Panic button with GPS locator, designed to look like a car remote. You can put one in your pocket, one on your keys, and stash the other two either in your house or your car." He handed me the fob. "What looks like the ignition button is actually a very loud alarm. The lock button dials my phone directly and transmits audio one-way from you to me and the unlock disconnects the call. The trunk release sends an alarm to my phone, and the car alarm is a silent all-hands-on-deck emergency distress call. I've got that one set up to go to my phone, my mobile team, and the vamps. They'll dispatch the closest pack of Hunters."

Hunters were dhampirs—half-vampires—with abnormally sharp senses of smell, sight, and hearing. They were also notoriously unstable, violent, and single-minded in pursuit of their targets and could go for a week or more without sleep or rest. If the vamps had committed multiple packs of Hunters, I doubted Stevens would be running around for very long unless he found a place to hole up and had someone to bring him food and supplies. All it would take is for one Hunter to catch his scent and they would likely be able to follow it directly to him. I would not want to be Stevens if and when the Hunters caught up to him. There was a very good chance he would be alive but not in one piece when they delivered him back to the vamps.

I looked over the panic button. It looked exactly like a car remote and even sported a Toyota insignia for additional camouflage. "Fancy," I said, tucking it into my jacket pocket. "I'll put one on my keys and figure out where to keep the others."

Sean picked up the bulletproof vest. I sighed. "I already have one."

"What kind?"

I took him to my storage room and showed him my vest, which he immediately deemed inadequate. "It's not designed to stop rifle rounds."

I poked at the vest he was holding. "This one is?"

"Yes. There are ballistic plates in the front and back."

"What about you?"

He pulled up his polo shirt and showed me his own vest. "Standard issue for everyone on the team."

Reluctantly, I took the vest from him. "Holy crap, this is heavy."

"Compared to the lightweight one you have, it is, but it's not nearly as heavy as it could be."

We went back to the kitchen and I took off my suit jacket and blouse. Sean unfastened one side of the vest and helped me put it on over my head. With practiced ease, he adjusted the Velcro fasteners on the sides and shoulders until the vest was snug. Without the ballistic plates, it might not have been too bad, but with them, it was far from comfortable. At least my posture would improve, I supposed.

I grimaced as I put my blouse and suit jacket back on. "Anything else?"

He kissed my forehead. "Not right now. Thank you for putting on the vest."

"If it makes you feel better, I suppose it's worth it."

He smiled and squeezed my hand. "I put Rogue out in the yard. Ready to go?"

"Yep." I picked up my briefcase and headed for the front door.

He pulled a small walkie-talkie radio from his belt. "Mobile team, we're heading out now. Are we clear? Over."

My stomach roiled. I wasn't sure why until I realized that on the rare occasions that I left Moses's compound in Baltimore, our security escort had gone through the same routine with the guards outside the gate. I pretended to check something inside my briefcase so Sean couldn't see my eyes.

A short pause, then the male voice replied, "Clear to go. Over."

"Ten-four." He stuck the radio back on his belt and moved to the door. "Stay between me and the house and let me open your car door for you. Once you're in, I'll go around to the driver's side."

"Okay. Ready when you are."

Sean opened the door, looked around, then stepped out onto the porch. I followed him, allowing him to shield my body with his as we stepped outside.

I didn't like the feeling of being guarded, for a lot of reasons, but my rational side knew that I would be safer with extra eyes watching my back. At least two of those eyes belonged to Sean, and that helped. It was the first time I'd seen him in professional bodyguard mode. As much as it rankled me to do so, I had to follow his instructions and let him do his job. I locked the door and hurried down the steps and over to his SUV, staying in his shadow. I felt furtive and jumpy, and I hated it.

Sean had the SUV unlocked and already running when we got to it. He opened the door, I climbed in, and he shut it firmly. As he was walking around to the driver's side, I closed my eyes and blew out a breath, feeling squashed inside the tight-fitting vest. I thought of the packs of Hunters combing the city for Stevens and wished they would hurry up. I hadn't been under Sean's protection for six hours and already I felt smothered.

Sean climbed into the SUV and buckled in. I followed suit and he backed out of my driveway. Another black SUV followed as we headed down the street. "That your mobile team?" I asked.

"Team One, the eight a.m. to four p.m. shift. Jack and Karen."

I remembered that he'd said some members of his pack worked for him at the security company. "Is that the same Jack who's your beta?"

He glanced at me. "Yes."

"How many of your employees are members of your pack?"

"Just four in the field: Jack, Karen, Karen's brother Patrick, and Phillip. Ben Cooper is my installation manager."

We drove for a while in silence. Finally, Sean said, "Adri told me if you wanted to take a vacation, there's a jet waiting at the airport to take us anywhere you want to go. First-class travel and accommodations for two, courtesy of the Court."

"I'm not running. If I want to take a vacation, I'll take one, but it won't be because of Kent Stevens."

"I figured you'd say that," he said wryly. "I thought I'd ask anyway."

"We have work," I reminded him. "Esther Aldridge, namesake of the Aldridge Art Museum, the Aldridge Concert Hall, and a half-dozen other buildings in town, has a problem that needs fixing."

"Can't wait to find out what it is." Sean's eyes moved constantly, checking his mirrors and scanning around the vehicle as we drove toward downtown and the offices of Riddell, Ives, and McAllen.

I was relieved and eager to be back at work after being on the bombing case for so long. It felt like one more step toward normalcy, even if I had a security detail.

We arrived at the office building at one forty-five and turned into the parking garage. Mobile Team One—Jack and Karen—pulled in behind us as Sean headed up the ramp. He found two empty spots on the second level near the elevators. The mobile team parked next to us, on my side.

"Same drill as before, in reverse," Sean said. "I'll come around to open your door. Stay next to me. I'm going to introduce you to Jack and Karen and then Karen will stay here while Jack comes with us." He touched my hand. "Don't look Jack in the eye for more than a few seconds. His wolf is very dominant and aggressive. Karen's more submissive."

"Got it."

Sean got out of the vehicle and moved around to my side. When he opened the door, I stepped out with my briefcase.

The doors of the other SUV opened. The man who got out of the driver's seat was enormous, taller even than Sean, with a larger physique. His hair was blond, his eyes bright blue.

"Alice Worth, this is Jack Hastings," Sean said.

I shook hands with Sean's beta. "Nice to meet you," I said, my eyes fixed on his chin.

"Glad to meet you, Ms. Worth," Jack said gruffly. "We've all been anxious to meet the woman who's caught the eye of our alpha."

Was I imagining it, or was there a distinctive note of disapproval in his tone? I felt the weight of his appraising stare. I resisted the urge to meet his gaze, even though avoiding eye contact made me feel submissive and I didn't like it.

Jack's companion came around the back of the SUV. Karen was about my height and looked to be my age, with short dark hair and green eyes. I instinctively liked her.

Smiling, she held out her hand. "I'm Karen Williams. It's great to meet you, finally."

"Do we have any idea how long this meeting will last?" Jack asked.

I shrugged. "An initial client consultation usually takes forty-five minutes to an hour, but it's hard to say for sure. Once I talk with my client, I'll know more about what I'll need to do from there." I glanced at my phone. "We need to get moving."

"I'll keep an eye on our vehicles," Karen said. "See you in a bit."

Sean headed for the elevators and Jack gestured for me to walk between them. Having the beta at my back made me itch between my shoulder blades.

At the elevators, I hit the up button and we waited, Sean at my side as Jack guarded us. When the elevator arrived, we stepped inside and they maneuvered me to the back, blocking me in with four hundred pounds of werewolf.

"What floor?" Sean asked as the doors closed.

"Twenty."

Sean hit the button. As the elevator rose, he said, "Don't sit or stand near any windows. If I tell you to hit the floor or run, do it."

I blew out a breath. "Okay."

When the doors opened at the twentieth floor, we stepped out into the posh lobby of Riddell, Ives, and McAllen. I approached the reception desk, flanked by Sean and Jack.

The receptionist's gaze lingered on my entourage for a few extra beats before she looked at me. "Can I help you?"

I gave her a quick smile. "I have a two o'clock appointment with Aaron Riddell."

She checked her computer. "Ms. Worth and Mr. Maclin?"

"Yes."

"Follow me."

Jack took a seat in the reception area while Sean and I followed the receptionist down a long hallway. She stopped at a pair of doors and knocked twice.

"Come in," Aaron called.

The receptionist opened the door and ushered us inside, then closed the door behind us.

The conference room was enormous, with thick carpet, a long oval table ringed by eight leather chairs, a complete audio/visual system, and floor-to-ceiling windows overlooking downtown on two sides.

I could tell immediately that Sean did not like those windows. He moved slightly in front of me to block any shots from the building next to ours.

Three people rose as we entered the room: Aaron, his assistant, and a slim, gray-haired woman in a light blue designer pantsuit.

The woman and the assistant waited while Aaron came around the table to greet us with a smile. The tall African-American lawyer wore his usual tailored suit. He took my hand and kissed me lightly on the cheek. Next to me, Sean tensed.

"Alice, it's so good to see you," Aaron said. "You look lovely, as always."

"Good to see you, too, Aaron. It's been a while."

"Too long." Aaron and Sean shook hands. "Mr. Maclin, a pleasure to meet you. I've heard many good reports about your company."

"Call me Sean. It's good to meet you as well. Can we close these blinds?"

Aaron didn't hesitate. "Absolutely. Alex, if you would?"

Aaron's assistant did something on his tablet. The blinds closed with a quiet whir and the lights turned up.

Aaron gestured behind him. "I'd like to introduce my client, Ms. Esther Aldridge."

Esther was in her late sixties, with platinum hair in a neat twist and sharp blue eyes that raked me from head to foot as I approached her with my hand outstretched.

"Ms. Aldridge, it's an honor to meet you," I said. "The new exhibit hall in the museum is beautiful."

"I'm very proud of it," she said, shaking my hand with a surprisingly firm grip. "I've wanted to expand our collection of African art for years. I'm very pleased with our curator's work." She turned to Sean with narrowed eyes. "Mr. Maclin, I understand you're providing security for Ms. Worth."

"Yes, we are."

"Mr. Riddell has confidentiality agreements for both of you to sign, but I'm a bit old-fashioned. I would like your word as a gentleman that everything we discuss here today will remain confidential and that your employees will be required to maintain that same level of discretion."

"You have my word," Sean told her.

She studied him, then nodded briskly. "Fine. Let's get down to business."

We moved to the conference table. Esther sat on one side, with Aaron on her right and Alex next to him. Sean and I sat across from them.

Alex slid confidentiality agreements over to us. I scanned mine. It appeared identical to ones I had signed previously and I signed, initialed, and dated as required. Sean read his thoroughly, then signed and handed it back.

I took out a notepad and pen from my briefcase as Sean poured us each a glass of water from the pitcher on the table. Aaron's assistant poured water for his boss and Esther.

Aaron folded his hands on the table. "Ms. Aldridge has asked to meet you because she was recently the victim of a burglary that resulted in the theft of cash, jewelry, and several magical objects."

"When did the burglary take place?" I asked.

"Two nights ago, I believe," Esther said. "I was out of town for a few days and returned last night to discover I had been robbed. I called Mr. Riddell this morning and asked his advice on how to proceed. It was he who suggested I employ the services of a private investigator with experience in tracking magical objects—and whose discretion could be counted upon."

I nodded. "I understand. What can you tell me about the burglary itself?"

"My home has always had top-notch security and I've never had any problems. A few months ago, a friend told me he had recently added a different type of home security—one that utilized magic. I was skeptical, but wished to learn more."

Magic could certainly be used for home security; wards provided varying levels of protection and defense. While electronic systems could be circumvented or manipulated, wards were difficult to penetrate or break without causing serious harm to the interloper. I was somewhat surprised Esther had never considered their use before; her own art museum used wards to help protect its most valuable pieces.

Esther sipped her water and continued. "My friend showed me the protections at his home. It was a system of wards, 'anchored'—I believe that is the word—by a magical object provided by a mage. I saw for myself how effective the wards were and made an appointment to speak to the mage in question. He visited my home, assessed my needs, and recommended a similar system. I had it installed about six weeks ago and had no issues with its use. I believed my home to be secure until two nights ago, when someone, or perhaps a group of people, waltzed in right past the wards and my security system and robbed me blind."

"They broke the wards?"

"No, they simply passed through them, which I was led to believe was impossible."

I shook my head. "You were misled, unfortunately. The mage who set the wards could cross them. Also, there are 'passkey' spells that allow someone passage through a ward, but they have to be made by whoever created the wards in the first place."

"So this mage who set up the system has to be involved in the burglary?" Aaron interjected.

"More than likely. It's possible he had passkey spells on hand for some other reason, I suppose, and these thieves got hold of them, but the more likely scenario is that you were deliberately targeted and the mage who set your wards is in league with whoever burgled your house."

Esther's mouth compressed into an angry line. "I have attempted to call the mage several times and there was no answer."

"That's not a good sign," I said. "So, what is it you want me to do?"

"I doubt there's much chance of recovering any cash or the jewelry, but I want the magical objects recovered. I am willing to pay double your standard rate for your undivided attention and a fifty-percent bonus if all three objects are returned within the week."

"What about the wards the mage placed? Do you want me to remove them?"

Her eyes flashed. "I want those wards gone and replaced with a new security system." She turned to Sean. "I understand you own a security company, Mr. Maclin. How soon would your company be able to install a new system?"

"Let me look at our schedule." Sean pulled out his phone and checked a calendar. He looked up. "I can have our crew at your house by six o'clock."

"Do it," Esther said.

As he texted his staff to set up the installation, I turned to Esther. "Meanwhile, I'll need full access to your home and grounds, photos of the missing objects, and everything you have on the mage who set up the wards."

"Agreed," she said briskly.

Sean spoke up. "With your permission, I'll look into the breach of your security system, unless you would prefer that the company that installed it run the diagnostic?"

"The fewer people who know about the situation, the better, so I would prefer not to involve the other security company," she told him. "You have free access to the system. I'll see that you get the necessary codes."

"A question," I said. "Is it only the items you are interested in, or do you want the thieves found and arrested?"

"Only the items. I'm not interested in prosecuting the thieves or anyone else involved in the robbery; I want no part of any trial or publicity."

I'd expected as much. "Has your friend who recommended this mage also been a victim of a burglary?"

"I suppose it is possible, but I do not intend to ask, and nor should you."

I tilted my head. "Why is that?"

She set her water glass down. "Ms. Worth, there are good reasons I have called you and not the police to track down my missing items. First, I am a private person. Second, the missing objects are of questionable legal status. Third, they must be handled with care, by someone who understands magic. Fourth, I don't want anyone to know I was the victim of a burglary, and if my friends were also victims, they would feel the same way. If they *were* burgled, they may have hired someone like yourself to go after the thieves and their missing valuables. They are looking after their own interests; I must look after mine."

"I understand. Do you have the photos of the missing items?"

At Esther's nod, Aaron slid a folder over to me. I opened it.

The first magical object was a wide bronze or brass arm cuff. On the next page was a photo of a battered cup that looked to be made of pewter. The third item was a beautiful silver hand mirror.

I looked up at Esther. "What magical properties do these items have?"

She narrowed her eyes at me and said nothing.

I put down my pen. "I have to know what they do, Ms. Aldridge. Magic is volatile. Magical objects often have a mind of their own, sometimes quite literally. I'm not going to get killed because I don't know what I've got my hands on. I need full disclosure on this or I'm out. You can try to find someone else who's willing to go after magical objects without knowing what they do. Good luck with that."

We stared at each other across the table while the men were silent. Finally, she crossed her arms and spoke. "None of them are volatile. Drinking from the cup permits a vampire to walk in daylight for one hour. The mirror allows glimpses into one's forgotten memories. The cuff..." She coughed delicately. "The cuff belonged to my husband. It made him strong and quite virile."

Oh good Lord, I did *not* need any details. "Ms. Aldridge, just because their magic seems tame doesn't mean they aren't volatile." I was relieved, however, to hear that none of them contained the vengeful spirit of a five-hundred-year-old blood mage or the power to lay waste to a hundred square miles at a time. I could probably handle a cup, a mirror, and a magical Viagra bracelet, assuming I didn't break the damn mirror and net myself seven years of bad luck—or something much worse.

"Let's say I find one or more of these objects. There are a couple of possible scenarios for recovery." I ticked them off on my fingers. "One, someone is careless and leaves them lying around."

"Obviously, the ideal situation," Aaron said.

"Ideal, but unlikely. Two, they are available for purchase from someone who has acquired them."

"Safe to assume that said agent will not be willing to return them as stolen property." The lawyer exchanged a glance with his client. "Ms. Aldridge is willing to negotiate for the return of the items. Obviously, we want to limit both our expense and our exposure, so you are authorized to act as our agent if you believe the items can be bought for a reasonable amount."

"Define 'reasonable.'"

Esther spoke. "Six thousand for the mirror and cuff and ten thousand for the cup, to be paid in cash or bearer bonds. You will deliver the payment and collect the items yourself."

"The third possible scenario is that the items may be in a location that is very hard to get to. Before I or anyone else gets too deep in recovery efforts, I have to ask: what's special about these three items? Why not just buy new stuff? I get that the cuff belonged to your late husband, but—"

She interrupted me, her eyes flashing. "This is not about some sentimental attachment to a couple of knickknacks. Someone has stolen from me, and that cannot stand."

I raised my hands. "Okay, I can understand that. You want your stuff back, I'll get it back."

She gave me a nod. "Any special efforts required to reclaim the items will be justly compensated, as per our contract."

"Naturally, neither Ms. Aldridge nor I condone any actions that violate the law," Aaron said, his eyes twinkling.

"Naturally," I said dryly.

Esther leaned forward to pick up her glass of water. "So, how do we begin?"

"We need to sign a contract, and I need a retainer."

Alex produced paperwork and Aaron handed it to me. "I took the liberty of preparing a contract based on your standard terms and the special conditions we discussed here today."

I looked through it, then initialed, signed, and dated it and passed it back. He gave it to Esther, who signed and dated it as well.

Aaron slid an envelope across the table toward me. "Is this amount sufficient for a retainer?"

I opened the envelope, peeked at the check, and nodded. "Yes, that will work. I need all the information about the mage you hired to install the wards. Sean and I need to go to your house so he can see how they got past your security system and I can examine the wards and their anchor."

"Very well." Esther handed me a file. "This is my agreement with the mage who provided the wards. I'll let my assistant know you'll be by this afternoon. Her name is Christina Harris. If you need anything, she will provide it. I have meetings at the museum this afternoon and then dinner with friends, but I should be back home around seven."

I put the files and my notepad back into my briefcase and zipped it closed. We rose and shook hands. "Would you prefer that I call Aaron with updates?" I asked Esther.

She nodded. "Please. He will pass the information along to me."

We said our goodbyes. Alex escorted Sean and me back to the main lobby, where Jack sat leafing through a travel magazine.

He rose when we appeared. "Are we ready to go?"

Sean turned to me. "Where are we headed?"

"Home first so I can change, and then we'll head over to her house."

"By that point, it will be time for a shift change," Jack said as we entered the elevator and Sean hit the button for parking level two. "Should I have Team Two meet us at the nest?"

"Let's do that," Sean said. "I want to meet with both teams."

Jack pulled out his phone and sent a couple of texts as we descended in the elevator.

When we arrived on the parking deck, Karen waited by the SUVs. "Nothing to report," she said as we approached, giving me a smile. "All's quiet."

"Good. Let's head back to the nest, secondary route," Sean told Jack.

The blond man grunted assent and the mobile team got into their SUV as Sean loaded me into ours.

As we approached the exit of the parking garage, I said, "So, what have you been telling your pack about me?"

"Not as much as they would like," Sean said, turning onto the street. "I know you're a private person, so I really haven't said a lot. That's somewhat unusual; most werewolves bring their significant others around the pack so everyone can get used to each other."

"So, is keeping me away from them and not telling them about me causing friction?"

He hesitated. "Yes."

We drove in silence while I thought about that. On the one hand, I *was* a private person whose life depended on staying below the radar, but I didn't want to cause problems for Sean with his pack. If we were going to try to make this work, I would have to observe some shifter customs, including socializing, or at least interacting, with his pack.

"I guess I need to get to know your people," I said as we slowed and stopped at a traffic light.

Sean looked at me with a strange expression.

"What?" I asked, frowning.

"When we get home, I am going to kiss you," he said, his attention back on the traffic as we started to move again. "You don't know how happy I am to hear you say that, Alice."

"When we get home, I suppose I will permit you to kiss me," I said haughtily.

He gave me a wolfy grin that made me warm all the way down to my toes.

Things were changing between us. I'd once been so afraid of letting anyone in past the walls I'd built around myself that I'd driven him away. Now I realized that I very much liked the change he'd brought into my life, so much so that I was willing to put my fear aside and meet his pack. I'd been safe behind my walls, but I'd been very lonely too. I hadn't really been living then, only existing. In a way, it wasn't much different from my life with Moses.

Little by little, one step at a time, I was freeing myself from my past and the fortress I'd built for myself.

I smiled and gazed out the window as Sean drove us home.

6

THE CLOSER WE GOT TO MY HOUSE, THE MORE TENSE SEAN BECAME.

By the time we parked in the driveway, he was on high alert, his face hard and eyes golden. He moved quickly, exiting the driver's side of the SUV and coming around to mine. As soon as I stepped out of the vehicle, he was practically wrapped around me, hustling me up the sidewalk and the steps to the front door so quickly that I almost tripped several times.

I unlocked the door and in a flash we were inside. He shut and locked the door behind us, leaving Jack and Karen in the SUV outside on watch.

I scowled as I set down my briefcase and removed my jacket and blouse. "Why don't you just carry me inside next time?" I took off the bulletproof vest with a sigh of relief.

Sean took the vest from me and kissed me very thoroughly. "I need my hands free."

I sniffed and headed upstairs to change, carrying my jacket and top. "You're lucky I like you. Anybody else who tried to herd me like that would still be smoking on the ground outside."

When I came down fifteen minutes later, wearing a button-up shirt and khakis, Sean was in the living room with Jack, Karen, and two young men I took to be Team Two. Everyone was ominously silent.

The tension in the room went up a few notches as I reached the bottom of the stairs. Sean looked grim, Jack's expression was a combination of anger and annoyance, and none of the others looked at me. Fantastic. It wasn't hard to figure out what they'd been discussing before I came downstairs.

Sean spoke. "Alice, this is Team Two, Philip and Tom."

We exchanged subdued greetings.

"I've briefed them on who you're working for," Sean added. "Team One is going off duty, so Team Two will be accompanying us to the Aldridge home and standing watch while we work."

"Okay. I'm going to the basement while you guys wrap up your meeting. I'll be back up in a minute."

I headed for the basement door. Sean intercepted me and kissed my cheek. I felt the weight of Jack's stare as Sean squeezed my hand.

I opened the basement door, waited a moment in case Malcolm was in the middle of spellwork, then headed down the stairs, closing the door behind me. After a beat, I heard Jack's angry voice, but his words were indistinct.

Malcolm met me at the bottom of the stairs. He read my expression and asked, "You want me to go up there and find out what they're saying?"

I shook my head. "Shifters are more sensitive to the presence of ghosts, and I don't want them to know about you. I'll get the details from Sean later." And wouldn't that be a fun conversation?

I put that aside and focused on the task at hand. "Good news: we've got a case." I told Malcolm about Esther Aldridge's burglary and our mission to retrieve her stolen magical objects.

The ghost was even more excited than I was at the prospect of checking out the wards at Esther's house and going after the missing items. "A cup that lets vamps walk in daylight and a mirror that shows forgotten memories? Very cool."

"Very," I agreed. "I'm going to head there first and get a sense of what we're dealing with, but I might want help with the wards and the trace, if there is any. I'll summon you when I know the situation is secure."

"Sounds good. I'll hang out here until you're ready for me."

Back upstairs, I found Sean waiting alone in the foyer, holding my vest. "Team One left." His voice was tight with suppressed anger. "Philip and Tom are waiting in their SUV."

I took the vest from him and put it on. "You planning on telling me what's going on?"

"On the way, if that's okay."

"All right." I put on a blazer over the vest and checked my reflection in the mirror by the door. I made a face, picked up my shoulder bag, and sighed. "Ready."

Sean got the all-clear from the mobile team and we headed out.

We drove in silence for a while. Sean's jaw was so tight that it made mine ache.

"Let's hear it," I said finally.

He sighed. "I mentioned that my not being forthcoming about you has been causing some tension, but there's more to it than that. A few members of the pack would prefer I date a shifter. There's no rule saying an alpha has to have a werewolf mate, but it's traditional. It's only a couple of people causing problems; the rest have no issue with you being a human mage."

I said nothing.

"My relationship with you is not open to debate or contingent upon anyone's approval," Sean said flatly when I was quiet. "You have nothing to prove to them. All that matters is you and me."

"That's not exactly true, is it? If they don't like that you're dating someone who isn't a shifter—"

"Then they are more than welcome to take it up with me, in whatever manner they see fit," he broke in. "As I said, who I date is not subject to a vote. A pack is not a democracy. You don't need anyone's approval."

"Is Jack one of the people who wants you to have a werewolf mate?"

"Yes."

"Who else?"

"Jack's mate Delia. Eddie and his mate Thea. Caleb because he follows Jack's lead. A few others are concerned about it but haven't voiced objections."

"So, that's five or more out of how many total pack members?"

"Fifteen at the moment, not counting the kids or human spouses."

I stared out the window.

"What are you thinking?" Sean asked.

"Is this likely to cause someone to challenge you?"

He shook his head. "I doubt it. They may be angry, but they know it's not worth dying over. I'm sure once they get to know you, they'll come around."

"I don't think Jack is going to 'come around.' He seems to feel pretty strongly about it."

"Like I said, it doesn't matter," Sean stated. "If anyone has a problem, I'll deal with them."

In a werewolf pack, "dealing" with a problem almost always involved bloodshed. The question was, whose blood would be shed: Sean's, Jack's, or mine?

According to the paperwork Esther gave me, the mage who had installed her wards was a man named Joseph Kendall. Like many self-employed mage security consultants, he had a small office downtown. His website was very professional and he clearly catered to wealthy clients. His photo showed a smiling, dark-haired man of about forty-five in a tailored suit.

As Sean drove, I called Caitlyn Morse, a freelance researcher who used to work for Mark Dunlap Investigations but had quit after Mark's murder, unwilling to put up with the new management. As usual, I felt a stab of grief when I thought of my former mentor.

Cait's cheery voice distracted me from unpleasant memories. "Alice! How are you?"

"Doing well, Cait. You looking for a project?"

"Always. What do you have?"

"I need a background check on a man named Joseph Kendall." I gave her the information I had for him.

Computer keys clicked rapidly. "How deep do I need to go? Vitals only, or do you need his first-grade teacher's name?"

"I need the works," I said. "Particular emphasis on any known criminal associates and any past history of shenanigans. I'm on a time crunch and my client's paying for express service, so when you invoice me, figure your fees appropriately."

"That's what I like to hear. I'll get right on it and e-mail you the files when I've got them. Anything else?"

"Not at the moment. Happy searching." We said our goodbyes and I disconnected just as Sean and I arrived at our destination.

Sean turned into a long, winding driveway that led to an imposing mansion hidden from the street by trees. He parked out front and the mobile team pulled in next to us.

As we exited the SUV, the house wards tingled on my skin. Sean and I walked to the front door as Tom emerged from the mobile team SUV and took up a position next to it, scanning the yard.

The front door opened as we approached, revealing a stern ash-blonde woman in heels and a dark green suit.

I held out my hand. "I'm Alice Worth. Are you Ms. Aldridge's assistant?"

"Yes. I'm Christina Harris." Her handshake was brisk. "Ms. Aldridge told me to expect you. Please come in."

As I walked inside, I sensed only deterrent wards, set to incapacitate anyone who tried to get through, and no deadly black wards. Those were illegal, but some unscrupulous mages used them anyway if a client paid them enough. We stepped into an enormous entryway and Christina closed the door behind us.

As Sean examined the security system keypad by the door, I placed my hand against the wall and closed my eyes, assessing Kendall's magic.

He was an air mage. The wards were well-made but simplistic. That didn't necessarily mean he lacked skill, but considering the wealth and status of his client, they were woefully inadequate, even without taking into account the passkey spells. A loud sneeze could break them. The shoddy workmanship alone made me angry.

I sensed the trace linking the wards to their anchor. It was a pulsing white line leading somewhere in the house, to the item providing the wards' power. I followed that line to its source, expecting to find an object charged with Kendall's own magic, and instead found something else.

I sucked in a breath and yanked my hand off the wall.

"What's wrong?" Sean asked.

"I'm not sure," I lied. I turned to Christina. "Can you show me the anchor, please?"

"Of course. This way."

We followed her through the entryway, down a long hall, and around a corner. She opened a pair of doors and ushered us into a large office overlooking the garden behind the house.

Sean went to close the curtains immediately, but my attention was on a ceramic figure of a nude woman on a small table next to a wall of bookcases. It pulsed with magic.

The statue was about two feet tall and surprisingly heavy. I turned it around, then picked it up and checked the bottom.

I glanced at Christina. "Do you have something I can put down on the floor, like a drop cloth?"

Her eyebrows went up. "I can bring you something. One moment." She left the office. I listened to her heels clicking down the hallway.

"What's going on?" Sean asked in a low voice.

"We might have a problem. I need Malcolm." I closed my eyes, found the cool blue-green trace in my mind linking me to my ghost, and tugged. I felt a few seconds of dizziness, and then it faded.

About ten seconds later, I sensed Malcolm had jumped to a crystal on my bracelet. I touched the crystal with my other hand. "*Release*."

Malcolm appeared next to me. "Hey, Alice. Hey, Sean." He glanced around in appreciation. "Nice digs."

"I need your help," I said. "Tell me what you sense in this statue."

He stared at the ceramic figure, then cursed and flitted back four feet in the blink of an eye.

"What's in the statue?" Sean asked.

Malcolm was swearing a blue streak, so I answered. "There's a ghost trapped in the statue. That's what Kendall's using to power the wards instead of his own magic."

Sean stared at the statue in horror. "There's a *person* in there?"

Footsteps approached. "Malcolm," I hissed. I didn't know if Esther's assistant had any ability to sense a ghost but I didn't want to take any chances.

Malcolm cut himself off in mid-curse and went invisible.

Christina reentered the office, carrying a folded piece of heavy cloth like the kind used to drape over furniture in storage. She handed it to me. "Will this work?"

"Perfect." I unfolded the cloth and spread it on the floor. I glanced at Sean. "Would you mind?"

"Not at all," he said, picking up the statue.

"Wait," Christina began.

Sean raised the statue and smashed it on the cloth. Esther's assistant stumbled back, shocked, as pieces of ceramic scattered across the floor. "What are you doing?" she demanded.

"Ms. Aldridge instructed me to break the wards," I told her, using the toe of my boot to nudge the debris. "I'm working on doing that. You need to go into another part of the house while we work. We'll find you if we need anything."

Without a word, she spun on her heel and left.

Malcolm reappeared next to me. "Where's the crystal?"

I crouched and poked around carefully until I uncovered a marble-sized blue crystal embedded in a chunk of ceramic.

"How long do you think the ghost has been in there?" Malcolm asked me.

"I don't know. I can't tell how old this statue was. It could be months or years. Or decades."

We stared at the crystal.

"What do you want to do?" Malcolm asked.

"We have to release the ghost," I said. "We don't know what kind of shape it'll be in, so we need a circle to contain it. If it's gone wraith, I'll have to discorporate it." I looked at Sean. "You need to be outside the circle. Malcolm and I will handle this."

Reluctantly, he moved away. I took a piece of chalk from my bag and drew a circle around the drop cloth, closing myself and Malcolm inside.

"Charge the circle and hold it. Don't let the ghost break it," I told Malcolm. "Sean, stay out of the circle, no matter what."

The circle flared around us, its power tingling on my skin.

"What do you mean, no matter what?" Sean demanded.

"The ghost may be violent, but I won't let it hurt me." I crouched and picked up the piece of ceramic that contained the crystal. As I stood, the ghost's power buzzed on the edges of my senses. The question was: how stable would he or she be, after being trapped in the crystal for so long?

I pressed the crystal into the palm of my hand, and a jolt of power made my head jerk. I braced myself, focused on the crystal, and spooled my blood magic. With a single blow, I severed the binding spell holding the ghost in the crystal and released it.

A piercing scream filled the air as the ghost emerged in a wave of madness. The spirit wasn't a wraith yet, but it was only a matter of time. Like a poltergeist, she no longer looked human, but I saw two crazed eyes in a formless face a split second before she picked me up and slammed me against the barrier of the circle, my feet dangling eighteen inches from the floor.

Outside the circle, Sean growled and paced, but my attention was on the tormented spirit.

"You're all right," I told her, though she was too far gone to understand me. "You're free of the crystal now."

She made a heartbreaking keening sound. Sean couldn't hear it, but Malcolm and I could. A white ribbon of trace bound her to Kendall. She'd been his bound ghost and he'd trapped her in the crystal to use as a power source.

I felt a spike of fury and realized it was Malcolm's. "Discorporate her," my ghost pleaded. "Please. She's suffered enough. Do it before he realizes she's been released and summons her."

Malcolm was right; the moment Kendall sensed the ghost had been freed, he could pull her back to him and we might never find her again.

There was no time to be kind or gentle. "May you find rest," I whispered, and used my blood magic to pull her apart.

Her wail was excruciating. I dropped to the floor on my hands and knees as the ghost disintegrated. Kendall's binding broke with a sound like a snap.

A strange surge of familiar blue-green magic flared as Malcolm vanished. He was trying to follow the link back to Kendall.

"Malcolm, no!" I shouted. I grabbed my ghost and yanked him back. The hard ricochet of magic left me dazed.

I huddled on the floor, disoriented, trying to shake off the effects of the magic. Malcolm and Sean were shouting, but I couldn't understand what they were saying. Malcolm sounded angry with me and Sean was worried. I heard a female voice and Sean's angry reply, followed by the sound of a door slamming.

Malcolm broke the circle and Sean picked me up. "Alice, talk to me," he said urgently. He carried me over to a sofa and put me down.

I forced my eyes open and blinked slowly, focusing on Sean's face as he crouched next to me. "I'm okay," I told him, squeezing his hand.

Malcolm appeared in my line of sight. He was so furious he was flitting in place, flickering in and out. "Why didn't you let me go after him?" he shouted. "He had her trapped in there for years. Why did you pull me back?" His anger sizzled on my skin and I flinched.

Sean turned toward the sound of Malcolm's voice and snarled, "Back off, right now."

I pushed myself up until I was sitting. "He could have broken our binding," I told my ghost angrily. "He might have been able to take you from me, you idiot. What if he took you and put you in a crystal and I couldn't find you? You'd end up like her, or worse. Did you even think of that? I would never have forgiven myself!"

Malcolm disappeared. At first, I thought he'd jumped somewhere else, but I realized he was on the other side of the room, by the bookcases, his back to me.

I struggled to get to my feet. Sean helped me up and I stumbled across the room. "Malcolm, I'm sorry. I can't lose you like that. I can't."

The ghost turned around. He looked anguished. "She was suffering so much."

"I know. We did what we could to help her."

When he spoke again, it was in a tone of voice I'd never heard him use before. "We have to find this guy and make him pay for doing that to her."

"I agree, but for now we need to remove the house wards and Sean needs to figure out how the burglars got past the security system."

"Are you okay?" Sean asked me.

I took a deep breath and let it out. "I'm all right. Did Christina Harris come in here while we were dealing with the ghost?"

"She came running when we started yelling. I got her out of here."

"I'll have to go apologize for all the chaos. Malcolm, can you unweave the wards while I go find her?"

"I can do that. They're basic wards. It won't take me ten minutes."

"Thank you." I touched his hand. It was a strange feeling, like touching thick fog. "Be careful, you jerk."

He gave me a lopsided smile and turned to face the exterior wall, his fingers moving as he traced the wards.

Sean and I went in search of Christina Harris. We found her at a desk in a solarium down the hall, working on a laptop, a stack of papers at her side. She looked up as we entered and gave us a hard stare as Sean moved to stand between me and the windows.

"I apologize for all this," I told her sincerely. "We uncovered something very unpleasant in regard to the house wards and it was a difficult and dangerous situation to resolve."

She looked surprised. "I thought it would be a simple matter to deal with the wards."

"So did I, until we got in there," I said. "The mage who set up the wards was rather unethical in his methods. I'll report what we found to Ms. Aldridge."

"What can I help you with at this point?"

"Sean needs the information for the main security system, if you have that handy. Meanwhile, I'd like you to show me where the magical items were kept."

Christina rose and handed Sean a folder. "Those are the codes and the rest of the information about the security system."

"Thank you," Sean said. He squeezed my hand, then headed for the front door as I followed Esther's assistant back to the office.

Malcolm had gone invisible but I could sense his presence near the bookcases as he worked on unweaving Kendall's wards.

Christina led me to a corner of the room, where she slid a panel aside to reveal a large safe. She punched in an eight-digit code, turned the handle, and opened the door. The safe was empty.

"Was everything in the safe taken?" I asked.

She shook her head. "The only things taken were approximately five thousand dollars in cash, some heirloom jewelry, and the three magical objects. We cleaned everything else out and moved it to a different safe when this one was compromised."

The safe had no wards, which meant any mage who entered the house would probably be able to sense the magic trace emanating from the objects stored inside. I shook my head. This sort of thing happened often when people without magic dabbled in collecting magical objects as a hobby. They didn't really know what they had or how to keep the items safe and hidden.

I reached into the safe and closed my eyes so I could focus on what little magic trace was left behind by the missing items. The white air magic was undoubtedly an echo from the mirror, since memory spells were a form of air magic. The cup had left behind blood and earth magic, as I would have expected from an object designed for vampire use. The hint of fire magic was probably from the cuff. I committed the traces to memory so I could identify the objects when I found them.

The mirror seemed to be the strongest trace, so it had probably been in Esther's possession the longest. I wondered if she used it regularly, and if so, what memories it showed her. While the cup was intriguing and the cuff was maybe the oddest item I'd ever been hired to find, the mirror was certainly one magical object I wanted nothing to do with. My past had few good memories to offer. I had a hard enough time keeping the ones buried I remembered; I certainly didn't need to dredge up any of the ones I'd managed to forget.

When I opened my eyes, Christina Harris was sitting in a chair, leafing through an architecture magazine, and Malcolm had finished unweaving the house wards. I realized with a start that I'd been standing at the safe for almost fifteen minutes.

"I'm done with the safe for now," I said. "I think I'll go check on Sean."

As she closed up the safe, I headed down the hall, following the sound of voices. When I rounded the corner, I found Sean and a young, dark-haired man in a tool belt and a Maclin Security shirt by the security system keypad. The younger man had a small laptop.

Sean smiled as I approached. "Alice, this is Ben, head of our installation division and a member of the pack."

Ben shook my hand and gave me a cheery smile. "It's nice to meet you, Alice."

"Nice to meet you." I smiled back. "You guys getting to the bottom of the security system breach?"

"We're getting there," Sean said. "It looks like whoever got in here bypassed the system with some pretty advanced equipment. What did you find out?"

"The thieves cracked the safe to get to the missing items."

"What kind of safe? Biometric scanner? Fingerprint? Voice identification?"

"Eight-digit code."

Sean shook his head. "You're kidding me. Might as well have been keeping the stuff in a cardboard box labeled 'Valuables.'"

"I suppose if you've never had a break-in, you might get a little too complacent." I pulled the folder containing the pictures of the missing items from my bag. "I'm going to work in the office for a while and make some phone calls."

"I'll join you soon. The rest of the installation crew will be here any minute."

"Sounds good." I headed back to the office.

Christina had gone back to working in the solarium, so I sat down on one of the couches in the office.

Malcolm reappeared and floated over to me. "All done with the wards. They were a joke."

"I know. Thank you for unweaving them."

"You're welcome."

"You should probably jump back to the basement for now. I'll summon you if something comes up, or I'll see you when we get home later tonight."

"Okay." He hesitated. "I'm sorry I tried to follow the trace back to Kendall. That was stupid."

"It's okay. I understand why you did it. As awful as seeing her in that condition was for me, I'm sure it was ten times worse for you."

"That could have easily been me. If I'd ended up back at Bell's cabal as a bound ghost, that *would* have been me, trapped in a crystal until I went wraith. Remember what I told you when we first met, that I'd rather you discorporate me than let that happen to me?"

I nodded.

"Nothing's changed about that. If they ever come for me, send me on if you can, as long as it doesn't put you at risk."

"I will," I promised, though my stomach hurt to even think about doing to Malcolm what I'd just done to Kendall's bound ghost.

"Thanks, Alice. That lady's coming back. I'm out of here." He disappeared.

Christina appeared in the doorway. "I'm about to make some coffee. Would you like a cup?"

I sighed. "More than just about anything in the world. With cream and sugar, please and thank you."

As she headed back down the hall, I opened the folder Esther had given me and studied the pictures of the missing magical items. "Okay, my pretties. If I were a recently stolen magical object, where would I be?"

No answer from the photos, but it didn't take a rocket scientist to figure it out. I tapped my fingers on the arm of the sofa. "I'd be on my way to someone who could sell me, that's where I'd be."

This kind of hardware couldn't be fenced or sold very many places. If it was still in the city, there was a short list of possible buyers and sellers, and I knew a couple of them personally.

That was when I felt it: a distant surge of magic, not nearly as formidable as the one that had destroyed Darius Bell's cabal compound, but powerful and deadly nonetheless. It washed over the house like a gentle tide.

The other shoe had finally dropped.

"Oh, Moses, you old bastard," I whispered. "What have you done?"

7

Bell Industries was a metal-fabrication company headquartered next to the river. It was a major supplier of commercial construction materials in the city and one of Darius Bell's most profitable businesses—*was* being the operative word.

Earth mages had razed Bell's compound, but it was water mages who'd destroyed Bell Industries and a one-block radius around it. They pulled the river over its banks and into the company's facility, then used the force of the water to demolish all three main buildings.

Most of the employees had already left for the day, but early reports listed more than three dozen people missing and presumed dead. The damage was estimated to be in the tens of millions. The new police chief had already made a statement condemning both incidents and offering a substantial reward for information, a reward I was pretty sure would go unclaimed.

I doubted Bell had been there, so my grandfather's attack was probably designed to cripple Bell financially as well as send a message that any and all of Bell's assets and people were fair game.

Sean and I looked at news articles about the attack online. "These cabals are run by psychopaths," he said as we watched aerial footage of the widespread damage caused by the water mages. "They don't care about collateral damage or how many people they kill in their wars."

"No, they don't," I said bitterly. "Cabal leaders only care about money and power. People are expendable." I stopped before I gave anything away about my past involvement with cabals.

He squeezed my hand. "Are you going to be all right while I help with the security system installation?"

"I'm fine. Go help your people. I need to make some phone calls."

He kissed me and left the office in search of Ben's crew.

My first call was to Adri. The phone rang twice and then she answered. "Hello, Alice." Her cheerful tone seemed forced.

"Hey, Adri. How's Bryan?"

"I'll let him tell you himself. Hang on."

There was a rustle, as if Bryan was still recovering in bed. "Miss Alice." His voice was a shadow of its usual deep rumble.

"Hey, Bryan," I said, my throat tight with unexpected emotion. "It's really good to hear your voice."

"It's good to hear yours. The werewolf keeping you safe?"

"Yes, he is." I was so glad to talk to him that I didn't even chastise him for referring to Sean as "the werewolf." I cleared my throat. "I'm sorry I didn't call sooner."

"Don't worry about it. I hear you're back at work."

I blinked. "Wow, the vamp grapevine sure works fast."

"We're all very concerned about your safety, so of course we're keeping up with what's going on." A long pause. "I'm sorry I let him get away from me, Alice."

"Stop that right now," I snapped. I thought of the six bullets Stevens had put into him and couldn't stand to hear him blaming himself. "It wasn't your fault."

"Whose fault was it, then?" he retorted. "We should have captured him at the house. I shouldn't have let him get the drop on us last night. I underestimated him completely and now Fortune is dead because of it."

"We all underestimated him. There's a lot of blame to go around on this one, but I think you've more than paid your penance."

He did an impressive imitation of a werewolf growl. "Not until he's in a cell at the Vampire Court and facing justice for Fortune's murder and for shooting you."

"And for almost killing you," I said. "I hope you get him soon. I'm hip-deep in werewolves over here and they all think they're the boss of me."

Bryan snorted. "I'd pay real money to see them try to boss you, Alice. I appreciate you checking in on me. Was there something else you needed?"

"Yes, as a matter of fact. Could you ask Charles to call me when he's up and about?"

"Can I tell him what it's regarding?"

"Magical objects."

"Well, that will definitely intrigue him." I could hear the smile in his voice.

I sighed. "I guess I'll see you when this is all over. I doubt Charles will be leaving wherever you guys are holed up, unless he's thinking about trying to draw Stevens out?"

"There are several options on the table," Bryan said, demonstrating he hadn't lost his ability to be cagey.

"Well, whatever you decide to do, be careful."

"In the meantime, stay close to the werewolf. Let him do his job."

I huffed. "I do want to stay alive, you know."

"I know you do. I also know that sometimes you do what you think needs doing, and that's not always compatible with staying safe."

I started to protest and then had to admit he was right. "Well, with any luck, the Hunters will find Stevens soon and we can put all this behind us."

"You and I will raise a toast to that. Take care of yourself."

"You too."

Once we'd disconnected, I scrolled through my contacts and called a number I hadn't used in some time. The call went to voice mail. There was no recorded message, only a beep.

My message was terse. "This is Alice. Call me back."

My phone rang less than thirty seconds later. "Alice Worth," I said briskly.

"Girl, why you callin' me this early?" It was a familiar scratchy male voice. "Sun ain't even down yet."

"Sorry if I interrupted your beauty sleep, Phil. I'm on the trail of some hot merchandise, and the faster I find it, the bigger my payday. Thought I'd give you a call and see what you knew."

"Answers cost money. Fast answers cost more." There was no trace of Phil's good-ol'-boy persona now.

"You know I'm good for it. Cash or a favor?"

"Favor. I got some folks bothering me and I need some wards that bite." Phil was a pawn-shop owner and a fence. I wasn't surprised that he needed wards for protection.

"Done. I'm going to send you a couple of pictures. If you hear about anyone trying to buy or sell them, will you tag me in?"

"You got it. How hot are they?"

"Like a sidewalk in the summer."

"I'll call you if and when I hear something."

"You're a decent human being, Phil."

"Don't tell nobody that." He ended the call.

I took quick photos of Esther's missing items and sent them to Phil the fence, and then I made calls to two of his competitors and made similar deals with them for information. I'd just hung up from the second call when Sean came into the office.

"How goes the installation?" I asked him as he dropped onto the sofa next to me.

"Smoothly. We'll be ready to go soon. You running down some leads?" He laced his fingers with mine and kissed my knuckles.

"Putting out some feelers with some of the city's more upstanding citizens and waiting on a call back from my best potential source of information." I glanced at the sliver of fading daylight visible through a gap in the curtains.

Sean saw me look, put two and two together, and frowned.

"He's a broker," I reminded my disapproving bodyguard. "If those objects come on the market in this city, he'll know about it."

"You'll be asking him for a favor," Sean reminded me. "Vampires never do anything for free."

"All things considered, I think I might have some favors coming my way." That hole in my shoulder had to be worth something.

He squeezed my hand. "Speaking of sundown, we've been invited to dinner with Karen and her husband Cole tomorrow evening at their house. They've also invited Felicia Lowell, her mother, and her brother. I told them it would depend on how things are going with the case, so we're not locked into accepting."

Felicia had been kidnapped by the West-Addison harnad, who had attempted to manufacture a new drug using werewolf blood. Luckily, we'd taken them down before they were successful and rescued Felicia.

"That sounds nice," I said.

"We don't have to go. You've got an important case right now. We can always take a rain check for another time."

"Your pack is important too, Sean." I bumped him with my shoulder. "If we're not running down a hot lead, we'll go. Tell them we'll be there."

He narrowed his eyes at me. "Who are you, and what have you done with my girlfriend?"

I lunged at him and he pulled me close, laughing. "That's better," he said, kissing my hair. "For a minute there, I was worried about you."

"Jerk." I tried to pull away but he kissed me quickly before letting go and scooting over a few inches.

The reason for his quick movement became evident a few seconds later when I heard two sets of heels clicking briskly toward us. We got to our feet just as Esther Aldridge entered the office, followed by her assistant.

"Do you lovebirds need a few more minutes alone?" Esther asked as she strode over to her desk.

At our startled expressions, the older woman waved her hand dismissively and sat down. "It was rather obvious from the moment you arrived in Aaron Riddell's office that you're not merely her personal security. Do give me some credit for not having been born yesterday." She looked at me with an arched eyebrow. "I can't say I blame you, dear. He's quite a catch."

Before I could reply, Sean spoke up. "It's me who's lucky. *She's* the catch."

Esther let out a very unladylike snort. "If you weren't a werewolf, I'd call you 'silver-tongued,' young man."

I was taken aback that she knew Sean was a werewolf, but to my surprise, he chuckled.

She settled back in her chair and appraised us. "I understand from the nice young man out front that your installers will be done shortly. I appreciate your quick response and excellent service. What do you know about how the thieves got past the old system?"

"They're professionals with cutting-edge equipment," Sean told her. "The existing system had a flaw they were able to exploit. I'm sorry to say that your safe in here is woefully inadequate for its purpose. I would strongly recommend replacing it with a more modern version. I can make some recommendations, if you would like."

"Send me a proposal," Esther said.

I spoke up. "If and when the magical items are found and returned, you should have wards set around the safe to obscure the magical trace. Otherwise, anyone with magic will be able to sense exactly where the items are in your house and get a good idea of what they are, even without seeing them. That might be how you got on the thieves' radar; Kendall would have been able to sense the trace."

"Thank you. I will certainly consider it." Esther glanced at the drop cloth and chalk circle on the floor. "Ms. Harris tells me there was some excitement regarding the anchor."

"Joseph Kendall is a poor example of a mage security consultant," I told her frankly. "His wards were insufficient, in my opinion, but worse than that, instead of using his own magic, he trapped a ghost inside that statue and used her to power them."

Christina gasped. Esther stared at me. "There was a ghost inside the statue?"

"Yes, ma'am, there was. He'd had her in there for years, probably, using her for various purposes, until he brought her here."

"Is this sort of thing common?" Esther demanded.

I shook my head. "No. Most mages consider it reprehensible. Cabals use ghosts like that, but they're not really known for their morality. Please don't judge all mages by what Kendall did."

"Where is the ghost now?" Christina asked, scanning the room as if looking for the spirit.

"Once I released her, she passed on," I said, opting for partial truth. "She's gone. I am sorry about the mess in here, but I had no choice."

"You did what had to be done." Esther looked shaken. I couldn't blame her. "Do you have everything you need to begin looking for the stolen items?"

I nodded. "I think I do."

Christina handed me a card with her name and a phone number. "If you have any questions, or need to return to the house, please give me a call."

I put her number into my phone, then tucked the card in my bag. "With your permission, we'll take off. I'll keep Aaron posted on our progress."

"Thank you." Esther rose from her desk to give us each a handshake. We said good night and headed for the front door.

"So, where to?" Sean asked as we walked. "Looking for Kendall?"

I shook my head. "The goal is the missing items. I don't want to tip him off that we're snooping around. I think we head home for now."

Out front, two Maclin Security installation vans were parked beside our SUVs. Ben stood next to one of them, phone in hand. He looked up as we exited the house. "I was just about to message you that we've tested the system and everything's green across the board."

"Good work." Sean clapped Ben on the shoulder. "I appreciate the people who stayed late. If any of them want to go out for beers after, the first round is on me."

Ben grinned. "I'll make the offer. I'm sure a couple of them will take me up on it. I bet you get that Boss of the Year mug you've been wanting."

"Been waiting on that for a while," Sean joked. "You got it from here?"

"Yep. We'll button things up and head out." He held out his hand and we shook. "It was great to meet you, Alice. You coming to the pack's cookout next week?"

My eyebrows went up. The werewolves were having a cookout?

Part of me was apprehensive at the thought of facing the entire pack at once, but I was curious as to how many hamburgers a werewolf pack could eat. I'd seen how many Sean could put away at one sitting. It might be worth it to go just to get an answer to that question.

"I'm not sure yet," I told Ben with a smile. "My schedule is pretty erratic, but I'll be there if I can."

Ben's smile widened. "Awesome. My girlfriend Casey is helping coordinate the food. If you think you can make it, let me know so she can put you down for something."

"Will do."

Sean and I headed for our SUV. Once I was inside, he stopped to talk to the mobile team and then got in beside me. The sun was disappearing behind the horizon.

I cleared my throat. "So, there's a cookout?"

He sighed as he turned the key in the ignition and headed down the driveway with the other SUV right behind us. "I was going to wait to ask you about that until you'd had a chance to get used to the idea of being around the pack. I thought if we went to dinner at Karen and Cole's tomorrow night and it went well, that would be a good time to float the idea, but Ben stole my thunder." He glanced at me as we paused at the end of Esther's driveway. "This is all too much too soon, isn't it?"

"Well, it's a lot for someone who's been on her own for a while, but Karen and Ben have been very friendly and from what you've said about Felicia and her mother and brother, they seem like a nice family. It might not be so bad." I picked at a loose thread on my khakis.

"And?" Sean prompted.

I scowled. Sean was getting increasingly attuned to my emotions. That wasn't uncommon for a shifter, but it felt intrusive sometimes. "My birthday is coming up in a couple of d—" I caught myself. "Months."

Sean nodded. "I had it on my calendar, but I wasn't sure if you celebrated birthdays. It's a milestone, though, huh?"

"The big 3-0."

He reached over and squeezed my hand. "Are you having an existential crisis?" he teased. He saw my face and his smile vanished. "What's wrong?"

When I didn't say anything right away, he didn't press me for an answer. A few minutes later, as we were approaching a stoplight, I said, "I guess I've been thinking about family lately, or my lack of one. It's probably a direct result of my impending birthday because usually I don't dwell on that sort of thing. When I see big, happy families, it's hard. Your pack is like a family. Part of me wants to stay away because it hurts, but there's a part of me that wants that for myself."

"That's understandable."

I shrugged and stared out the window. "I'm sure it's just a temporary thing. Once this birthday is over, I'll go back to being my old solitary self."

"I don't think you will. You've changed since I met you. As rough as these last few months have been otherwise, look at all the connections you've made, the people you've gotten to know. You're not a loner anymore. You actually lit up at the idea of going to dinner at Karen's house tomorrow. When Ben mentioned the cookout, I thought you'd get that deer-in-the-headlights look. Instead, you looked like you were thinking about whether to bring potato salad or a dessert. I can tell you're intimidated by the thought of meeting the whole pack, but you didn't say no instantly like you would have done before."

"If I did volunteer to bring the potato salad, do they sell it in five-gallon buckets, and if so, how many are we talking?"

He laughed. I smiled and reached over the console to rest my hand on his thigh. It was something I'd never done before. There was something wonderful and comforting about such a casual intimacy.

When he didn't react, I started to pull my hand back, suddenly self-conscious.

"Leave it," Sean said. "Please."

I did.

When we got back to my house, we let Rogue in from the backyard and Sean fed him in the kitchen while I went upstairs to change into jeans and a T-shirt.

My phone rang as I was coming back downstairs. I glanced at the number, then answered. "Hello, Charles."

In the kitchen, Sean grumbled.

"Good evening, Alice." A shiver went down my spine at the sound of Charles's voice. I scowled. I was still feeling the effects of drinking his blood. "What a lovely surprise to hear you called. I can think of no better way to begin my day than by hearing your voice."

A low growl from the kitchen.

"My people tell me the werewolf is providing your protection detail," he continued. "If your security situation is not adequate, my invitation to join me remains open."

Another growl, much louder.

"My security is more than adequate," I assured him. "The reason I called is I'm looking for some magical objects that might be coming on the market and I wondered if you could keep an eye out for them."

"Intriguing." I could almost see his ears perk up. "What are these items?"

"I have photos I can send you, but briefly, there is a silver hand mirror, an antique pewter cup, and a fancy arm cuff."

"What do we know of their powers?"

"From what I've been told, the mirror supposedly lets you see forgotten memories. Drinking from the cup allows a vampire to walk in daylight for an hour. The cuff apparently increases male libido."

"Fascinating. I take it these objects are not being sold by their rightful owner?"

"They're not being sold by the person who had possession of them until a few nights ago. I'm not sure the term 'rightful owner' has much meaning when it comes to magical objects. I think the prevailing philosophy is more along the lines of 'possession is nine-tenths of the law.'"

He chuckled. "That is certainly true. Please send me the photos of the items in question and I will make discreet inquiries."

"Thank you. Any news on the manhunt?"

Rogue came into the living room and plopped down on his bed. In the kitchen, the coffee grinder fired up.

Charles made an odd sound that was almost a snarl. "Nothing substantial. Frankly, I expected to wake to the news he had been found and was quite dismayed to hear there are no leads thus far."

I sighed. "Well, it's only a matter of time. I doubt he's skipped town, so he's out there, somewhere. I'm assuming you're looking into weapons suppliers in town, in case he's in the market for more firepower?"

"That is one of the lines of inquiry Ms. Woodall is pursuing. Her work for us has thus far been exemplary."

"Excellent." I looked forward to teaming up with Arkady Woodall at some point for an investigation, assuming my sheep pajamas hadn't given her the wrong first impression. I grimaced. Maybe she'd forget about that.

"I will begin looking into the magical items you described." Charles sounded almost energized by the prospect. I wondered if he was already bored and stir-crazy. As antsy as I was surrounded by watchful werewolves, at least I wasn't trapped with him.

"Thanks, Charles. Call me anytime if you have news on either."

"Good night, my dear." We disconnected.

"You want a cup of coffee?" Sean called from the kitchen.

I snorted as I sent the pictures of the magical objects off to Charles. "You need to ask?"

He appeared carrying two cups of coffee. "It was pretty much a rhetorical question," he said, handing one to me and settling onto the couch. "No sign of Stevens, I take it?"

"None." I sipped my coffee. "In a way, it's surprising; with so many people looking for him, anyone else would probably already have been found. Then again, anyone else wouldn't have gotten away from the vamps in the first place."

My phone beeped with a text reply from Charles: *Photos received. I look forward to the hunt.*

"So, are we in for the evening?" he asked.

"I'm in a holding pattern until I hear back from either Cait with the background check or one of the people keeping an eye out for the magical objects." I yawned and took a couple of chugs of coffee. "I thought I'd look at some furniture options online, on the off-chance I get time to stop by the store tomorrow and make some purchases. If I knew what I wanted ahead of time, it wouldn't take long to make the final choices."

"That sounds like a plan. In the meantime, I'm going to see about getting us some food."

I reached for my bag. "We should try that new Italian place that delivers. I'm thinking lasagna. Let me give you my credit card."

"I've got this one. You got the pizza earlier."

I hesitated, then relented. "Okay, fair enough. Do we need to feed Philip and Tom?"

"I'll get something for them. A couple of meatball subs each should do it."

I laughed and shook my head. "Still getting used to werewolf appetites."

"We're pretty much always hungry, for all kinds of things," Sean said, his eyes gleaming. "Speaking of which, I'm very much looking forward to dessert."

"You *are* hungry," I teased.

"You have no idea." He took my coffee cup and set it on the floor with his own. "I'm a starving man, Alice. I haven't had a good meal in more than a week."

"You poor man." I climbed into his lap and held his face in my hands. "How about we just order subs for Team Two and skip straight to dessert?"

"You're going to need your energy for what I have in mind. As far as I know, all you've had all day is about a gallon of coffee and that one slice of pizza."

I gave him a look.

He turned serious. "Alice, I'm a shifter and an alpha. As long as we're together, there will never be a time when I'm not wanting to make sure you're safe and fed and happy."

I kissed him thoroughly and started to climb off his lap. "Then you'd best order the damn lasagna, because I am *starving*."

He laughed and reached for his phone.

Alice!

I heard Malcolm's panicked voice in my mind at the same moment I felt a yank on the blue-green magic trace that connected us. Someone was trying to pull my ghost away from me. Instinctively I yanked him back and it felt like someone drove a white-hot dagger through my skull—a blood magic attack that would have killed or incapacitated a weaker mage.

I made an involuntary sound that was half-gasp, half-cry and fell off the couch, my head bouncing on the wood floor.

"Alice!" Sean shouted. "What's happening?"

I couldn't talk because my jaw was clenched to hold in my screams. Through the agony, I realized a spell was trying to pull Malcolm away and someone with strong blood magic was attempting to sever the binding that connected us. Malcolm was resisting but he was losing his battle against the powerful spell.

I didn't recognize the magic but there was no time for me to think about who was on the other end of the attack. If whoever it was severed our binding, Malcolm would be lost to me forever—assuming I even survived. Stealing a bound ghost required the equivalent of a magical lobotomy and the pain was making it hard for me to think.

I heard Malcolm telling Sean someone was trying to take him from me and that if they succeeded I might die. Sean snarled at him to do something, but Malcolm wasn't a blood mage. He wasn't equipped for this fight, but I was.

From where I lay on the floor, I spooled my blood magic and yanked Malcolm to me. Startled, he tried to flit away, but I wrapped my magic around him like a cage. As he struggled to free himself, I thrust my hand into his body and ripped out the hidden spell that was trying to tear him away.

Malcolm yelped as the spell disintegrated. I released him and he flitted away from me, his eyes wide and horrified—whether at the attack or me or both, I couldn't tell.

The spell was gone, but I couldn't be sure there wouldn't be another attempt. Malcolm needed to be safe until I could figure out what the hell just happened.

"*Contain!*" I shouted.

With a tingle of magic, Malcolm went into a special crystal on my bracelet, one he couldn't jump out of or be taken from by anyone but me.

The stabbing pain in my head intensified as the blood mage stepped up his or her attack. Now that he or she had lost their ability to take Malcolm, they simply meant to kill me. Unfortunately for them, I was a better mage and a better killer.

I reached back through the magic trace and used my blood magic to kill my attacker. The dagger of blood magic in my head vanished with a sickening pop, leaving behind a vicious ache and a strange hollow feeling. Magic sizzled and then there was a familiar silence as somewhere the blood mage fell over dead.

And just like that, it was over.

Blood trickled from my nose. My arms and legs felt like they were full of lead. I tried to move but couldn't. My head hurt like it might split open.

"Alice," Sean said, his voice tight. "Alice, damn it, say something."

I opened my eyes. He was kneeling beside me, eyes bright with fury as he pulled me against his chest.

I forced myself to speak. "Nobody...takes...my ghost...from...me," I slurred, and then I passed out.

8

When I woke, I was in bed and very warm under what felt like a pile of blankets and quilts. Beyond my eyelids the room was dark, but I had no idea if it was day or night. My body ached down to the bones.

"*How* many dead?" The voice was more growl than human. It sounded like it was coming from the hallway outside my room.

A long pause.

"This has to be related to the Bell-Murphy war." Sean's anger prickled on my skin. "I don't know if it was a misfire of some magical weapon or these people were deliberately targeted. All she could tell me was someone tried to take away her ghost. Is it possible all of the victims—"

He broke off suddenly. I sensed movement before a warm hand brushed my forehead. "Alice? Are you awake?"

I made a small sound.

"I'll have to call you back." Sean put his phone on my nightstand. He pulled back the pile of blankets, scooped me up, and settled into the bed with me in his arms. I curled up against his chest and breathed in his scent, letting it ease the aches in my body.

He tucked my head under his chin. "Can you talk?" His voice was rough. "I need to know if you can understand me and how badly you're hurt."

I focused on putting syllables together. "Going...to be...all right."

He took a deep breath and squeezed me against his chest. "You're not lying to me, are you? We have an agreement: you don't tell me you're okay if you aren't."

"Feel like shit," I told him.

His laugh sounded strangled. I opened my eyes and moved my head so I could see him. He obviously hadn't slept and his eyes were bright, almost feverish, and shining gold, as if his wolf lurked just beneath his skin.

The curtains in my room were tightly closed but I saw daylight at the top and sides. "What time is it?" I asked.

"Almost noon." He kissed the top of my head. "It's been about fourteen hours since the attack."

I remembered what I'd heard him saying when I woke up. "What happened?"

"A lot of people died last night around the same time you were attacked and the hospitals are full of people in comas who aren't expected to survive. They don't even know how many victims there are yet; dozens, at least. People dropped unconscious or dead at home, in their cars, wherever they were, all over the city. There was a lot of panic at first, but things settled down when no one else seemed to be affected after the first wave hit."

"They tried to take Malcolm," I said. "There was some kind of spell inside him, hidden all this time. I broke it and killed the mage who tried to take him and kill me."

His chest rumbled with a low growl. "Good. So Malcolm is safe? I thought we'd lost him."

"I put him in my bracelet in case they tried again before I was recovered enough to defend us."

"Who do you think is responsible for this?"

"It has to be Bell. Malcolm died at the hands of one of his blood mages. I'm betting they spelled him before releasing him, so they could pull him back if and when they wanted to."

"But why release him at all? Isn't that unusual?"

"Very unusual; unheard-of, in fact. But if all of the dead and dying are people who had bound ghosts, then it's something Bell has been doing for a while." I laced my fingers with his. "Who was that on the phone?"

He squeezed my hand. "Adri Smith, calling to check on you when people started realizing that all the dead are mages. I don't think anyone has figured out the ghost connection, though."

"Bell has to be pulling in his ghosts because of Murphy's attacks," I said. "I don't know how or why, but he's either planning to use them as defense or offense."

"How would he do that?"

"Cabals use ghosts as energy sources, like Kendall used that ghost in the statue. They can amplify a mage's magic, be used as a focus for spellwork, and power wards, among other things. Maybe he's going to use them to strengthen the wards wherever he's holed up." I hesitated. "Or he's planning on using them to amplify a magical attack on Murphy or his people, either here or back in Baltimore."

"Why not just keep them stored at the cabal, in case something like this happens?"

My eyes widened. "Because they weaken if they're stored and go wraith over time. If they're free, they *gain* power, especially if they're bound to..." My voice trailed off.

"Bound to what?" he prompted.

"Strong mages," I whispered. "Son of a bitch, *that's* why he released Malcolm. We've been wondering all this time how Malcolm ended up with me when he died instead of at the cabal. Bell figured out a way to make his ghosts even stronger, by spelling them or arranging for them to be bound to mages and letting them build up power, then pulling them back when he's ready to use them, killing all those mages in the process. Not that he cared about that, obviously." My blood magic sizzled on my skin. "Murphy, Bell...they're all the same. Not an ounce of conscience among them."

Sean growled. "Is Bell likely to attack here, or back in Baltimore?"

"I'm betting Baltimore. Murphy took out Bell's compound and one of his most profitable businesses. If he can amass a cadre of mages like the one Murphy used to attack his compound, and he uses the ghosts to amplify their magic, and he doesn't care that it will kill most of them, he could obliterate Murphy's compound and everyone in it."

I turned my head away so he couldn't see my eyes, worried they would betray how I felt about that possibility. I'd fantasized about destroying the compound and killing Moses for most of my life, but it had seemed an impossible task. If Bell could do what I thought he could do, it might be the best chance anyone had of succeeding where so many others had failed. I tried not to get my hopes up, but my brain fixated on it and wouldn't let go.

"Murphy has to figure he'll be targeted," Sean said. "He might not know about the ghosts, but he's too smart to stay in his compound, knowing there's a target painted on it."

"He's arrogant. He thinks his wards will hold. No one has ever breached the perimeter walls, much less damaged the main building." Not from the outside, anyway, I thought, remembering the massive hole I'd blown in the compound on my way to freedom.

"So you think he'll stay home, despite the danger?"

"I guarantee he'll stay." I hesitated, then added, "Or at least that's my guess, based on what I've seen of him in the news."

"Well, you're probably right about that." He smoothed the hair back from my face. "Are you feeling any stronger?"

I nodded. "I'm a little foggy still, but I think it'll pass fairly soon. It's been a while since I had to fight a blood mage that way. Luckily, it's like riding a bicycle, I guess." I fell silent.

"You had no choice," he said firmly. "It was you or them, right?"

"Even after they couldn't get to Malcolm, they tried to kill me, I guess just on principle or in retaliation. They didn't have to, but they did and they paid for it."

"Will Bell's people be able to trace you through the dead mage?"

I shook my head. "No. What little trace of mine there was would have dissipated within moments. The only concern is whether Malcolm still has any of those spells hidden in him. I think it's best to leave him in the crystal for now, though, in case they're still trying to call him back. I need to be stronger before I let him out and try to look for more retrieval spells." I took a deep breath. "In the meantime, I'll get up and take a shower."

"Can you manage the shower by yourself?"

"I think so." Gingerly, I started to get up.

Sean resisted, holding me tight. "I thought I was going to lose you. I lay here all night, watching the news alerts about the dead and dying mages and wondering if you were going to wake up and what kind of shape you'd be in when you did."

"I'm not so easy to kill," I reminded him, then touched his face when his eyes darkened. "Thank you for taking care of me."

He squeezed my hand, then kissed it. "It's my privilege to do so." He sighed. "I'll call Karen and let her know we're probably not going to make it over there tonight."

"No, we're going."

"Alice, you just almost died. This isn't the time—"

"This is *exactly* the time," I countered. "I know an invitation like this is significant in shifter culture. It's a family dinner and I've been invited to sit and eat with you. That's an honor and an opportunity I'm not going to miss."

He kissed me then, carefully, as if afraid I might break. I grabbed him and kissed him hard.

When I leaned back, he was smiling. "Now I know you're feeling better. You need some coffee and some food. While you're in the shower, I'll order us some lasagna. By the time you're downstairs, it'll be here."

My stomach growled. He chuckled. "Get up," he said, rolling me gently off his lap. "Get clean, then come downstairs and get coffee and food."

I lay sprawled on the bed and smiled up at him. "You're my favorite werewolf."

"You're my favorite mage." He poked me in the side. "Get in the shower."

When I got out of the shower, I discovered Cait had sent me her preliminary report on Joseph Kendall earlier in the day. I took my laptop downstairs and Sean and I read through it while standing at the kitchen counter eating salad, lasagna, and breadsticks as Jack and Karen ate meatball subs outside in their SUV.

Unsurprisingly, the person Esther Aldridge and the others knew as Joseph Kendall didn't really exist—not on this plane of existence, anyway. The Joseph Kendall tied to the Social Security and SPERA registration numbers this man used belonged to a man who died in Indiana five years before. The mage claiming to be Kendall had stolen the dead man's identity.

Cait's attempt to identify the con man using facial recognition software had turned up several additional cases of identity theft that placed him in Dallas, Boston, and Denver in the past four years. In each of those cities, there were probably a half-dozen victims just like Esther Aldridge who had retained the services of someone like me to look into the thefts instead of notifying law enforcement. At this point, the con man had to have a small flock of private investigators and other less-legal hunters hot on his trail. He might have eluded justice up to now, but those chickens were going to come home to roost sooner or later.

So far, Cait hadn't connected the con man, who I'd creatively dubbed John Doe, to a real identity, but she was looking into it. In the meantime, she was also digging into his known associates in the city. I wondered if John Doe or one of his agents found new B&E-slash-safecracking crews in each city or if he had a team he worked with who came in to commit the burglaries, then left again.

"I'd like to pass this info on to Cyro," I told Sean. "I want to see about hiring him to get John Doe's phone records." Cait was a great researcher, but she stayed on the good side of the law. Black-hat hacker Cyro was firmly on the dark side.

He took a burner cell from his duffel bag. He sent off a text, then set the phone on the counter to finish his lasagna. A few minutes later, the phone rang.

He answered. "Maclin."

My ears weren't as sharp as his, but I could hear an electronically altered voice on the other end offering a terse greeting.

Briefly, Sean outlined what I was looking for and what we knew about John Doe. When he was done, the voice spoke again. Looking surprised, Sean held out the phone. "He'd like to speak to you."

Startled, I took the phone. "Alice Worth."

"Ms. Worth, this is Cyro," the voice said. "I understand you would like to employ my services."

I tried not to be creeped out by the strange computerized voice. "I would, assuming you're available. If the fee will be similar to what you charged the last time, I have the funds available in my business checking account for immediate transfer."

Cyro quoted me a price for John Doe's home, office, and mobile records. "I'll give you an account number. I'll begin the work when the funds are received."

My retainer from Esther would easily cover that amount. "Give me the number."

Cyro's mechanical voice relayed the number, which Sean wrote on a piece of paper.

"How soon can I expect a reply?" I asked. "Just so I have an idea of the time frame."

"I have a few jobs ahead of this today," Cyro said. "It depends on the difficulty of obtaining the information, obviously. Later this evening is probably the earliest I'll be able to send anything back. Tomorrow morning is more realistic."

"That's perfect. Thanks."

"Goodbye." The call ended.

I handed the phone back to Sean. "Wonder why he wanted to talk to me."

"It makes sense, if he's working for you directly this time."

"I guess," I said dubiously.

My phone rang and I answered. "Hey, Phil. Got some news for me?"

The fence's voice was gruff. "I sure do. You gonna come do me a favor?"

Sean's brows drew together. I mouthed *Wards* at him and his scowl faded.

"You know I will," I assured Phil. "My schedule's tight because I'm on a case, but I'll get it done ASAP. What do you know?"

"Got a line on a sparkly hand mirror."

My pulse sped up. "Who's selling it?" I took Sean's pen and pulled a notepad over.

"It's already been sold to a woman named Dora Quinn. She co-owns an antique shop just east of the Heights called Walsh & Quinn."

"Did she buy anything else?"

"My friend said no, just the mirror. He was glad to be rid of it, he said. Not sure what that means."

Considering the mirror's ability to show forgotten memories, I had an idea of why he'd been glad to get it off his hands.

"Rumor has it she paid three thousand for the mirror," he added.

"Good work, Phil. Keep your ears open and let me know if anything else interesting comes on the market. Also, if you hear anything about the whereabouts of a shady mage calling himself Joseph Kendall, I'd like to know."

"Will do."

We hung up. Sean looked up the antique store's website. The proprietors were two women who looked to be in their early forties. The store specialized in high-end "one-of-a-kind" collectibles, which was often a code for magical objects. Judging by the website and the photos of the store, their clientele were more *nouveau riche* than the kind of old money represented by Esther Aldridge.

"What's the plan?" Sean asked.

"I go in as a customer. If the mirror is on the premises, I'll probably be able to locate it unless it's behind wards. Once we know if it's there and I get a read on Dora Quinn, I'll decide which recovery method makes the most sense. Meanwhile, I guess I'm going to need my other good suit. Tell the mobile team we're rolling out in ten."

An hour later, I strode into Walsh & Quinn, exuding the haughty confidence of Audrey Talbot, the persona I'd created for just this sort of reconnaissance mission. My skin buzzed with the obfuscation spell that disrupted the security camera's view of me. Sean was two steps behind me, radiating menace and wearing a Secret Service-style earpiece that connected him to Jack and Karen, who were in their SUV. He was taking his role as Audrey's hired muscle very seriously.

I didn't sense the mirror in the store, but that didn't mean it wasn't here, tucked away in the kind of warded safe that Esther Aldridge should have had.

One of the owners appeared from a back room and approached us. She wore a black short-sleeved sweater and slim black slacks with heels, her shoulder-length blonde hair held back in a silver clip.

She took one look at Sean's glower and her blue eyes widened. "Good afternoon," she said, holding out her hand. "Welcome to Walsh & Quinn. I'm Dora Quinn."

"Audrey Talbot." I shook her hand briskly. "I'm looking for a special gift, and I understand you might have something unique."

"We specialize in unique gifts." Dora's smile was wide, but her eyes were calculating. "Can I ask how you heard about us?"

"A party, of course. I think it was the opera gala in March." I waved my hand as if the details were unimportant. "I heard your store is a place to find something special." I took a step closer and lowered my voice. "The gift is for my fiancé's mother. She has a small collection of one-of-a-kind items. We're...not close, but I hoped that if I could find something to add to her collection, it might smooth the waters. The wedding's only two months away, and I don't want her to cause trouble." I let my eyes water a bit, then bravely blinked away the unshed tears. "I love Dean *so much*."

"There, there," Dora said, patting my arm as she glanced at the large fake diamond engagement ring on my left hand. "I might have a few possibilities. What kinds of collectibles does your future mother-in-law like?"

"I haven't seen her collection," I sniffled, following Dora back toward the counter. "Dean's told me about it. That's what gave me the idea. I want something really special, something thoughtful."

"Wait here. I'll bring a few options out to show you." Dora disappeared into a back room.

Sean sidled up to me and lowered his head so that his mouth was near my ear. "Who's Dean?"

"Just some guy on a TV show," I murmured, my lips barely moving.

His fingertips slid over the small of my back, making me shiver. "Good," he said softly. He stepped back.

Dora returned carrying a small black velvet box. She set it on the counter in front of me. I sensed magic trace, but it wasn't from the mirror.

She opened the box and folded back a linen wrapping. I gasped. "Oh."

It was a statement necklace, made of swirling silver vines and diamonds. Fire magic danced along my senses. "Oh," I said again, my eyes wide. "What does it do?"

Her eyes sparkled with humor. "I haven't worn it myself, but I understand that its previous owner never left a party alone while wearing it."

A lust spell, then, held in the red crystal near the top of the necklace. "It's beautiful," I said, then shook my head regretfully. "My mother-in-law doesn't strike me as the sort who would wear it, though."

"She might like it simply as a collector's piece," Dora suggested. "Perhaps an item she could loan out for special occasions."

"Maybe," I mused. "She's very old-fashioned. Everything she has is antique. She even has one of those vintage dressing tables, like they had *ages* ago." I wrinkled my nose, showing my disdain for such a bizarre item, and hoping she'd take the bait and bring out the hand mirror.

Dora wrapped up the necklace. "Let me look and see what else I have." She closed the box and headed into the back room again.

We waited. This time, when she returned, she was carrying another flat box, and this one emanated familiar magic trace. She set it on the counter, lifted the lid, and unwrapped the mirror.

A sheet of tissue paper covered the mirror's reflective surface. "It's gorgeous," I breathed. "Why is it covered?"

Dora held out to her hand. "Don't get too close. It's—"

Without warning, the ground heaved beneath our feet as a wave of magical energy washed over us and an earthquake shook the shop.

Dora stumbled back with a startled shriek as items fell off the walls and tables. Everything on the counter slid off and fell. I grabbed for the mirror, afraid of what would happen if it shattered on the floor and released its magic.

The tissue paper fell away, revealing my reflection in the mirror. I tried to look away but it was too late. I felt a surge of magic and the shop and everything else faded into soft darkness.

I woke from a familiar nightmare, my heart pounding. I whimpered into the darkness of my room in my grandfather's compound. I expected my mother to come in to comfort me as she usually did, but she didn't appear.

I crawled out of bed, clutching Bernie, my stuffed rabbit, and crept down the hall. I could sneak into bed with my parents and they would hold me until I could fall asleep again.

As I approached their room, however, I heard voices. My parents weren't asleep and Mom sounded upset. I paused outside the door, trying to figure out if I should go in.

"She told me he made her do something that killed two people yesterday," my mother sobbed. "He's made her a killer, John. She's a baby."

I pressed my face against Bernie. Why did my mom call me a baby? I'm not a baby, I thought resentfully. Grandfather says I'm not a baby.

"We'll get her away from here as soon as we have a chance," my dad said. "I've been setting something up with some people from Paris. We'll get her out of the country, but we have to wait until the right time, until we know we can get there without leaving a trail. I know it's hard, Moira. You've got to hang on."

"I want to protect her from him, but I can't." My mother's voice was tight with pain. "Everything I've ever done, I did to keep her safe, but it wasn't enough. I can't even tell her who her father is, because if my father knew the truth he'd kill us all."

"You know you can't tell her, not yet," my dad said gently. "She's a child. She'd never be able to keep that a secret. Someday, once we're away from here and she can understand, you can tell her about Daniel."

Mom took a deep breath. "I've never forgiven myself for not telling him, but he was getting out, leaving this nightmare behind. He bought a bookstore in California. He never would have left if he'd known I was pregnant."

"If he'd stayed, you'd all three probably be dead." The bedding rustled. "Maybe she can find him when she's older, if she wants to. In the meantime, I love her like she's my own. You know that. She's my daughter and I'm her dad. And I swear I will get us all away from here just as soon as I can."

"I know." My mother started to cry again.

My dad made soothing sounds. My mother's crying was muffled, as if she was weeping against his chest.

I tiptoed back down the hall to my room and slipped into bed, squeezing Bernie tightly. My parents' conversation didn't make sense, and I resented that my mother had called me a baby. Magic sparked on my fingertips as a breeze blew through my room.

I fell asleep, still frowning, the whispered conversation between my parents a fading fragment of a memory in the mind of a child who, at age six, had already killed on the orders of her own grandfather.

I found myself huddled on the floor of Dora Quinn's wrecked antique shop, clutching the hand mirror so hard that my fingers were cramping. Someone had wrapped it in a cloth to cover the glass.

Sean was crouched next to me, his hand on my shoulder. "Audrey? Can you hear me?"

The memory was already fading, but I clung to pieces of it.

I can't even tell her who her father is, because if my father knew the truth he'd kill us all.
Someday, once we're away from here and she can understand, you can tell her about Daniel.
He never would have left if he'd known I was pregnant.
I love her like she's my own.

I let out a strangled sob.

Sean gently pried the mirror out of my grasp, put it in the box, and closed the lid. He slid it over so that it was next to him, then folded me in his arms. I trembled so hard that my teeth chattered.

Dora Quinn appeared, looking shell-shocked. I dimly recalled an earthquake and realized she was probably reeling from the damage to the shop's inventory.

"I have to call our insurance company and my business partner," she said shakily. "So many things are destroyed. I'll take this." She reached for the box.

Sean snarled. She jumped back with a frightened sound.

"That mirror is stolen property," I rasped. "You bought it from a fence. I'm returning it to its rightful owner. Be thankful the owner doesn't want to press charges. Receiving stolen property is a felony."

Dora's face turned beet red. "I have no idea what you are talking about. I have *never*—"

"Ms. Quinn, this is the best offer you could hope to receive under the circumstances," Sean said. "Now, why don't you go into the back and make those calls and Ms. Talbot and I will leave."

Dora took one look at Sean's golden eyes and made the right decision. "Fine," she snapped. She turned and stomped into the back office, slamming the door behind her.

Sean nuzzled my hair and held me. "Alice, whatever it was you saw, I'm sorry."

I shivered as a dozen emotions clashed inside me. How could I have forgotten something like that? I had other memories from when I was six; why didn't I remember that I'd heard my parents talking about my real father?

A thought occurred to me: was the supposed "lost memory" even real, or was it a cruel trick by the magic mirror? I'd been thinking about family lately. I'd encountered a lot of magical objects and many of them had had a mind of their own. Some were kind; others were malicious. The mirror might have plucked a real memory from my head, combined it with my longing for family, and generated a false recollection.

"We need to leave," Sean told me, interrupting my thoughts. He kissed my temple. "Can you walk?"

"I can walk." My voice was hoarse. "Get that box, and let's get the hell out of here."

9

On the way home, we found out the earthquake was the result of another magical attack. This one destroyed two buildings only a mile away from the antique shop. Earth mages had taken out one of Darius Bell's smaller holdings. There was little structural damage to other buildings, but a lot of broken store windows and loss of shop inventory in the Heights.

When we returned to my house, I carried the box inside, holding it like it was full of angry bees. While Sean let Rogue in from the backyard, I took the box down to the basement, locked it in one of my cupboards, then went upstairs to my room to change.

When I came out of the bathroom in jeans and a T-shirt, Sean was waiting in my bedroom, standing at the foot of my bed. We stared at each other.

The tension in his shoulders and worry in his eyes told me he wanted to ask what I'd seen, but he didn't.

I wanted to tell him, but I couldn't. The secret was too big and too dangerous.

Was this what it was going to be like for as long as we were together? Secrets, half-truths, and lies? I tried to imagine how I would feel if our situation was reversed and it was Sean who refused to tell me anything about himself, who radiated guilt and anger, but wouldn't explain why. Would I be as patient as him? When would his patience run out?

Before he left for Seattle, Special Agent Trent Lake of SPEMA had figured out I wasn't who I claimed to be. He'd seen enough to know he didn't want to know any more than that. How long before Sean came to the same conclusion? He'd already inferred that I'd been a killer before I came to the city. It wasn't much of a leap from that to realizing my whole identity was a lie.

I looked at him and wondered—would there be a point when I'd trust him enough to tell him the truth? And if not, what was I doing having dinner with members of his pack and making him think there was a chance for something long-term between us?

"Penny for your thoughts," he said.

I took a deep, shaky breath. "I'm not sure they're worth even that much."

"If I can guess what you're thinking about, do I win a prize?"

I eyed him uneasily.

"You were thinking that you want to tell me what you saw, but you can't. Then you started wondering if you'll ever be able to tell me your secrets and you're not sure, so now you're asking yourself if there's any point to this." He gestured between us. "Am I right?"

"Something like that," I admitted.

He crossed the room and stood in front of me, pinning me with those beautiful golden-brown eyes. "Then let me be clear: I am not angry or resentful toward you because of your secrets. I am angry that there is someone out there who is a danger to you, forcing you to keep these secrets while they eat you up from the inside. At some point, I hope you will trust me enough to share those secrets with me, but I understand we are not there yet."

"Thank you," I said quietly.

"If it had been me who'd looked into that mirror, I can't say for sure if I would want to tell you what I saw, so let's put that aside for now and talk about what *does* frustrate me." His gaze hardened. "We've had this conversation before, but you don't seem to believe me when I say I am with you because I want to be here. Your secrets, whatever they are, have convinced you that you are not worthy of being cared for. Stop second-guessing how I feel about you. There's a lot of crazy shit going on the world, but if there is one thing you can count on, Alice Worth, it's me." His eyes blazed.

"It's probably hard to tell sometimes, but I hope you know I trust you more than I've trusted anyone in a very long time," I told him. "As for the rest...it's all just the bullshit in my head."

His expression softened and he laced his fingers through mine. "There's bullshit in my head too, but when I'm with you, it's better." Something dark lurked in his eyes.

"Tell me," I said. "Please." Maybe it wasn't fair of me to ask since I wasn't telling him my secrets, but if he had a burden and I could help carry it, I would.

He ran his nose along my hairline. I leaned my head against his chest and listened to the sound of his heart.

He took a deep breath. "A couple of years ago, I got wind of trouble in a smaller pack about two hundred miles from here. The rumor was the new alpha was abusing the women and girls in the pack and the local LEOs were the sort who weren't interested in helping any kind of shifters, even if they were minors. None of the other packs in the area wanted to get involved; we tend to stay out of each other's business, generally speaking. I wasn't in a hurry to get involved either until I got an e-mail from a woman named Jean, begging me for help because the alpha had raped her daughter and nearly killed her son when he tried to stop the assault."

I flinched.

"The next day, I went out there with Jack and a couple other members of my pack, but it was too late. The alpha had discovered Jean's e-mail and killed her." His voice was flat. "I killed the alpha. Jack killed the beta. Jean's children joined our pack. You've met them: Karen and Patrick."

I thought of Karen's kind eyes and magic sizzled on my skin.

Sean squeezed me tighter. "If I'd acted sooner, Jean might still be alive and Karen and Patrick might not have been hurt. I live with that, every day."

"A lot of packs wouldn't have done anything or even taken in the refugees, much less gone out there and challenged the alpha," I pointed out.

"I know that, Alice," he said patiently. "But that doesn't change the guilt I feel and it's precious little comfort when I go to Karen's house and see pictures of Jean. I know Karen and Patrick don't blame me for her death, but I blame myself and I always will."

We stood silently for a while. Sean slid his hand under my T-shirt and pulled me against his body, wrapping his arm tightly around my waist. The feeling of his skin against mine and his familiar scent comforted me.

"The memory I saw...I don't know if it's real," I said. "Magical objects aren't always what they seem. I only have Esther Aldridge's word that the mirror shows forgotten memories. It could just as easily have created something from bits and pieces in my head."

Sean stroked my hair. "Is there any way to know for sure?"

"Maybe."

I had a first name: Daniel. He'd been associated with Moses's cabal but left around the time I was born, heading—according to the memory—for California. A good researcher might be able to find him, if he existed. It wasn't that simple, though. If the memory *was* real, and I did have a biological father somewhere, he had no idea I existed. Who was I to go in and potentially turn his life upside down?

I had no idea who this Daniel might have been, but my mother seemed to think that if Moses knew he was my real father, he would have killed all three of us. If I tracked him down, would I be putting his life at risk still? Why would Moses kill Daniel for having a baby with my mother? And why would he kill me for simply existing? Who was this Daniel?

A father. I couldn't get the possibility out of my head. Would we resemble each other? I'd looked a lot like my mother, before the surgery that turned me into Alice Worth, but maybe I'd looked like Daniel too. My mind started conjuring images of how he might look, who he might be.

If I did find him, what would I even say to him? *Hi, you don't know me, but about thirty years ago you had a relationship with Moses Murphy's daughter Moira, and, well...ta-dah!* I let out an almost hysterical half-laugh. The entire situation was beyond surreal.

Sean held me tightly, kissing the top of my head. "If I can help, let me know."

"Thanks." I smiled up at him. "You were pretty menacing as Audrey's bodyguard, by the way. I've never seen that side of you. I gotta be honest...it was really sexy."

"I could tell you liked it."

I wound my arms around his neck. "Oh, yeah? How could you tell?"

He ran his lips along my jaw and nipped my earlobe. "Your scent," he murmured into my ear. "It was making me crazy. It *is* making me crazy."

I shivered. "It is?"

"It certainly is." He inhaled deeply and growled low in his throat. "Whatever you're thinking about, you need to either stop or take off your clothes."

"What time do we need to leave for Karen's?"

He grinned and glanced at the clock. "Seven."

It was almost four. "Plenty of time for you to nap, then."

His grin became a frown.

"You didn't sleep last night," I reminded him. "You can't be an effective bodyguard on no sleep. You look tired."

He didn't argue, which meant he really was worn out. "What are you going to do?"

"I think I'm recovered enough now to let Malcolm out of my bracelet, check him for any more hidden spells, and talk to him about what happened last night." I remembered the way the ghost had looked at me after I'd ripped the spell out of his body and wondered how he'd react to seeing me. It had been almost a full day since a blood mage had tried to steal him away, but for him it had only been seconds.

"You won't go outside." He looked uneasy.

"I promise I won't go outside. I'll be in the basement until I know Malcolm is safe from Bell." I kissed him deeply. "Get some rest."

He sighed and ran his hands through his hair. "I'd sleep better if you were next to me."

I hesitated. I could let Malcolm out when we got back from Karen's. I'd be more recovered by then, and it would be safer for both of us. Plus, the thought of napping wrapped in Sean's arms was just too good an offer to pass up. "Okay," I said reluctantly. I wagged my finger at him. "But we're going to *nap*. No funny business."

"No funny business," he promised.

I got my pajamas from the back of the bathroom door and brought them into the bedroom. Sean's reaction was very different from Arkady Woodall's. "I like the sheep." His eyes glinted. "Wolves like sheep. Very tasty."

I bared my teeth at him. He laughed and headed into the bathroom.

While he was in the bathroom, the mobile team radioed in to report a shift change. I hadn't realized that Jack's presence outside my house was causing me to feel tense until I thought about him leaving and my shoulders relaxed.

I changed into the pajamas and looked at myself in the mirror over my dresser. Part of me wanted to throw our "no funny business" agreement to the wind, but Sean needed his sleep.

I sighed. "Cold showers and baseball," I told my reflection.

"What was that?" he asked from the bathroom.

"Nothing. Just talking to myself."

By the time Sean came back out wearing lounge pants and a faded Quiet Riot T-shirt, I was already in bed. What little daylight there was sneaking past the curtains reflected gold in his eyes as he crossed the room and climbed in next to me.

I rolled onto my side and Sean curled around me, wrapping his arm around my waist and pulling me against his body. We fit together like pieces of a puzzle, I thought to myself. I wriggled in closer.

Sean buried his face in the back of my neck and kissed me. "I'm here and I'm not going anywhere," he murmured, his breath tickling my skin. "But you're going to have to stop wiggling or that promise I made about no funny business is going to get broken."

I stilled. His skin was hot and the warmth seeped into me.

I worried we wouldn't be able to relax, but it didn't turn out to be a problem. Within minutes, we were both asleep.

We arrived at Karen's house at seven thirty on the dot. Sean parked his SUV in the driveway of a two-story farmhouse not far outside the city limits and the mobile team parked off to the side of the driveway, next to a sporty red car and a smaller SUV. He escorted me to the front door, carrying a bottle of Karen's favorite wine that we'd picked up on the way.

As we walked up the sidewalk, he bent down to murmur in my ear, "You look beautiful."

I wore a blue sundress and sandals with my monogram pendant, dangly earrings, and my charm bracelet. Despite the warm summer evening, I'd decided to wear my hair down. The look was somewhat spoiled by the bulletproof vest, but at least I'd get to take it off once we were inside.

The door opened as we approached and a smiling man who looked to be in his early thirties stepped aside to let us into the house. "Come on in, you two," he said warmly, shaking Sean's hand as he closed the door. "Everyone's in the living room." He turned to me and offered his hand. "Alice, it's great to meet you. I'm Cole, Karen's husband."

"Nice to meet you too," I said, shaking his hand. Sean had told me on the way to the house that Karen's husband was human. Several members of the pack had human spouses. It gave me hope that I might be more accepted at some point. Some packs didn't permit human mates, but the Tomb Mountain pack had always been more progressive, Sean said.

I took off the vest and Cole stuck it in the coat closet. I smoothed my dress, making a face at the wrinkles. As Cole turned to lead us to the living room, Sean squeezed my hand.

Four people were waiting for us. Karen was the first to greet me as we entered. "Alice!" She hurried to meet me and gave me a quick hug. I'd worried I would be underdressed, but she was wearing a light summer dress and sandals. She took the wine Sean had brought and set it on the table.

I recognized Felicia Lowell, though she looked very different than the last time I'd seen her, which was after several days of captivity and torture at the hands of the West-Addison harnad. She wore capri pants and a cute top, her long blonde hair in a neat braid.

"Alice, it's so good to get to meet you finally," she said, offering me her hand. "I never got a chance to thank you personally for rescuing me."

As we shook, I noticed faint scars on her wrists and ankles from the silver cuffs that had restrained her. Even werewolf healing abilities had their limits.

I shook hands with Felicia's brother David next. Then Karen introduced Nan, Felicia and David's mother.

The older woman threw her arms around me and hugged me tightly. "Thank you for saving my daughter," she told me as my ribs creaked.

"You're welcome," I wheezed.

Karen offered us something to drink. I requested a lemonade and Sean asked for a beer.

As Karen went to the kitchen, Sean glanced out the patio door to the deck, where a long table was set up for dinner. He counted the chairs and frowned. "Who else are we expecting?" he asked as Karen returned with our drinks.

She paused as she handed him a bottle. "Did Jack not tell you he was coming with Delia and they're bringing Caleb?"

At his expression, Karen took a step back and the others tensed. "I thought he told you," she said. "He said he was going to."

"It must have slipped his mind." Sean smiled at Karen. "Not your fault."

I wasn't sure how to react to the news of the unexpected guests. I didn't know enough about Sean's pack politics to think Jack had deliberately not told his alpha about his plans to crash the dinner party, but I suspected that might be the case. The tension in Sean's shoulders indicated that despite his reassurance, he wasn't very happy about this turn of events.

Felicia asked about my dress and we conversed for a few minutes, but the atmosphere in the room had turned noticeably edgy. I was angry at Jack for spoiling the mood but tried not to let it show. Sean would deal with the situation.

When all of the shifters turned toward the door at the same time, I guessed they'd heard someone pull up out front. Cole started for the foyer, but Sean held up his hand. "Let me," he said. It was phrased as a request, but Cole deferred to Sean immediately.

"Why don't we go out on the deck?" Karen suggested cheerfully as Sean headed for the front door.

We filed out the patio door and Cole closed it behind us. The back of the house faced east, so it was delightfully shady and cool.

"It's beautiful out here," I told my hosts, moving to stand at the railing and look out over their enormous backyard. "I love it. So peaceful."

"Where do you live?" Felicia asked, joining me at the railing.

"In town, on the east side. It's a quiet neighborhood, thankfully."

We chatted as the minutes ticked by. If the shifters could hear anything that was going on out front, they didn't let on. Finally, just when I was starting to wonder if one of us should go check on the rest of the dinner party, a group of people crossed the living room toward the patio doors with Sean in the lead.

When Sean slid the door open and stepped out onto the deck, I moved to join him. He was angry; I could see it in his eyes and in the tension in his shoulders, but when he kissed me, his mouth was gentle. I wasn't sure if he was staking a claim or if I was, but the kiss certainly made a statement.

The reaction among the shifters was palpable. I sensed pleasant surprise from Nan, Felicia, David, Karen, and Cole, and open hostility from the others. Jack's blue eyes were amber, a sign that his wolf was near his skin and angry.

The woman standing next to Jack, who I assumed was his wife, was much shorter than her husband, with shoulder-length curly brown hair and brown eyes. She wore slacks and a teal sleeveless top that showed off her toned arms. Behind them was a tall, surly young man with dark hair that hung in his eyes, wearing a black T-shirt and jeans.

Sean rested his hand on my lower back and turned to the others. "Alice, you've met Jack already. This is Delia, Jack's wife."

"Nice to meet you," I said, extending my hand.

After a beat, she took it. Her handshake was brief and she squeezed more forcefully than was necessary. "You too," she said shortly. Our eyes met and hers dropped before she looked back up, startled. Delia's wolf had recognized a more dominant female and indicated submissiveness.

Sean turned to the young man standing apart from the rest of the group. "Caleb Jennings, this is Alice Worth."

Grudgingly, he shuffled toward me, hand outstretched. As I shook his hand, he leaned close and sniffed.

Taken aback, I let go of his hand. "Hey."

"Caleb," Sean said sharply.

"Sorry," the young werewolf muttered. He stepped back and resumed staring at the ground.

"Well, we're all here, so let's eat!" Karen suggested.

We sat down as Karen and Cole brought out covered trays laden with pieces of chicken and steaks that looked like they had been placed on the grill just long enough to get them warm.

Before I could figure out how to politely request a salad, Cole set a plate down in front of me with a moderately sized steak cooked medium. "Wouldn't expect you to eat like a wolf," he joked, settling in across from me with his own steak. "It'll be nice to share a meal with someone else who doesn't like their steaks still mooing."

"Don't knock it till you've tried it." Sean looked over the table appreciatively. "Everything looks fantastic, guys. Thank you for inviting us."

"Our pleasure. Dig in!" Cole said.

The meal turned out to be pleasant, despite the unexpected guests. Whether by accident or design, Sean and I sat at one end of the table and Jack, Delia, and Caleb at the other end. I sat between Sean and Karen and across from Cole and Felicia. Our conversation was easy and cheerful. I answered questions about my work and chatted with the others as Sean ate and talked quietly with Nan. Several times during the meal, I sensed pointed stares from the other end of the table, but ignored them.

As I ate, I slid my foot out of my sandal and slowly ran my toes along Sean's calf. He calmly ate his food without so much as a glance in my direction, but I saw a gold sheen in his eyes. Nan's eyes twinkled as she watched us.

I started to get a sense of the pack hierarchy, at least among those at the table, based on nonverbal cues and the conversations around me. My brief exchange with Delia earlier had shown I had a relative position in the pack, despite being human and not a member, and the others had adjusted accordingly.

The mountain of food on the table disappeared at an alarming rate. The speed and single-minded efficiency with which they put food away was impressive and this was less than half the pack. Suddenly, my quip about needing five-gallon buckets of potato salad for the cookout seemed more like something I would have to actually look into.

Sean and I offered to help clear the table but Karen and Cole insisted on doing it themselves before bringing out dessert, which turned out to be homemade brownies with ice cream. I managed to eat almost half of mine before I couldn't take one more bite without risking busting a seam on my dress. It had been a little loose when we arrived but now felt a bit tight in the middle.

As we were drinking coffee and letting our food settle, Jack tossed his napkin on his empty plate, put down his coffee cup, and turned his piercing blue gaze on me. "So, I saw some interesting pictures online. You were quite the little hell-raiser back in Chicago, weren't you, Alice?"

Startled, I jerked and glared at him. We stared at each other. Amber rolled over Jack's eyes.

Sean's hand moved to my thigh and squeezed. "Lower your eyes, Alice," he said softly.

I resisted, not wanting to show submissiveness to Jack. A second ticked by. Two. Sean took my hand, lacing his fingers through mine.

The others watched Sean's beta warily as the large man leaned forward in his chair. No one breathed.

"Jack, stand down," Sean commanded.

"She's disrespectful," Jack growled.

"She's not pack," Sean said flatly. "She's shown you respect until now, but you were rude. You know as well as I do humans who don't spend much time around shifters don't react with the same instincts."

Jack's posture remained aggressive. "If she's with you, she needs to learn."

I bristled.

Sean's hand tightened on mine. "When she's around pack members, Alice will—"

"Don't talk about me like I'm not sitting here," I said.

The others looked startled that I'd interrupted their alpha. When Sean gestured for me to speak, I glanced at each of them. "When I'm around members of the pack I'll do the best I can to interact with you on your terms, but I'm sure we'll run into issues sometimes because I'm not a werewolf. You'll have to meet me partway."

"We don't have to meet you anywhere," Delia said curtly.

"You do," Sean said. If there had been a hint of his power in his tone before, now it was pure steel. "Because when you speak to Alice, you speak to me."

The werewolves around the table reacted as one, surprise rippling out in an almost visible wave.

"Is she your mate?" Jack demanded.

"Not yet," Sean said. He raised our entwined hands and put them deliberately on top of the table. "But I'm hoping." He stared at Jack as the others exchanged glances.

We'd have to talk about that later. For now, I looked around the table again, letting them see that I wasn't afraid. I even met Jack's eyes briefly. I wasn't trying to start a fight, but I wasn't going to be run over, by Jack or anyone else.

Finally, Sean defused the situation by rising from the table. The others followed suit, their eyes not meeting his. Even Cole, who wasn't a shifter, avoided Sean's hot golden gaze.

"Thank you for having us over," Sean told Karen with a smile. "Everything was excellent. Can we help you with the cleanup?"

"My kids and I are staying to help," Nan told him, winking at me. "We'll have it all done in a jiffy. You two run along."

"I don't think I'll be running anywhere anytime soon," I said, making a face. "I might need someone to roll me out to the SUV."

"I've got a wheelbarrow in the shed," Cole offered.

Everyone but Jack and Delia laughed at that. Even Caleb smiled fleetingly, though his face returned to its customary scowl quickly.

As evening turned to night, we filed inside carrying our dishes and made sure everything was in neat piles in the kitchen. I excused myself to use the restroom before we left.

When I came out, Sean waited by the front door with my vest. I groaned. "Oh, please don't make me put that on. I'm so full."

He looked sympathetic but stubborn. "It's adjustable. We'll leave it a little loose."

I grumbled as he slipped the vest over my head and fastened the straps. True to his word, he didn't tighten it as much as before, but I was instantly miserable and in no mood for any more trouble when Jack, Delia, and Caleb joined us in the foyer, which suddenly felt much too small.

Caleb stood next to me, bumping my arm with his. "Why does she have to wear a bulletproof vest?"

"It's a safety precaution," Sean said. "Alice is in a dangerous line of work."

His eyes lit up. "Cool." For the first time all evening, the young werewolf looked interested instead of surly. He brushed against me, jostling me deliberately again.

I held my ground. "Back up, Caleb. You're in my space."

Caleb growled. His fists clenched and his eyes went golden. Fury and resentment rolled off him in waves as shifter magic surged. I tensed, spooling magic in case he shifted and attacked.

Instantly, Sean was between us. The force of his alpha magic made the others take a step back. "You will not shift in this house," he told Caleb. "If you can't control your temper and your shifting, you'll have to go out to the pack land until you can. You endanger all of us by acting like this and I will not have you threaten Alice. Is that clear?"

There was a long pause as Caleb fought to control his wolf. When he replied, his voice had an edge of growl in it. "Yes."

Sean turned to Jack. "Can he stay with you tonight?"

"Yes." Jack put a hand on Caleb's shoulder and the younger man seemed to relax. The surge of shifter magic dissipated.

"Good. Take him home and keep an eye on him."

Jack gave Sean a nod. However strained the relationship between Sean and his beta might be because of me, they seemed united in their concern about the pack's youngest wolf, and for good reason. I'd only spent a few hours around Caleb, but it was obvious he was far from stable. The phrase "ticking time bomb" came to mind, and those were not words you wanted to use when describing a werewolf.

We moved to the door, Sean staying between Caleb and me. He took the radio off his belt and told the mobile team we were heading out. Once we'd gotten the all-clear from Philip, Sean reached for the door.

"Alice!"

I turned at the sound of Karen's voice. She hurried over to me with a small gift bag. "This is for you."

I blinked in surprise and took the bag. "What's this?"

"Just a little gift from us." She hugged me and then stepped back.

"Are we set?" Sean asked, his hand on my waist.

"All set." I smiled at Karen. "Thanks again for having us."

"It was our pleasure. Come back and see us again soon."

"I will," I promised as Sean ushered me out the door.

Without being told, I stayed in Sean's shadow as we went to the SUV and let him load me into the passenger seat. I felt Jack's gaze on me as clearly as if he were touching me, drilling twin holes between my shoulder blades until the SUV door slammed closed.

As Sean went over to talk to the mobile team, I let out the breath I'd been holding and reached into the gift bag. I pulled out a small, heavy item wrapped in tissue paper. When I unwrapped it, I found a snow globe. Inside the glass dome was a tiny forest covered in white snow and a group of wolves, their muzzles raised toward the sky as if in mid-howl. In the center of the group was a black-and-gray wolf, a little larger than the others, with golden-brown eyes and big, magnificent teeth.

Inside the bag, I also found a card that read simply *Welcome to the pack*. It was signed by Karen, Cole, Nan, Felicia, and David.

I smiled and shook the globe, watching the snow dance.

10

"You did good," Sean said as he turned the key in the ignition.

I gave him a flat look.

He heaved a sigh. "I didn't mean it like that. You don't need my approval. What I meant was that you showed them you aren't to be pushed around by anyone—not even me, and I'm glad you did."

I raised one shoulder in a half-shrug. "I didn't like the way Jack was treating me."

"I'm sorry." Sean squeezed my hand.

"Not your fault he's acting this way. Everyone else was wonderful. I just wonder how many other members of the pack are going to resent me as much as he and Delia do."

"They'll just have to get over it. Nothing matters but you and me." He grimaced and gestured in the direction of the mobile team's SUV. "Well, once this business with Kent Stevens is over."

I smiled and leaned over to kiss him, the mobile team, Jack, and Delia be damned. I grabbed a handful of his hair and teased his tongue with mine, turning up the heat. If they were looking over here, I wanted them to get their money's worth.

Finally, I pulled back, the skin around my mouth burning a bit from his beard stubble. Totally worth it.

Sean's eyes twinkled. "Trying to make a point?"

I settled back in my seat and belted in. "Maybe."

He chuckled and drove toward the main road. As we bumped down the gravel drive, he grew serious again. "If you ever feel threatened by anyone in the pack, no matter who it is, defend yourself. I hope it doesn't come to that, but if it does, do what you have to."

"That was my plan."

The corners of his mouth turned up. "I thought as much, but I figured it wouldn't hurt to say it out loud."

As we turned out onto the highway and accelerated, he said, "I noticed what happened when you met Delia. You don't seem surprised by her reaction. I didn't expect you to fall into the pack hierarchy so easily." He paused. "You know I want to ask."

I shrugged. "You already know I've spent time around shifters. It's not my first interaction with a group of werewolves and not the first time I've been recognized as a more dominant female. You could say I have a fairly well-developed sense of how pack hierarchy works, for a human."

"It's more than fairly well-developed. I'd say you have an instinct for it. Is it possible you have some shifter blood in your family?"

"Not that I'm aware of, but it would explain a few...oddities with my magic. It would have to be at least three generations back or more, though." I smiled. "It would be funny if I were part cat shifter."

Sean groaned. "Oh, please, *anything* but a cat shifter." He pondered that for a moment, then added, "It would explain a few things, however."

I poked him in the side, which had little effect through his vest. We drove in companionable silence for a while.

When we were about ten minutes from my house, my phone rang. I glanced at the screen and answered. "Hello, Charles."

"Alice, my dear, how was your meal with the wolves?" he purred. "Was dinner served on the hoof or were they actually quite civilized?"

There was no chance he didn't hear Sean's growl. I made an exasperated sound. "The meal was wonderful. Do you have any news? Is Stevens in custody?"

"Not yet." Charles's voice lost its mocking tone. "Our people are searching the city, but have found no trace of him."

I sighed and pulled unhappily at the side strap of my vest. "Then why are you calling?"

"I may have located one of your missing items."

I perked up, the vest and my discomfort forgotten. "Which one? Where is it?"

"I believe I know where your magic cup will be tonight."

"Where?"

"An auction."

I blinked. "An auction? What kind of auction?"

"A very exclusive auction." Charles's voice held a note of amusement.

"*How* exclusive?" I asked impatiently.

"Invitation only. Impenetrable security. Location known only to a handful of carefully selected individuals whose discretion is beyond reproach."

My eyes narrowed. "So you know where it is."

"I do."

I was in no mood for Charles's games. "Can you get me in or not?"

"Get *us* in," Sean interjected.

Charles overheard Sean's comment. "You, yes," he said. "The werewolf, on the other hand—"

"Vampire, where she goes, *I* go," Sean stated flatly.

"Well, you heard him," I told Charles. "So, what's your plan for sneaking Sean and me into this super-secret, ultra-exclusive auction?"

"I will not be sneaking you in," Charles said.

Sean growled.

The vampire chuckled. One of these days, he was going to find out why it was a bad idea to bait a werewolf. "You will be walking in through the front door."

I walked in through the front door.

Charles handed our invitations to the enormous tuxedo-clad security guard and rested his hand on mine where it was curled around his arm.

As the doorman looked over the invitations, I took the opportunity to glance around. The auction was taking place at a private mansion not far from Northbourne Manor, headquarters of the Vampire Court of the Northwestern United States. The interior of the house looked more like a museum than a residence.

The man-mountain at the door slipped our invitations into the basket at his elbow and gave Charles a small bow. "Welcome, Mr. Vaughan, Ms. Worth. You may wait in the main hall. The event starts promptly at twelve. Please be in your seats in the salon before it begins."

Charles inclined his head and we moved into the foyer. Behind us, Sean and Bryan, our escorts, stepped inside and the doorman greeted the next couple.

The entryway led to a wide hall. Paintings covered the walls and antiques and relics took up every available surface. Some held magic. I gave those a wide berth. About a dozen well-dressed vampires and a few humans sipped wine and champagne, browsed the art on display, and conversed quietly. Wait staff circulated among the guests, offering drinks and hors d'oeuvres.

Charles and I each took a glass of champagne. His was pink. Not rosé champagne, though, I decided immediately, as my magic tingled—champagne with a few drops of blood added for color and taste.

Bryan and Sean stood behind us, silent and watchful. Charles, like the other guests, had been limited to one security escort per person. Bryan appeared to have healed from his wounds, though his eyes were shadowed and he'd been uncharacteristically quiet since Charles's limo had picked Sean and me up at my house.

The forty-minute drive from my house to the mansion had been tense. When Sean had asked Charles where the vampire was residing since the ambush at his gate, Charles had evaded the question and repeated his invitation for me to stay with him. Sean had not taken that well. We'd avoided bloodshed, but only just.

Charles raised my hand to his cool lips. "You look divine, my dear."

I wore a floor-length, shimmery midnight-blue dress that clung like a second skin. Though it covered my back and arms, hiding my scars and tattoos, the front showcased my cleavage. The slit in the front went to mid-thigh. The dress and the four-inch stiletto heels had been supplied by Charles and both were a perfect fit. They'd arrived at my house less than fifteen minutes after we'd returned from Karen's house, accompanied by a professional makeup and hair stylist who trapped me in my bathroom for over an hour. I looked sultry and bronzed and not at all like myself.

I sipped my champagne. "I'm here to work, Charles. Stop flirting."

"One does not necessarily preclude the other," he said easily, exchanging a nod with a passing male vampire I didn't recognize. "We have little opportunity to see one another in a social setting. I have certainly never seen you wearing anything so alluring."

"It's a costume, nothing more," I said, my voice pitched so only Charles's ears could hear me. "I'm arm candy, as far as everyone here is concerned."

Charles leaned close, his lips a millimeter from my ear. "It is expected I should flirt outrageously with my 'arm candy,'" he murmured. "They will presume we are lovers, and suspect nothing of you." He slid his arm around my waist, brushing my butt with his fingertips as he did so.

"If you do that again, you may lose a hand," I muttered.

He arched an imperious eyebrow. "Your werewolf would be foolish to attack over so little a provocation."

I smiled with my teeth and tapped his glass with mine. "I wasn't talking about Sean."

He chuckled. "Oh, Alice, I do believe you mean it."

"I assure you I do."

Charles finished his champagne and a server appeared as if by magic to exchange his empty glass for a full one. I continued to sip my own drink slowly. I needed to keep my head clear and my senses sharp.

An unfamiliar vampire approached us, glass in hand. I didn't recognize him, but Charles apparently did.

"Vincent," my companion said, his voice suddenly glacial. "I was led to believe this was an *exclusive* affair, but your presence leads me to conclude that standards have slipped somewhat."

The tall, dark-skinned vampire chuckled. "Vaughan, how nice to see you again. And who is this lovely woman?" He turned to me and extended his hand. "Vincent Barclay, at your service."

I offered my hand. He caught it in his cool grasp, bowed, and brushed his lips across my skin.

"May I present my guest this evening, Ms. Alice Worth," Charles said formally. "Alice, Mr. Barclay is visiting from Seattle."

"Pleased to meet you," I murmured.

The other vampire released my hand almost reluctantly, sliding his fingers through mine in a deliberate provocation. Charles drew me possessively against his side.

"Have you ever visited Seattle, Alice?" Barclay asked. He lingered over my name, as if savoring it, and I didn't like the sound of my name in his mouth.

"I didn't care for it," I said shortly. "Far too much rain."

He chuckled. "Perhaps you have not adequately explored the pleasures of being wet."

Charles's anger became white-hot fury. Behind us, both Sean and Bryan took a step closer.

"I do hope your stay is brief," Charles told the visiting vamp before I could respond. "I am sure you are needed back home. Safe travels." It was a clear dismissal.

Barclay's eyes glowed silver in anger. He and Charles eyed each other for several long moments. Finally, the other vampire bowed to me, turned, and departed.

"Well, that was interesting," I said.

Stay away from him, Charles said in my head. *He is known to take women by force for both blood and sex.*

Why does that not surprise me? I responded.

Barclay rejoined a small group of vampires standing near a grotesque painting of a group of young women being led to an altar that dripped blood. He caught my eye and raised his glass in my direction.

I deliberately turned away and leaned my head toward my companion. *Ten bucks he calls his home his lair*, I said to Charles.

He chuckled aloud, but his eyes remained fixed on the Seattle vamp. I had rarely seen Charles lose his trademark cool, but clearly Barclay was odious enough to rate overt loathing.

Why hasn't the Court dealt with him, if they know this about him? I asked. *Drinking blood from non-consenting donors is a violation of both vampire and human law.* And a capital crime in many states, though not in California or Washington state.

Charles finally returned his attention to me. *He is not without allies in both the human and vampire world. The situation is complex.*

I scowled and sipped my drink. I still had Trent Lake's phone number; he'd insisted I keep it after he moved to Seattle to become the assistant director of the SPEMA field office there. Barclay was from Seattle. I was willing to bet Trent would go after Barclay, regardless of whatever allies the vampire had. I didn't think about it too much now, not in such close proximity to Charles, who might overhear a stray thought, but it might be worth giving Trent a call to see if anything could be done about Barclay.

I longed to turn around and look at Sean, but I kept my attention on Charles and the scene in front of me. Around the room, the guests chatted quietly among themselves, but no one paid the least attention to their security. Doing so might jeopardize my cover as Charles's arm candy.

More importantly, Sean was wearing a tailored tuxedo and I was trying very hard not to think about how good he looked and how much I wanted to get him home and take that tuxedo off with my teeth.

I sipped my champagne and focused on the other guests before my hormones got the best of me and Charles mistook my body's reaction to Sean in a tux as a response to his flirting. I recognized a few faces in the crowd, but most of them were vampires and not ones I knew personally.

So, besides the cup, what are the other items up for bid tonight? I asked Charles. I disliked talking to Charles telepathically since the ability to do so was a result of him biting me without my consent, but with so many sharp ears around us, this conversation was better had in our heads.

I understand there are six lots, all collector's pieces. I am interested in a few for my own collection. Neither of the other items you are seeking is among them.

I've already obtained the hand mirror, so after this, the only thing I'm missing is the cuff. For the record, I'm authorized to bid on the cup, up to ten thousand dollars.

He tilted his head. *If I may, perhaps it would be more seemly if I were to bid on your behalf.*

When I started to object, Charles added, *You are here as my guest, as my 'arm candy,' as you so colorfully put it. If you were to bid, you would attract quite a lot of attention, which I am sure you would prefer to avoid.*

He wasn't wrong about that, but I frowned. *If you win the bidding, you'll have possession of the cup. What guarantee do I have you'll turn it over to me or my client?*

Charles smiled and flashed his fangs. *Perhaps you will have to take my word?*

Only Herculean effort kept me from scowling. *That is not very reassuring.*

He grew serious. *You wound me. Have I not kept my word in all our dealings, from the moment you first began working for the Court?*

He had me there, though I might have pointed out that drinking my blood while I was in a coma might not have been a violation of his word, but it had been a terrible violation nonetheless. We'd come to a kind of fragile understanding about that, however, and there was little point in revisiting that discussion since each of us possessed the means of the other's destruction. He knew I wasn't the mid-level earth and air mage I claimed to be, and I could use our connection to control his body or even kill him. Neither of us was anxious for anyone else to know about either of those facts.

I could tell by Charles's expression that he knew what I was thinking, and he sensed I'd chosen not to bring it up. He gave me an almost imperceptible nod and turned his attention back to watching the room.

At ten minutes to midnight, two doors opened at the end of the hall and a man appeared. "If you would all please follow me," he said.

Charles offered his arm. I set my glass down on a table and we joined the rest of the guests.

As we approached the doors to the salon, there was something of a bottleneck and our movement halted. A familiar warm body moved up directly behind me. I knew without turning who it was.

It was a risk, but I reached back with my free hand. Strong fingers caressed mine and hot golden shifter magic ran over my skin as Sean squeezed my hand. The scent of forest filled my nose and a little of the tension drained out of my shoulders. Then we were moving again and he let go. I missed his touch immediately.

I wasn't sure if Charles had seen or sensed our brief contact, but he covered my hand with his and drew me closer.

Stop provoking Sean, I snapped. *You're being childish, and I'm not a prize for you to be fighting over.*

I have no idea what you are referring to, Charles replied, his voice in my head pure innocence. *I am merely concerned that you may lose your footing on the marble floor. It appears to be treacherous.*

My response was brief and quite profane. Charles shook with silent laughter.

Game face, I told myself as we reached the doors of the salon.

At an ordinary auction, the goal was to win the bidding on the item you wanted.

At this midnight gathering, the goal was to bid, win, and get out alive.

It became quickly apparent the kind of auctions Charles regularly attended were very different from any I'd seen before.

There were sixteen bidders in attendance, plus that many security escorts lined up along the walls in the salon. A solemn vampire named Marcus introduced each item, opened the bidding, and acknowledged bidders with a somber "Sir" or "Madame" rather than by name. There was certainly no crass, loud, fast-paced auctioneering; this was a high-class affair where all the bidders were deadly serious about their bids.

The hosts of the event were equally serious about security. As we entered the salon, we crossed strong wards and a magic suppression spell settled over us like an invisible, prickly blanket. It didn't smother my magic entirely, but neither I nor anyone else would be able to unleash any strong magic or spells without first breaking the wards, which I assumed were full of landmines designed to incapacitate or kill anyone who tried. Considering the kind of clientele who came to these events and the powerful nature of the items for sale, it made sense the hosts would do everything in their power to ensure both the safety of the participants and the security of the valuables.

Lot 1201, the first item up for bid, was a dagger resonant with blood magic. Marcus informed us the weapon would drain the magical energy of its victim into the person who wielded it. A low murmur ran through the assembled guests, and then the bidding began at the reserve price of five thousand dollars.

Charles didn't bid on the dagger and I tuned out as the bids went back and forth, climbing in increments of five hundred dollars.

Despite my resolve to not think about it, my brain returned to the alleged "lost" memory conjured up by the hand mirror and the possibility that my biological father might still be alive. I made sure my shields were strong so Charles didn't accidentally overhear any unguarded thoughts and tried to put it out of my mind. There was nothing I could do about it right now; there would be time to think about it all later, when I wasn't sitting in a room full of vampires.

The sudden sound of wood striking wood startled me out of my reverie. Instead of a traditional gavel, Marcus had a fist-sized wooden ball that he tapped on his podium to close the bidding. The dagger had been sold for ten thousand dollars, to a beautiful female vampire I didn't recognize. Assistants took the dagger backstage and Marcus informed the winning bidder she would be able to take possession of the dagger at her time of departure, once payment was made in full.

Lot 1202 was a vampire relic: a wine bottle spelled to preserve the life energy in human blood kept inside. Lot 1203 was far more intriguing to me. It was an object of power, a flat golden ring about eighteen inches wide designed to focus a mage's power. They went for twelve and eighteen thousand dollars respectively. A male vampire I didn't recognize bought the bottle. The ring went to a human man in a dark suit who looked to be either a broker or someone's proxy. Charles bid on each, but only at the beginning and never seriously. Court mages were capable of creating bottles like Lot 1202 and presumably the profit margin on objects like the ring were too small to make it worth his while.

Most of the audience appeared to be here as spectators rather than active bidders. Perhaps none of the items offered so far were of interest to them, or events like this were a place to be seen as much or more than a way to acquire magical items of, as my client had put it, "questionable legal status."

Lot 1204 was Esther's cup.

It was presented in a velvet-lined wooden box by a silent assistant. As the assistant walked the cup past the assembled bidders, Marcus spoke. "This cup is a unique item dating from, we believe, the early sixteenth century. While it is rather plain in appearance, the cup is quite remarkable. Drinking from it permits a vampire to remain awake for one hour past dawn and to walk without harm in direct sunlight."

A murmur ran through the guests. I almost sighed aloud. I'd hoped the cup's power would remain a mystery, but someone had recognized its magic. If I got outbid, I'd have to either attempt to recover the cup some other way or report to Esther that it had gone for more than I'd been authorized to spend. Though she had seemed far more interested in recovering the cuff, I wanted a one hundred percent success rate for this job.

That's the cup, I told Charles.

Understood.

The bidding began at the reserve price of five thousand dollars. The female vampire who had won Lot 1201 opened the bidding. Charles inclined his head and Marcus accepted his bid for five thousand five hundred dollars. The female vamp bid again, and again Charles put in a bid. Back and forth it went, until the price reached ten thousand dollars and the female vamp declined to offer another bid.

I was about to breathe a sigh of relief when I glimpsed movement out of the corner of my eye and Marcus said, "A new bidder. Ten thousand five hundred. Thank you, sir."

Vincent Barclay. Son of a bitch.

Marcus looked at Charles questioningly. Without hesitation, Charles nodded.

"The bid is eleven thousand," Marcus said.

Charles, what are you doing? I asked. *Ten-thousand-dollar limit, remember?*

No response.

To our left, a deeper nod from Barclay. "Twelve thousand," Marcus said, reading the other vampire's body language.

Charles inclined his head again. "Thirteen thousand."

Charles.

Barclay raised his index finger. "Fifteen thousand."

Charles raised two fingers. "Twenty thousand."

Barclay made the same gesture. "Twenty-five thousand."

Charles again. "Thirty thousand."

I started to sweat. *Charles?*

Barclay raised his eyebrows. "Forty thousand," Marcus said.

Charles followed suit. "Fifty thousand."

Barclay hesitated for a fraction of a second, then nodded. Something flashed in his eyes: frustration, maybe, or irritation. Either way, he looked to be reaching his limit.

Charles made a kind of seated half-bow. "Sixty-five thousand," Marcus intoned. He looked at Barclay.

No response. The Seattle vamp was expressionless and still.

A few beats passed. Marcus tapped his ball. "Bidding is complete."

Mindful of the many vampires in the room, I'd kept my breathing slow and steady, but as the assistant vanished behind the red velvet curtain with the cup, it was everything I could do to stay calm. *Charles, what the hell? I was only authorized to spend ten thousand dollars.*

Then the cup is mine, he replied, his voice in my head as emotionless as I'd ever heard him be. *You were outbid by a factor of six. Your client will hardly be able to complain.*

I seethed. *Your little pissing contest with Mr. Vincent Barclay just cost me a big bonus.*

No response. I chanted swear words in my head and hoped he was hearing them.

Lot 1205 was already on exhibit: a wide gold cuff covered in a delicate vine pattern, with a network of tiny red crystals forming four stylized flowers. As the assistant passed me, I sensed ancient blood magic.

Marcus addressed the audience. "This cuff is believed to have belonged to the Borgia family, but its age is estimated to be more than two thousand years old. Its purpose is to rein in a newly risen vampire's bloodlust, ensuring a smoother transition. Bidding will begin at the reserve price of five thousand dollars."

Charles won the cuff, agreeing to shell out nineteen grand for it. I wondered if he intended to use it himself when he created new vamps or resell it. If I ever decided to speak to him again, I'd ask.

The auction paused for a brief interlude before the final lot was presented. Wait staff circulated with trays of champagne and hors d'oeuvres. I took a glass when it became clear I would be the only one who didn't, and a cracker topped with fancy cheese and a thin slice of smoked salmon.

When everyone was settled and the wait staff had departed, Marcus reappeared behind his podium. "Honored guests, I am pleased to present the evening's featured item, Lot 1206."

The crown jewel of the auction turned out to be a painted stone that had once belonged to Vlad Tepes when he resided at Poenari, his fortress in Romania. Where Vlad currently resided was one of the vampire world's most closely guarded secrets. Charles had told me once that humans should hope they never found out.

Marcus cleared his throat and the low murmur of conversation faded to silence. "Ladies and gentlemen, the bidding shall commence at the reserve price of twenty thousand dollars."

The bidding was intense and Charles was in the thick of it. By the time the sale price surpassed eighty thousand dollars, most of the bidders had dropped out and it was down to Charles, the female vampire who had won Lot 1201, and—of course—Vincent Barclay.

Barclay hadn't wanted to spend more than sixty grand on the cup, perhaps because he was here for the stone. Judging by the bidding frenzy, there had to be more to that stone than its value as having once belonged to Vlad Tepes, but I sensed no magic from it. The stone was about four inches long and roughly oval-shaped. It had originally been brightly painted, but now the paint was mostly gone, making it impossible to discern what the image had once been.

At seventy-five thousand, the female vamp dropped out and once again the bidding was between Charles and Barclay.

Back and forth they went. One hundred thousand. One-ten. One-twenty. I discovered I was holding my breath. Vampires didn't breathe, of course, but even the fangy undead appeared to be watching the bidding war with bated breath.

I was watching Barclay when Charles bid one-fifty and saw the almost imperceptible tightening of his eyes that signaled the Seattle vamp was reaching his limit. This was looking to be an expensive night for Charles if he won.

Barclay bid one-sixty, but a heartbeat too slow if he wanted Charles to think he wasn't backing down. Charles went in for the kill and bid one-eighty.

After a pause, Barclay demurred. Marcus tapped his strangely shaped gavel and bidding ended.

My curiosity got the better of me. *What is that doohickey, anyway?* I asked Charles as everyone rose. *I don't sense any magic.*

Not all objects of power use the same kinds of magic, he replied.

At Charles's summons, Bryan and Sean approached. "Stay with her," Charles instructed Sean. "I must render payment and arrange to take possession of my purchases. We will return in a few minutes."

Sean gave him a nod. Charles and Bryan disappeared behind the red curtain, along with the other winning bidders and their escorts. I feigned the bored expression of a piece of brainless arm candy left with the hired help.

Sean leaned close, his lips almost brushing my ear. "I thought you had a spending limit of ten grand for that cup."

"That was all Charles," I murmured, my eyes scanning the room as the other guests filed out. "Believe me, we're going to talk about it once we're in the car."

I was about to apologize for the way Charles had been needling him when my eyes met those of Vincent Barclay.

The Seattle vamp was standing by the doors with an enormous bodyguard who looked, impossible as it might seem, larger than Bryan. I had the thought, and not for the first time, that bodyguard physiques were a kind of power-play thing for vamps. When it came to hand-to-hand combat, size wasn't the deciding factor for enforcers whose reflexes, strength, and stamina were enhanced by regularly drinking vampire blood. I'd seen Adri beat the stuffing out of men twice her size, so having the biggest bodyguard was less a matter of security than good, old-fashioned dick-measuring.

It wasn't the size of the enforcer that made me pause, however; it was Barclay's eyes. They were pure black and filled with hate. After years of torture and abuse at the hands of my grandfather, few things frightened me anymore, but I would be lying if I said I didn't feel a chill as the Seattle vamp glowered at me.

Beside me, Sean went still. Shifter magic rose and he stared at Barclay, his eyes going bright gold. Two vampire security guards appeared from behind the red curtain and watched the stare-down, ready to intervene if a fight broke out.

Finally, Barclay turned away from us and left the salon with his enforcer. The security guards followed, apparently wanting to ensure that Barclay left the property without causing trouble.

"Does Vaughan have a history with this guy?" Sean asked, his voice growly.

"I think so," I murmured. "Not sure what it is, but I'm pretty sure the hate is mutual."

With the drama over, a passing waiter offered me champagne. I took a glass to have something to do with my hands, but found myself drinking it as the minutes ticked by. The female vamp left with a long wooden box tucked under her arm. The other winning bidders left a few minutes after that with their purchases, and still there was no sign of Charles and Bryan.

Nearly fifteen minutes after they'd disappeared behind the curtain, Charles and Bryan reappeared. Charles carried the wooden box that contained Esther's cup and another I assumed held the vampire cuff, but there was no sign of the stone.

The vampire gestured at the doors. "Shall we?"

When we'd entered, Charles and I had gone first with our escorts behind us. On the way out, Sean walked in front of us and Bryan followed.

When we reached the front doors, our limo waited with Adri at the wheel. It looked like we were the last to leave; no other vehicles remained in front of the mansion. A doorman opened the rear door and Charles offered me his hand as our escorts guarded us. As I settled myself into the seat, the vampire got in, followed by Sean and finally Bryan. Sean sat next to me and Bryan sat next to Charles.

As soon as the door closed, Adri pulled away, gliding around the circular drive and accelerating smoothly down the long driveway toward the main road. Charles put the wooden boxes next to him on the seat. The cup's magic teased my senses, reminding me that I'd failed my client, through no fault of my own.

Before I could bring it up, Sean spoke, addressing Charles. "You want to tell us about this vamp from Seattle?"

"Vincent Barclay is contemptible," Charles replied, his voice cold. "He trafficks people throughout the region for sex, blood, and other purposes. It is known that his companions are not always willing. He is not welcome in this city, which he knows very well. He risks much to defy the Court in this way."

That settled things, as far as I was concerned. When I got home, I'd put in a call to Trent Lake about Vincent Barclay. "He came for the Tepes stone, that much was obvious. Speaking of which, where is the stone? Did you not bring it with you?"

"I have it with me." He looked out the window as the limo slowed, turned onto the main road, and accelerated.

"Where are we headed?" Sean asked.

"You asked where I am staying," Charles said, his eyes on the scenery. "We are going to visit my temporary place of residence."

I started to object. Sean was tired after being up all night and only getting a few hours of sleep this afternoon. Plus, going to wherever Charles was staying seemed like a recipe for more of the same hostility that had made our ride out to the auction so tense. There was something in Charles's tone that made me stay quiet, however. I couldn't quite put a name to it, but he sounded almost...wistful?

Sean covered my hand with his. Charles's eyes flicked to our hands, then back to the window. I suppressed a smile. After spending most of the night needling Sean, he could hardly object to—

The limo swerved sharply, throwing us violently against one another. Sean dove on top of me, knocking me flat as the others hit the floor next to us.

A second vehicle plowed into ours, its engine roaring. Metal crunched, glass exploded, and the limo went sideways, the entire side caved in where Charles had been sitting a fraction of a second earlier. Sean curled around me, trying to shield me with his body as glass and broken pieces of the limo's interior pelted us.

The other vehicle's momentum pushed our limo sideways, tires squealing, as Adri fought in vain to keep us from going off the road. At the edge of the pavement the car turned on its side and we fell in a pile against the undamaged side of the limo. The limo teetered for a heartbeat before the other vehicle pushed us over and we began to roll down the steep embankment.

Seats, roof, floor, glass, grass, sky, and bodies whirled around me for what felt like an eternity as the limo rolled. Sean lost his grip on me when Bryan collided with us in midair. The four of us smashed into each other, our elbows, knees, and skulls battering each other's bodies relentlessly.

Through the broken window, I glimpsed the tree line approaching fast. If we'd been sliding down the hill I could have used my air or earth magic to slow or halt our movement, but since we were rolling there was little I could do but try to hang on to something.

The second impact was only slightly less terrible than the first and our roll down the hill came to an abrupt halt when we hit the trees. Someone grabbed my arm, but not fast enough. My face smashed into something hard and then there was only darkness.

11

When I woke, at first all I could see, taste, and smell was blood. Judging by the traces of shifter and vamp I could sense, not all of it was mine, but I suspected most of it was. It bubbled from my lips, trickled from my nose, ran down my face.

Disoriented and confused, I wiped the blood from my eyes. I recognized the effects of shock and possibly a mild concussion. My body ached like I'd been beaten up, which wasn't far from the truth. The worst pain radiated from the middle of my back, where Bryan's knee had hit me during the rollover, and I wasn't sure if I'd be able to stand up or walk if I tried. My left arm ached. Someone had grabbed me just before we hit the trees and my shoulder felt like it had almost been wrenched from its socket.

I managed to focus and discovered I was alone inside what remained of the limo, which was upside-down and smashed to hell.

Charles? I asked. Even my mental voice sounded woozy.

A pause, then a terse reply: *Stay where you are.* He cut our connection so abruptly that I winced.

I couldn't see what was going on outside, but I heard the distinctive sound of fighting. That meant Charles, Sean, and the enforcers were facing whoever—or whatever—had run us off the road, and they were having to fight hand-to-hand.

I forced myself to move, crawling toward the opening where a door had either been torn off or kicked out. Broken glass cut into my hands and knees, but I ignored the pain and focused on finding out what the hell was going on and where Sean was.

Finally, I emerged from the wrecked limo and tried to figure out what I was seeing.

To my left, Charles appeared to be fighting two other vampires. No wonder he'd blocked me out so he could concentrate; they moved so fast that all I saw was a blur. I couldn't tell who he was fighting or if I recognized them, but he appeared to be holding his own.

Meanwhile, Bryan and Adri, both bloody from the crash, battled two black-clad men who, based on their size and speed, appeared to be enforcers. They moved almost as fast as the vampires. One of them was bigger than Bryan, and I suspected I knew who had attacked us.

As I watched, Adri knocked her opponent down. He flipped back to his feet, a blade in his hand. In a blur of movement, she kicked the blade away and met his charge with a boot to the face. He went back down, dazed.

I heard a growl and turned to my right.

Sean, in wolf form, his fur standing up, ears back, and teeth bared, stood between me and a third vampire. I pushed bloody hair out of my eyes and looked up.

"Alice, my dear," Vincent Barclay said, his eyes silver. He looked me over and made a *tsk* sound. "Look at all that wasted blood. Such a shame."

I pulled myself to my feet, unwilling to face him on my hands and knees, no matter how much it hurt to stand up.

Barclay smiled, revealing his fangs. "Yes, do stand, love. No need to crawl to me. Not yet, anyway."

Sean snarled and snapped his teeth. On my left, one of the vampires went down and didn't get back up. Yay, Charles.

Barclay didn't bother to check on his fallen buddy. "What a lovely woman you are. I can't decide if I want to keep you for myself or see how much you might be worth on the open market. How much *are* you worth, Alice Worth?" He chuckled.

"Not funny," I muttered.

He tilted his head. "What did you say?"

I raised my head, my hands tingling with spooled magic, and met his glowing eyes with my own. "I said, that's not funny."

He came for me, vamp-fast. Sean met him in midair with a vicious snarl, his teeth sinking into the vampire's throat, and the fight was on. Sean was a blur of teeth and claws. While Barclay got in a few hits, the wolf was tearing him apart. Blood sprayed across the grass and it wasn't Sean's.

A strange pulse of magic from my left made me glance over just in time to see Charles pinning the second vamp to the ground, his palm against the other vamp's chest. A tendril of dark magic was coiled around Charles's arm. As I watched, the vamp on the ground convulsed, his back arching as a wave of energy ran up Charles's arm and disappeared. The vamp went still and Charles smiled, his eyes shining silver.

Before I could figure out what that was about, Barclay tore free of Sean's teeth and came after me.

The vamp's momentum drove me back into the side of the limo so hard that it knocked the wind out of me. Barclay's mouth was open, fangs extended, as he went for my throat.

I wrapped my hands around his torn neck and sliced through it with my spooled blood magic just as Sean hit him from the side. Barclay's head went one way and his body went another. Cool vampire blood fountained across my face and down the front of my dress.

Barclay's head rolled and came to a stop next to my bare foot, his face frozen in an expression of shock.

Sean stood over him and snarled as the Seattle vamp's body and head turned to ash. A frisson of cold gray vamp magic tingled on my skin and faded as Barclay died.

"Alice."

I wiped blood out of my eyes and looked up at the sound of Charles's voice. He,

Bryan, and Adri were bloody but in better shape than I was. Barclay's enforcers were either unconscious or dead. The other two vamps were still down and not moving.

The wind sent some of the ash swirling into the air and it stuck to my bloody dress. "Am I going to be in trouble for this?" I asked Charles, gesturing at what was left of Barclay.

"He stated his intention to kill us and take you and the Tepes stone," he said. "There will be a hearing before the Court, but I have no doubt your actions will be deemed justified."

"That's good to hear." I leaned back against the limo. The shock was beginning to wear off and I was acutely aware that I was hurting all over, except the parts that were numb.

Three black SUVs screeched to a stop up on the road next to the mangled stretch Hummer that had smashed our limo. Black-clad Vamp Court enforcers spilled out and rushed down the embankment.

Charles's people cleaned up Barclay's remains and loaded the unconscious vamps and enforcers into the SUVs. I crouched to burn my blood and ended up sitting against the side of the wrecked limo, unable to rise because my back had become a giant knot of pain. I pulled a few shards of glass from my knees and palms that looked like what was left of the highball glasses from the limo's minibar.

Charles tried to approach me. Sean moved between us and gave him a warning growl. "I mean her no harm, wolf," the vampire said.

Another growl, this time with more teeth.

"I'm all right," I said. "He's on edge because of Kent Stevens. You'd best give him some space and go see if you can find the stuff you bought at the auction somewhere in this wreck."

You are injured and require healing, Charles said in my head, annoyed. *This is no time for such behavior.*

He's just protecting me. Get Barclay's cronies out of here and he'll shift back. I hoped so, anyway.

Sure enough, as soon as two of the SUVs left with the prisoners, Sean shifted back to human. I knew I was in bad shape when the sight of him naked failed to elicit the usual response from me.

He crouched and touched my face. "How badly are you hurt?"

I thought about that. "Pretty badly." I lowered my voice. "I can't stand up."

He scooped me up and headed for the road, where two more SUVs had arrived with reinforcements. I spotted one of my missing shoes halfway up the hill, where it had apparently fallen out of the limo during our roll down the embankment.

"Why didn't you stay in the limo?" he asked as he carried me.

I rested my head against his chest. "Would you have stayed put if it was me facing some unknown attacker?"

"No," he said automatically.

"Well, there's your answer."

He kissed me then, vampire blood and ash and all.

The bathroom door opened and closed. Familiar footsteps crossed the tile floor. "Aren't you clean yet?"

I didn't open my eyes as Sean came to sit on the side of the gigantic tub where I'd been soaking for a very long time. "Don't rush me," I murmured, sliding a little farther down under the bubbles. "This tub is amazing." Not to mention the hot water and massage jets did wonders for my battered body.

He brushed hair back from my face, careful to avoid tender bruised areas. "How do you feel?"

"Sore." Which was the understatement of the year.

It turned out Charles was staying with Niara of the Vampire Court. As soon as we arrived at her home, a human physician examined me and determined I had no broken bones and had not been concussed. I did, however, have dozens of cuts and bruises, and my back hurt like I'd been kicked by a mule. The doctor removed shards of glass from my arms, legs, and hands and cleaned the wounds with what I could only assume was battery acid.

I'd refused both Charles's and Niara's offers of blood in favor of a mid-range air magic healing spell, which had helped but not healed me completely. My decision had angered Charles and left Sean conflicted. He didn't like seeing me hurting, but he didn't want me drinking from Charles again any more than I did.

Sean stayed at my side until I'd showered and climbed into the tub for an extended soak. He finally agreed to go shower and put on clothes when Bryan promised to guard the door.

He leaned down and kissed me. "If Malcolm were here, he would be able to heal your injuries."

"When I get home, I'll use a stronger healing spell and then I'll be fine." I opened my eyes and stared. "*That's* what they gave you to wear?"

He grinned down at me. "I always thought the enforcer look was unimaginative." He inhaled deeply and his eyes turned golden. "But if me wearing all black gets you this turned on, I might make this my standard attire when I'm not at work."

"There's no way you can smell anything from me over this bubble bath," I retorted, raising my hand and blowing some frothy bubbles in his direction. "Niara's housekeeper poured half a bottle of the stuff into the tub. It smells like a florist shop in here."

"It does," he agreed. "But I'd know your scent anywhere."

I pulled him down again for another kiss. When we broke apart, he reached for a towel, draped it over his knees, and gently lifted me out of the tub. I sat on his lap as he dried me carefully. Then he kissed me thoroughly enough to make me wish we were at home instead of a bathroom in Niara's house with Bryan standing outside the door. I was sitting on ample evidence that Sean agreed.

Finally, he nudged me off his lap. "Get dressed and let's find out why Vaughan brought us here."

"And what the hell that stone is." I caught a glimpse of myself in the mirror and winced. I was covered in bruises and half-healed cuts that stood out as angry red lines all over my skin. A knot on my forehead marked where I'd been knocked out, and my right knee had gotten twisted in the rollover and was now painful and stiff.

Sean made a growly sound and gently put his hand on my bruised back. "You'll finish healing yourself when we get home."

"I will," I promised. "Believe me, I have no desire to go around any longer than I have to feeling like a three-hundred-pound enforcer kicked me in the back. I'm almost afraid to ask, but what clothes did Charles give you for me?"

He gestured at a stack of folded clothes on the counter. "These are from Niara, actually."

The clothes turned out to be a pretty, sleeveless purple top that left my midriff bare and a colorful, multi-layered ankle-length wrap skirt.

Sean raised his eyebrows at the sheer black bra and matching skimpy undies, both of which fit too well to be coincidence. "Anything I should know about this?" he asked, gesturing at my sexy lingerie.

I hesitated.

His eyebrows went higher. "Really. And here I thought Vaughan was the only member of the Court I had to keep an eye on."

"No need to worry. I made it clear I wasn't interested," I told him as I tied the skirt around my hips. I pulled the top on over my head and stepped into a pair of sandals.

"And vampires are always *so* respectful of boundaries when it comes to these things," he said dryly. "As evidenced by that very lovely lingerie, which she must have had on hand and which I look forward to taking off later."

I started combing through my wet hair. "Speaking of which, I'm sorry your clothes were ruined in the wreck and then finished off when you shifted. I wanted to take that tux off of you myself."

"I know." He kissed me. "You'll have to settle for taking off this enforcer uniform, I guess."

I looked him over and decided I could make do with that.

When we emerged from the bathroom, Bryan was waiting on us. We followed the enforcer through a maze of hallways and out onto the back patio, where Charles and Niara waited.

Niara's residence was as beautiful and colorful as Charles's was elegant and understated. She'd decorated her veranda in bright fabrics and rattan furniture. Beyond stretched an enormous garden. The scent of flowers filled the air.

Dark shadows moved along the walls of the garden: heavily armed Vampire Court security watching for trouble. I'd almost forgotten Kent Stevens in all the excitement of the auction and Barclay's attack, but the sight of the guards brought all the tension and uneasiness back in a rush.

Charles had changed into a light gray summer suit. He rose as we approached, looking me over appreciatively, but his eyes were dark with anger. *You are limping*, he said in my head. *Why do you refuse my offer of healing?*

It's only cuts and bruises, Charles, not a bullet wound. Nothing a strong healing spell can't fix.

Out loud, I said, "It's beautiful out here, Niara."

Tonight, her hair was in long, tiny braids and held back from her face with a colorful scarf. She wore a long purple shift dress and her feet were bare except for a gold anklet and toe rings.

I no longer had Niara's blood in me, but the warm copper glow in her eyes made me remember the feeling of her hands on me in the stairwell at Hawthorne's the night it was bombed. I'd be lying if I said there wasn't a spark of attraction there, but even if it weren't for Sean, vampires of either sex were a no-fly zone for a list of reasons longer than my arm—not that either she or Charles seemed put off in the least by my repeated refusals. I got the impression that one or both of them were simply in no rush to force the issue. And why should they? Vampires had all the time in the world to plot and wait until they thought the time was right.

Niara smiled. "My refuge from the world," she said, her voice low-pitched and musical. "No matter the ugliness beyond those walls, I am surrounded by beauty here. Your presence makes it all the more lovely. Please, sit." She gestured at the two empty chairs.

Sean and I sat as Charles reseated himself next to Niara. The table held a bottle of champagne in a bucket of ice, four glasses, and the box containing Esther's cup.

As Charles reached for the champagne, I asked, "What are we celebrating?"

"Many things," he said, removing the foil and *muselet* with practiced ease. "My success at the auction, our survival, and Vincent Barclay's long-overdue true death."

The cork slid free of the bottle with a muffled *pop*. He divided the champagne among the four glasses.

We raised our glasses in a toast. As we enjoyed the champagne, I spoke up. "Speaking of Barclay's attack, what exactly *is* that stone, and what did it do to that vamp?"

"As you heard at the auction, the stone was one of many that once belonged to Vlad Tepes," Charles said. "The magic is ancient. Few know its origin. I know only that it predates our earliest records. Tepes's collection of vampire objects of power was the largest ever known. Pieces from the collection become available on occasion. Their powers vary, but the object I purchased tonight possesses the ability to transfer life energy to the one who wields it."

I stared at him. "That's what I saw you do to that vamp on the side of the road. You took his life energy. Did it kill him?"

"No. A vampire's immortality cannot be taken in that way. He is merely very weakened and mortal for a time."

"But if you used that weapon on a human or a shifter?" Sean asked.

"They would most likely die." Charles sipped his champagne.

"Do you plan on reselling the object or keeping it?" I asked.

"I have not decided. I must study the market, determine if it could be sold for a sufficient profit at this time. If not, I will keep it in my collection until such time as I can make an adequate profit, or I choose to keep it."

"And the cup?" I gestured at the box on the table. "What's your plan for that, now that you've got it?"

"I plan to use it," he said matter-of-factly.

I almost dropped my glass.

Niara's expression was grim. "You risk much." Her tone indicated they'd already argued about this before Sean and I came outside. "You have not seen it used. You have only the word of the expert brought in by the broker as to what its power is. If they are wrong—if Alice's client is wrong—you may die under the sun."

"I have not stood in the sun for more than two hundred years," Charles said. "Perhaps I am willing to risk much to feel that warmth once again."

Her gaze became distant as she toyed with her champagne glass. "I have felt the sun," she said, her voice softening. "Not so long ago, I was tempted, as you are now, by magic and the promise of walking in the daylight. It had been so very long since I had felt the caress of the sun that once blessed me as I walked the plains of home. My people called themselves children of the sun. I thought I was parted from it forever, and then I received a great gift: a magical talisman that allowed me to see the sun again, as if I had not become a vampire and a child of the night. It was not long before I knew it was a great folly."

"You regret that you walked beneath the sun?" Charles asked in disbelief.

Niara seemed to be considering what to say. Finally, she said, "Perhaps I cannot explain in a way you would believe. But if you do this, you risk more than you know." She glanced at the eastern horizon. "Dawn comes within the hour. You have time to consider this decision, but I will leave you to it." She rose.

We stood as well. It took some effort on my part since my back and knee had stiffened again. Niara brushed her lips across Charles's mouth, then disappeared into the house.

"Well, that was sobering," I said as we reseated ourselves. "Are you reconsidering?"

"No," Charles said firmly.

"Niara's right that we don't know for certain what the cup's power is. I have only my client's word, and any expert the seller called in can only give their best guess at what the spell will do. What if they're half right and the spell only lasts thirty minutes?"

"I will put on sunscreen."

I stared at him, nonplussed. "You don't seem to be taking Niara's warning very seriously."

He finished the last of his champagne and set the glass on the table. "I take her warning very seriously. Still, I choose to accept the risk for the chance to walk in these gardens in the sunlight."

"Sir."

We all looked up at the unexpected sound of Bryan's voice. The enforcer stood in his customary spot to Charles's right. "I will accompany you with a large umbrella or a covering," he said. "If the spell fails, I'll do my best to see that you are returned to the safety of the house and healed, should it be necessary."

Charles inclined his head. "Thank you, Mr. Smith. Your offer is greatly appreciated but unnecessary. Alice alone will accompany me."

Bryan stiffened, Sean made a low growly noise, and I jerked in surprise. "Me?" My voice had a hint of squeak in it.

"She wouldn't be able to protect you from the sun or return you to the house," Bryan objected.

"This is true," Charles acknowledged. "But I wish to take a walk in a garden in the sunlight accompanied by a beautiful woman."

Bryan looked at me, clearly unhappy. "Then ask Adri," I suggested. "She's gorgeous, and she'd be able to bring you back to the house if—"

"It is your company I desire," Charles interrupted. "If you wish, you may consider it a last request."

My stomach lurched. "Damn it, Charles," I ground out. I reached for the box, flipped open the lid, and grabbed the cup.

It wasn't really a good idea to pick up a magical object, but I was angry and more than a little uneasy at the thought I might witness Charles cindered by the morning sun. We might have had a difficult relationship and I didn't doubt that he wouldn't hesitate to sell me out if he ever figured out who I was, but that didn't mean I wanted to watch him burn to death in front of me.

The magic in the cup seared my senses. My head jerked back and my vision faded as I lowered my shields and plunged headlong into the cup's magic.

I knew the spellwork that would allow a vampire to walk in daylight by heart; my grandfather had me learn it not long after my blood magic manifested when I was twelve, because vampires would pay astronomical sums for the chance to experience daylight after decades or centuries—or millennia—of moonlight. I found the spell easily, woven through the blood magic and the peaceful green of the earth magic, and traced its lines and runes, feeling their familiar curves and edges. Finally, I raised my shields slowly, disengaged from the cup's magic, and returned to awareness.

I opened my eyes and found myself staring into Sean's fiery golden gaze. He was crouched in front of my chair, gripping the armrests. "I have been trying to get you to respond for almost five minutes," he snapped. "What the hell did you think you were doing?"

"Trying to find out if this cup is the real deal," I said, my voice uneven. I looked past Sean at Charles, who sat on the edge of his chair watching me. "As far as I can tell, the cup is exactly as advertised: a spell that keeps you awake past sunrise and permits you to be exposed to the sun without burning."

"As far as you can tell?" Bryan asked skeptically.

"I'm familiar with this kind of spell," I said. "That's what it is."

"For one hour?" Charles asked.

"I'm reasonably certain the spell will last for one hour, but it's not as if there's a timer in the spellwork. 'Reasonably certain' is as good as it's going to get on the timing. I can't guarantee anything, Charles."

"There are no guarantees, in this life or any other," he told me. "Your 'reasonably certain' is enough for me. I accept the risk."

"I'm not sure I do. If I'm wrong—"

"Then I was sufficiently warned and chose to proceed against the advice of my companions." He regarded me. "I cannot force you to join me, but I would be...grateful if you would."

Sean and Bryan were plainly displeased, although for very different reasons. I didn't need to be able to read his mind to know Sean was thinking about who might be blamed if the spell didn't work the way it was supposed to and Charles ended up severely burned or turned to ash.

Bryan was no doubt thinking that his entire job—his life, in fact—was dedicated to keeping Charles safe from harm, and I'd caused all this by bringing Charles into my search for the missing magical objects. If something did go wrong, I'd have to answer to Bryan before I even got a chance to answer to the Court.

But I saw something in Charles's eyes that I'd not seen in the five years I'd known him: a glimmer of life. Even in moments of levity, which were few and far between, Charles's eyes had never belied any hint of humanity. And yet, when he looked at the cup, I saw an echo of the man he must have once been, before he'd been turned.

Maybe it was stupid and sentimental of me—in fact, it almost certainly was incredibly stupid, given the possible consequences I might face if the spell failed—but I was having a difficult time talking myself into refusing his request.

I put the cup on the table. "I accept. There's only one important question left to answer."

Charles ignored the low growl from Sean and Bryan's frown. He tilted his head. "And that would be...?"

"What do you want to drink?"

After browsing Niara's well-stocked cellar, Charles chose a 1914 merlot and brought the bottle up to the sitting room that overlooked the veranda.

Ten minutes before the sun was expected to rise, he pulled the cork from the bottle and poured wine into the cup and a wineglass. He handed me the glass and we walked to the doors that looked out over Niara's garden.

Charles touched the rim of the cup gently to my glass. "To you," he said. We drank.

Magic coiled down Charles's arm as he swallowed the wine. It faded and his aura changed from its usual cool gray to peaceful earth-magic green.

I lowered my shields and touched him. "How do you feel?"

"Warm," he said.

We turned to face the eastern horizon. When he took my hand, I didn't pull away.

It began as gradual lightening of the sky over the hills and then dawn broke in a spectacular array of oranges, reds, and yellows. Charles flinched as the first rays of sunlight touched us, but the spell held and he was unharmed. We stood motionless as the sun peeked over the top of the hill and the day began.

Slowly, as if in a dream, Charles reached out and opened the door. I followed him out onto the veranda, my hand in his. We left our glasses on the table and descended to the garden. The grass and flowers sparkled with morning dew.

I wondered what Charles was thinking about as we strolled down the path, heading away from the house. His face was impassive and I couldn't read his eyes. Sean and Bryan stood at the edge of the veranda, watching us.

When we reached a point about three-quarters of the way across the garden, Charles stopped and turned to me. His mask of impassivity vanished and he raised his face to the sky, his eyes full of wonder. "So bright."

"It's a beautiful sunrise," I said.

"It is perhaps the most beautiful I have ever seen." He fell silent.

We started walking again, wandering between rows of flowers and neatly trimmed hedges. He seemed lost in thought and I stayed quiet, not wanting to intrude on this miraculous daytime excursion.

He surprised me when he spoke. "Have I ever told you of my life before I was turned?"

"A little. When we first met, five years ago or so, you told me you fought in the Revolutionary War as a teenager. That's all I know." Well, and that he'd been eviscerated before his death, but I didn't want to bring that up. He might regret revealing that to me. I knew very well the emotional weight of scars.

"Many years ago, before I was turned, I was married."

My steps faltered. He smiled slightly and pulled on my hand, urging me to resume walking. "Her name was Emma. We married when I was seventeen and she was fifteen. Such things were common in those days. Our families had little money, but we were very much in love."

We turned away from the house, wandering nearer to the far end of the garden. "We had a small home near her parents' residence where we lived for fourteen years. She bore me six children, three of whom lived past infancy: two daughters and a son. Our lives were difficult. We were not always happy, but we were always in love. I considered myself quite fortunate to be wealthy in love, if not in worldly goods."

Charles paused to run his fingertips over the warm brick of the garden wall. "In the year 1792, I was returning to my home from visiting a friend when I was arrested on suspicion of committing a murder. The victim was the pregnant wife of the local magistrate. A witness described a man seen fleeing from the scene. I had the great misfortune of wearing similar clothing and resembling the man who was described. The magistrate believed me guilty. I was tortured in order to obtain a confession. You have seen the scar."

I nodded.

"I survived the wound, but once I had confessed, though it was under duress, my guilt was decided. I asked to see my wife and was told her parents had taken her and my children away to another town so they would be spared the infamy of having a murderer for a husband and father. My own parents wanted nothing to do with me. I was branded a rapist and a killer. Even the minister of our church refused to visit my bedside. I was forsaken by everyone. My execution was to be held as soon as I was able to climb the steps to the gallows. Had the situation gone on much longer, I am sure the magistrate would have simply dragged me up the steps and put the noose around my neck himself."

We walked on in silence. I snuck glimpses at the watch I'd borrowed, watching as the minutes ticked by.

"One night as I lay in my bed in the jail, delirious with fever, as the wound had become infected, the bars were torn from the window. The smell of my blood had drawn a newly risen vampire. I could see little through my delirium, but I felt the pain when he bit my throat. I could not fight back, but neither did I desire to do so. It would be, I decided, a death preferable to hanging in front of my neighbors and those I had once called friends."

My stomach twisted. I squeezed his hand, but he did not return the gesture, as if too caught up in his memories to notice it.

Charles continued, "My attacker drained me to the point of death. Just as I felt myself slipping away, the door burst open and two more vampires rushed in. They pulled him away from me and I lost consciousness. The next night, I rose as a vampire."

"One of the other vamps turned you?"

"Yes. They could not leave me behind, for my wound would have been proof vampires lived nearby. The elder of the two took me to his home. They decided because I had so stubbornly clung to life despite my grievous wound, I would be likely to rise as a vampire. And since I was a condemned man with no friends or family to claim me, I would not be missed by anyone."

Though we had made a final turn back toward the house, Charles continued to walk slowly. There was only twenty minutes until the hour was up, but he was in no hurry.

"What about your wife? Did you ever see her again?"

"Some months later, when I had control of my bloodlust, I followed her to a village where she had gone to live with her new husband. I observed her caring for our children and keeping the house. She was with child, the child of her new husband. I watched as he returned home from working in the fields and she greeted him with a smile and a kiss. I left then and did not return."

We walked in silence back toward the house. When I looked at Charles's face, I was startled. "Charles, you have a sunburn!"

He smiled, but it didn't reach his eyes. "Do I?"

I remembered something he'd said before the bombing, when he'd visited my house and found me drunk on my back porch. "The night you showed me your scar, you said part of the reason you kept it was to remind you of a lesson you'd learned. What was the lesson?"

"That those you love and trust can and will turn against you," he said quietly. "And people will commit great evil and call it justice."

We climbed the steps to the veranda. Sean and Bryan watched us pass as we walked to the table, where the cup and my wineglass waited. Charles picked up the cup and regarded it.

I stole another glance at my watch. Nine minutes before the spell would break. My stomach churned as the seconds ticked by and the vampire made no move to return to the house.

Finally, Charles held the cup out. *Return this to your client,* he said in my head. *Take it far from me and never tell me who possesses it.*

Why? I asked, stunned.

Because I think I have come to understand what Niara was attempting to tell me when I was too stubborn to hear her words. I have walked in the sun and remembered what it was like to be human. I will never be human. If I were to use this cup again, I believe I might not return to the safety of my home before the hour ended.

My stomach contracted. *You wouldn't commit suicide by sunlight, Charles. I know you.*

He smiled without humor. *You do not know me, Alice. Never presume to know what is in my heart. Take the cup away.*

I can't repay the sixty-five grand, I reminded him.

This hour with you has been repayment enough. He kissed my cheek, startling me with the warmth of his usually cool lips. *I feel the pull of sleep. My stolen hour is almost gone.*

I took the cup. This use had depleted its magic, but it would regenerate. My fingers brushed his and he paused, savoring the moment.

Finally, Charles released my hand and went inside. I followed, but he'd already vanished into the recesses of Niara's mansion. Somewhere in the house, a heavy door closed and locked.

Sean came inside and picked up the wooden box. I nestled the cup in its velvet-lined interior and closed the lid. I looked up at him.

He used his thumb to wipe the single tear off my cheek. "Let's go home."

12

Adri drove us home. Sean contacted Mobile Team One, Jack and Karen, and gave them our ETA. He'd put his shoulder rig back on and we both wore our bulletproof vests again. I was too tired and emotionally drained to waste energy thinking about how uncomfortable I was. Our drive was silent.

When we pulled into my driveway, Jack and Karen were already parked in front of my house. Sean gave the mobile team a wave and escorted me inside. He locked the door behind us as Adri backed down the driveway and I tossed my vest in the coat closet.

While he let the dog in and checked the doors and windows, I took the cup down to the basement and put it in the cabinet with the hand mirror.

Back upstairs, I stifled a grimace as I sat on the couch and called Aaron Riddell. My back and knee ached mercilessly.

"I have good news," I told the attorney when he came on the line. "I've got two out of three. The cup and the hand mirror are in my hands."

"Two days and two down. I knew you were the best in the business," Aaron said. I could hear the smile in his voice. "You sound kind of rough. Did you have to get them the hard way?"

"You don't really want any details, do you?"

"No, I do not, but if you end up needing legal representation—"

"—I'll have to call someone else. There's no way I'd be able to afford your rates."

He chuckled. "I'm sure I could offer you a discount. And what about item number three?"

Sean came downstairs and headed for the kitchen, still wearing his all-black enforcer clothes. My eyes followed him. Yum.

"Alice?" Aaron prodded.

"Yes?" I shook myself as Sean disappeared into the kitchen. "Yes, sorry, I was distracted." I heard him pouring dog food into Rogue's bowl.

"You'll let me know as soon as you have any news on the cuff?"

"Yep. You'll be the first to know as soon as I've got it."

"Great. I'll let my client know about your success. I'm sure she'll be very happy to hear it."

We said our goodbyes.

Sean stuck his head out of the kitchen. "Do you want coffee?"

I shook my head. "I'm recovered enough to release Malcolm from my bracelet and check him for hidden spells. Once that's done, I'm going to finish healing myself and take a nap for a few hours."

He came into the living room and sat on the couch next to me. "Are you all right?"

I hesitated. "How much did you hear of what Charles was telling me?"

"Very little. I did hear the last bit about learning a couple of lessons."

I stared in the direction of the fireplace. "He told me how, when, and why he was turned."

"Oh." He put his hand on my thigh and squeezed. "It wasn't a happy story, I take it. Those stories seldom are." Something about the tone of his voice made me look up. His eyes were haunted.

Though I'd never asked Sean if he'd been born a werewolf or been bitten, I'd assumed the latter, and the way he spoke more or less confirmed it.

Sean figured out what I was thinking. "I will tell you, Alice," he said quietly. "You only have to ask."

I read his expression and knew it wasn't the right time. "I want to hear the story, but it can wait until another day," I told him, leaning over to give him a quick kiss.

When I sat back, I shook my head. "One thing I have to remember is that no matter what stories he tells me, he's still Charles Vaughan of the Vampire Court. I can't forget either where his loyalties lie or that he's dangerous. He never does anything without a reason. If he told me that story—assuming any of it is true—he did it because he thinks it was to his advantage to do so."

"That's my Alice," Sean teased, lifting my hand and pressing a kiss to my knuckles. "You never allow sentiment to cloud your vision. It's one of the things I love most about you."

"I don't know if that's true," I countered, while my stomach did a somersault and then tied itself into a pretzel. "I feel like I've let Charles pull the wool over my eyes a couple of times. Maybe I've finally learned from those mistakes, though." I started to push myself to my feet.

Sean rose and pulled me up carefully to minimize the strain on my sore back. I rested my forehead against his chest.

He hadn't said he loved me; he said there were things about me he loved. It wasn't much of a difference, but I wondered if he was trying out the word to see how I would react.

There was love in the way he cared for me when I was hurt, the way he both protected and supported me in front of his pack, the way my well-being and happiness were essential for his own. There was love in everything he did.

He hadn't come out and said it, but I was pretty sure he loved me. Did I love him? Did I even know what love felt like? I remembered loving my parents, but that was a long time ago, and not the same kind of love. Was I even capable of loving someone? I hoped I was, but I was very much afraid that I couldn't.

He kissed the top of my head. "You're awfully quiet all of a sudden."

"I got lost in thought." I gave him a quick squeeze and headed for the basement door. "I'm going downstairs to check on Malcolm. It might take a little while."

"Alice."

I paused with my hand on the doorknob. "What's up?"

"I understand why you need those wards on your basement and why you haven't granted me passage through them." His eyes glowed. "I'm not asking you to change that, but I want you to know if you get hurt down there or I think you're in danger, I'm coming through those wards."

He wouldn't get through them, but he wouldn't let that keep him from trying. He'd fight them until he was either unconscious or dead.

I'd been thinking of my basement as some kind of retreat or escape and not from Sean's perspective. To him, it was a source of worry and that worst of emotions for an alpha: helplessness. It must have been gnawing on him constantly since we'd gotten back together, and the close call with the blood mage had made it impossible for him to stay quiet anymore. He was probably imagining what might happen if someone else tried to take Malcolm and I ended up unconscious or worse and he couldn't get to me.

I couldn't do that to him. As much as I needed my own space and a place to retreat, it didn't have be locked to him. In fact, it *shouldn't* be.

"Come give me your hand," I said softly.

"Alice—"

"Sean, give me your hand."

He joined me at the door. I traced four runes on the doorframe and the wards hummed. As I had done once before, I took his hand and drew two more runes with our index fingers. The wards chimed as magic ran through us.

"They feel powerful," he said. "I wish I could see them."

"I can show them to you." I placed my palm on the doorframe and suspended the obfuscation spells, revealing the wards.

Sean caught his breath.

Hundreds of layers of wards appeared, colorful and neon-bright: white air magic, green earth magic, and purple, red, and black blood magic, interwoven in seemingly endless chains of runes and spells that ran along the walls, floor, and ceiling of the basement.

As we watched, a golden thread—Sean's shifter trace—snaked its way along the existing wards, weaving itself through the spellwork until it was visible throughout, permitting him to enter the basement unharmed.

"I've never seen anything like this," he said, looking over the wards in awe. "This is a masterpiece. You are the most incredible woman I've ever known."

I took my hand off the doorway and the wards vanished, once again hidden by their powerful obfuscation spells. "You are welcome in the basement, but don't come down unannounced in case I'm doing spellwork or if I'm down there because I need alone time. You remember what to touch down there and what not to?"

"I remember." He took me in his arms and held me. "Thank you. This means a lot to me."

"It means a lot to me too." I kissed him, then reached for the doorknob. "I'm going to let Malcolm out and check him for spells. I'll be back upstairs when that's done."

"Let me know if you need me." He let go of my hand and headed for the kitchen. "In the meantime, I'm going to make an omelet for breakfast. I'll make yours when you're done."

"Thanks." I hesitated. "I love the way you make omelets."

He paused at the doorway to the kitchen and turned around. His grin made my heart skip a beat.

Smiling, I opened the basement door, pushed through the wards, and headed downstairs.

Since I didn't know whether Malcolm still had any of those retrieval spells hidden in him, I spent a good twenty minutes drawing runes and turning the three inlaid concentric circles into a fortress that even a team of blood mages wouldn't be able to get through.

When I charged the circles, the power level made my hair stick out. I took a deep breath, exhaled, and touched the blue crystal on my bracelet. "*Release.*"

Malcolm popped into existence, his eyes wide and full of panic. He saw me, flitted back, and hit the inner circle, which zapped him and sent a bolt of magic back into me. He bounced away from the circle and flitted around me in a whirlwind.

"Malcolm, it's okay," I said, trying to keep track of him as he moved. "It's okay. We're in my basement. No one's going to take you."

He stopped as suddenly as he'd appeared, flickering with anger. "What the *hell*, Alice?" he yelled.

I blinked at him. "What did I do?"

"What did you do?" Malcolm moved as far from me as he could within the small circle. He'd gone from panicked to furious in record time. "You caged me in blood magic and ripped a spell out of me!"

"You were trying to get away—"

"From the blood magic! Which is how I *died*, if you'll recall, so I'm a little edgy about it!"

"—and if I hadn't gotten that spell out of you, they would have taken you and I would have probably died, and you'd be in a crystal at Bell's cabal like all the other ghosts!"

"Like all the other...? What other ghosts?" Malcolm floated back and forth in confusion. "Wait, whose clothes are those? Why is your face all bruised? How long have I been in your bracelet?"

I hesitated. "Don't get mad."

Malcolm's irritation buzzed on my skin. "Alice, when you say that, I feel like I will probably have a good reason to be mad."

I sighed. "It's been about thirty-six hours since the attack."

"*Thirty-six hours?*"

"A really crazy thirty-six hours."

He closed his eyes, appeared to count to ten, then reopened them. "Okay, let's hear it."

I told him about the attacks on mages, my theory that Bell had pulled back all his bound ghosts, our outing to find the mirror, my dinner with the pack, the auction, Vincent Barclay's attack, our visit to Niara's mansion, and Charles's walk in the sun. Malcolm listened with varying levels of anger, disbelief, sympathy, shock, and surprise.

When I finished, he was quiet. "Is that all?" he asked finally, his tone dry.

I rubbed my forehead. "I intended to take you out of the bracelet last night after dinner with the pack, but then Charles called about the auction."

"It's okay." Malcolm's anger had faded. "You did what you had to do under the circumstances. Thank you for not letting me end up back at the cabal, stuck in a crystal for all eternity. Also, I'm glad you're not dead."

"Hey, me too. Speaking of which, I need to make sure you don't have any more of those spells hidden in you."

He floated back and forth nervously. "How are you going to do that?"

"There's only one way. I need to search by hand."

He flitted back to the far side of the circle. "Alice...please."

"There's no other way. Neither you or I sensed the one that almost got you the other night. The only way to be sure there aren't more of those spells hidden in you is for me to look really, really closely. You know I'm right."

"I know," he said miserably. "It's not that I feel pain, exactly, but it's like I'm being cut open over and over again."

I hated that I had no choice but to do this to him. "I'll wait until you're ready," I promised.

He floated over to me. "Can you talk and search at the same time?"

"Yes. What do you want me to say?"

"Tell me more about your dinner with Sean's pack."

"Okay." I rolled my shoulders. "Let me know when you're ready."

"Just do it."

I started at his feet, passing my hands slowly through his non-corporeal form, my shields down and senses wide open, searching for any trace of another hidden spell.

I talked as I worked, describing my visit to Cole and Karen's house, the surprise visit by Jack, Delia, and Caleb, Jack's hostility, Sean's statement that he hoped I might be his mate, and the snow globe I'd been given. Malcolm shuddered as I passed my hands through his body, but didn't make a sound.

I found two more hidden spells, one of which was another retrieval spell. Since I had the luxury of time, I unwove it instead of tearing it out. When I finished, the spell dissipated in a puff of blood magic.

The second spell gave me pause.

It wasn't a retrieval spell; it was the spell that bound Malcolm to me. I'd theorized to Sean that Bell had found a way to have his ghosts bound to high-level mages in the area, but Malcolm had been bound to me specifically. When he'd first manifested in my office, he'd told me he'd been assigned to haunt me because of my past. The spell that bound us wasn't made of blood magic. The magic was silver—afterlife magic—and nothing on this plane of existence had made it. I could not unweave or break it, since that kind of magic was beyond even my abilities.

Strangely, the spellwork contained an element I couldn't identify. I sifted through the magic until I figured it out. The spell wasn't permanent; there was a condition that, once it was met, would free Malcolm and me from each other. What that condition was, I couldn't tell. I wondered if Malcolm knew, but this didn't seem like the time to ask.

"Alice?" he asked, his voice hollow. "Are you finished?"

"I'm finished." I raised my shields and withdrew my hands. They were bluish with cold and almost numb. "I found another retrieval spell and the spell that binds you to me. Other than that, I'm pretty sure you're free of hidden spells."

"Okay. Can you break the circles, please?"

I'd never seen him so subdued. There was no snark, no sarcastic quip, not even a smirk. I hesitated to use the word, but he looked...haunted.

I dropped the circles and he floated toward the steps. "I need to go out for a while and clear my head," he told me. "Is that okay?"

"Take as much time as you need. If something comes up, I'll summon you." I paused. "I'd break our binding and free you if I could."

He shook his head. "I don't want you to. If I have to be a bound ghost, I want to be bound to you. I need some space right now, that's all."

I didn't know what to say to make him feel better, so I just said, "Okay."

He vanished. My house wards tingled as he crossed them.

With a heavy heart, I cleaned up the runes I'd drawn in the circles, then slowly climbed the stairs, enduring stabbing pains in my back and knee with each step.

When I opened the basement door, I found Sean sitting on the couch. He took one look at my face and put his phone down. "What's wrong?"

"I found another of those spells in Malcolm." I pulled the door closed and headed for the stairs. "I got rid of it and he's clean of spells now, as far as I can tell. He needed some alone time after we finished, so he went out for a while."

Sean met me at the foot of the steps. "Let me make you breakfast. I've got everything ready. It'll only take a few minutes."

The thought of food made my stomach churn. "I'm really not hungry. I need to use a healing spell and then rest if I'm going to be able to do anything later today about tracking down that cuff."

I expected him to argue, but he didn't. He touched my hand and recoiled. "Why are you so cold?"

"Occupational hazard when working with ghosts." I headed up the stairs.

Sean followed me to my room and stood quietly while I changed into pajamas and a tank top. I washed my face, got my first aid box from the drawer in the bathroom, and returned to the bedroom.

Sean was sitting on the bed. "I have to use a blood magic healing spell," I told him, tracing runes on the lid of the box and opening it. "It's going to be painful."

"I know." His voice was gruff.

I selected a strong spell in a blue crystal, closed the box, and put it on my nightstand. "I'd rather you didn't watch."

"I'd rather you not go through it alone." He rose and moved to my side, taking the hand that didn't hold the spell crystal. "That's what this is about, you know: not having to face anything by yourself. I can ease your pain; I've done it before."

He'd used his alpha shifter magic to take away my pain on several occasions and had even been able to relieve my cravings for Black Fire after I'd been exposed to the drug.

"Don't make me stand by helplessly while you're hurting." He squeezed my hand. "It was damn near impossible when we first met after you'd been burned. Now I won't be able to bear it." The growl in his voice told me his wolf was close to his skin and very unhappy.

"All right." I climbed onto the bed as he moved to the other side and lay down facing me. "Don't touch me until I tell you the spell is done," I reminded him as we settled in.

"I remember the rules." He leaned over and kissed me. When he withdrew, his eyes were bright. "Do you trust me?"

"Yes."

A rush of golden shifter magic rolled through me, taking away the pain in my back, arms, and legs.

I lifted my tank top, pressed the crystal to my stomach, and invoked the spell. "*Helios.*"

Healing magic pulsed through my body. Instead of the agony I was used to, the pain was distant, muted by Sean's magic. I locked my eyes on his and lost myself in their glow. Sean's jaw tightened as the strong healing spell rolled through me in waves.

I lost track of time in the haze of magic. When the last of the pulses faded and the spell crystal was empty, I dropped it on the bed. I was dazed and shaking, but not nauseous or hurting except for a dull, distant ache.

Sean's shifter magic dissipated. He touched my face. "Alice?"

"Why didn't you tell me my pain became yours?" I asked, my voice tight.

He set his jaw. "I'm an alpha. It's part of my role. I take pain from a new wolf who's learning to shift, from a mother giving birth to a child, from a pack member who's grieving or injured."

My stomach knotted. "Every time you've done this for me, you've suffered? When you took away my cravings for Black Fire, they didn't just go away? You felt them instead?" The need had been so terrible, and he'd taken it. The thought of him suffering on my behalf made me feel sicker than any healing spell had ever done.

His eyes darkened. "Alice—"

I started to get up. I don't know why or where I intended to go, but he caught my arm and held on. "Stop, please. Don't run. Hear me out."

I pulled away but sat on the bed, my arms wrapped around my knees. "I'm listening."

He leaned against the headboard. "I don't feel the pain or the addiction as badly as you would, but that's not the point. Even if it was ten times worse, I would still do it. I do it for my pack because I am their alpha. For you, I do it because I can't bear to see you hurting." His eyes searched my face. "If that's not enough to convince you, I can tell you it would hurt me more to see your pain than to take it for myself. You are worth that much to me."

"You should have told me," I protested. It was surely the height of hypocrisy for me to fuss at him for holding things back from me, but I couldn't help it.

He didn't point out my double standard. "If I had, would you have let me do it?"

"Maybe," I hedged.

He shook his head. "I know you better than that. You'd have refused on principle and suffered. Or you would have given in to the cravings and found a Black Fire dealer." His face was grave. "I could tell you were close to the breaking point several times. You had no choice about being exposed to the drug and you would have had little choice about whether to use it again. I could save you from that, and whatever discomfort I felt was well worth it to know that I'd never have to see you trapped in addiction. What was a brief sick feeling for me might have been devastating to you. I didn't even have to think about it."

I rubbed my face with my hands. "I know I said thank you for helping me through that, but now I realize how woefully inadequate that was. I can't ever make it up to you."

"Stop." He took my hands. "You owe me *nothing*. Our relationship does not have a ledger of debts and credits. It never has and it never will."

When I said nothing, he let go of my hands and sat back. "You've been keeping track, haven't you? All this time, you've been counting up all the things I've done for you and you think you're in my debt."

I didn't have to admit it; he saw it in my face.

He looked like he'd been slapped. "Damn it, Alice, I don't care what kind of life you had before you came here, where no one gave you anything unless you earned it or offered you anything without getting something in return. That is not what love is. Love is taking care of each other and not keeping score. If you need me, I'm here. If I need you, you're here. That is what this is. *There are no ledgers.*"

"It's all I've ever known," I confessed.

"I know." He pulled me into his arms and pressed a kiss into my hair, then rested his cheek on my head. "There may come a time when I'll need you to be my strength. I know you'll be there when I need you because somehow, despite everything you've been through, or maybe because of it, you are a good and unselfish person. You put everyone else ahead of your own safety. I worry that you'll give too much of yourself again, like when you sacrificed yourself to destroy the *Kasten* or used the Black Fire overdose to take out Spencer Addison and his wards."

We sat quietly. Finally, he asked, "Can you bring up your cold fire in your hand?"

Puzzled at his request, I raised my right hand and spooled earth magic. Green flames appeared on my fingertips, then spread to engulf my whole hand. We watched the fire dance.

"Take our ledger and put it in the fire," he told me. "Burn it. No more keeping score."

I closed my eyes and envisioned the list of things Sean had done for me since the night we met at Hawthorne's. It was a long list. I hesitated.

"Burn it, Alice," he murmured, his lips against my ear. "Please."

In my head, I dropped the list into the fire and watched it turn to ash. I snuffed out the fire on my hand.

"No more ledgers, no more keeping score," he said. "No more owing. Take what you need when you need it and know that I am happy to give."

I looked up at him. "Take what I need?"

"Whenever you need it."

"And if I need something now?"

"Whenever you need it," he repeated.

I kissed him with all my pent-up desire and he made that growly sound I liked, the one that made me crazy. I pulled his tight black shirt out of his pants and he slid it off over his head, tossing it to the floor. My tank top followed a second later.

I straddled his lap and cupped his face with my hands. "How much do you like these pants?" he asked me, his voice half-growl.

I shrugged. "They're not my favorite."

He tore them off, leaving me naked. He toed off his shoes and unfastened his belt.

"How much do you like these pants?" I asked him.

"I thought you liked the way they looked," he said, his eyes twinkling.

"I did, very much, but right now they're in the way."

Fabric ripped and the pants were gone. As I'd suspected, he hadn't been wearing anything under them. I rose up on my knees and lowered myself slowly, teasing him until I couldn't stand it anymore and slid down. I cried out and he groaned, pulling me down until I was full of him.

He held me still and looked in my eyes. "I love the way you feel."

I kissed him deeply and rested my forehead on his. "I love how you know what I need, even before I do."

He released my waist and guided me with his hands on my hips. Though it had been nearly two weeks since we'd made love—an eternity for us—we moved slowly, enjoying every moment, every touch, every little bit of sensation.

When I started moving faster, he slipped a hand between us and stroked me softly. I gasped, my head falling back as his gentle movements became more earnest and deliberate. My legs began to shake and he pulled me close to carefully bite my shoulder.

When the wave of bliss broke over me, he held me against his chest as I shuddered. A tiny sound that was almost a sob escaped and he kissed me, his hand cupping the back of my head. He moved his lips along my jaw to my ear. "My beautiful Alice," he murmured.

He rolled us over so that he was above me and took control of our pace, his movements catching the last of my aftershocks and drawing them out until I trembled and gasped for air. He was tender and patient, exactly what I needed at this moment to feel whole again.

The healing spell had mended my cuts and bruises, but it was Sean who repaired my heart. I didn't know how to say that, so I tried to show him with my eyes how much that meant to me.

He leaned down and ran his nose along my hairline, drinking in my scent. "I'm yours, Alice. Never doubt it."

When we finally went over the edge together, I released my magic and it swirled around us in a gentle storm of green, white, black, red, and purple, with traces of golden shifter magic.

The release of energy helped me regenerate the magic I'd expended dealing with Vincent Barclay and helping Malcolm. Its return made Sean stronger and increased his alpha magic, which gave him more power to strengthen and lead his pack. It also brought a second wave of pleasure that we shared.

Beyond the practical benefits, Sean had confessed that he enjoyed seeing our magic blended together, and I'd realized I did as well. We watched the magic swirl around the bed, then held each other as it rolled back through us.

Afterward, I lay in his arms and listened to his heart. "I love the way you smell after sex," he told me, nuzzling my hair.

I smiled lazily and poked him in the side. "Because I smell like you?"

He nipped my earlobe lightly with his teeth. "Because you smell like *us*."

"What do I smell like normally?"

"Honey and vanilla and that body wash you use. And magic."

"What does magic smell like?"

He thought about that. "It's hard to describe. Sometimes it's like how the air smells when it rains. When you're angry, your blood magic smells like a high-voltage wire."

I nestled deeper into his arms. "You smell like a forest to me."

"I smell like a forest?" He sounded surprised.

"Like green leaves and shade and earth." I rolled over and he curled around me, pulling me close with his arm around my middle. "It's the most wonderful smell."

He kissed my shoulder. "A forest. I didn't know that."

"A forest in spring," I murmured, and fell asleep.

13

THE MAN CALLING HIMSELF JOSEPH KENDALL HAD BEEN LIVING IN A 2,400-SQUARE-foot condo just north of downtown, in the trendy Castle View neighborhood. Apparently, being a con man and criminal mastermind paid fairly well.

At the moment, however, we were far from the condo and its posh uptown address. Instead, Sean and I were in his SUV, parked across the street from a seedy motel near the airport, watching the door to room 220. Light peeked through a gap in the curtains and the television was on, but we'd seen no hint of movement in the room since we arrived several hours earlier.

Phil texted me mid-afternoon to pass along a tip that Kendall/John Doe was staying here. A motel like this was a perfect place to lay low, but it seemed like such a step down from his Castle digs that I was skeptical. Still, we'd come to check it out.

Sean went into the motel office, showed John Doe's picture to the clerk, and traded cash for a room number and some information. According to the desk clerk, who spoke to Sean from behind bulletproof glass, our shady mage had checked in as Tom Nelson last night and paid for three days in cash with the stipulation that housekeeping not enter his room. The clerk hadn't seen him since. Sean returned to the SUV, where I'd waited under the watchful eyes of Mobile Team Two.

As the hours passed and we saw no sign of anyone moving in the room, it became increasingly likely the room was empty. We'd debated whether Sean should walk past to see if he could get a glimpse through the gap in the curtain, but decided to wait until after dark.

In the meantime, I looked through the phone records Cyro had sent over earlier in the day. In addition to the raw records from the cell and landline phone companies, Cyro had provided a report identifying the numbers that had called and been called from John Doe's home, cell, and business lines. Sean loaned me a tablet so I could see the reports better than on my phone screen and highlight names and numbers of interest.

The report was a list of people who were probably clients and potential victims of

John Doe's crime spree. I wasn't sure what good those names would do me, but I noted them anyway.

Since John Doe had been staying ahead of the law and anyone else who had been chasing him for so long, I had to assume he was meticulous and probably paranoid about leaving any kind of trail someone like me could follow. That meant burner phones, VPNs, and probably no paper trail, but a good investigator always did due diligence because even the best criminals made mistakes. I wasn't seeing any so far, though.

As I picked up my coffee and drank the last of it, I glanced at Mobile Team Two's SUV. "I hope Philip and Tom brought magazines or something. This might be a long, dull night if we decide to stick around for a while."

"I hope they *didn't*," Sean said. "They need to be vigilant. You're looking for signs of John Doe. They're watching for Stevens."

I propped my elbow on the door and rubbed my forehead. "This is driving me crazy."

"Do you feel self-conscious or guilty because all of these people are focused on protecting you?"

"Yes," I said reluctantly.

"You have to get over that. They're doing their job. It's what they love to do. Ask any of my people if they'd rather be doing anything else and they'll tell you no. Protecting an asset is way more interesting than most of the other work they do. I know you think they're over there bored out of their minds, but I can promise you they aren't. They're on alert, watching everyone and everything around us. This is a challenge for them. Most of them are adrenaline junkies. When I asked for volunteers for the mobile teams and told them what we were up against, I had three times more people wanting the gig than I had spots available. So relax; nobody's here because I forced them to be."

I stared at him. I hadn't really thought of it that way. I'd felt like I was imposing on Sean and his people from the moment he showed up on my doorstep. How had he known that?

He put his hand on my thigh. "I think there's some part of you that questions whether you're worth all this." At my look of surprise, he smiled. "I know a little bit about how you think."

"Thanks," I said softly. "That helps. But I'm never going to be comfortable being the center of attention." Not when my life depended on staying below the radar.

"I know." Sean rubbed my leg. His touch felt good. "I wish I could make this go away, but I can't. The best I can do is keep you safe while the vamps and the feds look for Stevens."

"I wonder where he is. I wish he'd go after Charles again. It might even be worth it for Charles to leave Niara's house and visit a couple of his businesses to try to draw him out."

"I suggested that to Bryan Smith," he said, surprising me. "He's pretty certain Stevens won't be able to evade the Hunters for much longer. If Stevens is smart, he won't fall for an obvious trap. Hell, if he's smart, he headed to another country after he missed Vaughan the other night."

"He won't run. He's still here. He wants Charles dead. He wants Julie Day dead. Maybe..." My voice trailed off.

Sean's hand froze on my thigh. "Don't even think about it."

"I could do it," I argued. "I could go back to the hotel where Julie was staying. With your people around, and the vamps and the Hunters—"

"No. You are not going to offer yourself as bait."

"You just suggested Charles do it."

"Vaughan is a vampire. He can heal virtually any injury. Stevens can't kill him unless he puts a stake in his heart or cuts off his head or drags him out into the sunlight. You... you, he can kill a hundred ways." His eyes shone gold. "You are *not* bait, Alice. They'll get him some other way."

"If I'm not bait, I'm going to be a sitting duck. I don't know how Stevens might figure out who I am, but if he does, wouldn't it be better to have him find me when we control the situation, instead of waiting to be surprised? I could go back to the hotel or Mike Robinson's house. We could arrange to have gaps in the security. He'll never be able to resist coming after me and the Hunters will get him."

Sean's eyes glowed gold. "No," he growled.

"You're not thinking like a professional right now," I accused him. "You're letting your feelings for me cloud your judgment. If I were a different client—"

"I don't care *who* you are. No client of mine is going to set themselves up as bait for a highly trained Marine."

"You're treating me like I'm a fragile flower who needs protecting," I protested. "I'm a high-level mage and a private investigator. My whole life I've been in danger in one way or another and I survived. Stevens is no more of a threat than John West or Spencer Addison or a dozen other people I've faced. Why is this any different from a month ago, when I posed as a prostitute to get myself kidnapped and taken to the harnad warehouse?"

Sean took a deep breath, exhaled, and gripped the steering wheel until his knuckles turned white. "Alice, you know I don't think you're any kind of fragile flower. I didn't try to talk you out of going into that warehouse or out of any other dangerous situation. I do try to protect you when I can, because it's important to me that you're as safe as you can be given your line of work and the kinds of threats you face. What's different about Stevens versus someone like John West is that Stevens's weapons aren't magic—they're grenades and high-powered rifles. I believed you could beat John West and you did. But when it comes to the kinds of weapons Stevens has, what can you do against someone who could shoot you from a hundred yards away?"

"He won't shoot me from a hundred yards away. If I'm any judge of character, Stevens will want to be up close and personal when he tries to take me out. He'll want me to see him coming. He could have taken out Charles and Bryan that night from a distance if he'd wanted, but he came right at them. It's personal for him. And if he's anywhere near me, I can take him out before he gets me. I have more weapons at my disposal than my fire whip."

"You may be right about him wanting to face you." He rubbed his chin and stared ahead through the windshield. "You asked what's different now. It's not just that Stevens is coming after you with rifles. My wolf thinks of you as his mate and he knows you're in danger. He wants to kill the person who is a threat to you, but that isn't an option right now and it's hard for him to understand that. I want Stevens dead too, or at least taken off the board. We're both angry and unhappy with the situation."

"And to top it off, you're at odds with Jack and Delia because of me."

He took my hand, a sign that he needed my touch to calm himself and his wolf. "You aren't the cause of the trouble; the disagreement over my 'ideal' mate predates you by a couple of years. Jack and some of the others have different ideas about what's best for me and the pack and that's what's causing the conflict. What he can't understand is that I believe—I *know*—you would be good for all of us."

My stomach knotted. I didn't agree that I would necessarily be good for Sean or the pack as Sean's mate. I'd always been a loner and as nice as Karen, Cole, Nan, and the others were, I couldn't imagine ever being comfortable as part of a pack. Besides, I had a murderous crime lord grandfather. I was a danger to them, not a benefit.

While I was thinking about that, Sean continued. "The other thing Jack doesn't understand is human dating and human relationships. Both he and Delia were born shifters. They've never been human. Their courtship took all of a couple of weeks. The concept of dating for months or years before committing to a bond is as alien to them as the idea of the mating bond is to you. But I was human before I was a werewolf, and even if my wolf thinks of you as his mate, I'm not wired to think that way. I still think like a human most of the time, and my human self knows we've only been dating a couple of months—not nearly long enough for either of us to be sure about anything long-term."

He lifted my hand and kissed my knuckles. "Do I think you and I might have that bond someday? Yeah, I do. But I'm in no hurry to get there."

"Thank you." I squeezed his hand. "I am sorry about your pack troubles, though."

"They'll have to get used to you," he said firmly. "They'll come around, or they'll learn to live with it."

We sat in comfortable silence for a few minutes. Finally, I made a decision. "Let's go take a look at that motel room. He's either not there or he's in there dead. Either way, I'm ready to find out."

"I agree." He picked up his radio. "Mobile Unit."

Tom's response was immediate. "Go for Mobile Unit."

"We're getting a look at the room. Going to earpiece for contact. Keep your eyes open."

"Ten-four."

Sean stuck his earpiece in his left ear, turned down the volume of the walkie-talkie, and clipped it to his belt in the back under his jacket. I put my phone in my back pocket and waited while he exited the SUV and came around to my side.

We crossed the street and the motel parking lot to the stairs. I heard music playing and the sounds of televisions as we climbed up to the second floor and made our way down the walkway toward room 220.

When we passed the window, I caught a glimpse of the small room. The bed was unmade, a towel tossed on top of the rumpled covers. Two suitcases and a duffel bag were piled in the corner. The room appeared to be empty.

Sean touched his earpiece. "Raven and I are checking out the room. Keep an eye on traffic." I assumed that meant listen in on the police scanner in case someone saw us and called the cops. That didn't seem likely in this part of town, but I didn't want to have to explain to anyone in uniform why we were breaking into the room, especially if there was a body in there.

He slipped a small black case from his inside jacket pocket. I took it and crouched to look at the lock. "I'll get the door. You keep watch."

As I went to work with his lock picking tools, Sean murmured, "I do love a woman of many talents."

"Which of my many talents do you like the most?"

He pondered that. "It's a tough call. It might be a tie between your precision with your fire whip and that thing you do with my—"

The lock clicked. "Hold that thought," I said. I handed him back the lock pick set and we slipped inside room 220.

Sean closed the curtains as I took a quick look around. "No bodies," I announced after I checked the tiny bathroom. "But I wish I'd thought to bring some gloves. I'm going to take a bath in hand sanitizer after we get done searching this place."

He reached into an inside jacket pocket and took out two pairs of black latex gloves. He held them aloft and raised his eyebrows.

I sidled over and pulled him down for a kiss. "You know what I find sexy?" I asked softly, my lips against his.

He rested his hand on my butt. "What do you find sexy?"

"A man who knows not to leave fingerprints." I took a pair of gloves from him and pulled them on.

As the latex snapped against my hand, Sean grinned. "I don't know how, but you make those gloves look hot."

I winked at him. "I think we need to explore your latex kink later when we're somewhere a little more sanitary. You want to search the bags while I do the room?"

"Let's do it."

We worked in silence for a while. I started with the bed, checking between the sheets, inside the pillowcases, and even under the stained mattress. *My kingdom for a hazmat suit*, I thought as I dropped the mattress back onto the sagging box spring. I looked under the bed using my flashlight, then moved on to check the small dresser.

Meanwhile, Sean was looking through John Doe's suitcases and duffel bag. He was extremely thorough, checking each garment and even the lining of the suitcases and bag. Ordinarily, I would have felt compelled to double-check. It was nice to work with someone whose skills I could trust.

When my search of the dresser came up empty, I searched Doe's toiletries, which were expensive. "How many moisturizers do you have?" I asked as I rummaged through the bottles on the counter.

"Uh, one, I think. Why? How many does he have?"

"Three, and one of them has gold flakes in it." I waved the bottle. "Maybe you should try it. It might make you sparkly."

"Werewolves do not *sparkle* under any circumstances," he informed me. "You finding anything?"

"Not a damn thing," I said grumpily. "You?"

"Nope. Well-made but generic clothes only. No paperwork of any kind and nothing that might give us a hint to his identity. No identification. No pictures, nothing of any sentimental value."

"I'm not giving up. There's something here; there has to be." I searched under the sink, behind the toilet, and even inside the toilet tank, finding nothing.

When I came back into the bedroom, Sean was standing by the door. "Ready to head out?"

"In a second. There's one more place I haven't checked." I went to the window A/C unit. "Got something I can use to pry the cover off?"

He produced a pocketknife. I carefully slid the blade into the casing of the A/C. The plastic cover popped off easily. I handed Sean the knife and took the cover off. There was a key taped to the inside of the A/C cover.

"I'll be damned," Sean said, impressed. "What made you think to look in here?"

"It's the sort of place I'd hide something in a room like this." I pulled the key free and studied it. "Looks like the key to a heavy-duty disc padlock. He could have a storage unit somewhere, if this is his key."

He leaned in to get a closer look at the A/C cover. "There's no dust or dirt on top of the tape. I'd say there's a good chance this is John Doe's key."

"Yeah, but where's the lock it goes to?" I scrutinized the inside of the A/C but couldn't see anything else inside it. "I think that's all there is. We should probably skedaddle."

I pocketed the key and put the cover back on the A/C as Sean alerted the mobile team that we were heading out. Once we got the all-clear from Tom, we left the room and locked the door on the way out. We took off our gloves and I stuck mine in my pocket in case I needed them again. I was hoping for at least one more B&E opportunity in the near future.

By the time we got back to the SUV, I had a plan for that. I knew from Cait's report that John Doe had been leasing an Infiniti while in the city. The car was still parked in front of the condo, but it might still be of use.

"I have a job for Cyro," I told Sean as he got in and shut his door. "It's a long shot, but I'm sure John Doe's fancy car has a built-in navigation system."

He smiled. "And you're wondering if it could tell us if he's been visiting a self-storage facility?"

"Bingo."

"Let's find out." He took a burner phone from the center console and sent a text. "In the meantime, do we stay and watch the room or go home?"

I thought about it. "We should stay," I decided. "The towel on the bed was still damp, so he's been in the room recently."

"The only thing in that room worth going back for is the key," Sean pointed out. "The rest of it he could leave, but if that key goes to a storage unit, either he's going to need it or someone else is. Either way, it's your best lead unless something else turns up."

"Exactly. I hate to say it, but I think we have to stay."

Sean informed the mobile team that we were going to stay to watch the room. Tom had just radioed his acknowledgment when Sean's burner phone rang. He answered. "This is Sean."

I heard Cyro's familiar electronic voice on the other end. Sean explained what we needed, then held the phone out to me. "He'd like to speak to you."

I took the phone. "This is Alice."

"Hello, Alice," the electronic voice said. Keyboard keys clicked rapidly in the background. "I like this challenge. You bring me the most interesting projects."

"I do try."

"I'm intrigued by this man who calls himself Kendall. He's very good at covering his tracks and hiding his real identity—better than most people I run into. I might have to make identifying and finding him a personal project."

"He certainly has a lot to answer for."

"Oh, not because he's a thief," Cyro said. "I couldn't care less that he travels from city to city swindling rich people out of their junk. It's more about the challenge. I get bored."

"I can see that." I hesitated. "I don't know if it matters, but when I went to my client's home yesterday I discovered Kendall had been using a ghost trapped in a crystal as a power source. She'd been in there for years. It was his magic binding her to the crystal, so he's the one who put her in there."

A long pause. "Where is she now?" I could hear his anger even through the electronically modulated voice.

"She passed on and he won't be able to get her back."

"Thank you for that," Cyro said. "I'll bump this to top priority. You'll have the info from the car's navigation system as soon as I can get it. You're looking for a self-storage facility?"

"Thank you. Yes, we believe so. We have a key we think goes to a heavy-duty padlock. If you don't find a storage facility, I'll take the raw records. Maybe we can retrace his movements and figure out what the key goes to if it isn't storage."

"I'll see what I can do. Take care." The call ended.

I handed the phone back to Sean, who frowned. "What are you thinking about?" I asked.

He drummed his fingers on the steering wheel. "I've been talking to Cyro for almost five years. He's always been all business. He's never made small talk, revealed anything personal, or told me to 'take care.' And he's certainly never wanted to speak to anyone else when I ask about a project, even if it would be easier to get the information he needs directly from the client instead of relaying it through me. These conversations between you are completely different from any I've ever had and I'd like to know why."

"I'd like to know why too." I kept my tone light, but Sean's words were troubling.

I didn't need a hacker like Cyro sniffing around me. As secure as I felt that my identity was safely hidden, if anyone could uncover the truth—that I was not the real Alice Worth, or that I was Moses Murphy's granddaughter—it would be someone like Cyro. I was beginning to regret coming to his attention in any way. I did not want a talented hacker to find me interesting. I didn't want *anyone* to find me interesting.

Sean took my hand. "After this, we don't need to contact Cyro for anything anymore. We both have other resources we can call on. They might not be as good or as fast or as willing to break federal law as him, but they're a safer option. No case or client is worth endangering you."

For a moment, I didn't know what to say to that. Sean knew I had secrets. He'd figured out that I was probably hiding from someone and my life before I arrived in the city had been dangerous and violent. If I acknowledged that I needed to distance myself from Cyro, I was more or less confirming that I didn't want a hacker getting interested enough about me to dig into my past. I was so paranoid about revealing anything about my previous life that I didn't even want to confirm that I'd had one.

I should run.

The thought popped into my head out of nowhere. Just a few months ago, I'd felt reasonably secure in my new life. It had been lonely, but was as safe as I could be given the circumstances. Things changed quickly around the time I'd met Sean. Malcolm showed up, bound to me as a result of things I'd done while part of the cabal. Then Charles bit me and discovered I wasn't a mid-level mage. Federal agent Trent Lake figured out I wasn't really Alice Worth, and I worried Sean might be getting perilously close to coming to the same conclusion.

Now I'd come to the attention of a hacker who liked challenges and finding out people's real identities. If he figured out who I was, the best I could hope for was probably that I'd be blackmailed. At worst, he'd sell me out to Moses. And it wasn't even just my own life that might be in jeopardy—now it was Malcolm, Sean, and Sean's pack too. All those lives depended on Moses not finding me.

I didn't want to run. This mess with Kent Stevens aside, I liked my life as Alice Worth. I liked being a mage private investigator. I liked my home and the small group of people I called friends. I liked Sean. I liked the idea of having a family in the form of a pack, even if it scared me too.

If I had to run, I had options. Alice Worth wasn't the only identity I had. There were others, sitting on digital shelves across the country and even in Europe. I could leave Alice behind and become one of a dozen women anywhere from Dallas to Dublin.

I thought of John Doe, who ran from city to city with nothing but a couple of suitcases. Would that be my fate? Was it delusional of me to think I could have anything more than that? To think that I *deserved* to have anything more? Wasn't it entirely selfish of me to put everyone around me in danger by staying?

"Alice, please stop." Sean's firm voice broke into my thoughts. "I can feel how dark it just got in your head. I think I know what you're thinking about." He squeezed my hand. "I'm going to say this, even if it pisses you off. If someone comes looking for you, they will have to go through me. I don't care if it's an ex-Marine with a grudge or an army. Don't run because you think it's the best option you have. You have a better one: staying here. Out there, you're alone and vulnerable. Here, you are not alone."

"I'd only run if I had to."

His eyes went golden. "I'm telling you that you don't have to."

"Aren't I the best judge of that?"

"Aren't I the best judge of whether I want to fight for you or not?" he countered. "I thought we settled this when we faced the demon Ravan together. You told me it was my decision to make. You trusted me to make that choice then. Unless something's changed, you should still trust me now."

"I do trust you to make that decision. That doesn't mean it's ever going to be easy for me to see you put yourself in danger."

"It's never going to be easy for me to let you go into harm's way either. I guess the only thing we can do about it is face threats together."

I wanted to punch the dashboard in frustration. "Why is this so stressful?"

He grinned. "Us caring about each other is causing you stress?"

"Yes!"

He laughed. Despite the lead ball of worry in my stomach, I had to smile.

I took off my jacket, wadded it up, and put it on the center console between us. I laid down across the jacket, resting my head on Sean's thigh, and shifted with a pained grunt as the stupid vest and cup holders dug into various parts of my anatomy.

"That can't be comfortable," he said, gently brushing my hair back from my face. "Why don't you climb in the back seat for a bit and lie down if you're tired?"

"I'm not tired," I lied. "It's not even midnight." I wiggled a bit until I found a position that was merely uncomfortable instead of painful. "Tell me a story."

He rested his hand on my hip. "I'd like to tell you the story of how I became the alpha of our pack."

"I'd like that."

A pause. "In order to explain how I became the alpha, I have to tell you how I became a werewolf."

I put my hand on top of his. "If you're ready to tell me, I'm ready to hear it."

He took a deep breath. "I was twenty-two. My friends Danny and Matt and I decided to go camping. We packed up and drove out to the middle of nowhere, then hiked for a half a day to find the right spot to camp. Nobody had cell phones back then, not that you'd be able to get a signal out there. We had compasses and balls and we figured that was all we needed. We wanted to prove how tough we were, I guess."

When he went quiet, I glanced up at him. Sean was staring into space, as if looking back through time. "The first couple of days were great," he said. "We sat around and bullshitted each other the way twenty-two-year-olds do, with all our big plans for the future. We fished for food and swam in ice-cold water and shared the couple of bottles of vodka that we brought."

Another pause. I waited.

"It happened on the third night. We were asleep when they found us. It was two werewolves—a mated pair who didn't belong to any pack. They were lurking on the edge of the Tomb Mountain Pack's territory, hunting. It was a full moon."

I grimaced. At any other time, werewolves could shift back and forth between their human and wolf forms at will. But on the full moon, they were forced to shift at the moon's rise and stay in wolf form until dawn. They were at their most feral and violent.

"I didn't even know what happened for a long time," he said finally. "I was asleep when we were attacked. All I remembered was teeth and claws and blood and hearing Danny and Matt screaming. They tore us apart. The next morning, I woke up. The others didn't."

I squeezed his hand.

"When I came to, the first thing I saw was Henry, the Tomb Mountain Pack alpha, standing over me. The sunlight was blinding. I could hear every rustle, every little sound. I didn't understand what was going on. Then I saw his eyes. They were gold. He told me to sleep, and I did."

"The next couple of days were basically a blur. I shifted to my wolf and back a half-dozen times without having much control over it. Henry or his beta, Seth, were always with me. Without them, I don't know what I would have done. When I was finally able to stay in human form and think clearly, Henry told me Danny and Matt were dead. Apparently only one of the werewolves who attacked us was capable of transmitting the virus. Whichever one it was bit me. The other one killed Danny and Matt. That's why I lived and they didn't."

His voice was heavy with sorrow. I entwined our fingers and waited for him to continue.

"The werewolves who attacked us got away. They must have realized what they did and left the region. A park ranger found Danny and Matt's bodies two days later and called in the feds. They looked for me for a week. In the meantime, I stayed with Henry until I had enough control to go back. I went to the feds and told them what happened. They ran tests, determined I was newly turned and not responsible for my friends' deaths, and sent me on my way."

His hand tightened on mine until it hurt, but I stayed quiet. "I was so afraid to go home, afraid I wouldn't be able to control my shifting. I told my parents I was upset about Danny and Matt and I was going to take a road trip. I went back to the pack and stayed with them for six weeks. When I felt like I could control myself, I went back home."

"When did you finally tell your family?" I asked.

"Four months after the attack, when I hadn't shifted involuntarily in more than two months. They took the news pretty well, all things considered, except they were angry that I'd kept it from them for so long. I'm lucky. They accept me and they love me. A lot of werewolves get disowned by their families, or worse."

We sat quietly for a while, holding hands and lost in our own thoughts. I imagined Sean, young and afraid, a new werewolf who couldn't control his shifting, having to rely on complete strangers to help him adjust. "At least you had Henry and the pack," I said softly.

"Henry could tell my wolf was very dominant," he said. "He was old, and he knew someday soon he wouldn't be able to run the pack anymore. I'm not saying he helped me entirely for selfish reasons, but he knew what he was doing when he brought me into the pack. He told me later that he saw the potential for me to be the alpha someday, even in those first few days. If something happened to him, he needed to make sure Seth didn't become the alpha." His tone changed when he said Seth's name.

"What happened?"

"About ten years ago, Henry turned eighty. He was still strong and sharp and a good alpha, but Seth and a couple of the other younger males thought he was too old and weak. Seth ambushed Henry during a full moon and killed him. Technically it was his right to do so under shifter law, but most modern werewolf packs don't fight to the death to establish a new alpha. Simply defeating him would have been enough, but Seth wanted to make a point. He killed Henry, then dragged his body into the open so we could all see it. That was the sort of alpha Seth wanted to be. He liked to kill. He wanted to rule by fear, and he thought all the females in the pack should belong to him first, even before their spouses."

"And that's why Henry made sure you survived and joined his pack, so someday you could protect the others from Seth."

"And that's what I did. The same night Seth killed Henry, I fought Seth and I killed him." His fingers stroked mine. "Does that bother you?"

"Of course not." I squeezed his hand again. "It wouldn't have been enough just to beat him. Someone like that...they would never have accepted you as their alpha. He wouldn't have stopped trying to kill you." I looked up at him. "What made you want to tell me all this now?"

"I've been thinking about telling you for a while. After the conversations we've had tonight and given everything else that's going on, it seemed like the right time to put my cards on the table."

"I'm glad you told me." I wiggled until my head and neck were nestled comfortably against his leg. "Tell me about some of the people you've worked for. I bet you have all kinds of funny work stories."

Sean ran his fingers through my hair and told me about an investment banker who had three girlfriends who found out about each other when they showed up at his apartment at the same time. The catfight that ensued involved a lot of screaming and broken glassware.

I closed my eyes and laughed softly as he described how his employees tried to separate the women from the banker and each other.

"Three girlfriends at the same time? What an idiot," I murmured sleepily when he finished.

"I agree," Sean said. "You find the right woman, you only want the one."

"Mmmm. Tell me another story."

He described some of the misadventures his employees had while attempting to upgrade the surveillance cameras at Nyx, a vampire burlesque and sex club near downtown.

I dozed a bit as he talked, not wanting to sleep, but feeling secure with him watching over me. Eventually, not long after Team Three arrived at midnight, sleep stole me away.

14

I napped until three thirty, then stayed awake to watch for John Doe. We remained parked in front of the motel until just after dawn, but there was no sign of anyone trying to get into the room. At seven, with Team One getting ready to come on duty, I decided to call it off and we headed back to my house. Sean met briefly with his people, then joined me in bed for a few hours of sleep.

I was in the shower when Sean knocked on the bathroom door and stuck his head in. "Cyro just sent over the navigation records for John Doe's Infiniti."

I shut off the water and reached for a towel to wrap around my hair. "Tell me there's good news."

"What's that? I can't hear you through the shower curtain."

"Uh-huh. So much for werewolf hearing." I grabbed another towel off the rack and pulled the curtain back. He was leaning against the counter and grinning. I rolled my eyes and stepped out of the shower. "Can you hear me now?"

"Loud and clear." He kissed my forehead. "How are you feeling?"

"Better than you, I'm sure." Unlike me, Sean hadn't slept during the stakeout and we'd only napped a few hours at home. I sniffed the air. "Do I smell coffee?"

"There's a whole pot in the kitchen with your name on it."

"Awesome," I said fervently as I dried myself off. "What were you saying about the records from the car?"

"Cyro came through with the navigation data. It looks like John Doe regularly cleared his history in the car, but that data never really goes away. It's stored on a server somewhere."

I draped the towel over the rack and started dressing. "Well, don't keep me in suspense...where are we going?"

"A self-storage company on the west side. John Doe was last there two days ago. Cyro went ahead and got into the company's records and found out he's renting the unit under the name of Ted Nickerson."

"Tom Nelson, Ted Nickerson," I mused as I pulled my shirt on over my head. "Same initials. Might be a clue to his identity. Let me dry my hair and finish getting ready. We'll be able to roll out of here in about fifteen minutes if you'll pour that coffee into a travel mug for me."

Sean went back downstairs, humming "Eye of the Tiger" under his breath. I chuckled and reached for my hair dryer. It looked like I wasn't the only one excited about finding out what was in John Doe's storage unit.

Twenty minutes later, with Jack and Karen following us, Sean and I were on our way to the west side. I'd spent the extra five minutes consuming a breakfast burrito that he'd whipped up in the time it took me to dry my hair, put on makeup, and get downstairs.

"You're trying to fatten me up," I accused him as we drove. "I tasted butter in those eggs."

He gave me an innocent look. "How else are you supposed to make them?"

I sighed and guzzled coffee. "I don't have a werewolf's metabolism. If you keep feeding me like one of your pack, I won't be able to run after anyone if I have to."

"That was hardly a werewolf-sized meal. A werewolf would have eaten four of those burritos. Besides, you were hungry, and you ate every last bite."

"I was just being polite," I huffed.

He laughed. I put my hand on his leg and sipped my coffee.

Our destination turned out to be a medium-sized self-storage business that looked like it had been built in the late eighties.

"Interesting," I said as we pulled into the drive. "I was expecting something a lot more high-tech and secure for someone who runs a burglary ring."

"The high-end places have a lot more security and a lot more traffic," Sean pointed out. He pulled up to the gate, rolled down his window, and punched a four-digit code into the small keypad. The gate rolled open.

"You get that code from Cyro?"

He nodded. "Yes. When we're done here, I'll let him know and he'll erase the security cam footage of our visit."

"Great." I was still uneasy about Cyro, but I couldn't argue that having a master hacker on call was advantageous.

Sean drove through the gate and rolled slowly down the passageway between the long storage buildings. "We're looking for unit 303."

I looked around. "These look like buildings one and two. Building three is probably on the other side."

Behind us, Jack and Karen entered through the gate and followed us around the back. Building three was on the left. Unit 303 was third from the back.

Sean parked in front of the unit. Jack backed their vehicle against the fence so he and Karen had a clear line of sight down both passageways.

We got out of the SUV and went to the rolling door of the unit. Sean pulled the key from his pocket and reached for the padlock.

"Wait. There are wards." I placed my hand on the door and felt the wards pulsing against my skin. They were much more powerful and intricately made than the wards on Esther's house. "I need Malcolm's help."

"Has he been back since you took the other retrieval spell out of him yesterday?"

I shook my head. "No. I can still sense him, so he's okay. I guess he just needed some time alone. I'll see if he's ready to talk." I found the familiar blue-green trace in my mind that connected us and gave it two gentle tugs.

A few seconds later, I felt the telltale buzzing in the crystal on my bracelet as Malcolm jumped to me. I touched the crystal. *"Release."*

Malcolm appeared beside me. He looked better than yesterday, and some of the sparkle was back in his eyes. "Hey, Alice. Heya, Sean." He glanced around. "What are we doing here?"

I explained how we'd ended up at the storage unit and why I'd paged him.

He floated over to the wards and studied them. "It's air magic, obviously. More complex than the other ones, but not anywhere near expert level." He frowned. "These other wards are, though."

"What other wards?"

"There are black wards inside the door. They're masked to you, but I can see them."

I pinched the bridge of my nose. "Black wards. Fantastic."

"They aren't that bad. I'm thinking he hired someone; they seem...generic."

I tapped my lip with my index finger. "Do the wards go around the perimeter of the unit?"

"No, only along the door. How big of a circle can you cast without drawing a line?"

"Why?"

"If you can control the flare, I'm pretty sure I can break the wards rather than spending hours unweaving them."

"I can tap a ley line to hold a circle big enough, but what if there are landmines?" I worried aloud, thinking about the hidden curses that had almost taken me out the last time I'd tried unweaving someone else's wards.

He shrugged. "Landmines don't seem to affect me much. They'd have to be specifically made to target ghosts, and I doubt these were. I can't imagine he'd be too concerned about a ghost getting into the storage unit."

"As soon as we break the wards, he'll know we're here, assuming he's still alive, that is."

"How dangerous is what you're about to do?" Sean asked.

"About a three for her," Malcolm told him. "Unless I'm wrong about those landmines, about a one for me. Relax, dude. This is a walk in the park for a couple of bad-ass mages like us."

I was glad to see Malcolm getting back to his old self after the scare with the retrieval spell and yesterday's unpleasant search for additional spells. I didn't like seeing him upset, especially if I was the cause of it, either directly or indirectly.

I gestured. "Sean, you need to stand over by the SUV." He moved to where I pointed. "Let me know when you're ready," I said to Malcolm.

He gave me a grin. If I didn't know any better, I'd have said he was having fun. "Ready."

The city was located at the intersection of two ley lines, which was one of the reasons I'd chosen to move here after leaving my grandfather's compound. As an earth mage, I could make better use of the lines than air, fire, or water mages. I rarely did, however, because it hurt like hell and because I hadn't really had the need to siphon that much power. It also had the potential to attract attention, but I wasn't planning on tapping the line for very long.

I closed my eyes and reached out to find the closest ley line. It felt like a high-voltage wire on the edge of my awareness. I breathed deeply, exhaled, and grabbed the line.

The sensation was pure power, like one of those cartoons where someone gets electrocuted and they light up like an incandescent bulb. My hair stuck straight out with the force of it. Every cell in my body seemed to vibrate. It didn't hurt yet, but it would.

I envisioned the bubble I wanted to create around the door of the storage unit and focused my magic and the ley line energy. With a heavy *pop* sound that only I could hear, the bubble formed. Pain sizzled along my skin, a familiar sensation.

Malcolm didn't need me to tell him when the circle was in place. Only seconds after I'd formed the bubble, he broke the air magic wards. The energy hit the barrier of my bubble. I gritted my teeth as it crackled and faded. *That wasn't so bad*, I thought.

Then Malcolm broke through the layers of blood wards. It was like the difference between a little Fourth of July popper and three bundles of dynamite going off one after the other: blam, *blam, BLAM*. On the third wave, the discharge of energy made me stagger and fall to my hands and knees. I set my jaw and didn't yell, but that *hurt*. I barely registered the gravel that bit into my palms through the pain of the wards bursting against my containment bubble.

Despite their power, the broken wards dissipated quickly. As soon as the energy faded, I released the ley line and dropped the circle.

I couldn't get up right away, not because of the pain, but because conducting that much power and focusing it left me disoriented. When I'd lived at my grandfather's compound I'd worked with ley lines regularly, but since I'd been in the city, this was only the second time I'd tapped into one. Using ley lines regularly or for very long got you noticed by local mages and harnads, and I had no desire to come to their attention.

I heard Sean telling Jack over the radio that I was fine. They'd apparently seen me go down and wondered what had happened.

Malcolm's cold hand touched my shoulder. *How long has it been since you used a ley line?*

I took a deep breath. *Too long. I need to practice more often.*

Yeah, you do. You don't want to be in a situation where you need to tap a line and you can't do it. He took his hand off my shoulder.

"I'm all right," I said out loud as Sean came to stand next to me. My voice sounded a little wispy, but my head was clear.

"So that was a three?" he asked mildly, offering me a hand.

"Actually, yes." I pulled myself to my feet and gave him a quick smile to show I was okay. "The wards packed a little more of a punch than I expected, but the circle held without any trouble and now we can get into the unit."

"Without getting fried," Malcolm added.

"Thank you for helping us with the wards," Sean said. "You good?"

"Yeah, I'm good. Sorry I needed some space."

"Don't apologize," I told the ghost. "You can take some 'me' time whenever you need to. You mind sticking around? I'm not sure what we're going to find in there."

"Yeah, no problem. I got no place to be." Malcolm grinned at me and I smiled back.

Sean and I pulled on another pair of black latex gloves. He used the key we'd found to unlock the padlock. "Let's get in here and see what's what." He took the radio from his belt. "Going to check out the unit. Keep an eye out for visitors."

"Ten-four," Jack said briskly.

Sean raised the door halfway and we slipped inside. He found the light switch by the door and flipped it before rolling the door back down to hide us from anyone passing by.

The unit was about ten feet by ten feet and nearly full. Boxes of various sizes, all marked with runes, filled three tall metal shelves. A half-dozen large paintings wrapped in paper were stacked against the wall.

"This is the tidiest storage unit I've ever seen," Sean said, surveying the room. "Malcolm, do you sense any more wards?"

"Not from here, but you guys stay where you are and I'll do a more thorough search."

We waited by the door while Malcolm floated around, checking every inch of the storage unit. Finally, he came back to us. "No more wards I can sense," he reported. "Most of the boxes are spelled, but they should be pretty easy to unweave. Some of the boxes have containment spells, though, which means whatever is in them could go kaboom if we're not careful."

I pursed my lips. "Well, I don't want to open any of those boxes. There's no telling what's in them and I have no desire to blow up the building."

"So what's the plan?" Sean asked.

"See if we can find the cuff, I guess," I said. "Then we have a choice of whether to just leave things where they are and let the situation sort itself out, or tip off SPEMA about a cache of magical objects and let them look for John Doe."

"You could sell them to Charles," Malcolm said, half-jokingly.

I shook my head. "I'm not getting into the stolen magical objects trade. There are others hunting for these items and not all of them play nice. All I'm taking out of here is the cuff if we can find it."

"It's probably not in one of the containment boxes, so I'll start unweaving the spells on the other ones," Malcolm said. "Some of them have blood ward locks, so I'll start with those since it's safer for me to unweave them than you."

We went to work as Sean watched. While Malcolm focused on unweaving blood ward locks, I looked through the boxes that just had simple masking spells designed to hide the magic trace of their contents.

In the third box I opened, I found a bracelet that matched the lust-spell necklace Dora Quinn had shown me at Walsh & Quinn.

"That wench is selling all kinds of stolen goods," I fumed, showing Sean the bracelet. "I'm starting to think half the stuff in that shop was obtained in the same way she got Esther's hand mirror."

"Maybe we should drop a dime to SPEMA about the shop," Sean said.

"Maybe we should." I closed the box and put it back on the shelf before opening the next one.

Not all of the boxes housed magical objects; some contained antiques and jewelry. I checked to see if any of it belonged to Esther. If I managed to recover any of her missing jewelry, maybe she'd bump up that bonus. To my disappointment, none of it matched the photos of Esther's stolen pieces.

The pieces in the boxes with the blood ward locks were more expensive magical items. The boxes with containment spells had me worried; some of them might pack a wallop and I had no way of knowing what was in them. By the time I finished looking in all the boxes on the first and second shelving units, I'd decided we had to tip SPEMA off about this stash before those items fell into the wrong hands.

I was beginning to think we were going to come up empty in our search for Esther's cuff when I opened a medium-sized box and whooped. "Got it!"

"Excellent." Sean joined me and examined the cuff. It was about four inches wide and made of what looked like hammered brass. The edges were lined with runes, the fire magic spellwork that gave its wearer the extra zip that Esther and her husband had apparently enjoyed.

Sean's thoughts must have mirrored my own. "Maybe we should take this for a test drive before you give it back to your client," he said with a wink.

"You don't need any help in the virility department," I told him, patting his butt affectionately. "If you had any more sex drive, it might literally kill me. I can barely keep up with you as it is."

"Oh my God, you two. Get a room," Malcolm complained. He'd stopped unweaving blood ward locks when I found the cuff and was now floating by the door.

"I plan to." Sean grinned. "Alice and I are going to have a lot to celebrate once she gets this stuff back to her client. I can't believe Aldridge was willing to pay five or six grand for this thing. It sure doesn't look like much, does it?" He reached for the cuff.

It happened faster than any of us could react. As soon as Sean's fingers got near the cuff, it flipped and closed around his right forearm with a flare of magic.

He snarled and tried to pull the cuff off with his other hand, but it had closed completely around his wrist without even leaving a visible seam.

Magic pulsed from the cuff and each wave was stronger than the last. Sean staggered and grabbed the shelving unit for support as he went down. The shelf fell over, sending boxes crashing to the floor.

Whatever the cuff was doing to Sean, it sure as hell had nothing to do with his libido. He was on his hands and knees, his muscles straining as if he was fighting something. When I heard joints popping, I realized he was trying not to shift. It had to be agonizing.

"Alice, get this thing off me," he growled.

"Hold still," I told him. My earth magic spiraled out of my hand and formed a short, thin whip. I lashed the cuff with the power and precision of someone who'd been practicing that skill her entire life.

The cuff should have split instantly. Instead, a backlash of magic traveled up my whip and punched me in the chest so hard that my heart stuttered. The blast knocked the wind out of me and sent me crashing to my knees.

As I went down, Malcolm zipped to Sean and tried to unweave the spells on the cuff. The moment he made contact with the spells, a powerful flare of magic disrupted his form.

"No," I gasped as he fractured before my eyes. I'd never seen magic affect a ghost that way. "Malcolm!"

He vanished. Fear gripped me until I recognized the tingle of magic as the spell he used to jump back to one of the crystals in my basement. He would be protected there and hopefully regenerate and heal whatever damage the cuff had done to him.

"Get...Jack," Sean ground out, his eyes bright gold. His voice was more than half growl.

As I reached for the radio on his belt, the rolling door was yanked up so quickly that I heard metal bending.

Jack appeared in the doorway, framed by sunlight. He must have sensed trouble through the pack bonds. He slammed the door back down and crouched at Sean's side. "What happened?"

"The cuff—" I began.

"I wasn't asking you," Jack snarled.

He grabbed the cuff with both hands, attempting to tear it apart, but was knocked back by a burst of magic. The damn thing was warded against magic *and* physical force. What the hell *was* that thing?

Sean was growling now, his eyes golden as he fought to stay human. "Lead...the...pack," he ordered Jack. "Protect...Alice. Even...from me."

"I will," Jack said. "Shift now before resisting it kills you."

Sean looked at me, his eyes almost full wolf. There was no fear in them, only anger and pain. I wanted to take the pain from him, but I couldn't and it was breaking my heart.

"I will get the cuff off you," I promised him.

He held his human form for one more second, and then he shifted with the sound of bones popping and a pulse of golden magic.

Sean's wolf was enormous, black and silver with golden eyes. I'd hoped that when he shifted the cuff would fall off, but instead it appeared to have changed sizes so that now it fit snugly on the wolf's front leg.

My thoughts raced. Clearly, the cuff was much more than a libido-enhancing accessory. Perhaps that was its effect when worn by a human, but its effect on a shifter was dramatic.

"Sean?" I asked tentatively.

The wolf lowered his head and growled softly, his eyes on me. Sean had told me that though the wolf was in the driver's seat when he was in wolf form, he was aware of everything that was going on and could speak to the wolf.

Jack turned on me, his eyes bright. "What the fuck is that thing on his leg?"

The wolf snarled at him and snapped his teeth. He moved between Jack and me and growled warningly at his beta. The message was clear: back off.

Jack's demeanor instantly changed. His posture became less aggressive and the glow in his eyes diminished. "I'm not going to attack her," he said calmly. "I'm just trying to figure out what happened."

The wolf seemed to not understand what Jack was saying. He bared his teeth, his ears back as if preparing to attack.

"Sean, everything is okay," I said, trying to make my voice soothing. "Can you hear me? We're going to help you."

The wolf stood his ground, watching Jack closely and growling. I started to move around to his side, thinking if he could see my eyes and body language I might be able to communicate better.

The wolf turned his head and snapped his teeth at me. I froze.

In the blink of an eye, Jack pulled out a gun and shot the wolf.

The dart hit the wolf in the neck. He whipped his head around and snarled at Jack, who held his ground as the wolf tried to leap. Instead, his legs went out from under him and he fell.

Stunned, I asked, "Why did you have that gun?"

Jack stuck the gun back in the holster at the small of his back. "It was for Caleb," he said shortly.

I went to the wolf on my hands and knees. His eyes were half-closed but he managed to look at me. I saw pain, worry, and anger.

I ran my fingers through the wolf's fur and lowered my forehead to his. "I will get that cuff off you," I told him again. "Just hang on."

The wolf let out a tiny, almost imperceptible whine. Then his eyes closed and he went limp.

I laid my head against his side and listened to the steady, slow beating of his heart. He was so warm. I wanted to cry. I wanted to tear something or someone apart. But mostly I wanted to find out what the hell this cuff was and how to get it off him.

Jack pulled his radio from his belt. "Mobile Unit, back our vehicle up to the door and open the back."

"Ten-four," Karen replied, her voice strained. I wondered if everyone in the pack could sense what had happened to Sean.

I raised my head. "What are you doing?"

"Taking my alpha somewhere safe, somewhere far away from you."

I was on my feet before I realized I'd moved. My magic surged and the ground trembled beneath us. "The hell you are."

His fury was so intense that it scoured my skin like a sandstorm. "That tranquilizer won't last more than an hour or two, and you have no way of caging a werewolf."

"I have to get that cuff off of him," I argued.

"We'll get the cuff off. If you're too stupid and weak to do it, we'll find a mage who can."

My rage went ice-cold. "I am neither stupid nor weak. I just need time. That cuff is heavily warded, but every spell has counter-spells. Every ward can be broken, eventually."

Tires crunched outside as Karen backed their SUV up to the rolling door. A door slammed and footsteps approached.

"We'll find someone who can remove the cuff. It's no longer of any concern to you." Jack crouched and picked up the wolf's unconscious body. "Open the door," he called to Karen.

As she rolled the door up, I said, "That's not your decision to make, Jack. Sean and I are a couple whether you like it or not, and his well-being is of great concern to me, as mine is to him."

"Which is why you're still in one piece," Jack snapped. "Now move out of the way."

"What happened?" Karen asked, her eyes wide and horrified as she watched Jack carry Sean to the open back of the SUV.

"I'll explain later," Jack told her, placing the wolf carefully into the cargo area. "You drive the other vehicle and follow me."

Karen froze. "And leave Alice here alone?"

"I'll send personnel from Maclin Security to come get her. She can wait here." Jack shut the back of the SUV.

Karen hesitated, looking at me helplessly.

"Get his phone and radio. We need to go *now*," Jack ordered.

"It's okay," I told Karen. "Go. I'll be all right."

As she bent to pick up Sean's things, Jack snarled at me. "Don't give her permission to obey an order. She's pack."

"I wasn't giving her permission; I was reassuring her. There's a difference." I approached the open door where Jack was waiting for Karen. "When I figure out how to remove that cuff, I will come for him. Don't get in my way."

Karen seemed to shrink as Jack loomed over me. "Are you threatening me?"

The last time Jack and I had squared off, at Karen's house, Sean had advised me to avoid looking his beta in the eye. It had felt wrong then and it felt wrong now. My gut told me facing him was the only way to show Jack he had no authority over me and never would.

I met his gaze and didn't back down. "I'm making it clear where we stand. Take it however you want."

We stared at each other. His hands curled into fists and he made a low growl. Shifter magic rose.

I pushed my blood magic through my fingertips, forming razor-like claws. I kept my hand at my side, but he saw the blades.

Someday, Jack and I might have to settle our differences, but today was not that day. Sean was more important. As much as it rankled me to do so, I took a step back to show that I didn't want to fight. "Take him somewhere safe."

Jack turned on his heel and left with Karen behind him. She sent me an apologetic look just before Jack reached up and pulled the door down. He slammed it closed, leaving me alone in the semi-darkness.

Moments later, an engine started and the SUVs drove away.

15

There was so much I needed to do. I had to get home to check on Malcolm. I needed to figure out what the hell the cuff was and how to get it off Sean. Then I'd have to deal with Jack, assuming Sean didn't kill him outright for leaving me high and dry.

First, in the privacy of John Doe's storage unit, I sat down on a cardboard box, put my head in my hands, and gave myself exactly sixty seconds to break down.

In the space of just a few minutes, the ground had been yanked out from under my feet. Malcolm was hurt. Sean was possibly stuck in wolf form as the cuff did God-knew-what to him.

The wolf's final whine echoed in my ears. I doubted I'd ever forget that sound. I'd only heard it once before: when the demon Ravan broke his ribs while they were fighting in my backyard. Hearing Sean in pain did something to me that I'd never felt before. It made me furious beyond what I would have thought possible. I supposed that was a taste of what Sean felt when he saw me hurt or in danger. I rubbed my face with my hands.

My phone buzzed. I dug it out of my pocket. The caller ID read *C Rose Calling*. I didn't recognize the name or number.

Frowning, I answered. "Alice Worth."

"This is Cyro." The electronic voice was tense. "What is your status?"

Sean had told me a while back that Cyro's full pseudonym was Cyanide Rose. That explained the caller ID, though not why he was calling me now.

When I didn't respond immediately, he spoke again, more urgently. "Ms. Worth? Are you all right?"

"I'm fine," I said. "Why are you calling me?"

"I saw what looked like trouble and the Maclin Security SUVs left without you. What's going on?"

I blinked. "Were you watching the security cameras?"

"Yes, obviously." Cyro sounded irritated. "Why is Maclin in wolf form and unconscious, and why did his beta leave you there alone and unprotected?"

"There was a medical emergency and they had to leave." I didn't want Cyro involved any more than he already was. "I have someone coming to pick me up."

"Ms. Worth—"

"I need to make some calls, Cyro," I told him. "Once I'm gone, please erase the security footage of us being here. I'm going to tip the feds off about what we found in the storage unit and I don't want anyone to know we were here."

"Consider it done," he said briskly. "Do you want me to send an anonymous tip to SPEMA instead so it can't be traced back to you? No charge."

I couldn't think of a downside to accepting. "Okay. I appreciate it."

"I'll keep an eye on the cameras until you're safely away."

"Thank you."

"Goodbye." Cyro disconnected.

I scrolled through my contacts and made a call. The phone rang once. "Miss Alice," Bryan rumbled.

I took a deep breath. "I need your help."

About thirty minutes later, tires crunched in the gravel outside the storage unit. My phone buzzed with a text message. *Bryan: Your ride has arrived.*

I texted back an acknowledgment and opened the rolling door. A black Vampire Court SUV was backed up to the storage unit, its engine running. I rolled the door closed, locked the padlock, and went around to the passenger door. I opened it and blinked in surprise.

"Hop in," Arkady Woodall said. She was wearing a black jacket over a black shirt, black jeans, and tall black boots. Her blonde hair was back in a ponytail. The butt of a gun peeked out from under her left arm and I saw another in a holster on her right ankle.

"Sorry. I was expecting Adri." I climbed into the passenger seat, put the box that had held the cuff on the floor at my feet, and dropped my messenger bag next to it. My door shut with a heavy sound. The Court had sent me an armored vehicle with bulletproof glass. Fancy.

She headed for the main gate. "I asked to come instead. Seatbelt."

I buckled in. "Bryan told you why I needed a ride?"

"Yes. He let Maclin Security know the Court is taking over your personal safety until further notice."

She slowed as she approached the gate. A second Court SUV waited on the street. Like ours, its windows were darkly tinted. I could only make out two hulking shadows in the front seats. The gate rolled aside slowly.

I glanced up at the security camera mounted above us. Somewhere, Cyro was watching and hopefully ready to erase the footage of our visit as soon as we were out of sight.

As we drove through the gate, she asked, "Where to?"

"My house, please." My worry about Malcolm gnawed at me. Our link felt thin in a way it never had before and I feared for him. I needed to know how he was doing before I could do anything else.

Arkady turned left out of the drive and accelerated. The backup SUV fell in behind us as we headed east across the city.

"Catch me up on your case," she said. "How did we end up here?"

I gave her an abbreviated version of what had happened since I was hired to recover the three magic objects. I left out the identity of my client and didn't mention Malcolm.

As she listened, her eyes swept our surroundings as Sean's did when he drove. I felt hollow without him next to me.

"What happens if you figure out how to get that cuff off and Jack Hastings tries to block access to Sean?" Arkady asked.

"I would hope he wouldn't, for the simple fact that his alpha's well-being should be more important to him than his objection to me. But if he does interfere, I'll have to go through him."

She glanced at me. "I'm your security against Kent Stevens, but I won't be able to help you with Hastings if it comes down to that. As an employee of the Court, I can't interfere in a pack disagreement."

I'd figured as much. Interfering with pack business was a quick way for the Vampire Court to get sideways with the Were Ruling Council. "I don't need your help against Jack Hastings."

She smiled. "You don't really think you need my help with Stevens either, but you need a ride home because you're not sure if you can trust Maclin Security or anyone else from the pack without Sean in charge. I get it. If I were in your shoes, I'd be pissed about the whole thing too. That's part of the reason I asked for this gig."

"What's the other reason?"

"Curiosity." She slowed to make a turn. "Mr. Vaughan mentioned that he offered you a chance to be a Court investigator but you turned it down."

I was somewhat surprised Charles had revealed that fact to her. "Did he say why I turned it down?"

"He said you preferred to run your own company and remain an independent associate of the Court. I assume there's more to the story than that, since I've never known vampires to care very much about what a human prefers."

In fact, he'd attempted to blackmail me into accepting, forcing me to turn the tables and do some blackmail of my own. Naturally, I didn't reveal that to Arkady.

When I didn't comment, she added, "I also found it rather interesting that after Stevens almost took him out, Mr. Vaughan's first priority after saving Bryan Smith's life was to come to your home to check on your welfare, in direct violation of Valas's orders."

"He disobeyed Valas to come to my house?" Hoo boy. I could only imagine how tongues wagged about that back at Vamp Court headquarters. This was not good news. I didn't need anyone associated with the Court wondering too much about the exact nature of my relationship with Charles, or asking questions about why he'd allowed me to turn down his job offer.

"Valas ordered him to either come to Northbourne or go to Niara's home. Instead, he jumped into the vehicle with Matthias and me and headed straight for you without even waiting for additional backup. And you answered the door in sheep pajamas." Her eyes twinkled.

I crossed my arms. "I apologize for nothing. I love those pajamas."

"I have a pair with cats sleeping on clouds. If you tell anybody that, I will shoot you."

We exchanged a smile.

"So you were curious enough about me to take babysitting duty." I dug in my bag until I found my bottle of water. "I'm not that interesting, honestly."

"I'm also hoping Stevens shows up so I can shoot him in his kneecaps," she said conversationally. "I liked Fortune."

I took a deep breath and exhaled. I'd buried my grief over Fortune's death by keeping busy, but her words brought it back full force. "He was a good guy."

"We were sleeping together." Her voice was flat, unemotional. I recognized that tone; I'd used it often enough myself when I didn't want others to know I was hurting.

I stuck the water bottle back in my bag. "I didn't know that. I'm sorry, Arkady."

She gripped the steering wheel and stared straight ahead. "I'm okay. I'll be better when Stevens is dead."

I remembered the night Fortune died and Bryan was shot, when Charles had brought Arkady to my house. She had been entirely professional, hiding her pain from all of us while we dealt with the aftermath of Kent Stevens's attack and the logistics of arranging protection for Charles and me.

I was no longer ambivalent about wanting Stevens to find me. Between Arkady's guns and my magic, I liked our chances versus the former Marine. Sean hadn't wanted me to use myself as bait, but something told me my new bodyguard might not object quite as strenuously to the idea.

First things first, though: check on Malcolm and try to figure out how to get the cuff off Sean. Then we'd see about arranging some payback.

When we got to my house, Arkady escorted me to my front door. I dropped the house wards briefly to grant her passage. Once we were safe inside, I gave her clearance through the wards, figuring my bodyguard needed to be able to get in and out freely without getting fried.

Once we were inside, Sean's absence was like a punch in my gut. Everywhere I looked, I saw signs of his presence in my life, from the coffee mugs on the kitchen counter to the dishes in the sink and his clothes in the laundry room.

"Make yourself at home," I told Arkady as I headed for the basement door. "I have to do some work downstairs. If you need me, call or text. Don't try to come through the wards."

"Got it. I'm going to make some coffee, if that's all right."

My chest hurt. I forced myself not to think about how Sean usually made coffee for us. "Help yourself. There's some whole beans in the cabinet above the coffeemaker. The grinder is on the counter. Mugs are to the right of the sink."

I left Arkady upstairs, closing the basement door behind me.

When he needed to jump to the safety of my basement, Malcolm ended up in a medium-sized blue crystal I kept on the work table. Unlike the crystal I'd kept him in after the blood mage's failed attempt to recall him, he could release himself from the crystal in the basement. My worry grew when I realized he hadn't this time.

When I picked it up, the crystal buzzed against my skin. Malcolm was still inside it. The buzzing felt thready, though. Something was terribly wrong.

I closed my fist around the crystal, shut my eyes, and carefully funneled energy into it. I sensed a tug on the flow of power, as if Malcolm was trying to draw more energy from me. He'd always said that being in the crystal was like being asleep, but he still had some level of awareness. He might be drawing on my energy out of instinct rather than consciously. Either way, if he needed more, he could have it.

I funneled energy into the crystal until I wasn't sure how much more it could contain. My connection to Malcolm was stronger, but something was still off.

For better or worse, I had to know what kind of shape he was in. I took a deep breath, exhaled, and spoke. "*Release*."

Malcolm appeared beside me. He was jumbled, like a puzzle still in pieces in its box. Slowly, as if it took a lot of effort, he reformed in human shape, but maybe half as opaque as normal and with hollow eyes.

"Are you all right?" I asked, my heart in my throat.

"I feel thin, like I'm not all here," he said, his voice faint. "Where's Sean?"

"I couldn't get the cuff off him. It forced him to shift and he became aggressive. Jack darted him and took him somewhere."

"Alice, I'm so sorry." He floated back and forth slowly, as if trying to figure out how to move. "What should we do?"

"I'm going to figure out what that cuff is and how to get it off of him. What happened to you?"

"I tried to unweave the spells on the cuff and hit wards I've never felt before. The cuff was warded against ghosts or anyone who tried to interfere with the spellwork. I felt myself disintegrating." He went quiet. "I thought I was a goner. When I jumped here, I didn't know if I'd make it to the crystal or if I'd go poof and wake up somewhere else. Then, when I got here, I didn't start regenerating like I normally do, and even with all the energy you gave me, I'm still not whole."

His vulnerability and powerlessness made my heart ache. "We'll figure out how to get you back to one hundred percent. What can you tell me about the magic on the cuff?"

"I didn't recognize it."

I frowned. "You mean you didn't recognize the spellwork?"

He shook his head. "No, I mean I didn't recognize the *magic*. The fire magic spellwork was easy to see and feel. What zapped me, and what made the cuff latch itself onto Sean, is some kind of magic I've never encountered before. It felt ancient. It wasn't fire magic, or air, or earth, or water, or even blood magic."

I recalled something Charles had said to me after the auction: *Not all objects of power use the same kind of magic*. I hadn't sensed the magic in the Tepes stone, but it had power; I'd seen it with my own eyes when Charles used it to drain the vamp on the side of the road. I hadn't sensed anything but fire magic on the cuff, but it clearly had much more than that in it. My studies in magic were extensive, but I'd encountered two new forms of magic in as many days and I needed to know more about both.

At this point, I'd take any clues I could get. "What color was the magic?"

He thought about it. "Brown? No, not brown. More like copper."

Copper-colored magic? I'd never heard of such a thing. I didn't know of any magic that was any shade of brown, but if Malcolm said it was copper-colored, that's what it was.

Maybe the clue wasn't the brown, but its variant shade. "So, it was a kind of dark golden brown?"

He nodded slowly. "You could say that. What are you thinking?"

"Shifter magic is golden. You said the magic felt ancient. What if it's some kind of ancient shifter magic?"

Despite his depleted condition, Malcolm's eyes lit up. "Maybe it was some kind of old shifter magical object and someone added the fire magic spellwork later?"

"That's what I'm leaning toward at this point. It makes sense. The cuff didn't react to me, so the spells must only activate when in the presence of a shifter." I rubbed my forehead.

"Do you think Esther Aldridge knew the cuff was a shifter relic?"

I thought about it, then shook my head. "I don't think she did. I didn't sense any trace of shifter magic in her safe, which means that aspect of the cuff hadn't been used while it was in her possession. She probably thought of it only in terms of what it did for her husband and never suspected it was anything more than that. Yet another good reason for non-mages to leave magic objects the hell alone."

"The thing I don't understand is what the damn thing is supposed to do. What's the benefit of forcing a shifter to go furry and making him more aggressive?"

"Not all magical objects are designed to be beneficial." I headed for my bookcases. "It could be punishment, or it could have been designed to harm the wearer outright. Or it might just have a mind of its own and do whatever it wants. If we're right and it's ancient magic, there's no telling what it's designed to do, or what it might be doing to him."

"Do you want me to try to check on Sean?" he asked. "I have enough juice to get to him. I could keep an eye on him and let you know if there are any...developments."

My heart hurt. I wanted to know that Sean was all right. My only other option was to call someone in the pack for updates, like Karen or Nan, but that might put them crossways with Jack. Despite what I'd declared to Jack about Sean and I being a couple, I had no formal claim on him, no authority to ask a member of the pack to go against the acting alpha.

"Please check on him for me," I said finally. "Be careful and don't let them sense you."

He floated over to me. "You'll figure this out, Alice. You'll get that cuff off him and then you'll deal with Jack. You and Sean are the real thing. You can't let some stupid bracelet and a jerk beta mess up the second-best thing you've got going for you."

"What's the first-best thing I have going for me?" I asked, not quite sniffling.

He grinned. "Me, of course."

I couldn't help but smile at that. With a wink, he disappeared.

When he was gone, I went to work pulling books from the shelves and stacking them on the table. I grabbed anything on shifter magic or forms of ancient magic. I didn't have much. When I finished looking through my library, I had only ten books in the pile, and I wasn't sure any of them would have information that would be helpful to me. At times like this I sorely missed my library back at my grandfather's cabal, which had been enormous. No doubt I could have found what I needed there. I sat down at the table and started skimming.

An hour later, I set the tenth book aside and sighed. As I'd feared, nothing in my library had anything helpful in the way of information about ancient shifter magic. I was also curious about the magic of the Tepes stone, but that had to go to the back burner for now.

I pushed my chair back, stretched, and headed for the steps. I'd almost forgotten I had a houseguest.

When I emerged from the basement, I found Arkady sitting on the couch. The TV was on, tuned to a news channel and muted.

She put down her phone as I closed the door. "Any luck?"

I didn't tell her about Malcolm; the fewer people who knew about my ghost sidekick, the better. I shook my head. "I have a theory about what the cuff might be, but I'm having a hard time finding any information that might be helpful."

"You could call Kim Dade, the Vampire Court researcher, and see if she has any ideas," she suggested. "I'm not sure what she's working on right now, but I know you two are good friends."

On the surface that sounded like a good idea, but I was reluctant to reveal too many details about the situation to the Court. Information was a valuable commodity, as Charles liked to remind me. There were other packs in the area, and any one of them might be interested in knowing the alpha of the Tomb Mountain Pack was temporarily out of commission. If that news got out, one of the other packs might try to make a move, and though Jack was no pushover, a beta—even a strong one—was not an alpha.

On the other hand, I could ask Kim about ancient shifter magical objects in general and see what resources she could point me toward.

"Not a bad idea," I said finally. I sent her a text asking her to call me when she had a moment.

My phone rang as I was in the kitchen pouring myself a cup of coffee. "Hey, Alice," Kim greeted me. "How are you holding up with all this mess with Kent Stevens?"

I added milk and sugar to my coffee and stirred it. "I'm hanging in there. I've got plenty of security keeping an eye on me. Arkady Woodall is over here now."

"Stevens better hope the Hunters catch him before she does," she said ominously. "What can I do for you?"

"This might be outside your area of expertise, but I'm needing to find some information about shifter magical objects, possibly of ancient origin. What are my best resources for that?"

"The Court has a pretty extensive library, of course. Do you know what you're looking for? I could run a search."

"I'm not exactly sure yet," I hedged. "I don't suppose I could access the library and do some searching?"

"Unfortunately, not without clearance," Kim said, sounding regretful. "Is it Court business? You could ask Juliet LaRoche or Ezekiel Monroe for authorization if so." LaRoche and Monroe were the daytime representatives of Niara and Valas, respectively.

"It's actually personal. If I can't get into the Court library, what's the next-best thing?"

"Have you tried the MOP website?"

I frowned. "Really? The last time I used that, it was a mess. There was more false information on it than real."

"It used to be a dumpster fire, but about a year ago a group of mages took it over and became full-time administrators. They cleaned it up, took down the fake stuff, and started moderating posts. It's actually a pretty good resource now. You have to register to use it, but it's worth it for you, in my opinion."

"That's an idea. I'll check it out."

"Let me know if you find what you're looking for and I might be able to dig something up in our library. In the meantime, stay safe."

"You too. Thanks, Kim."

We said our goodbyes and disconnected. I topped off my coffee and took it into the living room.

As I settled onto the other end of the couch with my laptop, Arkady asked, "Was she able to help?"

"She suggested I look in the MOP database." I opened the laptop and searched for the website.

"I'm assuming that has nothing to do with actual mops."

I smiled. "It stands for Magic and Objects of Power. It's basically an online database resource for mages and researchers to find information. It used to be about as helpful and trustworthy as the walls of a public bathroom, but Kim says they've cleaned it up and it's reliable now, so I'm going to give it a try."

When I found the website, it looked nothing like what I remembered. Instead of disorganized pages full of links to error-filled articles written by anyone with access to the internet, I found a very authoritative site with public pages offering helpful information to non-mages and a registration system for mages wanting access to the database.

I opted for a premium membership, which allowed me full access to the site. I was still skeptical, but I figured I could cancel my membership if the site didn't live up to expectations.

Once I was logged in, I was amazed at the amount of information and how well it was organized. The site was hosted by a foundation with a board of directors who were all credentialed mages. Many articles were written by authors affiliated with the site, while others were written by members of the public and then fact-checked by employees of the foundation. The forums were moderated, and I saw quite a few discussion threads where the questions and comments seemed insightful and accurate.

As a test, I searched for a cup like the one that had granted Charles an hour in daylight and found an entry that described a cup very like the one I'd recovered for Esther. The photo was of a different cup, but the description of the spellwork was consistent with what I knew.

To my surprise, a recent update to the article noted that one such cup had just sold at auction for more than sixty thousand dollars, though that was considered anomalous and nearly five times the expected price. The database's sources were clearly up-to-date on recent transactions in the world of magical objects, since that sale had taken place less than forty-eight hours before. I was impressed.

A second search led me to a section of the site devoted to mirrors. Mirrors had countless uses in magic, from divination to spirit communication. Some could be used as portals between realms, offering passage at a price to the demon realm, fae realm, or the in-between places. Wall and floor-length mirrors were most often used in magic, but hand mirrors were no less powerful because of their size.

After some reading, I found an entry on hand mirrors spelled to reveal hidden memories. I'd set the possible memory the mirror had shown me aside to think about later, half-convinced the mirror had invented it from bits and pieces in my head. According to the database, the spellwork was real and a double-edged sword capable of uncovering repressed and traumatic memories. The article's author included a heartfelt warning about using such mirrors. Reading between the lines, I wondered if she had found out the hard way that some memories were better off left buried. If my own recovered memory was true, I would have a lot to think about once this mess with the cuff was resolved.

Having verified that the database was in fact a much-improved and useful resource, I began my search for information about ancient shifter magic and magical objects. Shifter magic was as complex and varied as my own, and some objects dated back hundreds or even thousands of years. These objects varied in strength, purpose, and application, and ranged from stone teeth to obelisks and everything in between.

I had a better understanding of shifter magic than the average mage, but only as much as I'd needed to do spellwork, such as wards within my grandfather's cabal compound that blocked shifters from gaining access to certain areas. I understood how magic allowed shifters to change from human form to furry form and back again, and how the pack bonds allowed shifters to sense each other and draw strength from their alpha. Having spent time around Sean, I had a better understanding of how an alpha's magic differed from members of the pack, and how he could draw power from the pack if needed. Shifter physiology included abilities like faster healing and enhanced senses, but the magic of the shift itself was powerful enough to heal injuries, even potentially fatal ones.

When it came to shifter magic objects, however, I knew next to nothing. No human magic could create them and they could not be used by anyone who was not a shifter. Human magic could hide them or contain their power, but that was the extent to which a non-shifter could interact with them. As such, I had never studied them and found myself engrossed in reading basic shifter magic theory in order to understand the source of their power and the mechanics of their spellwork. I hadn't done this sort of research in a very long time, but it didn't take long to remember how much I enjoyed it. Learning about magic was more than a hobby or a job; it was part of who I was.

I took a break after a while to refill my coffee cup and to let Rogue into the backyard so he could potty and run off some of his seemingly boundless energy.

As I closed the back door, Arkady looked up from her phone. "So, do you mind if I ask what's up with your garden back there? I went out on the back porch earlier when I let the dog in and if I didn't know better, I'd say the plants leaned in my direction like they were sizing me up."

I stretched, putting my coffee cup on the floor so I could bend over and touch my toes. My back popped. "It's kind of a long story, but the short version is that the plants are magical and probably hungry, so you should keep a safe distance."

Her eyebrows went up, but she seemed to take that bit of news in stride. "What do you feed hungry plants? I'm guessing not normal plant food."

"They seem to be carnivorous, so I'm thinking I might have to run by a butcher shop and pick something up."

"There are a couple of shops in town that deliver. You can order on their website and they'll bring you what you need."

I hadn't thought of that. "Good point." I didn't have a good sense yet of how much I might need or how often I'd need to feed the garden, but I could start with a small whole hog, the kind you'd buy if you were going to have a barbecue, and go from there.

I found the website of a local carnicería and put in an order, then returned to reading about shifter magic.

My search for cuffs with shifter magic turned up a surprisingly high number of hits.

It appeared that cuffs were a common type of magical object for shifters, which made sense. The cuff that had latched onto Sean's arm had changed size when he shifted.

The question was: what type of spellwork was on the cuff? If the magic had been natural human magic, I could have explored it as I had the spellwork on the cup and probably determined its purpose. But between those heavy-duty wards and my unfamiliarity with shifter magic, I was at something of a loss.

My best option at the moment seemed to be reading through the entries on magical cuffs on the MOP website. If that didn't pan out, I'd be forced to decide whether to ask Charles for authorization to search the Court library. No doubt he would find out what had happened at the storage unit as soon as he woke at sunset.

Most of the entries in the database had pictures or drawings of the cuffs. That was enormously helpful, but I didn't go by the images alone. The appearance of the cuff might have been altered along the way, so I read through each article, looking for hints as to what this particular cuff might be. It felt like I was looking for a needle in a pile of needles.

By late afternoon, my eyes were bleary and I hadn't found any answers. I was just getting up to refill my coffee cup when I sensed Malcolm cross the wards as he jumped to his crystal downstairs.

I put my cup on the counter and headed for the basement door. "I need to go downstairs for a few minutes."

"Okay." Arkady was watching the news and snacking on some chips she'd found in the pantry.

When I got downstairs, I found Malcolm floating by the work table. He was still distressingly weak, so much so that I felt guilty for asking him to go check on Sean. Normally when I was near the ghost, his aura buzzed on my skin and the blue-green thread that connected us hummed with energy. Since the run-in with the wards on the cuff, our connection had felt almost completely diminished, and even standing two feet away, I couldn't sense his energy at all.

Judging by his expression, the news was grim. "How is he?" I asked.

Malcolm didn't even try to sugar-coat his response. "Not good. They've got him at Jack and Delia's house, in a cage they apparently keep on hand for when they've got a wolf who's gone mad. As soon as the tranquilizer wore off, he went berserk and Jack had to dose him again. Not to knock him out, but enough to make him too tired to hurt himself trying to get out of the cage."

"Why is he being so violent? Is it the cuff?"

"Everyone thinks so. The wolf almost took a chunk out of Jack's arm when he got too close to the cage. I think he knows Jack was responsible for carting him off and leaving you unprotected. If—*when* Sean shifts back to human, he's gonna have Jack's ass for that."

"I was hoping that since you were gone so long, no news was good news." I sat on the work table, my legs dangling.

Malcolm shook his head. "Jack called a pack meeting. That's why I was gone all afternoon; I wanted to stay until the end and see what was decided. It got pretty ugly."

I could only imagine. "Let's hear it."

"Everyone's upset and angry about Sean's condition and Jack blamed you for everything. He basically said that either you knew what the cuff would do and let Sean get trapped on purpose, or that you were incompetent. Either way, he's got some of them believing you're the worst thing that's ever happened to Sean. He brought up how

Sean ended up in Vamp Court custody after he got in a fight with Charles and blamed you for that too. Some of the pack seem to agree."

"What about Karen, Nan, and Felicia?"

"They don't believe you did it on purpose, and Nan told Jack he was wrong to have separated Sean from you. Ben said so too."

"Ben said that?" I was surprised. I'd only met Ben once, at Esther's house, and I certainly hadn't expected to hear him speak up on my behalf.

"Yep, he came to your defense pretty strongly. He seems to be third in the pack hierarchy, just below Jack, so his voice carries weight. He reminded Jack and the rest of the pack that Sean had stated his feelings about you quite clearly and it wasn't their place to interfere with the alpha's courtship of a potential mate. He also reminded Jack that Sean told him to protect you and that he left you stranded in the storage unit without so much as a sharp stick. The others didn't take kindly to that. Criticizing you is one thing, but Jack basically disobeyed a direct order from Sean. Jack tried to say he had no choice, but the others didn't buy it. Even the ones who don't seem to think you'd be a good mate didn't think Jack should have gone against Sean's directive. It reflects poorly not just on the pack, but on Maclin Security as well."

That was something, at least. "So where did it end up?"

"Jack's determined to find out what the cuff is and how to get it off. He's made some calls to experts and the Were Ruling Council. In the meantime, he's decreed that you're not allowed any contact with Sean. The others argued that letting you visit him might calm him down, but Jack's word is law until Sean is better and he wasn't budging an inch on that."

"They can't keep Sean drugged the whole time," I protested.

"Ben pointed that out. Jack said they'll have the cuff off before it becomes an issue." He floated over to me. "Here's what's really got me worried, Alice. Once the pack meeting broke up, Jack and Delia were talking about what's going to happen once Sean shifts back. Delia asked what Jack will do if Sean still wants you as his mate. Jack said, and I quote, 'Then we'll have to deal with her some other way.'"

I took a deep breath and exhaled. "In a weird way, I'm kind of relieved to hear that. Before, I wasn't sure exactly where we stood. Now I know. It's always better to know for sure who your enemies are. If Jack comes for me, I'll be waiting."

"You want me to go back there and keep an eye on things?"

"I'm worried about you. I don't know what those wards did to you, but you're down in power by at least half and you aren't regenerating like you should. You're vulnerable right now until we figure out how to undo the damage. As glad as I am to know how Sean is doing and how the pack meeting went, it was selfish and dangerous of me to ask you to leave the safety of the house and go out there."

"Well, the good news is that I can pretty much jump between Sean and here now, so that limits my exposure. None of the shifters seemed to sense my presence, so my masking and obfuscation spells seem to be holding up well. I *am* running on about half power. Other than siphoning power from you, the fastest way I know to regenerate is in a crystal."

I held out my arm. "Take what you need."

He shook his head. "Without Sean here, you can't regenerate magical energy like you normally could."

I gave him a look.

He sighed. "Alice, sex regenerates magical energy; everyone knows that. I'm not trying to embarrass you by bringing it up, but I'm not going to siphon energy from you and risk leaving you vulnerable right now with everything that's going on."

"Fine. If you want to regenerate in the crystal, I can at least speed up the process." I gestured at the circles inlaid in the floor.

He nodded slowly. "A power circle? That would work. Good thinking, Alice."

"I have my moments." I picked up Malcolm's crystal and held it out. "Hop in. When you feel like you're back to full strength, you can jump out and break the circle."

"Thanks." Malcolm hesitated. "Everything is going to be all right. Just don't go up against Jack without me, okay?"

"I'll try not to," I promised.

Malcolm vanished. The crystal buzzed faintly in my palm.

I put the crystal in the center of the smallest circle on the floor, grabbed a piece of chalk, and went to work drawing runes. When the spellwork was complete, it formed a web with the crystal at the nexus. I placed my palm on the circle and fed energy into the web until every line and rune pulsed with power. The energy formed a loop, feeding power into Malcolm's crystal and hopefully speeding up his regeneration.

I got to my feet and took a moment to just breathe. The news about Sean and the pack was bad, but not as bad as I'd feared. Jack could be as angry as he wanted, but I wasn't going to be intimidated. It had never been my nature to back down and I wasn't going to start now. Sean was worth fighting for.

Jack might think he knew what he was up against by picking a fight with me, but he had no idea what I was capable of, or what I would be willing to do to hold onto one of the few chances at happiness I had ever had.

16

When I got back upstairs, I found Arkady in the kitchen. "So, I couldn't help but notice that you seemed to be talking to someone downstairs," she said as I got a glass and filled it from the sink.

I'd wanted to keep Malcolm under wraps, but unless I wanted to claim I was having a conversation with voices in my head, I didn't have much choice but to acknowledge that there had been someone else in the basement.

"I was getting a report from a ghost," I said.

"As one does," she said dryly. "Is he keeping an eye on Sean for you?"

She put two and two together faster than about anybody I'd ever known. "Yes."

"How are things going?"

I drained the water and set the glass in the sink. "Not well. Speaking of which, I should get back to my research."

She glanced out the window. The sun was beginning to set. "You'll probably be getting a call soon."

Somewhere in or below Niara's home, Charles would be waking soon, if he hadn't already. "I figured as much. When's your shift change, by the way? I just want to get a sense of how this is going to work."

She smiled. "There is no shift change, Alice. I'm with you twenty-four seven until this situation is resolved. The team out in the SUV will switch off every six to eight hours, depending, but you and I are best buddies until Kent Stevens is on ice."

"I had a thought about that," I said.

We headed back to the living room and settled on the couch. She muted the television and looked at me expectantly. "What's on your mind?"

"What are your thoughts on trying to draw Stevens out?"

She tilted her head. "My orders are to keep you out of harm's way and leave the search to others." After a pause, she added, "However, with the hunt for Stevens dragging into its fourth day, there might be some flexibility there. If nothing else, your case might take us near some of the locations Stevens could be watching, like Mr.

Vaughan's new wine and cocktail bar, where his temporary offices are located while Hawthorne's is being rebuilt."

"That wasn't a spontaneous suggestion, was it?"

"Not entirely, no. I wasn't going to bring it up, but I thought you might suggest something along those lines. I'm kind of surprised you didn't before now."

"I did bring it up, actually, but my previous bodyguard vetoed the idea."

She nodded slowly. "I can see that. An alpha werewolf wouldn't like the idea of his girlfriend using herself as bait. In that case, maybe we should hold off and let the Hunters find him."

"Sean's not here," I pointed out. "And I'm the one who makes decisions about what I do and don't do. I guess I *am* wondering why Charles isn't willing to do it."

"Oh, he *is* willing, very much so," Arkady assured me. "But Valas has forbidden him to go near any of his properties. He hasn't left Niara's house since Fortune was killed, except to attend the auction with you the other night. Valas wasn't very happy about that either, especially given what happened afterward."

"Charles was hardly to blame for that," I protested. "That creepy Seattle vamp attacked *us* trying to steal the item Charles bought at the auction."

"And you as well, from what I understand. Well done dealing with him, by the way. It's another reason I like the idea of stopping by the wine bar and seeing if Stevens is hanging around. I get the impression you're a force to be reckoned with. If you can take out a vampire, you can deal with Stevens, especially if I'm there too. The Hunters can have him when we're done."

The more I thought about it, the more I liked her plan. As much as it had bothered me to be under guard these last few days, what had frustrated me more was that we had been doing nothing to take Stevens out. The Court had dispatched Hunters and other resources to find him, but sitting on my hands while someone else acted had never been my style. I did feel some guilt about doing this against Sean's wishes, but if we could eliminate Stevens that would be one less problem for Sean to deal with. It looked like Sean was going to have his hands full with Jack as it was without also worrying about whether Stevens was still out there gunning for me.

"How about this," I said. "Let me keep researching for about another hour or so. That will give you time to think about our strategy and contact whoever you need to coordinate with about baiting a trap tonight at the bar. When the pieces are in place, we'll head out."

She grinned. "I like how you don't even hesitate once you've made up your mind. I'll start making some calls. One thing: the bar has a dress code. I'm assuming you've got something appropriate to wear?"

"I have a couple of options. What about you?"

"I'll have someone bring me what I need." She cracked her knuckles and reached for her phone. "Let's do it."

While Arkady went to the kitchen to make phone calls, I got back to the database and its entries on magical cuffs. I noticed that a number of the articles were by the same person, an Ella Potter from Portland. She seemed to have quite a bit of knowledge about shifter magic, particularly spelled arm cuffs. If I couldn't find what I needed in the database, I might be able to contact her for information. Her webpage invited inquiries by e-mail.

My phone rang about a half-hour into my reading. I took a deep breath and answered it. "Hello, Charles."

"I should never have left your safety in the hands of the wolves." His voice was as cold as I had ever heard him be. He wasn't just angry; he was livid.

I found myself trying to defuse the situation. "It was my decision to hire Maclin Security, and it was the right one. Sean and his employees provided excellent security up until this afternoon. It was also my decision to ask Bryan to send someone from the Court to take over this afternoon instead of waiting for a replacement team from Maclin Security. I'm grateful to the Court for responding so quickly. I'm not going to defend what Jack did because he went against Sean's orders and he'll have to answer for that to both the pack and his employers."

"Mr. Hastings's actions constitute a breach of contract." His tone was icy. "I have instructed one of my attorneys to proceed with legal action on the matter."

I sighed. "Charles—"

"Alice, *this is not acceptable!*" he thundered.

I stared at the phone in shock. I'd only heard Charles raise his voice one other time in the entire five years I had known him, and that incident occurred on the first night we met, when he thought I'd killed a Court mage without warning or provocation.

He lowered his voice, but his fury was still evident. "The Court placed an enormously valuable asset in the hands of a contractor and you were left unarmed, without so much as a vehicle with which to transport yourself to a safe location. Other companies who work for the Court must understand that such a violation of trust will not be tolerated."

"I'm never unarmed, Charles," I reminded him. "I have magic. The storage facility was a pretty secure location, all things considered. I was less vulnerable there than almost anywhere else. I'm not telling you not to be angry, because I'm angry too, but don't assume I was defenseless and left out in the open, because I wasn't."

Silence.

"Arkady is here with me now," I said when he didn't reply. "There's an SUV full of Bryan-sized enforcers parked outside. I'm safe."

"A condition which you must find irksome, as I understand you wish to use yourself as bait for Kent Stevens." He was still angry, but his tone was dry.

"I'm tired of hiding, Charles. I'm a mage, Arkady's got two really big guns, and we have the full force of the Court as backup. I want this over with. I want him to come at me and I want Arkady to have the chance to put bullets in both of his kneecaps."

His tone hardened. "As much as I endorse Ms. Woodall's desire to do so, I would have refused her request for the operation, which is why she asked Valas instead."

I smiled to myself. Crafty Arkady. "The sooner we nail this bastard, the sooner we can all get back to our normal lives, including you."

"If you are harmed in any way, I will hold Ms. Woodall responsible."

That got my hackles up. "Don't be ridiculous. It was my idea. The only person responsible for my safety is me."

"Ms. Woodall cleared this plan with Valas last night," Charles informed me.

That changed nothing, as far as I was concerned. All it proved was that Arkady had been planning a way to get to Stevens, probably since the moment she found out Fortune was dead. I would have done the same.

"She didn't bring it up; I did this afternoon. I've been wanting to do something to draw him out but Sean wouldn't go for it."

"How very annoying to find myself agreeing with the wolf."

I paused. "You haven't asked about Sean's condition, so you must know what happened."

"I understand the cuff attached itself to his arm and forced him to shift. He was taken to a place of safety, where his condition has deteriorated to the point that he must be sedated to prevent him from harming himself or others."

I wasn't surprised he knew the details; the Court had eyes and ears all over the place. I did, however, take exception to the cold way he said it, as if it hadn't turned my life upside down. "Then there's nothing more you and I need to talk about."

"Alice." Charles's voice stopped me before I could end the call. "There is no love between the wolf and I, as you well know. But I would not have you suffer, and I know his condition weighs heavily upon you. What assistance can I offer?"

"What would you want in return for your assistance?"

His response was exactly what I expected. "The answer would depend on what was required."

I sighed. "What would it cost to give me access to the Vamp Court library so I can try to find out what this cuff is and how to remove it?"

"That is not a simple request. A great deal of the information we possess is considered confidential and our resources are designated for Court business only. However, the welfare of an alpha like Maclin is of interest to the Court because the stability of local packs benefits us as well. As such, I believe that as a gesture of goodwill it would be possible to assign one of our researchers to the task."

I closed my eyes. A Court researcher was more than I could have hoped for. I might have an answer in minutes or hours instead of days.

Charles's next words, however, brought me crashing back down to earth. "If we do this research on behalf of the shifters, we will have to share our findings with Maclin's pack as well. It cannot be given to you alone."

My heart sank. "So if you find out what the cuff is, you'll have to call Jack?"

A pause. "We would pass the information to the Were Ruling Council, who would no doubt pass it on to Mr. Hastings, as he is currently acting as the head of the Tomb Mountain Pack."

I read between the lines and recognized an opportunity for negotiation. "How much of a head start can you give me with the info before you contact the Council?"

I heard the smile in Charles's voice when he replied. "Perhaps a few hours. Communication between the Court and the Council is a delicate matter that must be handled carefully. It will take some time to compose the document and have it reviewed by the necessary personnel."

"Do it," I said. "Please."

"I will see if Ms. Dade is available, since you have worked with her before. Would you prefer to be alerted as soon as she has discovered something?"

"Yes, anytime day or night." I took a deep breath. A little of the weight lifted off my chest. "Thank you, Charles."

"I would prefer to be with you during this operation tonight," he said quietly. "You are not merely an asset of the Court to me, nor is your safety purely a matter of protecting a resource. Others may look at you as such, but I do not. Some may consider it a higher priority to apprehend Stevens than to ensure your safety. I do not believe Ms. Woodall is one of the latter, or I would send Adri Smith in her place. Even so, be cautious."

I'd been thinking about that in the back of my mind since I'd first proposed using myself as bait to Arkady. The Court wanted Stevens. They wanted to protect me too because I was useful to them, but if it came down to it there were undoubtedly some who would throw me under the bus if it meant getting Stevens. Like Charles, I didn't think Arkady would be among them, despite the fact Stevens had killed Fortune.

I might have even wondered about Adri and Bryan if it came down to it. Arkady worked for the Court; Adri and Bryan *belonged* to the Court. I hadn't known Arkady long, but I was usually pretty good about reading people. You got good at that sort of thing when you were a prisoner of an organized crime syndicate and surrounded by enemies. My instincts told me Arkady wanted Stevens's hide, but not at the expense of mine.

"Thanks for the warning," I said finally. "Wish me luck."

"I do not believe in luck, only in planning and strength. I wish you success and a safe return."

"Good night."

We disconnected. Arkady appeared in the kitchen doorway. "What was the warning about?" she asked.

I put my laptop aside and stood. "There's a chance some of our backup tonight might want Stevens in custody more than they want me to come out unscathed."

She snorted. "As I'm sure you'd already guessed. Good thing I've got your back."

"And I've got yours. If he does show up, he'll never know what hit him."

My perimeter wards tingled, signaling a visitor's arrival. "Are we expecting someone?" I asked.

She didn't ask how I knew. "That's my change of clothes. We're due at the bar by nine-thirty, so we'd better get moving."

I frowned. "It's not even seven yet. How long will it take you to get ready?"

Arkady headed for the front door just as footsteps crossed the porch and someone knocked loudly. "Oh, honey, you have no idea."

Up until two nights ago, I had wondered how Charles's newest wine and cocktail bar had gotten its name. Thanks to our walk in the sun and the story he'd told me, now I knew: it was the year he'd become a vampire.

Our SUV pulled up in front of 1792 at precisely nine thirty. Our driver was a Court enforcer named Kirwin. I'd met him not long after I moved to the city and saw him occasionally at Northbourne. Our other escort was Matthias, who'd accompanied Charles and Arkady to my house the night Fortune was killed—and who, unless I was very much mistaken, had a bit of a crush on Arkady. I hadn't noticed it that night, but I caught him making googly eyes at her at least twice during our drive from my house to the bar.

Matthias opened the rear door and gallantly offered his hand to help Arkady out of the back. She was wearing an emerald green pantsuit with heels, her hair back in a loose twist. The matching jacket covered her shoulder holster and the long pants hid her ankle holster. She had the skills of a professional makeup artist and put them to good use on both of us. She looked absolutely gorgeous, like a Norse goddess.

I'd resigned myself to wearing something that would hide my vest, but Arkady had surprised me with a form-fitting and very feminine vest shaped like a corset. She assured me it would stop rifle rounds. It was no more comfortable than the one Sean had given me, but at least I didn't look like I was wearing a vest. I quickly made up my mind to try to keep it when this was over.

Though his eyes were on Arkady, Matthias helped me out of the SUV. I wore a short purple dress with over-the-knee boots. Like Arkady, I'd styled my hair up. I wore diamond earrings and a charm bracelet with Malcolm's crystal on it, but the ghost was still in his crystal in my basement, regenerating slowly. The crystal would allow him to jump to me, or for me to stash him in it, should trouble arise.

Matthias stayed with us as Kirwin drove away to park nearby. Well-dressed couples came and went through the front door of the club. We waited outside for a few seconds to make sure Stevens saw me, if he was watching.

I felt exposed on the sidewalk with tall buildings on all sides, offering Stevens an almost infinite selection of sniper nests. But as I'd told Sean, I doubted Stevens would try to take me out from a distance. He'd want me to see his face. I felt no itchiness between my shoulder blades, however. That wasn't a surefire way of knowing whether we were being watched, but I was willing to bet Stevens wasn't here, not right now. I couldn't help but be disappointed, but the night was only just getting started.

At Arkady's nod, Matthias opened the door to the club and ushered us inside. 1792 reminded me immediately of Hawthorne's: dark wood, subdued lighting, and private booths along the walls with tables in the middle of the floor.

The bar had the well-deserved reputation of serving the finest martinis in the city and its wine list was second to none. A pianist provided quiet music from a nook near the front windows. The men wore jackets, the women evening wear. The bar certainly catered to a much different clientele than Hawthorne's, where I had been comfortable wearing jeans and a T-shirt and hanging out for an hour or two nursing a Scotch or beers. I doubted I'd be returning here anytime soon unless it was for business.

We approached the host with Matthias behind us. Arkady unleashed a smile that could only be described as her third-most-lethal weapon, possibly her second. The host looked positively gobsmacked and couldn't take his eyes off her.

"We have a table reserved under the name of Vaughan," she told him. "Party of two."

It took him several seconds to process her words and realize who we were. His eyes widened. "Yes, of course. This way, please."

He led us to one of the best tables in the club, a corner booth with an excellent view of the entire room. It had no clear line of sight to the front window, eliminating the threat of a sniper shot through the glass. Once we sat, I realized the lighting ensured we could see the room while we remained in shadow. The booth also had dark red velvet curtains that could be drawn for additional privacy. Very nice. Being guests of the owner certainly had its perks.

The host had only taken two steps away from our booth when a tuxedo-clad young man appeared and presented us with menus. "Ms. Woodall, Ms. Worth, welcome to 1792. My name is Anthony. What may we serve you tonight?"

I scanned my menu. There were several pages of martinis that were specialties of the house, and then the wine list. I'd never been much of a wine drinker, and I wouldn't know a good martini if it walked up and introduced itself.

I glanced at Arkady over the top of my menu. Her expression mirrored mine.

Our dismay must have been obvious. Before either of us could speak, our server gestured at another young man standing off to the side holding a tray with two glasses on it.

"With the compliments of the owner." He placed one of the glasses in front of me with a flourish. "A fifty-year Glenfiddich single malt Scotch whisky, neat." The second glass went to Arkady. "And a sixty-month tequila for Ms. Woodall."

I raised my eyebrows. "I didn't see any whisky or tequila on the menu."

Anthony smiled. "Mr. Vaughan anticipated your desires and sent some from his private stock. Would you like me to draw the curtains?"

"Not at the moment," I said. "I think I'll people-watch for a bit."

"Thank you, Anthony," Arkady added.

He gave us a small bow and retreated. I didn't see Matthias, but I assumed he was somewhere nearby, keeping an eye on us and listening in on the conversation among the various members of the Court security team positioned in and around the building.

Arkady raised her glass. "To revenge."

I tapped her glass with mine. "May we serve it cold tonight."

My Scotch was almost unbelievably smooth, with a seemingly endless finish. I hadn't been drinking much lately, so the whisky was a rare treat on multiple levels. I didn't even realize I'd closed my eyes until Arkady chuckled. "I take it yours was good too?"

I opened my eyes and set my glass back on the table. "Very, very good. I think I need a cigarette."

She surprised me by saying, "Me too." She leaned forward conspiratorially. "What do you think they'd do if we both lit one?"

"I think we'd see how quickly and politely Anthony could ask us to put them out."

She sighed. "Maybe later we can smoke in celebration back at your house."

"Any sign of Stevens?" I asked.

She shook her head. Like Matthias, she wore an earpiece so she could listen to the security teams outside. "No sign of him. Trust me, I'd tell you if there was."

"Maybe this was too obvious of a setup," I ventured. "He'd have to know we wouldn't be dumb enough to show up at Charles's place practically wearing targets around our necks unless it was part of a plan to draw him out."

"Of course he'll know it's a setup." Arkady leaned back in the booth, crossed her legs, and sipped her tequila. "Part of what I've been doing the last couple of days is reading everything the Court has dug up on Stevens, from his military record to his involvement with fringe 'Human rights' groups since his brother died. This is about the psychology of a man who's not just bent on revenge, but to whom a trap is a challenge —especially a trap laid by women. He has a history of domestic violence. He never went to jail for it because the women always dropped the charges, but his misogyny is another factor I'm counting on. The only thing better than what we've laid out tonight would be if it was Adri Smith instead of Matthias with us. If he lets us leave here unscathed, it's a blow to every part of his ego. He won't be able to walk away, even if he knows it's a trap. And that's why we'll get him."

"I hope I'm right about Stevens wanting to look me in the eye," I confessed. "If he does decide to snipe me instead from the building across the street, my last thought in this life is probably going to be 'Oops.'"

She smiled without humor. "I think you're right, for what it's worth. He didn't open fire on Mr. Vaughan's vehicle the other night until he was in sight of its passengers. He could have taken them out before they'd known what hit them, but then what would be the point?"

We sipped our drinks and waited for word from the security teams outside. I wondered if Arkady was thinking about Fortune. My own thoughts kept drifting back to Sean. Part of me felt guilty for being here while he was lying drugged in a cage, but there was a Court researcher working on finding out about the cuff and I had no doubt Kim Dade would get the answers many times faster than I could. Since I could do little to help Sean until I got some answers from Kim, I might as well stay busy and do whatever was in my power to eliminate a different kind of threat.

As for setting myself up as bait against his wishes, I reminded myself that it was better to have the situation resolved so he wouldn't have to deal with Stevens once we got the cuff off. He'd have enough on his plate dealing with Jack. I was surrounded by Court security and I had my magic.

To distract myself, I sipped my Scotch and scanned the people sitting at the tables and in the row of booths behind Arkady. I saw no empty chairs anywhere. I made a mental note to compliment Charles on the bar's success. It might not be my scene, but I recognized a well-run and high-quality establishment when I saw one. In this city, it was no small feat to reach this kind of success and maintain it.

As my eyes passed over the couples and small groups in the booths, I caught sight of a red-haired woman in a green cocktail dress sitting with her back to me a couple of booths away. She was slim, wearing diamond drop earrings that had to be several carats each. She gestured dramatically as she spoke to her companions and a diamond tennis bracelet sparkled on her wrist. But that wasn't what made me pause with my drink halfway to my mouth.

It was her ring.

She waved her right hand and the ring glittered. From here, it appeared to be made of white gold with black diamonds forming an *M*.

I put my drink on the table before I dropped it.

No, it can't be her.

Just as that desperate thought crossed my mind, she turned and signaled to a passing server, allowing me to see her face in profile.

Time seemed to slow and then stop. I went cold all over faster than if someone had dumped a bucket of ice water over my head. My heart pounded in my ears loudly enough to drown out everything else.

I suddenly knew who my grandfather had sent to the city to lead the war against Darius Bell: his oldest daughter, Catherine Murphy Atwood. My mother's sister.

My aunt.

17

As much as my mother had abhorred my grandfather's cabal and everything he did, Catherine had always embraced her role as one of his lieutenants. Though I was her only niece, I had never been anything more than a tool or a weapon to her, something to be used in whatever way was needed to make money and gain more power for the syndicate. I was not allowed to refer to her as "Aunt Catherine," only Catherine.

In the days and weeks after Moses murdered my parents, I'd tried, out of desperation, to turn to Catherine for love and comfort, but there was none to be had. I'd realized later that she blamed me for my mother's death, since my parents had been attempting to flee with me when Moses was tipped off to their plan and burned them alive. Her sister's horrible death had been my fault, as far as she was concerned, and if she'd treated me with indifference before my mother died, her coldness had become outright hatred afterward.

Like Moses, she was a high-level fire mage. Unlike Moses, she'd never tortured me herself; she left that to others. But she didn't mind watching, and she hadn't offered any care after. She also didn't have blood magic, which was why she thought Moses was reluctant to name her as his successor. The real reason was that she didn't command the same level of fear that he did, and since the big cabals ran on fear and loyalty, that was a serious strike against her case for becoming the new Davo. She was a perfectly competent lieutenant, however, and followed Moses's orders to the letter.

It hadn't occurred to me that Moses would send Catherine here, but it should have. The more I thought about it, the more it made sense. Catherine was less well-known than some of Moses's other senior lieutenants, despite being his daughter. She stayed under the radar. People underestimated her and her ruthlessness. She would be able to go unnoticed for longer than the others. If Darius Bell was looking for Moses's people in the city, he wouldn't be looking for a woman in her mid-fifties who could pass as anything from a teacher to a lawyer without attracting attention. She could smile convincingly at bank managers, hotel concierges, even restaurant servers, and no one would suspect who she was or what she was capable of doing.

Catherine ordered another round of drinks for her group. The server scurried away to the bar to put the order in. I wondered who she was sitting with. I didn't recognize the man across from her, but I couldn't see who else was in the booth.

I had to regroup before Arkady or anyone else who was watching us wondered why I was staring at that booth and its occupants. There would time enough later to think about Catherine and the danger she represented. For now, I needed to be thinking about our current mission to catch Kent Stevens.

I picked up my glass and took a much-needed drink. "How long do you think we should stay here?"

Arkady raised her shoulder in a half-shrug. "An hour at least. If he's not here, he may be watching this location via some kind of surveillance camera. If he saw us go in, he'll be headed this way. He's probably already staked out several ways of approaching the bar. We need to give him time to get here."

"That makes sense." I picked up the menu and glanced at the first page. My stomach growled, reminding me that I'd had nothing to eat since the breakfast burrito Sean made this morning. That meal felt like an eternity ago. "Some of these appetizers look interesting. Are you hungry at all? I could snack."

"I am actually starving to death." She picked up her own menu and read through the options. "Seared tuna, mini-croquettes, artisanal cheeses…what I wouldn't give for a pepperoni pizza," she muttered.

It was hard to ignore Catherine and I didn't want anyone from her group noticing me looking at her. I scooted over so she was no longer in my line of sight. "Well, the croquettes sound good, and I'm thinking the meat and cheese board is the closest we're going to get to a pizza. Unless you think the thing I can't pronounce with the marinated olives sounds good."

"No, I do not." Arkady raised her hand.

Anthony materialized almost out of thin air. "What may I bring out for you?"

"We're hungry," Arkady told him. "How about two orders of the croquettes and a meat and cheese board? What else do you recommend?"

He didn't even blink at the amount of food we were ordering. "I can highly recommend either the empanadas or the seared tuna."

"Empanadas. Thank you."

He left in the direction of the kitchen.

I reached for my water. "Well, you read my dossier, but I know next to nothing about you. How did you end up working for the Court?"

"It's kind of a long story, but the short version is that I got kicked out of the Army for punching my CO when he tried to pressure me into sex. After that, I went into private security while I got my PI license."

"Did you like private security?"

She nodded. "I did, actually, though I liked the investigative work a lot more. I worked with a friend of Fortune's, and when the Court let it be known that they were looking for investigators, I sent in my résumé and Fortune put in a good word. I interviewed with Mr. Vaughan and Bryan Smith, and then with Niara and her head of security, Nadya."

"Have you met Valas?"

She shook her head. "I've spoken with Juliet LaRoche, Valas's daytime representative. I haven't been invited to actually meet Valas yet, though I understand that she ultimately made the decision to hire me. I hear she's quite impressive."

"That she is." And also more than a bit terrifying.

We chatted about the members of the Court until our food arrived. Mindful that there was a chance our booth was bugged and our conversation was not private, we kept the conversation light. Once the food arrived, however, if anyone was listening all they would have heard was the sound of two hungry women eating everything in sight.

Anthony reappeared as we were finishing the last of the meat and cheese tray. He looked suitably impressed by the way we'd cleaned our plates. "May I bring you anything else? Perhaps a dessert?"

Arkady covered her mouth to hide a burp. "I think I'll pass. Alice?"

"No, thank you. Could you point me toward the ladies' room?"

He smiled and gestured grandly toward the back of the club. "Allow me to escort you."

"Me too," Arkady added quickly. Apparently I wasn't allowed to use the bathroom by myself.

We slid from our booth, purses in hand, and followed Anthony along the booths to the end, where two hallways branched in opposite directions. Anthony indicated the hallway on the left. "Second door on the right, ladies."

The bathroom was worthy of a two-page spread in a design magazine, but I couldn't really appreciate it fully until I'd relieved my bladder. While we were in the stalls, someone else entered the bathroom and took the stall farthest from the door.

Business concluded, I flushed the toilet, double-checked to make sure my undergarments were in place and my dress wasn't tucked into my underwear, and emerged from the stall to find Arkady already washing her hands at the sink.

I joined her. "This place is really nice," I said as I washed my hands. The soap smelled like lilacs.

Arkady took a folded paper towel from a basket and dried her hands. "That was the best tequila I've ever had. I was about to ask Anthony how Mr. Vaughan knew what my favorite drink was, but then I realized there's probably nothing about me that Mr. Vaughan doesn't know, down to my bra size and what kind of ice cream I have in the freezer."

"More than likely." I took some lipstick from my bag and applied it as the toilet flushed in the last stall. "You don't seem upset about that."

She took out her own lipstick. "Bra size and favorite ice cream flavor, no. But every girl has secrets she wants and needs to keep buried, and there are some invasions of privacy I won't accept. This is a good job, but it's a job. I won't hesitate to walk away if certain lines get crossed. I made that pretty clear."

I wondered what kinds of secrets Arkady might have buried and how she intended to keep the vamps from digging them up. I knew all too well what a minefield secrets were. I hoped she would have more luck protecting hers than I'd had.

The stall door opened and Catherine emerged. Our eyes met in the mirror.

Hers were the same gray as my mother's had been, the same as Moses's were. Mine were dark brown, a gift from my dad, my mother had always said. She'd loved my brown eyes. I'd never understood why, really, until I figured out that the things she loved most about me were the things that weren't part of the Murphy family legacy. I'd always thought my eyes were a darker version of my dad's, but now I had to question that given what the mirror had revealed to me. Perhaps they reminded her of my biological father, Daniel.

I dropped my lipstick back into my purse and stepped aside to allow Catherine to reach the sink.

"Excuse me," she said, reaching for the soap dispenser and turning her attention to washing her hands.

The sound of her voice made the hair stand up on the back of my neck. I hadn't heard her voice in more than five years, but it sounded exactly as I remembered it.

I wanted nothing more than to run from that bathroom and then away from the bar as fast as I could, but I forced myself to smile at Arkady and walk leisurely out into the hall, as if I couldn't sense my life crumbling around me.

"Is it about time to leave?" I asked as we returned to our booth and slid into the seats.

She checked the time. "It's been a little over an hour. Let's give it another fifteen minutes, shall we? I'll let them know we're almost ready to leave."

As Arkady texted the security team, Catherine walked past me on her way back to her table. Her hand passed within inches of my arm. I held still as she went by.

I looked nothing like her niece anymore, thanks to surgery. My magic was unrecognizable under so many layers of spells. There was absolutely no cause for her to suspect I was even alive, as far as I knew, much less reason to think I might be here now in the same bar, mere feet away. It was sheer paranoia to think that she had passed by me so closely on purpose to try to sense my magic or that she'd gone to the restroom at the same time I had to engineer an encounter.

It was equally paranoid for me to think the reason her attractive male companion had glanced at me twice since we'd come back to our seats was because she had mentioned me. At any other time, I would have thought his glances were simply admiring a woman in a bar, but I couldn't help but wonder.

He caught my eye and smiled. I gave him a slight shake of my head to indicate that I wasn't interested and turned my attention to Arkady, hoping for an all-clear signal to move out. The sooner we were out of here, the better.

Arkady raised her eyebrows. "Is someone checking you out?"

"Yeah, but he's not my type. Plus I've got a werewolf boyfriend, you know?" I realized I'd just referred to Sean as my "werewolf boyfriend." Suddenly I was a character in a teen shifter romance. Ugh. I picked up my Scotch and tossed back the remainder.

Arkady tilted her head, listening to the voices on her earpiece. "Well, we have people in place all around. The net is set. I'll have Kirwin bring the car to the front."

"Let's walk to the car."

She studied me. "That was not the plan."

"New plan. Let's make the bait super-shiny."

She sent a text, received one, and then sent another. "They don't like it, but they're ready. The SUV is parked in a lot two blocks to the north."

My heart raced in anticipation. "Then let's go."

I'd once told Charles that I was addicted to danger, and it was true. I needed the adrenaline, the risk, and yes, even the pain of fights. Thanks to my grandfather, I'd known little else since I was a child. The need for danger had become a part of me. I couldn't get rid of it any more than I could my magic.

Until Sean, I felt most alive when my life was on the line. Now I felt that way when we were together, too, but I still felt compelled to run toward danger rather than away from it. Sean would need to accept that about me, as difficult as it would be for him to do so. He could stand beside me if he wanted, but I wouldn't be left behind or kept safely put away. It just wasn't in me.

As much as I'd enjoyed our conversation and my drink, Arkady and I were here on a mission. Catherine's sudden appearance had unnerved me, but that was a problem I would have to think about and deal with later. Right now, we had business outside.

We got up from our booth and headed out to meet it.

"Why the hell didn't it work?" I demanded.

Arkady tapped her foot, clearly irritated, as Matthias drove us back to my house. Kirwin had received a request for him to return to Northbourne, so we'd left him at 1792. Most of our drive had been ominously silent.

"Heck if I know," she said finally. "I thought we had him figured out. There's no way he could have resisted that bait if he saw you, and I would have bet real money he'd be there. It's the obvious best spot for him to find Vaughan or you. We'll just have to try again tomorrow, I guess."

I didn't punch the seat in frustration, but I wanted to. I worried that I might bust the leather upholstery wide open if I did. I'd spooled magic during the walk, preparing to face Stevens, and now all of that power sizzled on my skin, refusing to be put back in the bottle.

Like me, Arkady was restless and short-tempered. I was starting to think she might love a good fight as much or more than I did, and we were both all wound up with no one to pound. Maybe we could take turns punching my heavy bag when we got home.

I also hadn't gotten a call yet from Kim Dade about the cuff, which gnawed on my already-frayed nerves. My fingers itched to call her, but she'd said she'd let me know as soon as she found something. A phone call would do nothing but interrupt her research.

The SUV turned onto my street. "I'm going to stay and watch the house until dawn," Matthias told Arkady, catching her eye in the rearview mirror. "If Ms. Worth needs to leave for any reason, we'll be her escorts."

"Good." Arkady's attention was out the window as the SUV pulled into my driveway and parked, so she missed the look Matthias gave her. Poor guy had it bad. I wondered if she'd noticed it yet.

Matthias left the engine running but opened his door. "I'll escort you into the house."

"Wait for us to come around to your side," Arkady reminded me, opening her door.

"I remember," I said, hoping I didn't sound as sullen as I felt.

They got out. Matthias opened my door and offered me his hand as Arkady kept watch on our surroundings. He flinched when my spooled magic gave him a little zap, but he didn't let go until both of my feet were on the ground.

Arkady and I headed toward my front door with Matthias at our six. I opened my handbag and reached for my keys.

Behind me, I heard four quick, heavy *thumps*. Matthias grunted, staggered, and fell.

In the time that it took me to realize he'd been shot, Arkady spun around, her gun raised as she searched for a target. "Take cover!" she ordered me.

Thump thump. She went down with a pained sound, two neat holes punched in the front of her jumpsuit right above her heart. The bullets hit her vest, but their impact knocked the wind out of her. She lay crumpled on the lawn, struggling to breathe.

Matthias, bleeding from at least a couple of wounds, crawled to her and shielded her with his body. "Get inside," he rasped.

If I went into the house I'd be safe behind my wards, but the shooter might pick me off before I could get the door open. Besides, I wasn't about to leave Arkady and Matthias wounded and undefended.

I dropped to a crouch just as bullets hit the sidewalk next to me, pelting me with pieces of cement. The shots seemed to have come from the direction of the carport, but I couldn't see anyone. More bullets peppered the sidewalk in front of me. Were there two shooters? Did Stevens have a partner, or a whole team?

I was a sitting duck in the middle of my walkway, so I scuttled behind the SUV just as three or four rounds hit the bullet-resistant glass above my head. I realized now that my escorts were down, all of the shots were directed at me. Clearly I was the primary target. I needed to draw their fire farther away from Arkady and Matthias.

I got up and ran for the backyard gate as bullets thumped into the grass behind me. I expected to feel shots in my back at any moment as I got the gate unlatched, swung it open, and dashed into the darkness of my backyard. I left the gate ajar, hoping Stevens would follow me and leave Arkady and Matthias alone.

Sean had told me that the vamps had people watching my house, so where the hell were they? Why hadn't they found the shooters and taken them out? What were they waiting for?

There wasn't much cover in my backyard except for some bushes, a couple of skinny trees, and my new garden. The plants rustled in excitement as I ran around to the side of the garden and put the mass of swaying greenery between me and the backyard gate. I peered through the plants, watching the side of the house and waiting for Stevens to show his face or for the Vamp Court's team to find Stevens and whoever was helping him.

I sensed an obfuscation spell break behind me. I spun and raised my left hand, forming an air magic shield, as my cold-fire whip spiraled out of my right palm.

Kent Stevens appeared seemingly out of thin air, gun in hand, and fired five shots straight at me. All five hit the shield and were deflected away.

I lashed out with my fire whip, striking Stevens across the chest and throwing him back into the bushes. To my surprise, he held onto his gun and fired several more shots before I could get my shield back in place. Angry hornets tore past my upper left arm and hip. I ignored the flashes of heat and pain and raised my shield, sending the rest of the bullets into the fence on my left.

Stevens rolled to his feet—

—and vanished.

Shit.

Obfuscation spells powerful enough to make someone invisible were rare and very, very expensive for non-mages. Now I knew how he'd slipped past the Vamp Court team watching the house and made it seem like there were multiple shooters instead of just one.

These spells were air magic, though, so as an air mage I had a slight advantage. I'd also been practicing engaging an invisible target with Malcolm, and I had a second to be thankful for our recent sparring sessions before I sensed magic to my left. I raised my shield just in time to block three shots. I lashed out with my whip, but missed him.

Footsteps rustled in the grass to my right; I lashed again and this time my cold fire whip made contact, sending him flying backward. Blood splattered on the fence and something hit the ground and became visible: his gun, a Glock with a suppressor and extended magazine. I lashed it with my whip and the barrel bent, rendering the firearm useless.

Silence.

Breathing hard, I backed up against the fence and tried to sense where he was, but it was hard to focus with the pain in my arm and side and the sensation of blood dripping down my leg.

The sharp point of a knife punctured my right side, just below the edge of my vest. A spell broke and I found myself staring into Stevens's eyes from inches away. I hadn't seen him since that day at Robinson's house, but he looked almost like a different person. His face was a cold mask, his eyes dark and murderous. I was right; he wanted to look me in the eye, up close and personal, when he took me out. That decision doomed him.

I didn't wait for him to speak or drive his knife farther into my flesh. I pushed my blood magic out through my fingertips and plunged the wide red-and-black blade deep into his gut, twisting it as hard as I could.

He grunted and dropped his Ka-Bar knife. Hot blood poured over my fingers. I pulled my magic blade out and hit him on the chest with both hands. Air magic sent him flying back to land on the grass next to the garden. He lay stunned, his hands on the bloody, gaping wound in his stomach. I backed toward my house, watching him.

Two figures ran through my backyard gate, moving too quickly to be human. A pair of Hunters—one male, one female. They must not have been able to find him when he was using the obfuscation spells, but the smell of blood had drawn them like a magnet.

They headed straight for Stevens, fangs bared and eyes black. If they got hold of him, they would tear him to shreds.

I raised my hand. Red, purple, and black blood magic flared on my fingers. I sensed the dark magic of the Hunters and grabbed it with my mind, bending their will to mine. "*Stop*," I commanded.

They stopped, frozen, staring at me in a combination of fury and confusion.

Arkady appeared, walking unsteadily, her gun still in her hand and her breathing labored. She gave the Hunters a wide berth and joined me in the middle of the yard.

"The Hunters," she rasped. "How...*why* are you stopping them?"

How was not an answer I was willing to share with her, but the *why* was important. "Because he's yours to take down," I told her. "Two in the kneecaps, remember? For Fortune."

She swallowed hard. I saw a flash of something in her eyes—grief, maybe, or pain—and then it was gone. Despite the soreness in her chest, she straightened. "Thank you."

Stevens must have moved, because when I'd left him lying on the ground, he hadn't been within reach of the garden. Somehow, despite his guts spilling out, he was able to move. Maybe he was going for another weapon; maybe he was trying to get back on his feet.

Either way, he didn't get very far.

The plants moved fast. One moment, Stevens was on the ground next to the flowerbed; the next, a thick vine wrapped around his legs and yanked him into the garden. His short scream ended abruptly in a wet gurgle.

Arkady and I ran for the garden, but it was too late. The plants thrashed wildly and

I heard a sound that was somewhere between chewing and slurping. The thrashing subsided, but the sound continued. I had a feeling I'd be hearing it in my nightmares for a while.

Finally, Arkady stuck her gun back in her shoulder holster and studied the plants as they enjoyed their dinner. "I really wanted to shoot him, but I think I like this even more. Do you think the plants will eat everything, or—?"

The garden rustled and a gloppy wet boot plopped on the grass at my feet, followed by its mate. A thick leather belt landed next to them a moment later, still buckled. It had been chewed in half.

Arkady turned a little green. "I think I'm going to be sick."

I pressed a hand to my bloody side and glared at her. "Don't you dare."

We turned and headed for the front of the house. Behind us, the garden slurped and sighed.

It was a well-planned ambush, and it had almost worked.

Matthias swore we hadn't been followed from the bar, so at first it was a mystery how Stevens found me. Not long after we returned to 1792 for medical attention and a debriefing, however, the vamps found Stevens's vehicle, a stolen truck, two streets away from my house. In it was a prepaid mobile phone with one incoming message from a blocked number that read simply *Identity Confirmed: Alice Evelyn Worth* and gave my address. They speculated that someone working for Stevens had surveillance in place at 1792 and used facial recognition software to identify me. There wasn't much chance of figuring out who had sent the text that directed Stevens to my home, but the vamps were on it. They were also looking into where he might have bought the obfuscation spells.

Charles and Bryan arrived at 1792 at the same time we did. Matthias had taken four shots in the back. Two hit his vest, but one hit him in the neck and the other his upper left arm. He lost a lot of blood, but he lived, thanks to a little luck and Charles's blood.

Arkady had a spectacular and very painful bruise on her chest from the bullets that hit her vest. She declined all offers of healing and said she'd be fine with some aspirin and an ice pack. We made plans to meet for drinks soon and she went home to recuperate. Matthias watched her go with a hangdog look, then left as well, headed for Northbourne.

My own wounds were fairly minor. One bullet had grazed my upper left arm and the second left a slightly deeper trench across my hip. I had an inch-deep puncture in my right side from Stevens's knife. Like Arkady, I declined Charles's blood, preferring standard first-aid remedies. I'd heal the injuries myself at home with spells later.

Bryan, a former Army medic, dressed my wounds, gave me ibuprofen and a bottle of fancy water, and hovered next to me like a very large, very stern mother hen as I reclined on one of the enormous overstuffed sofas in Charles's office above 1792.

It was my first visit to the office Charles was using as his primary workspace while his former digs were being rebuilt. This room was more spacious than his office above Hawthorne's had been, with a large sitting area, a full bar, and an enormous L-shaped desk. The walls were lined with bookcases and display cases full of antiques and artifacts.

"I like the sofas," I said, wincing as I adjusted the pillows I was leaning against. "Super-comfy. I could almost fall asleep right here."

"You are welcome to do so, or you may stay in one of the furnished apartments upstairs," Charles said. He'd been in a good mood since he'd heard what had happened to Stevens. He was less happy about my refusal to let him heal my wounds and frowned when I grimaced.

The ibuprofen took the edge off the pain, but my arm, side, and hip throbbed mercilessly. Bryan had offered me stronger pain meds, but I declined. If Kim called about the cuff, I wanted a clear head.

I finished the last of the fancy water and handed the bottle to Bryan. "Thanks for the offer, but I'd rather sleep at home in my own bed. I'll get up and go here in a minute." Maybe five or ten minutes. The couch was ridiculously plush and I strongly suspected I was going to need help getting up.

"There is no hurry. May I offer you a drink?" Charles asked.

I shook my head. "I better not. Thanks, though, and thank you very much for the fantastic Scotch you served me down in the bar earlier. That was quite a special treat."

"I suspected neither you nor Ms. Woodall would find much on the drink menu downstairs that was to your liking." Charles poured himself three fingers of whiskey and joined me in the sitting area, settling into the armchair across from me so we could converse easily. "What is your assessment of Ms. Woodall?"

"You knew I'd like her. Crack shot, highly trained, cool as a cucumber under pressure, fearless, driven, total adrenaline junkie."

He smiled. "Those words describe someone else I know."

I scoffed. "That last thing maybe."

He waved his hand. "This is unnecessary modesty. We are well aware of your skills, Alice—though not all of them, it would seem. I speculated that you might be able to control Hunters, but it is quite something else when it happens."

Before Charles had bitten me, I'd kept the fact I was a blood mage hidden from him, as well as some of the more unique skills I had developed. He now knew I was a high-level blood mage, however, and some powerful blood mages shared an affinity for the dark magic that bound Hunters to their master. My ability to command Hunters was rare but not unique. I hadn't planned on revealing it, but I had weighed the value of keeping that ability a secret from Charles versus permitting Arkady the opportunity to take her revenge and decided her need was greater.

Charles contemplated his Scotch. "As I am sure you recall, the first night we met, five years ago, I engineered an encounter between you and two Hunters. I suspected then that you had blood magic, though you had so carefully hidden it. The Hunters' reactions to you—and your reaction to them—was further evidence of this. Amira, their Master, thought so as well." He studied me. "I cannot help but wonder what else you are capable of."

"Well, I've been known to make a mean grilled cheese." I shifted position again and stifled a groan.

At least 1792 had an elevator so I didn't have to either climb stairs or suffer the indignities of being carried as a result of my injured hip. I hoped Charles had added one to the new Hawthorne's. He disliked elevators as a rule, but had acknowledged that not all of his visitors appreciated having to climb several flights of stairs to visit his office, especially if they were a bit worse for wear.

As I was debating whether to force myself to get up or lie on the couch for a few more minutes, my cell phone rang. I dug around in the couch until I found it. The screen read *Kim Dade Calling*.

My discomfort forgotten, I sat up and answered. "Hi, Kim."

"Hi, Alice."

I knew her well enough to recognize that tone. My heart sank. "You have bad news."

She sighed. "Well, the good news is that I did find out what that cuff is. The fire magic spellwork you sensed must have been added sometime in the past twenty years or so. The original shifter magic dates back at least a thousand years."

So our guess about its age and origin were correct. That was something, at least. "What's its purpose?"

"It's designed to be worn by the alpha of a pack. The original spellwork is supposed to strengthen the alpha and bolster the pack bonds, thus fortifying the pack and assuring strong leadership and dominance."

"The hell it is," I said hotly. "That cuff forced Sean to shift and made him violent and irrational."

"That's because you've only got one cuff." She took a deep breath. "That's the bad news. It's one of a pair, Alice. There's a second cuff that's supposed to be worn by the alpha's mate. Together, the cuffs reinforce their bond and provide strength and stability to the pack. That cuff Sean is wearing is not supposed to be used individually. The magic is incomplete, and you know how dangerous broken spellwork can be."

Shock left me speechless for a moment. "What will happen to Sean if someone doesn't put on the other cuff?"

Her voice was full of sorrow. "Without a mate to wear the matching cuff, Sean is going to die."

18

My world shrank to the feeling of the phone in my hand and the pain in my chest. "How long?" I asked hoarsely.

"Days at most. Maybe less. He's probably weak already and going downhill rapidly. I'm sorry, Alice."

And Jack had dosed him with a sedative. I felt a surge of rage and fought to focus on figuring out what to do. "How do we get the cuff off of him?"

"As far as I know, you can't. The magic is bound to him. It only comes off if he dies, so it can be passed to the next alpha."

That settled that. "Then we have to find the other cuff. Do you know where it is?"

"I've been looking, but there's no trace of where it might be. It's not in a museum as far as I can tell, so it's probably in a private collection. It could be here, or it might be on the other side of the world. I'll keep trying, though. If it's out there, I'll try like hell to find it."

"Thank you, Kim. Please call me the second you know something."

We disconnected.

I put my phone in my lap and looked up to find Charles and Bryan standing in front of me. "I have to get to Sean," I said, struggling to rise.

"Miss Alice, let me help you." Bryan took me by my right arm and lifted me to my feet. "You're in no condition to confront a pack of werewolves."

"He's dying alone in a cage," I said, pushing Bryan away. I was well aware that he moved only because he chose to do so. "I can't leave him like that. He needs me."

"He needs someone to find the other cuff and put it on," Charles said. "Are you willing to do that, Alice?"

I hesitated.

It made me sick to my stomach, but I hesitated. Sean loved me. I didn't want him to die. I would give almost anything, *do* almost anything, to save him. But at the thought of putting on the other cuff and binding myself to him for the rest of our lives, even if it was to save his life, I hesitated.

I hated myself so much in that moment that I was sure Charles sensed it.

I tried to remember how Sean and I had talked about a mate bond only yesterday. He'd said he thought we might have such a bond someday, but not yet. Though his wolf wanted me as a mate, Sean knew we'd only been dating a few months and neither of us were ready for that level of commitment.

And then there was my grandfather, who had quickly gone from distant danger to imminent threat. It was one thing if I told Sean the truth about Moses and he chose to accept that risk, but putting the cuff on meant Sean had no say in whether he would become a target.

Even knowing that, we were talking about life and death. If I found the other cuff— and that was a mighty big *if*—I'd have to choose whether to put it on and save Sean's life, or refuse and watch him die. I knew couldn't watch him die, but I didn't think I could put the cuff on.

The debate was academic unless we found the second cuff. Sean's current condition was much more critical.

I swallowed hard and turned to Charles. "Please call Jack and tell him what we know. When you're done, I would like to speak to him."

"I do not believe he will allow you to see the wolf," he told me gently. "I cannot ask him to grant you access. It is a pack matter and the Court has no authority."

"I have to get in to see Sean." I paced, limping from one side of the sitting area to the other. "I have to tell him that I'm trying to find the other cuff. I have to tell him... something important. And if I can get into the cage, touch the cuff, and sense the magic, I might be able to use the trace to locate the second cuff."

"That magic could have killed you the first time," he reminded me. "It may kill you outright if you touch it now that the spellwork has degraded further. You cannot risk it."

"I have to. I have no choice." I took a shaky breath. "Please call Jack, Charles. Before it's too late."

Left hook, right hook. Left hook, right hook. Jab, cross, jab. Left hook, right hook. Left hook again. *Bam bam bam*. My gloved fists pounded the bag. I reset my feet and started again. Left hook, right hook. Jab, cross, jab.

Malcolm hovered in the hallway outside the spare bedroom, his worry a faint buzz on the edges of my senses. "Alice, you've got to stop this. You just got shot twice, for Pete's sake. Why aren't you resting?"

"You think I can rest right now?" I delivered three quick punches to the bag and wiped sweat off my face. My arms and shoulders were screaming. "Do you really believe I could go lie down and sleep while Sean is locked in a cage dying and Jack Hastings won't let me see him?"

"Okay, maybe you can't sleep, but you sure as hell don't have to be in here running yourself into the ground. I thought you were past doing this sort of bullshit."

Left hook, right hook. Jab, cross, jab. "What bullshit am I doing, Malcolm?"

"Damn it, you know exactly what I mean. You're punishing yourself because you think this is your fault. It's four o'clock in the morning and you've been punching that bag since you got home and healed your arm and side. What would Sean say if he were here?"

I turned on him, my gloves raised. "He's *not* here, Malcolm. That's the point!" I turned and punched the bag three more times, my eyes stinging.

Malcolm floated over next to me. "Alice, stop," he pleaded.

One second, I was pulling my arm back to deliver another set of punches, and the next I was sitting on the floor, dazed.

Malcolm floated above me, looking furious. "I said *stop!*" he yelled.

I blinked up at him. My butt hurt from landing on the floor but I had no memory of going down. My chest felt kind of tingly. "Did you just zap me?" I asked in confusion.

He crossed his arms, still angry. "Did you just spend the last forty-five minutes doing the closest thing to beating the crap out of yourself and ignoring me when I told you to stop?"

"What do you want me to do?" I rested my gloved hands in my lap as sweat trickled down my face. "You said I couldn't go out to Jack's house and cut my way through the pack to get to Sean."

"I'm pretty sure Charles told you that too," he pointed out. "I'm equally sure you know you can't do that, not if you want any kind of future with Sean. I know your usual solution to a situation like this is to go in with magic blazing, but that's not going to work this time. You have to go a different route."

"I wish I knew what route to take. Jack won't even talk to me, much less let me see Sean, even when Charles said I might be able to trace the second cuff if I could touch the one Sean's wearing. He just said they'll find the other cuff and it's no longer any business of the Court's, or mine."

"What good will it do them if they find the other cuff?" Malcolm asked. "You're Sean's mate. They'll have to let you put it on if they find it, right?"

When I frowned at him, he looked surprised, then thoughtful. "Oh."

"What do you mean, 'oh'?" I demanded.

"You're not sure if you want to put it on." When I started to protest, he shook his head. "No, I get it. You're not Sean's mate, not yet. You've only been dating a couple of months. But you have to put the cuff on, or Sean dies." He grimaced. "Crap, Alice, that's tough."

"This is all speculative anyway, probably. I don't see any way we could find the other cuff, especially if Jack won't let me use the trace."

"That magic would probably kill you if you touched it anyway. It's undoubtedly warded against doing exactly what you want to do: use the trace to find the other cuff. Everything about it is designed not to let anyone mess with the spellwork or the cuffs themselves. We're both lucky we're not dead from it already." He made a face. "Well, in my case, deader."

I suddenly felt every ounce of the exhaustion I'd been trying to ignore. I pulled off my gloves and started unwrapping my hands. Malcolm watched me, floating back and forth.

When my hands were free, I left the gloves and the hand-wraps on the floor and got to my feet. I started toward the door, then paused and turned back. "I'm a bad person, aren't I?"

He stared at me, nonplussed. "Of course you aren't. Why would you think that?"

My eyes burned. "Because Sean will die if I don't find that cuff and put it on, and I'm not sure I can put it on, not even to save his life."

He floated over to me. "Alice, you are absolutely, positively *not* a bad person. I may not know anything about what happened to you before you moved here, but I am one hundred percent certain that you are a good person and that you will save Sean's life, whether that means putting on the cuff or figuring out some other way."

"There is no other way, apparently," I said wearily. "Find and put on the other cuff, or Sean dies. The cuff only comes off if Sean dies."

"Well, so says Kim Dade," Malcolm pointed out. "Maybe you need to get a second opinion. Is there anyone else you can ask?"

"Maybe." I told him about Ella Potter, the shifter magic expert from Portland who seemed to know a bit about magic cuffs.

"Send her an e-mail right now, then go to bed," Malcolm told me. "You can try to catch a little bit of rest until you hear from her. Take something to help you sleep if you have to. You got almost no sleep last night and if you don't get at least a couple of hours tonight, you'll be useless if you've got to swing into action later."

I couldn't argue with that, though I found it highly unlikely I'd be able to fall asleep anytime soon.

I went downstairs and fetched my laptop, then took a shower because I was sweaty and gross. I put on my sheep pajamas—the ones Sean liked, because wolves thought sheep were tasty—and sat on the bed with the computer in my lap. Malcolm had gone downstairs to give me some space.

I found Ella Potter's e-mail address on the MOP website and wrote a detailed message explaining the situation. I attached a photo of the cuff, explained what another researcher had uncovered, and asked if she knew anything more that might help us. Though I knew it was a very long shot, I also asked if she had any idea where the second cuff might be or how else it might be traced if I didn't have access to the magic on the one Sean was wearing.

I read back over my message to make sure it was clear that my inquiry was urgent but didn't sound like I was begging for help. I decided it was reasonably professional and hit Send.

With that done, I closed the laptop and turned off my lamp. I slid down under the covers and curled into a ball. I couldn't remember my room ever feeling so empty and silent.

After a few minutes, I rolled over to the other side of the bed, the side closer to the bathroom where Sean usually slept. The forest scent was much stronger on that side of the bed. I buried my nose in the pillow and inhaled.

This morning, in the minutes before we fell asleep together, I'd laid in his arms thinking about the story he'd revealed to me while we were staking out John Doe's motel room. It was the most painful and personal story a werewolf could tell: how he'd become a shifter. It was proof of his trust in me. He was waiting for me to tell him my story, but in the meantime, he offered me his. He'd put his cards on the table, hoping I might do the same.

For the first time I thought I might be able to tell him my story someday soon. When, I wasn't sure, but soon, assuming I figured out a way to save him.

With my nose filled with the scent of a forest in spring, I could almost feel his arm around my middle and his nose against the back of my neck. I wrapped my arms around myself and slept.

I dreamed of the wolf.

He lay on his side in a glass cage in the middle of an empty, dark room, his golden eyes full of pain and hurt. Need mate, *he said in my head.*

I pounded my fists against the glass walls. I'm trying to get to you, *I told him.*

He summoned up enough strength to bite at the cuff on his front leg, but it held fast. He lay his head back down and showed his teeth. Bad magic.

I know. There's another cuff that matches that one. If I can find it, I can save you. You've got to hang on. Please don't give up.

A clawed hand grabbed me by the shoulder, spun me around, and slammed me up against the glass wall of the cage. Jack's face was half-wolf, half-human, with an oversize jaw and huge teeth. His eyes were bright gold with fury. "I told you to stay away," *he snarled in my face. His breath was hot.*

The wolf growled and snapped his teeth. Protect mate, not hurt, *he commanded.*

Jack ignored the wolf and grabbed me by the throat. I pushed my blood magic out through my fingertips and slashed his face, opening four long, bloody gashes.

With a snarl, he flung me down and towered over me, his face twisted with rage. Blood dripped down the front of his shirt. "You are not welcome in our pack," *he growled.*

My pack, *the wolf snarled. He struggled to his feet and moved stiffly to the glass wall.* My mate, my pack.

Jack turned on him with a growl. I slashed at his legs with my blood magic and he came at me, teeth bared. The last thing I felt was the pain as he sank his canines deep into the soft flesh of my throat.

I woke with a short scream, my hands on my throat as I shook uncontrollably. The dream had seemed so real that it took several seconds to process that I was in my own bedroom and not the eerie, empty room with Jack and Sean's wolf.

Strangely, my shoulder hurt where Jack had grabbed it in the dream, and my neck was sore. I must have been sleeping in an uncomfortable position, I reasoned. There was obviously no way I had actually been interacting with either the wolf or Jack in a dream.

With my blackout curtains closed I couldn't tell what time it was, but I sensed that it was late morning and my bedside clock confirmed it. The message light was blinking on my phone, indicating I had two voicemails from my office line.

The first message was from Aaron Riddell, inquiring on the status of my search for the cuff. He asked me to give him a call at his office. With everything that had happened, I hadn't even given any thought to what I would tell him or Esther about the cuff. If I was able to somehow get it off Sean, I had no idea if I would be able to return it to my client, or if the pack would want to keep it in case the second cuff turned up. I wasn't even going to consider the possibility that it would fall off on its own. I wasn't going to let that happen to Sean.

When I played the second message, I got a surprise. "Alice, this is Karen Williams from Sean's pack." Her voice was tense and angry. "I didn't have your cell, so I'm trying your office number. Jack ordered us not to contact you, but you deserve to know what's happening."

My stomach knotted.

"Sean is...in really bad shape," she continued, her voice breaking. "He can barely eat or drink and he isn't moving around very much. I know you're trying to find the second cuff. Please hurry. I don't know how much longer he can hang on. We've tried to talk Jack into letting you come see him, but he won't even consider it."

She took a deep breath. "You need to know what Jack's trying to do. A year or so ago, he and Delia set Sean up on a date with Lily Anderson, a female shifter from another pack. They dated for a while but Sean wasn't all that taken with her. She fell in love with him, though, and their alpha has kept in touch with Jack, hoping they might get back together even though Sean has said he's not interested. Well, Jack is looking for that other cuff too, and if he finds it he's going to have Lily put it on and make her Sean's mate."

For a moment, I couldn't get a breath. A bubble of rage filled my chest and threatened to burst through my skin. How dare Jack even think about binding Sean to someone for life without his consent, whether or not it would save his life to do so? The thought made me sick to my stomach.

Karen went on. "Jack says that if they're bound together, whether it was Sean's choice or not, he'll have to accept Lily or risk war with her pack. He's probably right. Sean won't have any choice. I'm so sorry about this, Alice. I know you care about Sean very much and he cares about you. That's why I'm calling to warn you. Please, *please* find that cuff before Jack does. It will break our hearts if he does this to Sean and to you. I know this probably isn't how you envisioned your relationship would go, but I believe that you'll find the cuff and save Sean. Just *hurry*, Alice. Please hurry." *Beep.*

I put the phone on the bed and sat with my legs dangling over the side, too stunned to move at first. I'd never even considered that Jack might give the cuff to another woman if he found it. He had to know how angry Sean would be if he was bound to this other woman. I couldn't imagine Sean not killing him over it.

I remembered Jack's size and felt a sudden rush of fear. Sean was weakened tremendously by the cuff. What if Sean challenged Jack and lost? In fact, what if Jack was counting on Sean to fight him in a weakened condition so he could kill Sean and become the new alpha?

I rubbed my face. Was Jack that ruthless and disloyal? He just might be. I'd been wondering how he thought he was going to get away with everything he'd done since the cuff got onto Sean's arm. Maybe he was well aware of how angry Sean would be and he was planning to use that anger to his advantage.

My search for the cuff had just taken on additional urgency. I grabbed my laptop, hoping to find an e-mail reply from Ella Potter, the shifter magic expert.

I opened my e-mail and found three messages in my inbox. One of them was from Ella, sent about twenty minutes ago. My heart in my throat, I opened the message.

Hi, Alice. Thanks so much for contacting me! I'm so sorry to hear about what the cuff is doing to your friend.

First, the bad news: I don't have any information about where the other cuff might be. I've seen cuffs like this before, but not this particular set. I can confirm what your researcher has told you about their purpose and that the cuff's magic will keep it affixed to the alpha's arm until either he or his mate dies, in which case both cuffs fall off so they can go to the new alpha pair. The spellwork is potentially deadly to anyone who attempts to remove the cuff, either physically or by interfering with the magic. It sounds like you know that already from personal experience.

I do have some potentially good news for you, however. Since you can't touch the magic on the cuff you have, I do know of a spell that might work to help you find the cuff you need. I've attached a copy of the spell and the instructions for using it. I'm hoping you have enough of your friend's shifter magic that it will work. I don't know if you are a mid or high-level mage, but obviously the more powerful you are, the more likely you'll be able to get it to work.

Just so you know, I was contacted via e-mail this morning by a shifter named Jack Hastings, who told me essentially the same story you did, except his version wasn't very complimentary toward you. I told him that as far as I knew his information about the cuff was correct and that I didn't know where the other cuff might be. I didn't tell him that you had also contacted me, or about the spell. I didn't much like the way he spoke about you.

I sincerely hope you can find the other cuff. I will ask around and see if anyone I know has any information that might be helpful, either about the cuff or ways of locating the other one. In the meantime, good luck with the spell and let me know if I can do anything else to help. Peace and best wishes, Ella.

I opened the attached image and studied the spellwork. Most of the runes were new to me, but the basic structure was familiar and based on air magic, as most tracking spells were. The accompanying instructions stated that the probability of the spell working increased based on the power of the mage using it, the amount of shifter magic they could draw upon, and how much—if any—of the trace from the known cuff was available.

I was a high-level air mage, so that would help. Sean and I blended our magic on a regular basis, as Malcolm had recently—and so awkwardly—pointed out, so I had that going for me. I did have the box the cuff had been stored in, and if anything would have some of the cuff's trace, it would be that box.

I also had Malcolm, whose magic skills were better in some areas than my own. If there was a way to increase the chances of the spell working, he would know how.

There was no time to waste with Sean's condition deteriorating rapidly and Jack hunting for the other cuff too. There was a good chance he would find out about the tracking spell some other way and there were other high-level mages around who might be able to use it. Time was ticking.

I printed off the spellwork and the instructions Ella had sent, e-mailed back a quick and heartfelt thanks for her help, got dressed, and hurried down to the main floor. "Malcolm!" I called.

He came up through the floor from the basement. "I'm glad you got at least a little bit of sleep," he said. "What have you got?"

I told him what I'd received from Ella and showed him the spellwork. We studied the diagram together in the kitchen while coffee brewed and I made a couple of pieces of toast with jelly for breakfast. Magic took energy, so I needed food even if it tasted like sawdust.

"Holy crap, this might work," Malcolm said finally as I licked jelly off my fingers. "I take back all the complaining I did about you guys going at it like bunnies, because all that shifter magic in your aura is going to really help us out here."

"I swear, if I hear you say one more thing about bunnies, you will be sorry." I poured my coffee into a large tumbler, snapped on the lid, and headed for the basement. "Let's get a move on. We've got to hurry."

On the way downstairs, I told him about Karen's warning and Jack's plan to find the cuff and put it on Lily Anderson.

As I'd expected, Malcolm went nuclear at the news. By the time he got done swearing, I was on my hands and knees in the smallest circle on the basement floor, using chalk to draw the spellwork.

Malcolm hovered nearby, watching me work. "I'm thinking we can increase the chances of this working with two sets of amplification spells in the second and third circles. I can close and power them while you focus on the tracking spell and channeling the shifter trace. You'll have to be in the center circle anyway."

That was a hell of a lot of spellwork and it would take hours to draw it all, but Malcolm was right: it was our best chance of getting the spell to work. Magic like this would take a lot out of me, so everything would have to be right the first time because I might not have enough juice to try again.

It took well over an hour just to draw out the spellwork for the tracking spell. It was intricate and a lot of the runes were new to me because it was based on shifter magic. Malcolm watched, learning the new spellwork along with me.

I had to take a short break before I started the first set of amplification spells. I used the time to sit on the couch for a few minutes and call Aaron.

He greeted me warmly. "Alice, thank you for returning my call. I hadn't heard from you in a day or two, so I just wanted to touch base and see how things were going."

"I'm still hunting for the cuff," I told him. I disliked lying to Aaron, but the situation left me little choice at the moment. "If you want me to hand the cup and the mirror over while I'm looking for the cuff, you could send a courier to my house with a check from Ms. Aldridge and I'll box them up."

"Let me ask my client what she prefers and I'll get back to you. Are you doing all right? You sound tired."

"I've been putting in some long hours on this," I said truthfully. "I had a couple of leads that didn't pan out, but I'm not giving up."

"Don't forget about that bonus for wrapping the case up within a week," he reminded me. "I know you're working as fast as you can, but that extra cash could pay for a nice vacation for you and Sean."

I thought of the trip to the Bahamas that Sean had been trying to talk me into taking. If we got out of this mess—*when* we got out of it—I thought I just might take him up on the offer. Goodness knows we'd deserve some real rest and relaxation after this.

"That's a good way to look at it," I said, hoping he didn't notice the way my voice trembled. "I'll keep looking for the cuff. Just let me know if you're sending someone to pick up the other two items."

"I will. Take care of yourself, Alice. I know you forget to do that sometimes."

"I'll try. Bye, Aaron." We ended the call.

Aaron was a good man. Our affair had been short but passionate. I'd broken things off when I sensed he was starting to want more than just a physical relationship. Back then, two years ago or so, I would never have considered allowing someone to get as close to me as Sean was. Every once in a while, I felt guilty about kicking Aaron to the curb just because he'd started having feelings for me. We'd both moved on, however, and luckily we were still friends.

Arkady texted to ask how I was feeling. I told her I was fine. She sent a photo of what the bruise on her chest looked like today. I winced, then texted back that if she needed company while she recuperated, Matthias might be willing to help nurse her back to health. She replied with a "Wow" emoji.

Me: How did you NOT notice that??

Arkady: I was busy trying not to get killed!

Huh. Maybe Arkady wasn't quite as observant as I'd thought.

Having gotten my second wind, I went back downstairs with a tumbler full of ice water and a turkey sandwich. I needed to be at my best for this to work, which meant more real food and drinking something other than just coffee.

I worked on the first set of amplification spells, which would fill the second circle on the basement floor. That went much faster than the tracking spell even though it was larger, since I'd been doing these spells since I was six. I took a quick break, and then drew the amplification spells in the enormous third circle. That took longer just because the area was so large, but I worked quickly.

When I finally finished, it was late afternoon and I had three circles full of intricately drawn spellwork ready to be used. My fingers were cramping from holding the chalk and my knees hurt from crawling around on the floor, so I sat on the work table for a few minutes to rest and drink more water before doing the final steps for the spell.

Something had been bothering Malcolm for a while, but he hadn't brought it up while I was working. I figured he'd speak up when I took a break and I was right.

"Alice, I'm really sorry for knocking you down last night," he said, looking ashamed. "It was wrong of me to do that. I've been feeling horrible about it ever since. It doesn't matter how frustrated I was; violence is never the answer. I deserve for you to rip me a new one, so have at it. I'm ready." He braced himself.

I smiled. "I accept your apology. I'm not going to rip you a new one. Neither of us were our best selves at that moment. Let's just both learn our lessons and move on. Sound fair?"

Relieved, he returned my smile. "Sounds more than fair."

My phone rang. The screen read *C Rose Calling*. I debated sending it to voicemail, then decided Cyro wouldn't be calling if it wasn't important. I answered and put the call on speaker so Malcolm could hear. "Alice Worth," I said cautiously.

"Congratulations on taking down Kent Stevens last night," the electronic voice said. "You and Ms. Woodall make a good team."

I blinked. "You saw us? How?"

"The Vampire Court had video surveillance in place at your home. I hacked into the feed after you left 1792. I was concerned when it looked like he got the drop on you, but you handled the situation."

"How did you know we were springing a trap on Stevens?" I asked suspiciously.

"I didn't," Cyro said. "I've been keeping an eye on the area around 1792, using facial recognition software in case Stevens showed up, and got a ding when you arrived at the bar. The only reasonable explanation for you being there was to set a trap for him, and it worked. Well done."

"Thanks."

"The main reason I'm calling is the cops found a body in a dumpster behind a motel near the airport early this morning. It's in pretty bad shape, but there's a good chance it's your guy who called himself Kendall. Somebody worked him over with a baseball bat or a pipe with particular attention to his face. The M.E. thinks the body's been in the dumpster since yesterday. They're running fingerprints but no hits so far. I just thought you should know."

I exhaled. "I'm not surprised at all. If you go around stealing from people long enough, it's going to catch up with you sooner or later. The cops have any leads?"

"There's a rumor it might have something to do with the Murphy cabal."

In shock, I blurted out, "*What?*" I calmed myself and added, "Why would they think so?"

"A security camera caught the license plate of a vehicle that might have dumped the body and it traces back to someone who is a known associate of the cabal, Darren Walker. He's been seen hanging around with Catherine Atwood, who is Moses Murphy's only surviving daughter. She's been in town for a couple of weeks, coordinating the attacks on Darius Bell's cabal. Now she's hunting for Bell himself, but he's gone into hiding since his HQ was destroyed."

It was surreal to hear Cyro talking about Catherine, but it did confirm why my aunt was in the city.

"But what's the connection to John Doe?" I asked.

"You know the magical objects you found yesterday in the storage unit? I tipped off SPEMA, as we discussed, and they confiscated the whole stash. There are some items in the collection that are listed in the SPEMA reports as 'highly volatile magic weapons.' If I had to guess, I'd say maybe John Doe was procuring those weapons for Murphy's cabal and when the feds got them instead, Atwood or someone else working for Murphy was pissed and put him out of business permanently."

That made as much sense as anything. Now I was doubly glad we'd given the magical objects to the feds instead of letting my aunt get her hands on them. A powerful magic weapon in the hands of a high-level fire mage was a disaster waiting to happen.

There was a good chance Catherine would find another supplier, obtain weapons, and go after Bell with them. I'd been thinking it had been too quiet in the city these last few days; now perhaps I knew why.

I had my own problems to deal with at the moment, however. Catherine had to stay on the back burner for now. "Thank you for letting me know about John Doe, Cyro. I appreciate the call."

"You're welcome. Take care." The call ended.

I put the phone down on the table, stood up, and stretched. "Well, RIP John Doe, I guess."

"I guess so," Malcolm said. "Idiot got mixed up with Murphy's cabal. How did he think that was going to end? Murphy kills everybody, sooner or later. Everyone knows that."

"Some people think they can make a lot of money getting involved with cabals and find out too late that they've gotten in too deeply to get out." I took off my shirt and put it on the table. I was wearing a sports bra underneath. "Okay, enough delays. We need to get this show on the road."

Malcolm hovered next to me as I used a tube of henna to draw the rest of the tracking spell on my arms and chest. That done, I went to one of the cupboards along the wall, took out the box that had contained the cuff, and set it on top of the spellwork in the center circle.

Barefoot, I sat in the center circle in front of the box. In my head, I ran through the steps I would need to follow for the spell to work. I had used tracking spells many times before, but the inclusion of the shifter magic was new.

Finally, I rolled my shoulders and gave Malcolm a nod. "Ready."

"All right. Let's do this."

I shut my eyes. It wasn't necessary to do so, but I always saw magic and spellwork a little better with my other senses. I closed the inner circle and fed energy into it until my skin buzzed.

I sensed Malcolm close the second circle and then charge the amplification spellwork within it. A second wave of energy followed as he closed the third circle and charged the second set of amplification spells. The power buzzed, waiting for me to use it.

Most tracking spells acted like homing beacons, allowing the user to follow the trace to the object. Instead, this one was designed to show me the cuff's location, which made sense since it could be—though hopefully wasn't—thousands of miles away. I was far more familiar with the former type of tracking spell than the latter, but I had plenty of experience with both.

I held the tracking spell in my mind and drew on the shifter magic in my aura. Suddenly the white lines of air magic spellwork ignited bright gold. I'd never used shifter magic before, but it was beautiful. I sensed the tracking spell forming, waiting for its target, waiting to be unleashed.

Carefully, I opened the box that had held the cuff and put my hand inside.

Before, I'd only sensed the trace of fire magic, but now I had shifter magic coursing through me and the residual golden magic in the box blazed in response.

I had all of the components. Now to put them together and light the fuse.

I grabbed the power from the amplification spellwork and fed it into the tracking spell underneath me. The surge of energy was incredible. Once I had control of the power, I fed the shifter magic into the tracking spell, then drew the power through me to the spellwork drawn on my chest and arms. The sensation was of enormous pressure, like a wave about to break, or a gun about to go off.

I took a deep breath, exhaled, and connected the trace from the box to the tracking spell. "*Adinvenire*."

With the power of the amplification spells behind it, invoking the spell felt like being fired from a cannon. Images flew past my inner eye like a movie being fast-forwarded. Buildings, streets, grass, pavement, cars, and trees flashed by as the spell searched for the missing cuff at metaphysical speeds with my consciousness along for the ride.

To my surprise, the search seemed to take only a few seconds of real time. That meant the cuff was relatively close by. I barely had time to register relief about that before the spell slammed me face-first—metaphysically speaking—into a wall made of wards.

I fell back with a startled sound, banging the back of my head on the concrete floor. The tracking spell fractured, threatening to release all of its energy in a giant flare. Instinctively, I broke the spell and the inner circle, dropped the amplification spells, and lay dazed, staring up at the basement ceiling.

Malcolm broke the second and third circles and appeared above me, worried. "What happened?"

I tried to process what I'd seen in the last milliseconds before the spell hit the wards and broke. There was a house, and a hallway, and a door, and a room, and then a wall safe. The wards were on the safe, so the cuff must be inside.

I ran the movie backward, trying to recall the room it was in and the outside of the house. I remembered lots of dark wood inside the house and large rooms. It was very elegant...and somehow familiar.

I sucked in a breath and sat up.

"Alice, you okay? Did you see where the cuff is?"

"Yeah, I saw it." I staggered to my feet. The back of my head hurt and my body ached like I'd gone ten rounds with a professional boxer, but at the moment, I didn't care.

Blood magic ignited on my hands. "It's in a safe at Charles's house. That fangy son of a bitch has the cuff."

19

Not long after sunset, I pulled up to the gate of Charles's estate.

The gates swung open as I reached for the button to roll my window down. I drove up the long driveway and parked in front of the mansion's front steps next to two black SUVs. I got out of the car and headed for the front door.

The door opened, revealing Bryan. "Miss Alice."

"Bryan. I assume he's here?"

He stepped aside to let me walk past and closed the door behind me. "He is. Would you care to wait in the office? He'll be with you in a few minutes."

"All right." I followed Bryan through the foyer and down a hall to a pair of doors. He opened them and ushered me into the office.

Charles's home office was large enough to accommodate a game of field hockey, with room left over. Two stories tall, it boasted floor-to-ceiling bookcases on two walls. The third wall was a two-level art gallery. Narrow wrought-iron staircases led up to a walkway that ran around the three interior walls. Tall west-facing windows offered a panoramic view of the estate's backyard.

Like his office above 1792, the room was divided into three main areas: the desk area, a sitting area with several couches and chairs, and the bar, with its enormous granite counter and tall chairs.

Everything about this meeting was part of a chess match, from the timing of my arrival to the room Charles had chosen for our meeting and my choice of where I sat. With that in mind, I settled into one of the chairs in front of the desk.

Bryan headed for the bar. "What can I get you to drink?"

"Just water, please."

He selected a bottle from the fridge, removed the cap, and brought it to me wrapped in a cloth napkin. He placed a coaster on the table at my right and set the bottle down. "You look like you've recovered from last night. How are your arm and side?"

"All healed. Neither were all that serious." I picked up the bottle and took a drink.

"I'm sure you're all relieved to have the Kent Stevens situation resolved and be back home."

"Very much so." Bryan moved around in front of me, leaning against Charles's desk. "It was very courageous of you to risk your life to draw Stevens out. Mr. Vaughan and I would have preferred to have done that ourselves."

"So I gathered." I crossed my legs and studied him. "I meant to ask before, but will there be a funeral for Fortune? I'd like to attend."

"His family requested a private service, from what I understand. Mr. Vaughan is covering the costs of the funeral and burial, naturally, but the Court is respecting their wishes."

"Oh." I set the bottle down on the table. "The construction project looks like it's going well. Any idea when Hawthorne's will reopen?"

The answer came from behind me. "We hope to reopen in two months."

Charles strode into the office. He wore a gray summer suit, with a purple tie and matching silk handkerchief perfectly folded in the breast pocket. It was the color combination he knew I liked most on him and another deliberate choice in our chess match.

He walked around the desk and settled into the oversize leather chair as Bryan returned to the bar to pour his employer two fingers of Scotch from a crystal decanter. He brought the glass to Charles and set it on the leather desk pad.

"Thank you," Charles said. "If you will excuse us?"

"Of course." Bryan inclined his head and turned to me. His expression was carefully neutral, but I read concern in his eyes. If I'd had any question of whether he knew the reason for my visit, that look dispelled it. Everyone in the room knew why I was here and what was at stake. He departed, closing the doors behind him.

Charles and I studied one another, reading each other's body language. To the untrained eye he might have seemed as expressive as a rock, but I knew him well enough to see he had anticipated this meeting. Arkady loved a physical fight. Charles enjoyed a battle of wits.

I had come prepared for both.

In the hours between my realization that Charles had the cuff and my arrival at his house, I had allowed myself to be angry. I embraced the fury, and then I let it go. I could not afford to allow anger to be a part of this chess match. Anger made you stupid. It sucked away your ability to think five steps ahead and strategize. I wasn't here to lash out or retaliate or even demand explanations. Charles would be coldly strategic, so I couldn't afford to be any less calculating. My years as a prisoner in my grandfather's cabal had taught me many things, but perhaps the most valuable lesson of all was to never let the bastards see that they got to you. Show your enemies no anger, no grief, no hurt, and no happiness, because they will use your feelings as a weapon against you.

I spoke first. "How long have you had the cuff?"

He picked up the glass and took a sip. "Since early this morning."

"How long have you known there was a second cuff?"

"For certain, since the night of the auction."

"When did you suspect there were two?"

"From the moment you sent me the images of the items you had been hired to locate."

"And when did you find out the second cuff was the cause of Sean's condition?"

He put the glass back on the desk. "Last evening, while you and Ms. Woodall were at 1792."

His responses felt like truth. "So Kim found out about the second cuff and told you, and you held back that information until after the operation to catch Stevens was over. You had her call me with the news once the dust had settled."

He gave me a nod.

"So I wasn't distracted during the operation, or so I went ahead with it instead of backing out to focus on looking for the second cuff?"

"Both."

In other words, it was more important to Charles that Stevens be caught than for me to know about and begin my search for the second cuff. I was not in the least surprised by that, nor by any of his other responses. I had expected as much.

I took a drink of water. "What made you suspect there was a second cuff to begin with?"

"When I saw the picture of the cuff you sent, I recalled selling a similar object a few years ago to a client from another city. There was, of course, a chance it had since changed hands, or that your client was in fact the person I had sold it to, but the cuff I had seen did not have the additional spellwork. It required some time to ascertain that they were, indeed, two different cuffs."

"And when did you begin the process of obtaining the other cuff?"

"The moment I suspected they were likely a pair: the night of the auction."

I hadn't thought it would be possible for me to be any angrier than I was, but I went even colder at the realization that the chess match had started days ago, even before Sean and I went to John Doe's storage unit.

"You couldn't have known the cuff would end up attaching itself to Sean, so why not just tell me about the second cuff to begin with? Why keep it a secret and go to all the trouble to obtain the second one?" I studied him and thought about it. "Were you hoping to find my client's missing cuff before I did and then sell the set to the highest bidder?"

He inclined his head. "Unfortunately, my agents were not able to locate it before you did. The man calling himself Joseph Kendall left little trail for them to follow. Once the cuff had affixed itself to Maclin, I accelerated my plan to obtain the second cuff and adjusted my strategy accordingly."

I had one last question. "Does Jack Hastings know you have the cuff?"

"I have not yet revealed that fact to him, nor has he contacted me to request a meeting."

Charles's deliberate word choice was not lost on me. He had not *yet* told Jack about the cuff, but that was on the table.

Our relative positions in this match were complex. We both knew I wanted the cuff, and that my need for it was great. We also knew Jack wanted the cuff. I assumed Charles already knew what he planned to do with it and what the possible fallout from that might be.

On the surface, those facts seemed to put me at a disadvantage. Charles had something I wanted and there was another interested party. But because of my magic coursing through his veins and his knowledge about my power, and because I had something *he* wanted just as much, nothing was as simple as it might appear.

One point to Charles for keeping the cuff at his house so that I would come here to get it. One point to me for being calm instead of furious at the games he'd played. He'd chosen to meet me in the office, as opposed to another room or on the back patio, knowing I'd decide to sit across from each other at the desk rather than at the bar or in the sitting area. He'd chosen our battlefield and I'd accepted his terms in that regard.

The office setting told me he was approaching our discussion as a business negotiation. The cuff was for sale if we could decide on terms.

I didn't inquire about his asking price; he would have declined to name a figure. I'd heard someone once say that in a dark room, the ceiling was always higher. Besides, we both knew quite well what he wanted in return for the cuff. Like chess strategy, we had to follow a series of expected moves…at least, up until a certain point.

I rested my hands on the arms of the chair. "According to my sources, the fair market value for the cuff, given its age and purpose, is twelve thousand dollars." That number came from Ella, with whom I had exchanged several e-mails before I arrived at Charles's house. "I am willing to offer fourteen thousand four hundred dollars, or twenty percent above market value."

He remained impassive. "And if Mr. Hastings were to offer more?"

"Then I will exceed his best offer by the same percentage."

I was not at all surprised when he replied, "Perhaps cash is less interesting to me than the services I might receive from a potential buyer. No doubt the pack could provide many benefits whose value far exceeds that of the cuff's potential sale price. What might your counteroffer be?"

I paused a moment as if contemplating my answer, when in fact I'd had it prepared knowing he wouldn't accept a cash offer.

"Your new building will be completed soon and no doubt you'll require a great deal of wards and spellwork to protect it. You know very well both the cost of creating wards on that scale and the value of it. In exchange for the cuff, I will provide the wards for your new building, to your specifications, as expediently as my physical ability will allow."

That got a reaction. It was only a slight narrowing of his eyes, but I'd surprised and impressed him with my second offer. He'd set the stage for me to offer my magic skills by mentioning what the pack might be able to do, but he hadn't expected me to make such a large bid. It was big enough to throw him slightly off his game. He'd been prepared to pretend to consider and then reject my proposal, but it was a hell of an offer and he hesitated just a little too long if he'd wanted me to think he wasn't tempted by it. Point to me.

The question was, was it big enough to derail his plans for how this negotiation was going to go?

The answer, it turned out, was no, but it had made the train wobble a bit.

Charles steepled his fingers. "That is quite a tempting offer, but I would prefer to pay you a fair price for that work rather than set the rather dangerous precedent of you bartering your services to a member of the Court. Others on the Court might see it as an opportunity to exploit you in the future, and I am loath to be the cause of it."

It was a nice parry; I had to give him credit. There was just enough truth in his reasoning that it wasn't an outright lie.

So here we were, arriving at exactly the place Charles had wanted this negotiation to go. That might have seemed like a failure on my part, but I'd known from the beginning this was where we'd end up, and I'd come prepared for it.

Part of Charles's game plan was for me to be the one who made the offer. He wanted me to say the words. I had no doubt it would give him pleasure to hear them.

As such, I was willing to do what he wanted, because it would be to my advantage in the end...if I acted the part and made just the right moves.

I took a deep breath, as if steeling myself, and thought about Sean so I felt a stab of pain, fear, and anger that Charles could sense. It was pure method acting. "In return for the cuff, I will let you drink from me."

Charles raised an eyebrow, feigning surprise. "That is a very generous offer."

"You know I want the cuff," I told him, leaning forward. "And we both know you'd like to drink from me again, especially if I'm awake and able to share the experience, unlike last time."

Judging by the flash of surprise in Charles's eyes, I scored a palpable hit with that comment. Charles had indeed already bitten me, but I was in a coma at the time and unaware of it. Part of his reason for biting me was to discover what secrets my blood held—that I was a high-level mage, not the mid-level mage I'd claimed to be—and to establish a kind of dominance over me.

A not-insignificant purpose for a vampire's bite is the intimacy of it; not just the physical and sexual intimacy, but the emotional one. Charles wanted to bite me with my consent not just because he enjoyed the taste of my blood and would benefit from the power of my magic, but because he believed it would bind us together, much like that walk in the sun and his seemingly spontaneous story were designed to do. He hadn't known I was onto his game until this moment. As I'd told Sean, I'd suspected Charles's decision to share his story of how he became a vampire had an ulterior motive, but it wasn't until I knew he had the other cuff that I put it all together.

Charles wanted me; he'd been clear about that since our first meeting when I'd smirked in his face and then threatened to burn down Vampire Court headquarters. He'd bided his time for the last five years, playing a long, carefully calculated game as I settled into my new life and the walls I'd built around myself started to come down. He'd even let me leave Hawthorne's with Sean the night we'd first met, when he could have covertly interfered. He'd wagered my relationship with Sean wouldn't last. He was still betting on that, even to the point that he was willing to hand over the cuff, because he was sure I wouldn't put it on. My reaction to him asking me if I would do so last night had no doubt confirmed that belief.

He was banking on that walk in the sun, his story, and his bite to strengthen the bond between us just as my conflict with Jack and the problems caused by the cuff made my future with Sean even less certain.

I had no doubt that he'd considered selling the cuff to Jack. It had to have been an attractive prospect, at least at first. If Jack put the cuff on Lily Anderson and bound her and Sean together for life, Sean was no longer a rival for my affections. Hard on the heels of that thought must have been the realization that if word got out that Jack had obtained the cuff from Charles, it would torpedo once and for all any chance of me ever being interested in him.

At the same time, he couldn't just keep the cuff hidden until Sean died. If the other members of the Court or the Were Ruling Council discovered Charles caused Sean's death, either directly or indirectly, there would be hell to pay and the Court wouldn't protect him. They'd throw him to the wolves, quite literally.

So he'd arrived at the only logical conclusion: a business transaction. A drink of my blood for the cuff. I get what I want, Charles gets what he wants, Sean lives, and because I wouldn't be putting the cuff on—or so he believed—Charles's plans to add me to his collection were coming along nicely.

He might suspect I had figured some of this out, but his surprise at my reference to his earlier bite told me he hadn't credited me with deciphering his motives. My advantage was my past as a prisoner of my grandfather's cabal, where there were plots within plots within plots and no one's motivations were simple. Charles was very, very good at 12-D chess, but so was I, as he was about to find out. Magic and sarcasm weren't my only weapons.

"I confess you are correct," he said, choosing to acknowledge that I'd accurately assumed he wanted to share the intimacy of his bite with me. "While I found your blood sweeter than any wine I have ever tasted, and the power of your magic strengthened me more than I could have imagined, I found the experience unsatisfying. In some circumstances, a vampire's bite is not merely for sustenance. You are as far from a food source as could be, Alice. For me, you are a joy."

Time to negotiate. "Then let's come to an agreement. You will hand over the cuff to me, with no strings attached. In return, you may bite me and drink from me once, at a time of my choosing but within the month."

"Very well, but I will choose the time," Charles said. "I choose tonight, before I present you with the cuff."

I had expected that counteroffer, but I pretended to be insulted. "Do you think I'll go back on my word?"

"Not at all, but I strongly suspect that the wolf will object most strenuously to our agreement and I think you will agree that it would be much easier for all concerned if our transaction is completed prior to his recovery."

I couldn't disagree with that. "All right; agreed. You can bite my wrist."

He smiled. "My terms are for your throat only. On this I will not negotiate."

Again, not a surprise, but I didn't accept right away. It was time to play a very big card. "In return for biting my throat, you will not bring any pleasure with your bite."

His poker face disappeared. I saw surprise, anger, concern, and dismay before he managed to get his mask back in place.

He'd counted on the intense pleasure of the bite to make it intimate, and he certainly hadn't thought I would figure that out and refuse it. I knew very well, though not from my own experience, that a vampire could bring their food source to climax with a bite, and it would not have surprised me in the least if Charles had planned to do that to me.

I was willing to trade a bite and pint for the cuff and let it be a business transaction, but I wouldn't allow Charles to give me an orgasm. The bite was intimate enough. At the moment, there was only one person who was allowed to see and share my pleasure, and that was Sean.

"If there is no pleasure, there will be only pain," Charles said finally. "I do not wish to hurt you."

He'd hurt me plenty by keeping his knowledge of the cuff a secret, but it would do no good to point that out. That was in the past and dwelling on it would not help me negotiate with him now.

"Those are my terms, Charles. One bite, right now, on my throat, with no pleasure. You will not attempt to turn me. I will stay fully dressed. Then you will hand over the cuff and allow me to leave without any delay. You will do me no harm, physical or otherwise, other than the bite. And though it goes without saying, any attempt to deviate from our terms will end very badly for you."

His face darkened. "I have never reneged on an agreement, Alice, and I do not intend to start now."

"Good. Then we have a deal?"

"We do."

"Shall we drink on it?"

"Indeed." Charles rose and moved to the bar. He selected a glass and poured two fingers of Scotch.

While his back was turned, I entertained a brief fantasy of reaching into my boot, pulling out the stake I'd hidden inside, and planting it right in his lying, scheming heart. My fingers itched. I tapped them on the arm of my chair and put the fantasy aside...for now.

He brought me my glass and picked up his own. "To you. A masterful negotiation."

I rose and tapped the rim of my glass to his. "And to you, for a masterful scheme."

We drank.

For all of my careful negotiations, I had overlooked one detail: where Charles would administer his bite. That would teach me to think I could ever completely outmaneuver a vampire. I'd thought he'd given in on the no-pleasure debate too quickly; perhaps now I knew why.

I'd planned to sit on one of the sofas in the office while he bit me. Unfortunately, since I hadn't made that part of our agreed-upon terms, we had to hash it out after the fact, which meant I had little bargaining power when push came to shove on the topic of location.

As a result, we ended up in bed.

Actually, *on* a bed, and not Charles's own, not that he hadn't tried his damnedest to talk me into doing precisely that.

He escorted me to one of the mansion's many guest rooms. Before I surrendered to the inevitable, as it were, I took a moment to "compose myself" in the adjoining bathroom while Charles presumably set the mood.

I ran water in the sink while I let Malcolm out of my earring and gave him instructions on what to do if Charles deviated from the terms we'd agreed upon—up to and including the separation of his head from his body if he tried to turn me. I was ninety-nine percent certain he wouldn't attempt it, but if he did, I wanted to make sure it didn't happen.

Malcolm, needless to say, was extremely unhappy about the entire situation. He'd already voiced his objections back at home, so he had nothing to add now except to glare in the direction of the bedroom. Even my assurance that I was fine with the way our negotiations had turned out wasn't enough to lessen his anger at Charles. I figured I'd be hearing about all this later too.

I washed my hands, turned the light off, and opened the bathroom door.

I'd half-expected Charles to have changed into a silk robe and turned the room into a candlelit, rose-petal-strewn love nest while I'd been in the bathroom. Indeed, he'd turned off the overhead light in favor of a bedside Tiffany lamp that cast a rosy glow, but there were no candles and no actual roses. Nor was he undressed, other than he'd removed his suit jacket and tie and draped them neatly over the back of a chair. His shoes waited next to the bed.

He stood in his socks, collar unbuttoned and hands behind his back, as I emerged from the bathroom. At my surprise, the corners of his mouth turned up. "You were expecting something quite different?"

"I wasn't expecting you to be wearing checkered socks."

He glanced at his feet. "I do allow myself a bit of whimsy on occasion."

"You're on a slippery slope with this, Charles. Today, it's checkered socks. Tomorrow, who knows, a polka-dot bow tie?"

"I said whimsy, Alice, not lunacy." He gestured grandly at the bed. "Please, be comfortable."

I intended to stay fully dressed, but I couldn't bring myself to put my dirty boots on the very expensive-looking comforter. I unzipped them and steadied myself against one of the bedposts as I toed them off. I wasn't exactly stalling, but I didn't rush the process either.

With my boots lying beside Charles's shoes on the floor, I sat on the side of the bed. "Okay, I'm ready."

"You should lie down," Charles advised gently. "If you remain sitting up, you may faint."

That was a fair point. Feeling self-conscious, I swung my feet up onto the bed and lay back, my head resting on a pillow as light and airy as a cloud. The comforter was silk and velvet and somehow almost as weightless as the pillow. I lay with my arms at my sides and spine as straight as a board, my gaze fixed on the ceiling.

His eyes glowing softly, Charles walked around to the other side of the bed. He moved like silk himself, somehow making the climb onto and across the bed look elegant instead of awkward. Despite everything, my heart raced as he lay down at my side.

I cursed my failure to think about where he would want to be while he bit me and returned my gaze to the ceiling. Trying to slow my heart rate, I pictured myself standing in an ice-cold shower while someone read me baseball scores.

He chuckled. "A cold shower, Alice?"

Too late, I realized I might have been focusing a little *too* hard on that image. "Damn it, Charles, stay out of my head," I snapped.

"You broadcast your thoughts," he countered. "I made no attempt to eavesdrop, as you call it."

"Whatever. Let's just do this." I turned my face away.

Carefully, he used his fingertips to turn my head back. "I am open to renegotiating our terms," he said quietly. "Specifically, your edict that I cannot mitigate the pain of the bite. I have not bitten anyone in such a way in a very long time. I told you that I do not wish to hurt you, and I spoke the truth."

He might truly not want to hurt me, but he was willing to do so to get what he wanted. I would not have expected any different. "You've seen the scars on my back. You know I'm no stranger to pain."

His eyes darkened. "If I ever encounter the person or persons who inflicted those wounds on you, I will show them their own entrails before they die. I have no desire to be remembered in the same category as your past tormentors."

I kept my mind carefully blank so Charles didn't catch any stray memories or thoughts of Moses. "I offered you my throat, Charles. It's not the same category at all." I turned my head again. "Please just bite me and let's get this over with. I have a life to save."

He brushed hair back from my neck and leaned close, his lips cool against my skin. My pulse raced and I knew he could sense my blood rushing millimeters away from his fangs. I shivered.

"Sweet Alice," he murmured, and bit me.

The pain of his fangs piercing my skin made my vision go white. I managed not to cry out but I couldn't do anything about my flinch. He held me still so I didn't jerk away and tear my own flesh.

The agony did not lessen; if anything, it increased. My chest heaved and my breathing became ragged, almost like sobs. I felt a strange pulling sensation in the midst of the pain and realized Charles was drinking.

The pain was so great that I almost told him I'd changed my mind about the pleasure, but I pictured Sean and that killed the impulse. If I could withstand hours of torture by a blood mage, I could hold up under a few minutes of pain from a vampire bite, or had I grown weak? The fear that I'd become cowardly was enough to banish all thoughts of asking him to ease the pain.

Charles made a sound low in his throat. I'd heard it once or twice before, a kind of sensual growl. I realized my body was responding in a very unexpected way to the pain of his bite. Whether my arousal was a result of his or vice-versa, no amount of imagining a cold shower had any effect on the growing heat between my legs.

At first, I thought he'd broken his word and given me pleasure, but there was nothing but pain. I'd always liked a little pain with my pleasure—sometimes more than a little—but this was the first time I'd become so aroused by pain alone. I'd experienced agony before and never had this reaction.

Unless it was Charles I was reacting to.

I banished the thought as quickly as it popped into my head. We were lying in bed and he was drinking my blood. It was by definition an intimate act and it had triggered an automatic response. There was nothing more to it than that.

Then why was my hand on his, where it rested on my hip?

I wanted to let go of him, but I couldn't. My hand wouldn't obey; instead, my fingers tightened around his and he made that low sound again. Dimly, I realized the pain had indeed diminished as endorphins kicked in and my arousal grew. I couldn't stifle a moan. His hand squeezed my hip, though I had long since stopped struggling to get away.

I lost track of time as he drank, drifting in and out of awareness and caught between pain and pleasure. It was something of a surprise when his fangs slid out of my flesh. His cool tongue laved my neck, cleaning up the blood that trickled from the bite and healing the punctures. I realized then that I'd forgotten a second item while negotiating. Vampires often branded their cattle by leaving visible bite marks. Charles had healed the wound of his own accord.

I sensed my magic coursing through his body, blending with his own. He would be stronger for a time because of it. More importantly, my influence over him increased as well, and that would not fade away. It shifted the balance of power between us ever so slightly in my favor—another reason I'd been willing to make this trade.

Finally, he raised his head. His eyes were deep black. He looked fully sated, his skin slightly pink. He was also quite aroused, but so was I, so I couldn't fault him for it. To his credit, he kept a little space between us and ignored the visible evidence of his excitement.

I wanted to get up and leave, but I couldn't, not just yet. Not until I thought I could stand up without falling.

He took my warm hand in his cool one. "Your blood tasted slightly of whisky."

"I wondered why you gave me a glass of that fifty-year single malt to seal our agreement. Now I understand." My voice was stronger than I would have expected, all things considered.

We stared at each other. I wondered if he would mention my reaction to his bite.

Instead, he raised my hand to his lips and kissed it. "I would give you the world, if you would take it from me."

"I don't want the world," I said, pulling my hand out of his grip. "I've been offered that before and turned it down. It would never be worth the price I'd have to pay."

"Perhaps the price is negotiable. You drive a hard bargain, as they say. I have no doubt you would come out the winner."

"I highly doubt I would." I pushed myself up until I was sitting. I had a moment of lightheadedness and then it passed.

Charles watched as I swung my legs over the side of the bed, picked up my boots, and put them on. When I started to stand, he rose and moved vamp-fast around to my side. "Slowly," he cautioned me.

"It ain't my first rodeo with blood loss," I told him. I lowered my feet to the floor and carefully stood.

He cupped my face with his hand. "You should eat a meal and drink water. May I call for some food?"

"No, thank you. I have to be going." I pushed his hand away. "Can I have the cuff, please?"

"It is on its way. I can have a light meal here in moments."

"I really don't have time. Sean's dying, remember? I'm in a bit of a rush."

"What will you do with the cuff once you have it?"

"Whatever I have to do to save Sean."

He studied me. "Perhaps it would best not to disclose how you came into possession of the cuff. I am sure you can concoct a reasonable explanation for obtaining it that does not mention my name."

"I'm sure I can."

Someone knocked at the door. I suspected it was Bryan, and when the door opened, I found I was right.

He didn't look surprised or relieved, so I assumed Charles had already told him that I was fine. He carried a wooden box with runes inscribed on all six sides.

Charles took the box and handed it to me. "The spellwork hides the contents from tracking spells until the box is opened. As such, you should not open the box until you reach your destination."

At my raised eyebrow, he sighed. "I give you my word the cuff is in the box."

"Good." I picked up my messenger bag and put the box inside it. I touched my right earring, as if checking to make sure it was still there. At that prearranged signal, Malcolm jumped into the earring.

With my ghost safely stashed, I turned to Charles. "I'll be in touch."

"I have no doubt we will speak again soon." He glanced at Bryan. "Please escort Alice to her car."

"Yes, sir." Bryan headed for the door. "Miss Alice, please follow me."

I headed for the door. At the threshold, I paused and turned back. Charles was watching me, standing in his checkered socks next to the rumpled bed.

I didn't thank him, nor did I tell him what a bastard he was for keeping the information about the cuff from me. He knew how I felt and that I wouldn't forget or forgive what he'd done anytime soon. He didn't tell me he didn't think I'd put the cuff on, or that he wouldn't forget my reaction to his bite. Everything we didn't say hung in the air between us.

"Good night, Charles," I said finally.

"Good night, Alice."

I followed Bryan into the hall and closed the door behind me.

20

About ninety minutes later, scrubbed clean and wearing different clothes, I pulled up in front of another enormous gate and rolled down my window.

A black-clad Court enforcer approached my vehicle. "Ms. Worth, what brings you to Northbourne tonight?"

I recognized him. "Hello, Carlos. I'd like to see Valas."

"Do you have an appointment?"

He knew very well I didn't, or I'd have been expected. "No, I don't, but I have with me the only way to save Sean Maclin's life and if I don't see her, he'll die."

He got a faraway look that told me he was speaking to someone telepathically. I waited.

The metal barricades in front of the gate retracted into the ground and the gate began to swing open. "Proceed directly to the main entrance," he instructed me. "Someone will meet you there."

I thanked him and passed through the gate. Northbourne's driveway was nearly a quarter of a mile long. As I drove, my earring buzzed reassuringly, reminding me that I was not going into Northbourne alone.

I'd let Malcolm out when we got home. To his credit, he'd said nothing about what he'd seen and heard while Charles was drinking from me. Instead, he asked me if I was sure I was going through with my "crazy" plan to ask Valas for help. When I said yes, he told me in no uncertain terms that he was coming along. I surprised him by readily agreeing. If any part of my plan did go sideways, I might need his help just to survive.

While I showered, I'd sent Malcolm to do a quick check on Sean's condition. He reported that Sean was weak but aware enough that when Malcolm got near him he raised his head slightly and appeared to hear the ghost when he spoke. Malcolm told the wolf that I was coming and that he needed to hang on. The wolf seemed to understand.

He'd also overheard Jack shouting at someone on the phone, a mage he'd hired to locate the other cuff. The hired mage wasn't having any luck. According to Malcolm,

Jack and Delia were discussing whether I had the cuff and had found some way of hiding it from anyone else. That was uncomfortably accurate. They were debating whether to come to my house looking for it when Malcolm jumped home to warn me that we'd better get moving.

Ahead loomed Northbourne, the headquarters of the Vampire Court of the Northwestern United States. The estate had once belonged to a shipping magnate. The Court had renovated it into a fortress that was part residence, part courthouse, part magic workshop, and part prison. Though Valas was the only member of the Court who resided there full time, the others had apartments where they stayed when they needed additional security or when their Court duties required them to be close at hand.

From what I understood, Valas had not left Northbourne in years. How many was a matter of conjecture, but the consensus was that she did not pass its gate except on the rarest of occasions.

I was hoping that tonight would be one of those occasions.

When I parked in front of the estate's wide front steps, a Court enforcer I didn't recognize opened my door. "Ms. Worth, this way, please."

We entered Northbourne's enormous main lobby, with its marble floor, soaring rotunda, and sweeping grand staircase. The enforcer led me to the right of the stairs and down a long hall lined with artwork. I'd never been down this corridor before.

"What's your name?" I asked, scurrying to keep up with his long strides.

He looked straight ahead. "Hanson, like the band."

"There's a band called Hanson?"

A pause. "Never mind."

"Okay. Where are we headed, Hanson?"

"You asked to see Valas. We are going to her audience chamber."

Of course Valas had an audience chamber.

At the end of the hallway we encountered a pair of doors. Hanson paused outside, presumably asking permission to enter. After a moment, he turned the handles and swung them open.

The room was less ostentatious than I had imagined, but it still made Charles's home office look like a broom closet by comparison. High above us, the chandelier glowed dimly, leaving the room in near darkness. Two large chairs sat in front of an enormous stone fireplace. Despite the warm night, a fire burned in the fireplace. A long and very heavy-looking conference table ringed with ornately carved chairs took up a good part of the other side of the room. The large open area in between must be for gatherings or ceremonies. The deep carpet seemed to swallow my boots.

I expected to be led to the conference table. Instead, Hanson directed me to sit in one of the chairs by the fire. I wondered at this choice of seating. The conference table signaled a business meeting; the chairs, a cozy fireside chat. I doubted my conversation with Valas would be anything close to cozy.

I perched on the edge of the chair. "Shouldn't I stand and wait for Valas?"

Before Hanson could reply, a familiar voice answered from the shadows. "I do not think you care much for such proprieties."

Hanson bowed in the direction of the voice. "Madame Valas, Ms. Worth."

I rose as the tall, slim vampire seemed to appear out of the shadows themselves. Her long, straight black hair framed her hawklike face. Tonight, she wore a floor-length midnight-blue dress. Her slippered feet made no noise as she crossed the floor.

The one and only time I had met her before now was when I gave a progress report to the entire Court during my investigation into the West-Addison harnad. At that time, I'd been some twenty feet away, far enough that I hadn't sensed her dark magic until she wished for me to do so—and then she almost crushed me with it, or tried to.

Tonight, as she sat in the chair across from me, her power felt like I was standing too near an open furnace. As she was perfectly capable of containing her magic behind her shields, I assumed she was reminding me, and none too subtly, of her power.

"Please sit," Valas said graciously, indicating my chair.

It was a far cry from the last time, when she'd used her power to drop me into a chair like a marionette with its strings cut. She'd been trying to make a point then. Tonight, she'd agreed to see me without an appointment. I must have piqued her interest when we'd met before, or perhaps my reference to saving Sean's life had been intriguing. Either way, I had my audience. Now I had to make it count.

Unlike Charles and Niara and every other vamp I'd ever encountered, the head of the Court had not one scent but many. She was ancient. Before I'd met her, I'd heard she was at least a thousand years old, but her power felt much older than that. Her accent sounded vaguely Middle Eastern or eastern European. I had not been able to identify her accent, probably because the language she had spoken when alive no longer existed.

"You have come to me for help," she said without preamble.

When I started to object, she raised her hand. "Ms. Worth, your situation is a desperate one. You have obtained the cuff that is the mate to the one currently draining the life from your lover, but his beta, Jack Hastings, has declared you *persona non grata*. You cannot reach him without risking great harm to yourself or members of his pack. All this is known to me. What I do not know is why you have come to me, or what you believe I can or will do to assist you. The Court, as you know, cannot interfere in a pack matter."

It would appear there was little I could tell Valas that she didn't already know. "If no one knew or suspected anyone from the Court was involved, you'd have nothing to worry about in that regard."

She raised an imperious eyebrow. "Perhaps that is true, but again I ask: why would I risk war with the Were Ruling Council to help you?"

"Because Sean is a good alpha and the stability of his pack benefits the Court. Jack may have designs on taking Sean's position. You and I both know he'd make a very bad alpha. Their troubles will become your troubles sooner or later—probably sooner."

She regarded me. "He schemes to unite his pack with another through a mate bond with the daughter of another alpha."

"True, but there's no way that goes the way he wants it to. Sean loves me. He'll never accept Lily Anderson without making Jack pay dearly for what he's done."

Valas nodded slowly. "You fear for Maclin's life if he challenges Hastings."

"He's weakened because of the cuff, but he wouldn't let that stop him from challenging Jack for stranding me, barring me from seeing him, and trying to get the cuff before I could. Again, it's in the Court's best interest to do what it can to keep that from happening, even it means covertly helping me."

"Let us stipulate that I do not disagree with your assessment of the situation. I am still unclear as to what you want of me." She leaned forward, her eyes so dark that they seemed eternal. Her ancient scent enveloped me and the air became thick with power. "And I wonder, Alice, what you offer me in return."

Earlier, I sat across the table from Charles and painstakingly negotiated for possession of the cuff. Those stakes had been high, but I had prevailed.

For the second time in a single night, I opened negotiations with a vampire, with Sean's life—and mine—hanging in the balance.

The speeding car hit a pothole and the bone-jarring impact rattled my teeth.

"Perhaps your speed is excessive," my companion suggested, her hands folded neatly in her lap. "The road conditions do not appear ideal for your vehicle. Had I known, I would have insisted on taking a different mode of transportation."

"We're in stealth mode," I reminded her, narrowly avoiding another pothole as my car flew down the country road. "The Court SUVs and limos might have better suspensions, but they aren't stealthy. I promise we'll get there in one piece."

"Do humans find that comment reassuring?" Valas asked. "'In one piece' could mean many things."

I slowed as a couple of deer ran across the road. "Generally it's meant to be somewhat tongue-in-cheek."

"Ah, a form of sarcasm. I see." She nodded and continued looking out the window, studying the houses and empty fields as we passed.

My navigation app informed me that we were a little over a mile away from our destination. "We're getting close. I'll park a little ways up the road and we can go in on foot."

"You will park directly in front of the residence," she told me. "Additional 'stealth' will not be required."

"Are you sure?"

The scent of lost empires filled my car, indicating her displeasure. "You will trust and obey."

I wasn't very good at doing either of those things, but I didn't have a hell of a lot of choice in the matter. "Okay," I said, hoping I sounded more certain than I felt.

Ahead in the darkness, I saw a two-story house set back from road. Despite it being the middle of the night, all the lights were on. Almost a dozen trucks, SUVs, and cars were parked out front. It looked like the whole damn pack was at Jack and Delia's. That was a lot of werewolves to wade through.

Hoping Valas was right about not needing to sneak up on the house, I turned into the driveway. There were so many other vehicles already here that the only empty space was directly in front of the garage, blocking in a large truck I assumed was Jack's. I parked and turned off the car, leaving the key in the ignition in case I had to leave quickly. I got out, put my messenger bag on my shoulder, and listened.

The house was eerily quiet. I expected pack meetings to be loud events, but I heard nothing but nighttime insects and the wind.

"We must go inside," Valas said, closing her door. She'd opted to wear the same long blue dress to come with me to Jack's house. My suggestion that she change into something less formal had been met with an imperious stare.

I headed for the front door with Valas behind me. Perhaps it would have made more sense to send the immortal and immensely powerful vampire in first, given we might be walking into a den of very angry werewolves, but hiding behind someone else had never been my style. It was bad enough that I'd had to ask for her help; I wasn't going to cower behind her too.

I opened the door, stopped, and stared.

The front room was a large formal living space. Beyond it, through a wide arched doorway, I saw a family room. I counted well over a dozen men and women—most or all of the adults in Sean's pack—in the two rooms.

And they were all unconscious.

"What did you do?" I breathed.

"What you requested that I do." Valas moved past me into the house and closed the door behind us. "You wished to get to your lover without confronting members of his pack and to execute your plan without their interference. This was the easiest and most efficient way to accomplish both."

Jack, Delia, Ben, and Nan were in the front room, along with an older man and woman I didn't recognize. In the family room I found Karen, Felicia, Felicia's brother David, and several others. Some were sprawled on the floor, others slumped over in chairs or sofas. Jack, Delia, and Ben seemed to be in a tight group in the middle of the living room, as if they had been standing close to each other, perhaps arguing, when Valas's magic had hit and dropped them where they stood.

One pack member who was conspicuously absent was Caleb. I wondered if Jack had decided it was best to keep the volatile young werewolf far away from such a stressful and emotional situation. I hated to agree with Jack on anything, but it was probably the right call.

I became aware of a strange keening sound drifting up from below. By the time my brain processed what it was, I was already in motion, headed for a door just off the enormous kitchen. I flung the door open and ran down the stairs.

Patrick, Karen's brother, lay unconscious on the floor near the foot of the stairs. I stopped short when I realized Jack and Delia's basement was large and unfinished—an enormous, nearly empty concrete space that was straight out of my dream.

The wolf, however, was not in a glass cage. It was made of steel and looked like the sort used to hold lions or tigers. I shook myself and went to the cage.

The wolf stopped keening when I appeared. He'd apparently sensed the rest of the pack being spelled and dragged himself to the side of the cage to throw himself weakly against the bars. He'd been too feeble to injure himself very badly, for which I was grateful. He lay on his side, his golden eyes full of fury and pain.

"Sean, I'm here," I told him, my voice sounding choked. "I'm here, I'm here."

If the wolf understood what I was saying, he didn't react except for a heartbreaking whine. I went to open the door of the cage, but it was padlocked.

The wolf raised his head and growled. I turned to find Valas right behind me. I hadn't heard her come down the stairs.

She held out a key. "From the pocket of the beta. He did not entrust it to this one." She nodded at Patrick. "He is a poor beta if he mistrusts his pack. As an alpha, he would spell disaster. You were correct in coming to me with this matter."

"You got all that from a key?"

"Much can be learned from apparent trifles. Go to your wolf."

I took the key and unlocked the padlock. The wolf raised his head as I opened the door and entered the cage.

"Don't try to get up. Save your strength," I told him.

He settled back but kept a wary eye on Valas as I knelt beside him. She stayed outside the cage, watching us.

I buried my face in the wolf's fur and drank in his scent. There was a part of me that had worried I would never smell him again, never hold him in my arms in either form. I realized my face was wet with tears. It was a hell of a thing to care about someone so much that it gave you pain to see them hurt.

"I'm here. I'm here." I repeated the words like a mantra. It still didn't feel real to be reunited with Sean. The situation had seemed so hopeless only hours ago, until I'd discovered Charles had the cuff.

"Ms. Worth, I cannot hold the spell indefinitely, and there is other magic to be done that will require a great deal of power. We must not delay."

I let myself hold the wolf for a little longer before I sat up. I opened my messenger bag and took out the box that held the second cuff.

"If you wish to change our plans, you must do so now," Valas told me. "There will be no going back. Only death will remove the cuff."

"I never go back." I wiped my tears away and set the box in my lap. "The only way is forward."

I opened the box. The spellwork that hid the box's contents from tracking spells broke when I lifted the lid. Inside the wooden box was a second box identical to the one that had held the cuff now affixed to the wolf's front leg. I opened that box and found the second cuff inside. Charles had indeed kept his word.

I picked up the cuff. Golden magic pulsed.

The wolf raised his head and gave a short yip. I couldn't tell if it was concern, a question, or a warning.

I lowered my face to his. "You have to trust me. It's the only way to save you. We'll be okay. I know what I'm doing."

Charles had bet I wouldn't put the cuff on. He'd been so certain of it that he'd handed it over without an ounce of hesitation. I guess he didn't know me quite as well as he thought.

I slid the cuff onto my right forearm. The cold metal made me shiver. I sensed shifter magic, but it was dormant. I wasn't a shifter, so the cuff didn't react.

The wolf whined.

"The only way is forward," I whispered, and touched my cuff to his. "*Este comparia*."

The cuff closed tightly around my wrist. My world turned gold. Shifter magic seared my skin, traveling through my bones. I threw my head back and screamed. Beside me, the wolf raised his head and howled.

The magic was pure golden power. It pulsed between the wolf and me and filled me up, igniting every cell and synapse. The wolf staggered to his feet. I wondered if the magic was having the same effect on him. I hoped so. He would need every bit of strength he could get.

Then I felt the pack.

The pack bonds were like doors opening in my head. I sensed Jack, Delia, Ben, Nan, Felicia...one by one I became aware of them all. They were all still unconscious, except for two who weren't at the house: Caleb and one other. In those lying upstairs, I sensed an echo of fear, as if they'd had just enough time to realize what was happening before they lost consciousness.

I also sensed that they'd become aware, in a distant way, that something big had just happened. There was a kind of restlessness in their sleep and I wondered if Valas's spell was about to break.

A voice cut through the chaos in my head. *Alice, what have you done?* It was Charles. He sounded furious...and fearful. I had never heard fear from Charles before, not once in five years. Did he fear that he had lost me, or did he fear for my life?

I owed him no explanation and I had no time to waste; the wolves were beginning to stir. I shut the link between us and opened my eyes.

Valas knelt outside the cage. She'd closed the door but not locked it, shutting me inside with the wolf. He paced and growled, but not in anger. Through our new bond, I sensed confusion and wonder and fierce protectiveness.

Mate, the wolf said in my head, his voice a growl. *Mine*.

"Our time grows short," Valas said. "The spell is finished?"

"Yes." My eyes felt warm and I wondered if they were golden like Sean's. "The cuff's magic is complete. The bond is set."

"Remember our arrangement." Her eyes turned dark and the shadows gathered around her. "The terms we agreed upon must be fulfilled."

"I know what I agreed to. Now hold up your end of the bargain."

She smiled slightly. "You have no fear. I should like to know how you came to be so fearless."

Above us, in the house, I heard movement and voices. The werewolves were waking up.

"That's a story for another day." I met her ancient, fathomless eyes with my own. "Make it quick."

"As you wish." She reached through the bars and touched my chest.

Behind me, the wolf snarled and leaped at her, but it was too late.

Dark magic rose. My vision went black. My breathing ceased. My heart stopped. My thoughts became dust.

And I died.

21

I WAS NO STRANGER TO DEATH. I'D DIED A NUMBER OF TIMES UNDER TORTURE AT MY grandfather's cabal, only to be revived either by magic or medical intervention each time. The only thing that hurt worse than dying was coming back.

When I'd died after fighting Amelia Wharton and the *Kasten*, I had felt no pain, only serenity. My return to life was equally peaceful, like waking from a long sleep. Then I'd wandered alone in darkness for what felt like an eternity while my body lay in a coma in Charles's care.

My demise at Valas's hands was so fast that I scarcely had time to realize what was happening before it was over—which was, I supposed, the point of asking for a quick death. I had no idea what magic she used, but it was sharper and faster than the finest blade.

I woke much the same way, like a switch had been flipped from off to on.

As my senses came back online, I realized my ears were filled with the sound of howling. A dozen voices were raised in what could only be described as a chorus of grief. It was strangely beautiful. The sound was definitely wolf in nature, but something about the intonation made me think the howls came from human throats. That didn't seem possible, but I'd given up on the concepts of possible and impossible long ago.

"*Quiet!*" Sean thundered.

The howling cut off instantly.

Someone picked up my arm and pressed two fingers into my wrist, searching for a pulse. I felt a weight on my chest, as if they were listening for a heartbeat or for the sound of me breathing.

The weight lifted off my chest. "Alice, can you hear me?" The hope in Sean's voice made my heart hurt.

Speech seemed beyond my ability at the moment, but sensation was creeping back into my limbs and I could remember how to move.

I opened my eyes.

I heard several gasps and a voice I thought was Nan's whisper, "Thank God." Clearly we were not alone, but the only thing I cared about was the familiar face above mine and the red-rimmed golden eyes that stared back at me in disbelief.

And then Sean kissed me so hard, and for so long, that I almost passed out from lack of air.

When he finally raised his head, he smoothed my hair back and held my face in his hands. Neither of us spoke for a very long time. For me, it was enough to see him back in human form, and—I glanced at his bare arm to confirm it—without that damn cuff.

I became aware that we were still in the cage in Jack and Delia's basement and the entire pack was gathered around outside it, watching us in stunned silence. It felt like a punch in the stomach when I realized they'd all been howling over my death.

I didn't know I was crying until Sean used his thumbs to wipe away my tears. He kissed the tip of my nose. "My Alice," he murmured.

For the first time, I didn't feel weird when he said it, not even in front of an audience.

"I missed you." My voice sounded wispy, not surprising since I'd been stone-cold dead only moments ago.

He smiled. I loved the way his eyes crinkled when he smiled. "I missed you, too."

"Where are they?" I asked.

He figured out what I meant and hooked his thumb over his shoulder. "Over there, in their boxes, where they'll stay."

"What are you going to do with them?"

"I haven't decided. Maybe melt them down. Maybe put them in a safe, fill the safe with concrete, and then drop the safe over the side of a boat a hundred miles out into the Pacific."

That made me smile back at him. "It sounds like you've given this some thought."

"Trust me, I had a lot of time to think about how to dispose of those damn things." He pressed his forehead to mine the way I'd touched my face to the wolf's. His skin felt blazingly hot against mine. "I thought I'd lost you for good this time," he said roughly.

Before I had a chance to reply, someone spoke. "I believe the decision of what to do with those cuffs is something the pack should discuss." The speaker was behind me, but I recognized Jack's voice.

Sean's eyes blazed. He raised his head and shot Jack the deadliest stare I'd ever seen from him. His fury seared my skin and alpha power rose until the air crackled around us. "This topic is not open for debate." The words were clipped and full of warning.

It was a warning that went unheeded. "The cuffs are a source of enormous power," Jack said.

"The cuffs are a prison." Sean looked down at me. "Can you stand?"

It didn't matter if I could or couldn't; I was going to. Sean and I would face Jack together. "Yes."

He offered me his hand. I took it and he lifted me to my feet. Everything got a bit hazy and he steadied me by my upper arms until my ears stopped ringing and I could see clearly again. He was naked, but nudity mattered little to werewolves, especially in front of the pack.

When I was standing on my own, he opened the door of the cage and ushered me out. I made it one slow step at a time, letting him half-support me with one arm around my waist. I was happy that Sean seemed to have recovered from his ordeal. If he felt any weakness or shakiness, I couldn't see it. The power we'd shared after I put on the cuff must have helped him regain his strength.

Valas was long gone. Her part in this was over. Whatever the magic was that killed me and then resurrected me once the cuff fell off, she hadn't needed to be physically present for it to finish its work. All that remained was for me to fulfill my obligations to her. I put aside thoughts of our bargain until this mess was cleaned up.

Nan pushed her way through the group and met us just outside the cage door. I thought she was there to greet Sean, but instead she put her arms around me and squeezed gently. "Alice."

I returned her hug a bit awkwardly. "Hey, Nan."

She released me and smiled tearfully up at Sean. He smiled back briefly. His expression hardened as Jack moved to the front of the group. For the first time since I woke up, I got a good look at the beta's face.

Four faint scars cut across the left side of his face, slashing diagonally like someone had clawed him exactly how and where I had in my dream. With their ability to heal it was rare to see a shifter with scars, but wounds left by magic were the hardest to heal completely, as the scars on my back could attest. It didn't seem possible that I had inflicted physical harm on him in a dream, but what other explanation could there be?

While I was processing that, Sean stepped forward to meet Jack toe-to-toe. Jack had a couple of inches and maybe twenty pounds on Sean, but Sean still seemed larger somehow.

"Where did those scars come from?" Sean asked.

Jack jerked his head at me. "Ask *her*."

Sean glanced my way. "Alice?"

Maybe they would be able to explain how it happened. "Last night I had a dream that I was here speaking to your wolf. Jack attacked me in the dream. I slashed his face in self-defense. I had no idea it was anything but just a dream until now."

"You found a way to use the pack bonds against us," Jack snarled at me. "I was defending our pack."

"I wasn't attacking you or anyone else in the pack. I didn't even do it on purpose. I was asleep."

"It shouldn't be possible for you to contact Sean through the pack bonds," Ben said, moving to stand next to Sean and Jack. "You're human and you're not his mate—not yet, anyway."

I raised my hand and concentrated. Golden magic ran along my fingertips. "I'm no ordinary human." I'd only just learned how to use shifter magic, but they didn't need to know that.

My simple demonstration had a seismic effect on the pack. On the faces of those I knew, I saw astonishment, wonder, and happiness. Several others seemed equally pleased. The older couple whose names I didn't know exchanged a glance. Jack, of course, only grew angrier.

Delia stepped out of the group to stand next to her husband. The look she gave me was pure venom. "So she knows a few magic tricks. That doesn't make her worthy of you *or* the pack, and it sure as hell doesn't give her the right to wear the cuff."

"Watch yourself," Sean warned. "A month ago, Alice risked her life to save Felicia from the West-Addison harnad. She just died for me and the pack. Everyone here is in her debt, twice over."

"She doesn't look dead to me," Delia retorted. "It was just some cheap stunt, Sean. She's trying to trick you and all of us."

"You felt her die, Delia," Ben said. "We all did. That was no stunt. I don't know how she did it; maybe she'll tell us someday. But the fact of the matter is, she was dead for close to seven minutes in order to free Sean from that cuff."

Holy shit, seven minutes? Not only had I been dead, I'd started going cold before the damn cuffs fell off and Valas brought me back. That wasn't mostly dead; that was *all the way* dead. Hearing news like that was enough to make me need a stiff drink or three.

I wondered if the cuffs had been spelled to wait a certain amount of time before falling off to prevent someone from doing what I'd just done. I felt a bit smug that I'd tricked that blasted shifter magic.

"Our pack would benefit from those cuffs," Jack told Sean. "If the right people wore them, we'd be stronger. Faster. More stable. Our dominance over the other packs would be beyond questioning. You felt the power, all of you." He turned his bright amber stare on the others. "Tell me you don't all want that power for our pack."

No one spoke at first. Several of them exchanged glances, even Felicia, Karen, and David. I remembered the power too, how it filled me and made me feel like I could face anything or anyone, as if my magic was endless.

Power like that was a drug; I'd learned that the hard way. Once you got a taste of it, you could never have enough. You'd kill for it, betray anyone and everyone, inflict unimaginable suffering to get more. My grandfather was a prime example. So were Adelbert and the *Kasten* and the harnad blood mages John West and Spencer Addison. Even I had felt a taste of that desire for power when I'd been injected with the drug Black Fire and experienced what it was like to have so much magic that my body couldn't even contain it all.

Sean wanted his pack to be safe and strong. Jack wanted power and to bring other packs to heel. That and his lack of compassion would make him a disastrous alpha.

Karen spoke. "Not if it means locking those cuffs on Sean and his mate." Her voice was quiet but firm.

Jack glared at her, but then Nan said, "Not if Sean says it's the wrong choice for us."

Ben joined in. "Not if the purpose of that power is to subjugate anyone else."

Karen's brother Patrick spoke up. "Power like that will only end up destroying us."

One by one the rest of the pack shook their heads, leaving Jack and Delia alone in their desire to use the cuffs.

"You got your discussion," Sean told Jack. He addressed the rest of the pack. "While I'm glad to hear that almost everyone is in agreement, the decision about what to do about the cuffs is mine to make, with Alice's input because there is magic involved and because she has earned the right to have a say."

Jack's anger was still palpable, but he said nothing. His silence worried me. Delia tried to stare me down, but she couldn't hold my gaze for more than a few seconds before she looked away.

"Everyone, please go upstairs so I can speak to Alice privately," Sean said. "Those who need to leave may do so. Ben, I'd like you to stay, and Karen too."

"I'll tell Cole I'll be a bit longer," she said. "It's no problem."

"I'll stay," Ben added. "I'll let Casey know not to wait up."

The pack headed for the stairs. Karen squeezed my hand as she passed.

When the door closed behind Ben, leaving us alone in the basement, Sean rubbed his face and turned to me. "Where do things stand with Kent Stevens?"

I might have known that would be his first question. "He's dead."

He stilled. "Alice, tell me you didn't use yourself as bait."

"It was a Court-run operation. I was safe—"

"Don't lie to me, Alice. Not about this."

I was starting to feel a little wobbly. Being dead could take a lot out of you. I glanced at the couch. "Can we sit, please?"

We moved to the couch and sat. "Tell me what happened," he said.

I told him the whole story, from when Arkady picked me up at the storage unit through Stevens getting munched by the garden. He inspected my arm and hip and saw for himself that the wounds were healed.

He got up and paced, his anger prickling on my arms. "You knew I didn't want you to do that. It was the Court's responsibility to catch him. It should have been Vaughan out there, not you."

"Stevens escaped me too, that first day at Mike Robinson's house," I reminded him. "And as long as it was my life on the line, that made it my responsibility to help catch him. Do I think Charles should have been the bait? Yes, but that wasn't my call. It was Valas who decided he needed to stay sequestered. I don't know why, and they're not likely to tell me."

When he didn't reply, I added, "I needed him caught or dead, Sean. I knew that cuff was hurting you and I couldn't save you and watch out for him too. I couldn't do what I needed to do to help you with bodyguards dogging my every step. I was tired of waiting."

"Do you think it was easy for me to wait it out on the sidelines?" he demanded. "Don't you know how badly I wanted to find Stevens and tear him apart for hurting you?"

"Of course I did; that's why I took care of it. You have enough trouble with Jack and the cuffs without having to worry about Stevens and me too."

He spun around to face me, his eyes bright and furious. "Alice, damn it, do you think I couldn't handle Stevens *and* my own pack? You're always reminding me that you're a high-level mage and I should treat you as one, but you don't treat me as an alpha. You keep thinking that you have to protect me. It's not just an insult; it diminishes me in front of my pack and in the eyes of others, from the vampires to the Were Ruling Council."

Shocked, I said, "I never meant it as an insult or to make you look weak."

"Of course you didn't. You're too busy thinking that you have to save everyone and protect everyone. I love that about you, but sometimes there are other considerations beyond your compulsive need to throw yourself on every grenade."

Still angry, he returned to the couch and touched my face. I leaned into the warmth of his hand. Finally, he exhaled. "You put on the matching cuff and then died for seven minutes so we'd both be free of them. I want to be angry with you for doing that, but I can't. Just tell me it was the only way."

I covered his hand with mine. "It was the only way."

"Whatever magic you used to kill and then resurrect yourself, you could have used it on me."

I realized then that he had no idea that Valas had been here. Had she wiped his memory somehow, or had he not been aware of her presence?

"The hell I could," I snapped. "As if I would ever have done that to you."

"Yet you have no problem doing it to yourself." He shook his head. "All right. Now explain how you found the second cuff."

This was the part I had been dreading. "After Kim Dade, the Court researcher, found out there was a matching cuff, I did some research online and found an expert in shifter magic who had a tracking spell. I found out that it was here, in the city."

He read my expression. "Tell me what you're not telling me, Alice."

"Charles had the cuff."

His face was like a glacier. "Did he know all along?"

"He suspected there was a second cuff and tried to find it before I did so he could sell the set to whichever pack would pay him the most. He only found out last night, just before we set the trap for Kent Stevens, that without it you would die. As soon as that was over, he had Kim call me with the news."

"And how long did he have the second cuff?"

"Since this morning, he said. The second the sun set tonight, I went to get it from him."

Sean leaned forward and inhaled.

Shocked and furious, I jumped up and nearly fell when a wave of dizziness made me grab for the arm of the couch. "What did you think, that I had sex with Charles to get the cuff?"

He shook his head. "I didn't think that, but there is no way in hell Vaughan gave you that cuff without getting something big in return." He read my eyes and his expression went flat. "He bit you."

"Sean—"

He stood, his hands balled into fists and fury rolling off him in waves. "The first time he bit you, it was an unforgivable violation—you said so yourself. And now you let him bite you again?"

He turned and punched the door of what turned out to be a storage closet. He pulled his fist out and punched it again, demolishing it completely.

"Sean, hear me out. I knew that was what he wanted and I was ready to negotiate. He drank from me, but it was just a bite, nothing else. We were fully dressed. I didn't allow him to give me any pleasure with the bite. It was nothing but...nothing but pain for me. When it was done, he handed over the cuff and I left. It was a business transaction."

No answer.

His silence infuriated me. "Damn it, you were *dying*. I had no choice."

He spun around, his eyes flashing fire, but I kept talking. "It was nothing but a bite and a pint of blood. You would have done the same for me, if our roles were reversed. Look me in the eye and tell me you wouldn't."

"That would be different."

I put my hands on my hips. "How would it be different? Because you're a man, or because you're an alpha?"

He ran his hands through his hair. I'd just caught him in a double standard and he knew it. "You are a high-level mage and an associate of the pack. You are not just some vampire's meal."

"No, I'm not a meal. I've never allowed any vampire to bite me, not ever. I've been offered sums of money that you wouldn't believe. Gifts fit for kings. I turned them all down. But I did this *for you*, because..." I stopped.

"Because why, Alice?" he asked. "Tell me why."

"Because the thought of losing you was more than I could bear. Because Charles thought he had me right where he wanted me and I showed him he was wrong. Because you are the one chance at happiness I've ever had, and I'd be damned if I was going to let you down when you needed me." When he didn't respond, I added, "And because if he got hold of the cuff first, Jack was going to put it on Lily Anderson."

Sean's face went blank. Alpha magic rose and I stumbled, almost falling to one knee.

Finally, he spoke. "Jack was going to put the second cuff on Lily?" His voice was deadly.

"Yes. Jack wouldn't let me come see you, but Karen called and warned me that—"

Ben's voice interrupted me, calling to us through the basement door. "Sean? A Vamp Court SUV just parked in the driveway and there's a vampire—"

CRASH. It sounded like someone had come through the front door without bothering to open it.

"Where is Alice?" It was Charles, upstairs. His voice was almost a roar. "*Where is her body?*"

Sean started for the stairs, still cold with fury.

"Wait," I said.

He turned around. "What?"

"He doesn't know I'm alive," I said softly. "That means he's lost his connection to me, the one he got by biting me while I was in a coma. He felt me die and he still thinks I'm dead." I smiled. "He's not in my head anymore, Sean. I'm free of him."

"Good." He came back and scooped me up. "You're in no shape to climb stairs."

I would have protested except he was right, so I let him carry me up the steps. When we got to the top, he pressed his lips to my ear. "Our conversation is not finished," he murmured. "But I have a beta I have to deal with, and a vampire who needs to understand once and for all that three's a crowd."

He kicked the basement door open and stepped into the kitchen.

22

Charles had indeed broken through Jack and Delia's solid oak front door, reducing it to a pile of splintered wood and broken glass. He stood in the front room with Bryan at his side, facing off with Jack, Delia, Ben, and Karen.

Gone was his trademark icy calm. He was shrouded in shadow, his face a mask of pure rage and eyes pitch black. Dark magic made the air heavy.

The werewolves' eyes were golden but they held their ground and their human forms—at least for now. I had to grudgingly give Jack credit for not attacking Charles, despite the vampire's intrusion into his home.

When Sean stepped into view, Charles looked past the others and spotted us. It took several seconds for him to process the sight of me alive. His anger gave way to relief and then confusion.

Bryan, for his part, looked as close to nonplussed as I'd ever seen him. He stared at me like he thought I was a ghost.

Sean spoke first. "Get out of this house, Vaughan. You'll be hearing from my attorney about the damages to the Hastingses' property."

If Charles heard what Sean said, he didn't acknowledge it. "Alice," he said, his voice rough with only a hint of its usual suave tones. "I do not understand."

Sean lowered me down carefully and steadied me with one hand on my back. He knew me well enough to know I wanted to face Charles on my own two feet. His touch made my skin warm and tingly. Maybe a fragment of our bond from the cuffs remained, or maybe the magic of the cuffs had awakened some trace of shifter blood in my veins. If so, that was something I would have to figure out later once Charles and Jack were dealt with.

"What don't you understand, Charles?" I asked. "I told you I would do whatever I had to do to save Sean's life."

"A statement that turned out to be far from mere hyperbole." He took a few steps toward the kitchen. At Sean's nod, the others reluctantly moved aside so Charles could approach us.

He entered the kitchen and stopped on the other side of the center island. "I felt your death, but not your return to life. Our link has been terminated as if it never existed. No human magic I have ever known would be capable of this. How is this possible?"

I'd been wondering that myself. Valas must have severed the connection, but I hadn't thought to ask her to do so; I hadn't even known it was possible. Why she'd done it was a question I wanted an answer to. She must have thought it would benefit her in some way. That would be something else I'd have to fret about later.

"You have no idea what I'm capable of," I told Charles truthfully. We might no longer share a telepathic link, but he could still sense emotions and deception. Good thing I excelled at partial truths and evasive answers.

"I certainly never thought you capable of giving your life for his." Charles glowered at Sean, who returned his gaze impassively. "There was no guarantee that your life could be restored. You might have truly died. He is not worthy of such a sacrifice. You are worth ten of him."

I opened my mouth to object, but Sean spoke first. "On that we agree," he said. "Regardless of how you or I feel about it, the choice was Alice's to make. Her choice seems clear, doesn't it, Vaughan?" In other words: *Alice chose me.*

Something dark flashed in Charles's eyes. His anger began to give way to the cool calculation I was used to seeing. I suspected he was about to go on the attack, and I was right.

"Did Alice tell you how she came to be in possession of the second cuff?" he purred.

I almost smiled. Charles had advised me not to tell Sean that I'd obtained the cuff from him. Even then I'd thought that he intended to use it against me at his first opportunity. I'd never considered holding that information back. As angry as Sean had been at the news that I'd traded a bite for the cuff, it would have been far worse if he'd learned of our arrangement from Charles instead.

"Of course she told me," Sean snapped. "First you bite her while she's in a coma and defenseless, and now you coerce her and try to pass it off as just another business transaction. Even for you, this was a new low."

The corners of Charles's mouth turned up and his eyes glowed silver. "But did she tell you how much she enjoyed my bite? The scent of her arousal still lingers on my bed."

In the front room, Jack and Delia looked at me with contempt. Neither Ben nor Karen reacted visibly; either they assumed Charles was lying or they were taking their cue from Sean, who just shook his head. "It means nothing," he said. "It was an involuntary physiological response. Don't delude yourself into thinking it was anything more than that."

"Perhaps it is you who is deluded." Charles studied Sean. "She saved your life because she owes you her own. She chose to risk death rather than wear the cuff and bind herself to you."

"You know nothing of Alice if you think that was her motivation," Sean said coldly.

I'd had enough of them talking about me as if I wasn't standing right there, and I wanted Charles gone before I lost my tight control over my anger and found myself tempted to fry him where he stood. "Now you know I'm not dead, and you're trespassing on private property. You need to leave before this becomes an incident and the Court gets involved in a dispute with the Were Ruling Council."

"As you wish." Charles gave us a slight bow and backed toward the front doorway. "I can see that you all have much to discuss. I will compensate you for the damages to your home, Mr. Hastings, and please accept my apology for my intrusion. Good night."

Bryan watched the werewolves as Charles departed, one hand near his gun. He glanced at me, his face unreadable, then followed his employer down the front steps and out of my line of sight.

Jack went to the door as Charles and Bryan got into their SUV. Tires crunched on gravel as they backed down the driveway.

When the sound of the engine faded, Jack turned around to find Sean advancing on him, radiating alpha power and fury. The force of it scoured my flesh. Wincing, I rubbed my arms and leaned against the kitchen island.

Before Jack had a chance to react, Sean had him by the throat. "Before I shifted, I gave you an order to protect Alice." He slammed the larger man against the wall hard enough to shake the house as Delia looked on in shock. "You stranded her at the storage unit without any weapons or even a vehicle. As your boss and your alpha, I gave you a clear directive and you deliberately refused to obey it. The Court will sue Maclin Security for breach of contract because we were hired to provide security and we left an asset vulnerable to assassination. But more to the point, I trusted you to carry out my orders and you betrayed me."

"You ordered me to lead the pack and that's what I did," Jack growled.

"And your plan to find the second cuff and give it to Lily Anderson?" Sean demanded. "Was that your way of leading the pack? To bind me for life to a woman you know I don't love and never will, without any regard whatsoever for what I wanted?"

"Better that than let you be bound to *her*." Jack jerked his head in my direction. "She's not pack and she never will be. She's a human and a vampire's whore."

The last word hadn't even left his mouth before Sean picked Jack up and threw him out the front door.

I felt a strange pull and the others staggered slightly. By the time I realized he'd drawn power from the pack to shift faster, Sean—already in wolf form—was out the front door with Ben, Delia, and Karen right behind him.

I was still shaky and Sean had used some of my energy to shift, so I lurched through the kitchen and front room using walls, furniture, and then finally the doorframe to steady myself.

By the time I made it to the front porch, the fight was already underway in the yard. Jack's wolf was larger than Sean's and tawny brown with darker coloring on his ears, face, and tail. The fight was vicious; both wolves were already bloodied before I got to the door.

I worried that his ordeal in the cage had weakened Sean more than he'd let on, and the fast shift couldn't have helped even if he'd drawn on the pack bonds. As we watched from the porch, Jack ripped at Sean's leg with his teeth. Sean snarled and came up limping, his leg bloody and torn.

Delia turned on me as the wolves growled and circled each other. "You're the cause of all this, Alice. We were fine before you got your hooks in Sean. Get out."

"What exactly is your problem with me, Delia?" I asked. "Is it that I'm human, or that you can't push me around like you do the others?"

Delia's eyes went bright yellow. Karen took a step back, but Ben stared Delia down. "You know damn well Sean and Jack had their problems long before Alice even met Sean. And it doesn't matter one bit what Jack thinks about Alice; his orders were to protect her and he didn't."

"Sean told Jack to lead the pack," Delia argued, echoing her husband's earlier argument. "The pack comes first."

"Sean told Jack to protect Alice and Jack said he would," Karen said, her voice gaining some strength despite the more dominant woman's glower. "If we can't trust Jack to keep his word, he's not the beta this pack needs. In fact, maybe he's not a wolf this pack needs."

Furious, Delia started to go after Karen, but Ben caught Delia's wrist. "Stop," he warned her. "If you have a problem with a member of the pack, you talk to Sean."

Delia pulled away and crossed her arms. "Fine."

We turned back to the fight in time to see Sean's wolf leap at Jack and take him down. Jack might be bigger, but Sean was the alpha and despite the injured leg and smaller size, he was stronger and his fury gave him the advantage.

Delia made a fearful sound when Sean's teeth closed on Jack's throat, but Sean didn't intend to kill Jack. The brown wolf let out a short whine, signaling surrender. Sean shook him none too gently, then let go and backed away. Jack rolled onto his side to show Sean his belly, and then crouched with his tail tucked in a submissive posture. Beside me, Delia took a few steps back and bowed her head, echoing her husband's pose.

The wolves shifted back to human, their wounds healing in a pulse of golden shifter magic. Sean watched as Jack got to his feet. Both men were breathing heavily and sweating, but Jack seemed the worse for wear.

When Jack was standing, Sean approached him. "You are never to speak to or about Alice that way again," he said coldly. "When I give you an order, I expect to be obeyed. You've never disobeyed me before and I need to know you never will again if I'm even going to consider giving you a second chance."

"You have my word," Jack said.

Jack had his back to me, so I couldn't see his face or read his body language except the deliberate hunch of his shoulders and the way he seemed to shrink in size in the face of Sean's anger. He certainly appeared and sounded submissive and contrite, but appearances could be deceiving.

Sean studied his beta. Finally, he said, "You're suspended without pay from Maclin Security for two weeks. What happens after that may depend on the legal action the Court takes. As far as your role with the pack goes, this is my last warning. If we have to have this discussion again, there will be a different and more permanent solution. Am I clear?"

"Perfectly clear."

"Good." Sean glanced up. "Everyone, please go inside. I'll join you in a few minutes." He looked at me. "Alice, a word?"

"Sure." I leaned against the wall as the others filed past. Ben and Karen gave me small smiles. Delia and Jack ignored me altogether.

When they were inside the house, Sean opened the back of the Maclin Security SUV parked off to the side of the driveway. He found his duffel bag and pulled on a pair of jeans and a company polo shirt.

I made it down the front steps and joined him just as he closed the back of the SUV. I put my hand on his back.

When he turned, his eyes were hard, his face expressionless. He'd never looked at me like that. "Alice, don't." He stepped away.

Stung, I dropped my hand to my side. "Charles was just trying to get a rise out of you by bringing up the bite. He made it sound like I enjoyed it, but it wasn't like that at all."

"This isn't about him biting you." He walked around to the other side of the SUV, putting the vehicle between us and the house to keep our conversation private. "I'm disgusted at him for that, not at you."

"Then why—?"

"Because I asked you not to use yourself as bait for Kent Stevens, and the first thing you did as soon as I was out of the picture was do exactly that." He was furious with me, his words clipped and angry. "You very nearly died. You had two bullet wounds. The Vampire Court manipulated you into risking your life. They kept Vaughan safe while you walked around with a target on your back. They knew you'd eventually volunteer to draw him out because that's the sort of person you are."

"The plan to catch him was my idea," I argued.

"Stop defending them," he said harshly. "Damn it, Alice, can't you see when you're being used by those bloodsuckers? They don't care if you live or die. You're nothing but an asset to them, except for Vaughan, who still thinks he has a shot with you if he's just patient enough. Even then you're just a meal and a prize to him, something he wants to add to his collection."

"He doesn't have a shot with me and never will. He can plot and scheme all he wants; it won't get him anywhere."

"This isn't about you and Vaughan. It's about you keeping ledgers."

I blinked. "You lost me."

He paced, too angry to stand still. "You said you had to get Stevens out of the way so you could focus on helping me, but I think you did it for the same basic reason you sacrificed yourself to destroy the *Kasten* and almost died taking out the West-Addison harnad. You may have burned the ledger of things you think you owe me for, but you've got another ledger, a much bigger one, and it's full of the things you did before you moved here. You're trying to offset that list of sins by saving everyone and taking out as many bad guys as you can, no matter what it costs you or those who care about you. You've put Malcolm and me through so much in these past few months, and I don't think you even think about that at all unless we bring it up."

Sean came back to stand in front of me again. "I don't know what's in that ledger. You won't tell me and I'm not going to beg you to reveal your secrets. What I *do* know is that you'll do anything to try to balance the scales, running yourself into the ground and almost dying over and over, and it's still not enough. I don't know if it will *ever* be enough, and as much as I care about you, I don't think I can keep doing this."

"What are you saying?" I didn't even recognize my own voice.

He rubbed his face with both hands. When he looked back at me, his eyes were hollow. "I'm saying I need some time."

If he'd punched me in the gut, it wouldn't have hurt half as much. "Sean, please."

He gripped my hand and his eyes searched my face. "If you could go back to yesterday and do it all again, knowing now how I'd feel about it, would you do the same thing? Would you put yourself in the line of fire to catch Stevens? Would you die to get the cuff off me?"

I couldn't lie to him. "Yes, I would, because there was no other way."

He let go of my hand. "I know. You'll throw yourself on every grenade because you think you're the only one who can and maybe walk away from it. But the thing about just barely surviving every time is that you're not the only one who gets hurt."

My chest ached like someone was standing on it. "Don't do this. We...I..."

"Go home and rest," he told me gently. "Do you want to give the cuff back your client so you can get your bonus?"

In that moment, I couldn't have cared less about Esther Aldridge or her damned bonus. "No. The cuffs are too dangerous to just let them be bought and sold by people who have no idea what they are. No one should have those cuffs. Patrick was right; power like that only ever ends up destroying everyone and everything around it."

"Then I'll make sure they disappear forever." He took a couple of steps back. The physical distance between us was only a few feet, but it felt like miles. "Do you need a ride home?"

"No." I didn't know *what* I needed, but I could get myself home. After that, I had no idea what I would do.

Of all the possible outcomes I had foreseen, Sean asking me to go home without him had never been one of them. I'd predicted he'd be angry, but not that I would push him to his breaking point.

I'd been worried my secrets would be the thing he couldn't live with. I'd never considered that it would be my willingness to risk my life. Maybe I should have seen it when he reacted so angrily to my initial suggestion about using myself as bait the night we were staking out John Doe's motel room, but I hadn't.

For all my planning and dealing, I'd never even thought about how he would react to shifting back to his human form next to my dead body, or how the members of the pack would feel after sharing his pain and grief over my death. Like a vampire—like my grandfather—I'd thought the ends justified the means. Maybe I shared more attributes with Charles and Moses than I'd ever been willing to admit, even to myself.

I wanted to beg. I wanted to rage. I wanted to punch him, then kiss him and hold him and never let him go.

Instead, I got in my car and went home.

23

Thanks to exhaustion and a glass of Scotch, I managed to sleep until almost noon, when Aaron Riddell woke me with a phone call and a request for an update.

I told him the cuff had been bought by a mage who'd accidentally destroyed it while attempting to intensify the spellwork, but that I could deliver the mirror and cup either to his office or Esther's home. I was too emotionally drained to feel any pang of conscience for lying to him.

He checked with Esther, then called back a few minutes later to say he would be sending a courier over to pick up the items and deliver a check if I'd e-mail my invoice to his assistant. According to Aaron, Esther was unhappy that I'd failed to recover the cuff, but grateful that I'd found the other two items. She'd offered to add a small bonus anyway, despite my only partial success. Aaron advised me to accept graciously, so I did.

I put Sean's toiletries in a bin under the sink so I didn't have to look at them and took a long shower. My emotions were all over the place. I was hurt, sad, confused, and angry in turns. I was deeply hurt that Sean had sent me away, but most of my anger was directed at myself. He'd been so patient and understanding for so long, waiting for me to realize how my actions hurt the people who cared about me, but he'd finally reached the end of his rope. I should have apologized the second I came to and saw the pain I'd caused, but instead I'd acted like it was all business as usual.

Maybe my life with my grandfather was partially to blame for my difficulty in understanding and accounting for other people's feelings. I'd certainly never learned empathy from him, and caring about others was a vulnerability I couldn't afford back then. But I'd been away from the cabal for five years now, and this wasn't the first time Malcolm and Sean had called me out for hurting them with my actions. I couldn't blame Moses for this, as much as I wished I could. No, this one was on me.

After my shower, I sat on my bed in my bathrobe, my hair wrapped in a towel, and finalized my invoice for Esther while Rogue snoozed over by the window. The bill was a nice chunk of change, but I couldn't feel anything close to happy about it. I e-mailed the paperwork to Aaron's assistant and said I'd have the items ready for pick-up within the hour.

I dried my hair and dressed, then put Sean's clothes in a box in the closet. I had no idea what the protocol was for what to do with his things. Should I mail them to his house? Offer to drop them off? Keep them in hopes that we'd forgive each other and fix what I'd broken?

I wiped my eyes, picked up my laptop, and opened my bedroom door to find Malcolm waiting in the hallway. "Hey, Alice," he said somberly.

I'd told him what happened when I got home, over Scotch on my back porch. I could tell he wasn't surprised by Sean's reaction to what I'd done.

To make matters worse, my last thoughts before I fell asleep were that if I'd wronged Sean so badly, I'd done the same to my ghost.

"I'm sorry for everything, Malcolm," I said, leaning against my bedroom doorway. "I'm sorry for every time I didn't think about how much you worried about me, or about how me putting myself in danger affected you. I don't even know how many times I've done that."

"About ten times in the past week alone," he said half-jokingly, but his light tone was forced.

He grew serious. "The thing is, I don't think you have any idea how to let people care about you. We made some progress on that recently, but the bigger problem is that you don't put much value on your own life. Just because *you're* cavalier about it doesn't mean other people are too. Your life isn't just a tool you can use to solve problems and neither is your death, but that's how you act."

I wished I could tell him that I'd been raised to think of myself as literally a tool and a weapon and not as having inherent value beyond my usefulness, but I wasn't ready to reveal that about myself.

Besides, I was beginning to understand that I didn't listen enough when Malcolm talked, so I shut up and listened.

When I said nothing, he went on. "It hurts us when you don't seem to notice how much we worry about you or you brush us off when we express concern. I'm sure this is all a result of what you went through before you came here, but it makes it hard to be around you sometimes. Feeling you die and then you acting like it was no big deal was the last straw for Sean."

"Did you talk to him?"

He nodded. "After you fell asleep, I went to check on him and we talked for a bit. I'm sorry, but as much as I hate what happened between you, I can't blame him for feeling the way he does."

"Neither can I."

"You don't?"

I shrugged wearily and rubbed my eyes. "Everything you both said to me is true. I don't know how to fix this about myself, but I do know I screwed up. I can't turn back time and do it over, and though I owe Sean an apology for not thinking more about his feelings, I'm not sorry for what I did with the cuff or that I helped get Stevens even though he didn't want me to."

"Yeah, he's pretty angry about the Stevens situation." He made a face. "He cares about you a lot, Alice. Maybe you should give him a call and tell him what you just told me about realizing you messed up."

"He told me he needed time. I'm no expert in this sort of thing, but I'm pretty sure that meant more than eight hours." I headed downstairs with Malcolm following as Rogue ran ahead of us to stand by the back door. "In the meantime, I've got plenty of stuff to do to keep me busy."

"Like what?"

"Clean up all that spellwork in the basement, for starters. Aaron will be sending a courier over in a bit to drop off a check from Esther and pick up the mirror and the cup, so I need to get those boxed up. Then I'm going shopping for new living room furniture. Maybe some new patio furniture too, if I can find some that I like."

"Well, that does sound like a full day," Malcolm said, watching me with narrowed eyes. "And then what?"

"Then I'll find more stuff to do." I let Rogue out into the backyard and headed for the kitchen to make coffee. "Oh, hey—there's something I meant to ask you the other day, but I forgot. When I was checking you for more of those hidden retrieval spells, I found the spell that links us together. I think there's a condition that will break the spell. Do you know what it is?"

He looked bemused and shook his head. "No, I have no idea. I would tell you if I did."

I sighed. "I guess that'll stay a mystery for now. Come on—let's go to the basement and get to cleaning."

That night, I was on my back porch in shorts and a T-shirt, drinking Scotch and relaxing on one of my new chaise lounges, when the perimeter wards tingled. I didn't bother to get up; if it was who I thought it was, my visitors knew where to find me.

The back gate creaked open and closed. Charles appeared out of the darkness, wearing a dark gray suit. I didn't see anyone with him, but either Bryan or Adri was somewhere close by, watching us.

The garden rustled ominously when he came into view. Charles paused to study the plants, then turned to me with raised eyebrows. "Fascinating. Your garden recently consumed an entire human body, and yet it seems interested in eating me as well."

I sipped my whisky and set the glass down on the table. "It likes blood—the more powerful, the better. I'm sure it would find you to be quite a delicacy. Strange to be the food for a change, isn't it?"

"You must share your gardening tips with me."

"Why, what are you thinking about growing? A conscience?"

He chuckled and climbed the steps to where I was reclining. "You have new furniture."

"You're very observant." I gestured at the second chaise lounge. "Take a load off."

He unbuttoned his suit jacket and settled into the lounge, crossing his ankles. "Surprisingly comfortable." He glanced at the table between us, where a second, unused glass waited next to the bottle of Dalwhinnie. "Did you anticipate my arrival?"

"Let's just say I had a feeling you'd be coming around. Help yourself."

As he poured himself two fingers of Scotch, I toyed with my glass. "I finally had a few minutes today to do a bit of reading on vampire objects of power, particularly the Tepes stone you purchased at the auction. You've got a tiger by the tail, don't you?"

He sipped his whisky. "It would seem so, yes."

"And you don't think it's going to turn around and bite you?"

"Perhaps I believe it is better I should have possession of this tiger than someone like Vincent Barclay or one of his associates. But I did not come here to discuss the stone." He studied me. "Are you recovered from last night's unpleasantness?"

"Still recovering." I shrugged. "I get dizzy if I stand up too fast and I have a weird headache. I'm sure it will pass."

Charles rested his glass on his thigh and watched the plants in my garden swaying back and forth. "I have heard a rumor that your sacrifice was not as well-received as it might have been and you were sent away."

Of course he'd heard about what happened between Sean and me. "Did you come here to gloat?"

"No."

Oddly, I believed him.

He glanced at me. "Your hurt weighs heavily on me. I can no longer share my thoughts with you, but I sense the pain this rejection has caused you. I do not understand the cause of the wolf's decision to end your relationship, especially so soon after you saved his life at great personal cost."

I didn't bother explaining that requesting time apart wasn't the same as an outright breakup. "He appreciated what I did, but not how I did it."

"He objected to how you obtained the second cuff?"

"He objected to how I died and didn't apologize when I woke up."

He frowned and tilted his head. "You should have apologized for dying?"

"Yep." I sipped my whisky.

"If this is a joke, I do not understand the humor in it."

"It's pretty damn far from a joke." My voice was bitter. "If you didn't come here to gloat, why are you here?"

He rotated the glass in his hands, watching the reflection of the moonlight in the amber liquid. "I have been preoccupied with the question of how you survived and how you severed our connection so thoroughly. I believe I have uncovered the explanation for how it was accomplished."

"Oh, yeah? What's that?"

"You did not do it yourself."

When I didn't reply, he said, "I understand you went to Northbourne and requested an audience with Valas after you left my home. Approximately one hour later, you departed in your vehicle, seemingly alone. Not long after your departure, a Court-owned limousine left the estate. It returned to Northbourne an hour later and unloaded its passenger via a private entrance."

He put his glass on the table and turned to face me, sitting up with his feet on the concrete. "I must conclude that you went to the Hastingses' home with Valas. She not only assisted you in reaching Maclin, but she also caused both your death and your return to life. It was Valas who severed our connection. Was it at your request?"

If I denied that Valas had been involved, Charles would sense my deception, so I went with evasion. "The Court can't interfere in a pack matter; you said so yourself."

His eyes went silver. He caught my wrist and held it. "You have placed yourself in Valas's debt. I can think of no greater folly than what you have done. She is no kind benefactor."

"And *you* are?" I pulled my arm from his grip. "If I made a deal, it was worth it to save Sean. It didn't turn out exactly how I planned, but he's alive and that's what matters."

"Did you tell Maclin about your agreement with Valas?"

Blood magic spooled around my hands as my eyes grew warm and glowed. "If you breathe a word of this to anyone, especially Sean, I will kill you. And now you know that I don't make idle threats."

"Tell me the terms of your agreement with Valas. I will assist you in renegotiating the deal if I can."

"The terms of our agreement are confidential. I'm courting trouble even by having this discussion with you." I drained the last of my whisky. "If you'd told me about the second cuff from the beginning, maybe none of this would have happened. I'm not saying you're to blame because I made my own choices, but I wouldn't have ended up in Valas's audience chamber last night if it hadn't been for your games."

Charles said nothing for several long moments. His face was blank. I couldn't tell if he felt bad about what he'd done, or if he was merely trying to work out what kind of deal I might have struck with the head of the Vamp Court.

When he spoke, I decided it had been the latter. "If Valas severed the connection between us, it was because she did not want me to interfere with her plans. Perhaps she did not wish you to be able to call to me for help." His eyes widened. "Or perhaps... Alice, if you fail to meet your obligations to Valas, is the price your life?"

I said nothing.

He tried to take my face in his hands, but I knocked them away. "You are mad," he said roughly. "She means to turn you. Whatever you have agreed to do in return for her assistance, she will ensure that you fail so you will become a vampire of her line. It would not be the first time she has done such a thing." His eyes glowed in anger. "Why did you not tell me that you intended to go to her? I would have found another way to save the wolf."

"Yes, I'm sure you would have done that out of the goodness of your heart," I scoffed.

"Perhaps not, but I would not have tricked you into making a deal that would cost you your life."

"So you say now." I shook my head. "What's done is done, Charles. We've all made our beds and now we get to lie in them. I won't forget that you kept the second cuff a secret or that you tried to torpedo my relationship by telling Sean about my reaction to your bite."

"I spoke out of jealousy and anger. I am not proud of what I said." He leaned forward. "Allow me to drink from you again and reinstate our link."

Infuriated, I rose. "You are the most shameless—"

He stood and caught my wrist again. "Not for my benefit; for yours," he snapped. "Without our link, you will not be able to call on me to help you. Now you cannot rely on Maclin or his pack to protect you. You have only your ghost and his powers are limited. How will you protect yourself if you are alone?"

"The same way I always have. Let go of me."

He released my arm. "I will not let you face Valas alone."

"You don't seem to understand that you don't get a say in what I do. I've said it before and I'll say it again: I am not yours to protect, and I sure as hell don't need you to *let* me do anything. Now, please leave."

He studied me. "Very well, but should you need assistance, you know how to reach me." He drank the remainder of his whisky and set the glass on the table. "Maclin is a fool to send you away. You were willing to give your life to save his, and he behaves as though he has been wronged. If you had made such a sacrifice for me, all that I have and all of eternity would be yours."

There was little point trying to explain Sean's point of view to Charles. He had even less capacity for empathy than me. "Good night, Charles."

He met my eyes. I read in them his intent to say something in confidence. Since we could no longer share our thoughts, I reluctantly presented my cheek for a good-night kiss.

He brushed his cool lips along my jaw. "Good night, Alice." With his mouth near my ear, he breathed words so softly that I barely heard them. "She is not invincible. Should you need to know how to defeat her, you have only to ask." He took two steps back, then turned to cross my porch and walk down the steps. He joined Bryan, who had appeared, as usual, out of the shadows.

I watched as they crossed my backyard. Halfway to the gate, Charles glanced back. I leaned against the porch railing and gave him a slight nod. He nodded back and they disappeared around the corner of the house. The gate didn't creak, but a few moments later I felt the wards tingle as they left my property.

No doubt Charles's information would come with a price, but it was a good option to keep in my back pocket for when Valas tried to turn our deal against me. That she would was inevitable, but maybe I'd have a few surprises in store for her when she did.

Several days passed with no word from Sean. Workmen sent by Charles came to repair the hole in the wall he'd made the night Fortune was killed. I deposited Esther's check, took delivery of my new living room furniture, deep-cleaned the house room by room, punched the heavy bag for at least an hour each day, created wards for my informant Phil, and utterly failed to not think about Sean every damn minute.

In the meantime, the city was eerily quiet. There hadn't been any more magic attacks since the one that damaged the Heights the day Sean and I had visited Walsh & Quinn to get the mirror. The feds and the mayor were still demanding answers and accountability for the attacks on Darius Bell's cabal, but no one had been charged or even arrested. I assumed Catherine was trying to track Bell down and once she found him, all bets were off. Moses had to be apoplectic that she'd failed to kill him. My grandfather was not renowned for his patience. If she didn't deliver Bell's body soon, she risked being recalled to Baltimore to face Moses's wrath in person.

On the fourth day, I got a call from a woman who wanted wards around the new home she'd just bought with her fiancé. The property backed up to a cemetery and she worried that ghosts and other spirits would haunt the house. That project kept me busy and distracted for the rest of that day and most of the next. The only downside was that Malcolm couldn't help with the wards—ghost-proof wards meant no ghost assistant.

Once the project was complete, I went out and had drinks with Arkady at a dive bar. She listened sympathetically to my tale of woe and bought me shots while I talked about Sean. We both got drunk and sang karaoke. She chose a Stevie Nicks song and sounded pretty great. I went with "Heartache Tonight" by the Eagles.

We had so much fun that we decided to come back the following week. We also made plans to visit her favorite gun range over the weekend and maybe have brunch after. I had no idea how to do the "bestie" thing, but thought maybe I was getting the hang of it.

When I got home that night, Malcolm was out "doing ghost stuff," as he called wandering around the city. The house was dark and quiet. I sat in the living room with the lights off, curled up on my new sofa.

I looked up when Rogue whined, thinking he was at the back door asking to be let into the yard. Instead, he sat in the foyer, staring at the leash on the hook by the front door. It wasn't hard to figure out what was upsetting him.

"He's not coming over tonight," I told the dog. I rose and headed for the stairs. "Come on. Let's go to bed."

Reluctantly, Rogue followed me upstairs and lay in his bed by the window while I washed my face and brushed my teeth. When I crawled into bed, he came over and put his chin on the mattress.

We generally didn't let the dog up onto the bed, but what the hell. I patted the bed. "Come on up, fur-face."

Rogue jumped up onto the bed and immediately settled down on the side closest to the bathroom, the side that still smelled like Sean.

I sat on my side of the bed for a while, listening to the dog's light snore and wondering what Sean was doing right now. Once or twice I started to reach for my phone, but I stopped myself from calling. He'd asked me for time. I didn't know if that meant days or weeks or forever, but I'd give him at least a little more time before I tried calling him.

Finally, I went downstairs, leaving Rogue on the bed still asleep. I poured myself a glass of my best whisky, got the last two chocolate chip cookies out of the package I'd bought the day before, grabbed a dog biscuit from the box in the pantry, and took it all back upstairs.

I sat cross-legged on the bed and poked the dog's nose with the biscuit. "Hey, fur-face. Wake up."

Rogue sat up and took the biscuit, eyeing me suspiciously. He was normally not allowed to eat anything on the bed and it took some encouragement to get him to start gnawing on his treat.

I ate the cookies and drank my whisky and watched Rogue eat. When he was done, he curled up with his back against Sean's pillow and closed his eyes.

"Happy birthday to me," I said to the dog. He was already snoring again.

I put my empty glass on the nightstand and pulled the covers up to my chin.

Hours later, something roused me from a sound sleep.

Groggy, I tried to figure out if I'd heard something. Rogue was asleep in the bed next to me, though, and if it had been a noise in the house he would have woken up.

I was just about to turn over and go back to sleep when I sensed Malcolm cross the house wards as he jumped into one of the crystals in the basement.

Less than a second later, he appeared next to my bed. "Alice!" he shouted frantically. "Alice, Alice, wake up! Everything's on fire!"

I was out of bed in a flash, wide awake, my heart thundering in my ears. "The house is on fire?"

"No, the *city* is on fire!" He pointed at my bedroom windows.

I ran to the curtains and flung them open. In the distance, I saw an orange glow in the direction of downtown. It sure as hell wasn't sunrise at four in the morning. "Oh my God," I breathed. "What happened?"

"There was another magic shockwave. Did you feel it?"

"Something woke me up just before you jumped home. That must have been the wave."

I went to my dresser, pulling my tank top off over my head. Malcolm quickly turned away, but I was in too much of a hurry to care about modesty right now. I put on a bra and a T-shirt and a pair of jeans. I grabbed my socks, boots, and phone, and ran downstairs.

"Did you see what happened?" I asked as I sat on the couch and put my boots on.

"I couldn't get too close, but I saw a woman standing on a rooftop right smack in the center of the fire. She was holding something that looked like a gold ring and it seemed to be focusing the fire."

A ring was bad news; the most powerful magical objects were circles because they channeled power, like the circles in my basement.

My fumbling fingers pulled up the zipper on the second boot. "What did she look like?"

"Um, dark clothes, red hair? In her forties or fifties, maybe?"

"Catherine," I breathed.

Malcolm stopped flitting and hovered in front of me. "Do you know who she is?"

Oops. "You remember what Cyro said about John Doe trying to get weapons for Catherine Atwood, Moses Murphy's daughter? I bet it's her."

I finished putting on my boots and went to the front closet for a black hoodie sweatshirt. I grabbed my keys on the way out the door.

"What are you going to do? Alice, wait." Malcolm followed me down the sidewalk toward my car. "Alice!"

"She'll burn the whole city down if it means killing Darius Bell," I said as I got to my car. "Let's go, Malcolm. We have to stop her."

"We have to—*what?* Alice, damn it, she's a high-level fire mage with some kind of mega-weapon, and we're one mage and one ghost!"

"*Get in the car, Malcolm!*" I slammed my door closed, turned my key in the ignition, and hit the gas just as Malcolm appeared in the passenger seat area.

"You remember how I said it sucks when I try to warn you about doing dangerous stuff and you ignore me?" He crossed his arms and glared at me. "This is exactly what I was talking about. This right here."

I backed onto the street, shifted gears, and floored it in the direction of the fire. "I know. I apologize in advance for what I'm about to do."

"Oh, God, she apologized," Malcolm muttered. "Now I *know* this is going to end badly."

24

A LOCAL RADIO STATION REPORTED THAT THE FIRE WAS CONSUMING APPROXIMATELY four blocks just west of downtown. Luckily, many of the structures involved were office buildings with few people at work in the middle of the night, but the fire was threatening to spread to nearby apartment buildings. A dozen fire crews were on scene, attempting to contain the blaze, but the fire was far too intense.

As I drove, Malcolm told me Catherine was on the roof of a building that overlooked a luxury condo. There was a good chance she'd tracked Bell to that condo and had used whatever weapon she'd obtained to create a perimeter of fire before torching the condo itself. Or maybe she was waiting for him to try to escape along with everyone else and target him then. Either way, many people were going to die horribly unless I could figure out a way to stop her.

I picked up my cell phone, scrolled through my recent calls, and dialed a number from the list. I left it in the holder and turned on the speaker so I could keep both hands on the wheel.

The phone rang once before an electronic voice answered. "This is Cyro."

I exhaled. "Cyro, it's Alice Worth. I'm sorry to bother—"

"You're heading downtown toward the fire. What do you need?"

I had no idea how he was tracking my movements—maybe my phone? Or was there a tracking device on my car? Damn it, something else I'd have to worry about later. "I'm sure what I'm asking for is out of my price range, but how much would it cost for you to shut down all the surveillance cameras you can around the scene? I'm going to try to do something about the fire and I don't want to be seen."

I heard keys clicking rapidly in the background. "This one's on the house, unless you die trying to save the city, in which case I'll subtract my fee from your bank account."

I blinked. "Okay. I guess I can live with that—or not, as the case may be. What's a good vantage point close to Ground Zero? I need a rooftop with a good view of the fire, preferably somewhere without people around."

As Cyro searched for an appropriate destination, I thought about what Sean and Malcolm had said about facing danger on my own and how my decisions affected the people who cared about me.

I muted my call with Cyro and glanced over at Malcolm. "We're doing this together, all right? Team effort. Nobody's going Lone Ranger."

"The Lone Ranger had Tonto," Malcolm pointed out.

"Shut up. You know what I mean."

"Yeah, I know what you mean. Way to show personal growth."

I rolled my eyes and unmuted my phone.

"There's a six-story private parking garage about a block north of the fire," Cyro said. "It's at the corner of Twenty-third and Burgess Avenue. I'll cut the cameras and raise the gate for you."

"Holy shit," Malcolm muttered. "Who *is* this guy?"

I took a deep breath. "Thank you, Cyro. If this goes sideways, I want you to know how much I've appreciated your help."

"Just try not to die," he said. "I'd like more interesting projects in the future."

"I'll certainly do my best to survive." I hesitated. "Do you have eyes on the cause of the fire?"

"Yes. It's Catherine Atwood, Moses Murphy's daughter. She's on the roof of an office building next door to the parking garage with some kind of magical object. I'm running a search on it, but I don't have any information yet about what it is or where she got it. Anything else?"

"Yeah, one more thing. If I don't make it out, will you arrange to get my car out of the garage and back to my house?"

"I can do that. I thought you were going to ask me to clear your browser history."

That made me laugh, despite the fear and adrenaline coursing through my veins. "Thanks, Cyro. I gotta go."

"Good luck." The call ended.

"So, do you have a plan or are we just winging it like usual?" Malcolm asked as I turned onto Twenty-third. Ahead of us, the fire raged against the night sky.

"I'm thinking." I hit a dip going too fast and the car's bumper scraped. I winced. "We won't be able to get close enough to her to take out that weapon, so we need options for containing the fire."

"Neither of us has fire magic," Malcolm pointed out. "I have water and you have air and we both have earth magic, but I don't know how that's going to help."

"We'll come up with something." I spotted the garage entrance and slowed to turn. Sure enough, the gate was up.

The garage belonged to one of the office buildings and it was almost completely empty in the middle of the night. I parked on the first level, jumped from the car, and ran for the stairs with Malcolm right behind me. My eyes burned from the heavy smoke and the garage echoed with the deafening sound of a dozen sirens.

By the time I made it to the third floor, I had to pull myself up the stairs using the handrail. "I need to do more cardio," I panted.

Malcolm snorted. "Or maybe the fact that you died a couple of days ago and haven't fully recovered from that yet has something to do with it."

"Maybe." I focused on breathing and making my legs keep climbing the steps.

When I reached the top of the stairs, my legs felt like they were made of rubber and

I was gasping for air. I emerged onto the rooftop parking deck and took a moment to bend over and put my hands on my knees, sucking in air and swearing under my breath.

"Alice?"

An unexpected—but very familiar—voice made me jump and look up. I gaped at the sight of Sean, wearing a dark jacket and jeans, striding toward me across the parking deck. He didn't look angry or even surprised to see me. My heart skipped a beat and it had nothing to do with physical exertion.

"What are you doing here?" I asked, trying to catch my breath.

"Karen's brother Patrick lives in that condo with his girlfriend," he told me, joining me at the top of the stairs. "I came to see if I could help get people out, but there's no way through the fire. Cyro called me and suggested I come up here to meet you and get a bird's-eye view."

I set my worries about where we stood aside to focus on the deadly problem in front of us. "Malcolm's with me," I told him, since he couldn't see the ghost.

Sean and Malcolm exchanged greetings as I half-dragged my leaden legs across the parking deck to the waist-high concrete ledge.

We were upwind and a full block away from the blaze, but even at this distance the heat and smoke were nearly unbearable. I counted eight buildings completely engulfed in flames, forming a perimeter around a twelve-story condo. Emergency vehicles packed the nearby streets, filling the sky with red and blue flashing lights. Fire trucks aimed a dozen jets of water at the burning buildings, but they weren't making any headway. The magic-enhanced fires were just too massive.

I moved to the far end of the parking deck and finally spotted Catherine on the roof of an adjacent building. She faced the fire, holding the gold ring Malcolm had described. I couldn't be sure from this distance, but it looked very much like the ring I'd seen bought at the auction. Somehow it had made its way into Catherine's hands, presumably after we'd had Kendall's stash of stolen weapons and artifacts seized by SPEMA.

At the moment, the weapon was not in use; she'd apparently used it to start the blaze by focusing her fire magic at the targeted buildings.

"What do you know about this?" Sean asked me.

"Cyro says that's Catherine Atwood, Moses Murphy's daughter. My guess is she found out Darius Bell is holed up in that condo and she's trying to flush him out."

"By burning all these buildings down and killing everyone?" His anger prickled on my skin.

"She doesn't care. Moses probably told her to take Bell out or else."

Catherine set the ring at her feet and raised her arms. The fire responded by surging in the buildings closest to the condo. Several thundering crashes indicated that floors were collapsing in those buildings. The fires grew and licked at the exterior walls of the condo. I could see people in the windows and more trying to escape through the various street-level doors, only to be driven back by the fire.

A police helicopter approached us. I ducked my head to avoid being photographed as it flew overhead.

"Oh, shit," Malcolm breathed.

I looked up just in time to see Catherine send a plume of fire toward the helicopter. It avoided the flames and accelerated away, circling at a safe distance as the fire grew and spread.

"Well, that explains why all the news helicopters are keeping their distance," Malcolm said.

"She's going to burn everyone in that condo alive," Sean said grimly.

"No, she's not," I stated. "We won't let her."

Despite how certain I sounded, I wasn't sure what we could do. Neither Malcolm nor I could control fire. We both had earth magic, but that wouldn't help. I had air magic, but even if I tapped a ley line to boost my power I wouldn't be able to do anything but fan the flames more. Malcolm's water magic wouldn't be enough to pull the river this far and we'd flood the city in the attempt. My blood magic could do nothing from this distance without a focus.

Lightning flashed on the horizon. There was a rainstorm north of us, but it was too far away and moving in the wrong direction—not that a storm that small would do much against a fire this size, anyway. But if it were bigger, and it turned south...

"I have an idea," I said to Malcolm. I pointed.

He frowned at the storm and then at me. "I don't get it."

"We need to bring that storm here."

"What are you suggesting? That we do a rain dance?"

"No. I've got air magic. You've got water magic. We just need to work together."

He shook his head. "Water magic can make a storm stronger, but I'm not powerful enough to do it. I know you're strong, but even you can't move a storm against the wind."

"I can if I pull energy from the two ley lines that intersect here."

"Even if you *could* do that, that little bit of rain isn't enough to put this fire out."

"I can make the storm big and strong enough. All you have to do is share my body and let me use your magic."

"*Are you insane?*" He flitted back and forth so quickly that I couldn't track him with my eyes. "Are you out of your damn mind? You can't summon a thunderstorm!"

"Yes, I can," I said calmly. "I've done it before. Not for a while, but I've done it. I just need your water magic."

He stopped directly in front of me. "There's no way in hell I'm going to do this. Just touching me makes your hands turn blue. If I share your body, you'll freeze to death in minutes."

"I only need a few minutes. The storm isn't that far away. It's the only—"

"I swear to God, Alice, don't you dare say it's the only way!" he yelled. "It is *not* the only way!"

"Then give me another idea," I begged. "Name anything else we can do to save the people in that condo and in these other buildings."

Malcolm crossed his arms. "We can't save everyone every time. Some things are just beyond what anyone can do."

"This isn't beyond what I can do. I've done it before. Granted, not by sharing my body with a ghost, but I've used a ghost with water magic in a focus to summon a storm."

"A ghost in a focus?" He hovered right in front of me, his eyes dark with fury. "So you've used ghosts trapped in crystals, just like the ghost Kendall was using in that statue?"

"Not by choice," I snapped. "You know I used to belong to a cabal. Do you think I did it because I *wanted* to? You know me, Malcolm. You don't believe for one minute that I did it by choice."

Sean's attention was still on the fire, but he glanced at me when I mentioned the cabal. He didn't look surprised, however. No doubt he'd already surmised that I'd once belonged to one; few high-level mages escaped their clutches, and he'd probably picked up enough clues over the past few months to figure it out. The scars on my back showed I'd been tortured by a blood mage, as was common with cabal mages who refused to obey orders. I'd basically just confirmed what he already knew.

"No, I don't believe you did it by choice," Malcolm said grimly. "I know you only did it because you had to. But you don't have to do this. This isn't a grenade you have to fall on."

"This is different. This one *is* my grenade to fall on. This time it's not just me trying to balance the scales. It's personal."

"In what way is this personal?" Malcolm asked.

I couldn't very well tell him that was my aunt over there burning the city down. "One of Sean's pack members is in there, along with probably a hundred other people. Isn't that enough?"

"If I share your body, it will freeze you from the inside out. I refuse to help you kill yourself."

"I'm not asking you to kill me. I'm just asking you to let me use your water magic long enough to summon that storm. You can jump out of me before I get to the point where we have to worry about me freezing to death."

Sean had been watching Catherine and listening to us argue. He turned to me, his expression grim. I thought he was going to side with Malcolm, but instead he said, "Let's do it. What can I do to help?"

Malcolm gaped at him. "You're not serious. After everything you said about her falling on grenades, you're going to ask her to do this?"

"She says she can do it." Sean met my eyes. I saw worry and anger, but I also saw his confidence in me.

"I can do this," I told him. "I can save Patrick and the other people in the condo, and I can do it without dying." Tentatively, I reached out and took his hand.

He lifted it to his lips and pressed a kiss to my knuckles. "Then let's save them."

Malcolm swore. "The second you start getting too cold, I'm jumping out, whether it's done or not," he warned me.

"Agreed. Hurry." I squeezed Sean's hand, then let go and stepped back.

Malcolm muttered something I couldn't hear, braced himself, and dove straight at me.

I'd never shared my body with a ghost before. It felt like being dunked in a frozen lake. The shock drove me to my knees. I cried out involuntarily as his non-corporeal form moved under my skin. He settled into my body and my temperature began to drop. The chill was uncomfortable, but not yet debilitating or dangerous.

Sean crouched in front of me. "Are you okay?"

"I'm okay," I said shakily. "This feels really, really weird."

You're telling me, Malcolm said in my head. *Let's do this before you freeze to death.*

Sean helped me to my feet just as a gust of wind blew a thick cloud of smoke in our direction. I coughed and blinked away tears. "I'll be focused on the magic and the storm," I told him. "Keep us safe."

"Always." He squeezed my hands and flinched. "You're already getting cold."

"I know. I need to hurry." I hesitated, then added, "When this is over, I'd like to talk."

"When this is over, I'd like to listen." He let go of my hands. "Bring the thunder, Miss Magic."

I gave him a small smile, turned to face the storm, and closed my eyes.

Malcolm's magic pulsed though me. The unfamiliar sensation of water tugged at my awareness. I'd always had an affinity to the earth and air because of my own magic, but now I could feel the water the fire crews were using to fight the blaze. The sensation was wonderful, like standing in a cool stream.

With Malcolm's water magic now part of me, I sensed the far-off thunderstorm. It was too far away for me to summon, however. I needed a power boost.

Now the ley lines, Malcolm said in my head. *Be careful.*

Brace yourself, I told him.

I'd certainly never imagined that I'd need the lines to fight my aunt or save the city from fire. By doing so I risked outing myself, but it appeared I had little choice unless I was willing to let everyone in that condo, including Patrick, burn to death.

I sensed the ley line energy pulsing on the edge of my senses. We weren't far from their intersection; only a mile or so. I took several deep breaths and grabbed the lines.

Everything went white. For a moment, I thought my chest might explode at the sheer force of the power I was conducting. I gasped for air and fought to contain the energy. Pain seared every nerve and I set my jaw to keep from crying out.

You're getting cold, Malcolm said. I couldn't feel anything but the ley-line power and pain, so his words were a surprise. *And the condo just caught fire, so you've got to hurry.*

Okay. Here goes, I told him.

I let the water and air magic rise until it filled me and danced on my skin. The cool blue and white energy of the storm crackled on the edge of my senses, pulling at me like a magnet. I used the ley line power to enhance our magic, raised my arms, and pulled the storm toward us.

With so much power behind it, our magic brought the storm faster than I'd thought possible. The air changed and became heavy as the rain approached the city. I pushed Malcolm's water magic into the storm and used my enhanced air magic to build it to near-hurricane strength.

"Here it comes," Sean warned me.

The storm arrived with a roar. The wall of wind and rain pushed me back several steps and nearly knocked me over. Sean wrapped his arms around me and braced me, planting his feet and pushing back against the force of the wind.

The rain was so heavy that I thought I might drown standing up in it. The wind made Sean stagger but he stayed on his feet.

I forced my eyes open. I was soaked to my skin, but my hoodie kept enough of the rain out of my eyes that I could see. Despite the power of the magic that created the fires, the deluge began to drown the flames in the buildings around us.

Down at street level, the fire crews took advantage of breaks in the wall of fire surrounding the condo to move people to safety away from the blaze. Residents emerged from various doors and ran to the first responders.

Suddenly, Sean dove to the pavement and covered my body with his as a fireball passed over us. Catherine had spotted us and attacked.

He rolled us behind the concrete barrier along the edge of the roof. Another fireball, this one much larger, blasted over our heads.

"How is she using fire in this rain?" Sean shouted over the roar of the storm.

I was now shivering violently. "It's m-m-magic."

You're getting too cold, Malcolm said in my head. *I'm jumping out.*

No, wait, I told him. *I need your magic still. The storm will dissipate if I let up, and without water magic I can't defend us against Catherine's fire.*

You agreed that I would get out of your body when you started to get too cold, he snapped. *That's the only reason I said I'd do this.*

Just one more minute. I promise I won't—

A fireball arced over the concrete wall and landed right on top of us. Sean snarled and rolled us into a deep puddle to try to put out the flames, but it was fire magic, not normal fire. Stop, drop, and roll would do us no good.

I used Malcolm's water magic to smother the flames. Our clothes were half-burned and my skin was angry red in places. I couldn't feel the pain yet because I was so cold.

"Are you all right?" Sean asked. His arms and back were burned where he'd been trying to shield me. Some of the burns looked like they might be second-degree. It had to be excruciating, but as always, his concern was for me.

It was seeing him hurt that flipped the switch inside me. I hadn't come down here to confront Catherine directly; my goal was to save the people in the condo and the other buildings around us. But she'd hurt Sean, and I'd be damned if that bitch was going to get away with it.

"G-g-get m-m-me up," I said, my teeth chattering. "St-stay b-b-b-behind me and d-don't let her s-see your f-face."

Sean didn't argue. Malcolm, however, did. As Sean lifted me to my feet, the ghost demanded, *What are you doing? She's got fire, Alice!*

Wait 'til you see what I've got, I told him.

With Sean behind me, holding me up as the rain pounded us and the wind roared across the top deck of the parking garage, I looked over at the building next to ours.

Catherine stood facing us, soaked to the skin and struggling against the wind and rain. I could see her fury even from thirty feet away. Orange flames danced on her hands and arms. She looked so much like Moses that bile rose in my throat.

She bent down to pick up the magical weapon at her feet. At this distance, it would turn us both to ash in an instant.

Sean braced himself, his arms tightening around me. "Get behind me," he growled in my ear.

"No, *you* stay behind *me*." *Go to hell, Catherine*, I thought, and raised my arms toward the sky.

My air magic, enhanced by the ley lines, arced through the rain. I seized the power of the storm itself—not the rain, but the charged particles in the air—and the energy was like grabbing a third ley line. The surge of pure power and pain made me scream.

What the f— Malcolm began.

I formed the power into a bolt and brought it down on Catherine's head with all my might and magic. A brilliant flash of white blinded me and a deafening thunderclap shook the parking garage.

Sean dropped us to the pavement again, but this time I didn't even feel the impact when we hit the concrete. I was numb from cold and drained of magic. I landed in a heap and stayed down, too dazed to move or react.

With no more air or water magic to use, I let go of the ley lines. The sudden loss of power and absence of pain made me feel hollow, like a husk with nothing inside.

Nothing inside me but a ghost, anyway.

You conjured lightning, Malcolm said in awe. *I've never seen anyone...Alice?*

I couldn't respond, not even a thought. I was too cold, too drained, too exhausted.

Malcolm swore. I felt a strange popping sensation and realized he'd jumped from my body.

"Alice?" Sean asked. I vaguely sensed him brushing wet hair back from my face. "Jesus, she's blue. Malcolm?"

"Yeah, I'm here," Malcolm said tersely. "She's got severe hypothermia. We need to get her warmed up and into dry clothes before she dies of exposure."

Sean picked me up and ran. I nestled my face against his chest, breathing in his scent as we crossed the parking deck to the stairs.

The rain was gentle now. The storm would fade soon. I hoped it had done enough that the firefighters could put the fires out without too much trouble. In any case, by bringing the storm, I'd done what I could to save the people in the condo. The rest would be up to others; I had nothing left to give.

As he rushed down the steps, I heard Sean ask Malcolm, "Did she just do what I think she did?"

"Yep. She fried someone with a bolt of lightning." A pause. "It was awesome."

"Did you know she could do that?"

"Nope, but it doesn't surprise me. If anyone could smite someone with lightning, it would be Alice."

We reached the bottom of the stairs. "Alice, can you hear me?" Sean asked.

I was shivering so hard that I could barely speak. "C-cold," I managed to say.

He squeezed me tightly against his chest. "I'm taking you to my house to get you warmed up. Hang on."

I mumbled something unintelligible. He carried me to my car and laid me down in the back seat. He disappeared for a few moments and returned with a blanket I assumed he'd gotten from his truck. He removed my boots, ripped off my soaked clothes, and wrapped me in some kind of blanket that smelled like dirt and grass. Maybe a picnic blanket? Did werewolves go on picnics?

"Yes, we do," Sean said. I hadn't realized I'd spoken out loud. He kissed my forehead. "Werewolves like picnics a lot. Rest now. I've got you."

Werewolves liked picnics. Who would have thunk it?

Smiling, I faded out.

25

Strange sensations and sounds pulled me from my rest. I thought at first that hands were caressing my body, but somehow I knew that wasn't what was happening. I was miserably cold, deeper than my bones, all the way down to my core. I couldn't even remember what it felt like to be warm. My heartbeat was a slow *lub-dub* in my chest.

The soft noises became recognizable as water sloshing. The sensation of caresses was actually the water tugging at the traces of magic left behind by Malcolm. I realized I was submerged in water, my body against someone I instinctively recognized as Sean even before I detected the scent of forest. He was in the water with me, holding me against his body, my head tucked under his chin as I shivered. I couldn't open my eyes, but I sensed a lot of bare skin between us.

"Alice, are you awake?" Sean asked. His voice echoed, like we were in a bathroom.

I tried to speak. "Ssss..."

He squeezed me. "We're at my house, in a tub full of hot water. I'm trying to warm you up but you still feel like a block of ice."

I tried again. "Sssss...Sean."

He moved a little and I heard the water running. "I've never been more thankful for my tankless water heater and soaker tub. We've been in here over an hour."

"Rrrrr...wrinkly," I said.

He shook with laughter. "My Alice."

My heart soared. "Your Alice," I agreed.

The water shut off and he wrapped his arms around me again. "Malcolm went back to the fire scene to keep an eye on things. Patrick and his girlfriend are fine, but they'll have to find another place to live. The condo took heavy damage from the fire. There were some injuries, but everyone got out of the condo alive and casualties in the other buildings were minimal, thanks to you." He kissed my hair.

I sensed he was holding something back. "What else?" I murmured.

"A stringer got some footage of us on the roof of the parking garage. The quality is terrible because of the storm, but the local and national news channels picked it up. I doubt there's any chance of us being identified, but the video does show you controlling the storm. Thankfully, the recording cuts out before the end."

I was too cold to feel much of anything about that unwelcome news. I'd known there was a chance I'd out myself, but not trying to help was never an option. At least the video hadn't shown me taking out Catherine with the lightning.

"Worth the risk," I said softly.

"The only person who got any kind of look at us was Catherine Atwood, and I doubt she's in any condition to talk about what she saw." He cupped my head with his hand and held me close. "I've heard that air mages could summon lightning, but I've never seen anyone do it before."

It wasn't really summoning—more like conjuring or conducting—but I was too tired to explain the difference. Here I was, reunited with Sean after several days of wishing desperately for a chance to fix things between us, and I didn't have the strength to talk. I snuggled deeper against his chest and made a little unhappy sound.

He tightened his arms around me. "Is there nothing else I can do? Malcolm healed your burns but he said healing spells wouldn't help with hypothermia." He took a deep breath. "Could Vaughan heal you?"

I could only imagine what asking that had cost him. "Don't want his help." My voice was faint, but firm. "Just hold me, please."

"That I can do." He settled deeper into the water so it covered me up to my chin. "I know you said you wanted to talk and I told you I wanted to listen, and I do, but I have something I need to tell you. Maybe this isn't the time and maybe I'm a bastard to say it when you're in this condition, but I'm going to anyway."

My stomach flip-flopped. His tone was strange. I wasn't sure what he was going to say, and I feared very much that I wouldn't like it.

"I've been doing a lot of thinking these last couple of days. There's a lot about you I don't know; too much, to be honest, but here's what I *do* know. I know you're not the Alice Worth who was the daughter of Henry and Laura Worth of Chicago. I know you're powerful and dangerous and that you're on the run from someone who means you harm. I also know you're the most selfless and brave person I have ever met, and you'll never stop saving the world. And I know that I love you, not in spite of all that, but because of it."

I'd feared he would figure out that I wasn't who I said I was. I'd also known he loved me and it was only a matter of time before he said the words out loud. I expected to feel panicky on both counts, like I wanted to run for the hills and never look back.

Instead, what I felt was...relief. And happiness.

My reaction startled me so much that I didn't notice I was slipping away again until my hand slid across his chest and splashed into the water.

"Alice?" he asked worriedly. "I said, I love you."

Just before I drifted off, I smiled and whispered, "I know."

I woke up in the middle of a pile of werewolves.

Five of them, to be exact. Two were gray, one was solid black, one was brown with black and dark brown markings, and the fifth was gray and white. None of them was

Sean, but as I blinked blearily and focused on my surroundings, I found that we were all lying on a king-sized mattress on the floor in one of the spare bedrooms in his house.

I was wearing long-sleeved flannel pajamas over what felt like thermal long underwear and two pairs of thick socks, and I was wedged between two very large wolves weighing about two hundred pounds each. Miraculously, I was no longer freezing. I'd thought I'd never be warm again.

When I pushed myself up onto my elbows and moved to relieve a cramp in one leg, all of the wolves raised their heads. The larger of the gray wolves stared at me, as if daring me to move. I froze.

Sean appeared in the doorway, wearing a green button-up shirt and jeans. "You're safe with them, Alice."

I eyed the gray wolf. "I know, but she doesn't seem like she wants me going anywhere."

He came over to the side of the bed. "That's Nan's wolf, and no, she doesn't. When she saw the shape you were in, I got an earful about taking better care of you. And she's been giving me dirty looks every time I come in here to check on you."

In fact, the wolf was giving him one now, presumably for not telling me to lie down and go back to sleep. I'd seldom seen such disapproval on a wolf's face. I giggled before I could stop myself.

"How do you feel?" He leaned over to touch my face. "You're still a little cold."

"I feel good," I assured him. "I'm hungry, actually. I bet a pot of coffee and a hot breakfast would fix me right up."

He chuckled. "When you ask for food and coffee, then I know you're on the mend."

I rubbed my eyes and looked out the window. It was a bright and sunny afternoon, but I had no idea how much time had passed since we'd gotten to Sean's house. "So, how long was I out?"

"It's almost five o'clock. It's been about eleven hours since you put the fire out."

Well, that wasn't so bad. I'd expected it to be at least the next day. I felt low on magic, but plenty rested.

I looked at the werewolves piled on the bed around me. "Thank you so much for this," I said a little awkwardly, wondering how much their wolves would even understand me. "Thanks for taking care of me. I—" I broke off. I'd been about to say that I owed them, but that didn't seem like the right thing to say. Instead, I said, "I don't think I've ever slept better than I did with all of you on this bed."

Sean smiled. "I wasn't sure how you'd react to finding yourself up to your ears in werewolves, but I needed to keep you safe and warm and this seemed the best way to do that. Besides, Nan wouldn't take no for an answer, and I learned long ago to take her advice on such things."

Smart man. "Who else is here?"

"The other gray wolf is Felicia. The black wolf is David, her brother. The brown is Patrick, and the gray and white wolf is Karen."

One by one, the wolves got to their feet and stretched. Each carefully nuzzled my face with theirs before trotting out of the room, presumably to shift back to their human forms and give us some time to talk.

When we were alone, Sean shut the bedroom door and helped me to my feet and off the mattress. When we were standing on the hardwood floor, he took my face in his hands and kissed me very thoroughly.

I rested my forehead on his chest and let his familiar scent envelop me. "Where's Malcolm?" I asked.

"Back at your place. He said he didn't want the other wolves to sense him, and he wanted to keep an eye on the house."

"Any news?"

"Some. Should I fill you in over omelets and coffee?"

His guarded tone made me think that it wasn't good news. "You'd better just tell me now."

"Darius Bell survived the fire, so that's a plus for those of us who don't want Moses Murphy taking over the city. Bell's organization is crippled, but not giving up. Just before noon, there was an attack on Murphy's compound near Baltimore. The building sustained some damage and there were a few casualties, but none of them were Murphy."

I was disappointed but not surprised. It would be difficult or nearly impossible to take Moses out when he was in his compound, but I supposed Bell was angry enough to make an attempt, even if all it accomplished was to make the point that he was willing and able to take the fight to Moses.

"Hopefully he'll have better luck next time," I said. "What else?"

Sean took out his phone and handed it to me. The screen showed a still image from the video of us on the roof of the parking garage. We were little more than two small, dark, faceless figures in the pouring rain, recorded from a rooftop several buildings away. There was no way anyone would be able to identify us from that image.

Then I noticed the headline. "Oh, you have *got* to be kidding me. 'Storm Girl'?"

He frowned and took the phone back to look at the picture. "What?"

"They're calling me Storm Girl," I fumed. "Maybe the hoodie made me look young. I'm a high-level mage and a licensed private investigator. I'm on a first-name basis with five of the nine members of the Vampire Court. I'm *thirty years old*, for crying out loud. Storm *Girl?*"

Sean's mouth twitched. "And?"

I crossed my arms. "Damn it, I should at least be Storm Woman."

He couldn't contain himself anymore and burst out laughing. I scowled and he kissed my forehead, still chuckling. "It's a terrible superhero name," he admitted. "We need to come up with something better."

My scowl deepened. "I don't want a superhero name. I'm not a superhero, or even a hero."

"You are most definitely a hero, but we'll save that debate for another day. I've got one more piece of news." He took a deep breath. "I got a call from Cyro about an hour ago. A jet belonging to Moses Murphy took off from a private airport this morning headed for Baltimore. Cyro managed to get surveillance footage from the hangar showing them loading Catherine Atwood onto the plane. She was in bad shape, but it looks like she survived somehow."

I went cold all over—much colder than when I'd shared my body with Malcolm. Next to Moses himself arriving in the city, Catherine being alive was the worst news I could have gotten. Actually, it might be worse than finding out my grandfather was here. She'd gotten a glimpse of me up on the roof, and if she recognized me as the woman she'd encountered at 1792, there was a chance she'd be able to figure out who I was. Even if she didn't make that connection, she still might be able to track me down if she got a good enough look at me.

I must not have hit her directly with the lightning. It was nearly impossible to hit a target that small with a lightning strike; unlike a bolt of magic, which I could aim, lightning was an imprecise weapon. Even if I'd missed, though, Catherine had been standing in ankle-deep rainwater, a perfect conductor for the electricity in the lightning. She should have been fried to a crisp. I wondered if she'd been using some kind of protection spells, or if she'd just gotten lucky. Either way, it was not what I wanted to hear, not by a long shot.

There was always the chance she'd die from her injuries, hopefully without having a chance to tell anyone about who or what she'd seen on the rooftop. I couldn't very well bank on that, though. I had to assume I was now in imminent danger of discovery.

What surprised me most about my reaction to the news was that I didn't immediately want to run. Even six months ago, that would have been my first thought. Instead, I was angry that Catherine and Moses were threats to the life I had built here. Maybe defiance had overpowered my fear because I'd just summoned a thunderstorm and reminded myself of how powerful I was. Maybe it was because I had allies who I believed would have my back if I had to fight, or because I had so much more to fight for now. Maybe it was because Sean had told me he loved me—an important moment that I hadn't even had a chance to really process yet. Maybe it was all of the above. Instead of mentally lacing up my shoes to run, I sensed myself digging in my heels.

Sean startled me by picking me up around the waist and kissing me fiercely. When he put me down, I was breathless. "What was that for?" I asked.

"For deciding to stay and fight instead of cut and run."

I frowned at him. "You don't know what's going on in my head."

He grinned. "Oh yes, I do. I've seen that stubborn look in your eyes a hundred times. Plus, you just smote someone with lightning. A woman who does that isn't the type to turn tail and run, not when she has so many good reasons to stay."

"The last time we spoke, at Jack's house, you said you didn't think you could do this." I gestured between us. "I have to ask: what changed your mind?"

"I didn't so much change my mind as come to terms with what I already knew." He wrapped his arms around me and rested his chin on top of my head. "What I figured out was that it didn't matter if I thought I couldn't do this; the fact is that I *have* to. You are part of my soul. I had so many people around me wondering if you were strong enough to be my partner that I didn't think to ask if I was strong enough to be *yours*. It's me who needs to be stronger, not you."

When I started to object, he moved so he could see my face, his eyes softly golden. "I've always told myself that I wanted a partner and a mate who would stand beside me and who would fight with and for my pack, but I don't think I ever really understood what that meant until now. The night I met you at Hawthorne's, you sat across the booth from me and stared me down. It was your fearlessness that drew me to you as much as anything else. You are exactly what I'd wished and waited for, and I almost blew it because I didn't know how to deal with your power, your courage, and your need to protect others. You face your enemies as though you were the alpha of a pack. You are fierce and you'll fight until you have nothing left. I don't know how, but you can even use shifter magic. Your strength knows no bounds."

He squeezed my hand. "The other members of the pack already recognize your strength. I shouldn't have advised you not to look Jack in the eye. Your place is at my side, within the pack hierarchy—not outside it. Like an alpha, you will never stop trying to save people, even if it means endangering yourself. It's as much a part of you as your magic. The minute I figured out that I had to stop trying to force you to be someone else, the answers fell into place, and I knew I should never have sent you home the other night without talking everything through."

"So why didn't you come over or call me once you'd figured all this out?" I demanded.

He smiled ruefully. "I had that epiphany all of forty-five minutes before Patrick called to say he and Amanda were trapped in their apartment and their entire neighborhood was on fire."

"Speaking of epiphanies..." I took a deep breath. "I apologize for not thinking about how you and the pack would feel about me dying. I'm not sorry that I did it and I'd do it again, but not without leaving a note telling you what was going on, or at least apologizing when I woke up."

"Both of those would have been good choices," he said mildly.

Might as well tell him the rest of what I'd figured out during our time apart. "I know it comes across like I'm cavalier about my life, but I'm really not. The only reason I did what I did was that I knew I'd make it back. But I *was* cavalier about your feelings, and for that I am truly sorry."

He wrapped me in his arms again. "Thank you for saying that. On the way to my house from the parking garage, Malcolm let me know that you and he had talked about some of this already."

"That meddling ghost," I muttered.

He chuckled. "More like matchmaking ghost. He doesn't like seeing you unhappy, and I think he was afraid that one or both of us would bungle this conversation." He squeezed me gently. "I don't believe in giving ultimatums, but here's what I need from you going forward. Remember your life has value and Malcolm and I care very much that you stay alive. Things that hurt you hurt us. I'm not asking you not to throw yourself on any more grenades, but before you do, remember you are loved and you don't have to face anything by yourself ever again. That includes whoever you're running from."

"I'm not running anymore. If they come looking for me, I'll be waiting."

"And I'll be waiting too, right by your side." He kissed my temple. "You still haven't brought up what I said to you in the tub, right before you passed out again. Nice *Star Wars* reference, by the way."

"What *Star Wars* reference?"

Sean made a choking sound.

I laughed. "I'm kidding. Yes, I quoted *Star Wars*. Well, *The Empire Strikes Back*, actually."

He heaved a sigh of relief. "That was going to be a deal-breaker for me, Alice. I can take a lot of things in stride, but missing obvious *Star Wars* references is just more than anyone can take." He tipped my chin up. "I love you."

"I might be too broken to love you back," I admitted. That could have been the most honest thing I'd ever said to him.

"I know that's what you believe, but I know you well enough to know you're not as broken as you think. In any case, I don't need you to say the words to know how you feel. I see it in your eyes and I feel it when you're near me. That's worth more to me than words."

"Then let me put a couple of cards on the table." I took a deep breath. "You saw me use shifter magic at Jack's house. I don't have any answers for how that might be possible, unless it's related to what I learned from Esther's magic mirror the other day."

He waited while I struggled to force the words out.

Finally, I cleared my throat and continued. "The mirror showed me something that might have taken place when I was about six or seven. I overheard my parents talking. It's possible the man I thought was my father wasn't really my biological father. If it's true, then maybe that has something to do with my ability to use shifter magic and the way I relate to the members of your pack. Maybe my real...real father was a shifter, or had shifter blood."

He held me tightly. "That's a hell of lot to process by yourself, and I know it was hard to tell me about it. I'm glad that you did. What are you going to do about it, now that you know?"

"I don't know. If the memory is real, all I have is a first name. The situation is really complicated. I'm going to have to think about what I want to do, if anything. If I start nosing around, I'm not sure what I'll find. I might be putting him at risk just by looking."

"I think you're right to think about it before you make any decisions. There's no rush."

Some of the tension went out of my shoulders. Sean's reassurance had come to mean something to me.

That left one more card to put on the table. It was even harder to put down than the first one, so I spoke quickly, before I had a chance to talk myself out of it. "You said you know I'm not the same Alice Worth who grew up in Chicago. You're right."

Sean stilled.

"That's who I am now, but once upon a time I used to be someone else, someone who got away from a cabal and needed a new identity and a new life. I had a chance to become Alice Worth, so that's what I did. I've been Alice for more than five years. I *am* Alice."

"And the first Alice Worth?" he asked, his voice quiet.

"Dead. I didn't kill her," I added quickly. "I had nothing to do with her death except be in a position to take advantage of it. That sounds cold, I know, but I was desperate to escape my old life." I took a deep, shaky breath. "I'm not ready to talk about that other life, not yet, but I'm getting there. I have no right to ask you to give me more time on that, but that's what I'm asking for."

I didn't breathe until he answered. "Take as much time as you need until you're ready to tell me," Sean said. I almost sagged in relief. He held me close and nuzzled my hair. "I can wait to hear the rest of the story because I know who you are, even if I don't know who you were before."

"Can I tell you something?" I asked suddenly.

"Of course."

"Yesterday was my birthday, my real birthday. I turned thirty yesterday." I blurted it out in a rush.

"Oh, Alice." He kissed me hard, his hands on my face. When he moved back, he looked stricken. "I am so sorry. I should have been there with you. Did Malcolm know?"

I shook my head. "Nobody knew. Well, except Rogue. We celebrated my birthday on the bed with cookies and a dog biscuit."

"Cookie *and* dog biscuit crumbs in the bed." Sean shook his head with feigned disgust. He grew serious again. "We'll have another celebration, you and I. A real date for once, with dinner and a movie, or whatever else you'd like to do. We'll have a cake and ice cream too."

"I don't need any of that. One thirtieth birthday was enough, thank you very much. But I'll tell you what I *do* want."

"Tell me."

"I want to go to the pack's cookout that's coming up in a couple of days." I took a deep breath. "And I want to go with you to the Bahamas."

His grin made my stomach flutter. "When do you want to go?"

"As soon as you can get the time off. I got paid for finding Esther's cup and mirror, so it will be my treat."

He eyed me. "We'll split it, fifty-fifty."

I relented. "Fine. Don't forget that you said you'd bring me all the umbrella drinks I wanted, whenever I wanted them. And food. And you have to put sunscreen on my back and shake the sand out of my shoes."

"Your wish is my command, my lady," he said. "Now, let's go downstairs so I can fix you some breakfast. Your stomach is growling so loudly that I'm sure Nan can hear it from the living room, and I'm going to catch hell if I don't feed you soon. Do you want to change first?"

I shook my head. "I'm enjoying being warm. I like the jammies. Whose are they?"

"Felicia's, I think. Nan brought them." He took my hand. "She's going to fuss over you until it drives you crazy, so just be prepared."

I smiled up at him. "I'm okay with that."

He raised my hand to his lips, kissed my knuckles, and opened the bedroom door.

How many hamburgers *can* a pack of werewolves eat? I lost count at fifty, so the world may never know.

By ten o'clock, most of the food was gone and the pack was gathered around the bonfire, talking and laughing and drinking beer while the kids ran through Cole and Karen's backyard chasing each other in some version of tag that involved climbing trees.

I'd socialized before and during dinner, but even with Sean at my side to make sure I didn't get too crowded, it became overwhelming and I had to take refuge on our picnic blanket on the edge of the clearing. I'd worried that my retreat would come across as unfriendly or aloof, but everyone was good-natured about it.

Everyone but Jack, Delia, and Caleb, that was.

I wasn't sure if Sean had warned them not to talk to me or if they chose to avoid me on their own, but the three of them stayed as far from me as they could get from the moment they arrived. Jack and Delia ignored me altogether, but Caleb glared at me throughout the evening. I didn't let it bother me and had a good time talking and laughing with Nan, Felicia, Karen, Cole, and the others.

The older couple I'd seen at Jack's house were Eddie and his wife Thea. They seemed lukewarm toward me; Sean told me that like Jack and Delia, they wanted him to find a shifter mate.

The other pack member I hadn't met yet because he wasn't at Jack's that night was John, who came to the cookout with his husband Brandon and their three kids. John and Brandon warmed up quickly and we chatted all through dinner. All in all, I felt very welcomed by most of the pack, so Jack and Delia's indifference and Caleb's animosity meant little to me other than it irritated Sean.

Sean left the group by the fire and joined me on the blanket. He took a bottle of beer from our cooler and settled in next to me, his leg against mine. "Hey," he said, bumping me with his shoulder. "Are you warm enough?"

"Yep." Despite the warm summer evening, I wore a sweatshirt over a T-shirt and jeans with thick socks and boots and held a tumbler of hot tea. I was still not fully recovered, but with enough layers and a hot werewolf by my side—wink, wink—I felt plenty toasty.

I leaned against him and smiled as the kids ran past us, headed for the trees. "Don't they ever get tired?"

"They'll crash hard before too long. Even shifter kids run out of steam eventually." He took a drink. "Do you remember having that much energy?"

I shook my head. "No, but I'm sure I did at some point. I'm old now, though, so I'm just going to sit here and drink my tea."

"Hey, watch it," he said with mock outrage. "I'm a decade older than you."

"That's why you're over here with me. This is the seniors section."

He kissed me hard. "Seniors," he scoffed, reaching for his beer. "Hardly."

We watched the others while I rested my head on his shoulder and he put his arm around me. Finally, he asked, "Did you have fun tonight?"

"I really did. I'm sorry I had to leave the group."

"It's all right. You handled everything even better than I thought you would. I know these things aren't easy for someone who's used to being on her own." He ran his nose along my hairline. "I did let them know that you'll need some time to adjust to hanging around a big group."

"I figured you did. Thank you."

I noticed that Jack and Delia were standing together with Caleb on one side of the fire. As Jack and Caleb talked, Delia watched us with narrowed eyes.

"Jack and Delia aren't going to accept me," I said quietly. "I don't know about Eddie and Thea either."

"They *will* accept you. They might not like you, but they will accept you." Sean's voice was firm.

I thought about telling him what Malcolm had overheard Jack say to Delia about getting rid of me, but decided against it. No need to stir up trouble unless it looked like Jack might actually be trying to follow through on the threat.

"By the way, I bought our plane tickets to Nassau," Sean said. "And I found us a deal on a little cabana with its own private beach."

"When do we leave?"

He checked his phone. "In nine hours."

My mouth fell open. "Sean Maclin, when am I supposed to pack?"

"All you need is a swimsuit, a toothbrush, and your passport. We're leaving everything else behind." His voice was firm. He was obviously referring to more than just clothes and toiletries.

We'd been unable to find out anything more about Catherine's condition; even Cyro couldn't get any information other than she'd been taken to Moses's compound. Malcolm and I had been on high alert for the past several days, watching for anything or anyone suspicious, but everything seemed normal.

In the meantime, the city was obsessed with identifying "Storm Girl" and the mysterious man with her. Darius Bell even offered a substantial reward for information. His attorney released a statement claiming Bell wanted to reward the woman who'd saved him and dozens of others from the fire, but I knew better. Bell wanted a powerful mage on his side in the war against Moses. He might not be the butcher Moses was, but he was still the head of his cabal and he would be every bit as ruthless as my grandfather. He'd had Malcolm tortured to death and recalled all of his bound ghosts, killing dozens of mages in the process. I harbored no illusions that I would be any better off as his prisoner than if Moses got me.

And then there was my agreement with Valas...

"Hey." Sean kissed my temple. "Don't let it get too dark in there, Miss Magic. Think about sunshine and umbrella drinks and crystal-blue Caribbean water. Can't you almost smell the sea?"

I closed my eyes and nestled my head against his chest, my nose filled with the scent of forest. "Paradise, here we come."

EPILOGUE

"Can you *believe* this place?"

I looked up from my umbrella drink as a tall black woman with a halo of curls slid onto the barstool next to me. She wore a teal bikini with a wrap tied around her hips and oversized sunglasses.

She grinned at me and signaled to the bartender. "Give me one of those," she said, pointing to my drink.

The bartender gave her a smile and began mixing her drink.

"What are you drinking, anyway?" she asked me, peering at the coconut on the bar in front of me.

"It's rum punch, and it's the best rum punch on the island."

"I love rum punch." She pushed her sunglasses up onto her head. "I'm Ree."

"Alice. Are you from the States?"

"Yep, California."

"Me too. What city?"

"San Francisco area." She took her drink from the bartender and handed him a twenty from a little pouch around her neck. "Keep the change," she told him.

We drank for a bit. I gazed through the palm trees at the ocean and marveled that there could be so many different shades of blue all in one place.

"Hey, I love your bracelet," she said.

I smiled self-consciously. "Thank you."

On our first day on the island, Sean had given me a bracelet made of tiny seashells. I told him I didn't want anything for my birthday. He informed me that it was an "I love you" present. I said I didn't think that was a real thing people did, but he insisted it was. The bracelet was the first gift I'd ever allowed him to give me, and I was trying not to be weirded out about it.

"What brings you to the Bahamas?" I asked as I finished my drink and signaled for another.

"I just had to get away." Ree nursed her drink. "Work has been absolutely insane lately. I'm so busy that I hardly ever get to take a vacation. Then yesterday I decided either I had to take a break or I'd go bonkers, so I booked a flight and *voilà!*" She used her coconut to gesture around us at the palm trees, beach, and sea. "Here I am, in paradise."

"What kind of work do you do?"

"I'm in IT. Yeah, I know, I'm a nerd." She laughed. "Computers and networks and stuff like that. Super boring. What do you do?"

"I'm an administrative assistant." That was my go-to answer when strangers asked what I did. Telling people I was a private investigator usually resulted in a million nosy questions and I just wanted to enjoy the sunshine and my rum punch.

"Sounds about as interesting as my job. You here by yourself?"

"No. My boyfriend had to make a phone call, so he went to our room for a few minutes. He'll be back soon."

"He left you here by yourself?" she teased. "He must trust you not to get into any trouble."

"I'm not sure what kind of trouble I could get into around here, unless it involved falling out of a palm tree or stepping on a sea urchin."

"Hey, you never know," Ree pointed out. "Some people can find trouble anywhere."

"Not me. I stay far away from trouble." I managed to say it with a straight face. I took my new drink from the bartender.

"How long are you here for?" my drinking companion asked. She placed her empty coconut back on the bar and shook her head when the bartender asked if she wanted another.

"Four more days. It's been heavenly to just get away." In fact, I was starting to wonder why on earth I would want to ever go back, despite the dangers of spiny sea urchins and having sand in places I didn't know you could get sand.

"Oh, I agree." Ree put her sunglasses back on. "Having a getaway is crucial, especially when life spins out of control. Hey, is that your boyfriend?" She pointed over my shoulder.

I turned. Sean waved as he headed for the little bar where I'd parked myself while he'd gone to make his daily phone call to the office. He wore a brightly colored shirt, left unbuttoned, and board shorts. He'd managed to turn dark brown in just the three days we'd been here. I couldn't help but notice how many stares he got from other women as he strode across the sand.

I watched him approach and decided we needed to return to our cabana so we could get back to what we'd been doing for most of the past three days.

When Sean joined me at the bar, he gave me a sizzling kiss that sent liquid heat rushing through me. He inhaled and his eyes went golden. "You know how much I love how you look in that bikini," he murmured, his lips near my ear. "But I love how you look even more without it."

Oh, we *definitely* needed to get back to the cabana.

I didn't want to be rude, so I turned back to where Ree had been standing to introduce Sean, but she'd vanished. Huh. Well, I *had* been ogling him for much longer than was necessary. She probably got bored and left.

"How were the drinks?" Sean asked, nuzzling my neck.

I shivered at the feeling of his breath on my sun-warmed skin. "Really great. Rum punch might be my new favorite beverage. Next to Scotch, of course."

"I think I'll order one to take back." He moved away to get the bartender's attention.

I slid down off my barstool and reached for my drink. A small folded piece of paper was tucked under the coconut.

The outside flap had a little drawing of a bottle with a skull and crossbones on the label and a long-stemmed rose.

With a frown, I opened the note. Inside was a short message, written in a neat, feminine hand. *Catherine is awake. If you need help, call me.*

Beside that message was a single word—the name of a woman everyone thought had been killed five years ago in an accident at Moses Murphy's cabal headquarters. It was a name I hadn't used since the night I fled the compound and left that life behind.

I stood frozen in shock, the note crumpled in my hand, my heart pounding so hard that I was sure everyone on the island could hear it.

Bottle of poison. A rose. Cyanide Rose. Cyro.

I looked around but saw no sign of Ree. Her empty coconut remained on the bar, but the straw was gone. She'd taken it with her. No DNA left behind.

Sean joined me, a coconut in each hand and a big grin on his face. "I figured we both needed one for the walk back." His smile faded. "Everything all right?"

"Fine." I forced a smile and took the coconut he was offering, the note hidden in my other hand. "Thank you. I was just thinking I could really use a drink."

He laughed and put his arm around my waist as we headed down the path that led to our cabana. I finished my drink before we got halfway there and left the empty coconut on another of the hotel's many bars.

The note I tore into tiny pieces and flushed down the toilet when I got back to the cabana. I washed my face at the sink and stared at myself in the mirror. My eyes looked shadowed.

Having a getaway is crucial, she'd said.

Catherine is awake.

If you need help, call me.

I heard Sean's voice in my head. *Remember you are loved and you don't have to face anything by yourself ever again.*

"Alice?" Sean called through the door. "You okay?"

I dried my face and opened the door. "I'm fine," I assured him. "Too much rum punch. Race you to the hammock!" I took off running down the hall.

With a laugh, he gave chase. I let him catch me before we got to the door.

We never did make it out to the hammock.

THE END

Thank you for reading! Did you enjoy?

Please Add Your Review! And don't miss book 4 coming this spring from City Owl Press! Sign up for our mailing list to get all the latest info!

ABOUT THE AUTHOR

LISA EDMONDS was born and raised in Kansas, and studied English and forensic criminology at Wichita State University. After acquiring her Bachelor's and Master's degrees, she considered a career in law enforcement as a behavioral analyst before earning a Ph.D. in English from Texas A&M University. She is currently an associate professor of English at a college in Texas and teaches both writing and literature courses. When not in the classroom, she shares a quiet country home with her husband Bill D'Amico and their cats, and enjoys writing, reading, traveling, spoiling her nephew, and singing karaoke.

© *Madison Hurley Photography*

Want an exclusive look at the playlists for the Alice Worth novels? Check out her website: www.lisaedmonds.com

And be sure to find Lisa Edmonds across social media.
Facebook: www.facebook.com/Edmonds411
Instagram: www.instagram.com/edmonds411/
Twitter: www.twitter.com/Edmonds411

ABOUT THE PUBLISHER

City Owl Press is a cutting edge indie publishing company, bringing the world of romance and speculative fiction to discerning readers.

www.cityowlpress.com

CPSIA information can be obtained
at www.ICGtesting.com
Printed in the USA
LVHW081515111222
734991LV00016B/349/J